Guy de Maupassant: The Complete Novels and Short Stories + A Biography of the Author

Guy de Maupassant

GRAPEVINE INDIA

Published by

GRAPEVINE INDIA PUBLISHERS PVT LTD

www.grapevineindia.com
Delhi | Mumbai
email: grapevineindiapublishers@gmail.com

Ordering Information:
Quantity sales: Special discounts are available on quantity purchases by corporations, associations, and others.
For details, reach out to the publisher.

First published by Grapevine India 2023

STRONG AS DEATH

By Guy De Maupassant

PART I

CHAPTER I

A DUEL OF HEARTS

Broad daylight streamed down into the vast studio through a skylight in the ceiling, which showed a large square of dazzling blue, a bright vista of limitless heights of azure, across which passed flocks of birds in rapid flight. But the glad light of heaven hardly entered this severe room, with high ceilings and draped walls, before it began to grow soft and dim, to slumber among the hangings and die in the portieres, hardly penetrating to the dark corners where the gilded frames of portraits gleamed like flame. Peace and sleep seemed imprisoned there, the peace characteristic of an artist's dwelling, where the human soul has toiled. Within these walls, where thought abides, struggles, and becomes exhausted in its violent efforts, everything appears weary and overcome as soon as the energy of action is abated; all seems dead after the great crises of life, and the furniture, the hangings, and the portraits of great personages still unfinished on the canvases, all seem to rest as if the whole place had suffered the master's fatigue and had toiled with him, taking part in the daily renewal of his struggle. A vague, heavy odor of paint, turpentine, and tobacco was in the air, clinging to the rugs and chairs; and no sound broke the deep silence save the sharp short cries of the swallows that flitted above the open skylight, and the dull, ceaseless roar of Paris, hardly heard above the roofs. Nothing moved except a little cloud of smoke that rose intermittently toward the ceiling with every puff that Olivier Bertin, lying upon his divan, blew slowly from a cigarette between his lips.

With gaze lost in the distant sky, he tried to think of a new subject for a painting. What should he do? As yet he did not know. He was by no means resolute and sure of himself as an artist, but was of an uncertain, uneasy spirit, whose undecided inspiration ever hesitated among all the manifestations of art. Rich, illustrious, the gainer of all honors, he nevertheless remained, in these his later years, a man who did not know exactly toward what ideal he had been aiming. He had won the Prix of Rome, had been the defender of traditions, and had evoked, like so many others, the great scenes of history; then, modernizing his tendencies, he had painted living men, but in a way that showed the influence of classic memories. Intelligent, enthusiastic, a worker that clung to his changing dreams, in love with his art, which he knew to perfection, he had acquired, by reason of the delicacy of his mind, remarkable executive ability and great versatility, due in some degree to his hesitations and his experiments in all styles of his art. Perhaps, too, the sudden admiration of the world for his works, elegant, correct, and full of distinctions, influenced his nature and prevented him from becoming what he naturally might have been. Since the triumph of his first success, the desire to please always made him anxious, without his being conscious of it; it influenced his actions and weakened his convictions. This desire to please was apparent in him in many ways, and had contributed much to his glory.

His grace of manner, all his habits of life, the care he devoted to his person, his long-standing reputation for strength and agility as a swordsman and an equestrian, had added further attractions to his steadily growing fame. After his Cleopatra, the first picture that had made him illustrious, Paris suddenly became enamored of him, adopted him, made a pet of him; and all at once he became one of those brilliant, fashionable artists one meets in the Bois, for whose presence hostesses maneuver, and whom the Institute welcomes thenceforth. He had entered it as a conqueror, with the approval of all Paris.

Thus Fortune had led him to the beginning of old age, coddling and caressing him.

Under the influence of the beautiful day, which he knew was glowing without, Bertin sought a poetic subject. He felt somewhat dreamy, however, after his breakfast and his cigarette; he pondered awhile, gazing into space, in fancy sketching rapidly against the blue sky the figures of graceful women in the Bois or on the sidewalk of a street, lovers by the water—all the pleasing fancies in which his thoughts reveled. The changing images stood out against the bright sky, vague and fleeting in the hallucination of his eye, while the swallows, darting through space in ceaseless flight, seemed trying to efface them as if with strokes of a pen.

He found nothing. All these half-seen visions resembled things that he had already done; all the women appeared to be the daughters or the sisters of those that had already been born of his artistic fancy; and the vague fear, that had haunted him for a year, that he had lost the power to create, had made the round of all subjects and exhausted his inspiration, outlined itself distinctly before this review of his work—this lack of power to dream anew, to discover the unknown.

He arose quietly to look among his unfinished sketches, hoping to find something that would inspire him with a new idea.

Still puffing at his cigarette, he proceeded to turn over the sketches, drawings, and rough drafts that he kept in a large old closet; but, soon becoming disgusted with this vain quest, and feeling depressed by the lassitude of his spirits, he tossed away his cigarette, whistled a popular street-song, bent down and picked up a heavy dumb-bell that lay under a chair. Having raised with the other hand a curtain that draped a mirror, which served him in judging the accuracy of a pose, in verifying his perspectives and testing the truth, he placed himself in front of it and began to swing the dumb-bell, meanwhile looking intently at himself.

He had been celebrated in the studios for his strength; then, in the gay world, for his good looks. But now the weight of years was making him heavy. Tall, with broad shoulders and full chest, he had acquired the protruding stomach of an old wrestler, although he kept up his fencing every day and rode his horse with assiduity. His head was still remarkable and as handsome as ever, although in a style different from that of his earlier days. His thick and short white hair set off the black eyes beneath heavy gray eyebrows, while his luxuriant moustache—the moustache of an old soldier—had remained quite dark, and it gave to his countenance a rare characteristic of energy and pride.

Sstanding before the mirror, with heels together and body erect, he went through the usual movements with the two iron balls, which he held out at the end of his muscular arm, watching with a complacent expression its evidence of quiet power.

But suddenly, in the glass, which reflected the whole studio, he saw one of the portieres move; then appeared a woman's head—only a head, peeping in. A voice behind him asked:

"Anyone here?"

"Present!" he responded promptly, turning around. Then, throwing his dumb-bell on the floor, he hastened toward the door with an appearance of youthful agility that was slightly affected.

A woman entered attired in a light summer costume. They shook hands.

"You were exercising, I see," said the lady.

"Yes," he replied; "I was playing peacock, and allowed myself to be surprised."

The lady laughed, and continued:

"Your concierge's lodge was vacant, and as I know you are always alone at this hour I came up without being announced."

He looked at her.

"Heavens, how beautiful you are! What chic!"

"Yes, I have a new frock. Do you think it pretty?"

"Charming, and perfectly harmonious. We can certainly say that nowadays it is possible to give expression to the lightest textiles."

He walked around her, gently touching the material of the gown, adjusting its folds with the tips of his fingers, like a man that knows a woman's toilet as the modiste knows it, having all his life employed his artist's taste and his athlete's muscles in depicting with slender brush changing and delicate fashions, in revealing feminine grace enclosed within a prison of velvet and silk, or hidden by snowy laces. He finished his scrutiny by declaring: "It is a great success, and it becomes you perfectly!"

The lady allowed herself to be admired, quite content to be pretty and to please him.

No longer in her first youth, but still beautiful, not very tall, somewhat plump, but with that freshness which lends to a woman of forty an appearance of having only just reached full maturity, she seemed like one of those roses that flourish for an indefinite time up to the moment when, in too full a bloom, they fall in an hour.

Beneath her blonde hair she possessed the shrewdness to preserve all the alert and youthful grace of those Parisian women who never grow old; who carry within themselves a surprising vital force, an indomitable power of resistance, and who remain for twenty years triumphant and indestructible, careful above all things of their bodies and ever watchful of their health.

She raised her veil and murmured:

"Well, you do not kiss me!"

"I have been smoking."

"Pooh!" said the lady. Then, holding up her face, she added, "So much the worse!"

Their lips met.

He took her parasol and divested her of her spring jacket with the prompt, swift movement indicating familiarity with this service. As she seated herself on the divan, he asked with an air of interest:

"Is all going well with your husband?"

"Very well; he must be making a speech in the House at this very moment."

"Ah! On what, pray?"

"Oh—no doubt on beets or on rape-seed oil, as usual!"

Her husband, the Comte de Guilleroy, deputy from the Eure, made a special study of all questions of agricultural interest.

Perceiving in one corner a sketch that she did not recognize, the lady walked across the studio, asking, "What is that?"

"A pastel that I have just begun—the portrait of the Princesse de Ponteve."

"You know," said the lady gravely, "that if you go back to painting portraits of women I shall close your studio. I know only too well to what that sort of thing leads!"

"Oh, but I do not make twice a portrait of Any!" was the answer.

"I hope not, indeed!"

She examined the newly begun pastel sketch with the air of a woman that understands the technic of art. She stepped back, advanced, made a shade of her hand, sought the place where the best light fell on the sketch, and finally expressed her satisfaction.

"It is very good. You succeed admirably with pastel work."

"Do you think so?" murmured the flattered artist.

"Yes; it is a most delicate art, needing great distinction of style. It cannot be handled by masons in the art of painting."

For twelve years the Countess had encouraged the painter's leaning toward the distinguished in art, opposing his occasional return to the simplicity of realism; and, in consideration of the demands of fashionable modern elegance, she had tenderly urged him toward an ideal of grace that was slightly affected and artificial.

"What is the Princess like?" she asked.

He was compelled to give her all sorts of details—those minute details in which the jealous and subtle curiosity of women delights, passing from remarks upon her toilet to criticisms of her intelligence.

Suddenly she inquired: "Does she flirt with you?"

He laughed, and declared that she did not.

Then, putting both hands on the shoulders of the painter, the Countess gazed fixedly at him. The ardor of her questioning look caused a quiver in the pupils of her blue eyes, flecked with almost imperceptible black points, like tiny ink-spots.

Again she murmured: "Truly, now, she is not a flirt?"

"No, indeed, I assure you!"

"Well, I am quite reassured on another account," said the Countess. "You never will love anyone but me now. It is all over for the others. It is too late, my poor dear!"

The painter experienced that slight painful emotion which touches the heart of middle-aged men when some one mentions their age; and he murmured: “To-day and to-morrow, as yesterday, there never has been in my life, and never will be, anyone but you, Any.”

She took him by the arm, and turning again toward the divan made him sit beside her.

“Of what were you thinking?” she asked.

“I am looking for a subject to paint.”

“What, pray?”

“I don’t know, you see, since I am still seeking it.”

“What have you been doing lately?”

He was obliged to tell her of all the visits he had received, about all the dinners and soirees he had attended, and to repeat all the conversations and chit-chat. Both were really interested in all these futile and familiar details of fashionable life. The little rivalries, the flirtations, either well known or suspected, the judgments, a thousand times heard and repeated, upon the same persons, the same events and opinions, were bearing away and drowning both their minds in that troubled and agitated stream called Parisian life. Knowing everyone in all classes of society, he as an artist to whom all doors were open, she as the elegant wife of a Conservative deputy, they were experts in that sport of brilliant French chatter, amiably satirical, banal, brilliant but futile, with a certain shibboleth which gives a particular and greatly envied reputation to those whose tongues have become supple in this sort of malicious small talk.

“When are you coming to dine?” she asked suddenly.

“Whenever you wish. Name your day.”

“Friday. I shall have the Duchesse de Mortemain, the Corbelles, and Musadieu, in honor of my daughter’s return—she is coming this evening. But do not speak of it, my friend. It is a secret.”

“Oh, yes, I accept. I shall be charmed to see Annette again. I have not seen her in three years.”

“Yes, that is true. Three years!”

Though Annette, in her earliest years, had been brought up in Paris in her parents’ home, she had become the object of the last and passionate affection of her grandmother, Madame Paradin, who, almost blind, lived all the year round on her son-in-law’s estate at the castle of Roncieres, on the Eure. Little by little, the old lady had kept the child with her more and more, and as the De Guilleroys passed almost half their time in this domain, to which a variety of interests, agricultural and political, called them frequently, it ended in taking the little girl to Paris on occasional visits, for she herself preferred the free and active life of the country to the cloistered life of the city.

For three years she had not visited Paris even once, the Countess having preferred to keep her entirely away from it, in order that a new taste for its gaieties should not be awakened in her before the day fixed for her debut in society. Madame de Guilleroy had given her in the country two governesses, with unexceptionable diplomas, and had visited her mother and her daughter more frequently than before. Moreover, Annette’s sojourn at the castle was rendered almost necessary by the presence of the old lady.

Formerly, Olivier Bertin had passed six weeks or two months at Roncieres every year; but in the past three years rheumatism had sent him to watering-places at some distance, which had so much revived his love for Paris that after his return he could not bring himself to leave it.

As a matter of custom, the young girl should not have returned home until autumn, but her father had suddenly conceived a plan for her marriage, and sent for her that she might meet immediately the Marquis de Farandal, to whom he wished her to be betrothed. But this plan was kept quite secret, and Madame de Guilleroy had told only Olivier Bertin of it, in strict confidence.

"Then your husband's idea is quite decided upon?" said he at last.

"Yes; I even think it a very happy idea."

Then they talked of other things.

She returned to the subject of painting, and wished to make him decide to paint a Christ. He opposed the suggestion, thinking that there was already enough of them in the world; but she persisted, and grew impatient in her argument.

"Oh, if I knew how to draw I would show you my thought: it should be very new, very bold. They are taking him down from the cross, and the man who has detached the hands has let drop the whole upper part of the body. It has fallen upon the crowd below, and they lift up their arms to receive and sustain it. Do you understand?"

Yes, he understood; he even thought the conception quite original; but he held himself as belonging to the modern style, and as his fair friend reclined upon the divan, with one daintily-shod foot peeping out, giving to the eye the sensation of flesh gleaming through the almost transparent stocking, he said: "Ah, that is what I should paint! That is life—a woman's foot at the edge of her skirt! Into that subject one may put everything—truth, desire, poetry. Nothing is more graceful or more charming than a woman's foot; and what mystery it suggests: the hidden limb, lost yet imagined beneath its veiling folds of drapery!"

Sitting on the floor, a la Turque, he seized her shoe and drew it off, and the foot, coming out of its leather sheath, moved about quickly, like a little animal surprised at being set free.

"Isn't that elegant, distinguished, and material—more material than the hand? Show me your hand, Any!"

She wore long gloves reaching to the elbow. In order to remove one she took it by the upper edge and slipped it down quickly, turning it inside out, as one would skin a snake. The arm appeared, white, plump, round, so suddenly bared as to produce an idea of complete and bold nudity.

She gave him her hand, which drooped from her wrist. The rings sparkled on her white fingers, and the narrow pink nails seemed like amorous claws protruding at the tips of that little feminine paw.

Olivier Bertin handled it tenderly and admiringly. He played with the fingers as if they were live toys, while saying:

"What a strange thing! What a strange thing! What a pretty little member, intelligent and adroit, which executes whatever one wills—books, laces, houses, pyramids, locomotives, pastry, or caresses, which last is its pleasantest function."

He drew off the rings one by one, and as the wedding-ring fell in its turn, he murmured smilingly:

"The law! Let us salute it!"

"Nonsense!" said the Countess, slightly wounded.

Bertin had always been inclined to satirical banter, that tendency of the French to mingle irony with the most serious sentiments, and he had often unintentionally made her sad, without knowing how to understand the subtle distinctions of women, or to discern the border of sacred ground, as he himself said. Above all things it vexed her whenever he alluded with a touch of familiar lightness to their attachment, which was an affair of such long standing that he declared it the most beautiful example of love in the nineteenth century. After a silence, she inquired:

"Will you take Annette and me to the varnishing-day reception?"

"Certainly."

Then she asked him about the best pictures to be shown in the next exposition, which was to open in a fortnight.

Suddenly, however, she appeared to recollect something she had forgotten.

"Come, give me my shoe," she said. "I am going now."

He was playing dreamily with the light shoe, turning it over abstractedly in his hands. He leaned over, kissed the foot, which appeared to float between the skirt and the rug, and which, a little chilled by the air, no longer moved restlessly about; then he slipped on the shoe, and Madame de Guilleroy, rising, approached the table, on which were scattered papers, open letters, old and recent, beside a painter's inkstand, in which the ink had dried. She looked at it all with curiosity, touched the papers, and lifted them to look underneath.

Bertin approached her, saying:

"You will disarrange my disorder."

Without replying to this, she inquired:

"Who is the gentleman that wishes to buy your Baigneuses?"

"An American whom I do not know."

"Have you come to an agreement about the Chanteuse des rues?"

"Yes. Ten thousand."

"You did well. It was pretty, but not exceptional. Good-by, dear."

She presented her cheek, which he brushed with a calm kiss; then she disappeared through the portieres, saying in an undertone:

"Friday—eight o'clock. I do not wish you to go with me to the door—you know that very well. Good-by!"

When she had gone he first lighted another cigarette, then he began to pace slowly to and fro in his studio. All the past of this liaison unrolled itself before him. He recalled all its details, now long remote, sought them and put them together, interested in this solitary pursuit of reminiscences.

It was at the moment when he had just risen like a star on the horizon of artistic Paris, when the painters were monopolizing the favor of the public, and had built up a quarter with magnificent dwellings, earned by a few strokes of the brush.

After his return from Rome, in 1864, he had lived for some years without success or renown; then suddenly, in 1868, he exhibited his Cleopatra, and in a few days was being praised to the skies by both critics and public.

In 1872, after the war, and after the death of Henri Regnault had made for all his brethren, a sort of pedestal of glory, a Jocaste a bold subject, classed Bertin among the daring, although his wisely original execution made him acceptable even to the Academicians. In 1873 his first medal placed him beyond competition with his Juive d'Alger, which he exhibited on his return from a trip to Africa, and a portrait of the Princesse de Salia, in 1874, made him considered by the fashionable world the first portrait painter of his day. From that time he became the favorite painter of Parisian women of that class, the most skilful and ingenious interpreter of their grace, their bearing, and their nature. In a few months all the distinguished women in Paris solicited the favor of being reproduced by his brush. He was hard to please, and made them pay well for that favor.

After he had become the rage, and was received everywhere as a man of the world he saw one day, at the Duchesse de Mortemain's house, a young woman in deep mourning, who was just leaving as he entered, and who, in this chance meeting in a doorway, dazzled him with a charming vision of grace and elegance.

On inquiring her name, he learned that she was the Comtesse de Guilleroy, wife of a Normandy country squire, agriculturist and deputy; that she was in mourning for her husband's father; and that she was very intellectual, greatly admired, and much sought after.

Struck by the apparition that had delighted his artist's eye, he said:

"Ah, there is some one whose portrait I should paint willingly!"

This remark was repeated to the young Countess the next day; and that evening Bertin received a little blue-tinted note, delicately perfumed, in a small, regular handwriting, slanting a little from left to right, which said:

"MONSIEUR:

"The Duchesse de Mortemain, who has just left my house, has assured me that you would be disposed to make, from my poor face, one of your masterpieces. I would entrust it to you willingly if I were certain that you did not speak idly, and that you really see in me something that you could reproduce and idealize.

"Accept, Monsieur, my sincere regards.

"ANNE DE GUILLEROY."

He answered this note, asking when he might present himself at the Countess's house, and was very simply invited to breakfast on the following Monday.

It was on the first floor of a large and luxurious modern house in the Boulevard Malesherbes. Traversing a large salon with blue silk walls, framed in white and gold, the painter was shown into a sort of boudoir hung with tapestries of the last century, light and coquettish, those tapestries a la Watteau, with their dainty coloring and graceful figures, which seem to have been designed and executed by workmen dreaming of love.

He had just seated himself when the Countess appeared. She walked so lightly that he had not heard her coming through the next room, and was surprised when he saw her. She extended her hand in graceful welcome.

"And so it is true," said she, "that you really wish to paint my portrait?"

"I shall be very happy to do so, Madame."

Her close-fitting black gown made her look very slender and gave her a youthful appearance though a grave air, which was belied, however, by her smiling face, lighted up by her bright golden hair. The Count entered, leading by the hand a little six-year-old girl.

Madame de Guilleroy presented him, saying, "My husband."

The Count was rather short, and wore no moustache; his cheeks were hollow, darkened under the skin by his close-shaven beard. He had somewhat the appearance of a priest or an actor; his hair was long and was tossed back carelessly; his manner was polished, and around the mouth two large circular lines extended from the cheeks to the chin, seeming to have been acquired from the habit of speaking in public.

He thanked the painter with a flourish of phrases that betrayed the orator. He had wished for a long time to have a portrait of his wife, and certainly he would have chosen M. Olivier Bertin, had he not feared a refusal, for he well knew that the painter was overwhelmed with orders.

It was arranged, then, with much ceremony on both sides, that the Count should accompany the Countess to the studio the next day. He asked, however, whether it would not be better to wait, because of the Countess's deep mourning; but the painter declared that he wished to translate the first impression she had made upon him, and the striking contrast of her animated, delicate head, luminous under the golden hair, with the austere black of her garments.

She came, then, the following day, with her husband, and afterward with her daughter, whom the artist seated before a table covered with picture-books.

Olivier Bertin, following his usual custom, showed himself very reserved. Fashionable women made him a little uneasy, for he hardly knew them. He supposed them to be at once immoral and shallow, hypocritical and dangerous, futile and embarrassing. Among the women of the demi-monde he had had some passing adventures due to his renown, his lively wit, his elegant and athletic figure, and his dark and animated face. He preferred them, too; he liked their free ways and frank speech, accustomed as he was to the gay and easy manners of the studios and green-rooms he frequented. He went into the fashionable world for the glory of it, but his heart was not in it; he enjoyed it through his vanity, received congratulations and commissions, and played the gallant before charming ladies who flattered him, but never paid court to any. As he did not allow himself to indulge in daring pleasantries and spicy jests in their society, he thought them all prudes, and himself was considered as having good taste. Whenever one of them came to pose at his studio, he felt, in spite of any advances she might make to please him, that disparity of rank which prevents any real unity between artists and fashionable people, no matter how much they may be thrown together. Behind the smiles and the admiration which among women are always a little artificial, he felt the indefinable mental reserve of the being that judges itself of superior essence. This brought about in him an abnormal feeling of pride, which showed itself in a bearing of haughty respect, dissembling the vanity of the parvenu who is treated as an equal by princes and princesses, who owes to his talent the honor accorded to others by their birth. It was said of him with slight surprise: "He is really very well bred!" This surprise, although it flattered him, also wounded him, for it indicated a certain social barrier.

The admirable and ceremonious gravity of the painter a little annoyed Madame de Guilleroy, who could find nothing to say to this man, so cold, yet with a reputation for cleverness.

After settling her little daughter, she would come and sit in an armchair near the newly begun sketch, and tried, according to the artist's recommendation, to give some expression to her physiognomy.

In the midst of the fourth sitting, he suddenly ceased painting and inquired:

"What amuses you more than anything else in life?"

She appeared somewhat embarrassed.

"Why, I hardly know. Why this question?"

"I need a happy thought in those eyes, and I have not seen it yet."

"Well, try to make me talk; I like very much to chat."

"Are you gay?"

"Very gay."

"Well, then, let us chat, Madame."

He had said "Let us chat, Madame," in a very grave tone; then, resuming his painting, he touched upon a variety of subjects, seeking something on which their minds could meet. They began by exchanging observations on the people that both knew; then they talked of themselves—always the most agreeable and fascinating subject for a chat.

When they met again the next day they felt more at ease, and Bertin, noting that he pleased and amused her, began to relate some of the details of his artist life, allowing himself to give free scope to his reminiscences, in a fanciful way that was peculiar to him.

Accustomed to the dignified presence of the literary lights of the salons, the Countess was surprised by this almost wild gaiety, which said unusual things quite frankly, enlivening them with irony; and presently she began to answer in the same way, with a grace at once daring and delicate.

In a week's time she had conquered and charmed him by her good humor, frankness, and simplicity. He had entirely forgotten his prejudices against fashionable women, and would willingly have declared that they alone had charm and fascination. As he painted, standing before his canvas, advancing and retreating, with the movements of a man fighting, he allowed his fancy to flow freely, as if he had known for a long time this pretty woman, blond and black, made of sunlight and mourning, seated before him, laughing and listening, answering him gaily with so much animation that she lost her pose every moment.

Sometimes he would move far away from her, closing one eye, leaning over for a searching study of his model's pose; then he would draw very near to her to note the slightest shadows of her face, to catch the most fleeting expression, to seize and reproduce that which is in a woman's face beyond its more outward appearance; that emanation of ideal beauty, that reflection of something indescribable, that personal and intimate charm peculiar to each, which causes her to be loved to distraction by one and not by another.

One afternoon the little girl advanced, and, planting herself before the canvas, inquired with childish gravity:

"That is mamma, isn't it?"

The artist took her in his arms to kiss her, flattered by that naïve homage to the resemblance of his work.

Another day, when she had been very quiet, they suddenly heard her say, in a sad little voice:

"Mamma, I am so tired of this!"

The painter was so touched by this first complaint that he ordered a shopful of toys to be brought to the studio the following day.

Little Annette, astonished, pleased, and always thoughtful, put them in order with great care, that she might play with them one after another, according to the desire of the moment. From the date of this gift, she loved the painter as little children love, with that caressing, animal-like affection which makes them so sweet and captivating.

Madame de Guilleroy began to take pleasure in the sittings. She was almost without amusement or occupation that winter, as she was in mourning; so that, for lack of society and entertainments, her chief interest was within the walls of Bertin's studio.

She was the daughter of a rich and hospitable Parisian merchant, who had died several years earlier, and of his ailing wife, whose lack of health kept her in bed six months out of the twelve, and while still very young she had become a perfect hostess, knowing how to receive, to smile, to chat, to estimate character, and how to adapt herself to everyone; thus she early became quite at her ease in society, and was always far-seeing and compliant. When the Count de Guilleroy was presented to her as her betrothed, she understood at once the advantages to be gained by such a marriage, and, like a sensible girl, admitted them without constraint, knowing well that one cannot have everything and that in every situation we must strike a balance between good and bad.

Launched in the world, much sought because of her beauty and brilliance, she was admired and courted by many men without ever feeling the least quickening of her heart, which was as reasonable as her mind.

She possessed a touch of coquetry, however, which was nevertheless prudent and aggressive enough never to allow an affair to go too far. Compliments pleased her, awakened desires, fed her vanity, provided she might seem to ignore them; and when she had received for a whole evening the incense of this sort of homage, she slept quietly, as a woman who has accomplished her mission on earth. This existence, which lasted seven years, did not weary her nor seem monotonous, for she adored the incessant excitement of society, but sometimes she felt that she desired something different. The men of her world, political advocates, financiers, or wealthy idlers, amused her as actors might; she did not take them too seriously, although she appreciated their functions, their stations, and their titles.

The painter pleased her at first because such a man was entirely a novelty to her. She found the studio a very amusing place, laughed gaily, felt that she, too, was clever, and felt grateful to him for the pleasure she took in the sittings. He pleased her, too, because he was handsome, strong, and famous, no woman, whatever she may pretend, being indifferent to physical beauty and glory. Flattered at having been admired by this expert, and disposed, on her side, to think well of him, she had discovered in him an alert and cultivated mind, delicacy, fancy, the true charm of intelligence, and an eloquence of expression that seemed to illumine whatever he said.

A rapid friendship sprang up between them, and the hand-clasp exchanged every day as she entered seemed more and more to express something of the feeling in their hearts.

Then, without deliberate design, with no definite determination, she felt within her heart a growing desire to fascinate him, and yielded to it. She had foreseen nothing, planned nothing; she was only coquettish with added grace, as a woman always is toward a man who pleases her more than all others; and in her manner with him, in her glances and smiles, was that seductive charm that diffuses itself around a woman in whose breast has awakened a need of being loved.

She said flattering things to him which meant "I find you very agreeable, Monsieur;" and she made him talk at length in order to show him, by her attention, how much he aroused her interest. He would cease to paint and sit beside her; and in that mental exaltation due to an intense desire to please, he had crises of poetry, of gaiety or of philosophy, according to his state of mind that day.

She was merry when he was gay; when he became profound she tried to follow his discourse, though she did not always succeed; and when her mind wandered to other things, she appeared to listen with so perfect an air of comprehension and such apparent enjoyment of this initiation, that he felt his spirit exalted in noting her attention to his words, and was touched to have discovered a soul so delicate, open, and docile, into which thought fell like a seed.

The portrait progressed, and was likely to be good, for the painter had reached the state of emotion that is necessary in order to discover all the qualities of the model, and to express them with that convincing ardor which is the inspiration of true artists.

Leaning toward her, watching every movement of her face, all the tints of her flesh, every shadow of her skin, all the expression and the translucence of her eyes, every secret of her physiognomy, he had become saturated with her personality as a sponge absorbs water; and, in transferring to canvas that emanation of disturbing charm which his eye seized, and which flowed like a wave from his thought to his brush, he was overcome and intoxicated by it, as if he had drunk deep of the beauty of woman.

She felt that he was drawn toward her, and was amused by this game, this victory that was becoming more and more certain, animating even her own heart.

A new feeling gave fresh piquancy to her existence, awaking in her a mysterious joy. When she heard him spoken of her heart throbbed faster, and she longed to say—a longing that never passed her lips—"He is in love with me!" She was glad when people praised his talent, and perhaps was even more pleased when she heard him called handsome. When she was alone, thinking of him, with no indiscreet babble to annoy her, she really imagined that in him she had found merely a good friend, one that would always remain content with a cordial hand-clasp.

Often, in the midst of a sitting, he would suddenly put down his palette on the stool and take little Annette in his arms, kissing her tenderly on her hair, and his eyes, while gazing at the mother, said, "It is you, not the child, that I kiss in this way."

Occasionally Madame de Guilleroy did not bring her daughter, but came alone. On these days he worked very little, and the time was spent in talking.

One afternoon she was late. It was a cold day toward the end of February. Olivier had come in early, as was now his habit whenever she had an appointment with him, for he always hoped she would arrive before the usual hour. While waiting he paced to and fro, smoking, and asking himself the question that he was surprised to find himself asking for the hundredth time that week: "Am I in love?" He did not know, never having been really in love. He had had his caprices, certainly, some of which had lasted a long time, but never had he mistaken them for love. To-day he was astonished at the emotion that possessed him.

Did he love her? He hardly desired her, certainly, never having dreamed of the possibility of possessing her. Heretofore, as soon as a woman attracted him he had desired to make a conquest of her, and had held out his hand toward her as if to gather fruit, but without feeling his heart affected profoundly by either her presence or her absence.

Desire for Madame de Guilleroy hardly occurred to him; it seemed to be hidden, crouching behind another and more powerful feeling, which was still uncertain and hardly awakened. Olivier had believed that love began with reveries and with poetic exaltations. But his feeling, on the contrary, seemed to come from an indefinable emotion, more physical than mental. He was nervous and restless, as if under the shadow of threatening illness, though nothing painful entered into this fever of the blood which by contagion stirred his mind also. He was quite aware that Madame de Guilleroy was the cause of his agitation; that it was due to the memories she left him and to the expectation of her return. He did not feel drawn to her by an impulse of his whole being, but he felt her always near him, as if she never had left him; she left to him something of herself when she departed—something subtle and inexpressible. What was it? Was it love? He probed deep in his heart in order to see, to understand. He thought her charming, but she was not at all the type of ideal woman that his blind hope had created. Whoever calls upon love has foreseen the moral traits and physical charms of her who will enslave him; and Madame de Guilleroy, although she pleased him infinitely, did not appear to him to be that woman.

But why did she thus occupy his thought, above all others, in a way so different, so unceasing? Had he simply fallen into the trap set by her coquetry, which he had long before understood, and, circumvented by his own methods, was he now under the influence of that special fascination which gives to women the desire to please?

He paced here and there, sat down, sprang up, lighted cigarettes and threw them away, and his eyes every instant looked at the clock, whose hands moved toward the usual hour in slow, unhurried fashion.

Several times already he had almost raised the convex glass over the two golden arrows turning so slowly, in order to push the larger one on toward the figure it was approaching so lazily. It seemed to him that this would suffice to make the door open, and that the expected one would appear, deceived and brought to him by this ruse. Then he smiled at this childish, persistent, and unreasonable desire.

At last he asked himself this question: "Could I become her lover?" This idea seemed strange to him, indeed hardly to be realized or even pursued, because of the complications it might bring into his life. Yet she pleased him very much, and he concluded: "Decidedly I am in a very strange state of mind."

The clock struck, and this reminder of the hour made him start, striking on his nerves rather than his soul. He awaited her with that impatience which delay increases from second to second. She was always prompt, so that before ten minutes should pass he would see her enter. When the ten minutes had elapsed, he felt anxious, as at the approach of some grief, then irritated because she had made him lose time; finally, he realized that if she failed to come it would cause him actual suffering. What should he do? Should he wait for her? No; he would go out, so that if, by chance, she should arrive very late, she would find the studio empty.

He would go out, but when? What latitude should he allow her? Would it not be better to remain and to make her comprehend, by a few coldly polite words, that he was not one to be kept waiting. And suppose she did not come? Then he would receive a despatch, a card, a servant or a messenger. If she did not come, what should he do? It would be a day lost; he could not work. Then? Well, then he would go to seek news of her, for see her he must!

It was quite true; he felt a profound, tormenting, harassing necessity for seeing her. What did it mean? Was it love? But he felt no mental exaltation, no intoxication of the senses; it awakened no reverie of the soul, when he realized that if she did not come that day he should suffer keenly.

The door-bell rang on the stairway of the little hotel, and Olivier Bertin suddenly found himself somewhat breathless, then so joyous that he executed a pirouette and flung his cigarette high in the air.

She entered; she was alone! Immediately he was seized with a great audacity.

"Do you know what I asked myself while waiting for you?"

"No, indeed, I do not."

"I asked myself whether I were not in love with you?"

"In love with me? You must be mad!"

But she smiled, and her smile said: That is very pretty; I am glad to hear it! However, she said: "You are not serious, of course; why do you make such a jest?"

"On the contrary, I am absolutely serious," he replied. "I do not declare that I am in love with you; but I ask myself whether I am not well on the way to become so."

"What has made you think so?"

"My emotion when you are not here; my happiness when you arrive."

She seated herself.

"Oh, don't disturb yourself over anything so trifling! As long as you sleep well and have an appetite for dinner, there will be no danger!"

He began to laugh.

"And if I lose my sleep and no longer eat?"

"Let me know of it."

"And then?"

"I will allow you to recover yourself in peace."

"A thousand thanks!"

And on the theme of this uncertain love they spun theories and fancies all the afternoon. The same thing occurred on several successive days. Accepting his statement as a sort of jest, of no real importance, she would say gaily on entering: "Well, how goes your love to-day?"

He would reply lightly, yet with perfect seriousness, telling her of the progress of his malady, in all its intimate details, and of the depth of the tenderness that had been born and was daily increasing. He analyzed himself minutely before her, hour by hour, since their separation the evening before, with the air of a professor giving a lecture; and she listened with interest, a little moved, and somewhat disturbed by this story which seemed that in a book of which she was the heroine. When he had enumerated, in his gallant and easy manner, all the anxieties of which he had become the prey, his voice sometimes trembled in expressing by a word, or only by an intonation, the tender aching of his heart.

And she persisted in questioning him, vibrating with curiosity, her eyes fixed upon him, her ear eager for those things that are disturbing to know but charming to hear.

Sometimes when he approached her to alter a pose he would seize her hand and try to kiss it. With a swift movement she would draw away her fingers from his lips, saying, with a slight frown:

"Come, come—work!"

He would begin his work again, but within five minutes she would ask some adroit question that led him back to the sole topic that interested them.

By this time she began to feel some fear deep in her heart. She longed to be loved—but not too much! Sure of not being led away, she yet feared to allow him to venture too far, thereby losing him, since then she would be compelled to drive him to despair after seeming to encourage him. Yet, should it become necessary to renounce this tender and delicate friendship, this stream of pleasant converse which rippled along bearing nuggets of love like a river whose sand is full of gold, it would cause her great sorrow—a grief that would be heart-breaking.

When she set out from her own home to go to the painter's studio, a wave of joy, warm and penetrating, overflowed her spirit, making it light and happy. As she laid her hand on Olivier's bell, her breast throbbed with impatience, and the stair-carpet seemed the softest her feet ever had pressed. But Bertin became gloomy, a little nervous, often irritable. He had his moments of impatience, soon repressed, but frequently recurring.

One day, when she had just entered, he sat down beside her instead of beginning to paint, saying:

"Madame, you can no longer ignore the fact that what I have said is not a jest, and that I love you madly."

Troubled by this beginning and seeing that the dreaded crisis had arrived, she tried to stop him, but he listened to her no longer. Emotion overflowed his heart, and she must hear him, pale, trembling, and anxious as she listened. He spoke a long time, demanding nothing, tenderly, sadly, with despairing resignation; and she allowed him to take her hands, which he kept in his. He was kneeling before her without her taking any notice of his attitude, and with a far-away look upon his face he begged her not to work him any harm. What harm? She did not understand nor try to understand, overcome by the cruel grief of seeing him suffer, yet that grief was almost happiness. Suddenly she saw tears in his eyes and was so deeply moved that she exclaimed: "Oh!"—ready to embrace him as one embraces a crying child. He repeated in a very soft tone: "There, there! I suffer too much;" then, suddenly, won by his sorrow, by the contagion of tears, she sobbed, her nerves quivering, her arms trembling, ready to open.

When she felt herself suddenly clasped in his embrace and kissed passionately on the lips, she wished to cry out, to struggle, to repulse him; but she judged herself lost, for she consented while resisting, she yielded even while she struggled, pressing him to her as she cried: "No, no, I will not!"

Then she was overcome with the emotion of that moment; she hid her face in her hands, then she suddenly sprang to her feet, caught up her hat which had fallen to the floor, put it on her head and rushed away, in spite of the supplications of Olivier, who held a fold of her skirt.

As soon as she was in the street, she had a desire to sit down on the curbstone, her limbs were so exhausted and powerless. A cab was passing; she called to it and said to the driver: "Drive slowly, and take me wherever you like." She threw herself into the carriage, closed the door, sank back in one corner, feeling herself alone behind the raised windows—alone to think.

For some minutes she heard only the sound of the wheels and the jarring of the cab. She looked at the houses, the pedestrians, people in cabs and omnibuses, with a blank gaze that saw nothing; she thought of nothing, as if she were giving herself time, granting herself a respite before daring to reflect upon what had happened.

Then, as she had a practical mind and was not lacking in courage, she said to herself: "I am a lost woman!" For some time she remained under that feeling of certainty that irreparable misfortune had befallen her, horror-struck, like a man fallen from a roof, knowing that his legs are broken but dreading to prove it to himself.

But, instead of feeling overwhelmed by the anticipation of suffering, her heart remained calm and peaceful after this catastrophe; it beat slowly, softly, after the fall that had terrified her soul, and seemed to take no part in the perturbation of her mind.

She repeated aloud, as if to understand and convince herself: "Yes, I am a lost woman." No echo of suffering responded from her heart to this cry of her conscience.

She allowed herself to be soothed for some time by the movement of the carriage, putting off a little longer the necessity of facing this cruel situation. No, she did not suffer. She was afraid to think, that was all; she feared to know, to comprehend, and to reflect; on the contrary, in that mysterious and impenetrable being created within us by the incessant struggle between our desires and our will, she felt an indescribable peace.

After perhaps half an hour of this strange repose, understanding at last that the despair she had invoked would not come, she shook off her torpor and murmured: "It is strange: I am hardly sorry even!"

Then she began to reproach herself. Anger awakened within her against her own blindness and her weakness. How had she not foreseen this, not comprehended that the hour for that struggle must come; that this man was so dear to her as to render her cowardly, and that sometimes in the purest hearts desire arises like a gust of wind, carrying the will before it?

But, after she had judged and reprimanded herself severely, she asked herself what would happen next?

Her first resolve was to break with the painter and never to see him again. Hardly had she formed this resolution before a thousand reasons sprang up as quickly to combat it. How could she explain such a break? What should she say to her husband? Would not the suspected truth be whispered, then spread abroad?

Would it not be better, for the sake of appearances, to act, with Olivier Bertin himself, the hypocritical comedy of indifference and forgetfulness, to show him that she had effaced that moment from her memory and from her life?

But could she do it? Would she have the audacity to appear to recollect nothing, to assume a look of indignant astonishment in saying: "What would you with me?" to the man with whom she had actually shared that swift and ardent emotion?

She reflected a long time, and decided that any other solution was impossible.

She would go to him courageously the next day, and make him understand as soon as she could what she desired him to do. She must not use a word, an allusion, a look, that could recall to him that moment of shame.

After he had suffered—for assuredly he would have his share of suffering, as a loyal and upright man—he would remain in future that which he had been up to the present.

As soon as this new resolution was formed, she gave her address to the coachman and returned home, profoundly depressed, with a desire to take to her bed, to see no one, to sleep and forget. Having shut herself up in her room, she remained there until the dinner hour, lying on a couch, benumbed, not wishing to agitate herself longer with that thought so full of danger.

She descended at the exact hour, astonished to find herself so calm, and awaited her husband with her ordinary demeanor. He appeared, carrying their little one in his arms; she pressed his hand and kissed the child, and felt no pang of anguish.

Monsieur de Guilleroy inquired what she had been doing. She replied indifferently that she had been posing, as usual.

"And the portrait—is it good?" he asked.

"It is coming on very well."

He spoke of his own affairs, in his turn; he enjoyed talking, while dining, of the sitting of the Chamber, and of the discussion of the proposed law on the adulteration of food-stuffs.

This rather tiresome talk, which she usually endured amiably, now irritated her, and made her look with closer attention at the man who was vulgarly loquacious in his interest in such things; but she smiled as she listened, and replied pleasantly, more gracious even than usual, more indulgent toward these banalities. As she looked at him she thought: "I have deceived him! He is my husband, and I have deceived him! How strange it is! Nothing can change that fact, nothing can obliterate it! I closed my eyes. I submitted for a few seconds, a few seconds only, to a man's kisses, and I am no longer a virtuous woman. A few seconds in my life—seconds that never can be effaced—have brought into it that little irreparable fact, so grave, so short, a crime, the most shameful one for a woman—and yet I feel no despair! If anyone had told me that yesterday, I should not have believed it. If anyone had convinced me that it would indeed come to pass, I should have thought instantly of the terrible remorse that would fill my heart to-day."

Monsieur de Guilleroy went out after dinner, as he did almost every evening. Then the Countess took her little daughter on her lap, weeping over her and kissing her; the tears she shed were sincere, coming from her conscience, not from her heart.

But she slept very little. Amid the darkness of her room, she tormented herself afresh as to the dangers of the attitude toward the painter that she purposed to assume; she dreaded the interview that must take place the following day, and the things that he must say to her, looking her in the face meanwhile.

She arose early, but remained lying on her couch all the morning, forcing herself to foresee what it was she had to fear and what she must say in reply, in order to be ready for any surprise.

She went out early, that she might yet think while walking.

He hardly expected her, and had been asking himself, since the evening before, what he should do when he met her.

After her hasty departure—that flight which he had not dared to oppose—he had remained alone, still listening, although she was already far away, for the sound of her step, the rustle of her skirt, and the closing of the door, touched by the timid hand of his goddess.

He remained standing, full of deep, ardent, intoxicating joy. He had won her, her! That had passed between them! Was it possible? After the surprise of this triumph, he gloated over it, and, to realize it more keenly, he sat down and almost lay at full length on the divan where he had made her yield to him.

He remained there a long time, full of the thought that she was his mistress, and that between them, between the woman he had so much desired and himself, had been tied in a few moments that mysterious bond which secretly links two beings to each other. He retained in his still quivering body the piercingly sweet remembrance of that wild, fleeting moment when their lips had met, when their beings had united and mingled, thrilling together with the deepest emotion of life.

He did not go out that evening, in order to live over again that rapturous moment; he retired early, his heart vibrating with happiness. He had hardly awakened the next morning before he asked himself what he should do. To a cocotte or an actress he would have sent flowers or even a jewel; but he was tortured with perplexity before this new situation.

He wished to express, in delicate and charming terms, the gratitude of his soul, his ecstasy of mad tenderness, his offer of a devotion that should be eternal; but in order to intimate all these passionate and high-souled thoughts he could find only set phrases, commonplace expressions, vulgar and puerile.

Assuredly, he must write—but what? He scribbled, erased, tore up and began anew twenty letters, all of which seemed to him insulting, odious, ridiculous.

He gave up the idea of writing, therefore, and decided to go to see her, as soon as the hour for the sitting had passed, for he felt very sure that she would not come.

Shutting himself up in his studio, he stood in mental exaltation before the portrait, his lips longing to press themselves on the painting, whereon something of herself was fixed; and again and again he looked out of the window into the street. Every gown he saw in the distance made his heart throb quickly. Twenty times he believed that he saw her; then when the approaching woman had passed he sat down again, as if overcome by a deception.

Suddenly he saw her, doubted, then took his opera-glass, recognized her, and, dizzy with violent emotion, sat down once more to await her.

When she entered he threw himself on his knees and tried to take her hands, but she drew them away abruptly, and, as he remained at her feet, filled with anguish, his eyes raised to hers, she said haughtily:

"What are you doing, Monsieur? I do not understand that attitude."

"Oh, Madame, I entreat you—"

She interrupted him harshly:

"Rise! You are ridiculous!"

He rose, dazed, and murmured:

"What is the matter? Do not treat me in this way—I love you!"

Then, in a few short, dry phrases, she signified her wishes, and decreed the situation.

"I do not understand what you wish to say. Never speak to me of your love, or I shall leave this studio never to return. If you forget for a single moment this condition of my presence here, you never will see me again."

He looked at her, crushed by this unexpected harshness; then he understood, and murmured:

"I shall obey, Madame."

"Very well," she rejoined; "I expected that of you! Now work, for you are long in finishing that portrait."

He took up his palette and began to paint, but his hand trembled, his troubled eyes looked without seeing; he felt a desire to weep, so deeply wounded was his heart.

He tried to talk to her; she barely answered him. When he attempted to pay her some little compliment on her color, she cut him short in a tone so brusque that he felt suddenly one of those furies of a lover that change tenderness to hatred. Through soul and body he felt a nervous shock, and in a moment he detested her. Yes, yes, that was, indeed, woman! She, too, was like all the others! Why not? She, too, was false, changeable, and weak, like all of them. She had attracted him, seduced him with girlish ruses, trying to overcome him without intending to give him anything in return, enticing him only to refuse him, employing toward him all the tricks of cowardly coquettes who seem always on the point of yielding so long as the man who cringes like a dog before them dares not carry out his desire.

But the situation was the worse for her, after all; he had taken her, he had overcome her. She might try to wash away that fact and answer him insolently; she could efface nothing, and he—he would forget it! Indeed, it would have been a fine bit of folly to embarrass himself with this sort of mistress, who would eat into his artist life with the capricious teeth of a pretty woman.

He felt a desire to whistle, as he did in the presence of his models, but realized that his nerve was giving way and feared to commit some stupidity. He cut short the sitting under pretense of having an appointment. When they bowed at parting they felt themselves farther apart than the day they first met at the Duchesse de Mortemain's.

As soon as she had gone, he took his hat and topcoat and went out. A cold sun, in a misty blue sky, threw over the city a pale, depressing, unreal light.

After he had walked a long time, with rapid and irritated step, elbowing the passers-by that he need not deviate from a straight line, his great fury against her began to change into sadness and regret. After he had repeated to himself all the reproaches he had poured upon her, he remembered, as he looked at the women that passed him, how pretty and charming she was. Like many others who do not admit it, he had always been waiting to meet the "impossible she," to find the rare, unique, poetic and passionate being, the dream of whom hovers over our hearts. Had he not almost found it? Was it not she who might have given him this almost impossible happiness? Why, then, is it true that nothing is realized? Why can one seize nothing of that which he pursues, or can succeed only in grasping a phantom, which renders still more grievous this pursuit of illusions?

He was no longer resentful toward her; it was life itself that made him bitter. Now that he was able to reason, he asked himself what cause for anger he had against her? With what could he reproach her, after all?—with being amiable, kind, and gracious toward him, while she herself might well reproach him for having behaved like a villain!

He returned home full of sadness. He would have liked to ask her pardon, to devote himself to her, to make her forget; and he pondered as to how he might enable her to comprehend that henceforth, until death, he would be obedient to all her wishes.

The next day she arrived, accompanied by her daughter, with a smile so sad, an expression so pathetic, that the painter fancied he could see in those poor blue eyes, that had always been so merry, all the pain, all the remorse, all the desolation of that womanly heart. He was moved to pity, and, in order that she might forget, he showed toward her with delicate reserve the most thoughtful attentions. She acknowledged them with gentleness and kindness, with the weary and languid manner of a woman who suffers.

And he, looking at her, seized again with a mad dream of loving and of being loved, asked himself why she was not more indignant at his conduct, how she could still come to his studio, listen to him and answer him, with that memory between them.

Since she could bear to see him again, however, could endure to hear his voice, having always in her mind the one thought which she could not escape, it must be that this thought had not become intolerable to her. When a woman hates the man who has conquered her thus, she cannot remain in his presence without showing her hatred, but that man never can remain wholly indifferent to her. She must either detest him or pardon him. And when she pardons that transgression, she is not far from love!

While he painted slowly, he arrived at this conclusion by small arguments, precise, clear, and sure; he now felt himself strong, steady, and master of the situation. He had only to be prudent, patient, devoted, and one day or another she would again be his.

He knew how to wait. In order to reassure her and to conquer her once more, he practised ruses in his turn; he assumed a tenderness restrained by apparent remorse, hesitating attentions, and indifferent attitudes. Tranquil in the certainty of approaching happiness, what did it matter whether it arrived a little sooner, a little later? He even experienced a strange, subtle pleasure in delay, in watching her, and saying to himself, "She is afraid!" as he saw her coming always with her child.

He felt that between them a slow work of reconciliation was going on, and thought that in the Countess's eyes was something strange: constraint, a sweet sadness, that appeal of a struggling soul, of a faltering will, which seems to say: "But—conquer me, then!"

After a while she came alone once more, reassured by his reserve. Then he treated her as a friend, a comrade; he talked to her of his life, his plans, his art, as to a brother.

Deluded by this attitude, she assumed joyfully the part of counselor, flattered that he distinguished her thus above other women, and convinced that his talent would gain in delicacy through this intellectual intimacy. But, from consulting her and showing deference to her, he caused her to pass naturally from the functions of a counselor to the sacred office of inspirer. She found it charming to use her influence thus over the great man, and almost consented that he should love her as an artist, since it was she that gave him inspiration for his work!

It was one evening, after a long talk about the loves of illustrious painters, that she let herself glide into his arms. She rested there this time, without trying to escape, and gave him back his kisses.

She felt no remorse now, only the vague consciousness of a fall; and to stifle the reproaches of her reason she attributed it to fatality.

Drawn toward him by her virgin heart and her empty soul, the flesh overcome by the slow domination of caresses, little by little she attached herself to him, as do all tender women who love for the first time.

With Olivier it was a crisis of acute love, sensuous and poetic. It seemed to him sometimes that one day he had taken flight, with hands extended, and that he had been able to clasp in full embrace that winged and magnificent dream which is always hovering over our hopes.

He had finished the Countess's portrait, the best, certainly, that he ever had painted, for he had discovered and crystallized that inexpressible something which a painter seldom succeeds in unveiling—that reflection, that mystery, that physiognomy of the soul, which passes intangibly across a face.

Months rolled by, then years, which hardly loosened the tie that united the Comtesse de Guilleroy and the painter, Olivier Bertin. With him it was no longer the exaltation of the beginning, but a calm, deep affection, a sort of loving friendship that had become a habit.

With her, on the contrary, the passionate, persistent attachment of certain women who give themselves to a man wholly and forever was always growing. Honest and straight in adulterous love as they might have been in marriage, they devote themselves to a single object with a tenderness from which nothing can turn them. Not only do they love the lover, but they wish to love him, and, with eyes on him alone, they so fill their hearts with thoughts of him that nothing strange can thenceforth enter there. They have bound their lives resolutely, as one who knows how to swim, yet wishes to die, ties his hands together before leaping from a high bridge into the water.

But from the moment when the Countess had yielded, she was assailed by fears for Bertin's constancy. Nothing held him but his masculine will, his caprice, his passing fancy for a woman he had met one day just as he had already met so many others! She realized that he was so free, so susceptible to temptation—he who lived without duties, habits, or scruples, like all men! He was handsome, celebrated, much sought after, having, to respond to his easily awakened desires, fashionable women, whose modesty is so fragile, women of the demi-monde of the theater, prodigal of their favors with such men as he. One of them, some evening after supper, might follow him and please him, take him and keep him.

Thus she lived in terror of losing him, watching his manner, his attitudes, startled by a word, full of anguish when he admired another woman, praised the charm of her countenance or her grace of bearing. All of which she was ignorant in his life made her tremble, and all of which she was cognizant alarmed her. At each of their meetings she questioned him ingeniously, without his perceiving it, in order to make him express his opinion on the people he had seen, the houses where he had dined, in short, the lightest expression of his mind. As soon as she fancied she detected the influence of some other person, she combated it with prodigious astuteness and innumerable resources.

Oh, how often did she suspect those brief intrigues, without depth, lasting perhaps a week or two, from time to time, which come into the life of every prominent artist!

She had, as it were, an intuition of danger, even before she detected the awakening of a new desire in Olivier, by the look of triumph in his eyes, the expression of a man when swayed by a gallant fancy.

Then she would suffer; her sleep would be tortured by doubts. In order to surprise him, she would appear suddenly in his studio, without giving him notice of her coming, put questions that seemed naïve, tested his tenderness while listening to his thoughts, as we test while listening to detect hidden illness in the body. She would weep as soon as she found herself sure that some one would take him from her this time, robbing her of that love to which she clung so passionately because she had staked upon it all her will, her strength of affection, all her hopes and dreams.

Then, when she saw that he came back to her, after these brief diversions, she experienced, as she drew close to him again, took possession of him as of something lost and found, a deep, silent happiness which sometimes, when she passed a church, urged her go in and thank God.

Her preoccupation in ever making herself pleasing to him above all others, and of guarding him against all others, had made her whole life become a combat interrupted by coquetry. She had ceaselessly struggled for him, and before him, with her grace, her beauty and elegance. She wished that wherever he went he should hear her praised for her charm, her taste, her wit, and her toilets. She wished to please others for his sake, and to attract them so that he should be both proud and jealous of her. And every time that she succeeded in arousing his jealousy, after making him suffer a little, she allowed him the triumph of winning her back, which revived his love in exciting his vanity. Then, realizing that it was always possible for a man to meet in society a woman whose physical charm would be greater than her own, being a novelty, she resorted to other means: she flattered and spoiled him. Discreetly but continuously she heaped praises upon him; she soothed him with admiration and enveloped him in flattery, so that he might find all other friendship, all other love, even, a little cold and incomplete, and that if others also loved him he would perceive at last that she alone of them all understood him.

She made the two drawing-rooms in her house, which he entered so often, a place as attractive to the pride of the artist as to the heart of the man, the place in all Paris where he liked best to come, because there all his cravings were satisfied at the same time.

Not only did she learn to discover all his tastes, in order that, while gratifying them in her own house, she might give him a feeling of well-being that nothing could replace, but she knew how to create new tastes, to arouse appetites of all kinds, material and intellectual, habits of little attentions, of affections, of adoration and flattery! She tried to charm his eye with elegance, his sense of smell with perfumes, and his taste with delicate food.

But when she had planted in the soul and in the senses of a selfish bachelor a multitude of petty, tyrannical needs, when she had become quite certain that no mistress would trouble herself as she did to watch over and maintain them, in order to surround him with all the little pleasures of life, she suddenly feared, as she saw him disgusted with his own home, always complaining of his solitary life, and, being unable to come into her home except under all the restraints imposed by society, going to the club, seeking every means to soften his lonely lot—she feared lest he thought of marriage.

On some days she suffered so much from all these anxieties that she longed for old age, to have an end of this anguish and rest in a cooler and calmer affection.

Years passed, however, without disuniting them. The chain wherewith she had attached him to her was heavy, and she made new links as the old ones wore away. But, always solicitous, she watched over the painter's heart as one guards a child crossing a street full of vehicles, and day by day she lived in expectation of the unknown danger, the dread of which always hung over her.

The Count, without suspicion or jealousy, found this intimacy of his wife with a famous and popular artist a perfectly natural thing. Through continually meeting, the two men, becoming accustomed to each other, finally became excellent friends.

CHAPTER II

TWIN ROSES FROM A SINGLE STEM

When Bertin entered, on Friday evening, the house of his friend, where he was to dine in honor of the return of Antoinette de Guilleroy, he found in the little Louis XV salon only Monsieur de Musadieu, who had just arrived.

He was a clever old man, who perhaps might have become of some importance, and who now could not console himself for not having attained to something worth while.

He had once been a commissioner of the imperial museums, and had found means to get himself reappointed Inspector of Fine Arts under the Republic, which did not prevent him from being, above all else, the friend of princes, of all the princes, princesses, and duchesses of European aristocracy, and the sworn protector of artists of all sorts. He was endowed with an alert mind and quick perceptions, with great facility of speech that enabled him to say agreeably the most ordinary things, with a suppleness of thought that put him at ease in any society, and a subtle diplomatic scent that gave him the power to judge men at first sight; and he strolled from salon to salon, morning and evening, with his enlightened, useless, and gossiping activity.

Apt at everything, as he appeared, he would talk on any subject with an air of convincing competence and familiarity that made him greatly appreciated by fashionable women, whom he served as a sort of traveling bazaar of erudition. As a matter of fact, he knew many things without ever having read any but the most indispensable books; but he stood very well with the five Academies, with all the savants, writers, and learned specialists, to whom he listened with clever discernment. He knew how to forget at once explanations that were too technical or were useless to him, remembered the others very well, and lent to the information thus gleaned an easy, clear, and good-natured rendering that made them as readily comprehensible as the popular presentation of scientific facts. He gave the impression of being a veritable storehouse of ideas, one of those vast places wherein one never finds rare objects but discovers a multiplicity of cheap productions of all kinds and from all sources, from household utensils to the popular instruments for physical culture or for domestic surgery.

The painters, with whom his official functions brought him in continual contact, made sport of him but feared him. He rendered them some services, however, helped them to sell pictures, brought them in contact with fashionable persons, and enjoyed presenting them, protecting them, launching them. He seemed to devote himself to a mysterious function of fusing the fashionable and the artistic worlds, pluming himself on his intimate acquaintance with these, and of his familiar footing with those, on breakfasting with the Prince of Wales, on his way through Paris, or dining, the same evening, with Paul Adelmant, Olivier Bertin, and Amaury Maldant.

Bertin, who liked him well enough, found him amusing, and said of him: "He is the encyclopedia of Jules Verne, bound in ass's skin!"

The two men shook hands and began to talk of the political situation and the rumors of war, which Musadieu thought alarming, for evident reasons which he explained very well, Germany having every interest in crushing us and in hastening that moment for which M. de Bismarck had been waiting eighteen years; while Olivier Bertin proved by irrefutable argument that these fears were chimerical, it being impossible for Germany to be foolish enough to risk her conquest in an always doubtful venture, or for the Chancelor to be imprudent enough to risk, in the latter years of his life, his achievements and his glory at a single blow.

M. de Musadieu, however, seemed to know something of which he did not wish to speak. Furthermore, he had seen a Minister that morning and had met the Grand Duke Vladimir, returning from Cannes, the evening before.

The artist was unconvinced by this, and with quiet irony expressed doubt of the knowledge of even the best informed. Behind all these rumors was the influence of the Bourse! Bismarck alone might have a settled opinion on the subject.

M. de Guilleroy entered, shook hands warmly, excusing himself in unctuous words for having left them alone.

"And you, my dear Deputy," asked the painter, "what do you think of these rumors of war?"

M. de Guilleroy launched into a discourse. As a member of the Chamber, he knew more of the subject than anyone else, though he held an opinion differing from that of most of his colleagues. No, he did not believe in the probability of an approaching conflict, unless it should be provoked by French turbulence and by the rodomontades of the self-styled patriots of the League. And he painted Bismarck's portrait in striking colors, a portrait a la Saint-Simon. The man Bismarck was one that no one wished to understand, because one always lends to others his own ways of thinking, and credits them with a readiness to do that which he would do were he placed in their situation. M. de Bismarck was not a false and lying diplomatist, but frank and brutal, always loudly proclaiming the truth and announcing his intentions. "I want peace!" said he. That was true; he wanted peace, nothing but peace, and everything had proved it in a blinding fashion for eighteen years; everything—his arguments, his alliances, that union of peoples banded together against our impetuosity. M. de Guilleroy concluded in a tone of profound conviction: "He is a great man, a very great man, who desires peace, but who has faith only in menaces and violent means as the way to obtain it. In short, gentlemen, a great barbarian."

"He that wishes the end must take the means," M. de Musadieu replied. "I will grant you willingly that he adores peace if you will concede to me that he always wishes to make war in order to obtain it. But that is an indisputable and phenomenal truth: In this world war is made only to obtain peace!"

A servant announced: "Madame la Duchesse de Mortemain."

Between the folding-doors appeared a tall, large woman, who entered with an air of authority.

Guilleroy hastened to meet her, and kissed her hand, saying:

"How do you do, Duchess?"

The other two men saluted her with a certain distinguished familiarity, for the Duchess's manner was both cordial and abrupt.

She was the widow of General the Duc de Mortemain, mother of an only daughter married to the Prince de Salia; daughter of the Marquis de Farandal, of high family and royally rich, and received at her mansion in the Rue de Varenne all the celebrities of the world, who met and complimented one another there. No Highness passed through Paris without dining at her table; no man could attract public attention that she did not immediately wish to know him. She must see him, make him talk to her, form her own judgment of him. This amused her greatly, lent interest to life, and fed the flame of imperious yet kindly curiosity that burned within her.

She had hardly seated herself when the same servant announced:

"Monsieur le Baron and Madame la Baronne de Corbelle."

They were young; the Baron was bald and fat, the Baroness was slender, elegant, and very dark.

This couple occupied a peculiar situation in the French aristocracy due solely to a scrupulous choice of connections. Belonging to the polite world, but without value or talent, moved in all their actions by an immoderate love of that which is select, correct, and distinguished; by dint of visiting only the most princely houses, of professing their royalist sentiments, pious and correct to a supreme degree; by respecting all that should be respected, by condemning all that should be condemned, by never being mistaken on a point of worldly dogma or hesitating over a detail of etiquette, they had succeeded in passing in the eyes of many for the finest flower of high life. Their opinion formed a sort of code of correct form and their presence in a house gave it a true title of distinction.

The Corbelles were relatives of the Comte de Guilleroy.

"Well," said the Duchess in astonishment, "and your wife?"

"One instant, one little instant," pleaded the Count. "There is a surprise: she is just about to come."

When Madame de Guilleroy, as the bride of a month, had entered society, she was presented to the Duchesse de Mortemain, who loved her immediately, adopted her, and patronized her.

For twenty years this friendship never had diminished, and when the Duchess said, "Ma petite," one still heard in her voice the tenderness of that sudden and persistent affection. It was at her house that the painter and the Countess had happened to meet.

Musadieu approached the group. "Has the Duchess been to see the exposition of the Intemperates?" he inquired.

"No; what is that?"

"A group of new artists, impressionists in a state of intoxication. Two of them are very fine."

The great lady murmured, with disdain: "I do not like the jests of those gentlemen."

Authoritative, brusque, barely tolerating any other opinion than her own, and founding hers solely on the consciousness of her social station, considering, without being able to give a good reason for it, that artists and learned men were merely intelligent mercenaries charged by God to amuse society or to render service to it, she had no other basis for her judgments than the degree of astonishment or of pleasure she experienced at the sight of a thing, the reading of a book, or the recital of a discovery.

Tall, stout, heavy, red, with a loud voice, she passed as having the air of a great lady because nothing embarrassed her; she dared to say anything and patronized the whole world, including dethroned princes, with her receptions in their honor, and even the Almighty by her generosity to the clergy and her gifts to the churches.

"Does the Duchess know," Musadieu continued, "that they say the assassin of Marie Lambourg has been arrested?"

Her interest was awakened at once.

"No, tell me about it," she replied.

He narrated the details. Musadieu was tall and very thin; he wore a white waistcoat and little diamond shirt-studs; he spoke without gestures, with a correct air which allowed him to say the daring things which he took delight in uttering. He was very near-sighted, and appeared, notwithstanding his eye-glass, never to see anyone; and when he sat down his whole frame seemed to accommodate itself to the shape of the chair. His figure seemed to shrink into folds, as if his spinal column were made of rubber; his legs, crossed one over the other, looked like two rolled ribbons, and his long arms, resting on the arms of the chair, allowed to droop his pale hands with interminable fingers. His hair and moustache, artistically dyed, with a few white locks cleverly forgotten, were a subject of frequent jests.

While he was explaining to the Duchess that the jewels of the murdered prostitute had been given as a present by the suspected murderer to another girl of the same stamp, the door of the large drawing-room opened wide once more, and two blond women in white lace, a creamy Mechlin, resembling each other like two sisters of different ages, the one a little too mature, the other a little too young, one a trifle too plump, the other a shade too slender, advanced, clasping each other round the waist and smiling.

The guests exclaimed and applauded. No one, except Olivier Bertin, knew of Annette de Guilleroy's return, and the appearance of the young girl beside her mother, who at a little distance seemed almost as fresh and even more beautiful—for, like a flower in full bloom, she had not ceased to be brilliant, while the child, hardly budding, was only beginning to be pretty—made both appear charming.

The Duchess, delighted, clapped her hands, exclaiming: "Heavens! How charming and amusing they are, standing beside each other! Look, Monsieur de Musadieu, how much they resemble each other!"

The two were compared, and two opinions were formed. According to Musadieu, the Corbelles, and the Comte de Guilleroy, the Countess and her daughter resembled each other only in coloring, in the hair, and above all in the eyes, which were exactly alike, both showing tiny black points, like minute drops of ink, on the blue iris. But it was their opinion that when the young girl should have become a woman they would no longer resemble each other.

According to the Duchess, on the contrary, and also Olivier Bertin, they were similar in all respects, and only the difference in age made them appear unlike.

"How much she has changed in three years!" said the painter. "I should not have recognized her, and I don't dare to tutoyer the young lady!"

The Countess laughed. "The idea! I should like to hear you say 'you' to Annette!"

The young girl, whose future gay audacity was already apparent under an air of timid playfulness, replied: "It is I who shall not dare to say 'thou' to Monsieur Bertin."

Her mother smiled.

"Yes, continue the old habit—I will allow you to do so," she said. "You will soon renew your acquaintance with him."

But Annette shook her head.

"No, no, it would embarrass me," she said.

The Duchess embraced her, and examined her with all the interest of a connoisseur.

"Look me in the face, my child," she said. "Yes, you have exactly the same expression as your mother; you won't be so bad by-and-by, when you have acquired more polish. And you must grow a little plumper—not very much, but a little. You are very thin."

"Oh, don't say that!" exclaimed the Countess.

"Why not?"

"It is so nice to be slender. I intend to reduce myself at once."

But Madame de Mortemain took offense, forgetting in her anger the presence of a young girl.

"Oh, of course, you are all in favor of bones, because you can dress them better than flesh. For my part, I belong to the generation of fat women! To-day is the day of thin ones. They make me think of the lean kine of Egypt. I cannot understand how men can admire your skeletons. In my time they demanded more!"

She subsided amid the smiles of the company, but added, turning to Annette:

"Look at your mamma, little one; she does very well; she has attained the happy medium—imitate her."

They passed into the dining-room. After they were seated, Musadieu resumed the discussion.

"For my part, I say that men should be thin, because they are formed for exercises that require address and agility, incompatible with corpulency. But the women's case is a little different. Don't you think so, Corbelle?"

Corbelle was perplexed, the Duchess being stout and his own wife more than slender. But the Baroness came to the rescue of her husband, and resolutely declared herself in favor of slimness. The year before that, she declared, she had been obliged to struggle with the beginning of embonpoint, over which she soon triumphed.

"Tell us how you did it," demanded Madame de Guilleroy.

The Baroness explained the method employed by all the fashionable women of the day. One must never drink while eating; but an hour after the repast a cup of tea may be taken, boiling hot. This method succeeded with everyone. She cited astonishing cases of fat women who in three months had become more slender than the blade of a knife. The Duchess exclaimed in exasperation:

"Good gracious, how stupid to torture oneself like that! You like nothing any more—nothing—not even champagne. Bertin, as an artist, what do you think of this folly?"

"Mon Dieu, Madame, I am a painter and I simply arrange the drapery, so it is all the same to me. If I were a sculptor I might complain."

"But as a man, which do you prefer?"

"I? Oh, a certain rounded slimness—what my cook calls a nice little corn-fed chicken. It is not fat, but plump and delicate."

The comparison caused a laugh; but the incredulous Countess looked at her daughter and murmured:

"No, it is very much better to be thin; slender women never grow old."

This point also was discussed by the company; and all agreed that a very fat person should not grow thin too rapidly.

This observation gave place to a review of women known in society and to new discussions on their grace, their chic and beauty. Musadieu pronounced the blonde Marquise de Lochrist incomparably charming, while Bertin esteemed as a beauty Madame Mandeliere, with her brunette complexion, low brow, her dusky eyes and somewhat large mouth, in which her teeth seemed to sparkle.

He was seated beside the young girl, and said suddenly, turning to her:

"Listen to me, Nanette. Everything that we have just been saying you will hear repeated at least once a week until you are old. In a week you will know all that society thinks about politics, women, plays, and all the rest of it. Only an occasional change of names will be necessary—names of persons and titles of works. When you have heard us all express and defend our opinions, you will quietly choose your own among those that one must have, and then you need never trouble yourself to think of anything more, never. You will only have to rest in that opinion."

The young girl, without replying, turned upon him her mischievous eyes, wherein sparkled youthful intelligence, restrained, but ready to escape.

But the Duchess and Musadieu, who played with ideas as one tosses a ball, without perceiving that they continually exchanged the same ones, protested in the name of thought and of human activity.

Then Bertin attempted to show how the intelligence of fashionable people, even the brightest of them, is without value, foundation, or weight; how slight is the basis of their beliefs, how feeble and indifferent is their interest in intellectual things, how fickle and questionable are their tastes.

Warmed by one of those spasms of indignation, half real, half assumed, aroused at first by a desire to be eloquent, and urged on by the sudden prompting of a clear judgment, ordinarily obscured by an easy-going nature, he showed how those persons whose sole occupation in life is to pay visits and dine in town find themselves becoming, by an irresistible fatality, light and graceful but utterly trivial beings, vaguely agitated by superficial cares, beliefs, and appetites.

He showed that none of that class has either depth, ardor, or sincerity; that, their intellectual culture being slight and their erudition a simple varnish, they must remain, in short, manikins who produce the effect and make the gesture of the enlightened beings that they are not. He proved that, the frail roots of their instincts having been nourished on conventionalities instead of realities, they love nothing sincerely, that even the luxury of their existence is a satisfaction of vanity and not the gratification of a refined bodily necessity, for usually their table is indifferent, their wines are bad and very dear.

They live, as he said, beside everything, but see nothing and study nothing; they are near science, of which they are ignorant; nature, at which they do not know how to look; outside of true happiness, for they are powerless to enjoy it; outside of the beauty of the world and the beauty of art, of which they chatter without having really discovered it, or even believing in it, for they are ignorant of the intoxication of tasting the joys of life and of intelligence. They are incapable of attaching themselves in anything to that degree that existence is illumined by the happiness of comprehending it.

The Baron de Corbelle thought that it was his duty to come to the defense of society. This he did with inconsistent and irrefutable arguments, which melt before reason as snow before the fire, yet which cannot be disproved—the absurd and triumphant arguments of a country curate who would demonstrate the existence of God. In concluding, he compared fashionable people to race-horses, which, in truth, are good for nothing, but which are the glory of the equine race.

Bertin, irritated by this adversary, preserved a politely disdainful silence. But suddenly the Baron's imbecilities exasperated him, and, interrupting him adroitly, he recounted the life of a man of fashion from his rising to his going to rest, without omitting anything. All the details, cleverly described, made up an irresistibly amusing silhouette. Once could see the fine gentleman dressed by his valet, first expressing a few general ideas to the hairdresser that came to shave him; then, when taking his morning stroll, inquiring of the grooms about the health of the horses; then trotting through the avenues of the Bois, caring only about saluting and being saluted; then breakfasting opposite his wife, who in her turn had been out in her coupe, speaking to her only to enumerate the names of the persons he had met that morning; then passing from drawing-room to drawing-room until evening, refreshing his intelligence by contact with others of his circle, dining with a prince, where the affairs of Europe were discussed, and finishing the evening behind the scenes at the Opera, where his timid pretensions at being a gay dog were innocently satisfied by the appearance of being surrounded by naughtiness.

The picture was so true, although its satire wounded no one present, that laughter ran around the table.

The Duchess, shaken by the suppressed merriment of fat persons, relieved herself by discreet chuckles.

"Really, you are too funny!" she said at last; "you will make me die of laughter."

Bertin replied, with some excitement:

"Oh, Madame, in the polite world one does not die of laughter! One hardly laughs, even. We have sufficient amiability, as a matter of good taste, to pretend to be amused and appear to laugh. The grimace is imitated well enough, but the real thing is never done. Go to the theaters of the common people—there you will see laughter. Go among the bourgeoisie, when they are amusing themselves; you will see them laugh to suffocation. Go to the soldiers' quarters, you will see men choking, their eyes full of tears, doubled up on their beds over the jokes of some funny fellow. But in our drawing-rooms we never laugh. I tell you that we simulate everything, even laughter."

Musadieu interrupted him:

"Permit me to say that you are very severe. It seems to me that you yourself, my dear fellow, do not wholly despise this society at which you rail so bitterly."

Bertin smiled.

"I? I love it!" he declared.

"But then——"

"I despise myself a little, as a mongrel of doubtful race."

"All that sort of talk is nothing but a pose," said the Duchess.

And, as he denied having any intention of posing, she cut short the discussion by declaring that all artists try to make people believe that chalk is cheese.

The conversation then became general, touching upon everything, ordinary and pleasant, friendly and critical, and, as the dinner was drawing toward its end, the Countess suddenly exclaimed, pointing to the full glasses of wine that were ranged before her plate:

"Well, you see that I have drunk nothing, nothing, not a drop! We shall see whether I shall not grow thin!"

The Duchess, furious, tried to make her swallow some mineral water, but in vain; then she exclaimed:

"Oh, the little simpleton! That daughter of hers will turn her head. I beg of you, Guilleroy, prevent your wife from committing this folly."

The Count, who was explaining to Musadieu the system of a threshing-machine invented in America, had not been listening.

"What folly, Duchess?"

"The folly of wishing to grow thin."

The Count looked at his wife with an expression of kindly indifference.

"I never have formed the habit of opposing her," he replied.

The Countess had risen, taking the arm of her neighbor; the Count offered his to the Duchess, and they passed into the large drawing-room, the boudoir at the end being reserved for use in the daytime.

It was a vast and well lighted room. On the four walls the large and beautiful panels of pale blue silk, of antique pattern, framed in white and gold, took on under the light of the lamps and the chandelier a moonlight softness and brightness. In the center of the principal one, the portrait of the Countess by Olivier Bertin seemed to inhabit, to animate the apartment. It had a look of being at home there, mingling with the air of the salon its youthful smile, the grace of its pose, the bright charm of its golden hair. It had become almost a custom, a sort of polite ceremony, like making the sign of the cross on entering a church, to compliment the model on the work of the painter whenever anyone stood before it.

Musadieu never failed to do this. His opinion as a connoisseur commissioned by the State having the value of that of an official expert, he regarded it as his duty to affirm often, with conviction, the superiority of that painting.

"Indeed," said he, "that is the most beautiful modern portrait I know. There is prodigious life in it."

The Comte de Guilleroy, who, through hearing this portrait continually praised, had acquired a rooted conviction that he possessed a masterpiece, approached to join him, and for a minute or two they lavished upon the portrait all the art technicalities of the day in praise of the apparent qualities of the work, and also of those that were suggested.

All eyes were lifted toward the portrait, apparently in a rapture of admiration, and Olivier Bertin, accustomed to these eulogies, to which he paid hardly more attention than to questions about his health when meeting some one in the street, nevertheless adjusted the reflector lamp placed before the portrait in order to illumine it, the servant having carelessly set it a little on one side.

Then they seated themselves, and as the Count approached the Duchess, she said to him:

"I believe that my nephew is coming here for me, and to ask you for a cup of tea."

Their wishes, for some time, had been mutually understood and agreed, without either side ever having exchanged confidences or even hints.

The Marquis de Farandal, who was the brother of the Duchesse de Mortemain, after almost ruining himself at the gaming table, had died of the effects of a fall from his horse, leaving a widow and a son. This young man, now nearly twenty-eight years of age, was one of the most popular leaders of the cotillion in Europe, for he was sometimes requested to go to Vienna or to London to crown in the waltz some princely ball. Although possessing very small means, he remained, through his social station, his family, his name, and his almost royal connections, one of the most popular and envied men in Paris.

It was necessary to give a solid foundation to this glory of his youth, and after a rich, a very rich marriage, to replace social triumphs by political success. As soon as the Marquis should become a deputy, he would become also, by that attainment alone, one of the props of the future throne, one of the counselors of the King, one of the leaders of the party.

The Duchess, who was well informed, knew the amount of the enormous fortune of the Comte de Guilleroy, a prudent hoarder of money, who lived in a simple apartment when he was quite able to live like a great lord in one of the handsomest mansions of Paris. She knew about his always successful speculations, his subtle scent as a financier, his share in the most fruitful schemes of the past ten years, and she had cherished the idea of marrying her nephew to the daughter of the Norman deputy, to whom this marriage would give an immense influence in the aristocratic society of the princely circle. Guilleroy, who had made a rich marriage, and had thereby increased a large personal fortune, now nursed other ambitions.

He had faith in the return of the King, and wished, when that event should come, to be so situated as to derive from it the largest personal profit.

As a simple deputy, he did not cut a prominent figure. As a father-in-law of the Marquis of Farandal, whose ancestors had been the faithful and chosen familiars of the royal house of France, he might rise to the first rank.

The friendship of the Duchess for his wife lent to this union an element of intimacy that was very precious; and, for fear some other young girl might appear who would please the Marquis, he had brought about the return of his own daughter in order to hasten events.

Madame de Mortemain, foreseeing and divining his plans, lent him her silent complicity; and on that very day, although she had not been informed of the sudden return of the young girl, she had made an appointment with her nephew to meet her at the Guilleroys, so that he might gradually become accustomed to visit that house frequently.

For the first time, the Count and the Duchess spoke of their mutual desires in veiled terms; and when they parted, a treaty of alliance had been concluded.

At the other end of the room everyone was laughing at a story M. de Musadieu was telling to the Baroness de Corbelle about the presentation of a negro ambassador to the President of the Republic, when the Marquis de Farandal was announced.

He appeared in the doorway and paused. With a quick and familiar gesture, he placed a monocle on his right eye and left it there, as if to reconnoiter the room he was about to enter, but perhaps to give those that were already there the time to see him and to observe his entrance. Then by an imperceptible movement of cheek and eyebrow, he allowed to drop the bit of glass at the end of a black silk hair, and advanced quickly toward Madame de Guilleroy, whose extended hand he kissed, bowing very low. He saluted his aunt likewise, then shook hands with the rest of the company, going from one to another with easy elegance of manner.

He was a tall fellow, with a red moustache, and was already slightly bald, with the figure of an officer and the gait of an English sportsman. It was evident, at first sight of him, that all his limbs were better exercised than his head, and that he cared only for such occupations as developed strength and physical activity. He had some education, however, for he had learned, and was learning every day, by much mental effort, a great deal that would be useful to him to know later: history, studying dates unweariedly, but mistaking the lesson to be learned from facts and the elementary notions of political economy necessary to a deputy, the A B C of sociology for the use of the ruling classes.

Musadieu esteemed him, saying: “He will be a valuable man.” Bertin appreciated his skill and his vigor. They went to the same fencing-hall, often hunted together, and met while riding in the avenues of the Bois. Between them, therefore, had been formed a sympathy of similar tastes, that instinctive free-masonry which creates between two men a subject of conversation, as agreeable to one as to the other.

When the Marquis was presented to Annette de Guilleroy, he immediately had a suspicion of his aunt’s designs, and after saluting her he ran his eyes over her, with the rapid glance of a connoisseur.

He decided that she was graceful, and above all full of promise, for he had led so many cotillions that he knew young girls well, and could predict almost to a certainty the future of their beauty, as an expert who tastes a wine as yet too new.

He exchanged only a few unimportant words with her, then seated himself near the Baroness de Corbelle, so that he could chat with her in an undertone.

Everyone took leave at an early hour, and when all had gone, when the child was in her bed, the lamps were extinguished, the servants gone to their own quarters, the Comte de Guilleroy, walking across the drawing-room, lighted now by only two candles, detained for a long time the Countess, who was half asleep in an armchair, to tell her of his hopes, to suggest the attitude for themselves to assume, to forecast all combinations, the chances and the precautions to be taken.

It was late when he retired, charmed, however, with this evening, and murmuring, "I believe that that affair is a certainty."

CHAPTER III

A FLAME REKINDLED

"When will you come, my friend? I have not seen you for three days, and that seems a long time to me. My daughter occupies much of my time, but you know that I can no longer do without you."

The painter, who was drawing sketches, ever seeking a new subject re-read the Countess's note, then, opening the drawer of a writing-desk, he deposited it on a heap of other letters, which had been accumulating there since the beginning of their love-affair.

Thanks to the opportunities given them by the customs of fashionable society, they had grown used to seeing each other almost every day. Now and then she visited him, and sat for an hour or two in the armchair in which she had posed, while he worked. But, as she had some fear of the criticisms of the servants, she preferred to receive him at her own house, or to meet him elsewhere, for that daily interview, that small change of love.

These meetings would be agreed upon beforehand, and always seemed perfectly natural to M. de Guilleroy.

Twice a week at least the painter dined at the Countess's house, with a few friends; on Monday nights he visited her in her box at the Opera; then they would agree upon a meeting at such or such a house, to which chance led them at the same hour. He knew the evenings that she did not go out, and would call then to have a cup of tea with her, feeling himself very much at home even near the folds of her robe, so tenderly and so surely settled in that ripe affection, so fixed in the habit of finding her somewhere, of passing some time by her side, or exchanging a few words with her and of mingling a few thoughts, that he felt, although the glow of his passion had long since faded, an incessant need of seeing her.

The desire for family life, for a full and animated household, for the family table, for those evenings when one talks without fatigue with old friends, that desire for contact, for familiarity, for human intercourse, which dwells dormant in every human heart, and which every old bachelor carries from door to door to his friends, where he installs something of himself, added a strain of egoism to his sentiments of affection. In that house, where he was loved and spoiled, where he found everything, he could still rest and nurse his solitude.

For three days he had not seen his friends, who must be very much occupied by the return of the daughter of the house; and he was already feeling bored, and even a little offended because they had not sent for him sooner, but not wishing, as a matter of discretion, to be the first to make an approach.

The Countess's letter aroused him like the stroke of a whip. It was three o'clock in the afternoon. He decided to go immediately to her house, that he might find her before she went out.

The valet appeared, summoned by the sound of Olivier's bell.

"What sort of weather is it, Joseph?"

"Very fine, Monsieur."

"Warm?"

"Yes, Monsieur."

"White waistcoat, blue jacket, gray hat."

He always dressed with elegance, but although his tailor turned him out in correct styles, the very way in which he wore his clothes, his manner of walking, his comfortable proportions encased in a white waistcoat, his high gray felt hat, tilted a little toward the back of his head, seemed to reveal at once that he was both an artist and a bachelor.

When he reached the Countess's house, he was told that she was dressing for a drive in the Bois. He was a little vexed at this, and waited.

According to his habit, he began to pace to and fro in the drawing-room, going from one seat to another, or from the windows to the wall, in the large drawing-room darkened by the curtains. On the light tables with gilded feet, trifles of various kinds, useless, pretty, and costly, lay scattered about in studied disorder. There were little antique boxes of chased gold, miniature snuff-boxes, ivory statuettes, objects in dull silver, quite modern, of an exaggerated severity, in which English taste appeared: a diminutive kitchen stove, and upon it a cat drinking from a pan, a cigarette-case simulating a loaf of bread, a coffee-pot to hold matches, and in a casket a complete set of doll's jewelry—necklaces, bracelets, rings, brooches, ear-rings set with diamonds, sapphires, rubies, emeralds, a microscopic fantasy that seemed to have been executed by Lilliputian jewelers.

From time to time he touched some object, given by himself on some anniversary; he lifted it, handled it, examining it with dreamy indifference, then put it back in its place.

In one corner some books that were luxuriously bound but seldom opened lay within easy reach on a round table with a single leg for a foundation, which stood before a little curved sofa. The Revue des Deux Mondes lay there also, somewhat worn, with turned-down pages, as if it had been read and re-read many times; other publications lay near it, some of them uncut: the Arts modernes, which is bought only because of its cost, the subscription price being four hundred francs a year; and the Feuille libre, a thin volume between blue covers, in which appear the more recent poets, called "les enerves."

Between the windows stood the Countess's writing-desk, a coquettish piece of furniture of the last century, on which she wrote replies to those hurried questions handed to her during her receptions. A few books were on that, also, familiar books, index to the heart and mind of a woman: Musset, Manon Lescaut, Werther; and, to show that she was not a stranger to the complicated sensations and mysteries of psychology, Les Fleurs du Mal, Le Rouge et le Noir, La Femme au XVIII Siecle, Adolphe.

Beside the books lay a charming hand-mirror, a masterpiece of the silversmith's art, the glass being turned down upon a square of embroidered velvet, in order to allow one to admire the curious gold and silver workmanship on the back. Bertin took it up and looked at his own reflection. For some years he had been growing terribly old in appearance, and although he thought that his face showed more originality than when he was younger, the sight of his heavy cheeks and increasing wrinkles saddened him.

A door opened behind him.

"Good morning, Monsieur Bertin," said Annette.

"Good morning, little one; are you well?"

"Very well; and you?"

"What, are you not saying 'thou' to me, then, after all?"

"No, indeed! It would really embarrass me."

"Nonsense!"

"Yes, it would. You make me feel timid."

"And why, pray?"

"Because—because you are neither young enough nor old enough—"

The painter laughed.

"After such a reason as that I will insist no more."

She blushed suddenly, up to the white brow, where the waves of hair began to ripple, and resumed, with an air of slight confusion:

"Mamma told me to say to you that she will be down immediately, and to ask you whether you will go to the Bois de Boulogne with us."

"Yes, certainly. You are alone?"

"No; with the Duchesse de Mortemain."

"Very well; I will go."

"Then will you allow me to go and put on my hat?"

"Yes, go, my child."

As Annette left the room the Countess entered, veiled, ready to set forth. She extended her hands cordially.

"We never see you any more. What are you doing?" she inquired.

"I did not wish to trouble you just at this time," said Bertin.

In the tone with which she spoke the word "Olivier!" she expressed all her reproaches and all her attachment.

"You are the best woman in the world," he said, touched by the tender intonation of his name.

This little love-quarrel being finished and settled, the Countess resumed her light, society tone.

"We shall pick up the Duchess at her hotel and then make a tour of the Bois. We must show all that sort of thing to Nanette, you know."

The landau awaited them under the porte-cochere.

Bertin seated himself facing the two ladies, and the carriage departed, the pawing of the horses making a resonant sound against the over-arching roof of the porte-cochere.

Along the grand boulevard descending toward the Madeleine all the gaiety of the springtime seemed to have fallen upon the tide of humanity.

The soft air and the sunshine lent to the men a festive air, to the women a suggestion of love; the bakers' boys deposited their baskets on the benches to run and play with their brethren, the street urchins; the dogs appeared in a great hurry to go somewhere; the canaries hanging in the boxes of the concierges trilled loudly; only the ancient cab-horses kept their usual sedate pace.

"Oh, what a beautiful day! How good it is to live!" murmured the Countess.

The painter contemplated both mother and daughter in the dazzling light. Certainly, they were different, but at the same time so much alike that the latter was veritably a continuation of the former, made of the same blood, the same flesh, animated by the same life. Their eyes, above all, those blue eyes flecked with tiny black drops, of such a brilliant blue in the daughter, a little faded in the mother, fixed upon him a look so similar that he expected to hear them make the same replies. And he was surprised to discover, as he made them laugh and talk, that before him were two very distinct women, one who had lived and one who was about to live. No, he did not foresee what would become of that child when her young mind, influenced by tastes and instincts that were as yet dormant, should have expanded and developed amid the life of the world. This was a pretty little new person, ready for chances and for love, ignored and ignorant, who was sailing out of port like a vessel, while her mother was returning, having traversed life and having loved!

He was touched at the thought that she had chosen himself, and that she preferred him still, this woman who had remained so pretty, rocked in that landau, in the warm air of springtime.

As he expressed his gratitude to her in a glance, she divined it, and he thought he could feel her thanks in the rustle of her robe.

In his turn he murmured: "Oh, yes, what a beautiful day!"

When they had taken up the Duchess, in the Rue de Varenne, they spun along at a swift pace toward the Invalides, crossed the Seine, and reached the Avenue des Champs-Elysees, going up toward the Arc de triomphe de l'Etoile in the midst of a sea of carriages.

The young girl was seated beside Olivier, riding backward, and she opened upon this stream of equipages wide and wondering eager eyes. Occasionally, when the Duchess and the Countess acknowledged a salutation with a short movement of the head, she would ask "Who is that?" Bertin answered: "The Pontaiglin," "the Puicelci," "the Comtesse de Lochrist," or "the beautiful Madame Mandeliere."

Now they were following the Avenue of the Bois de Boulogne, amid the noise and the rattling of wheels. The carriages, a little less crowded than below the Arc de Triomphe, seemed to struggle in an endless race. The cabs, the heavy landaus, the solemn eight-spring vehicles, passed one another over and over again, distanced suddenly by a rapid victoria, drawn by a single trotter, bearing along at a reckless pace, through all that rolling throng, bourgeois and aristocratic, through all societies, all classes, all hierarchies, an indolent young woman, whose bright and striking toilette diffused among the carriages it touched in passing a strange perfume of some unknown flower.

"Who is that lady?" Annette inquired.

"I don't know," said Bertin, at which reply the Duchess and the Countess exchanged a smile.

The leaves were opening, the familiar nightingales of that Parisian garden were singing already among the tender verdure, and when, as the carriage approached the lake, it joined the long file of other vehicles at a walk, there was an incessant exchange of salutations, smiles, and friendly words, as the wheels touched. The procession seemed now like the gliding of a flotilla in which were seated very well-bred ladies and gentlemen. The Duchess, who was bowing every moment before raised hats or inclined heads, appeared to be passing them in review, calling to mind what she knew, thought, or supposed of these people, as they defiled before her.

"Look, dearest, there is the lovely Madame Mandeliere again—the beauty of the Republic."

In a light and dashing carriage, the beauty of the Republic allowed to be admired, under an apparent indifference to this indisputable glory, her large dark eyes, her low brow beneath a veil of dusky hair, and her mouth, which was a shade too obstinate in its lines.

"Very beautiful, all the same," said Bertin.

The Countess did not like to hear him praise other women. She shrugged her shoulders slightly, but said nothing.

But the young girl, in whom the instinct of rivalry suddenly awoke, ventured to say: "I do not find her beautiful at all."

"What! You do not think her beautiful?" said the painter.

"No; she looks as if she had been dipped in ink."

The Duchess, delighted, burst into laughter.

"Bravo, little one!" she cried. "For the last six years half the men in Paris have been swooning at the feet of that negress! I believe that they sneer at us. Look at the Comtesse de Lochrist instead."

Alone, in a landau with a white poodle, the Countess, delicate as a miniature, a blond with brown eyes, whose grace and beauty had served for five or six years as the theme for the admiration of her partisans, bowed to the ladies, with a fixed smile on her lips.

But Nanette exhibited no greater enthusiasm than before.

"Oh," she said, "she is no longer young!"

Bertin, who usually did not at all agree with the Countess in the daily discussions of these two rivals, felt a sudden irritation at the stupid intolerance of this little simpleton.

"Nonsense!" he said. "Whether one likes her or not, she is charming; and I only hope that you may become as pretty as she."

"Pooh! pooh!" said the Duchess. "You notice women only after they have passed the thirtieth year. The child is right. You admire only passee beauty."

"Pardon me!" he exclaimed; "a woman is really beautiful only after maturing, when the expression of her face and eyes has become fully developed!"

He enlarged upon this idea that the first youthful freshness is only the gloss of riper beauty; he demonstrated that men of the world were wise in paying but little attention to young girls in their first season, and that they were right in proclaiming them beautiful only when they passed into their later period of bloom.

The Countess, flattered, murmured: "He is right; he speaks as an artist. The youthful countenance is very charming, but it is always a trifle commonplace."

The painter continued to urge his point, indicating at what moment a face that was losing, little by little, the undecided grace of youth, really assumed its definite form, its true character and physiognomy.

At each word the Countess said "Yes," with a little nod of conviction; and the more he affirmed, with all the heat of a lawyer making a plea, with the animation of the accused pleading his own cause, the more she approved, by glance and gesture, as if they two were allied against some danger, and must defend themselves against some false and menacing opinion. Annette hardly heard them, she was so engrossed in looking about her. Her usually smiling face had become grave, and she said no more, carried away by the pleasure of the rapid driving. The sunlight, the trees, the carriage, this delightful life, so rich and gay—all this was for her!

Every day she might come here, recognized in her turn, saluted and envied; and perhaps the men, in pointing her out to one another, would say that she was beautiful. She noticed all those that appeared to her distinguished among the throng and inquired their names, without thinking of anything beyond the mere sound of the syllables, though sometimes they awoke in her an echo of respect and admiration, when she realized that she had seen them often in the newspapers or heard stories concerning them. She could not become accustomed to this long procession of celebrities; it seemed unreal to her, as if she were a part of some stage spectacle. The cabs filled her with disdain mingled with disgust; they annoyed and irritated her, and suddenly she said:

"I think they should not allow anything but private carriages to come here."

"Indeed, Mademoiselle!" said Bertin; "and then what becomes of our equality, liberty and fraternity?"

Annette made a moue that signified "Don't talk about that!" and continued:

"They should have a separate drive for cabs—that of Vincennes, for instance."

"You are behind the times, little one, and evidently do not know that we are swimming in the full tide of democracy. But, if you wish to see this place free from any mingling of the middle class, come in the morning, and then you will find only the fine flower of society."

He proceeded to describe graphically, as he knew well how to do, the Bois in the morning hours with its gay cavaliers and fair Amazons, that club where everyone knows everyone else by their Christian names, their pet names, their family connections, titles, qualities, and vices, as if they all lived in the same neighborhood or in the same small town.

"Do you come here often at that hour?" Annette inquired.

"Very often; there is no more charming place in Paris."

"Do you come on horseback in the mornings?"

"Yes."

"And in the afternoon you pay visits?"

"Yes."

"Then, when do you work?"

"Oh, I work—sometimes; and besides, you see, I have chosen a special entertainment suited to my tastes. As I paint the portraits of beautiful women, it is necessary that I should see them and follow them everywhere."

"On foot and on horseback!" murmured Annette, with a perfectly serious face.

He threw her a sidelong glance of appreciation, which seemed to say: "Ah! you are witty, even now! You will do very well."

A breath of cold air from far away, from the country that was hardly awake as yet, swept over the park, and the whole Bois, coquettish, frivolous, and fashionable, shivered under its chill. For some seconds it caused the tender leaves to tremble on the trees, and garments on shoulders. All the women, with a movement almost simultaneous, drew up over their arms and chests their wraps lying behind them; and the horses began to trot, from one end of the avenue to the other, as if the keen wind had flicked them like a whip.

The Countess's party returned quickly, to the silvery jingle of the harness, under the slanting red rays of the setting sun.

"Shall you go home?" inquired the Countess of Bertin, with whose habits she was familiar.

"No, I am going to the club."

"Then, shall we set you down there in passing?"

"Thank you, that will be very convenient."

"And when shall you invite us to breakfast with the Duchess?"

"Name your day."

This painter in ordinary to the fair Parisians, whom his admirers christened "a Watteau realist" and his detractors a "photographer of gowns and mantles," often received at breakfast or at dinner the beautiful persons whose feature he had reproduced, as well as the celebrated and the well known, who found very amusing these little entertainments in a bachelor's establishment.

"The day after to-morrow, then. Will the day after to-morrow suit you, my dear Duchess?" asked Madame de Guilleroy.

"Yes, indeed; you are charming! Monsieur Bertin never thinks of me when he has his little parties. It is quite evident that I am no longer young."

The Countess, accustomed to consider the artist's home almost the same as her own, replied:

"Only we four, the four of the landau—the Duchess, Annette, you and I, eh, great artist?"

"Only ourselves," said he, alighting from the carriage, "and I will have prepared for you some crabs a l'alsacienne."

"Oh, you will awaken a desire for luxury in the little one!"

He bowed to them, standing beside the carriage door, then entered quickly the vestibule of the main entrance to the club, threw his topcoat and cane to a group of footmen, who had risen like soldiers at the passing of an officer; mounted the broad stairway, meeting another brigade of servants in knee-breeches, pushed open a door, feeling himself suddenly as alert as a young man, as he heard at the end of the corridor a continuous clash of foils, the sound of stamping feet, and loud exclamations: "Touche!" "A moi." "Passe!" "J'en ai!" "Touche!" "A vous!"

In the fencing-hall the swordsmen, dressed in gray linen, with leather vests, their trousers tight around the ankles, a sort of apron falling over the front of the body, one arm in the air, with the hand thrown backward, and in the other hand, enormous in a large fencing-glove, the thin, flexible foil, extended and recovered with the agile swiftness of mechanical jumping-jacks.

Others rested and chatted, still out of breath, red and perspiring, with handkerchief in hand to wipe off faces and necks; others, seated on a square divan that ran along the four sides of the hall, watched the fencing—Liverdy against Landa, and the master of the club, Taillade, against the tall Rocdiane.

Bertin, smiling, quite at home, shook hands with several men.

"I choose you!" cried the Baron de Baverie.

"I am with you, my dear fellow," said Bertin, passing into the dressing-room to prepare himself.

He had not felt so agile and vigorous for a long time, and, guessing that he should fence well that day, he hurried as impatiently as a schoolboy ready for play. As soon as he stood before his adversary he attacked him with great ardor, and in ten minutes he had touched him eleven times and had so fatigued him that the Baron cried for quarter. Then he fenced with Punisimont, and with his colleague, Amaury Maldant.

The cold douche that followed, freezing his palpitating flesh, reminded him of the baths of his twentieth year, when he used to plunge head first into the Seine from the bridges in the suburbs, in order to amaze the bourgeois passers-by.

"Shall you dine here?" inquired Maldant.

"Yes."

"We have a table with Liverdy, Rocdiane, and Landa; make haste; it is a quarter past seven."

The dining-room was full, and there was a continuous hum of men's voices.

There were all the nocturnal vagabonds of Paris, idlers and workers, all those who from seven o'clock in the evening know not what to do and dine at the club, ready to catch at anything or anybody that chance may offer to amuse them.

When the five friends were seated the banker Liverdy, a vigorous and hearty man of forty, said to Bertin:

"You were in fine form this evening."

"Yes, I could have done surprising things to-day," Bertin replied.

The others smiled, and the landscape painter, Amaury Maldant, a thin little bald-headed man with a gray beard, said, with a sly expression:

"I, too, always feel the rising of the sap in April; it makes me bring forth a few leaves—half a dozen at most—then it runs into sentiment; there never is any fruit."

The Marquis de Rocdiane and the Comte Landa sympathized with him. Both were older than he, though even a keen eye could not guess their age; clubmen, horsemen, swordsmen, whose incessant exercise had given them bodies of steel, they boasted of being younger in every way than the enervated good-for-nothings of the new generation.

Rocdiane, of good family, with the entree to all salons, though suspected of financial intrigues of many kinds (which, according to Bertin, was not surprising, since he had lived so much in the gaming-houses), married, but separated from his wife, who paid him an annuity, a director of Belgian and Portuguese banks, carried boldly upon his energetic, Don Quixote-like face the somewhat tarnished honor of a gentleman, which was occasionally brightened by the blood from a thrust in a duel.

The Comte de Landa, a good-natured colossus, proud of his figure and his shoulders, although married and the father of two children, found it difficult to dine at home three times a week; he remained at the club on the other days, with his friends, after the session in the fencing-hall.

"The club is a family," he said, "the family of those who as yet have none, of those who never will have one, and of those who are bored by their own."

The conversation branched off on the subject of women, glided from anecdotes to reminiscences, from reminiscences to boasts, and then to indiscreet confidences.

The Marquis de Rocdiane allowed the names of his inamoratas to be guessed by unmistakable hints—society women whose names he did not utter, so that their identity might be the better surmised. The banker Liverdy indicated his flames by their first names. He would say: "I was at that time the best of friends with the wife of a diplomat. Now, one evening when I was leaving her, I said to her, 'My little Marguerite'"—then he checked himself, amid the smiles of his fellows, adding "Ha! I let something slip. One should form a habit of calling all women Sophie."

Olivier Bertin, very reserved, was accustomed to declare, when questioned:

"For my part, I content myself with my models."

They pretended to believe him, and Landa, who was frankly a libertine, grew quite excited at the idea of all the pretty creatures that walked the streets and all the young persons who posed undraped before the painter at ten francs an hour.

As the bottle became empty, all these gray-beards, as the younger members of the club called them, acquired red faces, and their kindling ardor awakened new desires.

Rocdiane, after the coffee, became still more indiscreet, and forgot the society women to celebrate the charms of simple cocottes.

"Paris!" said he, a glass of kummel in his hand, "The only city where a man never grows old, the only one where, at fifty, if he is sound and well preserved, he will always find a young girl, as pretty as an angel, to love him."

Landa, finding again his Rocdiane after the liqueurs, applauded him enthusiastically, and mentioned the young girls who still adored him every day.

But Liverdy, more skeptical, and pretending to know exactly what women were worth, murmured: "Yes, they tell you that they adore you!"

"They prove it to me, my dear fellow," exclaimed Landa.

"Such proofs don't count."

"They suffice me!"

"But, sacrebleu! they do mean it," cried Rocdiane. "Do you believe that a pretty little creature of twenty, who has been going the rounds in Paris for five or six years already, where all our moustaches have taught her kisses and spoiled her taste for them, still knows how to distinguish a man of thirty from a man of sixty? Pshaw! what nonsense! She has seen and known too many of them. Now, I'll wager that, down in the bottom of her heart, she actually prefers an old banker to a young stripling. Does she know or reflect upon that? Have men any age here? Oh, my dear fellow, we grow young as we grow gray, and the whiter our hair becomes the more they tell us they love us, the more they show it, and the more they believe it."

They rose from the table, their blood warmed and lashed by alcohol, ready to make any conquest; and they began to deliberate how to spend the evening, Bertin mentioning the Cirque, Rocdiane the Hippodrome, Maldant the Eden, and Landa the Folies-Bergere, when a light and distant sound of the tuning of violins reached their ears.

"Ah, there is music at the club to-day, it seems," said Rocdiane.

"Yes," Bertin replied. "Shall we listen for ten minutes before going out?"

"Agreed."

They crossed a salon, a billiard-room, a card-room, and finally reached a sort of box over the gallery of the musicians. Four gentlemen, ensconced in armchairs, were waiting there already, in easy attitudes, while below, among rows of empty seats, a dozen others were chatting, sitting or standing.

The conductor tapped his desk with his bow; the music began.

Olivier adored music as an opium-eater adores opium. It made him dream.

As soon as the sonorous wave from the instruments reached him he felt himself borne away in a sort of nervous intoxication, which thrilled body and mind indescribably. His imagination ran riot, made drunk by melody, and carried him along through sweet dreams and charming reveries. With closed eyes, legs crossed, and folded arms, he listened to the strains, and gave himself up to the visions that passed before his eyes and into his mind.

The orchestra was playing one of Haydn's symphonies, and when Bertin's eyelids drooped over his eyes, he saw again the Bois, the crowd of carriages around him, and facing him in the landau the Countess and her daughter. He heard their voices, followed their words, felt the movement of the carriage, inhaled the air, filled with the odor of young leaves.

Three times, his neighbor, speaking to him, interrupted this vision, which three times he began again, as the rolling of the vessel seems to continue when, after crossing the ocean, one lies motionless in bed.

Then it extended itself to a long voyage, with the two women always seated before him, sometimes on the railway, again at the table of strange hotels. During the whole execution of the symphony they accompanied him, as if, while driving with him in the sunshine, they had left the image of their two faces imprinted on his vision.

Silence followed; then came a noise of seats being moved and chattering of voices, which dispelled this vapor of a dream, and he perceived, dozing around him, his four friends, relaxed from a listening attitude to the comfortable posture of sleep.

"Well, what shall we do now?" he asked, after he had roused them.

"I should like to sleep here a little longer," replied Rocdiane frankly.

"And I, too," said Landa.

Bertin rose.

"Well, I shall go home," he said. "I am rather tired."

He felt very animated, on the contrary, but he wished to go, fearing the end of the evening around the baccarat-table of the club, which unfortunately he knew so well.

He went home, therefore, and the following day, after a nervous night, one of those nights that put artists in that condition of cerebral activity called inspiration, he decided not to go out, but to work until evening.

It was an excellent day, one of those days of facile production, when ideas seem to descend into the hands and fix themselves upon the canvas.

With doors shut, far from the world, in the quiet of his own dwelling, closed to everyone, in the friendly peace of his studio, with clear eye, lucid mind, enthusiastic, alert, he tasted that happiness given only to artists, the happiness of bringing forth their work in joy. Nothing existed any more for him in such hours of work except the piece of canvas on which was born an image under the caress of his brush; and he experienced, in these crises of productiveness, a strange and delicious sensation of abounding life which intoxicated him. When evening came he was exhausted as by healthful fatigue, and went to sleep with agreeable anticipation of his breakfast the next morning.

The table was covered with flowers, the menu was carefully chosen, for Madame de Guilleroy's sake, as she was a refined epicure; and in spite of strong but brief resistance, the painter compelled his guests to drink champagne.

"The little one will get intoxicated," protested the Countess.

"Dear me! there must be a first time," replied the indulgent Duchess.

Everyone, as the party returned to the studio, felt stirred by that light gaiety which lifts one as if the feet had wings.

The Duchess and the Countess, having an engagement at a meeting of the Committee of French Mothers, were to take Annette home before going to the meeting; but Bertin offered to take her for a walk, and then to the Boulevard Malesherbes; so both ladies left them.

"Let us take the longest way," said Annette.

"Would you like to stroll about the Monceau Park?" asked Bertin. "It is a very pretty place; we will look at the babies and nurses."

"Yes, I should like that."

They passed through the Avenue Velasquez and entered the gilded and monumental gate that serves as a sign and an entrance to that exquisite jewel of a park, displaying in the heart of Paris its verdant and artificial beauty, surrounded by a belt of princely mansions.

Along the wide walks, which unroll their massive and artistic curves through grassy lawns, throngs of people, sitting on iron chairs, watch the passers; while in the little paths, deep in shade and winding like streams, groups of children crawl in the sand, run about, or jump the rope under the indolent eyes of nurses or the anxious watchfulness of mothers. Two enormous trees, rounded into domes, like monuments of leaves, the gigantic horse-chestnuts, whose heavy verdure is lighted up by red and white clusters, the showy sycamores, the graceful plane-trees with their trunks designedly polished, set off in a charming perspective the tall, undulating grass.

The weather was warm, the turtle-doves were cooing among the branches, and flying to meet one another from the tree-tops, while the sparrows bathed in the rainbow formed by the sunshine and the spray thrown over the smooth turf. White statues on their pedestals seemed happy in the midst of the green freshness. A little marble boy was drawing from his foot an invisible thorn, as if he had just pricked himself in running after the Diana fleeing toward the little lake, imprisoned by the woods that screened the ruins of a temple.

Other statues, amorous and cold, embraced one another on the borders of the groves, or dreamed there, holding one knee in the hand. A cascade foamed and rolled over the pretty rocks; a tree, truncated like a column, supported an ivy; a tombstone bore an inscription. The stone shafts erected on the lawns hardly suggest better the Acropolis than this elegant little park recalled wild forests. It is the charming and artificial place where city people go to look at flowers grown in hot-houses, and to admire, as one admires the spectacle of life at the theater, that agreeable representation of the beauties of nature given in the heart of Paris.

Olivier Bertin had come almost every day for years to this favorite spot to look at the fair Parisians moving in their appropriate setting. "It is a park made for toilettes," he would say; "Badly dressed people are horrible in it." He would rove about there for hours, knowing all the plants and all the habitual visitors.

He now strolled beside Annette along the avenues, his eye distracted by the motley and animated crowd in the gardens.

"Oh, the little love!" exclaimed Annette. She was gazing at a tiny boy with blond curls, who was looking at her with his blue eyes full of surprise and delight.

Then she passed all the children in review, and the pleasure she felt in seeing those living dolls, decked out in their dainty ribbons, made her talkative and communicative.

She walked slowly, chatting to Bertin, giving him her reflections on the children, the nurses, and the mothers. The larger children drew from her little exclamations of joy, while the little pale ones touched her sympathy.

Bertin listened, more amused by her than by the little ones, and, always remembering his work, he murmured, "That is delicious!" thinking that he must make an exquisite picture, with one corner of this park and a bouquet of nurses, mothers and children. Why had he never thought of it before?

"You like those little ones?" he inquired.

"I adore them!"

He felt, from her manner of looking at them, that she longed to take them in her arms, to hug and kiss them—the natural and tender longing of a future mother; and he was surprised at this secret instinct hidden in this little woman.

As she appeared ready to talk, he questioned her about her tastes. She admitted, with pretty naivete, that she had hopes of social success and glory, and that she desired to have fine horses, which she knew almost as well as a horse-dealer, for a part of the farm at Roncieres was devoted to breeding; but she appeared to trouble her head no more about a fiance than one is concerned about an apartment, which is always to be found among the multitude of houses to rent.

They approached the lake, where two swans and six ducks were quietly floating, as clean and calm as porcelain birds, and they passed before a young woman sitting in a chair, with an open book lying on her knees, her eyes gazing upward, her soul having apparently taken flight in a dream.

She was as motionless as a wax figure. Plain, humble, dressed as a modest girl who has no thought of pleasing, she had gone to the land of Dreams, carried away by a phrase or a word that had bewitched her heart. Undoubtedly she was continuing, according to the impulse of her hopes, the adventure begun in the book.

Bertin paused, surprised. "How beautiful to dream like that!" said he.

They had passed before her; now they turned and passed her again without her perceiving them, so attentively did she follow the distant flight of her thought.

"Tell me, little one," said the painter to Annette, "would it bore you very much to pose for me once or twice?"

"No, indeed! Quite the contrary."

"Look well at that young lady who is roaming in the world of fancy."

"The lady there, in that chair?"

"Yes. Well, you, too, will sit on a chair, you will have an open book on your knee, and you will try to do as she does. Have you ever had daydreams?"

"Yes, indeed."

"Of what?"

He tried to confess her as to her aerial flights, but she would make no reply, evaded his questions, looked at the ducks swimming after some bread thrown to them by a lady, and seemed embarrassed, as if he had touched upon a subject that was a sensitive point with her.

Then, to change the conversation, she talked about her life at Roncieres, spoke of her grandmother, to whom she read aloud a long time every day, and who must now feel very lonely and sad.

As he listened, the painter felt as gay as a bird, gay as he never had been. All that she had said, all the doings, the trifling everyday details of the simple life of a young girl, amused and interested him.

"Let us sit down," he said.

They seated themselves near the water, and the two swans came floating toward them, expecting some fresh dainty.

Bertin felt recollections awakening within him—those faded remembrances that are drowned in forgetfulness, and which suddenly return, one knows not why. They surged up rapidly, of all sorts, and so numerous at the same time that it seemed to him a hand was stirring the miry depths of his memory.

He tried to guess the reasons of this rising up of his former life which several times already, though never so insistently as to-day, he had felt and remarked. A cause always existed for these sudden evocations—a natural and simple cause, an odor, perhaps, often a perfume. How many times a woman's draperies had thrown to him in passing, with the evaporating breath of some essence, a host of forgotten events. At the bottom of old perfume-bottles he had often found bits of his former existence; and all wandering odors—of streets, fields, houses, furniture, sweet or unsavory, the warm odors of summer evenings, the cold breath of winter nights, revived within him far-off reminiscences, as if odors kept embalmed within him these dead-and-gone memories, as aromatics preserve mummies.

Was it the damp grass or the chestnut blossoms that thus reanimated the past? No. What, then?

Was it his eye to which he owed this alertness? What had he seen? Nothing. Among the persons he had met, perhaps one might have resembled some one he had known, and, although he had not recognized it, it might have rung in his heart all the chords of the past.

Was it not a sound, rather? Very often he had heard by chance a piano, an unknown voice, even a hand-organ in the street playing some old air, which had suddenly made him feel twenty years younger, filling his breast with tender recollections, long buried.

But this appeal, continued, incessant, intangible, almost irritating! What was there near him to revive thus his extinct emotions?

"It is growing a little cool; we must go home," he said.

They rose, and resumed their walk.

He looked at the poor people sitting on benches, for whom a chair was too great an expense.

Annette also observed them, and felt disturbed at the thought of their lives, their occupations, surprised that they should come to lounge in this beautiful public garden, when their own appearance was so forlorn.

More than ever was Olivier now dreaming over past years. It seemed to him that a fly was humming in his ear, filling it with a buzzing song of bygone days.

The young girl, observing his dreamy air, asked:

"What is the matter? You seem sad."

His heart thrilled within him. Who had said that? She or her mother? Not her mother with her present voice but with her voice of long ago, so changed that he had only just recognized it.

"Nothing," he replied, smiling. "You entertain me very much; you are very charming, and you remind me of your mother."

How was it that he had not sooner remarked this strange echo of a voice once so familiar, now coming from these fresh lips?

"Go on talking," he said.

"Of what?"

"Tell me what your teachers have taught you. Did you like them?"

She began again to chat pleasantly. He listened, stirred by a growing anxiety; he watched and waited to detect, among the phrases of this young girl, almost a stranger to his heart, a word, a sound, a laugh, that seemed to have been imprisoned in her throat since her mother's youth. Certain intonations made him tremble with astonishment. Of course there were differences in their tones, the resemblance of which he had not remarked immediately, and which were in some ways so dissimilar that he had not confounded them at all; but these differences rendered all the more striking this sudden reproduction of the maternal speech. He had noted their facial resemblance with a friendly and curious eye, but now the mystery of this resuscitated voice mingled them in such a way that, turning away his head that he might no longer see the young girl, he asked himself whether it were not the Countess who was speaking thus to him, twelve years earlier.

Then when he had woven this hallucination, he turned toward her again, and found, as their eyes met, a little of the shy hesitation with which the mother's gaze had met his in the first days of their love.

They had already walked three times around the park, passing always before the same persons, the same nurses and children.

Annette was now inspecting the buildings surrounding the garden, inquiring the names of their owners. She wished to know all about them, asked questions with eager curiosity, seeming to fill her feminine mind with these details, and, with interested face, listening with her eyes as much as with her ears.

But when they arrived at the pavilion that separates the two gates of the outer boulevard, Bertin perceived that it was almost four o'clock.

"Oh," he said, "we must go home."

They walked slowly toward the Boulevard Malesherbes.

After the painter had left Annette at her home he proceeded toward the Place de la Concorde.

He sang to himself softly, longed to run, and would have been glad to jump over the benches, so agile did he feel. Paris seemed radiant to him, more beautiful than ever. "Decidedly the springtime revarnishes the whole world," was his reflection.

He was in one of those periods of mental excitement when one understands everything with more pleasure, when the vision is clearer and more comprehensive, when one feels a keener joy in seeing and feeling, as if an all-powerful hand had brightened all the colors of earth, reanimated all living creatures, and had wound up in us, as in a watch that has stopped, the activity of sensation.

He thought, as his glance took in a thousand amusing things: "And I said that there were moments when I could no longer find subjects to paint!"

He felt such a sensation of freedom and clear-sightedness that all his artistic work seemed commonplace to him, and he conceived a new way of expressing life, truer and more original; and suddenly he was seized with a desire to return home and work, so he retraced his steps and shut himself up in his studio.

But as soon as he was alone, before a newly begun picture, the ardor that had burned in his blood began to cool. He felt tired, sat down on his divan, and again gave himself up to dreaming.

The sort of happy indifference in which he lived, that carelessness of the satisfied man whose almost every need is gratified, was leaving his heart by degrees, as if something were still lacking. He realized that his house was empty and his studio deserted. Then, looking around him, he fancied he saw pass by him the shadow of a woman whose presence was sweet. For a long time he had forgotten the sensation of impatience that a lover feels when awaiting the coming of his mistress, and now he suddenly felt that she was far away, and he longed, with the ardor of a young man, to have her near him.

He was moved in thinking how much they had loved each other; and in that vast apartment he found once more, where she had come so often, innumerable reminders of her, her gestures, words, and kisses. He recalled certain days, certain hours, certain moments, and he felt around him the sweetness of her early caresses.

He got up, unable to sit quietly any longer, and began to walk, thinking again that, in spite of this intimacy that had so filled his life, he still remained alone, always alone. After the long hours of work, when he looked around him, dazed by the reawakening of the man who returns to life, he saw and felt only walls within reach of his hand and voice. Not having any woman in his home, and not being able to meet the one he loved except with the precautions of a thief, he had been compelled to spend his leisure time in public places where one finds or purchases the means of killing time. He was accustomed to going to the club, to the Cirque and the Hippodrome, on fixed days, to the Opera, and to all sorts of places, so that he should not be compelled to go home, where no doubt he would have lived in perfect happiness had he only had her beside him.

Long before, in certain hours of tender abandon, he had suffered cruelly because he could not take her and keep her with him; then, as his ardor cooled, he had accepted quietly their separation and his own liberty; now he regretted them once more, as if he were again beginning to love her. And this return of tenderness invaded his heart so suddenly, almost without reason, because the weather was fine, and possibly because a little while ago he had recognized the rejuvenated voice of that woman! How slight a thing it takes to move a man's heart, a man who is growing old, with whom remembrance turns into regret!

As in former days, the need of seeing her again came to him, entering body and mind, like a fever; and he began to think after the fashion of a young lover, exalting her in his heart, and feeling himself exalted in his desire for her; then he decided, although he had seen her only that morning, to go and ask for a cup of tea that same evening.

The hours seemed long to him, and as he set out for the Boulevard Malesherbes he was seized with a fear of not finding her, which would force him still to pass the evening alone, as he had passed so many others.

To his query: "Is the Countess at home?" the servant's answer, "Yes, Monsieur," filled him with joy.

He said, with a radiant air: "It is I again!" as he appeared at the threshold of the smaller drawing-room where the two ladies were working, under the pink shade of a double lamp of English metal, on a high and slender standard.

"What, is it you? How fortunate!" exclaimed the Countess.

"Well, yes. I feel very lonely, so I came."

"How nice of you!"

"You are expecting someone?"

"No—perhaps—I never know."

He had seated himself and now looked scornfully at the gray knitting-work that mother and daughter were swiftly making from heavy wool, working at it with long needles.

"What is that?" he asked.

"Coverlets."

"For the poor?"

"Yes, of course."

"It is very ugly."

"It is very warm."

"Possibly, but it is very ugly, especially in a Louis Fifteenth apartment, where everything else charms the eye. If not for your poor, you really ought to make your charities more elegant, for the sake of your friends."

"Oh, heavens, these men!" said the Countess, with a shrug of her shoulders. "Why, everyone is making this kind of coverlets just now."

"I know that; I know it only too well! Once cannot make an evening call now without seeing that frightful gray stuff dragged over the prettiest gowns and the most elegant furniture. Bad taste seems to be the fashion this spring."

To judge whether he spoke the truth, the Countess spread out her knitting on a silk-covered chair beside her; then she assented indifferently:

"Yes, you are right—it is ugly."

Then she resumed her work. Upon the two bent heads fell a stream of light; a rosy radiance from the lamp illumined their hair and complexions, extending to their skirts and their moving fingers. They watched their work with that attention, light but continuous, given by women to this labor of the fingers which the eye follows without a thought.

At the four corners of the room four other lamps of Chinese porcelain, borne by ancient columns of gilded wood, shed upon the hangings a soft, even light, modified by lace shades thrown over the globes.

Bertin took a very low seat, a dwarf armchair, in which he could barely seat himself, but which he had always preferred when talking with the Countess because it brought him almost at her feet.

"You took a long walk with Nane this afternoon in the park," said the Countess.

"Yes. We chatted like old friends. I like your daughter very much. She resembles you very strongly. When she pronounces certain phrases, one would believe that you had left your voice in her mouth."

"My husband has already said that very often."

He watched the two women work, bathed in the lamplight, and the thought that had often made him suffer, which had given him suffering that day, even—the recollection of his desolate home, still, silent, and cold, whatever the weather, whatever fire might be lighted in chimney or furnace—saddened him as if he now understood his bachelor's isolation for the first time.

Oh, how deeply he longed to be the husband of this woman, and not her lover! Once he had desired to carry her away, to take her from that man, to steal her altogether. To-day he was jealous of him, that deceived husband who was installed beside her forever, in the habits of her household and under the sweet influence of her presence. In looking at her he felt his heart full of old things revived, of which he wished to speak. Certainly, he still loved her very much, even a little more to-day than he had for some time; and the desire to tell her of this return of youthful feeling, which would be sure to delight her, made him wish that she would send the young girl to bed as soon as possible.

Obsessed by this strong desire to be alone with her, to sit near her and lay his head on her knee, to take the hands from which would slip the quilt for the poor, the needles, and the ball of wool, which would roll under a sofa at the end of a long, unwound thread, he looked at the time, relapsed into almost complete silence, and thought that it was a great mistake to allow young girls to pass the evening with grown-up persons.

Presently a sound of footsteps was heard in the next room, and a servant appeared at the door announcing:

"Monsieur de Musadieu."

Olivier Bertin felt a spasm of anger, and when he shook hands with the Inspector of Fine Arts he had a great desire to take him by the shoulders and throw him into the street.

Musadieu was full of news; the ministry was about to fall, and there was a whisper of scandal about the Marquis de Rocdiane. He looked at the young girl, adding: "I will tell you about that a little later."

The Countess raised her eyes to the clock and saw that it was about to strike ten.

"It is time to go to bed, my child," she said to her daughter.

Without replying, Annette folded her knitting-work, rolled up her ball of wool, kissed her mother on the cheeks, gave her hand to the two gentlemen, and departed quickly, as if she glided away without disturbing the air as she went.

"Well, what is your scandal?" her mother demanded, as soon as she had gone.

It appeared that rumor said that the Marquis de Rocdiane, amicably separated from his wife, who paid to him an allowance that he considered insufficient, had discovered a sure if singular means to double it. The Marquise, whom he had had watched, had been surprised in flagrante delictu, and was compelled to buy off, with an increased allowance, the legal proceedings instituted by the police commissioner.

The Countess listened with curious gaze, her idle hands holding the interrupted needle-work on her knee.

Bertin, who was still more exasperated by Musadieu's presence since Annette had gone, was incensed at this recital, and declared, with the indignation of one who had known of the scandal but did not wish to speak of it to anyone, that the story was an odious falsehood, one of those shameful lies which people of their world ought neither to listen to nor repeat. He appeared greatly wrought up over the matter, as he stood leaning against the mantelpiece and speaking with the excited manner of a man disposed to make a personal question of the subject under discussion.

Rocdiane was his friend, he said; and, though he might be criticised for frivolity in certain respects, no one could justly accuse him or even suspect him of any really unworthy action. Musadieu, surprised and embarrassed, defended himself, tried to explain and to excuse himself.

"Allow me to say," he remarked at last, "that I heard this story just before I came here, in the drawing-room of the Duchesse de Mortemain."

"Who told it to you? A woman, no doubt," said Bertin.

"No, not at all; it was the Marquis de Farandal."

The painter, irritated still further, retorted: "That does not astonish me—from him!"

There was a brief silence. The Countess took up her work again. Presently Olivier said in a calmer voice: "I know for a fact that that story is false."

In reality, he knew nothing whatever about it, having heard it mentioned then for the first time.

Musadieu thought it wise to prepare the way for his retreat, feeling the situation rather dangerous; and he was just beginning to say that he must pay a visit at the Corbelles' that evening when the Comte de Guilleroy appeared, returning from dining in the city.

Bertin sat down again, overcome, and despairing now of getting rid of the husband.

"You haven't heard, have you, of the great scandal that is running all over town this evening?" inquired the Count pleasantly.

As no one answered, he continued: "It seems that Rocdiane surprised his wife in a criminal situation, and has made her pay dearly for her indiscretion."

Then Bertin, with his melancholy air, with grief in voice and gesture, placing one hand on Guilleroy's shoulder, repeated in a gentle and amicable manner all that he had just said so roughly to Musadieu.

The Count, half convinced, annoyed to have allowed himself to repeat so lightly a doubtful and possibly compromising thing, pleaded his ignorance and his innocence. The gossips said so many false and wicked things!

Suddenly, all agreed upon this statement: the world certainly accused, suspected, and calumniated with deplorable facility! All four appeared to be convinced, during the next five minutes, that all the whispered scandals were lies; that the women did not have the lovers ascribed to them; that the men never committed the sins they were accused of; and, in short, that the outward appearance of things was usually much worse than the real situation.

Bertin, who no longer felt vexed with Musadieu since De Guilleroy's arrival, was now very pleasant to him, led him to talk on his favorite subjects, and opened the sluices of his eloquence. The Count wore the contented air of a man who carries everywhere with him an atmosphere of peace and cordiality.

Two servants noiselessly entered the drawing-room, bearing the tea-table, on which the boiling water steamed in a pretty, shining kettle over the blue flame of an alcohol lamp.

The Countess rose, prepared the hot beverage with the care and precaution we have learned from the Russians, then offered a cup to Musadieu, another to Bertin, following this with plates containing sandwiches of pate de foies gras and little English and Austrian cakes.

The Count approached the portable table, where was also an assortment of syrups, liqueurs, and glasses; he mixed himself a drink, then discreetly disappeared into the next room.

Bertin found himself again facing Musadieu, and felt once more the sudden desire to thrust outside this bore, who, now put on his mettle, talked at great length, told stories, repeated jests, and made some himself. The painter glanced continually at the clock, the hands of which approached midnight. The Countess noticed his glances, understood that he wished to speak to her alone, and, with that ability of a clever woman of the world to change by indescribable shades of tone the whole atmosphere of a drawing-room, to make it understood, without saying anything, whether one is to remain or to go, she diffused about her, by her attitude alone, by the bored expression of her face and eyes, a chill as if she had just opened a window.

Musadieu felt this chilly current freezing his flow of ideas; and, without asking himself the reason, he felt a sudden desire to rise and depart.

Bertin, as a matter of discretion, followed his example. The two men passed through both drawing-rooms together, followed by the Countess, who talked to the painter all the while. She detained him at the threshold of the ante-chamber to make some trifling explanation, while Musadieu, assisted by a footman, put on his topcoat. As Madame de Guilleroy continued to talk to Bertin, the Inspector of Fine Arts, having waited some seconds before the front door, held open by another servant, decided to depart himself rather than stand there facing the footman any longer.

The door was closed softly behind him, and the Countess said to the artist in a perfectly easy tone:

"Why do you go so soon? It is not yet midnight. Stay a little longer."

They reentered the smaller drawing-room together and seated themselves.

"My God! how that animal set my teeth on edge!" said Bertin.

"Why, pray?"

"He took you away from me a little."

"Oh, not very much."

"Perhaps not, but he irritated me."

"Are you jealous?"

"It is not being jealous to find a man a bore."

He had taken his accustomed armchair, and seated close beside her now he smoothed the folds of her robe with his fingers as he told her of the warm breath of tenderness that had passed through his heart that day.

The Countess listened, surprised, charmed, and gently laid her hand on his white locks, which she caressed tenderly, as if to thank him.

"I should like so much to live always near you!" he sighed.

He was thinking of her husband, who had retired to rest, asleep, no doubt, in some neighboring chamber, and he continued:

"It is undoubtedly true that marriage is the only thing that really unites two lives."

"My poor friend!" she murmured, full of pity for him and also for herself.

He had laid his cheek against the Countess's knees, and he looked up at her with a tenderness touched with sadness, less ardently than a short time before, when he had been separated from her by her daughter, her husband, and Musadieu.

"Heavens! how white your hair has grown!" said the Countess with a smile, running her fingers lightly over Olivier's head. "Your last black hairs have disappeared."

"Alas! I know it. Everything goes so soon!"

She was concerned lest she had made him sad.

"Oh, but your hair turned gray very early, you know," she said. "I have always known you with pepper-and-salt locks."

"Yes, that is true."

In order to dispel altogether the slight cloud of regret she had evoked, she leaned over him and, taking his head between her hands, kissed him slowly and tenderly on the forehead, with long kisses that seemed as if they never would end. Then they gazed into each other's eyes, seeking therein the reflection of their mutual fondness.

"I should like so much to pass a whole day with you," Bertin continued. He felt himself tormented obscurely by an inexpressible necessity for close intimacy. He had believed, only a short time ago, that the departure of those who had been present would suffice to realize the desire that had possessed him since morning; and now that he was alone with his mistress, now that he felt on his brow the touch of her hands, and, against his cheek, through the folds of her skirt, the warmth of her body, he felt the same agitation reawakened, the same longing for a love hitherto unknown and ever fleeing him. He now fancied that, away from that house—perhaps in the woods where they would be absolutely alone—this deep yearning of his heart would be calmed and satisfied.

"What a boy you are!" said the Countess. "Why, we see each other almost every day."

He begged her to devise a plan whereby she might breakfast with him, in some suburb of Paris, as she had already done four or five times.

The Countess was astonished at his caprice, so difficult to realize now that her daughter had returned. She assured him that she would try to do it as soon as her husband should go to Ronces; but that it would be impossible before the varnishing-day reception, which would take place the following Saturday.

"And until then when shall I see you?" he asked.

"To-morrow evening at the Corbelles'. Come over here Thursday, at three o'clock, if you are free; and I believe that we are to dine together with the Duchess on Friday."

"Yes, exactly."

He arose.

"Good-by!"

"Good-by, my friend."

He remained standing, unable to decide to go, for he had said almost nothing of all that he had come to say, and his mind was still full of unsaid things, his heart still swelled with vague desires which he could not express.

"Good-bye!" he repeated, taking her hands.

"Good-by, my friend!"

"I love you!"

She gave him one of those smiles with which a woman shows a man, in a single instant, all that she has given him.

With a throbbing heart he repeated for the third time, "Good-by!" and departed.

CHAPTER IV

A DOUBLE JEALOUSY

One would have said that all the carriages in Paris were making a pilgrimage to the Palais de l'Industrie that day. As early as nine o'clock in the morning they began to drive, by way of all streets, avenues, and bridges, toward that hall of the fine arts where all artistic Paris invites all fashionable Paris to be present at the pretended varnishing of three thousand four hundred pictures.

A long procession of visitors pressed through the doors, and, disdaining the exhibition of sculpture, hastened upstairs to the picture gallery. Even while mounting the steps they raised their eyes to the canvases displayed on the walls of the staircase, where they hang the special category of decorative painters who have sent canvases of unusual proportions or works that the committee dare not refuse.

In the square salon a great crowd surged and rustled. The artists, who were in evidence until evening, were easily recognized by their activity, the sonorousness of their voices, and the authority of their gestures. They drew their friends by the sleeve toward the pictures, which they pointed out with exclamations and mimicry of a connoisseur's energy. All types of artists were to be seen—tall men with long hair, wearing hats of mouse-gray or black and of indescribable shapes, large and round like roofs, with their turned-down brims shadowing the wearer's whole chest. Others were short, active, slight or stocky, wearing foulard cravats and round jackets, or the sack-like garment of the singular costume peculiar to this class of painters.

There was the clan of the fashionables, of the curious, and of artists of the boulevard; the clan of Academicians, correct, and decorated with red rosettes, enormous or microscopic, according to individual conception of elegance and good form; the clan of bourgeois painters, assisted by the family surrounding the father like a triumphal chorus.

On the four great walls the canvases admitted to the honor of the square salon dazzled one at the very entrance by their brilliant tones, glittering frames, the crudity of new color, vivified by fresh varnish, blinding under the pitiless light poured from above.

The portrait of the President of the Republic faced the entrance; while on another wall a general bedizened with gold lace, sporting a hat decorated with ostrich plumes, and wearing red cloth breeches, hung in pleasant proximity to some naked nymphs under a willow-tree, and near by was a vessel in distress almost engulfed by a great wave. A bishop of the early Church excommunicating a barbarian king, an Oriental street full of dead victims of the plague, and the Shade of Dante in Hell, seized and captivated the eye with irresistible fascination.

Other paintings in the immense room were a charge of cavalry; sharpshooters in a wood; cows in a pasture; two noblemen of the eighteenth century fighting a duel on a street corner; a madwoman sitting on a wall; a priest administering the last rites to a dying man; harvesters, rivers, a sunset, a moonlight effect—in short, samples of everything that artists paint, have painted, and will paint until the end of the world.

Olivier, in the midst of a group of celebrated brother painters, members of the Institute and of the jury, exchanged opinions with them. He was oppressed by a certain uneasiness, a dissatisfaction with his own exhibited work, of the success of which he was very doubtful, in spite of the warm congratulations he had received.

Suddenly he sprang forward; the Duchesse de Mortemain had appeared at the main entrance.

"Hasn't the Countess arrived yet?" she inquired of Bertin.

"I have not seen her."

"And Monsieur de Musadieu?"

"I have not seen him either."

"He promised me to be here at ten o'clock, at the top of the stairs, to show me around the principal galleries."

"Will you permit me to take his place, Duchess?"

"No, no. Your friends need you. We shall see each other again very soon, for I shall expect you to lunch with us."

Musadieu hastened toward them. He had been detained for some minutes in the hall of sculpture, and excused himself, breathless already.

"This way, Duchess, this way," said he. "Let us begin at the right."

They were just disappearing among the throng when the Comtesse de Guilleroy, leaning on her daughter's arm, entered and looked around in search of Olivier Bertin.

He saw them and hastened to meet them. As he greeted the two ladies, he said:

"How charming you look to-day. Really, Nanette has improved very much. She has actually changed in a week."

He regarded her with the eye of a close observer, adding: "The lines of her face are softer, yet more expressive; her complexion is clearer. She is already something less of a little girl and somewhat more of a Parisian."

Suddenly he bethought himself of the grand affair of the day.

"Let us begin at the right," said he, "and we shall soon overtake the Duchess."

The Countess, well informed on all matters connected with painting, and as preoccupied as if she were herself on exhibition, inquired: "What do they say of the exposition?"

"A fine one," Bertin replied. "There is a remarkable Bonnat, two excellent things by Carolus Duran, an admirable Puvis de Chavannes, a very new and astonishing Roll, an exquisite Gervex, and many others, by Beraud, Cazin, Duez—in short, a heap of good things."

"And you?" said the Countess.

"Oh, they compliment me, but I am not satisfied."

"You never are satisfied."

"Yes, sometimes. But to-day I really feel that I am right."

"Why?"

"I do not know."

"Let us go to see it."

When they arrived before Bertin's picture—two little peasant-girls taking a bath in a brook—they found a group admiring it. The Countess was delighted, and whispered: "It is simply a delicious bit—a jewel! You never have done anything better."

Bertin pressed close to her, loving her and thanking her for every word that calmed his suffering and healed his aching heart. Through his mind ran arguments to convince him that she was right, that she must judge accurately with the intelligent observation of an experienced Parisian. He forgot, so desirous was he to reassure himself, that for at least twelve years he had justly reproached her for too much admiring the dainty trifles, the elegant nothings, the sentimentalities and nameless trivialities of the passing fancy of the day, and never art, art alone, art detached from the popular ideas, tendencies, and prejudices.

"Let us go on," said he, drawing them away from his picture. He led them for a long time from gallery to gallery, showing them notable canvases and explaining their subjects, happy to be with them.

"What time is it?" the Countess asked suddenly.

"Half after twelve."

"Oh, let us hasten to luncheon then. The Duchess must be waiting for us at Ledoyen's, where she charged me to bring you, in case we should not meet her in the galleries."

The restaurant, in the midst of a little island of trees and shrubs, seemed like an overflowing hive. A confused hum of voices, calls, the rattling of plates and glasses came from the open windows and large doors. The tables, set close together and filled with people eating, extended in long rows right and left of a narrow passage, up and down which ran the distracted waiters, holding along their arms dishes filled with meats, fish, or fruit.

Under the circular gallery there was such a throng of men and women as to suggest a living pate. Everyone there laughed, called out, drank and ate, enlivened by the wines and inundated by one of those waves of joy that sweep over Paris, on certain days, with the sunshine.

An attendant showed the Countess, Annette, and Bertin upstairs into a reserved room, where the Duchess awaited them. As they entered, the painter observed, beside his aunt, the Marquis de Farandal, attentive and smiling, and extending his hand to receive the parasols and wraps of the Countess and her daughter. He felt again so much displeasure that he suddenly desired to say rude and irritating things.

The Duchess explained the meeting of her nephew and the departure of Musadieu, who had been carried off by the Minister of the Fine Arts, and Bertin, at the thought that this insipidly good-looking Marquis might marry Annette, that he had come there only to see her, and that he regarded her already as destined to share his bed, unnerved and revolted him, as if some one had ignored his own rights—sacred and mysterious rights.

As soon as they were at table, the Marquis, who sat beside the young girl, occupied himself in talking to her with the devoted air of a man authorized to pay his addresses.

He assumed a curious manner, which seemed to the painter bold and searching; his smiles were satisfied and almost tender, his gallantry was familiar and officious. In manner and word appeared already something of decision, as if he were about to announce that he had won the prize.

The Duchess and the Countess seemed to protect and approve this attitude of a pretender, and exchanged glances of complicity.

As soon as the luncheon was finished the party returned to the Exposition. There was such a dense crowd in the galleries, it seemed impossible to penetrate it. An odor of perspiring humanity, a stale smell of old gowns and coats, made an atmosphere at once heavy and sickening. No one looked at the pictures any more, but at faces and toilets, seeking out well-known persons; and at times came a great jostling of the crowd as it was forced to give way before the high double ladder of the varnishers, who cried: "Make way, Messieurs! Make way, Mesdames!"

At the end of ten minutes, the Countess and Olivier found themselves separated from the others. He wished to find them immediately, but, leaning upon him, the Countess said: "Are we not very well off as it is? Let them go, since it is quite natural that we should lose sight of them; we will meet them again in the buffet at four o'clock."

"That is true," he replied.

But he was absorbed by the idea that the Marquis was accompanying Annette and continuing his attempts to please her by his fatuous and affected gallantry.

"You love me always, then?" murmured the Countess.

"Yes, certainly," he replied, with a preoccupied air, trying to catch a glimpse of the Marquis's gray hat over the heads of the crowd.

Feeling that he was abstracted, and wishing to lead him back to her own train of thought, the Countess continued:

"If you only knew how I adore your picture of this year! It is certainly your chef-d'oeuvre."

He smiled, suddenly, forgetting the young people in remembering his anxiety of the morning.

"Do you really think so?" he asked.

"Yes, I prefer it above all others."

With artful wheedling, she crowned him anew, having known well for a long time that nothing has a stronger effect on an artist than tender and continuous flattery. Captivated, reanimated, cheered by her sweet words, he began again to chat gaily, seeing and hearing only her in that tumultuous throng.

By way of expressing his thanks, he murmured in her ear: "I have a mad desire to embrace you!"

A warm wave of emotion swept over her, and, raising her shining eyes to his, she repeated her question: "You love me always, then?"

He replied, with the intonation she wished to hear, and which she had not heard before:

"Yes, I love you, my dear Any."

"Come often to see me in the evenings," she said. "Now that I have my daughter I shall not go out very much."

Since she had recognized in him this unexpected reawakening of tenderness, her heart was stirred with great happiness. In view of Olivier's silvery hair, and the calming touch of time, she had not suspected that he was fascinated by another woman, but she was terribly afraid that, from pure dread of loneliness, he might marry. This fear, which was of long standing, increased constantly, and set her wits to contriving plans whereby she might have him near her as much as possible, and to see that he should not pass long evenings alone in the chill silence of his empty rooms. Not being always able to hold and keep him, she would suggest amusements for him, sent him to the theater, forced him to go into society, being better pleased to know that he was mingling with many other women than alone in his gloomy house.

She resumed, answering his secret thought: "Ah, if I could only have you always with me, how I should spoil you! Promise me to come often, since I hardly go out at all now."

"I promise it."

At that moment a voice murmured "Mamma!" in her ear.

The Countess started and turned. Annette, the Duchess, and the Marquis had just rejoined them.

"It is four o'clock," said the Duchess. "I am very tired and I wish to go now."

"I will go, too; I have had enough of it," said the Countess.

They reached the interior stairway which divides the galleries where the drawings and water-colors are hung, overlooking the immense garden inclosed in glass, where the works of sculpture are exhibited.

From the platform of this stairway they could see from one end to the other of this great conservatory, filled with statues set up along the pathway around large green shrubs, and below was the crowd which covered the paths like a moving black wave. The marbles rose from this mass of dark hats and shoulders, piercing it in a thousand places, and seeming almost luminous in their dazzling whiteness.

As Bertin took leave of the ladies at the door of exit, Madame de Guilleroy whispered:

"Then—will you come this evening?"

"Yes, certainly."

Bertin reentered the Exposition, to talk with the artists over the impressions of the day.

Painters and sculptors stood talking in groups around the statues and in front of the buffet, upholding or attacking the same ideas that were discussed every year, using the same arguments over works almost exactly similar. Olivier, who usually took a lively share in these disputes, being quick in repartee and clever in disconcerting attacks, besides having a reputation as an ingenious theorist of which he was proud, tried to urge himself to take an active part in the debates, but the things he said interested him no more than those he heard, and he longed to go away, to listen no more, to understand no more, knowing beforehand as he did all that anyone could say on those ancient questions of art, of which he knew all sides.

He loved these things, however, and had loved them until now in an almost exclusive way; but to-day he was distracted by one of those slight but persistent preoccupations, one of those petty anxieties which are so small we ought not to allow ourselves to be troubled by them, but which, in spite of all we do or say, prick through our thoughts like an invisible thorn buried in the flesh.

He had even forgotten his anxiety over his little peasant bathers in the remembrance of the displeasing idea of the Marquis approaching Annette. What did it matter to him, after all? Had he any right? Why should he wish to prevent this precious marriage, already arranged, and suitable from every point of view? But no reasoning could efface that impression of uneasiness and discontent which had seized him when he had beheld Farandal talking and smiling like an accepted suitor, caressing with his glances the fair face of the young girl.

When he entered the Countess's drawing-room that evening, and found her alone with her daughter, continuing by the lamplight their knitting for the poor, he had great difficulty in preventing himself from saying sneering things about the Marquis, and from revealing to Annette his real banality, veiled by a mask of elegance and good form.

For a long time, during these after-dinner evening visits, he had often allowed himself to lapse into occasional silence that was slightly somnolent, and was accustomed to fall into the easy attitudes of an old friend who does not stand on ceremony. But now he seemed suddenly to rouse himself and to show the alertness of men who do their best to be agreeable, who take thought as to what they wish to say, and who, before certain persons, seek for the best phrases in which to express their ideas and render them attractive. No longer did he allow the conversation to lag, but did his best to keep it bright and interesting; and when he had made the Countess and her daughter laugh gaily, when he felt that he had touched their emotions, or when they ceased to work in order to listen to him, he felt a thrill of pleasure, an assurance of success, which rewarded him for his efforts.

He came now every time that he knew they were alone, and never, perhaps, had he passed such delightful evenings.

Madame de Guilleroy, whose continual fears were soothed by this assiduity, made fresh efforts to attract him and to keep him near her. She refused invitations to dinners in the city, she did not go to balls, nor to the theaters, in order to have the joy of throwing into the telegraph-box, on going out at three o'clock, a little blue despatch which said: "Come to-night." At first, wishing to give him earlier the tete-a-tete that he desired, she had sent her daughter to bed as soon as it was ten o'clock. Then after one occasion when he had appeared surprised at this and had begged laughingly that Annette should not be treated any longer like a naughty little girl, she had allowed her daughter a quarter of an hour's grace, then half an hour, and finally a whole hour. Bertin never remained long after the young girl had retired; it was as if half the charm that held him there had departed with her. He would soon take the little low seat that he preferred beside the Countess and lay his cheek against her knee with a caressing movement. She would give him one of her hands, which he clasped in his, and the fever of his spirit would suddenly be abated; he ceased to talk, and appeared to find repose in tender silence from the effort he had made.

Little by little the Countess, with the keenness of feminine instinct, comprehended that Annette attracted him almost as much as she herself. This did not anger her; she was glad that between them he could find something of that domestic happiness which he lacked; and she imprisoned him between them, as it were, playing the part of tender mother in such a way that he might almost believe himself the young girl's father; and a new bond of tenderness was added to that which had always held him to this household.

Her personal vanity, always alert, but disturbed since she had felt in several ways, like almost invisible pin-pricks, the innumerable attacks of advancing age, took on a new allurement. In order to become as slender as Annette, she continued to drink nothing, and the real slimness of her figure gave her the appearance of a young girl. When her back was turned one could hardly distinguish her from Annette; but her face showed the effect of this regime. The plump flesh began to be wrinkled and took on a yellowish tint which rendered more dazzling by contrast the superb freshness of the young girl's complexion. Then the Countess began to make up her face with theatrical art, and, though in broad daylight she produced an effect that was slightly artificial, in the evening her complexion had that charmingly soft tint obtained by women who know how to make up well.

The realization of her fading beauty, and the employment of artificial aid to restore it, somewhat changed her habits. As much as possible, she avoided comparison with her daughter in the full light of day, but rather sought it by lamplight, which, if anything, showed herself to greater advantage. When she was fatigued, pale, and felt that she looked older than usual, she had convenient headaches by reason of which she excused herself from going to balls and theaters; but on days when she knew she looked well she triumphed again and played the elder sister with the grave modesty of a little mother. In order always to wear gowns like those of her daughter, she made Annette wear toilettes suitable for a fully-grown young woman, a trifle too old for her; and Annette who showed more and more plainly her joyous and laughing disposition, wore them with sparkling vivacity that rendered her still more attractive. She lent herself with all her heart to the coquettish arts of her mother, acting with her, as if by instinct, graceful little domestic scenes; she knew when to embrace her at the effective moment, how to clasp her tenderly round the waist, and to show by a movement, a caress, or some ingenious pose, how pretty both were and how much they resembled each other.

From seeing the two so much together, and from continually comparing them, Olivier Bertin sometimes actually confused them in his own mind. Sometimes, when Annette spoke, and he happened to be looking elsewhere, he was compelled to ask: "Which of you said that?" He often amused himself by playing this game of confusion when all three were alone in the drawing-room with the Louis XV tapestries. He would close his eyes and beg them to ask him the same question, the one after the other, and then change the order of the interrogations, so that he might recognize their voices. They did this with so much cleverness in imitating each other's intonations, in saying the same phrases with the same accents, that often he could not tell which spoke. In fact, they had come to speak so much alike that the servants answered "Yes, Madame" to the daughter and "Yes, Mademoiselle" to the mother.

From imitating each other's voices and movements for amusement, they acquired such a similarity of gait and gesture that Monsieur de Guilleroy himself, when he saw one or the other pass through the shadowy end of the drawing-room, confounded them for an instant and asked: "Is that you, Annette, or is it your mamma?"

From this resemblance, natural and assumed, was engendered in the mind and heart of the painter a strange impression of a double entity, old and young, wise yet ignorant, two bodies made, the one after the other, with the same flesh; in fact, the same woman continued, but rejuvenated, having become once more what she was formerly. Thus he lived near them, shared between them, uneasy, troubled, feeling for the mother his old ardor awakened, and for the daughter an indefinable tenderness.

PART II
CHAPTER I

A WILLING ENVOY

"Paris, July 20, 11 P. M.

"MY FRIEND: My mother has just died at Roncieres. We shall leave here at midnight. Do not come, for we have told no one. But pity me and think of me. YOUR ANY."

"July 21, 12 M.

"MY POOR FRIEND: I should have gone, notwithstanding what you wrote, if I had not become used to regarding all your wishes as commands. I have thought of you with poignant grief ever since last night. I think of that silent journey you made, sitting opposite your daughter and your husband, in that dimly-lighted carriage, which bore you toward your dead. I could see all three of you under the oil lamp, you weeping and Annette sobbing. I saw your arrival at the station, the entrance of the castle in the midst of a group of servants, your rush up the stairs toward that room, toward that bed where she lies, your first look at her, and your kiss on her thin, motionless face. And I thought of your heart, your poor heart—that poor heart, of which half belongs to me and which is breaking, which suffers so much, which stifles you, making me suffer also at this moment.

"With profound pity, I kiss your eyes filled with tears.

"OLIVIER."

"Roncieres, July 24.

"Your letter would have done me good, my friend, if anything could do me good in the horrible situation into which I have fallen. We buried her yesterday, and since her poor lifeless body has gone out of this house it seems to me that I am alone in the world. We love our mothers almost without knowing or feeling it, for such love is as natural as it is to live, and we do not realize how deep-rooted is that love until the moment of final separation. No other affection is comparable to that, for all others come by chance, while this begins at birth; all the others are brought to us later by the accidents of life, while this has lived in our very blood since our first day on earth. And then, and there, we have lost not only a mother but our childhood itself, which half disappears, for our little life of girlhood belonged to her as much as to ourselves. She alone knew it as we knew it; she knew about innumerable things, remote, insignificant and dear, which are and which were the first sweet emotions of our heart. To her alone I could still say: 'Do you remember, mother, the day when—? Do you remember, mother, the china doll that grandmother gave me?' Both of us murmured to each other a long, sweet chapter of trifling childish memories, which no one on earth now knows of but me. So it is a part of myself that is dead—the older, the better. I have lost the poor heart wherein the little girl I was once still lived. Now no one knows her any more; no one remembers the little Anne, her short skirts, her laughter and her faces.

"And a day will come—and perhaps it is not far away—when in my turn I too shall go, leaving my dear Annette alone in the world, as mamma has left me to-day. How sad all this is, how hard, and cruel! Yet one never thinks about it; we never look about us to see death take someone every instant, as it will soon take us. If we should look at it, if we should think of it, if we were not distracted, rejoiced, or blinded by all that passes before us, we could no longer live, for the sight of this endless massacre would drive us mad.

"I am so crushed, so despairing, that I have no longer strength to do anything. Day and night I think of my poor mamma, nailed in that box, buried beneath that earth, in that field, under the rain, whose old face, which I used to kiss with so much happiness, is now only a mass of frightful decay! Oh, what horror!

"When I lost papa, I was just married, and I did not feel all these things as I do to-day. Yes, pity me, think of me, write to me. I need you so much just now.

"ANNE."

"Paris, July 25.

"MY POOR FRIEND: Your grief gives me horrible pain, and life no longer seems rosy to me. Since your departure I am lost, abandoned, without ties or refuge. Everything fatigues me, bores me and irritates me. I am ceaselessly thinking of you and Annette; I feel that you are both far, far away when I need you near me so much.

"It is extraordinary how far away from me you seem to be, and how I miss you. Never, even in my younger days, have you been my all, as you are at this moment. I have foreseen for some time that I should reach this crisis, which must be a sun-stroke in Indian summer. What I feel is so very strange that I wish to tell you about it. Just fancy that since your absence I cannot take walks any more! Formerly, and even during the last few months, I liked very much to set out alone and stroll along the street, amusing myself by looking at people and things, and enjoying the mere sight of everything and the exercise of walking. I used to walk along without knowing where I was going, simply to walk, to breathe, to dream. Now, I can no longer do this. As soon as I reach the street I am oppressed by anguish, like the fear of a blind man that has lost his dog. I become uneasy, exactly like a traveler that has lost his way in the wood, and I am compelled to return home. Paris seems empty, frightful, alarming. I ask myself: 'Where am I going?' I answer myself: 'Nowhere, since I am still walking.' Well, I cannot, for I can no longer walk without some aim. The bare thought of walking straight before me wearies and bores me inexpressibly. Then I drag my melancholy to the club.

"And do you know why? Only because you are no longer here. I am certain of this. When I know that you are in Paris, my walks are no longer useless, for it is possible that I may meet you in the first street I turn into. I can go anywhere because you may go anywhere. If I do not see you, I may at least find Annette, who is an emanation of yourself. You and she fill the streets full of hope for me—the hope of recognizing you, whether you approach me from a distance, or whether I divine your identity in following you. And then the city becomes charming to me, and the women whose figures resemble yours stir my heart with all the liveliness of the streets, hold my attention, occupy my eyes, and give me a sort of hunger to see you.

"You will consider me very selfish, my poor friend, to speak to you in this way of the solitude of an old cooing pigeon when you are shedding such bitter tears. Pardon me! I am so used to being spoiled by you that I cry 'Help! Help!' when I have you no longer.

"I kiss your feet so that you may have pity on me.

"OLIVIER."

"Roncieres, July 30.

"MY FRIEND: Thanks for your letter. I need so much to know that you love me! I have just passed some frightful days. Indeed, I believed that grief would kill me in my turn.

"It was like a block of suffering in my breast, growing larger and larger, stifling me, strangling me. The physician that was called to treat me for the nervous crisis I was enduring, which recurred four or five times a day, injected morphine, which made me almost wild, and the great heat we have had aggravated my condition and threw me into a state of over-excitement that was almost delirium. I am a little more calm since the great storm of Friday. I must tell you that since the day of the funeral I could weep no more, but during the storm, the approach of which upset me, I suddenly felt the tears beginning to flow from my eyes, slow, small, burning. Oh, those first tears, how they hurt me! They seemed to tear me, as if they had claws, and my throat was so choked that I could hardly breathe. Then the tears came faster, larger, cooler. They ran from my eyes as from a spring, and came so fast that my handkerchief was saturated and I had to take another. The great block of grief seemed to soften and to flow away through my eyes.

"From that moment I have been weeping from morning till night, and that is saving me. One would really end by going mad or dying, if one could not weep. I am all alone, too. My husband is making some little trips around the country, and I insisted that he should take Annette with him, to distract and console her a little. They go in the carriage or on horseback as far as eight or ten leagues from Roncieres, and she returns to me rosy with youth, in spite of her sadness, her eyes shining with life, animated by the country air and the excursion she has had. How beautiful it is to be at that age! I think that we shall remain here a fortnight or three weeks longer; then, although it will be August, we shall return to Paris for the reason you know.

"I send to you all that remains to me of my heart.

"ANY."

"Paris, August 4th.

"I can bear this no longer, my dear friend; you must come back, for something is certainly going to happen to me. I ask myself whether I am not already ill, so great a dislike have I for everything I used to take pleasure in doing, or did with indifferent resignation. For one thing, it is so warm in Paris that every night means a Turkish bath of eight or nine hours. I get up overcome by the fatigue of this sleep in a hot bath, and for an hour or two I walk about before a white canvas, with the intention to draw something. But mind, eye, and hand are all empty. I am no longer a painter! This futile effort to work is exasperating. I summon my models; I place them, and they give me poses, movements, and expressions that I have painted to satiety. I make them dress again and let them go. Indeed, I can no longer see anything new, and I suffer from this as if I were blind. What is it? Is it fatigue of the eye or of the brain, exhaustion of the artistic faculty or of the optic nerve? Who knows? It seems to me that I have ceased to discover anything in the unexplored corner that I have been permitted to visit. I no longer perceive anything but that which all the world knows; I do the things that all poor painters have done; I have only one subject now, and only the observation of a vulgar pedant. Once upon a time, and not so very long ago, either, the number of new subjects seemed to me unlimited, and in order to express them I had such a variety of means the difficulty of making a choice made me hesitate. But now, alas! Suddenly the world of half-seen subjects has become depopulated, my study has become powerless and useless. The people that pass have no more sense for me. I no longer find in every human being the character and savor which once I liked so much to discern and reveal. I believe, however, that I could make a very pretty portrait of your daughter. Is it because she resembles you so much that I confound you both in my mind? Yes, perhaps.

"Well, then, after forcing myself to sketch a man or a woman who does not resemble any of the familiar models, I decide to go and breakfast somewhere, for I no longer have the courage to sit down alone in my own dining-room. The Boulevard Malesherbes seems like a forest path imprisoned in a dead city. All the houses smell empty. On the street the sprinklers throw showers of white rain, splashing the wooden pavement whence rises the vapor of damp tar and stable refuse; and from one end to the other of the long descent from the Parc Monceau to Saint Augustin, one sees five or six black forms, unimportant passers, tradesmen or domestics. The shade of the plane-trees spreads over the burning sidewalks, making a curious spot, looking almost like liquid, as if water spilled there were drying. The stillness of the leaves on the branches, and of their gray silhouettes on the asphalt, expresses the fatigue of the roasted city, slumbering and perspiring like a workman asleep on a bench in the sun. Yes, she perspires, the beggar, and she smells frightfully through her sewer mouths, the vent-holes of sinks and kitchens, the streams through which the filth of her streets is running. Then I think of those summer mornings in your orchard full of little wild-flowers that flavor the air with a suggestion of honey. Then I enter, sickened already, the restaurant where bald, fat, tired-looking men are eating, with half-opened waistcoats and moist, shining foreheads. The food shows the effect of heat—the melon growing soft under the ice, the soft bread, the flabby filet, the warmed-over vegetables, the purulent cheese, the fruits ripened on the premises. I go out, nauseated, and go home to try to sleep a little until the hour for dinner, which I take at the club.

"There I always find Adelmans, Maldant, Rocdiane, Landa, and many others, who bore and weary me as much as hand-organs. Each one has his own little tune, or tunes, which I have heard for fifteen years, and they play them all together every evening in that club, which is apparently a place where one goes to be entertained. Someone should change my own generation for my benefit, for my eyes, my ears, and my mind have had enough of it. They still make conquests, however, they boast of them and congratulate one another on them!

"After yawning as many times as there are minutes between eight o'clock and midnight, I go home and go to bed, and while I undress I think that the same thing will begin over again the next day.

"Yes, my dear friend, I am at the age when a bachelor's life becomes intolerable, because there is nothing new for me under the sun. An unmarried man should be young, curious, eager. When one is no longer all that, it becomes dangerous to remain free. Heavens! how I loved my liberty, long ago, before I loved you more! How burdensome it is to me to-day! For an old bachelor like me, liberty is an empty thing, empty everywhere; it is the path to death, with nothing in himself to prevent him from seeing the end; it is the ceaseless query: 'What shall I do? Whom can I go to see, so that I shall not be alone?' And I go from one friend to another, from one handshake to the next, begging for a little friendship. I gather up my crumbs, but they do not make a loaf. You, I have You, my friend, but you do not belong to me. Perhaps it is because of you that I suffer this anguish, for it is the desire for contact with you, for your presence, for the same roof over our heads, for the same walls inclosing our lives, the same interests binding our hearts together, the need of that community of hopes, griefs, pleasures, joys, sadness, and also of material things, that fills me with so much yearning. You do belong to me—that is to say, I steal a little of you from time to time. But I long to breathe forever the same air that you breathe, to share everything with you, to possess nothing that does not belong to both of us, to feel that all which makes up my own life belongs to you as much as to me—the glass from which I drink, the chair on which I sit, the bread I eat and the fire that warms me.

"Adieu! Return soon. I suffer too much when you are far away.

"OLIVIER."

"Roncieres, August 8th.

"MY FRIEND: I am ill, and so fatigued that you would not recognize me at all. I believe that I have wept too much. I must rest a little before I return, for I do not wish you to see me as I am. My husband sets out for Paris the day after to-morrow, and will give you news of us. He expects to take you to dinner somewhere, and charges me to ask you to wait for him at your house about seven o'clock.

"As for me, as soon as I feel a little better, as soon as I have no more this corpse-like face which frightens me, I will return to be near you. In all the world, I have only Annette and you, and I wish to offer to each of you all that I can give without robbing the other.

"I hold out my eyes, which have wept so much, so that you may kiss them.

"ANY."

When he received this letter announcing the still delayed return, Olivier was seized with an immoderate desire to take a carriage for the railway station to catch a train for Roncieres; then, thinking that M. de Guilleroy must return the next day, he resigned himself, and even began to wish for the arrival of the husband with almost as much impatience as if it were that of the wife herself.

Never had he liked Guilleroy as during those twenty-four hours of waiting. When he saw him enter, he rushed toward him, with hands extended, exclaiming:

"Ah, dear friend! how happy I am to see you!"

The other also seemed very glad, delighted above all things to return to Paris, for life was not gay in Normandy during the three weeks he had passed there.

The two men sat down on a little two-seated sofa in a corner of the studio, under a canopy of Oriental stuffs, and again shook hands with mutual sympathy.

"And the Countess?" asked Bertin, "how is she?"

"Not very well. She has been very much affected, and is recovering too slowly. I must confess that I am a little anxious about her."

"But why does she not return?"

"I know nothing about it. It was impossible for me to induce her to return here."

"What does she do all day?"

"Oh, heavens! She weeps, and thinks of her mother. That is not good for her. I should like very much to have her decide to have a change of air, to leave the place where that happened, you understand?"

"And Annette?"

"Oh, she is a blooming flower."

Olivier smiled with joy.

"Was she very much grieved?" he asked again.

"Yes, very much, very much, but you know that the grief of eighteen years does not last long."

After a silence Guilleroy resumed:

"Where shall we dine, my dear fellow? I need to be cheered up, to hear some noise and see some movement."

"Well, at this season, it seems to me that the Cafe des Ambassadeurs is the right place."

So they set out, arm in arm, toward the Champs-Elysees. Guilleroy, filled with the gaiety of Parisians when they return, to whom the city, after every absence, seems rejuvenated and full of possible surprises, questioned the painter about a thousand details of what people had been doing and saying; and Olivier, after indifferent replies which betrayed all the boredom of his solitude, spoke of Roncieres, tried to capture from this man, in order to gather round him that almost tangible something left with us by persons with whom we have recently been associated, that subtle emanation of being one carries away when leaving them, which remains with us a few hours and evaporates amid new surroundings.

The heavy sky of a summer evening hung over the city and over the great avenue where, under the trees, the gay refrains of open-air concerts were beginning to sound. The two men, seated on the balcony of the Cafe des Ambassadeurs, looked down upon the still empty benches and chairs of the inclosure up to the little stage, where the singers, in the mingled light of electric globes and fading day, displayed their striking costumes and their rosy complexions. Odors of frying, of sauces, of hot food, floated in the slight breezes from the chestnut-trees, and when a woman passed, seeing her reserved chair, followed by a man in a black coat, she diffused on her way the fresh perfume of her dress and her person.

Guilleroy, who was radiant, murmured:

"Oh, I like to be here much better than in the country!"

"And I," Bertin replied, "should like it much better to be there than here."

"Nonsense!"

"Heavens, yes! I find Paris tainted this summer."

"Oh, well, my dear fellow, it is always Paris, after all."

The Deputy seemed to be enjoying his day, one of those rare days of effervescence and gaiety in which grave men do foolish things. He looked at two cocottes dining at a neighboring table with three thin young men, superlatively correct, and he slyly questioned Olivier about all the well-known girls, whose names were heard every day. Then he murmured in a tone of deep regret:

"You were lucky to have remained a bachelor. You can do and see many things."

But the painter did not agree with him, and, as a man will do when haunted by a persistent idea, he took Guilleroy into his confidence on the subject of his sadness and isolation. When he had said everything, had recited to the end of his litany of melancholy, and, urged by the longing to relieve his heart, had confessed naively how much he would have enjoyed the love and companionship of a woman installed in his home, the Count, in his turn, admitted that marriage had its advantages. Recovering his parliamentary eloquence in order to sing the praises of his domestic happiness, he eulogized the Countess in the highest terms, to which Olivier listened gravely with frequent nods of approval.

Happy to hear her spoken of, but jealous of that intimate happiness which Guilleroy praised as a matter of duty, the painter finally murmured, with sincere conviction:

"Yes, indeed, you were the lucky one!"

The Deputy, flattered, assented to this; then he resumed:

"I should like very much to see her return; indeed, I am a little anxious about her just now. Wait—since you are bored in Paris, you might go to Roncieres and bring her back. She will listen to you, for you are her best friend; while a husband—you know——"

Delighted, Olivier replied: "I ask nothing better. But do you think it would not annoy her to see me arriving in that abrupt way?"

"No, not at all. Go, by all means, my dear fellow."

"Well, then, I will. I will leave to-morrow by the one o'clock train. Shall I send her a telegram?"

"No, I will attend to that. I will telegraph, so that you will find a carriage at the station."

As they had finished dinner, they strolled again up the Boulevard, but in half an hour the Count suddenly left the painter, under the pretext of an urgent affair that he had quite forgotten.

CHAPTER II

SPRINGTIME AND AUTUMN

The Countess and her daughter, dressed in black crape, had just seated themselves opposite each other, for breakfast, in the large dining-room at Roncieres. The portraits of many ancestors, crudely painted, one in a cuirass, another in a tight-fitting coat, this a powdered officer of the French Guards, that a colonel of the Restoration, hung in line on the walls, a collection of deceased Guilleroys, in old frames from which the gilding was peeling. Two servants, stepping softly, began to serve the two silent women, and the flies made a little cloud of black specks, dancing and buzzing around the crystal chandelier that hung over the center of the table.

"Open the windows," said the Countess, "It is a little cool here."

The three long windows, reaching from the floor to the ceiling, and large as bay-windows, were opened wide. A breath of soft air, bearing the odor of warm grass and the distant sounds of the country, swept in immediately through these openings, mingling with the slightly damp air of the room, inclosed by the thick walls of the castle.

"Ah, that is good!" said Annette, taking a full breath.

The eyes of the two women had turned toward the outside and now gazed, beneath the blue sky, lightly veiled by the midday haze which was reflected on the meadows impregnated with sunshine, at the long and verdant lawns of the park, with its groups of trees here and there, and its perspective opening to the yellow fields, illuminated as far as the eye could see by the golden gleam of ripe grain.

"We will take a long walk after breakfast," said the Countess. "We might walk as far as Berville, following the river, for it will be too warm on the plain."

"Yes, mamma, and let us take Julio to scare up some partridges."

"You know that your father forbids it."

"Oh, but since papa is in Paris!—it is so amusing to see Julio pointing after them. There he is now, worrying the cows! Oh, how funny he is, the dear fellow!"

Pushing back her chair, she jumped up and ran to the window, calling out: "Go on, Julio! After them!"

Upon the lawn three heavy cows, gorged with grass and overcome with heat, lay on their sides, their bellies protruding from the pressure of the earth. Rushing from one to another, barking and bounding wildly, in a sort of mad abandon, partly real, partly feigned, a hunting spaniel, slender, white and red, whose curly ears flapped at every bound, was trying to rouse the three big beasts, which did not wish to get up. It was evidently the dog's favorite sport, with which he amused himself whenever he saw the cows lying down. Irritated, but not frightened, they gazed at him with their large, moist eyes, turning their heads to watch him.

Annette, from her window, cried:

"Fetch them, Julio, fetch them!"

The excited spaniel, growing bolder, barked louder and ventured as far as their cruppers, feigning to be about to bite them. They began to grow uneasy, and the nervous twitching of their skin, to get rid of the flies, became more frequent and protracted.

Suddenly the dog, carried along by the impetus of a rush that he could not check in time, bounced so close to one cow that, in order not to fall against her, he was obliged to jump over her. Startled by the bound, the heavy animal took fright, and first raising her head she finally raised herself slowly on her four legs, sniffing loudly. Seeing her erect, the other two immediately got up also, and Julio began to prance around them in a dance of triumph, while Annette praised him.

"Bravo, Julio, bravo!"

"Come," said the Countess, "come to breakfast, my child."

But the young girl, shading her eyes with one hand, announced:

"There comes a telegraph messenger!"

Along the invisible path among the wheat and the oats a blue blouse appeared to be gliding along the top of the grain, and it came toward the castle with the firm step of a man.

"Oh, heavens!" murmured the Countess; "I hope he does not bring bad news!"

She was still shaken with that terror which remains with us a long time after the death of some loved one has been announced by a telegram. Now she could not remove the gummed band to open the little blue paper without feeling her fingers tremble and her soul agitated, believing that from those folds which it took so long to open would come a grief that would cause her tears to flow afresh.

Annette, on the contrary, full of girlish curiosity, was delighted to meet with the unknown mystery that comes to all of us at times. Her heart, which life had just saddened for the first time, could anticipate only something joyful from that black and ominous bag hanging from the side of the mail-carrier, who saw so many emotions through the city streets and the country lanes.

The Countess ceased to eat, concentrating her thoughts on the man who was approaching, bearer of a few written words that might wound her as if a knife had been thrust in her throat. The anguish of having known that experience made her breathless, and she tried to guess what this hurried message might be. About what? From whom? The thought of Olivier flashed through her mind. Was he ill? Dead, perhaps, too!

The ten minutes she had to wait seemed interminable to her; then, when she had torn open the despatch and recognized the name of her husband, she read: "I telegraph to tell you that our friend Bertin leaves for Roncieres on the one o'clock train. Send Phaeton station. Love."

"Well, mamma?" said Annette.

"Monsieur Olivier Bertin is coming to see us."

"Ah, how lucky! When?"

"Very soon."

"At four o'clock?"

"Yes."

"Oh, how kind he is!"

But the Countess had turned pale, for a new anxiety had lately troubled her, and the sudden arrival of the painter seemed to her as painful a menace as anything she might have been able to foresee.

"You will go to meet him with the carriage," she said to her daughter.

"And will you not come, too, mamma?"

"No, I will wait for you here."

"Why? That will hurt him."

"I do not feel very well."

"You wished to walk as far as Berville just now."

"Yes, but my breakfast has made me feel ill."

"You will feel better between now and the time to go."

"No, I am going up to my room. Let me know as soon as you arrive."

"Yes, mamma."

After giving orders that the phaeton should be ready at the proper hour, and that a room be prepared, the Countess returned to her own room, and shut herself in.

Up to this time her life had passed almost without suffering, affected only by Olivier's love and concerned only by her anxiety to retain it. She had succeeded, always victorious in that struggle. Her heart, soothed by success and by flattery, had become the exacting heart of a beautiful worldly woman to whom are due all the good things of earth, and, after consenting to a brilliant marriage, with which affection had nothing to do, after accepting love later as the complement of a happy existence, after taking her part in a guilty intimacy, largely from inclination, a little from a leaning toward sentiment itself as a compensation for the prosaic hum-drum of daily life, had barricaded itself in the happiness that chance had offered her, with no other desire than to defend it against the surprises of each day. She had therefore accepted with the complacency of a pretty woman the agreeable events that occurred; and, though she ventured little, and was troubled little by new necessities and desires for the unknown; though she was tender, tenacious, and farseeing, content with the present, but naturally anxious about the morrow, she had known how to enjoy the elements that Destiny had furnished her with wise and economical prudence.

Now, little by little, without daring to acknowledge it even to herself, the vague preoccupation of passing time, of advancing age, had glided into her soul. In her consciousness it had the effect of a gnawing trouble that never ceased. But, knowing well that this descent of life was without an end, that once begun it never could be stopped, and yielding to the instinct of danger, she closed her eyes in letting herself glide along, that she might retain her dream, that she might not be seized with dizziness at sight of the abyss or be made desperate by her impotence.

She lived, then, smiling, with a sort of factitious pride in remaining beautiful so long, and when Annette appeared at her side with the freshness of her eighteen years, instead of suffering from this contrast, she was proud, on the contrary, of being able to command preference, in the ripe grace of her womanhood, over that blooming young girl in the radiant beauty of first youth.

She had even believed that she had entered upon the beginning of a happy, tranquil period when the death of her mother struck a blow at her heart. During the first few days she was filled with that profound despair that leaves no room for any other thought. She remained from morning until night buried in grief, trying to recall a thousand things of the dead, her familiar words, her face in earlier days, the gowns she used to wear, as if she had stored her memory with relics; and from the now buried past she gathered all the intimate and trivial recollections with which to feed her cruel reveries. Then, when she had arrived at such paroxysms of despair that she fell into hysterics and swooned, all her accumulated grief broke forth in tears, flowing from her eyes by day and by night.

One morning, when her maid entered, and opened the shutters after raising the shades, asking: "How does Madame feel to-day?" she answered, feeling exhausted from having wept so much: "Oh, not at all well! Indeed, I can bear no more."

The servant, who was holding a tea-tray, looked at her mistress, and, touched to see her lying so pale amide the whiteness of the bed, she stammered, in a tone of genuine sadness: "Madame really looks very ill. Madame would do well to take care of herself."

The tone in which this was said pierced the Countess's heart like a sharp needle, and as soon as the maid had gone she rose to go and look at her face in her large dressing-mirror.

She was stupefied at the sight of herself, frightened by her hollow cheeks, her red eyes, the ravages produced in her by these days of suffering. Her face, which she knew so well, which she had often looked at in so many different mirrors, of which she knew all the expressions, all the smiles, the pallor which she had already corrected so many times, smoothing away the marks of fatigue, and the tiny wrinkles at the corners of the eyes, visible in too strong a light—her face suddenly seemed to her that of another woman, a new face that was distorted and irreparably ill.

In order to see herself better, to be surer with regard to this unexpected misfortune, she approached near enough to the mirror to touch it with her forehead, so that her breath, spreading a light mist over the glass, almost obscured the pale image she was contemplating. She was compelled to take a handkerchief to wipe away this mist, and, trembling with a strange emotion, she made a long and patient examination of the alterations in her face. With a light finger she stretched the skin of her cheeks, smoothed her forehead, pushed back her hair, and turned the eyelids to look at the whites of her eyes. Then she opened her mouth and examined her teeth which were a little tarnished where the gold fillings shone, and she was disturbed to note the livid gums and the yellow tint of the flesh above the cheeks and at the temples.

She was so lost in this examination of her fading beauty that she did not hear the door open, and was startled when her maid, standing behind her, said:

"Madame has forgotten to take her tea."

The Countess turned, confused, surprised, ashamed, and the servant, guessing her thoughts continued:

"Madame has wept too much; there is nothing worse to spoil the skin. One's blood turns to water."

And as the Countess added sadly: "There is age also," the maid exclaimed: "Oh, but Madame has not reached that time yet! With a few days of rest not a trace will be left. But Madame must go to walk, and take great care not to weep."

As soon as she was dressed the Countess descended to the park, and for the first time since her mother's death she visited the little orchard where long ago she had liked to cultivate and gather flowers; then she went to the river and strolled beside the stream until the hour for breakfast.

She sat down at the table opposite her husband, and beside her daughter, and remarked, that she might know what they thought: "I feel better today. I must be less pale."

"Oh, you still look very ill," said the Count.

Her heart contracted and she felt like weeping, for she had fallen into the habit of it.

Until evening, and the next day, and all the following days, whether she thought of her mother or of herself, every moment she felt her throat swelling with sobs and her eyes filling with tears, but to prevent them from overflowing and furrowing her cheeks she repressed them, and by a superhuman effort of will turned her thoughts in other directions, mastered them, ruled them, separated them from her sorrow, forced herself to feel consoled, tried to amuse herself and to think of sad things no more, in order to regain the hue of health.

Above all, she did not wish to return to Paris and to receive Olivier Bertin until she had become more like her former self. Realizing that she had grown too thin, that the flesh of women of her age needs to be full in order to keep fresh, she sought to create appetite by walking in the woods and along the roads; and though she returned weary and not hungry she forced herself to eat a great deal.

The Count, who wished to go away, could not understand her obstinacy. Finally, as her resistance seemed invincible, he declared that he would go alone, leaving the Countess free to return when she might feel so disposed.

The next day she received the telegram announcing Olivier's arrival.

A desire to flee seized her, so much did she fear his first look. She would have preferred to wait another week or two. In a week, with care one may change the face completely, since women, even when young and in good health, under the least change of influence become unrecognizable from one day to another. But the idea of appearing in broad daylight before Olivier, in the open fields, in the heat of August, beside Annette, so fresh and blooming, disturbed her so much that she decided immediately not to go to the station, but to await him in the half-darkened drawing-room.

She went up to her room and fell into a dream. Breaths of warm air stirred the curtains from time to time; the song of the crickets filled the air. Never before had she felt so sad. It was no more the great grief that had shattered her heart, overwhelming her before the soulless body of her beloved old mother. That grief, which she had believed incurable, had in a few days become softened, and was now but a sorrow of the memory; but now she felt herself swept away on a deep wave of melancholy into which she had entered gradually, and from which she never would emerge.

She had an almost irresistible desire to weep—and would not. Every time she felt her eyelids grow moist she wiped them away quickly, rose, paced about the room, looked out into the park and gazed at the tall trees, watched the slow, black flight of the crows against the background of blue sky. Then she passed before her mirror, judged her appearance with one glance, effaced the trace of a tear by touching the corner of her eye with rice powder, and looked at the clock, trying to guess at what point of the route he must have reached.

Like all women who are carried away by a distress of soul, whether real or unreasonable, she clung to her lover with a sort of frenzy. Was he not her all—all, everything, more than life, all that anyone must be who has come to be the sole affection of one who feels the approach of age?

Suddenly she heard in the distance the crack of a whip; she ran to the window and saw the phaeton as it made the turn round the lawn, drawn by two horses. Seated beside Annette, in the back seat of the carriage, Olivier waved his handkerchief as he saw the Countess, to which she responded by waving him a salutation from the window. Then she went down stairs with a heart throbbing fast but happy now, thrilled with joy at knowing him so near, of speaking to him and seeing him.

They met in the antechamber, before the drawing-room door.

He opened his arms to her with an irresistible impulse, and in a voice warmed by real emotion, exclaimed: "Ah, my poor Countess, let me embrace you!"

She closed her eyes, leaned toward him and pressed against him, lifted her cheek to him, and as he pressed his lips upon it, she murmured in his ear: "I love thee!"

Then Olivier, without dropping the hands he clasped in his own, looked at her, saying: "Let us see that sad face."

She felt ready to faint.

"Yes, a little pale," said he, "but that is nothing."

To thank him for saying that, she said brokenly,

"Ah, dear friend, dear friend!" finding nothing else to say.

But he turned, looking behind her in search of Annette, who had disappeared.

"Is it not strange," he said abruptly, "to see your daughter in mourning?"

"Why?" inquired the Countess.

"What? You ask why?" he exclaimed, with extraordinary animation. "Why, it is your own portrait painted by me—it is my portrait. It is yourself, such as you were when I met you long ago when I entered the Duchess's house! Ah, do you remember that door where you passed under my gaze, as a frigate passes under a cannon of a fort? Good heavens! when I saw the little one, just now, at the railway station, standing on the platform, all in black, with the sun shining on her hair massed around her face, the blood rushed to my head. I thought I should weep. I tell you, it is enough to drive one mad, when one has known you as I have, who has studied you as no one else has, and reproduced you in painting, Madame. Ah, I thought that you had sent her alone to meet me at the station in order to give me that surprise. My God! but I was surprised, indeed! I tell you, it is enough to drive one mad."

He called: "Annette! Nane!"

The young girl's voice replied from outside, where she was giving sugar to the horses:

"Yes, yes, I am here!"

"Come in here!"

She entered quickly.

"Here, stand close beside your mother."

She obeyed, and he compared the two, but repeated mechanically, "Yes, it is astonishing, astonishing!" for they resembled each other less when side by side than they did before leaving Paris, the young girl having acquired a new expression of luminous youth in her black attire, while the mother had for a long time lost that radiance of hair and complexion that had dazzled and entranced the painter when they met for the first time.

Then the Countess and Olivier entered the drawing-room. He seemed in high spirits.

"Ah, what a good plan it was to come here!" he said. "But it was your husband's idea that I should come, you know. He charged me to take you back with me. And I—do you know what I propose? You have no idea, have you? Well, I propose, on the contrary, to remain here! Paris is odious in this heat, while the country is delicious. Heavens! how sweet it is here!"

The dews of evening impregnated the park with freshness, the soft breeze made the trees tremble, and the earth exhaled imperceptible vapors which threw a light, transparent veil over the horizon. The three cows, standing with drooping heads, cropped the grass with avidity, and four peacocks, with a loud rustling of wings, flew up into their accustomed perch in a cedar-tree under the windows of the castle. The barking of dogs in the distance came to the ear, and in the quiet air of the close of day the calls of human voices were heard, in phrases shouted across the fields, from one meadow to another, and in those short, guttural cries used in driving animals.

The painter, with bared head and shining eyes, breathed deeply, and, as he met the Countess's look, he said:

"This is happiness!"

"It never lasts," she answered, approaching nearer.

"Let us take it when it comes," said he.

"You never used to like the country until now," the Countess replied, smiling.

"I like it to-day because I find you here. I do not know how to live any more where you are not. When one is young, he may be in love though far away, through letters, thoughts, or dreams, perhaps because he feels that life is all before him, perhaps too because passion is stronger than pure affection; at my age, on the contrary, love has become like the habit of an invalid; it is a binding up of the soul, which flies now with only one wing, and mounts less frequently into the ideal. The heart knows no more ecstasy, only selfish wants. And then I know quite well that I have no time to lose to enjoy what remains for me."

"Oh, old!" she remonstrated, taking his hand tenderly.

"Yes, yes, I am old," he repeated. "Everything shows it, my hair, my changing character, the coming sadness. Alas! that is something I never have known till now—sadness. If someone had told me when I was thirty that a time would come when I should be sad without cause, uneasy, discontented with everything, I should not have believed it. That proves that my heart also has grown old."

The Countess replied with an air of profound certainty:

"Oh, as for me, my heart is still young. It never has changed. Yes, it has grown younger, perhaps. Once it was twenty; now it is only sixteen!"

They remained a long while thus, talking in the open window, mingled with the spirit of evening, very near each other, nearer than they ever had been, in this hour of tenderness, this twilight of love, like that of the day.

A servant entered, announcing:

"Madame la Comtesse is served."

"Have you called my daughter?" the Countess asked.

"Mademoiselle is in the dining-room."

All three sat down at the table. The shutters were closed, and two large candelabra with six candles each illumined Annette's face and seemed to powder her hair with gold dust. Bertin, smiling, looked at her continually.

"Heavens, now pretty she is in black!" he said.

And he turned toward the Countess while admiring the daughter, as if to thank the mother for having given him this pleasure.

When they returned to the drawing-room the moon had risen above the trees in the park. Their somber mass appeared like a great island, and the country round about like a sea hidden under the light mist that floated over the plains.

"Oh, mamma, let us take a walk," said Annette.

The Countess consented.

"I will take Julio."

"Very well, if you wish."

They set out. The young girl walked in front, amusing herself with the dog. When they crossed the lawn they heard the breathing of the cows, which, awake and scenting their enemy, raised their heads to look. Under the trees, farther away, the moon was pouring among the branches a shower of fine rays that fell to earth, seeming to wet the leaves that were spread out on the path in little patches of yellow light. Annette and Julio ran along, each seeming to have on this serene night, the same joyful and unburdened hearts, the gaiety of which expressed itself in graceful gambols.

In the little openings, where the wave of moonlight descended as into a well, the young girl looked like a spirit, and the painter called her back, marveling at this dark vision with its clear and brilliant face. Then when she darted away again, he took the Countess's hand

and pressed it, often seeking her lips as they traversed the deeper shadows, as if the sight of Annette had revived the impatience of his heart.

At last they reached the edge of the plain, where they could just discern, afar, here and there, the groups of trees belonging to the farms. Through the milky mist that bathed the fields the horizon appeared illimitable, and the soft silence, the living silence of that vast space, so warm and luminous, was full of inexpressible hope, of that indefinable expectancy which makes summer nights so sweet. Far up in the heavens a few long slender clouds looked like silver shells. Standing still for a few seconds, one could hear in that nocturnal peace a confused, continuous murmur of life, a thousand slight sounds, the harmony of which seemed like silence.

A quail in a neighboring field uttered her double cry, and Julio, his ears erect, glided furtively toward the two flute-like notes of the bird, Annette following, as softly as he, holding her breath and crouching low.

"Ah," said the Countess, standing alone with the painter, "why do moments like this pass so quickly? We can hold nothing, keep nothing. We have not even time to taste what is good. It is over already."

Olivier kissed her hand, and replied, smiling:

"Oh, I cannot philosophize this evening! I belong to the present hour entirely."

"You do not love me as I love you," she murmured.

"Ah, do not—"

"No," she interrupted, "in me you love, as you said very truly before dinner, a woman who satisfies the needs of your heart, a woman who never has caused you a pain, and who has put a little happiness into your life. I know that; I feel it. Yes, I have the good consciousness, the ardent joy of having been good, useful, and helpful to you. You have loved, you still love all that you find agreeable in me, my attentions to you, my admiration, my wish to please you, my passion, the complete gift I made to you of my whole being. But it is not I you really love, do you know? Oh, I feel that as one feels a cold current of air. You love a thousand things about me—my beauty, which is fast leaving me, my devotion, the wit they say I possess, the opinion the world has of me, and that which I have of you in my heart; but it is not I—I, nothing but myself—do you understand?"

He laughed in a soft and friendly way.

"No, I do not understand you very well. You make a reproachful attack which is quite unexpected."

"Oh, my God! I wish I could make you understand how I love you! I am always seeking, but cannot find a means. When I think of you—and I am always thinking of you—I feel in the depths of my being an unspeakable intoxication of longing to be yours, an irresistible need of giving myself to you even more completely. I should like to sacrifice myself in some absolute way, for there is nothing better, when one loves, than to give, to give always, all, all, life, thought, body, all that one has, to feel that one is giving, to be ready to risk anything to give still more. I love you so much that I love to suffer for you, I love even my anxieties, my torments, my jealousies, the pain I feel when I realize that you are not longer tender toward me. I love in you a someone that only I have discovered, a you which is not the you of the world that is admired and known, a you which is mine, which cannot change nor grow old, which I cannot cease to love, for I have, to look at it, eyes that see it alone. But one cannot say these things. There are no words to express them."

He repeated softly, over and over:

"Dear, dear, dear Any!"

Julio came back, bounding toward them, without having found the quail, which had kept still at his approach; Annette followed him, breathless from running.

"I can't run any more," said she. "I will prop myself up with you, Monsieur painter!"

She leaned on Olivier's free arm, and they returned, walking thus, he between them, under the shadow of the trees. They spoke no more. He walked on, possessed by them, penetrated by a sort of feminine essence with which their contact filled him. He did not try to see them, since he had them near him; he even closed his eyes that he might feel their proximity the better. They guided him, conducted him, and he walked straight before him, fascinated by them, with the one on the left as well as the one on the right, without knowing, indeed, which was on the left or which on the right, which was mother, which was daughter. He abandoned himself willingly to the pleasure of unpremeditated and exquisite sensuous delight. He even tried to mingle them in his heart, not to distinguish them in his thought, and quieted desire with the charm of this confusion. Was it not only one woman beside him, composed of this mother and daughter, so much alike? And did not the daughter seem to have come to earth only for the purpose of reanimating his former love for the mother?

When he opened his eyes on entering the castle, it seemed to him that he had just passed through the most delicious moments of his life; that he had experienced the strangest, the most puzzling, yet complete emotion a man might feel, intoxicated with the same love by the seductiveness emanating from two women.

"Ah, what an exquisite evening!" said he, as soon as he found himself between them in the lamplight.

"I am not at all sleepy," said Annette; "I could pass the whole night walking when the weather is fine."

The Countess looked at the clock.

"Oh, it is half after eleven. You must go to bed, my child."

They separated, and went to their own apartments. The young girl who did not wish to go to bed was the only one that went to sleep at once.

The next morning, at the usual hour, when the maid, after opening the curtains and the shutters, brought the tea and looked at her mistress, who was still drowsy, she said:

"Madame looks better to-day, already."

"Do you think so?"

"Oh, yes. Madame's face looks more rested."

Though she had not yet looked at herself, the Countess knew that this was true. Her heart was light, she did not feel it throb, and she felt once more as if she lived. The blood flowing in her veins was no longer coursing so rapidly as on the day before, hot and feverish, sending nervousness and restlessness through all her body, but gave her a sense of well-being and happy confidence.

When the maid had gone she went to look at herself in the mirror. She was a little surprised, for she felt so much better that she expected to find herself rejuvenated by several years in a single night. Then she realized the childishness of such a hope, and, after another glance, resigned herself to the knowledge that her complexion was only clearer, her eyes less fatigued, her lips a little redder than on the day before. As her soul was content, she could not feel sad, and she smiled, thinking: "Yes, in a few days I shall be quite myself again. I have gone through too much to recover so quickly."

But she remained seated a very long time before her toilet-table, upon which were laid out in graceful order on a muslin scarf bordered with lace, before a beautiful mirror of cut crystal, all her little ivory-handled instruments of coquetry, bearing her arms surmounted by a coronet. There they were, innumerable, pretty, all different, destined for delicate and secret use, some of steel, fine and sharp, of strange shapes, like surgical instruments for operations on children, others round and soft, of feathers, of down, of the skins of unknown animals, made to lay upon the tender skin the caresses of fragrant powders or of powerful liquid perfumes.

She handled them a long time with practised fingers, carrying them from her lips to her temples with touches softer than a kiss, correcting imperfections, underlining the eyes, beautifying the eyelashes. At last, when she went down stairs, she felt almost sure that the first glance cast upon her would not be too unfavorable.

"Where is Monsieur Bertin?" she inquired of a servant she met in the vestibule.

"Monsieur Bertin is in the orchard, playing tennis with Mademoiselle," the man replied.

She heard them from a distance counting the points. One after the other, the deep voice of the painter and the light one of the young girl, called: "Fifteen, thirty, forty, vantage, deuce, vantage, game!"

The orchard, where a space had been leveled for a tennis-court, was a great, square grass-plot, planted with apple-trees, inclosed by the park, the vegetable-garden, and the farms belonging to the castle. Along the slope that formed a boundary on three sides, like the defenses of an intrenched camp, grew borders of various kinds of flowers, wild and cultivated, roses in masses, pinks, heliotrope, fuchsias, mignonnette, and many more, which as Bertin said gave the air a taste of honey. Besides this, the bees, whose hives, thatched with straw, lined the wall of the vegetable-garden, covered the flowery field in their yellow, buzzing flight.

In the exact center of this orchard a few apple-trees had been cut down, in order to make a good court for tennis, and a tarry net, stretched across this space, separated it into two camps.

Annette, on one side, with bare head, her black skirt caught up, showing her ankles and half way up to her knee when she ran to catch a ball, dashed to and fro, with sparkling eyes and flushed cheeks, tired, out of breath with the sure and practised play of her adversary.

He, in white flannels, fitting tightly over the hips, a white shirt, and a white tennis cap, his abdomen somewhat prominent in that costume, awaited the ball coolly, judged its fall with precision, received and returned it without haste, without running, with the elegant pose, the passionate attention, and professional skill which he displayed in all athletic sports.

It was Annette that spied her mother first.

"Good morning, mamma!" she cried, "wait till we have finished this play."

That second's distraction lost her the game. The ball passed against her, almost rolling, touched the ground and went out of the game.

Bertin shouted "Won!" and the young girl, surprised, accused him of having profited by her inattention. Julio, trained to seek and find the lost balls, as if they were partridges fallen among the bushes, sprang behind her to get the ball rolling in the grass, seized it in his jaws, and brought it back, wagging his tail.

The painter now saluted the Countess, but, urged to resume the game, animated by the contest, pleased to find himself so agile, he threw only a short, preoccupied glance at the face prepared so carefully for him, asking:

"Will you allow me, dear Countess? I am afraid of taking cold and having neuralgia."

"Oh, yes," the Countess replied.

She sat down on a hay-stack, mowed that morning in order to give a clear field to the players, and, her heart suddenly touched with sadness, looked on at the game.

Her daughter, irritated at losing continually, grew more animated, excited, uttered cries of vexation or of triumph, and flew impetuously from one end of the court to the other. Often, in her swift movements, little locks of hair were loosened, rolled down and fell upon her shoulders. She seized them with impatient movements, and, holding the racket between her knees, fastened them up in place, thrusting hairpins into the golden mass.

And Bertin, from his position, cried to the Countess:

"Isn't she pretty like that, and fresh as the day?"

Yes, she was young, she could run, grow warm, become red, let her hair fly, brave anything, dare everything, for all that only made her more beautiful.

Then, when they resumed their play with ardor, the Countess, more and more melancholy, felt that Olivier preferred that game, that childish sport, like the play of kittens jumping after paper balls, to the sweetness of sitting beside her that warm morning, and feeling her loving pressure against him.

When the bell, far away, rang the first signal for breakfast, it seemed to her that someone had freed her, that a weight had been lifted from her heart. But as she returned, leaning on his arm, he said to her:

"I have been amusing myself like a boy. It is a great thing to be, or to feel oneself, young. Ah, yes, there is nothing like that. When we do not like to run any more, it is all over with us."

When they left the table the Countess, who on the preceding day had for the first time omitted her daily visit to the cemetery, proposed that they should go there together; so all three set out for the village.

They were obliged to go through some woods, through which ran a stream called "La Rainette," no doubt because of the frogs that peopled it; then they had to cross the end of a plain before arriving at the church, situated in the midst of a group of houses that sheltered the grocer, the baker, the butcher, the wine-merchant, and several other modest tradesmen who supplied the needs of the peasants.

The walk was made in thoughtful silence, the recollection of the dead weighing on their spirits. Arrived at the grave, the women knelt and prayed a long time. The Countess, motionless, bent low, her handkerchief at her eyes, for she feared to weep lest her tears run down her cheeks. She prayed, but not as she had prayed before this day, in a sort of invocation to her mother, a despairing appeal penetrating under the marble of the tomb until she seemed to feel by the poignancy of her own anguish that the dead must hear her, listen to her, but a simple, hesitating, and earnest utterance of the consecrated words of the Pater Noster and the Ave Maria. She would not have had that day sufficient strength and steadiness of nerve necessary for that cruel communion that brought no response with what remained of that being who had disappeared in the tomb where all that was left of her was concealed. Other anxieties had penetrated her woman's heart, had agitated, wounded, and distracted her; and her fervent prayer rose to Heaven, full of vague supplications. She offered her adoration to God, the inexorable God who has made all poor creatures on the earth, and begged Him to take pity on her as well as on the one He had recalled to Himself.

She could not have told what she had asked of God, so vague and confused were her fears still; but she felt the need of Divine aid, of a superhuman support against approaching dangers and inevitable sorrows.

Annette, with closed eyes, having also murmured the formulas, sank into a reverie, for she did not wish to rise before her mother.

Olivier Bertin looked at them, thinking that he never had seen a more ravishing picture, and somewhat regretful that it was out of the question for him to be permitted to make a sketch of the scene.

On their way back they talked of human life, softly stirring those bitter and poetic ideas of a tender but pessimistic philosophy, which is a frequent subject of conversation between men and women whom life has wounded a little, and whose hearts mingle as they sympathize with each other's grief.

Annette, who was not ripe for such thoughts, left them frequently to gather wild flowers beside the road.

But Olivier, desiring to keep her near him, nervous at seeing her continually darting away, never removed his eyes from her. He was irritated that she should show more interest in the colors of the plants than in the words he spoke. He experienced an inexpressible dissatisfaction at not being able to charm her, to dominate her, as he had captivated her mother; and he felt a desire to hold out his hand and seize her, hold her, forbid her to go away. He felt that she was too alert, too young, too indifferent, too free—free as a bird, or like a little dog that will not come back, will not obey, which has independence in its veins, that sweet instinct of liberty which neither voice nor whip has yet vanquished.

In order to attract her he talked of gayer things, and at times he questioned her, trying to awaken her feminine curiosity so that she would listen; but one would think that the capricious wind of heaven was blowing through Annette's head that day, as it blew across the undulating grain, carrying away and dispersing her attention into space, for she hardly uttered even the commonplace replies expected of her, between her short digressions, and made them with an absent air, then returned to her flowers. Finally he became exasperated, filled with a childish impatience, and as she ran up to beg her mother to carry her first bouquet so that she could gather another, he caught her by the elbow and pressed her arm, so that she could not escape again. She struggled, laughing, pulling with all her strength to get away from him; then, moved by masculine instinct, he tried gentler means, and, not being able to win her attention he tried to purchase it by tempting her coquetry.

"Tell me," said he, "what flower you prefer, and I will have a brooch made of it for you."

She hesitated, surprised.

"What, a brooch?"

"In stones of the same color; in rubies if it is the poppy; in sapphires if it is the cornflower, with a little leaf in emeralds."

Annette's face lighted up with that affectionate joy with which promises and presents animate a woman's countenance.

"The cornflower," said she, "it is so pretty."

"The cornflower it shall be. We will go to order it as soon as we return to Paris."

She no longer tried to leave him, attracted by the thought of the jewel she already tried to see, to imagine.

"Does it take very long to make a thing like that?" she asked.

He laughed, feeling that he had caught her.

"I don't know; it depends upon the difficulties. We will make the jeweler do it quickly."

A dismal thought suddenly crossed her mind.

"But I cannot wear it since I am in deep mourning!"

He had passed his arm under that of the young girl, and pressed it against him.

"Well, you will keep the brooch until you cease to wear mourning," said he; "that will not prevent you from looking at it."

As on the preceding evening, he was walking between them, held captive between their shoulders, and in order to see their eyes, of a similar blue dotted with tiny black spots, raised to his, he spoke to them in turn, moving his head first toward the one, then toward the other. As the bright sunlight now shone on them, he did not so fully confound the Countess with Annette, but he did more and more associate the daughter with the new-born remembrances of what the mother had been. He had a strong desire to embrace both, the one to find again upon cheek and neck a little of that pink and white freshness which he had already tasted, and which he saw now reproduced as by a miracle; the other because he loved her as he always had, and felt that from her came the powerful appeal of long habit. He even realized at that moment that his desire and affection for her, which for some time had been waning, had revived at the sight of her resuscitated youth.

Annette went away again to gather more flowers. This time Olivier did not call her back; it was as if the contact of her arm and the satisfaction of knowing that he had given her pleasure had quieted him; but he followed all her movements with the pleasure one feels in seeing the persons or things that captivate and intoxicate our eyes. When she returned, with a large cluster of flowers, he drew a deep breath, seeking unconsciously to inhale something of her, a little of her breath or the warmth of her skin in the air stirred by her running. He looked at her, enraptured, as one watches the dawn, or listens to music, with thrills of delight when she bent, rose again, or raised her arms to arrange her hair. And then, more and more, hour by hour, she evoked in him the memory of the past! Her laughter, her pretty ways, her motions, brought back to his lips the savor of former kisses given and returned; she made of the far-off past, of which he had forgotten the precise sensation, something like a dream in the present; she confused epochs, dates, the ages of his heart, and rekindling the embers of cooled emotions, she mingled, without his realizing it, yesterday with to-morrow, recollection with hope.

He asked himself as he questioned his memory whether the Countess in her brightest bloom had had that fawn-like, supple grace, that bold, capricious, irresistible charm, like the grace of a running, leaping animal. No. She had had a riper bloom but was less untamed. First, a child of the city, then a woman, never having imbibed the air of the fields and lived in the grass, she had grown pretty under the shade of the walls and not in the sunlight of heaven.

When they reentered the castle the Countess began to write letters at her little low table in the bay-window; Annette went up to her own room, and the painter went out again to walk slowly, cigar in mouth, hands clasped behind him, through the winding paths of the park. But he did not go away so far that he lost sight of the white facade or the pointed roof of the castle. As soon as it disappeared behind groups of trees or clusters of shrubbery, a shadow seemed to fall over his heart, as when a cloud hides the sun; and when it reappeared through the apertures in the foliage he paused a few seconds to contemplate the two rows of tall windows. Then he resumed his walk. He felt agitated, but content. Content with what? With everything.

The air seemed pure to him, life was good that day. His body felt once more the liveliness of a small boy, a desire to run, to catch the yellow butterflies fluttering over the lawn, as if they were suspended at the end of elastic threads. He sang little airs from the opera. Several times he repeated the celebrated phrase by Gounod: “Laisse-moi contempler ton visage,” discovering in it a profoundly tender expression which never before he had felt in the same way.

Suddenly he asked himself how it was that he had so soon become different from his usual self. Yesterday, in Paris, dissatisfied with everything, disgusted, irritated; to-day calm, satisfied with everything—one would say that some benevolent god had changed his soul. “That same kind god,” he thought, “might well have changed my body at the same time, and rejuvenated me a little.” Suddenly he saw Julio hunting among the bushes. He called him, and when the dog ran up to put his finely formed head, with its curly ears, under his hand, he sat down on the grass to pet him more comfortably, spoke gentle words to him, laid him on his knees, and growing tender as he caressed the animal, he kissed it, after the fashion of women whose hearts are easily moved to demonstration.

After dinner, instead of going out as on the evening before, they spent the hours in the drawing-room.

Suddenly the Countess said: “We must leave here soon.”

“Oh, don’t speak of that yet!” Olivier exclaimed. “You would not leave Roncieres when I was not here; now what I have come, you think only of going away.”

“But, my dear friend,” said she, “we three cannot remain here indefinitely.”

“It does not necessarily follow that we need stay indefinitely, but just a few days. How many times have I stayed at your house for whole weeks?”

“Yes, but in different circumstances, when the house was open to everyone.”

“Oh, mamma,” said Annette, coaxingly, “let us stay a few days more, just two or three. He teaches me so well how to play tennis. It annoys me to lose, but afterward I am glad to have made such progress.”

Only that morning the Countess had been planning to make this mysterious visit of her friend’s last until Sunday, and now she wished to go away, without knowing why. That day which she had hoped would be such a happy one had left in her soul an inexpressible but poignant sadness, a causeless apprehension, as tenacious and confused as a presentiment.

When she was once more alone in her room she even sought to define this new access of melancholy.

Had she experienced one of those imperceptible emotions whose touch has been so slight that reason does not remember it, but whose vibrations still stir the most sensitive chords of the heart? Perhaps? Which? She recalled, certainly, some little annoyances, in the thousand degrees of sentiment through which she had passed, each minute having its own. But they were too petty to have thus disheartened her. “I am exacting,” she thought. “I have no right to torment myself in this way.”

She opened her window, to breathe the night air, and leaned on the window-sill, gazing at the moon.

A slight noise made her look down. Olivier was pacing before the castle. “Why did he say that he was going to his room?” she thought; “why did he not tell me he was going out again? Why did he not ask me to come with him? He knows very well that it would have made me so happy. What is he thinking of now?”

This idea that he had not wished to have her with him on his walk, that he had preferred to go out alone this beautiful night, alone, with a cigar in his mouth, for she could see its fiery-red point—alone, when he might have given her the joy of taking her with him; this idea that he had not continual need of her, that he did not desire her always, created within her soul a new fermentation of bitterness.

She was about to close the window, that she might not see him or be tempted to call to him, when he raised his eyes and saw her.

“Well, are you star-gazing, Countess?”

“Yes,” she answered. “You also, as it appears.”

“Oh, I am simply smoking.”

She could not resist the desire to ask: “Why did you not tell me you were going out?”

“I only wanted to smoke a cigar. I am coming in now.”

“Then good-night, my friend.”

“Good-night, Countess.”

She retired as far as her low chair, sat down in it and wept; and her maid, who was called to assist her to bed, seeing her red eyes said with compassion:

"Ah, Madame is going to make a sad face for herself again to-morrow."

The Countess slept badly; she was feverish and had nightmare. As soon as she awoke she opened her window and her curtains to look at herself in the mirror. Her features were drawn, her eyelids swollen, her skin looked yellow; and she felt such violent grief because of this that she wished to say she was ill and to keep her bed, so that she need not appear until evening.

Then, suddenly, the necessity to go away entered her mind, to depart immediately, by the first train, to quit the country, where one could see too clearly by the broad light of the fields the ineffaceable marks of sorrow and of life itself. In Paris one lives in the half shadow of apartments, where heavy curtains, even at noontime, admit only a softened light. She would herself become beautiful again there, with the pallor one should have in that discreetly softened light. Then Annette's face rose before her eyes—so fresh and pink, with slightly disheveled hair, as when she was playing tennis. She understood then the unknown anxiety from which her soul had suffered. She was not jealous of her daughter's beauty! No, certainly not; but she felt, she acknowledged for the first time that she must never again show herself by Annette's side in the bright sunlight.

She rang, and before drinking her tea she gave orders for departure, wrote some telegrams, even ordering her dinner for that evening by telegraph, settled her bills in the country, gave her final instructions, arranged everything in less than an hour, a prey to feverish and increasing impatience.

When she went down stairs, Annette and Olivier, who had been told of her decision, questioned her with surprise. Then, seeing that she would not give any precise reason for this sudden departure, they grumbled a little and expressed their dissatisfaction until they separated at the station in Paris.

The Countess, holding out her hand to the painter, said: "Will you dine with us to-morrow?"

"Certainly, I will come," he replied, rather sulkily. "All the same, what you have done was not nice. We were so happy down there, all three of us."

CHAPTER III

A DANGEROUS WARNING

As soon as the Countess was alone with her daughter in her carriage, which was taking her back to her home, she suddenly felt tranquil and quieted, as if she had just passed through a serious crisis. She breathed easier, smiled at the houses, recognized with joy the look of the city, whose details all true Parisians seem to carry in their eyes and hearts. Each shop she passed suggested the ones beyond, on a line along the Boulevard, and the tradesman's face so often seen behind his show-case. She felt saved. From what? Reassured. Why? Confident. Of what?

When the carriage stopped under the arch of the porte-cochere, she alighted quickly and entered, as if flying, the shadow of the stairway; then passed to the shadow of her drawing-room, then to that of her bedroom. There she remained standing a few moments, glad to be at home, in security, in the dim and misty daylight of Paris, which, hardly brightening, compels one to guess as well as to see, where one may show what he pleases and hide what he will; and the unreasoning memory of the dazzling glare that bathed the country remained in her like an impression of past suffering.

When she went down to dinner, her husband, who had just arrived at home, embraced her affectionately, and said, smiling: "Ah, ha! I knew very well that our friend Bertin would bring you back. It was very clever of me to send him after you."

Annette responded gravely, in the peculiar tone she affected when she said something in jest without smiling:

"Oh, he had a great deal of trouble. Mamma could not decide for herself."

The Countess said nothing, but felt a little confused.

The doors being closed to visitors, no one called that evening. Madame de Guilleroy passed the whole of the following day in different shops, choosing or ordering what she needed. She had loved, from her youth, almost from her infancy, those long sittings before the mirrors of the great shops. From the moment of entering one, she took delight in thinking of all the details of that minute rehearsal in the green-room of Parisian life. She adored the rustle of the dresses worn by the salesgirls, who hastened forward to meet her, all smiles, with their offers, their queries; and Madame the dressmaker, the milliner, or corset-maker, was to her a person of consequence, whom she treated as an artist when she expressed an opinion in asking advice. She enjoyed even more to feel herself in the skilful hands of the young girls who undressed her and dressed her again, causing her to turn gently around before her own gracious reflection. The little shiver that the touch of their fingers produced on her skin, her neck, or in her hair, was one of the best and sweetest little pleasures that belonged to her life of an elegant woman.

This day, however, she passed before those candid mirrors, without her veil or hat, feeling a certain anxiety. Her first visit, at the milliner's, reassured her. The three hats which she chose were wonderfully becoming; she could not doubt it, and when the milliner said, with an air of conviction, "Oh, Madame la Comtesse, blondes should never leave off mourning" she went away much pleased, and entered other shops with a heart full of confidence.

Then she found at home a note from the Duchess, who had come to see her, saying that she would return in the evening; then she wrote some letters; then she fell into dreamy reverie for some time, surprised that this simple change of place had caused to recede into a past that already seemed far away the great misfortune that had overwhelmed her. She could not even convince herself that her return from Roncieres dated only from the day before, so much was the condition of her soul modified since her return to Paris, as if that little change had healed her wounds.

Bertin, arriving at dinner-time, exclaimed on seeing her:

"You are dazzling this evening!"

And this exclamation sent a warm wave of happiness through her being.

When they were leaving the table, the Count, who had a passion for billiards, offered to play a game with Bertin, and the two ladies accompanied them to the billiard-room, where the coffee was served.

The men were still playing when the Duchess was announced, and they all returned to the drawing-room. Madame de Corbelle and her husband presented themselves at the same time, their voices full of tears. For some minutes it seemed, from the doleful tones, that everyone was about to weep; but little by little, after a few tender words and inquiries, another current of thought set in; the voices took on a more cheerful tone, and everyone began to talk naturally, as if the shadow of the misfortune that had saddened them had suddenly been dissipated.

Then Bertin rose, took Annette by the hand, led her under the portrait of her mother, in the ray of light from the reflector, and said:

"Isn't this stupefying?"

The Duchess was so greatly surprised that she seemed dazed; she repeated many times: "Heavens! is it possible? Heavens! is it possible? It is like someone raised from the dead. To think that I did not see that when I came in! Oh, my little Any, I find you again, I, who knew you so well then in your first mourning as a woman—no, in your second, for you had already lost your father. Oh, that Annette, in black like that—why, it is her mother come back to earth! What a miracle! Without that portrait we never should have perceived it. Your daughter resembles you very much, but she resembles that portrait much more."

Musadieu now appeared, having heard of Madame de Guilleroy's return, as he wished to be one of the first to offer her the "homage of his sorrowful sympathy."

He interrupted his first speech on perceiving the young girl standing against the frame, illumined by the same ray of light, appearing like the living sister of the painting.

"Ah, that is certainly one of the most astonishing things I ever have seen," he exclaimed.

The Corbelles, whose convictions always followed established opinions, marveled in their turn with a little less exuberant ardor.

The Countess's heart seemed to contract, little by little, as if all these exclamations of astonishment had hurt it. Without speaking, she looked at her daughter standing by the image of herself, and a sudden feeling of weakness came over her. She longed to cry out: "Say no more! I know very well that she resembles me!"

Until the end of the evening she remained in a melancholy mood, having lost once more the confidence she had felt the day before.

Bertin was chatting with her when the Marquis de Farandal was announced. As soon as the painter saw him enter and approach the hostess he rose and glided behind her armchair, murmuring: "This is delightful! There comes that great animal now." Then, making a detour of the apartment, he reached the door and departed.

After receiving the salutations of the newcomer, the Countess looked around to find Olivier, to resume with him the talk in which she had been interested. Not seeing him, she asked:

"What, has the great man gone?"

"I believe so, my dear," her husband answered; "I just saw him going away in the English fashion."

She was surprised, reflected a few moments, and then began to talk to the Marquis.

Her intimate friends, however, discreetly took their leave early, for, so soon after her affliction, she had only half-opened her door, as it were.

When she found herself again lying on her bed, all the griefs that had assailed her in the country reappeared. They took a more distinct form; she felt them more keenly. She realized that she was growing old!

That evening, for the first time, she had understood that, in her own drawing-room, where until now she alone had been admired, complimented, flattered, loved, another, her daughter, was taking her place. She had comprehended this suddenly, when feeling that everyone's homage was paid to Annette. In that kingdom, the house of a pretty woman, where she will permit no one to overshadow her, where she eliminated with discreet and unceasing care all disadvantageous comparisons, where she allows the entrance of her equals only to attempt to make them her vassals, she saw plainly that her daughter was about to become the sovereign. How strange had been that contraction of her heart when all eyes were turned upon Annette as Bertin held her by the hand standing before the portrait! She herself felt as if she had suddenly disappeared, dispossessed, dethroned. Everyone looked at Annette; no one had a glance for her any more! She was so accustomed to hear compliments and flattery, whenever her portrait was admired, she was so sure of eulogistic phrases, which she had little regarded but which pleased her nevertheless, that this desertion of herself, this unexpected defection, this admiration intended wholly for her daughter, had moved, astonished, and hurt her more than if it had been a question of no matter what rivalry under any kind of conditions.

But, as she had one of those natures which, in all crises, after the first blow, react, struggle, and find arguments for consolation, she reasoned that, once her dear little daughter should be married, when they should no longer live under the same roof, she herself would no longer be compelled to endure that incessant comparison which was beginning to be too painful for her under the eyes of her friend Olivier.

But the shock had been too much for her that evening. She was feverish and hardly slept at all. In the morning she awoke weary and overcome by extreme lassitude, and then within her surged up an irresistible longing to be comforted again, to be succored, to ask help from someone who could cure all her ills, all her moral and physical ailments.

Indeed, she felt so ill at ease and weak that she had an idea of consulting her physician. Perhaps she was about to be seriously affected, for it was not natural that in a few hours she should pass through those successive phases of suffering and relief. So she sent him a telegram, and awaited his coming.

He arrived about eleven o'clock. He was one of those dignified, fashionable physicians whose decorations and titles guarantee their ability, whose tact at least equals mere skill, and who have, above all, when treating women, an adroitness that is surer than medicines.

He entered, bowed, looked at his patient, and said with a smile: "Come, this is not a very grave case. With eyes like yours one is never very ill."

She felt immediate gratitude to him for this beginning, and told him of her troubles, her weakness, her nervousness and melancholy; then she mentioned, without laying too much stress on the matter, her alarmingly ill appearance. After listening to her with an attentive air, though asking no questions except as to her appetite, as if he knew well the secret nature of this feminine ailment, he sounded her, examined her, felt of her shoulders with the tips of his fingers, lifted her arms, having undoubtedly met her thought and understood with the shrewdness of a practitioner who lifts all veils that she was consulting him more for her beauty than for her health. Then he said:

"Yes, we are a little anemic, and have some nervous troubles. That is not surprising, since you have experienced such a great affliction. I will write you a little prescription that will set you right again. But above all, you must eat strengthening food, take beef-tea, no water, but drink beer. I will indicate an excellent brand. Do not tire yourself by late hours, but walk as much as you can. Sleep a good deal and grow a little plumper. This is all that I can advise you, my fair patient."

She had listened to him with deep interest, trying to guess at what his words implied. She caught at the last word.

"Yes, I am too thin," said she. "I was a little too stout at one time, and perhaps I weakened myself by dieting."

"Without any doubt. There is no harm in remaining thin when one has always been so; but when one grows thin on principle it is always at the expense of something else. Happily, that can be soon remedied. Good-bye, Madame."

She felt better already, more alert; and she wished to send for the prescribed beer for her breakfast, at its headquarters, in order to obtain it quite fresh.

She was just leaving the table when Bertin was announced.

"It is I, again," said he, "always I. I have come to ask you something. Have you anything particular to do this afternoon?"

"No, nothing. Why?"

"And Annette?"

"Nothing, also."

"Then, can you come to the studio about four o'clock?"

"Yes, but for what purpose?"

"I am sketching the face of my Reverie, of which I spoke to you when I asked you whether Annette might pose for me a few moments. It would render me a great service if I could have her for only an hour to-day. Will you?"

The Countess hesitated, annoyed, without knowing the reason why. But she replied:

"Very well, my friend; we shall be with you at four o'clock."

"Thank you! You are goodness itself!"

He went away to prepare his canvas and study his subject, so that he need not tire his model too much.

Then the Countess went out alone, on foot, to finish her shopping. She went down to the great central streets, then walked slowly up the Boulevard Malesherbes, for she felt as if her limbs were breaking. As she passed Saint Augustin's, she was seized with a desire to enter the church and rest. She pushed open the door, sighed with satisfaction in breathing the cool air of the vast nave, took a chair and sat down.

She was religious as very many Parisians are religious. She believed in God without a doubt, not being able to admit the existence of the universe without the existence of a creator. But associating, as does everyone, the attributes of divinity with the nature of the created matter that she beheld with her own eyes, she almost personified the Eternal God with what she knew of His work, without having a very clear idea as to what this mysterious Maker might really be.

She believed in Him firmly, adored Him theoretically, feared Him very vaguely, for she did not profess to understand His intentions or His will, having a very limited confidence in the priests, whom she regarded merely as the sons of peasants revolting from military service. Her father, a middle-class Parisian, never had imposed upon her any particular principles of devotion, and she had lived on thinking little about religious matters until her marriage. Then, her new station in life indicating more strictly her apparent duties toward the Church, she had conformed punctiliously to this light servitude, as do so many of her station.

She was lady patroness to numerous and very well known infant asylums, never failed to attend mass at one o'clock on Sundays, gave alms for herself directly, and for the world by means of an abbe, the vicar of her parish.

She had often prayed, from a sense of duty, as a soldier mounts guard at a general's door. Sometimes she had prayed because her heart was sad, especially when she suspected Olivier of infidelity to her. At such times, without confiding to Heaven the cause for her appeal, treating God with the same naïve hypocrisy that is shown to a husband, she asked Him to succor her. When her father died, long before, and again quite recently, at her mother's death, she had had violent crises of religious fervor, and had passionately implored Him who watches over us and consoles us.

And, now behold! to-day, in that church where she had entered by chance, she suddenly felt a profound need to pray, not for some one nor for some thing, but for herself, for herself alone, as she had already prayed the other day at her mother's grave. She must have help from some source, and she called on God now as she had summoned the physician that very morning.

She remained a long time on her knees, in the deep silence of the church, broken only by the sound of footsteps. Then suddenly, as if a clock had struck in her heart, she awoke from her memories, drew out her watch and started to see that it was already four o'clock. She hastened away to take her daughter to the studio, where Olivier must already be expecting them.

They found the artist in his studio, studying upon the canvas the pose of his Reverie. He wished to reproduce exactly what he had seen in the Parc Monceau while walking with Annette: a young girl, dreaming, with an open book upon her knees. He had hesitated as to whether he should make her plain or pretty. If she were ugly she would have more character, would arouse more thought and emotion, would contain more philosophy. If pretty, she would be more seductive, would diffuse more charm, and would please better.

The desire to make a study after his little friend decided him. The Reveuse should be pretty, and therefore might realize her poetic vision one day or other; whereas if ugly she would remain condemned to a dream without hope and without end.

As soon as the two ladies entered Olivier said, rubbing his hands:

"Well, Mademoiselle Nane, we are going to work together, it seems!"

The Countess seemed anxious. She sat in an armchair, and watched Olivier as he placed an iron garden-chair in the right light. He opened his bookcase to get a book, then asked, hesitating:

"What does your daughter read?"

"Dear me! anything you like! Give her a volume of Victor Hugo."

"'La Legende des Siecles?'"

"That will do."

"Little one, sit down here," he continued, "and take this volume of verse. Look for page—page 336, where you will find a poem entitled 'Les Pauvres Gens.' Absorb it, as one drinks the best wines, slowly, word by word, and let it intoxicate you and move you. Then close the book, raise your eyes, think and dream. Now I will go and prepare my brushes."

He went into a corner to put the colors on his palette, but while emptying on the thin board the leaden tubes whence issued slender, twisting snakes of color, he turned from time to time to look at the young girl absorbed in her reading.

His heart was oppressed, his fingers trembled; he no longer knew what he was doing, and he mingled the tones as he mixed the little piles of paste, so strongly did he feel once more before this apparition, before that resurrection, in that same place, after twelve years, an irresistible flood of emotion overwhelming his heart.

Now Annette had finished her reading and was looking straight before her. Approaching her, Olivier saw in her eyes two bright drops which, breaking forth, ran down her cheeks. He was startled by one of those shocks that make a man forget himself, and turning toward the Countess he murmured:

"God! how beautiful she is!"

But he remained stupefied before the livid and convulsed face of Madame de Guilleroy. Her large eyes, full of a sort of terror, gazed at her daughter and the painter. He approached her, suddenly touched with anxiety.

"What is the matter?" he asked.

"I wish to speak to you."

Rising, she said quickly to Annette; "Wait a moment, my child; I have a word to say to Monsieur Bertin."

She passed swiftly into the little drawing-room near by, where he often made his visitors wait. He followed her, his head confused, understanding nothing. As soon as they were alone, she seized his hands and stammered:

"Olivier! Olivier, I beg you not to make her pose for you!"

"But why?" he murmured, disturbed.

"Why? Why?" she said precipitately. "He asks it! You do not feel it, then yourself? Why? Oh, I should have guessed it sooner myself, but I only discovered it this moment. I cannot tell you anything now. Go and find my daughter. Tell her that I am ill; fetch a cab, and come to see me in an hour. I will receive you alone."

"But, really, what is the matter with you?"

She seemed on the verge of hysterics.

"Leave me! I cannot speak here. Get my daughter and call a cab."

He had to obey and reentered the studio. Annette, unsuspicious, had resumed her reading, her heart overflowing with sadness by the poetic and lamentable story.

"Your mother is indisposed," said Olivier. "She became very ill when she went into the other room. I will take some ether to her."

He went out, ran to get a flask from his room and returned.

He found them weeping in each other's arms. Annette, moved by "Les Pauvres Gens," allowed her feelings full sway, and the Countess was somewhat solaced by blending her grief with that sweet sorrow, in mingling her tears with those of her daughter.

He waited for some time, not daring to speak; he looked at them, his own heart oppressed with an incomprehensible melancholy.

"Well," said he at last. "Are you better?"

"Yes, a little," the Countess replied. "It was nothing. Have you ordered a carriage?"

"Yes, it will come directly."

"Thank you, my friend—it is nothing. I have had too much grief for a long time."

"The carriage is here," a servant announced.

And Bertin, full of secret anguish, escorted his friend, pale and almost swooning, to the door, feeling her heart throb against his arm.

When he was alone he asked himself what was the matter with her, and why had she made this scene. And he began to seek a reason, wandering around the truth without deciding to discover it. Finally, he began to suspect. "Well," he said to himself, "is it possible she believes that I am making love to her daughter? No, that would be too much!" And, combating with ingenious and loyal arguments that supposititious conviction, he felt indignant that she had lent for an instant to this healthy and almost paternal affection any suspicion of gallantry. He became more and more irritated against the Countess, utterly unwilling to concede that she had dared suspect him of such villainy, of an infamy so unqualifiable; and he resolved, when the time should come for him to answer her, that he would not soften the expression of his resentment.

He soon left his studio to go to her house, impatient for an explanation. All along the way he prepared, with a growing irritation, the arguments and phrases that must justify him and avenge him for such a suspicion.

He found her on her lounge, her face changed by suffering.

"Well," said he, drily, "explain to me, my dear friend, the strange scene that has just occurred."

"What, you have not yet understood it?" she said, in a broken voice.

"No, I confess I have not."

"Come, Olivier, search your own heart well."

"My heart?"

"Yes, at the bottom of your heart."

"I don't understand. Explain yourself better."

"Look well into the depths of your heart, and see whether you find nothing there that is dangerous for you and for me."

"I repeat that I do not comprehend you. I guess that there is something in your imagination, but in my own conscience I see nothing."

"I am not speaking of your conscience, but of your heart."

"I cannot guess enigmas. I entreat you to be more clear."

Then, slowing raising her hands, she took the hands of the painter and held them; then, as if each word broke her heart, she said:

"Take care, my friend, or you will fall in love with my daughter!"

He withdrew his hands abruptly, and with the vivacity of innocence which combats a shameful accusation, with animated gesture and increasing excitement, he defended himself, accusing her in her turn of having suspected him unjustly.

She let him talk for some time, obstinately incredulous, sure of what she had said. Then she resumed:

"But I do not suspect you, my friend. You were ignorant of what was passing within you, as I was ignorant of it until this morning. You treat me as if I had accused you of wishing to seduce Annette. Oh, no, no! I know how loyal you are, worthy of all esteem and of every confidence. I only beg you, I entreat you to look into the depths of your heart and see whether the affection which, in spite of yourself, you are beginning to have for my daughter, has not a characteristic a little different from simple friendship."

Now he was offended, and, growing still more excited, he began once more to plead his loyalty, just as he argued all alone in the street.

She waited until he had finished his defense; then, without anger, but without being shaken in her conviction, though frightfully pale, she murmured:

"Olivier, I know very well all that you have just said to me, and I think as you do. But I am sure that I do not deceive myself. Listen, reflect, understand. My daughter resembles me too much, she is too much what I was once when you began to love me, that you should not begin to love her, too."

"Then," he exclaimed, "you dare to throw in my face such a thing as that on this simple supposition and ridiculous reasoning: 'He loves me; my daughter resembles me; therefore he will love her'!"

But seeing the Countess's face changing more and more, he continued in a softer tone:

"Now, my dear Any, it is precisely because I do find you once more in her that this young girl pleases me so much. It is you, you alone, that I love when I look at her."

"Yes, and it is just that from which I begin to suffer, and which makes me so anxious. You are not yet aware of what you feel, but by and by you will no longer be able to deceive yourself regarding it."

"Any, I assure you that you are mad."

"Do you wish proofs?"

"Yes."

"You had not come to Roncieres for three years, in spite of my desire to have you come. But you rushed down there when it was proposed that you should come to fetch us."

"Oh, indeed! You reproach me for not leaving you alone down there, knowing that you were ill, after your mother's death!"

"So be it! I do not insist. But look: the desire to see Annette again is so imperious with you that you could not pass this day without asking me to take her to your studio, under the pretext of posing her."

"And do you not suppose it was you I wished to see?"

"At this moment you are arguing against yourself, trying to convince yourself—but you do not deceive me. Listen again: Why did you leave abruptly, the night before last, when the Marquis de Farandal entered? Do you know why?"

He hesitated, very much surprised, disturbed, disarmed by this observation. Then he said slowly:

"But—I hardly know—I was tired, and then, to be candid, that imbecile makes me nervous."

"Since when?"

"Always."

"Pardon me, I have heard you sing his praises. You liked him once. Be quite sincere, Olivier."

He reflected a few moments; then, choosing his words, he said:

"Yes, it is possible that the great love I have for you makes me love so much everything that belongs to you as to modify my opinion of that bore, whom I might meet occasionally with indifference, but whom I should not like to see in your house almost every day."

"My daughter's house will not be mine. But this is sufficient. I know the uprightness of your heart. I know that you will reflect deeply on what I have just said to you. When you have reflected you will understand that I have pointed out a great danger to you, while yet there is time to escape it. And you will beware. Now let us talk of something else, will you?"

He did not insist, but he was much disturbed; he no longer knew what to think, though indeed he had need for reflection. He went away after a quarter of an hour of unimportant conversation.

CHAPTER IV

SWEET POISON

With slow steps, Olivier returned to his own house, troubled as if he had just learned some shameful family secret. He tried to sound his heart, to see clearly within himself, to read those intimate pages of the inner book which seemed glued together, and which sometimes only a strange hand can turn over by separating them. Certainly he did not believe himself in love with Annette. The Countess, whose watchful jealousy never slept, had foreseen this danger from afar, and had signaled it before it even existed. But might that peril exist to-morrow, the day after, in a month? It was the frank question that he tried to answer sincerely. It was true that the child stirred his instincts of tenderness, but these instincts in men are so numerous that the dangerous ones should not be confounded with the inoffensive. Thus he adored animals, especially cats, and could not see their silky fur without being seized with an irresistible sensuous desire to caress their soft, undulating backs and kiss their electric fur.

The attraction that impelled him toward this girl a little resembled those obscure yet innocent desires that go to make up part of all the ceaseless and unappeasable vibrations of human nerves. His eye of the artist, as well as that of the man, was captivated by her freshness, by that springing of beautiful clear life, by that essence of youth that glowed in her; and his heart, full of memories of his long intimacy with the Countess, finding in the extraordinary resemblance of Annette to her mother a reawakening of old feelings, of emotions sleeping since the beginning of his love, had been startled perhaps by the sensation of an awakening. An awakening? Yes. Was it that? This idea illumined his mind. He felt that he had awakened after years of sleep. If he had loved the young girl without being aware of it, he should have experienced near her that rejuvenation of his whole being which creates a different man as soon as the flame of a new desire is kindled within him. No, the child had only breathed upon the former fire. It had always been the mother that he loved, but now a little more than recently, no doubt, because of her daughter, this reincarnation of herself. And he formulated this decision with the reassuring sophism: "One loves but once! The heart may often be affected at meeting some other being, for everyone exercises on others either attractions or repulsions. All these influences create friendship, caprices, desire for possession, quick and fleeting ardors, but not real love. That this love may exist it is necessary that two beings should be so truly born for each other, should be linked together in so many different ways, by so many similar tastes, by so many affinities of body, of mind, and of character, and so many ties of all kinds that the whole shall form a union of bonds. That which we love, in short, is not so much Madame X. or Monsieur Z.; it is a women or a man, a creature without a name, something sprung from Nature, that great female, with organs, a form, a heart, a mind, a combination of attributes which like a magnet attract our organs, our eyes, our lips, our hearts, our thoughts, all our appetites, sensual as well as intellectual. We love a type, that is, the reunion in one single person of all the human qualities that may separately attract us in others."

For him, the Comtesse de Guilleroy had been this type, and their long-standing liaison, of which he had not wearied, proved it to him beyond doubt. Now, Annette so much resembled physically what her mother had been as to deceive the eye; so there was nothing astonishing in the fact that this man's heart had been surprised, if even it had not been wholly captured. He had adored one woman! Another woman was born of her, almost her counterpart. He could not prevent himself from bestowing on the latter a little tender remnant of the passionate attachment he had had for the former. There was no harm nor danger in that. Only his eyes and his memory allowed themselves to be deluded by this appearance of resurrection; but his instinct never had been affected, for never had he felt the least stirring of desire for the young girl.

However, the Countess had reproached him with being jealous of the Marquis! Was it true? Again he examined his conscience severely, and decided that as a matter of fact he was indeed a little jealous. What was there astonishing in that, after all? Are we not always being jealous of men who pay court to no matter what woman? Does not one experience in the street, at a restaurant, or a theater, a little feeling of enmity toward the gentleman who is passing or who enters with a lovely girl on his arm? Every possessor of a woman is a rival, a triumphant male, a conqueror envied by all the other males. And then, without considering these physiological reasons, if it was natural that he should have for Annette a sympathy a little excessive because of his love for her mother, was it not natural also that he should feel in his heart a little masculine hatred of the future husband? He could conquer this unworthy feeling without much trouble.

But in the depths of his heart he still felt a sort of bitter discontent with himself and with the Countess. Would not their daily intercourse be made disagreeable by the suspicion that he would be aware of in her? Should he not be compelled to watch with tiresome and scrupulous attention all that he said and did, his very looks, his slightest approach toward the young girl? for all that he might do or say would appear suspicious to the mother. He reached his home in a gloomy mood and began to smoke cigarettes, with the vehemence of an irritated man who uses ten matches to light his tobacco. He tried in vain to work. His hand, his eye, and his brain seemed to have lost the knack of painting, as if they had forgotten it, or never had known and practised the art. He had taken up to finish a little sketch on canvas—a street corner, at which a blind man stood singing—and he looked at it with unconquerable indifference, with such a lack of power to continue it that he sat down before it, palette in hand, and forgot it, though continuing to gaze at it with attention and abstracted fixity.

Then, suddenly, impatience at the slowness of time, at the interminable minutes, began to gnaw him with its intolerable fever. What should he do until he could go to the club for dinner, since he could not work at home? The thought of the streets tired him only to think of, filled him with disgust for the sidewalks, the pedestrians, the carriages and shops; and the idea of paying visits that day, to no matter whom, aroused in him an instantaneous hatred for everyone he knew.

Then, what should he do? Should he pace to and fro in his studio, looking at the clock at every turn, watching the displacement of the long hand every few seconds? Ah, he well knew those walks from the door to the cabinet, covered with ornaments. In his hours of excitement, impulse, ambition, of fruitful and facile execution, these pacings had been delicious recreation—these goings and comings across the large room, brightened, animated, and warmed by work; but now, in his hours of powerlessness and nausea, the miserable hours, when nothing seemed worth the trouble of an effort or a movement, it was like the terrible tramping of a prisoner in his cell. If only he could have slept, even for an hour, on his divan! But no, he should not sleep; he should only agitate himself until he trembled with exasperation. Whence came this sudden attack of bad temper? He thought: "I am becoming excessively nervous to have worked myself into such a state for so insignificant a cause."

Then he thought he would take a book. The volume of La Legende des Siecles had remained on the iron chair where Annette had laid it. He opened it and read two pages of verse without understanding them. He understood them no more than if they had been written in a foreign tongue. He was determined, however, and began again, only to find that what he read had not really penetrated to his mind. "Well," said he to himself, "it appears that I am becoming imbecile!" But a sudden inspiration reassured him as to how he should fill the two hours that must elapse before dinner-time. He had a hot bath prepared, and there he remained stretched out, relaxed and soothed by the warm water, until his valet, bringing his clothes, roused him from a doze. Then he went to the club, where he found the usual companions. He was received with open arms and exclamations, for they had not seen him for several days.

"I have just returned from the country," he explained.

All those men, except Musadieu, the landscape painter, professed a profound contempt for the fields. Rocdiane and Landa, to be sure, went hunting there, but among plains or woods they only enjoyed the pleasure of seeing pheasants, quail, or partridges falling like handfuls of feathers under their bullets, or little rabbits riddled with shot, turning somersaults like clowns, going heels over head four or five times, showing their white bellies and tails at every bound. Except for these sports of autumn and winter, they thought the country a bore. As Rocdiane would say: "I prefer little women to little peas!"

The dinner was lively and jovial as usual, animated by discussions wherein nothing unforeseen occurs. Bertin, to arouse himself, talked a great deal. They found him amusing, but as soon as he had had coffee, and a sixty-point game of billiards with the banker Liverdy, he went out, rambling from the Madeleine to the Rue Taitbout; after passing three times before the Vaudeville, he asked himself whether he should enter; almost called a cab to take him to the Hippodrome; changed his mind and turned toward the Nouveau Cirque, then made an abrupt half turn, without motive, design, or pretext, went up the Boulevard Malesherbes, and walked more slowly as he approached the dwelling of the Comtesse de Guilleroy. "Perhaps she will think it strange to see me again this evening," he thought. But he reassured himself in reflecting that there was nothing astonishing in his coming a second time to inquire how she felt.

She was alone with Annette, in the little back drawing-room, and was still working on her coverlets for the poor.

She said simply, on seeing him enter: "Ah, is it you, my friend?"

"Yes, I felt anxious; I wished to see you. How are you?"

"Thank you, very well."

She paused a moment, then added, significantly:

"And you?"

He began to laugh unconcernedly, as he replied: "Oh. I am very well, very well. Your fears were entirely without foundation."

She raised her eyes, pausing in her work, and fixed her gaze upon him, a gaze full of doubt and entreaty.

"It is true," said he.

"So much the better," she replied, with a smile that was slightly forced.

He sat down, and for the first time in that house he was seized with irresistible uneasiness, a sort of paralysis of ideas, still greater than that which had seized him that day as he sat before his canvas.

"You may go on, my child; it will not annoy him," said the Countess to her daughter.

"What was she doing?"

"She was studying a fantaisie."

Annette rose to go to the piano. He followed her with his eyes, unconsciously, as he always did, finding her pretty. Then he felt the mother's eye upon him, and turned his head abruptly, as if he were seeking something in the shadowy corner of the drawing-room.

The Countess took from her work-table a little gold case that he had given her, opened it, and offered him some cigarettes.

"Pray smoke, my friend," said she; "you know I like it when we are alone here."

He obeyed, and the music began. It was the music of the distant past, graceful and light, one of those compositions that seem to have inspired the artist on a soft moonlight evening in springtime.

"Who is the composer of that?" asked Bertin.

"Schumann," the Countess replied. "It is little known and charming."

A desire to look at Annette grew stronger within him, but he did not dare. He would have to make only a slight movement, merely a turn of the neck, for he could see out of the corner of his eye the two candles lighting the score; but he guessed so well, read so clearly, the watchful gaze of the Countess that he remained motionless, his eyes looking straight before him, interested apparently in the gray thread of smoke from his cigarette.

"Was that all you had to say to me?" Madame de Guilleroy murmured to him.

He smiled.

"Don't be vexed with me. You know that music hypnotizes me; it drinks my thoughts. I will talk soon."

"I must tell you," said the Countess, "that I had studied something for you before mamma's death. I never had you hear it, but I will play it for you immediately, as soon as the little one has finished; you shall see how odd it is."

She had real talent, and a subtle comprehension of the emotion that flows through sounds. It was indeed one of her surest powers over the painter's sensibility.

As soon as Annette had finished the pastoral symphony by Mehul, the Countess rose, took her place, and awakened a strange melody with her fingers, a melody of which all the phrases seemed complaints, divers complaints, changing, numerous, interrupted by a single note, beginning again, falling into the midst of the strains, cutting them short, scanning them, crashing into them, like a monotonous, incessant, persecuting cry, an unappeasable call of obsession.

But Olivier was looking at Annette, who had sat down facing him, and he heard nothing, comprehended nothing.

He looked at her, without thinking, indulging himself with the sight of her, as a good and habitual possession of which he had been deprived, drinking her youthful beauty wholesomely, as we drink water when thirsty.

"Well," said the Countess, "was not that beautiful?"

"Admirable! Superb!" he said, aroused. "By whom?"

"You do not know it?"

"No."

"What, really, you do not know it?"

"No, indeed."

"By Schubert."

"That does not astonish me at all," he said, with an air of profound conviction. "It is superb! You would be delightful if you would play it over again."

She began once more, and he, turning his head, began again to contemplate Annette, but listened also to the music, that he might taste two pleasures at the same time.

When Madame de Guilleroy had returned to her chair, in simple obedience to the natural duplicity of man he did not allow his gaze to rest longer on the fair profile of the young girl, who knitted opposite her mother, on the other side of the lamp.

But, though he did not see her, he tasted the sweetness of her presence, as one feels the proximity of a fire on the hearth; and the desire to cast upon her swift glances only to transfer them immediately to the Countess, tormented him—the desire of the schoolboy who climbs up to the window looking into the street as soon as the master's back is turned.

He went away early, for his power of speech was as paralyzed as his mind, and his persistent silence might be interpreted.

As soon as he found himself in the street a desire to wander took possession of him, for whenever he heard music it remained in his brain a long time, threw him into reveries that seemed the music itself in a dream, but in a clearer sequel. The sound of the notes returned, intermittent and fugitive, bringing separate measures, weakened, and far off as an echo; then, sinking into silence, appeared to leave it to the mind to give a meaning to the themes, and to seek a sort of tender and harmonious ideal. He turned to the left on reaching the outer Boulevard, perceiving the fairylike illumination of the Parc Monceau, and entered its central avenue, curving under the electric moons. A policeman was slowly strolling along; now and then a belated cab passed; a man, sitting on a bench in a bluish bath of electric light, was reading a newspaper, at the foot of a bronze mast that bore the dazzling globe. Other lights on the broad lawns, scattered among the trees, shed their cold and powerful rays into the foliage and on the grass, animating this great city garden with a pale life.

Bertin, with hands behind his back, paced the sidewalk, thinking of his walk with Annette in this same park when he had recognized in her the voice of her mother.

He let himself fall upon a bench, and, breathing in the cool freshness of the dewy lawns, he felt himself assailed by all the passionate expectancy that transforms the soul of youth into the incoherent canvas of an unfinished romance of love. Long ago he had known such evenings, those evenings of errant fancy, when he had allowed his caprice to roam through imaginary adventures, and he was astonished to feel a return of sensations that did not now belong to his age.

But, like the persistent note in the Schubert melody, the thought of Annette, the vision of her face bent beside the lamp, and the strange suspicion of the Countess, recurred to him at every instant. He continued, in spite of himself, to occupy his heart with this question, to sound the impenetrable depths where human feelings germinate before being born. This obstinate research agitated him; this constant preoccupation regarding the young girl seemed to open to his soul the way to tender reveries. He could not drive her from his mind; he bore within himself a sort of evocation of her image, as once he had borne the image of the Countess after she had left him; he often had the strange sensation of her presence in the studio.

Suddenly, impatient at being dominated by a memory, he arose, muttering: "Any was stupid to say that to me. Now she will make me think of the little one!"

He went home, disturbed about himself. After he had gone to bed he felt that sleep would not come to him, for a fever coursed in his veins, and a desire for reverie fermented in his heart. Dreading a wakeful night, one of those enervating attacks of insomnia brought about by agitation of the spirit, he thought he would try to read. How many times had a short reading served him as a narcotic! So he got up and went into his library to choose a good and soporific work; but his mind, aroused in spite of himself, eager for any emotion it could find, sought among the shelves for the name of some author that would respond to his state of exaltation and expectancy. Balzac, whom he loved, said nothing to him; he disdained Hugo, scorned Lamartine, who usually touched his emotions, and fell eagerly upon Musset, the poet of youth. He took the volume and carried it to bed, to read whatever he might chance to find.

When he had settled himself in bed, he began to drink, as with the thirst of a drunkard, those flowing verses of an inspired being who sang, like a bird, of the dawn of existence, and having breath only for the morning, was silent in the arid light of day; those verses of a poet who above all mankind was intoxicated with life, expressing his intoxication in fanfares of frank and triumphant love, the echo of all young hearts bewildered with desires.

Never had Bertin so perfectly comprehended the physical charm of those poems, which move the senses but hardly touch the intelligence. With his eyes on those vibrating stanzas, he felt that his soul was but twenty years old, radiant with hopes, and he read the volume through in a state of youthful intoxication. Three o'clock struck, and he was astonished to find that he had not yet grown sleepy. He rose to shut his window and to carry his book to a table in the middle of the room; but at the contact of the cold air a pain, of which several seasons at Aix had not cured him, ran through his loins, like a warning or a recall; and he threw aside the poet with an impatient movement, muttering: "Old fool!" Then he returned to bed and blew out his light.

He did not go to see the Countess the next day, and he even made the energetic resolution not to return there for two days. But whatever he did, whether he tried to paint or to walk, whether he bore his melancholy mood with him from house to house, his mind was everywhere harassed by the preoccupation of those two women, who would not be banished.

Having forbidden himself to go to see them, he solaced himself by thinking of them, and he allowed both mind and heart to give themselves up to memories of both. It happened often that in that species of hallucination in which he lulled his isolation the two faces approached each other, different, such as he knew them; then, passing one before the other, mingled, blended together, forming only one face, a little confused, a face that was no longer the mother's, not altogether that of the daughter, but the face of a woman loved madly, long ago, in the present, and forever.

Then he felt remorse at having abandoned himself to the influence of these emotions, which he knew were powerful and dangerous. To escape them, to drive them away, to deliver his soul from this sweet and captivating dream, he directed his mind toward all imaginable ideas, all possible subjects of reflection and meditation. Vain efforts! All the paths of distraction that he took led him back to the same point, where he met a fair young face that seemed to be lying in wait for him. It was a vague and inevitable obsession that floated round him, recalling him, stopping him, no matter what detour he might make in order to fly from it.

The confusion of these two beings, which had so troubled him on the evening of their walk at Roncieres, rose again in his memory as soon as he evoked them, after ceasing to reflect and reason, and he attempted to comprehend what strange emotion was this that stirred his being. He said to himself: "Now, have I for Annette a more tender feeling than I should have?" Then, probing his heart, he felt it burning with affection for a woman who was certainly young, who had Annette's features, but who was not she. And he reassured himself in a cowardly way by thinking: "No, I do not love the little one; I am the victim of a resemblance."

However, those two days at Roncieres remained in his soul like a source of heat, of happiness, of intoxication; and the least details of those days returned to him, one by one, with precision, sweeter even than at the time they occurred. Suddenly, while reviewing the course of these memories, he saw once more the road they had followed on leaving the cemetery, the young girl plucking flowers, and he recollected that he had promised her a cornflower in sapphires as soon as they returned to Paris.

All his resolutions took flight, and without struggling longer he took his hat and went out, rejoiced at the thought of the pleasure he was about to give her.

The footman answered him, when he presented himself:

"Madame is out, but Mademoiselle is at home."

Again he felt a thrill of joy.

"Tell her that I should like to speak to her."

Annette appeared very soon.

"Good-day, dear master," said she gravely.

He began to laugh, shook hands with her, and sitting near her, said:

"Guess why I have come."

She thought a few seconds.

"I don't know."

"To take you and your mother to the jeweler's to choose the sapphire cornflower I promised you at Roncieres."

The young girl's face was illumined with delight.

"Oh, and mamma has gone out," said she. "But she will return soon. You will wait for her, won't you?"

"Yes, if she is not too long."

"Oh, how insolent! Too long, with me! You treat me like a child."

"No, not so much as you think," he replied.

He felt in his heart a longing to please her, to be gallant and witty, as in the most successful days of his youth, one of those instinctive desires that excite all the faculties of charming, that make the peacock spread its tail and the poet write verses. Quick and vivacious phrases rose to his lips, and he talked as he knew how to talk when he was at his best. The young girl, animated by his vivacity, answered him with all the mischief and playful shrewdness that were in her.

Suddenly, while he was discussing an opinion, he exclaimed: "But you have already said that to me often, and I answered you—"

She interrupted him with a burst of laughter.

"Ah, you don't say 'tu' to me any more! You take me for mamma!"

He blushed and was silent, then he stammered:

"Your mother has already sustained that opinion with me a hundred times."

His eloquence was extinguished; he knew no more what to say, and he now felt afraid, incomprehensibly afraid, of this little girl.

"Here is mamma," said she.

She had heard the door open in the outer drawing-room, and Olivier, disturbed as if some one had caught him in a fault, explained how he had suddenly bethought him of his promise, and had come for them to take them to the jeweler's.

"I have a coupe," said he. "I will take the bracket seat."

They set out, and a little later they entered Montara's.

Having passed all his life in the intimacy, observation, study, and affection of women, having always occupied his mind with them, having been obliged to sound and discover their tastes, to know the details of dress and fashion as they knew them, being familiar with the minute details of their private life, he had arrived at a point that enabled him often to share certain of their sensations, and he always experienced, when entering one of the great shops where the charming and delicate accessories of their beauty are to be found, an emotion of pleasure that almost equaled that which stirred their hearts. He interested himself as they did in those coquettish trifles with which they set forth their beauty; the stuffs pleased his eyes; the laces attracted his hands; the most insignificant furbelows held his attention. In jewelers' shops he felt for the showcases a sort of religious respect, as if before a sanctuary of opulent seduction; and the counter, covered with dark cloth, upon which the supple fingers of the goldsmith make the jewels roll, displaying their precious reflections, filled him with a certain esteem.

When he had seated the Countess and her daughter before this severe piece of furniture, on which each, with a natural movement, placed one hand, he indicated what he wanted, and they showed him models of little flowers.

Then they spread sapphires before him, from which it was necessary to choose four. This took a long time. The two women turned them over on the cloth with the tips of their fingers, then lifted them carefully, looked through them at the light, studying them with knowing and passionate attention. When they had laid aside those they had chosen, three emeralds had to be selected to make the leaves, then a tiny diamond that would tremble in the center like a drop of dew.

Then Olivier, intoxicated with the joy of giving, said to the Countess:

"Will you do me the favor to choose two rings?"

"I?"

"Yes. One for you, one for Annette. Let me make you these little presents in memory of the two days I passed at Roncieres."

She refused. He insisted. A long discussion followed, a struggle of words and arguments, which ended, not without difficulty, in his triumph.

Rings were brought, some, the rarest, alone in special cases; others arranged in similar groups in large square boxes, wherein all the fancifulness of their settings were displayed in alignment on the velvet. The painter was seated between the two women, and began, with the same ardent curiosity, to take up the gold rings, one by one, from the narrow slits that held them. He deposited them before him on the cloth-covered counter where they were massed in two groups, those that had been rejected at first sight and those from which a choice would be made.

Time was passing, insensibly and sweetly, in this pretty work of selection, more captivating than all the pleasures of the world, distracting and varied as a play, stirring also an exquisite and almost sensuous pleasure in a woman's heart.

Then they compared, grew animated, and, after some hesitation, the choice of the three judges settled upon a little golden serpent holding a beautiful ruby between his thin jaws and his twisted tail.

Olivier, radiant, now arose.

"I will leave you my carriage," said he; "I have something to look after, and I must go."

But Annette begged her mother to walk home, since the weather was so fine. The Countess consented, and, having thanked Bertin, went out into the street with her daughter.

They walked for some time in silence, enjoying the sweet realization of presents received; then they began to talk of all the jewels they had seen and handled. Within their minds still lingered a sort of glittering and jingling, an echo of gaiety. They walked quickly through the crowd which fills the street about five o'clock on a summer evening. Men turned to look at Annette, and murmured in distinct words of admiration as they passed. It was the first time since her mourning, since black attire had added brilliancy to her daughter's beauty, that the Countess had gone out with her in the streets of Paris; and the sensation of that street success, that awakened attention, those whispered compliments, that little wake of flattering emotion which the passing of a pretty woman leaves in a crowd of men, contracted her heart little by little with the same painful feeling she had had the other evening in her drawing-room, when her guests had compared the little one with her own portrait. In spite of herself, she watched for those glances that Annette attracted; she felt them coming from a distance, pass over her own face without stopping and suddenly settle upon the fair face beside her own. She guessed, she saw in the eyes the rapid and silent homage to this blooming youth, to the powerful charm of that radiant freshness, and she thought: "I was as pretty as she, if not prettier." Suddenly the thought of Olivier flashed across her mind, and she was seized, as at Roncieres, with a longing to flee.

She did not wish to feel herself any longer in this bright light, amid this stream of people, seen by all those men who yet did not look at her. Those days seemed far away, though in reality quite recent, when she had sought and provoked comparison with her daughter. Who, to-day, among the passers, thought of comparing them? Only one person had thought of it, perhaps, a little while ago, in the jeweler's shop. He? Oh, what suffering! Could it be that he was thinking continually of that comparison? Certainly he could not see them together without thinking of it, and without remembering the time when she herself had entered his house, so fresh, so pretty, so sure of being loved!

"I feel ill," said she. "We will take a cab, my child."

Annette was uneasy.

"What is the matter, mamma?" she asked.

"It is nothing; you know that since your grandmother's death I often have these moments of weakness."

CHAPTER V

A WANING MOON

Fixed ideas have the tenacity of incurable maladies. Once entered in the soul they devour it, leaving it no longer free to think of anything, or to have a taste for the least thing. Whatever she did, or wherever she was, alone or surrounded by friends, she could no longer rid herself of the thought that had seized her in coming home side by side with her daughter. Could it be that Olivier, seeing them together almost every day, thought continually of the comparison between them?

Surely he must do it in spite of himself, incessantly, himself haunted by that unforgettable resemblance, accentuated still further by the imitation of tone and gesture they had tried to produce. Every time he entered she thought of that comparison; she read it in his eyes, guessed it and pondered over it in her heart and in her mind. Then she was tortured by a desire to hide herself, to disappear, never to show herself again beside her daughter.

She suffered, too, in all ways, not feeling at home any more in her own house. That pained feeling of dispossession which she had had one evening, when all eyes were fixed on Annette under her portrait, continued, stronger and more exasperating than before. She reproached herself unceasingly for feeling that yearning need for deliverance, that unspeakable desire to send her daughter away from her, like a troublesome and tenacious guest; and she labored against it with unconscious skill, convinced of the necessity of struggling to retain, in spite of everything, the man she loved.

Unable to hasten Annette's marriage too urgently, because of their recent mourning, she feared, with a confused yet dominating fear, anything that might defeat that plan; and she sought, almost in spite of herself, to awaken in her daughter's heart some feeling of tenderness for the Marquis.

All the resourceful diplomacy she had employed so long to hold Olivier now took with her a new form, shrewder, more secret, exerting itself to kindle affection between the young people, and to keep the two men from meeting.

As the painter, who kept regular hours of work, never breakfasted away from home, and usually gave only his evenings to his friends, she often invited the Marquis to breakfast. He would arrive, spreading around him the animation of his ride, a sort of breath of morning air. And he talked gaily of all those worldly things that seem to float every day upon the autumnal awakening of brilliant and horse-loving Paris in the avenues of the Bois. Annette was amused in listening to him, acquired some taste for those topics of the days that he recounted to her, fresh and piquant as they were. An intimacy of youth sprang up between them, a pleasant companionship which a common and passionate love for horses naturally fostered. When he had gone the Countess and the Count would artfully praise him, saying everything necessary to let the young girl know that it depended only upon herself to marry him if he pleased her.

She had understood very quickly, however, and reasoning frankly with herself, judged it a very simple thing to take for a husband this handsome fellow, who would give her, besides other satisfactions, that which she preferred above all others, the pleasure of galloping beside him every morning on a thoroughbred.

They found themselves betrothed one day, quite naturally, after a clasp of the hand and a smile, and the marriage was spoken of as something long decided. Then the Marquis began to bring gifts, and the Duchess treated Annette like her own daughter. The whole affair, then, had been fostered by common accord, warmed over the fire of a little intimacy, during the quiet hours of the day; and the Marquis, having many other occupations, relatives, obligations and duties, rarely came in the evening.

That was Olivier's time. He dined regularly every week with his friends, and also continued to appear without appointment to ask for a cup of tea between ten o'clock and midnight.

As soon as he entered the Countess watched him, devoured by a desire to know what was passing in his heart. He gave no glance, made no gesture that she did not immediately interpret, and she was tortured by this thought: "It is impossible that he is not in love with her, seeing us so close together."

He, too, brought gifts. Not a week passed that he did not appear bearing two little packages in his hands, offering one to the mother, the other to the daughter; and the Countess, opening the boxes, which often held valuable objects, felt again that contraction of the heart. She knew so well that desire to give which, as a woman, she never had been able to satisfy—that desire to bring something that would give pleasure, to purchase for someone, to find in the shops some trifle that would please.

The painter had already been through this phase, and she had seen him come in many times with that same smile, that same gesture, a little packet in his hand. That habit had ceased after awhile, and now it had begun again. For whom? She had no matter of doubt. It was not for her!

He appeared fatigued and thin. She concluded that he was suffering. She compared his entrances, his manner, his bearing with the attitude of the Marquis, who was also beginning to be attracted by Annette's grace. It was not at all the same thing: Monsieur de Farandal admired her, Olivier Bertin loved! She believed this at least during her hours of torture; then, in quieter moments she still hoped that she had deceived herself.

Oh, often she could hardly restrain herself from questioning him when she was alone with him, praying, entreating him to speak, to confess all, to hide nothing! She preferred to know and to weep under certainty than to suffer thus under doubt, not able to read that closed heart, wherein she felt another love was growing.

That heart, which she prized more highly than her life, over which she had watched, and which she had warmed and animated with her love for twelve years, of which she had believed herself sure, which she had hoped was definitely hers, conquered, submissive, passionately devoted for the rest of their lives, behold! now that heart was escaping her by an inconceivable, horrible, and monstrous fatality! Yes, it had suddenly closed itself, upon a secret. She could no longer penetrate it by a familiar word, or hide therein her own affection as in a faithful retreat open for herself alone. What is the use of loving, of giving oneself without reserve, if suddenly he to whom one has offered her whole being, her entire existence, all, everything she had in the world, is to escape thus because another face has pleased him, transforming him in a few days almost into a stranger?

A stranger! He, Olivier? He spoke to her, as always, with the same words, the same voice, the same tone. And yet there was something between them, something inexplicable, intangible, invincible, almost nothing—that almost nothing that causes a sail to float away when the wind turns.

He was drifting, in fact, drifting away from her a little more each day, by all the glances he cast upon Annette. He himself did not attempt to see clearly into the depths of his heart.

He felt, indeed, that fermentation of love, that irresistible attraction; but he would not understand, he trusted to events, to the unforeseen chances of life.

He had no longer any other interest than that of his dinners and his evenings between those two women, separated from the gay world by their mourning. Meeting only indifferent faces at their house—those of the Corbelles, and Musadieu oftener—he fancied himself almost alone in the world with them; and as he now seldom saw the Duchess and the Marquis, for whom the morning and noontimes were reserved, he wished to forget them, suspecting that the marriage had been indefinitely postponed.

Besides, Annette never spoke of Monsieur de Farandal before him. Was this because of a sort of instinctive modesty, or was it perhaps from one of those secret intuitions of the feminine heart which enable them to foretell that of which they are ignorant?

Weeks followed weeks, without changing this manner of life, and autumn came, bringing the reopening of the Chamber, earlier than usual because of certain political dangers.

On the day of the reopening, the Comte de Guilleroy was to take to the meeting of Parliament Madame de Mortemain, the Marquis, and Annette, after a breakfast at his own house. The Countess alone, isolated in her sorrow, which was steadily increasing, had declared that she would remain at home.

They had left the table and were drinking coffee in the large drawing-room, in a merry mood. The Count, happy to resume parliamentary work, his only pleasure, talked very well concerning the existing situation and of the embarrassments of the Republic; the Marquis, unmistakably in love, answered him brightly, while gazing at Annette; and the Duchess was almost equally pleased with the emotion of her nephew and the distress of the government. The air of the drawing-room was warm with that first concentrated heat of newly-lighted furnaces, the heat of draperies, carpets, and walls, in which the perfumes of asphyxiated flowers was evaporating. There was in this closely shut room, filled with the aroma of coffee, an air of comfort, intimate, familiar, and satisfied, when the door was opened before Olivier Bertin.

He paused at the threshold, so surprised that he hesitated to enter, surprised as a deceived husband who beholds his wife's crime. A confusion of anger and mingled emotion suffocated him, revealing to him the fact that his heart was worm-eaten with love! All that they had hidden from him, and all that he had concealed from himself appeared before him as he perceived the Marquis installed in the house, as a betrothed lover!

He understood, in a transport of exasperation, all that which he would rather not have known and all that the Countess had not dared to tell him. He did not ask himself why all those preparations for marriage had been concealed from him. He guessed it, and his eyes, growing hard, met those of the Countess, who blushed. They understood each other.

When he was seated, everyone was silent for a few seconds, his unexpected entrance having paralyzed their flow of spirits; then the Duchess began to speak to him, and he replied in a brief manner, his voice suddenly changed.

He looked around at these people who were now chatting again, and said to himself: "They are making game of me. They shall pay for it." He was especially vexed with the Countess and Annette, whose innocent dissimulation he suddenly understood.

"Oh, oh! it is time to go," exclaimed the Count, looking at the clock. Turning to the painter, he added: "We are going to the opening of Parliament. My wife will remain here, however.

Will you accompany us? It would give me great pleasure."

"No, thanks," replied Olivier drily. "Your Chamber does not tempt me."

Annette approached in a playful way, saying: "Oh, do come, dear master! I am sure that you would amuse us much more than the deputies."

"No, indeed. You will amuse yourself very well without me."

Seeing him discontented and chagrined, she insisted, to show that she felt kindly toward him.

"Yes, come, sir painter! I assure you that as for myself I cannot do without you."

His next words escaped him so quickly that he could nether check them as he spoke nor soften their tone:

"Bah! You do well enough without me, just as everyone else does!"

A little surprised at his tone, she exclaimed: "Come, now! Here he is beginning again to leave off his 'tu' to me!"

His lips were curled in one of those smiles that reveal the suffering of a soul, and he said with a slight bow: "It will be necessary for me to accustom myself to it one day or another."

"Why, pray?"

"Because you will marry, and your husband, whoever he may be, would have the right to find that word rather out of place coming from me."

"It will be time enough then to think about that," the Countess hastened to say. "But I trust that Annette will not marry a man so susceptible as to object to such familiarity from so old a friend."

"Come, come!" cried the Count; "let us go. We shall be late."

Those who were to accompany him, having risen, went out after him, after the usual handshakes and kisses which the Duchess, the Countess, and her daughter exchanged at every meeting as at every parting.

They remained alone, She and He, standing, behind the draperies over the closed door.

"Sit down, my friend," said she softly.

But he answered, almost violently: "No, thanks! I am going, too."

"Oh, why?" she murmured, entreatingly.

"Because this is not my hour, it appears. I ask pardon for having come without warning."

"Olivier, what is the matter with you?"

"Nothing. I only regret having disturbed an organized pleasure party."

She seized his hand.

"What do you mean?" she asked. "They were just about to set out, since they were going to be present at the opening of the session. I intended to stay at home. Contrary to what you said just now, you were really inspired in coming to-day when I am alone."

He sneered.

"Inspired? Yes, I was inspired!"

She seized his wrists, and looking deep into his eyes she murmured very low:

"Confess to me that you love her!"

He withdrew his hands, unable to control his impatience any longer.

"But you are simply insane with that idea!"

She seized him again by the arm and, tightening her hold on his sleeve, she implored:

"Olivier! Confess, confess! I would rather know. I am certain of it, but I would rather know. I would rather—Oh, you do not comprehend what my life has become!"

He shrugged his shoulders.

"What would you have me do? Is it my fault if you lose your head?"

She held him, drawing him toward the other salon at the back, where they could not be heard. She drew him by his coat, clinging to him and panting. When she had led him as far as the little circular divan, she made him let himself fall upon it; then she sat down beside him.

"Olivier, my friend, my only friend, I pray you to tell me that you love her. I know it, I feel it from all that you do. I cannot doubt it. I am dying of it, but I wish to know it from your own lips."

As he still resisted, she fell on her knees at his feet. Her voice shook.

"Oh, my friend, my only friend! Is it true that you love her?"

"No, no, no!" he exclaimed, as he tried to make her rise. "I swear to you that I do not."

She reached up her hand to his mouth and pressed it there tight, stammering: "Oh, do not lie! I suffer too much!"

Then, letting her head fall on this man's knees, she sobbed.

He could see only the back of her neck, a mass of blond hair, mingled with many white threads, and he was filled with immense pity, immense grief.

Seizing that heavy hair in both hands he raised her head violently, turning toward himself two bewildered eyes, from which tears were flowing. And then on those tearful eyes he pressed his lips many times, repeating:

"Any! Any! My dear, my dear Any!"

Then she, attempting to smile, and speaking in that hesitating voice of children when choking with grief, said:

"Oh, my friend, only tell me that you still love me a little."

He embraced her again, even more tenderly than before.

"Yes, I love you, my dear Any."

She arose, sat down beside him again, seized his hands, looked at him, and said tenderly:

"It is such a long time that we have loved each other. It should not end like this."

He pressed her close to him, asking:

"Why should it end?"

"Because I am old, and because Annette resembles too much what I was when you first knew me."

Now it was his turn to close her sad lips with his fingers, saying:

"Again! I beg that you will speak no more of that. I swear to you that you deceive yourself."

"Oh, if you will only love me a little," she repeated.

"Yes, I love you," he said again.

They remained a long time without speaking, hands clasped in hands, deeply moved and very sad. At last she broke the silence, murmuring:

"Oh, the hours that remain for me to live will not be gay!"

"I will try to make them sweet to you."

The shadow of the clouded sky that precedes the twilight by two hours was darkening the drawing-room, burying them little by little in the gray dimness of an autumn evening.

The clock struck.

"It is a long time since we came in here," said she. "You must go, for someone might come, and we are not calm."

He arose, clasped her close, kissing her half-open lips, as he used to do; then they crossed the two drawing-rooms, arm in arm, like a newly-married pair.

"Good-by, my friend."

"Good-by, my friend."

And the portiere fell behind him.

He went downstairs, turned toward the Madeleine, and began to walk without knowing what he was doing, dazed as if from a blow, his legs weak, his heart hot and palpitating as if something burning shook within his breast. For two or three hours, perhaps four, he walked straight before him, in a sort of moral stupor and physical prostration which left him only just strength enough to put one foot before the other. Then he went home to reflect.

He loved this little girl, then. He comprehended now all that he had felt near her since that walk in the Parc Monceau, when he found in her mouth the call from a voice hardly recognized, the voice that long ago had awakened his heart; then all that slow, irresistible renewal of a love not yet extinct, not yet frozen, which he persisted in not acknowledging to himself.

What should he do? But what could he do? When she was married he would avoid seeing her often, that was all. Meantime, he would continue to return to the house, so that no one should suspect anything, and he would hide his secret from everyone.

He dined at home, which he very seldom did. Then he had a fire made in the large stove in his studio, for the night promised to be very cold. He even ordered the chandeliers to be lighted, as if he disliked the dark corners, and then he shut himself in. What strange emotion, profound, physical, frightfully sad, had seized him! He felt it in his throat, in his breast, in all his relaxed muscles as well as in his fainting soul. The walls of the apartment oppressed him; all his life was inclosed therein—his life as an artist, his life as a man. Every painted study hanging there recalled a success, each piece of furniture spoke of some memory. But successes and memories were things of the past. His life? How short, how empty it seemed to him, yet full. He had made pictures, and more pictures, and always pictures, and had loved one woman. He recalled the evenings of exaltation, after their meetings, in this same studio. He had walked whole nights with his being on fire with fever. The joy of happy love, the joy of worldly success, the unique intoxication of glory, had caused him to taste unforgettable hours of inward triumph.

He had loved a woman, and that woman had loved him. Through her he had received that baptism which reveals to man the mysterious world of emotions and of love. She had opened his heart almost by force, and now he could no longer close it. Another love had entered, in spite of him, through this opening—another, or rather the same relighted by a new face; the same, stronger by all the force which this need to adore takes on in old age. So he loved this little girl! He need no longer struggle, resist, or deny; he loved her with the despairing knowledge that he should not even gain a little pity from her, that she would always be ignorant of his terrible torment, and that another would marry her! At this thought constantly recurring, impossible to drive away, he was seized with an animal-like desire to howl like chained dogs, for like them he felt powerless, enslaved, imprisoned. Becoming more and more nervous, the longer he thought, he walked with long strides through the vast room, lighted up as if for a celebration. At last, unable to tolerate longer the pain of that reopened wound, he wished to try to calm it with the recollection of his early love, to drown it in evoking his first and great passion. From the closet where he kept it he took the copy of the Countess's portrait that he had made formerly for himself, then he put it on his easel, and sitting down in front of it, gazed at it. He tried to see her again, to find her living again, such as he had loved her before. But it was always Annette that rose upon the canvas. The mother had disappeared, vanished, leaving in her place that other face which resembled hers so strangely. It was the little one, with her hair a little lighter, her smile a little more mischievous, her air a little more mocking; and he felt that he belonged body and soul to that young being, as he never had belonged to the other, as a sinking vessel belongs to the waves!

Then he arose, and in order to see this apparition no more he turned the painting around; then, as he felt his heart full of sadness, he went to his chamber to bring into the studio the drawer of his desk, wherein were sleeping all the letters of the mistress of his heart. There they lay, as if in a bed, one upon the other, forming a thick layer of little thin papers. He thrust his hands among the mass, among all that which spoke of both of them, deep into that bath of their long intimacy. He looked at that narrow board coffin in which lay the mass of piled-up envelopes, on which his name, his name alone, was always written. He reflected that the love, the tender attachment of two beings, one for the other, were recounted therein, among that yellowish wave of papers spotted by red seals, and he inhaled, in bending over it, the old melancholy odor of letters that have been packed away.

He wished to re-read them, and feeling in the bottom of the drawer, he drew out a handful of the earlier ones. As soon as he opened them vivid memories emerged from them, which stirred his soul. He recognized many that he had carried about on his person for whole weeks, and found again, throughout the delicate handwriting that said such sweet things to him, the forgotten emotions of early days. Suddenly he found under his fingers a fine embroidered handkerchief. What was that? He pondered a few minutes, then he remembered! One day, at his house, she had wept because she was a little jealous, and he had stolen and kept her handkerchief, moist with her tears!

Ah, what sad things! What sad things! The poor woman!

From the depths of that drawer, from the depths of his past, all these reminiscences rose like a vapor, but it was only the impalpable vapor of a reality now dead. Nevertheless, he suffered and wept over the letters, as one weeps over the dead because they are no more.

But the remembrance of all his early love awakened in him a new and youthful ardor, a wave of irresistible tenderness which called up in his mind the radiant face of Annette. He had loved the mother, through a passionate impulse of voluntary servitude; he was beginning to love this little girl like a slave, a trembling old slave on whom fetters are riveted that he never can break. He felt this in the depths of his being, and was terrified. He tried to understand how and why she possessed him thus. He knew her so little! She was hardly a woman as yet; her heart and soul still slept with the sleep of youth.

He, on the other hand, was now almost at the end of his life. How, then, had this child been able to capture him with a few smiles and locks of her hair? Ah, the smiles, the hair of that little blonde maiden made him long to fall on his knees and strike the dust with his head!

Does one know, does one ever know why a woman's face has suddenly the power of poison upon us? It seems as if one had been drinking her with the eyes, that she had become one's mind and body. We are intoxicated with her, mad over her; we live of that absorbed image and would die of it!

How one suffers sometimes from this ferocious and incomprehensible power of a certain face on a man's heart!

Olivier Bertin began to pace his room again; night was advancing, his fire had gone out. Through the window-panes the cold air penetrated from outside. Then he went back to bed, where he continued to think and suffer until daylight.

He rose early, without knowing why, nor what he was going to do, agitated by his nervousness, irresolute as a whirling weather-vane.

In seeking some distraction for his mind, some occupation for his body, he recollected that on that particular day of the week certain members of his club had the habit of meeting regularly at the Moorish Baths, where they breakfasted after the massage. So he dressed quickly, hoping that the hot room and the shower would calm him, and he went out.

As soon as he found himself in the street, he felt the cold air, that first crisp cold of the early frost, which destroys in a single night the last trances of summer.

All along the Boulevards fell a thick shower of large yellow leaves which rustled down with a dry sound. As far as could be seen, they fell from one end of the broad avenue to the other, between the facades of the houses, as if all their stems had just been cut from the branches by a thin blade of ice. The road and the sidewalks were already covered with them, resembling for a few hours the paths in the woods at the beginning of winter. All that dead foliage crackled under the feet, and massed itself, from time to time, in light waves under the gusts of wind.

This was one of those days of transition which mark the end of one season and the beginning of another, which have a savor or a special sadness—the sadness of the death-struggle or the savor of rising sap.

In crossing the threshold of the Moorish Baths, the thought of the heat that would soon penetrate his flesh after his walk in the cold air gave a feeling of satisfaction to Olivier's sad heart.

He undressed quickly, wrapping around his body the light scarf the attendant handed to him, and disappeared behind the padded door open before him.

A warm, oppressive breath, which seemed to come from a distant furnace, made him pant as if he needed air while traversing a Moorish gallery lighted by two Oriental lanterns. Then a negro with woolly head, attired only in a girdle, with shining body and muscular limbs, ran before him to raise a curtain at the other end; and Bertin entered the large hot-air room, round, high-studded, silent, almost as mystic as a temple. Daylight fell from above through a cupola and through trefoils of colored glass into the immense circular room, with paved floor and walls covered with pottery decorated after the Arab fashion.

Men of all ages, almost naked, walked slowly about, grave and silent; others were seated on marble benches, with arms crossed; others still chatted in low tones.

The burning air made one pant at the very entrance. There was, within that stifling and decorated circular room, where human flesh was heated, where black and yellow attendants with copper-colored legs moved about, something antique and mysterious.

The first face the painter saw was that of the Comte de Landa. He was promenading around like a Roman wrestler, proud of his enormous chest and of his great arms crossed over it. A frequenter of the hot baths, he felt when there like an admired actor on the stage, and he criticised like an expert the muscles of all the strong men in Paris.

"Good-morning, Bertin," said he.

They shook hands; then Landa continued: "Splendid weather for sweating!"

"Yes, magnificent."

"Have you seen Rocdiane? He is down there. I was at his house just as he was getting out of bed. Oh, look at that anatomy!"

A little gentleman was passing, bow-legged, with thin arms and flanks, the sight of whom caused the two old models of human vigor to smile disdainfully.

Rocdiane approached them, having perceived the painter. They sat down on a long marble table and began to chat quite as if they were in a drawing-room. The attendants moved about, offering drinks. One could hear the clapping of the masseurs' hands on bare flesh and the sudden flow of the shower-baths. A continuous pattering of water, coming from all corners of the great amphitheater, filled it also with a sound like rain.

At every instant some newcomer saluted the three friends, or approached them to shake hands. Among them were the big Duke of Harrison, the little Prince Epilati, Baron Flach, and others.

Suddenly Rocdiane said: "How are you, Farandal?"

The Marquis entered, his hands on his hips, with the easy air of well-made men, who never feel embarrassed at anything.

"He is a gladiator, that chap!" Landa murmured.

Rocdiane resumed, turning toward Bertin: "Is it true that he is to marry the daughter of your friend?"

"I think so," said the painter.

But the question, before that man, in that place, gave to Olivier's heart a frightful shock of despair and revolt. The horror of all the realities he had foreseen appeared to him for a second with such acuteness that he struggled an instant or so against an animal-like desire to fling himself on Farandal.

He arose.

"I am tired," said he. "I am going to the massage now."

An Arab was passing.

"Ahmed, are you at liberty?"

"Yes, Monsieur Bertin."

And he went away quickly in order to avoid shaking hands with Farandal, who was approaching slowly in making the rounds of the Hammam.

He remained barely a quarter of an hour in the large quiet resting-room, in the center of a row of cells containing the beds, with a parterre of African plants and a little fountain in the center. He had a feeling of being pursued, menaced, that the Marquis would join him, and that he should be compelled, with extended hand, to treat him as a friend, when he longed to kill him.

He soon found himself again on the Boulevard, covered with dead leaves. They fell no more, the last ones having been detached by a long blast of wind. Their red and yellow carpet shivered, stirred, undulated from one sidewalk to another, blown by puffs of the rising wind.

Suddenly a sort of roaring noise glided over the roofs, the animal-like sound of a passing tempest, and at the same time a furious gust of wind that seemed to come from the Madeleine swept through the Boulevard.

All the fallen leaves, which appeared to have been waiting for it, rose at its approach. They ran before it, massing themselves, whirling, and rising in spirals up to the tops of the buildings. The wind chased them like a flock, a mad flock that fled before it, flying toward the gates of Paris and the free sky of the suburbs. And when the great cloud of leaves and dust had disappeared on the heights of the Quartier Malesherbes, the sidewalks and roads remained bare, strangely clean and swept.

Bertin was thinking: "What will become of me? What shall I do? Where shall I go?" And he returned home, unable to think of anything.

A news-stand attracted his eye. He bought seven or eight newspapers, hoping that he might find in them something to read for an hour or two.

"I will breakfast here," said he, as he entered, and went up to his studio.

But as he sat down he felt that he could not stay there, for throughout his body surged the excitement of an angry beast.

The newspapers, which he glanced through, could not distract his mind for a minute, and the news he read met his eye without reaching his brain. In the midst of an article which he was not trying to comprehend, the name of Guilleroy made him start. It was about the session of the Chamber, where the Count had spoken a few words.

His attention, aroused by that call, was now arrested by the name of the celebrated tenor Montrose, who was to give, about the end of December, a single performance at the Opera. This would be, the newspaper stated, a magnificent musical solemnity, for the tenor Montrose, who had been absent six years from Paris, had just won, throughout Europe and America, a success without precedent; moreover, he would be supported by the illustrious Swedish singer, Helsson, who had not been heard in Paris for five years.

Suddenly Olivier had an idea, which seemed to spring from the depths of his heart—he would give Annette the pleasure of seeing this performance. Then he remembered that the Countess's mourning might be an obstacle to this scheme, and he sought some way to realize it in spite of the difficulty. Only one method presented itself. He must take a stage-box where one may be almost invisible, and if the Countess should still not wish to go, he would have Annette accompanied by her father and the Duchess. In that case, he would have to offer his box to the Duchess. But then he would be obliged to invite the Marquis!

He hesitated and reflected a long time.

Certainly, the marriage was decided upon; no doubt the date was settled. He guessed the reason for his friend's haste in having it finished soon; he understood that in the shortest time possible she would give her daughter to Farandal. He could not help it. He could neither prevent, nor modify, nor delay this frightful thing. Since he must bear it, would it not be better for him to try to master his soul, to hide his suffering, to appear content, and no longer allow himself to be carried away by his rage, as he had done?

Yes, he would invite the Marquis, and so allay the Countess's suspicions, and keep for himself a friendly door in the new establishment.

As soon as he had breakfasted, he went down to the Opera to engage one of the boxes hidden by the curtain. It was promised to him. Then he hastened to the Guilleroys'.

The Countess appeared almost immediately, apparently still a little moved by their tender interview of the day before.

"How kind of you to come again to-day!" said she.

"I am bringing you something," he faltered.

"What is it?"

"A stage-box at the Opera for the single performance of Helsson and Montrose."

"Oh, my friend, what a pity! And my mourning?"

"Your mourning has lasted for almost four months."

"I assure you that I cannot."

"And Annette? Remember that she may never have such an opportunity again."

"With whom could she go?"

"With her father and the Duchess, whom I am about to invite. I intend also to offer a seat to the Marquis."

She gazed deep into his eyes, and a wild desire to kiss him rose to her lips. Hardly believing her ears, she repeated: "To the Marquis?"

"Why, yes."

She consented at once to this arrangement.

He continued, in an indifferent tone: "Have you fixed the date of their marriage?"

"Oh, yes, almost. We have reasons for hastening it very much, especially as it was decided upon before my mother's death. You remember that?"

"Yes, perfectly. And when will it take place?"

"About the beginning of January. I ask your pardon for not having told you of it sooner."

Annette entered. He felt his heart leap within him as if on springs, and all the tenderness that drew him toward her suddenly became bitter, arousing in his heart that strange, passionate animosity into which love changes when lashed by jealousy.

"I have brought you something," he said.

"So we have decided to say 'you'?" she replied.

He assumed a paternal tone.

"Listen, my child, I know all about the event that is soon to occur. I assure you that then it will be indispensable. Better say 'you' now than later."

She shrugged her shoulders with an air of discontent, while the Countess remained silent, looking afar off, her thoughts preoccupied.

"Well, what have you brought me?" inquired Annette.

He told her about the performance, and the invitations he intended to give. She was delighted, and, throwing her arms around his neck with the manner of a little girl, she kissed him on both cheeks.

He felt ready to sink, and understood, when he felt the light caresses of that little mouth with its sweet breath, that he never should be cured of his passion.

The Countess, annoyed, said to her daughter: "You know that your father is waiting for you."

"Yes, mamma, I am going."

She ran away, still throwing kisses from the tips of her fingers.

As soon as she had gone, Olivier asked: "Will they travel?"

"Yes, for three months."

"So much the better," he murmured in spite of himself.

"We will resume our former life," said the Countess.

"Yes, I hope so," said he, hesitatingly.

"But do not neglect me meanwhile."

"No, my friend."

The impulse he had shown the evening before, when seeing her weep, and the intention which he had just expressed of inviting the Marquis to the performance at the Opera, had given new hope to the Countess.

But it was short. A week had not passed ere she was again following the expression of this man's face with tortured and jealous attention, watching every stage of his suffering. She could ignore nothing, herself enduring all the pain that she guessed at in him; and Annette's constant presence reminded her at every moment of the day of the hopelessness of her efforts.

Everything oppressed her at the same time—her age and her mourning. Her active, intelligent, and ingenious coquetry, which all her life had given her triumph, found itself paralyzed by that black uniform which marked her pallor and the change in her features, while it rendered the adolescence of her daughter absolutely dazzling. The time seemed far away, though it was quite recent, when, on Annette's return to Paris, she had proudly sought similar toilets which at that time were favorable to her. Now she had a furious longing to tear from her body those vestments of death which made her ugly and tortured her.

If she had felt that all the resources of elegance were at her service, if she had been able to choose and use delicately shaded stuffs, in harmony with her coloring, which would have lent a studied power to her fading charms, as captivating as the inert grace of her daughter, she would no doubt have known how to remain still the more charming.

She knew so well the influences of the fever-giving costume of evening, and the soft sensuousness of morning attire, of the disturbing deshabille worn at breakfast with intimate friends, which lend to a woman until noontime a sort of reminiscence of her rising, the material and warm impression of the bed and of her perfumed room!

But what could she attempt under that sepulchral robe, that convict's dress, which must cover her for a whole year? A year! She must remain a year imprisoned in that black attire, inactive and vanquished. For a whole year she would feel herself growing old, day by day, hour by hour, minute by minute, under that sheath of crape! What would she be in a year if her poor ailing body continued to alter thus under the anguish of her soul?

These thoughts never left her, and spoiled for her everything she might have enjoyed, turned into sadness things that would have given her joy, leaving her not a pleasure, a contentment, or a gaiety intact. She was agitated incessantly by an exasperating need to shake off this weight of misery that crushed her, for without this tormenting obsession she would still have been so happy, alert, and healthy! She felt that her soul was still fresh and bright, her heart still young, the ardor of a being that is beginning to live, an insatiable appetite for happiness, more voracious even than before, and a devouring desire to love.

And now, all good things, all things sweet, delicious and poetic, which embellish life and make it enjoyable, were withdrawing from her, because she was growing old! It was all finished! Yet she still found within her the tenderness of the young girl and the passionate impulses of the young woman. Nothing had grown old but her body, that miserable skin, that stuff over the bones, fading little by little like the covering of a piece of furniture. The curse of this decay had attached itself to her, and had become almost a physical suffering. This fixed idea had created a sensation of the epidermis, the sensation of growing old, continuous and imperceptible, like that of cold or of heat. She really believed that she felt an indescribable sort of itching, the slow march of wrinkles upon her forehead, the weakening of the tissues of the cheeks and throat, and the multiplication of those innumerable little marks that wear out the tired skin. Like some one afflicted with a consuming disease, whom a continual prurience induces to scratch himself, the perception and terror of that abominable, swift and secret work of time filled her soul with an irresistible need of verifying it in her mirrors. They called her, drew her, forced her to come, with fixed eyes, to see, to look again, to recognize incessantly, to touch with her finger, as if to assure herself, the indelible mark of the years. At first this was an intermittent thought, returning whenever she saw the polished surface of the dreaded crystal, at home or abroad. She paused in the street to gaze at herself in the shop-windows, hanging as if by one hand to all the glass plates with which merchants ornament their facades. It became a disease, an obsession. She carried in her pocket a dainty little ivory powder-box, as large as a nut, the interior of which contained a tiny mirror; and often, while walking, she held it open in her hand and raised it to her eyes.

When she sat down to read or write in the tapestried drawing-room, her mind, distracted for the time by a new occupation, would soon return to its obsession. She struggled, tried to amuse herself, to have other ideas, to continue her work. It was in vain; the prick of desire tormented her, and soon dropping her book or her pen, her hand would steal out, by an irresistible impulse, toward the little hand-glass mounted in antique silver that lay upon her desk. In this oval, chiseled frame her whole face was inclosed, like a face of days gone by, a portrait of the last century, or a once fresh pastel now tarnished by the sun. Then after gazing at herself a long time, she laid, with a weary movement, the little glass upon the desk and tried to resume her work; but ere she had read two pages or written twenty lines, she was again seized with the invincible and torturing need of looking at herself, and once more would extend her hand to take up the mirror.

She now handled it like an irritating and familiar toy that the hand cannot let alone, used it continually even when receiving her friends, and made herself nervous enough to cry out, hating it as if it were a sentient thing while turning it in her fingers.

One day, exasperated by this struggle between herself and this bit of glass, she threw it against the wall, where it was broken to pieces.

But after a time her husband, who had it repaired, brought it back to her, clearer than ever; and she was compelled to take it, to thank him, and resign herself to keep it.

Every evening, too, and every morning, shut up in her own room, she resumed, in spite of herself, that minute and patient examination of the quiet, odious havoc.

When she was in bed she could not sleep; she would light a candle again and lie, wide-eyed, thinking how insomnia and grief hasten irremediably the horrible work of fleeting time. She listened in the silence of the night to the ticking of the clock, which seemed to murmur, in its monotonous and regular tic-tac: "It goes, it goes, it goes!" and her heart shrank with such suffering that, with the sheet gripped between her teeth, she groaned in despair.

Once, like everyone else, she had some notion of the passing years and of the changes they bring. Like everyone else, she had said to herself every winter, every spring, and every summer, "I have changed very much since last year." But, always beautiful, with a changing beauty, she was never uneasy about it. Now, however, suddenly, instead of admitting peacefully the slow march of the seasons, she had just discovered and understood the formidable flight of the minutes. She had had a sudden revelation of the gliding of the hour, of that imperceptible race, maddening when we think of it—of that infinite defile of little hurrying seconds, which nibble at the body and the life of men.

After these miserable nights, she had long periods of somnolence that made her more tranquil, in the warmth of her bed, when her maid had opened the curtains and lighted the morning fire. She lay there tired, drowsy, neither awake nor asleep, in the torpor of thought which brings about the revival of that instinctive and providential hope which gives light and life to the hearts of men up to their last days.

Every morning now, as soon as she had risen from her bed, she felt moved by a powerful desire to pray to God, to obtain from Him a little relief and consolation.

She would kneel, then, before a large figure of Christ carved in oak, a gift from Olivier, a rare work he had discovered; and, with lips closed, but imploring with that voice of the soul with which we speak to ourselves, she lifted toward the Divine martyr a sorrowful supplication. Distracted by the need of being heard and succored, naïve in her distress, as are all faithful ones on their knees, she could not doubt that He heard her, that He was attentive to her request, and was perhaps touched at her grief. She did not ask Him to do for her that which He never had done for anyone—to leave her until death all her charm, her freshness and grace; she begged only a little repose, a little respite. She must grow old, of course, just as she must die. But why so soon? Some women remain beautiful so long! Could He not grant that she should be one of these? How good He would be, He who had also suffered so much, if only He would let her keep for two or three years still the little charm she needed in order to be pleasing.

She did not say these things to Him, of course, but she sighed them forth, in the confused plaint of her being.

Then, having risen, she would sit before her toilet-table, and with a tension of thought as ardent as in her prayer, she would handle the powders, the pastes, the pencils, the puffs and brushes, which gave her once more a plaster-like beauty, fragile, lasting only for a day.

CHAPTER VI

THE ASHES OF LOVE

On the Boulevard two names were heard from all lips: “Emma Helsson” and “Montrose.” The nearer one approached the Opera, the oftener he heard those names repeated. Immense posters, too, affixed to the Morris columns, announced them in the eyes of passers, and in the evening air could be felt the excitement of an approaching event.

That heavy monument called the National Academy of Music, squatted under the black sky, exhibited to the crowd before its doors the pompous, whitish facade and marble colonnade of its balcony, illuminated like a stage setting by invisible electric lights.

In the square the mounted Republican guards directed the movement of the crowds, and the innumerable carriages coming from all parts of Paris allowed glimpses of creamy light stuff and fair faces behind their lowered windows.

The coupes and landaus formed in line under the reserved arcades, and stopped for a moment, and from them alighted fashionable and other women, in their opera-cloaks, trimmed with fur, feathers, and rare laces—precious bodies, divinely set forth!

All the way along the celebrated stairway was a sort of fairy flight, an uninterrupted mounting of ladies dressed like queens, whose throats and ears scattered flashing rays from their diamonds, and whose long trains swept the stairs.

The theater was filling early, for no one wished to lose a note of the two illustrious artists; and throughout the vast amphitheater, under the dazzling electric light from the great chandelier, a throng of people were seating themselves amid an uproar of voices.

From the stage-box, already occupied by the Duchess, Annette, the Count, the Marquis, Bertin and Musadieu, one could see nothing but the wings, where men were talking, running about, and shouting, machinists in blouses, gentlemen in evening dress, actors in costume. But behind the great curtain one heard the deep sound of the crowd, one felt the presence of a mass of moving, over-excited beings, whose agitation seemed to penetrate the curtain, and to extend even to the decorations.

They were about to present Faust.

Musadieu was relating anecdotes about the first representatives of this work at the Theatre Lyrique, of its half success in the beginning followed by brilliant triumph, of the original cast, and their manner of singing each aria. Annette, half turned toward him, listened with that eager, youthful curiosity with which she regarded the whole world; and at times she cast a tender glance at her fiance, who in a few days would be her husband. She loved him, now, as innocent hearts love; that is to say she loved in him all the hopes she had for the future. The intoxication of the first feasts of life, and the ardent longing to be happy, made her tremble with joy and expectation.

And Olivier, who saw all, and knew all, who had sounded all the depths of secret, helpless, and jealous love, down in the furnace of human suffering, where the heart seems to crackle like flesh over hot coals, stood in the back of the box looking at them with eyes that betrayed his torture.

The three blows were struck, and suddenly the sharp little tap of a bow on the leader’s desk stopped short all movement, all coughing and whispering; then, after a brief and profound silence, the first measure of the introduction arose, filling the house with the invisible and irresistible mystery of the music that penetrates our bodies, thrills our nerves and souls with a poetic and sensuous fever, mingling with the limpid air we breathe a wave of sound to which we listen.

Olivier took a seat at the back of the box, painfully affected, as if his heart's wounds had been touched by those accents. But when the curtain rose he stood up again, and saw Doctor Faust, lost in sorrowful meditation, seated in his alchemist's laboratory.

He had already heard the opera twenty times, and almost knew it by heart, and his attention soon wandered from the stage to the audience. He could see only a small part of it behind the frame of the stage which concealed their box, but the angle that was visible, extending from the orchestra to the top gallery, showed him a portion of the audience in which he recognized many faces. In the orchestra rows, the men in white cravats, sitting side by side, seemed a museum of familiar countenances, society men, artists, journalists, the whole category of those that never fail to go where everyone else goes. In the balcony and in the boxes he noted and named to himself the women he recognized. The Comtesse de Lochrist, in a proscenium box, was absolutely ravishing, while a little farther on a bride, the Marquise d'Ebelin, was already looking through her lorgnette. "That is a pretty debut," said Bertin to himself.

The audience listened with deep attention and evident sympathy to the tenor Montrose, who was lamenting over his waning life.

Olivier thought: "What a farce! There is Faust, the mysterious and sublime Faust who sings the horrible disgust and nothingness of everything; and this crowd are asking themselves anxiously whether Montrose's voice has not changed!" Then he listened, like the others, and behind the trivial words of the libretto, through that music which awakens profound perception in the soul, he had a sort of revelation as to how Goethe had been able to conceive the heart of Faust.

He had read the poem some time before, and thought it very beautiful without being moved by it, but now he suddenly realized its unfathomable depth, for it seemed to him that on that evening he himself had become a Faust.

Leaning lightly upon the railing of the box, Annette was listening with all her ears; and murmurs of satisfaction were beginning to be heard from the audience, for Montrose's voice was better and richer than ever!

Bertin had closed his eyes. For a whole month, all that he had seen, all that he had felt, everything that he had encountered in life he had immediately transformed into a sort of accessory to his passion. He threw the world and himself as nourishment to this fixed idea. All that he saw that was beautiful or rare, all that he imagined that was charming, he mentally offered to his little friend; and he had no longer an idea that he did not in some way connect with his love.

Now he listened from the depths of his soul to the echo of Faust's lamentations, and the desire to die surged up within him, the desire to have done with all his grief, with all the misery of his hopeless love. He looked at Annette's delicate profile, and saw the Marquis de Farandal, seated behind her, also looking at it. He felt old, lost, despairing. Ah, never to await anything more, never to hope for anything more, no longer to have even the right to desire, to feel himself outside of everything, in the evening of life, like a superannuated functionary whose career is ended—what intolerable torture!

Applause burst forth; Montrose had triumphed already. And Labarriere as Mephistopheles sprang up from the earth.

Olivier, who never had heard him in this role, listened with renewed attention. The remembrance of Aubin, so dramatic with his bass voice, then of Faure, so seductive with his baritone, distracted him a short time.

But suddenly a phrase sung by Montrose with irresistible power stirred him to the heart. Faust was saying to Satan:

> "Je veux un tresor qui les contient tous—
>
> Je veux la jeunesse."

And the tenor appeared in silken doublet, a sword by his side, a plumed cap on his head, elegant, young, and handsome, with the affectations of a handsome singer.

A murmur arose. He was very attractive and the women were pleased with him. But Olivier felt some disappointment, for the poignant evocation of Goethe's dramatic poem disappeared in this metamorphosis. Thenceforth he saw before him only a fairy spectacle, filled with pretty little songs, and actors of talent whose voices were all he listened to. That man in a doublet, that pretty youth with his roulades, who showed his thighs and displayed his voice, displeased him. This was not the real, irresistible, and sinister Chevalier Faust, who was about to seduce the fair Marguerite.

He sat down again, and the phrase he had just heard returned to his mind:

"I would have a treasure that embraces all—Youth!"

He murmured it between his teeth, sang it sadly in the depths of his soul, and, with eyes fixed always upon Annette's blonde head, which rose in the square opening of the box, he felt all the bitterness of that desire that never could be realized.

But Montrose had just finished the first act with such perfection that enthusiasm broke forth. For several minutes, the noise of clapping, stamping, and bravos swept like a storm through the theater. In all the boxes the women clapped their gloved hands, while the men standing behind them shouted as they applauded.

The curtain fell, but it was raised twice before the applause subsided. Then, when the curtain had fallen for the third time, separating the stage and the interior boxes from the audience, the Duchess and Annette continued their applause a few moments, and were specially thanked by a discreet bow from the tenor.

"Oh, he looked at us!" said Annette.

"What an admirable artist!" said the Duchess.

And Bertin, who had been leaning over, looked with a mingled feeling of irritation and disdain at the admired actor as he disappeared between two wings, waddling a little, his legs stiff, one hand on his hip, in the affected pose of a theatrical hero.

They began to talk of him. His social successes had made him as famous as his talent. He had visited every capital, in the midst of feminine ecstasies of those who, hearing before he appeared that he was irresistible, had felt their hearts throb as he appeared upon the stage. But it was said that he appeared to care very little for all this sentimental delirium, and contented himself with his musical triumphs. Musadieu related, in veiled language because of Annette's presence, details of the life of this handsome singer, and the Duchess, quite carried away, understood and approved all the follies that he was able to create, so seductive, elegant, and distinguished did she consider this exceptional musician! She concluded, laughing: "And how can anyone resist that voice!"

Olivier felt angry and bitter. He did not understand how anyone could really care for a mere actor, for that perpetual representation of human types which never resembled himself in the least; that illusory personification of imaginary men, that nocturnal and painted manikin who plays all his characters at so much a night.

"You are jealous of them!" said the Duchess. "You men of the world and artists all have a grudge against actors because they are more successful than you." Turning to Annette, she added: "Come, little one, you who are entering life and look at it with healthy eyes, what do you think of this tenor?"

"I think he is very good indeed," Annette replied, with an air of conviction.

The three strokes sounded for the second act, and the curtain rose on the Kermesse.

Helsson's passage was superb. She seemed to have more voice than formerly, and to have acquired more certainty of method. She had, indeed, become the great, excellent, exquisite singer, whose worldly fame equaled that of Bismarck or De Lesseps.

When Faust rushed toward her, when he sang in his bewitching voice phrases so full of charm and when the pretty blonde Marguerite replied so touchingly the whole house was moved with a thrill of pleasure.

When the curtain fell, the applause was tremendous, and Annette applauded so long that Bertin wished to seize her hands to make her stop. His heart was stung by a new torment. He did not speak between the acts, for he was pursuing into the wings, his fixed thought now become absolute hatred, following to his box, where he saw, putting more white powder on his cheeks, the odious singer who was thus over-exciting this child!

Then the curtain rose on the garden scene. Immediately a sort of fever of love seemed to spread through the house, for never had that music, which seems like the breath of kisses, been rendered by two such interpreters. It was no longer two illustrious actors, Montrose and Helsson; they became two beings from the ideal world, hardly two beings, indeed, but two voices: the eternal voice of the man that loves, the eternal voice of the woman that yields; and together they sighed forth all the poetry of human tenderness.

When Faust sang:

"Laisse-moi, laisse-moi contempler ton visage,"

in the notes that soared from his mouth there was such an accent of adoration, of transport and supplication that for a moment a desire to love filled every heart.

Olivier remembered that he had murmured that phrase himself in the park at Roncieres, under the castle windows.

Until then he had thought it rather ordinary; but now it rose to his lips like a last cry of passion, a last prayer, the last hope and the last favor he might expect in this life.

Then he listened no more, heard nothing more. A sharp pang of jealousy tore his heart, for he had just seen Annette carry her handkerchief to her eyes.

She wept! Then her heart was awakening, becoming animated and moved, her little woman's heart which as yet knew nothing! There, very near him, without giving a thought to him, she had a revelation of the way in which love may overwhelm a human being; and this revelation, this initiation had come to her from that miserable strolling singer!

Ah, he felt very little anger now toward the Marquis de Farandal, that stupid creature who saw nothing, who did not know, did not understand! But how he execrated that man in tights, who was illuminating the soul of that young girl!

He longed to throw himself upon her, as one throws himself upon a person in danger of being run over by a fractious horse, to seize her by the arm and drag her away, and say to her: "Let us go! let us go! I entreat you!"

How she listened, how she palpitated! And how he suffered. He had suffered thus before, but less cruelly. He remembered it, for the stings of jealousy smart afresh like reopened wounds. He had first felt it at Roncieres, in returning from the cemetery, when he felt for the first time that she was escaping from him, that he could not control her, that young girl as independent as a young animal. But down there, when she had irritated him by leaving him to pluck flowers, he had experienced chiefly a brutal desire to check her playful flights, to compel her person to remain beside him; to-day it was her fleeting, intangible soul that was escaping. Ah, that gnawing irritation which he had just recognized, how often he had experienced it by the indescribable little wounds which seem to be always bruising a loving heart. He recalled all the painful impressions of petty jealousy that he had endured, in little stings, day after day. Every time that she had remarked, admired, liked, desired something, he had been jealous of it; jealous in an imperceptible but continuous fashion, jealous of all that absorbed the time, the looks, the attention, the gaiety, the astonishment or affection of Annette, for all that took a little of her away from him. He had been jealous of all that she did without him, of all that he did not know, of her going about, her reading, of everything that seemed to please her, jealous even of a heroic officer wounded in Africa, of whom Paris talked for a week, of the author of a much praised romance, of a young unknown poet she never had seen, but whose verses Musadieu had recited; in short, of all men that anyone praised before her, even carelessly, for when one loves a woman one cannot tolerate without anguish that she should even think of another with an appearance of interest. In one's heart is felt the imperious need of being for her the only being in the world. One wishes her to see, to know, to appreciate no one else. So soon as she shows an indication of turning to look at or recognize some person, one throws himself before her, and if one cannot turn aside or absorb her interest he suffers to the bottom of his heart.

Olivier suffered thus in the presence of this singer, who seemed to scatter and to gather love in that opera-house, and he felt vexed with everyone because of the tenor's triumph, with the women whom he saw applauding him from their boxes, with the men, those idiots who were giving a sort of apotheosis to that coxcomb!

An artist! They called him a artist, a great artist! And he had successes, this paid actor, interpreter of another's thought, such as no creator had ever known! Ah, that was like the justice and the intelligence of the fashionable world, those ignorant and pretentious amateurs for whom the masters of human art work until death. He looked at them, applauding, shouting, going into ecstasies; and the ancient hostility that had always seethed at the bottom of his proud heart of a parvenu became a furious anger against those imbeciles, all-powerful only by right of birth and wealth.

Until the end of the performance he remained silent, a prey to thought; then when the storm of enthusiasm had at last subsided he offered his arm to the Duchess, while the Marquis took Annette's. They descended the grand stairway again, in the midst of a stream of men and women, in a sort of slow and magnificent cascade of bare shoulders, sumptuous gowns, and black coats. Then the Duchess, the young girl, her father, and the Marquis entered the same landau, and Olivier Bertin remained alone with Musadieu in the Place de l'Opera.

Suddenly he felt a sort of affection for this man, or rather that natural attraction one feels for a fellow-countryman met in a distant land, for he now felt lost in that strange, indifferent crowd, whereas with Musadieu he might still speak of her.

So he took his arm.

"You are not going home now?" said he. "It is a fine night; let us take a walk."

"Willingly."

They went toward the Madeleine, in the mist of the nocturnal crowd possessed by that short and violent midnight excitement which stirs the Boulevards when the theaters are being emptied.

Musadieu had a thousand things in his mind, all his subjects for conversation from the moment when Bertin should name his preference; and he let his eloquence loose upon the two or three topics that interested him most. The painter allowed him to run on without listening to him, and holding him by the arm, sure of being able soon to lead him to talk of Annette, he walked along without noticing his surroundings, imprisoned within his love. He walked, exhausted by that fit of jealousy which had bruised him like a fall, overcome by the conviction that he had nothing more to do in the world.

He should go on suffering thus, more and more, without expecting anything. He should pass empty days, one after another, seeing her from afar, living, happy, loved and loving, without doubt. A lover! Perhaps she would have a lover, as her mother had had one! He felt within him sources of suffering so numerous, diverse, and complicated, such an afflux of miseries, such inevitable tortures, he felt so lost, so far overwhelmed, from this moment, by a wave of unimaginable agony that he could not suppose anyone ever had suffered as he did. And he suddenly thought of the puerility of poets who have invented the useless labor of Sisyphus, the material thirst of Tantalus, the devoured heart of Prometheus! Oh, if they had foreseen, if they had experienced the mad love of an elderly man for a young girl, how would they had expressed the painful and secret effort of a being who can no longer inspire love, the tortures of fruitless desire, and, more terrible than a vulture's beak, a little blonde face rending a heart!

Musadieu talked without stopping, and Bertin interrupted him, murmuring almost in spite of himself, under the impulse of his fixed idea:

"Annette was charming this evening."

"Yes, delicious!"

The painter added, to prevent Musadieu from taking up the broken thread of his ideas: "She is prettier than her mother ever was."

To this the other agreed absent-mindedly, repeating "Yes, yes, yes!" several times in succession, without his mind having yet settled itself on this new idea.

Olivier endeavored to continue the subject, and in order to attract his attention by one of Musadieu's own favorite fads, he continued:

"She will have one of the first salons in Paris after her marriage."

That was enough, and, the man of fashion being convinced, as well as the Inspector of Fine Arts, he began to talk wisely of the social footing on which the Marquise de Farandal would stand in French society.

Bertin listened to him, and fancied Annette in a large salon full of light, surrounded by men and women. This vision, too, made him jealous.

They were now going up the Boulevard Malesherbes. As they passed the Guilleroys' house the painter looked up. Lights seemed to be shining through the windows, among the openings in the curtains. He suspected that the Duchess and the Marquis had been invited to come and have a cup of tea. And a burning rage made him suffer terribly.

He still held Musadieu by the arm, and once or twice attempted to continue, by contradicting Musadieu's opinions, the talk about the future Marquise. Even that commonplace voice in speaking of her caused her charming image to flit beside them in the night.

When they arrived at the painter's door, in the Avenue de Villiers, Bertin asked: "Will you come in?"

"No, thank you. It is late, and I am going to bed."

"Oh, come up for half an hour, and we'll have a little more talk."

"No, really. It is too late."

The thought of staying there alone, after the anguish he had just endured, filled Olivier's soul with horror. He had someone with him; he would keep him.

"Do come up; I want you to choose a study that I have intended for a long time to offer you."

The other, knowing that painters are not always in a giving mood, and that the remembrance of promises is short, seized the opportunity. In his capacity as Inspector of Fine Arts, he possessed a gallery that had been furnished with skill.

"I am with you," said he.

They entered.

The valet was aroused and soon brought some grog; and the talk was for some time all about painting. Bertin showed some studies, and begged Musadieu to take the one that pleased him best; Musadieu hesitated, disturbed by the gaslight, which deceived him as to tones. At last he chose a group of little girls jumping the rope on a sidewalk; and almost at once he wished to depart, and to take his present with him.

"I will have it taken to your house," said the painter.

"No; I should like better to have it this very evening, so that I may admire it while I am going to bed," said Musadieu.

Nothing could keep him, and Olivier Bertin found himself again alone in his house, that prison of his memories and his painful agitation.

When the servant entered the next morning, bringing tea and the newspapers, he found his master sitting up in bed, so pale and shaken that he was alarmed.

"Is Monsieur indisposed?" he inquired.

"It is nothing—only a little headache."

"Does not Monsieur wish me to bring him something?"

"No. What sort of weather is it?"

"It rains, Monsieur."

"Very well. That is all."

The man withdrew, having placed on the little table the tea-tray and the newspapers.

Olivier took up the Figaro and opened it. The leading article was entitled "Modern Painting." It was a dithyrambic eulogy on four or five young painters who, gifted with real ability as colorists, and exaggerating them for effect, now pretended to be revolutionists and renovators of genius.

As did all the older painters, Bertin sneered at these newcomers, was irritated at their assumption of exclusiveness, and disputed their doctrines. He began to read the article, then, with the rising anger so quickly felt by a nervous person; at last, glancing a little further down, he saw his own name, and these words at the end of a sentence struck him like a blow of the fist full in the chest: "The old-fashioned art of Olivier Bertin."

He had always been sensitive to either criticism or praise, but, at the bottom of his heart, in spite of his legitimate vanity, he suffered more from being criticised than he enjoyed being praised, because of the uneasiness concerning himself which his hesitations had always encouraged. Formerly, however, at the time of his triumphs, the incense offered was so frequent that it made him forget the pin-pricks. To-day, before the ceaseless influx of new artists and new admirers, congratulations were more rare and criticism was more marked. He felt that he had been enrolled in the battalion of old painters of talent, whom the younger ones do not treat as masters; and as he was as intelligent as he was perspicacious he suffered now from the least insinuations as much as from direct attacks.

But never had any wound to his pride as an artist hurt him like this. He remained gasping, and reread the article in order to grasp its every meaning. He and his equals were thrown aside with outrageous disrespect; and he arose murmuring those words, which remained on his lips: "The old-fashioned art of Olivier Bertin."

Never had such sadness, such discouragement, such a sensation of having reached the end of everything, the end of his mental and physical being, thrown him into such desperate distress of soul. He sat until two o'clock in his armchair, before the fireplace, his legs extended toward the fire, not having strength to move, or to do anything. Then the need of being consoled rose within him, the need to clasp devoted hands, to see faithful eyes, to be pitied, succored, caressed with friendly words. So he went, as usual, to the Countess.

When he entered Annette was alone in the drawing-room, standing with her back toward him, hastily writing the address on a letter. On a table beside her lay a copy of Figaro. Bertin saw the journal at the moment that he saw the young girl and was bewildered, not daring to advance! Oh, if she had read it! She turned, and in a preoccupied, hurried way, her mind haunted with feminine cares, she said to him:

"Ah, good-morning, sir painter! You will excuse me if I leave you? I have a dressmaker upstairs who claims me. You understand that a dressmaker, at the time of a wedding, is very important. I will lend you mamma, who is talking and arguing with my artist. If I need her I will call her for a few minutes."

And she hastened away, running a little, to show how much she was hurried.

This abrupt departure, without a word of affection, without a tender look for him who loved her so much—so much!—quite upset him. His eyes rested again on the Figaro, and he thought: "She has read it! They laugh at me, they deny me. She no longer believes in me. I am nothing to her any more."

He took two steps toward the journal, as one walks toward a man to strike him. Then he said to himself: "Perhaps she has not read it, after all. She is so preoccupied to-day. But someone will undoubtedly speak of it before her, perhaps this evening, at dinner, and that will make her curious to read it."

With a spontaneous, almost unthinking, movement he took the copy, closed it, folded it, and slipped it into his pocket with the swiftness of a thief.

The Countess entered. As soon as she saw Olivier's convulsed and livid face, she guessed that he had reached the limit of suffering.

She hastened toward him, with an impulse from all her poor soul, so agonized also, and from her poor body, that was itself so wounded. Throwing her hands upon his shoulders, and plunging her glance into the depths of his eyes, she said:

"Oh, how unhappy you are!"

This time he did not deny it; his throat swelled with a spasm of pain, and he stammered:

"Yes—yes—yes!"

She felt that he was near weeping, and led him into the darkest corner of the drawing-room, toward two armchairs hidden by a small screen of antique silk. They sat down behind this slight embroidered wall, veiled also by the gray shadow of a rainy day.

She resumed, pitying him, deeply moved by his grief:

"My poor Olivier, how you suffer!"

He leaned his white head on the shoulder of his friend.

"More than you believe!" he said.

"Oh, I knew it! I have felt it all. I saw it from the beginning and watched it grow."

He answered as if she had accused him: "It is not my faulty, Any."

"I know it well; I do not reproach you for it."

And softly, turning a little, she laid her lips on one of Olivier's eyes, where she found a bitter tear.

She started, as if she had just tasted a drop of despair, and repeated several times:

"Ah, poor friend—poor friend—poor friend!"

Then after a moment of silence she added: "It is the fault of our hearts, which never have grown old. I feel that my own is full of life!"

He tried to speak but could not, for now his sobs choked him. She listened, as he leaned against her, to the struggle in his breast. Then, seized by the selfish anguish of love, which had gnawed at her heart so long, she said in the agonized tone in which one realizes a horrible misfortune:

"God! how you love her!"

Again he confessed: "Ah, yes! I love her!"

She reflected a few moments, then continued: "You never have loved me thus?"

He did not deny it, for he was passing through one of those periods in which one speaks with absolute truth, and he murmured:

"No, I was too young then."

She was surprised.

"Too young? Why?"

"Because life was too sweet. It is only at our age that one loves despairingly."

"Does the love you feel for her resemble that which you felt for me?" the Countess asked.

"Yes and no—and yet it is almost the same thing. I have loved you as much as anyone can love a woman. As for her, I love her just as I loved you, since she is yourself; but this love has become something irresistible, destroying, stronger than death. I belong to it as a burning house belongs to the fire."

She felt her sympathy wither up under a breath of jealousy; but, assuming a consoling tone, she said:

"My poor friend! In a few days she will be married and gone. When you see her no more no doubt you will be cured of this fancy."

He shook his head.

"Oh, I am lost, lost, lost!"

"No, no, I say! It will be three months before you see her again. That will be sufficient. Three months were quite enough for you to love her more than you love me, whom you have known for twelve years!"

Then, in his infinite distress, he implored: "Any, do not abandon me!"

"What can I do, my friend?"

"Do not leave me alone."

"I will go to see you as often as you wish."

"No. Keep me here as much as possible."

"But then you would be near her."

"And near you!"

"You must not see her any more before her marriage."

"Oh, Any!"

"Well, at least, not often."

"May I stay here this evening?"

"No, not in your present condition. You must divert your mind; go to the club, or the theater—no matter where, but do not stay here."

"I entreat you—"

"No, Olivier, it is impossible. And, besides, I have guests coming to dinner whose presence would agitate you still more."

"The Duchess and—he!"

"Yes."

"But I spent last evening with them."

"And you speak of it! You are in a fine state to-day."

"I promise you to be calm."

"No, it is impossible."

"Then I am going away."

"Why do you hurry now?"

"I must walk."

"That is right! Walk a great deal, walk until evening, kill yourself with fatigue and then go to bed."

He had risen.

"Good-by, Any!"

"Good-by, dear friend. I will come to see you to-morrow morning. Would you like me to do something very imprudent, as I used to do—pretend to breakfast here at noon, and then go and have breakfast with you at a quarter past one?"

"Yes, I should like it very much. You are so good!"

"It is because I love you."

"And I love you, too."

"Oh, don't speak of that any more!"

"Good-by, Any."

"Good-by, dear friend, till to-morrow."

"Good-by!"

He kissed her hands many times, then he kissed her brow, then the corner of her lips. His eyes were dry now, his bearing resolute. Just as he was about to go, he seized her, clasped her close in both arms, and pressing his lips to her forehead, he seemed to drink in, to inhale from her all the love she had for him.

Then he departed quickly, without turning toward her again.

When she was alone she let herself sink, sobbing, upon a chair. She would have remained there till night if Annette had not suddenly appeared in search of her. In order to gain time to dry her red eyelids, the Countess answered: "I have a little note to write, my child. Go up-stairs, and I will join you in a few seconds."

She was compelled to occupy herself with the great affair of the trousseau until evening.

The Duchess and her nephew dined with the Guilleroys, as a family party. They had just seated themselves at table, and were speaking of the opera of the night before, when the butler appeared, carrying three enormous bouquets.

Madame de Mortemain was surprised.

"Good gracious! What is that?"

"Oh, how lovely they are!" exclaimed Annette; "who can have sent them?"

"Olivier Bertin, no doubt," replied her mother.

She had been thinking of him since his departure. He had seemed so gloomy, so tragic, she understood so clearly his hopeless sorrow, she felt so keenly the counter-stroke of that grief, she loved him so much, so entirely, so tenderly, that her heart was weighed down by sad presentiments.

In the three bouquets were found three of the painter's cards. He had written on them in pencil, respectively, the names of the Countess, the Duchess, and Annette.

"Is he ill, your friend Bertin?" the Duchess inquired. "I thought he looked rather bad last night."

"Yes, I am a little anxious about him, although he does not complain," Madame de Guilleroy answered.

"Oh, he is growing old, like all the rest of us," her husband interposed. "He is growing old quite fast, indeed. I believe, however, that bachelors usually go to pieces suddenly. Their breaking-up comes more abruptly than ours. He really is very much changed."

"Ah, yes!" sighed the Countess.

Farandal suddenly stopped his whispering to Annette to say: "The Figaro has a very disagreeable article about him this morning."

Any attack, any criticism or allusion unfavorable to her friend's talent always threw the Countess into a passion.

"Oh," said she, "men of Bertin's importance need not mind such rudeness."

Guilleroy was astonished.

"What!" he exclaimed, "a disagreeable article about Olivier! But I have not read it. On what page?"

The Marquis informed him: "The first page, at the top, with the title, 'Modern Painting.'"

And the deputy ceased to be astonished. "Oh, exactly! I did not read it because it was about painting."

Everyone smiled, knowing that apart from politics and agriculture M. de Guilleroy was interested in very few things.

The conversation turned upon other subjects until they entered the drawing-room to take coffee. The Countess was not listening and hardly answered, being pursued by anxiety as to what Olivier might be doing. Where was he? Where had he dined? Where had he taken his hopeless heart at that moment? She now felt a burning regret at having let him go, not to have kept him; and she fancied him roving the streets, so sad and lonely, fleeing under his burden of woe.

Up to the time of the departure of the Duchess and her nephew she had hardly spoken, lashed by vague and superstitious fears; then she went to bed and lay there long, her eyes wide open in the darkness, thinking of him!

A very long time had passed when she thought she heard the bell of her apartment ring. She started, sat up and listened. A second time the vibrating tinkle broke the stillness of the night.

She leaped out of bed, and with all her strength pressed the electric button that summoned her maid. Then, candle in hand, she ran to the vestibule.

Through the door she asked: "Who is there?"

"It is a letter," an unknown voice replied.

"A letter! From whom?"

"From a physician."

"What physician?"

"I do not know; it is about some accident."

Hesitating no more, she opened the door, and found herself facing a cab-driver in an oilskin cap. He held a paper in his hand, which he presented to her. She read: "Very urgent—Monsieur le Comte de Guilleroy."

The writing was unknown.

"Enter, my good man," said she; "sit down, and wait for me."

When she reached her husband's door her heart was beating so violently that she could not call him. She pounded on the wood with her metal candlestick. The Count was asleep and did not hear.

Then, impatient, nervous, she kicked the door, and heard a sleepy voice asking: "Who is there? What time is it?"

"It is I," she called. "I have an urgent letter for you, brought by a cabman. There has been some accident."

"Wait! I am getting up. I'll be there," he stammered from behind his bed-curtains.

In another minute he appeared in his dressing-gown. At the same time two servants came running, aroused by the ringing of the bell. They were alarmed and bewildered, having seen a stranger sitting on a chair in the dining-room.

The Count had taken the letter and was turning it over in his fingers, murmuring: "What is that? I cannot imagine."

"Well, read it, then!" said the Countess, in a fever.

He tore off the envelope, unfolded the paper, uttered an exclamation of amazement, then looked at his wife with frightened eyes.

"My God! what is it?" said she.

He stammered, hardly able to speak, so great was his emotion: "Oh, a great misfortune—a great misfortune! Bertin has fallen under a carriage!"

"Dead?" she cried.

"No, no!" said he; "read for yourself."

She snatched from his hand the letter he held out and read:

"MONSIEUR: A great misfortune has just happened. Your friend, the eminent artist, M. Olivier Bertin, has been run over by an omnibus, the wheel of which passed over his body. I cannot as yet say anything decisive as to the probable result of this accident, which may not be serious, although it may have an immediate and fatal result. M. Bertin begs you earnestly and entreats Madame la Comtesse de Guilleroy to come to him at once. I hope, Monsieur, that Madame la Comtesse and yourself will grant the desire of our friend in common, who before daylight may have ceased to live.

"DR. DE RIVIL."

The Countess stared at her husband with great, fixed eyes, full of terror. Then suddenly she experienced, like an electric shock, an awakening of that courage which comes to women at times, which makes them in moments of terror the most valiant of creatures.

Turning to her maid she said: "Quick! I am going to dress."

"What will Madame wear?" asked the servant.

"Never mind that. Anything you like. James," she added, "be ready in five minutes."

Returning toward her room, her soul overwhelmed, she noticed the cabman, still waiting, and said to him: "You have your carriage?"

"Yes, Madame."

"That is well; we will take that."

Wildly, with precipitate haste, she threw on her clothes, hooking, clasping, tying, and fastening at hap-hazard; then, before the mirror, she lifted and twisted her hair without a semblance of order, gazing without thinking of what she was doing at the reflection of her pale face and haggard eyes.

When her cloak was over her shoulders, she rushed to her husband's room, but he was not yet ready. She dragged him along.

"Come, come!" said she; "remember, he may die!"

The Count, dazed, followed her stumblingly, feeling his way with his feet on the dark stairs, trying to distinguish the steps, so that he should not fall.

The drive was short and silent. The Countess trembled so violently that her teeth rattled, and through the window she saw the flying gas-jets, veiled by the falling rain. The sidewalks gleamed, the Boulevard was deserted, the night was sinister. On arriving, they found that the painter's door was open, and that the concierge's lodge was lighted but empty.

At the top of the stairs the physician, Dr. de Rivil, a little gray man, short, round, very well dressed, extremely polite, came to meet them. He bowed low to the Countess and held out his hand to the Count.

She asked him, breathing rapidly as if climbing the stairs had exhausted her and put her out of breath:

"Well, doctor?"

"Well, Madame, I hope that it will be less serious than I thought at first."

"He will not die?" she exclaimed.

"No. At least, I do not believe so."

"Will you answer for that?"

"No. I only say that I hope to find only a simple abdominal contusion without internal lesions."

"What do you call lesions?"

"Lacerations."

"How do you know that there are none?"

"I suppose it."

"And if there are?"

"Oh, then it would be serious."

"He might die of them?"

"Yes."

"Very soon?"

"Very soon. In a few minutes or even seconds. But reassure yourself, Madame; I am convinced that he will be quite well again in two weeks."

She had listened, with profound attention, to know all and understand all.

"What laceration might he have?"

"A laceration of the liver, for instance."

"That would be very dangerous?"

"Yes—but I should be surprised to find any complication now. Let us go to him. It will do him good, for he awaits you with great impatience."

On entering the room she saw first a pale face on a white pillow. Some candles and the firelight illumined it, defined the profile, deepened the shadows; and in that pale face the Countess saw two eyes that watched her coming.

All her courage, energy, and resolution fell, so much did those hollow and altered features resemble those of a dying man. He, whom she had seen only a little while ago, had become this thing, this specter! "Oh, my God!" she murmured between her teeth, and she approached him, palpitating with horror.

He tried to smile, to reassure her, and the grimace of that attempt was frightful.

When she was beside the bed, she put both hands gently on one of Olivier's, which lay along his body, and stammered: "Oh, my poor friend!"

"It is nothing," said he, in a low tone, without moving his head.

She now looked at him closely, frightened at the change in him. He was so pale that he seemed no longer to have a drop of blood under his skin. His hollow cheeks seemed to have been sucked in from the interior of his face, and his eyes were sunken as if drawn by a string from within.

He saw the terror of his friend, and sighed: "Here I am in a fine state!"

"How did it happen?" she asked, looking at him with fixed gaze.

He was making a great effort to speak, and his whole face twitched with pain.

"I was not looking about me—I was thinking of something else—something very different—oh, yes!—and an omnibus knocked me down and ran over my abdomen."

As she listened she saw the accident, and shaking with terror, she asked: "Did you bleed?"

"No. I am only a little bruised—a little crushed."

"Where did it happen?" she inquired.

"I do not know exactly," he answered in a very low voice; "it was far away from here."

The physician rolled up an armchair, and the Countess sank into it. The Count remained standing at the foot of the bed, repeating between his teeth: "Oh, my poor friend! my poor friend! What a frightful misfortune!"

And he was indeed deeply grieved, for he loved Olivier very much.

"But where did it happen?" the Countess repeated.

"I know hardly anything about it myself, or rather I do not understand it at all," the physician replied. "It was at the Gobelins, almost outside of Paris! At least, the cabman that brought him home declared to me that he took him in at a pharmacy of that quarter, to which someone had carried him, at nine o'clock in the evening!" Then, leaning toward Olivier, he asked: "Did the accident really happen near the Gobelins?"

Bertin closed his eyes, as if to recollect; then murmured: "I do not know."

"But where were you going?"

"I do not remember now. I was walking straight before me."

A groan that she could not stifle came from the Countess's lips; then oppressed with a choking that stopped her breathing a few seconds, she drew out her handkerchief, covered her eyes, and wept bitterly.

She knew—she guessed! Something intolerable, overwhelming had just fallen on her heart—remorse for not keeping Olivier near her, for driving him away, for throwing him into the street, where, stupefied with grief, he had fallen under the omnibus.

He said in that colorless voice he now had: "Do not weep. It distresses me."

By a tremendous effort of will, she ceased to sob, uncovered her eyes and fixed them, wide open, upon him, without a quiver of her face, whereon the tears continued slowly to roll down.

They looked at each other, both motionless, their hands clasped under the coverlet. They gazed at each other, no longer knowing that any other person was in the room; and that gaze carried a superhuman emotion from one heart to the other.

They gazed upon each other, and the need of talking, unheard, of hearing the thousand intimate things, so sad, which they had still to say, rose irresistibly to their lips. She felt that she must at any price send away the two men that stood behind her; she must find a way, some ruse, some inspiration, she, the woman, fruitful in resources! She began to reflect, her eyes always fixed on Olivier.

Her husband and the doctor were talking in undertones, discussing the care to be given. Turning her head the Countess said to the doctor: "Have you brought a nurse?"

"No, I prefer to send a hospital surgeon, who will keep a better watch over the case."

"Send both. One never can be too careful. Can you still get them to-night, for I do not suppose you will stay here till morning?"

"Indeed, I was just about to go home. I have been here four hours already."

"But on your way back you will send us the nurse and the surgeon?"

"It will be difficult in the middle of the night. But I shall try."

"You must!"

"They may promise, but will they come?"

"My husband will accompany you and will bring them back either willingly or by force."

"You cannot remain here alone, Madame!"

"I?" she exclaimed with a sort of cry of defiance, of indignant protest against any resistance to her will. Then she pointed out, in that authoritative tone to which no one ventures a reply, the necessities of the situation. It was necessary that the nurse and the surgeon should be there within an hour, to forestall all accident. To insure this, someone must get out of bed and bring them. Her husband alone could do that. During this time she would remain near the injured man, she, for whom it was a duty and a right. She would thereby simply fulfil her role of friend, her role of woman. Besides, this was her will, and no one should dissuade her from it.

Her reasoning was sensible. They could only agree upon that, and they decided to obey her.

She had risen, full of the thought of their departure, impatient to know that they were off and that she was left alone. Now, in order that she should commit no error during their absence, she listened, trying to understand perfectly, to remember everything, to forget nothing of the physician's directions. The painter's valet, standing near her, listened also, and behind him his wife, the cook, who had helped in the first binding of the patient, indicated by nods of the head that she too understood. When the Countess had recited all the instructions like a lesson, she urged the two men to go, repeating to her husband:

"Return soon, above all things, return soon!"

"I will take you in my coupe," said the doctor to the Count. "It will bring you back quicker. You will be here again in an hour."

Before leaving, the doctor again carefully examined the wounded man, to assure himself that his condition remained satisfactory.

Guilleroy still hesitated.

"You do not think that we are doing anything imprudent?" he asked.

"No," said the doctor. "He needs only rest and quiet. Madame de Guilleroy will see that he does not talk, and will speak to him as little as possible."

The Countess was startled, and said:

"Then I must not talk to him?"

"Oh, no, Madame! Take an armchair and sit beside him. He will not feel that he is alone and will be quite content; but no fatigue of words, or even of thoughts. I will call about nine o'clock to-morrow morning. Good-bye, Madame. I salute you!"

He left the room with a low bow, followed by the Count who repeated:

"Do not worry yourself, my dear. Within an hour I shall return, and then you can go home."

When they were gone, she listened for the sound of the door below being closed, then to the rolling wheels of the coupe in the street.

The valet and the cook still stood there, awaiting orders. The Countess dismissed them.

"You may go now," said she; "I will ring if I need anything."

They too withdrew, and she remained alone with him.

She had drawn quite near to the bed, and putting her hands on the two edges of the pillow, on both sides of that dear face, she leaned over to look upon it. Then, with her face so close to his that she seemed to breathe her words upon it, she whispered:

"Did you throw yourself under that carriage?"

He tried to smile still, saying: "No, it was that which threw itself upon me."

"That is not true; it was you."

"No, I swear to you it was it!"

After a few moments of silence, those instants when souls seem mingled in glances, she murmured: "Oh, my dear, dear Olivier, to think that I let you go, that I did not keep you with me!"

"It would have happened just the same, some day or another," he replied with conviction.

They still gazed at each other, seeking to read each other's inmost thoughts.

"I do not believe that I shall recover," he said at last. "I suffer too much."

"Do you suffer very much?" she murmured.

"Oh, yes!"

Bending a little lower, she brushed his forehead, then his eyes, then his cheeks with slow kisses, light, delicate as her care for him. She barely touched him with her lips, with that soft little breath that children give when they kiss. This lasted a long time, a very long time. He let that sweet rain of caresses fall on him, and they seemed to soothe and refresh him, for his drawn face twitched less than before.

"Any!" he said finally.

She ceased her kissing to listen to him.

"What, my friend?"

"You must make me a promise."

"I will promise anything you wish."

"If I am not dead before morning, swear to me that you will bring Annette to me, just once, only once! I cannot bear to die without seeing her again. . . . Think that . . . to-morrow . . . at this time perhaps I shall have . . . shall surely have closed my eyes forever and that I never shall see you again. I . . . nor you . . . nor her!"

She stopped him; her heart was breaking.

"Oh, hush . . . hush! Yes, I promise you to bring her!"

"You swear it?"

"I swear it, my friend. But hush, do not talk any more. You hurt me frightfully—hush!"

A quick convulsion passed over his face; when it had passed he said:

"Since we have only a few minutes more to remain together, do not let us lose them; let us seize them to bid each other good-by. I have loved you so much——"

"And I," she sighed, "how I still love you!"

He spoke again:

"I never have had real happiness except through you. Only these last days have been hard. . . . It was not your fault. . . . Ah, my poor Any, how sad life is! . . . and how hard it is to die!"

"Hush, Olivier, I implore you!"

He continued, without listening to her: "I should have been a happy man if you had not had your daughter. . . ."

"Hush! My God! Hush! . . ."

He seemed to dream rather than speak.

"Ah, he that invented this existence and made men was either blind or very wicked. . . ."

"Olivier, I entreat you . . . if you ever have loved me, be quiet, do not talk like that any more!"

He looked at her, leaning over him, she herself so pale that she looked as if she were dying, too; and he was silent.

Then she seated herself in the armchair, close to the bed, and again took the hand on the coverlet.

"Now I forbid you to speak," said she. "Do not stir, and think of me as I think of you."

Again they looked at each other, motionless, joined together by the burning contact of their hands. She pressed, with gentle movement, the feverish hand she clasped, and he answered these calls by tightening his fingers a little. Each pressure said something to them, evoked some period of their finished past, revived in their memory the stagnant recollections of their love. Each was a secret question, each was a mysterious reply, sad questions and sad replies, those "do you remembers?" of a bygone love.

Their minds, in this agonizing meeting, which might be the last, traveled back through the years, through the whole history of their passion; and nothing was audible in the room save the crackling of the fire.

Suddenly, as if awakening from a dream, he said, with a start of terror:

"Your letters!"

"What? My letters?" she queried.

"I might have died without destroying them!"

"Oh, what does that matter to me? That is of no consequence now. Let them find them and read them—I don't care!"

"I will not have that," he said. "Get up, Any; open the lowest drawer of my desk, the large one; they are all there, all. You must take them and throw them into the fire."

She did not move at all, but remained crouching, as if he had counseled her to do something cowardly.

"Any, I entreat you!" he continued; "if you do not do this, you will torture me, unnerve me, drive me mad. Think—they may fall into anyone's hands, a notary, a servant, or even your husband. . . . I do not wish. . . ."

She rose, still hesitating, and repeating:

"No, that is too hard, too cruel! I feel as if you were compelling me to burn both our hearts!"

He supplicated her, his face drawn with pain.

Seeing him suffer thus, she resigned herself and walked toward the desk. On opening the drawer, she found it filled to the edge with a thick packet of letters, piled one on top of another, and she recognized on all the envelopes the two lines of the address she had written so often. She knew them—those two lines—a man's name, the name of a street—as well as she knew her own name, as well as one can know the few words that have represented to us in life all hope and all happiness. She looked at them, those little square things that contained all she had known how to express of her love, all that she could take of herself to give to him, with a little ink on a bit of white paper.

He had tried to turn his head on the pillow that he might watch her, and again he said: "Burn them, quick!"

Then she took two handfuls, holding them a few seconds in her grasp. They seemed heavy to her, painful, living, at the same time dead, so many different things were in them, so many things that were now over—so sweet to feel, to dream! It was the soul of her soul, the heart of her heart, the essence of her loving self that she was holding there; and she remembered with what delirium she had scribbled some of them, with what exaltation, what intoxication of living and of adoring some one, and of expressing it.

"Burn them! Burn them, Any!" Olivier repeated.

With the same movement of both hands, she cast into the fireplace the two packets of papers, which became scattered as they fell upon the wood. Then she seized those that remained in the desk and threw them on top of the others, then another handful, with swift movements, stooping and rising again quickly, to finish as soon as might be this terrible task.

When the fireplace was full and the drawer empty, she remained standing, waiting, watching the almost smothered flames as they crept up from all sides on that mountain of envelopes. They attacked them first at the edges, gnawed at the corners, ran along the edge of the paper, went out, sprang up again, and went creeping on and on. Soon, all around that white pyramid glowed a vivid girdle of clear fire which filled the room with light; and this light, illuminating the woman standing and the man dying, was their burning love, their love turned to ashes.

The Countess turned, and in the dazzling light of that fire she beheld her friend leaning with a haggard face on the edge of the bed.

"Are they all there?" he demanded.

"Yes, all."

But before returning to him she cast a last look upon that destruction, and on that mass of papers, already half consumed, twisting and turning black, and she saw something red flowing. It looked like drops of blood, and seemed to come out of the very heart of the letters, as from a wound; it ran slowly toward the flames, leaving a purple train.

The Countess received in her soul the shock of supernatural terror, and recoiled as if she had seen the assassination of a human being; then she suddenly understood that she had seen simply the melting of the wax seals.

She returned to the wounded man, and lifting his head tenderly laid it back in the center of the pillow. But he had moved, and his pain increased. He was panting now, his face drawn by fearful suffering, and he no longer seemed to know that she was there.

She waited for him to become a little calmer, to open his eyes, which remained closed, to be able to say one word more to her.

Presently she asked: "Do you suffer much?"

He did not reply.

She bent over him and laid a finger on his forehead to make him look at her. He opened his eyes then, but they were wild and dazed.

Terrified, she repeated: "Do you suffer? Olivier! Answer me! Shall I call? Make an effort! Say something to me!"

She thought she heard him murmur: "Bring her . . . you swore to me."

Then he writhed under the bedclothes, his body grew rigid, his face convulsed with awful grimaces.

"Olivier! My God! Olivier!" she cried. "What is the matter? Shall I call?"

This time he heard her, for he replied, "No . . . it is nothing."

He appeared to grow easier, in fact, to suffer less, to fall suddenly into a sort of drowsy stupor. Hoping that he would sleep, she sat down again beside the bed, took his hand, and waited. He moved no more, his chin had dropped to his breast, his mouth was half opened by his short breath, which seemed to rasp his throat in passing. Only his fingers moved involuntarily now and then, with slight tremors which the Countess felt to the roots of her hair, making her long to cry out. They were no more the tender little meaning pressures which, in place of the weary lips, told of all the sadness of their hearts; they were spasms of pain which spoke only of the torture of the body.

Now she was frightened, terribly frightened, and had a wild desire to run away, to ring, to call, but she dared not move, lest she might disturb his repose.

The far-off sound of vehicles in the streets penetrated the walls; and she listened to hear whether that rolling of wheels did not stop before the door, whether her husband were not coming to deliver her, to tear her away at last from this sad tete-a-tete.

As she tried to draw her hand from Olivier's, he pressed it, uttering a deep sigh! Then she resigned herself to wait, so that she should not trouble him.

The fire was dying out on the hearth, under the black ashes of the letters; two candles went out; some pieces of furniture cracked.

All was silent in the house; everything seemed dead except a tall Flemish clock on the stairs, which regularly chimed the hour, the half hour, and the quarter, singing the march of time in the night, modulating it in divers tones.

The Countess, motionless, felt an intolerable terror rising in her soul. Nightmare assailed her; fearful thoughts filled her mind; and she thought she could feel that Olivier's fingers were growing cold within her own. Was that true? No, certainly not. But whence had come that sensation of inexpressible, frozen contact? She roused herself, wild with terror, to look at his face. It was relaxed, impassive, inanimate, indifferent to all misery, suddenly soothed by the Eternal Oblivion.

NOTRE CŒUR OR

A WOMAN'S PASTIME

By

GUY DE MAUPASSANT

CHAPTER I.

THE INTRODUCTION

One day Massival, the celebrated composer of "Rebecca," who for fifteen years, now, had been known as "the young and illustrious master," said to his friend André Mariolle:

"Why is it that you have never secured a presentation to Mme. Michèle de Burne? Take my word for it, she is one of the most interesting women in new Paris."

"Because I do not feel myself at all adapted to her surroundings."

"You are wrong, my dear fellow. It is a house where there is a great deal of novelty and originality; it is wide-awake and very artistic. There is excellent music, and the conversation is as good as in the best salons of the last century. You would be highly appreciated—in the first place because you play so well on the violin, then because you have been very favorably spoken of in the house, and finally because you have the reputation of being select in your choice of friends."

Flattered, but still maintaining his attitude of resistance, supposing, moreover, that this urgent invitation was not given without the young woman being aware of it, Mariolle ejaculated a "Bah! I shall not bother my head at all about it," in which, through the disdain that he intended to express, was evident his foregone acceptance.

Massival continued: "Would you like to have me present you some of these days? You are already known to her through all of us who are on terms of intimacy with her, for we talk about you often enough. She is a very pretty woman of twenty-eight, abounding in intelligence, who will never take a second husband, for her first venture was a very unfortunate one. She has made her abode a rendezvous for agreeable men. There are not too many club-men or society-men found there—just enough of them to give the proper effect. She will be delighted to have me introduce you."

Mariolle was vanquished; he replied: "Very well, then; one of these days."

At the beginning of the following week the musician came to his house and asked him: "Are you disengaged to-morrow?"

"Why, yes."

"Very well. I will take you to dine with Mme. de Burne; she requested me to invite you. Besides, here is a line from her."

After a few seconds' reflection, for form's sake, Mariolle answered: "That is settled!"

André Mariolle was about thirty-seven years old, a bachelor without a profession, wealthy enough to live in accordance with his likings, to travel, and even to indulge himself in collecting modern paintings and ancient knickknacks. He had the reputation of being a man of intelligence, rather odd and unsociable, a little capricious and disdainful, who affected the hermit through pride rather than through timidity. Very talented and acute, but indolent, quick to grasp the meaning of things, and capable, perhaps, of accomplishing something great, he had contented himself with enjoying life as a spectator, or rather as a dilettante. Had he been poor, he would doubtless have turned out to be a remarkable or celebrated man; born with a good income, he was eternally reproaching himself that he could never be anything better than a nobody.

It is true that he had made more than one attempt in the direction of the arts, but they had lacked vigor. One had been in the direction of literature, by publishing a pleasing book of travels, abounding in incident and correct in style; one toward music by his violin-playing, in which he had gained, even among professional musicians, a respectable reputation; and, finally, one at sculpture, that art in which native aptitude and the faculty of rough-hewing striking and deceptive figures atone in the eyes of the ignorant for deficiencies in study and knowledge. His statuette in terra-cotta, "Masseur Tunisien," had even been moderately successful at the Salon of the preceding year. He was a remarkable horseman, and was also, it was said, an excellent fencer, although he never used the foils in public, owing, perhaps, to the same self-distrustful feeling which impelled him to absent himself from society resorts where serious rivalries were to be apprehended.

His friends appreciated him, however, and were unanimous in extolling his merits, perhaps for the reason that they had little to fear from him in the way of competition. It was said of him that in every case he was reliable, a devoted friend, extremely agreeable in manner, and very sympathetic in his personality.

Tall of stature, wearing his black beard short upon the cheeks and trained down to a fine point upon the chin, with hair that was beginning to turn gray but curled very prettily, he looked one straight in the face with a pair of clear, brown, piercing eyes in which lurked a shade of distrust and hardness.

Among his intimates he had an especial predilection for artists of every kind—among them Gaston de Lamarthe the novelist, Massival the musician, and the painters Jobin, Rivollet, De Mandol—who seemed to set a high value on his reason, his friendship, his intelligence, and even his judgment, although at bottom, with the vanity that is inseparable from success achieved, they set him down as a very agreeable and very intelligent man who had failed to score a success.

Mariolle's haughty reserve seemed to say: "I am nothing because I have not chosen to be anything." He lived within a narrow circle, therefore, disdaining gallantry and the great frequented salons, where others might have shone more brilliantly than he, and might have obliged him to take his place among the lay-figures of society. He visited only those houses where appreciation was extended to the solid qualities that he was unwilling to display; and though he had consented so readily to allow himself to be introduced to Mme. Michèle de Burne, the reason was that his best friends, those who everywhere proclaimed his hidden merits, were the intimates of this young woman.

She lived in a pretty entresol in the Rue du Général-Foy, behind the church of Saint Augustin. There were two rooms with an outlook on the street—the dining-room and a salon, the one in which she received her company indiscriminately—and two others that opened on a handsome garden of which the owner of the property had the enjoyment. Of the latter the first was a second salon of large dimensions, of greater length than width, with three windows opening on the trees, the leaves of which brushed against the awnings, a room which was embellished with furniture and ornaments exceptionally rare and simple, in the purest and soberest taste and of great value. The tables, the chairs, the little cupboards or étagères, the pictures, the fans and the porcelain figures beneath glass covers, the vases, the statuettes, the great clock fixed in the middle of a panel, the entire decoration of this young woman's apartment attracted and held attention by its shape, its age, or its elegance. To create for herself this home, of which she was almost as proud as she was of her own person, she had laid under contribution the knowledge, the friendship, the good nature, and the rummaging instinct of every artist of her acquaintance. She was rich and willing to pay well, and her friends had discovered for her many things, distinguished by originality, which the mere vulgar amateur would have passed by with contempt. Thus, with their assistance, she had furnished this dwelling, to which access was obtained with difficulty, and where she imagined that her friends received more pleasure and returned more gladly than elsewhere.

It was even a favorite hobby of hers to assert that the colors of the curtains and hangings, the comfort of the seats, the beauty of form, and the gracefulness of general effect are of as much avail to charm, captivate, and acclimatize the eye as are pretty smiles. Sympathetic or antipathetic rooms, she would say, whether rich or poor, attract, hold, or repel, just like the people who live in them. They awake the feelings or stifle them, warm or chill the mind, compel one to talk or be silent, make one sad or cheerful; in a word, they give every visitor an unaccountable desire to remain or to go away.

About the middle of this dimly lighted gallery a grand piano, standing between two jardinières filled with flowers, occupied the place of honor and dominated the room. Beyond this a lofty door with two leaves opened gave access to the bedroom, which in turn communicated with a dressing-room, also very large and elegant, hung with chintz like a drawing-room in summer, where Mme. de Burne generally kept herself when she had no company.

Married to a well-mannered good-for-nothing, one of those domestic tyrants before whom everything must bend and yield, she had at first been very unhappy. For five years she had had to endure the unreasonable exactions, the harshness, the jealousy, even the violence of this intolerable master, and terrified, beside herself with astonishment, she had submitted without revolt to this revelation of married life, crushed as she was beneath the despotic and torturing will of the brutal man whose victim she had become.

He died one night, from an aneurism, as he was coming home, and when she saw the body of her husband brought in, covered with a sheet, unable to believe in the reality of this deliverance, she looked at his corpse with a deep feeling of repressed joy and a frightful dread lest she might show it.

Cheerful, independent, even exuberant by nature, very flexible and attractive, with bright flashes of wit such as are shown in some incomprehensible way in the intellects of certain little girls of Paris, who seem to have breathed from their earliest childhood the stimulating air of the boulevards—where every evening, through the open doors of the theaters, the applause or the hisses that greet the plays come forth, borne on the air—she nevertheless retained from her five years of servitude a strange timidity grafted upon her old-time audacity, a great fear lest she might say too much, do too much, together with a burning desire for emancipation and a stern resolve never again to do anything to imperil her liberty.

Her husband, a man of the world, had trained her to receive like a mute slave, elegant, polite, and well dressed. The despot had numbered among his friends many artists, whom she had received with curiosity and listened to with delight, without ever daring to allow them to see how she understood and appreciated them.

When her period of mourning was ended she invited a few of them to dinner one evening. Two of them sent excuses; three accepted and were astonished to find a young woman of admirable intelligence and charming manners, who immediately put them at their ease and gracefully told them of the pleasure that they had afforded her in former days by coming to her house. From among her old acquaintances who had ignored her or failed to recognize her qualities she thus gradually made a selection according to her inclinations, and as a widow, an enfranchised woman, but one determined to maintain her good name, she began to receive all the most distinguished men of Paris whom she could bring together, with only a few women. The first to be admitted became her intimates, formed a nucleus, attracted others, and gave to the house the air of a small court, to which every habitué contributed either personal merit or a great name, for a few well-selected titles were mingled with the intelligence of the commonalty.

Her father, M. de Pradon, who occupied the apartment over hers, served as her chaperon and "sheep-dog." An old beau, very elegant and witty, and extremely attentive to his daughter, whom he treated rather as a lady acquaintance than as a daughter, he presided at the Thursday dinners that were quickly known and talked of in Paris, and to which invitations were much sought after. The requests for introductions and invitations came in shoals, were discussed, and very frequently rejected by a sort of vote of the inner council. Witty sayings that had their origin in this circle were quoted and obtained currency in the city. Actors, artists, and young poets made their débuts there, and received, as it were, the baptism of their future greatness. Longhaired geniuses, introduced by Gaston de Lamarthe, seated themselves at the piano and replaced the Hungarian violinists that Massival had presented, and foreign ballet-dancers gave the company a glimpse of their graceful steps before appearing at the Eden or the Folies-Bergères.

Mme. de Burne, over whom her friends kept jealous watch and ward and to whom the recollection of her commerce with the world under the auspices of marital authority was loathsome, was sufficiently wise not to enlarge the circle of her acquaintance to too great an extent. Satisfied and at the same time terrified as to what might be said and thought of her, she abandoned herself to her somewhat Bohemian inclinations with consummate prudence. She valued her good name, and was fearful of any rashness that might jeopardize it; she never allowed her fancies to carry her beyond the bounds of propriety, was moderate in her audacity and careful that no liaison or small love affair should ever be imputed to her.

All her friends had made love to her, more or less; none of them had been successful. They confessed it, admitted it to each other with surprise, for men never acknowledge, and perhaps they are right, the power of resistance of a woman who is her own mistress. There was a story current about her. It was said that at the beginning of their married life her husband had exhibited such revolting brutality toward her that she had been forever cured of the love of men. Her friends would often discuss the case at length. They inevitably arrived at the conclusion that a young girl who has been brought up in the dream of future tenderness and the expectation of an awe-inspiring mystery must have all her ideas completely upset when her initiation into the new life is committed to a clown. That worldly philosopher, George de Maltry, would give a gentle sneer and add: "Her hour will strike; it always does for women like her, and the longer it is in coming the louder it strikes. With our friend's artistic tastes, she will wind up by falling in love with a singer or a pianist."

Gaston de Lamarthe's ideas upon the subject were quite different. As a novelist, observer, and psychologist, devoted to the study of the inhabitants of the world of fashion, of whom he drew ironical and lifelike portraits, he claimed to analyze and know women with infallible and unique penetration. He put Mme. de Burne down among those flighty creatures of the time, the type of whom he had given in his interesting novel, "Une d'Elles." He had been the first to diagnose this new race of women, distracted by the nerves of reasoning, hysterical patients, drawn this way and that by a thousand contradictory whims which never ripen into desires, disillusioned of everything, without having enjoyed anything, thanks to the times, to the way of living, and to the modern novel, and who, destitute of all ardor and enthusiasm, seem to combine in their persons the capricious, spoiled child and the old, withered sceptic. But he, like the rest of them, had failed in his love-making.

For all the faithful of the group had in turn been lovers of Mme. de Burne, and after the crisis had retained their tenderness and their emotion in different degrees. They had gradually come to form a sort of little church; she was its Madonna, of whom they conversed constantly among themselves, subject to her charm even when she was not present. They praised, extolled, criticised, or disparaged her, according as she had manifested irritation or gentleness, aversion or preference. They were continually displaying their jealousy of each other, played the spy on each other a little, and above all kept their ranks well closed up, so that no rival might get near her who could give them any cause for alarm.

These assiduous ones were few in number: Massival, Gaston de Lamarthe, big Fresnel, George de Maltry, a fashionable young philosopher, celebrated for his paradoxes, for his eloquent and involved erudition that was always up to date though incomprehensible even to the most impassioned of his female admirers, and for his clothes, which were selected with as much care as his theories. To this tried band she had added a few more men of the world who had a reputation for wit, the Comte de Marantin, the Baron de Gravil, and two or three others.

The two privileged characters of this chosen battalion seemed to be Massival and Lamarthe, who, it appears, had the gift of being always able to divert the young woman by their artistic unceremoniousness, their chaff, and the way they had of making fun of everybody, even of herself, a little, when she was in humor to tolerate it. The care, whether natural or assumed, however, that she took never to manifest a marked and prolonged predilection for any one of her admirers, the unconstrained air with which she practiced her coquetry and the real impartiality with which she dispensed her favors maintained between them a friendship seasoned with hostility and an alertness of wit that made them entertaining.

One of them would sometimes play a trick on the others by presenting a friend; but as this friend was never a very celebrated or very interesting man, the rest would form a league against him and quickly send him away.

It was in this way that Massival brought his comrade André Mariolle to the house. A servant in black announced these names: "Monsieur Massival! Monsieur Mariolle!"

Beneath a great rumpled cloud of pink silk, a huge shade that was casting down upon a square table with a top of ancient marble the brilliant light of a lamp supported by a lofty column of gilded bronze, one woman's head and three men's heads were bent over an album that Lamarthe had brought in with him. Standing between them, the novelist was turning the leaves and explaining the pictures.

As they entered the room, one of the heads was turned toward them, and Mariolle, as he stepped forward, became conscious of a bright, blond face, rather tending to ruddiness, upon the temples of which the soft, fluffy locks of hair seemed to blaze with the flame of burning brushwood. The delicate retroussé nose imparted a smiling expression to this countenance, and the clean-cut mouth, the deep dimples in the cheeks, and the rather prominent cleft chin, gave it a mocking air, while the eyes, by a strange contrast, veiled it in melancholy. They were blue, of a dull, dead blue as if they had been washed out, scoured, used up, and in the center the black pupils shone, round and dilated. The strange and brilliant glances that they emitted seemed to tell of dreams of morphine, or perhaps, more simply, of the coquettish artifice of belladonna.

Mme. de Burne arose, gave her hand, thanked and welcomed them.

"For a long time I have been begging my friends to bring you to my house," she said to Mariolle, "but I always have to tell these things over and over again in order to get them done."

She was tall, elegantly shaped, rather deliberate in her movements, modestly décolletée, scarcely showing the tips of her handsome shoulders, the shoulders of a red-headed woman, that shone out marvelously under the light. And yet her hair was not red, but of the inexpressible color of certain dead leaves that have been burned by the frosts of autumn.

She presented M. Mariolle to her father, who bowed and shook hands.

The men were conversing familiarly together in three groups; they seemed to be at home, in a kind of club that they were accustomed to frequent, to which the presence of a woman imparted a note of refinement.

Big Fresnel was chatting with the Comte de Marantin. Fresnel's frequent visits to this house and the preference that Mme. de Burne evinced for him shocked and often provoked her friends. Still young, but with the proportions of a drayman, always puffing and blowing, almost beardless, his head lost in a vague cloud of light, soft hair, commonplace, tiresome, ridiculous, he certainly could have but one merit in the young woman's eyes, a merit that was displeasing to the others but indispensable to her,—that of loving her blindly. He had received the nickname of "The Seal." He was married, but never said anything about bringing his wife to the house. It was said that she was very jealous in her seclusion.

Lamarthe and Massival especially evinced their indignation at the evident sympathy of their friend for this windy person, and when they could no longer refrain from reproaching her with this reprehensible inclination, this selfish and vulgar liking, she would smile and answer:

"I love him as I would love a great, big, faithful dog."

George de Maltry was entertaining Gaston de Lamarthe with the most recent discovery, not yet fully developed, of the micro-biologists. M. de Maltry was expatiating on his theme with many subtile and far-reaching theories, and the novelist accepted them enthusiastically, with the facility with which men of letters receive and do not dispute everything that appears to them original and new.

The philosopher of "high life," fair, of the fairness of linen, slender and tall, was incased in a coat that fitted very closely about the hips. Above, his pale, intelligent face emerged from his white collar and was surmounted by smooth, blond hair, which had the appearance of being glued on.

As to Lamarthe, Gaston de Lamarthe, to whom the particle that divided his name had imparted some of the pretensions of a gentleman and man of the world, he was first, last, and all the time a man of letters, a terrible and pitiless man of letters. Provided with an eye that gathered in images, attitudes, and gestures with the rapidity and accuracy of the photographer's camera, and endowed with penetration and the novelist's instinct, which were as innate in him as the faculty of scent is in a hound, he was busy from morning till night storing away impressions to be used afterward in his profession. With these two very simple senses, a distinct idea of form and an intuitive one of substance, he gave to his books, in which there appeared none of the ordinary aims of psychological writers, the color, the tone, the appearance, the movement of life itself.

Each one of his novels as it appeared excited in society curiosity, conjecture, merriment, or wrath, for there always seemed to be prominent persons to be recognized in them, only faintly disguised under a torn mask; and whenever he made his way through a crowded salon he left a wake of uneasiness behind him. Moreover, he had published a volume of personal recollections, in which he had given the portraits of many men and women of his acquaintance, without any clearly defined intention of unkindness, but with such precision and severity that they felt sore over it. Some one had applied to him the sobriquet, "Beware of your friends." He kept his secrets close-locked within his breast and was a puzzle to his intimates. He was reputed to have once passionately loved a woman who caused him much suffering, and it was said that after that he wreaked his vengeance upon others of her sex.

Massival and he understood each other very well, although the musician was of a very different disposition, more frank, more expansive, less harassed, perhaps, but manifestly more impressible. After two great successes—a piece performed at Brussels and afterward brought to Paris, where it was loudly applauded at the Opéra-Comique; then a second work that was received and interpreted at the Grand Opéra as soon as offered—he had yielded to that species of cessation of impulse that seems to smite the greater part of our contemporary artists like premature paralysis. They do not grow old, as their fathers did, in the midst of their renown and success, but seem threatened with impotence even when in the very prime of life. Lamarthe was accustomed to say: "At the present day there are in France only great men who have gone wrong."

Just at this time Massival seemed very much smitten with Mme. de Burne, so that every eye was turned upon him when he kissed her hand with an air of adoration. He inquired:

"Are we late?"

She replied:

"No, I am still expecting the Baron de Gravil and the Marquise de Bratiane."

"Ah, the Marquise! What good luck! We shall have some music this evening, then."

"I hope so."

The two laggards made their appearance. The Marquise, a woman perhaps a little too diminutive, Italian by birth, of a lively disposition, with very black eyes and eyelashes, black eyebrows, and black hair to match, which grew so thick and so low down that she had no forehead to speak of, her eyes even being threatened with invasion, had the reputation of possessing the most remarkable voice of all the women in society.

The Baron, a very gentlemanly man, hollow-chested and with a large head, was never really himself unless he had his violoncello in his hands. He was a passionate melomaniac, and only frequented those houses where music received its due share of honor.

Dinner was announced, and Mme. de Burne, taking André Mariolle's arm, allowed her guests to precede her to the dining-room; then, as they were left together, the last ones in the drawing-room, just as she was about to follow the procession she cast upon him an oblique, swift glance from her pale eyes with their dusky pupils, in which he thought that he could perceive more complexity of thought and more curiosity of interest than pretty women generally bestow upon a strange gentleman when receiving him at dinner for the first time.

The dinner was monotonous and rather dull. Lamarthe was nervous, and seemed ill disposed toward everyone, not openly hostile, for he made a point of his good-breeding, but displaying that almost imperceptible bad humor that takes the life out of conversation. Massival, abstracted and preoccupied, ate little, and from time to time cast furtive glances at the mistress of the house, who seemed to be in any place rather than at her own table. Inattentive, responding to remarks with a smile and then allowing her face to settle back to its former intent expression, she appeared to be reflecting upon something that seemed greatly to preoccupy her, and to interest her that evening more than did her friends. Still she contributed her share to the conversation—very amply as regarded the Marquise and Mariolle,—but she did it from habit, from a sense of duty, visibly absent from herself and from her abode. Fresnel and M. de Maltry disputed over contemporary poetry. Fresnel held the opinions upon poetry that are current among men of the world, and M. de Maltry the perceptions of the spinners of most complicated verse—verse that is incomprehensible to the general public.

Several times during the dinner Mariolle had again encountered the young woman's inquiring look, but more vague, less intent, less curious. The Marquise de Bratiane, the Comte de Marantin, and the Baron de Gravil were the only ones who kept up an uninterrupted conversation, and they had quantities of things to say.

After dinner, during the course of the evening, Massival, who had kept growing more and more melancholy, seated himself at the piano and struck a few notes, whereupon Mme. de Burne appeared to awake and quickly organized a little concert, the numbers of which comprised the pieces that she was most fond of.

The Marquise was in voice, and, animated by Massival's presence, she sang like a real artist. The master accompanied her, with that dreamy look that he always assumed when he sat down to play. His long hair fell over the collar of his coat and mingled with his full, fine, shining, curling beard. Many women had been in love with him, and they still pursued him with their attentions, so it was said. Mme. de Burne, sitting by the piano and listening with all her soul, seemed to be contemplating him and at the same time not to see him, and Mariolle was a little jealous. He was not particularly jealous because of any relation that there was between her and him, but in presence of that look of a woman fixed so intently upon one of the Illustrious he felt himself humiliated in his masculine vanity by the consciousness of the rank that They bestow on us in proportion to the renown that we have gained. Often before this he had secretly suffered from contact with famous men whom he was accustomed to meet in the presence of those beings whose favor is by far the dearest reward of success.

About ten o'clock the Comtesse de Frémines and two Jewesses of the financial community arrived, one after the other. The talk was of a marriage that was on the carpet and a threatened divorce suit. Mariolle looked at Madame de Burne, who was now seated beneath a column that sustained a huge lamp. Her well-formed, tip-tilted nose, the dimples in her cheeks, and the little indentation that parted her chin gave her face the frolicsome expression of a child, although she was approaching her thirtieth year, and something in her glance that reminded one of a withering flower cast a shade of melancholy over her countenance. Beneath the light that streamed upon it her skin took on tones of blond velvet, while her hair actually seemed colored by the autumnal sun which dyes and scorches the dead leaves.

She was conscious of the masculine glance that was traveling toward her from the other end of the room, and presently she arose and went to him, smiling, as if in response to a summons from him.

"I am afraid you are somewhat bored," she said. "A person who has not got the run of a house is always bored."

He protested the contrary. She took a chair and seated herself by him, and at once the conversation began to be animated. It was instantaneous with both of them, like a fire that blazes up brightly as soon as a match is applied to it. It seemed as if they had imparted their sensations and their opinions to each other beforehand, as if a similarity of disposition and education, of tastes and inclinations, had predisposed them to a mutual understanding and fated them to meet.

Perhaps there may have been a little artfulness on the part of the young woman, but the delight that one feels in encountering one who is capable of listening, who can understand you and reply to you and whose answers give scope for your repartees, put Mariolle into a fine glow of spirits. Flattered, moreover, by the reception which she had accorded him, subjugated by the alluring favor that she displayed and by the charm which she knew how to use so adroitly in captivating men, he did his best to exhibit to her that shade of subdued but personal and delicate wit which, when people came to know him well, had gained for him so many and such warm friendships.

She suddenly said to him:

"Really, it is very pleasant to converse with you, Monsieur. I had been told that such was the case, however."

He was conscious that he was blushing, and replied at a venture:

"And I had been told, Madame, that you were——"

She interrupted him:

"Say a coquette. I am a good deal of a coquette with people whom I like. Everyone knows it, and I do not attempt to conceal it from myself, but you will see that I am very impartial in my coquetry, and this allows me to keep or to recall my friends without ever losing them, and to retain them all about me."

She said this with a sly air which was meant to say: "Be easy and don't be too presumptuous. Don't deceive yourself, for you will get nothing more than the others."

He replied:

"That is what you might call warning your guests of the perils that await them here. Thank you, Madame: I greatly admire your mode of procedure."

She had opened the way for him to speak of herself, and he availed himself of it. He began by paying her compliments and found that she was fond of them; then he aroused her woman's curiosity by telling her what was said of her in the different houses that he frequented. She was rather uneasy and could not conceal her desire for further information, although she affected much indifference as to what might be thought of herself and her tastes. He drew for her a charming portrait of a superior, independent, intelligent, and attractive woman, who had surrounded herself with a court of eminent men and still retained her position as an accomplished member of society. She disclaimed his compliments with smiles, with little disclaimers of gratified egotism, all the while taking much pleasure in the details that he gave her, and in a playful tone kept constantly asking him for more, questioning him artfully, with a sensual appetite for flattery.

As he looked at her, he said to himself, "She is nothing but a child at heart, just like all the rest of them"; and he went on to finish a pretty speech in which he was commending her love for art, so rarely found among women. Then she assumed an air of mockery that he had not before suspected in her, that playfully tantalizing manner that seems inherent in the French. Mariolle had overdone his eulogy; she let him know that she was not a fool.

"Mon Dieu!" she said, "I will confess to you that I am not quite certain whether it is art or artists that I love."

He replied: "How could one love artists without being in love with art?"

"Because they are sometimes more comical than men of the world."

"Yes, but they have more unpleasant failings."

"That is true."

"Then you do not love music?"

She suddenly dropped her bantering tone. "Excuse me! I adore music; I think that I am more fond of it than of anything else. And yet Massival is convinced that I know nothing at all about it."

"Did he tell you so?"

"No, but he thinks so."

"How do you know?"

"Oh! we women guess at almost everything that we don't know."

"So Massival thinks that you know nothing of music?"

"I am sure of it. I can see it only by the way that he has of explaining things to me, by the way in which he underscores little niceties of expression, all the while saying to himself: 'That won't be of any use, but I do it because you are so nice.'"

"Still he has told me that you have the best music in your house of any in Paris, no matter whose the other may be."

"Yes, thanks to him."

"And literature, are you not fond of that?"

"I am very fond of it; and I am even so audacious as to claim to have a very good perception of it, notwithstanding Lamarthe's opinion."

"Who also decides that you know nothing at all about it?"

"Of course."

"But who has not told you so in words, any more than the other."

"Pardon me; he is more outspoken. He asserts that certain women are capable of showing a very just and delicate perception of the sentiments that are expressed, of the truthfulness of the characters, of psychology in general, but that they are totally incapable of discerning the superiority that resides in his profession, its art. When he has once uttered this word, Art, all that is left one to do is to show him the door."

Mariolle smiled and asked:

"And you, Madame, what do you think of it?"

She reflected for a few seconds, then looked him straight in the face to see if he was in a frame of mind to listen and to understand her.

"I believe that sentiment, you understand—sentiment—can make a woman's mind receptive of everything; only it is frequently the case that what enters does not remain there. Do you follow me?"

"No, not fully, Madame."

"Very well! To make us comprehensive to the same degree as you, our woman's nature must be appealed to before addressing our intelligence. We take no interest in what a man has not first made sympathetic to us, for we look at all things through the medium of sentiment. I do not say through the medium of love; no,—but of sentiment, which has shades, forms, and manifestations of every sort. Sentiment is something that belongs exclusively to our domain, which you men have no conception of, for it befogs you while it enlightens us. Oh! I know that all this is incomprehensible to you, the more the pity! In a word, if a man loves us and is agreeable to us, for it is indispensable that we should feel that we are loved in order to become capable of the effort—and if this man is a superior being, by taking a little pains he can make us feel, know, and possess everything, everything, I say, and at odd moments and by bits impart to us the whole of his intelligence. That is all often blotted out afterward; it disappears, dies out, for we are forgetful. Oh! we forget as the wind forgets the words that are spoken to it. We are intuitive and capable of enlightenment, but changeable, impressionable, readily swayed by our surroundings. If I could only tell you how many states of mind I pass through that make of me entirely different women, according to the weather, my health, what I may have been reading, what may have been said to me! Actually there are days when I have the feelings of an excellent mother without children, and others when I almost have those of a cocotte without lovers."

Greatly pleased, he asked: "Is it your opinion that intelligent women generally are gifted with this activity of thought?"

"Yes," she said. "Only they allow it to slumber, and then they have a life shaped for them which draws them in one direction or the other."

Again he questioned: "Then in your heart of hearts it is music that you prefer above all other distractions?"

"Yes! But what I was telling you just now is so true! I should certainly never have enjoyed it as I do enjoy it, adored it as I do adore it, had it not been for that angelic Massival. He seems to have given me the soul of the great masters by teaching me to play their works, of which I was passionately fond before. What a pity that he is married!"

She said these last words with a sprightly air, but so regretfully that they threw everything else into shadow, her theories upon women and her admiration for art.

Massival was, in fact, married. Before the days of his success he had contracted one of those unions that artists make and afterward trail after them through their renown until the day of their death. He never mentioned his wife's name, never presented her in society, which he frequented a great deal; and although he had three children the fact was scarcely known.

Mariolle laughed. She was decidedly nice, was this unconventional woman, pretty, and of a type not often met with. Without ever tiring, with a persistency that seemed in no wise embarrassing to her, he kept gazing upon that face, grave and gay and a little self-willed, with its audacious nose and its sensual coloring of a soft, warm blonde, warmed by the midsummer of a maturity so tender, so full, so sweet that she seemed to have reached the very year, the month, the minute of her perfect flowering. He wondered: "Is her complexion false?" And he looked for the faint telltale line, lighter or darker, at the roots of her hair, without being able to discover it.

Soft footsteps on the carpet behind him made him start and turn his head. It was two servants bringing in the tea-table. Over the blue flame of the little lamp the water bubbled gently in a great silver receptacle, as shining and complicated as a chemist's apparatus.

"Will you have a cup of tea?" she asked.

Upon his acceptance she arose, and with a firm step in which there was no undulation, but which was rather marked by stiffness, proceeded to the table where the water was simmering in the depths of the machine, surrounded by a little garden of cakes, pastry, candied fruits, and bonbons. Then, as her profile was presented in clear relief against the hangings of the salon, Mariolle observed the delicacy of her form and the thinness of her hips beneath the broad shoulders and the full chest that he had been admiring a moment before. As the train of her light dress unrolled and dragged behind her, seemingly prolonging upon the carpet a body that had no end, this blunt thought arose to his mind: "Behold, a siren! She is altogether promising." She was now going from one to another, offering her refreshments with gestures of exquisite grace. Mariolle was following her with his eyes; but Lamarthe, who was walking about with his cup in his hand, came up to him and said:

"Shall we go, you and I?"

"Yes, I think so."

"We will go at once, shall we not? I am tired."

"At once. Come."

They left the house. When they were in the street, the novelist asked:

"Are you going home or to the club?"

"I think that I will go and spend an hour at the club."

"At the Tambourins?"

"Yes."

"I will go as far as the door with you. Those places are tiresome to me; I never put my foot in them. I join them only because they enable me to economize in hack-hire."

They locked arms and went down the street toward Saint Augustin. They walked a little way in silence; then Mariolle said:

"What a singular woman! What do you think of her?"

Lamarthe began to laugh outright. "It is the commencement of the crisis," he said. "You will have to pass through it, just as we have all done. I have had the malady, but I am cured of it now. My dear friend, the crisis consists of her friends talking of nothing but of her when they are together, whenever they chance to meet, wherever they may happen to be."

"At all events, it is the first time in my case, and it is very natural for me to ask for information, since I scarcely know her."

"Let it be so, then; we will talk of her. Well, you are bound to fall in love with her. It is your fate, the lot that is shared by all."

"She is so very seductive, then?"

"Yes and no. Those who love the women of other days, women who have a heart and a soul, women of sensibility, the women of the old-fashioned novel, cannot endure her and execrate her to such a degree as to speak of her with ignominy. We, on the other hand, who are disposed to look favorably upon what is modern and fresh, are compelled to confess that she is delicious, provided always that we don't fall in love with her. And that is just exactly what everybody does. No one dies of the complaint, however; they do not even suffer very acutely, but they fume because she is not other than she is. You will have to go through it all if she takes the fancy; besides, she is already preparing to snap you up."

Mariolle exclaimed, in response to his secret thought:

"Oh! I am only a chance acquaintance for her, and I imagine that she values acquaintances of all sorts and conditions."

"Yes, she values them, parbleu! and at the same time she laughs at them. The most celebrated, even the most distinguished, man will not darken her door ten times if he is not congenial to her, and she has formed a stupid attachment for that idiotic Fresnel, and that tiresome De Maltry. She inexcusably suffers herself to be carried away by those idiots, no one knows why; perhaps because she gets more amusement out of them than she does out of us, perhaps because their love for her is deeper; and there is nothing in the world that pleases a woman so much as to be loved like that."

And Lamarthe went on talking of her, analyzing her, pulling her to pieces, correcting himself only to contradict himself again, replying with unmistakable warmth and sincerity to Mariolle's questions, like a man who is deeply interested in his subject and carried away by it; a little at sea also, having his mind stored with observations that were true and deductions that were false. He said:

"She is not the only one, moreover; at this minute there are fifty women, if not more, who are like her. There is the little Frémines who was in her drawing-room just now; she is Mme. de Burne's exact counterpart, save that she is more forward in her manners and married to an outlandish kind of fellow, the consequence of which is that her house is one of the most entertaining lunatic asylums in Paris. I go there a great deal."

Without noticing it, they had traversed the Boulevard Malesherbes, the Rue Royale, the Avenue des Champs-Élysées, and had reached the Arc de Triomphe, when Lamarthe suddenly pulled out his watch.

"My dear fellow," he said, "we have spent an hour and ten minutes in talking of her; that is sufficient for to-day. I will take some other occasion of seeing you to your club. Go home and go to bed; it is what I am going to do."

CHAPTER II.

"WILL YOU WALK INTO MY PARLOR?"

The room was large and well lighted, the walls and ceiling hung with admirable hangings of chintz that a friend of hers in the diplomatic service had brought home and presented to her. The ground was yellow, as if it had been dipped in golden cream, and the designs of all colors, in which Persian green was predominant, represented fantastic buildings with curving roofs, about which monstrosities in the shape of beasts and birds were running and flying: lions wearing wigs, antelopes with extravagant horns, and birds of paradise.

The furniture was scanty. Upon three long tables with tops of green marble were arranged all the implements requisite for a pretty woman's toilette. Upon one of them, the central one, were the great basins of thick crystal; the second presented an array of bottles, boxes, and vases of all sizes, surmounted by silver caps bearing her arms and monogram; while on the third were displayed all the tools and appliances of modern coquetry, countless in number, designed to serve various complex and mysterious purposes. The room contained only two reclining chairs and a few low, soft, and luxurious seats, calculated to afford rest to weary limbs and to bodies relieved of the restraint of clothing.

Covering one entire side of the apartment was an immense mirror, composed of three panels. The two wings, playing on hinges, allowed the young woman to view herself at the same time in front, rear, and profile, to envelop herself in her own image. To the right, in a recess that was generally concealed by hanging draperies, was the bath, or rather a deep pool, reached by a descent of two steps. A bronze Love, a charming conception of the sculptor Prédolé, poured hot and cold water into it through the seashells with which he was playing. At the back of this alcove a Venetian mirror, composed of smaller mirrors inclined to each other at varying angles, ascended in a curved dome, shutting in and protecting the bath and its occupant, and reflecting them in each one of its many component parts. A little beyond the bath was her writing-desk, a plain and handsome piece of furniture of modern English manufacture, covered with a litter of papers, folded letters, little torn envelopes on which glittered gilt initials, for it was in this room that she passed her time and attended to her correspondence when she was alone.

Stretched at full length upon her reclining-chair, enveloped in a dressing-gown of Chinese silk, her bare arms—and beautiful, firm, supple arms they were—issuing forth fearlessly from out the wide folds of silk, her hair turned up and burdening the head with its masses of blond coils, Mme. de Burne was indulging herself with a gentle reverie after the bath. The chambermaid knocked, then entered, bringing a letter. She took it, looked at the writing, tore it open, and read the first lines; then calmly said to the servant: "I will ring for you in an hour."

When she was alone she smiled with the delight of victory. The first words had sufficed to let her understand that at last she had received a declaration of love from Mariolle. He had held out much longer than she had thought he was capable of doing, for during the last three months she had been besieging him with such attentions, such display of grace and efforts to charm, as she had never hitherto employed for anyone. He had seemed to be distrustful and on his guard against her, against the bait of insatiable coquetry that she was continually dangling before his eyes.

It had required many a confidential conversation, into which she had thrown all the physical seduction of her being and all the captivating efforts of her mind, many an evening of music as well, when, seated before the piano that was ringing still, before the leaves of the scores that were full of the soul of the tuneful masters, they had both thrilled with the same emotion, before she at last beheld in his eyes that avowal of the vanquished man, the mendicant supplication of a love that can no longer be concealed. She knew all this so well, the rouée! Many and many a time, with feline cunning and inexhaustible curiosity, she had made this secret, torturing plea rise to the eyes of the men whom she had succeeded in beguiling. It afforded her so much amusement to feel that she was gaining them, little by little, that they were conquered, subjugated by her invincible woman's might, that she was for them the Only One, the sovereign Idol whose caprices must be obeyed.

It had all grown up within her almost imperceptibly, like the development of a hidden instinct, the instinct of war and conquest. Perhaps it was that a desire of retaliation had germinated in her heart during her years of married life, a dim longing to repay to men generally that measure of ill which she had received from one of them, to be in turn the strongest, to make stubborn wills bend before her, to crush resistance and to make others, as well as she, feel the keen edge of suffering. Above all else, however, she was a born coquette, and as soon as her way in life was clear before her she applied herself to pursuing and subjugating lovers, just as the hunter pursues the game, with no other end in view than the pleasure of seeing them fall before her.

And yet her heart was not eager for emotion, like that of a tender and sentimental woman; she did not seek a man's undivided love, nor did she look for happiness in passion. All that she needed was universal admiration, homage, prostrations, an incense-offering of tenderness. Whoever frequented her house had also to become the slave of her beauty, and no consideration of mere intellect could attach her for any length of time to those who would not yield to her coquetry, disdainful of the anxieties of love, their affections, perhaps, being placed elsewhere.

In order to retain her friendship it was indispensable to love her, but that point once reached she was infinitely nice, with unimaginable kindnesses and delightful attentions, designed to retain at her side those whom she had captivated. Those who were once enlisted in her regiment of adorers seemed to become her property by right of conquest. She ruled them with great skill and wisdom, according to their qualities and their defects and the nature of their jealousy. Those who sought to obtain too much she expelled forthwith, taking them back again afterward when they had become wiser, but imposing severe conditions. And to such an extent did this game of bewitchment amuse her, perverse woman that she was, that she found it as pleasurable to befool steady old gentlemen as to turn the heads of the young.

It might even have been said that she regulated her affection by the fervency of the ardor that she had inspired, and that big Fresnel, a dull, heavy companion who was of no imaginable benefit to her, retained her favor thanks to the mad passion by which she felt that he was possessed. She was not entirely indifferent to men's merits, either, and more than once had been conscious of the commencement of a liking that no one divined except herself, and which she quickly ended the moment it became dangerous.

Everyone who had approached her for the first time and warbled in her ear the fresh notes of his hymn of gallantry, disclosing to her the unknown quantity of his nature—artists more especially, who seemed to her to possess more subtile and more delicate shades of refined emotion—had for a time disquieted her, had awakened in her the intermittent dream of a grand passion and a long liaison. But swayed by prudent fears, irresolute, driven this way and that by her distrustful nature, she had always kept a strict watch upon herself until the moment she ceased to feel the influence of the latest lover.

And then she had the sceptical vision of the girl of the period, who would strip the greatest man of his prestige in the course of a few weeks. As soon as they were fully in her toils, and in the disorder of their heart had thrown aside their theatrical posturings and their parade manners, they were all alike in her eyes, poor creatures whom she could tyrannize over with her seductive powers. Finally, for a woman like her, perfect as she was, to attach herself to a man, what inestimable merits he would have had to possess!

She suffered much from ennui, however, and was without fondness for society, which she frequented for the sake of appearances, and the long, tedious evenings of which she endured with heavy eyelids and many a stifled yawn. She was amused only by its refined trivialities, by her own caprices and by her quickly changing curiosity for certain persons and certain things, attaching herself to it in such degree as to realize that she had been appreciated or admired and not enough to receive real pleasure from an affection or a liking—suffering from her nerves and not from her desires. She was without the absorbing preoccupations of ardent or simple souls, and passed her days in an ennui of gaieties, destitute of the simple faith that attends on happiness, constantly on the lookout for something to make the slow hours pass more quickly, and sinking with lassitude, while deeming herself contented.

She thought that she was contented because she was the most seductive and the most sought after of women. Proud of her attractiveness, the power of which she often made trial, in love with her own irregular, odd, and captivating beauty, convinced of the delicacy of her perceptions, which allowed her to divine and understand a thousand things that others were incapable of seeing, rejoicing in the wit that had been appreciated by so many superior men, and totally ignoring the limitations that bounded her intelligence, she looked upon herself as an almost unique being, a rare pearl set in the midst of this common, workaday world, which seemed to her slightly empty and monotonous because she was too good for it.

Not for an instant would she have suspected that in her unconscious self lay the cause of the melancholy from which she suffered so continuously. She laid the blame upon others and held them responsible for her ennui. If they were unable sufficiently to entertain and amuse or even impassion her, the reason was that they were deficient in agreeableness and possessed no real merit in her eyes. "Everyone," she would say with a little laugh, "is tiresome. The only endurable people are those who afford me pleasure, and that solely because they do afford me pleasure."

And the surest way of pleasing her was to tell her that there was no one like her. She was well aware that no success is attained without labor, and so she gave herself up, heart and soul, to her work of enticement, and found nothing that gave her greater enjoyment than to note the homage of the softening glance and of the heart, that unruly organ which she could cause to beat violently by the utterance of a word.

She had been greatly surprised by the trouble that she had had in subjugating André Mariolle, for she had been well aware, from the very first day, that she had found favor in his eyes. Then, little by little, she had fathomed his suspicious, secretly envious, extremely subtile, and concentrated disposition, and attacking him on his weak side, she had shown him so many attentions, had manifested such preference and natural sympathy for him, that he had finally surrendered.

Especially in the last month had she felt that he was her captive; he was agitated in her presence, now taciturn, now feverishly animated, but would make no avowal. Oh, avowals! She really did not care very much for them, for when they were too direct, too expressive, she found herself obliged to resort to severe measures. Twice she had even had to make a show of being angry and close her door to the offender. What she adored were delicate manifestations, semi-confidences, discreet allusions, a sort of moral getting-down-on-the-marrow-bones; and she really showed exceptional tact and address in extorting from her admirers this moderation in their expressions.

For a month past she had been watching and waiting to hear fall from Mariolle's lips the words, distinct or veiled, according to the nature of the man, which afford relief to the overburdened heart.

He had said nothing, but he had written. It was a long letter: four pages! A thrill of satisfaction crept over her as she held it in her hands. She stretched herself at length upon her lounge so as to be more comfortable and kicked the little slippers from off her feet upon the carpet; then she proceeded to read. She met with a surprise. In serious terms he told her that he did not desire to suffer at her hands, and that he already knew her too well to consent to be her victim. With many compliments, in very polite words, which everywhere gave evidence of his repressed love, he let her know that he was apprised of her manner of treating men—that he, too, was in the toils, but that he would release himself from the servitude by taking himself off. He would just simply begin his vagabond life of other days over again. He would leave the country. It was a farewell, an eloquent and firm farewell.

Certainly it was a surprise as she read, re-read, and commenced to read again these four pages of prose that were so full of tender irritation and passion. She arose, put on her slippers, and began to walk up and down the room, her bare arms out of her turned-back sleeves, her hands thrust halfway into the little pockets of her dressing-gown, one of them holding the crumpled letter.

Taken all aback by this unforeseen declaration, she said to herself: "He writes very well, very well indeed; he is sincere, feeling, touching. He writes better than Lamarthe; there is nothing of the novel sticking out of his letter."

She felt like smoking, went to the table where the perfumes were and took a cigarette from a box of Dresden china; then, having lighted it, she approached the great mirror in which she saw three young women coming toward her in the three diversely inclined panels. When she was quite near she halted, made herself a little bow with a little smile, a friendly little nod of the head, as if to say: "Very pretty, very pretty." She inspected her eyes, looked at her teeth, raised her arms, placed her hands on her hips and turned her profile so as to behold her entire person in the three mirrors, bending her head slightly forward. She stood there amorously facing herself surrounded by the threefold reflection of her own being, which she thought was charming, filled with delight at sight of herself, engrossed by an egotistical and physical pleasure in presence of her own beauty, and enjoying it with a keen satisfaction that was almost as sensual as a man's.

Every day she surveyed herself in this manner, and her maid, who had often caught her at it, used to say, spitefully:

"Madame looks at herself so much that she will end up by wearing out all the looking-glasses in the house."

In this love of herself, however, lay all the secret of her charm and the influence that she exerted over men. Through admiring herself and tenderly loving the delicacy of her features and the elegance of her form, by constantly seeking for and finding means of showing them to the greatest advantage, through discovering imperceptible ways of rendering her gracefulness more graceful and her eyes more fascinating, through pursuing all the artifices that embellished her to her own vision, she had as a matter of course hit upon that which would most please others. Had she been more beautiful and careless of her beauty, she would not have possessed that attractiveness which drew to her everyone who had not from the beginning shown himself unassailable.

Wearying soon a little of standing thus, she spoke to her image that was smiling to her still, and her image in the threefold mirror moved its lips as if to echo: "We will see about it." Then she crossed the room and seated herself at her desk. Here is what she wrote:

"DEAR MONSIEUR MARIOLLE: Come to see me to-morrow at four o'clock. I shall be alone, and hope to be able to reassure you as to the imaginary danger that alarms you.

"I subscribe myself your friend, and will prove to you that I am.....

MICHÈLE DE BURNE."

How plainly she dressed next day to receive André Mariolle's visit! A little gray dress, of a light gray bordering on lilac, melancholy as the dying day and quite unornamented, with a collar fitting closely to the neck, sleeves fitting closely to the arms, corsage fitting closely to the waist and bust, and skirt fitting closely to the hips and legs.

When he made his appearance, wearing rather a solemn face, she came forward to meet him, extending both her hands. He kissed them, then they seated themselves, and she allowed the silence to last a few moments in order to assure herself of his embarrassment.

He did not know what to say, and was waiting for her to speak. She made up her mind to do so.

"Well! let us come at once to the main question. What is the matter? Are you aware that you wrote me a very insolent letter?"

"I am very well aware of it, and I render my most sincere apology. I am, I have always been with everyone, excessively, brutally frank. I might have gone away without the unnecessary and insulting explanations that I addressed to you. I considered it more loyal to act in accordance with my nature and trust to your understanding, with which I am acquainted."

She resumed with an expression of pitying satisfaction:

"Come, come! What does all this folly mean?"

He interrupted her: "I would prefer not to speak of it."

She answered warmly, without allowing him to proceed further:

"I invited you here to discuss it, and we will discuss it until you are quite convinced that you are not exposing yourself to any danger." She laughed like a little girl, and her dress, so closely resembling that of a boarding-school miss, gave her laughter a character of childish youth.

He hesitatingly said: "What I wrote you was the truth, the sincere truth, the terrifying truth."

Resuming her seriousness, she rejoined: "I do not doubt you: all my friends travel that road. You also wrote that I am a fearful coquette. I admit it, but then no one ever dies of it; I do not even believe that they suffer a great deal. There is, indeed, what Lamarthe calls the crisis. You are in that stage now, but that passes over and subsides into—what shall I call it?—into the state of chronic love, which does no harm to a body, and which I keep simmering over a slow fire in all my friends, so that they may be very much attached, very devoted, very faithful to me. Am not I, also, sincere and frank and nice with you? Eh? Have you known many women who would dare to talk as I have talked to you?"

She had an air of such drollness, coupled with such decision, she was so unaffected and at the same time so alluring, that he could not help smiling in turn. "All your friends," he said, "are men who have often had their fingers burned in that fire, even before it was done at your hearth. Toasted and roasted already, it is easy for them to endure the oven in which you keep them; but for my part, I, Madame, have never passed through that experience, and I have felt for some time past that it would be a dreadful thing for me to give way to the sentiment that is growing and waxing in my heart."

Suddenly she became familiar, and bending a little toward him, her hands clasped over her knees: "Listen to me," she said, "I am in earnest. I hate to lose a friend for the sake of a fear that I regard as chimerical. You will be in love with me, perhaps, but the men of this generation do not love the women of to-day so violently as to do themselves any actual injury. You may believe me; I know them both." She was silent; then with the singular smile of a woman who utters a truth while she thinks she is telling a fib, she added: "Besides, I have not the necessary qualifications to make men love me madly; I am too modern. Come, I will be a friend to you, a real nice friend, for whom you will have affection, but nothing more, for I will see to it." She went on in a more serious tone: "In any case I give you fair warning that I am incapable of feeling a real passion for anyone, let him be who he may; you shall receive the same treatment as the others, you shall stand on an equal footing with the most favored, but never on any better; I abominate despotism and jealousy. I have had to endure everything from a husband, but from a friend, a simple friend, I do not choose to accept affectionate tyrannizings, which are the bane of all cordial relations. You see that I am just as nice as nice can be, that I talk to you like a comrade, that I conceal nothing from you. Are you willing loyally to accept the trial that I propose? If it does not work well, there will still be time enough for you to go away if the gravity of the situation demands it. A lover absent is a lover cured."

He looked at her, already vanquished by her voice, her gestures, all the intoxication of her person; and quite resigned to his fate, and thrilling through every fiber at the consciousness that she was sitting there beside him, he murmured:

"I accept, Madame, and if harm comes to me, so much the worse! I can afford to endure a little suffering for your sake."

She stopped him.

"Now let us say nothing more about it," she said; "let us never speak of it again." And she diverted the conversation to topics that might calm his agitation.

In an hour's time he took his leave; in torments, for he loved her; delighted, for she had asked and he had promised that he would not go away.

CHAPTER III.

THE THORNS OF THE ROSE

He was in torments, for he loved her. Differing in this from the common run of lovers, in whose eyes the woman chosen of their heart appears surrounded by an aureole of perfection, his attachment for her had grown within him while studying her with the clairvoyant eyes of a suspicious and distrustful man who had never been entirely enslaved. His timid and sluggish but penetrating disposition, always standing on the defensive in life, had saved him from his passions. A few intrigues, two brief liaisons that had perished of ennui, and some mercenary loves that had been broken off from disgust, comprised the history of his heart. He regarded women as an object of utility for those who desire a well-kept house and a family, as an object of comparative pleasure to those who are in quest of the pastime of love.

Before he entered Mme. de Burne's house his friends had confidentially warned him against her. What he had learned of her interested, puzzled, and pleased him, but it was also rather distasteful to him. As a matter of principle he did not like those gamblers who never pay when they lose. After their first few meetings he had decided that she was very amusing, and that she possessed a special charm that had a contagion in it. The natural and artificial beauties of this charming, slender, blond person, who was neither fat nor lean, who was furnished with beautiful arms that seemed formed to attract and embrace, and with legs that one might imagine long and tapering, calculated for flight, like those of a gazelle, with feet so small that they would leave no trace, seemed to him to be a symbol of hopes that could never be realized.

He had experienced, moreover, in his conversation with her a pleasure that he had never thought of meeting with in the intercourse of fashionable society. Gifted with a wit that was full of familiar animation, unforeseen and mocking and of a caressing irony, she would, notwithstanding this, sometimes allow herself to be carried away by sentimental or intellectual influences, as if beneath her derisive gaiety there still lingered the secular shade of poetic tenderness drawn from some remote ancestress. These things combined to render her exquisite.

She petted him and made much of him, desirous of conquering him as she had conquered the others, and he visited her house as often as he could, drawn thither by his increasing need of seeing more of her. It was like a force emanating from her and taking possession of him, a force that lay in her charm, her look, her smile, her speech, a force that there was no resisting, although he frequently left her house provoked at something that she had said or done.

The more he felt working on him that indescribable influence with which a woman penetrates and subjugates us, the more clearly did he see through her, the more did he understand and suffer from her nature, which he devoutly wished was different. It was certainly true, however, that the very qualities which he disapproved of in her were the qualities that had drawn him toward her and captivated him, in spite of himself, in spite of his reason, and more, perhaps, than her real merits.

Her coquetry, with which she toyed, making no attempt at concealing it, as with a fan, opening and folding it in presence of everybody according as the men to whom she was talking were pleasing to her or the reverse; her way of taking nothing in earnest, which had seemed droll to him upon their first acquaintance, but now seemed threatening; her constant desire for distraction, for novelty, which rested insatiable in her heart, always weary—all these things would so exasperate him that sometimes upon returning to his house he would resolve to make his visits to her more infrequent until such time as he might do away with them altogether. The very next day he would invent some pretext for going to see her. What he thought to impress upon himself, as he became more and more enamored, was the insecurity of this love and the certainty that he would have to suffer for it.

He was not blind; little by little he yielded to this sentiment, as a man drowns because his vessel has gone down under him and he is too far from the shore. He knew her as well as it was possible to know her, for his passion had served to make his mental vision abnormally clairvoyant, and he could not prevent his thoughts from going into indefinite speculations concerning her. With indefatigable perseverance, he was continually seeking to analyze and understand the obscure depths of this feminine soul, this incomprehensible mixture of bright intelligence and disenchantment, of sober reason and childish triviality, of apparent affection and fickleness, of all those ill-assorted inclinations that can be brought together and co-ordinated to form an unnatural, perplexing, and seductive being.

But why was it that she attracted him thus? He constantly asked himself this question, and was unable to find a satisfactory answer to it, for, with his reflective, observing, and proudly retiring nature, his logical course would have been to look in a woman for those old-fashioned and soothing attributes of tenderness and constancy which seem to offer the most reliable assurance of happiness to a man. In her, however, he had encountered something that he had not expected to find, a sort of early vegetable of the human race, as it were, one of those creatures who are the beginning of a new generation, exciting one by their strange novelty, unlike anything that one has ever known before, and even in their imperfections awakening the dormant senses by a formidable power of attraction.

To the romantic and dreamily passionate women of the Restoration had succeeded the gay triflers of the imperial epoch, convinced that pleasure is a reality; and now, here there was afforded him a new development of this everlasting femininity, a woman of refinement, of indeterminate sensibility, restless, without fixed resolves, her feelings in constant turmoil, who seemed to have made it part of her experience to employ every narcotic that quiets the aching nerves: chloroform that stupefies, ether and morphine that excite to abnormal reverie, kill the senses, and deaden the emotions.

He relished in her that flavor of an artificial nature, the sole object of whose existence was to charm and allure. She was a rare and attractive bauble, exquisite and delicate, drawing men's eyes to her, causing the heart to throb, and desire to awake, as one's appetite is excited when he looks through the glass of the shop-window and beholds the dainty viands that have been prepared and arranged for the purpose of making him hunger for them.

When he was quite assured that he had started on his perilous descent toward the bottom of the gulf, he began to reflect with consternation upon the dangers of his infatuation. What would happen him? What would she do with him? Most assuredly she would do with him what she had done with everyone else: she would bring him to the point where a man follows a woman's capricious fancies as a dog follows his master's steps, and she would classify him among her collection of more or less illustrious favorites. Had she really played this game with all the others? Was there not one, not a single one, whom she had loved, if only for a month, a day, an hour, in one of those effusions of feeling that she had the faculty of repressing so readily? He talked with them interminably about her as they came forth from her dinners, warmed by contact with her. He felt that they were all uneasy, dissatisfied, unstrung, like men whose dreams have failed of realization.

No, she had loved no one among these paraders before public curiosity. But he, who was a nullity in comparison with them, he, to whom it was not granted that heads should turn and wondering eyes be fixed on him when his name was mentioned in a crowd or in a salon,—what would he be for her? Nothing, nothing; a mere supernumerary upon her scene, a Monsieur, the sort of man that becomes a familiar, commonplace attendant upon a distinguished woman, useful to hold her bouquet, a man comparable to the common grade of wine that one drinks with water. Had he been a famous man he might have been willing to accept this rôle, which his celebrity would have made less humiliating; but unknown as he was, he would have none of it. So he wrote to bid her farewell.

When he received her brief answer he was moved by it as by the intelligence of some unexpected piece of good fortune, and when she had made him promise that he would not go away he was as delighted as a schoolboy released for a holiday.

Several days elapsed without bringing any fresh development to their relations, but when the calm that succeeds the storm had passed, he felt his longing for her increasing within him and burning him. He had promised that he would never again speak to her on the forbidden topic, but he had not promised that he would not write, and one night when he could not sleep, when she had taken possession of all his faculties in the restless vigil of his insomnia of love, he seated himself at his table, almost against his will, and set himself to put down his feelings and his sufferings upon fair, white paper. It was not a letter; it was an aggregation of notes, phrases, thoughts, throbs of moral anguish, transmuting themselves into words. It soothed him; it seemed to him to give him a little comfort in his suffering, and lying down upon his bed, he was at last able to obtain some sleep.

Upon awaking the next morning he read over these few pages and decided that they were sufficiently harrowing; then he inclosed and addressed them, kept them by him until evening, and mailed them very late so that she might receive them when she arose. He thought that she would not be alarmed by these innocent sheets of paper. The most timorous of women have an infinite kindness for a letter that speaks to them of a sincere love, and when these letters are written by a trembling hand, with tearful eyes and melancholy face, the power that they exercise over the female heart is unbounded.

He went to her house late that afternoon to see how she would receive him and what she would say to him. He found M. de Pradon there, smoking cigarettes and conversing with his daughter. He would often pass whole hours with her in this way, for his manner toward her was rather that of a gentleman visitor than of a father. She had brought into their relations and their affection a tinge of that homage of love which she bestowed upon herself and exacted from everyone else.

When she beheld Mariolle her face brightened with delight; she shook hands with him warmly and her smile told him: "You have afforded me much pleasure."

Mariolle was in hopes that the father would go away soon, but M. de Pradon did not budge. Although he knew his daughter thoroughly, and for a long time past had placed the most implicit confidence in her as regarded her relations with men, he always kept an eye on her with a kind of curious, uneasy, somewhat marital attention. He wanted to know what chance of success there might be for this newly discovered friend, who he was, what he amounted to. Would he be a mere bird of passage, like so many others, or a permanent member of their usual circle?

He intrenched himself, therefore, and Mariolle immediately perceived that he was not to be dislodged. The visitor made up his mind accordingly, and even resolved to gain him over if it were possible, considering that his good-will, or at any rate his neutrality, would be better than his hostility. He exerted himself and was brilliant and amusing, without any of the airs of a sighing lover. She said to herself contentedly: "He is not stupid; he acts his part in the comedy extremely well"; and M. de Pradon thought: "This is a very agreeable man, whose head my daughter does not seem to have turned."

When Mariolle decided that it was time for him to take his leave, he left them both delighted with him.

But he left that house with sorrow in his soul. In the presence of that woman he felt deeply the bondage in which she held him, realizing that it would be vain to knock at that heart, as a man imprisoned fruitlessly beats the iron door with his fist. He was well assured that he was entirely in her power, and he did not try to free himself. Such being the case, and as he could not avoid this fatality, he resolved that he would be patient, tenacious, cunning, dissembling, that he would conquer by address, by the homage that she was so greedy of, by the adoration that intoxicated her, by the voluntary servitude to which he would suffer himself to be reduced.

His letter had pleased her; he would write. He wrote. Almost every night, when he came home, at that hour when the mind, fresh from the influence of the day's occurrences, regards whatever interests or moves it with a sort of abnormally developed hallucination, he would seat himself at his table by his lamp and exalt his imagination by thoughts of her. The poetic germ, that so many indolent men suffer to perish within them from mere slothfulness, grew and throve under this regimen. He infused a feverish ardor into this task of literary tenderness by means of constantly writing the same thing, the same idea, that is, his love, in expressions that were ever renewed by the constantly fresh-springing, daily renewal of his desire. All through the long day he would seek for and find those irresistible words that stream from the brain like fiery sparks, compelled by the over-excited emotions. Thus he would breathe upon the fire of his own heart and kindle it into raging flames, for often love-letters contain more danger for him who writes than for her who receives them.

By keeping himself in this continuous state of effervescence, by heating his blood with words and peopling his brain with one solitary thought, his ideas gradually became confused as to the reality of this woman. He had ceased to entertain the opinion of her that he had first held, and now beheld her only through the medium of his own lyrical phrases, and all that he wrote of her night by night became to his heart so many gospel truths. This daily labor of idealization displayed her to him as in a dream. His former resistance melted away, moreover, in presence of the affection that Mme. de Burne undeniably evinced for him. Although no word had passed between them at this time, she certainly showed a preference for him beyond others, and took no pains to conceal it from him. He therefore thought, with a kind of mad hope, that she might finally come to love him.

The fact was that the charm of those letters afforded her a complicated and naïve delight. No one had ever flattered and caressed her in that manner, with such mute reserve. No one had ever had the delicious idea of sending to her bedside, every morning, that feast of sentiment in paper wrapping that her maid presented to her on the little silver salver. And what made it all the dearer in her eyes was that he never mentioned it, that he seemed to be quite unaware of it himself, that when he visited her salon he was the most undemonstrative of her friends, that he never by word or look alluded to those showers of tenderness that he was secretly raining down upon her.

Of course she had had love-letters before that, but they had been pitched in a different key, had been less reserved, more pressing, more like a summons to surrender. For the three months that his "crisis" had lasted Lamarthe had dedicated to her a very nice correspondence from a much-smitten novelist who maunders in a literary way. She kept in her secretary, in a drawer specially allotted to them, these delicate and seductive epistles from a writer who had shown much feeling, who had caressed her with his pen up to the very day when he saw that he had no hope of success.

Mariolle's letters were quite different; they were so strong in their concentrated desire, so deep in the expression of their sincerity, so humble in their submissiveness, breathing a devotion that promised to be lasting, that she received and read them with a delight that no other writings could have afforded her.

It was natural that her friendly feeling for the man should increase under such conditions. She invited him to her house the more frequently because he displayed such entire reserve in his relations toward her, seeming not to have the slightest recollection in conversation with her that he had ever taken up a sheet of paper to tell her of his adoration. Moreover she looked upon the situation as an original one, worthy of being celebrated in a book; and in the depths of her satisfaction in having at her side a being who loved her thus, she experienced a sort of active fermentation of sympathy which caused her to measure him by a standard other than her usual one.

Up to the present time, notwithstanding the vanity of her coquetry she had been conscious of preoccupations that antagonized her in all the hearts that she had laid waste. She had not held undisputed sovereignty over them, she had found in them powerful interests that were entirely dissociated from her. Jealous of music in Massival's case, of literature in Lamarthe's, always jealous of something, discontented that she only obtained partial successes, powerless to drive all before her in the minds of these ambitious men, men of celebrity, or artists to whom their profession was a mistress from whom nobody could part them, she had now for the first time fallen in with one to whom she was all in all. Certainly big Fresnel, and he alone, loved her to the same degree. But then he was big Fresnel. She felt that it had never been granted her to exercise such complete dominion over anyone, and her selfish gratitude for the man who had afforded her this triumph displayed itself in manifestations of tenderness. She had need of him now; she had need of his presence, of his glance, of his subjection, of all this domesticity of love. If he flattered her vanity less than the others did, he flattered more those supreme exactions that sway coquettes body and soul—her pride and her instinct of domination, her strong instinct of feminine repose.

Like an invader she gradually assumed possession of his life by a series of small incursions that every day became more numerous. She got up fêtes, theater-parties, and dinners at the restaurant, so that he might be of the party. She dragged him after her with the satisfaction of a conqueror; she could not dispense with his presence, or rather with the state of slavery to which he was reduced. He followed in her train, happy to feel himself thus petted, caressed by her eyes, her voice, by her every caprice, and he lived only in a continuous transport of love and longing that desolated and burned like a wasting fever.

CHAPTER IV.

THE BENEFIT OF CHANGE OF SCENE

One day Mariolle had gone to her house. He was awaiting her, for she had not come in, although she had sent him a telegram to tell him that she wanted to see him that morning. Whenever he was alone in this drawing-room which it gave him such pleasure to enter and where everything was so charming to him, he nevertheless was conscious of an oppression of the heart, a slight feeling of affright and breathlessness that would not allow him to remain seated as long as she was not there. He walked about the room in joyful expectation, dashed by the fear that some unforeseen obstacle might intervene to detain her and cause their interview to go over until next day. His heart gave a hopeful bound when he heard a carriage draw up before the street door, and when the bell of the apartment rang he ceased to doubt.

She came in with her hat on, a thing which she was not accustomed to do, wearing a busy and satisfied look. "I have some news for you," she said.

"What is it, Madame?"

She looked at him and laughed. "Well! I am going to the country for a while."

Her words produced in him a quick, sharp shock of sorrow that was reflected upon his face. "Oh! and you tell me that as if you were glad of it!"

"Yes. Sit down and I will tell you all about it. I don't know whether you are aware that M. Valsaci, my poor mother's brother, the engineer and bridge-builder, has a country-place at Avranches where he spends a portion of his time with his wife and children, for his business lies mostly in that neighborhood. We pay them a visit every summer. This year I said that I did not care to go, but he was greatly disappointed and made quite a time over it with papa. Speaking of scenes, I will tell you confidentially that papa is jealous of you and makes scenes with me, too; he says that I am entangling myself with you. You will have to come to see me less frequently. But don't let that trouble you; I will arrange matters. So papa gave me a scolding and made me promise to go to Avranches for a visit of ten days, perhaps twelve. We are to start Tuesday morning. What have you got to say about it?"

"I say that it breaks my heart."

"Is that all?"

"What more can I say? There is no way of preventing you from going."

"And nothing presents itself to you?"

"Why, no; I can't say that there does. And you?"

"I have an idea; it is this: Avranches is quite near Mont Saint-Michel. Have you ever been at Mont Saint-Michel?"

"No, Madame."

"Well, something will tell you next Friday that you want to go and see this wonder. You will leave the train at Avranches; on Friday evening at sunset, if you please, you will take a walk in the public garden that overlooks the bay. We will happen to meet there. Papa will grumble, but I don't care for that. I will make up a party to go and see the abbey next day, including all the family. You must be enthusiastic over it, and very charming, as you can be when you choose; be attentive to my aunt and gain her over, and invite us all to dine at the inn where we alight. We will sleep there, and will have all the next day to be together. You will return by way of Saint Malo, and a week later I shall be back in Paris. Isn't that an ingenious scheme? Am I not nice?"

With an outburst of grateful feeling, he murmured: "You are dearer to me than all the world."

"Hush!" said she.

They looked each other for a moment in the face. She smiled, conveying to him in that smile—very sincere and earnest it was, almost tender—all her gratitude, her thanks for his love, and her sympathy as well. He gazed upon her with eyes that seemed to devour her. He had an insane desire to throw himself down and grovel at her feet, to kiss the hem of her robe, to cry aloud and make her see what he knew not how to tell in words, what existed in all his form from head to feet, in every fiber of his body as well as in his heart, paining him inexpressibly because he could not display it—his love, his terrible and delicious love.

There was no need of words, however; she understood him, as the marksman instinctively feels that his ball has penetrated the bull's-eye of the target. Nothing any longer subsisted within this man, nothing, nothing but her image. He was hers more than she herself was her own. She was satisfied, and she thought he was charming.

She said to him, in high good-humor: "Then that is settled; the excursion is agreed on."

He answered in a voice that trembled with emotion: "Why, yes, Madame, it is agreed on."

There was another interval of silence. "I cannot let you stay any longer to-day," she said without further apology. "I only ran in to tell you what I have told you, since I am to start day after to-morrow. All my time will be occupied to-morrow, and I have still half-a-dozen things to attend to before dinner-time."

He arose at once, deeply troubled, for the sole desire of his heart was to be with her always; and having kissed her hands, went his way, sore at heart, but hopeful nevertheless.

The four intervening days were horribly long ones to him. He got through them somehow in Paris without seeing a soul, preferring silence to conversation, and solitude to the company of friends.

On Friday morning, therefore, he boarded the eight-o'clock express. The anticipation of the journey had made him feverish, and he had not slept a wink. The darkness of his room and its silence, broken only by the occasional rattling of some belated cab that served to remind him of his longing to be off, had weighed upon him all night long like a prison.

At the earliest ray of light that showed itself between his drawn curtains, the gray, sad light of early morning, he jumped from his bed, opened the window, and looked at the sky. He had been haunted by the fear that the weather might be unfavorable. It was clear. There was a light floating mist, presaging a warm day. He dressed more quickly than was needful, and in his consuming impatience to get out of doors and at last begin his journey he was ready two hours too soon, and nothing would do but his valet must go out and get a cab lest they should all be gone from the stand. As the vehicle jolted over the stones, its movements were so many shocks of happiness to him, but when he reached the Mont Parnasse station and found that he had fifty minutes to wait before the departure of the train, his spirits fell again.

There was a compartment disengaged; he took it so that he might be alone and give free course to his reveries. When at last he felt himself moving, hurrying along toward her, soothed by the gentle and rapid motion of the train, his eagerness, instead of being appeased, was still further excited, and he felt a desire, the unreasoning desire of a child, to push with all his strength against the partition in front of him, so as to accelerate their speed. For a long time, until midday, he remained in this condition of waiting expectancy, but when they were past Argentan his eyes were gradually attracted to the window by the fresh verdure of the Norman landscape.

The train was passing through a wide, undulating region, intersected by valleys, where the peasant holdings, mostly in grass and apple-orchards, were shut in by great trees, the thick-leaved tops of which seemed to glow in the sunlight. It was late in July, that lusty season when this land, an abundant nurse, gives generously of its sap and life. In all the inclosures, separated from each other by these leafy walls, great light-colored oxen, cows whose flanks were striped with undefined figures of odd design, huge, red, wide-fronted bulls of proud and quarrelsome aspect, with their hanging dewlaps of hairy flesh, standing by the fences or lying down among the pasturage that stuffed their paunches, succeeded each other, until there seemed to be no end to them in this fresh, fertile land, the soil of which appeared to exude cider and fat sirloins. In every direction little streams were gliding in and out among the poplars, partially concealed by a thin screen of willows; brooks glittered for an instant among the herbage, disappearing only to show themselves again farther on, bathing all the scene in their vivifying coolness. Mariolle was charmed at the sight, and almost forgot his love for a moment in his rapid flight through this far-reaching park of apple-trees and flocks and herds.

When he had changed cars at Folligny station, however, he was again seized with an impatient longing to be at his destination, and during the last forty minutes he took out his watch twenty times. His head was constantly turned toward the window of the car, and at last, situated upon a hill of moderate height, he beheld the city where she was waiting for his coming. The train had been delayed, and now only an hour separated him from the moment when he was to come upon her, by chance, on the public promenade.

He was the only passenger that climbed into the hotel omnibus, which the horses began to drag up the steep road of Avranches with slow and reluctant steps. The houses crowning the heights gave to the place from a distance the appearance of a fortification. Seen close at hand it was an ancient and pretty Norman city, with small dwellings of regular and almost similar appearance built closely adjoining one another, giving an aspect of ancient pride and modern comfort, a feudal yet peasant-like air.

As soon as Mariolle had secured a room and thrown his valise into it, he inquired for the street that led to the Botanical Garden and started off in the direction indicated with rapid strides, although he was ahead of time. But he was in hopes that perhaps she also would be on hand early. When he reached the iron railings, he saw at a glance that the place was empty or nearly so. Only three old men were walking about in it, bourgeois to the manner born, who probably were in the habit of coming there daily to cheer their leisure by conversation, and a family of English children, lean-legged boys and girls, were playing about a fair-haired governess whose wandering looks showed that her thoughts were far away.

Mariolle walked straight ahead with beating heart, looking scrutinizingly up and down the intersecting paths. He came to a great alley of dark green elms which cut the garden in two portions crosswise and stretched away in its center, a dense vault of foliage; he passed through this, and all at once, coming to a terrace that commanded a view of the horizon, his thoughts suddenly ceased to dwell upon her whose influence had brought him hither.

From the foot of the elevation upon which he was standing spread an illimitable sandy plain that stretched away in the distance and blended with sea and sky. Through it rolled a stream, and beneath the azure, aflame with sunlight, pools of water dotted it with luminous sheets that seemed like orifices opening upon another sky beneath. In the midst of this yellow desert, still wet and glistening with the receding tide, at twelve or fifteen kilometers from the shore rose a pointed rock of monumental profile, like some fantastic pyramid, surmounted by a cathedral. Its only neighbor in these immense wastes was a low, round backed reef that the tide had left uncovered, squatting among the shifting ooze: the reef of Tombelaine. Farther still away, other submerged rocks showed their brown heads above the bluish line of the waves, and the eye, continuing to follow the horizon to the right, finally rested upon the vast green expanse of the Norman country lying beside this sandy waste, so densely covered with trees that it had the aspect of a limitless forest. It was all Nature offering herself to his vision at a single glance, in a single spot, in all her might and grandeur, in all her grace and freshness, and the eye turned from those woodland glimpses to the stern apparition of the granite mount, the hermit of the sands, rearing its strange Gothic form upon the far-reaching strand.

The strange pleasure which in other days had often made Mariolle thrill, in the presence of the surprises that unknown lands preserve to delight the eyes of travelers, now took such sudden possession of him that he remained motionless, his feelings softened and deeply moved, oblivious of his tortured heart. At the sound of a striking bell, however, he turned, suddenly repossessed by the eager hope that they were about to meet. The garden was still almost untenanted. The English children had gone; the three old men alone kept up their monotonous promenade. He came down and began to walk about like them.

Immediately—in a moment—she would be there. He would see her at the end of one of those roads that centered in this wondrous terrace. He would recognize her form, her step, then her face and her smile; he would soon be listening to her voice. What happiness! What delight! He felt that she was near him, somewhere, invisible as yet, but thinking of him, knowing that she was soon to see him again.

With difficulty he restrained himself from uttering a little cry. For there, down below, a blue sunshade, just the dome of a sunshade, was visible, gliding along beneath a clump of trees. It must be she; there could be no doubt of it. A little boy came in sight, driving a hoop before him; then two ladies,—he recognized her,—then two men: her father and another gentleman. She was all in blue, like the heavens in springtime. Yes, indeed! he recognized her, while as yet he could not distinguish her features; but he did not dare to go toward her, feeling that he would blush and stammer, that he would be unable to account for this chance meeting beneath M. de Pradon's suspicious glances.

He went forward to meet them, however, keeping his field-glass to his eye, apparently quite intent on scanning the horizon. She it was who addressed him first, not even taking the trouble to affect astonishment.

"Good day, M. Mariolle," she said. "Isn't it splendid?"

He was struck speechless by this reception, and knew not what tone to adopt in reply. Finally he stammered: "Ah, it is you, Madame; how glad I am to meet you! I wanted to see something of this delightful country."

She smiled as she replied: "And you selected the very time when I chanced to be here. That was extremely kind of you." Then she proceeded to make the necessary introductions. "This is M. Mariolle, one of my dearest friends; my aunt, Mme. Valsaci; my uncle, who builds bridges."

When salutations had been exchanged. M. de Pradon and the young man shook hands rather stiffly and the walk was continued.

She had made room for him between herself and her aunt, casting upon him a very rapid glance, one of those glances which seem to indicate a weakening determination.

"How do you like the country?" she asked.

"I think that I have never beheld anything more beautiful," he replied.

"Ah! if you had passed some days here, as I have just been doing, you would feel how it penetrates one. The impression that it leaves is beyond the power of expression. The advance and retreat of the sea upon the sands, that grand movement that is going on unceasingly, that twice a day floods all that you behold before you, and so swiftly that a horse galloping at top speed would scarce have time to escape before it—this wondrous spectacle that Heaven gratuitously displays before us, I declare to you that it makes me forgetful of myself. I no longer know myself. Am I not speaking the truth, aunt?"

Mme. Valsaci, an old, gray-haired woman, a lady of distinction in her province and the respected wife of an eminent engineer, a supercilious functionary who could not divest himself of the arrogance of the school, confessed that she had never seen her niece in such a state of enthusiasm. Then she added reflectively: "It is not surprising, however, when, like her, one has never seen any but theatrical scenery."

"But I go to Dieppe and Trouville almost every year."

The old lady began to laugh. "People only go to Dieppe and Trouville to see their friends. The sea is only there to serve as a cloak for their rendezvous." It was very simply said, perhaps without any concealed meaning.

People were streaming along toward the terrace, which seemed to draw them to it with an irresistible attraction. They came from every quarter of the garden, in spite of themselves, like round bodies rolling down a slope. The sinking sun seemed to be drawing a golden tissue of finest texture, transparent and ethereally light, behind the lofty silhouette of the abbey, which was growing darker and darker, like a gigantic shrine relieved against a veil of brightness. Mariolle, however, had eyes for nothing but the adored blond form walking at his side, wrapped in its cloud of blue. Never had he beheld her so seductive. She seemed to him to have changed, without his being able to specify in what the change consisted; she was bright with a brightness he had never seen before, which shone in her eyes and upon her flesh, her hair, and seemed to have penetrated her soul as well, a brightness emanating from this country, this sky, this sunlight, this verdure. Never had he known or loved her thus.

He walked at her side and could find no word to say to her. The rustle of her dress, the occasional touch of her arm, the meeting, so mutely eloquent, of their glances, completely overcame him. He felt as if they had annihilated his personality as a man—felt himself suddenly obliterated by contact with this woman, absorbed by her to such an extent as to be nothing; nothing but desire, nothing but appeal, nothing but adoration. She had consumed his being, as one burns a letter.

She saw it all very clearly, understood the full extent of her victory, and thrilled and deeply moved, feeling life throb within her, too, more keenly among these odors of the country and the sea, full of sunlight and of sap, she said to him: "I am so glad to see you!" Close upon this, she asked: "How long do you remain here?"

He replied: "Two days, if to-day counts for a day." Then, turning to the aunt: "Would Mme. Valsaci do me the honor to come and spend the day to-morrow at Mont Saint-Michel with her husband?"

Mme. de Burne made answer for her relative: "I will not allow her to refuse, since we have been so fortunate as to meet you here."

The engineer's wife replied: "Yes, Monsieur, I accept very gladly, upon the condition that you come and dine with me this evening."

He bowed in assent. All at once there arose within him a feeling of delirious delight, such a joy as seizes you when news is brought that the desire of your life is attained. What had come to him? What new occurrence was there in his life? Nothing; and yet he felt himself carried away by the intoxication of an indefinable presentiment.

They walked upon the terrace for a long time, waiting for the sun to set, so as to witness until the very end the spectacle of the black and battlemented mount drawn in outline upon a horizon of flame. Their conversation now was upon ordinary topics, such as might be discussed in presence of a stranger, and from time to time Mme. de Burne and Mariolle glanced at each other. Then they all returned to the villa, which stood just outside Avranches in a fine garden, overlooking the bay.

Wishing to be prudent, and a little disturbed, moreover, by M. de Pradon's cold and almost hostile attitude toward him, Mariolle withdrew at an early hour. When he took Mme. de Burne's hand to raise it to his lips, she said to him twice in succession, with a peculiar accent: "Till to-morrow! Till to-morrow!"

As soon as he was gone M. and Mme. Valsaci, who had long since habituated themselves to country ways, proposed that they should go to bed.

"Go," said Mme. de Burne. "I am going to take a walk in the garden."

"So am I," her father added.

She wrapped herself in a shawl and went out, and they began to walk side by side upon the white-sanded alleys which the full moon, streaming over lawn and shrubbery, illuminated as if they had been little winding rivers of silver.

After a silence that had lasted for quite a while, M. de Pradon said in a low voice: "My dear child, you will do me the justice to admit that I have never troubled you with my counsels?"

She felt what was coming, and was prepared to meet his attack. "Pardon me, papa," she said, "but you did give me one, at least."

"I did?"

"Yes, yes."

"A counsel relating to your way of life?"

"Yes; and a very bad one it was, too. And so, if you give me any more, I have made up my mind not to follow them."

"What was the advice that I gave you?"

"You advised me to marry M. de Burne. That goes to show that you are lacking in judgment, in clearness of insight, in acquaintance with mankind in general and with your daughter in particular."

"Yes I made a mistake on that occasion; but I am sure that I am right in the very paternal advice that I feel called upon to give you at the present juncture."

"Let me hear what it is. I will accept as much of it as the circumstances call for."

"You are on the point of entangling yourself."

She laughed with a laugh that was rather too hearty, and completing the expression of his idea, said: "With M. Mariolle, doubtless?"

"With M. Mariolle."

"You forget," she rejoined, "the entanglements that I have already had with M. de Maltry, with M. Massival, with M. Gaston de Lamarthe, and a dozen others, of all of whom you have been jealous; for I never fall in with a man who is nice and willing to show a little devotion for me but all my flock flies into a rage, and you first of all, you whom nature has assigned to me as my noble father and general manager."

"No, no, that is not it," he replied with warmth; "you have never compromised your liberty with anyone. On the contrary you show a great deal of tact in your relations with your friends."

"My dear papa, I am no longer a child, and I promise you not to involve myself with M. Mariolle any more than I have done with the rest of them; you need have no fears. I admit, however, that it was at my invitation that he came here. I think that he is delightful, just as intelligent as his predecessors and less egotistical; and you thought so too, up to the time when you imagined that you had discovered that I was showing some small preference for him. Oh, you are not so sharp as you think you are! I know you, and I could say a great deal more on this head if I chose. As M. Mariolle was agreeable to me, then, I thought it would be very nice to make a pleasant excursion in his company, quite by chance, of course. It is a piece of stupidity to deprive ourselves of everything that can amuse us when there is no danger attending it. And I incur no danger of involving myself, since you are here."

She laughed openly as she finished, knowing well that every one of her words had told, that she had tied his tongue by the adroit imputation of a jealousy of Mariolle that she had suspected, that she had instinctively scented in him for a long time past, and she rejoiced over this discovery with a secret, audacious, unutterable coquetry. He maintained an embarrassed and irritated silence, feeling that she had divined some inexplicable spite underlying his paternal solicitude, the origin of which he himself did not care to investigate.

"There is no cause for alarm," she added. "It is quite natural to make an excursion to Mont Saint-Michel at this time of the year in company with you, my father, my uncle and aunt, and a friend. Besides no one will know it; and even if they do, what can they say against it? When we are back in Paris I will reduce this friend to the ranks again, to keep company with the others."

"Very well," he replied. "Let it be as if I had said nothing."

They took a few steps more; then M. de Pradon asked:

"Shall we return to the house? I am tired; I am going to bed."

"No; the night is so fine. I am going to walk awhile yet."

He murmured meaningly: "Do not go far away. One never knows what people may be around."

"Oh, I will be right here under the windows."

"Good night, then, my dear child."

He gave her a hasty kiss upon the forehead and went in. She took a seat a little way off upon a rustic bench that was set in the ground at the foot of a great oak. The night was warm, filled with odors from the fields and exhalations from the sea and misty light, for beneath the full moon shining brightly in the cloudless sky a fog had come up and covered the waters of the bay. Onward it slowly crept, like white smoke-wreaths, hiding from sight the beach that would soon be covered by the incoming tide.

Michèle de Burne, her hands clasped over her knees and her dreamy eyes gazing into space, sought to look into her heart through a mist that was as impenetrable and pale as that which lay upon the sands. How many times before this, seated before her mirror in her dressing-room at Paris, had she questioned herself:

"What do I love? What do I desire? What do I hope for? What am I?"

Apart from the pleasure of being beautiful, and the imperious necessity which she felt of pleasing, which really afforded her much delight, she had never been conscious of any appeal to her heart beyond some passing fancy that she had quickly put her foot upon. She was not ignorant of herself, for she had devoted too much of her time and attention to watching and studying her face and all her person not to have been observant of her feelings as well. Up to the present time she had contented herself with a vague interest in that which is the subject of emotion in others, but was powerless to impassion her, or capable at best of affording her a momentary distraction.

And yet, whenever she had felt a little warmer liking for anyone arising within her, whenever a rival had tried to take away from her a man whom she valued, and by arousing her feminine instincts had caused an innocuous fever of attachment to simmer gently in her veins, she had discovered that these false starts of love had caused her an emotion that was much deeper than the mere gratification of success. But it never lasted. Why? Perhaps because she was too clear-sighted; because she allowed herself to become wearied, disgusted. Everything that at first had pleased her in a man, everything that had animated, moved, and attracted her, soon appeared in her eyes commonplace and divested of its charm. They all resembled one another too closely, without ever being exactly similar, and none of them had yet presented himself to her endowed with the nature and the merits that were required to hold her liking sufficiently long to guide her heart into the path of love.

Why was this so? Was it their fault or was it hers? Were they wanting in the qualities which she was looking for, or was it she who was deficient in the attribute that makes one loved? Is love the result of meeting with a person whom one believes to have been created expressly for himself, or is it simply the result of having been born with the faculty of loving? At times it seemed to her that everyone's heart must be provided with arms, like the body, loving, outstretching arms to attract, embrace, and enfold, and that her heart had only eyes and nothing more.

Men, superior men, were often known to become madly infatuated with women who were unworthy of them, women without intelligence, without character, often without beauty. Why was this? Wherein lay the mystery? Was such a crisis in the existence of two beings not to be attributed solely to a providential meeting, but to a kind of seed that everyone carries about within him, and that puts forth its buds when least expected? She had been intrusted with confidences, she had surprised secrets, she had even beheld with her own eyes the swift transfiguration that results from the breaking forth of this intoxication of the feelings, and she had reflected deeply upon it.

In society, in the unintermitting whirl of visiting and amusement, in all the small tomfooleries of fashionable existence by which the wealthy beguile their idle hours, a feeling of envious, jealous, and almost incredulous astonishment had sometimes been excited in her at the sight of men and women in whom some extraordinary change had incontestably taken place. The change might not be conspicuously manifest, but her watchful instinct felt it and divined it as the hound holds the scent of his game. Their faces, their smiles, their eyes especially would betray something that was beyond expression in words, an ecstasy, a delicious, serene delight, a joy of the soul made manifest in the body, illuming look and flesh.

Without being able to account for it she was displeased with them for this. Lovers had always been disagreeable objects to her, and she imagined that the deep and secret feeling of irritation inspired in her by the sight of people whose hearts were swayed by passion was simply disdain. She believed that she could recognize them with a readiness and an accuracy that were exceptional, and it was a fact that she had often divined and unraveled liaisons before society had even suspected their existence.

When she reflected upon all this, upon the fond folly that may be induced in woman by the contact of some neighboring existence, his aspect, his speech, his thought, the inexpressible something in the loved being that robs the heart of tranquillity, she decided that she was incapable of it. And yet, weary of everything, oppressed by ineffable yearnings, tormented by a haunting longing after change and some unknown state, feelings which were, perhaps, only the undeveloped movements of an undefined groping after affection, how often had she desired, with a secret shame that had its origin in her pride, to meet with a man, who, for a time, were it only for a few months, might by his sorceries raise her to an abnormally excited condition of mind and body—for it seemed to her that life must assume strange and attractive forms of ecstasy and delight during these emotional periods. Not only had she desired such an encounter, but she had even sought it a little—only a very little, however—with an indolent activity that never devoted itself for any length of time to one pursuit.

In all her inchoate attachments for the men called "superior," who had dazzled her for a few weeks, the short-lived effervescence of her heart had always died away in irremediable disappointment. She looked for too much from their dispositions, their characters, their delicacy, their renown, their merits. In the case of everyone of them she had been compelled to open her eyes to the fact that the defects of great men are often more prominent than their merits; that talent is a special gift, like a good digestion or good eyesight, an isolated gift to be exercised, and unconnected with the aggregate of personal charm that makes one's relations cordial and attractive.

Since she had known Mariolle, however, she was otherwise attached to him. But did she love him, did she love him with the love of woman for man? Without fame or prestige, he had conquered her affections by his devotedness, his tenderness, his intelligence, by all the real and unassuming attractions of his personality. He had conquered, for he was constantly present in her thoughts; unremittingly she longed for his society; in all the world there was no one more agreeable, more sympathetic, more indispensable to her. Could this be love?

She was not conscious of carrying in her soul that divine flame that everyone speaks of, but for the first time she was conscious of the existence there of a sincere wish to be something more to this man than merely a charming friend. Did she love him? Does love demand that a man appear endowed with exceptional attractions, that he be different from all the world and tower above it in the aureole that the heart places about its elect, or does it suffice that he find favor in your eyes, that he please you to that extent that you scarce know how to do without him? In the latter event she loved him, or at any rate she was very near loving him. After having pondered deeply on the matter with concentrated attention, she at length answered herself: "Yes, I love him, but I am lacking in warmth; that is the defect of my nature."

Still, she had felt some warmth a little while before when she saw him coming toward her upon the terrace in the garden of Avranches. For the first time she had felt that inexpressible something that bears us, impels us, hurries us toward some one; she had experienced great pleasure in walking at his side, in having him near her, burning with love for her, as they watched the sun sinking behind the shadow of Mont Saint-Michel, like a vision in a legend. Was not love itself a kind of legend of the soul, in which some believe through instinct, and in which others sometimes also come to believe through stress of pondering over it? Would she end by believing in it? She had felt a strange, half-formed desire to recline her head upon the shoulder of this man, to be nearer to him, to seek that closer union that is never found, to give him what one offers vainly and always retains: the close intimacy with one's inner self.

Yes, she had experienced a feeling of warmth toward him, and she still felt it there at the bottom of her heart, at that very moment. Perhaps it would change to passion should she give way to it. She opposed too much resistance to men's powers of attraction; she reasoned on them, combated them too much. How sweet it would be to walk with him on an evening like this along the river-bank beneath the willows, and allow him to taste her lips from time to time in recompense of all the love he had given her!

A window in the villa was flung open. She turned her head. It was her father, who was doubtless looking to see if she were there. She called to him: "You are not asleep yet?"

He replied: "If you don't come in you will take cold."

She arose thereupon and went toward the house. When she was in her room she raised her curtains for another look at the mist over the bay, which was becoming whiter and whiter in the moonlight, and it seemed to her that the vapors in her heart were also clearing under the influence of her dawning tenderness.

For all that she slept soundly, and her maid had to awake her in the morning, for they were to make an early start, so as to have breakfast at the Mount.

A roomy wagonette drew up before the door. When she heard the rolling of the wheels upon the sand she went to her window and looked out, and the first thing that her eyes encountered was the face of André Mariolle who was looking for her. Her heart began to beat a little more rapidly. She was astonished and dejected as she reflected upon the strange and novel impression produced by this muscle, which palpitates and hurries the blood through the veins merely at the sight of some one. Again she asked herself, as she had done the previous night before going to sleep: “Can it be that I am about to love him?” Then when she was seated face to face with him her instinct told her how deeply he was smitten, how he was suffering with his love, and she felt as if she could open her arms to him and put up her mouth. They only exchanged a look, however, but it made him turn pale with delight.

The carriage rolled away. It was a bright summer morning; the air was filled with the melody of birds and everything seemed permeated by the spirit of youth. They descended the hill, crossed the river, and drove along a narrow, rough, stony road that set the travelers bumping upon their seats. Mme. de Burne began to banter her uncle upon the condition of this road; that was enough to break the ice, and the brightness that pervaded the air seemed to be infused into the spirit of them all.

As they emerged from a little hamlet the bay suddenly presented itself again before them, not yellow as they had seen it the evening before, but sparkling with clear water which covered everything, sands, salt-meadows, and, as the coachman said, even the very road itself a little way further on. Then, for the space of an hour they allowed the horses to proceed at a walk, so as to give this inundation time to return to the deep.

The belts of elms and oaks that inclosed the farms among which they were now passing momentarily hid from their vision the profile of the abbey standing high upon its rock, now entirely surrounded by the sea; then all at once it was visible again between two farmyards, nearer, more huge, more astounding than ever. The sun cast ruddy tones upon the old crenelated granite church, perched on its rocky pedestal. Michèle de Burne and André Mariolle contemplated it, both mingling with the newborn or acutely sensitive disturbances of their hearts the poetry of the vision that greeted their eyes upon this rosy July morning.

The talk went on with easy friendliness. Mme. Valsaci told tragic tales of the coast, nocturnal dramas of the yielding sands devouring human life. M. Valsaci took up arms for the dike, so much abused by artists, and extolled it for the uninterrupted communication that it afforded with the Mount and for the reclaimed sand-hills, available at first for pasturage and afterward for cultivation.

Suddenly the wagonette came to a halt; the sea had invaded the road. It did not amount to much, only a film of water upon the stony way, but they knew that there might be sink-holes beneath, openings from which they might never emerge, so they had to wait. “It will go down very quickly,” M. Valsaci declared, and he pointed with his finger to the road from which the thin sheet of water was already receding, seemingly absorbed by the earth or drawn away to some distant place by a powerful and mysterious force.

They got down from the carriage for a nearer look at this strange, swift, silent flight of the sea, and followed it step by step. Now spots of green began to appear among the submerged vegetation, lightly stirred by the waves here and there, and these spots broadened, rounded themselves out and became islands. Quickly these islands assumed the appearance of continents, separated from each other by miniature oceans, and finally over the whole expanse of the bay it was a headlong flight of the waters retreating to their distant abode. It resembled nothing so much as a long silvery veil withdrawn from the surface of the earth, a great, torn, slashed veil, full of rents, which left exposed the wide meadows of short grass as it was pulled aside, but did not yet disclose the yellow sands that lay beyond.

They had climbed into the carriage again, and everyone was standing in order to obtain a better view. The road in front of them was drying and the horses were sent forward, but still at a walk, and as the rough places sometimes caused them to lose their equilibrium,

André Mariolle suddenly felt Michèle de Burne's shoulder resting against his. At first he attributed this contact to the movement of the vehicle, but she did not stir from her position, and at every jolt of the wheels a trembling started from the spot where she had placed herself and shook all his frame and laid waste his heart. He did not venture to look at the young woman, paralyzed as he was by this unhoped-for familiarity, and with a confusion in his brain such as arises from drunkenness, he said to himself: "Is this real? Can it be possible? Can it be that we are both losing our senses?"

The horses began to trot and they had to resume their seats. Then Mariolle felt some sudden, mysterious, imperious necessity of showing himself attentive to M. de Pradon, and he began to devote himself to him with flattering courtesy. Almost as sensible to compliments as his daughter, the father allowed himself to be won over and soon his face was all smiles.

At last they had reached the causeway and were advancing rapidly toward the Mount, which reared its head among the sands at the point where the long, straight road ended. Pontorson river washed its left-hand slope, while, to the right, the pastures covered with short grass, which the coachman wrongly called "samphire," had given way to sand-hills that were still trickling with the water of the sea. The lofty monument now assumed more imposing dimensions upon the blue heavens, against which, very clear and distinct now in every slightest detail, its summit stood out in bold relief, with all its towers and belfries, bristling with grimacing gargoyles, heads of monstrous beings with which the faith and the terrors of our ancestors crowned their Gothic sanctuaries.

It was nearly one o'clock when they reached the inn, where breakfast had been ordered. The hostess had delayed the meal for prudential reasons; it was not ready. It was late, therefore, when they sat down at table and everyone was very hungry. Soon, however, the champagne restored their spirits. Everyone was in good humor, and there were two hearts that felt that they were on the verge of great happiness. At dessert, when the cheering effect of the wine that they had drunk and the pleasures of conversation had developed in their frames the feeling of well-being and contentment that sometimes warms us after a good meal, and inclines us to take a rosy view of everything, Mariolle suggested: "What do you say to staying over here until to-morrow? It would be so nice to look upon this scene by moonlight, and so pleasant to dine here together this evening!"

Mme. de Burne gave her assent at once, and the two men also concurred. Mme. Valsaci alone hesitated, on account of the little boy that she had left at home, but her husband reassured her and reminded her that she had frequently remained away before; he at once sat down and dispatched a telegram to the governess. André Mariolle had flattered him by giving his approval to the causeway, expressing his judgment that it detracted far less than was generally reported from the picturesque effect of the Mount, thereby making himself persona grata to the engineer.

Upon rising from table they went to visit the monument, taking the road of the ramparts. The city, a collection of old houses dating back to the Middle Ages and rising in tiers one above the other upon the enormous mass of granite that is crowned by the abbey, is separated from the sands by a lofty crenelated wall. This wall winds about the city in its ascent with many a twist and turn, with abrupt angles and elbows and platforms and watchtowers, all forming so many surprises for the eye, which, at every turn, rests upon some new expanse of the far-reaching horizon. They were silent, for whether they had seen this marvelous edifice before or not, they were equally impressed by it, and the substantial breakfast that they had eaten, moreover, had made them short-winded. There it rose above them in the sky, a wondrous tangle of granite ornamentation, spires, belfries, arches thrown from one tower to another, a huge, light, fairy-like lace-work in stone, embroidered upon the azure of the heavens, from which the fantastic and bestial-faced array of gargoyles seemed to be preparing to detach themselves and wing their flight away. Upon the northern flank of the Mount, between the abbey and the sea, a wild and almost perpendicular descent that is called the Forest, because it is covered with ancient trees, began where the houses ended and formed a speck of dark green coloring upon the limitless expanse of yellow sands. Mme. de Burne and Mariolle, who headed the little procession, stopped to enjoy the view. She leaned upon his arm, her senses steeped in a rapture such as she had never known before. With light steps she pursued her upward way, willing to keep on climbing forever in his company toward this fabric of a vision, or indeed toward any other end. She would have been glad that the steep way should never have an ending, for almost for the first time in her life she knew what it was to experience a plenitude of satisfaction.

"Heavens! how beautiful it is!" she murmured.

Looking upon her, he answered: "I can think only of you."

She continued, with a smile: "I am not inclined to be very poetical, as a general thing, but this seems to me so beautiful that I am really moved."

He stammered: "I—I love you to distraction."

He was conscious of a slight pressure of her arm, and they resumed the ascent.

They found a keeper awaiting them at the door of the abbey, and they entered by that superb staircase, between two massive towers, which leads to the Hall of the Guards. Then they went from hall to hall, from court to court, from dungeon to dungeon, listening, wondering, charmed with everything, admiring everything, the crypt, with its huge pillars, so beautiful in their massiveness, which sustains upon its sturdy arches all the weight of the choir of the church above, and all of the Wonder, an awe-inspiring edifice of three stories of Gothic monuments rising one above the other, the most extraordinary masterpiece of the monastic and military architecture of the Middle Ages.

Then they came to the cloisters. Their surprise was so great that they involuntarily came to a halt at sight of this square court inclosing the lightest, most graceful, most charming of colonnades to be seen in any cloisters in the world. For the entire length of the four galleries the slender shafts in double rows, surmounted by exquisite capitals, sustain a continuous garland of flowers and Gothic ornamentation of infinite variety and constantly changing design, the elegant and unaffected fancies of the simple-minded old artists who thus worked out their dreams in stone beneath the hammer.

Michèle de Burne and André Mariolle walked completely around the inclosure, very slowly, arm in arm, while the others, somewhat fatigued, stood near the door and admired from a distance.

"Heavens! what pleasure this affords me!" she said, coming to a stop.

"For my part, I neither know where I am nor what my eyes behold. I am conscious that you are at my side, and that is all."

Then smiling, she looked him in the face and murmured: "André!"

He saw that she was yielding. No further word was spoken, and they resumed their walk. The inspection of the edifice was continued, but they hardly had eyes to see anything.

Nevertheless their attention was attracted for the space of a moment by the airy bridge, seemingly of lace, inclosed within an arch thrown across space between two belfries, as if to afford a way to scale the clouds, and their amazement was still greater when they came to the "Madman's Path," a dizzy track, devoid of parapet, that encircles the farthest tower nearly at its summit.

"May we go up there?" she asked.

"It is forbidden," the guide replied.

She showed him a twenty-franc piece. All the members of the party, giddy at sight of the yawning gulf and the immensity of surrounding space, tried to dissuade her from the imprudent freak.

She asked Mariolle: "Will you go?"

He laughed: "I have been in more dangerous places than that." And paying no further attention to the others, they set out.

He went first along the narrow cornice that overhung the gulf, and she followed him, gliding along close to the wall with eyes downcast that she might not see the yawning void beneath, terrified now and almost ready to sink with fear, clinging to the hand that he held out to her; but she felt that he was strong, that there was no sign of weakening there, that he was sure of head and foot; and enraptured for all her fears, she said to herself: "Truly, this is a man." They were alone in space, at the height where the sea-birds soar; they were contemplating the same horizon that the white-winged creatures are ceaselessly scouring in their flight as they explore it with their little yellow eyes.

Mariolle felt that she was trembling; he asked: "Do you feel dizzy?"

"A little," she replied in a low voice; "but in your company I fear nothing."

At this he drew near and sustained her by putting his arm about her, and this simple assistance inspired her with such courage that she ventured to raise her head and take a look at the distance. He was almost carrying her and she offered no resistance, enjoying the protection of those strong arms which thus enabled her to traverse the heavens, and she was grateful to him with a romantic, womanly gratitude that he did not mar their sea-gull flight by kisses.

When they had rejoined the others of the party, who were awaiting them with the greatest anxiety, M. de Pradon angrily said to his daughter: "Dieu! what a silly thing to do!"

She replied with conviction: "No, it was not, papa, since it was successfully accomplished. Nothing that succeeds is ever stupid."

He merely gave a shrug of the shoulders, and they descended the stairs. At the porter's lodge there was another stoppage to purchase photographs, and when they reached the inn it was nearly dinner-time. The hostess recommended a short walk upon the sands, so as to obtain a view of the Mount toward the open sea, in which direction, she said, it presented its most imposing aspect. Although they were all much fatigued, the band started out again and made the tour of the ramparts, picking their way among the treacherous downs, solid to the eye but yielding to the step, where the foot that was placed upon the pretty yellow carpet that was stretched beneath it and seemed solid would suddenly sink up to the calf in the deceitful golden ooze.

Seen from this point the abbey, all at once losing the cathedral-like appearance with which it astounded the beholder on the mainland, assumed, as if in menace of old Ocean, the martial appearance of a feudal manor, with its huge battlemented wall picturesquely pierced with loop-holes and supported by gigantic buttresses that sank their Cyclopean stone foundations in the bosom of the fantastic mountain. Mme. de Burne and André Mariolle, however, were not heedless of all that. They were thinking only of themselves, caught in the meshes of the net that they had set for each other, shut up within the walls of that prison to which no sound comes from the outer world, where the eye beholds only one being.

When they found themselves again seated before their well-filled plates, however, beneath the cheerful light of the lamps, they seemed to awake, and discovered that they were hungry, just like other mortals.

They remained a long time at table, and when the dinner was ended the moonlight was quite forgotten in the pleasure of conversation. There was no one, moreover, who had any desire to go out, and no one suggested it. The broad moon might shed her waves of poetic light down upon the little thin sheet of rising tide that was already creeping up the sands with the noise of a trickling stream, scarcely perceptible to the ear, but sinister and alarming; she might light up the ramparts that crept in spirals up the flanks of the Mount and illumine the romantic shadows of all the belfries of the old abbey, standing in its wondrous setting of a boundless bay, in the bosom of which were quiveringly reflected the lights that crawled along the downs—no one cared to see more.

It was not yet ten o'clock when Mme. Valsaci, overcome with sleep, spoke of going to bed, and her proposition was received without a dissenting voice. Bidding one another a cordial good night, each withdrew to his chamber.

André Mariolle knew well that he would not sleep; he therefore lighted his two candles and placed them on the mantelpiece, threw open his window, and looked out into the night.

All the strength of his body was giving way beneath the torture of an unavailing hope. He knew that she was there, close at hand, that there were only two doors between them, and yet it was almost as impossible to go to her as it would be to dam the tide that was coming in and submerging all the land. There was a cry in his throat that strove to liberate itself, and in his nerves such an unquenchable and futile torment of expectation that he asked himself what he was to do, unable as he was longer to endure the solitude of this evening of sterile happiness.

Gradually all the sounds had died away in the inn and in the single little winding street of the town. Mariolle still remained leaning upon his window-sill, conscious only that time was passing, contemplating the silvery sheet of the still rising tide and rejecting the idea of going to bed as if he had felt the undefined presentiment of some approaching, providential good fortune.

All at once it seemed to him that a hand was fumbling with the fastening of his door. He turned with a start: the door slowly opened and a woman entered the room, her head veiled in a cloud of white lace and her form enveloped in one of those great dressing-gowns that seem made of silk, cashmere, and snow. She closed the door carefully behind her; then, as if she had not seen him where he stood motionless—as if smitten with joy—in the bright square of moonlight of the window, she went straight to the mantelpiece and blew out the two candles.

CHAPTER V.

CONSPIRACY

They were to meet next morning in front of the inn to say good-bye to one another. André, the first one down, awaited her coming with a poignant feeling of mixed uneasiness and delight. What would she do? What would she be to him? What would become of her and of him? In what thrice-happy or terrible adventure had he engaged himself? She had it in her power to make of him what she would, a visionary, like an opium-eater, or a martyr, at her will. He paced to and fro beside the two carriages, for they were to separate, he, to continue the deception, ending his trip by way of Saint Malo, they returning to Avranches.

When would he see her again? Would she cut short her visit to her family, or would she delay her return? He was horribly afraid of what she would first say to him, how she would first look at him, for he had not seen her and they had scarcely spoken during their brief interview of the night before. There remained to Mariolle from that strange, fleeting interview the faint feeling of disappointment of the man who has been unable to reap all that harvest of love which he thought was ready for the sickle, and at the same time the intoxication of triumph and, resulting from that, the almost assured hope of finally making himself complete master of her affections.

He heard her voice and started; she was talking loudly, evidently irritated at some wish that her father had expressed, and when he beheld her standing at the foot of the staircase there was a little angry curl upon her lips that bespoke her impatience.

Mariolle took a couple of steps toward her; she saw him and smiled. Her eyes suddenly recovered their serenity and assumed an expression of kindliness which diffused itself over the other features, and she quickly and cordially extended to him her hand, as if in ratification of their new relations.

"So then, we are to separate?" she said to him.

"Alas! Madame, the thought makes me suffer more than I can tell."

"It will not be for long," she murmured. She saw M. de Pradon coming toward them, and added in a whisper: "Say that you are going to take a ten days' trip through Brittany, but do not take it."

Mme. de Valsaci came running up in great excitement. "What is this that your father has been telling me—that you are going to leave us day after to-morrow? You were to stay until next Monday, at least."

Mme. de Burne replied, with a suspicion of ill humor: "Papa is nothing but a bungler, who never knows enough to hold his tongue. The sea-air has given me, as it does every year, a very unpleasant neuralgia, and I did say something or other about going away so as not to have to be ill for a month. But this is no time for bothering over that."

Mariolle's coachman urged him to get into the carriage and be off, so that they might not miss the Pontorson train.

Mme. de Burne asked: "And you, when do you expect to be back in Paris?"

He assumed an air of hesitancy: "Well, I can't say exactly; I want to see Saint Malo, Brest, Douarnenez, the Bay des Trépassés, Cape Raz, Audierne, Penmarch, Morbihan, all this celebrated portion of the Breton country, in a word. That will take me say—" after a silence devoted to feigned calculation, he exceeded her estimate—"fifteen or twenty days."

"That will be quite a trip," she laughingly said. "For my part, if my nerves trouble me as they did last night, I shall be at home before I am two days older."

His emotion was so great that he felt like exclaiming: "Thanks!" He contented himself with kissing, with a lover's kiss, the hand that she extended to him for the last time, and after a profuse exchange of thanks and compliments with the Valsacis and M. de Pradon, who seemed to be somewhat reassured by the announcement of his projected trip, he climbed into his vehicle and drove off, turning his head for a parting look at her.

He made no stop on his journey back to Paris and was conscious of seeing nothing on the way. All night long he lay back in the corner of his compartment with eyes half closed and folded arms, his mind reverting to the occurrences of the last few hours, and all his thoughts concentrated upon the realization of his dream.

Immediately upon his arrival at his own abode, upon the cessation of the noise and bustle of travel, in the silence of the library where he generally passed his time, where he worked and wrote, and where he almost always felt himself possessed by a restful tranquillity in the friendly companionship of his books, his piano, and his violin, there now commenced in him that unending torment of impatient waiting which devours, as with a fever, insatiable hearts like his. He was surprised that he could apply himself to nothing, that nothing served to occupy his mind, that reading and music, the occupations that he generally employed to while away the idle moments of his life, were unavailing, not only to afford distraction to his thoughts, but even to give rest and quiet to his physical being, and he asked himself what he was to do to appease this new disturbance. An inexplicable physical need of motion seemed to have taken possession of him—of going forth and walking the streets, of constant movement, the crisis of that agitation that is imparted by the mind to the body and which is nothing more than an instinctive and unappeasable longing to seek and find some other being.

He put on his hat and overcoat, and as he was descending the stairs he asked himself: "In which direction shall I go?" Thereupon an idea occurred to him that he had not yet thought of: he must procure a pretty and secluded retreat to serve them as a trysting place.

He pursued his investigations in every quarter, ransacking streets, avenues, and boulevards, distrustfully examining concierges with their servile smiles, lodging-house keepers of suspicious appearance and apartments with doubtful furnishings, and at evening he returned to his house in a state of discouragement. At nine o'clock the next day he started out again, and at nightfall he finally succeeded in discovering at Auteuil, buried in a garden that had three exits, a lonely pavilion which an upholsterer in the neighborhood promised to render habitable in two days. He ordered what was necessary, selecting very plain furniture of varnished pine and thick carpets. A baker who lived near one of the garden gates had charge of the property, and an arrangement was completed with his wife whereby she was to care for the rooms, while a gardener of the quarter also took a contract for filling the beds with flowers.

All these arrangements kept him busy until it was eight o'clock, and when at last he got home, worn out with fatigue, he beheld with a beating heart a telegram lying on his desk. He opened it and read:

"I will be home to-morrow. Await instructions. "MICHE."

He had not written to her yet, fearing that as she was soon to leave Avranches his letter might go astray, and as soon as he had dined he seated himself at his desk to lay before her what was passing in his mind. The task was a long and difficult one, for all the words and phrases that he could muster, and even his ideas, seemed to him weak, mediocre, and ridiculous vehicles in which to convey to her the delicacy and passionateness of his thanks.

The letter that he received from her upon waking next morning confirmed the statement that she would reach home that evening, and begged him not to make his presence known to anyone for a few days, in order that full belief might be accorded to the report that he was traveling. She also requested him to walk upon the terrace of the Tuileries garden that overlooks the Seine the following day at ten o'clock.

He was there an hour before the time appointed, and to kill time wandered about in the immense garden that was peopled only by a few early pedestrians, belated officeholders on their way to the public buildings on the left bank, clerks and toilers of every condition. It was a pleasure to him to watch the hurrying crowds driven by the necessity of earning their daily bread to brutalizing labors, and to compare his lot with theirs, on this spot, at the minute when he was awaiting his mistress—a queen among the queens of the earth. He felt himself so fortunate a being, so privileged, raised to such a height beyond their petty struggles, that he felt like giving thanks to the blue sky, for to him Providence was but a series of alternations of sunshine and of rain due to Chance, mysterious ruler over weather and over men.

When it wanted a few minutes of ten he ascended to the terrace and watched for her coming. "She will be late!" he thought. He had scarcely more than heard the clock in an adjacent building strike ten when he thought he saw her at a distance, coming through the garden with hurrying steps, like a working-woman in haste to reach her shop. "Can it indeed be she?" He recognized her step but was astonished by her changed appearance, so unassuming in a neat little toilette of dark colors. She was coming toward the stairs that led up to the terrace, however, in a bee-line, as if she had traveled that road many times before.

"Ah!" he said to himself, "she must be fond of this place and come to walk here sometimes." He watched her as she raised her dress to put her foot on the first step and then nimbly flew up the remaining ones, and as he eagerly stepped forward to meet her she said to him as he came near with a pleasant smile, in which there was a trace of uneasiness: "You are very imprudent! You must not show yourself like that; I saw you almost from the Rue de Rivoli Come, we will go and take a seat on a bench yonder. There is where you must wait for me next time."

He could not help asking her: "So you come here often?"

"Yes, I have a great liking for this place, and as I am an early walker I come here for exercise and to look at the scenery, which is very pretty. And then one never meets anybody here, while the Bois is out of the question on just that account. But you must be careful not to give away my secret."

He laughed: "I shall not be very likely to do that." Discreetly taking her hand, a little hand that was hanging at her side conveniently concealed in the folds of her dress, he sighed: "How I love you! My heart was sick with waiting for you. Did you receive my letter?"

"Yes; I thank you for it. It was very touching."

"Then you have not become angry with me yet?"

"Why no! Why should I? You are just as nice as you can be."

He sought for ardent words, words that would vibrate with his emotion and his gratitude. As none came to him, and as he was too deeply moved to permit of the free expression of the thought that was within him, he simply said again: "How I love you!"

She said to him: "I brought you here because there are water and boats in this place as well as down yonder. It is not at all like what we saw down there; still it is not disagreeable."

They were sitting on a bench near the stone balustrade that runs along the river, almost alone, invisible from every quarter. The only living beings to be seen on the long terrace at that hour were two gardeners and three nursemaids. Carriages were rolling along the quay at their feet, but they could not see them; footsteps were resounding upon the adjacent sidewalk, over against the wall that sustained the promenade; and still unable to find words in which to express their thoughts, they let their gaze wander over the beautiful Parisian landscape that stretches from the Île Saint-Louis and the towers of Nôtre-Dame to the heights of Meudon. She repeated her thought: "None the less, it is very pretty, isn't it?"

But he was suddenly seized by the thrilling remembrance of their journey through space up on the summit of the abbey tower, and with a regretful feeling for the emotion that was past and gone, he said: "Oh, Madame, do you remember our escapade of the 'Madman's Path?'"

"Yes; but I am a little afraid now that I come to think of it when it is all over. Dieu! how my head would spin around if I had it to do over again! I was just drunk with the fresh air, the sunlight, and the sea. Look, my friend, what a magnificent view we have before us. How I do love Paris!"

He was surprised, having a confused feeling of missing something that had appeared in her down there in the country. He murmured: "It matters not to me where I am, so that I am only near you!"

Her only answer was a pressure of the hand. Inspired with greater happiness, perhaps, by this little signal than he would have been by a tender word, his heart relieved of the care that had oppressed it until now, he could at last find words to express his feelings. He told her, slowly, in words that were almost solemn, that he had given her his life forever that she might do with it what she would.

She was grateful; but like the child of modern scepticism that she was and willing captive of her iconoclastic irony, she smiled as she replied: "I would not make such a long engagement as that if I were you!"

He turned and faced her, and, looking her straight in the eyes with that penetrating look which is like a touch, repeated what he had just said at greater length, in a more ardent, more poetical form of expression. All that he had written in so many burning letters he now expressed with such a fervor of conviction that it seemed to her as she listened that she was sitting in a cloud of incense. She felt herself caressed in every fiber of her feminine nature by his adoring words more deeply than ever before.

When he had ended she simply said: "And I, too, love you dearly!"

They were still holding each other's hand, like young folks walking along a country road, and watching with vague eyes the little steamboats plying on the river. They were alone by themselves in Paris, in the great confused uproar, whether remote or near at hand, that surrounded them in this city full of all the life of all the world, more alone than they had been on the summit of their aerial tower, and for some seconds they were quite oblivious that there existed on earth any other beings but their two selves.

She was the first to recover the sensation of reality and of the flight of time. "Shall we see each other again to-morrow?" she said.

He reflected for an instant, and abashed by what he had in mind to ask of her: "Yes—yes—certainly," he replied. "But—shall we never meet in any other place? This place is unfrequented. Still—people may come here."

She hesitated. "You are right. Still it is necessary also that you should not show yourself for at least two weeks yet, so that people may think that you are away traveling. It will be very nice and mysterious for us to meet and no one know that you are in Paris. Meanwhile, however, I cannot receive you at my house, so—I don't see——"

He felt that he was blushing, and continued: "Neither can I ask you to come to my house. Is there nothing else—is there no other place?"

Being a woman of practical sense, logical and without false modesty, she was neither surprised nor shocked.

"Why, yes," she said, "only we must have time to think it over."

"I have thought it over."

"What! so soon?"

"Yes, Madame."

"Well?"

"Are you acquainted with the Rue des Vieux-Champs at Auteuil?"

"No."

"It runs into the Rue Tournemine and the Rue Jean-de-Saulge."

"Well?"

"In this street, or rather lane, there is a garden, and in this garden a pavilion that also communicates with the two streets that I mentioned."

"What next?"

"That pavilion awaits you."

She reflected, still with no appearance of embarrassment, and then asked two or three questions that were dictated by feminine prudence. His explanations seemed to be satisfactory, for she murmured as she arose:

"Well, I will go to-morrow."

"At what time?"

"Three o'clock."

"Seven is the number; I will be waiting for you behind the door. Do not forget. Give a knock as you pass."

"Yes, my friend. Adieu, till to-morrow."

"Till to-morrow, adieu. Thanks; I adore you."

They had risen to their feet. "Do not come with me," she said. "Stay here for ten minutes, and when you leave go by the way of the quay."

"Adieu!"

"Adieu!"

She started off very rapidly, with such a modest, unassuming air, so hurriedly, that actually she might have been mistaken for one of Paris' pretty working-girls, who trot along the streets in the morning on the way to their honest labors.

He took a cab to Auteuil, tormented by the fear that the house might not be ready against the following day. He found it full of workmen, however; the hangings were all in place upon the walls, the carpets laid upon the floors. Everywhere there was a sound of pounding, hammering, beating, washing. In the garden, which was quite large and rather pretty, the remains of an ancient park, containing a few large old trees, a thick clump of shrubbery that stood for a forest, two green tables, two grass-plots, and paths twisting about among the beds, the gardener of the vicinity had set out rose-trees, geraniums, pinks, reseda, and twenty other species of those plants, the growth of which is advanced or retarded by careful attention, so that a naked field may be transformed in a day into a blooming flower garden.

Mariolle was as delighted as if he had scored another success with his Michèle, and having exacted an oath from the upholsterer that all the furniture should be in place the next day before noon, he went off to various shops to buy some bric-à-brac and pictures for the adornment of the interior of this retreat. For the walls he selected some of those admirable photographs of celebrated pictures that are produced nowadays, for the tables and mantelshelves some rare pottery and a few of those familiar objects that women always like to have about them. In the course of the day he expended the income of three months, and he did it with great pleasure, reflecting that for the last ten years he had been living very economically, not from penuriousness, but because of the absence of expensive tastes, and this circumstance now allowed him to do things somewhat magnificently.

He returned to the pavilion early in the morning of the following day, presided over the arrival and placing of the furniture, climbed ladders and hung the pictures, burned perfumes and vaporized them upon the hangings and poured them over the carpets. In his feverish joy, in the excited rapture of all his being, it seemed to him that he had never in his life been engaged in such an engrossing, such a delightful labor. At every moment he looked to see what time it was, and calculated how long it would be before she would be there; he urged on the workmen, and stimulated his invention so to arrange the different objects that they might be displayed in their best light.

In his prudence he dismissed everyone before it was two o'clock, and then, as the minute-hand of the clock tardily made its last revolution around the dial, in the silence of that house where he was awaiting the greatest happiness that ever he could have wished for, alone with his reverie, going and coming from room to room, he passed the minutes until she should be there.

Finally he went out into the garden. The sunlight was streaming through the foliage upon the grass and falling with especially charming brilliancy upon a bed of roses. The very heavens were contributing their aid to embellish this trysting-place. Then he went and stood by the gate, partially opening it to look out from time to time for fear she might mistake the house.

Three o'clock rang out from some belfry, and forthwith the sounds were echoed from a dozen schools and factories. He stood waiting now with watch in hand, and gave a start of surprise when two little, light knocks were given against the door, to which his ear was closely applied, for he had heard no sound of footsteps in the street.

He opened: it was she. She looked about her with astonishment. First of all she examined with a distrustful glance the neighboring houses, but her inspection reassured her, for certainly she could have no acquaintances among the humble bourgeois who inhabited the quarter. Then she examined the garden with pleased curiosity, and finally placed the backs of her two hands, from which she had drawn her gloves, against her lover's mouth; then she took his arm. At every step she kept repeating: "My! how pretty it is! how unexpected! how attractive!" Catching sight of the rose-bed that the sun was shining upon through the branches of the trees, she exclaimed: "Why, this is fairyland, my friend!"

She plucked a rose, kissed it, and placed it in her corsage. Then they entered the pavilion, and she seemed so pleased with everything that he felt like going down on his knees to her, although he may have felt at the bottom of his heart that perhaps she might as well have shown more attention to him and less to the surroundings. She looked about her with the pleasure of a child who has received a new plaything, and admired and appreciated the elegance of the place with the satisfaction of a connoisseur whose tastes have been gratified. She had feared that she was coming to some vulgar, commonplace resort, where the furniture and hangings had been contaminated by other rendezvous, whereas all this, on the contrary, was new, unforeseen, and alluring, prepared expressly for her, and must have cost a lot of money. Really he was perfect, this man. She turned to him and extended her arms, and their lips met in one of those long kisses that have the strange, twofold sensation of self-effacement and unadulterated bliss.

When, at the end of three hours, they were about to separate, they walked through the garden and seated themselves in a leafy arbor where no eye could reach them. André addressed her with an exuberance of feeling, as if she had been an idol that had come down for his sake from her sacred pedestal, and she listened to him with that fatigued languor which he had often seen reflected in her eyes after people had tired her by too long a visit. She continued affectionate, however, her face lighted up by a tender, slightly constrained smile, and she clasped the hand that she held in hers with a continuous pressure that perhaps was more studied than spontaneous.

She could not have been listening to him, for she interrupted one of his sentences to say: "Really, I must be going. I was to be at the Marquise de Bratiane's at six o'clock, and I shall be very late."

He conducted her to the gate by which she had obtained admission. They gave each other a parting kiss, and after a furtive glance up and down the street, she hurried away, keeping close to the walls.

When he was alone he felt within him that sudden void that is ever left by the disappearance of the woman whose kiss is still warm upon your lips, the queer little laceration of the heart that is caused by the sound of her retreating footsteps. It seemed to him that he was abandoned and alone, that he was never to see her again, and he betook himself to pacing the gravel-walks, reflecting upon this never-ceasing contrast between anticipation and realization. He remained there until it was dark, gradually becoming more tranquil and yielding himself more entirely to her influence, now that she was away, than if she had been there in his arms. Then he went home and dined without being conscious of what he was eating, and sat down to write to her.

The next day was a long one to him, and the evening seemed interminable. Why had she not answered his letter, why had she sent him no word? The morning of the second day he received a short telegram appointing another rendezvous at the same hour. The little blue envelope speedily cured him of the heart-sickness of hope deferred from which he was beginning to suffer.

She came, as she had done before, punctual, smiling, and affectionate, and their second interview in the little house was in all respects similar to the first. André Mariolle, surprised at first and vaguely troubled that the ecstatic passion he had dreamed of had not made itself felt between them, but more and more overmastered by his senses, gradually forgot his visions of anticipation in the somewhat different happiness of possession. He was becoming attached to her by reason of her caresses, an invincible tie, the strongest tie of all, from which there is no deliverance when once it has fully possessed you and has penetrated through your flesh, into your veins.

Twenty days rolled by, such sweet, fleeting days. It seemed to him that there was to be no end to it, that he was to live forever thus, nonexistent for all and living for her alone, and to his mental vision there presented itself the seductive dream of an unlimited continuance of this blissful, secret way of living.

She continued to make her visits at intervals of three days, offering no objections, attracted, it would seem, as much by the amusement she derived from their clandestine meetings—by the charm of the little house that had now been transformed into a conservatory of rare exotics and by the novelty of the situation, which could scarcely be called dangerous, since she was her own mistress, but still was full of mystery—as by the abject and constantly increasing tenderness of her lover.

At last there came a day when she said to him: "Now, my dear friend, you must show yourself in society again. You will come and pass the afternoon with me to-morrow. I have given out that you are at home again."

He was heartbroken. "Oh, why so soon?" he said.

"Because if it should leak out by any chance that you are in Paris your absence would be too inexplicable not to give rise to gossip."

He saw that she was right and promised that he would come to her house the next day. Then he asked her: "Do you receive to-morrow?"

"Yes," she replied. "It will be quite a little solemnity."

He did not like this intelligence. "Of what description is your solemnity?"

She laughed gleefully. "I have prevailed upon Massival, by means of the grossest sycophancy, to give a performance of his 'Dido,' which no one has heard yet. It is the poetry of antique love. Mme. de Bratiane, who considered herself Massival's sole proprietor, is furious. She will be there, for she is to sing. Am I not a sly one?"

"Will there be many there?"

"Oh, no, only a few intimate friends. You know them nearly all."

"Won't you let me off? I am so happy in my solitude."

"Oh! no, my friend. You know that I count on you more than all the rest."

His heart gave a great thump. "Thank you," he said; "I will come."

CHAPTER VI.

QUESTIONINGS

Good day, M. Mariolle."

Mariolle noticed that it was no longer the "dear friend" of Auteuil, and the clasp of the hand was a hurried one, the hasty pressure of a busy woman wholly engrossed in her social functions. As he entered the salon Mme. de Burne was advancing to speak to the beautiful Mme. le Prieur, whose sculpturesque form, and the audacious way that she had of dressing to display it, had caused her to be nicknamed, somewhat ironically, "The Goddess." She was the wife of a member of the Institute, of the section of Inscriptions and Belles-Lettres.

"Ah, Mariolle!" exclaimed Lamarthe, "where do you come from? We thought that you were dead."

"I have been making a trip through Finistère."

He was going on to relate his impressions when the novelist interrupted him: "Are you acquainted with the Baronne de Frémines?"

"Only by sight; but I have heard a good deal of her. They say that she is queer."

"The very queen of crazy women, but with an exquisite perfume of modernness. Come and let me present you to her." Taking him by the arm he led him toward a young woman who was always compared to a doll, a pale and charming little blond doll, invented and created by the devil himself for the damnation of those larger children who wear beards on their faces. She had long, narrow eyes, slightly turned up toward the temples, apparently like the eyes of the Chinese; their soft blue glances stole out between lids that were seldom opened to their full extent, heavy, slowly-moving lids, designed to veil and hide this creature's mysterious nature.

Her hair, very light in color, shone with silky, silvery reflections, and her delicate mouth, with its thin lips, seemed to have been cut by the light hand of a sculptor from the design of a miniature-painter. The voice that issued from it had bell-like intonations, and the audacity of her ideas, of a biting quality that was peculiar to herself, smacking of wickedness and drollery, their destructive charm, their cold, corrupting seductiveness, all the complicated nature of this full-grown, mentally diseased child acted upon those who were brought in contact with her in such a way as to produce in them violent passions and disturbances.

She was known all over Paris as being the most extravagant of the mondaines of the real monde, and also the wittiest, but no one could say exactly what she was, what were her ideas, what she did. She exercised an irresistible sway over mankind in general. Her husband, also, was quite as much of an enigma as she. Courteous and affable and a great nobleman, he seemed quite unconscious of what was going on. Was he indifferent, or complaisant, or was he simply blind? Perhaps, after all, there was nothing in it more than those little eccentricities which doubtless amused him as much as they did her. All sorts of opinions, however, were prevalent in regard to him, and some very ugly reports were circulated. Rumor even went so far as to insinuate that his wife's secret vices were not unprofitable to him.

Between her and Mme. de Burne there were natural attractions and fierce jealousies, spells of friendship succeeded by crises of furious enmity. They liked and feared each other and mutually sought each other's society, like professional duelists, who appreciate at the same time that they would be glad to kill each other.

It was the Baronne de Frémines who was having the upper hand at this moment. She had just scored a victory, an important victory: she had conquered Lamarthe, had taken him from her rival and borne him away ostentatiously to domesticate him in her flock of acknowledged followers. The novelist seemed to be all at once smitten, puzzled, charmed, and stupefied by the discoveries he had made in this creature sui generis, and he could not help talking about her to everybody that he met, a fact which had already given rise to much gossip.

Just as he was presenting Mariolle he encountered Mme. de Burne's look from the other end of the room; he smiled and whispered in his friend's ear: "See, the mistress of the house is angry."

André raised his eyes, but Madame had turned to meet Massival, who just then made his appearance beneath the raised portière. He was followed almost immediately by the Marquise de Bratiane, which elicited from Lamarthe: "Ah! we shall only have a second rendition of 'Dido'; the first has just been given in the Marquise's coupé."

Mme. de Frémines added: "Really, our friend De Burne's collection is losing some of its finest jewels."

Mariolle felt a sudden impulse of anger rising in his heart, a kind of hatred against this woman, and a brusque sensation of irritation against these people, their way of life, their ideas, their tastes, their aimless inclinations, their childish amusements. Then, as Lamarthe bent over the young woman to whisper something in her ear, he profited by the opportunity to slip away.

Handsome Mme. le Prieur was sitting by herself only a few steps away; he went up to her to make his bow. According to Lamarthe she stood for the old guard among all this irruption of modernism. Young, tall, handsome, with very regular features and chestnut hair through which ran threads of gold, extremely affable, captivating by reason of her tranquil, kindly charm of manner, by reason also of a calm, well-studied coquetry and a great desire to please that lay concealed beneath an outward appearance of simple and sincere affection, she had many firm partisans, whom she took good care should never be exposed to dangerous rivalries. Her house had the reputation of being a little gathering of intimate friends, where all the habitués, moreover, concurred in extolling the merits of the husband.

She and Mariolle now entered into conversation. She held in high esteem this intelligent and reserved man, who gave people so little cause to talk about him and who was perhaps of more account than all the rest.

The remaining guests came dropping in: big Fresnel, puffing and giving a last wipe with his handkerchief to his shining and perspiring forehead, the philosophic George de Maltry, finally the Baron de Gravil accompanied by the Comte de Marantin. M. de Pradon assisted his daughter in doing the honors of the house; he was extremely attractive to Mariolle.

But Mariolle, with a heavy heart, saw her going and coming and bestowing her attentions on everyone there more than on him.

Twice, it is true, she had thrown him a swift look from a distance which seemed to say, "I am not forgetting you," but they were so fleeting that perhaps he had failed to catch their meaning. And then he could not be unconscious to the fact that Lamarthe's aggressive assiduities to Mme. de Frémines were displeasing to Mme. de Burne. "That is only her coquettish feeling of spite," he said to himself, "a woman's irritation from whose salon some valuable trinket has been spirited away." Still it made him suffer, and his suffering was the greater since he saw that she was constantly watching them in a furtive, concealed kind of way, while she did not seem to trouble herself a bit at seeing him sitting beside Mme. le Prieur.

The reason was that she had him in her power, she was sure of him, while the other was escaping her. What, then, could be to her that love of theirs, that love which was born but yesterday, and which in him had banished and killed every other idea?

M. de Pradon had called for silence, and Massival was opening the piano, which Mme. de Bratiane was approaching, removing her gloves meanwhile, for she was to sing the woes of "Dido," when the door again opened and a young man appeared upon whom every eye was immediately fixed. He was tall and slender, with curling side-whiskers, short, blond, curly hair, and an air that was altogether aristocratic. Even Mme. le Prieur seemed to feel his influence.

"Who is it?" Mariolle asked her.

"What! is it possible that you do not know him?"

"No, I do not."

"It is Comte Rudolph de Bernhaus."

"Ah! the man who fought a duel with Sigismond Fabre."

"Yes."

The story had made a great noise at the time. The Comte de Bernhaus, attached to the Austrian embassy and a diplomat of the highest promise, an elegant Bismarck, so it was said, having heard some words spoken in derogation of his sovereign at an official reception, had fought the next day with the man who uttered them, a celebrated fencer, and killed him. After this duel, in respect to which public opinion had been divided, the Comte acquired between one day and the next a notoriety after the manner of Sarah Bernhardt, but with this difference, that his name appeared in an aureole of poetic chivalry. He was in addition a man of great charm, an agreeable conversationalist, a man of distinction in every respect. Lamarthe used to say of him: "He is the one to tame our pretty wild beasts."

He took his seat beside Mme. de Burne with a very gallant air, and Massival sat down before the keyboard and allowed his fingers to run over the keys for a few moments.

Nearly all the audience changed their places and drew their chairs nearer so as to hear better and at the same time have a better view of the singer. Thus Mariolle and Lamarthe found themselves side by side.

There was a great silence of expectation and respectful attention; then the musician began with a slow, a very slow succession of notes, something like a musical recitative. There were pauses, then the air would be lightly caught up in a series of little phrases, now languishing and dying away, now breaking out in nervous strength, indicative, it would seem, of distressful emotion, but always characterized by originality of invention. Mariolle gave way to reverie. He beheld a woman, a woman in the fullness of her mature youth and ripened beauty, walking slowly upon a shore that was bathed by the waves of the sea. He knew that she was suffering, that she bore a great sorrow in her soul, and he looked at Mme. de Bratiane.

Motionless, pale beneath her wealth of thick black hair that seemed to have been dipped in the shades of night, the Italian stood waiting, her glance directed straight before her. On her strongly marked, rather stern features, against which her eyes and eyebrows stood out like spots of ink, in all her dark, powerful, and passionate beauty, there was something that struck one, something like the threat of the coming storm that we read in the blackening sky.

Massival, slightly nodding his head with its long hair in cadence with the rhythm, kept on relating the affecting tale that he was drawing from the resonant keys of ivory.

A shiver all at once ran through the singer; she partially opened her mouth, and from it there proceeded a long-drawn, heartrending wail of agony. It was not one of those outbursts of tragic despair that divas give utterance to upon the stage, with dramatic gestures, neither was it one of those pitiful laments for love betrayed that bring a storm of bravos from an audience; it was a cry of supreme passion, coming from the body and not from the soul, wrung from her like the roar of a wounded animal, the cry of the feminine animal betrayed. Then she was silent, and Massival again began to relate, more animatedly, more stormily, the moving story of the miserable queen who was abandoned by the man she loved. Then the woman's voice made itself heard again. She used articulate language now; she told of the intolerable torture of solitude, of her unquenchable thirst for the caresses that were hers no more, and of the grief of knowing that he was gone from her forever.

Her warm, ringing voice made the hearts of her audience beat beneath the spell. This somber Italian, with hair like the darkness of the night, seemed to be suffering all the sorrows that she was telling, she seemed to love, or to have the capacity of loving, with furious ardor. When she ceased her eyes were full of tears, and she slowly wiped them away. Lamarthe leaned over toward Mariolle and said to him in a quiver of artistic enthusiasm: "Good heavens! how beautiful she is just now! She is a woman, the only one in the room." Then he added, after a moment of reflection: "After all, who can tell? Perhaps there is nothing there but the mirage of the music, for nothing has real existence except our illusions. But what an art to produce illusions is that of hers!"

There was a short intermission between the first and the second parts of the musical poem, and warm congratulations were extended to the composer and his interpreter. Lamarthe in particular was very earnest in his felicitations, and he was really sincere, for he was endowed with the capacity to feel and comprehend, and beauty of all kinds appealed strongly to his nature, under whatever form expressed. The manner in which he told Mme. de Bratiane what his feelings had been while listening to her was so flattering that it brought a slight blush to her face and excited a little spiteful feeling among the other women who heard it. Perhaps he was not altogether unaware of the feeling that he had produced.

When he turned around to resume his chair, he perceived Comte de Bernhaus just in the act of seating himself beside Mme. de Frémines. She seemed at once to be on confidential terms with him, and they smiled at each other as if this close conversation was particularly agreeable to them both. Mariolle, whose gloom was momentarily increasing, stood leaning against a door; the novelist came and stationed himself at his side. Big Fresnel, George de Maltry, the Baron de Gravil and the Comte de Marantin formed a circle about Mme. de Burne, who was going about offering tea. She seemed imprisoned in a crown of adorers. Lamarthe ironically called his friend's attention to it and added: "A crown without jewels, however, and I am sure that she would be glad to give all those rhinestones for the brilliant that she would like to see there."

"What brilliant do you mean?" inquired Mariolle.

"Why, Bernhaus, handsome, irresistible, incomparable Bernhaus, he in whose honor this fête is given, for whom the miracle was performed of inducing Massival to bring out his 'Dido' here."

André, though incredulous, was conscious of a pang of regret as he heard these words. "Has she known him long?" he asked.

"Oh, no; ten days at most. But she put her best foot foremost during this brief campaign, and her tactics have been those of a conqueror. If you had been here you would have had a good laugh."

"How so?"

"She met him for the first time at Mme. de Frémines's; I happened to be dining there that evening. Bernhaus stands very well in the good graces of the lady of that house, as you may see for yourself; all that you have to do is to look at them at the present moment; and behold, in the very minute that succeeded the first salutation that they ever made each other, there is our pretty friend De Burne taking the field to effect the conquest of the Austrian phœnix. And she is succeeding, and will succeed, although the little Frémines is more than a match for her in coquetry, real indifference, and perhaps perversity. But our friend De Burne uses her weapons more scientifically, she is more of a woman, by which I mean a modern woman, that is to say, irresistible by reason of that artificial seductiveness which takes the place in the modern woman of the old-fashioned natural charm of manner. And it is not her artificiality alone that is to be taken into account, but her æstheticism, her profound comprehension of feminine æsthetics; all her strength lies therein. She knows herself thoroughly, because she takes more delight in herself than in anything else, and she is never at fault as to the best means of subjugating a man and making the best use of her gifts in order to captivate men."

Mariolle took exception to this. "I think that you put it too strongly," he said. "She has always been very simple with me."

"Because simplicity is the right thing to meet the requirements of your case. I do not wish to speak ill of her, however. I think that she is better than most of her set. But they are not women."

Massival, striking a few chords on the piano, here reduced them to silence, and Mme. de Bratiane proceeded to sing the second part of the poem, in which her delineation of the title-role was a magnificent study of physical passion and sensual regret.

Lamarthe, however, never once took his eyes from Mme. de Frémines and the Comte de Bernhaus, where they were enjoying their tête-à-tête, and as soon as the last vibrations of the piano were lost in the murmurs of applause, he again took up his theme as if in continuation of an argument, or as if he were replying to an adversary: "No, they are not women. The most honest of them are coquettes without being aware of it. The more I know them the less do I find in them that sensation of mild exhilaration that it is the part of a true woman to inspire in us. They intoxicate, it is true, but the process wears upon our nerves, for they are too sophisticated. Oh, it is very good as a liqueur to sip now and then, but it is a poor substitute for the good wine that we used to have. You see, my dear fellow, woman was created and sent to dwell on earth for two objects only, and it is these two objects alone that can avail to bring out her true, great, and noble qualities—love and the family. I am talking like M. Prudhomme. Now the women of to-day are incapable of loving, and they will not bear children. When they are so inexpert as to have them, it is a misfortune in their eyes; then a burden. Truly, they are not women; they are monsters."

Astonished by the writer's violent manner and by the angry look that glistened in his eye, Mariolle asked him: "Why, then, do you spend half your time hanging to their skirts?"

Lamarthe hotly replied: "Why? Why? Because it interests me—parbleu! And then—and then—Would you prevent a physician from going to the hospitals to watch the cases? Those women constitute my clinic."

This reflection seemed to quiet him a little: he proceeded: "Then, too, I adore them for the very reason that they are so modern. At bottom I am really no more a man than they are women. When I am at the point of becoming attached to one of them, I amuse myself by investigating and analyzing all the resulting sensations and emotions, just like a chemist who experiments upon himself with a poison in order to ascertain its properties." After an interval of silence, he continued: "In this way they will never succeed in getting me into their clutches. I can play their game as well as they play it themselves, perhaps even better, and that is of use to me for my books, while their proceedings are not of the slightest bit of use to them. What fools they are! Failures, every one of them—charming failures, who will be ready to die of spite as they grow older and see the mistake that they have made."

Mariolle, as he listened, felt himself sinking into one of those fits of depression that are like the humid gloom with which a long-continued rain darkens everything about us. He was well aware that the man of letters, as a general thing, was not apt to be very far out of the way, but he could not bring himself to admit that he was altogether right in the present case. With a slight appearance of irritation, he argued, not so much in defense of women as to show the causes of the position that they occupy in contemporary literature. "In the days when poets and novelists exalted them, and endowed them with poetic attributes," he said, "they looked for in life, and seemed to find, that which their heart had discovered in their reading. Nowadays you persist in suppressing everything that has any savor of sentiment and poetry, and in its stead give them only naked, undeceiving realities. Now, my dear sir, the more love there is in books, the more love there is in life. When you invented the ideal and laid it before them, they believed in the truth of your inventions. Now that you give them nothing but stern, unadorned realism, they follow in your footsteps and have come to measure everything by that standard of vulgarity."

Lamarthe, who was always ready for a literary discussion, was about to commence a dissertation when Mme. de Burne came up to them. It was one of the days when she looked at her best, with a toilette that delighted the eye and with that aggressive and alluring air that denoted that she was ready to try conclusions with anyone. She took a chair. "That is what I like," she said; "to come upon two men and find that they are not talking about me. And then you are the only men here that one can listen to with any interest. What was the subject that you were discussing?"

Lamarthe, quite without embarrassment and in terms of elegant raillery, placed before her the question that had arisen between himself and Mariolle. Then he resumed his reasoning with a spirit that was inflamed by that desire of applause which, in the presence of women, always excites men who like to intoxicate themselves with glory.

She at once interested herself in the discussion, and, warming to the subject, took part in it in defense of the women of our day with a good deal of wit and ingenuity. Some remarks upon the faithfulness and the attachment that even those who were looked on with most suspicion might be capable of, incomprehensible to the novelist, made Mariolle's heart beat more rapidly, and when she left them to take a seat beside Mme. de Frémines, who had persistently kept the Comte de Bernhaus near her, Lamarthe and Mariolle, completely vanquished by her display of feminine tact and grace, were united in declaring that, beyond all question, she was exquisite.

"And just look at them!" said the writer.

The grand duel was on. What were they talking about now, the Austrian and those two women? Mme. de Burne had come up just at the right moment to interrupt a tête-à-tête which, however agreeable the two persons engaged in it might be to each other, was becoming monotonous from being too long protracted, and she broke it up by relating with an indignant air the expressions that she had heard from Lamarthe's lips. To be sure, it was all applicable to Mme. de Frémines, it all resulted from her most recent conquest, and it was all related in the hearing of an intelligent man who was capable of understanding it in all its bearings. The match was applied, and again the everlasting question of love blazed up, and the mistress of the house beckoned to Mariolle and Lamarthe to come to them; then, as their voices grew loud in debate, she summoned the remainder of the company.

A general discussion ensued, bright and animated, in which everyone had something to say. Mme. de Burne was witty and entertaining beyond all the rest, shifting her ground from sentiment, which might have been factitious, to droll paradox. The day was a triumphant one for her, and she was prettier, brighter, and more animated than she had ever been.

CHAPTER VII.

DEPRESSION

When André Mariolle had parted from Mme. de Burne and the penetrating charm of her presence had faded away, he felt within him and all about him, in his flesh, in his heart, in the air, and in all the surrounding world a sensation as if the delight of life which had been his support and animating principle for some time past had been taken from him.

What had happened? Nothing, or almost nothing. Toward the close of the reception she had been very charming in her manner toward him, saying to him more than once: "I am not conscious of anyone's presence here but yours." And yet he felt that she had revealed something to him of which he would have preferred always to remain ignorant. That, too, was nothing, or almost nothing; still he was stupefied, as a man might be upon hearing of some unworthy action of his father or his mother, to learn that during those twenty days which he had believed were absolutely and entirely devoted by her as well as by him, every minute of them, to the sentiment of their newborn love, so recent and so intense, she had resumed her former mode of life, had made many visits, formed many plans, recommenced those odious flirtations, had run after men and disputed them with her rivals, received compliments, and showed off all her graces.

So soon! All this she had done so soon! Had it happened later he would not have been surprised. He knew the world, he knew women and their ways of looking at things, he was sufficiently intelligent to understand it all, and would never have been unduly exacting or offensively jealous. She was beautiful; she was born—it was her allotted destiny—to receive the homage of men and listen to their soft nothings. She had selected him from among them all, and had bestowed herself upon him courageously, royally. It was his part to remain, he would remain in any event, a grateful slave to her caprices and a resigned spectator of her triumphs as a pretty woman. But it was hard on him; something suffered within him, in that obscure cavern down at the bottom of the heart where the delicate sensibilities have their dwelling.

No doubt he had been in the wrong; he had always been in the wrong since he first came to know himself. He carried too much sentimental prudence into his commerce with the world; his feelings were too thin-skinned. This was the cause of the isolated life that he had always led, through his dread of contact with the world and of wounded susceptibilities. He had been wrong, for this supersensitiveness is almost always the result of our not admitting the existence of a nature essentially different from our own, or else not tolerating it. He knew this, having often observed it in himself, but it was too late to modify the constitution of his being.

He certainly had no right to reproach Mme. de Burne, for if she had forbidden him her salon and kept him in hiding during those days of happiness that she had afforded him, she had done it to blind prying eyes and be more fully his in the end. Why, then, this trouble that had settled in his heart? Ah! why? It was because he had believed her to be wholly his, and now it had been made clear to him that he could never expect to seize and hold this woman of a many-sided nature who belonged to all the world.

He was well aware, moreover, that all our life is made up of successes relative in degree to the "almost," and up to the present time he had borne this with philosophic resignation, dissembling his dissatisfaction and his unsatisfied yearnings under the mask of an assumed unsociability. This time he had thought that he was about to obtain an absolute success—the "entirely" that he had been waiting and hoping for all his life. The "entirely" is not to be attained in this world.

His evening was a dismal one, spent in analyzing the painful impression that he had received. When he was in bed this impression, instead of growing weaker, took stronger hold of him, and as he desired to leave nothing unexplored, he ransacked his mind to ascertain the remotest causes of his new troubles. They went, and came, and returned again like little breaths of frosty air, exciting in his love a suffering that was as yet weak and indistinct, like those vague neuralgic pains that we get by sitting in a draft, presages of the horrible agonies that are to come.

He understood in the first place that he was jealous, no longer as the ardent lover only but as one who had the right to call her his own. As long as he had not seen her surrounded by men, her men, he had not allowed himself to dwell upon this sensation, at the same time having a faint prevision of it, but supposing that it would be different, very different, from what it actually was. To find the mistress whom he believed had cared for none but him during those days of secret and frequent meetings—during that early period that should have been entirely devoted to isolation and tender emotion—to find her as much, and even more, interested and wrapped up in her former and frivolous flirtations than she was before she yielded herself to him, always ready to fritter away her time and attention on any chance comer, thus leaving but little of herself to him whom she had designated as the man of her choice, caused him a jealousy that was more of the flesh than of the feelings, not an undefined jealousy, like a fever that lies latent in the system, but a jealousy precise and well defined, for he was doubtful of her.

At first his doubts were instinctive, arising in a sensation of distrust that had intruded itself into his veins rather than into his thoughts, in that sense of dissatisfaction, almost physical, of the man who is not sure of his mate. Then, having doubted, he began to suspect.

What was his position toward her after all? Was he her first lover, or was he the tenth? Was he the successor of M. de Burne, or was he the successor of Lamarthe, Massival, George de Maltry, and the predecessor as well, perhaps, of the Comte de Bernhaus? What did he know of her? That she was surprisingly beautiful, stylish beyond all others, intelligent, discriminating, witty, but at the same time fickle, quick to weary, readily fatigued and disgusted with anyone or anything, and, above all else, in love with herself and an insatiable coquette. Had she had a lover—or lovers—before him? If not, would she have offered herself to him as she did? Where could she have got the audacity that made her come and open his bedroom door, at night, in a public inn? And then after that, would she have shown such readiness to visit the house at Auteuil? Before going there she had merely asked him a few questions, such questions as an experienced and prudent woman would naturally ask. He had answered like a man of circumspection, not unaccustomed to such interviews, and immediately she had confidingly said "Yes," entirely reassured, probably benefiting by her previous experiences.

And then her knock at that little door, behind which he was waiting, with a beating heart, almost ready to faint, how discreetly authoritative it had been! And how she had entered without any visible display of emotion, careful only to observe whether she might be recognized from the adjacent houses! And the way that she had made herself at home at once in that doubtful lodging that he had hired and furnished for her! Would a woman who was a novice, how daring soever she might be, how superior to considerations of morality and regardless of social prejudices, have penetrated thus calmly the mystery of a first rendezvous? There is a trouble of the mind, a hesitation of the body, an instinctive fear in the very feet, which know not whither they are tending; would she not have felt all that unless she had had some experience in these excursions of love and unless the practice of these things had dulled her native sense of modesty?

Burning with this persistent, irritating fever, which the warmth of his bed seemed to render still more unendurable, Mariolle tossed beneath the coverings, constantly drawn on by his chain of doubts and suppositions; like a man that feels himself irrecoverably sliding down the steep descent of a precipice. At times he tried to call a halt and break the current of his thoughts; he sought and found, and was glad to find, reflections that were more just to her and reassuring to him, but the seeds of distrust had been sown in him and he could not help their growing.

And yet, with what had he to reproach her? Nothing, except that her nature was not entirely similar to his own, that she did not look upon life in the same way that he did and that she had not in her heart an instrument of sensibility attuned to the same key as his.

Immediately upon awaking next morning the longing to see her and to re-enforce his confidence in her developed itself within him like a ravening hunger, and he awaited the proper moment to go and pay her the visit demanded by custom. The instant that she saw him at the door of the little drawing-room devoted to her special intimates, where she was sitting alone occupied with her correspondence, she came to him with her two hands outstretched.

"Ah! Good day, dear friend!" she said, with so pleased and frank an air that all his odious suspicions, which were still floating indeterminately in his brain, melted away beneath the warmth of her reception.

He seated himself at her side and at once began to tell her of the manner in which he loved her, for their love was now no longer what it had been. He gently gave her to understand that there are two species of the race of lovers upon earth: those whose desire is that of madmen and whose ardor disappears when once they have achieved a triumph, and those whom possession serves to subjugate and capture, in whom the love of the senses, blending with the inarticulate and ineffable appeals that the heart of man at times sends forth toward a woman, gives rise to the servitude of a complete and torturing love.

Torturing it is, certainly, and forever so, however happy it may be, for nothing, even in the moments of closest communion, ever sates the need of her that rules our being.

Mme. de Burne was charmed and gratified as she listened, carried away, as one is carried away at the theater when an actor gives a powerful interpretation of his rôle and moves us by awaking some slumbering echo in our own life. It was indeed an echo, the disturbing echo of a real passion; but it was not from her bosom that this passion sent forth its cry. Still, she felt such satisfaction that she was the object of so keen a sentiment, she was so pleased that it existed in a man who was capable of expressing it in such terms, in a man of whom she was really very fond, for whom she was really beginning to feel an attachment and whose presence was becoming more and more a necessity to her—not for her physical being but for that mysterious feminine nature which is so greedy of tenderness, devotion, and subjection—that she felt like embracing him, like offering him her mouth, her whole being, only that he might keep on worshiping her in this way.

She answered him frankly and without prudery, with that profound artfulness that certain women are endowed with, making it clear to him that he too had made great progress in her affections, and they remained tête-à-tête in the little drawing-room, where it so happened that no one came that day until twilight, talking always upon the same theme and caressing each other with words that to them did not have the common significance.

The servants had just brought in the lamps, when Mme. de Bratiane appeared. Mariolle withdrew, and as Mme. de Burne was accompanying him to the door through the main drawing-room, he asked her: "When shall I see you down yonder?"

"Will Friday suit you?"

"Certainly. At what hour?"

"The same, three o'clock."

"Until Friday, then. Adieu. I adore you!"

During the two days that passed before this interview, he experienced a sensation of loneliness that he had never felt before in the same way. A woman was wanting in his life—she was the only existent object for him in the world, and as this woman was not far away and he was prevented by social conventions alone from going to her, and from passing a lifetime with her, he chafed in his solitude, in the interminable lapse of the moments that seemed at times to pass so slowly, at the absolute impossibility of a thing that was so easy.

He arrived at the rendezvous on Friday three hours before the time, but it was pleasing to him—it comforted his anxiety—to wait there where she was soon to come, after having already suffered so much in awaiting her mentally in places where she was not to come.

He stationed himself near the door long before the clock had struck the three strokes that he was expecting so eagerly, and when at last he heard them he began to tremble with impatience. The quarter struck. He looked out into the street, cautiously protruding his head between the door and the casing; it was deserted from one end to the other. The minutes seemed to stretch out in aggravating slowness. He was constantly drawing his watch from his pocket, and at last when the hand marked the half-hour it appeared to him that he had been standing there for an incalculable length of time. Suddenly he heard a faint sound upon the pavement outside, and the summons upon the door of the little gloved hand quickly made him forget his disappointment and inspired in him a feeling of gratitude toward her.

She seemed a little out of breath as she asked: "I am very late, am I not?"

"No, not very."

"Just imagine, I was near not being able to come at all. I had a houseful, and I was at my wits' end to know what to do to get rid of all those people. Tell me, do you go under your own name here?"

"No. Why do you ask?"

"So that I may send you a telegram if I should ever be prevented from coming."

"I am known as M. Nicolle."

"Very well; I won't forget. My! how nice it is here in this garden!"

There were five great splashes of perfumed, many-hued brightness upon the grass-plots of the flowers, which were carefully tended and constantly renewed, for the gardener had a customer who paid liberally.

Halting at a bench in front of a bed of heliotrope: "Let us sit here for a while," she said; "I have something funny to tell you."

She proceeded to relate a bit of scandal that was quite fresh, and from the effect of which she had not yet recovered. The story was that Mme. Massival, the ex-mistress whom the artist had married, had come to Mme. de Bratiane's, furious with jealousy, right in the midst of an entertainment in which the Marquise was singing to the composer's accompaniment, and had made a frightful scene: results, rage of the fair Italian, astonishment and laughter of the guests. Massival, quite beside himself, tried to take away his wife, who kept striking him in the face, pulling his hair and beard, biting him and tearing his clothes, but she clung to him with all her strength and held him so that he could not stir, while Lamarthe and two servants, who had hurried to them at the noise, did what they could to release him from the teeth and claws of this fury.

Tranquillity was not restored until after the pair had taken their departure. Since then the musician had remained invisible, and the novelist, witness of the scene, had been repeating it everywhere in a very witty and amusing manner. The affair had produced a deep impression upon Mme. de Burne; it preoccupied her thoughts to such an extent that she hardly knew what she was doing. The constant recurrence of the names of Massival and Lamarthe upon her lips annoyed Mariolle.

"You just heard of this?" he said.

"Yes, hardly an hour ago."

"And that is the reason why she was late," he said to himself with bitterness. Then he asked aloud, "Shall we go in?"

"Yes," she absently murmured.

When, an hour later, she had left him, for she was greatly hurried that day, he returned alone to the quiet little house and seated himself on a low chair in their apartment. The feeling that she had been no more his than if she had not come there left a sort of black cavern in his heart, in all his being, that he tried to probe to the bottom. He could see nothing there, he could not understand; he was no longer capable of understanding. If she had not abstracted herself from his kisses, she had at all events escaped from the immaterial embraces of his tenderness by a mysterious absence of the will of being his. She had not refused herself to him, but it seemed as if she had not brought her heart there with her; it had remained somewhere else, very far away, idly occupied, distracted by some trifle.

Then he saw that he already loved her with his senses as much as with his feelings, even more perhaps. The deprivation of her soulless caresses inspired him with a mad desire to run after her and bring her back, to again possess himself of her. But why? What was the use—since the thoughts of that fickle mind were occupied elsewhere that day? So he must await the days and the hours when, to this elusive mistress of his, there should come the caprice, like her other caprices, of being in love with him.

He returned wearily to his house, with heavy footsteps, his eyes fixed on the sidewalk, tired of life, and it occurred to him that he had made no appointment with her for the future, either at her house or elsewhere.

CHAPTER VIII.

NEW HOPES

Until the setting in of winter she was pretty faithful to their appointments; faithful, but not punctual. During the first three months her tardiness on these occasions ranged between three-quarters of an hour and two hours. As the autumnal rains compelled Mariolle to await her behind the garden gate with an umbrella over his head, shivering, with his feet in the mud, he caused a sort of little summer-house to be built, a covered and inclosed vestibule behind the gate, so that he might not take cold every time they met.

The trees had lost their verdure, and in the place of the roses and other flowers the beds were now filled with great masses of white, pink, violet, purple, and yellow chrysanthemums, exhaling their penetrating, balsamic perfume—the saddening perfume by which these noble flowers remind us of the dying year—upon the moist atmosphere, heavy with the odor of the rain upon the decaying leaves. In front of the door of the little house the inventive genius of the gardener had devised a great Maltese cross, composed of rarer plants arranged in delicate combinations of color, and Mariolle could never pass this bed, bright with new and constantly changing varieties, without the melancholy reflection that this flowery cross was very like a grave.

He was well acquainted now with those long watches in the little summer-house behind the gate. The rain would fall sullenly upon the thatch with which he had had it roofed and trickle down the board siding, and while waiting in this receiving-vault he would give way to the same unvarying reflections, go through the same process of reasoning, be swayed in turn by the same hopes, the same fears, the same discouragements. It was an incessant battle that he had to fight; a fierce, exhausting mental struggle with an elusive force, a force that perhaps had no real existence: the tenderness of that woman's heart.

What strange things they were, those interviews of theirs! Sometimes she would come in with a smile upon her face, full to overflowing with the desire of conversation, and would take a seat without removing her hat and gloves, without raising her veil, often without so much as giving him a kiss. It never occurred to her to kiss him on such occasions; her head was full of a host of captivating little preoccupations, each of them more captivating to her than the idea of putting up her lips to the kiss of her despairing lover. He would take a seat beside her, heart and mouth overrunning with burning words which could find no way of utterance; he would listen to her and answer, and while apparently deeply interested in what she was saying would furtively take her hand, which she would yield to him calmly, amicably, without an extra pulsation in her veins.

At other times she would appear more tender, more wholly his; but he, who was watching her with anxious and clear-sighted eyes, with the eyes of a lover powerless to achieve her entire conquest, could see and divine that this relative degree of affection was owing to the fact that nothing had occurred on such occasions of sufficient importance to divert her thoughts from him.

Her persistent unpunctuality, moreover, proved to Mariolle with how little eagerness she looked forward to these interviews. When we love, when anything pleases and attracts us, we hasten to the anticipated meeting, but once the charm has ceased to work, the appointed time seems to come too quickly and everything serves as a pretext to delay our loitering steps and put off the moment that has become indefinably distasteful to us. An odd comparison with a habit of his own kept incessantly returning to his mind. In summer-time the anticipation of his morning bath always made him hasten his toilette and his visit to the bathing establishment, while in the frosty days of winter he always found so many little things to attend to at home before going out that he was invariably an hour behind his usual time. The meetings at Auteuil were to her like so many winter shower-baths.

For some time past, moreover, she had been making these interviews more infrequent, sending telegrams at the last hour, putting them off until the following day and apparently seeking for excuses for dispensing with them. She always succeeded in discovering excuses of a nature to satisfy herself, but they caused him mental and physical worries and anxieties that were intolerable. If she had manifested any coolness, if she had shown that she was tiring of this passion of his that she felt and knew was constantly increasing in violence, he might at first have been irritated and then in turn offended, discouraged, and resigned, but on the contrary she manifested more affection for him than ever, she seemed more flattered by his love, more desirous of retaining it, while not responding to it otherwise than by friendly marks of preference which were beginning to make all her other admirers jealous.

She could never see enough of him in her own house, and the same telegram that would announce to André that she could not come to Auteuil would convey to him her urgent request to dine with her or come and spend an hour in the evening. At first he had taken these invitations as her way of making amends to him, but afterward he came to understand that she liked to have him near her and that she really experienced the need of him, more so than of the others. She had need of him as an idol needs prayers and faith in order to make it a god; standing in the empty shrine it is but a bit of carved wood, but let a believer enter the sanctuary, and kneel and prostrate himself and worship with fervent prayers, drunk with religion, it becomes the equal of Brahma or of Allah, for every loved being is a kind of god. Mme. de Burne felt that she was adapted beyond all others to play this rôle of fetich, to fill woman's mission, bestowed on her by nature, of being sought after and adored, and of vanquishing men by the arms of her beauty, grace, and coquetry.

In the meantime she took no pains to conceal her affection and her strong liking for Mariolle, careless of what folks might say about it, possibly with the secret desire of irritating and inflaming the others. They could hardly ever come to her house without finding him there, generally installed in the great easy-chair that Lamarthe had come to call the "pulpit of the officiating priest," and it afforded her sincere pleasure to remain alone in his company for an entire evening, talking and listening to him. She had taken a liking to this kind of family life that he had revealed to her, to this constant contact with an agreeable, well-stored mind, which was hers and at her command just as much as were the little trinkets that littered her dressing-table. In like manner she gradually came to yield to him much of herself, of her thoughts, of her deeper mental personality, in the course of those affectionate confidences that are as pleasant in the giving as in the receiving. She felt herself more at ease, more frank and familiar with him than with the others, and she loved him the more for it. She also experienced the sensation, dear to womankind, that she was really bestowing something, that she was confiding to some one all that she had to give, a thing that she had never done before.

In her eyes this was much, in his it was very little. He was still waiting and hoping for the great final breaking up of her being which should give him her soul beneath his caresses.

Caresses she seemed to regard as useless, annoying, rather a nuisance than otherwise. She submitted to them, not without returning them, but tired of them quickly, and this feeling doubtless engendered in her a shade of dislike to them. The slightest and most insignificant of them seemed to be irksome to her. When in the course of conversation he would take her hand and carry it to his lips and hold it there a little, she always seemed desirous of withdrawing it, and he could feel the movement of the muscles in her arm preparatory to taking it away.

He felt these things like so many thrusts of a knife, and he carried away from her presence wounds that bled unintermittently in the solitude of his love. How was it that she had not that period of unreasoning attraction toward him that almost every woman has when once she has made the entire surrender of her being? It may be of short duration, frequently it is followed quickly by weariness and disgust, but it is seldom that it is not there at all, for a day, for an hour! This mistress of his had made of him, not a lover, but a sort of intelligent companion of her life.

Of what was he complaining? Those who yield themselves entirely perhaps have less to give than she!

He was not complaining; he was afraid. He was afraid of that other one, the man who would spring up unexpectedly whenever she might chance to fall in with him, to-morrow, may be, or the day after, whoever he might be, artist, actor, soldier, or man of the world, it mattered not what, born to find favor in her woman's eyes and securing her favor for no other reason, because he was the man, the one destined to implant in her for the first time the imperious desire of opening her arms to him.

He was now jealous of the future as before he had at times been jealous of her unknown past, and all the young woman's intimates were beginning to be jealous of him. He was the subject of much conversation among them; they even made dark and mysterious allusions to the subject in her presence. Some said that he was her lover, while others, guided by Lamarthe's opinion, decided that she was only making a fool of him in order to irritate and exasperate them, as it was her habit to do, and that this was all there was to it. Her father took the matter up and made some remarks to her which she did not receive with good grace, and the more conscious she became of the reports that were circulating among her acquaintance, the more, by an odd contradiction to the prudence that had ruled her life, did she persist in making an open display of the preference that she felt for Mariolle.

He, however, was somewhat disturbed by these suspicious mutterings. He spoke to her of it.

"What do I care?" she said.

"If you only loved me, as a lover!"

"Do I not love you, my friend?"

"Yes and no; you love me well enough in your own house, but very badly elsewhere. I should prefer it to be just the opposite, for my sake, and even, indeed, for your own."

She laughed and murmured: "We can't do more than we can."

"If you only knew the mental trouble that I experience in trying to animate your love. At times I seem to be trying to grasp the intangible, to be clasping an iceberg in my arms that chills me and melts away within my embrace."

She made no answer, not fancying the subject, and assumed the absent manner that she often wore at Auteuil. He did not venture to press the matter further. He looked upon her a good deal as amateurs look upon the precious objects in a museum that tempt them so strongly and that they know they cannot carry away with them.

His days and nights were made up of hours of suffering, for he was living in the fixed idea, and still more in the sentiment than in the idea, that she was his and yet not his, that she was conquered and still at liberty, captured and yet impregnable. He was living at her side, as near her as could be, without ever reaching her, and he loved her with all the unsatiated longings of his body and his soul. He began to write to her again, as he had done at the commencement of their liaison. Once before with ink he had vanquished her early scruples; once again with ink he might be victorious over this later and obstinate resistance. Putting longer intervals between his visits to her, he told her in almost daily letters of the fruitlessness of his love. Now and then, when he had been very eloquent and impassioned and had evinced great sorrow, she answered him. Her letters, dated for effect midnight, or one, two, or three o'clock in the morning, were clear and precise, well considered, encouraging, and afflicting. She reasoned well, and they were not destitute of wit and even fancy, but it was in vain that he read them and re-read them, it was in vain that he admitted that they were to the point, well turned, intelligent, graceful, and satisfactory to his masculine vanity; they had in them nothing of her heart, they satisfied him no more than did the kisses that she gave him in the house at Auteuil.

He asked himself why this was so, and when he had learned them by heart he came to know them so well that he discovered the reason, for a person's writings always afford the surest clue to his nature. Spoken words dazzle and deceive, for lips are pleasing and eyes seductive, but black characters set down upon white paper expose the soul in all its nakedness.

Man, thanks to the artifices of rhetoric, to his professional address and his habit of using the pen to discuss all the affairs of life, often succeeds in disguising his own nature by his impersonal prose style, literary or business, but woman never writes unless it is of herself and something of her being goes into her every word. She knows nothing of the subtilities of style and surrenders herself unreservedly in her ignorance of the scope and value of words. Mariolle called to mind the memoirs and correspondence of celebrated women that he had read; how distinctly their characters were all set forth there, the précieuses, the witty, and the sensible! What struck him most in Mme. de Burne's letters was that no trace of sensibility was to be discovered in them. This woman had the faculty of thought but not of feeling. He called to mind letters that he had received from other persons; he had had many of them. A little bourgeoise that he had met while traveling and who had loved him for the space of three months had written delicious, thrilling notes, abounding in fresh and unexpected terms of sentiment; he had been surprised by the flexibility, the elegant coloring, and the variety of her style. Whence had she obtained this gift? From the fact that she was a woman of sensibility; there could be no other answer. A woman does not elaborate her phrases; they come to her intelligence straight from her emotions; she does not rummage the dictionary for fine words. What she feels strongly she expresses justly, without long and labored consideration, in the adaptive sincerity of her nature.

He tried to test the sincerity of his mistress's nature by means of the lines which she wrote him. They were well written and full of amiability, but how was it that she could find nothing better for him? Ah! for her he had found words that burned as living coals!

When his valet brought in his mail he would look for an envelope bearing the longed-for handwriting, and when he recognized it an involuntary emotion would arise in him, succeeded by a beating of the heart. He would extend his hand and grasp the bit of paper; again he would scrutinize the address, then tear it open. What had she to say to him? Would he find the word "love" there? She had never written or uttered this word without qualifying it by the adverb "well": "I love you well"; "I love you much"; "Do I not love you?" He knew all these formulas, which are inexpressive by reason of what is tacked on to them. Can there be such a thing as a comparison between the degrees of love when one is in its toils? Can one decide whether he loves well or ill? "To love much," what a dearth of love that expression manifests! One loves, nothing more, nothing less; nothing can be said, nothing expressed, nothing imagined that means more than that one simple sentence. It is brief, it is everything. It becomes body, soul, life, the whole of our being. We feel it as we feel the warm blood in our veins, we inhale it as we do the air, we carry it within us as we carry our thoughts, for it becomes the atmosphere of the mind. Nothing has existence beside it. It is not a word, it is an inexpressible state of being, represented by a few letters. All the conditions of life are changed by it; whatever we do, there is nothing done or seen or tasted or enjoyed or suffered just as it was before. Mariolle had become the victim of this small verb, and his eye would run rapidly over the lines, seeking there a tenderness answering to his own. He did in fact find there sufficient to warrant him in saying to himself: "She loves me very well," but never to make him exclaim: "She loves me!" She was continuing in her correspondence the pretty, poetical romance that had had its inception at Mont Saint-Michel. It was the literature of love, not of the love.

When he had finished reading and re-reading them, he would lock the precious and disappointing sheets in a drawer and seat himself in his easy-chair. He had passed many a bitter hour in it before this.

After a while her answers to his letters became less frequent; doubtless she was somewhat weary of manufacturing phrases and ringing the changes on the same stale theme. And then, besides, she was passing through a period of unwonted fashionable excitement, of which André had presaged the approach with that increment of suffering that such insignificant, disagreeable incidents can bring to troubled hearts.

It was a winter of great gaiety. A mad intoxication had taken possession of Paris and shaken the city to its depths; all night long cabs and coupés were rolling through the streets and through the windows were visible white apparitions of women in evening toilette. Everyone was having a good time; all the conversation was on plays and balls, matinées and soirées. The contagion, an epidemic of pleasure, as it were, had quickly extended to all classes of society, and Mme. de Burne also was attacked by it.

It had all been brought about by the effect that her beauty had produced at a dance at the Austrian embassy. The Comte de Bernhaus had made her acquainted with the ambassadress, the Princess de Malten, who had been immediately and entirely delighted with Mme. de Burne. Within a very short time she became the Princess's very intimate friend and thereby extended with great rapidity her relations among the most select diplomatic and aristocratic circles. Her grace, her elegance, her charming manners, her intelligence and wit quickly achieved a triumph for her and made her la mode, and many of the highest titles among the women of France sought to be presented to her. Every Monday would witness a long line of coupés with arms on their panels drawn up along the curb of the Rue du Général-Foy, and the footmen would lose their heads and make sad havoc with the high-sounding names that they bellowed into the drawing-room, confounding duchesses with marquises, countesses with baronnes.

She was entirely carried off her feet. The incense of compliments and invitations, the feeling that she was become one of the elect to whom Paris bends the knee in worship as long as the fancy lasts, the delight of being thus admired, made much of, and run after, were too much for her and gave rise within her soul to an acute attack of snobbishness.

Her artistic following did not submit to this condition of affairs without a struggle, and the revolution produced a close alliance among her old friends. Fresnel, even, was accepted by them, enrolled on the regimental muster and became a power in the league, while Mariolle was its acknowledged head, for they were all aware of the ascendency that he had over her and her friendship for him. He, however, watched her as she was whirled away in this flattering popularity as a child watches the vanishing of his red balloon when he has let go the string. It seemed to him that she was eluding him in the midst of this elegant, motley, dancing throng and flying far, far away from that secret happiness that he had so ardently desired for both of them, and he was jealous of everybody and everything, men, women, and inanimate objects alike. He conceived a fierce detestation for the life that she was leading, for all the people that she associated with, all the fêtes that she frequented, balls, theaters, music, for they were all in a league to take her from him by bits and absorb her days and nights, and only a few scant hours were now accorded to their intimacy. His indulgence of this unreasoning spite came near causing him a fit of sickness, and when he visited her he brought with him such a wan face that she said to him:

"What ails you? You have changed of late, and are very thin."

"I have been loving you too much," he replied.

She gave him a grateful look: "No one ever loves too much, my friend."

"Can you say such a thing as that?"

"Why, yes."

"And you do not see that I am dying of my vain love for you."

"In the first place it is not true that you love in vain; then no one ever dies of that complaint, and finally all our friends are jealous of you, which proves pretty conclusively that I am not treating you badly, all things considered."

He took her hand: "You do not understand me!"

"Yes, I understand very well."

"You hear the despairing appeal that I am incessantly making to your heart?"

"Yes, I have heard it."

"And——"

"And it gives me much pain, for I love you enormously."

"And then?"

"Then you say to me: 'Be like me; think, feel, express yourself as I do.' But, my poor friend, I can't. I am what I am. You must take me as God made me, since I gave myself thus to you, since I have no regrets for having done so and no desire to withdraw from the bargain, since there is no one among all my acquaintance that is dearer to me than you are."

"You do not love me!"

"I love you with all the power of loving that exists in me. If it is not different or greater, is that my fault?"

"If I was certain of that I might content myself with it."

"What do you mean by that?"

"I mean that I believe you capable of loving otherwise, but that I do not believe that it lies in me to inspire you with a genuine passion."

"My friend, you are mistaken. You are more to me than anyone has ever been hitherto, more than anyone will ever be in the future; at least that is my honest conviction. I may lay claim to this great merit: that I do not wear two faces with you, I do not feign to be what you so ardently desire me to be, when many women would act quite differently. Be a little grateful to me for this, and do not allow yourself to be agitated and unstrung; trust in my affection, which is yours, sincerely and unreservedly."

He saw how wide the difference was that parted them. "Ah!" he murmured, "how strangely you look at love and speak of it! To you, I am some one that you like to see now and then, whom you like to have beside you, but to me, you fill the universe: in it I know but you, feel but you, need but you."

She smiled with satisfaction and replied: "I know that; I understand. I am delighted to have it so, and I say to you: Love me always like that if you can, for it gives me great happiness, but do not force me to act a part before you that would be distressing to me and unworthy of us both. I have been aware for some time of the approach of this crisis; it is the cause of much suffering to me, for I am deeply attached to you, but I cannot bend my nature or shape it in conformity with yours. Take me as I am."

Suddenly he asked her: "Have you ever thought, have you ever believed, if only for a day, only for an hour, either before or after, that you might be able to love me otherwise?"

She was at a loss for an answer and reflected for a few seconds. He waited anxiously for her to speak, and continued: "You see, don't you, that you have had other dreams as well?"

"I may have been momentarily deceived in myself," she murmured, thoughtfully.

"Oh! how ingenious you are!" he exclaimed; "how psychological! No one ever reasons thus from the impulse of the heart."

She was reflecting still, interested in her thoughts, in this self-investigation; finally she said: "Before I came to love you as I love you now, I may indeed have thought that I might come to be more—more—more captivated with you, but then I certainly should not have been so frank and simple with you. Perhaps later on I should have been less sincere."

"Why less sincere later on?"

"Because all of love, according to your idea, lies in this formula: 'Everything or nothing,' and this 'everything or nothing' as far as I can see means: 'Everything at first, nothing afterward.' It is when the reign of nothing commences that women begin to be deceitful."

He replied in great distress: "But you do not see how wretched I am—how I am tortured by the thought that you might have loved me otherwise. You have felt that thought: therefore it is some other one that you will love in that manner."

She unhesitatingly replied: "I do not believe it."

"And why? Yes, why, I ask you? Since you have had the foreknowledge of love, since you have felt in anticipation the fleeting and torturing hope of confounding soul and body with the soul and body of another, of losing your being in his and taking his being to be portion of your own, since you have perceived the possibility of this ineffable emotion, the day will come, sooner or later, when you will experience it."

"No; my imagination deceived me, and deceived itself. I am giving you all that I have to give you. I have reflected deeply on this subject since I have been your mistress. Observe that I do not mince matters, not even my words. Really and truly, I am convinced that I cannot love you more or better than I do at this moment. You see that I talk to you just as I talk to myself. I do that because you are very intelligent, because you understand and can read me like a book, and the best way is to conceal nothing from you; it is the only way to keep us long and closely united. And that is what I hope for, my friend."

He listened to her as a man drinks when he is thirsty, then kneeled before her and laid his head in her lap. He took her little hands and pressed them to his lips, murmuring: "Thanks! thanks!" When he raised his eyes to look at her, he saw that there were tears standing in hers; then placing her arms in turn about André's neck, she gently drew him toward her, bent over and kissed him upon the eyelids.

"Take a chair," she said; "it is not prudent to be kneeling before me here."

He seated himself, and when they had contemplated each other in silence for a few moments, she asked him if he would take her some day to visit the exhibition that the sculptor Prédolé, of whom everyone was talking enthusiastically, was then giving of his works. She had in her dressing-room a bronze Love of his, a charming figure pouring water into her bath-tub, and she had a great desire to see the complete collection of the eminent artist's works which had been delighting all Paris for a week past at the Varin gallery. They fixed upon a date and then Mariolle arose to take leave.

"Will you be at Auteuil to-morrow?" she asked him in a whisper.

"Oh! Yes!"

He was very joyful on his way homeward, intoxicated by that "Perhaps?" which never dies in the heart of a lover.

CHAPTER IX.

DISILLUSION

Mme. de Burne's coupé was proceeding at a quick trot along the Rue de Grenelle. It was early April, and the hailstones of a belated storm beat noisily against the glasses of the carriage and rattled off upon the roadway which was already whitened by the falling particles. Men on foot were hurrying along the sidewalk beneath their umbrellas, with coat-collars turned up to protect their necks and ears. After two weeks of fine weather a detestable cold spell had set in, the farewell of winter, freezing up everything and bringing chapped hands and chilblains.

With her feet resting upon a vessel filled with hot water and her form enveloped in soft furs that warmed her through her dress with a velvety caress that was so deliciously agreeable to her sensitive skin, the young woman was sadly reflecting that in an hour at farthest she would have to take a cab to go and meet Mariolle at Auteuil. She was seized by a strong desire to send him a telegram, but she had promised herself more than two months ago that she would not again have recourse to this expedient unless compelled to, for she had been making a great effort to love him in the same manner that he loved her. She had seen how he suffered, and had commiserated him, and after that conversation when she had kissed him upon the eyes in an outburst of genuine tenderness, her sincere affection for him had, in fact, assumed a warmer and more expansive character. In her surprise at her involuntary coldness she had asked herself why, after all, she could not love him as other women love their lovers, since she knew that she was deeply attached to him and that he was more pleasing to her than any other man. This indifference of her love could only proceed from a sluggish action of the heart, which could be cured like any other sluggishness.

She tried it. She endeavored to arouse her feelings by thoughts of him, to be more demonstrative in his presence. She was successful now and then, just as one excites his fears at night by thinking of ghosts or robbers. Fired a little herself by this pretense of passion, she even forced herself to be more caressing; she succeeded very well at first, and delighted him to the point of intoxication.

She thought that this was the beginning in her of a fever somewhat similar to that with which she knew that he was consuming. Her old intermittent hopes of love, that she had dimly seen the possibility of realizing the night that she had dreamed her dreams among the white mists of Saint-Michel's Bay, took form and shape again, not so seductive as then, less wrapped in clouds of poetry and idealism, but more clearly defined, more human, stripped of illusion after the experience of her liaison. Then she had summoned up and watched for that irresistible impulse of all the being toward another being that arises, she had heard, when the emotions of the soul act upon two physical natures. She had watched in vain; it had never come.

She persisted, however, in feigning ardor, in making their interviews more frequent, in saying to him: "I feel that I am coming to love you more and more." But she became weary of it at last, and was powerless longer to impose upon herself or deceive him. She was astonished to find that the kisses that he gave her were becoming distasteful to her after a while, although she was not by any means entirely insensible to them.

This was made manifest to her by the vague lassitude that took possession of her from the early morning of those days when she had an appointment with him. Why was it that on those mornings she did not feel, as other women feel, all her nature troubled by the desire and anticipation of his embraces? She endured them, indeed she accepted them, with tender resignation, but as a woman conquered, brutally subjugated, responding contrary to her own will, never voluntarily and with pleasure. Could it be that her nature, so delicate, so exceptionally aristocratic and refined, had in it depths of modesty, the modesty of a superior and sacred animality, that were as yet unfathomed by modern perceptions?

Mariolle gradually came to understand this; he saw her factitious ardor growing less and less. He divined the nature of her love-inspired attempt, and a mortal, inconsolable sorrow took possession of his soul.

She knew now, as he knew, that the attempt had been made and that all hope was gone. The proof of this was that this very day, wrapped as she was in her warm furs and with her feet on her hot-water bottle, glowing with a feeling of physical comfort as she watched the hail beating against the windows of her coupé, she could not find in her the courage to leave this luxurious warmth to get into an ice-cold cab to go and meet the poor fellow.

The idea of breaking with him, of avoiding his caresses, certainly never occurred to her for a moment. She was well aware that to completely captivate a man who is in love and keep him as one's own peculiar private property in the midst of feminine rivalries, a woman must surrender herself to him body and soul. That she knew, for it is logical, fated, indisputable. It is even the loyal course to pursue, and she wanted to be loyal to him in all the uprightness of her nature as his mistress. She would go to him then, she would go to him always; but why so often? Would not their interviews even assume a greater charm for him, an attraction of novelty, if they were granted more charily, like rare and inestimable gifts presented to him by her and not to be used too prodigally?

Whenever she had gone to Auteuil she had had the impression that she was bearing to him a priceless gift, the most precious of offerings. In giving in this way, the pleasure of giving is inseparable from a certain sensation of sacrifice; it is the pride that one feels in being generous, the satisfaction of conferring happiness, not the transports of a mutual passion.

She even calculated that André's love would be more likely to be enduring if she abated somewhat of her familiarity with him, for hunger always increases by fasting, and desire is but an appetite. Immediately that this resolution was formed she made up her mind that she would go to Auteuil that day, but would feign indisposition. The journey, which a minute ago had seemed to her so difficult through the inclement weather, now appeared to her quite easy, and she understood, with a smile at her own expense and at this sudden revelation, why she made such a difficulty about a thing that was quite natural. But a moment ago she would not, now she would. The reason why she would not a moment ago was that she was anticipating the thousand petty disagreeable details of the rendezvous! She would prick her fingers with pins that she handled very awkwardly, she would be unable to find the articles that she had thrown at random upon the bedroom floor as she disrobed in haste, already looking forward to the hateful task of having to dress without an attendant.

She paused at this reflection, dwelling upon it and weighing it carefully for the first time. After all, was it not rather repugnant, rather vulgarizing, this idea of a rendezvous for a stated time, settled upon a day or two days in advance, just like a business appointment or a consultation with your doctor? There is nothing more natural, after a long and charming tête-à-tête, than that the lips which have been uttering warm, seductive words should meet in a passionate kiss; but how different that was from the premeditated kiss that she went there to receive, watch in hand, once a week. There was so much truth in this that on those days when she was not to see André she had frequently felt a vague desire of being with him, while this desire was scarcely perceptible at all when she had to go to him in foul cabs, through squalid streets, with the cunning of a hunted thief, all her feelings toward him quenched and deadened by these considerations.

Ah! that appointment at Auteuil! She had calculated the time on all the clocks of all her friends; she had watched the minutes that brought her nearer to it slip away at Mme. de Frémines's, at Mme. de Bratiane's, at pretty Mme. le Prieur's, on those afternoons when she killed time by roaming about Paris so as not to remain in her own house, where she might be detained by an inopportune visit or some other unforeseen obstacle.

She suddenly said to herself: "I will make to-day a day of rest; I will go there very late." Then she opened a little cupboard in the front of the carriage, concealed among the folds of black silk that lined the coupé, which was fitted up as luxuriously as a pretty woman's boudoir. The first thing that presented itself when she had thrown open the doors of this secret receptacle was a mirror playing on hinges that she moved so that it was on a level with her face. Behind the mirror, in their satin-lined niches, were various small objects in silver: a box for her rice-powder, a pencil for her lips, two crystal scent-bottles, an inkstand and penholder, scissors, a pretty paper-cutter to tear the leaves of the last novel with which she amused herself as she rolled along the streets. The exquisite clock, of the size and shape of a walnut, told her that it was four o'clock. Mme. de Burne reflected: "I have an hour yet, at all events," and she touched a spring that had the effect of making the footman who was seated beside the coachman stoop and take up the speaking-tube to receive her order. She pulled out the other end from where it was concealed in the lining of the carriage, and applying her lips to the mouthpiece of rock-crystal: "To the Austrian embassy!" she said.

Then she inspected herself in the mirror. The look that she gave herself expressed, as it always did, the delight that one feels in looking upon one's best beloved; then she threw back her furs to judge of the effect of her corsage. It was a toilette adapted to the chill days of the end of winter. The neck was trimmed with a bordering of very fine white down that shaded off into a delicate gray as it fell over the shoulders, like the wing of a bird. Upon her hat—it was a kind of toque—there towered an aigret of more brightly colored feathers, and the general effect that her costume inspired was to make one think that she had got herself up in this manner in preparation for a flight through the hail and the gray sky in company with Mother Carey's chickens.

She was still complacently contemplating herself when the carriage suddenly wheeled into the great court of the embassy.

Thereupon she arranged her wrap, lowered the mirror to its place, closed the doors of the little cupboard, and when the coupé had come to a halt said to her coachman: "You may go home; I shall not need you any more." Then she asked the footman who came forward from the entrance of the hotel: "Is the Princess at home?"

"Yes, Madame."

She entered and ascended the stairs and came to a small drawing-room where the Princess de Malten was writing letters.

The ambassadress arose with an appearance of much satisfaction when she perceived her friend, and they kissed each other twice in succession upon the cheek, close to the corner of the lips. Then they seated themselves side by side upon two low chairs in front of the fire. They were very fond of each other, took great delight in each other's society and understood each other thoroughly, for they were almost counterparts in nature and disposition, belonging to the same race of femininity, brought up in the same atmosphere and endowed with the same sensations, although Mme. de Malten was a Swede and had married an Austrian. They had a strange and mysterious attraction for each other, from which resulted a profound feeling of unmixed well-being and contentment whenever they were together. Their babble would run on for half a day on end, without once stopping, trivial, futile talk, interesting to them both by reason of their similarity of tastes.

"You see how I love you!" said Mme. de Burne. "You are to dine with me this evening, and still I could not help coming to see you. It is a real passion, my dear."

"A passion that I share," the Swede replied with a smile.

Following the habit of their profession, they put each her best foot foremost for the benefit of the other; coquettish as if they had been dealing with a man, but with a different style of coquetry, for the strife was different, and they had not before them the adversary, but the rival.

Madame de Burne had kept looking at the clock during the conversation. It was on the point of striking five. He had been waiting there an hour. "That is long enough," she said to herself as she arose.

"So soon?" said the Princess.

"Yes," the other unblushingly replied. "I am in a hurry; there is some one waiting for me. I would a great deal rather stay here with you."

They exchanged kisses again, and Mme. de Burne, having requested the footman to call a cab for her, drove away.

The horse was lame and dragged the cab after him wearily, and the animal's halting and fatigue seemed to have infected the young woman. Like the broken-winded beast, she found the journey long and difficult. At one moment she was comforted by the pleasure of seeing André, at the next she was in despair at the thought of the discomforts of the interview.

She found him waiting for her behind the gate, shivering. The biting blasts roared through the branches of the trees, the hailstones rattled on their umbrella as they made their way to the house, their feet sank deep into the mud. The garden was dead, dismal, miry, melancholy, and André was very pale. He was enduring terrible suffering.

When they were in the house: "Gracious, how cold it is!" she exclaimed.

And yet a great fire was blazing in each of the two rooms, but they had not been lighted until past noon and had not had time to dry the damp walls, and shivers ran through her frame. "I think that I will not take off my furs just yet," she added. She only unbuttoned her outer garment and threw it open, disclosing her warm costume and her plume-decked corsage, like a bird of passage that never remains long in one place.

He seated himself beside her.

"There is to be a delightful dinner at my house to-night," she said, "and I am enjoying it in anticipation."

"Who are to be there?"

"Why, you, in the first place; then Prédolé, whom I have so long wanted to know."

"Ah! Prédolé is to be there?"

"Yes; Lamarthe is to bring him."

"But Prédolé is not the kind of a man to suit you, not a bit! Sculptors in general are not so constituted as to please pretty women, and Prédolé less so than any of them."

"Oh, my friend, that cannot be. I have such an admiration for him!"

The sculptor Prédolé had gained a great success and had captivated all Paris some two months before by his exhibition at the Varin gallery. Even before that he had been highly appreciated; people had said of him, "His figurines are delicious"; but when the world of artists and connoisseurs had assembled to pass judgment upon his collected works in the rooms of the Rue Varin, the outburst of enthusiasm had been explosive. They seemed to afford the revelation of such an unlooked-for charm, they displayed such a peculiar gift in the translation of elegance and grace, that it seemed as if a new manner of expressing the beauty of form had been born to the world. His specialty was statuettes in extremely abbreviated costumes, in which his genius displayed an unimaginable delicacy of form and airy lightness. His dancing girls, especially, of which he had made many studies, displayed in the highest perfection, in their pose and the harmony of their attitude and motion, the ideal of female beauty and suppleness.

For a month past Mme. de Burne had been unceasing in her efforts to attract him to her house, but the artist was unsociable, even something of a bear, so the report ran. At last she had succeeded, thanks to the intervention of Lamarthe, who had made a touching, almost frantic appeal to the grateful sculptor.

"Whom have you besides?" Mariolle inquired.

"The Princess de Malten."

He was displeased; he did not fancy that woman. "Who else?"

"Massival, Bernhaus, and George de Maltry. That is all: only my select circle. You are acquainted with Prédolé, are you not?"

"Yes, slightly."

"How do you like him?"

"He is delightful; I never met a man so enamored of his art and so interesting when he holds forth on it."

She was delighted and again said: "It will be charming."

He had taken her hand under her fur cloak; he gave it a little squeeze, then kissed it. Then all at once it came to her mind that she had forgotten to tell him that she was ill, and casting about on the spur of the moment for another reason, she murmured: "Gracious! how cold it is!"

"Do you think so?"

"I am chilled to my very marrow."

He arose to take a look at the thermometer, which was, in fact, pretty low; then he resumed his seat at her side.

She had said: "Gracious! how cold it is!" and he believed that he understood her. For three weeks, now, at every one of their interviews, he had noticed that her attempt to feign tenderness was gradually becoming fainter and fainter. He saw that she was weary of wearing this mask, so weary that she could continue it no longer, and he himself was so exasperated by the little power that he had over her, so stung by his vain and unreasoning desire of this woman, that he was beginning to say to himself in his despairing moments of solitude: "It will be better to break with her than to continue to live like this."

He asked her, by way of fathoming her intentions: "Won't you take off your cloak now?"

"Oh, no," she said; "I have been coughing all the morning; this fearful weather has given me a sore throat. I am afraid that I may be ill." She was silent a moment, then added: "If I had not wanted to see you very much indeed I would not have come to-day." As he did not reply, in his grief and anger, she went on: "This return of cold weather is very dangerous, coming as it does after the fine days of the past two weeks."

She looked out into the garden, where the trees were already almost green despite the clouds of snow that were driving among their branches. He looked at her and thought: "So that is the kind of love that she feels for me!" and for the first time he began to feel a sort of jealous hatred of her, of her face, of her elusive affection, of her form, so long pursued, so subtle to escape him. "She pretends that she is cold," he said to himself. "She is cold only because I am here. If it were a question of some party of pleasure, some of those idiotic caprices that go to make up the useless existence of these frivolous creatures, she would brave everything and risk her life. Does she not ride about in an open carriage on the coldest days to show her fine clothes? Ah! that is the way with them all nowadays!"

He looked at her as she sat there facing him so calmly, and he knew that in that head, that dear little head that he adored so, there was one wish paramount, the wish that their tête-à-tête might not be protracted; it was becoming painful to her.

Was it true that there had ever existed, that there existed now, women capable of passion, of emotion, who weep, suffer, and bestow themselves in a transport, loving with heart and soul and body, with mouth that speaks and eyes that gaze, with heart that beats and hand that caresses; women ready to brave all for the sake of their love, and to go, by day or by night, regardless of menaces and watchful eyes, fearlessly, tremorously, to him who stands with open arms waiting to receive them, mad, ready to sink with their happiness?

Oh, that horrible love that which now held him in its fetters!—love without issue, without end, joyless and triumphless, eating away his strength and devouring him with its anxieties; love in which there was no charm and no delight, cause to him only of suffering, sorrow, and bitter tears, where he was constantly pursued by the intolerable regret of the impossibility of awaking responsive kisses upon lips that are as cold and dry and sterile as dead trees!

He looked at her as she sat there, so charming in her feathery dress. Were not her dresses the great enemy that he had to contend against, more than the woman herself, jealous guardians, coquettish and costly barriers, that kept him from his mistress?

"Your toilette is charming," he said, not caring to speak of the subject that was torturing him so cruelly.

She replied with a smile: "You must see the one that I shall wear to-night." Then she coughed several times in succession and said: "I am really taking cold. Let me go, my friend. The sun will show himself again shortly, and I will follow his example."

He made no effort to detain her, for he was discouraged, seeing that nothing could now avail to overcome the inertia of this sluggish nature, that his romance was ended, ended forever, and that it was useless to hope for ardent words from those tranquil lips, or a kindling glance from those calm eyes. All at once he felt rising with gathering strength within him the stern determination to end this torturing subserviency. She had nailed him upon a cross; he was bleeding from every limb, and she watched his agony without feeling for his suffering, even rejoicing that she had had it in her power to effect so much. But he would tear himself from his deathly gibbet, leaving there bits of his body, strips of his flesh, and all his mangled heart. He would flee like a wild animal that the hunters have wounded almost unto death, he would go and hide himself in some lonely place where his wounds might heal and where he might feel only those dull pangs that remain with the mutilated until they are released by death.

"Farewell, then," he said.

She was struck by the sadness of his voice and rejoined: "Until this evening, my friend."

"Until this evening," he re-echoed. "Farewell."

He saw her to the garden gate, and came back and seated himself, alone, before the fire.

Alone! How cold it was; how cold, indeed! How sad he was, how lonely! It was all ended! Ah, what a horrible thought! There was an end of hoping and waiting for her, dreaming of her, with that fierce blazing of the heart that at times brings out our existence upon this somber earth with the vividness of fireworks displayed against the blackness of the night. Farewell those nights of solitary emotion when, almost until the dawn, he paced his chamber thinking of her; farewell those wakings when, upon opening his eyes, he said to himself: "Soon I shall see her at our little house."

How he loved her! how he loved her! What a long, hard task it would be to him to forget her! She had left him because it was cold! He saw her before him as but now, looking at him and bewitching him, bewitching him the better to break his heart. Ah, how well she had done her work! With one single stroke, the first and last, she had cleft it asunder. He felt the old gaping wound begin to open, the wound that she had dressed and now had made incurable by plunging into it the knife of death-dealing indifference. He even felt that from this broken heart there was something distilling itself through his frame, mounting to his throat and choking him; then, covering his eyes with his hands, as if to conceal this weakness even from himself, he wept.

She had left him because it was cold! He would have walked naked through the driving snow to meet her, no matter where; he would have cast himself from the house top, only to fall at her feet. An old tale came to his mind, that has been made into a legend: that of the Côte des Deux Amans, a spot which the traveler may behold as he journeys toward Rouen. A maiden, obedient to her father's cruel caprice, which prohibited her from marrying the man of her choice unless she accomplished the task of carrying him, unassisted, to the summit of the steep mountain, succeeded in dragging him up there on her hands and knees, and died as she reached the top. Love, then, is but a legend, made to be sung in verse or told in lying romances!

Had not his mistress herself, in one of their earliest interviews, made use of an expression that he had never forgotten: "Men nowadays do not love women so as really to harm themselves by it. You may believe me, for I know them both." She had been wrong in his case, but not in her own, for on another occasion she had said: "In any event, I give you fair warning that I am incapable of being really smitten with anyone, be he who he may."

Be he who he may? Was that quite a sure thing? Of him, no; of that he was quite well assured now, but of another?

Of him? She could not love him. Why not?

Then the feeling that his life had been a wasted one, which had haunted him for a long time past, fell upon him as if it would crush him. He had done nothing, obtained nothing, conquered nothing, succeeded in nothing. When he had felt an attraction toward the arts he had not found in himself the courage that is required to devote one's self exclusively to one of them, nor the persistent determination that they demand as the price of success. There had been no triumph to cheer him; no elevated taste for some noble career to ennoble and aggrandize his mind. The only strenuous effort that he had ever put forth, the attempt to conquer a woman's heart, had proved ineffectual like all the rest. Take him all in all, he was only a miserable failure.

He was weeping still beneath his hands which he held pressed to his eyes. The tears, trickling down his cheeks, wet his mustache and left a salty taste upon his lips, and their bitterness increased his wretchedness and his despair.

When he raised his head at last he saw that it was night. He had only just sufficient time to go home and dress for her dinner.

CHAPTER X.

FLIGHT

André Mariolle was the first to arrive at Mme. de Burne's. He took a seat and gazed about him upon the walls, the furniture, the hangings, at all the small objects and trinkets that were so dear to him from their association with her—at the familiar apartment where he had first known her, where he had come to her so many times since then, and where he had discovered in himself the germs of that ill-starred passion that had kept on growing, day by day, until the hour of his barren victory. With what eagerness had he many a time awaited her coming in this charming spot which seemed to have been made for no one but her, an exquisite setting for an exquisite creature! How well he knew the pervading odor of this salon and its hangings; a subdued odor of iris, so simple and aristocratic. He grasped the arms of the great armchair, from which he had so often watched her smile and listened to her talk, as if they had been the hands of some friend that he was parting with forever. It would have pleased him if she could not come, if no one could come, and if he could remain there alone, all night, dreaming of his love, as people watch beside a dead man. Then at daylight he could go away for a long time, perhaps forever.

The door opened, and she appeared and came forward to him with outstretched hand. He was master of himself, and showed nothing of his agitation. She was not a woman, but a living bouquet—an indescribable bouquet of flowers.

A girdle of pinks enclasped her waist and fell about her in cascades, reaching to her feet. About her bare arms and shoulders ran a garland of mingled myosotis and lilies-of-the-valley, while three fairy-like orchids seemed to be growing from her breast and caressing the milk-white flesh with the rosy and red flesh of their supernal blooms. Her blond hair was studded with violets in enamel, in which minute diamonds glistened, and other diamonds, trembling upon golden pins, sparkled like dewdrops among the odorous trimming of her corsage.

"I shall have a headache," she said, "but I don't care; my dress is becoming."

Delicious odors emanated from her, like spring among the gardens. She was more fresh than the garlands that she wore. André was dazzled as he looked at her, reflecting that it would be no less brutal and barbarous to take her in his arms at that moment than it would be to trample upon a blossoming flower-bed. So their bodies were no longer objects to inspire love; they were objects to be adorned, simply frames on which to hang fine clothes. They were like birds, they were like flowers, they were like a thousand other things as much as they were like women. Their mothers, all women of past and gone generations, had used coquettish arts to enhance their natural beauties, but it had been their aim to please in the first place by their direct physical seductiveness, by the charm of native grace, by the irresistible attraction that the female form exercises over the heart of the males. At the present day coquetry was everything. Artifice was now the great means, and not only the means, but the end as well, for they employed it even more frequently to dazzle the eyes of rivals and excite barren jealousy than to subjugate men.

What end, then, was this toilette designed to serve, the gratification of the eyes of him, the lover, or the humiliation of the Princess de Malten?

The door opened, and the lady whose name was in his thoughts was announced.

Mme. de Burne moved quickly forward to meet her and gave her a kiss, not unmindful of the orchids during the operation, her lips slightly parted, with a little grimace of tenderness. It was a pretty kiss, an extremely desirable kiss, given and returned from the heart by those two pairs of lips.

Mariolle gave a start of pain. Never once had she run to meet him with that joyful eagerness, never had she kissed him like that, and with a sudden change of ideas he said to himself: "Women are no longer made to fulfill our requirements."

Massival made his appearance, then M. de Pradon and the Comte de Bernhaus, then George de Maltry, resplendent with English "chic."

Lamarthe and Prédolé were now the only ones missing. The sculptor's name was mentioned, and every voice was at once raised in praise of him. "He had restored to life the grace of form, he had recovered the lost traditions of the Renaissance, with something additional: the sincerity of modern art!" M. de Maltry maintained that he was the exquisite revealer of the suppleness of the human form. Such phrases as these had been current in the salons for the last two months, where they had been bandied about from mouth to mouth.

At last the great man appeared. Everyone was surprised. He was a large man of uncertain age, with the shoulders of a coal-heaver, a powerful face with strongly-marked features, surrounded by hair and beard that were beginning to turn white, a prominent nose, thick full lips, wearing a timid and embarrassed air. He held his arms away from his body in an awkward sort of way that was doubtless to be attributed to the immense hands that protruded from his sleeves. They were broad and thick, with hairy and muscular fingers; the hands of a Hercules or a butcher, and they seemed to be conscious of being in the way, embarrassed at finding themselves there and looking vainly for some convenient place to hide themselves. Upon looking more closely at his face, however, it was seen to be illuminated by clear, piercing, gray eyes of extreme expressiveness, and these alone served to impart some degree of life to the man's heavy and torpid expression. They were constantly searching, inquiring, scrutinizing, darting their rapid, shifting glances here, there, and everywhere, and it was plainly to be seen that these eager, inquisitive looks were the animating principle of a deep and comprehensive intellect.

Mme. de Burne was somewhat disappointed; she politely led the artist to a chair which he took and where he remained seated, apparently disconcerted by this introduction to a strange house.

Lamarthe, master of the situation, approached his friend with the intention of breaking the ice and relieving him from the awkwardness of his position. "My dear fellow," he said, "let me make for you a little map to let you know where you are. You have seen our divine hostess; now look at her surroundings." He showed him upon the mantelpiece a bust, authenticated in due form, by Houdon, then upon a cabinet in buhl a group representing two women dancing, with arms about each other's waists, by Clodion, and finally four Tanagra statuettes upon an étagère, selected for their perfection of finish and detail.

Then all at once Prédolé's face brightened as if he had found his children in the desert. He arose and went to the four little earthen figures, and when Mme. de Burne saw him grasp two of them at once in his great hands that seemed made to slaughter oxen, she trembled for her treasures. When he laid hands on them, however, it appeared that it was only for the purpose of caressing them, for he handled them with wonderful delicacy and dexterity, turning them about in his thick fingers which somehow seemed all at once to have become as supple as a juggler's. It was evident by the gentle way the big man had of looking at and handling them that he had in his soul and his very finger-ends an ideal and delicate tenderness for such small elegancies.

"Are they not pretty?" Lamarthe asked him.

The sculptor went on to extol them as if they had been his own, and he spoke of some others, the most remarkable that he had met with, briefly and in a voice that was rather low but confident and calm, the expression of a clearly defined thought that was not ignorant of the value of words and their uses.

Still under the guidance of the author, he next inspected the other rare bric-à-brac that Mme. de Burne had collected, thanks to the counsels of her friends. He looked with astonishment and delight at the various articles, apparently agreeably disappointed to find them there, and in every case he took them up and turned them lightly over in his hands, as if to place himself in direct personal contact with them. There was a statuette of bronze, heavy as a cannon-ball, hidden away in a dark corner; he took it up with one hand, carried it to the lamp, examined it at length, and replaced it where it belonged without visible effort. Lamarthe exclaimed: "The great, strong fellow! he is built expressly to wrestle with stone and marble!" while the ladies looked at him approvingly.

Dinner was now announced. The mistress of the house took the sculptor's arm to pass to the dining-room, and when she had seated him in the place of honor at her right hand, she asked him out of courtesy, just as she would have questioned a scion of some great family as to the exact origin of his name: "Your art, Monsieur, has also the additional honor, has it not, of being the most ancient of all?"

He replied in his calm deep voice: "Mon Dieu, Madame, the shepherds in the Bible play upon the flute, therefore music would seem to be the more ancient—although true music, as we understand it, does not go very far back, while true sculpture dates from remote antiquity."

"You are fond of music?"

"I love all the arts," he replied with grave earnestness.

"Is it known who was the inventor of your art?"

He reflected a moment, then replied in tender accents, as if he had been relating some touching tale: "According to Grecian tradition it was Dædalus the Athenian. The most attractive legend, however, is that which attributes the invention to a Sicyonian potter named Dibutades. His daughter Kora having traced her betrothed's profile with the assistance of an arrow, her father filled in the rude sketch with clay and modeled it. It was then that my art was born."

"Charming!" murmured Lamarthe. Then turning to Mme. de Burne, he said: "You cannot imagine, Madame, how interesting this man becomes when he talks of what he loves; what power he has to express and explain it and make people adore it."

But the sculptor did not seem disposed either to pose for the admiration of the guests or to perorate. He had tucked a corner of his napkin between his shirt-collar and his neck and was reverentially eating his soup, with that appearance of respect that peasants manifest for that portion of the meal. Then he drank a glass of wine and drew himself up with an air of greater ease, of making himself more at home. Now and then he made a movement as if to turn around, for he had perceived the reflection in a mirror of a modern group that stood on the mantelshelf behind him. He did not recognize it and was seeking to divine the author. At last, unable longer to resist the impulse, he asked: "It is by Falguière, is it not?"

Mme. de Burne laughed. "Yes, it is by Falguière. How could you tell, in a glass?"

He smiled in turn. "Ah, Madame, I can't explain how it is done, but I can tell at a glance the sculpture of those men who are painters as well, and the painting of those who also practice sculpture. It is not a bit like the work of a man who devotes himself to one art exclusively."

Lamarthe, wishing to show off his friend, called for explanations, and Prédolé proceeded to give them. In his slow, precise manner of speech he defined and illustrated the painting of sculptors and the sculpture of painters in such a clear and original way that he was listened to as much with eyes as with ears. Commencing his demonstration at the earliest period and pursuing it through the history of art and gathering examples from epoch to epoch, he came down to the time of the early Italian masters who were painters and sculptors at the same time, Nicolas and John of Pisa, Donatello, Lorenzo Ghiberti. He spoke of Diderot's interesting remarks upon the same subject, and in conclusion mentioned Ghiberti's bronze gates of the baptistry of Saint John at Florence, such living and dramatically forceful bas-reliefs that they seem more like paintings upon canvas. He waved his great hands before him as if he were modeling, with such ease and grace of motion as to delight every eye, calling up above the plates and glasses the pictures that his tongue told of, and reconstructing the work that he mentioned with such conviction that everyone followed the motions of his fingers with breathless attention. Then some dishes that he fancied were placed before him and he ceased talking and began eating.

He scarcely spoke during the remainder of the dinner, not troubling himself to follow the conversation, which ranged from some bit of theatrical gossip to a political rumor; from a ball to a wedding; from an article in the "Revue des Deux Mondes" to the horse-show that had just opened. His appetite was good, and he drank a good deal, without being at all affected by it, having a sound, hard head that good wine could not easily upset.

When they had returned to the drawing-room, Lamarthe, who had not drawn the sculptor out to the extent that he wished to do, drew him over to a glass case to show him a priceless object, a classic, historic gem: a silver inkstand carved by Benvenuto Cellini. The men listened with extreme interest to his long and eloquent rhapsody as they stood grouped about him, while the two women, seated in front of the fire and rather disgusted to see so much enthusiasm wasted upon the form of inanimate objects, appeared to be a little bored and chatted together in a low voice from time to time. After that conversation became general, but not animated, for it had been somewhat damped by the ideas that had passed into the atmosphere of this pretty room, with its furnishing of precious objects.

Prédolé left early, assigning as a reason that he had to be at work at daybreak every morning. When he was gone Lamarthe enthusiastically asked Mme. de Burne: "Well, how did you like him?"

She replied, hesitatingly and with something of an air of ill nature: "He is quite interesting, but prosy."

The novelist smiled and said to himself: "Parbleu, that is because he did not admire your toilette; and you are the only one of all your pretty things that he hardly condescended to look at." He exchanged a few pleasant remarks with her and went over and took a seat by Mme. de Malten, to whom he began to be very attentive. The Comte de Bernhaus approached the mistress of the house, and taking a small footstool, appeared sunk in devotion at her feet. Mariolle, Massival, Maltry, and M. de Pradon continued to talk of the sculptor, who had made a deep impression on their minds. M. de Maltry was comparing him to the old masters, for whom life was embellished and illuminated by an exclusive and consuming love of the manifestations of beauty, and he philosophized upon his theme with many very subtle and very tiresome observations.

Massival, quickly tiring of a conversation which made no reference to his own art, crossed the room to Mme. de Malten and seated himself beside Lamarthe, who soon yielded his place to him and went and rejoined the men.

"Shall we go?" he said to Mariolle.

"Yes, by all means!"

The novelist liked to walk the streets at night with some friend and talk, when the incisive, peremptory tones of his voice seemed to lay hold of the walls of the houses and climb up them. He had an impression that he was very eloquent, witty, and sagacious during these nocturnal tête-à-têtes, which were monologues rather than conversations so far as his part in them was concerned. The approbation that he thus gained for himself sufficed his needs, and the gentle fatigue of legs and lungs assured him a good night's rest.

Mariolle, for his part, had reached the limit of his endurance. The moment that he was outside her door all his wretchedness and sorrow, all his irremediable disappointment, boiled up and overflowed his heart. He could stand it no longer; he would have no more of it. He would go away and never return.

The two men found themselves alone with each other in the street. The wind had changed and the cold that had prevailed during the day had yielded; it was warm and pleasant, as it almost always is two hours after a snowstorm in spring. The sky was vibrating with the light of innumerable stars, as if a breath of summer in the immensity of space had lighted up the heavenly bodies and set them twinkling. The sidewalks were gray and dry again, while in the roadway pools of water reflected the light of the gas-lamps.

Lamarthe said: "What a fortunate man he is, that Prédolé! He lives only for one thing, his art; thinks but of that, loves but that; it occupies all his being; consoles and cheers him, and affords him a life of happiness and comfort. He is really a great artist of the old stock. Ah! he doesn't let women trouble his head, not much, our women of to-day with their frills and furbelows and fantastic disguises! Did you remark how little attention he paid to our two pretty dames? And yet they were rather seductive. But what he is looking for is the plastic—the plastic pure and simple; he has no use for the artificial. It is true that our divine hostess put him down in her books as an insupportable fool. In her estimation a bust by Houdon, Tanagra statuettes, and an inkstand by Cellini are but so many unconsidered trifles that go to the adornment and the rich and natural setting of a masterpiece, which is Herself; she and her dress, for dress is part and parcel of Herself; it is the fresh accentuation that she places on her beauty day by day. What a trivial, personal thing is woman!"

He stopped and gave the sidewalk a great thump with his cane, so that the noise resounded through the quiet street, then he went on.

"They have a very clear and exact perception of what adds to their attractions: the toilette and the ornaments in which there is an entire change of fashion every ten years; but they are heedless of that attribute which involves rare and constant power of selection, which demands from them keen and delicate artistic penetration and a purely æsthetic exercise of their senses. Their senses, moreover, are extremely rudimentary, incapable of high development, inaccessible to whatever does not touch directly the feminine egotism that absorbs everything in them. Their acuteness is the stratagem of the savage, of the red Indian; of war and ambush. They are even almost incapable of enjoying the material pleasures of the lower order, which require a physical education and the intelligent exercise of an organ, such as good living. When, as they do in exceptional cases, they come to have some respect for decent cookery, they still remain incapable of appreciating our great wines, which speak to masculine palates only, for wine does speak."

He again thumped the pavement with his cane, accenting his last dictum and punctuating the sentence, and continued.

"It won't do, however, to expect too much from them, but this want of taste and appreciation that so frequently clouds their intellectual vision when higher considerations are at stake often serves to blind them still more when our interests are in question. A man may have heart, feeling, intelligence, exceptional merits, and qualities of all kinds, they will all be unavailing to secure their favor as in bygone days when a man was valued for his worth and his courage. The women of to-day are actresses, second-rate actresses at that, who are merely playing for effect a part that has been handed down to them and in which they have no belief. They have to have actors of the same stamp to act up to them and lie through the rôle just as they do; and these actors are the coxcombs that we see hanging around them; from the fashionable world, or elsewhere."

They walked along in silence for a few moments, side by side. Mariolle had listened attentively to the words of his companion, repeating them in his mind and approving of his sentiments under the influence of his sorrow. He was aware also that a sort of Italian adventurer who was then in Paris giving lessons in swordsmanship, Prince Epilati by name, a gentleman of the fencing-schools, of considerable celebrity for his elegance and graceful vigor that he was in the habit of exhibiting in black-silk tights before the upper ten and the select few of the demimonde, was just then in full enjoyment of the attentions and coquetries of the pretty little Baronne de Frémines.

As Lamarthe said nothing further, he remarked to him:

"It is all our own fault; we make our selections badly; there are other women besides those."

The novelist replied: "The only ones now that are capable of real attachment are the shopgirls and some sentimental little bourgeoises, poor and unhappily married. I have before now carried consolation to one of those distressed souls. They are overflowing with sentiment, but such cheap, vulgar sentiment that to exchange ours against it is like throwing your money to a beggar. Now I assert that in our young, wealthy society, where the women feel no needs and no desires, where all that they require is some mild distraction to enable them to kill time, and where the men regulate their pleasures as scrupulously as they regulate their daily labors, I assert that under such conditions the old natural attraction, charming and powerful as it was, that used to bring the sexes toward each other, has disappeared."

"You are right," Mariolle murmured.

He felt an increasing desire to fly, to put a great distance between himself and these people, these puppets who in their empty idleness mimicked the beautiful, impassioned, and tender life of other days and were incapable of savoring its lost delights.

"Good night," he said; "I am going to bed." He went home and seated himself at his table and wrote:

"Farewell, Madame. Do you remember my first letter? In it too I said farewell, but I did not go. What a mistake that was! When you receive this I shall have left Paris; need I tell you why? Men like me ought never to meet with women like you. Were I an artist and were my emotions capable of expression in such manner as to afford me consolation, you would have perhaps inspired me with talent, but I am only a poor fellow who was so unfortunate as to be seized with love for you, and with it its accompanying bitter, unendurable sorrow.

"When I met you for the first time I could not have deemed myself capable of feeling and suffering as I have done. Another in your place would have filled my heart with divine joy in bidding it wake and live, but you could do nothing but torture it. It was not your fault, I know; I reproach you with nothing and I bear you no hard feeling; I have not even the right to send you these lines. Pardon me. You are so constituted that you cannot feel as I feel; you cannot even divine what passes in my breast when I am with you, when you speak to me and I look on you.

"Yes, I know; you have accepted me and offered me a rational and tranquil happiness, for which I ought to thank you on my knees all my life long, but I will not have it. Ah, what a horrible, agonizing love is that which is constantly craving a tender word, a warm caress, without ever receiving them! My heart is empty, empty as the stomach of a beggar who has long followed your carriage with outstretched hand and to whom you have thrown out pretty toys, but no bread. It was bread, it was love, that I hungered for. I am about to go away wretched and in need, in sore need of your love, a few crumbs of which would have saved me. I have nothing left in the world but a cruel memory that clings and will not leave me, and that I must try to kill.

"Adieu, Madame. Thanks, and pardon me. I love you still, this evening, with all the strength of my soul. Adieu.

CHAPTER XI.

LONELINESS

The city lay basking in the brightness of a sunny morning. Mariolle climbed into the carriage that stood waiting at his door with a traveling bag and two trunks on top. He had made his valet the night before pack the linen and other necessaries for a long absence, and now he was going away, leaving as his temporary address Fontainebleau post-office. He was taking no one with him, it being his wish to see no face that might remind him of Paris and to hear no voice that he had heard while brooding over certain matters.

He told the driver to go to the Lyons station and the cab started. Then he thought of that other trip of his, last spring, to Mont Saint-Michel; it was a year ago now lacking three months. He looked out into the street to drive the recollection from his mind.

The vehicle turned into the Avenue des Champs-Élysées, which was flooded with the light of the sun of early spring. The green leaves, summoned forth by the grateful warmth that had prevailed for a couple of weeks and not materially retarded by the cold storm of the last two days, were opening so rapidly on this bright morning that they seemed to impregnate the air with an odor of fresh verdure and of sap evaporating on the way to its work of building up new growths. It was one of those growing mornings when one feels that the dome-topped chestnut-trees in the public gardens and all along the avenues will burst into bloom in a single day through the length and breadth of Paris, like chandeliers that are lighted simultaneously. The earth was thrilling with the movement preparatory to the full life of summer, and the very street was silently stirred beneath its paving of bitumen as the roots ate their way through the soil. He said to himself as he jolted along in his cab: "At last I shall be able to enjoy a little peace of mind. I will witness the birth of spring in solitude deep in the forest."

The journey seemed long to him. The few hours of sleeplessness that he had spent in bemoaning his fate had broken him down as if he had passed ten nights at the bedside of a dying man. When he reached the village of Fontainebleau he went to a notary to see if there was a small house to be had furnished in the neighborhood of the forest. He was told of several. In looking over the photographs the one that pleased him most was a cottage that had just been given up by a young couple, man and wife, who had resided for almost the entire winter in the village of Montigny-sur-Loing. The notary smiled, notwithstanding that he was a man of serious aspect; he probably scented a love story.

"You are alone, Monsieur!" he inquired.

"I am alone."

"No servants, even?"

"No servants, even; I left them at Paris. I wish to engage some of the residents here. I am coming here to work in complete seclusion."

"You will have no difficulty in finding that, at this season of the year."

A few minutes afterward an open landau was whirling Mariolle and his trunks away to Montigny.

The forest was beginning to awake. The copses at the foot of the great trees, whose heads were covered with a light veil of foliage, were beginning to assume a denser aspect. The early birches, with their silvery trunks, were the only trees that seemed completely attired for the summer, while the great oaks only displayed small tremulous splashes of green at the ends of their branches and the beeches, more quick to open their pointed buds, were just shedding the dead leaves of the past year.

The grass by the roadside, unobscured as yet by the thick shade of the tree-tops, was growing lush and bright with the influx of new sap, and the odor of new growth that Mariolle had already remarked in the Avenue des Champs-Élysées, now wrapped him about and immersed him in a great bath of green life budding in the sunshine of the early season. He inhaled it greedily, like one just liberated from prison, and with the sensation of a man whose fetters have just been broken he luxuriously extended his arms along the two sides of the landau and let his hands hang down over the two wheels.

He passed through Marlotte, where the driver called his attention to the Hotel Corot, then just opened, of the original design of which there was much talk. Then the road continued, with the forest on the left hand and on the right a wide plain with trees here and there and hills bounding the horizon. To this succeeded a long village street, a blinding white street lying between two endless rows of little tile-roofed houses. Here and there an enormous lilac bush displayed its flowers over the top of a wall.

This street followed the course of a narrow valley along which ran a little stream. It was a narrow, rapid, twisting, nimble little stream, on one of its banks laving the foundations of the houses and the garden-walls and on the other bathing the meadows where the small trees were just beginning to put forth their scanty foliage. The sight of it inspired Mariolle with a sensation of delight.

He had no difficulty in finding his house and was greatly pleased with it. It was an old house that had been restored by a painter, who had tired of it after living there five years and offered it for rent. It was directly on the water, separated from the stream only by a pretty garden that ended in a terrace of lindens. The Loing, which just above this point had a picturesque fall of a foot or two over a dam erected there, ran rapidly by this terrace, whirling in great eddies. From the front windows of the house the meadows on the other bank were visible.

"I shall get well here," Mariolle thought.

Everything had been arranged with the notary in case the house should prove suitable. The driver carried back his acceptance of it. Then the housekeeping details had to be attended to, which did not take much time, the mayor's clerk having provided two women, one to do the cooking, the other to wash and attend to the chamber-work.

Downstairs there were a parlor, dining-room, kitchen, and two small rooms; on the floor above a handsome bedroom and a large apartment that the artist owner had fitted up as a studio. The furniture had all been selected with loving care, as people always furnish when they are enamored of a place, but now it had lost a little of its freshness and was in some disorder, with the air of desolation that is noticeable in dwellings that have been abandoned by their master. A pleasant odor of verbena, however, still lingered in the air, showing that the little house had not been long uninhabited. "Ah!" thought Mariolle, "verbena, that indicates simplicity of taste. The woman that preceded me could not have been one of those complex, mystifying natures. Happy man!"

It was getting toward evening, all these occupations having made the day pass rapidly. He took a seat by an open window, drinking in the agreeable coolness that exhaled from the surrounding vegetation and watching the setting sun as it cast long shadows across the meadows.

The two servants were talking while getting the dinner ready and the sound of their voices ascended to him faintly by the stairway, while through the window came the mingled sounds of the lowing of cows, the barking of dogs, and the cries of men bringing home the cattle or conversing with their companions on the other bank of the stream. Everything was peaceful and restful.

For the thousandth time since the morning Mariolle asked himself: "What did she think when she received my letter? What will she do?" Then he said to himself: "I wonder what she is doing now?" He looked at his watch; it was half past six. "She has come in from the street. She is receiving."

There rose before his mental vision a picture of the drawing-room, and the young woman chatting with the Princess de Malten, Mme. de Frémines, Massival, and the Comte de Bernhaus.

His soul was suddenly moved with an impulse that was something like anger. He wished that he was there. It was the hour of his accustomed visit to her, almost every day, and he felt within him a feeling of discomfort, not of regret. His will was firm, but a sort of physical suffering afflicted him akin to that of one who is denied his morphine at the accustomed time. He no longer beheld the meadows, nor the sun sinking behind the hills of the horizon; all that he could see was her, among her friends, given over to those cares of the world that had robbed him of her. "I will think of her no more," he said to himself.

He arose, went down to the garden and passed on to the terrace. There was a cool mist there rising from the water that had been agitated in its fall over the dam, and this sensation of chilliness, striking to a heart already sad, caused him to retrace his steps. His dinner was awaiting him in the dining-room. He ate it quickly; then, having nothing to occupy him, and feeling that distress of mind and body, of which he had had the presage, now increasing on him, he went to bed and closed his eyes in an attempt to slumber, but it was to no purpose. His thoughts refused to leave that woman; he beheld her in his thought and he suffered.

On whom would she bestow her favor now? On the Comte de Bernhaus, doubtless! He was just the man, elegant, conspicuous, sought after, to suit that creature of display. He had found favor with her, for had she not employed all her arts to conquer him even at a time when she was mistress to another man?

Notwithstanding that his mind was beset by these haunting thoughts, it would still keep wandering off into that misty condition of semi-somnolence in which the man and woman were constantly reappearing to his eyes. Of true sleep he got none, and all night long he saw them at his bedside, braving and mocking him, now retiring as if they would at last permit him to snatch a little sleep, then returning as soon as oblivion had begun to creep over him and awaking him with a spasm of jealous agony in his heart. He left his bed at earliest break of day and went away into the forest with a cane in his hand, a stout serviceable stick that the last occupant of the house had left behind him.

The rays of the newly risen sun were falling through the tops of the oaks, almost leafless as yet, upon the ground, which was carpeted in spots by patches of verdant grass, here by a carpet of dead leaves and there by heather reddened by the frosts of winter. Yellow butterflies were fluttering along the road like little dancing flames. To the right of the road was a hill, almost large enough to be called a mountain. Mariolle ascended it leisurely, and when he reached the top seated himself on a great stone, for he was quite out of breath. His legs were overcome with weakness and refused to support him; all his system seemed to be yielding to a sudden breaking down. He was well aware that this languor did not proceed from fatigue; it came from her, from the love that weighed him down like an intolerable burden, and he murmured: "What wretchedness! why does it possess me thus, me, a man who has always taken from existence only that which would enable him to enjoy it without suffering afterward?"

His attention was awakened by the fear of this malady that might prove so hard to cure, and he probed his feelings, went down to the very depths of his nature, endeavoring to know and understand it better, and make clear to his own eyes the reason of this inexplicable crisis. He said to himself: "I have never yielded to any undue attraction. I am not enthusiastic or passionate by nature; my judgment is more powerful than my instinct, my curiosity than my appetite, my fancy than my perseverance. I am essentially nothing more than a man that is delicate, intelligent, and hard to please in his enjoyments. I have loved the things of this life without ever allowing myself to become greatly attached to them, with the perceptions of an expert who sips and does not suffer himself to become surfeited, who knows better than to lose his head. I submit everything to the test of reason, and generally I analyze my likings too severely to submit to them blindly. That is even my great defect, the only cause of my weakness.

"And now that woman has taken possession of me, in spite of myself, in spite of my fears and of my knowledge of her, and she retains her hold as if she had plucked away one by one all the different aspirations that existed in me. That may be the case. Those aspirations of mine went out toward inanimate objects, toward nature, that entices and softens me, toward music, which is a sort of ideal caress, toward reflection, which is the delicate feasting of the mind, toward everything on earth that is beautiful and agreeable.

"Then I met a creature who collected and concentrated all my somewhat fickle and fluctuating likings, and directing them toward herself, converted them into love. Charming and beautiful, she pleased my eyes; bright, intelligent, and witty, she pleased my mind, and she pleased my heart by the mysterious charm of her contact and her presence and by the secret and irresistible emanation from her personality, until all these things enslaved me as the perfume of certain flowers intoxicates. She has taken the place of everything for me, for I no longer have any aspirations, I no longer wish or care for anything."

"In other days how my feelings would have thrilled and started in this forest that is putting forth its new life! To-day I see nothing of it, I am regardless of it; I am still at that woman's side, whom I desire to love no more.

"Come! I must kill these ideas by physical fatigue; unless I do I shall never get well."

He arose, descended the rocky hillside and resumed his walk with long strides, but still the haunting presence crushed him as if it had been a burden that he was bearing on his back. He went on, constantly increasing his speed, now and then encountering a brief sensation of comfort at the sight of the sunlight piercing through the foliage or at a breath of perfumed air from some grove of resinous pine-trees, which inspired in him a presentiment of distant consolation.

Suddenly he came to a halt. "I am not walking any longer," he said, "I am flying from something!" Indeed, he was flying, straight ahead, he cared not where, pursued by the agony of his love.

Then he started on again at a more reasonable speed. The appearance of the forest was undergoing a change. The growth was denser and the shadows deeper, for he was coming to the warmer portions of it, to the beautiful region of the beeches. No sensation of winter lingered there. It was wondrous spring, that seemed to have been the birth of a night, so young and fresh was everything.

Mariolle made his way among the thickets, beneath the gigantic trees that towered above him higher and higher still, and in this way he went on for a long time, an hour, two hours, pushing his way through the branches, through the countless multitudes of little shining leaves, bright with their varnish of new sap. The heavens were quite concealed by the immense dome of verdure, supported on its lofty columns, now perpendicular, now leaning, now of a whitish hue, now dark beneath the black moss that drew its nourishment from the bark.

Thus they towered, stretching away indefinitely in the distance, one behind the other, lording it over the bushy young copses that grew in confused tangles at their feet and wrapping them in dense shadow through which in places poured floods of vivid sunlight. The golden rain streamed down through all this luxuriant growth until the wood no longer remained a wood, but became a brilliant sea of verdure illumined by yellow rays. Mariolle stopped, seized with an ineffable surprise. Where was he? Was he in a forest, or had he descended to the bottom of a sea, a sea of leaves and light, an ocean of green resplendency?

He felt better—more tranquil; more remote, more hidden from his misery, and he threw himself down upon the red carpet of dead leaves that these trees do not cast until they are ready to put on their new garments. Rejoicing in the cool contact of the earth and the pure sweetness of the air, he was soon conscious of a wish, vague at first but soon becoming more defined, not to be alone in this charming spot, and he said to himself: "Ah! if she were only here, at my side!"

He suddenly remembered Mont Saint-Michel, and recollecting how different she had been down there to what she was in Paris, how her affection had blossomed out in the open air before the yellow sands, he thought that on that day she had surely loved him a little for a few hours. Yes, surely, on the road where they had watched the receding tide, in the cloisters where, murmuring his name: "André," she had seemed to say, "I am yours," and on the "Madman's Path," where he had almost borne her through space, she had felt an impulsion toward him that had never returned since she placed her foot, the foot of a coquette, on the pavement of Paris.

He continued to yield himself to his mournful reveries, still stretched at length upon his back, his look lost among the gold and green of the tree-tops, and little by little his eyes closed, weighed down with sleep and the tranquillity that reigned among the trees. When he awoke he saw that it was past two o'clock of the afternoon.

When he arose and proceeded on his way he felt less sad, less ailing. At length he emerged from the thickness of the wood and came to a great open space where six broad avenues converged and then stretched away and lost themselves in the leafy, transparent distance. A signboard told him that the name of the locality was "Le Bouquet-du-Roi." It was indeed the capital of this royal country of the beeches.

A carriage passed, and as it was empty and disengaged Mariolle took it and ordered the driver to take him to Marlotte, whence he could make his way to Montigny after getting something to eat at the inn, for he was beginning to be hungry.

He remembered that he had seen this establishment, which was only recently opened, the day before: the Hotel Corot, it was called, an artistic public-house in middle-age style of decoration, modeled on the Chat Noir in Paris. His driver set him down there and he passed through an open door into a vast room where old-fashioned tables and uncomfortable benches seemed to be awaiting drinkers of a past century. At the far end a woman, a young waitress, no doubt, was standing on top of a little folding ladder, fastening some old plates to nails that were driven in the wall and seemed nearly beyond her reach. Now raising herself on tiptoe on both feet, now on one, supporting herself with one hand against the wall while the other held the plate, she reached up with pretty and adroit movements; for her figure was pleasing and the undulating lines from wrist to ankle assumed changing forms of grace at every fresh posture. As her back was toward him she had been unaware of Mariolle's entrance, who stopped to watch her. He thought of Prédolé and his figurines; "It is a pretty picture, though!" he said to himself. "She is very graceful, that little girl."

He gave a little cough. She was so startled that she came near falling, but as soon as she had recovered her self-possession, she jumped down from her ladder as lightly as a rope dancer, and came to him with a pleasant smile on her face. "What will Monsieur have?" she inquired.

"Breakfast, Mademoiselle."

She ventured to say: "It should be dinner, rather, for it is half past three o'clock."

"We will call it dinner if you like. I lost myself in the forest."

Then she told him what dishes there were ready; he made his selection and took a seat. She went away to give the order, returning shortly to set the table for him. He watched her closely as she bustled around the table; she was pretty and very neat in her attire. She had a spry little air that was very pleasant to behold, in her working dress with skirt pinned up, sleeves rolled back, and neck exposed; and her corset fitted closely to her pretty form, of which she had no reason to be ashamed.

Her face was rather red, painted by exposure to the open air, and it seemed somewhat too fat and puffy, but it was as fresh as a new-blown rose, with fine, bright, brown eyes, a large mouth with its complement of handsome teeth, and chestnut hair that revealed by its abundance the healthy vigor of this strong young frame.

She brought radishes and bread and butter and he began to eat, ceasing to pay attention to the attendant. He called for a bottle of champagne and drank the whole of it, as he did two glasses of kummel after his coffee, and as his stomach was empty—he had taken nothing before he left his house but a little bread and cold meat—he soon felt a comforting feeling of tipsiness stealing over him that he mistook for oblivion. His griefs and sorrows were diluted and tempered by the sparkling wine which, in so short a time, had transformed the torments of his heart into insensibility. He walked slowly back to Montigny, and being very tired and sleepy went to bed as soon as it was dark, falling asleep as soon as his head touched the pillow.

He awoke after a while, however, in the dense darkness, ill at ease and disquieted as if a nightmare that had left him for an hour or two had furtively reappeared at his bedside to murder sleep. She was there, she, Mme. de Burne, back again, roaming about his bed, and accompanied still by M. de Bernhaus. "Come!" he said, "it must be that I am jealous. What is the reason of it?"

Why was he jealous? He quickly told himself why. Notwithstanding all his doubts and fears he knew that as long as he had been her lover she had been faithful to him—faithful, indeed, without tenderness and without transports, but with a loyal strength of resolution. Now, however, he had broken it all off, and it was ended; he had restored her freedom to her. Would she remain without a liaison? Yes, doubtless, for a while. And then? This very fidelity that she had observed toward him up to the present moment, a fidelity beyond the reach of suspicion, was it not due to the feeling that if she left him, Mariolle, because she was tired of him, she would some day, sooner or later, have to take some one to fill his place, not from passion, but from weariness of being alone?

Is it not true that lovers often owe their long lease of favor simply to the dread of an unknown successor? And then to dismiss one lover and take up with another would not have seemed the right thing to such a woman—she was too intelligent, indeed, to bow to social prejudices, but was gifted with a delicate sense of moral purity that kept her from real indelicacies. She was a worldly philosopher and not a prudish bourgeoise, and while she would not have quailed at the idea of a secret attachment, her nature would have revolted at the thought of a succession of lovers.

He had given her her freedom—and now? Now most certainly she would take up with some one else, and that some one would be the Comte de Bernhaus. He was sure of it, and the thought was now affording him inexpressible suffering. Why had he left her? She had been faithful, a good friend to him, charming in every way. Why? Was it because he was a brutal sensualist who could not separate true love from its physical transports? Was that it? Yes—but there was something besides. He had fled from the pain of not being loved as he loved, from the cruel feeling that he did not receive an equivalent return for the warmth of his kisses, an incurable affliction from which his heart, grievously smitten, would perhaps never recover. He looked forward with dread to the prospect of enduring for years the torments that he had been anticipating for a few months and suffering for a few weeks. In accordance with his nature he had weakly recoiled before this prospect, just as he had recoiled all his life long before any effort that called for resolution. It followed that he was incapable of carrying anything to its conclusion, of throwing himself heart and soul into such a passion as one develops for a science or an art, for it is impossible, perhaps, to have loved greatly without having suffered greatly.

Until daylight he pursued this train of thought, which tore him like wild horses; then he got up and went down to the bank of the little stream. A fisherman was casting his net near the little dam, and when he withdrew it from the water that flashed and eddied in the sunlight and spread it on the deck of his small boat, the little fishes danced among the meshes like animated silver.

Mariolle's agitation subsided little by little in the balmy freshness of the early morning air. The cool mist that rose from the miniature waterfall, about which faint rainbows fluttered, and the stream that ran at his feet in rapid and ceaseless current, carried off with them a portion of his sorrow. He said to himself: "Truly, I have done the right thing; I should have been too unhappy otherwise!" Then he returned to the house, and taking possession of a hammock that he had noticed in the vestibule, he made it fast between two of the lindens and throwing himself into it, endeavored to drive away reflection by fixing his eyes and thoughts upon the flowing stream.

Thus he idled away the time until the hour of breakfast, in an agreeable torpor, a physical sensation of well-being that communicated itself to the mind, and he protracted the meal as much as possible that he might have some occupation for the dragging minutes. There was one thing, however, that he looked forward to with eager expectation, and that was his mail. He had telegraphed to Paris and written to Fontainebleau to have his letters forwarded, but had received nothing, and the sensation of being entirely abandoned was beginning to be oppressive. Why? He had no reason to expect that there would be anything particularly pleasing or comforting for him in the little black box that the carrier bore slung at his side, nothing beyond useless invitations and unmeaning communications. Why, then, should he long for letters of whose contents he knew nothing as if the salvation of his soul depended on them? Was it not that there lay concealed in his heart the vainglorious expectation that she would write to him?

He asked one of his old women: "At what time does the mail arrive?"

"At noon, Monsieur."

It was just midday, and he listened with increased attention to the noises that reached him from outdoors. A knock at the outer door brought him to his feet; the messenger brought him only the newspapers and three unimportant letters. Mariolle glanced over the journals until he was tired, and went out.

What should he do? He went to the hammock and lay down in it, but after half an hour of that he experienced an uncontrollable desire to go somewhere else. The forest? Yes, the forest was very pleasant, but then the solitude there was even deeper than it was in his house, much deeper than it was in the village, where there were at least some signs of life now and then. And the silence and loneliness of all those trees and leaves filled his mind with sadness and regrets, steeping him more deeply still in wretchedness. He mentally reviewed his long walk of the day before, and when he came to the wide-awake little waitress of the Hotel Corot, he said to himself: "I have it! I will go and dine there." The idea did him good; it was something to occupy him, a means of killing two or three hours, and he set out forthwith.

The long village street stretched straight away in the middle of the valley between two rows of low, white, tile-roofed houses, some of them standing boldly up with their fronts close to the road, others, more retiring, situated in a garden where there was a lilac-bush in bloom and chickens scratching over manure-heaps, where wooden stairways in the open air climbed to doors cut in the wall. Peasants were at work before their dwellings, lazily fulfilling their domestic duties. An old woman, bent with age and with threads of gray in her yellow hair, for country folk rarely have white hair, passed close to him, a ragged jacket upon her shoulders and her lean and sinewy legs covered by a woolen petticoat that failed to conceal the angles and protuberances of her frame. She was looking aimlessly before her with expressionless eyes, eyes that had never looked on other objects than those that might be of use to her in her poor existence.

Another woman, younger than this one, was hanging out the family wash before her door. The lifting of her skirt as she raised her arms aloft disclosed to view thick, coarse ankles incased in blue knitted stockings, with great, projecting, fleshless bones, while the breast and shoulders, flat and broad as those of a man, told of a body whose form must have been horrible to behold.

Mariolle thought: "They are women! Those scarecrows are women!" The vision of Mme. de Burne arose before his eyes. He beheld her in all her elegance and beauty, the perfection of the human female form, coquettish and adorned to meet the looks of man, and again he smarted with the sorrow of an irreparable loss; then he walked on more quickly to shake himself free of this impression.

When he reached the inn at Marlotte the little waitress recognized him immediately, and accosted him almost familiarly: "Good day, Monsieur."

"Good day, Mademoiselle."

"Do you wish something to drink?"

"Yes, to begin with; then I will have dinner."

They discussed the question of what he should drink in the first place and what he should eat subsequently. He asked her advice for the pleasure of hearing her talk, for she had a nice way of expressing herself. She had a short little Parisian accent, and her speech was as unconstrained as was her movements. He thought as he listened: "The little girl is quite agreeable; she seems to me to have a bit of the cocotte about her."

"Are you a Parisian?" he inquired.

"Yes, sir."

"Have you been here long?"

"Two weeks, sir."

"And do you like it?"

"Not very well so far, but it is too soon to tell, and then I was tired of the air of Paris, and the country has done me good; that is why I made up my mind to come here. Then I shall bring you a vermouth, Monsieur?"

"Yes, Mademoiselle, and tell the cook to be careful and pay attention to my dinner."

"Never fear, Monsieur."

After she had gone away he went into the garden of the hotel, and took a seat in an arbor, where his vermouth was served. He remained there all the rest of the day, listening to a blackbird whistling in its cage, and watching the little waitress in her goings and comings. She played the coquette, and put on her sweetest looks for the gentleman, for she had not failed to observe that he found her to his liking.

He went away as he had done the day before after drinking a bottle of champagne to dispel gloom, but the darkness of the way and the coolness of the night air quickly dissipated his incipient tipsiness, and sorrow again took possession of his devoted soul. He thought: "What am I to do? Shall I remain here? Shall I be condemned for long to drag out this desolate way of living?" It was very late when he got to sleep

The next morning he again installed himself in the hammock, and all at once the sight of a man casting his net inspired him with the idea of going fishing. The grocer from whom he bought his lines gave him some instructions upon the soothing sport, and even offered to go with him and act as his guide upon his first attempt. The offer was accepted, and between nine o'clock and noon Mariolle succeeded, by dint of vigorous exertion and unintermitting patience, in capturing three small fish.

When he had dispatched his breakfast he took up his march again for Marlotte. Why? To kill time, of course.

The little waitress began to laugh when she saw him coming. Amused by her recognition of him, he smiled back at her, and tried to engage her in conversation. She was more familiar than she had been the preceding day, and met him halfway.

Her name was Elisabeth Ledru. Her mother, who took in dressmaking, had died the year before; then the husband, an accountant by profession, always drunk and out of work, who had lived on the little earnings of his wife and daughter, disappeared, for the girl could not support two persons, though she shut herself up in her garret room and sewed all day long. Tiring of her lonely occupation after a while, she got a position as waitress in a cook-shop, remained there a year, and as the hard work had worn her down, the proprietor of the Hotel Corot at Marlotte, upon whom she had waited at times, engaged her for the summer with two other girls who were to come down a little later on. It was evident that the proprietor knew how to attract customers.

Her little story pleased Mariolle, and by treating her with respect and asking her a few discriminating questions, he succeeded in eliciting from her many interesting details of this poor dismal home that had been laid in ruins by a drunken father. She, poor, homeless, wandering creature that she was, gay and cheerful because she could not help it, being young, and feeling that the interest that this stranger took in her was unfeigned, talked to him with confidence, with that expansiveness of soul that she could no more restrain than she could restrain the agile movements of her limbs.

When she had finished he asked her: "And—do you expect to be a waitress all your life?"

"I could not answer that question, Monsieur. How can I tell what may happen to me to-morrow?"

"And yet it is necessary to think of the future."

She had assumed a thoughtful air that did not linger long upon her features, then she replied: "I suppose that I shall have to take whatever comes to me. So much the worse!"

They parted very good friends. After a few days he returned, then again, and soon he began to go there frequently, finding a vague distraction in the girl's conversation, and that her artless prattle helped him somewhat to forget his grief.

When he returned on foot to Montigny in the evening, however, he had terrible fits of despair as he thought of Mme. de Burne. His heart became a little lighter with the morning sun, but with the night his bitter regrets and fierce jealousy closed in on him again. He had no intelligence; he had written to no one and had received letters from no one. Then, alone with his thoughts upon the dark road, his imagination would picture the progress of the approaching liaison that he had foreseen between his quondam mistress and the Comte de Bernhaus. This had now become a settled idea with him and fixed itself more firmly in his mind every day. That man, he thought, will be to her just what she requires; a distinguished, assiduous, unexacting lover, contented and happy to be the chosen one of this superlatively delicious coquette. He compared him with himself. The other most certainly would not behave as he had, would not be guilty of that tiresome impatience and of that insatiable thirst for a return of his affection that had been the destruction of their amorous understanding. He was a very discreet, pliant, and well-posted man of the world, and would manage to get along and content himself with but little, for he did not seem to belong to the class of impassioned mortals.

On one of André Mariolle's visits to Marlotte one day, he beheld two bearded young fellows in the other arbor of the Hotel Corot, smoking pipes and wearing Scotch caps on their heads. The proprietor, a big, broad-faced man, came forward to pay his respects as soon as he saw him, for he had an interested liking for this faithful patron of his dinner-table, and said to him: "I have two new customers since yesterday, two painters."

"Those gentlemen sitting there?"

"Yes. They are beginning to be heard of. One of them got a second-class medal last year."

And having told all that he knew about the embryo artists, he asked: "What will you take to-day, Monsieur Mariolle?"

"You may send me out a vermouth, as usual."

The proprietor went away, and soon Elisabeth appeared, bringing the salver, the glass, the carafe, and the bottle. Whereupon one of the painters called to her: "Well! little one, are we angry still?"

She did not answer and when she approached Mariolle he saw that her eyes were red.

"You have been crying," he said.

"Yes, a little," she simply replied.

"What was the matter?"

"Those two gentlemen there behaved rudely to me."

"What did they do to you?"

"They took me for a bad character."

"Did you complain to the proprietor?"

She gave a sorrowful shrug of the shoulders, "Oh! Monsieur—the proprietor. I know what he is now—the proprietor!"

Mariolle was touched, and a little angry; he said to her: "Tell me what it was all about."

She told him of the brutal conduct of the two painters immediately upon their arrival the night before, and then began to cry again, asking what she was to do, alone in the country and without friends or relatives, money or protection.

Mariolle suddenly said to her: "Will you enter my service? You shall be well treated in my house, and when I return to Paris you will be free to do what you please."

She looked him in the face with questioning eyes, and then quickly replied: "I will, Monsieur.

"How much are you earning here?"

"Sixty francs a month," she added, rather uneasily, "and I have my share of the pourboires besides; that makes it about seventy."

"I will pay you a hundred."

She repeated in astonishment: "A hundred francs a month?"

"Yes. Is that enough?"

"I should think that it was enough!"

"All that you will have to do will be to wait on me, take care of my clothes and linen, and attend to my room."

"It is a bargain, Monsieur."

"When will you come?"

"To-morrow, if you wish. After what has happened here I will go to the mayor and will leave whether they are willing or not."

Mariolle took two louis from his pocket and handed them to her. "There's the money to bind our bargain."

A look of joy flashed across her face and she said in a tone of decision: "I will be at your house before midday to-morrow, Monsieur."

CHAPTER XII.

CONSOLATION

Elisabeth came to Montigny next day, attended by a countryman with her trunk on a wheelbarrow. Mariolle had made a generous settlement with one of his old women and got rid of her, and the newcomer took possession of a small room on the top floor adjoining that of the cook. She was quite different from what she had been at Marlotte, when she presented herself before her new master, less effusive, more respectful, more self-contained; she was now the servant of the gentleman to whom she had been almost an humble friend beneath the arbor of the inn. He told her in a few words what she would have to do. She listened attentively, went and took possession of her room, and then entered upon her new service.

A week passed and brought no noticeable change in the state of Mariolle's feelings. The only difference was that he remained at home more than he had been accustomed to do, for he had nothing to attract him to Marlotte, and his house seemed less dismal to him than at first. The bitterness of his grief was subsiding a little, as all storms subside after a while; but in place of this aching wound there was arising in him a settled melancholy, one of those deep-seated sorrows that are like chronic and lingering maladies, and sometimes end in death. His former liveliness of mind and body, his mental activity, his interests in the pursuits that had served to occupy and amuse him hitherto were all dead, and their place had been taken by a universal disgust and an invincible torpor, that left him without even strength of will to get up and go out of doors. He no longer left his house, passing from the salon to the hammock and from the hammock to the salon, and his chief distraction consisted in watching the current of the Loing as it flowed by the terrace and the fisherman casting his net.

When the reserve of the first few days had begun to wear off, Elisabeth gradually grew a little bolder, and remarking with her keen feminine instinct the constant dejection of her employer, she would say to him when the other servant was not by: "Monsieur finds his time hang heavy on his hands?"

He would answer resignedly: "Yes, pretty heavy."

"Monsieur should go for a walk."

"That would not do me any good."

She quietly did many little unassuming things for his pleasure and comfort. Every morning when he came into his drawing-room, he found it filled with flowers and smelling as sweetly as a conservatory. Elisabeth must surely have enlisted all the boys in the village to bring her primroses, violets, and buttercups from the forest, as well as putting under contribution the small gardens where the peasant girls tended their few plants at evening. In his loneliness and distress he was grateful for her kind thoughtfulness and her unobtrusive desire to please him in these small ways.

It also seemed to him that she was growing prettier, more refined in her appearance, and that she devoted more attention to the care of her person. One day when she was handing him a cup of tea, he noticed that her hands were no longer the hands of a servant, but of a lady, with well-trimmed, clean nails, quite irreproachable. On another occasion he observed that the shoes that she wore were almost elegant in shape and material. Then she had gone up to her room one afternoon and come down wearing a delightful little gray dress, quite simple and in perfect taste. "Hallo!" he exclaimed, as he saw her, "how dressy you are getting to be, Elisabeth!"

She blushed up to the whites of her eyes. "What, I, Monsieur? Why, no. I dress a little better because I have more money."

"Where did you buy that dress that you have on?"

"I made it myself, Monsieur."

"You made it? When? I always see you busy at work about the house during the day."

"Why, during my evenings, Monsieur."

"But where did you get the stuff? and who cut it for you?"

She told him that the shopkeeper at Montigny had brought her some samples from Fontainebleau, that she had made her selection from them, and paid for the goods out of the two louis that he had paid her as advanced wages. The cutting and fitting had not troubled her at all, for she and her mother had worked four years for a ready-made clothing house. He could not resist telling her: "It is very becoming to you. You look very pretty in it." And she had to blush again, this time to the roots of her hair.

When she had left the room he said to himself: "I wonder if she is beginning to fall in love with me?" He reflected on it, hesitated, doubted, and finally came to the conclusion that after all it might be possible. He had been kind and compassionate toward her, had assisted her, and been almost her friend; there would be nothing very surprising in this little girl being smitten with the master, who had been so good to her. The idea did not strike him very disagreeably, moreover, for she was really very presentable, and retained nothing of the appearance of a servant about her. He experienced a flattering feeling of consolation, and his masculine vanity, that had been so cruelly wounded and trampled on and crushed by another woman, felt comforted. It was a compensation—trivial and unnoteworthy though it might be, it was a compensation—for when love comes to a man unsought, no matter whence it comes, it is because that man possesses the capacity of inspiring it. His unconscious selfishness was also gratified by it; it would occupy his attention and do him a little good, perhaps, to watch this young heart opening and beating for him. The thought never occurred to him of sending the child away, of rescuing her from the peril from which he himself was suffering so cruelly, of having more pity for her than others had showed toward him, for compassion is never an ingredient that enters into sentimental conquests.

So he continued his observations, and soon saw that he had not been mistaken. Petty details revealed it to him more clearly day by day. As she came near him one morning while waiting on him at table, he smelled on her clothing an odor of perfumery—villainous, cheap perfumery, from the village shopkeeper's, doubtless, or the druggist's—so he presented her with a bottle of Cyprus toilette-water that he had been in the habit of using for a long time, and of which he always carried a supply about with him. He also gave her fine soaps, tooth-washes, and rice-powder. He thus lent his assistance to the transformation that was becoming more apparent every day, watching it meantime with a pleased and curious eye. While remaining his faithful and respectful servant, she was thus becoming a woman in whom the coquettish instincts of her sex were artlessly developing themselves.

He, on his part, was imperceptibly becoming attached to her. She inspired him at the same time with amusement and gratitude. He trifled with this dawning tenderness as one trifles in his hours of melancholy with anything that can divert his mind. He was conscious of no other emotion toward her than that undefined desire which impels every man toward a prepossessing woman, even if she be a pretty servant, or a peasant maiden with the form of a goddess—a sort of rustic Venus. He felt himself drawn to her more than all else by the womanliness that he now found in her. He felt the need of that—an undefined and irresistible need, bequeathed to him by that other one, the woman whom he loved, who had first awakened in him that invincible and mysterious fondness for the nature, the companionship, the contact of women, for the subtle aroma, ideal or sensual, that every beautiful creature, whether of the people or of the upper class, whether a lethargic, sensual native of the Orient with great black eyes, or a blue-eyed, keen-witted daughter of the North, inspires in men in whom still survives the immemorial attraction of femininity.

These gentle, loving, and unceasing attentions that were felt rather than seen, wrapped his wound in a sort of soft, protecting envelope that shielded it to some extent from its recurrent attacks of suffering, which did return, nevertheless, like flies to a raw sore. He was made especially impatient by the absence of all news, for his friends had religiously respected his request not to divulge his address. Now and then he would see Massival's or Lamarthe's name in the newspapers among those who had been present at some great dinner or ceremonial, and one day he saw Mme. de Burne's, who was mentioned as being one of the most elegant, the prettiest, and best dressed of the women who were at the ball at the Austrian embassy. It sent a trembling through him from head to foot. The name of the Comte de Bernhaus appeared a few lines further down, and that day Mariolle's jealousy returned and wrung his heart until night. The suspected liaison was no longer subject for doubt for him now. It was one of those imaginary convictions that are even more torturing than reality, for there is no getting rid of them and they leave a wound that hardly ever heals.

No longer able to endure this state of ignorance and uncertainty, he determined to write to Lamarthe, who was sufficiently well acquainted with him to divine the wretchedness of his soul, and would be likely to afford him some clew as to the justice of his suspicions, even without being directly questioned on the subject. One evening, therefore, he sat down and by the light of his lamp concocted a long, artful letter, full of vague sadness and poetical allusions to the delights of early spring in the country and veiled requests for information. When he got his mail four days later he recognized at the very first glance the novelist's firm, upright handwriting.

Lamarthe sent him a thousand items of news that were of great importance to his jealous eyes. Without laying more stress upon Mme. de Burne and Bernhaus than upon any other of the crowd of people whom he mentioned, he seemed to place them in the foreground by one of those tricks of style characteristic of him, which led the attention to just the point where he wished to lead it without revealing his design. The impression that this letter, taken as a whole, left upon Mariolle was that his suspicions were at least not destitute of foundation. His fears would be realized to-morrow, if they had not been yesterday. His former mistress was always the same, leading the same busy, brilliant, fashionable life. He had been the subject of some talk after his disappearance, as the world always talks of people who have disappeared, with lukewarm curiosity.

After the receipt of this letter he remained in his hammock until nightfall; then he could eat no dinner, and after that he could get no sleep; he was feverish through the night. The next morning he felt so tired, so discouraged, so disgusted with his weary, monotonous life, between the deep silent forest that was now dark with verdure on the one hand and the tiresome little stream that flowed beneath his windows on the other, that he did not leave his bed.

When Elisabeth came to his room in response to the summons of his bell, she stood in the doorway pale with surprise and asked him: "Is Monsieur ill?"

"Yes, a little."

"Shall I send for the doctor?"

"No. I am subject to these slight indispositions."

"What can I do for Monsieur?"

He ordered his bath to be got ready, a breakfast of eggs alone, and tea at intervals during the day.

About one o'clock, however, he became so restless that he determined to get up. Elisabeth, whom he had rung for repeatedly during the morning with the fretful irresolution of a man who imagines himself ill and who had always come up to him with a deep desire of being of assistance, now, beholding him so nervous and restless, with a blush for her own boldness, offered to read to him.

He asked her: "Do you read well?"

"Yes, Monsieur; I gained all the prizes for reading when I was at school in the city, and I have read so many novels to mamma that I can't begin to remember the names of them."

He was curious to see how she would do, and he sent her into the studio to look among the books that he had packed up for the one that he liked best of all, "Manon Lescaut."

When she returned she helped him to settle himself in bed, arranged two pillows behind his back, took a chair, and began to read. She read well, very well indeed, intelligently and with a pleasing accent that seemed a special gift. She evinced her interest in the story from the commencement and showed so much feeling as she advanced in it that he stopped her now and then to ask her a question and have a little conversation about the plot and the characters.

Through the open windows, on the warm breeze loaded with the sweet odors of growing things, came the trills and roulades of the nightingales among the trees saluting their mates with their amorous ditties in this season of awakening love. The young girl, too, was moved beneath André's gaze as she followed with bright eyes the plot unwinding page by page.

She answered the questions that he put to her with an innate appreciation of the things connected with tenderness and passion, an appreciation that was just, but, owing to the ignorance natural to her position, sometimes crude. He thought: "This girl would be very intelligent and bright if she had a little teaching."

Her womanly charm had already begun to make itself felt in him, and really did him good that warm, still, spring afternoon, mingling strangely with that other charm, so powerful and so mysterious, of "Manon," the strangest conception of woman ever evoked by human ingenuity.

When it became dark after this day of inactivity Mariolle sank into a kind of dreaming, dozing state, in which confused visions of Mme. de Burne and Elisabeth and the mistress of Des Grieux rose before his eyes. As he had not left his room since the day before and had taken no exercise to fatigue him he slept lightly and was disturbed by an unusual noise that he heard about the house.

Once or twice before he had thought that he heard faint sounds and footsteps at night coming from the ground floor, not directly underneath his room, but from the laundry and bath-room, small rooms that adjoined the kitchen. He had given the matter no attention, however.

This evening, tired of lying in bed and knowing that he had a long period of wakefulness before him, he listened and distinguished something that sounded like the rustling of a woman's garments and the splashing of water. He decided that he would go and investigate, lighted a candle and looked at his watch; it was barely ten o'clock. He dressed himself, and having slipped a revolver into his pocket, made his way down the stairs on tiptoe with the stealthiness of a cat.

When he reached the kitchen, he was surprised to see that there was a fire burning in the furnace. There was not a sound to be heard, but presently he was conscious of something stirring in the bath-room, a small, whitewashed apartment that opened off the kitchen and contained nothing but the tub. He went noiselessly to the door and threw it open with a quick movement; there, extended in the tub, he beheld the most beautiful form that he had ever seen in his life.

It was Elisabeth.

CHAPTER XIII.

MARIOLLE COPIES MME DE BURNE

When she appeared before him next morning bringing him his tea and toast, and their eyes met, she began to tremble so that the cup and sugar-bowl rattled on the salver. Mariolle went to her and relieved her of her burden and placed it on the table; then, as she still kept her eyes fastened on the floor, he said to her: "Look at me, little one."

She raised her eyes to him; they were full of tears.

"You must not cry," he continued. As he held her in his arms, she murmured: "Oh! mon Dieu!" He knew that it was not regret, nor sorrow, nor remorse that had elicited from her those three agitated words, but happiness, true happiness. It gave him a strange, selfish feeling of delight, physical rather than moral, to feel this small person resting against his heart, to feel there at last the presence of a woman who loved him. He thanked her for it, as a wounded man lying by the roadside would thank a woman who had stopped to succor him; he thanked her with all his lacerated heart, and he pitied her a little, too, in the depths of his soul. As he watched her thus, pale and tearful, with eyes alight with love, he suddenly said to himself: "Why, she is beautiful! How quickly a woman changes, becomes what she ought to be, under the influence of the desires of her feelings and the necessities of her existence!"

"Sit down," he said to her. He took her hands in his, her poor toiling hands that she had made white and pretty for his sake, and very gently, in carefully chosen phrases, he spoke to her of the attitude that they should maintain toward each other. She was no longer his servant, but she would preserve the appearance of being so for a while yet, so as not to create a scandal in the village. She would live with him as his housekeeper and would read to him frequently, and that would serve to account for the change in the situation. He would have her eat at his table after a little, as soon as she should be permanently installed in her position as his reader.

When he had finished she simply replied: "No, Monsieur, I am your servant, and I will continue to be so. I do not wish to have people learn what has taken place and talk about it."

He could not shake her determination, although he urged her strenuously, and when he had drunk his tea she carried away the salver while he followed her with a softened look.

When she was gone he reflected. "She is a woman," he thought, "and all women are equal when they are pleasing in our eyes. I have made my waitress my mistress. She is pretty, she will be charming! At all events she is younger and fresher than the mondaines and the cocottes. What difference does it make, after all? How many celebrated actresses have been daughters of concierges! And yet they are received as ladies, they are adored like heroines of romance, and princes bow before them as if they were queens. Is this to be accounted for on the score of their talent, which is often doubtful, or of their beauty, which is often questionable? Not at all. But a woman, in truth, always holds the place that she is able to create for herself by the illusion that she is capable of inspiring."

He took a long walk that day, and although he still felt the same distress at the bottom of his heart and his legs were heavy under him, as if his suffering had loosened all the springs of his energy, there was a feeling of gladness within him like the song of a little bird. He was not so lonely, he felt himself less utterly abandoned; the forest appeared to him less silent and less void.

He returned to his house with the glad thought that Elisabeth would come out to meet him with a smile upon her lips and a look of tenderness in her eyes.

The life that he now led for about a month on the bank of the little stream was a real idyl. Mariolle was loved as perhaps very few men have ever been, as a child is loved by its mother, as the hunter is loved by his dog. He was all in all to her, her Heaven and earth, her charm and delight. He responded to all her ardent and artless womanly advances, giving her in a kiss her fill of ecstasy. In her eyes and in her soul, in her heart and in her flesh there was no object but him; her intoxication was like that of a young man who tastes wine for the first time. Surprised and delighted, he reveled in the bliss of this absolute self-surrender, and he felt that this was drinking of love at its fountain-head, at the very lips of nature.

Nevertheless he continued to be sad, sad, and haunted by his deep, unyielding disenchantment. His little mistress was agreeable, but he always felt the absence of another, and when he walked in the meadows or on the banks of the Loing and asked himself: "Why does this lingering care stay by me so?" such an intolerable feeling of desolation rose within him as the recollection of Paris crossed his mind that he had to return to the house so as not to be alone.

Then he would swing in the hammock, while Elisabeth, seated on a camp-chair, would read to him. As he watched her and listened to her he would recall to mind conversations in the drawing-room of Michèle, in the days when he passed whole evenings alone with her. Then tears would start to his eyes, and such bitter regret would tear his heart that he felt that he must start at once for Paris or else leave the country forever.

Elisabeth, seeing his gloom and melancholy, asked him: "Are you suffering? Your eyes are full of tears."

"Give me a kiss, little one," he replied; "you could not understand."

She kissed him, anxiously, with a foreboding of some tragedy that was beyond her knowledge. He, forgetting his woes for a moment beneath her caresses, thought: "Oh! for a woman who could be these two in one, who might have the affection of the one and the charm of the other! Why is it that we never encounter the object of our dreams, that we always meet with something that is only approximately like them?"

He continued his vague reflections, soothed by the monotonous sound of the voice that fell unheeded on his ear, upon all the charms that had combined to seduce and vanquish him in the mistress whom he had abandoned. In the besetment of her memory, of her imaginary presence, by which he was haunted as a visionary by a phantom, he asked himself: "Am I condemned to carry her image with me to all eternity?"

He again applied himself to taking long walks, to roaming through the thicknesses of the forest, with the vague hope that he might lose her somewhere, in the depths of a ravine, behind a rock, in a thicket, as a man who wishes to rid himself of an animal that he does not care to kill sometimes takes it away a long distance so that it may not find its way home.

In the course of one of these walks he one day came again to the spot where the beeches grew. It was now a gloomy forest, almost as black as night, with impenetrable foliage. He passed along beneath the immense, deep vault in the damp, sultry air, thinking regretfully of his earlier visit when the little half-opened leaves resembled a verdant, sunshiny mist, and as he was following a narrow path, he suddenly stopped in astonishment before two trees that had grown together. It was a sturdy beech embracing with two of its branches a tall, slender oak; and there could have been no picture of his love that would have appealed more forcibly and more touchingly to his imagination. Mariolle seated himself to contemplate them at his ease. To his diseased mind, as they stood there in their motionless strife, they became splendid and terrible symbols, telling to him, and to all who might pass that way, the everlasting story of his love.

Then he went on his way again, sadder than before, and as he walked along, slowly and with eyes downcast, he all at once perceived, half hidden by the grass and stained by mud and rain, an old telegram that had been lost or thrown there by some wayfarer. He stopped. What was the message of joy or sorrow that the bit of blue paper that lay there at his feet had brought to some expectant soul?

He could not help picking it up and opening it with a mingled feeling of curiosity and disgust. The words "Come—me—four o'clock—" were still legible; the names had been obliterated by the moisture.

Memories, at once cruel and delightful, thronged upon his mind of all the messages that he had received from her, now to appoint the hour for a rendezvous, now to tell him that she could not come to him. Never had anything caused him such emotion, nor startled him so violently, nor so stopped his poor heart and then set it thumping again as had the sight of those messages, burning or freezing him as the case might be. The thought that he should never receive more of them filled him with unutterable sorrow.

Again he asked himself what her thoughts had been since he left her. Had she suffered, had she regretted the friend whom her coldness had driven from her, or had she merely experienced a feeling of wounded vanity and thought nothing more of his abandonment? His desire to learn the truth was so strong and so persistent that a strange and audacious, yet only half-formed resolve, came into his head. He took the road to Fontainebleau, and when he reached the city went to the telegraph office, his mind in a fluctuating state of unrest and indecision; but an irresistible force proceeding from his heart seemed to urge him on. With a trembling hand, then, he took from the desk a printed blank and beneath the name and address of Mme. de Burne wrote this dispatch:

"I would so much like to know what you think of me! For my part I can forget nothing. ANDRÉ MARIOLLE."

Then he went out, engaged a carriage, and returned to Montigny, disturbed in mind by what he had done and regretting it already.

He had calculated that in case she condescended to answer him he would receive a letter from her two days later, but the fear and the hope that she might send him a dispatch kept him in his house all the following day. He was in his hammock under the lindens on the terrace, when, about three o'clock, Elisabeth came to tell him that there was a lady at the house who wanted to see him.

The shock was so great that his breath failed him for a moment and his legs bent under him, and his heart beat violently as he went toward the house. And yet he could not dare hope that it was she.

When he appeared at the drawing-room door Mme. de Burne arose from the sofa where she was sitting and came forward to shake hands with a rather reserved smile upon her face, with a slight constraint of manner and attitude, saying: "I came to see how you are, as your message did not give me much information on the subject."

He had become so pale that a flash of delight rose to her eyes, and his emotion was so great that he could not speak, could only hold his lips glued to the hand that she had given him.

"Dieu! how kind of you!" he said at last.

"No; but I do not forget my friends, and I was anxious about you."

She looked him in the face with that rapid, searching woman's look that reads everything, fathoms one's thoughts to their very roots, and unmasks every artifice. She was satisfied, apparently, for her face brightened with a smile. "You have a pretty hermitage here," she continued. "Does happiness reside in it?"

"No, Madame."

"Is it possible? In this fine country, at the side of this beautiful forest, on the banks of this pretty stream? Why, you ought to be at rest and quite contented here."

"I am not, Madame."

"Why not, then?"

"Because I cannot forget."

"Is it indispensable to your happiness that you should forget something?"

"Yes, Madame."

"May one know what?"

"You know."

"And then?"

"And then I am very wretched."

She said to him with mingled fatuity and commiseration: "I thought that was the case when I received your telegram, and that was the reason that I came, with the resolve that I would go back again at once if I found that I had made a mistake." She was silent a moment and then went on: "Since I am not going back immediately, may I go and look around your place? That little alley of lindens yonder has a very charming appearance: it looks as if it might be cooler out there than here in this drawing-room."

They went out. She had on a mauve dress that harmonized so well with the verdure of the trees and the blue of the sky that she appeared to him like some amazing apparition, of an entirely new style of beauty and seductiveness. Her tall and willowy form, her bright, clean-cut features, the little blaze of blond hair beneath a hat that was mauve, like the dress, and lightly crowned by a long plume of ostrich-feathers rolled about it, her tapering arms with the two hands holding the closed sunshade crosswise before her, the loftiness of her carriage, and the directness of her step seemed to introduce into the humble little garden something exotic, something that was foreign to it. It was a figure from one of Watteau's pictures, or from some fairy-tale or dream, the imagination of a poet's or an artist's fancy, which had been seized by the whim of coming away to the country to show how beautiful it was. As Mariolle looked at her, all trembling with his newly lighted passion, he recalled to mind the two peasant women that he had seen in Montigny village.

"Who is the little person who opened the door for me?" she inquired.

“She is my servant.”

“She does not look like a waitress.”

“No; she is very good looking.”

“Where did you secure her?”

“Quite near here; in an inn frequented by painters, where her innocence was in danger from the customers.”

“And you preserved it?”

He blushed and replied: “Yes, I preserved it.”

“To your own advantage, perhaps.”

“Certainly, to my own advantage, for I would rather have a pretty face about me than an ugly one.”

“Is that the only feeling that she inspires in you?”

“Perhaps it was she who inspired in me the irresistible desire of seeing you again, for every woman when she attracts my eyes, even if it is only for the duration of a second, carries my thoughts back to you.”

“That was a very pretty piece of special pleading! And does she love her preserver?”

He blushed more deeply than before. Quick as lightning the thought flashed through his mind that jealousy is always efficacious as a stimulant to a woman’s feelings, and decided him to tell only half a lie, so he answered, hesitatingly: “I don’t know how that is; it may be so. She is very attentive to me.”

Rather pettishly, Mme. de Burne murmured: “And you?”

He fastened upon her his eyes that were aflame with love, and replied: “Nothing could ever distract my thoughts from you.”

This was also a very shrewd answer, but the phrase seemed to her so much the expression of an indisputable truth, that she let it pass without noticing it. Could a woman such as she have any doubts about a thing like that? So she was satisfied, in fact, and had no further doubts upon the subject of Elisabeth.

They took two canvas chairs and seated themselves in the shade of the lindens over the running stream. He asked her: “What did you think of me?”

“That you must have been very wretched.”

“Was it through my fault or yours?”

“Through the fault of us both.”

“And then?”

“And then, knowing how beside yourself you were, I reflected that it would be best to give you a little time to cool down. So I waited.”

"What were you waiting for?"

"For a word from you. I received it, and here I am. Now we are going to talk like people of sense. So you love me still? I do not ask you this as a coquette—I ask it as your friend."

"I love you still."

"And what is it that you wish?"

"How can I answer that? I am in your power."

"Oh! my ideas are very clear, but I will not tell you them without first knowing what yours are. Tell me of yourself, of what has been passing in your heart and in your mind since you ran away from me."

"I have been thinking of you; I have had no other occupation." He told her of his resolution to forget her, his flight, his coming to the great forest in which he had found nothing but her image, of his days filled with memories of her, and his long nights of consuming jealousy; he told her everything, with entire truthfulness, always excepting his love for Elisabeth, whose name he did not mention.

She listened, well assured that he was not lying, convinced by her inner consciousness of her power over him, even more than by the sincerity of his manner, and delighted with her victory, glad that she was about to regain him, for she loved him still.

Then he bemoaned himself over this situation that seemed to have no end, and warming up as he told of all that he had suffered after having carried it so long in his thoughts, he again reproached her, but without anger, without bitterness, in terms of impassioned poetry, with that impotency of loving of which she was the victim. He told her over and over: "Others have not the gift of pleasing; you have not the gift of loving."

She interrupted him, speaking warmly, full of arguments and illustrations. "At least I have the gift of being faithful," she said. "Suppose I had adored you for ten months, and then fallen in love with another man, would you be less unhappy than you are?"

He exclaimed: "Is it, then, impossible for a woman to love only one man?"

But she had her answer ready for him: "No one can keep on loving forever; all that one can do is to be constant. Do you believe that that exalted delirium of the senses can last for years? No, no. As for the most of those women who are addicted to passions, to violent caprices of greater or less duration, they simply transform life into a novel. Their heroes are different, the events and circumstances are unforeseen and constantly changing, the dénouement varies. I admit that for them it is amusing and diverting, for with every change they have a new set of emotions, but for him—when it is ended, that is the last of it. Do you understand me?"

"Yes; what you say has some truth in it. But I do not see what you are getting at."

"It is this: there is no passion that endures a very long time; by that I mean a burning, torturing passion like that from which you are suffering now. It is a crisis that I have made hard, very hard for you to bear—I know it, and I feel it—by—by the aridity of my tenderness and the paralysis of my emotional nature. This crisis will pass away, however, for it cannot last forever."

"And then?" he asked with anxiety.

"Then I think that to a woman who is as reasonable and calm as I am you can make yourself a lover who will be pleasing in every way, for you have a great deal of tact. On the other hand you would make a terrible husband. But there is no such thing as a good husband, there never can be."

He was surprised and a little offended. "Why," he asked, "do you wish to keep a lover that you do not love?"

She answered, impetuously: "I do love him, my friend, after my fashion. I do not love ardently, but I love."

"You require above everything else to be loved and to have your lovers make a show of their love."

"It is true. That is what I like. But beyond that my heart requires a companion apart from the others. My vainglorious passion for public homage does not interfere with my capacity for being faithful and devoted; it does not destroy my belief that I have something of myself that I could bestow upon a lover that no other man should have: my loyal affection, the sincere attachment of my heart, the entire and secret trustfulness of my soul; in exchange for which I should receive from him, together with all the tenderness of a lover, the sensation, so sweet and so rare, of not being entirely alone upon the earth. That is not love from the way you look at it, but it is not entirely valueless, either."

He bent over toward her, trembling with emotion, and stammered: "Will you let me be that man?"

"Yes, after a little, when you are more yourself. In the meantime, resign yourself to a little suffering once in a while, for my sake. Since you have to suffer in any event, isn't it better to endure it at my side rather than somewhere far from me?" Her smile seemed to say to him: "Why can you not have confidence in me?" and as she eyed him there, his whole frame quivering with passion, she experienced through every fiber of her being a feeling of satisfied well-being that made her happy in her way, in the way that the bird of prey is happy when he sees his quarry lying fascinated beneath him and awaiting the fatal talons.

"When do you return to Paris?" she asked.

"Why—to-morrow!"

"To-morrow be it. You will come and dine with me?"

"Yes, Madame."

"And now I must be going," said she, looking at the watch set in the handle of her parasol.

"Oh! why so soon?"

"Because I must catch the five o'clock train. I have company to dinner to-day, several persons: the Princess de Malten, Bernhaus, Lamarthe, Massival, De Maltry, and a stranger, M. de Charlaine, the explorer, who is just back from upper Cambodia, after a wonderful journey. He is all the talk just now."

Mariolle's spirits fell; it hurt him to hear these names mentioned one after the other, as if he had been stung by so many wasps. They were poison to him.

"Will you go now?" he said, "and we can drive through the forest and see something of it."

"I shall be very glad to. First give me a cup of tea and some toast."

When the tea was served, Elisabeth was not to be found. The cook said that she had gone out to make some purchases. This did not surprise Mme. de Burne, for what had she to fear now from this servant? Then they got into the landau that was standing before the door, and Mariolle made the coachman take them to the station by a roundabout way which took them past the Gorge-aux-Loups. As they rolled along beneath the shade of the great trees where the nightingales were singing, she was seized by the ineffable sensation that the mysterious and all-powerful charm of nature impresses on the heart of man. "Dieu!" she said, "how beautiful it is, how calm and restful!"

He accompanied her to the station, and as they were about to part she said to him: "I shall see you to-morrow at eight o'clock, then?"

"To-morrow at eight o'clock, Madame."

She, radiant with happiness, went her way, and he returned to his house in the landau, happy and contented, but uneasy withal, for he knew that this was not the end.

Why should he resist? He felt that he could not. She held him by a charm that he could not understand, that was stronger than all. Flight would not deliver him, would not sever him from her, but would be an intolerable privation, while if he could only succeed in showing a little resignation, he would obtain from her at least as much as she had promised, for she was a woman who always kept her word.

The horses trotted along under the trees and he reflected that not once during that interview had she put up her lips to him for a kiss. She was ever the same; nothing in her would ever change and he would always, perhaps, have to suffer at her hands in just that same way. The remembrance of the bitter hours that he had already passed, with the intolerable certainty that he would never succeed in rousing her to passion, laid heavy on his heart, and gave him a clear foresight of struggles to come and of similar distress in the future. Still, he was content to suffer everything rather than lose her again, resigned even to that everlasting, ever unappeased desire that rioted in his veins and burned into his flesh.

The raging thoughts that had so often possessed him on his way back alone from Auteuil were now setting in again. They began to agitate his frame as the landau rolled smoothly along in the cool shadows of the great trees, when all at once the thought of Elisabeth awaiting him there at his door, she, too, young and fresh and pretty, her heart full of love and her mouth full of kisses, brought peace to his soul. Presently he would be holding her in his arms, and, closing his eyes and deceiving himself as men deceive others, confounding in the intoxication of the embrace her whom he loved and her by whom he was loved, he would possess them both at once. Even now it was certain that he had a liking for her, that grateful attachment of soul and body that always pervades the human animal as the result of love inspired and pleasure shared in common. This child whom he had made his own, would she not be to his dry and wasting love the little spring that bubbles up at the evening halting place, the promise of the cool draught that sustains our energy as wearily we traverse the burning desert?

When he regained the house, however, the girl had not come in. He was frightened and uneasy and said to the other servant: "You are sure that she went out?"

"Yes, Monsieur."

Thereupon he also went out in the hope of finding her. When he had taken a few steps and was about to turn into the long street that runs up the valley, he beheld before him the old, low church, surmounted by its square tower, seated upon a little knoll and watching the houses of its small village as a hen watches over her chicks. A presentiment that she was there impelled him to enter. Who can tell the strange glimpses of the truth that a woman's heart is capable of perceiving? What had she thought, how much had she understood? Where could she have fled for refuge but there, if the shadow of the truth had passed before her eyes?

The church was very dark, for night was closing in. The dim lamp, hanging from its chain, suggested in the tabernacle the ideal presence of the divine Consoler. With hushed footsteps Mariolle passed up along the lines of benches. When he reached the choir he saw a woman on her knees, her face hidden in her hands. He approached, recognized her, and touched her on the shoulder. They were alone.

She gave a great start as she turned her head. She was weeping.

"What is the matter?" he said.

She murmured: "I see it all. You came here because she had caused you to suffer. She came to take you away."

He spoke in broken accents, touched by the grief that he in turn had caused: "You are mistaken, little one. I am going back to Paris, indeed, but I shall take you with me."

She repeated, incredulously: "It can't be true, it can't be true."

"I swear to you that it is true."

"When?"

"To-morrow."

She began again to sob and groan: "My God! My God!"

Then he raised her to her feet and led her down the hill through the thick blackness of the night, but when they came to the river-bank he made her sit down upon the grass and placed himself beside her. He heard the beating of her heart and her quick breathing, and clasping her to his heart, troubled by his remorse, he whispered to her gentle words that he had never used before. Softened by pity and burning with desire, every word that he uttered was true; he did not endeavor to deceive her, and surprised himself at what he said and what he felt, he wondered how it was that, thrilling yet with the presence of that other one whose slave he was always to be, he could tremble thus with longing and emotion while consoling this love-stricken heart.

He promised that he would love her,—he did not say simply "love"—, that he would give her a nice little house near his own and pretty furniture to put in it and a servant to wait on her. She was reassured as she listened to him, and gradually grew calmer, for she could not believe that he was capable of deceiving her, and besides his tone and manner told her that he was sincere. Convinced at length and dazzled by the vision of being a lady, by the prospect—so undreamed of by the poor girl, the servant of the inn—of becoming the "good friend" of such a rich, nice gentleman, she was carried away in a whirl of pride, covetousness, and gratitude that mingled with her fondness for André. Throwing her arms about his neck and covering his face with kisses, she stammered: "Oh! I love you so! You are all in all to me!"

He was touched and returned her caresses. “Darling! My little darling!” he murmured.

Already she had almost forgotten the appearance of the stranger who but now had caused her so much sorrow. There must have been some vague feeling of doubt floating in her mind, however, for presently she asked him in a tremulous voice: “Really and truly, you will love me as you love me now?”

And unhesitatingly he replied: “I will love you as I love you now.”

THE OLIVE GROVE

AND

OTHER TALES

When the 'longshoremen of Garandou, a little port of Provence, situated in the bay of Pisca, between Marseilles and Toulon, perceived the boat of the Abbé Vilbois entering the harbor, they went down to the beach to help him pull her ashore.

The priest was alone in the boat. In spite of his fifty-eight years, he rowed with all the energy of a real sailor. He had placed his hat on the bench beside him, his sleeves were rolled up, disclosing his powerful arms, his cassock was open at the neck and turned over his knees, and he wore a round hat of heavy, white canvas. His whole appearance bespoke an odd and strenuous priest of southern climes, better fitted for adventures than for clerical duties.

He rowed with strong and measured strokes, as if to show the southern sailors how the men of the north handle the oars, and from time to time he turned around to look at the landing point.

The skiff struck the beach and slid far up, the bow plowing through the sand; then it stopped abruptly. The five men watching for the abbé drew near, jovial and smiling.

"Well!" said one, with the strong accent of Provence, "have you been successful, Monsieur le Curé?"

The abbé drew in the oars, removed his canvas head-covering, put on his hat, pulled down his sleeves, and buttoned his coat. Then having assumed the usual appearance of a village priest, he replied proudly: "Yes, I have caught three red-snappers, two eels, and five sunfish."

The fishermen gathered around the boat to examine, with the air of experts, the dead fish, the fat red-snappers, the flat-headed eels, those hideous sea-serpents, and the violet sunfish, streaked with bright orange-colored stripes.

Said one: "I'll carry them up to your house, Monsieur le Curé."

"Thank you, my friend."

Having shaken hands all around, the priest started homeward, followed by the man with the fish; the others took charge of the boat.

The Abbé Vilbois walked along slowly with an air of dignity. The exertion of rowing had brought beads of perspiration to his brow and he uncovered his head each time that he passed through the shade of an olive grove. The warm evening air, freshened by a slight breeze from the sea, cooled his high forehead covered with short, white hair, a forehead far more suggestive of an officer than of a priest.

The village appeared, built on a hill rising from a large valley which descended toward the sea.

It was a summer evening. The dazzling sun, traveling toward the ragged crests of the distant hills, outlined on the white, dusty road the figure of the priest, the shadow of whose three-cornered hat bobbed merrily over the fields, sometimes apparently climbing the trunks of the olive-trees, only to fall immediately to the ground and creep among them.

With every step he took, he raised a cloud of fine, white dust, the invisible powder which, in summer, covers the roads of Provence; it clung to the edge of his cassock turning it grayish white. Completely refreshed, his hands deep in his pockets, he strode along slowly and ponderously, like a mountaineer. His eyes were fixed on the distant village where he had lived twenty years, and where he hoped to die. Its church—his church—rose above the houses clustered around it; the square turrets of gray stone, of unequal proportions and quaint design, stood outlined against the beautiful southern valley; and their architecture suggested the fortifications of some old château rather than the steeples of a place of worship.

The abbé was happy; for he had caught three red-snappers, two eels, and five sunfish. It would enable him to triumph again over his flock, which respected him, no doubt, because he was one of the most powerful men of the place, despite his years. These little innocent vanities were his greatest pleasures. He was a fine marksman; sometimes he practiced with his neighbor, a retired army provost who kept a tobacco shop; he could also swim better than anyone along the coast.

In his day he had been a well-known society man, the Baron de Vilbois, but had entered the priesthood after an unfortunate love-affair. Being the scion of an old family of Picardy, devout and royalistic, whose sons for centuries had entered the army, the magistracy, or the Church, his first thought was to follow his mother's advice and become a priest. But he yielded to his father's suggestion that he should study law in Paris and seek some high office.

While he was completing his studies his father was carried off by pneumonia; his mother, who was greatly affected by the loss, died soon afterward. He came into a fortune, and consequently gave up the idea of following a profession to live a life of idleness. He was handsome and intelligent, but somewhat prejudiced by the traditions and principles which he had inherited, along with his muscular frame, from a long line of ancestors.

Society gladly welcomed him and he enjoyed himself after the fashion of a well-to-do and seriously inclined young man. But it happened that a friend introduced him to a young actress, a pupil of the Conservatoire, who was appearing with great success at the Odéon. It was a case of love at first sight.

His sentiment had all the violence, the passion of a man born to believe in absolute ideas. He saw her act the romantic rôle in which she had achieved a triumph the first night of her appearance. She was pretty, and, though naturally perverse, possessed the face of an angel.

She conquered him completely; she transformed him into a delirious fool, into one of those ecstatic idiots whom a woman's look will forever chain to the pyre of fatal passions. She became his mistress and left the stage. They lived together four years, his love for her increasing during the time. He would have married her in spite of his proud name and family traditions, had he not discovered that for a long time she had been unfaithful to him with the friend who had introduced them.

The awakening was terrible, for she was about to become a mother, and he was awaiting the birth of the child to make her his wife.

When he held the proof of her transgressions,—some letters found in a drawer,—he confronted her with his knowledge and reproached her with all the savageness of his uncouth nature for her unfaithfulness and deceit. But she, a child of the people, being as sure of this man as of the other, braved and insulted him with the inherited daring of those women, who, in times of war, mounted with the men on the barricades.

He would have struck her to the ground—but she showed him her form. As white as death, he checked himself, remembering that a child of his would soon be born to this vile, polluted creature. He rushed at her to crush them both, to obliterate this double shame. Reeling under his blows, and seeing that he was about to stamp out the life of her unborn babe, she realized that she was lost. Throwing out her hands to parry the blows, she cried:

"Do not kill me! It is his, not yours!"

He fell back, so stunned with surprise that for a moment his rage subsided. He stammered:

"What? What did you say?"

Crazed with fright, having read her doom in his eyes and gestures, she repeated: "It's not yours, it's his."

Through his clenched teeth he stammered:

"The child?"

"Yes."

"You lie!"

And again he lifted his foot as if to crush her, while she struggled to her knees in a vain attempt to rise. "I tell you it's his. If it was yours, wouldn't it have come much sooner?"

He was struck by the truth of this argument. In a moment of strange lucidity, his mind evolved precise, conclusive, irresistible reasons to disclaim the child of this miserable woman, and he felt so appeased, so happy at the thought, that he decided to let her live.

He then spoke in a calmer voice: "Get up and leave, and never let me see you again."

Quite cowed, she obeyed him and went. He never saw her again.

Then he left Paris and came south. He stopped in a village situated in a valley, near the coast of the Mediterranean. Selecting for his abode an inn facing the sea, he lived there eighteen months in complete seclusion, nursing his sorrow and despair. The memory of the unfaithful one tortured him; her grace, her charm, her perversity haunted him, and withal came the regret of her caresses.

He wandered aimlessly in those beautiful vales of Provence, baring his head, filled with the thoughts of that woman, to the sun that filtered through the grayish-green leaves of the olive-trees.

His former ideas of religion, the abated ardor of his faith, returned to him during his sorrowful retreat. Religion had formerly seemed a refuge from the unknown temptations of life, now it appeared as a refuge from its snares and tortures. He had never given up the habit of prayer. In his sorrow, he turned anew to its consolations, and often at dusk he would wander into the little village church, where in the darkness gleamed the light of the lamp hung above the altar, to guard the sanctuary and symbolize the Divine Presence.

He confided his sorrow to his God, told Him of his misery, asking advice, pity, help, and consolation. Each day, his fervid prayers disclosed stronger faith.

The bleeding heart of this man, crushed by love for a woman, still longed for affection; and soon his prayers, his seclusion, his constant communion with the Savior who consoles and cheers the weary, wrought a change in him, and the mystic love of God entered his soul, casting out the love of the flesh.

He then decided to take up his former plans and to devote his life to the Church.

He became a priest. Through family connections he succeeded in obtaining a call to the parish of this village which he had come across by chance. Devoting a large part of his fortune to the maintenance of charitable institutions, and keeping only enough to enable him to help the poor as long as he lived, he sought refuge in a quiet life filled with prayer and acts of kindness toward his fellow-men.

Narrow-minded but kind-hearted, a priest with a soldier's temperament, he guided his blind, erring flock forcibly through the mazes of this life in which every taste, instinct, and desire is a pitfall. But the old man in him never disappeared entirely. He continued to love out-of-door exercise and noble sports, but he hated every woman, having an almost childish fear of their dangerous fascination.

II.

The sailor who followed the priest, being a southerner, found it difficult to refrain from talking. But he did not dare start a conversation, for the abbé exerted a great prestige over his flock. At last he ventured a remark: "So you like your lodge, do you, Monsieur le Curé?"

This lodge was one of the tiny constructions that are inhabited during the summer by the villagers and the town people alike. It was situated in a field not far from the parish-house, and the abbé had hired it because the latter was very small and built in the heart of the village next to the church.

During the summer time, he did not live altogether at the lodge, but would remain a few days at a time to practice pistol-shooting and be close to nature.

"Yes, my friend," said the priest, "I like it very well."

The low structure could now be seen; it was painted pink, and the walls were almost hidden under the leaves and branches of the olive-trees that grew in the open field. A tall woman was passing in and out of the door, setting a small table at which she placed, at each trip, a knife and fork, a glass, a plate, a napkin, and a piece of bread. She wore the small cap of the women of Arles, a pointed cone of silk or black velvet, decorated with a white rosette.

When the abbé was near enough to make himself heard, he shouted:

"Eh! Marguerite!"

She stopped to ascertain whence the voice came, and recognizing her master: "Oh! it's you, Monsieur le Curé!"

"Yes. I have caught some fine fish, and want you to broil this sunfish immediately, do you hear?"

The servant examined, with a critical and approving glance, the fish that the sailor carried.

"Yes, but we are going to have a chicken for dinner," she said.

"Well, it cannot be helped. To-morrow the fish will not be as fresh as it is now. I mean to enjoy a little feast—it does not happen often—and the sin is not great."

The woman picked out a sunfish and prepared to go into the house. "Ah!" she said, "a man came to see you three times while you were out, Monsieur le Curé."

Indifferently he inquired: "A man! What kind of man?"

"Why, a man whose appearance was not in his favor."

"What! a beggar?"

"Perhaps—I don't know. But I think he is more of a 'maoufatan.'"

The abbé smiled at this word, which, in the language of Provence means a highwayman, a tramp, for he was well aware of Marguerite's timidity, and knew that every day and especially every night she fancied they would be murdered.

He handed a few sous to the sailor, who departed. And just as he was saying: "I am going to wash my hands,"—for his past dainty habits still clung to him,—Marguerite called to him from the kitchen where she was scraping the fish with a knife, thereby detaching its blood-stained, silvery scales:

"There he comes!"

The abbé looked down the road and saw a man coming slowly toward the house; he seemed poorly dressed, indeed, so far as he could distinguish. He could not help smiling at his servant's anxiety, and thought, while he waited for the stranger: "I think, after all, she is right; he does look like a 'maoufatan.'"

The man walked slowly, with his eyes on the priest and his hands buried deep in his pockets. He was young and wore a full, blond beard; strands of curly hair escaped from his soft felt hat, which was so dirty and battered that it was impossible to imagine its former color and appearance. He was clothed in a long, dark overcoat, from which emerged the frayed edge of his trousers; on his feet were bathing shoes that deadened his steps, giving him the stealthy walk of a sneak thief.

When he had come within a few steps of the priest, he doffed, with a sweeping motion, the ragged hat that shaded his brow. He was not bad looking, though his face showed signs of dissipation and the top of his head was bald, an indication of premature fatigue and debauch, for he certainly was not over twenty-five years old.

The priest responded at once to his bow, feeling that this fellow was not an ordinary tramp, a mechanic out of work, or a jail-bird, hardly able to speak any other tongue but the mysterious language of prisons.

"How do you do, Monsieur le Curé?" said the man. The priest answered simply, "I salute you," unwilling to address this ragged stranger as "Monsieur." They considered each other attentively; the abbé felt uncomfortable under the gaze of the tramp, invaded by a feeling of unrest unknown to him.

At last the vagabond continued: "Well, do you recognize me?"

Greatly surprised, the priest answered: "Why, no, you are a stranger to me."

"Ah! you do not know me? Look at me well."

"I have never seen you before."

"Well, that may be true," replied the man sarcastically, "but let me show you some one whom you will know better."

He put on his hat and unbuttoned his coat, revealing his bare chest. A red sash wound around his spare frame held his trousers in place. He drew an envelope from his coat pocket, one of those soiled wrappers destined to protect the sundry papers of the tramp, whether they be stolen or legitimate property, those papers which he guards jealously and uses to protect himself against the too zealous gendarmes. He pulled out a photograph about the size of a folded letter, one of those pictures which were popular long ago; it was yellow and dim with age, for he had carried it around with him everywhere and the heat of his body had faded it.

Pushing it under the abbé's eyes, he demanded:

"Do you know him?"

The priest took a step forward to look and grew pale, for it was his own likeness that he had given Her years ago.

Failing to grasp the meaning of the situation he remained silent.

The tramp repeated:

"Do you recognize him?"

And the priest stammered: "Yes."

"Who is it?"

"It is I."

"It is you?"

"Yes."

"Well, then, look at us both,—at me and at your picture!"

Already the unhappy man had seen that these two beings, the one in the picture and the one by his side, resembled each other like brothers; yet he did not understand, and muttered: "Well, what is it you wish?"

Then in an ugly voice, the tramp replied: "What do I wish? Why, first I wish you to recognize me."

"Who are you?"

"Who am I? Ask anybody by the roadside, ask your servant, let's go and ask the mayor and show him this; and he will laugh, I tell you that! Ah! you will not recognize me as your son, papa curé?"

The old man raised his arms above his head, with a patriarchal gesture, and muttered despairingly: "It cannot be true!"

The young fellow drew quite close to him.

"Ah! It cannot be true, you say! You must stop lying, do you hear?" His clenched fists and threatening face, and the violence with which he spoke, made the priest retreat a few steps, while he asked himself anxiously which one of them was laboring under a mistake.

Again he asserted: "I never had a child."

The other man replied: "And no mistress, either?"

The aged priest resolutely uttered one word, a proud admission:

"Yes."

"And was not this mistress about to give birth to a child when you left her?"

Suddenly the anger which had been quelled twenty-five years ago, not quelled, but buried in the heart of the lover, burst through the wall of faith, resignation, and renunciation he had built around it. Almost beside himself, he shouted:

"I left her because she was unfaithful to me and was carrying the child of another man; had it not been for this, I should have killed both you and her, sir!"

The young man hesitated, taken aback at the sincerity of this outburst. Then he replied in a gentler voice:

"Who told you that it was another man's child?"

"She told me herself and braved me."

Without contesting this assertion the vagabond assumed the indifferent tone of a loafer judging a case:

"Well, then, mother made a mistake, that's all!"

After his outburst of rage, the priest had succeeded in mastering himself sufficiently to be able to inquire:

"And who told you that you were my son?"

"My mother, on her deathbed, M'sieur le Curé. And then—this!" And he held the picture under the eyes of the priest.

The old man took it from him; and slowly, with a heart bursting with anguish, he compared this stranger with his faded likeness and doubted no longer—it was his son.

An awful distress wrung his very soul, a terrible, inexpressible emotion invaded him; it was like the remorse of some ancient crime. He began to understand a little, he guessed the rest. He lived over the brutal scene of the parting. It was to save her life, then, that the wretched and deceitful woman had lied to him, her outraged lover. And he had believed her. And a son of his had been brought into the world and had grown up to be this sordid tramp, who exhaled the very odor of vice as a goat exhales its animal smell.

He whispered: "Will you take a little walk with me, so that we can discuss these matters?"

The young man sneered: "Why, certainly! Isn't that what I came for?"

They walked side by side through the olive grove. The sun had gone down and the coolness of southern twilights spread an invisible cloak over the country. The priest shivered, and raising his eyes with a familiar motion, perceived the trembling gray foliage of the holy tree which had spread its frail shadow over the Son of Man in His great trouble and despondency.

A short, despairing prayer rose within him, uttered by his soul's voice, a prayer by which Christians implore the Savior's aid: "O Lord! have mercy on me."

Turning to his son he said: "So your mother is dead?"

These words, "Your mother is dead," awakened a new sorrow; it was the torment of the flesh which cannot forget, the cruel echo of past sufferings; but mostly the thrill of the fleeting, delirious bliss of his youthful passion.

The young man replied: "Yes, Monsieur le Curé, my mother is dead."

"Has she been dead a long while?"

"Yes, three years."

A new doubt entered the priest's mind. "And why did you not find me out before?"

The other man hesitated.

"I was unable to, I was prevented. But excuse me for interrupting these recollections—I will enter into more details later—for I have not had anything to eat since yesterday morning."

A tremor of pity shook the old man and holding forth both hands: "Oh! my poor child!" he said.

The young fellow took those big, powerful hands in his own slender and feverish palms.

Then he replied, with that air of sarcasm which hardly ever left his lips: "Ah! I'm beginning to think that we shall get along very well together, after all!"

The curé started toward the lodge.

"Let us go to dinner," he said.

He suddenly remembered, with a vague and instinctive pleasure, the fine fish he had caught, which, with the chicken, would make a good meal for the poor fellow.

The servant was in front of the door, watching their approach with an anxious and forbidding face.

"Marguerite," shouted the abbé, "take the table and put it into the dining-room, right away; and set two places, as quick as you can."

The woman seemed stunned at the idea that her master was going to dine with this tramp.

But the abbé, without waiting for her, removed the plate and napkin and carried the little table into the dining-room.

A few minutes later he was sitting opposite the beggar, in front of a soup-tureen filled with savory cabbage soup, which sent up a cloud of fragrant steam.

III.

When the plates were filled, the tramp fell to with ravenous avidity. The abbé had lost his appetite and ate slowly, leaving the bread in the bottom of his plate. Suddenly he inquired:

"What is your name?"

The man smiled; he was delighted to satisfy his hunger.

"Father unknown," he said, "and no other name but my mother's, which you probably remember. But I possess two Christian names, which, by the way, are quite unsuited to me—Philippe-Auguste."

The priest whitened.

"Why were you named thus?" he asked.

The tramp shrugged his shoulders. "I fancy you ought to know. After mother left you, she wished to make your rival believe that I was his child. He did believe it until I was about fifteen. Then I began to look too much like you. And he disclaimed me, the scoundrel. I had been christened Philippe-Auguste; now, if I had not resembled a soul, or if I had been the son of a third person, who had stayed in the background, to-day I should be the Vicomte Philippe-Auguste de Pravallon, son of the count and senator bearing this name. I have christened myself 'No-luck.'"

"How did you learn all this?"

"They discussed it before me, you know; pretty lively discussions they were, too. I tell you, that's what shows you the seamy side of life!"

Something more distressing than all he had suffered during the last half hour now oppressed the priest. It was a sort of suffocation which seemed as if it would grow and grow till it killed him; it was not due so much to the things he heard as to the manner in which they were uttered by this wayside tramp. Between himself and this beggar, between his son and himself, he was discovering the existence of those moral divergencies which are as fatal poisons to certain souls. Was this his son? He could not yet believe it. He wanted all the proofs, every one of them. He wanted to hear all, to listen to all. Again he thought of the olive-trees that shaded his little lodge, and for the second time he prayed: "O Lord! have mercy upon me."

Philippe-Auguste had finished his soup. He inquired: "Is there nothing else, abbé?"

The kitchen was built in an annex. Marguerite could not hear her master's voice. He always called her by striking a Chinese gong hung on the wall behind his chair. He took the brass hammer and struck the round metal plate. It gave a feeble sound, which grew and vibrated, becoming sharper and louder till it finally died away on the evening breeze.

The servant appeared with a frowning face and cast angry glances at the tramp, as if her faithful instinct had warned her of the misfortune that had befallen her master. She held a platter on which was the sunfish, spreading a savory odor of melted butter through the room. The abbé divided the fish lengthwise, helping his son to the better half: "I caught it a little while ago," he said, with a touch of pride in spite of his keen distress.

Marguerite had not left the room.

The priest added: "Bring us some wine, the white wine of Cape Corse."

She almost rebelled, and the priest, assuming a severe expression was obliged to repeat: "Now, go, and bring two bottles, remember," for, when he drank with anybody, a very rare pleasure, indeed, he always opened one bottle for himself.

Beaming, Philippe-Auguste remarked: "Fine! A splendid idea! It has been a long time since I've had such a dinner." The servant came back after a few minutes. The abbé thought it an eternity, for now a thirst for information burned his blood like infernal fire.

After the bottles had been opened, the woman still remained, her eyes glued on the tramp.

"Leave us," said the curé.

She intentionally ignored his command.

He repeated almost roughly: "I have ordered you to leave us."

Then she left the room.

Philippe-Auguste devoured the fish voraciously, while his father sat watching him, more and more surprised and saddened at all the baseness stamped on the face that was so like his own. The morsels the abbé raised to his lips remained in his mouth, for his throat could not swallow; so he ate slowly, trying to choose, from the host of questions which besieged his mind, the one he wished his son to answer first. At last he spoke:

"What was the cause of her death?"

"Consumption."

"Was she ill a long time?"

"About eighteen months."

"How did she contract it?"

"We could not tell."

Both men were silent. The priest was reflecting. He was oppressed by the multitude of things he wished to know and to hear, for since the rupture, since the day he had tried to kill her, he had heard nothing. Certainly, he had not cared to know, because he had buried her, along with his happiest days, in forgetfulness; but now, knowing that she was dead and gone, he felt within himself the almost jealous desire of a lover to hear all.

He continued: "She was not alone, was she?"

"No, she lived with him."

The old man started: "With him? With Pravallon?"

"Why, yes."

And the betrayed man rapidly calculated that the woman who had deceived him, had lived over thirty years with his rival.

Almost unconsciously he asked: "Were they happy?"

The young man sneered. "Why, yes, with ups and downs! It would have been better had I not been there. I always spoiled everything."

"How, and why?" inquired the priest.

"I have already told you. Because he thought I was his son up to my fifteenth year. But the old fellow wasn't a fool, and soon discovered the likeness. That created scenes. I used to listen behind the door. He accused mother of having deceived him. Mother would answer: 'Is it my fault? you knew quite well when you took me that I was the mistress of that other man.' You were that other man."

"Ah! They spoke of me sometimes?"

"Yes, but never mentioned your name before me, excepting toward the end, when mother knew she was lost. I think they distrusted me."

"And you—and you learned quite early the irregularity of your mother's position?"

"Why, certainly. I am not innocent and I never was. Those things are easy to guess as soon as one begins to know life."

Philippe-Auguste had been filling his glass repeatedly. His eyes now were beginning to sparkle, for his long fast was favorable to the intoxicating effects of the wine. The priest noticed it and wished to caution him. But suddenly the thought that a drunkard is imprudent and loquacious flashed through him, and lifting the bottle he again filled the young man's glass.

Meanwhile Marguerite had brought the chicken. Having set it on the table, she again fastened her eyes on the tramp, saying in an indignant voice: "Can't you see that he's drunk, Monsieur le Curé?"

"Leave us," replied the priest, "and return to the kitchen."

She went out, slamming the door.

He then inquired: "What did your mother say about me?"

"Why, what a woman usually says of a man she has jilted: that you were hard to get along with, very strange, and that you would have made her life miserable with your peculiar ideas."

"Did she say that often?"

"Yes, but sometimes only in allusions, for fear I would understand; but nevertheless I guessed all."

"And how did they treat you in that house?"

"Me? They treated me very well at first and very badly afterward. When mother saw that I was interfering with her, she shook me."

"How?"

"How? very easily. When I was about sixteen years old, I got into various scrapes, and those blackguards put me into a reformatory to get rid of me." He put his elbows on the table and rested his cheeks in his palms. He was hopelessly intoxicated, and felt the unconquerable desire of all drunkards to talk and boast about themselves.

He smiled sweetly, with a feminine grace, an arch grace the priest knew and recognized as the hated charm that had won him long ago, and had also wrought his undoing. Now it was his mother whom the boy resembled, not so much because of his features, but because of his fascinating and deceptive glance, and the seductiveness of the false smile that played around his lips, the outlet of his inner ignominy.

Philippe-Auguste began to relate: "Ah! Ah! Ah!—I've had a fine life since I left the reformatory! A great writer would pay a large sum for it! Why, old Père Dumas's Monte Cristo has had no stranger adventures than mine."

He paused to reflect with the philosophical gravity of the drunkard, then he continued slowly:

"When you wish a boy to turn out well, no matter what he has done, never send him to a reformatory. The associations are too bad. Now, I got into a bad scrape. One night about nine o'clock, I, with three companions—we were all a little drunk—was walking along the road near the ford of Folac. All at once a wagon hove in sight, with the driver and his family asleep in it. They were people from Martinon on their way home from town. I caught hold of the bridle, led the horse to the ferryboat, made him walk into it, and pushed the boat into the middle of the stream. This created some noise and the driver awoke. He could not see in the dark, but whipped up the horse, which started on a run and landed in the water with the whole load. All were drowned! My companions denounced me to the authorities, though they thought it was a good joke when they saw me do it. Really, we didn't think that it would turn out that way. We only wanted to give the people a ducking, just for fun. After that I committed worse offenses to revenge myself for the first one, which did not, on my honor, warrant the reformatory. But what's the use of telling them? I will speak only of the latest one, because I am sure it will please you. Papa, I avenged you!"

The abbé was watching his son with terrified eyes; he had stopped eating.

Philippe-Auguste was preparing to begin. "No, not yet," said the priest, "in a little while."

And he turned to strike the Chinese gong.

Marguerite appeared almost instantly. Her master addressed her in such a rough tone that she hung her head, thoroughly frightened and obedient: "Bring in the lamp and the dessert, and then do not appear until I summon you."

She went out and returned with a porcelain lamp covered with a green shade, and bringing also a large piece of cheese and some fruit.

After she had gone, the abbé turned resolutely to his son.

"Now I am ready to hear you."

Philippe-Auguste calmly filled his plate with dessert and poured wine into his glass. The second bottle was nearly empty, though the priest had not touched it.

His mouth and tongue, thick with food and wine, the man stuttered: "Well, now for the last job. And it's a good one. I was home again,—stayed there in spite of them, because they feared me,—yes, feared me. Ah! you can't fool with me, you know,—I'll do anything, when I'm roused. They lived together on and off. The old man had two residences. One official, for the senator, the other clandestine, for the lover. Still, he lived more in the latter than in the former, as he could not get along without mother. Mother was a sharp one—she knew how to hold a man! She had taken him body and soul, and kept him to the last! Well, I had come back and I kept them down by fright. I am resourceful at times—nobody can match me for sharpness and for strength, too—I'm afraid of no one. Well, mother got sick and the old man took her to a fine place in the country, near Meulan, situated in a park as big as a wood. She lasted about eighteen months, as I told you. Then we felt the end to be near. He came from Paris every day—he was very miserable—really.

"One morning they chatted a long time, over an hour, I think, and I could not imagine what they were talking about. Suddenly mother called me in and said:

"'I am going to die, and there is something I want to tell you beforehand, in spite of the Count's advice.' In speaking of him she always said 'the Count.' 'It is the name of your father, who is alive.' I had asked her this more than fifty times—more than fifty times—my father's name—more than fifty times—and she always refused to tell. I think I even beat her one day to make her talk, but it was of no use. Then, to get rid of me, she told me that you had died penniless, that you were worthless and that she had made a mistake in her youth, an innocent girl's mistake. She lied so well, I really believed you had died.

"Finally she said: 'It is your father's name.'

"The old man, who was sitting in an armchair, repeated three times, like this: 'You do wrong, you do wrong, you do wrong, Rosette.'

"Mother sat up in bed. I can see her now, with her flushed cheeks and shining eyes; she loved me, in spite of everything; and she said: 'Then you do something for him, Philippe!' In speaking to him she called him 'Philippe' and me 'Auguste.'

"He began to shout like a madman: 'Do something for that loafer—that blackguard, that convict? never!'

"And he continued to call me names, as if he had done nothing else all his life but collect them.

"I was angry, but mother told me to hold my tongue, and she resumed: 'Then you must want him to starve, for you know that I leave no money.'

"Without being deterred, he continued: 'Rosette, I have given you thirty-five thousand francs a year for thirty years,—that makes more than a million. I have enabled you to live like a wealthy, a beloved, and I may say, a happy woman. I owe nothing to that fellow, who has spoiled our late years, and he will not get a cent from me. It is useless to insist. Tell him the name of his father, if you wish. I am sorry, but I wash my hands of him.'

"Then mother turned toward me. I thought: 'Good! now I'm going to find my real father—if he has money, I'm saved.'

"She went on: 'Your father, the Baron de Vilbois, is to-day the Abbé Vilbois, curé of Garandou, near Toulon. He was my lover before I left him for the Count!'

"And she told me all, excepting that she had deceived you about her pregnancy. But women, you know, never tell the whole truth."

Sneeringly, unconsciously, he was revealing the depths of his foul nature. With beaming face he raised the glass to his lips and continued:

"Mother died two days—two days later. We followed her remains to the grave, he and I—say—wasn't it funny?—he and I—and three servants—that was all. He cried like a calf—we were side by side—we looked like father and son.

"Then he went back to the house alone. I was thinking to myself: 'I'll have to clear out now and without a penny, too.' I owned only fifty francs. What could I do to revenge myself?

"He touched me on the arm and said: 'I wish to speak to you.' I followed him into his office. He sat down in front of the desk and, wiping away his tears, he told me that he would not be as hard on me as he had said he would to mother. He begged me to leave you alone. That—that concerns only you and me. He offered me a thousand-franc note—a thousand—a thousand francs. What could a fellow like me do with a thousand francs?—I saw that there were very many bills in the drawer. The sight of the money made me wild. I put out my hand as if to take the note he offered me, but instead of doing so, I sprang at him, threw him to the ground and choked him till he grew purple. When I saw that he was going to give up the ghost, I gagged and bound him. Then I undressed him, laid him on his stomach and—ah! ah! ah!—I avenged you in a funny way!"

He stopped to cough, for he was choking with merriment. His ferocious, mirthful smile reminded the priest once more of the woman who had wrought his undoing.

"And then?" he inquired.

"Then,—ah! ah! ah!—There was a bright fire in the fireplace—it was in the winter—in December—mother died—a bright coal fire—I took the poker—I let it get red-hot—and I made crosses on his back, eight or more, I cannot remember how many—then I turned him over and repeated them on his stomach. Say, wasn't it funny, papa? Formerly they marked convicts in this way. He wriggled like an eel—but I had gagged him so that he couldn't scream. I gathered up the bills—twelve in all—with mine it made thirteen—an unlucky number. I left the house, after telling the servants not to bother their master until dinner-time, because he was asleep. I thought that he would hush the matter up because he was a senator and would fear the scandal. I was mistaken. Four days later I was arrested in a Paris restaurant. I got three years for the job. That is the reason why I did not come to you sooner." He drank again, and stuttering so as to render his words almost unintelligible, continued:

"Now—papa—isn't it funny to have one's papa a curé? You must be nice to me, very nice, because, you know, I am not commonplace,—and I did a good job—didn't I—on the old man?"

The anger which years ago had driven the Abbé Vilbois to desperation rose within him at the sight of this miserable man.

He, who in the name of the Lord, had so often pardoned the infamous secrets whispered to him under the seal of confession, was now merciless in his own behalf. No longer did he implore the help of a merciful God, for he realized that no power on earth or in the sky could save those who had been visited by such a terrible disaster.

All the ardor of his passionate heart and of his violent blood, which long years of resignation had tempered, awoke against the miserable creature who was his son. He protested against the likeness he bore to him and to his mother, the wretched mother who had formed him so like herself; and he rebelled against the destiny that had chained this criminal to him, like an iron ball to a galley-slave.

The shock roused him from the peaceful and pious slumber which had lasted twenty-five years; with a wonderful lucidity he saw all that would inevitably ensue.

Convinced that he must talk loud so as to intimidate this man from the first, he spoke with his teeth clenched with fury:

"Now that you have told all, listen to me. You will leave here to-morrow morning. You will go to a country that I shall designate, and never leave it without my permission. I will give you a small income, for I am poor. If you disobey me once, it will be withdrawn and you will learn to know me."

Though Philippe-Auguste was half dazed with wine, he understood the threat. Instantly the criminal within him rebelled. Between hiccoughs he sputtered: "Ah! papa, be careful what you say—you're a curé, remember—I hold you—and you have to walk straight, like the rest!"

The abbé started. Through his whole muscular frame crept the unconquerable desire to seize this monster, to bend him like a twig, so as to show him that he would have to yield.

Shaking the table, he shouted: "Take care, take care—I am afraid of nobody."

The drunkard lost his balance and seeing that he was going to fall and would forthwith be in the priest's power, he reached with a murderous look for one of the knives lying on the table. The abbé perceived his motion, and he gave the table a terrible shove; his son toppled over and landed on his back. The lamp fell with a crash and went out.

During a moment the clinking of broken glass was heard in the darkness, then the muffled sound of a soft body creeping on the floor, and then all was silent.

With the crashing of the lamp a complete darkness spread over them; it was so prompt and unexpected that they were stunned by it as by some terrible event. The drunkard, pressed against the wall, did not move; the priest remained on his chair in the midst of the night which had quelled his rage. The somber veil that had descended so rapidly, arresting his anger, also quieted the furious impulses of his soul; new ideas, as dark and dreary as the obscurity, beset him.

The room was perfectly silent, like a tomb where nothing draws the breath of life. Not a sound came from outside, neither the rumbling of a distant wagon, nor the bark of a dog, nor even the sigh of the wind passing through the trees.

This lasted a long time, perhaps an hour. Then suddenly the gong vibrated! It rang once, as if it had been struck a short, sharp blow, and was instantly followed by the noise of a falling body and an overturned chair.

Marguerite came running out of the kitchen, but as soon as she opened the door she fell back, frightened by the intense darkness. Trembling, her heart beating as if it would burst, she called in a low, hoarse voice: "M'sieur le Curé! M'sieur le Curé!"

Nobody answered, nothing stirred.

"Mon Dieu, mon Dieu," she thought, "what has happened, what have they done?"

She did not dare enter the room, yet feared to go back to fetch a light. She felt as if she would like to run away, to screech at the top of her voice, though she knew her legs would refuse to carry her. She repeated: "M'sieur le Curé! M'sieur le Curé! it is me, Marguerite."

But, notwithstanding her terror, the instinctive desire of helping her master and a woman's courage, which is sometimes heroic, filled her soul with a terrified audacity, and running back to the kitchen she fetched a lamp.

She stopped at the doorsill. First, she caught sight of the tramp lying against the wall, asleep, or simulating slumber; then she saw the broken lamp, and then, under the table, the feet and black-stockinged legs of the priest, who must have fallen backward, striking his head on the gong.

Her teeth chattering and her hands trembling with fright, she kept on repeating: "My God! My God! what is this?"

She advanced slowly, taking small steps, till she slid on something slimy and almost fell.

Stooping, she saw that the floor was red and that a red liquid was spreading around her feet toward the door. She guessed that it was blood. She threw down her light so as to hide the sight of it, and fled from the room out into the fields, running half crazed toward the village. She ran screaming at the top of her voice, and bumping against the trees she did not heed, her eyes fastened on the gleaming lights of the distant town.

Her shrill voice rang out like the gloomy cry of the night-owl, repeating continuously, "The maoufatan—the maoufatan—the maoufatan——"

When she reached the first house, some excited men came out and surrounded her; but she could not answer them and struggled to escape, for the fright had turned her head.

After a while they guessed that something must have happened to the curé, and a little rescuing party started for the lodge.

The little pink house standing in the middle of the olive grove had grown black and invisible in the dark, silent night. Since the gleam of the solitary window had faded, the cabin was plunged in darkness, lost in the grove, and unrecognizable for anyone but a native of the place.

Soon lights began to gleam near the ground, between the trees, streaking the dried grass with long, yellow reflections. The twisted trunks of the olive-trees assumed fantastic shapes under the moving lights, looking like monsters or infernal serpents. The projected reflections suddenly revealed a vague, white mass, and soon the low, square wall of the lodge grew pink from the light of the lanterns. Several peasants were carrying the latter, escorting two gendarmes with revolvers, the mayor, the garde-champêtre, and Marguerite, supported by the men, for she was almost unable to walk.

The rescuing party hesitated a moment in front of the open, grewsome door. But the brigadier, snatching a lantern from one of the men, entered, followed by the rest.

The servant had not lied, blood covered the floor like a carpet. It had spread to the place where the tramp was lying, bathing one of his hands and legs.

The father and son were asleep, the one with a severed throat, the other in a drunken stupor. The two gendarmes seized the latter and before he awoke they had him handcuffed. He rubbed his eyes, stunned, stupefied with liquor, and when he saw the body of the priest, he appeared terrified, unable to understand what had happened.

"Why did he not escape?" said the mayor.

"He was too drunk," replied the officer.

And every man agreed with him, for nobody ever thought that perhaps the Abbé Vilbois had taken his own life.

REVENGE

As they were still speaking of Pranzini, M. Maloureau, who had been Attorney-General under the Empire, said:

"I knew another case like that, a very curious affair, curious from many points, as you shall see.

"I was at that time Imperial attorney in the province, and stood very well at Court, thanks to my father, who was first President at Paris. I had charge of a still celebrated case, called 'The Affair of Schoolmaster Moiron.'

"M. Moiron, a schoolmaster in the north of France, bore an excellent reputation in all the country thereabout. He was an intelligent, reflective, very religious man, and had married in the district of Boislinot, where he practiced his profession. He had had three children, who all died in succession from weak lungs. After the loss of his own little ones, he seemed to lavish upon the urchins confided to his care all the tenderness concealed in his heart. He bought, with his own pennies, playthings for his best pupils, the diligent and good. He allowed them to have play dinners, and gorged them with dainties of candies and cakes. Everybody loved and praised this brave man, this brave heart, and it was like a blow when five of his pupils died of the same disease that had carried off his children. It was believed that an epidemic prevailed, caused by the water being made impure from drought. They looked for the cause, without discovering it, more than they did at the symptoms, which were very strange. The children appeared to be taken with a languor, could eat nothing, complained of pains in the stomach, and finally died in most terrible agony.

"An autopsy was made of the last to die, but nothing was discovered. The entrails were sent to Paris and analyzed, but showed no sign of any toxic substance.

"For one year no further deaths occurred; then two little boys, the best pupils in the class, favorites of father Moiron, expired in four days' time. An examination was ordered, and in each body fragments of pounded glass were found imbedded in the organs. They concluded that the two children had eaten imprudently of something carelessly prepared. Sufficient broken glass remained in the bottom of a bowl of milk to have caused this frightful accident, and the matter would have rested there had not Moiron's servant been taken ill in the interval. The physician found the same morbid signs that he observed in the preceding attacks of the children, and, upon questioning her, finally obtained the confession that she had stolen and eaten some bonbons, bought by the master for his pupils.

"Upon order of the court, the schoolhouse was searched and a closet was found, full of sweetmeats and dainties for the children. Nearly all these edibles contained fragments of glass or broken needles.

"Moiron was immediately arrested. He was so indignant and stupefied at the weight of suspicion upon him that he was nearly overcome. Nevertheless, the indications of his guilt were so apparent that they fought hard in my mind against my first conviction, which was based upon his good reputation, his entire life of truthfulness, and the absolute absence of any motive for such a crime.

"Why should this good, simple religious man kill children, and the children whom he seemed to love best? Why should he select those he had feasted with dainties, for whom he had spent in playthings and bonbons half his stipend?

"To admit this, it must be concluded that he was insane. But Moiron seemed so reasonable, so calm, so full of judgment and good sense! It was impossible to prove insanity in him.

"Proofs accumulated, nevertheless! Bonbons, cakes, pâtés of marshmallow, and other things seized at the shops where the schoolmaster got his supplies were found to contain no suspected fragment.

"He pretended that some unknown enemy had opened his closet with a false key and placed the glass and needles in the eatables. And he implied a story of heritage dependent on the death of a child, sought out and discovered by a peasant, and so worked up as to make the suspicion fall upon the schoolmaster. This brute, he said, was not interested in the other poor children who had to die also.

"This theory was plausible. The man appeared so sure of himself and so pitiful, that we should have acquitted him without doubt, if two overwhelming discoveries had not been made at one blow. The first was a snuffbox full of ground glass! It was his own snuffbox, in a secret drawer of his secretary, where he kept his money.

"He explained this in a manner not acceptable, by saying that it was the last ruse of an unknown guilty one. But a merchant of Saint-Marlouf presented himself at the house of the judge, telling him that Moiron had bought needles of him many times, the finest needles he could find, breaking them to see whether they suited him.

"The merchant brought as witnesses a dozen persons who recognized Moiron at first glance. And the inquest revealed the fact that the schoolmaster was at Saint-Marlouf on the days designated by the merchant.

"I pass over the terrible depositions of the children upon the master's choice of dainties, and his care in making the little ones eat in his presence and destroying all traces of the feast.

"Public opinion, exasperated, recalled capital punishment, and took on a new force from terror which permitted no delays or resistance.

"Moiron was condemned to death. His appeal was rejected. No recourse remained to him for pardon. I knew from my father that the Emperor would not grant it.

"One morning, as I was at work in my office, the chaplain of the prison was announced. He was an old priest who had a great knowledge of men and a large acquaintance among criminals. He appeared troubled and constrained. After talking a few moments of other things, he said abruptly, on rising:

"'If Moiron is decapitated, Monsieur Attorney-General, you will have allowed the execution of an innocent man.'

"Then, without bowing, he went out, leaving me under the profound effect of his words. He had pronounced them in a solemn, affecting fashion, opening lips, closed and sealed by confession, in order to save a life.

"An hour later I was on my way to Paris, and my father, at my request, asked an immediate audience with the Emperor.

"I was received the next day. Napoleon III. was at work in a little room when we were introduced. I exposed the whole affair, even to the visit of the priest, and, in the midst of the story, the door opened behind the chair of the Emperor, and the Empress, who believed in him alone, entered. His Majesty consulted her. When she had run over the facts, she exclaimed:

"'This man must be pardoned! He must, because he is innocent.'

"Why should this sudden conviction of a woman so pious throw into my mind a terrible doubt?

"Up to that time I had ardently desired a commutation of the sentence. And now I felt myself the puppet, the dupe of a criminal ruse, which had employed the priest and the confession as a means of defense.

"I showed some hesitation to their Majesties. The Emperor remained undecided, solicited on one hand by his natural goodness, and on the other held back by the fear of allowing himself to play a miserable part; but the Empress, convinced that the priest had obeyed a divine call, repeated: 'What does it matter? It is better to spare a guilty man than to kill an innocent one.' Her advice prevailed. The penalty of death was commuted, and that of hard labor was substituted.

"Some years after I heard that Moiron, whose exemplary conduct at Toulon had been made known again to the Emperor, was employed as a domestic by the director of the penitentiary. And then I heard no word of this man for a long time.

"About two years after this, when I was passing the summer at the house of my cousin, De Larielle, a young priest came to me one evening, as we were sitting down to dinner, and wished to speak to me.

"I told them to let him come in, and he begged me to go with him to a dying man, who desired, before all else, to see me. This had happened often, during my long career as judge, and, although I had been put aside by the Republic, I was still called upon from time to time in like circumstances.

"I followed the ecclesiastic, who made me mount into a little miserable lodging, under the roof of a high house. There, upon a pallet of straw, I found a dying man, seated with his back against the wall, in order to breathe. He was a sort of grimacing skeleton, with deep, shining eyes.

"When he saw me he murmured: 'You do not know me?'

"'No.'

"'I am Moiron.'

"I shivered, but said: 'The schoolmaster?'

"'Yes.'

"'How is it you are here?'

"'That would be too long—I haven't time—I am going to die—They brought me this curate—and as I knew you were here, I sent him for you—It is to you that I wish to confess—since you saved my life before—the other time——'

"He seized with his dry hands the straw of his bed, and continued, in a rasping, bass voice:

"'Here it is—I owe you the truth—to you, because it is necessary to tell it to some one before leaving the earth.

"'It was I who killed the children—all—it was I—for vengeance!

"'Listen. I was an honest man, very honest—very honest—very pure—adoring God—the good God—the God that they teach us to love, and not the false God, the executioner, the robber, the murderer who governs the earth—I had never done wrong, never committed a villainous act. I was pure as one unborn.

"'After I was married I had some children, and I began to love them as never father or mother loved their own. I lived only for them. I was foolish. They died, all three of them! Why? Why? What had I done? I? I had a change of heart, a furious change. Suddenly I opened my eyes as of one awakening; and I learned that God is wicked. Why had He killed my children? I opened my eyes and I saw that He loved to kill. He loves only that, Monsieur. He exists only to destroy! God is a murderer! Some death is necessary to Him every day. He causes them in all fashions, the better to amuse Himself. He has invented sickness and accident in order to divert Himself through all the long months and years. And, when He is weary, He has epidemics, pests, the cholera, quinsy, smallpox.

"'How do I know all that this monster has imagined? All these evils are not enough to suffice. From time to time He sends war, in order to see two hundred thousand soldiers laid low, bruised in blood and mire, with arms and legs torn off, heads broken by bullets, like eggs that fall along the road.

"'That is not all. He has made men who eat one another. And then, as men become better than He, He has made beasts to see the men chase them, slaughter, and nourish themselves with them. That is not all. He has made all the little animals that live for a day, flies which increase by myriads in an hour, ants, that one crushes, and others, many, so many that we cannot even imagine them. And all kill one another, chase one another, devour one another, murdering without ceasing. And the good God looks on and is amused, because He sees all for Himself, the largest as well as the smallest, those which are in drops of water, as well as those in the stars. He looks at them all and is amused! Ugh! Beast!

"'So I, Monsieur, I also have killed some children. I acted the part for Him. It was not He who had them. It was not He, it was I. And I would have killed still more, but you took me away. That's all!

"'I was going to die, guillotined. I! How He would have laughed, the reptile! Then I asked for a priest, and lied to him. I confessed. I lied, and I lived.

"'Now it is finished. I can no longer escape Him. But I have no fear of Him, Monsieur, I understand Him too well.'

"It was frightful to see this miserable creature, hardly able to breathe, talking in hiccoughs, opening an enormous mouth to eject some words scarcely heard, pulling up the cloth of his straw bed, and, under a cover nearly black, moving his meager limbs as if to save himself.

"Oh! frightful being and frightful remembrance!

"I asked him: 'You have nothing more to say?'

"'No, Monsieur.'

"'Then, farewell.'

"'Farewell, sir, one day or the other.'

“I turned toward the priest, whose somber silhouette was on the wall.

“’You will remain, M. Abbé?’

“’I will remain.’

“Then the dying man sneered: ‘Yes, yes, he sends crows to dead bodies.’

“As for me, I had seen enough. I opened the door and went away in self-protection.”

AN OLD MAID

In Argenteuil they called her Queen Hortense. No one ever knew the reason why. Perhaps because she spoke firmly, like an officer in command. Perhaps because she was large, bony, and imperious. Perhaps because she governed a multitude of domestic animals, hens, dogs, cats, canaries, and parrots,—those animals so dear to old maids. But she gave these familiar subjects neither dainties, nor pretty words, nor those tender puerilities which seem to slip from the lips of a woman to the velvety coat of the cat she is fondling. She governed her beasts with authority. She ruled.

She was an old maid, one of those old maids with cracked voice, and awkward gesture, whose soul seems hard. She never allowed contradiction from any person, nor argument, nor would she tolerate hesitation, or indifference, or idleness, or fatigue. No one ever heard her complain, or regret what was, or desire what was not. "Each to his part," she said, with the conviction of a fatalist. She never went to church, cared nothing for the priests, scarcely believed in God, and called all religious things "mourning merchandise."

For thirty years she had lived in her little house, with its tiny garden in front, extending along the street, never modifying her garments, changing only maids, and that mercilessly, when they became twenty-one years old.

She replaced, without tears and without regrets, her dogs or cats or birds, when they died of old age, or by accident, and she buried trespassing animals in a flower-bed, heaping the earth above them and treading it down with perfect indifference.

She had in the town some acquaintances, the families of employers, whose men went to Paris every day. Sometimes they would invite her to go to the theater with them. She inevitably fell asleep on these occasions, and they were obliged to wake her when it was time to go home. She never allowed anyone to accompany her, having no fear by night or day. She seemed to have no love for children.

She occupied her time with a thousand masculine cares, carpentry, gardening, cutting or sawing wood, repairing her old house, even doing mason's work when it was necessary.

She had some relatives who came to see her twice a year. Her two sisters, Madame Cimme and Madame Columbel, were married, one to a florist, the other to a small householder. Madame Cimme had no children; Madame Columbel had three: Henry, Pauline, and Joseph. Henry was twenty-one, Pauline and Joseph were three, having come when one would have thought the mother past the age. No tenderness united this old maid to her kinsfolk.

In the spring of 1882, Queen Hortense became suddenly ill. The neighbors went for a physician, whom she drove away. When the priest presented himself she got out of bed, half naked, and put him out of doors. The little maid, weeping, made gruel for her.

After three days in bed, the situation became so grave that the carpenter living next door, after counsel with the physician (now reinstated with authority), took it upon himself to summon the two families.

They arrived by the same train, about ten o'clock in the morning; the Columbels having brought their little Joseph.

When they approached the garden gate, they saw the maid seated in a chair against the wall, weeping. The dog lay asleep on the mat before the door, under a broiling sun; two cats, that looked as if dead, lay stretched out on the window-sills, with eyes closed and paws and tails extended at full length. A great glossy hen was promenading before the door, at the head of a flock of chickens, covered with yellow down, and in a large cage hung against the wall, covered with chickweed, were several birds, singing themselves hoarse in the light of this hot spring morning.

Two others, inseparable, in a little cage in the form of a cottage, remained quiet, side by side on their perch.

M. Cimme, a large, wheezy personage, who always entered a room first, putting aside men and women when it was necessary, remarked to the maid: "Eh, Celeste! Is it so bad as that?"

The little maid sobbed through her tears:

"She doesn't know me any more. The doctor says it is the end."

They all looked at one another.

Madame Cimme and Madame Columbel embraced each other instantly, not saying a word.

They resembled each other much, always wearing braids of hair and shawls of red cashmere, as bright as hot coals.

Cimme turned toward his brother-in-law, a pale man, yellow and thin, tormented by indigestion, who limped badly, and said to him in a serious tone:

"Gad! It was time!"

But no one dared to go into the room of the dying woman situated on the ground floor. Cimme himself stopped at that step. Columbel was the first to decide upon it; he entered, balancing himself like the mast of a ship, making a noise on the floor with the iron of his cane.

The two women ventured to follow, and M. Cimme brought up the line.

Little Joseph remained outside, playing with the dog.

A ray of sunlight fell on the bed, lighting up the hands which moved nervously, opening and shutting without ceasing. The fingers moved as if a thought animated them, as if they would signify something, indicate some idea, obey some intelligence. The rest of the body remained motionless under the covers. The angular figure gave no start. The eyes remained closed.

The relatives arranged themselves in a semicircle and, without saying a word, regarded the heaving breast and the short breathing. The little maid had followed them, still shedding tears.

Finally, Cimme asked: "What was it the doctor said?"

The servant whispered: "He said we should leave her quiet, that nothing more could be done."

Suddenly the lips of the old maid began to move. She seemed to pronounce some silent words, concealed in her dying brain, and her hands quickened their singular movement.

Then she spoke in a little, thin voice, quite unlike her own, an utterance that seemed to come from far off, perhaps from the bottom of that heart always closed.

Cimme walked upon tiptoe, finding this spectacle painful. Columbel, whose lame leg wearied him, sat down.

The two women remained standing.

Queen Hortense muttered something quickly, which they were unable to understand. She pronounced some names, called tenderly some imaginary persons:

"Come here, my little Philip, kiss your mother. You love mamma, don't you, my child? You, Rose, you will watch your little sister while I am out. Especially, don't leave her alone, do you hear? And I forbid you to touch matches."

She was silent some seconds; then, in a loud tone, as if she would call, she said: "Henrietta!" She waited a little and continued: "Tell your father to come and speak to me before going to his office." Then suddenly: "I am suffering a little to-day, dear; promise me you will not return late; you will tell your chief that I am ill. You know it is dangerous to leave the children alone when I am in bed. I am going to make you a dish of rice and sugar for dinner. The little ones like it so much. Claire will be the happy one!"

She began to laugh, a young and noisy laugh, as she had never laughed before. "Look, John," she said, "what a droll head he has. He has smeared himself with the sugarplums, the dirty thing! Look! my dear, how funny he looks!"

Columbel, who changed the position of his lame leg every moment, murmured: "She is dreaming that she has children and a husband; the end is near."

The two sisters did not move, but seemed surprised and stupid.

The little maid said: "Will you take off your hats and your shawls, and go into the other room?"

They went out without having said a word. And Columbel followed them limping, leaving the dying woman alone again.

When they were relieved of their outer garments, the women seated themselves. Then one of the cats left the window, stretched herself, jumped into the room, then upon the knees of Madame Cimme, who began to caress her.

They heard from the next room the voice of agony, living, without doubt, in this last hour, the life she had expected, living her dreams at the very moment when all would be finished for her.

Cimme, in the garden, played with the little Joseph and the dog, amusing himself much, with the gaiety of a great man in the country, without thought of the dying woman.

But suddenly he entered, addressing the maid: "Say, then, my girl, are you going to give us some luncheon? What are you going to eat, ladies?"

They decided upon an omelet of fine herbs, a piece of fillet with new potatoes, a cheese, and a cup of coffee.

And as Madame Columbel was fumbling in her pocket for her purse: Cimme stopped her, and turning to the maid said, “You need money?” and she answered: “Yes, sir.”

“How much?”

“Fifteen francs.”

“Very well. Make haste, now, my girl, because I am getting hungry.”

Madame Cimme, looking out at the climbing flowers bathed in the sunlight, and at two pigeons making love on the roof opposite, said, with a wounded air: “It is unfortunate to have come for so sad an event. It would be nice in the country, to-day.”

Her sister sighed without response, and Columbel murmured, moved perhaps by the thought of a walk:

“My leg plagues me awfully.”

Little Joseph and the dog made a terrible noise, one shouting with joy and the other barking violently. They played at hide-and-seek around the three flower-beds, running after each other like mad.

The dying woman continued to call her children, chatting with each, imagining that she was dressing them, that she caressed them, that she was teaching them to read: “Come, Simon, repeat, A, B, C, D. You do not say it well; see, D, D, D, do you hear? Repeat, then——”

Cimme declared: “It is curious what she talks about at this time.”

Then said Madame Columbel: “It would be better, perhaps, to go in there.”

But Cimme dissuaded her from it:

“Why go in, since we are not able to do anything for her? Besides we are as well off here.”

No one insisted. Madame observed the two green birds called inseparable. She remarked pleasantly upon this singular fidelity, and blamed men for not imitating these little creatures. Cimme looked at his wife and laughed, singing with a bantering air, “Tra-la-la, Tra-la-la,” as if to say he could tell some things about her fidelity to him.

Columbel, taken with cramps in his stomach, struck the floor with his cane. The other cat entered, tail in the air. They did not sit down at table until one o’clock.

When he had tasted the wine, Columbel, whom some one had recommended to drink only choice Bordeaux, called the servant:

“Say, is there nothing better than this in the cellar?”

“Yes, sir; there is some of the wine that was served to you when you were here before.”

“Oh, well, go and bring three bottles.”

They tasted this wine, which seemed excellent. Not that it proved to be remarkable, but it had been fifteen years in the cellar. Cimme declared it was just the wine for sickness.

Columbel, seized with a desire of possessing some of it, asked of the maid: “How much is left of it, my girl?”

"Oh, nearly all, sir; Miss never drinks any of it. It is the heap at the bottom."

Then Columbel turned toward his brother-in-law: "If you wish, Cimme, I will take this wine instead of anything else; it agrees with my stomach wonderfully."

The hen, in her turn, had entered with her troop of chickens; the two women amused themselves by throwing crumbs to them. Joseph and the dog, who had eaten enough, returned to the garden.

Queen Hortense spoke continually, but the voice was lower now, so that it was no longer possible to distinguish the words.

When they had finished the coffee, they all went in to learn the condition of the sick one. She seemed calm.

They went out and seated themselves in a circle in the garden, to aid digestion.

Presently the dog began to run around the chairs with all speed, carrying something in his mouth. The child ran after him violently. Both disappeared into the house. Cimme fell asleep, with his stomach in the sun.

The dying one began to speak loud again. Then suddenly she shouted.

The two women and Columbel hastened in to see what had happened. Cimme awakened but did not move, liking better things as they were.

The dying woman was sitting up, staring with haggard eyes. Her dog, to escape the pursuit of little Joseph, had jumped upon the bed, startling her from the death agony. The dog was intrenched behind the pillow, peeping at his comrade with eyes glistening, ready to jump again at the least movement. He held in his mouth one of the slippers of his mistress, shorn of its heel in the hour he had played with it.

The child, intimidated by the woman rising so suddenly before him, remained motionless before the bed.

The hen, having just entered, had jumped upon a chair, frightened by the noise. She called desperately to her chickens, which peeped, frightened, from under the four legs of the seat.

Queen Hortense cried out with a piercing tone: "No, no, I do not wish to die! I am not willing! Who will bring up my children? Who will care for them? Who will love them? No, I am not willing! I am not——"

She turned on her back. All was over.

The dog, much excited, jumped into the room and skipped about.

Columbel ran to the window and called his brother-in-law: "Come quickly! come quickly! I believe she is gone."

Then Cimme got up and resolutely went into the room, muttering: "It was not as long as I should have believed."

COMPLICATION

After swearing for a long time that he would never marry, Jack Boudillère suddenly changed his mind. It happened one summer at the seashore, quite unexpectedly.

One morning, as he was extended on the sand, watching the women come out of the water, a little foot caught his attention, because of its slimness and delicacy. Raising his eyes higher, the entire person seemed attractive. Of this entire person he had, however, seen only the ankles and the head, emerging from a white flannel bathing suit, fastened with care. He may be called sensuous and impressionable, but it was by grace of form alone that he was captured. Afterward, he was held by the charm and sweet spirit of the young girl, who was simple and good and fresh, like her cheeks and her lips.

Presented to the family, he was pleased, and straightway became love-mad. When he saw Bertha Lannis at a distance, on the long stretch of yellow sand, he trembled from head to foot. Near her he was dumb, incapable of saying anything or even of thinking, with a kind of bubbling in his heart, a humming in his ears, and a frightened feeling in his mind. Was this love?

He did not know, he understood nothing of it, but the fact remained that he was fully decided to make this child his wife.

Her parents hesitated a long time, deterred by the bad reputation of the young man. He had a mistress, it was said,—an old mistress, an old and strong entanglement, one of those chains that is believed to be broken, but which continues to hold, nevertheless. Beyond this, he had loved, for a longer or shorter period, every woman who had come within reach of his lips.

But he withdrew from the woman with whom he had lived, not even consenting to see her again. A friend arranged her pension, assuring her a subsistence. Jack paid, but he did not wish to speak to her, pretending henceforth that he did not know her name. She wrote letters which he would not open. Each week brought him a new disguise in the handwriting of the abandoned one. Each week a greater anger developed in him against her, and he would tear the envelope in two, without opening it, without reading a line, knowing beforehand the reproaches and complaints of the contents.

One could scarcely credit her perseverance, which lasted the whole winter long, and it was not until spring that her demand was satisfied.

The marriage took place in Paris during the early part of May. It was decided that they should not take the regular wedding journey. After a little ball, composed of a company of young cousins who would not stay past eleven o'clock, and would not prolong forever the cares of the day of ceremony, the young couple intended to pass their first night at the family home and to set out the next morning for the seaside, where they had met and loved.

The night came, and they were dancing in the great drawing-room. The newly-married pair had withdrawn from the rest into a little Japanese boudoir shut off by silk hangings, and scarcely lighted this evening, except by the dim rays from a colored lantern in the shape of an enormous egg, which hung from the ceiling. The long window was open, allowing at times a fresh breath of air from without to blow upon their faces, for the evening was soft and warm, full of the odor of springtime.

They said nothing, but held each other's hands, pressing them from time to time with all their force. She was a little dismayed by this great change in her life, but smiling, emotional, ready to weep, often ready to swoon from joy, believing the entire world changed because of what had come to her, a little disturbed without knowing the reason why, and feeling all her body, all her soul, enveloped in an indefinable, delicious lassitude.

Her husband she watched persistently, smiling at him with a fixed smile. He wished to talk but found nothing to say, and remained quiet, putting all his ardor into the pressure of the hand. From time to time he murmured "Bertha!" and each time she raised her eyes to his with a sweet and tender look. They would look at each other a moment, then his eyes, fascinated by hers, would fall.

They discovered no thought to exchange. But they were alone, except as a dancing couple would sometimes cast a glance at them in passing, a furtive glance, as if it were the discreet and confidential witness of a mystery.

A door at the side opened, a domestic entered, bearing upon a tray an urgent letter which a messenger had brought. Jack trembled as he took it, seized with a vague and sudden fear, the mysterious, abrupt fear of misfortune.

He looked long at the envelope, not knowing the handwriting, nor daring to open it, wishing not to read, not to know the contents, desiring to put it in his pocket and to say to himself: "To-morrow, to-morrow, I shall be far away and it will not matter!" But upon the corner were two words underlined: very urgent, which frightened him. "You will permit me, my dear," said he, and he tore off the wrapper. He read the letter, growing frightfully pale, running over it at a glance, and then seeming to spell it out.

When he raised his head his whole countenance was changed. He stammered: "My dear little one, a great misfortune has happened to my best friend. He needs me immediately, in a matter of—of life and death. Allow me to go for twenty minutes. I will return immediately."

She, trembling and affrighted, murmured: "Go, my friend!" not yet being enough of a wife to dare to ask or demand to know anything. And he disappeared. She remained alone, listening to the dance music in the next room.

He had taken a hat, the first he could find, and descended the staircase upon the run. As soon as he was mingled with the people on the street, he stopped under a gaslight in a vestibule and re-read the letter. It said:

"SIR: The Ravet girl, your old mistress, has given birth to a child which she asserts is yours. The mother is dying and implores you to visit her. I take the liberty of writing to you to ask whether you will grant the last wish of this woman, who seems to be very unhappy and worthy of pity. "Your servant, D. BONNARD."

When he entered the chamber of death, she was already in the last agony. He would not have known her. The physician and the two nurses were caring for her, dragging across the room some buckets full of ice and linen.

Water covered the floor, two tapers were burning on a table; behind the bed, in a little wicker cradle, a child was crying, and, with each of its cries, the mother would try to move, shivering under the icy compresses.

She was bleeding, wounded to death, killed by this birth. Her life was slipping away; and, in spite of the ice, in spite of all care, the hemorrhage continued, hastening her last hour.

She recognized Jack, and tried to raise her hand. She was too weak for that, but the warm tears began to glide down her cheeks.

He fell on his knees beside the bed, seized one of her hands and kissed it frantically; then, little by little, he approached nearer to the wan face which strained to meet him. One of the nurses, standing with a taper in her hand, observed them, and the doctor looked at them from the remote corner of the room.

With a far-off voice, breathing hard, she said: "I am going to die, my dear; promise me you will remain till the end. Oh! do not leave me now, not at the last moment!"

He kissed her brow, her hair with a groan. "Be tranquil!" he murmured, "I will stay."

It was some minutes before she was able to speak again, she was so weak and overcome. Then she continued: "It is yours, the little one. I swear it before God, I swear it to you upon my soul, I swear it at the moment of death. I have never loved any man but you—promise me not to abandon it——" He tried to take in his arms the poor, weak body, emptied of its life blood. He stammered, excited by remorse and chagrin: "I swear to you I will bring it up and love it. It shall never be separated from me." Then she held Jack in an embrace. Powerless to raise her head, she held up her blanched lips in an appeal for a kiss. He bent his mouth to receive this poor, suppliant caress.

Calmed a little, she murmured in a low tone: "Take it, that I may see that you love it."

He went to the cradle and took up the child.

He placed it gently on the bed between them. The little creature ceased to cry. She whispered: "Do not stir!" And he remained motionless. There he stayed, holding in his burning palms a hand that shook with the shiver of death, as he had held, an hour before, another hand that had trembled with the shiver of love. From time to time he looked at the hour, with a furtive glance of the eye, watching the hand as it passed midnight, then one o'clock, then two.

The doctor retired. The two nurses, after roaming around for some time with light step, slept now in their chairs. The child slept, and the mother, whose eyes were closed, seemed to be resting also.

Suddenly, as the pale daylight began to filter through the torn curtains, she extended her arms with so startling and violent a motion that she almost threw the child upon the floor. There was a rattling in her throat; then she turned over motionless, dead.

The nurses hastened to her side, declaring: "It is over."

He looked once at this woman he had loved, then at the hand that marked four o'clock, and, forgetting his overcoat, fled in his evening clothes with the child in his arms.

After she had been left alone, his young bride had waited calmly at first, in the Japanese boudoir. Then, seeing that he did not return, she went back to the drawing-room, indifferent and tranquil in appearance, but frightfully disturbed. Her mother, perceiving her alone, asked where her husband was. She replied: "In his room; he will return presently."

At the end of an hour, as everybody asked about him, she told of the letter, of the change in Jack's face, and her fears of some misfortune.

They still waited. The guests had gone; only the parents and near relatives remained. At midnight, they put the bride in her bed, shaking with sobs. Her mother and two aunts were seated on the bed listening to her weeping. Her father had gone to the police headquarters to make inquiries. At five o'clock a light sound was heard in the corridor. The door opened and closed softly. Then suddenly a cry, like the miauling of a cat, went through the house, breaking the silence.

All the women of the house were out with one bound, and Bertha was the first to spring forward, in spite of her mother and her aunts, clothed only in her night-robe.

Jack, standing in the middle of the room, livid, breathing hard, held the child in his arms.

The four women looked at him frightened; but Bertha suddenly became rash, her heart wrung with anguish, and ran to him saying: "What is it? What have you there?"

He had a foolish air, and answered in a husky voice: "It is—it is—I have here a child, whose mother has just died." And he put into her arms the howling little marmot.

Bertha, without saying a word, seized the child and embraced it, straining it to her heart. Then, turning toward her husband with her eyes full of tears, she said: "The mother is dead, you say?" He answered: "Yes, just died—in my arms—I had broken with her since last summer—I knew nothing about it—only the doctor sent for me and——"

Then Bertha murmured: "Well, we will bring up this little one."

FORGIVENESS

She had been brought up in one of those families who live shut up within themselves, entirely apart from the rest of the world. They pay no attention to political events, except to chat about them at table, and changes in government seem so far, so very far away that they are spoken of only as a matter of history—like the death of Louis XVI., or the advent of Napoleon.

Customs change, fashions succeed each other, but changes are never perceptible in this family, where old traditions are always followed. And if some impossible story arises in the neighborhood, the scandal of it dies at the threshold of this house.

The father and mother, alone in the evening, sometimes exchange a few words on such a subject, but in an undertone, as if the walls had ears.

With great discretion, the father says: "Do you know about this terrible affair in the Rivoil family?"

And the mother replies: "Who would have believed it? It is frightful!"

The children doubt nothing, but come to the age of living, in their turn, with a bandage over their eyes and minds, without a suspicion of any other kind of existence, without knowing that one does not always think as he speaks, nor speak as he acts, without knowing that it is necessary to live at war with the world, or at least, in armed peace, without surmising that the ingenuous are frequently deceived, the sincere trifled with, and the good wronged.

Some live until death in this blindness of probity, loyalty, and honor; so upright that nothing can open their eyes. Others, undeceived, without knowing much, are weighed down with despair, and die believing that they are the puppets of an exceptional fatality, the miserable victims of unlucky circumstance or particularly bad men.

The Savignols arranged a marriage for their daughter when she was eighteen. She married a young man from Paris, George Barton, whose business was on the Exchange. He was an attractive youth, with a smooth tongue, and he observed all the outward proprieties necessary. But at the bottom of his heart he sneered a little at his guileless parents-in-law, calling them, among his friends, "My dear fossils."

He belonged to a good family, and the young girl was rich. He took her to live in Paris.

She became one of the provincials of Paris, of whom there are many. She remained ignorant of the great city, of its elegant people, of its pleasures and its customs, as she had always been ignorant of the perfidy and mystery of life.

Shut up in her own household, she scarcely knew the street she lived in, and when she ventured into another quarter, it seemed to her that she had journeyed far, into an unknown, strange city. She would say in the evening:

"I crossed the boulevards to-day."

Two or three times a year, her husband took her to the theater. These were feast-days not to be forgotten, which she recalled continually.

Sometimes at table, three months afterward, she would suddenly burst out laughing and exclaim:

"Do you remember that ridiculous actor who imitated the cock's crowing?"

All her interests were within the boundaries of the two allied families, who represented the whole of humanity to her. She designated them by the distinguishing prefix "the," calling them respectively "the Martinets," or "the Michelins."

Her husband lived according to his fancy, returning whenever he wished, sometimes at daybreak, pretending business, and feeling in no way constrained, so sure was he that no suspicion would ruffle this candid soul.

But one morning she received an anonymous letter. She was too much astonished and dismayed to scorn this letter, whose author declared himself to be moved by interest in her happiness, by hatred of all evil and love of truth. Her heart was too pure to understand fully the meaning of the accusations.

But it revealed to her that her husband had had a mistress for two years, a young widow, Mrs. Rosset, at whose house he passed his evenings.

She knew neither how to pretend, nor to spy, nor to plan any sort of ruse. When he returned for luncheon, she threw him the letter, sobbing, and then fled to her room.

He had time to comprehend the matter and prepare his response before he rapped at his wife's door. She opened it immediately, without looking at him. He smiled, sat down, and drew her to his knee. In a sweet voice, and a little jocosely, he said:

"My dear little one, Mrs. Rosset is a friend of mine. I have known her for ten years and like her very much. I may add that I know twenty other families of whom I have not spoken to you, knowing that you care nothing for the world or for forming new friendships. But in order to finish, once for all, these infamous lies, I will ask you to dress yourself, after luncheon, and we will go to pay a visit to this young lady, who will become your friend at once, I am sure." She embraced her husband eagerly; and, from feminine curiosity, which no sooner sleeps than wakes again, she did not refuse to go to see this unknown woman, of whom, in spite of all, she was still suspicious. She felt by instinct that a known danger is sooner overcome.

They were ushered into a little apartment on the fourth floor of a handsome house. It was a coquettish little place, full of bric-à-brac and ornamented with works of art. After about five minutes' waiting, in a drawing-room where the light was dimmed by its generous window draperies and portières, a door opened and a young woman appeared. She was very dark, small, rather plump, and looked astonished, although she smiled. George presented them. "My wife, Madame Julie Rosset."

The young widow uttered a little cry of astonishment and joy, and came forward with both hands extended. She had not hoped for this happiness, she said, knowing that Madame Barton saw no one. But she was so happy! She was so fond of George! (She said George quite naturally, with sisterly familiarity.) And she had had great desire to know his young wife, and to love her, too.

At the end of a month these two friends were never apart from each other. They met every day, often twice a day, and nearly always dined together, either at one house or at the other. George scarcely ever went out now, no longer pretended delay on account of business, but said he loved his own chimney corner.

Finally, an apartment was left vacant in the house where Madame Rosset resided. Madame

Barton hastened to take it in order to be nearer her new friend.

During two whole years there was a friendship between them without a cloud, a friendship of heart and soul, tender, devoted, and delightful. Bertha could not speak without mentioning Julie's name, for to her Julie represented perfection. She was happy with a perfect happiness, calm and secure.

But Madame Rosset fell ill. Bertha never left her. She passed nights of despair; her husband, too, was broken-hearted.

One morning, in going out from his visit the doctor took George and his wife aside, and announced that he found the condition of their friend very grave.

When he had gone out, the young people, stricken down, looked at each other and then began to weep. They both watched that night near the bed. Bertha would embrace the sick one tenderly, while George, standing silently at the foot of her couch, would look at them with dogged persistence. The next day she was worse.

Finally, toward evening, she declared herself better, and persuaded her friends to go home to dinner.

They were sitting sadly at table, scarcely eating anything, when the maid brought George an envelope. He opened it, turned pale, and rising, said to his wife, in a constrained way: "Excuse me, I must leave you for a moment. I will return in ten minutes. Please don't go out." And he ran into his room for his hat.

Bertha waited, tortured by a new fear. But, yielding in all things, she would not go up to her friend's room again until he had returned.

As he did not re-appear, the thought came to her to look in his room to see whether he had taken his gloves, which would show whether he had really gone somewhere.

She saw them there, at first glance. Near them lay a rumpled paper.

She recognized it immediately; it was the one that had called George away.

And a burning temptation took possession of her, the first of her life, to read—to know. Her conscience struggled in revolt, but curiosity lashed her on and grief directed her hand. She seized the paper, opened it, recognized the trembling handwriting as that of Julie, and read:

"Come alone and embrace me, my poor friend; I am going to die."

She could not understand it all at once, but stood stupefied, struck especially by the thought of death. Then, suddenly, the familiarity of it seized upon her mind. This came like a great light, illuminating her whole life, showing her the infamous truth, all their treachery, all their perfidy. She saw now their cunning, their sly looks, her good faith played with, her confidence turned to account. She saw them looking into each other's faces, under the shade of her lamp at evening, reading from the same book, exchanging glances at the end of certain pages.

And her heart, stirred with indignation, bruised with suffering, sunk into an abyss of despair that had no boundaries.

When she heard steps, she fled and shut herself in her room.

Her husband called her: "Come quickly, Madame Rosset is dying!"

Bertha appeared at her door and said with trembling lip:

"Go alone to her; she has no need of me."

He looked at her sheepishly, careless from anger, and repeated:

"Quick, quick! She is dying!"

Bertha answered: "You would prefer it to be I."

Then he understood, probably, and left her to herself, going up again to the dying one.

There he wept without fear, or shame, indifferent to the grief of his wife, who would no longer speak to him, nor look at him, but who lived shut in with her disgust and angry revolt, praying to God morning and evening.

They lived together, nevertheless, eating together face to face, mute and hopeless.

After a time, he tried to appease her a little. But she would not forget. And so the life continued, hard for them both.

For a whole year they lived thus, strangers one to the other. Bertha almost became mad.

Then one morning, having set out at dawn, she returned toward eight o'clock carrying in both hands an enormous bouquet of roses, of white roses, all white.

She sent word to her husband that she would like to speak to him. He came in disturbed, troubled.

"Let us go out together," she said to him. "Take these flowers, they are too heavy for me."

He took the bouquet and followed his wife. A carriage awaited them, which started as soon as they were seated.

It stopped before the gate of a cemetery. Then Bertha, her eyes full of tears, said to George: "Take me to her grave."

He trembled, without knowing why, but walked on before, holding the flowers in his arms. Finally he stopped before a shaft of white marble and pointed to it without a word.

She took the bouquet from him, and, kneeling, placed it at the foot of the grave. Then her heart was raised in suppliant, silent prayer.

Her husband stood behind her, weeping, haunted by memories.

She arose and put out her hands to him.

"If you wish, we will be friends," she said.

THE WHITE WOLF

This is the story the old Marquis d'Arville told us after a dinner in honor of Saint-Hubert, at the house of Baron des Ravels. They had run down a stag that day. The Marquis was the only one of the guests who had not taken part in the chase. He never hunted.

During the whole of the long repast, they had talked of scarcely anything but the massacre of animals. Even the ladies interested themselves in the sanguinary and often unlikely stories, while the orators mimicked the attacks and combats between man and beast, raising their arms and speaking in thunderous tones.

M. d'Arville talked much, with a certain poesy, a little flourish, but full of effect. He must have repeated this story often, it ran so smoothly, never halting at a choice of words in which to clothe an image.

"Gentlemen, I never hunt, nor did my father, nor my grandfather, nor my great-great-grandfather. The last named was the son of a man who hunted more than all of you. He died in 1764. I will tell you how. He was named John, and was married, and became the father of the man who was my great-great-grandfather. He lived with his younger brother, Francis d'Arville, in our castle, in the midst of a deep forest in Lorraine.

"Francis d'Arville always remained a boy through his love for hunting. They both hunted from one end of the year to the other without cessation or weariness. They loved nothing else, understood nothing else, talked only of this, and lived for this alone.

"They were possessed by this terrible, inexorable passion. It consumed them, having taken entire control of them, leaving no place for anything else. They had agreed not to put off the chase for any reason whatsoever. My great-great-grandfather was born while his father was following a fox, but John d'Arville did not interrupt his sport, and swore that the little beggar might have waited until after the death-cry! His brother Francis showed himself still more hot-headed than he. The first thing on rising, he would go to see the dogs, then the horses; then he would shoot some birds about the place, even when about to set out hunting big game.

"They were called in the country Monsieur the Marquis and Monsieur the Cadet, noblemen then not acting as do those of our time, who wish to establish in their titles a descending scale of rank, for the son of a marquis is no more a count, or the son of a viscount a baron, than the son of a general is a colonel by birth. But the niggardly vanity of the day finds profit in this arrangement. To return to my ancestors:

"They were, it appears, immoderately large, bony, hairy, violent, and vigorous. The younger one was taller than the elder, and had such a voice that, according to a legend he was very proud of, all the leaves of the forest moved when he shouted.

"And when mounted, ready for the chase, it must have been a superb sight to see these two giants astride their great horses.

"Toward the middle of the winter of that year, 1764, the cold was excessive and the wolves became ferocious.

"They even attacked belated peasants, roamed around houses at night, howled from sunset to sunrise, and ravaged the stables.

"At one time a rumor was circulated. It was said that a colossal wolf, of grayish-white color, which had eaten two children, devoured the arm of a woman, strangled all the watchdogs of the country, was now coming without fear into the house inclosures and smelling around the doors. Many inhabitants affirmed that they had felt his breath, which made the lights flicker. Shortly a panic ran through all the province. No one dared to go out after nightfall. The very shadows seemed haunted by the image of this beast.

"The brothers D'Arville resolved to find and slay him. So they called together for a grand chase all the gentlemen of the country.

"It was in vain. They had beaten the forests and scoured the thickets, but had seen nothing of him. They killed wolves, but not that one. And each night after such a chase, the beast, as if to avenge himself, attacked some traveler, or devoured some cattle, always far from the place where they had sought him.

"Finally, one night he found a way into the swine-house of the castle D'Arville and ate two beauties of the best breed.

"The two brothers were furious, interpreting the attack as one of bravado on the part of the monster—a direct injury, a defiance. Therefore, taking all their best-trained hounds, they set out to run down the beast, with courage excited by anger.

"From dawn until the sun descended behind the great nut-trees, they beat about the forests with no result.

"At last, both of them, angry and disheartened, turned their horses' steps into a bypath bordered by brushwood. They were marveling at the baffling power of this wolf, when suddenly they were seized with a mysterious fear.

"The elder said:

"'This can be no ordinary beast. One might say he can think like a man.'

"The younger replied:

"'Perhaps we should get our cousin, the Bishop, to bless a bullet for him, or ask a priest to pronounce some words to help us.'

"Then they were silent.

"John continued: 'Look at the sun, how red it is. The great wolf will do mischief to-night.'

"He had scarcely finished speaking when his horse reared. Francis's horse started to run at the same time. A large bush covered with dead leaves rose before them, and a colossal beast, grayish white, sprang out, scampering away through the wood.

"Both gave a grunt of satisfaction, and bending to the necks of their heavy horses, they urged them on with the weight of their bodies, exciting them, hastening with voice and spur, until these strong riders seemed to carry the weight of their beasts between their knees, carrying them by force as if they were flying.

"Thus they rode, crashing through forests, crossing ravines, climbing up the sides of steep gorges, and sounding the horn, at frequent intervals, to arouse the people and the dogs of the neighborhood.

"But suddenly, in the course of this breakneck ride, my ancestor struck his forehead against a large branch and fractured his skull. He fell to the ground as if dead, while his frightened horse disappeared in the surrounding thicket.

"The younger D'Arville stopped short, sprang to the ground, seized his brother in his arms, and saw that he had lost consciousness.

"He sat down beside him, took his disfigured head upon his knees, looking earnestly at the lifeless face. Little by little a fear crept over him, a strange fear that he had never before felt, fear of the shadows, of the solitude, of the lonely woods, and also of the chimerical wolf, which had now come to be the death of his brother.

"The shadows deepened, the branches of the trees crackled in the sharp cold. Francis arose shivering, incapable of remaining there longer, and already feeling his strength fail. There was nothing to be heard, neither the voice of dogs nor the sound of a horn; all within this invisible horizon was mute. And in this gloomy silence and the chill of evening there was something strange and frightful.

"With his powerful hands he seized John's body and laid it across the saddle to take it home; then mounted gently behind it, his mind troubled by horrible, supernatural images, as if he were possessed.

"Suddenly, in the midst of these fears, a great form passed. It was the wolf. A violent fit of terror seized upon the hunter; something cold, like a stream of ice-water seemed to glide through his veins, and he made the sign of the cross, like a monk haunted with devils, so dismayed was he by the reappearance of the frightful wanderer. Then, his eyes falling upon the inert body before him, his fear was quickly changed to anger, and he trembled with inordinate rage.

"He pricked his horse and darted after him.

"He followed him through copses, over ravines, and around great forest trees, traversing woods that he no longer recognized, his eye fixed upon a white spot, which was ever flying from him as night covered the earth.

"His horse also seemed moved by an unknown force. He galloped on with neck extended, crashing over small trees and rocks, with the body of the dead stretched across him on the saddle. Brambles caught in his mane; his head, where it had struck the trunks of trees, was spattered with blood; the marks of the spurs were over his flanks.

"Suddenly the animal and its rider came out of the forest, rushing through a valley as the moon appeared above the hills. This valley was stony and shut in by enormous rocks, over which it was impossible to pass; there was no other way for the wolf but to turn on his steps.

"Francis gave such a shout of joy and revenge that the echo of it was like the roll of thunder. He leaped from his horse, knife in hand.

"The bristling beast, with rounded back, was awaiting him; his eyes shining like two stars. But before joining in battle, the strong hunter, grasping his brother, seated him upon a rock, supporting his head, which was now but a mass of blood, with stones, and cried aloud to him, as to one deaf: 'Look, John! Look here!'

"Then he threw himself upon the monster. He felt himself strong enough to overthrow a mountain, to crush the very rocks in his hands. The beast meant to kill him by sinking his claws in his vitals; but the man had seized him by the throat, without even making use of his weapon, and strangled him gently, waiting until his breath stopped and he could hear the death-rattle at his heart. And he laughed, with the joy of dismay, clutching more and more with a terrible hold, and crying out in his delirium: 'Look, John! Look!' All resistance ceased. The body of the wolf was limp. He was dead.

"Then Francis, taking him in his arms, threw him down at the feet of his elder brother, crying out in expectant voice: 'Here, here, my little John, here he is!'

"Then he placed upon the saddle the two bodies, the one above the other, and started on his way.

"He returned to the castle laughing and weeping, like Gargantua at the birth of Pantagruel, shouting in triumph and stamping with delight in relating the death of the beast, and moaning and tearing at his beard in calling the name of his brother.

"Often, later, when he recalled this day, he would declare, with tears in his eyes: 'If only poor John had seen me strangle the beast, he would have died content, I am sure!'

"The widow of my ancestor inspired in her son a horror of the chase, which was transmitted from father to son down to myself."

The Marquis d'Arville was silent. Some one asked: "Is the story a legend or not?"

And the narrator replied:

"I swear to you it is true from beginning to end."

Then a lady, in a sweet little voice, declared:

"It is beautiful to have passions like that."

Pierre & Jean

by Guy de Maupassant

Translated by Clara Bell

CHAPTER I

"Tschah!" exclaimed old Roland suddenly, after he had remained motionless for a quarter of an hour, his eyes fixed on the water, while now and again he very slightly lifted his line sunk in the sea.

Mme. Roland, dozing in the stern by the side of Mme. Rosémilly, who had been invited to join the fishing-party, woke up, and turning her head to look at her husband, said:

"Well, well! Gérome."

And the old fellow replied in a fury:

"They do not bite at all. I have taken nothing since noon. Only men should ever go fishing. Women always delay the start till it is too late."

His two sons, Pierre and Jean, who each held a line twisted round his forefinger, one to port and one to starboard, both began to laugh, and Jean remarked:

"You are not very polite to our guest, father."

M. Roland was abashed, and apologized.

"I beg your pardon, Mme. Rosémilly, but that is just like me. I invite ladies because I like to be with them, and then, as soon as I feel the water beneath me, I think of nothing but the fish."

Mme. Roland was now quite awake, and gazing with a softened look at the wide horizon of cliff and sea.

"You have had good sport, all the same," she murmured.

But her husband shook his head in denial, though at the same time he glanced complacently at the basket where the fish caught by the three men were still breathing spasmodically, with a low rustle of clammy scales and struggling fins, and dull, ineffectual efforts, gasping in the fatal air. Old Roland took the basket between his knees and tilted it up, making the silver heap of creatures slide to the edge that he might see those lying at the bottom, and their death-throes became more convulsive, while the strong smell of their bodies, a wholesome reek of brine, came up from the full depths of the creel. The old fisherman sniffed it eagerly, as we smell at roses, and exclaimed:

"Cristi! But they are fresh enough!" and he went on: "How many did you pull out, doctor?"

His eldest son, Pierre, a man of thirty, with black whiskers trimmed square like a lawyer's, his mustache and beard shaved away, replied:

"Oh, not many; three or four."

The father turned to the younger. "And you, Jean?" said he.

Jean, a tall fellow, much younger than his brother, fair, with a full beard, smiled and murmured:

"Much the same as Pierre—four or five."

Every time they told the same fib, which delighted father Roland. He had hitched his line round a row-lock, and folding his arms he announced:

"I will never again try to fish after noon. After ten in the morning it is all over. The lazy brutes will not bite; they are taking their siesta in the sun." And he looked round at the sea on all sides, with the satisfied air of a proprietor.

He was a retired jeweller who had been led by an inordinate love of seafaring and fishing to fly from the shop as soon as he had made enough money to live in modest comfort on the interest of his savings. He retired to le Havre, bought a boat, and became an amateur skipper. His two sons, Pierre and Jean, had remained at Paris to continue their studies, and came for the holidays from time to time to share their father's amusements.

On leaving school, Pierre, the elder, five years older than Jean, had felt a vocation to various professions and had tried half a dozen in succession, but, soon disgusted with each in turn, he started afresh with new hopes. Medicine had been his last fancy, and he had set to work with so much ardour that he had just qualified after an unusually short course of study, by a special remission of time from the minister. He was enthusiastic, intelligent, fickle, but obstinate, full of Utopias and philosophical notions.

Jean, who was as fair as his brother was dark, as deliberate as his brother was vehement, as gentle as his brother was unforgiving, had quietly gone through his studies for the law and had just taken his diploma as a licentiate, at the time when Pierre had taken his in medicine. So they were now having a little rest at home, and both looked forward to settling in Havre if they could find a satisfactory opening.

But a vague jealousy, one of those dormant jealousies which grow up between brothers or sisters and slowly ripen till they burst, on the occasion of a marriage perhaps, or of some good fortune happening to one of them, kept them on the alert in a sort of brotherly and non-aggressive animosity. They were fond of each other, it is true, but they watched each other. Pierre, five years old when Jean was born, had looked with the eyes of a little petted animal at that other little animal which had suddenly come to lie in his father's and mother's arms and to be loved and fondled by them. Jean, from his birth, had always been a pattern of sweetness, gentleness, and good temper, and Pierre had by degrees begun to chafe at everlastingly hearing the praises of this great lad, whose sweetness in his eyes was indolence, whose gentleness was stupidity, and whose kindliness was blindness. His parents, whose dream for their sons was some respectable and undistinguished calling, blamed him for so often changing his mind, for his fits of enthusiasm, his abortive beginnings, and all his ineffectual impulses towards generous ideas and the liberal professions.

Since he had grown to manhood they no longer said in so many words: "Look at Jean and follow his example," but every time he heard them say "Jean did this—Jean does that," he understood their meaning and the hint the words conveyed.

Their mother, an orderly person, a thrifty and rather sentimental woman of the middle class, with the soul of a soft-hearted book-keeper, was constantly quenching the little rivalries between her two big sons to which the petty events of their life constantly gave rise. Another little circumstance, too, just now disturbed her peace of mind, and she was in fear of some complications; for in the course of the winter, while her boys were finishing their studies, each in his own line, she had made the acquaintance of a neighbour, Mme. Rosémilly, the widow of a captain of a merchantman who had died at sea two years before. The young widow—quite young, only three-and-twenty—a woman of strong intellect who knew life by instinct as the free animals do, as though she had seen, gone through, understood, and weighted every conceivable contingency, and judged them with a wholesome, strict, and benevolent mind, had fallen into the habit of calling to work or chat for an hour in the evening with these friendly neighbours, who would give her a cup of tea.

Father Roland, always goaded on by his seafaring craze, would question their new friend about the departed captain; and she would talk of him, and his voyages, and his old-world tales, without hesitation, like a resigned and reasonable woman who loves life and respects death.

The two sons on their return, finding the pretty widow quite at home in the house, forthwith began to court her, less from any wish to charm her than from the desire to cut each other out.

Their mother, being practical and prudent, sincerely hoped that one of them might win the young widow, for she was rich; but then she would have liked that the other should not be grieved.

Mme. Rosémilly was fair, with blue eyes, a mass of light waving hair, fluttering at the least breath of wind, and an alert, daring, pugnacious little way with her, which did not in the least answer to the sober method of her mind.

She already seemed to like Jean best, attracted, no doubt, by an affinity of nature. This preference, however, she betrayed only by an almost imperceptible difference of voice and look and also by occasionally asking his opinion. She seemed to guess that Jean's views would support her own, while those of Pierre must inevitably be different. When she spoke of the doctor's ideas on politics, art, philosophy, or morals, she would sometimes say: "Your crotchets." Then he would look at her with the cold gleam of an accuser drawing up an indictment against women—all women, poor weak things

Never till his sons came home had M. Roland invited her to join his fishing expeditions, nor had he ever taken his wife; for he liked to put off before daybreak, with his ally, Captain Beausire, a master mariner retired, whom he had first met on the quay at high tides and with whom he had struck up an intimacy, and the old sailor Papagris, known as Jean Bart, in whose charge the boat was left.

But one evening of the week before, Mme. Rosémilly, who had been dining with them, remarked, "It must be great fun to go out fishing." The jeweller, flattered by her interest and suddenly fired with the wish to share his favourite sport with her, and to make a convert after the manner of priests, exclaimed: "Would you like to come?"

"To be sure I should."

"Next Tuesday?"

"Yes, next Tuesday."

"Are you the woman to be ready to start at five in the morning?"

She exclaimed in horror:

"No, indeed: that is too much."

He was disappointed and chilled, suddenly doubting her true vocation. However, he said:

"At what hour can you be ready?"

"Well—at nine?"

"Not before?"

"No, not before. Even that is very early."

The old fellow hesitated; he certainly would catch nothing, for when the sun has warmed the sea the fish bite no more; but the two brothers had eagerly pressed the scheme, and organized and arranged everything there and then.

So on the following Tuesday the Pearl had dropped anchor under the white rocks of Cape la Hève; they had fished till midday, then they had slept awhile, and then fished again without catching anything; and then it was that father Roland, perceiving, rather late, that all that Mme. Rosémilly really enjoyed and cared for was the sail on the sea, and seeing that his lines hung motionless, had uttered in a spirit of unreasonable annoyance, that vehement "Tschah!" which applied as much to the pathetic widow as to the creatures he could not catch.

Now he contemplated the spoil—his fish—with the joyful thrill of a miser; seeing as he looked up at the sky that the sun was getting low: "Well, boys," said he, "suppose we turn homeward."

The young men hauled in their lines, coiled them up, cleaned the hooks and stuck them into corks, and sat waiting.

Roland stood up to look out like a captain.

"No wind," said he. "You will have to pull, young 'uns."

And suddenly extending one arm to the northward, he exclaimed:

"Here comes the packet from Southampton."

Away over the level sea, spread out like a blue sheet, vast and sheeny and shot with flame and gold, an inky cloud was visible against the rosy sky in the quarter to which he pointed, and below it they could make out the hull of the steamer, which looked tiny at such a distance. And to southward other wreaths of smoke, numbers of them, could be seen, all converging towards the Havre pier, now scarcely visible as a white streak with the lighthouse, upright, like a horn, at the end of it.

Roland asked: "Is not the Normandie due to-day?" And Jean replied:

"Yes, to-day."

"Give me my glass. I fancy I see her out there."

The father pulled out the copper tube, adjusted it to his eye, sought the speck, and then, delighted to have seen it, exclaimed:

"Yes, yes, there she is. I know her two funnels. Would you like to look, Mme. Rosémilly?"

She took the telescope and directed it towards the Atlantic horizon, without being able, however, to find the vessel, for she could distinguish nothing—nothing but blue, with a coloured halo round it, a circular rainbow—and then all manner of queer things, winking eclipses which made her feel sick.

She said as she returned the glass:

"I never could see with that thing. It used to put my husband in quite a rage; he would stand for hours at the windows watching the ships pass."

Old Roland, much put out, retorted:

"Then it must be some defect in your eye, for my glass is a very good one."

Then he offered it to his wife.

"Would you like to look?"

"No, thank you. I know beforehand that I could not see through it."

Mme. Roland, a woman of eight-and-forty but who did not look it, seemed to be enjoying this excursion and this waning day more than any of the party.

Her chestnut hair was only just beginning to show streaks of white. She had a calm, reasonable face, a kind and happy way with her which it was a pleasure to see. Her son Pierre was wont to say that she knew the value of money, but this did not hinder her from enjoying the delights of dreaming. She was fond of reading, of novels, and poetry, not for their value as works of art, but for the sake of the tender melancholy mood they would induce in her. A line of poetry, often but a poor one, often a bad one, would touch the little chord, as she expressed it, and give her the sense of some mysterious desire almost realized. And she delighted in these faint emotions which brought a little flutter to her soul, otherwise as strictly kept as a ledger.

Since settling at Havre she had become perceptibly stouter, and her figure, which had been very supple and slight, had grown heavier.

This day on the sea had been delightful to her. Her husband, without being brutal, was rough with her, as a man who is the despot of his shop is apt to be rough, without anger or hatred; to such men to give an order is to swear. He controlled himself in the presence of strangers, but in private he let loose and gave himself terrible vent, though he was himself afraid of every one. She, in sheer horror of the turmoil, of scenes, of useless explanations, always gave way and never asked for anything; for a very long time she had not ventured to ask Roland to take her out in the boat. So she had joyfully hailed this opportunity, and was keenly enjoying the rare and new pleasure.

From the moment when they started she surrendered herself completely, body and soul, to the soft, gliding motion over the waves. She was not thinking; her mind was not wandering through either memories or hopes; it seemed to her as though her heart, like her body, was floating on something soft and liquid and delicious which rocked and lulled it.

When their father gave the word to return, "Come, take your places at the oars!" she smiled to see her sons, her two great boys, take off their jackets and roll up their shirt-sleeves on their bare arms.

Pierre, who was nearest to the two women, took the stroke oar, Jean the other, and they sat waiting till the skipper should say: "Give way!" For he insisted on everything being done according to strict rule.

Simultaneously, as if by a single effort, they dipped the oars, and lying back, pulling with all their might, began a struggle to display their strength. They had come out easily, under sail, but the breeze had died away, and the masculine pride of the two brothers was suddenly aroused by the prospect of measuring their powers. When they went out alone with their father they plied the oars without any steering, for Roland would be busy getting the lines ready, while he kept a lookout in the boat's course, guiding it by a sign or a word: "Easy, Jean, and you, Pierre, put your back into it." Or he would say, "Now, then, number one; come, number two—a little elbow grease." Then the one who had been dreaming pulled harder, the one who had got excited eased down, and the boat's head came round.

But to-day they meant to display their biceps. Pierre's arms were hairy, somewhat lean but sinewy; Jean's were round and white and rosy, and the knot of muscles moved under the skin.

At first Pierre had the advantage. With his teeth set, his brow knit, his legs rigid, his hands clinched on the oar, he made it bend from end to end at every stroke, and the Pearl was veering landward. Father Roland, sitting in the bows, so as to leave the stern seat to the two women, wasted his breath shouting, "Easy, number one; pull harder, number two!" Pierre pulled harder in his frenzy, and "number two" could not keep time with his wild stroke.

At last the skipper cried: "Stop her!" The two oars were lifted simultaneously, and then by his father's orders Jean pulled alone for a few minutes. But from that moment he had it all his own way; he grew eager and warmed to his work, while Pierre, out of breath and exhausted by his first vigorous spurt, was lax and panting. Four times running father Roland made them stop while the elder took breath, so as to get the boat into her right course again. Then the doctor, humiliated and fuming, his forehead dropping with sweat, his cheeks white, stammered out:

"I cannot think what has come over me; I have a stitch in my side. I started very well, but it has pulled me up."

Jean asked: "Shall I pull alone with both oars for a time?"

"No, thanks, it will go off."

And their mother, somewhat vexed, said:

"Why, Pierre, what rhyme or reason is there in getting into such a state. You are not a child."

And he shrugged his shoulders and set to once more.

Mme. Rosémilly pretended not to see, not to understand, not to hear. Her fair head went back with an engaging little jerk every time the boat moved forward, making the fine wayward hairs flutter about her temples.

But father Roland presently called out:

"Look, the Prince Albert is catching us up!"

They all looked round. Long and low in the water, with her two raking funnels and two yellow paddle-boxes like two round cheeks, the Southampton packet came ploughing on at full steam, crowded with passengers under open parasols. Its hurrying, noisy paddle-wheels beating up the water which fell again in foam, gave it an appearance of haste as of a courier pressed for time, and the upright stem cut through the water, throwing up two thin translucent waves which glided off along the hull.

When it had come quite near the Pearl, father Roland lifted his hat, the ladies shook their handkerchiefs, and half a dozen parasols eagerly waved on board the steamboat responded to this salute as she went on her way, leaving behind her a few broad undulations on the still and glassy surface of the sea.

There were other vessels, each with its smoky cap, coming in from every part of the horizon towards the short white jetty, which swallowed them up, one after another, like a mouth. And the fishing barks and lighter craft with broad sails and slender masts, stealing across the sky in tow of inconspicuous tugs, were coming in, faster and slower, towards the devouring ogre, who from time to time seemed to have had a surfeit, and spewed out to the open sea another fleet of steamers, brigs, schooners, and three-masted vessels with their tangled mass of rigging. The hurrying steamships flew off to the right and left over the smooth bosom of the ocean, while sailing vessels, cast off by the pilot-tugs which had hauled them out, lay motionless, dressing themselves from the main-mast to the fore-tops in canvas, white or brown, and ruddy in the setting sun.

Mme. Roland, with her eyes half-shut, murmured: "Good heavens, how beautiful the sea is!"

And Mme. Rosémilly replied with a long sigh, which, however, had no sadness in it:

"Yes, but it is sometimes very cruel, all the same."

Roland exclaimed:

"Look, there is the Normandie just going in. A big ship, isn't she?"

Then he described the coast opposite, far, far away, on the other side of the mouth of the Seine—that mouth extended over twenty kilometres, said he. He pointed out Villerville, Trouville, Houlgate, Luc, Arromanches, the little river of Caen, and the rocks of Calvados which make the coast unsafe as far as Cherbourg. Then he enlarged on the question of the sand-banks in the Seine, which shift at every tide so that even the pilots of Quillebœuf are at fault if they do not survey the channel every day. He bid them notice how the town of Havre divided Upper from Lower Normandy. In Lower Normandy the shore sloped down to the sea in pasture-lands, fields, and meadows. The coast of Upper Normandy, on the contrary, was steep, a high cliff, ravined, cleft and towering, forming an immense white rampart all the way to Dunkirk, while in each hollow a village or a port lay hidden: Étretat, Fécamp, Saint-Valery, Tréport, Dieppe, and the rest.

The two women did not listen. Torpid with comfort and impressed by the sight of the ocean covered with vessels rushing to and fro like wild beasts about their den, they sat speechless, somewhat awed by the soothing and gorgeous sunset. Roland alone talked on without end; he was one of those whom nothing can disturb. Women, whose nerves are more sensitive, sometimes feel, without knowing why, that the sound of useless speech is as irritating as an insult.

Pierre and Jean, who had calmed down, were rowing slowly, and the Pearl was making for the harbour, a tiny thing among those huge vessels.

When they came alongside of the quay, Papagris, who was waiting there, gave his hand to the ladies to help them out, and they took the way into the town. A large crowd, the crowd which haunts the pier every day at high tide—was also drifting homeward. Mme. Roland and Mme. Rosémilly led the way, followed by the three men. As they went up the Rue de Paris they stopped now and then in front of a milliner's or a jeweller's shop, to look at a bonnet or an ornament; then after making their comments they went on again. In front of the Place de la Bourse Roland paused, as he did every day, to gaze at the docks full of vessels—the Bassin du Commerce, with other docks beyond, where the huge hulls lay side by side, closely packed in rows, four or five deep. And masts innumerable; along several kilometres of quays the endless masts, with their yards, poles, and rigging, gave this great gap in the heart of the town the look of a dead forest. Above this leafless forest the gulls were wheeling, and watching to pounce, like a falling stone, on any scraps flung overboard; a sailor boy, fixing a pulley to a cross-beam, looked as if he had gone up there bird's-nesting.

"Will you dine with us without any sort of ceremony, just that we may end the day together?" said Mme. Roland to her friend.

"To be sure I will, with pleasure; I accept equally without ceremony. It would be dismal to go home and be alone this evening."

Pierre, who had heard, and who was beginning to be restless under the young woman's indifference, muttered to himself: "Well, the widow is taking root now, it would seem." For some days past he had spoken of her as "the widow." The word, harmless in itself, irritated Jean merely by the tone given to it, which to him seemed spiteful and offensive.

The three men spoke not another word till they reached the threshold of their own house. It was a narrow one, consisting of a ground-floor and two floors above, in the Rue Belle-Normande. The maid, Joséphine, a girl of nineteen, a rustic servant-of-all-work at low wages, gifted to excess with the startled animal expression of a peasant, opened the door, went up stairs at her master's heels to the drawing-room, which was on the first floor, and then said:

"A gentleman called—three times."

Old Roland, who never spoke to her without shouting and swearing, cried out:

"Who do you say called, in the devil's name?"

She never winced at her master's roaring voice, and replied:

"A gentleman from the lawyer's."

"What lawyer?"

"Why, M'sieu 'Canu—who else?"

"And what did this gentleman say?"

"That M'sieu 'Canu will call in himself in the course of the evening."

Maître Lecanu was M. Roland's lawyer, and in a way his friend, managing his business for him. For him to send word that he would call in the evening, something urgent and important must be in the wind; and the four Rolands looked at each other, disturbed by the announcement as folks of small fortune are wont to be at any intervention of a lawyer, with its suggestions of contracts, inheritance, lawsuits—all sorts of desirable or formidable contingencies. The father, after a few moments of silence, muttered:

"What on earth can it mean?"

Mme. Rosémilly began to laugh.

"Why, a legacy, of course. I am sure of it. I bring good luck."

But they did not expect the death of any one who might leave them anything.

Mme. Roland, who had a good memory for relationships, began to think over all their connections on her husband's side and on her own, to trace up pedigrees and the ramifications of cousin-ship.

Before even taking off her bonnet she said:

"I say, father" (she called her husband "father" at home, and sometimes "Monsieur Roland" before strangers), "tell me, do you remember who it was that Joseph Lebru married for the second time?"

"Yes—a little girl named Dumenil, a stationer's daughter."

"Had they any children?"

"I should think so! four or five at least."

"Not from that quarter, then."

She was quite eager already in her search; she caught at the hope of some added ease dropping from the sky. But Pierre, who was very fond of his mother, who knew her to be somewhat visionary and feared she might be disappointed, a little grieved, a little saddened if the news were bad instead of good, checked her:

"Do not get excited, mother; there is no rich American uncle. For my part, I should sooner fancy that it is about a marriage for Jean."

Every one was surprised at the suggestion, and Jean was a little ruffled by his brother's having spoken of it before Mme. Rosémilly.

"And why for me rather than for you? The hypothesis is very disputable. You are the elder; you, therefore, would be the first to be thought of. Besides, I do not wish to marry."

Pierre smiled sneeringly:

"Are you in love, then?"

And the other, much put out, retorted: "Is it necessary that a man should be in love because he does not care to marry yet?"

"Ah, there you are! That 'yet' sets it right; you are waiting."

"Granted that I am waiting, if you will have it so."

But old Roland, who had been listening and cogitating, suddenly hit upon the most probable solution.

"Bless me! what fools we are to be racking our brains. Maître Lecanu is our very good friend; he knows that Pierre is looking out for a medical partnership and Jean for a lawyer's office, and he has found something to suit one of you."

This was so obvious and likely that every one accepted it.

"Dinner is ready," said the maid. And they all hurried off to their rooms to wash their hands before sitting down to table.

Ten minutes later they were at dinner in the little dining-room on the ground-floor.

At first they were silent; but presently Roland began again in amazement at this lawyer's visit.

"For after all, why did he not write? Why should he have sent his clerk three times? Why is he coming himself?"

Pierre thought it quite natural.

"An immediate decision is required, no doubt; and perhaps there are certain confidential conditions which it does not do to put into writing."

Still, they were all puzzled, and all four a little annoyed at having invited a stranger, who would be in the way of their discussing and deciding on what should be done.

They had just gone upstairs again when the lawyer was announced. Roland flew to meet him.

"Good-evening, my dear Maître," said he, giving his visitor the title which in France is the official prefix to the name of every lawyer.

Mme. Rosémilly rose.

"I am going," she said. "I am very tired."

A faint attempt was made to detain her; but she would not consent, and went home without either of the three men offering to escort her, as they always had done.

Mme. Roland did the honours eagerly to their visitor.

"A cup of coffee, monsieur?"

"No, thank you. I have just had dinner."

"A cup of tea, then?"

"Thank you, I will accept one later. First we must attend to business."

The deep silence which succeeded this remark was broken only by the regular ticking of the clock, and below stairs the clatter of saucepans which the girl was cleaning—too stupid even to listen at the door.

The lawyer went on:

"Did you, in Paris, know a certain M. Maréchal—Léon Maréchal?"

M. and Mme. Roland both exclaimed at once: "I should think so!"

"He was a friend of yours?"

Roland replied: "Our best friend, monsieur, but a fanatic for Paris; never to be got away from the boulevard. He was a head clerk in the exchequer office. I have never seen him since I left the capital, and latterly we had ceased writing to each other. When people are far apart you know——"

The lawyer gravely put in:

"M. Maréchal is deceased."

Both man and wife responded with the little movement of pained surprise, genuine or false, but always ready, with which such news is received.

Maître Lecanu went on:

"My colleague in Paris has just communicated to me the main item of his will, by which he makes your son Jean—Monsieur Jean Roland—his sole legatee."

They were all too much amazed to utter a single word. Mme. Roland was the first to control her emotion and stammered out:

"Good heavens! Poor Léon—our poor friend! Dear me! Dear me! Dead!"

The tears started to her eyes, a woman's silent tears, drops of grief from her very soul, which trickle down her cheeks and seem so very sad, being so clear. But Roland was thinking less of the loss than of the prospect announced. Still, he dared not at once inquire into the clauses of the will and the amount of the fortune, so to work round to these interesting facts he asked:

"And what did he die of, poor Maréchal?"

Maître Lecanu did not know in the least.

"All I know is," said he, "that dying without any direct heirs, he has left the whole of his fortune—about twenty thousand francs a year ($3,840) in three per cents—to your second son, whom he has known from his birth up, and judges worthy of the legacy. If M. Jean should refuse the money, it is to go to the foundling hospitals."

Old Roland could not conceal his delight and exclaimed:

"Sacristi! It is the thought of a kind heart. And if I had had no heir I would not have forgotten him; he was a true friend."

The lawyer smiled.

"I was very glad," he said, "to announce the event to you myself. It is always a pleasure to be the bearer of good news."

It had not struck him that this good news was that of the death of a friend, of Roland's best friend; and the old man himself had suddenly forgotten the intimacy he had but just spoken of with so much conviction.

Only Mme. Roland and her sons still looked mournful. She, indeed, was still shedding a few tears, wiping her eyes with her handkerchief, which she then pressed to her lips to smother her deep sobs.

The doctor murmured:

"He was a good fellow, very affectionate. He often invited us to dine with him—my brother and me."

Jean, with wide-open, glittering eyes, laid his hand on his handsome fair beard, a familiar gesture with him, and drew his fingers down it to the tip of the last hairs, as if to pull it longer and thinner. Twice his lips parted to utter some decent remark, but after long meditation he could only say this:

"Yes, he was certainly fond of me. He would always embrace me when I went to see him."

But his father's thoughts had set off at a gallop—galloping round this inheritance to come; nay, already in hand; this money lurking behind the door, which would walk in quite soon, to-morrow, at a word of consent.

"And there is no possible difficulty in the way?" he asked. "No lawsuit—no one to dispute it?"

Maître Lecanu seemed quite easy.

"No; my Paris correspondent states that everything is quite clear. M. Jean has only to sign his acceptance."

"Good. Then—then the fortune is quite clear?"

"Perfectly clear."

"All the necessary formalities have been gone through?"

"All."

Suddenly the old jeweller had an impulse of shame—obscure, instinctive, and fleeting; shame of his eagerness to be informed, and he added:

"You understand that I ask all these questions immediately so as to save my son unpleasant consequences which he might not foresee. Sometimes there are debts, embarrassing liabilities, what not! And a legatee finds himself in an inextricable thorn-bush. After all, I am not the heir—but I think first of the little 'un."

They were accustomed to speak of Jean among themselves as the "little one," though he was much bigger than Pierre.

Suddenly Mme. Roland seemed to wake from a dream, to recall some remote fact, a thing almost forgotten that she had heard long ago, and of which she was not altogether sure. She inquired doubtingly:

"Were you not saying that our poor friend Maréchal had left his fortune to my little Jean?"

"Yes, madame."

And she went on simply:

"I am much pleased to hear it; it proves that he was attached to us."

Roland had risen.

"And would you wish, my dear sir, that my son should at once sign his acceptance?"

"No—no, M. Roland. To-morrow, at my office to-morrow, at two o'clock, if that suits you."

"Yes, to be sure—yes, indeed. I should think so."

Then Mme. Roland, who had also risen and who was smiling after her tears, went up to the lawyer, and laying her hand on the back of his chair while she looked at him with the pathetic eyes of a grateful mother, she said:

"And now for that cup of tea, Monsieur Lecanu?"

"Now I will accept it with pleasure, madame."

The maid, on being summoned, brought in first some dry biscuits in deep tin boxes, those crisp, insipid English cakes which seem to have been made for a parrot's beak, and soldered into metal cases for a voyage round the world. Next she fetched some little gray linen doilies, folded square, those tea-napkins which in thrifty families never get washed. A third time she came in with the sugar-basin and cups; then she departed to heat the water. They sat waiting.

No one could talk; they had too much to think about and nothing to say. Mme. Roland alone attempted a few commonplace remarks. She gave an account of the fishing excursion, and sang the praises of the Pearl and of Mme. Rosémilly.

"Charming, charming!" the lawyer said again and again.

Roland, leaning against the marble mantel-shelf as if it were winter and the fire burning, with his hands in his pockets and his lips puckered for a whistle, could not keep still, tortured by the invincible desire to give vent to his delight. The two brothers, in two arm-chairs that matched, one on each side of the centre-table, stared in front of them, in similar attitudes full of dissimilar expressions.

At last the tea appeared. The lawyer took a cup, sugared it, and drank it, after having crumbled into it a little cake which was too hard to crunch. Then he rose, shook hands, and departed.

"Then it is understood," repeated Roland. "To-morrow, at your place, at two?"

"Quite so. To-morrow, at two."

Jean had not spoken a word.

When their guest had gone, silence fell again till father Roland clapped his two hands on his younger son's shoulders, crying:

"Well, you devilish lucky dog! You don't embrace me!"

Then Jean smiled. He embraced his father, saying:

"It had not struck me as indispensable."

The old man was beside himself with glee. He walked about the room, strummed on the furniture with his clumsy nails, turned about on his heels, and kept saying:

"What luck! What luck! Now, that is really what I call luck!"

Pierre asked:

"Then you used to know this Maréchal well?"

And his father replied:

"I believe! Why, he used to spend every evening at our house. Surely you remember he used to fetch you from school on half-holidays, and often took you back again after dinner. Why, the very day when Jean was born it was he who went for the doctor. He had been breakfasting with us when your mother was taken ill. Of course we knew at once what it meant, and he set off post-haste. In his hurry he took my hat instead of his own. I remember that because we had a good laugh over it afterward. It is very likely that he may have thought of that when he was dying, and as he had no heir he may have said to himself: 'I remember helping to bring that youngster into the world, so I will leave him my savings.'"

Mme. Roland, sunk in a deep chair, seemed lost in reminiscences once more. She murmured, as though she were thinking aloud:

"Ah, he was a good friend, very devoted, very faithful, a rare soul in these days."

Jean got up.

"I shall go out for a little walk," he said.

His father was surprised and tried to keep him; they had much to talk about, plans to be made, decisions to be formed. But the young man insisted, declaring that he had an engagement. Besides, there would be time enough for settling everything before he came into possession of his inheritance. So he went away, for he wished to be alone to reflect. Pierre, on his part, said that he too was going out, and after a few minutes followed his brother.

As soon as he was alone with his wife, father Roland took her in his arms, kissed her a dozen times on each cheek, and, replying to a reproach she had often brought against him, said:

"You see, my dearest, that it would have been no good to stay any longer in Paris and work for the children till I dropped, instead of coming here to recruit my health, since fortune drops on us from the skies."

She was quite serious.

"It drops from the skies on Jean," she said. "But Pierre?"

"Pierre? But he is a doctor; he will make plenty of money; besides, his brother will surely do something for him."

"No, he would not take it. Besides, this legacy is for Jean, only for Jean. Pierre will find himself at a great disadvantage."

The old fellow seemed perplexed: "Well, then, we will leave him rather more in our will."

"No; that again would not be quite just."

"Drat it all!" he exclaimed. "What do you want me to do in the matter? You always hit on a whole heap of disagreeable ideas. You must spoil all my pleasures. Well, I am going to bed. Good-night. All the same, I call it good luck, jolly good luck!"

And he went off, delighted in spite of everything, and without a word of regret for the friend so generous in his death.

Mme. Roland sat thinking again in front of the lamp which was burning out.

CHAPTER II

As soon as he got out, Pierre made his way to the Rue de Paris, the high-street of Havre, brightly lighted up, lively and noisy. The rather sharp air of the seacoast kissed his face, and he walked slowly, his stick under his arm and his hands behind his back. He was ill at ease, oppressed, out of heart, as one is after hearing unpleasant tidings. He was not distressed by any definite thought, and he would have been puzzled to account, on the spur of the moment, for this dejection of spirit and heaviness of limb. He was hurt somewhere, without knowing where; somewhere within him there was a pin-point of pain—one of those almost imperceptible wounds which we cannot lay a finger on, but which incommode us, tire us, depress us, irritate us—a slight and occult pang, as it were a small seed of distress.

When he reached the square in front of the theatre, he was attracted by the lights in the Café Tortoni, and slowly bent his steps to the dazzling façade; but just as he was going in he reflected that he would meet friends there and acquaintances—people he would be obliged to talk to; and fierce repugnance surged up in him for this commonplace good-fellowship over coffee cups and liqueur glasses. So, retracing his steps, he went back to the high-street leading to the harbour.

"Where shall I go?" he asked himself, trying to think of a spot he liked which would agree with his frame of mind. He could not think of one, for being alone made him feel fractious, yet he could not bear to meet any one. As he came out on the Grand Quay he hesitated once more; then he turned towards the pier; he had chosen solitude.

Going close by a bench on the breakwater he sat down, tired already of walking and out of humour with his stroll before he had taken it.

He said to himself: "What is the matter with me this evening?" And he began to search in his memory for what vexation had crossed him, as we question a sick man to discover the cause of his fever.

His mind was at once irritable and sober; he got excited, then he reasoned, approving or blaming his impulses; but in time primitive nature at last proved the stronger; the sensitive man always had the upper hand over the intellectual man. So he tried to discover what had induced this irascible mood, this craving to be moving without wanting anything, this desire to meet some one for the sake of differing from him, and at the same time this aversion for the people he might see and the things they might say to him.

And then he put the question to himself, "Can it be Jean's inheritance?"

Yes, it was certainly possible. When the lawyer had announced the news he had felt his heart beat a little faster. For, indeed, one is not always master of one's self; there are sudden and pertinacious emotions against which a man struggles in vain.

He fell into meditation on the physiological problem of the impression produced on the instinctive element in man, and giving rise to a current of painful or pleasurable sensations diametrically opposed to those which the thinking man desires, aims at, and regards as right and wholesome, when he has risen superior to himself by the cultivation of his intellect. He tried to picture to himself the frame of mind of a son who had inherited a vast fortune, and who, thanks to that wealth, may now know many long-wished-for delights, which the avarice of his father had prohibited—a father, nevertheless, beloved and regretted.

He got up and walked on to the end of the pier. He felt better, and glad to have understood, to have detected himself, to have unmasked the other which lurks in us.

"Then I was jealous of Jean," thought he. "That is really vilely mean. And I am sure of it now, for the first idea which came into my head was that he would marry Mme. Rosémilly. And yet I am not in love myself with that priggish little goose, who is just the woman to disgust a man with good sense and good conduct. So it is the most gratuitous jealousy, the very essence of jealousy, which is merely because it is! I must keep an eye on that!"

By this time he was in front of the flag-staff, whence the depth of water in the harbour is signalled, and he struck a match to read the list of vessels signalled in the roadstead and coming in with the next high tide. Ships were due from Brazil, from La Plata, from Chili and Japan, two Danish brigs, a Norwegian schooner, and a Turkish steamship—which startled Pierre as much as if it had read a Swiss steamship; and in a whimsical vision he pictured a great vessel crowded with men in turbans climbing the shrouds in loose trousers.

"How absurd!" thought he. "But the Turks are a maritime people, too."

A few steps further on he stopped again, looking out at the roads. On the right, above Sainte-Adresse, the two electric lights of Cape la Hève, like monstrous twin Cyclops, shot their long and powerful beams across the sea. Starting from two neighbouring centres, the two parallel shafts of light, like the colossal tails of two comets, fell in a straight and endless slope from the top of the cliff to the uttermost horizon. Then, on the two piers, two more lights, the children of these giants, marked the entrance to the harbour; and far away on the other side of the Seine others were in sight, many others, steady or winking, flashing or revolving, opening and shutting like eyes—the eyes of the ports—yellow, red, and green, watching the night-wrapped sea covered with ships; the living eyes of the hospitable shore saying, merely by the mechanical and regular movement of their eye-lids: "I am here. I am Trouville; I am Honfleur; I am the Andemer River." And high above all the rest, so high that from this distance it might be taken for a planet, the airy lighthouse of Etouville showed the way to Rouen across the sand banks at the mouth of the great river.

Out on the deep water, the limitless water, darker than the sky, stars seemed to have fallen here and there. They twinkled in the night haze, small, close to shore or far away—white, red, and green, too. Most of them were motionless; some, however, seemed to be scudding onward. These were the lights of the ships at anchor or moving about in search of moorings.

Just at this moment the moon rose behind the town; and it, too, looked like some huge, divine pharos lighted up in the heavens to guide the countless fleet of stars in the sky. Pierre murmured, almost speaking aloud: "Look at that! And we let our bile rise for twopence!"

On a sudden, close to him, in the wide, dark ditch between the two piers, a shadow stole up, a large shadow of fantastic shape. Leaning over the granite parapet, he saw that a fishing-boat had glided in, without the sound of a voice or the splash of a ripple, or the plunge of an oar, softly borne in by its broad, tawny sail spread to the breeze from the open sea.

He thought to himself: "If one could but live on board that boat, what peace it would be—perhaps!"

And then again a few steps beyond, he saw a man sitting at the very end of the breakwater.

A dreamer, a lover, a sage—a happy or a desperate man? Who was it? He went forward, curious to see the face of this lonely individual, and he recognised his brother.

"What, is it you, Jean?"

"Pierre! You! What has brought you here?"

"I came out to get some fresh air. And you?"

Jean began to laugh.

"I too came out for fresh air." And Pierre sat down by his brother's side.

"Lovely—isn't it?"

"Oh, yes, lovely."

He understood from the tone of voice that Jean had not looked at anything. He went on:

"For my part, whenever I come here I am seized with a wild desire to be off with all those boats, to the north or the south. Only to think that all those little sparks out there have just come from the uttermost ends of the earth, from the lands of great flowers and beautiful olive or copper coloured girls, the lands of humming-birds, of elephants, of roaming lions, of negro kings, from all the lands which are like fairy-tales to us who no longer believe in the White Cat or the Sleeping Beauty. It would be awfully jolly to be able to treat one's self to an excursion out there; but, then, it would cost a great deal of money, no end—"

He broke off abruptly, remembering that his brother had that money now; and released from care, released from labouring for his daily bread, free, unfettered, happy, and light-hearted, he might go whither he listed, to find the fair-haired Swedes or the brown damsels of Havana. And then one of those involuntary flashes which were common with him, so sudden and swift that he could neither anticipate them, nor stop them, nor qualify them, communicated, as it seemed to him, from some second, independent, and violent soul, shot through his brain.

"Bah! He is too great a simpleton; he will marry that little Rosémilly." He was standing up now. "I will leave you to dream of the future. I want to be moving." He grasped his brother's hand and added in a heavy tone:

"Well, my dear old boy, you are a rich man. I am very glad to have come upon you this evening to tell you how pleased I am about it, how truly I congratulate you, and how much I care for you."

Jean, tender and soft-hearted, was deeply touched.

"Thank you, my good brother—thank you!" he stammered.

And Pierre turned away with his slow step, his stick under his arm, and his hands behind his back.

Back in the town again, he once more wondered what he should do, being disappointed of his walk and deprived of the company of the sea by his brother's presence. He had an inspiration. "I will go and take a glass of liqueur with old Marowsko," and he went off towards the quarter of the town known as Ingouville.

He had known old Marowsko-le père Marowsko, he called him—in the hospitals in Paris. He was a Pole, an old refugee, it was said, who had gone through terrible things out there, and who had come to ply his calling as a chemist and druggist in France after passing a fresh examination. Nothing was known of his early life, and all sorts of legends had been current among the indoor and outdoor patients and afterward among his neighbours. This reputation as a terrible conspirator, a nihilist, a regicide, a patriot ready for anything and everything, who had escaped death by a miracle, had bewitched Pierre Roland's lively and bold imagination; he had made friends with the old Pole, without, however, having ever extracted from him any revelation as to his former career. It was owing to the young doctor that this worthy had come to settle at Havre, counting on the large custom which the rising practitioner would secure him. Meanwhile he lived very poorly in his little shop, selling medicines to the small tradesmen and workmen in his part of the town.

Pierre often went to see him and chat with him for an hour after dinner, for he liked Marowsko's calm look and rare speech, and attributed great depth to his long spells of silence.

A simple gas-burner was alight over the counter crowded with phials. Those in the window were not lighted, from motives of economy. Behind the counter, sitting on a chair with his legs stretched out and crossed, an old man, quite bald, with a large beak of a nose which, as a prolongation of his hairless forehead, gave him a melancholy likeness to a parrot, was sleeping soundly, his chin resting on his breast. He woke at the sound of the shop-bell, and recognising the doctor, came forward to meet him, holding out both hands.

His black frock-coat, streaked with stains of acids and sirups, was much too wide for his lean little person, and looked like a shabby old cassock; and the man spoke with a strong Polish accent which gave the childlike character to his thin voice, the lisping note and intonations of a young thing learning to speak.

Pierre sat down, and Marowsko asked him: "What news, dear doctor?"

"None. Everything as usual, everywhere."

"You do not look very gay this evening."

"I am not often gay."

"Come, come, you must shake that off. Will you try a glass of liqueur?"

"Yes, I do not mind."

"Then I will give you something new to try. For these two months I have been trying to extract something from currants, of which only a sirup has been made hitherto—well, and I have done it. I have invented a very good liqueur—very good indeed; very good."

And quite delighted, he went to a cupboard, opened it, and picked out a bottle which he brought forth. He moved and did everything in jerky gestures, always incomplete; he never quite stretched out his arm, nor quite put out his legs; nor made any broad and definite movements. His ideas seemed to be like his actions; he suggested them, promised them, sketched them, hinted at them, but never fully uttered them.

And, indeed, his great end in life seemed to be the concoction of sirups and liqueurs. "A good sirup or a good liqueur is enough to make a fortune," he would often say.

He had compounded hundreds of these sweet mixtures without ever succeeding in floating one of them. Pierre declared that Marowsko always reminded him of Marat.

Two little glasses were fetched out of the back shop and placed on the mixing-board. Then the two men scrutinized the colour of the fluid by holding it up to the gas.

"A fine ruby," Pierre declared.

"Isn't it?" Marowsko's old parrot-face beamed with satisfaction.

The doctor tasted, smacked his lips, meditated, tasted again, meditated again, and spoke:

"Very good—capital; and quite new in flavour. It is a find, my dear fellow."

"Ah, really? Well, I am very glad."

Then Marowsko took counsel as to baptizing the new liqueur. He wanted to call it "Extract of currants," or else "Fine Groseille" or "Grosélia," or again "Groséline." Pierre did not approve of either of these names.

Then the old man had an idea:

"What you said just now would be very good, very good: 'Fine Ruby.'" But the doctor disputed the merit of this name, though it had originated with him. He recommended simply "Groseillette," which Marowsko thought admirable.

Then they were silent, and sat for some minutes without a word under the solitary gas-lamp. At last Pierre began, almost in spite of himself:

"A queer thing has happened at home this evening. A friend of my father's, who is lately dead, has left his fortune to my brother."

The druggist did not at first seem to understand, but after thinking it over he hoped that the doctor had half the inheritance. When the matter was clearly explained to him he appeared surprised and vexed; and to express his dissatisfaction at finding that his young friend had been sacrificed, he said several times over:

"It will not look well."

Pierre, who was relapsing into nervous irritation, wanted to know what Marowsko meant by this phrase.

Why would it not look well? What was there to look badly in the fact that his brother had come into the money of a friend of the family?

But the cautious old man would not explain further.

"In such a case the money is left equally to the two brothers, and I tell you, it will not look well."

And the doctor, out of all patience, went away, returned to his father's house, and went to bed. For some time afterward he heard Jean moving softly about the adjoining room, and then, after drinking two glasses of water, he fell asleep.

CHAPTER III

The doctor awoke next morning firmly resolved to make his fortune. Several times already he had come to the same determination without following up the reality. At the outset of all his trials of some new career the hopes of rapidly acquired riches kept up his efforts and confidence, till the first obstacle, the first check, threw him into a fresh path. Snug in bed between the warm sheets, he lay meditating. How many medical men had become wealthy in quite a short time! All that was needed was a little knowledge of the world; for in the course of his studies he had learned to estimate the most famous physicians, and he judged them all to be asses. He was certainly as good as they, if not better. If by any means he could secure a practice among the wealth and fashion of Havre, he could easily make a hundred thousand francs a year. And he calculated with great exactitude what his certain profits must be. He would go out in the morning to visit his patients; at the very moderate average of ten a day, at twenty francs each, that would mount up to seventy-two thousand francs a year at least, or even seventy-five thousand; for ten patients was certainly below the mark. In the afternoon he would be at home to, say, another ten patients, at ten francs each—thirty-six thousand francs. Here, then, in round numbers was an income of twenty thousand francs. Old patients, or friends whom he would charge only ten francs for a visit, or see at home for five, would perhaps make a slight reduction on this sum total, but consultations with other physicians and various incidental fees would make up for that.

Nothing could be easier than to achieve this by skilful advertising remarks in the Figaro to the effect that the scientific faculty of Paris had their eye on him, and were interested in the cures effected by the modest young practitioner of Havre! And he would be richer than his brother, richer and more famous; and satisfied with himself, for he would owe his fortune solely to his own exertions; and liberal to his old parents, who would be justly proud of his fame. He would not marry, would not burden his life with a wife who would be in his way, but he would choose his mistress from the most beautiful of his patients. He felt so sure of success that he sprang out of bed as though to grasp it on the spot, and he dressed to go and search through the town for rooms to suit him.

Then, as he wandered about the streets, he reflected how slight are the causes which determine our actions. Any time these three weeks he might and ought to have come to this decision, which, beyond a doubt, the news of his brother's inheritance had abruptly given rise to.

He stopped before every door where a placard proclaimed that "fine apartments" or "handsome rooms" were to be let; announcements without an adjective he turned from with scorn. Then he inspected them with a lofty air, measuring the height of the rooms, sketching the plan in his note-book, with the passages, the arrangement of the exits, explaining that he was a medical man and had many visitors. He must have a broad and well-kept stair-case; nor could he be any higher up than the first floor.

After having written down seven or eight addresses and scribbled two hundred notes, he got home to breakfast a quarter of an hour too late.

In the hall he heard the clatter of plates. Then they had begun without him! Why? They were never wont to be so punctual. He was nettled and put out, for he was somewhat thin-skinned. As he went in Roland said to him:

"Come, Pierre, make haste, devil take you! You know we have to be at the lawyer's at two o'clock. This is not the day to be dawdling."

Pierre sat down without replying, after kissing his mother and shaking hands with his father and brother; and he helped himself from the deep dish in the middle of the table to the cutlet which had been kept for him. It was cold and dry, probably the least tempting of them all. He thought that they might have left it on the hot plate till he came in, and not lose their heads so completely as to have forgotten their other son, their eldest.

The conversation, which his entrance had interrupted, was taken up again at the point where it had ceased.

"In your place," Mme. Roland was saying to Jean, "I will tell you what I should do at once. I should settle in handsome rooms so as to attract attention; I should ride on horseback and select one or two interesting cases to defend and make a mark in court. I would be a sort of amateur lawyer, and very select. Thank God you are out of all danger of want, and if you pursue a profession, it is, after all, only that you may not lose the benefit of your studies, and because a man ought never to sit idle."

Old Roland, who was peeling a pear, exclaimed:

"Christi! In your place I should buy a nice yacht, a cutter on the build of our pilot-boats. I would sail as far as Senegal in such a boat as that."

Pierre, in his turn, spoke his views. After all, said he, it was not his wealth which made the moral worth, the intellectual worth of a man. To a man of inferior mind it was only a means of degradation, while in the hands of a strong man it was a powerful lever. They, to be sure, were rare. If Jean were a really superior man, now that he could never want he might prove it. But then he must work a hundred times harder than he would have done in other circumstances. His business now must be not to argue for or against the widow and the orphan, and pocket his fees for every case he gained, but to become a really eminent legal authority, a luminary of the law. And he added in conclusion:

"If I were rich wouldn't I dissect no end of bodies!"

Father Roland shrugged his shoulders.

"That is all very fine," he said. "But the wisest way of life is to take it easy. We are not beasts of burden, but men. If you are born poor you must work; well, so much the worse; and you do work. But where you have dividends! You must be a flat if you grind yourself to death."

Pierre replied haughtily:

"Our notions differ. For my part, I respect nothing on earth but learning and intellect; everything else is beneath contempt."

Mme. Roland always tried to deaden the constant shocks between father and son; she turned the conversation, and began talking of a murder committed the week before at Bolbec Nointot. Their minds were immediately full of the circumstances under which the crime had been committed, and absorbed by the interesting horror, the attractive mystery of crime, which, however commonplace, shameful, and disgusting, exercises a strange and universal fascination over the curiosity of mankind. Now and again, however, old Roland looked at his watch. "Come," said he, "it is time to be going."

Pierre sneered.

"It is not yet one o'clock," he said. "It really was hardly worth while to condemn me to eat a cold cutlet."

“Are you coming to the lawyer’s?” his mother asked.

“I? No. What for?” he replied dryly. “My presence is quite unnecessary.”

Jean sat silent, as though he had no concern in the matter. When they were discussing the murder at Bolbec he, as a legal authority, had put forward some opinions and uttered some reflections on crime and criminals. Now he spoke no more; but the sparkle in his eye, the bright colour in his cheeks, the very gloss of his beard seemed to proclaim his happiness.

When the family had gone, Pierre, alone once more, resumed his investigations in the apartments to let. After two or three hours spent in going up and down stairs, he at last found, in the Boulevard François, a pretty set of rooms; a spacious entresol with two doors on two different streets, two drawing-rooms, a glass corridor, where his patients while they waited, might walk among flowers, and a delightful dining-room with a bow-window looking out over the sea.

When it came to taking it, the terms—three thousand francs—pulled him up; the first quarter must be paid in advance, and he had nothing, not a penny to call his own.

The little fortune his father had saved brought him in about eight thousand francs a year, and Pierre had often blamed himself for having placed his parents in difficulties by his long delay in deciding on a profession, by forfeiting his attempts and beginning fresh courses of study. So he went away, promising to send his answer within two days, and it occurred to him to ask Jean to lend him the amount of this quarter’s rent, or even of a half-year, fifteen hundred francs, as soon as Jean should have come into possession.

“It will be a loan for a few months at most,” he thought. “I shall repay him, very likely before the end of the year. It is a simple matter, and he will be glad to do so much for me.”

As it was not yet four o’clock, and he had nothing to do, absolutely nothing, he went to sit in the public gardens; and he remained a long time on a bench, without an idea in his brain, his eyes fixed on the ground, crushed by weariness amounting to distress.

And yet this was how he had been living all these days since his return home, without suffering so acutely from the vacuity of his existence and from inaction. How had he spent his time from rising in the morning till bed-time?

He had loafed on the pier at high tide, loafed in the streets, loafed in the cafés, loafed at Marowsko’s, loafed everywhere. And on a sudden this life, which he had endured till now, had become odious, intolerable. If he had had any pocket-money, he would have taken a carriage for a long drive in the country, along by the farm-ditches shaded by beech and elm trees; but he had to think twice of the cost of a glass of beer or a postage-stamp, and such an indulgence was out of his ken. It suddenly struck him how hard it was for a man of past thirty to be reduced to ask his mother, with a blush for a twenty-franc piece every now and then; and he muttered, as he scored the gravel with the ferule of his stick:

“Christi, if I only had money!”

And again the thought of his brother’s legacy came into his head like the sting of a wasp; but he drove it out indignantly, not choosing to allow himself to slip down that descent to jealousy.

Some children were playing about in the dusty paths. They were fair little things with long hair, and they were making little mounds of sand with the greatest gravity and careful attention, to crush them at once by stamping on them.

It was one of those gloomy days with Pierre when we pry into every corner of our souls and shake out every crease.

"All our endeavours are like the labours of those babies," thought he. And then he wondered whether the wisest thing in life were not to beget two or three of these little creatures and watch them grow up with complacent curiosity. A longing for marriage breathed on his soul. A man is not so lost when he is not alone. At any rate, he has some one stirring at his side in hours of trouble or of uncertainty; and it is something only to be able to speak on equal terms to a woman when one is suffering.

Then he began thinking of women. He knew very little of them, never having had any but very transient connections as a medical student, broken off as soon as the month's allowance was spent, and renewed or replaced by another the following month. And yet there must be some very kind, gentle, and comforting creatures among them. Had not his mother been the good sense and saving grace of his own home? How glad he would be to know a woman, a true woman!

He started up with a sudden determination to go and call on Mme. Rosémilly. But he promptly sat down again. He did not like that woman. Why not? She had too much vulgar and sordid common sense; besides, did she not seem to prefer Jean? Without confessing it to himself too bluntly, this preference had a great deal to do with his low opinion of the widow's intellect; for, though he loved his brother, he could not help thinking him somewhat mediocre and believing himself the superior. However, he was not going to sit there till nightfall; and as he had done on the previous evening, he anxiously asked himself: "What am I going to do?"

At this moment he felt in his soul the need of a melting mood, of being embraced and comforted. Comforted—for what? He could not have put it into words; but he was in one of these hours of weakness and exhaustion when a woman's presence, a woman's kiss, the touch of a hand, the rustle of a petticoat, a soft look out of black or blue eyes, seem the one thing needful, there and then, to our heart. And the memory flashed upon him of a little barmaid at a beer-house, whom he had walked home with one evening, and seen again from time to time.

So once more he rose, to go and drink a bock with the girl. What should he say to her? What would she say to him? Nothing, probably. But what did that matter? He would hold her hand for a few seconds. She seemed to have a fancy for him. Why, then, did he not go to see her oftener?

He found her dozing on a chair in the beer-shop, which was almost deserted. Three men were drinking and smoking with their elbows on the oak tables; the book-keeper in her desk was reading a novel, while the master, in his shirt-sleeves, lay sound asleep on a bench.

As soon as she saw him the girl rose eagerly, and coming to meet him, said:

"Good-day, monsieur—how are you?"

"Pretty well; and you?"

"I—oh, very well. How scarce you make yourself!"

"Yes. I have very little time to myself. I am a doctor, you know."

"Indeed! You never told me. If I had known that—I was out of sorts last week and I would have sent for you. What will you take?"

"A bock. And you?"

"I will have a bock, too, since you are willing to treat me."

She had addressed him with the familiar tu, and continued to use it, as if the offer of a drink had tacitly conveyed permission. Then, sitting down opposite each other, they talked for a while. Every now and then she took his hand with the light familiarity of girls whose kisses are for sale, and looking at him with inviting eyes she said:

"Why don't you come here oftener? I like you very much, sweetheart."

He was already disgusted with her; he saw how stupid she was, and common, smacking of low life. A woman, he told himself, should appear to us in dreams, or such a glory as may poetize her vulgarity.

Next she asked him:

"You went by the other morning with a handsome fair man, wearing a big beard. Is he your brother?"

"Yes, he is my brother."

"Awfully good-looking."

"Do you think so?"

"Yes, indeed; and he looks like a man who enjoys life, too."

What strange craving impelled him on a sudden to tell this tavern-wench about Jean's legacy? Why should this thing, which he kept at arm's length when he was alone, which he drove from him for fear of the torment it brought upon his soul, rise to his lips at this moment? And why did he allow it to overflow them as if he needed once more to empty out his heart to some one, gorged as it was with bitterness?

He crossed his legs and said:

"He has wonderful luck, that brother of mine. He had just come into a legacy of twenty thousand francs a year."

She opened those covetous blue eyes of hers very wide.

"Oh! and who left him that? His grandmother or his aunt?"

"No. An old friend of my parents'."

"Only a friend! Impossible! And you—did he leave you nothing?"

"No. I knew him very slightly."

She sat thinking some minutes; then, with an odd smile on her lips, she said:

"Well, he is a lucky dog, that brother of yours, to have friends of this pattern. My word! and no wonder he is so unlike you."

He longed to slap her, without knowing why; and he asked with pinched lips: "And what do you mean by saying that?"

She had put on a stolid, innocent face.

"O—h, nothing. I mean he has better luck than you."

He tossed a franc piece on the table and went out.

Now he kept repeating the phrase: "No wonder he is so unlike you."

What had her thought been, what had been her meaning under those words? There was certainly some malice, some spite, something shameful in it. Yes, that hussy must have fancied, no doubt, that Jean was Maréchal's son. The agitation which came over him at the notion of this suspicion cast at his mother was so violent that he stood still, looking about him for some place where he might sit down. In front of him was another café. He went in, took a chair, and as the waiter came up, "A bock," he said.

He felt his heart beating, his skin was gooseflesh. And then the recollection flashed upon him of what Marowsko had said the evening before. "It will not look well." Had he had the same thought, the same suspicion as this baggage? Hanging his head over the glass, he watched the white froth as the bubbles rose and burst, asking himself: "Is it possible that such a thing should be believed?"

But the reasons which might give rise to this horrible doubt in other men's minds now struck him, one after another, as plain, obvious, and exasperating. That a childless old bachelor should leave his fortune to a friend's two sons was the most simple and natural thing in the world; but that he should leave the whole of it to one alone—of course people would wonder, and whisper, and end by smiling. How was it that he had not foreseen this, that his father had not felt it? How was it that his mother had not guessed it? No; they had been too delighted at this unhoped-for wealth for the idea to come near them. And besides, how should these worthy souls have ever dreamed of anything so ignominious?

But the public—their neighbours, the shopkeepers, their own tradesmen, all who knew them—would not they repeat the abominable thing, laugh at it, enjoy it, make game of his father and despise his mother?

And the barmaid's remark that Jean was fair and he dark, that they were not in the least alike in face, manner, figure, or intelligence, would now strike every eye and every mind. When any one spoke of Roland's son, the question would be: "Which, the real or the false?"

He rose, firmly resolved to warn Jean, and put him on his guard against the frightful danger which threatened their mother's honour.

But what could Jean do? The simplest thing no doubt, would be to refuse the inheritance, which would then go to the poor, and to tell all friends or acquaintances who had heard of the bequest that the will contained clauses and conditions impossible to subscribe to, which would have made Jean not inheritor but merely a trustee.

As he made his way home he was thinking that he must see his brother alone, so as not to speak of such a matter in the presence of his parents. On reaching the door he heard a great noise of voices and laughter in the drawing-room, and when he went in he found Captain Beausire and Mme. Rosémilly, whom his father had brought home and engaged to dine with them in honour of the good news. Vermouth and absinthe had been served to whet their appetites, and every one had been at once put into good spirits. Captain Beausire, a funny little man who had become quite round by dint of being rolled about at sea, and whose ideas also seemed to have been worn round, like the pebbles of a beach, while he laughed with his throat full of r's, looked upon life as a capital thing, in which everything that might turn up was good to take. He clinked his glass against father Roland's, while Jean was offering two freshly filled glasses to the ladies. Mme. Rosémilly refused, till Captain Beausire, who had known her husband, cried:

"Come, come, madame, bis repetita placent, as we say in the lingo, which is as much as to say two glasses of vermouth never hurt any one. Look at me; since I have left the sea, in this way I give myself an artificial roll or two every day before dinner; I add a little pitching after my coffee, and that keeps things lively for the rest of the evening. I never rise to a hurricane, mind you, never, never. I am too much afraid of damage."

Roland, whose nautical mania was humoured by the old mariner, laughed heartily, his face flushed already and his eye watery from the absinthe. He had a burly shop-keeping stomach—nothing but stomach—in which the rest of his body seemed to have got stowed away; the flabby paunch of men who spend their lives sitting, and who have neither thighs, nor chest, nor arms, nor neck; the seat of their chairs having accumulated all their substance in one spot. Beausire, on the contrary, though short and stout, was as tight as an egg and as hard as a cannon-ball.

Mme. Roland had not emptied her glass and was gazing at her son Jean with sparkling eyes; happiness had brought a colour to her cheeks.

In him, too, the fulness of joy had now blazed out. It was a settled thing, signed and sealed; he had twenty thousand francs a year. In the sound of his laugh, in the fuller voice with which he spoke, in his way of looking at the others, his more positive manners, his greater confidence, the assurance given by money was at once perceptible.

Dinner was announced, and as the old man was about to offer his arm to Mme. Rosémilly, his wife exclaimed:

"No, no, father. Everything is for Jean to-day."

Unwonted luxury graced the table. In front of Jean, who sat in his father's place, an enormous bouquet of flowers—a bouquet for a really great occasion—stood up like a cupola dressed with flags, and was flanked by four high dishes, one containing a pyramid of splendid peaches; the second, a monumental cake gorged with whipped cream and covered with pinnacles of sugar—a cathedral in confectionery; the third, slices of pine-apple floating in clear sirup; and the fourth—unheard-of lavishness—black grapes brought from the warmer south.

"The devil!" exclaimed Pierre as he sat down. "We are celebrating the accession of Jean the rich."

After the soup, Madeira was passed round, and already every one was talking at once. Beausire was giving the history of a dinner he had eaten at San Domingo at the table of a negro general. Old Roland was listening, and at the same time trying to get in, between the sentences, his account of another dinner, given by a friend of his at Mendon, after which every guest was ill for a fortnight. Mme. Rosémilly, Jean, and his mother were planning an excursion to breakfast at Saint Jouin, from which they promised themselves the greatest pleasure; and Pierre was only sorry that he had not dined alone in some pot-house by the sea, so as to escape all this noise and laughter and glee which fretted him. He was wondering how he could now set to work to confide his fears to his brother, and induce him to renounce the fortune he had already accepted and of which he was enjoying the intoxicating foretaste. It would be hard on him, no doubt; but it must be done; he could not hesitate; their mother's reputation was at stake.

The appearance of an enormous shade-fish threw Roland back on fishing stories. Beausire told some wonderful tales of adventure on the Gaboon, at Sainte-Marie, in Madagascar, and above all, off the coasts of China and Japan, where the fish are as queer-looking as the natives. And he described the appearance of these fishes—their goggle gold eyes, their blue or red bellies, their fantastic fins like fans, their eccentric crescent-shaped tails—with such droll gesticulation that they all laughed till they cried as they listened.

Pierre alone seemed incredulous, muttering to himself: "True enough, the Normans are the Gascons of the north!"

After the fish came a vol-au-vent, then a roast fowl, a salad, French beans with a Pithiviers lark-pie. Mme. Rosémilly's maid helped to wait on them, and the fun rose with the number of glasses of wine they drank. When the cork of the first champagne-bottle was drawn with a pop, father Roland, highly excited, imitated the noise with his tongue and then declared: "I like that noise better than a pistol-shot."

Pierre, more and more fractious every moment, retorted with a sneer:

"And yet it is perhaps a greater danger for you."

Roland, who was on the point of drinking, set his full glass down on the table again, and asked:

"Why?"

He had for some time been complaining of his health, of heaviness, giddiness, frequent and unaccountable discomfort. The doctor replied:

"Because the bullet might very possibly miss you, while the glass of wine is dead certain to hit you in the stomach."

"And what then?"

"Then it scorches your inside, upsets your nervous system, makes the circulation sluggish, and leads the way to the apoplectic fit which always threatens a man of your build."

The jeweller's incipient intoxication had vanished like smoke before the wind. He looked at his son with fixed, uneasy eyes, trying to discover whether he was making game of him.

But Beausire exclaimed:

"Oh, these confounded doctors! They all sing the same tune—eat nothing, drink nothing, never make love or enjoy yourself; it all plays the devil with your precious health. Well, all I can say is, I have done all these things, sir, in every quarter of the globe, wherever and as often as I have had the chance, and I am none the worse."

Pierre answered with some asperity:

"In the first place, captain, you are a stronger man than my father; and in the next, all free livers talk as you do till the day when—when they come back no more to say to the cautious doctor: 'You were right.' When I see my father doing what is worst and most dangerous for him, it is but natural that I should warn him. I should be a bad son if I did otherwise."

Mme. Roland, much distressed, now put in her word: "Come, Pierre, what ails you? For once it cannot hurt him. Think of what an occasion it is for him, for all of us. You will spoil his pleasure and make us all unhappy. It is too bad of you to do such a thing."

He muttered, as he shrugged his shoulders.

"He can do as he pleases. I have warned him."

But father Roland did not drink. He sat looking at his glass full of the clear and luminous liquor while its light soul, its intoxicating soul, flew off in tiny bubbles mounting from its depths in hurried succession to die on the surface. He looked at it with the suspicious eye of a fox smelling at a dead hen and suspecting a trap. He asked doubtfully: "Do you think it will really do me much harm?" Pierre had a pang of remorse and blamed himself for letting his ill-humour punish the rest.

"No," said he. "Just for once you may drink it; but do not take too much, or get into the habit of it."

Then old Roland raised his glass, but still he could not make up his mind to put it to his lips. He contemplated it regretfully, with longing and with fear; then he smelt it, tasted it, drank it in sips, swallowing them slowly, his heart full of terrors, of weakness and greediness; and then, when he had drained the last drop, of regret.

Pierre's eye suddenly met that of Mme. Rosémilly; it rested on him clear and blue, far-seeing and hard. And he read, he knew, the precise thought which lurked in that look, the indignant thought of this simple and right-minded little woman; for the look said: "You are jealous—that is what you are. Shameful!"

He bent his head and went on with his dinner.

He was not hungry and found nothing nice. A longing to be off harassed him, a craving to be away from these people, to hear no more of their talking, jests, and laughter.

Father Roland meanwhile, to whose head the fumes of the wine were rising once more, had already forgotten his son's advice and was eyeing a champagne-bottle with a tender leer as it stood, still nearly full, by the side of his plate. He dared not touch it for fear of being lectured again, and he was wondering by what device or trick he could possess himself of it without exciting Pierre's remark. A ruse occurred to him, the simplest possible. He took up the bottle with an air of indifference, and holding it by the neck, stretched his arm across the table to fill the doctor's glass, which was empty; then he filled up all the other glasses, and when he came to his own he began talking very loud, so that if he poured anything into it they might have sworn it was done inadvertently. And in fact no one took any notice.

Pierre, without observing it, was drinking a good deal. Nervous and fretted, he every minute raised to his lips the tall crystal funnel where the bubbles were dancing in the living, translucent fluid. He let the wine slip very slowly over his tongue, that he might feel the little sugary sting of the fixed air as it evaporated.

Gradually a pleasant warmth glowed in his frame. Starting from the stomach as a centre, it spread to his chest, took possession of his limbs, and diffused itself throughout his flesh, like a warm and comforting tide, bringing pleasure with it. He felt better now, less impatient, less annoyed, and his determination to speak to his brother that very evening faded away; not that he thought for a moment of giving it up, but simply not to disturb the happy mood in which he found himself.

Beausire presently rose to propose a toast. Having bowed to the company, he began:

"Most gracious ladies and gentlemen, we have met to do honour to a happy event which has befallen one of our friends. It used to be said that Fortune was blind, but I believe that she is only short-sighted or tricksy, and that she has lately bought a good pair of glasses which enabled her to discover in the town of Havre the son of our worthy friend Roland, skipper of the Pearl."

Every one cried bravo and clapped their hands, and the elder Roland rose to reply. After clearing his throat, for it felt thick and his tongue was heavy, he stammered out:

"Thank you, captain, thank you—for myself and my son. I shall never forget your behaviour on this occasion. Here's good luck to you!"

His eyes and nose were full of tears, and he sat down, finding nothing more to say.

Jean, who was laughing, spoke in his turn:

"It is I," said he, "who ought to thank my friends here, my excellent friends," and he glanced at Mme. Rosémilly, "who have given me such a touching evidence of their affection. But it is not by words that I can prove my gratitude. I will prove it to-morrow, every hour of my life, always, for our friendship is not one of those which fade away."

His mother, deeply moved, murmured: "Well said, my boy."

But Beausire cried out:

"Come, Mme. Rosémilly, speak on behalf of the fair sex."

She raised her glass, and in a pretty voice, slightly touched with sadness, she said: "I will pledge you to the memory of M. Maréchal."

There was a few moments' lull, a pause for decent meditation, as after prayer. Beausire, who always had a flow of compliment, remarked:

"Only a woman ever thinks of these refinements." Then turning to Father Roland: "And who was this Maréchal, after all? You must have been very intimate with him."

The old man, emotional with drink, began to whimper, and in a broken voice he said:

"Like a brother, you know. Such a friend as one does not make twice—we were always together—he dined with us every evening—and would treat us to the play—I need say no more—no more—no more. A true friend—a real true friend—wasn't he, Louise?"

His wife merely answered: "Yes; he was a faithful friend."

Pierre looked at his father and then at his mother, then, as the subject changed he drank some more wine. He scarcely remembered the remainder of the evening. They had coffee, then liqueurs, and they laughed and joked a great deal. At about midnight he went to bed, his mind confused and his head heavy; and he slept like a brute till nine next morning.

CHAPTER IV

These slumbers, lapped in Champagne and Chartreuse, had soothed and calmed him, no doubt, for he awoke in a very benevolent frame of mind. While he was dressing he appraised, weighed, and summed up the agitations of the past day, trying to bring out quite clearly and fully their real and occult causes, those personal to himself as well as those from outside.

It was, in fact, possible that the girl at the beer-shop had had an evil suspicion—a suspicion worthy of such a hussy—on hearing that only one of the Roland brothers had been made heir to a stranger; but have not such natures as she always similar notions, without a shadow of foundation, about every honest woman? Do they not, whenever they speak, vilify, calumniate, and abuse all whom they believe to be blameless? Whenever a woman who is above imputation is mentioned in their presence, they are as angry as if they were being insulted, and exclaim: "Ah, yes, I know your married women; a pretty sort they are! Why, they have more lovers than we have, only they conceal it because they are such hypocrites. Oh, yes, a pretty sort, indeed!"

Under any other circumstances he would certainly not have understood, not have imagined the possibility of such an insinuation against his poor mother, who was so kind, so simple, so excellent. But his spirit seethed with the leaven of jealousy that was fermenting within him. His own excited mind, on the scent, as it were, in spite of himself, for all that could damage his brother, had even perhaps attributed to the tavern barmaid an odious intention of which she was innocent. It was possible that his imagination had, unaided, invented this dreadful doubt—his imagination, which he never controlled, which constantly evaded his will and went off, unfettered, audacious, adventurous, and stealthy, into the infinite world of ideas, bringing back now and then some which were shameless and repulsive, and which it buried in him, in the depths of his soul, in its most fathomless recesses, like something stolen. His heart, most certainly, his own heart had secrets from him; and had not that wounded heart discerned in this atrocious doubt a means of depriving his brother of the inheritance of which he was jealous? He suspected himself now, cross-examining all the mysteries of his mind as bigots search their consciences.

Mme. Rosémilly, though her intelligence was limited, had certainly a woman's instinct, scent, and subtle intuitions. And this notion had never entered her head, since she had, with perfect simplicity, drunk to the blessed memory of the deceased Maréchal. She was not the woman to have done this if she had had the faintest suspicion. Now he doubted no longer; his involuntary displeasure at his brother's windfall of fortune and his religious affection for his mother had magnified his scruples—very pious and respectable scruples, but exaggerated. As he put this conclusion into words in his own mind he felt happy, as at the doing of a good action; and he resolved to be nice to every one, beginning with his father, whose manias, and silly statements, and vulgar opinions, and too conspicuous mediocrity were a constant irritation to him.

He came in not late for breakfast, and amused all the family by his fun and good humour.

His mother, quite delighted, said to him:

"My little Pierre, you have no notion how humorous and clever you can be when you choose."

And he talked, putting things in a witty way, and making them laugh by ingenious hits at their friends. Beausire was his butt, and Mme. Rosémilly a little, but in a very judicious way, not too spiteful. And he thought as he looked at his brother: "Stand up for her, you muff. You may be as rich as you please, I can always eclipse you when I take the trouble."

As they drank their coffee he said to his father:

"Are you going out in the Pearl to-day?"

"No, my boy."

"May I have her with Jean Bart?"

"To be sure, as long as you like."

He bought a good cigar at the first tobacconist's and went down to the quay with a light step. He glanced up at the sky, which was clear and luminous, of a pale blue, freshly swept by the sea-breeze.

Papagris, the boatman, commonly called Jean Bart, was dozing in the bottom of the boat, which he was required to have in readiness every day at noon when they had not been out fishing in the morning.

"You and I together, mate," cried Pierre. He went down the iron ladder of the quay and leaped into the vessel.

"Which way is the wind?" he asked.

"Due east still, M'sieu Pierre. A fine breeze out at sea."

"Well, then, old man, off we go!"

They hoisted the foresail and weighed anchor; and the boat, feeling herself free, glided slowly down towards the jetty on the still water of the harbour. The breath of wind that came down the streets caught the top of the sail so lightly as to be imperceptible, and the Pearl seemed endowed with life—the life of a vessel driven on by a mysterious latent power. Pierre took the tiller, and, holding his cigar between his teeth, he stretched his legs on the bunk, and with his eyes half-shut in the blinding sunshine, he watched the great tarred timbers of the breakwater as they glided past.

When they reached the open sea, round the nose of the north pier which had sheltered them, the fresher breeze puffed in the doctor's face and on his hands, like a somewhat icy caress, filled his chest, which rose with a long sigh to drink it in, and swelling the tawny sail, tilted the Pearl on her beam and made her more lively. Jean Bart hastily hauled up the jib, and the triangle of canvas, full of wind, looked like a wing; then, with two strides to the stern, he let out the spinnaker, which was close-reefed against his mast.

Then, along the hull of the boat, which suddenly heeled over and was running at top speed, there was a soft, crisp sound of water hissing and rushing past. The prow ripped up the sea like the share of a plough gone mad, and the yielding water it turned up curled over and fell white with foam, as the ploughed soil, heavy and brown, rolls and falls in a ridge. At each wave they met—and there was a short, chopping sea—the Pearl shivered from the point of the bowsprit to the rudder, which trembled under Pierre's hand; when the wind blew harder in gusts, the swell rose to the gunwale as if it would overflow into the boat. A coal brig from Liverpool was lying at anchor, waiting for the tide; they made a sweep round her stern and went to look at each of the vessels in the roads one after another; then they put further out to look at the unfolding line of coast.

For three hours Pierre, easy, calm, and happy, wandered to and fro over the dancing waters, guiding the thing of wood and canvas, which came and went at his will, under the pressure of his hand, as if it were a swift and docile winged creature.

He was lost in day-dreams, the dreams one has on horseback or on the deck of a boat; thinking of his future, which should be brilliant, and the joys of living intelligently. On the morrow he would ask his brother to lend him fifteen hundred francs for three months, that he might settle at once in the pretty rooms on the Boulevard François.

Suddenly the sailor said: "The fog is coming up, M'sieu Pierre. We must go in."

He looked up and saw to the northward a gray shade, filmy but dense, blotting out the sky and covering the sea; it was sweeping down on them like a cloud fallen from above. He tacked for land and made for the pier, scudding before the wind and followed by the flying fog, which gained upon them. When it reached the Pearl, wrapping her in its intangible density, a cold shudder ran over Pierre's limbs, and a smell of smoke and mould, the peculiar smell of a sea-fog, made him close his mouth that he might not taste the cold, wet vapour. By the time the boat was at her usual moorings in the harbour the whole town was buried in this fine mist, which did not fall but yet wetted everything like rain, and glided and rolled along the roofs and streets like the flow of a river. Pierre, with his hands and feet frozen, made haste home and threw himself on his bed to take a nap till dinner-time. When he made his appearance in the dining-room his mother was saying to Jean:

"The glass corridor will be lovely. We will fill it with flowers. You will see. I will undertake to care for them and renew them. When you give a party the effect will be quite fairy-like."

"What in the world are you talking about?" the doctor asked.

"Of a delightful apartment I have just taken for your brother. It is quite a find; an entresol looking out on two streets. There are two drawing-rooms, a glass passage, and a little circular dining-room, perfectly charming for a bachelor's quarters."

Pierre turned pale. His anger seemed to press on his heart.

"Where is it?" he asked.

"Boulevard François."

There was no possibility for doubt. He took his seat in such a state of exasperation that he longed to exclaim: "This is really too much! Is there nothing for any one but him?"

His mother, beaming, went on talking: "And only fancy, I got it for two thousand eight hundred francs a year. They asked three thousand, but I got a reduction of two hundred francs on taking for three, six, or nine years. Your brother will be delightfully housed there. An elegant home is enough to make the fortune of a lawyer. It attracts clients, charms them, holds them fast, commands respect, and shows them that a man who lives in such good style expects a good price for his words."

She was silent for a few seconds and then went on:

"We must look out for something suitable for you; much less pretentious, since you have nothing, but nice and pretty all the same. I assure you it will be to your advantage."

Pierre replied contemptuously:

"For me! Oh, I shall make my way by hard work and learning."

But his mother insisted: "Yes, but I assure you that to be well lodged will be of use to you nevertheless."

About half-way through the meal he suddenly asked:

"How did you first come to know this man Maréchal?"

Old Roland looked up and racked his memory:

"Wait a bit; I scarcely recollect. It is such an old story now. Ah, yes, I remember. It was your mother who made the acquaintance with him in the shop, was it not, Louise? He first came to order something, and then he called frequently. We knew him as a customer before we knew him as a friend."

Pierre, who was eating beans, sticking his fork into them one by one as if he were spitting them, went on:

"And when was it that you made his acquaintance?"

Again Roland sat thinking, but he could remember no more and appealed to his wife's better memory.

"In what year was it, Louise? You surely have not forgotten, you who remember everything. Let me see—it was in—in—in fifty-five or fifty-six? Try to remember. You ought to know better than I."

She did in fact think it over for some minutes, and then replied in a steady voice and with calm decision:

"It was in fifty-eight, old man. Pierre was three years old. I am quite sure that I am not mistaken, for it was in that year that the child had scarlet fever, and Maréchal, whom we knew then but very little, was of the greatest service to us."

Roland exclaimed:

"To be sure—very true; he was really invaluable. When your mother was half-dead with fatigue and I had to attend to the shop, he would go to the chemist's to fetch your medicine. He really had the kindest heart! And when you were well again, you cannot think how glad he was and how he petted you. It was from that time that we became such great friends."

And this thought rushed into Pierre's soul, as abrupt and violent as a cannon-ball rending and piercing it: "Since he knew me first, since he was so devoted to me, since he was so fond of me and petted me so much, since I—I was the cause of his great intimacy with my parents, why did he leave all his money to my brother and nothing to me?"

He asked no more questions and remained gloomy; absent-minded rather than thoughtful, feeling in his soul a new anxiety as yet undefined, the secret germ of a new pain.

He went out early, wandering about the streets once more. They were shrouded in the fog which made the night heavy, opaque, and nauseous. It was like a pestilential cloud dropped on the earth. It could be seen swirling past the gas-lights, which it seemed to put out at intervals. The pavement was as slippery as on a frosty night after rain, and all sorts of evil smells seemed to come up from the bowels of the houses—the stench of cellars, drains, sewers, squalid kitchens—to mingle with the horrible savour of this wandering fog.

Pierre, with his shoulders up and his hands in his pockets, not caring to remain out of doors in the cold, turned into Marowsko's. The druggist was asleep as usual under the gas-light, which kept watch. On recognising Pierre for whom he had the affection of a faithful dog, he shook off his drowsiness, went for two glasses, and brought out the Groseillette.

"Well," said the doctor, "how is the liqueur getting on?"

The Pole explained that four of the chief cafés in the town had agreed to have it on sale, and that two papers, the Northcoast Pharos and the Havre Semaphore, would advertise it, in return for certain chemical preparations to be supplied to the editors.

After a long silence Marowsko asked whether Jean had come definitely into possession of his fortune; and then he put two or three other questions vaguely referring to the same subject. His jealous devotion to Pierre rebelled against this preference. And Pierre felt as though he could hear him thinking; he guessed and understood, read in his averted eyes and in the hesitancy of his tone, the words which rose to his lips but were not spoken—which the druggist was too timid or too prudent and cautious to utter.

At this moment, he felt sure, the old man was thinking: "You ought not to have suffered him to accept this inheritance which will make people speak ill of your mother."

Perhaps, indeed, Marowsko believed that Jean was Maréchal's son. Of course he believed it! How could he help believing it when the thing must seem so possible, so probable, self-evident? Why, he himself, Pierre, her son—had not he been for these three days past fighting with all the subtlety at his command to cheat his reason, fighting against this hideous suspicion?

And suddenly the need to be alone, to reflect, to discuss the matter with himself—to face boldly, without scruple or weakness, this possible but monstrous thing—came upon him anew, and so imperative that he rose without even drinking his glass of Groseillette, shook hands with the astounded druggist, and plunged out into the foggy streets again.

He asked himself: "What made this Maréchal leave all his fortune to Jean?"

It was not jealousy now which made him dwell on this question, not the rather mean but natural envy which he knew lurked within him, and with which he had been struggling these three days, but the dread of an overpowering horror; the dread that he himself should believe that Jean, his brother, was that man's son.

No. He did not believe it, he could not even ask himself the question which was a crime! Meanwhile he must get rid of this faint suspicion, improbable as it was, utterly and forever. He craved for light, for certainty—he must win absolute security in his heart, for he loved no one in the world but his mother. And as he wandered alone through the darkness he would rack his memory and his reason with a minute search that should bring out the blazing truth. Then there would be an end to the matter; he would not think of it again—never. He would go and sleep.

He argued thus: "Let me see: first to examine the facts; then I will recall all I know about him, his behaviour to my brother and to me. I will seek out the causes which might have given rise to the preference. He knew Jean from his birth? Yes, but he had known me first. If he had loved my mother silently, unselfishly, he would surely have chosen me, since it was through me, through my scarlet fever, that he became so intimate with my parents.

Logically, then, he ought to have preferred me, to have had a keener affection for me—unless it were that he felt an instinctive attraction and predilection for my brother as he watched him grow up."

Then, with desperate tension of brain and of all the powers of his intellect, he strove to reconstitute from memory the image of this Maréchal, to see him, to know him, to penetrate the man whom he had seen pass by him, indifferent to his heart during all those years in Paris.

But he perceived that the slight exertion of walking somewhat disturbed his ideas, dislocated their continuity, weakened their precision, clouded his recollection. To enable him to look at the past and at unknown events with so keen an eye that nothing should escape it, he must be motionless in a vast and empty space. And he made up his mind to go and sit on the jetty as he had done that other night. As he approached the harbour he heard, out at sea, a lugubrious and sinister wail like the bellowing of a bull, but more long-drawn and steady. It was the roar of a fog-horn, the cry of a ship lost in the fog. A shiver ran through him, chilling his heart; so deeply did this cry of distress thrill his soul and nerves that he felt as if he had uttered it himself. Another and a similar voice answered with such another moan, but farther away; then, close by, the fog-horn on the pier gave out a fearful sound in answer. Pierre made for the jetty with long steps, thinking no more of anything, content to walk on into this ominous and bellowing darkness.

When he had seated himself at the end of the breakwater he closed his eyes, that he might not see the two electric lights, now blurred by the fog, which make the harbour accessible at night, and the red glare of the light on the south pier, which was, however, scarcely visible. Turning half-round, he rested his elbows on the granite and hid his face in his hands.

Though he did not pronounce the words with his lips, his mind kept repeating: "Maréchal—Maréchal," as if to raise and challenge the shade. And on the black background of his closed eyelids, he suddenly saw him as he had known him: a man of about sixty, with a white beard cut in a point and very thick eyebrows, also white. He was neither tall nor short, his manner was pleasant, his eyes gray and soft, his movements gentle, his whole appearance that of a good fellow, simple and kindly. He called Pierre and Jean "my dear children," and had never seemed to prefer either, asking them both together to dine with him. And then Pierre, with the pertinacity of a dog seeking a lost scent, tried to recall the words, gestures, tones, looks, of this man who had vanished from the world. By degrees he saw him quite clearly in his rooms in the Rue Tronchet, where he received his brother and himself at dinner.

He was waited on by two maids, both old women who had been in the habit—a very old one, no doubt—of saying "Monsieur Pierre" and "Monsieur Jean." Maréchal would hold out both hands, the right hand to one of the young men, the left to the other, as they happened to come in.

"How are you, my children?" he would say. "Have you any news of your parents? As for me, they never write to me."

The talk was quiet and intimate, of commonplace matters. There was nothing remarkable in the man's mind, but much that was winning, charming, and gracious. He had certainly been a good friend to them, one of those good friends of whom we think the less because we feel sure of them.

Now, reminiscences came readily to Pierre's mind. Having seen him anxious from time to time, and suspecting his student's impecuniousness, Maréchal had of his own accord offered and lent him money, a few hundred francs perhaps, forgotten by both, and never repaid. Then this man must always have been fond of him, always have taken an interest in him, since he thought of his needs. Well then—well then—why leave his whole fortune to Jean? No, he had never shown more marked affection for the younger than for the elder, had never been more interested in one than in the other, or seemed to care more tenderly for this one or that one. Well then—well then—he must have had some strong secret reason for leaving everything to Jean—everything—and nothing to Pierre.

The more he thought, the more he recalled the past few years, the more extraordinary, the more incredible was it that he should have made such a difference between them. And an agonizing pang of unspeakable anguish piercing his bosom made his heart beat like a fluttering rag. Its springs seemed broken, and the blood rushed through in a flood, unchecked, tossing it with wild surges.

Then in an undertone, as a man speaks in a nightmare, he muttered: "I must know. My God! I must know."

He looked further back now, to an earlier time, when his parents had lived in Paris. But the faces escaped him, and this confused his recollections. He struggled above all to see Maréchal, with light, or brown, or black hair. But he could not; the later image, his face as an old man, blotted out all others. However, he remembered that he had been slighter, and had a soft hand, and that he often brought flowers. Very often—for his father would constantly say: "What, another bouquet! But this is madness, my dear fellow; you will ruin yourself in roses." And Maréchal would say: "No matter; I like it."

And suddenly his mother's voice and accent, his mother's as she smiled and said: "Thank you, my kind friend," flashed on his brain, so clearly that he could have believed he heard her. She must have spoken those words very often that they should remain thus graven on her son's memory.

So Maréchal brought flowers; he, the gentleman, the rich man, the customer, to the humble shop-keeper, the jeweller's wife. Had he loved her? Why should he have made friends with these tradespeople if he had not been in love with the wife? He was a man of education and fairly refined tastes. How many a time had he discussed poets and poetry with Pierre. He did not appreciate these writers from an artistic point of view, but with sympathetic and responsive feeling. The doctor had often smiled at his emotions which had struck him as rather silly, now he plainly saw that this sentimental soul could never, never have been the friend of his father, who was so matter-of-fact, so narrow, so heavy, to whom the word "Poetry" meant idiocy.

This Maréchal then, being young, free, rich, ready for any form of tenderness, went by chance into the shop one day, having perhaps observed its pretty mistress. He had bought something, had come again, had chatted, more intimately each time, paying by frequent purchases for the right of a seat in the family, of smiling at the young wife and shaking hands with the husband.

And what next—what next—good God—what next?

He had loved and petted the first child, the jeweller's child, till the second was born; then, till death, he had remained impenetrable; and when his grave was closed, his flesh dust, his name erased from the list of the living, when he himself was quiet and forever gone, having nothing to scheme for, to dread or to hide, he had given his whole fortune to the second child! Why?

The man had all his wits; he must have understood and foreseen that he might, that he almost infallibly must, give grounds for the supposition that the child was his. He was casting obloquy on a woman. How could he have done this if Jean were not his son?

And suddenly a clear and fearful recollection shot through his brain. Maréchal was fair—fair like Jean. He now remembered a little miniature portrait he had seen formerly in Paris, on the drawing-room chimney-shelf, and which had since disappeared. Where was it? Lost, or hidden away? Oh, if he could but have it in his hand for one minute! His mother kept it perhaps in the unconfessed drawer where love-tokens were treasured.

His misery in this thought was so intense that he uttered a groan, one of those brief moans wrung from the breast by a too intolerable pang. And immediately, as if it had heard him, as if it had understood and answered him, the fog-horn on the pier bellowed out close to him. Its voice, like that of a fiendish monster, more resonant than thunder—a savage and appalling roar contrived to drown the clamour of the wind and waves—spread through the darkness, across the sea, which was invisible under its shroud of fog. And again, through the mist, far and near, responsive cries went up to the night. They were terrifying, these calls given forth by the great blind steam-ships.

Then all was silent once more.

Pierre had opened his eyes and was looking about him, startled to find himself here, roused from his nightmare.

"I am mad," thought he, "I suspect my mother." And a surge of love and emotion, of repentance, and prayer, and grief, welled up in his heart. His mother! Knowing her as he knew her, how could he ever have suspected her? Was not the soul, was not the life of this simple-minded, chaste, and loyal woman clearer than water? Could any one who had seen and known her ever think of her but as above suspicion? And he, her son, had doubted her! Oh, if he could but have taken her in his arms at that moment, how he would have kissed and caressed her, and gone on his knees to crave pardon.

Would she have deceived his father—she?

His father!—A very worthy man, no doubt, upright and honest in business, but with a mind which had never gone beyond the horizon of his shop. How was it that this woman, who must have been very pretty—as he knew, and it could still be seen—gifted, too, with a delicate, tender emotional soul, could have accepted a man so unlike herself as a suitor and a husband? Why inquire? She had married, as young French girls do marry, the youth with a little fortune proposed to her by their relations. They had settled at once in their shop in the Rue Montmartre; and the young wife, ruling over the desk, inspired by the feeling of a new home, and the subtle and sacred sense of interests in common which fills the place of love, and even of regard, by the domestic hearth of most of the commercial houses of Paris, had set to work, with all her superior and active intelligence, to make the fortune they hoped for. And so her life had flowed on, uniform, peaceful and respectable, but loveless.

Loveless?—was it possible then that a woman should not love? That a young and pretty woman, living in Paris, reading books, applauding actresses for dying of passion on the stage, could live from youth to old age without once feeling her heart touched? He would not believe it of any one else; why should she be different from all others, though she was his mother?

She had been young, with all the poetic weaknesses which agitate the heart of a young creature. Shut up, imprisoned in the shop, by the side of a vulgar husband who always talked of trade, she had dreamed of moonlight nights, of voyages, of kisses exchanged in the shades of evening. And then, one day a man had come in, as lovers do in books, and had talked as they talk.

She had loved him. Why not? She was his mother. What then? Must a man be blind and stupid to the point of rejecting evidence because it concerns his mother? But did she give herself to him? Why yes, since this man had had no other love, since he had remained faithful to her when she was far away and growing old. Why yes, since he had left all his fortune to his son—their son!

And Pierre started to his feet, quivering with such rage that he longed to kill some one. With his arm outstretched, his hand wide open, he wanted to hit, to bruise, to smash, to strangle! Whom? Every one; his father, his brother, the dead man, his mother!

He hurried off homeward. What was he going to do?

As he passed a turret close to the signal mast the strident howl of the fog-horn went off in his very face. He was so startled that he nearly fell and shrank back as far as the granite parapet. He sat down half-stunned by the sudden shock. The steamer which was the first to reply seemed to be quite near and was already at the entrance, the tide having risen.

Pierre turned round and could discern its red eye dim through the fog. Then, in the broad light of the electric lanterns, a huge black shadow crept up between the piers. Behind him the voice of the look-out man, the hoarse voice of an old retired sea-captain, shouted:

"What ship?" And out of the fog the voice of the pilot standing on deck—not less hoarse—replied:

"The Santa Lucia."

"Where from?"

"Italy."

"What port?"

"Naples."

And before Pierre's bewildered eyes rose, as he fancied, the fiery pennon of Vesuvius, while, at the foot of the volcano, fire-flies danced in the orange-groves of Sorrento or Castellamare. How often had he dreamed of these familiar names as if he knew the scenery. Oh, if he might but go away, now at once, never mind whither, and never come back, never write, never let any one know what had become of him! But no, he must go home—home to his father's house, and go to bed.

He would not. Come what might he would not go in; he would stay there till daybreak. He liked the roar of the fog-horns. He pulled himself together and began to walk up and down like an officer on watch.

Another vessel was coming in behind the other, huge and mysterious. An English India-man, homeward bound.

He saw several more come in, one after another, out of the impenetrable vapour. Then, as the damp became quite intolerable, Pierre set out towards the town. He was so cold that he went into a sailors' tavern to drink a glass of grog, and when the hot and pungent liquor had scorched his mouth and throat he felt a hope revive within him.

Perhaps he was mistaken. He knew his own vagabond unreason so well! No doubt he was mistaken. He had piled up the evidence as a charge is drawn up against an innocent person, whom it is always so easy to convict when we wish to think him guilty. When he should have slept he would think differently.

Then he went in and to bed, and by sheer force of will he at last dropped asleep.

CHAPTER V

But the doctor's frame lay scarcely more than an hour or two in the torpor of troubled slumbers. When he awoke in the darkness of his warm, closed room he was aware, even before thought was awake in him, of the painful oppression, the sickness of heart which the sorrow we have slept on leaves behind it. It is as though the disaster of which the shock merely jarred us at first, had, during sleep, stolen into our very flesh, bruising and exhausting it like a fever. Memory returned to him like a blow, and he sat up in bed. Then slowly, one by one, he again went through all the arguments which had wrung his heart on the jetty while the fog-horns were bellowing. The more he thought the less he doubted. He felt himself dragged along by his logic to the inevitable certainty, as by a clutching, strangling hand.

He was thirsty and hot, his heart beat wildly. He got up to open his window and breathe the fresh air, and as he stood there a low sound fell on his ear through the wall. Jean was sleeping peacefully, and gently snoring. He could sleep! He had no presentiment, no suspicions! A man who had known their mother had left him all his fortune; he took the money and thought it quite fair and natural! He was sleeping, rich and contented, not knowing that his brother was gasping with anguish and distress. And rage boiled up in him against this heedless and happy sleeper.

Only yesterday he would have knocked at his door, have gone in, and sitting by the bed, would have said to Jean, scared by the sudden waking:

"Jean you must not keep this legacy which by to-morrow may have brought suspicion and dishonour on our mother."

But to-day he could say nothing; he could not tell Jean that he did not believe him to be their father's son. Now he must guard, must bury the shame he had discovered, hide from every eye the stain which he had detected and which no one must perceive, not even his brother—especially not his brother.

He no longer thought about the vain respect of public opinion. He would have been glad that all the world should accuse his mother if only he, he alone, knew her to be innocent! How could he bear to live with her every day, believing as he looked at her that his brother was the child of a stranger's love?

And how calm and serene she was, nevertheless, how sure of herself she always seemed! Was it possible that such a woman as she, pure of soul and upright in heart, should fall, dragged astray by passion, and yet nothing ever appear afterward of her remorse and the stings of a troubled conscience? Ah, but remorse must have tortured her, long ago in the earlier days, and then have faded out, as everything fades. She had surely bewailed her sin, and then, little by little, had almost forgotten it. Have not all women, all, this fault of prodigious forgetfulness which enables them, after a few years, hardly to recognise the man to whose kisses they have given their lips? The kiss strikes like a thunderbolt, the love passes away like a storm, and then life, like the sky, is calm once more, and begins again as it was before. Do we ever remember a cloud?

Pierre could no longer endure to stay in the room! This house, his father's house, crushed him. He felt the roof weigh on his head, and the walls suffocate him. And as he was very thirsty he lighted his candle to go to drink a glass of fresh water from the filter in the kitchen.

He went down the two flights of stairs; then, as he was coming up again with the water-bottle filled, he sat down, in his night-shirt, on a step of the stairs where there was a draught, and drank, without a tumbler, in long pulls like a runner who is out of breath. When he ceased to move the silence of the house touched his feelings; then, one by one, he could distinguish the faintest sounds. First there was the ticking of the clock in the dining-room which seemed to grow louder every second. Then he heard another snore, an old man's snore, short, laboured, and hard, his father beyond doubt; and he writhed at the idea, as if it had but this moment sprung upon him, that these two men, sleeping under the same room—father and son—were nothing to each other! Not a tie, not the very slightest, bound them together, and they did not know it! They spoke to each other affectionately, they embraced each other, they rejoiced and lamented together over the same things, just as if the same blood flowed in their veins. And two men born at opposite ends of the earth could not be more alien to each other than this father and son. They believed they loved each other, because a lie had grown up between them. This paternal love, this filial love, were the outcome of a lie—a lie which could not be unmasked, and which no one would ever know but he, the true son.

But yet, but yet—if he were mistaken? How could he make sure? Oh, if only some likeness, however slight, could be traced between his father and Jean, one of those mysterious resemblances which run from an ancestor to the great-great-grandson, showing that the whole race are the offspring of the same embrace. To him, a medical man, so little would suffice to enable him to discern this—the curve of a nostril, the space between the eyes, the character of the teeth or hair; nay less—a gesture, a trick, a habit, an inherited taste, any mark or token which a practised eye might recognise as characteristic.

He thought long, but could remember nothing; no, nothing. But he had looked carelessly, observed badly, having no reason for spying such imperceptible indications.

He got up to go back to his room and mounted the stairs with a slow step, still lost in thought. As he passed the door of his brother's room he stood stock still, his hand put out to open it. An imperative need had just come over him to see Jean at once, to look at him at his leisure, to surprise him in his sleep, while the calm countenance and relaxed features were at rest and all the grimace of life put off. Thus he might catch the dormant secret of his physiognomy, and if any appreciable likeness existed it would not escape him.

But supposing Jean were to wake, what could he say? How could he explain this intrusion?

He stood still, his fingers clinched on the door-handle, trying to devise a reason, an excuse. Then he remembered that a week ago he had lent his brother a phial of laudanum to relieve a fit of toothache. He might himself have been in pain this night and have come to find the drug. So he went in with a stealthy step, like a robber. Jean, his mouth open, was sunk in deep, animal slumbers. His beard and fair hair made a golden patch on the white linen; he did not wake, but he ceased snoring.

Pierre, leaning over him, gazed at him with hungry eagerness. No, this youngster was not in the least like Roland; and for the second time the recollection of the little portrait of Maréchal, which had vanished, recurred to his mind. He must find it! When he should see it perhaps he should cease to doubt!

His brother stirred, conscious no doubt of a presence, or disturbed by the light of the taper on his eyelids. The doctor retired on tip-toe to the door which he noiselessly closed; then he went back to his room, but not to bed again.

Day was long in coming. The hours struck one after another on the dining-room clock, and its tone was a deep and solemn one, as though the little piece of clockwork had swallowed a cathedral-bell. The sound rose through the empty staircase, penetrating through walls and doors, and dying away in the rooms where it fell on the torpid ears of the sleeping household. Pierre had taken to walking to and fro between his bed and the window. What was he going to do? He was too much upset to spend this day at home. He wanted still to be alone, at any rate till the next day, to reflect, to compose himself, to strengthen himself for the common every-day life which he must take up again.

Well, he would go over to Trouville to see the swarming crowd on the sands. That would amuse him, change the air of his thoughts, and give him time to inure himself to the horrible thing he had discovered. As soon as morning dawned he made his toilet and dressed. The fog had vanished and it was fine, very fine. As the boat for Trouville did not start till nine, it struck the doctor that he must greet his mother before starting.

He waited till the hour at which she was accustomed to get up, and then went downstairs. His heart beat so violently as he touched her door that he paused for breath. His hand as it lay on the lock was limp and tremulous, almost incapable of the slight effort of turning the handle to open it. He knocked. His mother's voice inquired:

"Who is there?"

"I—Pierre."

"What do you want?"

"Only to say good-morning, because I am going to spend the day at Trouville with some friends."

"But I am still in bed."

"Very well, do not disturb yourself. I shall see you this evening, when I come in."

He hoped to get off without seeing her, without pressing on her cheek the false kiss which it made his heart sick to think of. But she replied:

"No. Wait a moment. I will let you in. Wait till I get into bed again."

He heard her bare feet on the floor and the sound of the bolt drawn back. Then she called out:

"Come in."

He went in. She was sitting up in bed, while, by her side, Roland, with a silk handkerchief by way of night-cap and his face to the wall, still lay sleeping. Nothing ever woke him but a shaking hard enough to pull his arm off. On the days when he went fishing it was Joséphine, rung up by Papagris at the hour fixed, who roused her master from his stubborn slumbers.

Pierre, as he went towards his mother, looked at her with a sudden sense of never having seen her before. She held up her face, he kissed each cheek, and then sat down in a low chair.

"It was last evening that you decided on this excursion?" she asked.

"Yes, last evening."

"Will you return to dinner?"

"I do not know. At any rate do not wait for me."

He looked at her with stupefied curiosity. This woman was his mother! All those features, seen daily from childhood, from the time when his eye could first distinguish things, that smile, that voice—so well known, so familiar—abruptly struck him as new, different from what they had always been to him hitherto. He understood now that, loving her, he had never looked at her. All the same it was very really she, and he knew every little detail of her face; still, it was the first time he clearly identified them all. His anxious attention, scrutinizing her face which he loved, recalled a difference, a physiognomy he had never before discerned.

He rose to go; then, suddenly yielding to the invincible longing to know which had been gnawing at him since yesterday, he said:

"By the way, I fancy I remember that you used to have, in Paris, a little portrait of Maréchal, in the drawing-room."

She hesitated for a second or two, or at least he fancied she hesitated; then she said:

"To be sure."

"What has become of the portrait?"

She might have replied more readily:

"That portrait—stay; I don't exactly know—perhaps it is in my desk."

"It would be kind of you to find it."

"Yes, I will look for it. What do you want it for?"

"Oh, it is not for myself. I thought it would be a natural thing to give it to Jean, and that he would be pleased to have it."

"Yes, you are right; that is a good idea. I will look for it, as soon as I am up."

And he went out.

It was a blue day without a breath of wind. The folks in the streets seemed in good spirits, the merchants going to business, the clerks going to their office, the girls going to their shop. Some sang as they went, exhilarated by the bright weather.

The passengers were already going on board the Trouville boat; Pierre took a seat aft on a wooden bench.

He asked himself:

"Now was she uneasy at my asking for the portrait or only surprised? Has she mislaid it, or has she hidden it? Does she know where it is, or does she not? If she had hidden it—why?"

And his mind, still following up the same line of thought from one deduction to another, came to this conclusion:

That portrait—of a friend, of a lover, had remained in the drawing-room in a conspicuous place, till one day when the wife and mother perceived, first of all and before any one else, that it bore a likeness to her son. Without doubt she had for a long time been on the watch for this resemblance; then, having detected it, having noticed its beginnings, and understanding that any one might, any day, observe it too, she had one evening removed the perilous little picture and had hidden it, not daring to destroy it.

Pierre recollected quite clearly now that it was long, long before they left Paris that the miniature had vanished. It had disappeared, he thought, about the time that Jean's beard was beginning to grow, which had made him suddenly and wonderfully like the fair young man who smiled from the picture-frame.

The motion of the boat as it put off disturbed and dissipated his meditations. He stood up and looked at the sea. The little steamer, once outside the piers, turned to the left, and puffing and snorting and quivering, made for a distant point visible through the morning haze. The red sail of a heavy fishing-bark, lying motionless on the level waters, looked like a large rock standing up out of the sea. And the Seine, rolling down from Rouen, seemed a wide inlet dividing two neighbouring lands. They reached the harbour of Trouville in less than an hour, and as it was the time of day when the world was bathing, Pierre went to the shore.

From a distance it looked like a garden full of gaudy flowers. All along the stretch of yellow sand, from the pier as far as the Roches Noires, sun-shades of every hue, hats of every shape, dresses of every colour, in groups outside the bathing huts, in long rows by the margin of the waves, or scattered here and there, really looked like immense bouquets on a vast meadow. And the Babel of sounds—voices near and far ringing thin in the light atmosphere, shouts and cries of children being bathed, clear laughter of women—all made a pleasant, continuous din, mingling with the unheeding breeze, and breathed with the air itself.

Pierre walked among all this throng, more lost, more remote from them, more isolated, more drowned in his torturing thoughts, than if he had been flung overboard from the deck of a ship a hundred miles from shore. He passed by them and heard a few sentences without listening; and he saw, without looking, how the men spoke to the women, and the women smiled at the men. Then, suddenly, as if he had awoke, he perceived them all; and hatred of them all surged up in his soul, for they seemed happy and content.

Now, as he went, he studied the groups, wandering round them full of a fresh set of ideas. All these many-hued dresses which covered the sands like nosegays, those pretty stuffs, those showy parasols, the fictitious grace of tightened waists, all the ingenious devices of fashion from the smart little shoe to the extravagant hat, the seductive charm of gesture, voice, and smile, all the coquettish airs in short displayed on this seashore, suddenly struck him as stupendous efflorescences of female depravity. All these bedizened women aimed at pleasing, bewitching, and deluding some man. They had dressed themselves out for men—for all men—all excepting the husband whom they no longer needed to conquer. They had dressed themselves out for the lover of yesterday and the lover of to-morrow, for the stranger they might meet and notice or were perhaps on the lookout for.

And these men sitting close to them, eye to eye and mouth to mouth, invited them, desired them, hunted them like game, coy and elusive notwithstanding that it seemed so near and so easy to capture. This wide shore was, then, no more than a love-market where some sold, others gave themselves—some drove a hard bargain for their kisses while others promised them for love. All these women thought only of one thing, to make their bodies desirable—bodies already given, sold, or promised to other men. And he reflected that it was everywhere the same, all the world over.

His mother had done what others did—that was all. Others? These women he saw about him, rich, giddy, love-seeking, belonged on the whole to the class of fashionable and showy women of the world, some indeed to the less respectable sisterhood, for on these sands, trampled by the legion of idlers, the tribe of virtuous, home-keeping women were not to be seen.

The tide was rising, driving the foremost rank of visitors gradually landward. He saw the various groups jump up and fly, carrying their chairs with them, before the yellow waves as they rolled up edged with a lace-like frill of foam. The bathing-machines too were being pulled up by horses, and along the planked way which formed the promenade running along the shore from end to end, there was now an increasing flow, slow and dense, of well-dressed people in two opposite streams elbowing and mingling. Pierre, made nervous and exasperated by this bustle, made his escape into the town, and went to get his breakfast at a modest tavern on the skirts of the fields.

When he had finished with coffee, he stretched his legs on a couple of chairs under a lime-tree in front of the house, and as he had hardly slept the night before, he presently fell into a doze. After resting for some hours he shook himself, and finding that it was time to go on board again he set out, tormented by a sudden stiffness which had come upon him during his long nap. Now he was eager to be at home again; to know whether his mother had found the portrait of Maréchal. Would she be the first to speak of it, or would he be obliged to ask for it again? If she waited to be questioned further it must be because she had some secret reason for not showing the miniature.

But when he was at home again, and in his room, he hesitated about going down to dinner. He was too wretched. His revolted soul had not yet time to calm down. However, he made up his mind to it, and appeared in the dining-room just as they were sitting down.

All their faces were beaming.

"Well," said Roland, "are you getting on with your purchases? I do not want to see anything till it is all in its place."

And his wife replied: "Oh, yes. We are getting on. But it takes much consideration to avoid buying things that do not match. The furniture question is an absorbing one."

She had spent the day in going with Jean to cabinet-makers and upholsterers. Her fancy was for rich materials, rather splendid to strike the eye at once. Her son, on the contrary, wished for something simple and elegant. So in front of everything put before them they had each repeated their arguments. She declared that a client, a defendant, must be impressed; that as soon as he is shown into his counsel's waiting-room he should have a sense of wealth.

Jean, on the other hand, wishing to attract only an elegant and opulent class, was anxious to captivate persons of refinement by his quiet and perfect taste.

And this discussion, which had gone on all day, began again with the soup.

Roland had no opinion. He repeated: "I do not want to hear anything about it. I will go and see it when it is all finished."

Mme. Roland appealed to the judgment of her elder son.

"And you, Pierre, what do you think of the matter?"

His nerves were in a state of such intense excitement that he would have liked to reply with an oath. However, he only answered in a dry tone quivering with annoyance.

"Oh, I am quite of Jean's mind. I like nothing so well as simplicity, which, in matters of taste, is equivalent to rectitude in matters of conduct."

His mother went on:

"You must remember that we live in a city of commercial men, where good taste is not to be met with at every turn."

Pierre replied:

"What does that matter? Is that a reason for living as fools do? If my fellow-townsmen are stupid and ill-bred, need I follow their example? A woman does not misconduct herself because her neighbour has a lover."

Jean began to laugh.

"You argue by comparisons which seem to have been borrowed from the maxims of a moralist."

Pierre made no reply. His mother and his brother reverted to the question of stuffs and arm-chairs.

He sat looking at them as he had looked at his mother in the morning before starting for Trouville; looking at them as a stranger who would study them, and he felt as though he had really suddenly come into a family of which he knew nothing.

His father, above all, amazed his eyes and his mind. That flabby, burly man, happy and besotted, was his own father! No, no; Jean was not in the least like him.

His family!

Within these two days an unknown and malignant hand, the hand of a dead man, had torn asunder and broken, one by one, all the ties which had held these four human beings together. It was all over, all ruined. He had now no mother—for he could no longer love her now that he could not revere her with that perfect, tender, and pious respect which a son's love demands; no brother—since his brother was the child of a stranger; nothing was left him but his father, that coarse man whom he could not love in spite of himself.

And he suddenly broke out:

"I say, mother, have you found that portrait?"

She opened her eyes in surprise.

"What portrait?"

"The portrait of Maréchal."

"No—that is to say—yes—I have not found it, but I think I know where it is."

"What is that?" asked Roland. And Pierre answered:

"A little likeness of Maréchal which used to be in the dining-room in Paris. I thought that Jean might be glad to have it."

Roland exclaimed:

them into his creel. Mme. Rosémilly, surprised and delighted, remained at his side, almost forgetful of her promise to Jean, who followed them in a dream, giving herself up entirely to the childish enjoyment of pulling the creatures out from among the waving sea-grasses.

Roland suddenly exclaimed:

"Ah, here comes Mme. Roland to join us."

She had remained at first on the beach with Pierre, for they had neither of them any wish to play at running about among the rocks and paddling in the tide-pools; and yet they had felt doubtful about staying together. She was afraid of him, and her son was afraid of her and of himself; afraid of his own cruelty which he could not control. But they sat down side by side on the stones. And both of them, under the heat of the sun, mitigated by the sea-breeze, gazing at the wide, fair horizon of blue water streaked and shot with silver, thought as if in unison: "How delightful this would have been—once."

She did not venture to speak to Pierre, knowing that he would return some hard answer; and he dared not address his mother, knowing that in spite of himself he should speak violently. He sat twitching the water-worn pebbles with the end of his cane, switching them and turning them over. She, with a vague look in her eyes, had picked up three or four little stones and was slowly and mechanically dropping them from one hand into the other. Then her unsettled gaze, wandering over the scene before her, discerned, among the weedy rocks, her son Jean fishing with Mme. Rosémilly. She looked at them, watching their movements, dimly understanding, with motherly instinct, that they were talking as they did not talk every day. She saw them leaning over side by side when they looked into the water, standing face to face when they questioned their hearts, then scrambled up the rock and seated themselves to come to an understanding. Their figures stood out very sharply, looking as if they were alone in the middle of the wide horizon, and assuming a sort of symbolic dignity in that vast expanse of sky and sea and cliff.

Pierre, too, was looking at them, and a harsh laugh suddenly broke form his lips. Without turning to him Mme. Roland said:

"What is it?"

He spoke with a sneer.

"I am learning. Learning how a man lays himself out to be cozened by his wife."

She flushed with rage, exasperated by the insinuation she believed was intended.

"In whose name do you say that?"

"In Jean's, by Heaven! It is immensely funny to see those two."

She murmured in a low voice, tremulous with feeling: "O Pierre, how cruel you are! That woman is honesty itself. Your brother could not find a better."

He laughed aloud, a hard, satirical laugh:

"Ha! hah! Hah! Honesty itself! All wives are honesty itself—and all husbands are—betrayed." And he shouted with laughter.

She made no reply, but rose, hastily went down the sloping beach, and at the risk of tumbling into one of the rifts hidden by the sea-weed, of breaking a leg or an arm, she hastened, almost running, plunging through the pools without looking, straight to her other

"Why, yes, to be sure; I remember it perfectly. I saw it again last week. Your mother found it in her desk when she was tidying the papers. It was on Thursday or Friday. Do you remember, Louise? I was shaving myself when you took it out and laid in on a chair by your side with a pile of letters of which you burned half. Strange, isn't it, that you should have come across the portrait only two or three days before Jean heard of his legacy? If I believed in presentiments I should think that this was one."

Mme. Roland calmly replied:

"Yes, I know where it is. I will fetch it presently."

Then she had lied! When she had said that very morning to her son who had asked her what had become of the miniature: "I don't exactly know—perhaps it is in my desk"—it was a lie! She had seen it, touched it, handled it, gazed at it but a few days since; and then she had hidden it away again in the secret drawer with those letters—his letters.

Pierre looked at the mother who had lied to him; looked at her with the concentrated fury of a son who had been cheated, robbed of his most sacred affection, and with the jealous wrath of a man who, after long being blind, at last discovers a disgraceful betrayal. If he had been that woman's husband—and not her child—he would have gripped her by the wrists, seized her by the shoulders or the hair, have flung her on the ground, have hit her, hurt her, crushed her! And he might say nothing, do nothing, show nothing, reveal nothing. He was her son; he had no vengeance to take. And he had not been deceived.

Nay, but she had deceived his tenderness, his pious respect. She owed to him to be without reproach, as all mothers owe it to their children. If the fury that boiled within him verged on hatred it was that he felt her to be even more guilty towards him than toward his father.

The love of man and wife is a voluntary compact in which the one who proves weak is guilty only of perfidy; but when the wife is a mother her duty is a higher one, since nature has intrusted her with a race. If she fails, then she is cowardly, worthless, infamous.

"I do not care," said Roland suddenly, stretching out his legs under the table, as he did every evening while he sipped his glass of black-currant brandy. "You may do worse than live idle when you have a snug little income. I hope Jean will have us to dinner in style now. Hang it all! If I have indigestion now and then I cannot help it."

Then turning to his wife he added:

"Go and fetch that portrait, little woman, as you have done your dinner. I should like to see it again myself."

She rose, took a taper, and went. Then, after an absence which Pierre thought long, though she was not away more than three minutes, Mme. Roland returned smiling, and holding an old-fashioned gilt frame by the ring.

"Here it is," said she, "I found it at once."

The doctor was the first to put forth his hand; he took the picture, and holding it a little away from him, he examined it. Then, fully aware that his mother was looking at him, he slowly raised his eyes and fixed them on his brother to compare the faces. He could hardly refrain, in his violence, from saying: "Dear me! How like Jean!" And though he dared not utter the terrible words, he betrayed his thought by his manner of comparing the living face with the painted one.

They had, no doubt, details in common; the same beard, the same brow; but nothing sufficiently marked to justify the assertion: "This is the father and that the son." It was rather a family likeness, a relationship of physiognomies in which the same blood courses. But what to Pierre was far more decisive than the common aspect of the faces, was that his mother had risen, had turned her back, and was pretending, too deliberately, to be putting the sugar basin and the liqueur bottle away in a cupboard. She understood that he knew, or at any rate had his suspicions.

"Hand it on to me," said Roland.

Pierre held out the miniature and his father drew the candle towards him to see it better; then, he murmured in a pathetic tone:

"Poor fellow! To think that he was like that when we first knew him! Cristi! How time flies! He was a good-looking man, too, in those days, and with such a pleasant manner—was not he, Louise?"

As his wife made no answer he went on:

"And what an even temper! I never saw him put out. And now it is all at an end—nothing left of him—but what he bequeathed to Jean. Well, at any rate you may take your oath that that man was a good and faithful friend to the last. Even on his death-bed he did not forget us."

Jean, in his turn, held out his hand for the picture. He gazed at it for a few minutes and then said regretfully:

"I do not recognise it at all. I only remember him with white hair."

He returned the miniature to his mother. She cast a hasty glance at it, looking away as if she were frightened; then in her usual voice she said:

"It belongs to you now, my little Jean, as you are his heir. We will take it to your new rooms." And when they went into the drawing-room she placed the picture on the chimney-shelf by the clock, where it had formerly stood.

Roland filled his pipe; Pierre and Jean lighted cigarettes. They commonly smoked them, Pierre while he paced the room, Jean, sunk in a deep arm-chair, with his legs crossed. Their father always sat astride a chair and spat from afar into the fire-place.

Mme. Roland, on a low seat by a little table on which the lamp stood, embroidered, or knitted, or marked linen.

This evening she was beginning a piece of worsted work, intended for Jean's lodgings. It was a difficult and complicated pattern, and required all her attention. Still, now and again, her eye, which was counting the stitches, glanced up swiftly and furtively at the little portrait of the dead as it leaned against the clock. And the doctor, who was striding to and fro across the little room in four or five steps, met his mother's look at each turn.

It was as though they were spying on each other; and acute uneasiness, intolerable to be borne, clutched at Pierre's heart. He was saying to himself—at once tortured and glad:

"She must be in misery at this moment if she knows that I guess!" And each time he reached the fire-place he stopped for a few seconds to look at Maréchal's fair hair, and show quite plainly that he was haunted by a fixed idea. So that this little portrait, smaller than an opened palm, was like a living being, malignant and threatening, suddenly brought into this house and this family.

Presently the street-door bell rang. Mme. Roland, always so self-possessed, started violently, betraying to her doctor son the anguish of her nerves. Then she said: “It must be Mme. Rosémilly;” and her eye again anxiously turned to the mantel-shelf.

Pierre understood, or thought he understood, her fears and misery. A woman’s eye is keen, a woman’s wit is nimble, and her instincts suspicious. When this woman who was coming in should see the miniature of a man she did not know, she might perhaps at the first glance discover the likeness between this face and Jean. Then she would know and understand everything.

He was seized with dread, a sudden and horrible dread of this shame being unveiled, and, turning about just as the door opened, he took the little painting and slipped it under the clock without being seen by his father and brother.

When he met his mother’s eyes again they seemed to him altered, dim, and haggard.

“Good evening,” said Mme. Rosémilly. “I have come to ask you for a cup of tea.”

But while they were bustling about her and asking after her health, Pierre made off, the door having been left open.

When his absence was perceived they were all surprised. Jean, annoyed for the young widow, who, he thought, would be hurt, muttered: “What a bear!”

Mme. Roland replied: “You must not be vexed with him; he is not very well to-day and tired with his excursion to Trouville.”

“Never mind,” said Roland, “that is no reason for taking himself off like a savage.”

Mme. Rosémilly tried to smooth matters by saying: “Not at all, not at all. He has gone away in the English fashion; people always disappear in that way in fashionable circles if they want to leave early.”

“Oh, in fashionable circles, I dare say,” replied Jean. “But a man does not treat his family à l’Anglaise, and my brother has done nothing else for some time past.”

CHAPTER VI

For a week or two nothing occurred. The father went fishing; Jean, with his mother's help, was furnishing and settling himself; Pierre, very gloomy, never was seen excepting at meal-times.

His father having asked him one evening: "Why the deuce do you always come in with a face as cheerful as a funeral? This is not the first time I have remarked it."

The doctor replied: "The fact is I am terribly conscious of the burden of life."

The old man did not have a notion what he meant, and with an aggrieved look he went on: "It really is too bad. Ever since we had the good luck to come into this legacy, every one seems unhappy. It is as though some accident had befallen us, as if we were in mourning for some one."

"I am in mourning for some one," said Pierre.

"You are? For whom?"

"For some one you never knew, and of whom I was too fond."

Roland imagined that his son alluded to some girl with whom he had had some love passages, and he said:

"A woman, I suppose."

"Yes, a woman."

"Dead?"

"No. Worse. Ruined!"

"Ah!"

Though he was startled by this unexpected confidence, in his wife's presence too, and by his son's strange tone about it, the old man made no further inquiries, for in his opinion such affairs did not concern a third person.

Mme. Roland affected not to hear; she seemed ill and was very pale. Several times already her husband, surprised to see her sit down as if she were dropping into her chair, and to hear her gasp as if she could not draw her breath, had said:

"Really, Louise, you look very ill; you tire yourself too much with helping Jean. Give yourself a little rest. Sacristi! The rascal is in no hurry, as he is a rich man."

She shook her head without a word.

But to-day her pallor was so great that Roland remarked on it again.

"Come, come," said he, "this will not do at all, my dear old woman. You must take care of yourself." Then, addressing his son, "You surely must see that your mother is ill. Have you questioned her, at any rate?"

Pierre replied: "No; I had not noticed that there was anything the matter with her."

At this Roland was angry.

"But it stares you in the face, confound you! What on earth is the good of your being a doctor if you cannot even see that your mother is out of sorts? Why, look at her, just look at her. Really, a man might die under his very eyes and this doctor would never think there was anything the matter!"

Mme. Roland was panting for breath, and so white that her husband exclaimed:

"She is going to faint."

"No, no, it is nothing—I shall get better directly—it is nothing."

Pierre had gone up to her and was looking at her steadily.

"What ails you?" he said. And she repeated in an undertone:

"Nothing, nothing—I assure you, nothing."

Roland had gone to fetch some vinegar; he now returned, and handing the bottle to his son he said:

"Here—do something to ease her. Have you felt her heart?"

As Pierre bent over her to feel her pulse she pulled away her hand so vehemently that she struck it against a chair which was standing by.

"Come," said he in icy tones, "let me see what I can do for you, as you are ill."

Then she raised her arm and held it out to him. Her skin was burning, the blood throbbing in short irregular leaps.

"You are certainly ill," he murmured. "You must take something to quiet you. I will write you a prescription." And as he wrote, stooping over the paper, a low sound of choked sighs, smothered, quick breathing and suppressed sobs made him suddenly look round at her. She was weeping, her hands covering her face.

Roland, quite distracted, asked her:

"Louise, Louise, what is the mater with you? What on earth ails you?"

She did not answer, but seemed racked by some deep and dreadful grief. Her husband tried to take her hands from her face, but she resisted him, repeating:

"No, no, no."

He appealed to his son.

"But what is the matter with her? I never saw her like this."

"It is nothing," said Pierre, "she is a little hysterical."

And he felt as if it were a comfort to him to see her suffering thus, as if this anguish mitigated his resentment and diminished his mother's load of opprobrium. He looked at her as a judge satisfied with his day's work.

Suddenly she rose, rushed to the door with such a swift impulse that it was impossible to forestall or to stop her, and ran off to lock herself into her room.

Roland and the doctor were left face to face.

"Can you make head or tail of it?" said the father.

"Oh, yes," said the other. "It is a little nervous disturbance, not alarming or surprising; such attacks may very likely recur from time to time."

They did in fact recur, almost every day; and Pierre seemed to bring them on with a word, as if he had the clew to her strange and new disorder. He would discern in her face a lucid interval of peace and with the willingness of a torturer would, with a word, revive the anguish that had been lulled for a moment.

But he, too, was suffering as cruelly as she. It was dreadful pain to him that he could no longer love her nor respect her, that he must put her on the rack. When he had laid bare the bleeding wound which he had opened in her woman's, her mother's heart, when he felt how wretched and desperate she was, he would go out alone, wander about the town, so torn by remorse, so broken by pity, so grieved to have thus hammered her with his scorn as her son, that he longed to fling himself into the sea and put an end to it all by drowning himself.

Ah! How gladly now would he have forgiven her. But he could not, for he was incapable of forgetting. If only he could have desisted from making her suffer; but this again he could not, suffering as he did himself. He went home to his meals, full of relenting resolutions; then, as soon as he saw her, as soon as he met her eye—formerly so clear and frank, now so evasive, frightened, and bewildered—he struck at her in spite of himself, unable to suppress the treacherous words which would rise to his lips.

This disgraceful secret, known to them alone, goaded him up against her. It was as a poison flowing in his veins and giving him an impulse to bite like a mad dog.

And there was no one in the way now to hinder his reading her; Jean lived almost entirely in his new apartments, and only came home to dinner and to sleep every night at his father's.

He frequently observed his brother's bitterness and violence, and attributed them to jealousy. He promised himself that some day he would teach him his place and give him a lesson, for life at home was becoming very painful as a result of these constant scenes. But as he now lived apart he suffered less from this brutal conduct, and his love of peace prompted him to patience. His good fortune, too, had turned his head, and he scarcely paused to think of anything which had no direct interest for himself. He would come in full of fresh little anxieties, full of the cut of a morning-coat, of the shape of a felt hat, of the proper size for his visiting-cards. And he talked incessantly of all the details of his house—the shelves fixed in his bed-room cupboard to keep linen on, the pegs to be put up in the entrance hall, the electric bells contrived to prevent illicit visitors to his lodgings.

It had been settled that on the day when he should take up his abode there they should make an excursion to Saint Jouin, and return after dining there, to drink tea in his rooms. Roland wanted to go by water, but the distance and the uncertainty of reaching it in a sailing boat if there should be a head-wind, made them reject his plan, and a break was hired for the day.

They set out at ten to get there to breakfast. The dusty high road lay across the plain of Normandy, which, by its gentle undulations, dotted with farms embowered in trees, wears the aspect of an endless park. In the vehicle, as it jogged on at the slow trot of a pair of heavy horses, sat the four Rolands, Mme. Rosémilly, and Captain Beausire, all silent, deafened by the rumble of the wheels, and with their eyes shut to keep out the clouds of dust.

It was harvest-time. Alternating with the dark hue of clover and the raw green of beet-root, the yellow corn lighted up the landscape with gleams of pale gold; the fields looked as if they had drunk in the sunshine which poured down on them. Here and there the reapers were at work, and in the plots where the scythe had been put in the men might be seen see-sawing as they swept the level soil with the broad, wing-shaped blade.

After a two-hours' drive the break turned off to the left, past a windmill at work—a melancholy, gray wreck, half rotten and doomed, the last survivor of its ancient race; then it went into a pretty inn yard, and drew up at the door of a smart little house, a hostelry famous in those parts.

The mistress, well known as "La belle Alphonsine," came smiling to the threshold, and held out her hand to the two ladies who hesitated to take the high step.

Some strangers were already at breakfast under a tent by a grass-plot shaded by apple trees—Parisians, who had come from Étretat; and from the house came sounds of voices, laughter, and the clatter of plates and pans.

They were to eat in a room, as the outer dining-halls were all full. Roland suddenly caught sight of some shrimping nets hanging against the wall.

"Ah! ha!" cried he, "you catch prawns here?"

"Yes," replied Beausire. "Indeed it is the place on all the coast where most are taken."

"First-rate! Suppose we try to catch some after breakfast."

As it happened it would be low tide at three o'clock, so it was settled that they should all spend the afternoon among the rocks, hunting prawns.

They made a light breakfast, as a precaution against the tendency of blood to the head when they should have their feet in the water. They also wished to reserve an appetite for dinner, which had been ordered on a grand scale and to be ready at six o'clock when they came in.

Roland could not sit still for impatience. He wanted to buy the nets specially constructed for fishing prawns, not unlike those used for catching butterflies in the country. Their name on the French coast is lanets; they are netted bags on a circular wooden frame, at the end of a long pole. Alphonsine, still smiling, was happy to lend them. Then she helped the two ladies to make an impromptu change of toilet, so as not to spoil their dresses. She offered them skirts, coarse worsted stockings and hemp shoes. The men took off their socks and went to the shoemaker's to buy wooden shoes instead.

Then they set out, the nets over their shoulders and creels on their backs. Mme. Rosémilly was very sweet in this costume, with an unexpected charm of countrified audacity. The skirt which Alphonsine had lent her, coquettishly tucked up and firmly stitched so as to allow of her running and jumping fearlessly on the rocks, displayed her ankle and lower calf—the firm calf of a strong and agile little woman. Her dress was loose to give freedom to her movements, and to cover her head she had found an enormous garden hat of coarse yellow straw with an extravagantly broad brim; and to this, a bunch of tamarisk pinned in to cock it on one side, gave a very dashing and military effect.

Jean, since he had come into his fortune, had asked himself every day whether or no he should marry her. Each time he saw her he made up his mind to ask her to be his wife, and then, as soon as he was alone again, he considered that by waiting he would have time to reflect. She was now less rich than he, for she had but twelve thousand francs a year; but it was in real estate, in farms and lands near the docks in Havre; and this by-and-bye might be worth a great deal. Their fortunes were thus approximately equal, and certainly the young widow attracted him greatly.

As he watched her walking in front of him that day he said to himself:

"I must really decide; I cannot do better, I am sure."

They went down a little ravine, sloping from the village to the cliff, and the cliff, at the end of this comb, rose about eighty metres above the sea. Framed between the green slopes to the right and left, a great triangle of silvery blue water could be seen in the distance, and a sail, scarcely visible, looked like an insect out there. The sky, pale with light, was so merged into one with the water that it was impossible to see where one ended and the other began; and the two women, walking in front of the men, stood out against the bright background, their shapes clearly defined in their closely-fitting dresses.

Jean, with a sparkle in his eye, watched the smart ankle, the neat leg, the supple waist, and the coquettish broad hat of Mme. Rosémilly as they fled away from him. And this flight fired his ardour, urging him on to the sudden determination which comes to hesitating and timid natures. The warm air, fragrant with sea-coast odours—gorse, clover, and thyme, mingling with the salt smell of the rocks at low tide—excited him still more, mounting to his brain; and every moment he felt a little more determined, at every step, at every glance he cast at the alert figure; he made up his mind to delay no longer, to tell her that he loved her and hoped to marry her. The prawn-fishing would favour him by affording him an opportunity; and it would be a pretty scene too, a pretty spot for love-making—their feet in a pool of limpid water while they watched the long feelers of the shrimps lurking under the wrack.

When they had reached the end of the comb and the edge of the cliff, they saw a little footpath slanting down the face of it; and below them, about half-way between the sea and the foot of the precipice, an amazing chaos of enormous boulders tumbled over and piled one above the other on a sort of grassy and undulating plain which extended as far as they could see to the southward, formed by an ancient landslip. On this long shelf of brushwood and grass, disrupted, as it seemed, by the shocks of a volcano, the fallen rocks seemed the wreck of a great ruined city which had once looked out on the ocean, sheltered by the long white wall of the overhanging cliff.

"That is fine!" exclaimed Mme. Rosémilly, standing still. Jean had come up with her, and with a beating heart offered his hand to help her down the narrow steps cut in the rock.

They went on in front, while Beausire, squaring himself on his little legs, gave his arm to Mme. Roland, who felt giddy at the gulf before her.

Roland and Pierre came last, and the doctor had to drag his father down, for his brain reeled so that he could only slip down sitting, from step to step.

The two young people who led the way went fast till on a sudden they saw, by the side of a wooden bench which afforded a resting-place about half-way down the slope, a thread of clear water, springing from a crevice in the cliff. It fell into a hollow as large as a washing basin which it had worn in the stone; then, falling in a cascade, hardly two feet high, it trickled across the footpath which it had carpeted with cresses, and was lost among the briers and grass on the raised shelf where the boulders were piled.

"Oh, I am so thirsty!" cried Mme. Rosémilly.

But how could she drink? She tried to catch the water in her hand, but it slipped away between her fingers. Jean had an idea; he placed a stone on the path and on this she knelt down to put her lips to the spring itself, which was thus on the same level.

When she raised her head, covered with myriads of tiny drops, sprinkled all over her face, her hair, her eye-lashes, and her dress, Jean bent over her and murmured: "How pretty you look!"

She answered in the tone in which she might have scolded a child:

"Will you be quiet?"

These were the first words of flirtation they had ever exchanged.

"Come," said Jean, much agitated. "Let us go on before they come up with us."

For in fact they could see quite near them now Captain Beausire as he came down, backward, so as to give both hands to Mme. Roland; and further up, further off, Roland still letting himself slip, lowering himself on his hams and clinging on with his hands and elbows at the speed of a tortoise, Pierre keeping in front of him to watch his movements.

The path, now less steep, was here almost a road, zigzagging between the huge rocks which had at some former time rolled from the hill-top. Mme. Rosémilly and Jean set off at a run and they were soon on the beach. They crossed it and reached the rocks, which stretched in a long and flat expanse covered with sea-weed, and broken by endless gleaming pools. The ebbed waters lay beyond, very far away, across this plain of slimy weed, of a black and shining olive green.

Jean rolled up his trousers above his calf, and his sleeves to his elbows, that he might get wet without caring; then saying: "Forward!" he leaped boldly into the first tide-pool they came to.

The lady, more cautious, though fully intending to go in too, presently, made her way round the little pond, stepping timidly, for she slipped on the grassy weed.

"Do you see anything?" she asked.

"Yes, I see your face reflected in the water."

"If that is all you see, you will not have good fishing."

He murmured tenderly in reply:

"Of all fishing it is that I should like best to succeed in."

She laughed: "Try; you will see how it will slip through your net."

"But yet—if you will?"

"I will see you catch prawns—and nothing else—for the moment."

"You are cruel—let us go a little farther, there are none here."

He gave her his hand to steady her on the slippery rocks. She leaned on him rather timidly, and he suddenly felt himself overpowered by love and insurgent with passion, as if the fever that had been incubating in him had waited till to-day to declare its presence.

They soon came to a deeper rift, in which long slender weeds, fantastically tinted, like floating green and rose-coloured hair, were swaying under the quivering water as it trickled off to the distant sea through some invisible crevice.

Mme. Rosémilly cried out: "Look, look, I see one, a big one. A very big one, just there!" He saw it too, and stepped boldly into the pool, though he got wet up to the waist. But the creature, waving its long whiskers, gently retired in front of the net. Jean drove it towards the sea-weed, making sure of his prey. When it found itself blockaded it rose with a dart over the net, shot across the mere, and was gone. The young woman, who was watching the chase in great excitement, could not help exclaiming: "Oh! Clumsy!"

He was vexed, and without a moment's thought dragged his net over a hole full of weed. As he brought it to the surface again he saw in it three large transparent prawns, caught blindfold in their hiding-place.

He offered them in triumph to Mme. Rosémilly, who was afraid to touch them, for fear of the sharp, serrated crest which arms their heads. However, she made up her mind to it, and taking them up by the tip of their long whiskers she dropped them one by one into her creel, with a little seaweed to keep them alive. Then, having found a shallower pool of water, she stepped in with some hesitation, for the cold plunge of her feet took her breath away, and began to fish on her own account. She was dextrous and artful, with the light hand and the hunter's instinct which are indispensable. At almost every dip she brought up some prawns, beguiled and surprised by her ingeniously gentle pursuit.

Jean now caught nothing; but he followed her, step by step, touched her now and again, bent over her, pretended great distress at his own awkwardness, and besought her to teach him.

"Show me," he kept saying. "Show me how."

And then, as their two faces were reflected side by side in water so clear that the black weeds at the bottom made a mirror, Jean smiled at the face which looked up at him from the depth, and now and then from his finger-tips blew it a kiss which seemed to light upon it.

"Oh! how tiresome you are!" she exclaimed. "My dear fellow, you should never do two things at once."

He replied: "I am only doing one—loving you."

She drew herself up and said gravely:

"What has come over you these ten minutes; have you lost your wits?"

"No, I have not lost my wits. I love you, and at last I dare to tell you so."

They were at this moment both standing in the salt pool wet half-way up to their knees and with dripping hands, holding their nets. They looked into each other's eyes.

She went on in a tone of amused annoyance.

"How very ill-advised to tell me here and now! Could you not wait till another day instead of spoiling my fishing?"

"Forgive me," he murmured, "but I could not longer hold my peace. I have loved you a long time. To-day you have intoxicated me and I lost my reason."

Then suddenly she seemed to have resigned herself to talk business and think no more of pleasure.

"Let us sit down on that stone," said she, "we can talk more comfortably." They scrambled up a rather high boulder, and when they had settled themselves side by side in the bright sunshine, she began again:

"My good friend, you are no longer a child, and I am not a young girl. We both know perfectly well what we are about and we can weigh the consequences of our actions. If you have made up your mind to make love to me to-day I must naturally infer that you wish to marry me."

He was not prepared for this matter-of-fact statement of the case, and he answered blandly:

"Why, yes."

"Have you mentioned it to your father and mother?"

"No, I wanted to know first whether you would accept me."

She held out her hand, which was still wet, and as he eagerly clasped it:

"I am ready and willing," she said. "I believe you to be kind and true-hearted. But remember, I should not like to displease your parents."

"Oh, do you think that my mother has never foreseen it, or that she would not be as fond of you as she is if she did not hope that you and I should marry?"

"That is true. I am a little disturbed."

They said no more. He, for his part, was amazed at her being so little disturbed, so rational. He had expected pretty little flirting ways, refusals which meant yes, a whole coquettish comedy of love chequered by prawn-fishing in the splashing water. And it was all over; he was pledged, married with twenty words. They had no more to say about it since they were agreed, and they now sat, both somewhat embarrassed by what had so swiftly passed between them; a little perplexed, indeed, not daring to speak, not daring to fish, not knowing what to do.

Roland's voice rescued them.

"This way, this way, children. Come and watch Beausire. The fellow is positively clearing out the sea!"

The captain had, in fact, had a wonderful haul. Wet above his hips he waded from pool to pool, recognizing the likeliest spots at a glance, and searching all the hollows hidden under sea-weed, with a steady slow sweep of his net. And the beautiful transparent, sandy-gray prawns skipped in his palm as he picked them out of the net with a dry jerk and put

son.

Seeing her approach, Jean called out:

"Well, mother? So you have made the effort?"

Without a word she seized him by the arm, as if to say: "Save me, protect me!"

He saw her agitation, and greatly surprised he said:

"How pale you are! What is the matter?"

She stammered out:

"I was nearly falling; I was frightened at the rocks."

So then Jean guided her, supported her, explained the sport to her that she might take an interest in it. But as she scarcely heeded him, and as he was bursting with the desire to confide in some one, he led her away and in a low voice said to her:

"Guess what I have done!"

"But—what—I don't know."

"Guess."

"I cannot. I don't know."

"Well, I have told Mme. Rosémilly that I wish to marry her."

She did not answer, for her brain was buzzing, her mind in such distress that she could scarcely take it in. She echoed: "Marry her?"

"Yes. Have I done well? She is charming, do not you think?"

"Yes, charming. You have done very well."

"Then you approve?"

"Yes, I approve."

"But how strangely you say so! I could fancy that—that you were not glad."

"Yes, indeed, I am—very glad."

"Really and truly?"

"Really and truly."

And to prove it she threw her arms round him and kissed him heartily, with warm motherly kisses. Then, when she had wiped her eyes, which were full of tears, she observed upon the beach a man lying flat at full length like a dead body, his face hidden against the stones; it was the other one, Pierre, sunk in thought and desperation.

At this she led her little Jean farther away, quite to the edge of the waves, and there they talked for a long time of this marriage on which he had set his heart.

The rising tide drove them back to rejoin the fishers, and then they all made their way to the shore. They roused Pierre, who pretended to be sleeping; and then came a long dinner washed down with many kinds of wine.

CHAPTER VII

In the break, on their way home, all the men dozed excepting Jean. Beausire and Roland dropped every five minutes on to a neighbour's shoulder which repelled them with a shove. Then they sat up, ceased to snore, opened their eyes, muttered, "A lovely evening!" and almost immediately fell over on the other side.

By the time they reached Havre their drowsiness was so heavy that they had great difficulty in shaking it off, and Beausire even refused to go to Jean's rooms where tea was waiting for them. He had to be set down at his own door.

The young lawyer was to sleep in his new abode for the first time; and he was full of rather puerile glee which had suddenly come over him, at being able, that very evening, to show his betrothed the rooms she was so soon to inhabit.

The maid had gone to bed, Mme. Roland having declared that she herself would boil the water and make the tea, for she did not like the servants to be kept up for fear of fire.

No one had yet been into the lodgings but herself, Jean, and the workmen, that the surprise might be the greater at their being so pretty.

Jean begged them all to wait a moment in the ante-room. He wanted to light the lamps and candles, and he left Mme. Rosémilly in the dark with his father and brother; then he cried: "Come in!" opening the double door to its full width.

The glass gallery, lighted by a chandelier and little coloured lamps hidden among palms, india-rubber plants, and flowers, was first seen like a scene on the stage. There was a spasm of surprise. Roland, dazzled by such luxury, muttered an oath, and felt inclined to clap his hands as if it were a pantomime scene. They then went into the first drawing-room, a small room hung with dead gold and furnished to match. The larger drawing-room—the lawyer's consulting-room, very simple, hung with light salmon-colour—was dignified in style.

Jean sat down in his arm-chair in front of his writing-table loaded with books, and in a solemn, rather stilted tone, he began:

"Yes, madame, the letter of the law is explicit, and, assuming the consent I promised you, it affords me absolute certainty that the matter we discussed will come to a happy conclusion within three months."

He looked at Mme. Rosémilly, who began to smile and glanced at Mme. Roland. Mme. Roland took her hand and pressed it. Jean, in high spirits, cut a caper like a school-boy, exclaiming: "Hah! How well the voice carries in this room; it would be capital for speaking in."

And he declaimed:

"If humanity alone, if the instinct of natural benevolence which we feel towards all who suffer, were the motive of the acquittal we expect of you, I should appeal to your compassion, gentlemen of the jury, to your hearts as fathers and as men; but we have law on our side, and it is the point of law only which we shall submit to your judgment."

Pierre was looking at this home which might have been his, and he was restive under his brother's frolics, thinking him really too silly and witless.

Mme. Roland opened a door on the right.

"This is the bed-room," said she.

She had devoted herself to its decoration with all her mother's love. The hangings were of Rouen cretonne imitating old Normandy chintz, and the Louis XV. design—a shepherdess, in a medallion held in the beaks of a pair of doves—gave the walls, curtains, bed, and arm-chairs a festive, rustic style that was extremely pretty!

"Oh, how charming!" Mme. Rosémilly exclaimed, becoming a little serious as they entered the room.

"Do you like it?" asked Jean.

"Immensely."

"You cannot imagine how glad I am."

They looked at each other for a second, with confiding tenderness in the depths of their eyes.

She had felt a little awkward, however, a little abashed, in this room which was to be hers. She noticed as she went in that the bed was a large one, quite a family bed, chosen by Mme. Roland, who had no doubt foreseen and hoped that her son should soon marry; and this motherly foresight pleased her, for it seemed to tell her that she was expected in the family.

When they had returned to the drawing-room Jean abruptly threw open the door to the left, showing the circular dining-room with three windows, and decorated to imitate a Chinese lantern. Mother and son had here lavished all the fancy of which they were capable, and the room, with its bamboo furniture, its mandarins, jars, silk hangings glistening with gold, transparent blinds threaded with beads looking like drops of water, fans nailed to the wall to drape the hangings on, screens, swords, masks, cranes made of real feathers, and a myriad trifles in china, wood, paper, ivory, mother-of-pearl, and bronze, had the pretentious and extravagant aspect which unpractised hands and uneducated eyes inevitably stamp on things which need the utmost tact, taste, and artistic education. Nevertheless it was the most admired; only Pierre made some observations with rather bitter irony which hurt his brother's feelings.

Pyramids of fruit stood on the table and monuments of cakes. No one was hungry; they picked at the fruit and nibbled at the cakes rather than ate them. Then, at the end of about an hour, Mme. Rosémilly begged to take leave. It was decided that old Roland should accompany her home and set out with her forthwith; while Mme. Roland, in the maid's absence, should cast a maternal eye over the house and see that her son had all he needed.

"Shall I come back for you?" asked Roland.

She hesitated a moment and then said: "No, dear old man; go to bed. Pierre will see me home."

As soon as they were gone she blew out the candles, locked up the cakes, the sugar, and liqueurs in a cupboard of which she gave the key to Jean; then she went into the bed-room, turned down the bed, saw that there was fresh water in the water-bottle, and that the window was properly closed.

Pierre and Jean had remained in the little outer drawing-room; the younger still sore under the criticism passed on his taste, and the elder chafing more and more at seeing his brother in this abode. They both sat smoking without a word. Pierre suddenly started to his feet.

"Cristi!" he exclaimed. "The widow looked very jaded this evening. Long excursions do not improve her."

Jean felt his spirit rising with one of those sudden and furious rages which boil up in easy-going natures when they are wounded to the quick. He could hardly find breath to speak, so fierce was his excitement, and he stammered out:

"I forbid you ever again to say 'the widow' when you speak of Mme. Rosémilly."

Pierre turned on him haughtily:

"You are giving me an order, I believe. Are you gone mad by any chance?"

Jean had pulled himself up.

"I am not gone mad, but I have had enough of your manners to me."

Pierre sneered: "To you? And are you any part of Mme. Rosémilly?"

"You are to know that Mme. Rosémilly is about to become my wife."

Pierre laughed the louder.

"Ah! ha! very good. I understand now why I should no longer speak of her as 'the widow.' But you have taken a strange way of announcing your engagement."

"I forbid any jesting about it. Do you hear? I forbid it."

Jean had come close up to him, pale, and his voice quivering with exasperation at this irony levelled at the woman he loved and had chosen.

But on a sudden Pierre turned equally furious. All the accumulation of impotent rage, of suppressed malignity, of rebellion choked down for so long past, all his unspoken despair mounted to his brain, bewildering it like a fit.

"How dare you? How dare you? I order you to hold your tongue—do you hear? I order you."

Jean, startled by his violence, was silent for a few seconds, trying in the confusion of mind which comes of rage to hit on the thing, the phrase, the word, which might stab his brother to the heart. He went on, with an effort to control himself that he might aim true, and to speak slowly that the words might hit more keenly:

"I have known for a long time that you were jealous of me, ever since the day when you first began to talk of 'the widow' because you knew it annoyed me."

Pierre broke into one of those strident and scornful laughs which were common with him.

"Ah! ah! Good Heavens! Jealous of you! I? I? And of what? Good God! Of your person or your mind?"

But Jean knew full well that he had touched the wound in his soul.

"Yes, jealous of me—jealous from your childhood up. And it became fury when you saw that this woman liked me best and would have nothing to say to you."

Pierre, stung to the quick by this assumption, stuttered out:

"I? I? Jealous of you? And for the sake of that goose, that gaby, that simpleton?"

Jean, seeing that he was aiming true, went on:

"And how about the day when you tried to pull me round in the Pearl? And all you said in her presence to show off? Why, you are bursting with jealousy! And when this money was left to me you were maddened, you hated me, you showed it in every possible way, and made every one suffer for it; not an hour passes that you do not spit out the bile that is choking you."

Pierre clenched his fist in his fury with an almost irresistible impulse to fly at his brother and seize him by the throat.

"Hold your tongue," he cried. "At least say nothing about that money."

Jean went on:

"Why your jealousy oozes out at every pore. You never say a word to my father, my mother, or me that does not declare it plainly. You pretend to despise me because you are jealous. You try to pick a quarrel with every one because you are jealous. And now that I am rich you can no longer contain yourself; you have become venomous, you torture our poor mother as if she were to blame!"

Pierre had retired step by step as far as the fire-place, his mouth half open, his eyes glaring, a prey to one of those mad fits of passion in which a crime is committed.

He said again in a lower tone, gasping for breath: "Hold your tongue—for God's sake hold your tongue!"

"No! For a long time I have been wanting to give you my whole mind! You have given me an opening—so much the worse for you. I love the woman; you know it, and laugh her to scorn in my presence—so much the worse for you. But I will break your viper's fangs, I tell you. I will make you treat me with respect."

"With respect—you?"

"Yes—me."

"Respect you? You who have brought shame on us all by your greed."

"You say—? Say it again—again."

"I say that it does not do to accept one man's fortune when another is reputed to be your father."

Jean stood rigid, not understanding, dazed by the insinuation he scented.

"What? Repeat that once more."

"I say—what everybody is muttering, what every gossip is blabbing—that you are the son of the man who left you his fortune. Well, then—a decent man does not take the money which brings dishonour on his mother."

"Pierre! Pierre! Pierre! Think what you are saying. You? Is it you who give utterance to this infamous thing?"

"Yes, I. It is I. Have you not seen me crushed with woe this month past, spending my nights without sleep and my days in lurking out of sight like an animal? I hardly know what I am doing or what will become of me, so miserable am I, so crazed with shame and grief; for first I guessed—and now I know it."

"Pierre! Be silent. Mother is in the next room. Remember she may hear—she must hear."

But Pierre felt that he must unburden his heart. He told Jean all his suspicions, his arguments, his struggles, his assurance, and the history of the portrait—which had again disappeared. He spoke in short broken sentences almost without coherence—the language of a sleep-walker.

He seemed to have quite forgotten Jean, and his mother in the adjoining room. He talked as if no one were listening, because he must talk, because he had suffered too much and smothered and closed the wound too tightly. It had festered like an abscess and the abscess had burst, splashing every one. He was pacing the room in the way he almost always did, his eyes fixed on vacancy, gesticulating in a frenzy of despair, his voice choked with tearless sobs and revulsions of self-loathing; he spoke as if he were making a confession of his own misery and that of his nearest kin, as though he were casting his woes to the deaf, invisible winds which bore away his words.

Jean, distracted and almost convinced on a sudden by his brother's blind vehemence, was leaning against the door behind which, as he guessed, their mother had heard them.

She could not get out, she must come through his room. She had not come; then it was because she dare not.

Suddenly Pierre stamped his foot.

"I am a brute," he cried, "to have told you this."

And he fled, bare-headed, down the stairs.

The noise of the front-door closing with a slam roused Jean from the deep stupor into which he had fallen. Some seconds had elapsed, longer than hours, and his spirit had sunk into the numb torpor of idiocy. He was conscious, indeed, that he must presently think and act, but he would wait, refusing to understand, to know, to remember, out of fear, weakness, cowardice. He was one of those procrastinators who put everything off till to-morrow; and when he was compelled to come to a decision then and there, still he instinctively tried to gain a few minutes.

But the perfect silence which now reigned, after Pierre's vociferations, the sudden stillness of walls and furniture, with the bright light of six wax candles and two lamps, terrified him so greatly that he suddenly longed to make his escape too.

Then he roused his brain, roused his heart, and tried to reflect.

Never in his life had he had to face a difficulty. There are men who let themselves glide onward like running water. He had been duteous over his tasks for fear of punishment, and had got through his legal studies with credit because his existence was tranquil. Everything in the world seemed to him quite natural and never aroused his particular attention. He loved order, steadiness, and peace, by temperament, his nature having no complications; and face to face with this catastrophe, he found himself like a man who has fallen into the water and cannot swim.

At first he tried to be incredulous. His brother had told a lie, out of hatred and jealousy. But yet, how could he have been so vile as to say such a thing of their mother if he had not himself been distraught by despair? Besides, stamped on Jean's ear, on his sight, on his nerves, on the inmost fibres of his flesh, were certain words, certain tones of anguish, certain gestures of Pierre's, so full of suffering that they were irresistibly convincing; as incontrovertible as certainty itself.

He was too much crushed to stir or even to will. His distress became unbearable; and he knew that behind the door was his mother who had heard everything and was waiting.

What was she doing? Not a movement, not a shudder, not a breath, not a sigh revealed the presence of a living creature behind that panel. Could she have run away? But how? If she had run away—she must have jumped out of the window into the street. A shock of terror roused him—so violent and imperious that he drove the door in rather than opened it, and flung himself into the bed-room.

It was apparently empty, lighted by a single candle standing on the chest of drawers.

Jean flew to the window; it was shut and the shutters bolted. He looked about him, peering into the dark corners with anxious eyes, and he then noticed that the bed-curtains were drawn. He ran forward and opened them. His mother was lying on the bed, her face buried in the pillow which she had pulled up over her ears that she might hear no more.

At first he thought she had smothered herself. Then, taking her by the shoulders, he turned her over without her leaving go of the pillow, which covered her face, and in which she had set her teeth to keep herself from crying out.

But the mere touch of this rigid form, of those arms so convulsively clinched, communicated to him the shock of her unspeakable torture. The strength and determination with which she clutched the linen case full of feathers with her hands and teeth, over her mouth and eyes and ears, that he might neither see her nor speak to her, gave him an idea, by the turmoil it roused in him, of the pitch suffering may rise to, and his heart, his simple heart, was torn with pity. He was no judge, not he; not even a merciful judge; he was a man full of weakness and a son full of love. He remembered nothing of what his brother had told him; he neither reasoned nor argued, he merely laid his two hands on his mother's inert body, and not being able to pull the pillow away, he exclaimed, kissing her dress:

"Mother, mother, my poor mother, look at me!"

She would have seemed to be dead but that an almost imperceptible shudder ran through all her limbs, the vibration of a strained cord. And he repeated:

"Mother, mother, listen to me. It is not true. I know that it is not true."

A spasm seemed to come over her, a fit of suffocation; then she suddenly began to sob into the pillow. Her sinews relaxed, her rigid muscles yielded, her fingers gave way and left go of the linen; and he uncovered her face.

She was pale, quite colourless; and from under her closed lids tears were stealing. He threw his arms round her neck and kissed her eyes, slowly, with long heart-broken kisses, wet with her tears; and he said again and again:

"Mother, my dear mother, I know it is not true. Do not cry; I know it. It is not true."

She raised herself, she sat up, looked in his face, and with an effort of courage such as it must cost in some cases to kill one's self, she said:

"No, my child; it is true."

And they remained speechless, each in the presence of the other. For some minutes she seemed again to be suffocating, craning her throat and throwing back her head to get breath; then she once more mastered herself and went on:

"It is true, my child. Why lie about it? It is true. You would not believe me if I denied it."

She looked like a crazy creature. Overcome by alarm, he fell on his knees by the bedside, murmuring:

"Hush, mother, be silent." She stood up with terrible determination and energy.

"I have nothing more to say, my child. Good-bye." And she went towards the door.

He threw his arms about her exclaiming:

"What are you doing, mother; where are you going?"

"I do not know. How should I know—There is nothing left for me to do, now that I am alone."

She struggled to be released. Holding her firmly, he could find only words to say again and again:

"Mother, mother, mother!" And through all her efforts to free herself she was saying:

"No, no. I am not your mother now, poor boy—good-bye."

It struck him clearly that if he let her go now he should never see her again; lifting her up in his arms he carried her to an arm-chair, forced her into it, and kneeling down in front of her barred her in with his arms.

"You shall not quit this spot, mother. I love you and I will keep you! I will keep you always—I love you and you are mine."

She murmured in a dejected tone:

"No, my poor boy, it is impossible. You weep to-night, but to-morrow you would turn me out of the house. You, even you, could not forgive me."

He replied: "I? I? How little you know me!" with such a burst of genuine affection that, with a cry, she seized his head by the hair with both hands, and dragging him violently to her kissed him distractedly all over his face.

Then she sat still, her cheek against his, feeling the warmth of his skin through his beard, and she whispered in his ear: "No, my little Jean, you would not forgive me to-morrow. You think so, but you deceive yourself. You have forgiven me this evening, and that forgiveness has saved my life; but you must never see me again."

And he repeated, clasping her in his arms:

"Mother, do not say that."

"Yes, my child, I must go away. I do not know where, nor how I shall set about it, nor what I shall do; but it must be done. I could never look at you, nor kiss you, do you understand?"

Then he in his turn spoke into her ear:

"My little mother, you are to stay, because I insist, because I want you. And you must pledge your word to obey me, now, at once."

"No, my child."

"Yes, mother, you must; do you hear? You must."

"No, my child, it is impossible. It would be condemning us all to the tortures of hell. I know what that torment is; I have known it this month past. Your feelings are touched now, but when that is over, when you look on me as Pierre does, when you remember what I have told you—oh, my Jean, think—think—I am your mother!"

"I will not let you leave me, mother. I have no one but you."

"But think, my son, we can never see each other again without both of us blushing, without my feeling that I must die of shame, without my eyes falling before yours."

"But it is not so, mother."

"Yes, yes, yes, it is so! Oh, I have understood all your poor brother's struggles, believe me! All—from the very first day. Now, when I hear his step in the house my heart beats as if it would burst, when I hear his voice I am ready to faint. I still had you; now I have you no longer. Oh, my little Jean! Do you think I could live between you two?"

"Yes, I should love you so much that you would cease to think of it."

"As if that were possible!"

"But it is possible."

"How do you suppose that I could cease to think of it, with your brother and you on each hand? Would you cease to think of it, I ask you?"

"I? I swear I should."

"Why you would think of it at every hour of the day."

"No, I swear it. Besides, listen, if you go away I will enlist and get killed."

This boyish threat quite overcame her; she clasped Jean in a passionate and tender embrace. He went on:

"I love you more than you think—ah, much more, much more. Come, be reasonable. Try to stay for only one week. Will you promise me one week? You cannot refuse me that?"

She laid her two hands on Jean's shoulders, and holding him at arm's length she said:

"My child, let us try and be calm and not give way to emotions. First, listen to me. If I were ever to hear from your lips what I have heard for this month past from your brother, if I were once to see in your eyes what I read in his, if I could fancy from a word or a look that I was as odious to you as I am to him—within one hour, mark me—within one hour I should be gone forever."

"Mother, I swear to you—"

"Let me speak. For a month past I have suffered all that any creature can suffer. From the moment when I perceived that your brother, my other son, suspected me, that as the minutes went by, he guessed the truth, every moment of my life has been a martyrdom which no words could tell you."

Her voice was so full of woe that the contagion of her misery brought the tears to Jean's eyes.

He tried to kiss her, but she held him off.

"Leave me—listen; I still have so much to say to make you understand. But you never can understand. You see, if I stayed—I must—no, no. I cannot."

"Speak on, mother, speak."

"Yes, indeed, for at least I shall not have deceived you. You want me to stay with you? For what—for us to be able to see each other, speak to each other, meet at any hour of the day at home, for I no longer dare open a door for fear of finding your brother behind it. If we are to do that, you must not forgive me—nothing is so wounding as forgiveness—but you must owe me no grudge for what I have done. You must feel yourself strong enough, and so far unlike the rest of the world, as to be able to say to yourself that you are not Roland's son without blushing for the fact or despising me. I have suffered enough—I have suffered too much; I can bear no more, no indeed, no more! And it is not a thing of yesterday, mind you, but of long, long years. But you could never understand that; how should you! If you and I are to live together and kiss each other, my little Jean, you must believe that though I was your father's mistress I was yet more truly his wife, his real wife; that, at the bottom of my heart, I cannot be ashamed of it; that I have no regrets; that I love him still even in death; that I shall always love him and never loved any other man; that he was my life, my joy, my hope, my comfort, everything—everything in the world to me for so long! Listen, my boy, before God, who hears me, I should never have had a joy in my existence if I had not met him; never anything—not a touch of tenderness or kindness, not one of those hours which make us regret growing old—nothing. I owe everything to him! I had but him in the world, and you two boys, your brother and you. But for you, all would have been empty, dark, and void as the night. I should never have loved, or known, or cared for anything—I should not even have wept—for I have wept, my little Jean; oh, yes, and bitter tears, since we came to Havre. I was his wholly and forever; for ten years I was as much his wife as he was my husband before God who created us for each other. And then I began to see that he loved me less. He was always kind and courteous, but I was not what I had been to him. It was all over! Oh, how I have cried! How dreadful and delusive life is! Nothing lasts. Then we came here—I never saw him again; he never came. He promised it in every letter. I was always expecting him, and I never saw him again—and now he is dead! But he still cared for us since he remembered you. I shall love him to my latest breath, and I never will deny him, and I love you because you are his child, and I could never be ashamed of him before you. Do you understand? I could not. So if you wish me to remain you must accept the situation as his son, and we will talk of him sometimes; and you must love him a little and we must think of him when we look at each other. If you will not do this—if you cannot—then good-bye, my child; it is impossible that we should live together. Now, I will act by your decision."

Jean replied gently:

"Stay, mother."

She clasped him in her arms, and her tears flowed again; then, with her face against his, she went on:

"Well, but Pierre. What can we do about Pierre?"

Jean answered:

"We will find some plan! You cannot live with him any longer."

At the thought of her elder son she was convulsed with terror.

"No, I cannot; no, no!" And throwing herself on Jean's breast she cried in distress of mind:

"Save me from him, you, my little one. Save me; do something—I don't know what. Think of something. Save me."

"Yes, mother, I will think of something."

"And at once. You must, this minute. Do not leave me. I am so afraid of him—so afraid."

"Yes, yes; I will hit on some plan. I promise you I will."

"But at once; quick, quick! You cannot imagine what I feel when I see him."

Then she murmured softly in his ear: "Keep me here, with you."

He paused, reflected, and with his blunt good-sense saw at once the dangers of such an arrangement. But he had to argue for a long time, combating her scared, terror-stricken insistence.

"Only for to-night," she said. "Only for to-night. And to-morrow morning you can send word to Roland that I was taken ill."

"That is out of the question, as Pierre left you here. Come, take courage. I will arrange everything, I promise you, to-morrow; I will be with you by nine o'clock. Come, put on your bonnet. I will take you home."

"I will do just what you desire," she said with a childlike impulse of timidity and gratitude.

She tried to rise, but the shock had been too much for her; she could not stand.

He made her drink some sugared water and smell at some salts, while he bathed her temples with vinegar. She let him do what he would, exhausted, but comforted, as after the pains of child-birth. At last she could walk and she took his arm. The town hall struck three as they went past.

Outside their own door Jean kissed her, saying:

"Good-night, mother, keep up your courage."

She stealthily crept up the silent stairs, and into her room, undressed quickly, and slipped into bed with a reawakened sense of that long-forgotten sin. Roland was snoring. In all the house Pierre alone was awake, and had heard her come in.

CHAPTER VIII

When he got back to his lodgings Jean dropped on a sofa; for the sorrows and anxieties which made his brother long to be moving, and to flee like a hunted prey, acted differently on his torpid nature and broke the strength of his arms and legs. He felt too limp to stir a finger, even to get to bed; limp body and soul, crushed and heart-broken. He had not been hit, as Pierre had been, in the purity of filial love, in the secret dignity which is the refuge of a proud heart; he was overwhelmed by a stroke of fate which, at the same time, threatened his own nearest interests.

When at last his spirit was calmer, when his thoughts had settled like water that has been stirred and lashed, he could contemplate the situation which had come before him. If he had learned the secret of his birth through any other channel he would assuredly have been very wroth and very deeply pained, but after his quarrel with his brother, after the violent and brutal betrayal which had shaken his nerves, the agonizing emotion of his mother's confession had so bereft him of energy that he could not rebel. The shock to his feeling had been so great as to sweep away in an irresistible tide of pathos, all prejudice, and all the sacred delicacy of natural morality. Besides, he was not a man made for resistance. He did not like contending against any one, least of all against himself, so he resigned himself at once; and by instinctive tendency, a congenital love of peace, and of an easy and tranquil life, he began to anticipate the agitations which must surge up around him and at once be his ruin. He foresaw that they were inevitable, and to avert them he made up his mind to superhuman efforts of energy and activity. The knot must be cut immediately, this very day; for even he had fits of that imperious demand for a swift solution which is the only strength of weak natures, incapable of a prolonged effort of will. His lawyer's mind, accustomed as it was to disentangling and studying complicated situations and questions of domestic difficulties in families that had got out of gear, at once foresaw the more immediate consequences of his brother's state of mind. In spite of himself, he looked at the issue from an almost professional point of view, as though he had to legislate for the future relations of certain clients after a moral disaster. Constant friction against Pierre had certainly become unendurable. He could easily evade it, no doubt, by living in his own lodgings; but even then it was not possible that their mother should live under the same roof with her elder son. For a long time he sat meditating, motionless, on the cushions, devising and rejecting various possibilities, and finding nothing that satisfied him.

But suddenly an idea took him by storm. This fortune which had come to him. Would an honest man keep it?

"No," was the first immediate answer, and he made up his mind that it must go to the poor. It was hard, but it could not be helped. He would sell his furniture and work like any other man, like any other beginner. This manful and painful resolution spurred his courage; he rose and went to the window, leaning his forehead against the pane. He had been poor; he could become poor again. After all he should not die of it. His eyes were fixed on the gas lamp burning at the opposite side of the street. A woman, much belated, happened to pass; suddenly he thought of Mme. Rosémilly with a pang at his heart, the shock of deep feeling which comes of a cruel suggestion. All the dire results of his decision rose up before him together. He would have to renounce his marriage, renounce happiness, renounce everything. Could he do such a thing after having pledged himself to her? She had accepted him knowing him to be rich. She would take him still if he were poor; but had he any right to demand such a sacrifice? Would it not be better to keep this money in trust, to be restored to the poor at some future date.

And in his soul, where selfishness put on a guise of honesty, all these specious interests were struggling and contending. His first scruples yielded to ingenious reasoning, then came to the top again, and again disappeared.

He sat down again, seeking some decisive motive, some all-sufficient pretext to solve his hesitancy and convince his natural rectitude. Twenty times over had he asked himself this question: "Since I am this man's son, since I know and acknowledge it, is it not natural that I should also accept the inheritance?"

But even this argument could not suppress the "No" murmured by his inmost conscience.

Then came the thought: "Since I am not the son of the man I always believed to be my father, I can take nothing from him, neither during his lifetime nor after his death. It would be neither dignified nor equitable. It would be robbing my brother."

This new view of the matter having relieved him and quieted his conscience, he went to the window again.

"Yes," he said to himself, "I must give up my share of the family inheritance. I must let Pierre have the whole of it, since I am not his father's son. That is but just. Then is it not just that I should keep my father's money?"

Having discerned that he could take nothing of Roland's savings, having decided on giving up the whole of this money, he agreed; he resigned himself to keeping Maréchal's; for if he rejected both he would find himself reduced to beggary.

This delicate question being thus disposed of he came back to that of Pierre's presence in the family. How was he to be got rid of? He was giving up his search for any practical solution when the whistle of a steam-vessel coming into port seemed to blow him an answer by suggesting a scheme.

Then he threw himself on his bed without undressing, and dozed and dreamed till daybreak.

At a little before nine he went out to ascertain whether his plans were feasible. Then, after making sundry inquiries and calls, he went to his old home. His mother was waiting for him in her room.

"If you had not come," she said, "I should never have dared to go down."

In a minute Roland's voice was heard on the stairs: "Are we to have nothing to eat to-day, hang it all?"

There was no answer, and he roared out, with a thundering oath this time: "Joséphine, what the devil are you about?"

The girl's voice came up from the depths of the basement.

"Yes, M'sieu—what is it?"

"Where is your Miss'es?"

"Madame is upstairs with M'sieu Jean."

Then he shouted, looking up at the higher floor: "Louise!"

Mme. Roland half opened her door and answered:

"What is it, my dear?"

"Are we to have nothing to eat to-day, hang it all?"

"Yes, my dear, I am coming."

And she went down, followed by Jean.

Roland, as soon as he saw him, exclaimed:

"Hallo! There you are! Sick of your home already?"

"No, father, but I had something to talk over with mother this morning."

Jean went forward holding out his hand, and when he felt his fingers in the old man's fatherly clasp, a strange, unforeseen emotion thrilled through him, and a sense as of parting and farewell without return.

Mme. Roland asked:

"Pierre is not come down?"

Her husband shrugged his shoulders.

"No, but never mind him; he is always behind-hand. We will begin without him."

She turned to Jean:

"You had better go to call him, my child; it hurts his feelings if we do not wait for him."

"Yes, mother. I will go."

And the young man went. He mounted the stairs with the fevered determination of a man who is about to fight a duel and who is in a fright. When he knocked at the door Pierre said:

"Come in."

He went in. The elder was writing, leaning over his table.

"Good-morning," said Jean.

Pierre rose.

"Good-morning!" and they shook hands as if nothing had occurred.

"Are you not coming down to breakfast?"

"Well—you see—I have a good deal to do." The elder brother's voice was tremulous, and his anxious eye asked his younger brother what he meant to do.

"They are waiting for you."

"Oh! There is—is my mother down?"

"Yes, it was she who sent me to fetch you."

"Ah, very well; then I will come."

At the door of the dining-room he paused, doubtful about going in first; then he abruptly opened the door and saw his father and mother seated at the table opposite each other.

He went straight up to her without looking at her or saying a word, and bending over her, offered his forehead for her to kiss, as he had done for some time past, instead of kissing her on both cheeks as of old. He supposed that she put her lips near but he did not feel them on his brow, and he straightened himself with a throbbing heart after this feint of a caress. And he wondered:

"What did they say to each other after I had left?"

Jean constantly addressed her tenderly as "mother," or "dear mother," took care of her, waited on her, and poured out her wine.

Then Pierre understood that they had wept together, but he could not read their minds. Did Jean believe in his mother's guilt, or think his brother a base wretch?

And all his self-reproach for having uttered the horrible thing came upon him again, choking his throat and his tongue, and preventing his either eating or speaking.

He was now a prey to an intolerable desire to fly, to leave the house which was his home no longer, and these persons who were bound to him by such imperceptible ties. He would gladly have been off that moment, no matter whither, feeling that everything was over, that he could not endure to stay with them, that his presence was torture to them, and that they would bring on him incessant suffering too great to endure. Jean was talking, chatting with Roland. Pierre, as he did not listen, did not hear. But he presently was aware of a pointed tone in his brother's voice and paid more attention to his words. Jean was saying:

"She will be the finest ship in their fleet. They say she is of 6,500 tons. She is to make her first trip next month."

Roland was amazed.

"So soon? I thought she was not to be ready for sea this summer."

"Yes. The work has been pushed forward very vigorously, to get her through her first voyage before the autumn. I looked in at the Company's office this morning, and was talking to one of the directors."

"Indeed! Which of them?"

"M. Marchand, who is a great friend of the Chairman of the Board."

"Oh! Do you know him?"

"Yes. And I wanted to ask him a favour."

"Then you will get me leave to go over every part of the Lorraine as soon as she comes into port?"

"To be sure; nothing could be easier."

Then Jean seemed to hesitate, to be weighing his words, and to want to lead up to a difficult subject. He went on:

"On the whole, life is very endurable on board those great Transatlantic liners. More than half the time is spent on shore in two splendid cities—New York and Havre; and the remainder at sea with delightful company. In fact, very pleasant acquaintances are sometimes made among the passengers, and very useful in after-life—yes, really very useful. Only think, the captain, with his perquisites on coal, can make as much as twenty-five thousand francs a year or more."

Roland muttered an oath followed by a whistle, which testified to his deep respect for the sum and the captain.

Jean went on:

"The purser makes as much as ten thousand, and the doctor has a fixed salary of five thousand, with lodgings, keep, light, firing, service, and everything, which makes it up to ten thousand at least. That is very good pay."

Pierre raising his eyes met his brother's and understood.

Then, after some hesitation, he asked:

"Is it very hard to get a place as medical man on board a Transatlantic liner?"

"Yes—and no. It all depends on circumstances and recommendation."

There was a long pause; then the doctor began again.

"Next month, you say, the Lorraine is to sail?"

"Yes. On the 7th."

And they said nothing more.

Pierre was considering. It certainly would be a way out of many difficulties if he could embark as medical officer on board the steamship. By-and-by he could see; he might perhaps give it up. Meanwhile he would be gaining a living, and asking for nothing from his parents. Only two days since he had been forced to sell his watch, for he would no longer hold out his hand to beg of his mother. So he had no other resource left, no opening to enable him to eat the bread of any house but this which had become uninhabitable, or sleep in any other bed, or under any other roof. He presently said, with some little hesitation:

"If I could, I would very gladly sail in her."

Jean asked:

"What should hinder you?"

"I know no one in the Transatlantic Shipping Company."

Roland was astounded.

"And what has become of all your fine schemes for getting on?"

Pierre replied in a low voice:

"There are times when we must bring ourselves to sacrifice everything and renounce our fondest hopes. And after all it is only to make a beginning, a way of saving a few thousand francs to start fair with afterward."

His father was promptly convinced.

"That is very true. In a couple of years you can put by six or seven thousand francs, and that well laid out, will go a long way. What do you think of the matter, Louise?"

She replied in a voice so low as to be scarcely audible:

"I think Pierre is right."

Roland exclaimed:

"I will go and talk it over with M. Poulin: I know him very well. He is assessor of the Chamber of Commerce and takes an interest in the affairs of the Company. There is M. Lenient, too, the ship-owner, who is intimate with one of the vice-chairmen."

Jean asked his brother:

"Would you like me to feel my way with M. Marchand at once?"

"Yes, I should be very glad."

After thinking a few minutes Pierre added:

"The best thing I can do, perhaps, will be to write to my professors at the college of Medicine, who had a great regard for me. Very inferior men are sometimes shipped on board those vessels. Letters of strong recommendation from such professors as Mas-Roussel, Rémusot, Flanche, and Borriquel would do more for me in an hour than all the doubtful introductions in the world. It would be enough if your friend M. Marchand would lay them before the board."

Jean approved heartily.

"Your idea is really capital." And he smiled, quite reassured, almost happy, sure of success and incapable of allowing himself to be unhappy for long.

"You will write to-day?" he said.

"Directly. Now; at once. I will go and do so. I do not care for any coffee this morning; I am too nervous."

He rose and left the room.

Then Jean turned to his mother:

"And you, mother, what are you going to do?"

"Nothing. I do not know."

"Will you come with me to call on Mme. Rosémilly?"

"Why, yes—yes."

"You know I must positively go to see her to-day."

"Yes, yes. To be sure."

"Why must you positively?" asked Roland, whose habit it was never to understand what was said in his presence.

"Because I promised her I would."

"Oh, very well. That alters the case." And he began to fill his pipe, while the mother and son went upstairs to make ready.

When they were in the street Jean said:

"Will you take my arm, mother?"

He was never accustomed to offer it, for they were in the habit of walking side by side. She accepted and leaned on him.

For some time they did not speak; then he said:

"You see that Pierre is quite ready and willing to go away."

She murmured:

"Poor boy!"

"But why 'poor boy'? He will not be in the least unhappy on board the Lorraine."

"No—I know. But I was thinking of so many things."

And she thought for a long time, her head bent, accommodating her step to her son's; then, in the peculiar voice in which we sometimes give utterance to the conclusion of long and secret meditations, she exclaimed:

"How horrible life is! If by any chance we come across any sweetness in it, we sin in letting ourselves be happy, and pay dearly for it afterward."

He said in a whisper:

"Do not speak of that any more, mother."

"Is that possible? I think of nothing else."

"You will forget it."

Again she was silent; then with deep regret she said:

"How happy I might have been, married to another man!"

She was visiting it on Roland now, throwing all the responsibility of her sin on his ugliness, his stupidity, his clumsiness, the heaviness of his intellect, and the vulgarity of his person. It was to this that it was owing that she had betrayed him, had driven one son to desperation, and had been forced to utter to the other the most agonizing confession that can make a mother's heart bleed. She muttered: "It is so frightful for a young girl to have to marry such a husband as mine."

Jean made no reply. He was thinking of the man he had hitherto believed to be his father;

and possibly the vague notion he had long since conceived, of that father's inferiority, with his brother's constant irony, the scornful indifference of others, and the very maid-servant's contempt for Roland, had somewhat prepared his mind for his mother's terrible avowal. It had all made it less dreadful to him to find that he was another man's son; and if, after the great shock and agitation of the previous evening, he had not suffered the reaction of rage, indignation, and rebellion which Mme. Roland had feared, it was because he had long been unconsciously chafing under the sense of being the child of this well-meaning lout.

They had now reached the dwelling of Mme. Rosémilly.

She lived on the road to Sainte-Adresse, on the second floor of a large tenement which she owned. The windows commanded a view of the whole roadstead.

On seeing Mme. Roland, who entered first, instead of merely holding out her hands as usual, she put her arms round her and kissed her, for she divined the purpose of her visit.

The furniture of this drawing-room, all in stamped velvet, was always shrouded in chair-covers. The walls, hung with flowered paper, were graced by four engravings, the purchase of her late husband, the captain. They represented sentimental scenes of seafaring life. In the first a fisherman's wife was seen, waving a handkerchief on shore, while the vessel which bore away her husband vanished on the horizon. In the second the same woman, on her knees on the same shore, under a sky shot with lightning, wrung her arms as she gazed into the distance at her husband's boat which was going to the bottom amid impossible waves.

The others represented similar scenes in a higher rank of society. A young lady with fair hair, resting her elbows on the ledge of a large steamship quitting the shore, gazed at the already distant coast with eyes full of tears and regret. Whom is she leaving behind?

Then the same young lady sitting by an open widow with a view of the sea, had fainted in an arm-chair; a letter she had dropped lay at her feet. So he is dead! What despair!

Visitors were generally much moved and charmed by the commonplace pathos of these obvious and sentimental works. They were at once intelligible without question or explanation, and the poor women were to be pitied, though the nature of the grief of the more elegant of the two was not precisely known. But this very doubt contributed to the sentiment. She had, no doubt, lost her lover. On entering the room the eye was immediately attracted to these four pictures, and riveted as if fascinated. If it wandered it was only to return and contemplate the four expressions on the faces of the two women, who were as like each other as two sisters. And the very style of these works, in their shining frames, crisp, sharp, and highly finished, with the elegance of a fashion plate, suggested a sense of cleanliness and propriety which was confirmed by the rest of the fittings. The seats were always in precisely the same order, some against the wall and some round the circular centre-table. The immaculately white curtains hung in such straight and regular pleats that one longed to crumple them a little; and never did a grain of dust rest on the shade under which the gilt clock, in the taste of the first empire—a terrestrial globe supported by Atlas on his knees—looked like a melon left there to ripen.

The two women as they sat down somewhat altered the normal position of their chairs.

"You have not been out this morning?" asked Mme. Roland.

"No. I must own to being rather tired."

And she spoke as if in gratitude to Jean and his mother, of all the pleasure she had derived from the expedition and the prawn-fishing.

"I ate my prawns this morning," she added, "and they were excellent. If you felt inclined we might go again one of these days."

The young man interrupted her:

"Before we start on a second fishing excursion, suppose we complete the first?"

"Complete it? It seems to me quite finished."

"Nay, madame, I, for my part, caught something on the rocks of Saint Jouain which I am anxious to carry home with me."

She put on an innocent and knowing look.

"You? What can it be? What can you have found?"

"A wife. And my mother and I have come to ask you whether she had changed her mind this morning."

She smiled: "No, monsieur. I never change my mind."

And then he held out his hand, wide open, and she put hers into it with a quick, determined movement. Then he said: "As soon as possible, I hope."

"As soon as you like."

"In six weeks?"

"I have no opinion. What does my future mother-in-law say?"

Mme. Roland replied with a rather melancholy smile:

"I? Oh, I can say nothing. I can only thank you for having accepted Jean, for you will make him very happy."

"We will do our best, mamma."

Somewhat overcome, for the first time, Mme. Rosémilly rose, and throwing her arms round Mme. Roland, kissed her a long time as a child of her own might have done; and under this new embrace the poor woman's sick heart swelled with deep emotion. She could not have expressed the feeling; it was at once sad and sweet. She had lost her son, her big boy, but in return she had found a daughter, a grown-up daughter.

When they faced each other again, and were seated, they took hands and remained so, looking at each and smiling, while they seemed to have forgotten Jean.

Then they discussed a number of things which had to be thought of in view of an early marriage, and when everything was settled and decided Mme. Rosémilly seemed suddenly to remember a further detail and asked: "You have consulted M. Roland, I suppose?"

A flush of colour mounted at the same instant on the face of both mother and son. It was the mother who replied:

"Oh, no, it is quite unnecessary!" Then she hesitated, feeling that some explanation was needed, and added: "We do everything without saying anything to him. It is enough to tell him what we have decided on."

Mme. Rosémilly, not in the least surprised, only smiled, taking it as a matter of course, for the good man counted for so little.

When Mme. Roland was in the street again with her son she said:

"Suppose we go to your rooms for a little while. I should be glad to rest."

She felt herself homeless, shelterless, her own house being a terror to her.

They went into Jean's apartments.

As soon as the door was closed upon her she heaved a deep sigh, as if that bolt had placed her in safety, but then, instead of resting as she had said, she began to open the cupboards, to count the piles of linen, the pocket-handkerchiefs, and socks. She changed the arrangement to place them in more harmonious order, more pleasing to her housekeeper's eye; and when she had put everything to her mind, laying out the towels, the shirts, and the drawers on their several shelves and dividing all the linen into three principal classes, body-linen, household-linen, and table-linen, she drew back and contemplated the results, and called out:

"Come here, Jean, and see how nice it looks."

He went and admired it to please her.

On a sudden, when he had sat down again, she came softly up behind his arm-chair, and putting her right arm round his neck she kissed him, while she laid on the chimney-shelf a small packet wrapped in white paper which she held in the other hand.

"What is that?" he asked. Then, as she made no reply, he understood, recognising the shape of the frame.

"Give it me!" he said.

She pretended not to hear him, and went back to the linen cupboards. He got up hastily, took the melancholy relic, and going across the room, put it in the drawer of his writing-table, which he locked and double locked. She wiped away a tear with the tip of her finger, and said in a rather quavering voice: "Now I am going to see whether your new servant keeps the kitchen in good order. As she is out I can look into everything and make sure."

CHAPTER IX

Letters of recommendation from Professors Mas-Roussel, Rémusot, Flache, and Borriquel, written in the most flattering terms with regard to Dr. Pierre Roland, their pupil, had been submitted by M. Marchand to the directors of the Transatlantic Shipping Co., seconded by M. Poulin, judge of the Chamber of Commerce, M. Lenient, a great ship-owner, and Mr. Marival, deputy to the Mayor of Havre, and a particular friend of Captain Beausires's. It proved that no medical officer had yet been appointed to the Lorraine, and Pierre was lucky enough to be nominated within a few days.

The letter announcing it was handed to him one morning by Joséphine, just as he was dressed. His first feeling was that of a man condemned to death who is told that his sentence is commuted; he had an immediate sense of relief at the thought of his early departure and of the peaceful life on board, cradled by the rolling waves, always wandering, always moving. His life under his father's roof was now that of a stranger, silent and reserved. Ever since the evening when he allowed the shameful secret he had discovered to escape him in his brother's presence, he had felt that the last ties to his kindred were broken. He was harassed by remorse for having told this thing to Jean. He felt that it was odious, indecent, and brutal, and yet it was a relief to him to have uttered it.

He never met the eyes either of his mother or his brother; to avoid his gaze theirs had become surprisingly alert, with the cunning of foes who fear to cross each other. He was always wondering: "What can she have said to Jean? Did she confess or deny it? What does my brother believe? What does he think of her—what does he think of me?" He could not guess, and it drove him to frenzy. And he scarcely ever spoke to them, excepting when Roland was by, to avoid his questioning.

As soon as he received the letter announcing his appointment he showed it at once to his family. His father, who was prone to rejoicing over everything, clapped his hands. Jean spoke seriously, though his heart was full of gladness: "I congratulate you with all my heart, for I know there were several other candidates. You certainly owe it to your professors' letters."

His mother bent her head and murmured:

"I am very glad you have been successful."

After breakfast he went to the Company's offices to obtain information on various particulars, and he asked the name of the doctor on board the Picardie, which was to sail next day, to inquire of him as to the details of his new life and any details he might think useful.

Dr. Pirette having gone on board, Pierre went to the ship, where he was received in a little state-room by a young man with a fair beard, not unlike his brother. They talked together a long time.

In the hollow depths of the huge ship they could hear a confused and continuous commotion; the noise of bales and cases pitched down into the hold mingling with footsteps, voices, the creaking of the machinery lowering the freight, the boatswain's whistle, and the clatter of chains dragged or wound on to capstans by the snorting and panting engine which sent a slight vibration from end to end of the great vessel.

But when Pierre had left his colleague and found himself in the street once more, a new form of melancholy came down on him, enveloping him like the fogs which roll over the sea, coming up from the ends of the world and holding in their intangible density something mysteriously impure, as it were the pestilential breath of a far-away, unhealthy land.

In his hours of greatest suffering he had never felt himself so sunk in a foul pit of misery. It was as though he had given the last wrench; there was no fibre of attachment left. In tearing up the roots of every affection he had not hitherto had the distressful feeling which now came over him, like that of a lost dog. It was no longer a torturing mortal pain, but the frenzy of a forlorn and homeless animal, the physical anguish of a vagabond creature without a roof for shelter, lashed by the rain, the wind, the storm, all the brutal forces of the universe. As he set foot on the vessel, as he went into the cabin rocked by the waves, the very flesh of the man, who had always slept in a motionless and steady bed, had risen up against the insecurity henceforth of all his morrows. Till now that flesh had been protected by a solid wall built into the earth which held it, by the certainty of resting in the same spot, under a roof which could resist the gale. Now all that, which it was a pleasure to defy in the warmth of home, must become a peril and a constant discomfort. No earth under foot, only the greedy, heaving, complaining sea; no space around for walking, running, losing the way, only a few yards of planks to pace like a convict among other prisoners; no trees, no gardens, no streets, no houses; nothing but water and clouds. And the ceaseless motion of the ship beneath his feet. On stormy days he must lean against the wainscot, hold on to the doors, cling to the edge of the narrow berth to save himself from rolling out. On calm days he would hear the snorting throb of the screw, and feel the swift flight of the ship, bearing him on in its unpausing, regular, exasperating race.

And he was condemned to this vagabond convict's life solely because his mother had yielded to a man's caresses.

He walked on, his heart sinking with the despairing sorrow of those who are doomed to exile. He no longer felt a haughty disdain and scornful hatred of the strangers he met, but a woeful impulse to speak to them, to tell them all that he had to quit France, to be listened to and comforted. There was in the very depths of his heart the shame-faced need of a beggar who would fain hold out his hand—a timid but urgent need to feel that some one would grieve at his departing.

He thought of Marowsko. The old Pole was the only person who loved him well enough to feel true and keen emotion, and the doctor at once determined to go and see him.

When he entered the shop, the druggist, who was pounding powders in a marble mortar, started and left his work.

"You are never to be seen nowadays," said he.

Pierre explained that he had had a great many serious matters to attend to, but without giving the reason, and he took a seat, asking:

"Well, and how is business doing?"

Business was not doing at all. Competition was fearful, and rich folks rare in that workmen's quarter. Nothing would sell but cheap drugs, and the doctors did not prescribe the costlier and more complicated remedies on which a profit is made of five hundred per cent. The old fellow ended by saying: "If this goes on for three months I shall shut up shop. If I did not count on you, dear good doctor, I should have turned shoe-black by this time."

Pierre felt a pang, and made up his mind to deal the blow at once, since it must be done.

"I—oh, I cannot be of any use to you. I am leaving Havre early next month."

Marowsko took off his spectacles, so great was his agitation.

"You! You! What are you saying?"

"I say that I am going away, my poor friend."

The old man was stricken, feeling his last hope slipping from under him, and he suddenly turned against this man, whom he had followed, whom he loved, whom he had so implicitly trusted, and who forsook him thus.

He stammered out:

"You are surely not going to play me false—you?"

Pierre was so deeply touched that he felt inclined to embrace the old fellow.

"I am not playing you false. I have not found anything to do here, and I am going as medical officer on board a Transatlantic passenger boat."

"O Monsieur Pierre! And you always promised you would help me to make a living!"

"What can I do? I must make my own living. I have not a farthing in the world."

Marowsko said: "It is wrong; what you are doing is very wrong. There is nothing for me but to die of hunger. At my age this is the end of all things. It is wrong. You are forsaking a poor old man who came here to be with you. It is wrong."

Pierre tried to explain, to protest, to give reasons, to prove that he could not have done otherwise; the Pole, enraged by his desertion, would not listen to him, and he ended by saying, with an allusion no doubt to political events:

"You French—you never keep your word!"

At this Pierre rose, offended on his part, and taking rather a high tone he said:

"You are unjust, père Marowsko; a man must have very strong motives to act as I have done and you ought to understand that. Au revoir—I hope I may find you more reasonable." And he went away.

"Well, well," he thought, "not a soul will feel a sincere regret for me."

His mind sought through all the people he knew or had known, and among the faces which crossed his memory he saw that of the girl at the tavern who had led him to doubt his mother.

He hesitated, having still an instinctive grudge against her, then suddenly reflected on the other hand: "After all, she was right." And he looked about him to find the turning.

The beer-shop, as it happened, was full of people, and also full of smoke. The customers, tradesmen, and labourers, for it was a holiday, were shouting, calling, laughing, and the master himself was waiting on them, running from table to table, carrying away empty glasses and returning them crowned with froth.

When Pierre had found a seat not far from the desk he waited, hoping that the girl would see him and recognise him. But she passed him again and again as she went to and fro, pattering her feet under her skirts with a smart little strut. At last he rapped a coin on the table, and she hurried up.

"What will you take, sir?"

She did not look at him; her mind was absorbed in calculations of the liquor she had served.

"Well," said he, "this is a pretty way of greeting a friend."

She fixed her eyes on his face. "Ah!" said she hurriedly. "Is it you? You are pretty well? But I have not a minute to-day. A bock did you wish for?"

"Yes, a bock!"

When she brought it he said:

"I have come to say good-bye. I am going away."

And she replied indifferently:

"Indeed. Where are you going?"

"To America."

"A very fine country, they say."

And that was all!

Really, he was very ill-advised to address her on such a busy day; there were too many people in the café.

Pierre went down to the sea. As he reached the jetty he descried the Pearl; his father and Beausire were coming in. Papagris was pulling, and the two men, seated in the stern, smoked their pipes with a look of perfect happiness. As they went past the doctor said to himself: "Blessed are the simple-minded!" And he sat down on one of the benches on the breakwater, to try to lull himself in animal drowsiness.

When he went home in the evening his mother said, without daring to lift her eyes to his face:

"You will want a heap of things to take with you. I have ordered your under-linen, and I went into the tailor's shop about cloth clothes; but is there nothing else you need—things which I, perhaps, know nothing about?"

His lips parted to say, "No, nothing." But he reflected that he must accept the means of getting a decent outfit, and he replied in a very calm voice: "I hardly know myself, yet. I will make inquiries at the office."

He inquired, and they gave him a list of indispensable necessaries. His mother, as she took it from his hand, looked up at him for the first time for very long, and in the depths of her eyes there was the humble expression, gentle, sad, and beseeching, of a dog that has been beaten and begs forgiveness.

On the 1st of October the Lorraine from Saint-Nazaire, came into the harbour of Havre to sail on the 7th, bound for New York, and Pierre Roland was to take possession of the little floating cabin in which henceforth his life was to be confined.

Next day as he was going out, he met his mother on the stairs waiting for him, to murmur in an almost inaudible voice:

"You would not like me to help you to put things to rights on board?"

"No, thank you. Everything is done."

Then she said:

"I should have liked to see your cabin."

"There is nothing to see. It is very small and very ugly."

And he went downstairs, leaving her stricken, leaning against the wall with a wan face.

Now Roland, who had gone over the Lorraine that very day, could talk of nothing all dinnertime but this splendid vessel, and wondered that his wife should not care to see it as their son was to sail on board.

Pierre had scarcely any intercourse with his family during the days which followed. He was nervous, irritable, hard, and his rough speech seemed to lash every one indiscriminately. But the day before he left he was suddenly quite changed, and much softened. As he embraced his parents before going to sleep on board for the first time he said:

"You will come to say good-bye to me on board, will you not?"

Roland exclaimed:

"Why, yes, of course—of course, Louise?"

"Certainly, certainly," she said in a low voice.

Pierre went on: "We sail at eleven precisely. You must be there by half-past nine at the latest."

"Hah!" cried his father. "A good idea! As soon as we have bid you good-bye, we will make haste on board the Pearl, and look out for you beyond the jetty, so as to see you once more. What do you say, Louise?"

"Certainly."

Roland went on: "And in that way you will not lose sight of us among the crowd which throngs the breakwater when the great liners sail. It is impossible to distinguish your own friends in the mob. Does that meet your views?"

"Yes, to be sure; that is settled."

An hour later he was lying in his berth—a little crib as long and narrow as a coffin. There he remained with his eyes wide open for a long time, thinking over all that had happened during the last two months of his life, especially in his own soul. By dint of suffering and making others suffer, his aggressive and revengeful anguish had lost its edge, like a blunted sword. He scarcely had the heart left in him to owe any one or anything a grudge; he let his rebellious wrath float away down stream, as his life must. He was so weary of wrestling, weary of fighting, weary of hating, weary of everything, that he was quite worn out, and tried to stupefy his heart with forgetfulness as he dropped asleep. He heard vaguely, all about him, the unwonted noises of the ship, slight noises, and scarcely audible on this calm night in port; and he felt no more of the dreadful wound which had tortured him hitherto, but the discomfort and strain of its healing.

He had been sleeping soundly when the stir of the crew roused him. It was day; the tidal train had come down to the pier bringing the passengers from Paris. Then he wandered about the vessel among all these busy, bustling folks inquiring for their cabins, questioning and answering each other at random, in the scare and fuss of a voyage already begun. After greeting the Captain and shaking hands with his comrade the purser, he went into the saloon where some Englishmen were already asleep in the corners. The large low room, with its white marble panels framed in gilt beading, was furnished with looking-glasses, which prolonged, in endless perspective, the long tables, flanked by pivot-seats covered with red velvet. It was fit, indeed, to be the vast floating cosmopolitan dining-hall, where the rich natives of two continents might eat in common. Its magnificent luxury was that of great hotels, and theatres, and public rooms; the imposing and commonplace luxury which appeals to the eye of the millionaire.

The doctor was on the point of turning into the second-class saloon, when he remembered that a large cargo of emigrants had come on board the night before, and he went down to the lower deck. He was met by a sickening smell of dirty, poverty-stricken humanity, an atmosphere of naked flesh (far more revolting than the odour of fur or the skin of wild beasts). There, in a sort of basement, low and dark, like a gallery in a mine, Pierre could discern some hundreds of men, women, and children, stretched on shelves fixed one above another, or lying on the floor in heaps. He could not see their faces, but could dimly make out this squalid, ragged crowd of wretches, beaten in the struggle for life, worn out and crushed, setting forth, each with a starving wife and weakly children, for an unknown land where they hoped, perhaps, not to die of hunger. And as he thought of their past labour—wasted labour, and barren effort—of the mortal struggle taken up afresh and in vain each day, of the energy expended by this tattered crew who were going to begin again, not knowing where, this life of hideous misery, he longed to cry out to them:

"Tumble yourselves overboard, rather, with your women and your little ones." And his heart ached so with pity that he went away unable to endure the sight.

He found his father, his mother, Jean, and Mme. Rosémilly waiting for him in his cabin.

"So early!" he exclaimed.

"Yes," said Mme. Roland in a trembling voice. "We wanted to have a little time to see you."

He looked at her. She was dressed all in black as if she were in mourning, and he noticed that her hair, which only a month ago had been gray, was now almost white. It was very difficult to find space for four persons to sit down in the little room, and he himself got on to his bed. The door was left open, and they could see a great crowd hurrying by, as if it were a street on a holiday, for all the friends of the passengers and a host of inquisitive visitors had invaded the huge vessel. They pervaded the passages, the saloons, every corner of the ship; and heads peered in at the doorway while a voice murmured outside: "That is the doctor's cabin."

Then Pierre shut the door; but no sooner was he shut in with his own party than he longed to open it again, for the bustle outside covered their agitation and want of words.

Mme. Rosémilly at last felt she must speak.

"Very little air comes in through those little windows."

"Port-holes," said Pierre. He showed her how thick the glass was, to enable it to resist the most violent shocks, and took a long time explaining the fastening. Roland presently asked: "And you have your doctor's shop here?"

The doctor opened a cupboard and displayed an array of phials ticketed with Latin names on white paper labels. He took one out and enumerated the properties of its contents; then a second and a third, a perfect lecture on therapeutics, to which they all listened with great attention. Roland, shaking his head, said again and again: "How very interesting!" There was a tap at the door.

"Come in," said Pierre, and Captain Beausire appeared.

"I am late," he said as he shook hands, "I did not want to be in the way." He, too, sat down on the bed and silence fell once more.

Suddenly the Captain pricked his ears. He could hear the orders being given, and he said:

"It is time for us to be off if we mean to get on board the Pearl to see you once more outside, and bid you good-bye out on the open sea."

Old Roland was very eager about this, to impress the voyagers on board the Lorraine, no doubt, and he rose in haste.

"Good-bye, my boy." He kissed Pierre on the whiskers and then opened the door.

Mme. Roland had not stirred, but sat with downcast eyes, very pale. Her husband touched her arm.

"Come," he said, "we must make haste, we have not a minute to spare."

She pulled herself up, went to her son and offered him first one and then another cheek of white wax which he kissed without saying a word. Then he shook hands with Mme. Rosémilly and his brother, asking:

"And when is the wedding to be?"

"I do not know yet exactly. We will make it fit in with one of your return voyages."

At last they were all out of the cabin, and up on deck among the crowd of visitors, porters, and sailors. The steam was snorting in the huge belly of the vessel, which seemed to quiver with impatience.

"Good-bye," said Roland in a great bustle.

"Good-bye," replied Pierre, standing on one of the landing-planks lying between the deck of the Lorraine and the quay. He shook hands all round once more, and they were gone.

"Make haste, jump into the carriage," cried the father.

A fly was waiting for them and took them to the outer harbour, where Papagris had the Pearl in readiness to put out to sea.

There was not a breath of air; it was one of those crisp, still autumn days, when the sheeny sea looks as cold and hard as polished steel.

Jean took one oar, the sailor seized the other and they pulled off. On the breakwater, on the piers, even on the granite parapets, a crowd stood packed, hustling, and noisy, to see the Lorraine come out. The Pearl glided down between these two waves of humanity and was soon outside the mole.

Captain Beausire, seated between the two women, held the tiller, and he said:

"You will see, we shall be close in her way—close."

And the two oarsmen pulled with all their might to get out as far as possible. Suddenly Roland cried out:

"Here she comes! I see her masts and her two funnels! She is coming out of the inner harbour."

"Cheerily, lads!" cried Beausire.

Mme. Roland took out her handkerchief and held it to her eyes.

Roland stood up, clinging to the mast, and answered:

"At this moment she is working round in the outer harbour. She is standing still—now she moves again! She is taking the tow-rope on board no doubt. There she goes. Bravo! She is between the piers! Do you hear the crowd shouting? Bravo! The Neptune has her in tow. Now I see her bows—here she comes—here she is! Gracious Heavens, what a ship! Look! Look!"

Mme. Rosémilly and Beausire looked behind them, the oarsmen ceased pulling; only Mme. Roland did not stir.

The immense steamship, towed by a powerful tug, which, in front of her, looked like a caterpillar, came slowly and majestically out of the harbour. And the good people of Havre, who crowded the piers, the beach, and the windows, carried away by a burst of patriotic enthusiasm, cried: "Vive la Lorraine!" with acclamations and applause for this magnificent beginning, this birth of the beautiful daughter given to the sea by the great maritime town.

She, as soon as she had passed beyond the narrow channel between the two granite walls, feeling herself free at last, cast off the tow-ropes and went off alone, like a monstrous creature walking on the waters.

"Here she is—here she comes, straight down on us!" Roland kept shouting; and Beausire, beaming, exclaimed: "What did I promise you! Heh! Do I know the way?"

Jean in a low tone said to his mother: "Look, mother, she is close upon us!" And Mme. Roland uncovered her eyes, blinded with tears.

The Lorraine came on, still under the impetus of her swift exit from the harbour, in the brilliant, calm weather. Beausire, with his glass to his eye, called out:

"Look out! M. Pierre is at the stern, all alone, plainly to be seen! Look out!"

The ship was almost touching the Pearl now, as tall as a mountain and as swift as a train.

Mme. Roland, distraught and desperate, held out her arms towards it; and she saw her son, her Pierre, with his officer's cap on, throwing kisses to her with both hands.

But he was going away, flying, vanishing, a tiny speck already, no more than an imperceptible spot on the enormous vessel. She tried still to distinguish him, but she could not.

Jean took her hand.

"You saw?" he said.

"Yes, I saw. How good he is!"

And they turned to go home.

"Cristi! How fast she goes!" exclaimed Roland with enthusiastic conviction.

The steamer, in fact, was shrinking every second, as though she were melting away in the ocean. Mme. Roland, turning back to look at her, watched her disappearing on the horizon, on her way to an unknown land at the other side of the world.

In that vessel which nothing could stay, that vessel which she soon would see no more, was her son, her poor son. And she felt as though half her heart had gone with him; she felt, too, as if her life were ended; yes, and she felt as though she would never see the child again.

"Why are you crying?" asked her husband, "when you know he will be back again within a month."

She stammered out: "I don't know; I cry because I am hurt."

When they had landed, Beausire at once took leave of them to go to breakfast with a friend. Then Jean led the way with Mme. Rosémilly, and Roland said to his wife:

"A very fine fellow, all the same, is our Jean."

"Yes," replied the mother.

And her mind being too much bewildered to think of what she was saying, she went on:

"I am very glad that he is to marry Mme. Rosémilly."

The worthy man was astounded.

"Heh? What? He is to marry Mme. Rosémilly?"

"Yes, we meant to ask your opinion about it this very day."

"Bless me! And has this engagement been long in the wind?"

"Oh, no, only a very few days. Jean wished to make sure that she would accept him before consulting you."

Roland rubbed his hands.

"Very good. Very good. It is capital. I entirely approve."

As they were about to turn off from the quay down the Boulevard François, his wife once more looked back to cast a last look at the high seas, but she could see nothing now but a puff of gray smoke, so far away, so faint that it looked like a film of haze.

BEL AMI

OR

THE HISTORY OF A SCOUNDREL

CHAPTER I.

POVERTY

After changing his five-franc piece Georges Duroy left the restaurant. He twisted his mustache in military style and cast a rapid, sweeping glance upon the diners, among whom were three saleswomen, an untidy music-teacher of uncertain age, and two women with their husbands.

When he reached the sidewalk, he paused to consider what route he should take. It was the twenty-eighth of June and he had only three francs in his pocket to last him the remainder of the month. That meant two dinners and no lunches, or two lunches and no dinners, according to choice. As he pondered upon this unpleasant state of affairs, he sauntered down Rue Notre Dame de Lorette, preserving his military air and carriage, and rudely jostled the people upon the streets in order to clear a path for himself. He appeared to be hostile to the passers-by, and even to the houses, the entire city.

Tall, well-built, fair, with blue eyes, a curled mustache, hair naturally wavy and parted in the middle, he recalled the hero of the popular romances.

It was one of those sultry, Parisian evenings when not a breath of air is stirring; the sewers exhaled poisonous gases and the restaurants the disagreeable odors of cooking and of kindred smells. Porters in their shirt-sleeves, astride their chairs, smoked their pipes at the carriage gates, and pedestrians strolled leisurely along, hats in hand.

When Georges Duroy reached the boulevard he halted again, undecided as to which road to choose. Finally he turned toward the Madeleine and followed the tide of people.

The large, well-patronized cafes tempted Duroy, but were he to drink only two glasses of beer in an evening, farewell to the meager supper the following night! Yet he said to himself: "I will take a glass at the Americain. By Jove, I am thirsty."

He glanced at men seated at the tables, men who could afford to slake their thirst, and he scowled at them. "Rascals!" he muttered. If he could have caught one of them at a corner in the dark he would have choked him without a scruple! He recalled the two years spent in Africa, and the manner in which he had extorted money from the Arabs. A smile hovered about his lips at the recollection of an escapade which had cost three men their lives, a foray which had given his two comrades and himself seventy fowls, two sheep, money, and something to laugh about for six months. The culprits were never found; indeed, they were not sought for, the Arab being looked upon as the soldier's prey.

But in Paris it was different; there one could not commit such deeds with impunity. He regretted that he had not remained where he was; but he had hoped to improve his condition—and for that reason he was in Paris!

He passed the Vaudeville and stopped at the Cafe Americain, debating as to whether he should take that "glass." Before deciding, he glanced at a clock; it was a quarter past nine. He knew that when the beer was placed in front of him, he would drink it; and then what would he do at eleven o'clock? So he walked on, intending to go as far as the Madeleine and return.

When he reached the Place de l'Opera, a tall, young man passed him, whose face he fancied was familiar. He followed him, repeating: "Where the deuce have I seen that fellow?"

For a time he racked his brain in vain; then suddenly he saw the same man, but not so corpulent and more youthful, attired in the uniform of a Hussar. He exclaimed: "Wait, Forestier!" and hastening up to him, laid his hand upon the man's shoulder. The latter turned, looked at him, and said: "What do you want, sir?"

Duroy began to laugh: "Don't you remember me?"

"No."

"Not remember Georges Duroy of the Sixth Hussars."

Forestier extended both hands.

"Ah, my dear fellow, how are you?"

"Very well. And how are you?"

"Oh, I am not very well. I cough six months out of the twelve as a result of bronchitis contracted at Bougival, about the time of my return to Paris four years ago."

"But you look well."

Forestier, taking his former comrade's arm, told him of his malady, of the consultations, the opinions and the advice of the doctors and of the difficulty of following their advice in his position. They ordered him to spend the winter in the south, but how could he? He was married and was a journalist in a responsible editorial position.

"I manage the political department on 'La Vie Francaise'; I report the doings of the Senate for 'Le Salut,' and from time to time I write for 'La Planete.' That is what I am doing."

Duroy, in surprise, glanced at him. He was very much changed. Formerly Forestier had been thin, giddy, noisy, and always in good spirits. But three years of life in Paris had made another man of him; now he was stout and serious, and his hair was gray on his temples although he could not number more than twenty-seven years.

Forestier asked: "Where are you going?"

Duroy replied: "Nowhere in particular."

"Very well, will you accompany me to the 'Vie Francaise' where I have some proofs to correct; and afterward take a drink with me?"

"Yes, gladly."

They walked along arm-in-arm with that familiarity which exists between schoolmates and brother-officers.

"What are you doing in Paris?" asked Forestier, Duroy shrugged his shoulders.

"Dying of hunger, simply. When my time was up, I came hither to make my fortune, or rather to live in Paris—and for six months I have been employed in a railroad office at fifteen hundred francs a year."

Forestier murmured: "That is not very much."

"But what can I do?" answered Duroy. "I am alone, I know no one, I have no recommendations. The spirit is not lacking, but the means are."

His companion looked at him from head to foot like a practical man who is examining a subject; then he said, in a tone of conviction: "You see, my dear fellow, all depends on assurance, here. A shrewd, observing man can sometimes become a minister. You must obtrude yourself and yet not ask anything. But how is it you have not found anything better than a clerkship at the station?"

Duroy replied: "I hunted everywhere and found nothing else. But I know where I can get three thousand francs at least—as riding-master at the Pellerin school."

Forestier stopped him: "Don't do it, for you can earn ten thousand francs. You will ruin your prospects at once. In your office at least no one knows you; you can leave it if you wish to at any time. But when you are once a riding-master all will be over. You might as well be a butler in a house to which all Paris comes to dine. When you have given riding lessons to men of the world or to their sons, they will no longer consider you their equal."

He paused, reflected several seconds and then asked:

"Are you a bachelor?"

"Yes, though I have been smitten several times."

"That makes no difference. If Cicero and Tiberius were mentioned would you know who they were?"

"Yes."

"Good, no one knows any more except about a score of fools. It is not difficult to pass for being learned. The secret is not to betray your ignorance. Just maneuver, avoid the quicksands and obstacles, and the rest can be found in a dictionary."

He spoke like one who understood human nature, and he smiled as the crowd passed them by. Suddenly he began to cough and stopped to allow the paroxysm to spend itself; then he said in a discouraged tone:

"Isn't it tiresome not to be able to get rid of this bronchitis? And here is midsummer! This winter I shall go to Mentone. Health before everything."

They reached the Boulevarde Poissoniere; behind a large glass door an open paper was affixed; three people were reading it. Above the door was printed the legend, "La Vie Francaise."

Forestier pushed open the door and said: "Come in." Duroy entered; they ascended the stairs, passed through an antechamber in which two clerks greeted their comrade, and then entered a kind of waiting-room.

"Sit down," said Forestier, "I shall be back in five minutes," and he disappeared.

Duroy remained where he was; from time to time men passed him by, entering by one door and going out by another before he had time to glance at them.

Now they were young men, very young, with a busy air, holding sheets of paper in their hands; now compositors, their shirts spotted with ink—carefully carrying what were evidently fresh proofs. Occasionally a gentleman entered, fashionably dressed, some reporter bringing news.

Forestier reappeared arm-in-arm with a tall, thin man of thirty or forty, dressed in a black coat, with a white cravat, a dark complexion, and an insolent, self-satisfied air. Forestier said to him: "Adieu, my dear sir," and the other pressed his hand with: "Au revoir, my friend." Then he descended the stairs whistling, his cane under his arm.

Duroy asked his name.

"That is Jacques Rival, the celebrated writer and duelist. He came to correct his proofs. Garin, Montel and he are the best witty and realistic writers we have in Paris. He earns thirty thousand francs a year for two articles a week."

As they went downstairs, they met a stout, little man with long hair, who was ascending the stairs whistling. Forestier bowed low.

"Norbert de Varenne," said he, "the poet, the author of 'Les Soleils Morts,'—a very expensive man. Every poem he gives us costs three hundred francs and the longest has not two hundred lines. But let us go into the Napolitain, I am getting thirsty."

When they were seated at a table, Forestier ordered two glasses of beer. He emptied his at a single draught, while Duroy sipped his beer slowly as if it were something rare and precious. Suddenly his companion asked, "Why don't you try journalism?"

Duroy looked at him in surprise and said: "Because I have never written anything."

"Bah, we all have to make a beginning. I could employ you myself by sending you to obtain information. At first you would only get two hundred and fifty francs a month but your cab fare would be paid. Shall I speak to the manager?"

"If you will."

"Well, then come and dine with me to-morrow; I will only ask five or six to meet you; the manager, M. Walter, his wife, with Jacques Rival, and Norbert de Varenne whom you have just seen, and also a friend of Mme. Forestier, Will you come?"

Duroy hesitated, blushing and perplexed. Finally he, murmured: "I have no suitable clothes."

Forestier was amazed. "You have no dress suit? Egad, that is indispensable. In Paris, it is better to have no bed than no clothes." Then, fumbling in his vest-pocket, he drew from it two louis, placed them before his companion, and said kindly: "You can repay me when it is convenient. Buy yourself what you need and pay an installment on it. And come and dine with us at half past seven, at 17 Rue Fontaine."

In confusion Duroy picked up the money and stammered: "You are very kind—I am much obliged—be sure I shall not forget."

Forestier interrupted him: "That's all right, take another glass of beer. Waiter, two more glasses!" When he had paid the score, the journalist asked: "Would you like a stroll for an hour?"

"Certainly."

They turned toward the Madeleine. "What shall we do?" asked Forestier. "They say that in Paris an idler can always find amusement, but it is not true. A turn in the Bois is only enjoyable if you have a lady with you, and that is a rare occurrence. The cafe concerts may divert my tailor and his wife, but they do not interest me. So what can we do? Nothing! There ought to be a summer garden here, open at night, where a man could listen to good music while drinking beneath the trees. It would be a pleasant lounging place. You could walk in alleys bright with electric light and seat yourself where you pleased to hear the music. It would be charming. Where would you like to go?"

Duroy did not know what to reply; finally he said: "I have never been to the Folies Bergeres. I should like to go there."

His companion exclaimed: "The Folies Bergeres! Very well!"

They turned and walked toward the Faubourg Montmartre. The brilliantly illuminated building loomed up before them. Forestier entered, Duroy stopped him. "We forgot to pass through the gate."

The other replied in a consequential tone: "I never pay," and approached the box-office.

"Have you a good box?"

"Certainly, M. Forestier."

He took the ticket handed him, pushed open the door, and they were within the hall. A cloud of tobacco smoke almost hid the stage and the opposite side of the theater. In the spacious foyer which led to the circular promenade, brilliantly dressed women mingled with black-coated men.

Forestier forced his way rapidly through the throng and accosted an usher.

"Box 17?"

"This way, sir."

The friends were shown into a tiny box, hung and carpeted in red, with four chairs upholstered in the same color. They seated themselves. To their right and left were similar boxes. On the stage three men were performing on trapezes. But Duroy paid no heed to them, his eyes finding more to interest them in the grand promenade. Forestier remarked upon the motley appearance of the throng, but Duroy did not listen to him. A woman, leaning her arms upon the edge of her loge, was staring at him. She was a tall, voluptuous brunette, her face whitened with enamel, her black eyes penciled, and her lips painted. With a movement of her head, she summoned a friend who was passing, a blonde with auburn hair, likewise inclined to embonpoint, and said to her in a whisper intended to be heard; "There is a nice fellow!"

Forestier heard it, and said to Duroy with a smile: "You are lucky, my dear boy. My congratulations!"

The ci-devant soldier blushed and mechanically fingered the two pieces of gold in his pocket.

The curtain fell—the orchestra played a valse—and Duroy said:

"Shall we walk around the gallery?"

"If you like."

Soon they were carried along in the current of promenaders. Duroy drank in with delight the air, vitiated as it was by tobacco and cheap perfume, but Forestier perspired, panted, and coughed.

"Let us go into the garden," he said. Turning to the left, they entered a kind of covered garden in which two large fountains were playing. Under the yews, men and women sat at tables drinking.

"Another glass of beer?" asked Forestier.

"Gladly."

They took their seats and watched the promenaders. Occasionally a woman would stop and ask with a coarse smile: "What have you to offer, sir?"

Forestier's invariable answer was: "A glass of water from the fountain." And the woman would mutter, "Go along," and walk away.

At last the brunette reappeared, arm-in-arm with the blonde. They made a handsome couple. The former smiled on perceiving Duroy, and taking a chair she calmly seated herself in front of him, and said in a clear voice: "Waiter, two glasses."

In astonishment, Forestier exclaimed: "You are not at all bashful!"

She replied: "Your friend has bewitched me; he is such a fine fellow. I believe he has turned my head."

Duroy said nothing.

The waiter brought the beer, which the women swallowed rapidly; then they rose, and the brunette, nodding her head and tapping Duroy's arm with her fan, said to him: "Thank you, my dear! However, you are not very talkative."

As they disappeared, Forestier laughed and said: "Tell, me, old man, did you know that you had a charm for the weaker sex? You must be careful."

Without replying, Duroy smiled. His friend asked: "Shall you remain any longer? I am going; I have had enough."

Georges murmured: "Yes, I will stay a little longer: it is not late."

Forestier arose: "Very well, then, good-bye until to-morrow. Do not forget: 17 Rue Fontaine at seven thirty."

"I shall not forget. Thank you."

The friends shook hands and the journalist left Duroy to his own devices.

Forestier once out of sight, Duroy felt free, and again he joyously touched the gold pieces in his pocket; then rising, he mingled with the crowd.

He soon discovered the blonde and the brunette. He went toward them, but when near them dared not address them.

The brunette called out to him: “Have you found your tongue?”

He stammered: “Zounds!” too bashful to say another word. A pause ensued, during which the brunette took his arm and together they left the hall.

CHAPTER II.

MADAME FORESTIER

"Where does M. Forestier live?"

"Third floor on the left," said the porter pleasantly, on learning Duroy's destination.

Georges ascended the staircase. He was somewhat embarrassed and ill-at-ease. He had on a new suit but he was uncomfortable. He felt that it was defective; his boots were not glossy, he had bought his shirt that same evening at the Louvre for four francs fifty, his trousers were too wide and betrayed their cheapness in their fit, or rather, misfit, and his coat was too tight.

Slowly he ascended the stairs, his heart beating, his mind anxious. Suddenly before him stood a well-dressed gentleman staring at him. The person resembled Duroy so close that the latter retreated, then stopped, and saw that it was his own image reflected in a pier-glass! Not having anything but a small mirror at home, he had not been able to see himself entirely, and had exaggerated the imperfections of his toilette. When he saw his reflection in the glass, he did not even recognize himself; he took himself for some one else, for a man-of-the-world, and was really satisfied with his general appearance. Smiling to himself, Duroy extended his hand and expressed his astonishment, pleasure, and approbation. A door opened on the staircase, He was afraid of being surprised and began to ascend more rapidly, fearing that he might have been seen posing there by some of his friend's invited guests.

On reaching the second floor, he saw another mirror, and once more slackened his pace to look at himself. He likewise paused before the third glass, twirled his mustache, took off his hat to arrange his hair, and murmured half aloud, a habit of his: "Hall mirrors are most convenient."

Then he rang the bell. The door opened almost immediately, and before him stood a servant in a black coat, with a grave, shaven face, so perfect in his appearance that Duroy again became confused as he compared the cut of their garments.

The lackey asked:

"Whom shall I announce, Monsieur?" He raised a portiere and pronounced the name.

Duroy lost his self-possession upon being ushered into a world as yet strange to him. However, he advanced. A young, fair woman received him alone in a large, well-lighted room. He paused, disconcerted. Who was that smiling lady? He remembered that Forestier was married, and the thought that the handsome blonde was his friend's wife rendered him awkward and ill-at-ease. He stammered out:

"Madame, I am—"

She held out her hand. "I know, Monsieur—Charles told me of your meeting last night, and I am very glad that he asked you to dine with us to-day."

Duroy blushed to the roots of his hair, not knowing how to reply; he felt that he was being inspected from his head to his feet. He half thought of excusing himself, of inventing an explanation of the carelessness of his toilette, but he did not know how to touch upon that delicate subject.

He seated himself upon a chair she pointed out to him, and as he sank into its luxurious depths, it seemed to him that he was entering a new and charming life, that he would make his mark in the world, that he was saved. He glanced at Mme. Forestier. She wore a gown of pale blue cashmere which clung gracefully to her supple form and rounded outlines; her arms and throat rose in, lily-white purity from the mass of lace which ornamented the corsage and short sleeves. Her hair was dressed high and curled on the nape of her neck.

Duroy grew more at his ease under her glance, which recalled to him, he knew not why, that of the girl he had met the preceding evening at the Folies-Bergeres. Mme. Forestier had gray eyes, a small nose, full lips, and a rather heavy chin, an irregular, attractive face, full of gentleness and yet of malice.

After a short silence, she asked: "Have you been in Paris a long time?"

Gradually regaining his self-possession, he replied: "a few months, Madame. I am in the railroad employ, but my friend Forestier has encouraged me to hope that, thanks to him, I can enter into journalism."

She smiled kindly and murmured in a low voice: "I know."

The bell rang again and the servant announced: "Mme. de Marelle." She was a dainty brunette, attired in a simple, dark robe; a red rose in her black tresses seemed to accentuate her special character, and a young girl, or rather a child, for such she was, followed her.

Mme. Forestier said: "Good evening, Clotilde."

"Good evening, Madeleine."

They embraced each other, then the child offered her forehead with the assurance of an adult, saying:

"Good evening, cousin."

Mme. Forestier kissed her, and then made the introductions:

"M. Georges Duroy, an old friend of Charles. Mme. de Marelle, my friend, a relative in fact." She added: "Here, you know, we do not stand on ceremony."

Duroy bowed. The door opened again and a short man entered, upon his arm a tall, handsome woman, taller than he and much younger, with distinguished manners and a dignified carriage. It was M. Walter, deputy, financier, a moneyed man, and a man of business, manager of "La Vie Francaise," with his wife, nee Basile Ravalade, daughter of the banker of that name.

Then came Jacques Rival, very elegant, followed by Norbert de Varenne. The latter advanced with the grace of the old school and taking Mme. Forestier's hand kissed it; his long hair falling upon his hostess's bare arm as he did so.

Forestier now entered, apologizing for being late; he had been detained.

The servant announced dinner, and they entered the dining-room. Duroy was placed between Mme. de Marelle and her daughter. He was again rendered uncomfortable for fear of committing some error in the conventional management of his fork, his spoon, or his glasses, of which he had four. Nothing was said during the soup; then Norbert de Varenne asked a general question: "Have you read the Gauthier case? How droll it was!"

Then followed a discussion of the subject in which the ladies joined. Then a duel was mentioned and Jacques Rival led the conversation; that was his province. Duroy did not venture a remark, but occasionally glanced at his neighbor. A diamond upon a slight, golden thread depended from her ear; from time to time she uttered a remark which evoked a smile upon his lips. Duroy sought vainly for some compliment to pay her; he busied himself with her daughter, filled her glass, waited upon her, and the child, more dignified than her mother, thanked him gravely saying, "You are very kind, Monsieur," while she listened to the conversation with a reflective air. The dinner was excellent and everyone was delighted with it.

The conversation returned to the colonization of Algeria. M. Walter uttered several jocose remarks; Forestier alluded to the article he had prepared for the morrow; Jacques Rival declared himself in favor of a military government with grants of land to all the officers after thirty years of colonial service.

"In that way," said he, "you can establish a strong colony, familiar with and liking the country, knowing its language and able to cope with all those local yet grave questions which invariably confront newcomers."

Norbert de Varenne interrupted: "Yes, they would know everything, except agriculture. They would speak Arabic, but they would not know how to transplant beet-root, and how to sow wheat. They would be strong in fencing, but weak in the art of farming. On the contrary, the new country should be opened to everyone. Intelligent men would make positions for themselves; the others would succumb. It is a natural law."

A pause ensued. Everyone smiled. Georges Duroy, startled at the sound of his own voice, as if he had never heard it, said:

"What is needed the most down there is good soil. Really fertile land costs as much as it does in France and is bought by wealthy Parisians. The real colonists, the poor, are generally cast out into the desert, where nothing grows for lack of water."

All eyes turned upon him. He colored. M. Walter asked: "Do you know Algeria, sir?"

He replied: "Yes, sir, I was there twenty-eight months." Leaving the subject of colonization, Norbert de Varenne questioned him as to some of the Algerian customs. Georges spoke with animation; excited by the wine and the desire to please, he related anecdotes of the regiment, of Arabian life, and of the war.

Mme. Walter murmured to him in her soft tones: "You could write a series of charming articles."

Forestier took advantage of the situation to say to M. Walter: "My dear sir, I spoke to you a short while since of M. Georges Duroy and asked you to permit me to include him on the staff of political reporters. Since Marambot has left us, I have had no one to take urgent and confidential reports, and the paper is suffering by it."

M. Walter put on his spectacles in order to examine Duroy. Then he said: "I am convinced that M. Duroy is original, and if he will call upon me tomorrow at three o'clock, we will arrange matters." After a pause, turning to the young man, he said: "You may write us a short sketch on Algeria, M. Duroy. Simply relate your experiences; I am sure they will interest our readers. But you must do it quickly."

Mme. Walter added with her customary, serious grace: "You will have a charming title:

'Souvenirs of a Soldier in Africa.' Will he not, M. Norbert?"

The old poet, who had attained renown late in life, disliked and mistrusted newcomers. He replied dryly: "Yes, excellent, provided that it is written in the right key, for there lies the great difficulty."

Mme. Forestier cast upon Duroy a protecting and smiling glance which seemed to say: "You shall succeed." The servant filled the glasses with wine, and Forestier proposed the toast: "To the long prosperity of 'La Vie Francaise.'" Duroy felt superhuman strength within him, infinite hope, and invincible resolution. He was at his ease now among these people; his eyes rested upon their faces with renewed assurance, and for the first time he ventured to address his neighbor:

"You have the most beautiful earrings I have ever seen."

She turned toward him with a smile: "It is a fancy of mine to wear diamonds like this, simply on a thread."

He murmured in reply, trembling at his audacity: "It is charming—but the ear increases the beauty of the ornament."

She thanked him with a glance. As he turned his head, he met Mme. Forestier's eyes, in which he fancied he saw a mingled expression of gaiety, malice, and encouragement. All the men were talking at the same time; their discussion was animated.

When the party left the dining-room, Duroy offered his arm to the little girl. She thanked him gravely and stood upon tiptoe in order to lay her hand upon his arm. Upon entering the drawing-room, the young man carefully surveyed it. It was not a large room; but there were no bright colors, and one felt at ease; it was restful. The walls were draped with violet hangings covered with tiny embroidered flowers of yellow silk. The portieres were of a grayish blue and the chairs were of all shapes, of all sizes; scattered about the room were couches and large and small easy-chairs, all covered with Louis XVI. brocade, or Utrecht velvet, a cream colored ground with garnet flowers.

"Do you take coffee, M. Duroy?" Mme. Forestier offered him a cup, with the smile that was always upon her lips.

"Yes, Madame, thank you." He took the cup, and as he did so, the young woman whispered to him: "Pay Mme. Walter some attention." Then she vanished before he could reply.

First he drank his coffee, which he feared he should let fall upon the carpet; then he sought a pretext for approaching the manager's wife and commencing a conversation. Suddenly he perceived that she held an empty cup in her hand, and as she was not near a table, she did not know where to put it. He rushed toward her:

"Allow me, Madame."

"Thank you, sir."

He took away the cup and returned: "If you, but knew, Madame, what pleasant moments 'La Vie Francaise' afforded me, when I was in the desert! It is indeed the only paper one cares to read outside of France; it contains everything."

She smiled with amiable indifference as she replied: "M. Walter had a great deal of trouble in producing the kind of journal which was required."

They talked of Paris, the suburbs, the Seine, the delights of summer, of everything they could think of. Finally M. Norbert de Varenne advanced, a glass of liqueur in his hand, and Duroy discreetly withdrew. Mme. de Marelle, who was chatting with her hostess, called him: "So, sir," she said bluntly, "you are going to try journalism?" That question led to a renewal of the interrupted conversation with Mme. Walter. In her turn Mme. de Marelle related anecdotes, and becoming familiar, laid her hand upon Duroy's arm. He felt that he would like to devote himself to her, to protect her—and the slowness with which he replied to her questions indicated his preoccupation. Suddenly, without any cause, Mme. de Marelle called: "Laurine!" and the girl came to her. "Sit down here, my child, you will be cold near the window."

Duroy was seized with an eager desire to embrace the child, as if part of that embrace would revert to the mother. He asked in a gallant, yet paternal tone: "Will you permit me to kiss you, Mademoiselle?" The child raised her eyes with an air of surprise. Mme. de Marelle said with a smile: "Reply."

"I will allow you to-day, Monsieur, but not all the time."

Seating himself, Duroy took Laurine upon his knee, and kissed her lips and her fine wavy hair. Her mother was surprised: "Well, that is strange! Ordinarily she only allows ladies to caress her. You are irresistible, Monsieur!"

Duroy colored, but did not reply.

When Mme. Forestier joined them, a cry of astonishment escaped her: "Well, Laurine has become sociable; what a miracle!"

The young man rose to take his leave, fearing he might spoil his conquest by some awkward word. He bowed to the ladies, clasped and gently pressed their hands, and then shook hands with the men. He observed that Jacques Rival's was dry and warm and responded cordially to his pressure; Norbert de Varenne's was moist and cold and slipped through his fingers; Walter's was cold and soft, without life, expressionless; Forestier's fat and warm.

His friend whispered to him: "To-morrow at three o'clock; do not forget."

"Never fear!"

When he reached the staircase, he felt like running down, his joy was so great; he went down two steps at a time, but suddenly on the second floor, in the large mirror, he saw a gentleman hurrying on, and he slackened his pace, as much ashamed as if he had been surprised in a crime.

He surveyed himself some time with a complacent smile; then taking leave of his image, he bowed low, ceremoniously, as if saluting some grand personage.

CHAPTER III.

FIRST ATTEMPTS

When Georges Duroy reached the street, he hesitated as to what he should do. He felt inclined to stroll along, dreaming of the future and inhaling the soft night air; but the thought of the series of articles ordered by M. Walter occurred to him, and he decided to return home at once and begin work. He walked rapidly along until he came to Rue Boursault. The tenement in which he lived was occupied by twenty families—families of workingmen—and as he mounted the staircase he experienced a sensation of disgust and a desire to live as wealthy men do. Duroy's room was on the fifth floor. He entered it, opened his window, and looked out: the view was anything but prepossessing.

He turned away, thinking: "This won't do. I must go to work." So he placed his light upon the table and began to write. He dipped his pen into the ink and wrote at the head of his paper in a bold hand: "Souvenirs of a Soldier in Africa." Then he cast about for the first phrase. He rested his head upon his hand and stared at the blank sheet before him. What should he say? Suddenly he thought: "I must begin with my departure," and he wrote: "In 1874, about the fifteenth of May, when exhausted France was recruiting after the catastrophe of the terrible years—" Here he stopped short, not knowing how to introduce his subject. After a few minutes' reflection, he decided to lay aside that page until the following day, and to write a description of Algiers. He began: "Algiers is a very clean city—" but he could not continue. After an effort he added: "It is inhabited partly by Arabs." Then he threw his pen upon the table and arose. He glanced around his miserable room; mentally he rebelled against his poverty and resolved to leave the next day.

Suddenly the desire to work came on him, and he tried to begin the article again; he had vague ideas of what he wanted to say, but he could not express his thoughts in words. Convinced of his inability he arose once more, his blood coursing rapidly through his veins. He turned to the window just as the train was coming out of the tunnel, and his thoughts reverted to his parents. He saw their tiny home on the heights overlooking Rouen and the valley of the Seine. His father and mother kept an inn, La Belle-Vue, at which the citizens of the faubourgs took their lunches on Sundays. They had wished to make a "gentleman" of their son and had sent him to college. His studies completed, he had entered the army with the intention of becoming an officer, a colonel, or a general. But becoming disgusted with military life, he determined to try his fortune in Paris. When his time of service had expired, he went thither, with what results we have seen. He awoke from his reflections as the locomotive whistled shrilly, closed his window, and began to disrobe, muttering: "Bah, I shall be able to work better to-morrow morning. My brain is not clear to-night. I have drunk a little too much. I can't work well under such circumstances." He extinguished his light and fell asleep.

He awoke early, and, rising, opened his window to inhale the fresh air. In a few moments he seated himself at his table, dipped his pen in the ink, rested his head upon his hand and thought—but in vain! However, he was not discouraged, but in thought reassured himself: "Bah, I am not accustomed to it! It is a profession that must be learned like all professions. Some one must help me the first time. I'll go to Forestier. He'll start my article for me in ten minutes."

When he reached the street, Duroy decided that it was rather early to present himself at his friend's house, so he strolled along under the trees on one of the boulevards for a time. On arriving at Forestier's door, he found his friend going out.

"You here—at this hour! Can I do anything for you?"

Duroy stammered in confusion: "I—I—cannot write that article on Algeria that M. Walter wants. It is not very surprising, seeing that I have never written anything. It requires practice. I could write very rapidly, I am sure, if I could make a beginning. I have the ideas but I cannot express them." He paused and hesitated.

Forestier smiled maliciously: "I understand that."

Duroy continued: "Yes, anyone is liable to have that trouble at the beginning; and, well—I have come to ask you to help me. In ten minutes you can set me right. You can give me a lesson in style; without you I can do nothing."

The other smiled gaily. He patted his companion's arm and said to him: "Go to my wife; she will help you better than I can. I have trained her for that work. I have not time this morning or I would do it willingly."

But Duroy hesitated: "At this hour I cannot inquire for her."

"Oh, yes, you can; she has risen. You will find her in my study."

"I will go, but I shall tell her you sent me!"

Forestier walked away, and Duroy slowly ascended the stairs, wondering what he should say and what kind of a reception he would receive.

The servant who opened the door said: "Monsieur has gone out."

Duroy replied: "Ask Mme. Forestier if she will see me, and tell her that M. Forestier, whom I met on the street, sent me."

The lackey soon returned and ushered Duroy into Madame's presence. She was seated at a table and extended her hand to him.

"So soon?" said she. It was not a reproach, but a simple question.

He stammered: "I did not want to come up, Madame, but your husband, whom I met below, insisted—I dare scarcely tell you my errand—I worked late last night and early this morning, to write the article on Algeria which M. Walter wants—and I did not succeed—I destroyed all my attempts—I am not accustomed to the work—and I came to ask Forestier to assist me—his once."

She interrupted with a laugh: "And he sent you to me?"

"Yes, Madame. He said you could help me better than he—but—I dared not—I did not like to."

She rose.

"It will be delightful to work together that way. I am charmed with your idea. Wait, take my chair, for they know my handwriting on the paper—we will write a successful article."

She took a cigarette from the mantelpiece and lighted it. "I cannot work without smoking," she said; "what are you going to say?"

He looked at her in astonishment. "I do not know; I came here to find that out."

She replied: "I will manage it all right. I will make the sauce but I must have the dish." She questioned him in detail and finally said:

"Now, we will begin. First of all we will suppose that you are addressing a friend, which will allow us scope for remarks of all kinds. Begin this way: 'My dear Henry, you wish to know something about Algeria; you shall.'"

Then followed a brilliantly worded description of Algeria and of the port of Algiers, an excursion to the province of Oran, a visit to Saida, and an adventure with a pretty Spanish maid employed in a factory.

When the article was concluded, he could find no words of thanks; he was happy to be near her, grateful for and delighted with their growing intimacy. It seemed to him that everything about him was a part of her, even to the books upon the shelves. The chairs, the furniture, the air—all were permeated with that delightful fragrance peculiar to her.

She asked bluntly: "What do you think of my friend Mme. de Marelle?"

"I think her very fascinating," he said; and he would have liked to add: "But not as much so as you." He had not the courage to do so.

She continued: "If you only knew how comical, original, and intelligent she is! She is a true Bohemian. It is for that reason that her husband no longer loves her. He only sees her defects and none of her good qualities."

Duroy was surprised to hear that Mme. de Marelle was married.

"What," he asked, "is she married? What does her husband do?"

Mme. Forestier shrugged her shoulders. "Oh, he is superintendent of a railroad. He is in Paris a week out of each month. His wife calls it 'Holy Week.' or 'The week of duty.' When you get better acquainted with her, you will see how witty she is! Come here and see her some day."

As she spoke, the door opened noiselessly, and a gentleman entered unannounced. He halted on seeing a man. For a moment Mme. Forestier seemed confused; then she said in a natural voice, though her cheeks were tinged with a blush:

"Come in, my dear sir; allow me to present to you an old comrade of Charles, M. Georges Duroy, a future journalist." Then in a different tone, she said: "Our best and dearest friend, Count de Vaudrec."

The two men bowed, gazed into one another's eyes, and then Duroy took his leave. Neither tried to detain him.

On reaching the street he felt sad and uncomfortable. Count de Vaudrec's face was constantly before him. It seemed to him that the man was displeased at finding him tete-a-tete with Mme. Forestier, though why he should be, he could not divine.

To while away the time until three o'clock, he lunched at Duval's, and then lounged along the boulevard. When the clock chimed the hour of his appointment, he climbed the stairs leading to the office of "La Vie Francaise."

Duroy asked: "Is M. Walter in?"

"M. Walter is engaged," was the reply. "Will you please take a seat?"

Duroy waited twenty minutes, then he turned to the clerk and said: "M. Walter had an appointment with me at three o'clock. At any rate, see if my friend M. Forestier is here."

He was conducted along a corridor and ushered into a large room in which four men were writing at a table. Forestier was standing before the fireplace, smoking a cigarette. After listening to Duroy's story he said:

"Come with me; I will take you to M. Walter, or else you might remain here until seven o'clock."

They entered the manager's room. Norbert de Varenne was writing an article, seated in an easychair; Jacques Rival, stretched upon a divan, was smoking a cigar. The room had the peculiar odor familiar to all journalists. When they approached M. Walter, Forestier said: "Here is my friend Duroy."

The manager looked keenly at the young man and asked:

"Have you brought my article?"

Duroy drew the sheets of manuscript from his pocket.

"Here they are, Monsieur."

The manager seemed delighted and said with a smile: "Very good. You are a man of your word. Need I look over it, Forestier?"

But Forestier hastened to reply: "It is not necessary, M. Walter; I helped him in order to initiate him into the profession. It is very good." Then bending toward him, he whispered: "You know you promised to engage Duroy to replace Marambot. Will you allow me to retain him on the same terms?"

"Certainly."

Taking his friend's arm, the journalist drew him away, while M. Walter returned to the game of ecarte he had been engaged in when they entered. Forestier and Duroy returned to the room in which Georges had found his friend. The latter said to his new reporter:

"You must come here every day at three o'clock, and I will tell you what places to go to. First of all, I shall give you a letter of introduction to the chief of the police, who will in turn introduce you to one of his employees. You can arrange with him for all important news, official and semiofficial. For details you can apply to Saint-Potin, who is posted; you will see him to-morrow. Above all, you must learn to make your way everywhere in spite of closed doors. You will receive two hundred francs a months, two sous a line for original matter, and two sous a line for articles you are ordered to write on different subjects."

"What shall I do to-day?" asked Duroy.

"I have no work for you to-day; you can go if you wish to."

"And our—our article?"

"Oh, do not worry about it; I will correct the proofs. Do the rest to-morrow and come here at three o'clock as you did to-day."

And after shaking hands, Duroy descended the staircase with a light heart.

CHAPTER IV.

DUROY LEARNS SOMETHING

Georges Duroy did not sleep well, so anxious was he to see his article in print. He rose at daybreak, and was on the street long before the newsboys. When he secured a paper and saw his name at the end of a column in large letters, he became very much excited. He felt inclined to enact the part of a newsboy and cry out to the hurrying throng: "Buy this! it contains an article by me!" He strolled along to a cafe and seated himself in order to read the article through; that done he decided to go to the railroad office, draw his salary, and hand in his resignation.

With great pomposity he informed the chief clerk that he was on the staff of "La Vie Francaise," and by that means was avenged for many petty insults which had been offered him. He then had some cards written with his new calling beneath his name, made several purchases, and repaired to the office of "La Vie Francaise." Forestier received him loftily as one would an inferior.

"Ah, here you are! Very well; I have several things for you to do. Just wait ten minutes till I finish this work." He continued writing.

At the other end of the table sat a short, pale man, very stout and bald. Forestier asked him, when his letter was completed, "Saint-Potin, at what time shall you interview those people?"

"At four o'clock."

"Take Duroy, who is here, with you and initiate him into the business."

"Very well."

Then turning to his friend, Forestier added: "Have you brought the other paper on Algeria? The article this morning was very successful."

Duroy stammered: "No, I thought I should have time this afternoon. I had so much to do—I could not."

The other shrugged his shoulders. "If you are not more careful, you will spoil your future. M. Walter counted on your copy. I will tell him it will be ready to-morrow. If you think you will be paid for doing nothing, you are mistaken." After a pause, he added: "You should strike while the iron is hot."

Saint-Potin rose: "I am ready," said he.

Forestier turned around in his chair and said, to Duroy: "Listen. The Chinese general Li-Theng-Fao, stopping at the Continental, and Rajah Taposahib Ramaderao Pali, stopping at Hotel Bishop, have been in Paris two days. You must interview them." Addressing Saint-Potin, he said: "Do not forget the principal points I indicated to you. Ask the general and the rajah their opinions on the dealings of England in the extreme East, their ideas of their system of colonization and government, their hopes relative to the intervention of Europe and of France in particular." To Duroy he said: "Observe what Saint-Potin says; he is an excellent reporter, and try to learn how to draw out a man in five minutes." Then he resumed his work.

The two men walked down the boulevard together, while Saint-Potin gave Duroy a sketch of all the officials connected with the paper, sparing no one in his criticism. When he mentioned Forestier, he said: "As for him, he was fortunate in marrying his wife."

Duroy asked: "What about his wife?"

Saint-Potin rubbed his hands. "Oh, she is beloved by an old fellow named Vaudrec—he dotes upon her."

Duroy felt as if he would like to box Saint-Potin's ears. To change the subject he said: "It seems to me that it is late, and we have two noble lords to call upon!"

Saint-Potin laughed: "You are very innocent! Do you think that I am going to interview that Chinese and that Indian? As if I did not know better than they do what they should think to please the readers of 'La Vie Francaise'! I have interviewed five hundred Chinese, Prussians, Hindoos, Chilians, and Japanese. They all say the same thing. I need only copy my article on the last comer, word for word, changing the heading, names, titles, and ages: in that there must be no error, or I shall be hauled over the coals by the 'Figaro' or 'Gaulois.' But on that subject the porter of the hotels will post me in five minutes. We will smoke our cigars and stroll in that direction. Total—one hundred sous for cabfare. That is the way, my dear fellow."

When they arrived at the Madeleine, Saint-Potin said to his companion: "If you have anything to do, I do not need you."

Duroy shook hands with him and walked away. The thought of the article he had to write that evening haunted him. Mentally he collected the material as he wended his way to the cafe at which he dined. Then he returned home and seated himself at his table to work. Before his eyes was the sheet of blank paper, but all the material he had amassed had escaped him. After trying for an hour, and after filling five pages with sentences which had no connection one with the other, he said: "I am not yet familiar with the work. I must take another lesson."

At ten o'clock the following morning he rang the bell, at his friend's house. The servant who opened the door, said: "Monsieur is busy."

Duroy had not expected to find Forestier at home. However he said: "Tell him it is M. Duroy on important business."

In the course of five minutes he was ushered into the room in which he had spent so happy a morning. In the place Mme. Forestier had occupied, her husband was seated writing, while Mme. Forestier stood by the mantelpiece and dictated to him, a cigarette between her lips.

Duroy paused upon the threshold and murmured: "I beg your pardon, I am interrupting you."

His friend growled angrily: "What do you want again? Make haste; we are busy."

Georges stammered: "It is nothing."

But Forestier persisted: "Come, we are losing time; you did not force your way into the house for the pleasure of bidding us good morning."

Duroy, in confusion, replied: "No, it is this: I cannot complete my article, and you were—so—so kind the last time that I hoped—that I dared to come—"

Forestier interrupted with: "So you think I will do your work and that you have only to take the money. Well, that is fine!" His wife smoked on without interfering.

Duroy hesitated: "Excuse me. I believed—I—thought—" Then, in a clear voice, he said: "I beg a thousand pardons, Madame, and thank you very much for the charming article you wrote for me yesterday." Then he bowed, and said to Charles: "I will be at the office at three o'clock."

He returned home saying to himself: "Very well, I will write it alone and they shall see." Scarcely had he entered than he began to write, anger spurring him on. In an hour he had finished an article, which was a chaos of absurd matter, and took it boldly to the office. Duroy handed Forestier his manuscript. "Here is the rest of Algeria."

"Very well, I will hand it to the manager. That will do."

When Duroy and Saint-Potin, who had some political information to look up, were in the hall, the latter asked: "Have you been to the cashier's room?"

"No, why?"

"Why? To get your pay? You should always get your salary a month in advance. One cannot tell what might happen. I will introduce you to the cashier."

Duroy drew his two hundred francs together with twenty-eight francs for his article of the preceding day, which, in addition to what remained to him of his salary from the railroad office, left him three hundred and forty francs. He had never had so much, and he thought himself rich for an indefinite time. Saint-Potin took him to the offices of four or five rival papers, hoping that the news he had been commissioned to obtain had been already received by them and that he could obtain it by means of his diplomacy.

When evening came, Duroy, who had nothing more to do, turned toward the Folies-Bergeres, and walking up to the office, he said: "My name is Georges Duroy. I am on the staff of 'La Vie Francaise.' I was here the other night with M. Forestier, who promised to get me a pass. I do not know if he remembered it."

The register was consulted, but his name was not inscribed upon it. However, the cashier, a very affable man, said to him: "Come in, M. Duroy, and speak to the manager yourself; he will see that everything is all right."

He entered and almost at once came upon Rachel, the woman he had seen there before. She approached him: "Good evening, my dear; are you well?"

"Very well; how are you?"

"I am not ill. I have dreamed of you twice since the other night."

Duroy smiled. "What does that mean?"

"That means that I like you"; she raised her eyes to the young man's face, took his arm and leaning upon it, said: "Let us drink a glass of wine and then take a walk. I should like to go to the opera like this, with you, to show you off."

At daybreak he again sallied forth to obtain a "Vie Francaise." He opened the paper feverishly; his article was not there. On entering the office several hours later, he said to M. Walter: "I was very much surprised this morning not to see my second article on Algeria."

The manager raised his head and said sharply: "I gave it to your friend, Forestier, and asked him to read it; he was dissatisfied with it; it will have to be done over."

Without a word, Duroy left the room, and entering his friend's office, brusquely asked: "Why did not my article appear this morning?"

The journalist, who was smoking a cigar, said calmly: "The manager did not consider it good, and bade me return it to you to be revised. There it is." Duroy revised it several times, only to have it rejected. He said nothing more of his "souvenirs," but gave his whole attention to reporting. He became acquainted behind the scenes at the theaters, and in the halls and corridors of the chamber of deputies; he knew all the cabinet ministers, generals, police agents, princes, ambassadors, men of the world, Greeks, cabmen, waiters at cafes, and many others. In short he soon became a remarkable reporter, of great value to the paper, so M. Walter said. But as he only received ten centimes a line in addition to his fixed salary of two hundred francs and as his expenses were large, he never had a sou. When he saw certain of his associates with their pockets full of money, he wondered what secret means they employed in order to obtain it. He determined to penetrate that mystery, to enter into the association, to obtrude himself upon his comrades, and make them share with him. Often at evening, as he watched the trains pass his window, he dreamed of the conduct he might pursue.

CHAPTER V.

THE FIRST INTRIGUE

Two months elapsed. It was September. The fortune which Duroy had hoped to make so rapidly seemed to him slow in coming. Above all he was dissatisfied with the mediocrity of his position; he was appreciated, but was treated according to his rank. Forestier himself no longer invited him to dinner, and treated him as an inferior. Often he had thought of making Mme. Forestier a visit, but the remembrance of their last meeting restrained him. Mme. de Marelle had invited him to call, saying: "I am always at home about three o'clock." So one afternoon, when he had nothing to do, he proceeded toward her house. She lived on Rue Verneuil, on the fourth floor. A maid answered his summons, and said: "Yes, Madame is at home, but I do not know whether she has risen." She conducted Duroy into the drawing-room, which was large, poorly furnished, and somewhat untidy. The shabby, threadbare chairs were ranged along the walls according to the servant's fancy, for there was not a trace visible of the care of a woman who loves her home. Duroy took a seat and waited some time. Then a door opened and Mme. de Marelle entered hastily, clad in a Japanese dressing-gown. She exclaimed:

"How kind of you to come to see me. I was positive you had forgotten me." She held out her hand to him with a gesture of delight; and Duroy, quite at his ease in that shabby apartment, kissed it as he had seen Norbert de Varenne do.

Examining him from head to foot, she cried: "How you have changed! Well; tell me the news."

They began to chat at once as if they were old acquaintances, and in five minutes an intimacy, a mutual understanding, was established between those two beings alike in character and kind. Suddenly the young woman said in surprise: "It is astonishing how I feel with you. It seems to me as if I had known you ten years. We shall undoubtedly become good friends; would that please you?"

He replied: "Certainly," with a smile more expressive than words. He thought her very bewitching in her pretty gown. When near Mme. Forestier, whose impassive, gracious smile attracted yet held at a distance, and seemed to say: "I like you, yet take care," he felt a desire to cast himself at her feet, or to kiss the hem of her garment. When near Mme. de Marelle, he felt a more passionate desire.

A gentle rap came at the door through which Mme. de Marelle had entered, and she cried: "You may come in, my darling."

The child entered, advanced to Duroy and offered him her hand. The astonished mother murmured: "That is a conquest." The young man, having kissed the child, seated her by his side, and with a serious air questioned her as to what she had done since they last met. She replied in a flute-like voice and with the manner of a woman. The clock struck three; the journalist rose.

"Come often," said Mme. de Marelle; "it has been a pleasant causerie. I shall always be glad to welcome you. Why do I never meet you at the Forestiers?"

"For no particular reason. I am very busy. I hope, however, that we shall meet there one of these days."

In the course of a few days he paid another visit to the enchantress. The maid ushered him into the drawing-room and Laurine soon entered; she offered him not her hand but her forehead, and said: "Mamma wishes me to ask you to wait for her about fifteen minutes, for she is not dressed. I will keep you company."

Duroy, who was amused at the child's ceremonious manner, replied: "Indeed, Mademoiselle, I shall be enchanted to spend a quarter of an hour with you." When the mother entered they were in the midst of an exciting game, and Mme. de Marelle paused in amazement, crying: "Laurine playing? You are a sorcerer, sir!" He placed the child, whom he had caught in his arms, upon the floor, kissed the lady's hand, and they seated themselves, the child between them. They tried to converse, but Laurine, usually so silent, monopolized the conversation, and her mother was compelled to send her to her room.

When they were alone, Mme. de Marelle lowered her voice and said: "I have a great project. It is this: As I dine every week at the Foresters', I return it from time to time by inviting them to a restaurant. I do not like to have company at home; I am not so situated that I can have any. I know nothing about housekeeping or cooking. I prefer a life free from care; therefore I invite them to the cafe occasionally; but it is not lively when we are only three. I am telling you this in order to explain such an informal gathering. I should like you to be present at our Saturdays at the Cafe Riche at seven-thirty. Do you know the house?"

Duroy accepted gladly. He left her in a transport of delight and impatiently awaited the day of the dinner. He was the first to arrive at the place appointed and was shown into a small private room, in which the table was laid for four; that table looked very inviting with its colored glasses, silver, and candelabra.

Duroy seated himself upon a low bench. Forestier entered and shook hands with him with a cordiality he never evinced at the office.

"The two ladies will come together," said he. "These dinners are truly delightful."

Very soon the door opened and Mesdames Forestier and De Marelle appeared, heavily veiled, surrounded by the charming mystery necessary to a rendezvous in a place so public. As Duroy greeted the former, she took him to task for not having been to see her; then she added with a smile: "Ah, you prefer Mme. de Marelle; the time passes more pleasantly with her."

When the waiter handed the wine-list to Forestier, Mme. de Marelle exclaimed: "Bring the gentle-men whatever they want; as for us, we want nothing but champagne."

Forestier, who seemed not to have heard her, asked: "Do you object to my closing the window? My cough has troubled me for several days."

"Not at all."

His wife did not speak. The various courses were duly served and then the guests began to chat. They discussed a scandal which was being circulated about a society belle. Forestier was very much amused by it. Duroy said with a smile: "How many would abandon themselves to a caprice, a dream of love, if they did not fear that they would pay for a brief happiness with tears and an irremediable scandal?"

Both women glanced at him approvingly. Forestier cried with a sceptical laugh: "The poor husbands!" Then they talked of love. Duroy said: "When I love a woman, everything else in the world is forgotten."

Mme. Forestier murmured: "There is no happiness comparable to that first clasp of the hand, when one asks: 'Do you love me?' and the other replies: 'Yes, I love you.'" Mme. de Marelle cried gaily as she drank a glass of champagne: "I am less Platonic."

Forestier, lying upon the couch, said in serious tone: "That frankness does you honor and proves you to be a practical woman. But might one ask, what is M. de Marelle's opinion?"

She shrugged her shoulders disdainfully and said: "M. de Marelle has no opinion on that subject."

The conversation grew slow. Mme. de Marelle seemed to offer provocation by her remarks, while Mme. Forestier's charming reserve, the modesty in her voice, in her smile, all seemed to extenuate the bold sallies which issued from her lips. The dessert came and then followed the coffee. The hostess and her guests lighted cigarettes, but Forestier suddenly began to cough. When the attack was over, he growled angrily: "These parties are not good for me; they are stupid. Let us go home."

Mme. de Marelle summoned the waiter and asked for her bill. She tried to read it, but the figures danced before her eyes; she handed the paper to Duroy.

"Here, pay it for me; I cannot see." At the same time, she put her purse in his hand.

The total was one hundred and thirty francs. Duroy glanced at the bill and when it was settled, whispered: "How much shall I give the waiter?"

"Whatever you like; I do not know."

He laid five francs upon the plate and handed the purse to its owner, saying: "Shall I escort you home?"

"Certainly; I am unable to find the house."

They shook hands with the Forestiers and were soon rolling along in a cab side by side. Duroy could think of nothing to say; he felt impelled to clasp her in his arms. "If I should dare, what would she do?" thought he. The recollection of their conversation at dinner emboldened, but the fear of scandal restrained him. Mme. de Marelle reclined silently in her corner. He would have thought her asleep, had he not seen her eyes glisten whenever a ray of light penetrated the dark recesses of the carriage. Of what was she thinking? Suddenly she moved her foot, nervously, impatiently. That movement caused him to tremble, and turning quickly, he cast himself upon her, seeking her lips with his. She uttered a cry, attempted to repulse him and then yielded to his caresses as if she had not the strength to resist.

The carriage stopped at her door, but she did not rise; she did not move, stunned by what had just taken place. Fearing that the cabman would mistrust something, Duroy alighted from the cab first and offered his hand to the young woman. Finally she got out, but in silence. Georges rang the bell, and when the door was opened, he asked timidly: "When shall I see you again?"

She whispered so low that he could barely hear her: "Come and lunch with me to-morrow." With those words she disappeared.

Duroy gave the cabman a five-franc piece, and turned away with a triumphant, joyful air. He had at last conquered a married woman! A woman of the world! A Parisian! How easy it had been!

He was somewhat nervous the following day as he ascended Mme. de Marelle's staircase. How would she receive him? Suppose she forbade him to enter her house? If she had told—but no, she could not tell anything without telling the whole truth! He was master of the situation!

The little maid-servant opened the door. She was as pleasant as usual. Duroy felt reassured and asked: "Is Madame well?"

"Yes, sir; as well as she always is," was the reply, and he was ushered into the salon. He walked to the mantelpiece to see what kind of an appearance he presented: he was readjusting his cravat when he saw in the mirror the young woman standing on the threshold looking at him. He pretended not to have seen her, and for several moments they gazed at one another in the mirror. Then he turned. She had not moved; she seemed to be waiting. He rushed toward her crying: "How I love you!" He clasped her to his breast. He thought: "It is easier than I thought it would be. All is well." He looked at her with a smile, without uttering a word, trying to put into his glance a wealth of love. She too smiled and murmured: "We are alone. I sent Laurine to lunch with a friend."

He sighed, and kissing her wrists said: "Thanks; I adore you." She took his arm as if he had been her husband, and led him to a couch, upon which they seated themselves side by side. Duroy stammered, incoherently: "You do not care for me."

She laid her hand upon his lips. "Be silent!"

"How I love you!" said he.

She repeated: "Be silent!"

They could hear the servant laying the table in the dining-room. He rose: "I cannot sit so near you. I shall lose my head."

The door opened: "Madame is served!"

He offered her his arm gravely. They lunched without knowing what they were eating. The servant came and went without seeming to notice anything. When the meal was finished, they returned to the drawing-room and resumed their seats on the couch side by side. Gradually he drew nearer her and tried to embrace her.

"Be careful, some one might come in."

He whispered: "When can I see you alone to tell you how I love you?"

She leaned toward him and said softly: "I will pay you a visit one of these days."

He colored. "My rooms—are—are—very modest."

She smiled: "That makes no difference. I shall come to see you and not your rooms."

He urged her to tell him when she would come. She fixed a day in the following week, while he besought her with glowing eyes to hasten the day. She was amused to see him implore so ardently and yielded a day at a time. He repeated: "To-morrow, say—to-morrow." Finally she consented. "Yes, to-morrow at five o'clock."

He drew a deep breath; then they chatted together as calmly as if they had known one another for twenty years. A ring caused them to start; they separated. She murmured: "It is Laurine."

The child entered, paused in surprise, then ran toward Duroy clapping her hands, delighted to see him, and crying: "Ah, 'Bel-Ami!'"

Mme. de Marelle laughed. "Bel-Ami! Laurine has christened you. It is a pretty name. I shall call you Bel-Ami, too!"

He took the child upon his knee. At twenty minutes of three he rose to go to the office; at the half-open door he whispered: "To-morrow, five o'clock." The young woman replied: "Yes," with a smile and disappeared.

After he had finished his journalistic work, he tried to render his apartments more fit to receive his expected visitor. He was well satisfied with the results of his efforts and retired, lulled to rest by the whistling of the trains. Early the next morning he bought a cake and a bottle of Madeira. He spread the collation on his dressing-table which was covered with a napkin. Then he waited. She came at a quarter past five and exclaimed as she entered: "Why, it is nice here. But there were a great many people on the stairs."

He took her in his arms and kissed her hair. An hour and a half later he escorted her to a cab-stand on the Rue de Rome. When she was seated in the cab, he whispered: "Tuesday, at the same hour."

She repeated his words, and as it was night, she kissed him. Then as the cabman started up his horse, she cried: "Adieu, Bel-Ami!" and the old coupe rumbled off.

For three weeks Duroy received Mme. de Marelle every two or three days, sometimes in the morning, sometimes in the evening.

As he was awaiting her one afternoon, a noise on the staircase drew him to his door. A child screamed. A man's angry voice cried: "What is the brat howling about?"

A woman's voice replied: "Nicolas has been tripped up on the landing-place by the journalist's sweetheart."

Duroy retreated, for he heard the rustling of skirts. Soon there was a knock at his door, which he opened, and Mme. de Marelle rushed in, crying: "Did you hear?" Georges feigned ignorance of the matter.

"No; what?"

"How they insulted me?"

"Who?"

"Those miserable people below."

"Why, no; what is it? Tell me."

She sobbed and could not speak. He was forced to place her upon his bed and to lay a damp cloth upon her temples. When she grew calmer, anger succeeded her agitation. She wanted Duroy to go downstairs at once, to fight them, to kill them.

He replied: "They are working-people. Just think, it would be necessary to go to court where you would be recognized; one must not compromise oneself with such people."

She said: "What shall we do? I cannot come here again."

He replied: "That is very simple. I will move."

She murmured: "Yes, but that will take some time."

Suddenly she said: "Listen to me, I have found a means; do not worry about it. I will send you a 'little blue' to-morrow morning." She called a telegram a "little blue."

She smiled with delight at her plans, which she would not reveal. She was, however, very much affected as she descended the staircase and leaned with all her strength upon her lover's arm. They met no one.

He was still in bed the following morning when the promised telegram was handed him. Duroy opened it and read:

"Come at five o'clock to Rue de Constantinople, No. 127. Ask
for the room rented by Mme. Duroy. CLO."

At five o'clock precisely he entered a large furnished house and asked the janitor: "Has Mme. Duroy hired a room here?"

"Yes, sir."

"Will you show me to it, if you please?"

The man, accustomed no doubt to situations in which it was necessary to be prudent, looked him straight in the eyes; then selecting a key, he asked: "Are you M. Duroy?"

"Certainly."

He opened a small suite, comprising two rooms on the ground floor.

Duroy thought uneasily: "This will cost a fortune. I shall have to run into debt. She has done a very foolish thing."

The door opened and Clotilde rushed in. She was enchanted. "Is it not fine? There are no stairs to climb; it is on the ground floor! One could come and go through the window without the porter seeing one."

He embraced her nervously, not daring to ask the question that hovered upon his lips. She had placed a large package on the stand in the center of the room. Opening it she took out a tablet of soap, a bottle of Lubin's extract, a sponge, a box of hairpins, a button-hook, and curling-tongs. Then she amused herself by finding places in which to put them.

She talked incessantly as she opened the drawers: "I must bring some linen in order to have a change. We shall each have a key, besides the one at the lodge, in case we should forget ours. I rented the apartments for three months—in your name, of course, for I could not give mine."

Then he asked: "Will you tell me when to pay?"

She replied simply: "It is paid, my dear."

He made a pretense of being angry: "I cannot permit that."

She laid her hand upon his shoulder and said in a supplicatory tone: "Georges, it will give me pleasure to have the nest mine. Say that you do not care, dear Georges," and he yielded.

When she had left him, he murmured: "She is kind-hearted, anyway."

Several days later he received a telegram which read:

"My husband is coming home this evening. We shall therefore not meet for a week. What a bore, my dearest!"

"YOUR CLO."

Duroy was startled; he had not realized the fact that Mme. de Marelle was married. He impatiently awaited her husband's departure. One morning he received the following telegram:

"Five o'clock.—CLO."

When they met, she rushed into his arms, kissed him passionately, and asked: "After a while will you take me to dine?"

"Certainly, my darling, wherever you wish to go."

"I should like to go to some restaurant frequented by the working-classes."

They repaired to a wine merchant's where meals were also served. Clotilde's entrance caused a sensation on account of the elegance of her dress. They partook of a ragout of mutton and left that place to enter a ball-room in which she pressed more closely to his side. In fifteen minutes her curiosity was satisfied and he conducted her home. Then followed a series of visits to all sorts of places of amusement. Duroy soon began to tire of those expeditions, for he had exhausted all his resources and all means of obtaining money. In addition to that he owed Forestier a hundred francs, Jacques Rival three hundred, and he was hampered with innumerable petty debts ranging from twenty francs to one hundred sous.

On the fourteenth of December, he was left without a sou in his pocket. As he had often done before, he did not lunch, and spent the afternoon working at the office. At four o'clock he received a telegram from Mme. de Marelle, saying: "Shall we dine together and afterward have a frolic?"

He replied at once: "Impossible to dine," then he added: "But I will expect you at our apartments at nine o'clock." Having sent a boy with the note in order to save the money for a telegram, he tried to think of some way by which he could obtain his evening meal. He waited until all of his associates had gone and when he was alone, he rang for the porter, put his hand in his pocket and said: "Foucart, I have left my purse at home and I have to dine at the Luxembourg. Lend me fifty sous to pay for my cab."

The man handed him three francs and asked:

"Is that enough?"

"Yes, thank you." Taking the coins, Duroy rushed down the staircase and dined at a cookshop.

At nine o'clock, Mme. de Marelle, whom he awaited in the tiny salon, arrived. She wished to take a walk and he objected. His opposition irritated her.

"I shall go alone, then. Adieu!"

Seeing that the situation was becoming grave, he seized her hands and kissed them, saying:

"Pardon me, darling; I am nervous and out of sorts this evening. I have been annoyed by business matters."

Somewhat appeased but still, vexed, she replied:

"That does not concern me; I will not be the butt for your ill humor."

He clasped her in his arms and murmured his apologies. Still she persisted in her desire to go out.

"I beseech you, remain here by the fire with me. Say yes."

"No," she replied, "I will not yield to your caprices."

He insisted: "I have a reason, a serious reason—"

"If you will not go with me, I shall go alone. Adieu!"

She disengaged herself from his embrace and fled to the door. He followed her:

"Listen Clo, my little Clo, listen to me—"

She shook her head, evaded his caresses and tried to escape from his encircling arms.

"I have a reason—"

Looking him in the face, she said: "You lie! What is it?"

He colored, and in order to avoid a rupture, confessed in accents of despair: "I have no money!"

She would not believe him until he had turned all his pockets inside out, to prove his words. Then she fell upon his breast: "Oh, my poor darling! Had I known! How did it happen?"

He invented a touching story to this effect: That his father was in straitened circumstances, that he had given him not only his savings, but had run himself into debt.

"I shall have to starve for the next six months."

"Shall I lend you some?" she whispered.

He replied with dignity: "You are very kind, dearest; but do not mention that again; it wounds me."

She murmured: "You will never know how much I love you." On taking leave of him, she asked: "Shall we meet again the day after to-morrow?"

"Certainly."

"At the same time?"

"Yes, my darling."

They parted.

When Duroy opened his bedroom door and fumbled in his vest pocket for a match, he was amazed to find in it a piece of money—a twenty-franc piece! At first he wondered by what miracle it had got there; suddenly it occurred to him that Mme. de Marelle had given him alms! Angry and humiliated, he determined to return it when next they met. The next morning it was late when he awoke; he tried to overcome his hunger. He went out and as he passed the restaurants he could scarcely resist their temptations. At noon he said: "Bah, I shall lunch upon Clotilde's twenty francs; that will not hinder me from returning the money to-morrow."

He ate his lunch, for which he paid two francs fifty, and on entering the office of "La Vie Francaise" he repaid the porter the three francs he had borrowed from him. He worked until seven o'clock, then he dined, and he continued to draw upon the twenty francs until only four francs twenty remained. He decided to say to Mme. de Marelle upon her arrival:

"I found the twenty-franc piece you slipped into my pocket. I will not return the money to-day, but I will repay you when we next meet."

When Madame came, he dared not broach the delicate subject. They spent the evening together and appointed their next meeting for Wednesday of the following week, for Mme. de Marelle had a number of engagements. Duroy continued to accept money from Clotilde and quieted his conscience by assuring himself: "I will give it back in a lump. It is nothing but borrowed money anyway." So he kept account of all that he received in order to pay it back some day.

One evening, Mme. de Marelle said to him: "Would you believe that I have never been to the Folies-Bergeres; will you take me there?"

He hesitated, fearing a meeting with Rachel. Then he thought: "Bah, I am not married after all. If she should see me, she would take in the situation and not accost me. Moreover, we would have a box."

When they entered the hall, it was crowded; with difficulty they made their way to their seats. Mme. de Marelle did not look at the stage; she was interested in watching the women who were promenading, and she felt an irresistible desire to touch them, to see of what those beings were made. Suddenly she said:

"There is a large brunette who stares at us all the time. I think every minute she will speak to us. Have you seen her?"

He replied: "No, you are mistaken."

He told an untruth, for he had noticed the woman, who was no other than Rachel, with anger in her eyes and violent words upon her lips.

Duroy had passed her when he and Mme. de Marelle entered and she had said to him: "Good evening," in a low voice and with a wink which said "I understand." But he had not replied; for fear of being seen by his sweetheart he passed her coldly, disdainfully. The woman, her jealousy aroused, followed the couple and said in a louder key: "Good evening, Georges." He paid no heed to her. Then she was determined to be recognized and she remained near their box, awaiting a favorable moment. When she saw that she was observed by Mme. de Marelle, she touched Duroy's shoulder with the tip of her finger, and said:

"Good evening. How are you?"

But Georges did not turn his head.

She continued: "Have you grown deaf since Thursday?"

Still he did not reply. She laughed angrily and cried:

"Are you dumb, too? Perhaps Madame has your tongue?"

With a furious glance, Duroy then exclaimed:

"How dare you accost me? Go along or I will have you arrested."

With flaming eyes, she cried: "Ah, is that so! Because you are with another is no reason that you cannot recognize me. If you had made the least sign of recognition when you passed me, I would not have molested you. You did not even say good evening to me when you met me."

During that tirade Mme. de Marelle in affright opened the door of the box and fled through the crowd seeking an exit. Duroy rushed after her. Rachel, seeing him disappear, cried: "Stop her! she has stolen my lover!"

Two men seized the fugitive by the shoulder, but Duroy, who had caught up with her, bade them desist, and together he and Clotilde reached the street.

They entered a cab. The cabman asked: "Where shall I drive to?" Duroy replied: "Where you will!"

Clotilde sobbed hysterically. Duroy did not know what to say or do. At length he stammered:

"Listen Clo—my dearest Clo, let me explain. It is not my fault. I knew that woman—long ago—"

She raised her head and with the fury of a betrayed woman, she cried disconnectedly: "Ah, you miserable fellow—what a rascal you are! Is it possible? What disgrace, oh, my God! You gave her my money—did you not? I gave him the money—for that woman—oh, the wretch!"

For several moments she seemed to be vainly seeking an epithet more forcible. Suddenly leaning forward she grasped the cabman's sleeve. "Stop!" she cried, and opening the door, she alighted. Georges was about to follow her but she commanded: "I forbid you to follow me," in a voice so loud that the passers-by crowded around her, and Duroy dared not stir for fear of a scandal.

She drew out her purse, and taking two francs fifty from it, she handed it to the cabman, saying aloud: "Here is the money for your hour. Take that rascal to Rue Boursault at Batignolles!"

The crowd applauded; one man said: "Bravo, little one!" and the cab moved on, followed by the jeers of the bystanders.

CHAPTER VI.

A STEP UPWARD

The next morning Georges Duroy arose, dressed himself, and determined to have money; he sought Forestier. His friend received him in his study.

"What made you rise so early?" he asked.

"A very serious matter. I have a debt of honor."

"A gaming debt?"

He hesitated, then repeated: "A gaming debt."

"Is it large?"

"Five hundred francs." He only needed two hundred and eighty.

Forestier asked sceptically: "To whom do you owe that amount?"

Duroy did not reply at once. "To—to—a—M. de Carleville."

"Ah, where does he live?"

"Rue—Rue—"

Forestier laughed. "I know the gentleman! If you want twenty francs you can have them, but no more."

Duroy took the gold-piece, called upon more friends, and by five o'clock had collected eighty francs. As he required two hundred more, he kept what he had begged and muttered: "I shall not worry about it. I will pay it when I can."

For two weeks he lived economically, but at the end of that time, the good resolutions he had formed vanished, and one evening he returned to the Folies Bergeres in search of Rachel; but the woman was implacable and heaped coarse insults upon him, until he felt his cheeks tingle and he left the hall.

Forestier, out of health and feeble, made Duroy's existence at the office insupportable. The latter did not reply to his rude remarks, but determined to be avenged. He called upon Mme. Forestier. He found her reclining upon a couch, reading. She held out her hand without rising and said: "Good morning, Bel-Ami!"

"Why do you call me by that name?"

She replied with a smile: "I saw Mme. de Marelle last week and I know what they have christened you at her house."

He took a seat near his hostess and glanced at her curiously; she was a charming blonde, fair and plump, made for caresses, and he thought: "She is certainly nicer than the other one." He did not doubt that he would only have to extend his hand in order to gather the fruit. As he gazed upon her she chided him for his neglect of her.

He replied: "I did not come because it was for the best—"

"How? Why?"

"Why? Can you not guess?"

"No!"

"Because I loved you; a little, only a little, and I did not wish to love you any more."

She did not seem surprised, nor flattered; she smiled indifferently and replied calmly: "Oh, you can come just the same; no one loves me long."

"Why not?"

"Because it is useless, and I tell them so at once. If you had confessed your fears to me sooner, I would have reassured you. My dear friend, a man in love is not only foolish but dangerous. I cease all intercourse with people who love me or pretend to; firstly, because they bore me, and secondly, because I look upon them with dread, as I would upon a mad dog. I know that your love is only a kind of appetite; while with me it would be a communion of souls. Now, look me in the face—" she no longer smiled. "I will never be your sweetheart; it is therefore useless for you to persist in your efforts. And now that I have explained, shall we be friends?"

He knew that that sentence was irrevocable, and delighted to be able to form such an alliance as she proposed, he extended both hands, saying:

"I am yours, Madame, to do with as you will"

He kissed her hands and raising his head said: "If I had found a woman like you, how gladly would I have married her."

She was touched by those words, and in a soft voice, placing her hand upon his arm, she said: "I am going to begin my offices at once. You are not diplomatic—" she hesitated. "May I speak freely?"

"Yes."

"Call upon Mme. Walter who has taken a fancy to you. But be guarded as to your compliments, for she is virtuous. You will make a better impression there by being careful in your remarks. I know that your position at the office is unsatisfactory, but do not worry; all their employees are treated alike."

He said: "Thanks; you are an angel—a guardian angel."

As he took his leave, he asked again: "Are we friends—is it settled?"

"It is."

Having observed the effect of his last compliment, he said: "If you ever become a widow, I have put in my application!" Then he left the room hastily in order not to allow her time to be angry.

Duroy did not like to call on Mme. Walter, for he had never been invited, and he did not wish to commit a breach of etiquette. The manager had been kind to him, appreciated his services, employed him to do difficult work, why should he not profit by that show of favor to call at his house? One day, therefore, he repaired to the market and bought twenty-five pears. Having carefully arranged them in a basket to make them appear as if they came from a distance he took them to Mme. Walter's door with his card on which was inscribed:

"Georges Duroy begs Mme. Walter to accept the fruit which he received this morning from Normandy."

The following day he found in his letter-box at the office an envelope containing Mme, Walter's card on which was written:

"Mme. Walter thanks M. Georges Duroy very much, and is at home on Saturdays."

The next Saturday he called. M. Walter lived on Boulevard Malesherbes in a double house which he owned. The reception-rooms were on the first floor. In the antechamber were two footmen; one took Duroy's overcoat, the other his cane, put it aside, opened a door and announced the visitor's name. In the large mirror in the apartment Duroy could see the reflection of people seated in another room. He passed through two drawing-rooms and entered a small boudoir in which four ladies were gathered around a tea-table. Notwithstanding the assurance he had gained during his life in Paris, and especially since he had been thrown in contact with so many noted personages, Duroy felt abashed. He stammered:

"Madame, I took the liberty."

The mistress of the house extended her hand and said to him: "You are very kind, M. Duroy, to come to see me." She pointed to a chair. The ladies chatted on. Visitors came and went. Mme. Walter noticed that Duroy said nothing, that no one addressed him, that he seemed disconcerted, and she drew him into the conversation which dealt with the admission of a certain M. Linet to the Academy. When Duroy had taken his leave, one of the ladies said: "How odd he is! Who is he?"

Mme. Walter replied: "One of our reporters; he only occupies a minor position, but I think he will advance rapidly."

In the meantime, while he was being discussed, Duroy walked gaily down Boulevard Malesherbes.

The following week he was appointed editor of the "Echoes," and invited to dine at Mme. Walter's. The "Echoes" were, M. Walter said, the very pith of the paper. Everything and everybody should be remembered, all countries, all professions, Paris and the provinces, the army, the arts, the clergy, the schools, the rulers, and the courtiers. The man at the head of that department should be wide awake, always on his guard, quick to judge of what was best to be said and best to be omitted, to divine what would please the public and to present it well. Duroy was just the man for the place.

He was enjoying the fact of his promotion, when he received an engraved card which read:

"M. and Mme. Walter request the pleasure of M. Georges Duroy's company at dinner on Thursday, January 20."

He was so delighted that he kissed the invitation as if it had been a love-letter.

Then he sought the cashier to settle the important question of his salary. At first twelve hundred francs were allowed Duroy, who intended to save a large share of the money. He was busy two days getting settled in his new position, in a large room, one end of which he occupied, and the other end of which was allotted to Boisrenard, who worked with him.

The day of the dinner-party he left the office in good season, in order to have time to dress, and was walking along Rue de Londres when he saw before him a form which resembled Mme. de Marelle's. He felt his cheeks glow and his heart throb. He crossed the street in order to see the lady's face; he was mistaken, and breathed more freely. He had often wondered what he should do if he met Clotilde face to face. Should he bow to her or pretend not to see her? "I should not see her," thought he.

When Duroy entered his rooms he thought: "I must change my apartments; these will not do any longer." He felt both nervous and gay, and said aloud to himself: "I must write to my father." Occasionally he wrote home, and his letters always delighted his old parents. As he tied his cravat at the mirror he repeated: "I must write home to-morrow. If my father could see me this evening in the house to which I am going, he would be surprised. Sacristi, I shall soon give a dinner which has never been equaled!"

Then he recalled his old home, the faces of his father and mother. He saw them seated at their homely board, eating their soup. He remembered every wrinkle on their old faces, every movement of their hands and heads; he even knew what they said to each other every evening as they supped. He thought: "I will go to see them some day." His toilette completed, he extinguished his light and descended the stairs.

On reaching his destination, he boldly entered the antechamber, lighted by bronze lamps, and gave his cane and his overcoat to the two lackeys who approached him. All the salons were lighted. Mme. Walter received in the second, the largest. She greeted Duroy with a charming smile, and he shook hands with two men who arrived after him, M. Firmin and M. Laroche-Mathieu; the latter had especial authority at the office on account of his influence in the chamber of deputies.

Then the Forestiers arrived, Madeleine looking charming in pink. Charles had become very much emaciated and coughed incessantly.

Norbert de Varenne and Jacques Rival came together. A door opened at the end of the room, and M. Walter entered with two tall young girls of sixteen and seventeen; one plain, the other pretty. Duroy knew that the manager was a paterfamilias, but he was astonished. He had thought of the manager's daughters as one thinks of a distant country one will never see. Then, too, he had fancied them children, and he saw women. They shook hands upon being introduced and seated themselves at a table set apart for them. One of the guests had not arrived, and that embarrassing silence which precedes dinners in general reigned supreme.

Duroy happening to glance at the walls, M. Walter said: "You are looking at my pictures? I will show them all to you." And he took a lamp that they might distinguish all the details. There were landscapes by Guillemet; "A Visit to the Hospital," by Gervex; "A Widow," by Bouguereau; "An Execution," by Jean Paul Laurens, and many others.

Duroy exclaimed: "Charming, charming, char—" but stopped short on hearing behind him the voice of Mme. de Marelle who had just entered. M. Walter continued to exhibit and explain his pictures; but Duroy saw nothing—heard without comprehending. Mme. de Marelle was there, behind him. What should he do? If he greeted her, might she not turn her back upon him or utter some insulting remark? If he did not approach her, what would people think? He was so ill at ease that at one time he thought he should feign indisposition and return home.

The pictures had all been exhibited. M. Walter placed the lamp on the table and greeted the last arrival, while Duroy recommenced alone an examination of the canvas, as if he could not tear himself away. What should he do? He heard their voices and their conversation. Mme. Forestier called him; he hastened toward her. It was to introduce him to a friend who was on the point of giving a fete, and who wanted a description of it in "La Vie Francaise."

He stammered: "Certainly, Madame, certainly."

Madame de Marelle was very near him; he dared not turn to go away. Suddenly to his amazement, she exclaimed: "Good evening, Bel-Ami; do you not remember me?"

He turned upon his heel hastily; she stood before him smiling, her eyes overflowing with roguishness and affection. She offered him her hand; he took it doubtfully, fearing some perfidy. She continued calmly: "What has become of you? One never sees you!"

Not having regained his self-possession, he murmured: "I have had a great deal to do, Madame, a great deal to do. M. Walter has given me another position and the duties are very arduous."

"I know, but that is no excuse for forgetting your friends."

Their conversation was interrupted by the entrance of a large woman, decollette, with red arms, red cheeks, and attired in gay colors. As she was received with effusion, Duroy asked Mme. Forestier: "Who is that person?"

"Viscountess de Percemur, whose nom de plume is 'Patte Blanche.'"

He was surprised and with difficulty restrained a burst of laughter.

"Patte Blanche? I fancied her a young woman like you. Is that Patte Blanche? Ah, she is handsome, very handsome!"

A servant appeared at the door and announced: "Madame is served."

Duroy was placed between the manager's plain daughter, Mlle. Rose, and Mme. de Marelle. The proximity of the latter embarrassed him somewhat, although she appeared at ease and conversed with her usual spirit. Gradually, however, his assurance returned, and before the meal was over, he knew that their relations would be renewed. Wishing, too, to be polite to his employer's daughter, he addressed her from time to time. She responded as her mother would have done, without any hesitation as to what she should say. At M. Walter's right sat Viscountess de Percemur, and Duroy, looking at her with a smile, asked Mme. de Marelle in a low voice: "Do you know the one who signs herself 'Domino Rose'?"

"Yes, perfectly; Baroness de Livar."

"Is she like the Countess?"

"No. But she is just as comical. She is sixty years old, has false curls and teeth, wit of the time of the Restoration, and toilettes of the same period."

When the guests returned to the drawing-room, Duroy asked Mme. de Marelle: "May I escort you home?"

"No."

"Why not?"

"Because M. Laroche-Mathieu, who is my neighbor, leaves me at my door every time that

I dine here."

"When shall I see you again?"

"Lunch with me to-morrow."

They parted without another word. Duroy did not remain late; as he descended the staircase, he met Norbert de Varenne, who was likewise going away. The old poet took his arm; fearing no rivalry on the newspaper, their work being essentially different, he was very friendly to the young man.

"Shall we walk along together?"

"I shall be pleased to," replied Duroy.

The streets were almost deserted that night. At first the two men did not speak. Then Duroy, in order to make some remark, said: "That M. Laroche-Mathieu looks very intelligent."

The old poet murmured: "Do you think so?"

The younger man hesitated in surprise: "Why, yes! Is he not considered one of the most capable men in the Chamber?"

"That may be. In a kingdom of blind men the blind are kings. All those people are divided between money and politics; they are pedants to whom it is impossible to speak of anything that is familiar to us. Ah, it is difficult to find a man who is liberal in his ideas! I have known several, they are dead. Still, what difference does a little more or a little less genius make, since all must come to an end?" He paused, and Duroy said with a smile:

"You are gloomy to-night, sir!"

The poet replied: "I always am, my child; you will be too in a few years. While one is climbing the ladder, one sees the top and feels hopeful; but when one has reached that summit, one sees the descent and the end which is death. It is slow work ascending, but one descends rapidly. At your age one is joyous; one hopes for many things which never come to pass. At mine, one expects nothing but death."

Duroy laughed: "Egad, you make me shudder."

Norbert de Varenne continued: "You do not understand me now, but later on you will remember what I have told you. We breathe, sleep, drink, eat, work, and then die! The end of life is death. What do you long for? Love? A few kisses and you will be powerless. Money? What for? To gratify your desires. Glory? What comes after it all? Death! Death alone is certain."

He stopped, took Duroy by his coat collar and said slowly: "Ponder upon all that, young man; think it over for days, months, and years, and you will see life from a different standpoint. I am a lonely, old man. I have neither father, mother, brother, sister, wife, children, nor God. I have only poetry. Marry, my friend; you do not know what it is to live alone at my age. It is so lonesome. I seem to have no one upon earth. When one is old it is a comfort to have children."

When they reached Rue de Bourgogne, the poet halted before a high house, rang the bell, pressed Duroy's hand and said: "Forget what I have said to you, young man, and live according to your age. Adieu!" With those words he disappeared in the dark corridor.

Duroy felt somewhat depressed on leaving Varenne, but on his way a perfumed damsel passed by him and recalled to his mind his reconciliation with Mme. de Marelle. How delightful was the realization of one's hopes!

The next morning he arrived at his lady-love's door somewhat early; she welcomed him as if there had been no rupture, and said as she kissed him:

"You do not know how annoyed I am, my beloved; I anticipated a delightful honeymoon and now my husband has come home for six weeks. But I could not let so long a time go by without seeing you, especially after our little disagreement, and this is how I have arranged matters: Come to dinner Monday. I will introduce you to M. de Marelle, I have already spoken of you to him."

Duroy hesitated in perplexity; he feared he might betray something by a word, a glance. He stammered:

"No, I would rather not meet your husband."

"Why not? How absurd! Such things happen every day. I did not think you so foolish."

"Very well, I will come to dinner Monday."

"To make it more pleasant, I will have the Forestiers, though I do not like to receive company at home."

On Monday as he ascended Mme. de Marelle's staircase, he felt strangely troubled; not that he disliked to take her husband's hand, drink his wine, and eat his bread, but he dreaded something, he knew not what. He was ushered into the salon and he waited as usual. Then the door opened, and a tall man with a white beard, grave and precise, advanced toward him and said courteously:

"My wife has often spoken of you, sir; I am charmed to make your acquaintance."

Duroy tried to appear cordial and shook his host's proffered hand with exaggerated energy. M. de Marelle put a log upon the fire and asked:

"Have you been engaged in journalism a long time?"

Duroy replied: "Only a few months." His embarrassment wearing off, he began to consider the situation very amusing. He gazed at M. de Marelle, serious and dignified, and felt a desire to laugh aloud. At that moment Mme. de Marelle entered and approached Duroy, who in the presence of her husband dared not kiss her hand. Laurine entered next, and offered her brow to Georges. Her mother said to her:

"You do not call M. Duroy Bel-Ami to-day."

The child blushed as if it were a gross indiscretion to reveal her secret.

When the Forestiers arrived, Duroy was startled at Charles's appearance. He had grown thinner and paler in a week and coughed incessantly; he said they would leave for Cannes on the following Thursday at the doctor's orders. They did not stay late; after they had left, Duroy said, with a shake of his head:

"He will not live long."

Mme. de Marelle replied calmly: "No, he is doomed! He was a lucky man to obtain such a wife."

Duroy asked: "Does she help him very much?"

"She does all the work; she is well posted on every subject, and she always gains her point, as she wants it, and when she wants it! Oh, she is as maneuvering as anyone! She is a treasure to a man who wishes to succeed."

Georges replied: "She will marry very soon again, I have no doubt."

"Yes! I should not even be surprised if she had some one in view—a deputy! but I do not know anything about it."

M. de Marelle said impatiently: "You infer so many things that I do not like! We should never interfere in the affairs of others. Everyone should make that a rule."

Duroy took his leave with a heavy heart. The next day he called on the Forestiers, and found them in the midst of packing. Charles lay upon a sofa and repeated: "I should have gone a month ago." Then he proceeded to give Duroy innumerable orders, although everything had been arranged with M. Walter. When Georges left him, he pressed his comrade's hand and said:

"Well, old fellow, we shall soon meet again."

Mme. Forestier accompanied him to the door and he reminded her of their compact. "We are friends and allies, are we not? If you should require my services in any way, do not hesitate to call upon me. Send me a dispatch or a letter and I will obey."

She murmured: "Thank you, I shall not forget."

As Duroy descended the staircase, he met M. de Vaudrec ascending. The Count seemed sad—perhaps at the approaching departure.

The journalist bowed, the Count returned his salutation courteously but somewhat haughtily.

On Thursday evening the Forestiers left town.

CHAPTER VII.

A DUEL WITH AN END

Charles's absence gave Duroy a more important position on "La Vie Francaise." Only one matter arose to annoy him, otherwise his sky was cloudless.

An insignificant paper, "La Plume," attacked him constantly, or rather attacked the editor of the "Echoes" of "La Vie Francaise."

Jacques Rival said to him one day: "You are very forbearing."

"What should I do? It is no direct attack."

But, one afternoon when he entered the office, Boisrenard handed him a number of "La Plume."

"See, here is another unpleasant remark for you."

"Relative to what?"

"To the arrest of one Dame Aubert."

Georges took the paper and read a scathing personal denunciation. Duroy, it seems, had written an item claiming that Dame Aubert who, as the editor of "La Plume," claimed, had been put under arrest, was a myth. The latter retaliated by accusing Duroy of receiving bribes and of suppressing matter that should be published.

As Saint-Potin entered, Duroy asked him: "Have you seen the paragraph in 'La Plume'?"

"Yes, and I have just come from Dame Aubert's; she is no myth, but she has not been arrested; that report has no foundation."

Duroy went at once to M. Walter's office. After hearing the case, the manager bade him go to the woman's house himself, find out the details, and reply, to the article.

Duroy set out upon his errand and on his return to the office, wrote the following:

"An anonymous writer in 'La Plume' is trying to pick a quarrel with me on the subject of an old woman who, he claims, was arrested for disorderly conduct, which I deny. I have myself seen Dame Aubert, who is sixty years old at least; she told me the particulars of her dispute with a butcher as to the weight of some cutlets, which dispute necessitated an explanation before a magistrate. That is the whole truth in a nutshell. As for the other insinuations I scorn them. One never should reply to such things, moreover, when they are written under a mask.

GEORGES DUROY."

M. Walter and Jacques Rival considered that sufficient, and it was decided that it should be published in that day's issue.

Duroy returned home rather agitated and uneasy. What would this opponent reply? Who was he? Why that attack? He passed a restless night. When he re-read his article in the paper the next morning, he thought it more aggressive in print than it was in writing. He might, it seemed to him, have softened certain terms. He was excited all day and feverish during-the night. He rose early to obtain an issue of "La Plume" which should contain the reply to his note. He ran his eyes over the columns and at first saw nothing. He was beginning to breathe more freely when these words met his eye:

"M. Duroy of 'La Vie Francaise' gives us the lie! In doing so, he lies. He owns, however, that a woman named Aubert exists, and that she was taken before a magistrate by an agent. Two words only remain to be added to the word 'agent,' which are 'of morals' and all is told. But the consciences of certain journalists are on a par with their talents." "I sign myself, Louis Langremont."

Georges's heart throbbed violently, and he returned home in order to dress himself. He had been insulted and in such a manner that it was impossible to hesitate. Why had he been insulted? For nothing! On account of an old woman who had quarreled with her butcher.

He dressed hastily and repaired to M. Walter's house, although it was scarcely eight o'clock. M. Walter was reading "La Plume."

"Well," he said gravely, on perceiving Duroy, "you cannot let that pass." The young man did not reply.

The manager continued: "Go at once in search of Rival, who will look after your interests."

Duroy stammered several vague words and set out for Rival's house. Jacques was still in bed, but he rose when the bell rang, and having read the insulting paragraph, said: "Whom would you like to have besides me?"

"I do not know."

"Boisrenard?"

"Yes."

"Are you a good swordsman?"

"No."

"A good shot?"

"I have used a pistol a good deal."

"Good! Come and exercise while I attend to everything. Wait a moment."

He entered his dressing-room and soon reappeared, washed, shaven, and presentable.

"Come with me," said he. He lived on the ground floor, and he led Duroy into a cellar converted into a room for the practice of fencing and shooting. He produced a pair of pistols and began to give his orders as briefly as if they were on the dueling ground. He was well satisfied with Duroy's use of the weapons, and told him to remain there and practice until noon, when he would return to take him to lunch and tell him the result of his mission. Left to his own devices, Duroy aimed at the target several times and then sat down to reflect.

Such affairs were abominable anyway! What would a respectable man gain by risking his life? And he recalled Norbert de Varenne's remarks, made to him a short while before. "He was right!" he declared aloud. It was gloomy in that cellar, as gloomy as in a tomb. What o'clock was it? The time dragged slowly on. Suddenly he heard footsteps, voices, and Jacques Rival reappeared accompanied by Boisrenard. The former cried on perceiving Duroy: "All is settled!"

Duroy thought the matter had terminated with a letter of apology; his heart gave a bound and he stammered: "Ah—thank you!"

Rival continued: "M. Langremont has accepted every condition. Twenty-five paces, fire when the pistol is leveled and the order given." Then he added: "Now let us lunch; it is past twelve o'clock."

They repaired to a neighboring restaurant. Duroy was silent. He ate that they might not think he was frightened, and went in the afternoon with Boisrenard to the office, where he worked in an absent, mechanical manner. Before leaving, Jacques Rival shook hands with him and warned him that he and Boisrenard would call for him in a carriage the next morning at seven o'clock to repair to the wood at Vesinet, where the meeting was to take place.

All had been settled without his saying a word, giving his opinion, accepting or refusing, with such rapidity that his brain whirled and he scarcely knew what was taking place. He returned home about nine o'clock in the evening after having dined with Boisrenard, who had not left him all day. When he was alone, he paced the floor; he was too confused to think. One thought alone filled his mind and that was: a duel to-morrow! He sat down and began to meditate. He had thrown upon his table his adversary's card brought him by Rival. He read it for the twentieth time that day:

"Louis LANGREMONT,
176 Rue Montmartre."

Nothing more! Who was the man? How old was he? How tall? How did he look? How odious that a total stranger should without rhyme or reason, out of pure caprice, annoy him thus on account of an old, woman's quarrel with her butcher! He said aloud: "The brute!" and glared angrily at the card.

He began to feel nervous; the sound of his voice made him start; he drank a glass of water and laid down. He turned from his right side to his left uneasily. He was thirsty; he rose, he felt restless.

"Am I afraid?" he asked himself.

Why did his heart palpitate so wildly at the slightest sound? He began to reason philosophically on the possibility of being afraid. No, certainly he was not, since he was ready to fight. Still he felt so deeply moved that he wondered if one could be afraid in spite of oneself. What would happen if that state of things should exist? If he should tremble or lose his presence of mind? He lighted his candle and looked in the glass; he scarcely recognized his own face, it was so changed.

Suddenly he thought: "To-morrow at this time I may be dead." He turned to his couch and saw himself stretched lifeless upon it. He hastened to the window and opened it; but the night air was so chilly that he closed it, lighted a fire, and began to pace the floor once more, saying mechanically: "I must be more composed. I will write to my parents, in case of accident." He took a sheet of paper and after several attempts began:

"My dear father and mother:"

"At daybreak I am going to fight a duel, and as something might happen—"

He could write no more, he rose with a shudder. It seemed to him that notwithstanding his efforts, he would not have the strength necessary to face the meeting. He wondered if his adversary had ever fought before; if he were known? He had never heard his name. However, if he had not been a remarkable shot, he would not have accepted that dangerous weapon without hesitation. He ground his teeth to prevent his crying aloud. Suddenly he remembered that he had a bottle of brandy; he fetched it from the cupboard and soon emptied it. Now he felt his blood course more warmly through his veins. "I have found a means," said he.

Day broke. He began to dress; when his heart failed him, he took more brandy. At length there was a knock at the door. His friends had come; they were wrapped in furs. After shaking hands, Rival said: "It is as cold as Siberia. Is all well?"

"Yes."

"Are you calm?"

"Very calm."

"Have you eaten and drunk something?"

"I do not need anything."

They descended the stairs. A gentleman was seated in the carriage. Rival said: "Dr. Le Brument." Duroy shook hands with him and stammered: "Thank you," as he entered the carriage. Jacques Rival and Boisrenard followed him, and the coachman drove off. He knew where to go.

The conversation flagged, although the doctor related a number of anecdotes. Rival alone replied to him. Duroy tried to appear self-possessed, but he was haunted continually by the fear of showing his feelings or of losing his self-possession. Rival addressed him, saying: "I took the pistols to Gastine Renette. He loaded them. The box is sealed."

Duroy replied mechanically: "Thank you."

Then Rival proceeded to give him minute directions, that he might make no mistakes. Duroy repeated those directions as children learn their lessons in order to impress them upon his memory. As he muttered the phrases over and over, he almost prayed that some accident might happen to the carriage; if he could only break his leg!

At the end of a glade he saw a carriage standing and four gentlemen stamping their feet in order to keep them warm, and he was obliged to gasp in order to get breath. Rival and Boisrenard alighted first, then the doctor and the combatant.

Rival took the box of pistols, and with Boisrenard approached the two strangers, who were advancing toward them. Duroy saw them greet one another ceremoniously, then walk through the glade together as they counted the paces.

Dr. Le Brument asked Duroy: "Do you feel well? Do you not want anything?"

"Nothing, thank you." It seemed to him that he was asleep, that he was dreaming. Was he afraid? He did not know. Jacques Rival returned and said in a low voice: "All is ready. Fortune has favored us in the drawing of the pistols." That was a matter of indifference to

Duroy. They helped him off with his overcoat, led him to the ground set apart for the duel, and gave him his pistol. Before him stood a man, short, stout, and bald, who wore glasses. That was his adversary. A voice broke the silence—a voice which came from afar: "Are you ready, sirs?"

Georges cried: "Yes."

The same voice commanded: "Fire!"

Duroy heard nothing more, saw nothing more; he only knew that he raised his arm and pressed with all his strength upon the trigger. Soon he saw a little smoke before him; his opponent was still standing in the same position, and there was a small white cloud above his head. They had both fired. All was over! His second and the doctor felt him, unbuttoned his garments, and asked anxiously: "Are you wounded?" He replied: "No, I think not."

Langremont was not wounded either, and Jacques Rival muttered discontentedly: "That is always the way with those cursed pistols, one either misses or kills one's opponent."

Duroy was paralyzed with surprise and joy. All was over! He felt that he could fight the entire universe. All was over! What bliss! He felt brave enough to provoke anyone. The seconds consulted several moments, then the duelists and their friends entered the carriages and drove off. When the official report was drawn up, it was handed to Duroy who was to insert it in the "Echoes." He was surprised to find that two balls had been fired.

He said to Rival: "We only fired once!"

The latter smiled: "Yes—once—once each—that makes twice!"

And Duroy, satisfied with that explanation, asked no more questions. M. Walter embraced him.

"Bravo! you have defended the colors of 'La Vie Francaise'! Bravo!"

The following day at eleven o'clock in the forenoon, Duroy received a telegram:

"My God! I have been frightened. Come at once to Rue de Constantinople that I may embrace you, my love. How brave you are. I adore you. Clo."

He repaired to the place appointed, and Mme. de Marelle rushed into his arms, covering him with kisses.

"Oh, my darling, if you only knew how I felt when I read the morning papers! Tell me, tell me all about it."

Duroy was obliged to give her a detailed account.

"You must have had a terrible night before the duel!"

"Why, no; I slept very well."

"I should not have closed my eyes. Tell me what took place on the ground."

Forthwith he proceeded to give her a graphic description of the duel. When he had concluded, she said to him: "I cannot live without you! I must see you, and with my husband in Paris it is not very convenient. I often have an hour early in the morning when I could come and embrace you, but I cannot enter that horrible house of yours! What can we do?"

He asked abruptly: "How much do you pay here?"

"One hundred francs a month."

"Very well, I will take the apartments on my own account, and I will move at once. Mine are not suitable anyway for me now."

She thought a moment and then replied: "No I do not want you to."

He asked in surprise: "Why not?"

"Because!"

"That is no reason. These rooms suit me very well. I am here; I shall remain." He laughed. "Moreover, they were hired in my name!"

But she persisted: "No, no, I do not wish you to."

"Why not, then?"

She whispered softly, tenderly: "Because you would bring others here, and I do not wish you to."

Indignantly he cried: "Never, I promise you!"

"You would do so in spite of your promise."

"I swear I will not."

"Truly?"

"Truly—upon my word of honor. This is our nest—ours alone!"

She embraced him in a transport of delight. "Then I agree, my dearest. But if you deceive me once—just once, that will end all between us forever."

He protested, and it was agreed that he should settle in the rooms that same day. She said to him:

"You must dine with us Sunday. My husband thinks you charming."

He was flattered. "Indeed?"

"Yes, you have made a conquest. Did you not tell me that your home was in the country?"

"Yes; why?"

"Then you know something about agriculture?"

"Yes."

"Very well; talk to him of gardening and crops; he enjoys those subjects."

"All right. I shall not forget."

She left him, after lavishing upon him innumerable caresses.

CHAPTER VIII.

DEATH AND A PROPOSAL

Duroy moved his effects to the apartments in Rue de Constantinople. Two or three times a week, Mme. de-Marelle paid him visits. Duroy, to counterbalance them, dined at her house every Thursday, and delighted her husband by talking agriculture to him.

It was almost the end of February. Duroy was free from care. One night, when he returned home, he found a letter under his door. He examined the postmark; it was from Cannes. Having opened it, he read:

"Cannes, Villa Jolie."

"Dear sir and friend: You told me, did you not, that I could count upon you at any time? Very well. I have a favor to ask of you; it is to come and help me—not to leave me alone during Charles's last moments. He may not live through the week, although he is not confined to his bed, but the doctor has warned me. I have not the strength nor the courage to see that agony day and night, and I think with terror of the approaching end I can only ask such a thing of you, for my husband has no relatives. You were his comrade; he helped you to your position; come, I beg of you; I have no one else to ask."

"Your friend,"

"Madeleine Forestier."

Georges murmured: "Certainly I will go. Poor Charles!"

The manager, to whom he communicated the contents of that letter, grumblingly gave his consent. He repeated: "But return speedily, you are indispensable to us."

Georges Duroy left for Cannes the next day by the seven o'clock express, after having warned Mme. de Marelle by telegram. He arrived the following day at four o'clock in the afternoon. A commissionnaire conducted him to Villa Jolie. The house was small and low, and of the Italian style of architecture.

A servant opened the door and cried: "Oh, sir, Madame is awaiting you patiently."

Duroy asked: "How is your master?"

"Not very well, sir. He will not be here long."

The floor of the drawing-room which the young man entered was covered with a Persian rug; the large windows looked upon the village and the sea.

Duroy murmured: "How cozy it is here! Where the deuce do they get the money from?"

The rustling of a gown caused him to turn. Mme. Forestier extended both her hands, saying:

"How kind of you to come."

She was a trifle paler and thinner, but still as bright as ever, and perhaps prettier for being more delicate. She whispered: "It is terrible—he knows he cannot be saved and he tyrannizes over me. I have told him of your arrival. But where is your trunk?"

Duroy replied: "I left it at the station, not knowing which hotel you would advise me to stop at, in order to be near you."

She hesitated, then said: "You must stop here, at the villa. Your chamber is ready. He might die any moment, and if it should come in the night, I would be alone. I will send for your luggage."

He bowed. "As you will."

"Now, let us go upstairs," said she; he followed her. She opened a door on the first floor, and Duroy saw a form near a window, seated in an easy-chair, and wrapped in coverlets. He divined that it was his friend, though he scarcely recognized him. Forestier raised his hand slowly and with difficulty, saying:

"You are here; you have come to see me die. I am much obliged."

Duroy forced a smile. "To see you die? That would not be a very pleasant sight, and I would not choose that occasion on which to visit Cannes. I came here to rest."

"Sit down," said Forestier, and he bowed his head as if deep in hopeless meditation. Seeing that he did not speak, his wife approached the window and pointing to the horizon, said, "Look at that? Is it not beautiful?"

In spite of himself Duroy felt the grandeur of the closing day and exclaimed: "Yes, indeed, it is magnificent."

Forestier raised his head and said to his wife: "Give me more air."

She replied: "You must be careful; it is late, the sun is setting; you will catch more cold and that would be a serious thing in your condition."

He made a feeble gesture of anger with his right hand, and said: "I tell you I am suffocating! What difference does it make if I die a day sooner or later, since I must die?"

She opened the window wide. The air was soft and balmy. Forestier inhaled it in feverish gasps. He grasped the arms of his chair and said in a low voice: "Shut the window. I would rather die in a cellar."

His wife slowly closed the window, then leaned her brow against the pane and looked out. Duroy, ill at ease, wished to converse with the invalid to reassure him, but he could think of no words of comfort. He stammered: "Have you not been better since you are here?"

His friend shrugged his shoulders impatiently: "You will see very soon." And he bowed his head again.

Duroy continued: "At home it is still wintry. It snows, hails, rains, and is so dark that they have to light the lamps at three o'clock in the afternoon."

Forestier asked: "Is there anything new at the office?"

"Nothing. They have taken little Lacrin of the 'Voltaire' to fill your place, but he is incapable. It is time you came back."

The invalid muttered: "I? I will soon be writing under six feet of sod." A long silence ensued.

Mme. Forestier did not stir; she stood with her back to the room, her face toward the window. At length Forestier broke the silence in a gasping voice, heartrending to listen to: "How many more sunsets shall I see—eight—ten—fifteen—twenty—or perhaps thirty—no more. You have more time, you two—as for me—all is at an end. And everything will go on when I am gone as if I were here." He paused a few moments, then continued: "Everything that I see reminds me that I shall not see them long. It is horrible. I shall no longer see the smallest objects—the glasses—the dishes—the beds on which we rest—the carriages. It is fine to drive in the evening. How I loved all that."

Again Norbert de Varenne's words occurred to Duroy. The room grew dark. Forestier asked irritably:

"Are we to have no lamp to-night? That is what is called caring for an invalid!"

The form outlined against the window disappeared and an electric bell was heard to ring. A servant soon entered and placed a lamp upon the mantel-piece. Mme. Forestier asked her husband: "Do you wish to retire, or will you go downstairs to dinner?"

"I will go down to dinner."

The meal seemed to Duroy interminable, for there was no conversation, only the ticking of a clock broke the silence. When they had finished, Duroy, pleading fatigue, retired to his room and tried in vain to invent some pretext for returning home as quickly as possible. He consoled himself by saying: "Perhaps it will not be for long."

The next morning Georges rose early and strolled down to the beach. When he returned the servant said to him: "Monsieur has asked for you two or three times. Will you go upstairs?"

He ascended the stairs. Forestier appeared to be in a chair; his wife, reclining upon a couch, was reading. The invalid raised his head. Duroy asked:

"Well, how are you? You look better this morning."

Forestier murmured: "Yes, I am better and stronger. Lunch as hastily as you can with Madeleine, because we are going to take a drive."

When Mme. Forestier was alone with Duroy, she said to him: "You see, to-day he thinks he is better! He is making plans for to-morrow. We are now going to Gulf Juan to buy pottery for our rooms in Paris. He is determined to go, but he cannot stand the jolting on the road."

The carriage arrived, Forestier descended the stairs, step by step, supported by his servant. When he saw the closed landau, he wanted it uncovered. His wife opposed him: "It is sheer madness! You will take cold."

He persisted: "No, I am going to be better, I know it."

They first drove along a shady road and then took the road by the sea. Forestier explained the different points of interest. Finally they arrived at a pavilion over which were these words: "Gulf Juan Art Pottery," and the carriage drew up at the door. Forestier wanted to buy a vase to put on his bookcase. As he could not leave the carriage, they brought the pieces to him one by one. It took him a long time to choose, consulting his wife and Duroy: "You know it is for my study. From my easy-chair I can see it constantly. I prefer the ancient form—the Greek."

At length he made his choice. "I shall return to Paris in a few days," said he.

On their way home along the gulf a cool breeze suddenly sprang up, and the invalid began to cough. At first it was nothing, only a slight attack, but it grew worse and turned to a sort of hiccough—a rattle; Forestier choked, and every time he tried to breathe he coughed violently. Nothing quieted him. He had to be carried from the landau to his room. The heat of the bed did not stop the attack, which lasted until midnight. The first words the sick man uttered were to ask for a barber, for he insisted on being shaved every morning. He rose to be shaved, but was obliged to go to bed at once, and began to breathe so painfully that Mme. Forestier in affright woke Duroy and asked him to fetch the doctor. He returned almost immediately with Dr. Gavant who prescribed for the sick man. When the journalist asked him his opinion, he said: "It is the final stage. He will be dead to-morrow morning. Prepare that poor, young wife and send for a priest. I can do nothing more. However, I am entirely at your disposal" Duroy went to Mme. Forestier. "He is going to die. The doctor advises me to send for a priest. What will you do?"

She hesitated a moment and then said slowly:

"I will go and tell him that the cure wishes to see him. Will you be kind enough to procure one who will require nothing but the confession, and who will not make much fuss?"

The young man brought with him a kind, old priest who accommodated himself to circumstances. When he had entered the death chamber, Mme. Forestier went out and seated herself with Duroy in an adjoining room.

"That has upset him," said she. "When I mentioned the priest to him, his face assumed a scared expression. He knew that the end was near. I shall never forget his face."

At that moment they heard the priest saying to him: "Why no, you are not so low as that. You are ill, but not in danger. The proof of that is that I came as a friend, a neighbor." They could not hear his reply. The priest continued: "No, I shall not administer the sacrament. We will speak of that when you are better. If you will only confess, I ask no more. I am a pastor; I take advantage of every occasion to gather in my sheep."

A long silence followed. Then suddenly the priest said, in the tone of one officiating at the altar:

"The mercy of God is infinite; repeat the 'Confiteor,' my son. Perhaps you have forgotten it, I will help you. Repeat with me: 'Confiteor Deo omnipotenti; Beata Mariae semper virgini.'" He paused from time to time to permit the dying man to catch up to him.

Then he said: "Now, confess." The sick man murmured something. The priest repeated: "You have committed sins: of what kind, my son?"

The young woman rose and said simply: "Let us go into the garden. We must not listen to his secrets."

They seated themselves upon a bench before the door, beneath a blossoming rosebush. After several moments of silence Duroy asked: "Will it be some time before you return to Paris?"

"No," she replied; "when all is over, I will go back."

"In about ten days?"

"Yes, at most."

He continued; "Charles has no relatives then?"

"None, save cousins. His father and mother died when he was very young."

In the course of a few minutes, the servant came to tell them that the priest had finished, and together they ascended the stairs. Forestier seemed to have grown thinner since the preceding day. The priest was holding his hand.

"Au revoir, my son. I will come again to-morrow morning"; and he left. When he was gone, the dying man, who was panting, tried to raise his two hands toward his wife and gasped:

"Save me—save me, my darling. I do not want to die—oh, save me—go for the doctor. I will take anything. I do not want to die." He wept; the tears coursed down his pallid cheeks. Then his hands commenced to wander hither and thither continually, slowly, and regularly, as if gathering something on the coverlet. His wife, who was also weeping, sobbed:

"No, it is nothing. It is only an attack; you will be better to-morrow; you tired yourself with that drive."

Forestier drew his breath quickly and so faintly that one could scarcely hear him. He repeated:

"I do not want to die! Oh, my God—my God—what has happened to me? I cannot see. Oh, my God!" His staring eyes saw something invisible to the others; his hands plucked continually at the counterpane. Suddenly he shuddered and gasped: "The cemetery—me—my God!" He did not speak again. He lay there motionless and ghastly. The hours dragged on; the clock of a neighboring convent chimed noon.

Duroy left the room to obtain some food. He returned an hour later; Mme. Forestier would eat nothing. The invalid had not stirred. The young woman was seated in an easy-chair at the foot of the bed. Duroy likewise seated himself, and they watched in silence. A nurse, sent by the doctor, had arrived and was dozing by the window.

Duroy himself was almost asleep when he felt a presentiment that something was about to happen. He opened his eyes just in time to see Forestier close his. He coughed slightly, and two streams of blood issued from the corners of his mouth and flowed upon his night robe; his hands ceased their perpetual motion; he had breathed his last. His wife, perceiving it, uttered a cry and fell upon her knees by the bedside. Georges, in surprise and affright, mechanically made the sign of the cross.

The nurse, awakening, approached the bed and said: "It has come." Duroy, recovering his self-possession, murmured with a sigh of relief: "It was not as hard as I feared it would be."

That night Mme. Forestier and Duroy watched in the chamber of death. They were alone beside him who was no more. They did not speak, Georges's eyes seemed attracted to that emaciated face which the flickering light made more hollow. That was his friend, Charles Forestier, who the day before had spoken to him. For several years he had lived, eaten, laughed, loved, and hoped as did everyone—and now all was ended for him forever.

Life lasted a few months or years, and then fled! One was born, grew, was happy, and died. Adieu! man or woman, you will never return to earth! He thought of the insects which live several hours, of the feasts which live several days, of the men who live several years, of the worlds which last several centuries. What was the difference between one and the other? A few more dawns, that was all.

Duroy turned away his eyes in order not to see the corpse. Mme. Forestier's head was bowed; her fair hair enhanced the beauty of her sorrowful face. The young man's heart grew hopeful. Why should he lament when he had so many years still before him? He glanced at the handsome widow. How had she ever consented to marry that man? Then he pondered upon all the hidden secrets of their lives. He remembered that he had been told of a Count de Vaudrec who had dowered and given her in marriage. What would she do now? Whom would she marry? Had she projects, plans? He would have liked to know. Why that anxiety as to what she would do?

Georges questioned himself, and found that it was caused by a desire to win her for himself. Why should he not succeed? He was positive that she liked him; she would have confidence in him, for she knew that he was intelligent, resolute, tenacious. Had she not sent for him? Was not that a kind of avowal? He was impatient to question her, to find out her intentions. He would soon have to leave that villa, for he could not remain alone with the young widow; therefore he must find out her plans before returning to Paris, in order that she might not yield to another's entreaties. He broke the oppressive silence by saying:

"You must be fatigued."

"Yes, but above all I am grieved."

Their voices sounded strange in that room. They glanced involuntarily at the corpse as if they expected to see it move. Duroy continued:

"It is a heavy blow for you, and will make a complete change in your life."

She sighed deeply, but did not reply. He added:

"It is very sad for a young woman like you to be left alone." He paused; she still did not reply, and he stammered: "At any rate, you will remember the compact between us; you can command me as you will. I am yours."

She held out her hand to him and said mournfully and gently: "Thanks, you are very kind. If I can do anything for you, I say too: 'Count on me.'"

He took her proffered hand, gazed at it, and was seized with an ardent desire to kiss it. Slowly he raised it to his lips and then relinquished it. As her delicate fingers lay upon her knee the young widow said gravely:

"Yes, I shall be all alone, but I shall force myself to be brave."

He did not know how to tell her that he would be delighted to wed her. Certainly it was no time to speak to her on such a subject; however, he thought he might be able to express himself by means of some phrase which would have a hidden meaning and would infer what he wished to say. But that rigid corpse lay between them. The atmosphere became oppressive, almost suffocating. Duroy asked: "Can we not open the window a little? The air seems to be impure."

"Certainly," she replied; "I have noticed it too."

He opened the window, letting in the cool night air. He turned: "Come and look out, it is delightful."

She glided softly to his side. He whispered: "Listen to me. Do not be angry that I broach the subject at such a time, but the day after to-morrow I shall leave here and when you return to Paris it might be too late. You know that I am only a poor devil, who has his position to make, but I have the will and some intelligence, and I am advancing. A man who has attained his ambition knows what to count on; a man who has his way to make does not know what may come—it may be better or worse. I told you one day that my most cherished dream was to have a wife like you."

"I repeat it to you to-day. Do not reply, but let me continue. This is no proposal—the time and place would render it odious. I only wish to tell you that by a word you can make me happy, and that you can make of me as you will, either a friend or a husband—for my heart and my body are yours. I do not want you to answer me now. I do not wish to speak any more on the subject here. When we meet in Paris, you can tell me your decision."

He uttered these words without glancing at her, and she seemed not to have heard them, for she stood by his side motionless, staring vaguely and fixedly at the landscape before her, bathed in moonlight.

At length she murmured: "It is rather chilly," and turned toward the bed. Duroy followed her. They did not speak but continued their watch. Toward midnight Georges fell asleep. At daybreak the nurse entered and he started up. Both he and Mme. Forestier retired to their rooms to obtain some rest. At eleven o'clock they rose and lunched together; while through the open window was wafted the sweet, perfumed air of spring. After lunch, Mme. Forestier proposed that they take a turn in the garden; as they walked slowly along, she suddenly said, without turning her head toward him, in a low, grave voice:

"Listen to me, my dear friend; I have already reflected upon what you proposed to me, and I cannot allow you to depart without a word of reply. I will, however, say neither yes nor no. We will wait, we will see; we will become better acquainted. You must think it well over too. Do not yield to an impulse. I mention this to you before even poor Charles is buried, because it is necessary, after what you have said to me, that you should know me as I am, in order not to cherish the hope you expressed to me any longer, if you are not a man who can understand and bear with me."

"Now listen carefully: Marriage, to me, is not a chain but an association. I must be free, entirely unfettered, in all my actions—my coming and my going; I can tolerate neither control, jealousy, nor criticism as to my conduct. I pledge my word, however, never to compromise the name of the man I marry, nor to render him ridiculous in the eyes of the world. But that man must promise to look upon me as an equal, an ally, and not as an inferior, or as an obedient, submissive wife. My ideas, I know, are not like those of other people, but I shall never change them. Do not answer me, it would be useless. We shall meet again and talk it all over later. Now take a walk; I shall return to him. Good-bye until to-night."

He kissed her hand and left her without having uttered a word. That night they met at dinner; directly after the meal they sought their rooms, worn out with fatigue.

Charles Forestier was buried the next day in the cemetery at Cannes without any pomp, and Georges returned to Paris by the express which left at one-thirty. Mme. Forestier accompanied him to the station. They walked up and down the platform awaiting the hour of departure and conversing on indifferent subjects.

The train arrived, the journalist took his seat; a porter cried: "Marseilles, Lyons, Paris! All aboard!" The locomotive whistled and the train moved slowly out of the station.

The young man leaned out of the carriage, and looked at the youthful widow standing on the platform gazing after him. Just as she was disappearing from his sight, he threw her a kiss, which she returned with a more discreet wave of her hand.

CHAPTER IX.

MARRIAGE

Georges Duroy resumed his old habits. Installed in the cozy apartments on Rue de Constantinople, his relations with Mme. de Marelle became quite conjugal.

Mme. Forestier had not returned; she lingered at Cannes. He, however, received a letter from her announcing her return about the middle of April, but containing not a word as to their parting. He waited. He was resolved to employ every means to marry her if she seemed to hesitate; he had faith in his good fortune, in that power of attraction which he felt within him—a power so irresistible that all women yielded to it.

At length a short note admonished him that the decisive moment had arrived.

"I am in Paris. Come to see me."

"Madeleine Forestier."

Nothing more. He received it at nine o'clock. At three o'clock of the same day he called at her house. She extended both hands to him with a sweet smile, and they gazed into each other's eyes for several seconds, then she murmured:

"How kind of you to come!"

He replied: "I should have come, whensoever you bade me."

They sat down; she inquired about the Walters, his associates, and the newspaper.

"I miss that very much," said she. "I had become a journalist in spirit. I like the profession." She paused. He fancied he saw in her smile, in her voice, in her words, a kind of invitation, and although he had resolved not to hasten matters, he stammered:

"Well—why—why do you not resume—that profession—under—the name of Duroy?"

She became suddenly serious, and placing her hand on his arm, she said: "Do not let us speak of that yet."

Divining that she would accept him, he fell upon his knees, and passionately kissed her hands, saying:

"Thank you—thank you—how I love you."

She rose, she was very pale. Duroy kissed her brow. When she had disengaged herself from his embrace, she said gravely: "Listen, my friend, I have not yet fully decided; but my answer may be 'yes.' You must wait patiently, however, until I disclose the secret to you."

He promised and left her, his heart overflowing with joy. He worked steadily, spent little, tried to save some money that he might not be without a sou at the time of his marriage, and became as miserly as he had once been prodigal. Summer glided by; then autumn, and no one suspected the tie existing between Duroy and Mme. Forestier, for they seldom met in public.

One evening Madeleine said to him: "You have not yet told Mme. de Marelle our plans?"

"No, my dear; as you wished them kept secret, I have not mentioned them to a soul."

"Very well; there is plenty of time. I will tell the Walters."

She turned away her head and continued: "If you wish, we can be married the beginning of May."

"I obey you in all things joyfully."

"The tenth of May, which falls on Saturday, would please me, for it is my birthday."

"Very well, the tenth of May."

"Your parents live near Rouen, do they not?"

"Yes, near Rouen, at Canteleu."

"I am very anxious to see them!"

He hesitated, perplexed: "But—they are—" Then he added more firmly: "My dear, they are plain, country people, innkeepers, who strained every nerve to give me an education. I am not ashamed of them, but their—simplicity—their rusticity might annoy you."

She smiled sweetly. "No, I will love them very much. We will visit them; I wish to. I, too, am the child of humble parents—but I lost mine—I have no one in the world"—she held out her hand to him—"but you."

He was affected, conquered as he had never been by any woman.

"I have been thinking of something," said she, "but it is difficult to explain."

He asked: "What is it?"

"It is this: I am like all women. I have my—my weaknesses. I should like to bear a noble name. Can you not on the occasion of our marriage change your name somewhat?" She blushed as if she had proposed something indelicate.

He replied simply: "I have often thought of it, but it does not seem easy to me."

"Why not?"

He laughed. "Because I am afraid I should be ridiculed."

She shrugged her shoulders. "Not at all—not at all. Everyone does it, and no one laughs. Separate your name in this way: Du Roy. It sounds very well."

He replied: "No, that will not do; it is too common a proceeding. I have thought of assuming the name of my native place, first as a literary pseudonym and then as my surname in conjunction with Duroy, which might later on, as you proposed, be separated."

She asked: "Is your native place Canteleu?"

"Yes."

"I do not like the termination. Could we not modify it?"

She took a pen and wrote down the names in order to study them. Suddenly she cried: "Now I have it," and held toward him a sheet of paper on which was written: "Mme. Duroy de Cantel."

Gravely he replied: "Yes, it is very nice."

She was delighted, and repeated: "Duroy de Cantel. Mme. Duroy de Cantel. It is excellent, excellent!"

Then she added with an air of conviction: "You will see how easily it will be accepted by everyone! After to-morrow, sign your articles 'D. de Cantel,' and your 'Echoes' simply 'Duroy.' That is done on the press every day and no one will be surprised to see you take a nom de plume. What is your father's name?"

"Alexandre."

She murmured "Alexandre!" two or three times in succession; then she wrote upon a blank sheet:

"M. and Mme. Alexandre du Roy de Cantel announce the marriage of their son, M. Georges du Roy de Cantel with Mme. Forestier."

She examined her writing, and, charmed with the effect, exclaimed: "With a little method one can succeed in anything."

When Georges reached the street resolved to call himself, henceforth, "Du Roy," or even "Du Roy de Cantel," it seemed to him that he was of more importance. He swaggered more boldly, held his head more erect and walked as he thought gentlemen should. He felt a desire to inform the passers-by, "My name is Du Roy de Cantel."

Scarcely had he entered his apartments when the thought of Mme. de Marelle rendered him uneasy, and he wrote to her immediately, appointing a meeting for the following day.

"It will be hard," thought he. "There will be a quarrel surely."

The next morning he received a telegram from Madame, informing him that she would be with him at one o'clock. He awaited her impatiently, determined to confess at once and afterward to argue with her, to tell her that he could not remain a bachelor indefinitely, and that, as M. de Marelle persisted in living, he had been compelled to choose some one else as a legal companion. When the bell rang, his heart gave a bound.

Mme. de Marelle entered and cast herself into his arms, saying: "Good afternoon, Bel-Ami." Perceiving that his embrace was colder than usual, she glanced up at him and asked: "What ails you?"

"Take a seat," said he. "We must talk seriously."

She seated herself without removing her hat, and waited. He cast down his eyes; he was preparing to commence.

Finally he said slowly: "My dear friend, you see that I am very much perplexed, very sad, and very much embarrassed by what I have to confess to you. I love you; I love you with all my heart, and the fear of giving you pain grieves me more than what I have to tell you."

She turned pale, trembled, and asked: "What is it? Tell me quickly."

He said sadly but resolutely: "I am going to be married."

She sighed like one about to lose consciousness; then she gasped, but did not speak.

He continued: "You cannot imagine how much I suffered before taking that resolution. But I have neither position nor money. I am alone in Paris, I must have near me some one who can counsel, comfort, and support me. What I need is an associate, an ally, and I have found one!" He paused, hoping that she would reply, expecting an outburst of furious rage, reproaches, and insults. She pressed her hand to her heart and breathed with difficulty. He took the hand resting on the arm of the chair, but she drew it away and murmured as if stupefied: "Oh, my God!"

He fell upon his knees before her, without, however, venturing to touch her, more moved by her silence than he would have been by her anger.

"Clo, my little Clo, you understand my position. Oh, if I could have married you, what happiness it would have afforded me! But you were married! What could I do? Just think of it! I must make my way in the world and I can never do so as long as I have no domestic ties. If you knew. There are days when I should like to kill your husband." He spoke in a low, seductive voice. He saw two tears gather in Mme. de Marelle's eyes and trickle slowly down her cheeks. He whispered: "Do not weep, Clo, do not weep, I beseech you. You break my heart."

She made an effort to appear dignified and haughty, and asked, though somewhat unsteadily: "Who is it?"

For a moment he hesitated before he replied: "Madeleine Forestier!"

Mme. de Marelle started; her tears continued to flow. She rose. Duroy saw that she was going to leave him without a word of reproach or pardon, and he felt humbled, humiliated. He seized her gown and implored:

"Do not leave me thus."

She looked at him with that despairing, tearful glance so charming and so touching, which expresses all the misery pent-up in a woman's heart, and stammered: "I have nothing—to say; I can do nothing. You—you are right; you have made a good choice."

And disengaging herself she left the room.

With a sigh of relief at escaping so easily, he repaired to Mme. Forestier's, who asked him: "Have you told Mme. de Marelle?"

He replied calmly: "Yes."

"Did it affect her?"

"Not at all. On the contrary, she thought it an excellent plan."

The news was soon noised abroad. Some were surprised, others pretended to have foreseen it, and others again smiled, inferring that they were not at all astonished. The young man, who signed his articles, "D. de Cantel," his "Echoes," "Duroy," and his political sketches, "Du Roy," spent the best part of his time with his betrothed, who had decided that the date fixed for the wedding should be kept secret, that the ceremony should be celebrated in the presence of witnesses only, that they should leave the same evening for Rouen, and that the day following they should visit the journalist's aged parents and spend several days with them. Duroy had tried to persuade Madeleine to abandon that project, but not succeeding in his efforts he was finally compelled to submit.

The tenth of May arrived. Thinking a religious ceremony unnecessary, as they had issued no invitations, the couple were married at a magistrate's and took the six o'clock train for Normandy.

As the train glided along, Duroy seated in front of his wife, took her hand, kissed it, and said: "When we return we will dine at Chatou sometimes."

She murmured: "We shall have a great many things to do!" in a tone which seemed to say: "We must sacrifice pleasure to duty."

He retained her hand wondering anxiously how he could manage to caress her. He pressed her hand slightly, but she did not respond to the pressure.

He said: "It seems strange that you should be my wife."

She appeared surprised: "Why?"

"I do not know. It seems droll. I want to embrace you and I am surprised that I have the right."

She calmly offered him her cheek which he kissed as he would have kissed his sister's. He continued:

"The first time I saw you (you remember, at that dinner to which I was invited at Forestier's), I thought: 'Sacristi, if I could only find a wife like that!' And now I have one."

She glanced at him with smiling eyes.

He said to himself: "I am too cold. I am stupid. I should make more advances." And he asked: "How did you make Forestier's acquaintance?"

She replied with provoking archness: "Are we going to Rouen to talk of him?"

He colored. "I am a fool. You intimidate me."

She was delighted. "I? Impossible."

He seated himself beside her. She exclaimed: "Ah! a stag!" The train was passing through the forest of Saint-Germain and she had seen a frightened deer clear an alley at a bound. As she gazed out of the open window, Duroy bending over her, pressed a kiss upon her neck. For several moments she remained motionless, then raising her head, she said: "You tickle me, stop!"

But he did not obey her.

She repeated: "Stop, I say!"

He seized her head with his right hand, turned it toward him and pressed his lips to hers. She struggled, pushed him away and repeated: "Stop!"

He did not heed her. With an effort, she freed herself and rising, said: "Georges, have done. We are not children, we shall soon reach Rouen."

"Very well," said he, gaily, "I will wait."

Reseating herself near him she talked of what they would do on their return; they would keep the apartments in which she had lived with her first husband, and Duroy would receive Forestier's position on "La Vie Francaise." In the meantime, forgetting her injunctions and his promise, he slipped his arm around her waist, pressed her to him and murmured: "I love you dearly, my little Made."

The gentleness of his tone moved the young woman, and leaning toward him she offered him her lips; as she did so, a whistle announced the proximity of the station. Pushing back some stray locks upon her temples, she exclaimed:

"We are foolish."

He kissed her hands feverishly and replied:

"I adore you, my little Made."

On reaching Rouen they repaired to a hotel where they spent the night. The following morning, when they had drunk the tea placed upon the table in their room, Duroy clasped his wife in his arms and said: "My little Made, I feel that I love you very, very much."

She smiled trustfully and murmured as she returned his kisses: "I love you too—a little."

The visit to his parents worried Georges, although he had prepared his wife. He began again: "You know they are peasants, real, not sham, comic-opera peasants."

She smiled. "I know it, you have told me often enough."

"We shall be very uncomfortable. There is only a straw bed in my room; they do not know what hair mattresses are at Canteleu."

She seemed delighted. "So much the better. It would be charming to sleep badly—when—near you—and to be awakened by the crowing of the cocks."

He walked toward the window and lighted a cigarette. The sight of the harbor, of the river filled with ships moved him and he exclaimed: "Egad, but that is fine!"

Madeleine joined him and placing both of her hands on her husband's shoulder, cried: "Oh, how beautiful! I did not know that there were so many ships!"

An hour later they departed in order to breakfast with the old couple, who had been informed several days before of their intended arrival. Both Duroy and his wife were charmed with the beauties of the landscape presented to their view, and the cabman halted in order to allow them to get a better idea of the panorama before them. As he whipped up his horse, Duroy saw an old couple not a hundred meters off, approaching, and he leaped from the carriage crying: "Here they are, I know them."

The man was short, corpulent, florid, and vigorous, notwithstanding his age; the woman was tall, thin, and melancholy, with stooping shoulders—a woman who had worked from childhood, who had never laughed nor jested.

Madeleine, too, alighted and watched the couple advance, with a contraction of her heart she had not anticipated. They did not recognize their son in that fine gentleman, and they would never have taken that handsome lady for their daughter-in-law. They walked along, passed the child they were expecting, without glancing at the "city folks."

Georges cried with a laugh: "Good day, Father Duroy."

Both the old man and his wife were struck dumb with astonishment; the latter recovered her self-possession first and asked: "Is it you, son?"

The young man replied: "Yes, it is I, Mother Duroy," and approaching her, he kissed her upon both cheeks and said: "This is my wife."

The two rustics stared at Madeleine as if she were a curiosity, with anxious fear, combined with a sort of satisfied approbation on the part of the father and of jealous enmity on that of the mother.

M. Duroy, senior, who was naturally jocose, made so bold as to ask with a twinkle in his eye: "May I kiss you too?" His son uttered an exclamation and Madeleine offered her cheek to the old peasant; who afterward wiped his lips with the back of his hand. The old woman, in her turn, kissed her daughter-in-law with hostile reserve. Her ideal was a stout, rosy, country lass, as red as an apple and as round.

The carriage preceded them with the luggage. The old man took his son's arm and asked him: "How are you getting on?"

"Very well."

"That is right. Tell me, has your wife any means?"

Georges replied: "Forty thousand francs."

His father whistled softly and muttered: "Whew!" Then he added: "She is a handsome woman." He admired his son's wife, and in his day had considered himself a connoisseur.

Madeleine and the mother walked side by side in silence; the two men joined them. They soon reached the village, at the entrance to which stood M. Duroy's tavern. A pine board fastened over the door indicated that thirsty people might enter. The table was laid. A neighbor, who had come to assist, made a low courtesy on seeing so beautiful a lady appear; then recognizing Georges, she cried: "Oh Lord, is it you?"

He replied merrily: "Yes, it is I, Mother Brulin," and he kissed her as he had kissed his father and mother. Then he turned to his wife:

"Come into our room," said he, "you can lay aside your hat."

They passed through a door to the right and entered a room paved with brick, with whitewashed walls and a bed with cotton hangings.

A crucifix above a holy-water basin and two colored prints, representing Paul and Virginia beneath a blue palm-tree, and Napoleon I. on a yellow horse, were the only ornaments in that neat, but bare room.

When they were alone, Georges embraced Madeleine.

"Good morning, Made! I am glad to see the old people once more. When one is in Paris one does not think of this place, but when one returns, one enjoys it just the same."

At that moment his father cried, knocking on the partition with his fist: "Come, the soup is ready."

They re-entered the large public-room and took their seats at the table. The meal was a long one, served in a truly rustic fashion. Father Duroy, enlivened by the cider and several glasses of wine, related many anecdotes, while Georges, to whom they were all familiar, laughed at them.

Mother Duroy did not speak, but sat at the board, grim and austere, glancing at her daughter-in-law with hatred in her heart.

Madeleine did not speak nor did she eat; she was depressed. Wherefore? She had wished to come; she knew that she was coming to a simple home; she had formed no poetical ideas of those peasants, but she had perhaps expected to find them somewhat more polished, refined. She recalled her own mother, of whom she never spoke to anyone—a governess who had been betrayed and who had died of grief and shame when Madeleine was twelve years old. A stranger had had the little girl educated. Her father without doubt. Who was he? She did not know positively, but she had vague suspicions.

The meal was not yet over when customers entered, shook hands with M. Duroy, exclaimed on seeing his son, and seating themselves at the wooden tables began to drink, smoke, and play dominoes. The smoke from the clay pipes and penny cigars filled the room.

Madeleine choked and asked: "Can we go out? I cannot remain here any longer."

Old Duroy grumbled at being disturbed. Madeleine rose and placed her chair at the door in order to wait until her father-in-law and his wife had finished their coffee and wine.

Georges soon joined her.

"Would you like to stroll down to the Seine?"

Joyfully she cried: "Yes."

They descended the hillside, hired a boat at Croisset, and spent the remainder of the afternoon beneath the willows in the soft, warm, spring air, and rocked gently by the rippling waves of the river. They returned at nightfall. The evening repast by candle-light was more painful to Madeleine than that of the morning. Neither Father Duroy nor his wife spoke. When the meal was over, Madeleine drew her husband outside in order not to have to remain in that room, the atmosphere of which was heavy with smoke and the fumes of liquor.

When they were alone, he said: "You are already weary."

She attempted to protest; he interrupted her:

"I have seen it. If you wish we will leave tomorrow."

She whispered: "I should like to go."

They walked along and entered a narrow path among high trees, hedged in on either side by impenetrable brushwood.

She asked: "Where are we?"

He replied: "In the forest—one of the largest in France."

Madeleine, on raising her head, could see the stars between the branches and hear the rustling of the leaves. She felt strangely nervous. Why, she could not tell. She seemed to be lost, surrounded by perils, abandoned, alone, beneath that vast vaulted sky.

She murmured: "I am afraid; I should like to return."

"Very well, we will."

On their return they found the old people in bed. The next morning Madeleine rose early and was ready to leave at daybreak. When Georges told his parents that they were going to return home, they guessed whose wish it was.

His father asked simply: "Shall I see you soon again?"

"Yes—in the summer-time."

"Very well."

His mother grumbled: "I hope you will not regret what you have done."

Georges gave them two hundred francs to appease them, and the cab arriving at ten o'clock, the couple kissed the old peasants and set out.

As they were descending the side of the hill, Duroy laughed. "You see," said he, "I warned you. I should, however, not have presented you to M. and Mme. du Roy de Cantel, senior."

She laughed too and replied: "I am charmed now! They are nice people whom I am beginning to like very much. I shall send them confections from Paris." Then she murmured: "Du Roy de Cantel. We will say that we spent a week at your parents' estate," and drawing near him, she kissed him saying:

"Good morning, Georges."

He replied: "Good morning, Madeleine," as he slipped his arm around her waist.

CHAPTER X.

JEALOUSY

The Du Roys had been in Paris two days and the journalist had resumed work; he had given up his own especial province to assume that of Forestier, and to devote himself entirely to politics. On this particular evening he turned his steps toward home with a light heart. As he passed a florist's on Rue Notre Dame de Lorette he bought a bouquet of half-open roses for Madeleine. Having forgotten his key, on arriving at his door, he rang and the servant answered his summons.

Georges asked: "Is Madame at home?"

"Yes, sir."

In the dining-room he paused in astonishment to see covers laid for three: the door of the salon being ajar, he saw Madeleine arranging in a vase on the mantelpiece a bunch of roses similar to his.

He entered the room and asked: "Have you invited anyone to dinner?"

She replied without turning her head and continuing the arrangement of her flowers: "Yes and no: it is my old friend, Count de Vaudrec, who is in the habit of dining here every Monday and who will come now as he always has."

Georges murmured: "Very well."

He stopped behind her, the bouquet in his hand, the desire strong within him to conceal it—to throw it away. However, he said:

"Here, I have brought you some roses!"

She turned to him with a smile and said: "Ah, how thoughtful of you!" and she kissed him with such evident affection that he felt consoled.

She took the flowers, inhaled their perfume, and put them in an empty vase. Then she said as she noted the effect: "Now I am satisfied; my mantelpiece looks pretty," adding with an air of conviction:

"Vaudrec is charming; you will become intimate with him at once,"

A ring announced the Count. He entered as if he were at home. After gallantly kissing Mme. Du Roy's hand, he turned to her husband and cordially offered his hand, saying: "How are you, my dear Du Roy?"

He had no longer that haughty air, but was very affable. One would have thought in the course of five minutes, that the two men had known one another for ten years. Madeleine, whose face was radiant, said: "I will leave you together. I have work to superintend in the kitchen." The dinner was excellent and the Count remained very late. When he was gone, Madeleine said to her husband: "Is he not nice? He improves, too, on acquaintance. He is a good, true, faithful friend. Ah, without him—"

She did not complete her sentence and Georges replied: "Yes, he is very pleasant, I think we shall understand each other well."

“You do not know,” she said, “that we have work to do to-night before retiring. I did not have time to tell you before dinner, for Vaudrec came. Laroche-Mathieu brought me important news of Morocco. We must make a fine article of that. Let us set to work at once. Come, take the lamp.”

He carried the lamp and they entered the study. Madeleine leaned, against the mantelpiece, and having lighted a cigarette, told him the news and gave him her plan of the article. He listened attentively, making notes as she spoke, and when she had finished he raised objections, took up the question and, in his turn, developed another plan. His wife ceased smoking, for her interest was aroused in following Georges’s line of thought. From time to time she murmured: “Yes, yes; very good—excellent—very forcible—” And when he had finished speaking, she said: “Now let us write.”

It was always difficult for him to make a beginning and she would lean over his shoulder and whisper the phrases in his ear, then he would add a few lines; when their article was completed, Georges re-read it. Both he and Madeleine pronounced it admirable and kissed one another with passionate admiration.

The article appeared with the signature of “G. du Roy de Cantel,” and made a great sensation. M. Walter congratulated the author, who soon became celebrated in political circles. His wife, too, surprised him by the ingenuousness of her mind, the cleverness of her wit, and the number of her acquaintances. At almost any time upon returning home he found in his salon a senator, a deputy, a magistrate, or a general, who treated Madeleine with grave familiarity.

Deputy Laroche-Mathieu, who dined at Rue Fontaine every Tuesday, was one of the largest stockholders of M. Walter’s paper and the latter’s colleague and associate in many business transactions. Du Roy hoped, later on, that some of the benefits promised by him to Forestier might fall to his share. They would be given to Madeleine’s new husband—that was all—nothing was changed; even his associates sometimes called him Forestier, and it made Du Roy furious at the dead. He grew to hate the very name; it was to him almost an insult. Even at home the obsession continued; the entire house reminded him of Charles.

One evening Du Roy, who liked sweetmeats, asked:

“Why do we never have sweets?”

His wife replied pleasantly: “I never think of it, because Charles disliked them.”

He interrupted her with an impatient gesture: “Do you know I am getting tired of Charles? It is Charles here, Charles there, Charles liked this, Charles liked that. Since Charles is dead, let him rest in peace.”

Madeleine ascribed her husband’s burst of ill humor to puerile jealousy, but she was flattered and did not reply. On retiring, haunted by the same thought, he asked:

“Did Charles wear a cotton nightcap to keep the draft out of his ears?”

She replied pleasantly: “No, a lace one!”

Georges shrugged his shoulders and said scornfully: “What a bird!”

From that time Georges never called Charles anything but “poor Charles,” with an accent of infinite pity. One evening as Du Roy was smoking a cigarette at his window, toward the end of June, the heat awoke in him a desire for fresh air. He asked:

"My little Made, would you like to go as far as the Bois?"

"Yes, certainly."

They took an open carriage and drove to the Avenue du Bois de Boulogne. It was a sultry evening; a host of cabs lined the drive, one behind another. When the carriage containing Georges and Madeleine reached the turning which led to the fortifications, they kissed one another and Madeleine stammered in confusion: "We are as childish as we were at Rouen."

The road they followed was not so much frequented, a gentle breeze rustled the leaves of the trees, the sky was studded with brilliant stars and Georges murmured, as he pressed his wife to his breast: "Oh, my little Made."

She said to him: "Do you remember how gloomy the forest at Canteleu was? It seemed to me that it was full of horrible beasts and that it was interminable, while here it is charming. One can feel the caressing breezes, and I know that Sevres is on the other side."

He replied: "In our forests there are nothing but stags, foxes, roebucks, and boars, with here and there a forester's house." He paused for a moment and then asked: "Did you come here in the evening with Charles occasionally?"

She replied: "Frequently."

He felt a desire to return home at once. Forestier's image haunted him, however; he could think of nothing else. The carriage rolled on toward the Arc de Triomphe and joined the stream of carriages returning home. As Georges remained silent, his wife, who divined his thoughts, asked in her soft voice: "Of what are you thinking? For half an hour you have not uttered a word."

He replied with a sneer: "I am thinking of all those fools who kiss one another, and I believe truly that there is something else to be done in life."

She whispered: "Yes, but it is nice sometimes! It is nice when one has nothing better to do."

Georges' thoughts were busy with the dead; he said to himself angrily: "I am foolish to worry, to torment myself as I have done." After remonstrating thus with himself, he felt more reconciled to the thought of Forestier, and felt like exclaiming: "Good evening, old fellow!"

Madeleine, who was bored by his silence, asked: "Shall we go to Tortoni's for ices before returning home?"

He glanced at her from his corner and thought: "She is pretty; so much the better. Tit for tat, my comrade. But if they begin again to annoy me with you, it will get somewhat hot at the North Pole!"

Then he replied: "Certainly, my darling," and before she had time to think he kissed her. It seemed to Madeleine that her husband's lips were icy. However he smiled as usual and gave her his hand to assist her to alight at the cafe.

CHAPTER XI.

MADAME WALTER TAKES A HAND

On entering the office the following day, Du Roy sought Boisrenard and told him to warn his associates not to continue the farce of calling him Forestier, or there would be war. When Du Roy returned an hour later, no one called him by that name. From the office he proceeded to his home, and hearing the sound of ladies' voices in the drawing-room, he asked the servant: "Who is here?"

"Mme. Walter and Mme. de Marelle," was the reply.

His heart pulsated violently as he opened the door. Clotilde was seated by the fireplace; it seemed to Georges that she turned pale on perceiving him.

Having greeted Mme. Walter and her two daughters seated like sentinels beside her, he turned to his former mistress. She extended her hand; he took and pressed it as if to say: "I love you still!" She returned the pressure.

He said: "Have you been well since we last met?"

"Yes; have you, Bel-Ami?" And turning to Madeleine she added: "Will you permit me to call him Bel-Ami?"

"Certainly, my dear; I will permit anything you wish."

A shade of irony lurked beneath those words, uttered so pleasantly.

Mme. Walter mentioned a fencing-match to be given at Jacques Rival's apartments, the proceeds to be devoted to charities, and in which many society ladies were going to assist. She said: "It will be very entertaining; but I am in despair, for we have no one to escort us, my husband having an engagement."

Du Roy offered his services at once. She accepted, saying: "My daughters and I shall be very grateful."

He glanced at the younger of the two girls and thought: "Little Suzanne is not at all bad, not at all."

She resembled a doll, being very small and dainty, with a well-proportioned form, a pretty, delicate face, blue-gray eyes, a fair skin, and curly, flaxen hair. Her elder sister, Rose, was plain—one of those girls to whom no attention is ever paid. Her mother rose, and turning to Georges, said: "I shall count on you next Thursday at two o'clock."

He replied: "Count upon me, Madame."

When the door closed upon Mme. Walter, Mme. de Marelle, in her turn, rose.

"Au revoir, Bel-Ami."

This time she pressed his hand and he was moved by that silent avowal. "I will go to see her to-morrow," thought he.

Left alone with his wife, she laughed, and looking into his eyes said: "Mme. Walter has taken a fancy to you!"

He replied incredulously: "Nonsense!"

"But I know it. She spoke of you to me with great enthusiasm. She said she would like to find two husbands like you for her daughters. Fortunately she is not susceptible herself."

He did not understand her and repeated: "Susceptible herself?"

She replied in a tone of conviction: "Oh, Mme. Walter is irreproachable. Her husband you know as well as I. But she is different. Still she has suffered a great deal in having married a Jew, though she has been true to him; she is a virtuous woman."

Du Roy was surprised: "I thought her a Jewess."

"She a Jewess! No, indeed! She is the prime mover in all the charitable movements at the Madeleine. She was even married by a priest. I am not sure but that M. Walter went through the form of baptism."

Georges murmured: "And—she—likes—me—"

"Yes. If you were not married I should advise you to ask for the hand of—Suzanne—would you not prefer her to Rose?"

He replied as he twisted his mustache: "Eh! the mother is not so bad!"

Madeleine replied: "I am not afraid of her. At her age one does not begin to make conquests—one should commence sooner."

Georges thought: "If I might have had Suzanne, ah!" Then he shrugged his shoulders: "Bah, it is absurd; her father would not have consented."

He determined to treat Mme. Walter very considerately in order to retain her regard. All that evening he was haunted by recollections of his love for Clotilde; he recalled their escapades, her kindness. He repeated to himself: "She is indeed nice. Yes, I shall call upon her to-morrow."

When he had lunched the following morning he repaired to Rue Verneuil. The same maid opened the door, and with the familiarity of an old servant she asked: "Is Monsieur well?"

He replied: "Yes, my child," and entered the drawing-room in which some one was practising scales. It was Laurine. He expected she would fall upon his neck. She, however, rose ceremoniously, bowed coldly, and left the room with dignity; her manner was so much like that of an outraged woman that he was amazed. Her mother entered. He kissed her hand.

"How much I have thought of you," said he.

"And I of you," she replied.

They seated themselves and smiled as they gazed into one another's eyes.

"My dear little Clo, I love you."

"And I love you."

"Still—still—you did not miss me."

"Yes and no. I was grieved, but when I heard your reason, I said to myself: 'Bah, he will return to me some day.'"

"I dared not come. I did not know how I should be received. I dared not, but I longed to come. Now, tell me what ails Laurine; she scarcely bade me good morning and left the room with an angry air."

"I do not know, but one cannot mention you to her since your marriage; I really believe she is jealous."

"Nonsense."

"Yes, my dear, she no longer calls you Bel-Ami, but M. Forestier instead."

Du Roy colored, then drawing nearer the young woman, he said: "Kiss me."

She obeyed him.

"Where can we meet again?" he asked.

"At Rue de Constantinople."

"Ah, are the apartments not rented?"

"No, I kept them."

"You did?"

"Yes, I thought you would return."

His heart bounded joyfully. She loved him then with a lasting love! He whispered: "I adore you." Then he asked: "Is your husband well?"

"Yes, very well. He has just been home for a month; he went away the day before yesterday."

Du Roy could not suppress a smile: "How opportunely that always happens!"

She replied naively: "Yes, it happens opportunely, but he is not in the way when he is here; is he?"

"That is true; he is a charming man!"

"How do you like your new life?"

"Tolerably; my wife is a comrade, an associate, nothing more; as for my heart—"

"I understand; but she is good."

"Yes, she does not trouble me."

He drew near Clotilde and murmured: "When shall we meet again?"

"To-morrow, if you will."

"Yes, to-morrow at two o'clock."

He rose to take his leave somewhat embarrassed.

"You know I intend to take back the rooms on Rue de Constantinople myself. I wish to; it is not necessary for you to pay for them."

She kissed his hands, saying: "You may do as you like. I am satisfied to have kept them until we met again." And Du Roy took his leave very well satisfied.

When Thursday came, he asked Madeleine: "Are going to the fencing-match at Rival's?"

"No, I do not care about it. I will go to the chamber of deputies."

Georges called for Mme. Walter in an open carriage, for the weather was delightful. He was surprised to find her looking so handsome and so young. Never had she appeared so fresh. Her daughter, Suzanne, was dressed in pink; her sister looked like her governess. At Rival's door was a long line of carriages. Du Roy offered his arm to Mme. Walter and they entered.

The entertainment was for the benefit of the orphans of the Sixth Ward under the patronage of all the wiles of the senators and deputies who were connected with "La Vie Francaise."

Jacques Rival received the arrivals at the entrance to his apartments, then he pointed to a small staircase which led to the cellar in which were his shooting-gallery and fencing-room, saying: "Downstairs, ladies, downstairs. The match will take place in the subterranean apartments."

Pressing Du Roy's hand, he said: "Good evening, Bel-Ami."

Du Roy was surprised: "Who told you about that name?"

Rival replied: "Mme. Walter, who thinks it very pretty."

Mme. Walter blushed.

"Yes, I confess that if I knew you better, I should do as little Laurine, and I should call you Bel-Ami, too. It suits you admirably."

Du Roy laughed. "I beg you to do so, Madame."

She cast down her eyes. "No, we are not well enough acquainted."

He murmured: "Permit me to hope that we shall become so."

"Well, we shall see," said she.

They descended the stairs and entered a large room, which was lighted by Venetian lanterns and decorated with festoons of gauze. Nearly all the benches were filled with ladies, who were chatting as if they were at a theater. Mme. Walter and her daughters reached their seats in the front row.

Du Roy, having obtained their places for them, whispered: "I shall be obliged to leave you; men cannot occupy the seats."

Mme. Walter replied hesitatingly: "I should like to keep you, just the same. You could tell me the names of the participants. See, if you stand at the end of the seat, you will not annoy anyone." She raised her large, soft eyes to his and insisted: "Come, stay with us—Bel-Ami—we need you!"

He replied: "I obey with pleasure, Madame!"

Suddenly Jacques Rival's voice announced: "We will begin, ladies."

Then followed the fencing-match. Du Roy retained his place beside the ladies and gave them all the necessary information. When the entertainment was over and all expenses were paid, two hundred and twenty francs remained for the orphans of the Sixth Ward.

Du Roy, escorting the Walters, awaited his carriage. When seated face to face with Mme. Walter, he met her troubled but caressing glance.

"Egad, I believe she is affected," thought he; and he smiled as he recognized the fact that he was really successful with the female sex, for Mme. de Marelle, since the renewal of their relations, seemed to love him madly.

With a light heart he returned home. Madeleine was awaiting him in the drawing-room.

"I have some news," said she. "The affair with Morocco is becoming complicated. France may send an expedition out there in several months. In any case the ministry will be overthrown and Laroche will profit by the occasion."

Du Roy, in order to draw out his wife, pretended not to believe it. "France would not be silly enough to commence any folly with Tunis!"

She shrugged her shoulders impatiently. "I tell you she will! You do not understand that it is a question of money—you are as simple as Forestier."

Her object was to wound and irritate him, but he only smiled and replied: "What! as simple as that stupid fellow?"

She ceased and murmured: "Oh, Georges!"

He added: "Poor devil!" in a tone of profound pity.

Madeleine turned her back upon him scornfully; after a moment of silence, she continued: "We shall have some company Tuesday. Mme. Laroche-Mathieu is coming here to dine with Viscountess de Percemur. Will you invite Rival and Norbert de Varenne? I shall go to Mmes. Walter and de Marelle to-morrow. Perhaps, too, we may have Mme. Rissolin."

Du Roy replied: "Very well, I will see to Rival and Norbert."

The following day he thought he would anticipate his wife's visit to Mme. Walter and attempt to find out if she really was in love with him. He arrived at Boulevard Malesherbes at two o'clock. He was ushered into the salon and waited. Finally Mme. Walter appeared and offered him her hand cordially. "What good wind blows you here?"

"No good wind, but a desire to see you. Some power has impelled me hither, I do not know why; I have nothing to say except that I have come; here I am! Pardon the morning call and the candor of my explanation."

He uttered those words with a smile upon his lips and a serious accent in his voice.

In her astonishment, she stammered with a blush: "But indeed—I do not understand—you surprise me."

He added: "It is a declaration made in jest in order not to startle you."

They were seated near each other. She took the matter as a jest. "Is it a declaration—seriously?"

"Yes, for a long time I have wished to make it, but I dared not; they say you are so austere, so rigid."

She had recovered her self-possession and replied:

"Why did you choose to-day?"

"I do not know." Then he lowered his voice: "Or rather because I have thought only of you since yesterday."

Suddenly turning pale, she gasped: "Come, enough of this childishness! Let us talk of something else."

But he fell upon his knees before her. She tried to rise; he prevented her by twining his arms about her waist, and repeated in a passionate voice: "Yes, it is true that I have loved you madly for some time. Do not answer me. I am mad—I love you. Oh, if you knew how I love you!"

She could utter no sound; in her agitation she repulsed him with both hands, for she could feel his breath upon her cheek. He rose suddenly and attempted to embrace her, but gaining her liberty for a moment, she escaped him and ran from chair to chair. He, considering such pursuit beneath his dignity, sank into a chair, buried his face in his hands, and feigned to sob convulsively. Then he rose, cried:

"Adieu, adieu!" and fled.

In the hall he took his cane calmly and left the house saying: "Cristi! I believe she loves me!"

He went at once to the telegraph office to send a message to Clotilde, appointing a rendezvous for the next day.

On entering the house at his usual time, he said to his wife: "Well, is everyone coming to dinner?"

She replied: "Yes, all but Mme. Walter, who is uncertain as to whether she can come. She acted very strangely. Never mind, perhaps she can manage it anyway."

He replied: "She will come."

He was not, however, certain and was rendered uneasy until the day of the dinner. That morning Madeleine received a message from Mme. Walter to this effect: "I have succeeded in arranging matters and I shall be with you, but my husband cannot accompany me."

Du Roy thought: "I did right not to return there. She has calmed down." Still he awaited her arrival anxiously.

She appeared very composed, somewhat reserved, and haughty. He was very humble, very careful, and submissive. Mmes. Laroche-Mathieu and Rissolin were accompanied by their husbands. Mme. de Marelle looked bewitching in an odd combination of yellow and black.

At Du Roy's right sat Mme. Walter, and he spoke to her only of serious matters with exaggerated respect. From time to time he glanced at Clotilde.

"She is really very pretty and fresh looking," thought he. But Mme. Walter attracted him by the difficulty of the conquest. She took her leave early.

"I will escort you," said he.

She declined his offer. He insisted: "Why do you not want me? You wound me deeply. Do not let me feel that I am not forgiven. You see that I am calm."

She replied: "You cannot leave your guests thus."

He smiled: "Bah! I shall be absent twenty minutes. No one will even notice it; if you refuse me, you will break my heart."

"Very well," she whispered, "I will accept."

When they were seated in the carriage, he seized her hand, and kissing it passionately said: "I love you, I love you. Let me tell it to you. I will not touch you. I only wish to repeat that I love you."

She stammered: "After what you promised me—it is too bad—too bad."

He seemed to make a great effort, then he continued in a subdued voice: "See, how I can control myself—and yet—let me only tell you this—I love you—yes, let me go home with you and kneel before you five minutes to utter those three words and gaze upon your beloved face."

She suffered him to take her hand and replied in broken accents: "No, I cannot—I do not wish to. Think of what my servants, my daughters, would say—no—no—it is impossible."

He continued: "I cannot live without seeing you; whether it be at your house or elsewhere, I must see you for only a moment each day that I may touch your hand, breathe the air stirred by your gown, contemplate the outlines of your form, and see your beautiful eyes."

She listened tremblingly to the musical language of love, and made answer: "No, it is impossible. Be silent!"

He spoke very low; he whispered in her ear, comprehending that it was necessary to win that simple woman gradually, to persuade her to appoint a meeting where she willed at first, and later on where he willed.

"Listen: I must see you! I will wait at your door like a beggar. If you do not come down, I will come to you, but I shall see you to-morrow."

She repeated: "No, do not come. I shall not receive you. Think of my daughters!"

"Then tell me where I can meet you—in the street—it matters not where—at any hour you wish—provided that I can see you. I will greet you; I will say, I love you; and then go away."

She hesitated, almost distracted. As the coupe stopped at the door, she whispered hastily: "I will be at La Trinite to-morrow, at half past three."

After alighting, she said to her coachman: "Take M. du Roy home."

When he returned, his wife asked: "Where have you been?"

He replied in a low voice: "I have been to send an important telegram."

Mme. de Marelle approached him: "You must take me home, Bel-Ami; you know that I only dine so far from home on that condition." Turning to Madeleine, she asked: "You are not jealous?"

Mme. du Roy replied slowly: "No, not at all."

The guests departed. Clotilde, enveloped in laces, whispered to Madeleine at the door: "Your dinner was perfect. In a short while you will have the best political salon in Paris."

When she was alone with Georges, she said: "Oh, my darling Bel-Ami, I love you more dearly every day."

The cab rolled on, and Georges' thoughts were with Mme. Walter.

CHAPTER XII.

A MEETING AND THE RESULT

The July sun shone upon the Place de la Trinite, which was almost deserted. Du Roy drew out his watch. It was only three o'clock: he was half an hour too early. He laughed as he thought of the place of meeting. He entered the sacred edifice of La Trinite; the coolness within was refreshing. Here and there an old woman kneeled at prayer, her face in her hands. Du Roy looked at his watch again. It was not yet a quarter past three. He took a seat, regretting that he could not smoke. At the end of the church near the choir; he could hear the measured tread of a corpulent man whom he had noticed when he entered. Suddenly the rustle of a gown made him start. It was she. He arose and advanced quickly. She did not offer him her hand and whispered: "I have only a few minutes. You must kneel near me that no one will notice us."

She proceeded to a side aisle after saluting the Host on the High Altar, took a footstool, and kneeled down. Georges took one beside it and when they were in the attitude of prayer, he said: "Thank you, thank you. I adore you. I should like to tell you constantly how I began to love you, how I was conquered the first time I saw you. Will you permit me some day to unburden my heart, to explain all to you?"

She replied between her fingers: "I am mad to let you speak to me thus—mad to have come hither—mad to do as I have done, to let you believe that this—this adventure can have any results. Forget it, and never speak to me of it again." She paused.

He replied: "I expect nothing—I hope nothing—I love you—whatever you may do, I will repeat it so often, with so much force and ardor that you will finally understand me, and reply: 'I love you too.'"

He felt her frame tremble as she involuntarily repeated: "I love you too."

He was overcome by astonishment.

"Oh, my God!" she continued incoherently, "Should I say that to you? I feel guilty, despicable—I—who have two daughters—but I cannot—cannot—I never thought—it was stronger than I—listen—listen—I have never loved—any other but you—I swear it—I have loved you a year in secret—I have suffered and struggled—I can no longer; I love you." She wept and her bowed form was shaken by the violence of her emotion.

Georges murmured: "Give me your hand that I may touch, may press it."

She slowly took her hand from her face, he seized it saying: "I should like to drink your tears!"

Placing the hand he held upon his heart he asked: "Do you feel it beat?"

In a few moments the man Georges had noticed before passed by them. When Mme. Walter heard him near her, she snatched her fingers from Georges's clasp and covered her face with them. After the man had disappeared, Du Roy asked, hoping for another place of meeting than La Trinite: "Where shall I see you to-morrow?"

She did not reply; she seemed transformed into a statue of prayer. He continued: "Shall I meet you to-morrow at Park Monceau?"

She turned a livid face toward him and said unsteadily: "Leave me—leave me now—go—go away—for only five minutes—I suffer too much near you. I want to pray—go. Let me pray alone—five minutes—let me ask God—to pardon me—to save me—leave me—five minutes."

She looked so pitiful that he rose without a word and asked with some hesitation: "Shall I return presently?"

She nodded her head in the affirmative and he left her. She tried to pray; she closed her eyes in order not to see Georges. She could not pray; she could only think of him. She would rather have died than have fallen thus; she had never been weak. She murmured several words of supplication; she knew that all was over, that the struggle was in vain. She did not however wish to yield, but she felt her weakness. Some one approached with a rapid step; she turned her head. It was a priest. She rose, ran toward him, and clasping her hands, she cried: "Save me, save me!"

He stopped in surprise.

"What do you want, Madame?"

"I want you to save me. Have pity on me. If you do not help me, I am lost!"

He gazed at her, wondering if she were mad.

"What can I do for you?" The priest was a young man somewhat inclined to corpulence.

"Receive my confession," said she, "and counsel me, sustain me, tell me what to do."

He replied: "I confess every Saturday from three to six."

Seizing his arm she repeated: "No, now, at once—at once! It is necessary! He is here! In this church! He is waiting for me."

The priest asked: "Who is waiting for you?"

"A man—who will be my ruin if you do not save me. I can no longer escape him—I am too weak—too weak."

She fell upon her knees sobbing: "Oh, father, have pity upon me. Save me, for God's sake, save me!" She seized his gown that he might not escape her, while he uneasily glanced around on all sides to see if anyone noticed the woman at his feet. Finally, seeing that he could not free himself from her, he said: "Rise; I have the key to the confessional with me."

Du Roy having walked around the choir, was sauntering down the nave, when he met the stout, bold man wandering about, and he wondered: "What can he be doing here?"

The man slackened his pace and looked at Georges with the evident desire to speak to him. When he was near him, he bowed and said politely:

"I beg your pardon, sir, for disturbing you; but can you tell me when this church was built?"

Du Roy replied: "I do not know; I think it is twenty or twenty-five years. It is the first time I have been here. I have never seen it before." Feeling interested in the stranger, the journalist continued: "It seems to me that you are examining into it very carefully."

The man replied: "I am not visiting the church; I have an appointment." He paused and in a few moments added: "It is very warm outside."

Du Roy looked at him and suddenly thought that he resembled Forestier. "Are you from the provinces?" he asked.

"Yes, I am from Rennes. And did you, sir, enter this church from curiosity?"

"No, I am waiting for a lady." And with a smile upon his lips, he walked away.

He did not find Mme. Walter in the place in which he had left her, and was surprised. She had gone. He was furious. Then he thought she might be looking for him, and he walked around the church. Not finding her, he returned and seated himself on the chair she had occupied, hoping that she would rejoin him there. Soon he heard the sound of a voice. He saw no one; whence came it? He rose to examine into it, and saw in a chapel near by, the doors of the confessionals. He drew nearer in order to see the woman whose voice he heard. He recognized Mme. Walter; she was confessing. At first he felt a desire to seize her by the arm and drag her away; then he seated himself near by and bided his time. He waited quite awhile. At length Mme. Walter rose, turned, saw him and came toward him. Her face was cold and severe.

"Sir," said she, "I beseech you not to accompany me, not to follow me and not to come to my house alone. You will not be admitted. Adieu!" And she walked away in a dignified manner.

He permitted her to go, because it was against his principles to force matters. As the priest in his turn issued from the confessional, he advanced toward him and said: "If you did not wear a gown, I would give you a sound thrashing." Then he turned upon his heel and left the church whistling. In the doorway he met the stout gentleman. When Du Roy passed him, they bowed.

The journalist then repaired to the office of "La Vie Francaise." As he entered he saw by the clerks' busy air that something of importance was going on, and he hastened to the manager's room. The latter exclaimed joyfully as Du Roy entered: "What luck! here is Bel-Ami."

He stopped in confusion and apologized: "I beg your pardon, I am very much bothered by circumstances. And then I hear my wife and daughter call you Bel-Ami from morning until night, and I have acquired the habit myself. Are you displeased?"

Georges laughed. "Not at all."

M. Walter continued: "Very well, then I will call you Bel-Ami as everyone else does. Great changes have taken place. The ministry has been overthrown. Marrot is to form a new cabinet. He has chosen General Boutin d'Acre as minister of war, and our friend Laroche-Mathieu as minister of foreign affairs. We shall be very busy. I must write a leading article, a simple declaration of principles; then I must have something interesting on the Morocco question—you must attend to that."

Du Roy reflected a moment and then replied: "I have it. I will give you an article on the political situation of our African colony," and he proceeded to prepare M. Walter an outline of his work, which was nothing but a modification of his first article on "Souvenirs of a Soldier in Africa."

The manager having read the article said: "It is perfect; you are a treasure. Many thanks."

Du Roy returned home to dinner delighted with his day, notwithstanding his failure at La Trinite. His wife was awaiting him anxiously. She exclaimed on seeing him:

"You know that Laroche is minister of foreign affairs."

"Yes, I have just written an article on that subject."

"How?"

"Do you remember the first article we wrote on 'Souvenirs of a Soldier in Africa'? Well, I revised and corrected it for the occasion."

She smiled. "Ah, yes, that will do very well."

At that moment the servant entered with a dispatch containing these words without any signature:

"I was beside myself. Pardon me and come to-morrow at four o'clock to Park Monceau."

He understood the message, and with a joyful heart, slipped the telegram into his pocket. During dinner he repeated the words to himself; as he interpreted them, they meant, "I yield—I am yours where and when you will." He laughed.

Madeleine asked: "What is it?"

"Nothing much. I was thinking of a comical old priest I met a short while since."

Du Roy arrived at the appointed hour the following day. The benches were all occupied by people trying to escape from the heat and by nurses with their charges.

He found Mme. Walter in a little antique ruin; she seemed unhappy and anxious. When he had greeted her, she said: "How many people there are in the garden!"

He took advantage of the occasion: "Yes, that is true; shall we go somewhere else?"

"Where?"

"It matters not where; for a drive, for instance. You can lower the shade on your side and you will be well concealed."

"Yes, I should like that better; I shall die of fear here."

"Very well, meet me in five minutes at the gate which opens on the boulevard. I will fetch a cab."

When they were seated in the cab, she asked: "Where did you tell the coachman to drive to?"

Georges replied: "Do not worry; he knows."

He had given the man his address on the Rue de Constantinople.

Mme. Walter said to Du Roy: “You cannot imagine how I suffer on your account—how I am tormented, tortured. Yesterday I was harsh, but I wanted to escape you at any price. I was afraid to remain alone with you. Have you forgiven me?”

He pressed her hand. “Yes, yes, why should I not forgive you, loving you as I do?”

She looked at him with a beseeching air: “Listen: You must promise to respect me, otherwise I could never see you again.”

At first he did not reply; a smile lurked beneath his mustache; then he murmured: “I am your slave.”

She told him how she had discovered that she loved him, on learning that he was to marry Madeleine Forestier. Suddenly she ceased speaking. The carriage stopped. Du Roy opened the door.

“Where are we?” she asked.

He replied: “Alight and enter the house. We shall be undisturbed there.”

“Where are we?” she repeated.

“At my rooms; they are my bachelor apartments which I have rented for a few days that we might have a corner in which to meet.”

She clung to the cab, startled at the thought of a tete-a-tete, and stammered: “No, no, I do not want to.”

He said firmly: “I swear to respect you. Come, you see that people are looking at us, that a crowd is gathering around us. Make haste!” And he repeated, “I swear to respect you.”

She was terror-stricken and rushed into the house. She was about to ascend the stairs. He seized her arm: “It is here, on the ground floor.”

When he had closed the door, he showered kisses upon her neck, her eyes, her lips; in spite of herself, she submitted to his caresses and even returned them, hiding her face and murmuring in broken accents: “I swear that I have never had a lover”; while he thought: “That is a matter of indifference to me.”

CHAPTER XIII.

MADAME DE MARELLE

Autumn had come. The Du Roys had spent the entire summer in Paris, leading a vigorous campaign in "La Vie Francaise," in favor of the new cabinet. Although it was only the early part of October, the chamber was about to resume its sessions, for affairs in Morocco were becoming menacing. The celebrated speech made by Count de Lambert Sarrazin had furnished Du Roy with material for ten articles on the Algerian colony. "La Vie Francaise" had gained considerable prestige by its connection with the power; it was the first to give political news, and every newspaper in Paris and the provinces sought information from it. It was quoted, feared, and began to be respected: it was no longer the organ of a group of political intriguers, but the avowed mouthpiece of the cabinet. Laroche-Mathieu was the soul of the journal and Du Roy his speaking-trumpet. M. Walter retired discreetly into the background. Madeleine's salon became an influential center in which several members of the cabinet met every week. The president of the council had even dined there twice; the minister of foreign affairs was quite at home at the Du Roys; he came at any hour, bringing dispatches or information, which he dictated either to the husband or wife as if they were his secretaries. After the minister had departed, when Du Roy was alone with Madeleine, he uttered threats and insinuations against the "parvenu," as he called him. His wife simply shrugged her shoulders scornfully, repeating: "Become a minister and you can do the same; until then, be silent."

His reply was: "No one knows of what I am capable; perhaps they will find out some day."

She answered philosophically: "He who lives will see."

The morning of the reopening of the Chamber, Du Roy lunched with Laroche-Mathieu in order to receive instructions from him, before the session, for a political article the following day in "La Vie Francaise," which was to be a sort of official declaration of the plans of the cabinet. After listening to Laroche-Mathieu's eloquence for some time with jealousy in his heart, Du Roy sauntered slowly toward the office to commence his work, for he had nothing to do until four o'clock, at which hour he was to meet Mme. de Marelle at Rue de Constantinople. They met there regularly twice a week, Mondays and Wednesdays.

On entering the office, he was handed a sealed dispatch; it was from Mme. Walter, and read thus:

"It is absolutely necessary that I should see you to-day. It is important. Expect me at two o'clock at Rue de Constantinople. I can render you a great service; your friend until death,"

"VIRGINIE."

He exclaimed: "Heavens! what a bore!" and left the office at once, too much annoyed to work.

For six weeks he had ineffectually tried to break with Mme. Walter. At three successive meetings she had been a prey to remorse, and had overwhelmed her lover with reproaches. Angered by those scenes and already weary of the dramatic woman, he had simply avoided her, hoping that the affair would end in that way.

But she persecuted him with her affection, summoned him at all times by telegrams to meet her at street corners, in shops, or public gardens. She was very different from what he had fancied she would be, trying to attract him by actions ridiculous in one of her age. It disgusted him to hear her call him: "My rat—my dog—my treasure—my jewel—my bluebird"—and to see her assume a kind of childish modesty when he approached. It seemed to him that being the mother of a family, a woman of the world, she should have been more sedate, and have yielded With tears if she chose, but with the tears of a Dido and not of a Juliette. He never heard her call him "Little one" or "Baby," without wishing to reply "Old woman," to take his hat with an oath and leave the room.

At first they had often met at Rue de Constantinople, but Du Roy, who feared an encounter with Mme. de Marelle, invented a thousand and one pretexts in order to avoid that rendezvous. He was therefore obliged to either lunch or dine at her house daily, when she would clasp his hand under cover of the table or offer him her lips behind the doors. Above all, Georges enjoyed being thrown so much in contact with Suzanne; she made sport of everything and everybody with cutting appropriateness. At length, however, he began to feel an unconquerable repugnance to the love lavished upon him by the mother; he could no longer see her, hear her, nor think of her without anger. He ceased calling upon her, replying to her letters, and yielding to her appeals. She finally divined that he no longer loved her, and the discovery caused her unutterable anguish; but she watched him, followed him in a cab with drawn blinds to the office, to his house, in the hope of seeing him pass by. He would have liked to strangle her, but he controlled himself on account of his position on "La Vie Francaise" and he endeavored by means of coldness, and even at times harsh words, to make her comprehend that all was at an end between them.

Then, too, she persisted in devising ruses for summoning him to Rue de Constantinople, and he was in constant fear that the two women would some day meet face to face at the door.

On the other hand, his affection for Mme. de Marelle had increased during the summer. They were both Bohemians by nature; they took excursions together to Argenteuil, Bougival, Maisons, and Poissy, and when he was forced to return and dine at Mme. Walter's, he detested his mature mistress more thoroughly, as he recalled the youthful one he had just left. He was congratulating himself upon having freed himself almost entirely from the former's clutches, when he received the telegram above mentioned.

He re-read it as he walked along. He thought: "What does that old owl want with me? I am certain she has nothing to tell me except that she adores me. However, I will see, perhaps there is some truth in it. Clotilde is coming at four, I must get rid of the other one at three or soon after, provided they do not meet. What jades women are!"

As he uttered those words he was reminded of his wife, who was the only one who did not torment him; she lived by his side and seemed to love him very much at the proper time, for she never permitted anything to interfere with her ordinary occupations of life. He strolled toward the appointed place of meeting, mentally cursing Mme. Walter.

"Ah, I will receive her in such a manner that she will not tell me anything. First of all, I will give her to understand that I shall never cross her threshold again."

He entered to await her. She soon arrived and, seeing him, exclaimed: "Ah, you received my dispatch! How fortunate!"

"Yes, I received it at the office just as I was setting out for the Chamber. What do you want?" he asked ungraciously.

She had raised her veil in order to kiss him, and approached him timidly and humbly with the air of a beaten dog.

"How unkind you are to me; how harshly you speak! What have I done to you? You do not know what I have suffered for you!"

He muttered: "Are you going to begin that again?"

She stood near him awaiting a smile, a word of encouragement, to cast herself into his arms, and whispered: "You need not have won me to treat me thus; you might have left me virtuous and happy. Do you remember what you said to me in the church and how you forced me to enter this house? And now this is the way you speak to me, receive me! My God, my God, how you maltreat me!"

He stamped his foot and said violently: "Enough, be silent! I can never see you a moment without hearing that refrain. You were mature when you gave yourself to me. I am much obliged to you; I am infinitely grateful, but I need not be tied to your apron-strings until I die! You have a husband and I a wife. Neither of us is free; it was all a caprice, and now it is at an end!"

She said: "How brutal you are, how coarse and villainous! No, I was no longer a young girl, but I had never loved, never wavered in my dignity."

He interrupted her: "I know it, you have told me that twenty times; but you have had two children."

She drew back as if she had been struck: "Oh, Georges!" And pressing her hands to her heart, she burst into tears.

When she began to weep, he took his hat: "Ah, you are crying again! Good evening! Is it for this that you sent for me?"

She took a step forward in order to bar the way, and drawing a handkerchief from her pocket she wiped her eyes. Her voice grew steadier: "No, I came to—to give you—political news—to give you the means of earning fifty thousand francs—or even more if you wish to."

Suddenly softened he asked: "How?"

"By chance last evening I heard a conversation between my husband and Laroche. Walter advised the minister not to let you into the secret for you would expose it."

Du Roy placed his hat upon a chair and listened attentively.

"They are going to take possession of Morocco!"

"Why, I lunched with Laroche this morning, and he told me the cabinet's plans!"

"No, my dear, they have deceived you, because they feared their secret would be made known."

"Sit down," said Georges.

He sank into an armchair, while she drew up a stool and took her seat at his feet. She continued:

"As I think of you continually, I pay attention to what is talked of around me," and she proceeded to tell him what she had heard relative to the expedition to Tangiers which had been decided upon the day that Laroche assumed his office; she told him how they had little by little bought up, through agents who aroused no suspicions, the Moroccan loan, which had fallen to sixty-four or sixty-five francs; how when the expedition was entered upon the French government would guarantee the debt, and their friends would make fifty or sixty millions.

He cried: "Are you sure of that?"

She replied: "Yes, I am sure."

He continued: "That is indeed fine! As for that rascal of a Laroche, let him beware! I will get his ministerial carcass between my fingers yet!"

Then, after a moment's reflection, he muttered: "One might profit by that!"

"You too can buy some stock," said she; "it is only seventy-two francs."

He replied: "But I have no ready money."

She raised her eyes to his—eyes full of supplication.

"I have thought of that, my darling, and if you love me a little, you will let me lend it to you."

He replied abruptly, almost harshly: "No, indeed."

She whispered imploringly: "Listen, there is something you can do without borrowing money. I intended buying ten thousand francs' worth of the stock; instead, I will take twenty thousand and you can have half. There will be nothing to pay at once. If it succeeds, we will make seventy thousand francs; if not, you will owe me ten thousand which you can repay at your pleasure."

He said again: "No, I do not like those combinations."

She tried to persuade him by telling him that she advanced nothing—that the payments were made by Walter's bank. She pointed out to him that he had led the political campaign in "La Vie Francaise," and that he would be very simple not to profit by the results he had helped to bring about. As he still hesitated, she added: "It is in reality Walter who will advance the money, and you have done enough for him to offset that sum."

"Very well," said he, "I will do it. If we lose I will pay you back ten thousand francs."

She was so delighted that she rose, took his head between her hands, and kissed him. At first he did not repulse her, but when she grew more lavish with her caresses, he said:

"Come, that will do."

She gazed at him sadly. "Oh, Georges, I can no longer even embrace you."

"No, not to-day. I have a headache."

She reseated herself with docility at his feet and asked:

"Will you dine with us to-morrow? It would give me such pleasure,"

He hesitated at first, but dared not refuse.

"Yes, certainly."

"Thank you, dearest." She rubbed her cheek against the young man's vest; as she did so, one of her long black hairs caught on a button; she twisted it tightly around, then she twisted another around another button and so on. When he rose, he would tear them out of her head, and would carry away with him unwittingly a lock of her hair. It would be an invisible bond between them. Involuntarily he would think, would dream of her; he would love her a little more the next day.

Suddenly he said: "I must leave you, for I am expected at the Chamber for the close of the session. I cannot be absent to-day."

She sighed: "Already!" Then adding resignedly: "Go, my darling, but you will come to dinner tomorrow"; she rose abruptly. For a moment she felt a sharp, stinging pain, as if needles had been stuck into her head, but she was glad to have suffered for him.

"Adieu," said she.

He took her in his arms and kissed her eyes coldly; then she offered him her lips which he brushed lightly as he said: "Come, come, let us hurry; it is after three o'clock."

She passed out before him saying: "To-morrow at seven"; he repeated her words and they separated.

Du Roy returned at four o'clock to await his mistress. She was somewhat late because her husband had come home for a week. She asked:

"Can you come to dinner to-morrow? He will be delighted to see you."

"No; I dine at the Walters. We have a great many political and financial matters to talk over."

She took off her hat. He pointed to a bag on the mantelpiece: "I bought you some sweetmeats."

She clapped her hands. "What a darling you are!" She took them, tasted one, and said: "They are delicious. I shall not leave one. Come, sit down in the armchair, I will sit at your feet and eat my bonbons."

He smiled as he saw her take the seat a short while since occupied by Mme. Walter. She too, called him "darling, little one, dearest," and the words seemed to him sweet and caressing from her lips, while from Mme. Walter's they irritated and nauseated him.

Suddenly he remembered the seventy thousand francs he was going to make, and bluntly interrupting Mme. de Marelle's chatter, he said:

"Listen, my darling; I am going to intrust you with a message to your husband. Tell him from me to buy to-morrow ten thousand francs' worth of Moroccan stock which is at seventy-two, and I predict that before three months are passed he will have made eighty thousand francs. Tell him to maintain absolute silence. Tell him that the expedition to Tangiers, is decided upon, and that the French government will guarantee the Moroccan debt. It is a state secret I am confiding to you, remember!"

She listened to him gravely and murmured:

"Thank you. I will tell my husband this evening. You may rely upon him; he will not speak of it; he can be depended upon; there is no danger."

She had eaten all of her bonbons and began to toy with the buttons on his vest. Suddenly she drew a long hair out of the buttonhole and began to laugh.

"See! Here is one of Madeleine's hairs; you are a faithful husband!" Then growing serious, she examined the scarcely perceptible thread more closely and said: "It is not Madeleine's, it is dark."

He smiled. "It probably belongs to the housemaid."

But she glanced at the vest with the care of a police-inspector and found a second hair twisted around a second button; then she saw a third; and turning pale and trembling somewhat, she exclaimed: "Oh, some woman has left hairs around all your buttons."

In surprise, he stammered: "Why you—you are mad."

She continued to unwind the hairs and cast them upon the floor. With her woman's instinct she had divined their meaning and gasped in her anger, ready to cry:

"She loves you and she wished you to carry away with you something of hers. Oh, you are a traitor." She uttered a shrill, nervous cry: "Oh, it is an old woman's hair—here is a white one—you have taken a fancy to an old woman now. Then you do not need me—keep the other one." She rose.

He attempted to detain her and stammered: "No—Clo—you are absurd—I do not know whose it is—listen—stay—see—stay—"

But she repeated: "Keep your old woman—keep her—have a chain made of her hair—of her gray hair—there is enough for that—"

Hastily she donned her hat and veil, and when he attempted to touch her she struck him in the face, and made her escape while he was stunned by the blow. When he found that he was alone, he cursed Mme. Walter, bathed his face, and went out vowing vengeance. That time he would not pardon. No, indeed.

He strolled to the boulevard and stopped at a jeweler's to look at a chronometer he had wanted for some time and which would cost eighteen hundred francs. He thought with joy: "If I make my seventy thousand francs, I can pay for it"—and he began to dream of all the things he would do when he got the money. First of all he would become a deputy; then he would buy the chronometer; then he would speculate on 'Change, and then, and then—he did not enter the office, preferring to confer with Madeleine before seeing Walter again and writing his article; he turned toward home. He reached Rue Drouot when he paused; he had forgotten to inquire for Count de Vaudrec, who lived on Chaussee d'Antin. He retraced his steps with a light heart, thinking of a thousand things—of the fortune he would make,—of that rascal of a Laroche, and of old Walter.

He was not at all uneasy as to Clotilde's anger, knowing that she would soon forgive him.

When he asked the janitor of the house in which Count de Vaudrec lived: "How is M. de Vaudrec? I have heard that he has been ailing of late," the man replied; "The Count is very ill, sir; they think he will not live through the night; the gout has reached his heart."

Du Roy was so startled he did not know what to do! Vaudrec dying! He stammered:

"Thanks—I will call again"—unconscious of what he was saying. He jumped into a cab and drove home. His wife had returned. He entered her room out of breath: "Did you know? Vaudrec is dying!"

She was reading a letter and turning to him asked: "What did you say?"

"I said that Vaudrec is dying of an attack of gout."

Then he added: "What shall you do?"

She rose; her face was livid; she burst into tears and buried her face in her hands. She remained standing, shaken by sobs, torn by anguish. Suddenly she conquered her grief and wiping her eyes, said: "I am going to him—do not worry about me—I do not know what time I shall return—do not expect me."

He replied: "Very well. Go."

They shook hands and she left in such haste that she forgot her gloves. Georges, after dining alone, began to write his article. He wrote it according to the minister's instructions, hinting to the readers that the expedition to Morocco would not take place. He took it, when completed, to the office, conversed several moments with M. Walter, and set out again, smoking, with a light heart, he knew not why.

His wife had not returned. He retired and fell asleep. Toward midnight Madeleine came home. Georges sat up in bed and asked: "Well?"

He had never seen her so pale and agitated. She whispered: "He is dead!"

"Ah—and—he told you nothing?"

"Nothing. He was unconscious when I arrived."

Questions which he dared not ask arose to Georges' lips.

"Lie down and rest," said he.

She disrobed hastily and slipped into bed.

He continued: "Had he any relatives at his death-bed?"

"Only a nephew."

"Ah! Did he often see that nephew?"

"They had not met for ten years."

"Had he other relatives?"

"No, I believe not."

"Will that nephew be his heir?"

"I do not know."

"Was Vaudrec very rich?"

“Yes, very.”

“Do you know what he was worth?”

“No, not exactly—one or two millions perhaps.”

He said no more. She extinguished the light. He could not sleep. He looked upon Mme. Walter’s promised seventy thousand francs as very insignificant. Suddenly he thought he heard Madeleine crying. In order to insure himself he asked: “Are you asleep?”

“No.” Her voice was tearful and unsteady.

He continued: “I forgot to tell you that your minister has deceived us.”

“How?”

He gave her a detailed account of the combination prepared by Laroche and Walter. When he concluded she asked: “How did you know that?”

He replied: “Pardon me if I do not tell you! You have your means of obtaining information into which I do not inquire; I have mine which I desire to keep. I can vouch at any rate for the truth of my statements.”

She muttered: “It may be possible. I suspected that they were doing something without our knowledge.”

As she spoke Georges drew near her; she paid no heed to his proximity, however, and turning toward the wall, he closed his eyes and fell asleep.

CHAPTER XIV.

THE WILL

The church was draped in black, and over the door a large escutcheon surmounted by a coronet announced to the passers-by that a nobleman was being buried. The ceremony was just over; those present went out slowly, passing by the coffin, and by Count de Vaudrec's nephew, who shook hands and returned salutations.

When Georges du Roy and his wife left the church, they walked along side by side on their way home. They did not speak; they were both preoccupied. At length Georges said, as if talking to himself: "Truly it is very astonishing!"

Madeleine asked: "What, my friend?"

"That Vaudrec left us nothing."

She blushed and said: "Why should he leave us anything? Had he any reason for doing so?" Then after several moments of silence, she continued: "Perhaps there is a will at a lawyer's; we should not know of it."

He replied: "That is possible, for he was our best friend. He dined with us twice a week; he came at any time; he was at home with us. He loved you as a father; he had no family, no children, no brothers nor sisters, only a nephew. Yes, there should be a will. I would not care for much—a remembrance to prove that he thought of us—that he recognized the affection we felt for him. We should certainly have a mark of friendship."

She said with a pensive and indifferent air: "It is possible that there is a will."

When they entered the house, the footman handed Madeleine a letter. She opened it and offered it to her husband.

"OFFICE OF M. LAMANEUR,
Notary.
17 Rue des Vosges,"

"Madame: Kindly call at my office at a quarter past two o'clock Tuesday, Wednesday, or Thursday, on business which concerns you."

"Yours respectfully,"
"LAMANEUR."

Georges, in his turn, colored.

"That is as it should be. It is strange, however, that he should write to you and not to me, for I am the head of the family legally."

"Shall we go at once?" she asked.

"Yes, I should like to."

After luncheon they set out for M. Lamaneur's office.

The notary was a short, round man—round all over. His head looked like a ball fastened to another ball, which was supported by legs so short that they too almost resembled balls.

He bowed, as Du Roy and his wife were shown into his office, pointed to seats, and said, turning to Madeleine: "Madame, I sent for you in order to inform you of Count de Vaudrec's will, which will be of interest to you."

Georges could not help muttering: "I suspected that."

The notary continued: "I shall read you the document which is very brief."

"'I, the undersigned, Paul Emile Cyprien Gontran, Count de Vaudrec, sound both in body and mind, here express my last wishes. As death might take me away at any moment, I wish to take the precaution of drawing up my will, to be deposited with M. Lamaneur.'"

"'Having no direct heirs, I bequeath all my fortune, comprising stocks and bonds for six hundred thousand francs and landed property for five hundred thousand, to Mme. Claire Madeleine du Roy unconditionally. I beg her to accept that gift from a dead friend as a proof of devoted, profound, and respectful affection.'"

The notary said: "That is all. That document bears the date of August last, and took the place of one of the same nature made two years ago in the name of Mme. Claire Madeleine Forestier. I have the first will, which would prove, in case of contestation on the part of the family, that Count de Vaudrec had not changed his mind."

Madeleine cast down her eyes; her cheeks were pale. Georges nervously twisted his mustache.

The notary continued after a moment's pause: "It is of course understood that Madame cannot accept that legacy without your consent."

Du Roy rose and said shortly: "I ask time for reflection."

The notary smiled, bowed, and replied pleasantly: "I comprehend the scruples which cause you to hesitate. I may add that M. de Vaudrec's nephew, who was informed this morning of his uncle's last wishes, expresses himself as ready to respect them if he be given one hundred thousand francs. In my opinion the will cannot be broken, but a lawsuit would cause a sensation which you would probably like to avoid. The world often judges uncharitably. Can you let me have your reply before Saturday?"

Georges bowed, and together with his wife left the office. When they arrived home, Du Roy closed the door and throwing his hat on the bed, asked: "What were the relations between you and Vaudrec?"

Madeleine, who was taking off her veil, turned around with a shudder: "Between us?"

"Yes, between you and him! One does not leave one's entire fortune to a woman unless—"

She trembled, and could scarcely take out the pins which fastened the transparent tissue. Then she stammered in an agitated manner: "You are mad—you are—you are—you did not think—he would leave you anything!"

Georges replied, emphazing each word: "Yes, he could have left me something; me, your husband, his friend; but not you, my wife and his friend. The distinction is material in the eyes of the world."

Madeleine gazed at him fixedly: "It seems to me that the world would have considered a legacy from him to you very strange."

"Why?"

"Because,"—she hesitated, then continued: "Because you are my husband; because you were not well acquainted; because I have been his friend so long; because his first will, made during Forestier's lifetime, was already in my favor."

Georges began to pace to and fro. He finally said: "You cannot accept that."

She answered indifferently: "Very well; it is not necessary then to wait until Saturday; you can inform M. Lamaneur at once."

He paused before her, and they gazed into one another's eyes as if by that mute and ardent interrogation they were trying to examine each other's consciences. In a low voice he murmured: "Come, confess your relations."

She shrugged her shoulders. "You are absurd. Vaudrec was very fond of me, very, but there was nothing more, never."

He stamped his foot. "You lie! It is not possible."

She replied calmly: "It is so, nevertheless."

He resumed his pacing to and fro; then pausing again, he said: "Explain to me, then, why he left all his fortune to you."

She did so with a nonchalant air: "It is very simple. As you said just now, we were his only friends, or rather, I was his only friend, for he knew me when a child. My mother was a governess in his father's house. He came here continually, and as he had no legal heirs, he selected me. It is possible that he even loved me a little. But what woman has never been loved thus? He brought me flowers every Monday. You were never surprised at that, and he never brought you any. To-day he leaves me his fortune for the same reason, because he had no one else to leave it to. It would on the other hand have been extremely surprising if he had left it to you."

"Why?"

"What are you to him?"

She spoke so naturally and so calmly that Georges hesitated before replying: "It makes no difference; we cannot accept that bequest under those conditions. Everyone would talk about it and laugh at me. My fellow-journalists are already too much disposed to be jealous of me and to attack me. I have to be especially careful of my honor and my reputation. I cannot permit my wife to accept a legacy of that kind from a man whom rumor has already assigned to her as her lover. Forestier might perhaps have tolerated that, but I shall not."

She replied gently: "Very well, my dear, we will not take it; it will be a million less in our pockets, that is all."

Georges paced the room and uttered his thoughts aloud, thus speaking to his wife without addressing her:

"Yes, a million—so much the worse. He did not think when making his will what a breach of etiquette he was committing. He did not realize in what a false, ridiculous position he was placing me. He should have left half of it to me—that would have made matters right."

He seated himself, crossed his legs and began to twist the ends of his mustache, as was his custom when annoyed, uneasy, or pondering over a weighty question.

Madeleine took up a piece of embroidery upon which she worked occasionally, and said: "I have nothing to say. You must decide."

It was some time before he replied; then he said hesitatingly: "The world would never understand how it was that Vaudrec constituted you his sole heiress and that I allowed it. To accept that legacy would be to avow guilty relations on your part and an infamous lack of self-respect on mine. Do you know how the acceptance of it might be interpreted? We should have to find some adroit means of palliating it. We should have to give people to suppose, for instance, that he divided his fortune between us, giving half to you and half to me."

She said: "I do not see how that can be done, since there is a formal will."

He replied: "Oh, that is very simple. We have no children; you can therefore deed me part of the inheritance. In that way we can silence malignant tongues."

She answered somewhat impatiently: "I do not see how we can silence malignant tongues since the will is there, signed by Vaudrec."

He said angrily: "Do you need to exhibit it, or affix it to the door? You are absurd! We will say that the fortune was left us jointly by Count de Vaudrec. That is all. You cannot, moreover, accept the legacy without my authority; I will only consent on the condition of a partition which will prevent me from becoming a laughing-stock for the world."

She glanced sharply at him: "As you will. I am ready."

He seemed to hesitate again, rose, paced the floor, and avoiding his wife's piercing gaze, he said: "No—decidedly no—perhaps it would be better to renounce it altogether—it would be more correct—more honorable. From the nature of the bequest even charitably-disposed people would suspect illicit relations."

He paused before Madeleine. "If you like, my darling, I will return to M. Lamaneur's alone, to consult him and to explain the matter to him. I will tell him of my scruples and I will add that we have agreed to divide it in order to avoid any scandal. From the moment that I accept a portion of the inheritance it will be evident that there is nothing wrong. I can say: 'My wife accepts it because I, her husband, accept'—I, who am the best judge of what she can do without compromising herself."

Madeleine simply murmured: "As you wish."

He continued: "Yes, it will be as clear as day if that is done. We inherit a fortune from a friend who wished to make no distinction between us, thereby showing that his liking for you was purely Platonic. You may be sure that if he had given it a thought, that is what he would have done. He did not reflect—he did not foresee the consequences. As you said just now, he offered you flowers every week, he left you his wealth."

She interrupted him with a shade of annoyance:

"I understand. No more explanations are necessary. Go to the notary at once."

He stammered in confusion: "You are right; I will go." He took his hat, and, as he was leaving the room, he asked: "Shall I try to compromise with the nephew for fifty thousand francs?"

She replied haughtily: "No. Give him the hundred thousand francs he demands, and take them from my share if you wish."

Abashed, he murmured: "No, we will share it. After deducting fifty thousand francs each we will still have a million net." Then he added: "Until later, my little Made."

He proceeded to the notary's to explain the arrangement decided upon, which he claimed originated with his wife. The following day they signed a deed for five hundred thousand francs, which Madeleine du Roy gave up to her husband.

On leaving the office, as it was pleasant, Georges proposed that they take a stroll along the boulevards. He was very tender, very careful of her, and laughed joyously while she remained pensive and grave.

It was a cold, autumn day. The pedestrians seemed in haste and walked along rapidly.

Du Roy led his wife to the shop into the windows of which he had so often gazed at the coveted chronometer.

"Shall I buy you some trinket?" he asked.

She replied indifferently: "As you like."

They entered the shop: "What would you prefer, a necklace, a bracelet, or earrings?"

The sight of the brilliant gems made her eyes sparkle in spite of herself, as she glanced at the cases filled with costly baubles.

Suddenly she exclaimed: "There is a lovely bracelet."

It was a chain, very unique in shape, every link of which was set with a different stone.

Georges asked: "How much is that bracelet?"

The jeweler replied: "Three thousand francs, sir."

"If you will let me have it for two thousand five hundred, I will take it."

The man hesitated, then replied: "No, sir, it is impossible."

Du Roy said: "See here—throw in this chronometer at fifteen hundred francs; that makes four thousand, and I will pay cash. If you do not agree, I will go somewhere else."

The jeweler finally yielded. "Very well, sir."

The journalist, after leaving his address, said: "You can have my initials G. R. C. interlaced below a baron's crown, engraved on the chronometer."

Madeleine, in surprise, smiled, and when they left the shop, she took his arm quite affectionately. She thought him very shrewd and clever. He was right; now that he had a fortune he must have a title.

They passed the Vaudeville on their way arid, entering, secured a box. Then they repaired to Mme, de Marelle's at Georges' suggestion, to invite her to spend the evening with them. Georges rather dreaded the first meeting with Clotilde, but she did not seem to bear him any malice, or even to remember their disagreement. The dinner, which they took at a restaurant, was excellent, and the evening altogether enjoyable.

Georges and Madeleine returned home late. The gas was extinguished, and in order to light the way the journalist from time to time struck a match. On reaching the landing on the first floor they saw their reflections in the mirror. Du Roy raised his hand with the lighted match in it, in order to distinguish their images more clearly, and said, with a triumphant smile:

"The millionaires are passing by."

CHAPTER XV.

SUZANNE

Morocco had been conquered; France, the mistress of Tangiers, had guaranteed the debt of the annexed country. It was rumored that two ministers, Laroche-Mathieu being one of them, had made twenty millions.

As for Walter, in a few days he had become one of the masters of the world—a financier more omnipotent than a king. He was no longer the Jew, Walter, the director of a bank, the proprietor of a yellow newspaper; he was M. Walter the wealthy Israelite, and he wished to prove it.

Knowing the straitened circumstances of the Prince de Carlsbourg who owned one of the fairest mansions on Rue du Faubourg Saint-Honore, he proposed to buy it. He offered three million francs for it. The prince, tempted by the sum, accepted his offer; the next day, Walter took possession of his new dwelling. Then another idea occurred to him—an idea of conquering all Paris—an idea a la Bonaparte.

At that time everyone was raving over a painting by the Hungarian, Karl Marcovitch, exhibited by Jacques Lenoble and representing "Christ Walking on the Water." Art critics enthusiastically declared it to be the most magnificent painting of the age. Walter bought it, thereby causing entire Paris to talk of him, to envy him, to censure or approve his action. He issued an announcement in the papers that everyone was invited to come on a certain evening to see it.

Du Roy was jealous of M. Walter's success. He had thought himself wealthy with the five hundred thousand francs extorted from his wife, and now he felt poor as he compared his paltry fortune with the shower of millions around him. His envious rage increased daily. He cherished ill will toward everyone—toward the Walters, even toward his wife, and above all toward the man who had deceived him, made use of him, and who dined twice a week at his house. Georges acted as his secretary, agent, mouthpiece, and when he wrote at his dictation, he felt a mad desire to strangle him. Laroche reigned supreme in the Du Roy household, having taken the place of Count de Vaudrec; he spoke to the servants as if he were their master. Georges submitted to it all, like a dog which wishes to bite and dares not. But he was often harsh and brutal to Madeleine, who merely shrugged her shoulders and treated him as one would a fretful child. She was surprised, too, at his constant ill humor, and said: "I do not understand you. You are always complaining. Your position is excellent."

His only reply was to turn his back upon her. He declared that he would not attend M. Walter's fete—that he would not cross the miserable Jew's threshold. For two months Mme. Walter had written to him daily, beseeching him to come to see her, to appoint a meeting where he would, in order that she might give him the seventy thousand francs she had made for him. He did not reply and threw her letters into the fire. Not that he would have refused to accept his share of the profits, but he enjoyed treating her scornfully, trampling her under foot; she was too wealthy; he would be inflexible.

The day of the exhibition of the picture, as Madeleine chided him for not going, he replied: "Leave me in peace. I shall remain at home."

After they had dined, he said suddenly, "I suppose I shall have to go through with it. Get ready quickly."

"I shall be ready in fifteen minutes," she said.

As they entered the courtyard of the Hotel de Carlsbourg it was one blaze of light. A magnificent carpet was spread upon the steps leading to the entrance, and upon each one stood a man in livery, as rigid as marble.

Du Roy's heart was torn with jealousy. He and his wife ascended the steps and gave their wraps to the footmen who approached them.

At the entrance to the drawing-room, two children, one in pink, the other in blue, handed bouquets to the ladies.

The rooms were already well filled. The majority of the ladies were in street costumes, a proof that they came thither as they would go to any exhibition. The few who intended to remain to the ball which was to follow wore evening dress.

Mme. Walter, surrounded by friends, stood in the second salon and received the visitors. Many did not know her, and walked through the rooms as if in a museum—without paying any heed to the host and hostess.

When Virginie perceived Du Roy, she grew livid and made a movement toward him; then she paused and waited for him to advance. He bowed ceremoniously, while Madeleine greeted her effusively. Georges left his wife near Mme. Walter and mingled with the guests. Five drawing-rooms opened one into the other; they were carpeted with rich, oriental rugs, and upon their walls hung paintings by the old masters. As he made his way through the throng, some one seized his arm, and a fresh, youthful voice whispered in his ear: "Ah, here you are at last, naughty Bel-Ami! Why do we never see you any more?"

It was Suzanne Walter, with her azure eyes and wealth of golden hair. He was delighted to see her, and apologized as they shook hands.

"I have been so busy for two months that I have been nowhere."

She replied gravely: "That is too bad. You have grieved us deeply, for mamma and I adore you. As for myself, I cannot do without you. If you are not here, I am bored to death. You see I tell you so frankly, that you will not remain away like that any more. Give me your arm; I will show you 'Christ Walking on the Water' myself; it is at the very end, behind the conservatory. Papa put it back there so that everyone would be obliged to go through the rooms. It is astonishing how proud papa is of this house."

As they walked through the rooms, all turned to look at that handsome man and that bewitching girl. A well-known painter said: "There is a fine couple." Georges thought: "If my position had been made, I would have married her. Why did I never think of it? How could I have taken the other one? What folly! One always acts too hastily—one never reflects sufficiently." And longing, bitter longing possessed him, corrupting all his pleasure, rendering life odious.

Suzanne said: "You must come often, Bel-Ami; we can do anything we like now papa is rich."

He replied: "Oh, you will soon marry—some prince, perhaps, and we shall never meet any more."

She cried frankly: "Oh, oh, I shall not! I shall choose some one I love very dearly. I am rich enough for two."

He smiled ironically and said: "I give you six months. By that time you will be Madame la Marquise, Madame la Duchesse, or Madame la Princesse, and you will look down upon me, Mademoiselle."

She pretended to be angry, patted his arm with her fan, and vowed that she would marry according to the dictates of her heart.

He replied: "We shall see; you are too wealthy."

"You, too, have inherited some money."

"Barely twenty thousand livres a year. It is a mere pittance nowadays."

"But your wife has the same."

"Yes, we have a million together; forty thousand a year. We cannot even keep a carriage on that."

They had, in the meantime, reached the last drawing-room, and before them lay the conservatory with its rare shrubs and plants. To their left, under a dome of palms, was a marble basin, on the edges of which four large swans of delftware emitted the water from their beaks.

The journalist stopped and said to himself: "This is luxury; this is the kind of house in which to live. Why can I not have one?"

His companion did not speak. He looked at her and thought once more: "If I only had taken her!"

Suddenly Suzanne seemed to awaken from her reverie. "Come," said she, dragging Georges through a group which barred their way, and turning him to the right. Before him, surrounded by verdure on all sides, was the picture. One had to look closely at it in order to understand it. It was a grand work—the work of a master—one of those triumphs of art which furnishes one for years with food for thought.

Du Roy gazed at it for some time, and then turned away, to make room for others. Suzanne's tiny hand still rested upon his arm. She asked:

"Would you like a glass of champagne? We will go to the buffet; we shall find papa there."

Slowly they traversed the crowded rooms. Suddenly Georges heard a voice say: "That is Laroche and Mme. du Roy."

He turned and saw his wife passing upon the minister's arm. They were talking in low tones and smiling into each other's eyes. He fancied he saw some people whisper, as they gazed at them, and he felt a desire to fall upon those two beings and smite them to the earth. His wife was making a laughing-stock of him. Who was she? A shrewd little parvenue, that was all. He could never make his way with a wife who compromised him. She would be a stumbling-block in his path. Ah, if he had foreseen, if he had known. He would have played for higher stakes. What a brilliant match he might have made with little Suzanne! How could he have been so blind?

They reached the dining-room with its marble columns and walls hung with old Gobelins tapestry. Walter spied his editor, and hastened to shake hands. He was beside himself with joy. "Have you seen everything? Say, Suzanne, have you shown him everything? What a lot of people, eh? Have you seen Prince de Guerche? he just drank a glass of punch." Then he pounced upon Senator Rissolin and his wife.

A gentleman greeted Suzanne—a tall, slender man with fair whiskers and a worldly air. Georges heard her call him Marquis de Cazolles, and he was suddenly inspired with jealousy. How long had she known him? Since she had become wealthy no doubt. He saw in him a possible suitor. Some one seized his arm. It was Norbert de Varenne. The old poet said: "This is what they call amusing themselves. After a while they will dance, then they will retire, and the young girls will be satisfied. Take some champagne; it is excellent."

Georges scarcely heard his words. He was looking for Suzanne, who had gone off with the Marquis de Cazolles; he left Norbert de Varenne abruptly and went in pursuit of the young girl. The thirsty crowd stopped him; when he had made his way through it, he found himself face to face with M. and Mme. de Marelle. He had often met the wife, but he had not met the husband for some time; the latter grasped both of his hands and thanked him for the message he had sent him by Clotilde relative to the stocks.

Du Roy replied: "In exchange for that service I shall take your wife, or rather offer her my arm. Husband and wife should always be separated."

M. de Marelle bowed. "Very well. If I lose you we can meet here again in an hour."

The two young people disappeared in the crowd, followed by the husband. Mme. de Marelle said: "There are two girls who will have twenty or thirty millions each, and Suzanne is pretty in the bargain."

He made no reply; his own thought coming from the lips of another irritated him. He took Clotilde to see the painting. As they crossed the conservatory he saw his wife seated near Laroche-Mathieu, both of them almost hidden behind a group of plants. They seemed to say: "We are having a meeting in public, for we do not care for the world's opinion."

Mme. de Marelle admired Karl Marcovitch's painting, and they turned to repair to the other rooms. They were separated from M. de Marelle. He asked: "Is Laurine still vexed with me?"

"Yes. She refuses to see you and goes away when you are mentioned."

He did not reply. The child's sudden enmity grieved and annoyed him.

Suzanne met them at a door and cried: "Oh, here you are! Now, Bel-Ami, you are going to be left alone, for I shall take Clotilde to see my room." And the two women glided through the throng. At that moment a voice at his side murmured: "Georges!"

It was Mme. Walter. She continued in a low voice: "How cruel you are! How needlessly you inflict suffering upon me. I bade Suzanne take that woman away that I might have a word with you. Listen: I must speak to you this evening—or—or—you do not know what I shall do. Go into the conservatory. You will find a door to the left through which you can reach the garden. Follow the walk directly in front of you. At the end of it you will see an arbor. Expect me in ten minutes. If you do not meet me, I swear I will cause a scandal here at once!"

He replied haughtily: "Very well, I shall be at the place you named in ten minutes."

But Jacques Rival detained him. When he reached the alley, he saw Mme. Walter in front of him; she cried: "Ah, here you are! Do you wish to kill me?"

He replied calmly: "I beseech you, none of that, or I shall leave you at once."

Throwing her arms around his neck, she exclaimed: "What have I done to you that you should treat me so?"

He tried to push her away: "You twisted your hair around my coat buttons the last time we met, and it caused trouble between my wife and myself."

She shook her head: "Ah, your wife would not care. It was one of your mistresses who made a scene."

"I have none."

"Indeed! Why do you never come to see me? Why do you refuse to dine with me even once a week? I have no other thoughts than of you. I suffer terribly. You cannot understand that your image, always present, closes my throat, stifles me, and leaves me scarcely strength enough to move my limbs in order to walk. So I remain all day in my chair thinking of you."

He looked at her in astonishment. These were the words of a desperate woman, capable of anything. He, however, cherished a vague project and replied: "My dear, love is not eternal. One loves and one ceases to love. When it lasts it becomes a drawback. I want none of it! However, if you will be reasonable, and will receive and treat me as a friend, I will come to see you as formerly. Can you do that?"

She murmured: "I can do anything in order to see you."

"Then it is agreed that we are to be friends, nothing more."

She gasped: "It is agreed"; offering him her lips she cried in her despair: "One more kiss—one last kiss!"

He gently drew back. "No, we must adhere to our rules."

She turned her head and wiped away two tears, then drawing from her bosom a package of notes tied with pink ribbon, she held it toward Du Roy: "Here is your share of the profits in that Moroccan affair. I was so glad to make it for you. Here, take it."

He refused: "No, I cannot accept that money."

She became excited: "Oh, you will not refuse it now! It is yours, yours alone. If you do not take it, I will throw it in the sewer. You will not refuse it, Georges!"

He took the package and slipped it into his pocket "We must return to the house; you will take cold."

"So much the better; if I could but die!"

She seized his hand, kissed it passionately, and fled toward the house. He returned more leisurely, and entered the conservatory with head erect and smiling lips. His wife and Laroche were no longer there. The crowd had grown thinner. Suzanne, leaning on her sister's arm, advanced toward him. In a few moments, Rose, whom they teased about a certain Count, turned upon her heel and left them.

Du Roy, finding himself alone with Suzanne, said in a caressing voice: "Listen, my dear little one; do you really consider me a friend?"

"Why, yes, Bel-Ami."

"You have faith in me?"

"Perfect faith."

"Do you remember what I said to you a while since?"

"About what?"

"About your marriage, or rather the man you would marry."

"Yes."

"Well, will you promise me one thing?"

"Yes; what is it?"

"To consult me when you receive a proposal and to accept no one without asking my advice."

"Yes, I will gladly."

"And it is to be a secret between us—not a word to your father or mother."

"Not a word."

Rival approached them saying: "Mademoiselle, your father wants you in the ballroom."

She said: "Come, Bel-Ami," but he refused, for he had decided to leave at once, wishing to be alone with his thoughts. He went in search of his wife, and found her drinking chocolate at the buffet with two strange men. She introduced her husband without naming them.

In a short while, he asked: "Shall we go?"

"Whenever you like."

She took his arm and they passed through the almost deserted rooms.

Madeleine asked: "Where is Mme. Walter; I should like to bid her good-bye."

"It is unnecessary. She would try to keep us in the ballroom, and I have had enough."

"You are right."

On the way home they did not speak. But when they had entered their room, Madeleine, without even taking off her veil, said to him with a smile: "I have a surprise for you."

He growled ill-naturedly: "What is it?"

"Guess."

"I cannot make the effort."

"The day after to-morrow is the first of January."

"Yes."

"It is the season for New Year's gifts."

"Yes."

"Here is yours, which Laroche handed me just now." She gave him a small black box which resembled a jewel-casket.

He opened it indifferently and saw the cross of the Legion of Honor. He turned a trifle pale, then smiled, and said: "I should have preferred ten millions. That did not cost him much."

She had expected a transport of delight and was irritated by his indifference.

"You are incomprehensible. Nothing seems to satisfy you."

He replied calmly: "That man is only paying his debts; he owes me a great deal more."

She was astonished at his tone, and said: "It is very nice, however, at your age."

He replied: "I should have much more."

He took the casket, placed it on the mantelpiece, and looked for some minutes at the brilliant star within it, then he closed it with a shrug of his shoulders and began to prepare to retire.

"L'Officiel" of January 1 announced that M. Prosper Georges du Roy had been decorated with the Legion of Honor for exceptional services. The name was written in two words, and that afforded Georges more pleasure than the decoration itself.

An hour after having read that notice, he received a note from Mme. Walter, inviting him to come and bring his wife to dine with them that evening, to celebrate his distinction.

At first he hesitated, then throwing the letter in the fire, he said to Madeleine: "We shall dine at the Walters' this evening."

In her surprise she exclaimed: "Why, I thought you would never set your foot in their house again."

His sole reply was: "I have changed my mind."

When they arrived at Rue du Faubourg Saint-Honore, they found Mme. Walter alone in the dainty boudoir in which she received her intimate friends. She was dressed in black and her hair was powdered. At a distance she appeared like an old lady, in proximity, like a youthful one.

"Are you in mourning?" asked, Madeleine.

She replied sadly: "Yes and no. I have lost none of my relatives, but I have arrived at an age when one should wear somber colors. I wear it to-day to inaugurate it; hitherto I have worn it in my heart."

The dinner was somewhat tedious. Suzanne alone talked incessantly. Rose seemed preoccupied. The journalist was overwhelmed with congratulations, after the meal, when all repaired to the drawing-rooms. Mme. Walter detained him as they were about to enter the salon, saying: "I will never speak of anything to you again, only come to see me, Georges. It is impossible for me to live without you. I see you, I feel you, in my heart all day and all night. It is as if I had drunk a poison which preyed upon me. I cannot bear it. I would rather be as an old woman to you. I powdered my hair for that reason to-night; but come here—come from time to time as a friend."

He replied calmly: "Very well. It is unnecessary to speak of it again. You see I came to-day on receipt of your letter."

Walter, who had preceded them, with his two daughters and Madeleine, awaited Du Roy near the picture of "Christ Walking on the Water."

"Only think," said he, "I found my wife yesterday kneeling before that painting as if in a chapel. She was praying!"

Mme. Walter replied in a firm voice, in a voice in which vibrated a secret exaltation: "That Christ will save my soul. He gives me fresh courage and strength every time that I look at Him." And pausing before the picture, she murmured: "How beautiful He is! How frightened those men are, and how they love Him! Look at His head, His eyes, how simple and supernatural He is at the same time!"

Suzanne cried: "Why, He looks like you, Bel-Ami! I am sure He looks like you. The resemblance is striking."

She made him stand beside the painting and everyone recognized the likeness. Du Roy was embarrassed. Walter thought it very singular; Madeleine, with a smile, remarked that Jesus looked more manly. Mme. Walter stood by motionless, staring fixedly at her lover's face, her cheeks as white as her hair.

CHAPTER XVI.

DIVORCE

During the remainder of the winter, the Du Roys often visited the Walters. Georges, too, frequently dined there alone, Madeleine pleading fatigue and preferring to remain at home. He had chosen Friday as his day, and Mme. Walter never invited anyone else on that evening; it belonged to Bel-Ami. Often in a dark corner or behind a tree in the conservatory, Mme. Walter embraced the young man and whispered in his ear: "I love you, I love you! I love you desperately!"

But he always repulsed her coldly, saying: "If you persist in that, I will not come again."

Toward the end of March people talked of the marriage of the two sisters: Rose was to marry, Dame Rumor said, Count de Latour-Ivelin and Suzanne, the Marquis de Cazolles. The subject of Suzanne's possible marriage had not been broached again between her and Georges until one morning, the latter having been brought home by M. Walter to lunch, he whispered to Suzanne: "Come, let us give the fish some bread."

They proceeded to the conservatory in which was the marble basin containing the fish. As Georges and Suzanne leaned over its edge, they saw their reflections in the water and smiled at them. Suddenly, he said in a low voice: "It is not right of you to keep secrets from me, Suzanne."

She asked:

"What secrets, Bel-Ami?"

"Do you remember what you promised me here the night of the fete?"

"No."

"To consult me every time you received a proposal."

"Well?"

"Well, you have received one!"

"From whom?"

"You know very well."

"No, I swear I do not."

"Yes, you do. It is from that fop of a Marquis de Cazolles."

"He is not a fop."

"That may be, but he is stupid. He is no match for you who are so pretty, so fresh, so bright!"

She asked with a smile: "What have you against him?"

"I? Nothing!"

"Yes, you have. He is not all that you say he is."

"He is a fool, and an intriguer."

She glanced at him: "What ails you?"

He spoke as if tearing a secret from the depths of his heart: "I am—I am jealous of him."

She was astonished.

"You?"

"Yes, I."

"Why?"

"Because I love you and you know it"

Then she said severely: "You are mad, Bel-Ami!"

He replied: "I know that I am! Should I confess it—I, a married man, to you, a young girl? I am worse than mad—I am culpable, wretched—I have no possible hope, and that thought almost destroys my reason. When I hear that you are going to be married, I feel murder in my heart. You must forgive me, Suzanne."

He paused. The young girl murmured half sadly, half gaily: "It is a pity that you are married; but what can you do? It cannot be helped."

He turned toward her abruptly and said: "If I were free would you marry me?"

She replied: "Yes, Bel-Ami, I would marry you because I love you better than any of the others."

He rose and stammering: "Thanks—thanks—do not, I implore you, say yes to anyone. Wait a while. Promise me."

Somewhat confused, and without comprehending what he asked, she whispered: "I promise."

Du Roy threw a large piece of bread into the water and fled, without saying adieu, as if he were beside himself. Suzanne, in surprise, returned to the salon.

When Du Roy arrived home, he asked Madeleine, who was writing letters: "Shall you dine at the Walters' Friday? I am going."

She hesitated: "No, I am not well. I prefer to remain here."

"As you like. No one will force you." Then he took up his hat and went out.

For some time he had watched and followed her, knowing all her actions. The time he had awaited had come at length.

On Friday he dressed early, in order, as he said, to make several calls before going to M. Walter's. At about six o'clock, after having kissed his wife, he went in search of a cab. He said to the cabman: "You can stop at No. 17 Rue Fontaine, and remain there until I order you to go on. Then you can take me to the restaurant Du Coq-Faisan, Rue Lafayette."

The cab rolled slowly on; Du Roy lowered the shades. When in front of his house, he kept watch of it. After waiting ten minutes, he saw Madeleine come out and go toward the boulevards. When she was out of earshot, he put his head out of the window and cried: "Go on!"

The cab proceeded on its way and stopped at the Coq-Faisan. Georges entered the dining-room and ate slowly, looking at his watch from time to time. At seven-thirty he left and drove to Rue La Rochefoucauld. He mounted to the third story of a house in that street, and asked the maid who opened the door: "Is M. Guibert de Lorme at home?"

"Yes, sir."

He was shown into the drawing-room, and after waiting some time, a tall man with a military bearing and gray hair entered. He was the police commissioner.

Du Roy bowed, then said: "As I suspected, my wife is with her lover in furnished apartments they have rented on Rue des Martyrs."

The magistrate bowed: "I am at your service, sir."

"Very well, I have a cab below." And with three other officers they proceeded to the house in which Du Roy expected to surprise his wife. One officer remained at the door to watch the exit; on the second floor they halted; Du Roy rang the bell and they waited. In two or three minutes Georges rang again several times in succession. They heard a light step approach, and a woman's voice, evidently disguised, asked:

"Who is there?"

The police officer replied: "Open in the name of the law."

The voice repeated: "Who are you?"

"I am the police commissioner. Open, or I will force the door."

The voice continued: "What do you want?"

Du Roy interrupted: "It is I; it is useless to try to escape us."

The footsteps receded and then returned. Georges said: "If you do not open, we will force the door."

Receiving no reply he shook the door so violently that the old lock gave way, and the young man almost fell over Madeleine, who was standing in the antechamber in her petticoat, her hair loosened, her feet bare, and a candle in her hand.

He exclaimed: "It is she. We have caught them," and he rushed into the room. The commissioner turned to Madeleine, who had followed them through the rooms, in one of which were the remnants of a supper, and looking into her eyes said:

"You are Mme. Claire Madeleine du Roy, lawful wife of M. Prosper Georges du Roy, here present?"

She replied: "Yes, sir."

"What are you doing here?"

She made no reply. The officer repeated his question; still she did not reply. He waited several moments and then said: "If you do not confess, Madame, I shall be forced to inquire into the matter."

They could see a man's form concealed beneath the covers of the bed. Du Roy advanced softly and uncovered the livid face of M. Laroche-Mathieu.

The officer again asked: "Who are you?"

As the man did not reply, he continued: "I am the police commissioner and I call upon you to tell me your name. If you do not answer, I shall be forced to arrest you. In any case, rise. I will interrogate you when you are dressed."

In the meantime Madeleine had regained her composure, and seeing that all was lost, she was determined to put a brave face upon the matter. Her eyes sparkled with the audacity of bravado, and taking a piece of paper she lighted the ten candles in the candelabra as if for a reception. That done, she leaned against the mantelpiece, took a cigarette out of a case, and began to smoke, seeming not to see her husband.

In the meantime the man in the bed had dressed himself and advanced. The officer turned to him: "Now, sir, will you tell me who you are?"

He made no reply.

"I see I shall have to arrest you."

Then the man cried: "Do not touch me. I am inviolable."

Du Roy rushed toward him exclaiming: "I can have you arrested if I want to!" Then he added: "This man's name is Laroche-Mathieu, minister of foreign affairs."

The officer retreated and stammered: "Sir, will you tell me who you are?"

"For once that miserable fellow has not lied. I am indeed Laroche-Mathieu, minister," and pointing to Georges' breast, he added, "and that scoundrel wears upon his coat the cross of honor which I gave him."

Du Roy turned pale. With a rapid gesture he tore the decoration from his buttonhole and throwing it in the fire exclaimed: "That is what a decoration is worth which is given by a scoundrel of your order."

The commissioner stepped between them, as they stood face to face, saying: "Gentlemen, you forget yourselves and your dignity."

Madeleine smoked on calmly, a smile hovering about her lips. The officer continued: "Sir, I have surprised you alone with Mme. du Roy under suspicious circumstances; what have you to say?"

"Nothing; do your duty."

The commissioner turned to Madeleine: "Do you confess, Madame, that this gentleman is your lover?"

She replied boldly: "I do not deny it. That is sufficient."

The magistrate made several notes; when he had finished writing, the minister, who stood ready, coat upon arm, hat in hand, asked: "Do you need me any longer, sir? Can I go?"

Du Roy addressed him with an insolent smile: "Why should you go, we have finished; we will leave you alone together." Then, taking the officer's arm, he said: "Let us go, sir; we have nothing more to do in this place."

An hour later Georges du Roy entered the office of "La Vie Francaise." M. Walter was there; he raised his head and asked: "What, are you here? Why are you not dining at my house? Where have you come from?"

Georges replied with emphasis: "I have just found out something about the minister of foreign affairs."

"What?"

"I found him alone with my wife in hired apartments. The commissioner of police was my witness. The minister is ruined."

"Are you not jesting?"

"No, I am not. I shall even write an article on it."

"What is your object?"

"To overthrow that wretch, that public malefactor."

Georges placed his hat upon a chair and added: "Woe to those whom I find in my path. I never pardon."

The manager stammered: "But your wife?"

"I shall apply for a divorce at once."

"A divorce?"

"Yes, I am master of the situation. I shall be free. I have a stated income. I shall offer myself as a candidate in October in my native district, where I am known. I could not win any respect were I to be hampered with a wife whose honor was sullied. She took me for a simpleton, but since I have known her game, I have watched her, and now I shall get on, for I shall be free."

Georges rose.

"I will write the item; it must be handled prudently."

The old man hesitated, then said: "Do so: it serves those right who are caught in such scrapes."

CHAPTER XVII.

THE FINAL PLOT

Three months had elapsed. Georges du Roy's divorce had been obtained. His wife had resumed the name of Forestier.

As the Walters were going to Trouville on the fifteenth of July, they decided to spend a day in the country before starting.

The day chosen was Thursday, and they set out at nine o'clock in the morning in a large six-seated carriage drawn by four horses. They were going to lunch at Saint-Germain. Bel-Ami had requested that he might be the only young man in the party, for he could not bear the presence of the Marquis de Cazolles. At the last moment, however, it was decided that Count de Latour-Ivelin should go, for he and Rose had been betrothed a month. The day was delightful. Georges, who was very pale, gazed at Suzanne as they sat in the carriage and their eyes met.

Mme. Walter was contented and happy. The luncheon was a long and merry one. Before leaving for Paris, Du Roy proposed a walk on the terrace. They stopped on the way to admire the view; as they passed on, Georges and Suzanne lingered behind. The former whispered softly: "Suzanne, I love you madly."

She whispered in return: "I love you too, Bel-Ami."

He continued: "If I cannot have you for my wife, I shall leave the country."

She replied: "Ask papa. Perhaps he will consent."

He answered impatiently: "No, I repeat that it is useless; the door of the house would be closed against me. I would lose my position on the journal, and we would not even meet. Those are the consequences a formal proposal would produce. They have promised you to the Marquis de Cazolles; they hope you will finally say 'yes' and they are waiting."

"What can we do?"

"Have you the courage to brave your father and mother for my sake?"

"Yes."

"Truly?"

"Yes."

"Well! There is only one way. It must come from you and not from me. You are an indulged child; they let you say anything and are not surprised at any audacity on your part. Listen, then! This evening on returning home, go to your mother first, and tell her that you want to marry me. She will be very much agitated and very angry."

Suzanne interrupted him: "Oh, mamma would be glad."

He replied quickly: "No, no, you do not know her. She will be more vexed than your father. But you must insist, you must not yield; you must repeat that you will marry me and me alone. Will you do so?"

"I will."

"And on leaving your mother, repeat the same thing to your father very decidedly."

"Well, and then—"

"And then matters will reach a climax! If you are determined to be my wife, my dear, dear, little Suzanne, I will elope with you."

She clapped her hands, as all the charming adventures in the romances she had read occurred to her, and cried:

"Oh, what bliss! When will you elope with me?"

He whispered very low: "To-night!"

"Where shall we go?"

"That is my secret. Think well of what you are doing. Remember that after that flight you must become my wife. It is the only means, but it is dangerous—very dangerous—for you."

"I have decided. Where shall I meet you?"

"Meet me about midnight in the Place de la Concorde."

"I will be there."

He clasped her hand. "Oh, how I love you! How brave and good you are! Then you do not want to marry Marquis de Cazolles?"

"Oh, no!"

Mme. Walter, turning her head, called out: "Come, little one; what are you and Bel-Ami doing?"

They rejoined the others and returned by way of Chatou. When the carriage arrived at the door of the mansion, Mme. Walter pressed Georges to dine with them, but he refused, and returned home to look over his papers and destroy any compromising letters. Then he repaired in a cab with feverish haste to the place of meeting. He waited there some time, and thinking his ladylove had played him false, he was about to drive off, when a gentle voice whispered at the door of his cab: "Are you there, Bel-Ami?"

"Is it you, Suzanne?"

"Yes."

"Ah, get in." She entered the cab and he bade the cabman drive on.

He asked: "Well, how did it all pass off?"

She murmured faintly:

"Oh, it was terrible, with mamma especially."

"Your mamma? What did she say? Tell me!"

"Oh, it was frightful! I entered her room and made the little speech I had prepared. She turned pale and cried: 'Never!' I wept, I protested that I would marry only you; she was like a mad woman; she vowed I should be sent to a convent. I never saw her like that, never. Papa, hearing her agitated words, entered. He was not as angry as she was, but he said you were not a suitable match for me. As they had vexed me, I talked louder than they, and papa with a dramatic air bade me leave the room. That decided me to fly with you. And here I am; where shall we go?"

He replied, encircling her waist with his arm: "It is too late to take the train; this cab will take us to Sevres where we can spend the night, and to-morrow we will leave for La Roche-Guyon. It is a pretty village on the banks of the Seine between Mantes and Bonnieres."

The cab rolled on. Georges took the young girl's hand and kissed it respectfully. He did not know what to say to her, being unaccustomed to Platonic affection. Suddenly he perceived that she was weeping. He asked in affright:

"What ails you, my dear little one?"

She replied tearfully: "I was thinking that poor mamma could not sleep if she had found out that I was gone!"

Her mother indeed was not asleep.

When Suzanne left the room, Mine. Walter turned to her husband and asked in despair: "What does that mean?"

"It means that that intriguer has influenced her. It is he who has made her refuse Cazolles. You have flattered and cajoled him, too. It was Bel-Ami here, Bel-Ami there, from morning until night. Now you are paid for it!"

"I?"

"Yes, you. You are as much infatuated with him as Madeleine, Suzanne, and the rest of them. Do you think that I did not see that you could not exist for two days without him?"

She rose tragically: "I will not allow you to speak to me thus. You forget that I was not brought up like you, in a shop."

With an oath, he left the room, banging the door behind him.

When he was gone, she thought over all that had taken place. Suzanne was in love with Bel-Ami, and Bel-Ami wanted to marry Suzanne! No, it was not true! She was mistaken; he would not be capable of such an action; he knew nothing of Suzanne's escapade. They would take Suzanne away for six months and that would end it.

She rose, saying: "I cannot rest in this uncertainty. I shall lose my reason. I will arouse Suzanne and question her."

She proceeded to her daughter's room. She entered; it was empty; the bed had not been slept in. A horrible suspicion possessed her and she flew to her husband. He was in bed, reading.

She gasped: "Have you seen Suzanne?"

"No—why?"

"She is—gone! she is not in her room."

With one bound he was out of bed; he rushed to his daughter's room; not finding her there, he sank into a chair. His wife had followed him.

"Well?" she asked.

He had not the strength to reply: he was no longer angry; he groaned: "He has her—we are lost."

"Lost, how?"

"Why, he must marry her now!"

She cried wildly: "Marry her, never! Are you mad?"

He replied sadly: "It will do no good to yell! He has disgraced her. The best thing to be done is to give her to him, and at once, too; then no one will know of this escapade."

She repeated in great agitation: "Never; he shall never have Suzanne."

Overcome, Walter murmured: "But he has her. And he will keep her as long as we do not yield; therefore, to avoid a scandal we must do so at once."

But his wife replied: "No, no, I will never consent."

Impatiently he returned: "It is a matter of necessity. Ah, the scoundrel—how he has deceived us! But he is shrewd at any rate. She might have done better as far as position, but not intelligence and future, is concerned. He is a promising young man. He will be a deputy or a minister some day."

Mme. Walter, however, repeated wildly: "I will never let him marry Suzanne! Do you hear—never!"

In his turn he became incensed, and like a practical man defended Bel-Ami. "Be silent! I tell you he must marry her! And who knows? Perhaps we shall not regret it! With men of his stamp one never knows what may come about. You saw how he downed Laroche-Mathieu in three articles, and that with a dignity which was very difficult to maintain in his position as husband. So, we shall see."

Mme. Walter felt a desire to cry aloud and tear her hair. But she only repeated angrily: "He shall not have her!"

Walter rose, took up his lamp, and said: "You are silly, like all women! You only act on impulse. You do not know how to accommodate yourself to circumstances. You are stupid! I tell you he shall marry her; it is essential." And he left the room.

Mme. Walter remained alone with her suffering, her despair. If only a priest were at hand! She would cast herself at his feet and confess all her errors and her agony—he would prevent the marriage! Where could she find a priest? Where should she turn? Before her eyes floated, like a vision, the calm face of "Christ Walking on the Water," as she had seen it in the painting. He seemed to say to her: "Come unto Me. Kneel at My feet. I will comfort and instruct you as to what to do."

She took the lamp and sought the conservatory; she opened the door leading into the room which held the enormous canvas, and fell upon her knees before it. At first she prayed fervently, but as she raised her eyes and saw the resemblance to Bel-Ami, she murmured: "Jesus—Jesus—" while her thoughts were with her daughter and her lover. She uttered a wild cry, as she pictured them together—alone—and fell into a swoon. When day broke they found Mme. Walter still lying unconscious before the painting. She was so ill, after that, that her life was almost despaired of.

M. Walter explained his daughter's absence to the servants by saying to them that she had been sent to a convent for a short time. Then he replied to a long letter from Du Roy, giving his consent to his marriage with his daughter. Bel-Ami had posted that epistle when he left Paris, having prepared it the night of his departure. In it he said in respectful terms that he had loved the young girl a long time; that there had never been any understanding between them, but that as she came to him to say: "I will be your wife," he felt authorized in keeping her, in hiding her, in fact, until he had obtained a reply from her parents, whose wishes were to him of more value than those of his betrothed.

Georges and Suzanne spent a week at La Roche-Guyon. Never had the young girl enjoyed herself so thoroughly. As she passed for his sister, they lived in a chaste and free intimacy, a kind of living companionship. He thought it wiser to treat her with respect, and when he said to her: "We will return to Paris to-morrow; your father has bestowed your hand upon me" she whispered naively: "Already? This is just as pleasant as being your wife."

CHAPTER XVIII.

ATTAINMENT

It was dark in the apartments in the Rue de Constantinople, when Georges du Roy and Clotilde de Marelle, having met at the door, entered them. Without giving him time to raise the shades, the latter said:

"So you are going to marry Suzanne Walter?"

He replied in the affirmative, adding gently: "Did you not know it?"

She answered angrily: "So you are going to marry Suzanne Walter? For three months you have deceived me. Everyone knew of it but me. My husband told me. Since you left your wife you have been preparing for that stroke, and you made use of me in the interim. What a rascal you are!"

He asked: "How do you make that out? I had a wife who deceived me; I surprised her, obtained a divorce, and am now going to marry another. What is more simple than that?"

She murmured: "What a villain!"

He said with dignity: "I beg of you to be more careful as to what you say."

She rebelled at such words from him: "What! Would you like me to handle you with gloves? You have conducted yourself like a rascal ever since I have known you, and now you do not want me to speak of it. You deceive everyone; you gather pleasure and money everywhere, and you want me to treat you as an honest man."

He rose; his lips twitched: "Be silent or I will make you leave these rooms."

She cried: "Leave here—you will make me—you? You forget that it is I who have paid for these apartments from the very first, and you threaten to put me out of them. Be silent, good-for-nothing! Do you think I do not know how you stole a portion of Vaudrec's bequest from Madeleine? Do you think I do not know about Suzanne?"

He seized her by her shoulders and shook her. "Do not speak of that; I forbid you."

"I know you have ruined her!"

He would have taken anything else, but that lie exasperated him. He repeated: "Be silent—take care"—and he shook her as he would have shaken the bough of a tree. Still she continued; "You were her ruin, I know it." He rushed upon her and struck her as if she had been a man. Suddenly she ceased speaking, and groaned beneath his blows. Finally he desisted, paced the room several times in order to regain his self-possession, entered the bedroom, filled the basin with cold water and bathed his head. Then he washed his hands and returned to see what Clotilde was doing. She had not moved. She lay upon the floor weeping softly. He asked harshly:

"Will you soon have done crying?"

She did not reply. He stood in the center of the room, somewhat embarrassed, somewhat ashamed, as he saw the form lying before him. Suddenly he seized his hat. "Good evening. You can leave the key with the janitor when you are ready. I will not await your pleasure."

He left the room, closed the door, sought the porter, and said to him: "Madame is resting. She will go out soon. You can tell the proprietor that I have given notice for the first of October."

His marriage was fixed for the twentieth; it was to take place at the Madeleine. There had been a great deal of gossip about the entire affair, and many different reports were circulated. Mme. Walter had aged greatly; her hair was gray and she sought solace in religion.

In the early part of September "La Vie Francaise" announced that Baron du Roy de Cantel had become its chief editor, M. Walter reserving the title of manager. To that announcement were subjoined the names of the staff of art and theatrical critics, political reporters, and so forth. Journalists no longer sneered in speaking of "La Vie Francaise;" its success had been rapid and complete. The marriage of its chief editor was what was called a "Parisian event," Georges du Roy and the Walters having occasioned much comment for some time.

The ceremony took place on a clear, autumn day. At ten o'clock the curious began to assemble; at eleven o'clock, detachments of officers came to disperse the crowd. Soon after, the first guests arrived; they were followed by others, women in rich costumes, men, grave and dignified. The church slowly began to fill. Norbert de Varenne espied Jacques Rival, and joined him.

"Well," said he, "sharpers always succeed."

His companion, who was not envious, replied: "So much the better for him. His fortune is made."

Rival asked: "Do you know what has become of his wife?"

The poet smiled. "Yes and no—she lives a very retired life, I have been told, in the Montmartre quarter. But—there is a but—for some time I have read political articles in 'La Plume,' which resemble those of Forestier and Du Roy. They are supposed to be written by a Jean Le Dol, a young, intelligent, handsome man—something like our friend Georges—who has become acquainted with Mme. Forestier. From that I have concluded that she likes beginners and that they like her. She is, moreover, rich; Vaudrec and Laroche-Mathieu were not attentive to her for nothing."

Rival asked: "Tell me, is it true that Mme. Walter and Du Roy do not speak?"

"Yes. She did not wish to give him her daughter's hand. But he threatened the old man with shocking revelations. Walter remembered Laroche-Mathieu's fate and yielded at once; but his wife, obstinate like all women, vowed that she would never address a word to her son-in-law. It is comical to see them together! She looks like the statue of vengeance, and he is very uncomfortable, although he tries to appear at his ease."

Suddenly the beadle struck the floor three times with his staff. All the people turned to see what was coming, and the young bride appeared in the doorway leaning upon her father's arm. She looked like a beautiful doll, crowned with a wreath of orange blossoms. She advanced with bowed head. The ladies smiled and murmured as she passed them. The men whispered:

"Exquisite, adorable!"

M. Walter walked by her side with exaggerated dignity. Behind them came four maids of honor dressed in pink and forming a charming court for so dainty a queen.

Mme. Walter followed on the arm of Count de Latour-Ivelin's aged father. She did not walk; she dragged herself along, ready to faint at every step. She had aged and grown thinner.

Next came Georges du Roy with an old lady, a stranger. He held his head proudly erect and wore upon his coat, like a drop of blood, the red ribbon of the Legion of Honor.

He was followed by the relatives: Rose, who had been married six weeks, with a senator; Count de Latour-Ivelin with Viscountess de Percemur. Following them was a motley procession of associates and friends of Du Roy, country cousins of Mme. Walter's, and guests invited by her husband.

The tones of the organ filled the church; the large doors at the entrance were closed, and Georges kneeled beside his bride in the choir. The new bishop of Tangiers, cross in hand, miter on head, entered from the sacristy, to unite them in the name of the Almighty. He asked the usual questions, rings were exchanged, words pronounced which bound them forever, and then he delivered an address to the newly married couple.

The sound of stifled sobs caused several to turn their heads. Mme. Walter was weeping, her face buried in her hands. She had been obliged to yield; but since the day on which she had told Du Roy: "You are the vilest man I know; never speak to me again, for I will not answer you," she had suffered intolerable anguish. She hated Suzanne bitterly; her hatred was caused by unnatural jealousy. The bishop was marrying a daughter to her mother's lover, before her and two thousand persons, and she could say nothing; she could not stop him. She could not cry: "He is mine, that man is my lover. That union you are blessing is infamous."

Several ladies, touched by her apparent grief, murmured: "How affected that poor mother is!"

The bishop said: "You are among the favored ones of the earth. You, sir, who are raised above others by your talent—you who write, instruct, counsel, guide the people, have a grand mission to fulfill—a fine example to set."

Du Roy listened to him proudly. A prelate of the Roman Church spoke thus to him. A number of illustrious people had come thither on his account. It seemed to him that an invisible power was impelling him on. He would become one of the masters of the country—he, the son of the poor peasants of Canteleu. He had given his parents five thousand francs of Count de Vaudrec's fortune and he intended sending them fifty thousand more; then they could buy a small estate and live happily.

The bishop had finished his harangue, a priest ascended the altar, and the organ pealed forth. Suddenly the vibrating tones melted into delicate, melodious ones, like the songs of birds; then again they swelled into deep, full tones and human voices chanted over their bowed heads. Vauri and Landeck of the Opera were singing.

Bel-Ami, kneeling beside Suzanne, bowed his head. At that moment he felt almost pious, for he was filled with gratitude for the blessings showered upon him. Without knowing just whom he was addressing, he offered up thanks for his success. When the ceremony was over, he rose, and, giving his arm to his wife, they passed into the sacristy. A stream of people entered. Georges fancied himself a king whom the people were coming to greet. He shook hands, uttered words which signified nothing, and replied to congratulations with the words: “You are very kind.”

Suddenly he saw Mme. de Marelle, and the recollection of all the kisses he had given her and which she had returned, of all their caresses, of the sound of her voice, possessed him with the mad desire to regain her. She was so pretty, with her bright eyes and roguish air! She advanced somewhat timidly and offered him her hand. He took, retained, and pressed it as if to say: “I shall love you always, I am yours.”

Their eyes met, smiling, bright, full of love. She murmured in her soft tones: “Until we meet again, sir!” and he gaily repeated her words.

Others approached, and she passed on. Finally the throng dispersed. Georges placed Suzanne’s hand upon his arm to pass through the church with her. It was filled with people, for all had resumed their seats in order to see them leave the sacred edifice together. He walked along slowly, with a firm step, his head erect. He saw no one. He only thought of himself.

When they reached the threshold he saw a crowd gathered outside, come to gaze at him, Georges du Roy. The people of Paris envied him. Raising his eyes, he saw beyond the Place de la Concorde, the chamber of deputies, and it seemed to him that it was only a stone’s throw from the portico of the Madeleine to that of the Palais Bourbon.

Leisurely they descended the steps between two rows of spectators, but Georges did not see them; his thoughts had returned to the past, and before his eyes, dazzled by the bright sunlight, floated the image of Mme. de Marelle, rearranging the curly locks upon her temples before the mirror in their apartments.

MONT ORIOL

OR

A ROMANCE OF AUVERGNE

"HE HAD THOUGHT WITH DEEP ANXIETY OF THIS CHILD, OF WHICH HE WAS THE FATHER"

CHAPTER I.

THE SPA

The first bathers, the early risers, who had already been at the water, were walking slowly, in pairs or alone, under the huge trees along the stream which rushes down the gorges of Enval.

Others arrived from the village, and entered the establishment in a hurried fashion. It was a spacious building, the ground floor being reserved for thermal treatment, while the first story served as a casino, café, and billiard-room. Since Doctor Bonnefille had discovered in the heart of Enval the great spring, baptized by him the Bonnefille Spring, some proprietors of the country and the surrounding neighborhood, timid speculators, had decided to erect in the midst of this superb glen of Auvergne, savage and gay withal, planted with walnut and giant chestnut trees, a vast house for every kind of use, serving equally for the purpose of cure and of pleasure, in which mineral waters, douches, and baths were sold below, and beer, liqueurs, and music above.

A portion of the ravine along the stream had been inclosed, to constitute the park indispensable to every spa; and three walks had been made, one nearly straight, and the other two zigzag. At the end of the first gushed out an artificial spring detached from the parent spring, and bubbling into a great basin of cement, sheltered by a straw roof, under the care of an impassive woman, whom everyone called "Marie" in a familiar sort of way. This calm Auvergnat, who wore a little cap always as white as snow, and a big apron, perfectly clean at all times, which concealed her working-dress, rose up slowly as soon as she saw a bather coming along the road in her direction.

The bather would smile with a melancholy air, drink the water, and return her the glass, saying, "Thanks, Marie." Then he would turn on his heel and walk away. And Marie sat down again on her straw chair to wait for the next comer.

They were not, however, very numerous. The Enval station had just been six years open for invalids, and scarcely could count more patients at the end of these six years than it had at the start. About fifty had come there, attracted more than anything else by the beauty of the district, by the charm of this little village lost under enormous trees, whose twisted trunks seemed as big as the houses, and by the reputation of the gorges at the end of this strange glen which opened on the great plain of Auvergne and ended abruptly at the foot of the high mountain bristling with craters of unknown age—a savage and magnificent crevasse, full of rocks fallen or threatening, from which rushed a stream that cascaded over giant stones, forming a little lake in front of each.

This thermal station had been brought to birth as they all are, with a pamphlet on the spring by Doctor Bonnefille. He opened with a eulogistic description, in a majestic and sentimental style, of the Alpine seductions of the neighborhood. He selected only adjectives which convey a vague sense of delightfulness and enjoyment—those which produce effect without committing the writer to any material statement. All the surroundings were picturesque, filled with splendid sites or landscapes whose graceful outlines aroused soft emotions. All the promenades in the vicinity possessed a remarkable originality, such as would strike the imagination of artists and tourists. Then abruptly, without any transition, he plunged into the therapeutic qualities of the Bonnefille Spring, bicarbonate, sodium, mixed, lithineous, ferruginous, et cetera, et cetera, capable of curing every disease. He had, moreover, enumerated them under this heading: Chronic affections or acute specially associated with Enval. And the list of affections associated with Enval was long—long and varied, consoling for invalids of every kind. The pamphlet concluded with some information of practical utility, the cost of lodgings, commodities, and hotels—for three hotels had sprung up simultaneously with the casino-medical establishment. These were the Hotel Splendid, quite new, built on the slope of the glen looking down on the baths; the Thermal Hotel, an old inn with a new coat of plaster; and the Hotel Vidaillet, formed very simply by the purchase of three adjoining houses, which had been altered so as to convert them into one.

Then, all at once, two new doctors had installed themselves in the locality one morning, without anyone well knowing how they came, for at spas doctors seem to dart up out of the springs, like gas-jets. These were Doctor Honorat, a native of Auvergne, and Doctor Latonne, of Paris. A fierce antagonism soon burst out between Doctor Latonne and Doctor Bonnefille, while Doctor Honorat, a big, clean-shaven man, smiling and pliant, stretched forth his right hand to the first, and his left hand to the second, and remained on good terms with both. But Doctor Bonnefille was master of the situation, with his title of Inspector of the Waters and of the thermal establishment of Enval-les-Bains.

This title was his strength and the establishment his chattel. There he spent his days, and even his nights, it was said. A hundred times, in the morning, he would go from his house which was quite near in the village to his consultation-study fixed at the right-hand side facing the entrance to the thermal baths. Lying in wait there, like a spider in his web, he watched the comings and goings of the invalids, inspecting his own patients with a severe eye and those of the other doctors with a look of fury. He questioned everybody almost in the style of a ship's captain, and he struck terror into newcomers, unless it happened that he made them smile.

This day, as he arrived with rapid steps, which made the big flaps of his old frock coat fly up like a pair of wings, he was stopped suddenly by a voice exclaiming: "Doctor!"

He turned round. His thin face, full of big ugly wrinkles, and looking quite black at the end with a grizzled beard rarely cut, made an effort to smile; and he took off the tall silk hat, shabby, stained, and greasy, that covered his thick pepper-and-salt head of hair—"pepper and soiled, as his rival, Doctor Latonne, put it. Then he advanced a step, made a bow, and murmured:

"Good morning, Marquis—are you quite well this morning?"

The Marquis de Ravenel, a little man well preserved, stretched out his hand to the doctor, as he replied:

"Very well, doctor, very well, or, at least, not ill. I am always suffering from my kidneys; but indeed I am better, much better; and I am as yet only at my tenth bath. Last year I did not obtain the effect until the sixteenth, you recollect?"

"Yes, perfectly."

"But it is not about this I want to talk to you. My daughter has arrived this morning, and I wish to have a chat with you about her case first of all, because my son-in-law, William Andermatt, the banker——"

"Yes, I know."

"My son-in-law has a letter of recommendation addressed to Doctor Latonne. As for me, I have no confidence except in you, and I beg of you to have the kindness to come up to the hotel before—you understand? I prefer to say things to you candidly. Are you free at the present moment?"

Doctor Bonnefille had put on his hat again, and looked excited and troubled. He answered at once:

"Yes, I shall be free immediately. Do you wish me to accompany you?"

"Why, certainly."

And, turning their backs on the establishment, they directed their steps up a circular walk leading to the door of the Hotel Splendid, built on the slope of the mountain so as to offer a view of it to travelers.

They made their way to the drawing-room in the first story adjoining the apartments occupied by the Ravenel and Andermatt families, and the Marquis left the doctor by himself while he went to look for his daughter.

He came back with her presently. She was a fair young woman, small, pale, very pretty, whose features seemed like those of a child, while her blue eyes, boldly fixed, cast on people a resolute look that gave an alluring impression of firmness and a peculiar charm to this refined and fascinating creature. There was not much the matter with her—vague languors, sadnesses, bursts of tears without apparent cause, angry fits for which there seemed no season, and lastly anæmia. She craved above all for a child, which had been vainly looked forward to since her marriage, more than two years before.

Doctor Bonnefille declared that the waters of Enval would be effectual, and proceeded forthwith to write a prescription. The doctor's prescriptions had always the formidable aspect of an indictment. On a big white sheet of paper such as schoolboys use, his directions exhibited themselves in numerous paragraphs of two or three lines each, in an irregular handwriting, bristling with letters resembling spikes. And the potions, the pills, the powders, which were to be taken fasting in the morning, at midday, and in the evening, followed in ferocious-looking characters. One of these prescriptions might read:

"Inasmuch as M. X. is affected with a chronic malady, incurable and mortal, he will take, first, sulphate of quinine, which will render him deaf, and will make him lose his memory; secondly, bromide of potassium, which will destroy his stomach, weaken all his faculties, cover him with pimples, and make his breath foul; thirdly, salicylate of soda, whose curative effects have not yet been proved, but which seems to lead to a terrible and speedy death the patient treated by this remedy. And concurrently, chloral, which causes insanity, and belladonna, which attacks the eyes; all vegetable solutions and all mineral compositions which corrupt the blood, corrode the organs, consume the bones, and destroy by medicine those whom disease has spared."

For a long time he went on writing on the front page and on the back, then signed it just as a judge might have signed a death-sentence.

The young woman, seated opposite to him, stared at him with an inclination to laugh that made the corners of her lips rise up.

When, with a low bow, he had taken himself off, she snatched up the paper blackened with ink, rolled it up into a ball, and flung it into the fire. Then, breaking into a hearty laugh, said:

"Oh! father, where did you discover this fossil? Why, he looks for all the world like an old-clothesman. Oh! how clever of you to dig up a physician that might have lived before the Revolution! Oh! how funny he is, aye, and dirty—ah, yes! dirty—I believe really he has stained my penholder."

The door opened, and M. Andermatt's voice was heard saying, "Come in, doctor."

And Doctor Latonne appeared. Erect, slender, circumspect, comparatively young, attired in a fashionable morning-coat, and holding in his hand the high silk hat which distinguishes the practicing doctor in the greater part of the thermal stations of Auvergne, the physician from Paris, without beard or mustache, resembled an actor who had retired into the country.

The Marquis, confounded, did not know what to say or do, while his daughter put her handkerchief to her mouth to keep herself from bursting out laughing in the newcomer's face. He bowed with an air of self-confidence, and at a sign from the young woman took a seat.

M. Andermatt, who followed him, minutely detailed for him his wife's condition, her illnesses, together with their accompanying symptoms, the opinions of the physicians consulted in Paris, and then his own opinion based on special grounds which he explained in technical language.

He was a man still quite youthful, a Jew, who devoted himself to financial transactions. He entered into all sorts of speculations, and displayed in all matters of business a subtlety of intellect, a rapidity of penetration, and a soundness of judgment that were perfectly marvelous. A little too stout already for his figure, which was not tall, chubby, bald, with an infantile expression, fat hands, and short thighs, he looked much too greasy to be quite healthy, and spoke with amazing facility.

By means of tact he had been able to form an alliance with the daughter of the Marquis de Ravenel with a view to extending his speculations into a sphere to which he did not belong. The Marquis, besides, possessed an income of about thirty thousand francs, and had only two children; but, when M. Andermatt married, though scarcely thirty years of age, he owned already five or six millions, and had sown enough to bring him in a harvest of ten or twelve. M. de Ravenel, a man of weak, irresolute, shifting, and undecided character, at first angrily repulsed the overtures made to him with respect to this union, and was indignant at the thought of seeing his daughter allied to an Israelite. Then, after six months' resistance, he gave way, under the pressure of accumulated wealth, on the condition that the children should be brought up in the Catholic religion.

But they waited for a long time and no offspring was yet announced. It was then that the Marquis, enchanted for the past two years with the waters of Enval, recalled to mind the fact that Doctor Bonnefille's pamphlet also promised the cure for sterility.

Accordingly, he sent for his daughter, whom his son-in-law accompanied, in order to install her and to intrust her, acting on the advice of his Paris physician, to the care of Doctor Latonne. Therefore, Andermatt, since his arrival, had gone to look for this practitioner, and went on enumerating the symptoms which presented themselves in his wife's case. He finished by mentioning how much he had been pained at finding his hopes of paternity unrealized.

Doctor Latonne allowed him to go on to the end; then, turning toward the young woman: "Have you anything to add, Madame?"

She replied gravely: "No, Monsieur, nothing at all."

He went on: "In that case, I will trouble you to take off your traveling-dress and your corset, and to put on a simple white dressing-gown, all white."

She was astonished; he rapidly explained his system: "Good heavens, Madame, it is very simple. Formerly, the belief was that all diseases came from a poison in the blood or from an organic cause; to-day, we simply assume that, in many cases, and, above all, in your particular case, the uncertain ailments from which you suffer, and even certain serious troubles, very serious, mortal, may proceed only from the fact that some organ or other, having taken, under influences easy to determine, an abnormal development, to the detriment of the neighboring organs, destroys all the harmony, all the equilibrium of the human body, modifies or arrests its functions, and obstructs the play of all the other organs. A swelling of the stomach may be sufficient to make us believe in a disease of the heart, which, impeded in its movements, becomes violent, irregular, sometimes even intermittent. The dilatation of the liver or of certain glands may cause ravages which unobservant physicians attribute to a thousand different causes. Therefore, the first thing that we should do is to ascertain whether all the organs of a patient have their true compass and their normal position, for a very little thing is enough to upset a person's health. I am going, then, Madame, if you will allow me, to examine you with great care, and to mark out on your dressing-gown the limits, the dimensions, and the positions of your organs."

He had put down his hat on a chair, and he spoke in a facile manner. His large mouth, in opening and closing, made two deep hollows in his shaven cheeks, which gave him a certain ecclesiastical air.

Andermatt, delighted, exclaimed: "Capital, capital! That is very clever, very ingenious, very new, very modern."

"Very modern" in his mouth was the height of admiration.

The young woman, highly amused, rose and passed into her own apartment. She came back, after the lapse of a few minutes, in a white dressing-gown.

The physician made her lie down on a sofa, then, drawing from his pocket a pencil with three points, a black, a red, and a blue, he commenced to auscultate and to tap his new patient, riddling the dressing-gown all over with little dots of color by way of noting each observation.

She resembled, after a quarter of an hour of this work, a map indicating continents, seas, capes, rivers, kingdoms, and cities, and bearing the names of all these terrestrial divisions, for the doctor wrote on every line of demarcation two or three Latin words intelligible to himself alone.

Now, when he had listened to all the internal sounds in Madame Andermatt's body, and tapped on all the parts of her person that were irritated or hollow-sounding, he drew forth from his pocket a notebook of red leather with gold threads to fasten it, divided in alphabetical order, consulted the index, opened it, and wrote: "Observation 6347.—Madame A——, 21 years."

Then, collecting from her head to her feet the colored notes on her dressing-gown, and reading them as an Egyptologist deciphers hieroglyphics, he entered them in the notebook.

He observed, when he had finished: "Nothing disquieting, nothing abnormal, save a slight, a very slight deviation, which some thirty acidulated baths will cure. You will take furthermore three half-glasses of water each morning before noon. Nothing else. I will come back to see you in four or five days." Then he rose, bowed, and went out with such promptitude that everyone remained stupefied at it. This abrupt style of departure was a part of his mannerism, his tact, his special stamp. He considered it very good form, and thought it made a great impression on the patient.

Madame Andermatt ran to look at herself in the glass, and, shaking all over with a joyous burst of childlike laughter, said:

"Oh! how amusing they are, how droll they are! Tell me, is there not one more left of them? I want to see him immediately! Will, go and find him for me! We must have the third one here—I want to see him."

Her husband, surprised, asked:

"How, a third, a third what?"

The Marquis deemed it advisable to explain, while offering excuses, for he was a little afraid of his son-in-law. He related, therefore, how Doctor Bonnefille had come to see himself, and how he had introduced him to Christiane, in order to ascertain his opinion, as he had great confidence in the experience of the old physician, who was a native of the district, and who had discovered the spring.

Andermatt shrugged his shoulders, and declared that Doctor Latonne alone would take care of his wife, so that the Marquis, very uneasy, began to reflect on the best course to take in order to arrange matters without offending his irascible physician.

Christiane asked: "Is Gontran here?" This was her brother.

Her father replied: "Yes, for the past four days, with a friend of his of whom he has often spoken, M. Paul Bretigny. They are making a tour together in Auvergne. They have come from Mont Doré and from Bourboule, and will be setting out for Cantal at the end of next week."

Then he asked the young woman whether she desired to rest till luncheon after the night in the train; but she had slept perfectly in the sleeping car, and only required an hour for her toilette, after which she wished to visit the village and the establishment.

Her father and her husband went back to their rooms to wait till she was ready. She soon came out to call them, and they descended together. She grew enthusiastic at first sight over the aspect of the village, built in the middle of a wood in a deep valley, which seemed hemmed in on every side by chestnut-trees lofty as mountains. These could be seen everywhere, springing up just as they chanced to have shot forth here and there in a century, in front of doorways, in the courtyards, in the streets. Then, again, there were fountains everywhere made of a great black stone standing upright pierced with a small aperture, through which dashed a streamlet of clear water that whirled about in a circle before it fell into the trough. A fresh odor of grass and of stables floated over those masses of verdure; and they saw the peasant women of Auvergne standing in front of their dwellings, spinning at their distaffs with lively movements of their fingers the black wool attached to their girdles. Their short petticoats showed their thin ankles covered with blue stockings, and the bodies of their dresses fastened over their shoulders with straps left exposed the linen sleeves of their chemises, out of which stretched their hard, dry arms and bony hands.

But, suddenly, a queer lilting kind of music burst on the promenaders' ears. It was like a barrel-organ with piping sounds, a barrel-organ used up, broken-winded, invalided.

Christiane exclaimed: "What is that?"

Her father began to laugh: "It is the orchestra of the Casino. It takes four of them to make that noise."

And he led her up to a red bill affixed to a corner of a farmhouse, on which appeared in black letters:

CASINO OF ENVAL
UNDER THE DIRECTION OF M. PETRUS MARTEL,
OF THE ODÉON.

Saturday, 6th of July.

GRAND CONCERT
organized by the Maestro, Saint Landri, second grand prize winner at
the Conservatoire.

The piano will be presided over by M. Javel, grand laureate of the
Conservatoire.

Flute, M. Noirot, laureate of the Conservatoire.

Double-bass, M. Nicordi, laureate of the Royal Academy of Brussels.

After the Concert, grand representation of
Lost in the Forest,
a Comedy in one act, by M. Pointellet.

Characters:

Pierre de Lapointe	M. Petrus Martel, of the Odéon.
Oscar Léveillé	M. Petitnivelle, of the Vaudeville.
Jean	M. Lapalme, of the Grand Theater of Bordeaux.
Philippine	Mademoiselle Odelin, of the Odéon.

During the representation, the Orchestra will be likewise conducted by the Maestro, Saint Landri.

Christiane read this aloud, laughed, and was astonished.

Her father went on: "Oh! they will amuse you. Come and look at them."

They turned to the right, and entered the park. The bathers promenaded gravely, slowly, along the three walks. They drank their glasses of water, and then went away. Some of them, seated on benches, traced lines in the sand with the ends of their walking-sticks or their umbrellas. They did not talk, seemed not to think, scarcely to live, enervated, paralyzed by the ennui of the thermal station. Only the odd music of the orchestra broke the sweet silence as it leaped into the air, coming one knew not whence, produced one knew not how, passing under the foliage and appearing to stir up these melancholy walkers.

A voice cried: "Christiane!"

She turned round. It was her brother. He rushed toward her, embraced her, and, having pressed Andermatt's hand, took his sister by the arm, and drew her along with him, leaving his father and his brother-in-law in the rear.

They chatted. He was a tall, well-made young fellow, prone to laughter like her, light-hearted as the Marquis, indifferent to events, but always on the lookout for a thousand francs.

"I thought you were asleep," said he. "But for that I would have come to embrace you. And then Paul carried me off this morning to the château of Tournoel."

"Who is Paul? Oh, yes, your friend!"

"Paul Bretigny. It is true you don't know him. He is taking a bath at the present moment."

"He is a patient, then?"

"No, but he is curing himself, all the same. He is trying to get over a love episode."

"And so he's taking acidulated baths—they're called acidulated, are they not?—in order to restore himself."

"Yes. He's doing all I told him to do. Oh! he has been hit hard. He's a violent youth, terrible, and has been at death's door. He wanted to kill himself, too. It was an actress—a well-known actress. He was madly in love with her. And then she was not faithful to him, do you see? The result was a frightful drama. So I brought him away. He's going on better now, but he's still thinking about it."

She smiled for a moment, then, becoming grave, she returned:

"It will amuse me to see him."

For her, however, this thing, "Love," did not mean very much. She sometimes bestowed a thought on it, just as you think, when you are poor, now and then of a pearl necklace, of a diadem of brilliants, with a desire awakened in you for this thing—possible though far away. This fancy would come to her after reading some novel to kill time, without attaching to it, beyond that, any special importance. She had never dreamed about it much, having been born with a happy soul, tranquil and contented, and, although now two years and a half married, she had not yet awakened out of that sleep in which innocent young girls live, that sleep of the heart, of the mind, and of the senses, which, with some women, lasts until death. For her life was simple and good, without complications. She had never looked for the causes or the hidden meaning of things. She had lived on from day to day, slept soundly, dressed with taste, laughed, and felt satisfied. What more could she have asked for?

When Andermatt had been introduced to her as her future husband, she refused to wed him at first with a childish indignation at the idea of becoming the wife of a Jew. Her father and her brother, sharing her repugnance, replied with her and like her by formally declining the offer. Andermatt disappeared, acted as if he were dead, but, at the end of three months, had lent Gontran more than twenty thousand francs; and the Marquis, for other reasons, was beginning to change his opinion.

In the first place, he always on principle yielded when one persisted, through sheer egotistical desire not to be disturbed. His daughter used to say of him: "All papa's ideas are jumbled up together"; and this was true. Without opinions, without beliefs, he had only enthusiasms, which varied every moment. At one time, he would attach himself, with a transitory and poetic exaltation, to the old traditions of his race, and would long for a king, but an intellectual king, liberal, enlightened, marching along with the age. At another time, after he had read a book by Michelet or some democratic thinker, he would become a passionate advocate of human equality, of modern ideas, of the claims of the poor, the oppressed, and the suffering. He believed in everything, just as each thing harmonized with his passing moods; and, when his old friend, Madame Icardon, who, connected as she was with many Israelites, desired the marriage of Christiane and Andermatt, and began to preach in favor of it, she knew full well the kind of arguments with which she should attack him.

She pointed out to him that the Jewish race had arrived at the hour of vengeance. It had been a race crushed down as the French people had been before the Revolution, and was now going to oppress others by the power of gold. The Marquis, devoid of religious faith, but convinced that the idea of God was rather a legislative idea, which had more effect in keeping the foolish, the ignorant, and the timid in the right path than the simple notion of Justice, regarded dogmas with a respectful indifference, and held in equal and sincere esteem Confucius, Mohammed, and Jesus Christ. Accordingly, the fact that the latter was crucified did not at all present itself as an original wrongdoing but as a gross, political blunder. In consequence it only required a few weeks to make him admire the toil, hidden, incessant, and all-powerful, of the persecuted Jews everywhere. And, viewing with different eyes their brilliant triumph, he looked upon it as a just reparation for the indignities that so long had been heaped upon them. He saw them masters of kings, who are the masters of the people—sustaining thrones or allowing them to collapse, able to make a nation bankrupt as one might a wine-merchant, proud in the presence of princes who had grown humble, and casting their impure gold into the half-open purses of the most Catholic sovereigns, who thanked them by conferring on them titles of nobility and lines of railway. So he consented to the marriage of William Andermatt with Christiane de Ravenel.

As for Christiane, under the unconscious pressure of Madame Icardon, her mother's old companion, who had become her intimate adviser since the Marquise's death, a pressure to which was added that of her father and the interested indifference of her brother, she consented to marry this big, overrich youth, who was not ugly but scarcely pleased her, just as she would have consented to spend a summer in a disagreeable country.

She found him a good fellow, kind, not stupid, nice in intimate relations; but she frequently laughed at him along with Gontran, whose gratitude was of the perfidious order.

He would say to her: "Your husband is rosier and balder than ever. He looks like a sickly flower, or a sucking pig with its hair shaved off. Where does he get these colors?"

She would reply: "I assure you I have nothing to do with it. There are days when I feel inclined to paste him on a box of sugar-plums."

But they had arrived in front of the baths. Two men were seated on straw chairs with their backs to the wall, smoking their pipes, one at each side of the door.

Said Gontran: "Look, here are two good types. Watch the fellow at the right, the hunchback with the Greek cap! That's Père Printemps, an ex-jailer from Riom, who has become the guardian, almost the manager, of the Enval establishment. For him nothing is changed, and he governs the invalids just as he did his prisoners in former days. The bathers are always prisoners, their bathing-boxes are cells, the douche-room a black-hole, and the place where Doctor Bonnefille practices his stomach-washings with the aid of the Baraduc sounding-line a chamber of mysterious torture. He does not salute any of the men on the strength of the principle that all convicts are contemptible beings. He treats women with much more consideration, upon my honor—a consideration mingled with astonishment, for he had none of them under his control in the prison of Riom. That retreat being destined for males only, he has not yet got accustomed to talking to members of the fair sex. The other fellow is the cashier. I defy you to make him write your name. You are just going to see."

And Gontran, addressing the man at the left, slowly said:

"Monsieur Seminois, this is my sister, Madame Andermatt, who wants to subscribe for a dozen baths."

The cashier, very tall, very thin, with a poor appearance, rose up, went into his office, which exactly faced the study of the medical inspector, opened his book, and asked:

"What name?"

"Andermatt."

"What did you say?"

"Andermatt."

"How do you spell it?"

"A-n-d-e-r-m-a-t-t."

"All right."

And he slowly wrote it down. When he had finished, Gontran asked:

"Would you kindly read over my sister's name?"

"Yes, Monsieur! Madame Anterpat."

Christiane laughed till the tears came into her eyes, paid for her tickets, and then asked:

"What is it that one hears up there?"

Gontran took her arm in his. Two angry voices reached their ears on the stairs. They went up, opened a door, and saw a large coffee-room with a billiard table in the center. Two men in their shirt-sleeves at opposite sides of the billiard-table, each with a cue in his hand, were furiously abusing one another.

"Eighteen!"

"Seventeen!"

"I tell you I'm eighteen."

"That's not true—you're only seventeen!"

It was the director of the Casino, M. Petrus Martel of the Odéon, who was playing his ordinary game with the comedian of his company, M. Lapalme of the Grand Theater of Bordeaux.

Petrus Martel, whose stomach, stout and inactive, swayed underneath his shirt above a pair of pantaloons fastened anyhow, after having been a strolling player in various places, had undertaken the directorship of the Casino of Enval, and spent his days in drinking the allowances intended for the bathers. He wore an immense mustache like a dragoon, which was steeped from morning till night in the froth of bocks and the sticky syrup of liqueurs, and he had aroused in the old comedian whom he had enlisted in his service an immoderate passion for billiards.

As soon as they got up in the morning, they proceeded to play a game, insulted and threatened one another, expunged the record, began over again, scarcely gave themselves time for breakfast, and could not tolerate two clients coming to drive them away from their green cloth.

They soon put everyone to flight, and did not find this sort of existence unpleasant, though Petrus Martel always found himself at the end of the season in a bankrupt condition.

The female attendant, overwhelmed, would have to look on all day at this endless game, listen to the interminable discussion, and carry from morning till night glasses of beer or half-glasses of brandy to the two indefatigable players.

But Gontran carried off his sister: "Come into the park. 'Tis fresher."

At the end of the establishment they suddenly perceived the orchestra under a Chinese kiosque. A fair-haired young man, frantically playing the violin, was conducting with movements of his head. His hair was shaking from one side to the other in the effort to keep time, and his entire torso bent forward and rose up again, swaying from left to right, like the stick of the leader of an orchestra. Facing him sat three strange-looking musicians. This was the maestro, Saint Landri.

He and his assistants—a pianist, whose instrument, mounted on rollers, was wheeled each morning from the vestibule of the baths to the kiosque; an enormous flautist, who presented the appearance of sucking a match while tickling it with his big swollen fingers, and a double-bass of consumptive aspect—produced with much fatigue this perfect imitation of a bad barrel-organ, which had astonished Christiane in the village street.

As she stopped to look at them, a gentleman saluted her brother.

"Good day, my dear Count."

"Good day, doctor."

And Gontran introduced them: "My sister—Doctor Honorat."

She could scarcely restrain her merriment at the sight of this third physician. The latter bowed and made some complimentary remark.

"I hope that Madame is not an invalid?"

"Yes—slightly."

He did not go farther with the matter, and changed the subject.

"You are aware, my dear Count, that you will shortly have one of the most interesting spectacles that could await you on your arrival in this district."

"What is it, pray, doctor?"

"Père Oriol is going to blast his hill. This is of no consequence to you, but for us it is a big event."

And he proceeded to explain. "Père Oriol—the richest peasant in this part of the country—he is known to be worth over fifty thousand francs a year—owns all the vineyards along the plain up to the outlet of Enval. Now, just as you go out from the village at the division of the valley, rises a little mountain, or rather a high knoll, and on this knoll are the best vineyards of Père Oriol. In the midst of two of them, facing the road, at two paces from the stream, stands a gigantic stone, an elevation which has impeded the cultivation and put into the shade one entire side of the field, on which it looks down. For six years, Père Oriol has every week been announcing that he was going to blast his hill; but he has never made up his mind about it.

"Every time a country boy went to be a soldier, the old man would say to him: 'When you're coming home on furlough, bring me some powder for this rock of mine.' And all the young soldiers would bring back in their knapsacks some powder that they stole for Père Oriol's rock. He has a chest full of this powder, and yet the hill has not been blasted. At last, for a week past, he has been noticed scooping out the stone, with his son, big Jacques, surnamed Colosse, which in Auvergne is pronounced 'Coloche.' This very morning they filled with powder the empty belly of the enormous rock; then they stopped up the mouth of it, only letting in the fuse bought at the tobacconist's. In two hours' time they will set fire to it. Then, five or ten minutes afterward, it will go off, for the end of the fuse is pretty long."

Christiane was interested in this narrative, amused already at the idea of this explosion, finding here again a childish sport that pleased her simple heart. They had now reached the end of the park.

"Where do you go now?" she said.

Doctor Honorat replied: "To the End of the World, Madame; that is to say, into a gorge that has no outlet and which is celebrated in Auvergne. It is one of the loveliest natural curiosities in the district."

But a bell rang behind them. Gontran cried:

"Look here! breakfast-time already!"

They turned back. A tall, young man came up to meet them.

Gontran said: "My dear Christiane, let me introduce to you M. Paul Bretigny." Then, to his friend: "This is my sister, my dear boy."

She thought him ugly. He had black hair, close-cropped and straight, big, round eyes, with an expression that was almost hard, a head also quite round, very strong, one of those heads that make you think of cannon-balls, herculean shoulders; a rather savage expression, heavy and brutish. But from his jacket, from his linen, from his skin perhaps, came a very subtle perfume, with which the young woman was not familiar, and she asked herself:

"I wonder what odor that is?"

He said to her: "You arrived this morning, Madame?" His voice was a little hollow.

She replied: "Yes, Monsieur."

But Gontran saw the Marquis and Andermatt making signals to them to come in quickly to breakfast.

Doctor Honorat took leave of them, asking as he left whether they really meant to go and see the hill blasted. Christiane declared that she would go; and, leaning on her brother's arm, she murmured as she dragged him along toward the hotel:

"I am as hungry as a wolf. I shall be very much ashamed to eat as much as I feel inclined before your friend."

CHAPTER II.

THE DISCOVERY

The breakfast was long, as the meals usually are at a table d'hôte. Christiane, who was not familiar with all the faces of those present, chatted with her father and her brother. Then she went up to her room to take a rest till the time for blasting the rock.

She was ready long before the hour fixed, and made the others start along with her so that they might not miss the explosion. Just outside the village, at the opening of the glen, stood, as they had heard, a high knoll, almost a mountain, which they proceeded to climb under a burning sun, following a little path through the vine-trees. When they reached the summit the young woman uttered a cry of astonishment at the sight of the immense horizon displayed before her eyes. In front of her stretched a limitless plain, which immediately gave her soul the sensation of an ocean. This plain, overhung by a veil of light blue vapor, extended as far as the most distant mountain-ridges, which were scarcely perceptible, some fifty or sixty kilometers away. And under the transparent haze of delicate fineness, which floated above this vast stretch, could be distinguished towns, villages, woods, vast yellow squares of ripe crops, vast green squares of herbage, factories with long, red chimneys and blackened steeples and sharp-pointed structures, with the solidified lava of dead volcanoes.

"Turn around," said her brother.

She turned around. And behind she saw the mountain, the huge mountain indented with craters. This was the entrance to the foundation on which Enval stood, a great expanse of greenness in which one could scarcely trace the hidden gash of the gorge. The trees in a waving mass scaled the high slope as far as the first crater and shut out the view of those beyond. But, as they were exactly on the line that separated the plains from the mountain, the latter stretched to the left toward Clermont-Ferrand, and, wandering away, unrolled over the blue sky their strange mutilated tops, like monstrous blotches—extinct volcanoes, dead volcanoes. And yonder—over yonder, between two peaks—could be seen another, higher still, more distant still, round and majestic, and bearing on its highest pinnacle something of fantastic shape resembling a ruin. This was the Puy de Dome, the king of the mountains of Auvergne, strong and unwieldy, wearing on its head, like a crown placed thereon by the mightiest of peoples, the remains of a Roman temple.

Christiane exclaimed: "Oh! how happy I shall be here!"

And she felt herself happy already, penetrated by that sense of well-being which takes possession of the flesh and the heart, makes you breathe with ease, and renders you sprightly and active when you find yourself in a spot which enchants your eyes, charms and cheers you, seems to have been awaiting you, a spot for which you feel that you were born.

Some one called out to her: "Madame, Madame!" And, at some distance away, she saw Doctor Honorat, recognizable by his big hat. He rushed across to them, and conducted the family toward the opposite side of the hill, over a grassy slope beside a grove of young trees, where already some thirty persons were waiting, strangers and peasants mingled together.

Beneath their feet, the steep hillside descended toward the Riom road, overshadowed by willows that sheltered the shallow river; and in the midst of a vineyard at the edge of this stream rose a sharp-pointed rock before which two men on bended knees seemed to be praying. This was the scene of action.

The Oriols, father and son, were attaching the fuse. On the road, a crowd of curious spectators had stationed themselves, with a line of people lower down in front, among whom village brats were scampering about.

Doctor Honorat chose a convenient place for Christiane to sit down, and there she waited with a beating heart, as if she were going to see the entire population blown up along with the rock.

The Marquis, Andermatt, and Paul Bretigny lay down on the grass at the young woman's side, while Gontran remained standing. He said, in a bantering tone:

"My dear doctor, you must be much less busy than your brother-practitioners, who apparently have not an hour to spare to attend this little fête?"

Honorat replied in a good-humored tone:

"I am not less busy; only my patients occupy less of my time. And again I prefer to amuse my patients rather than to physic them."

He had a quiet manner which greatly pleased Gontran. Other persons now arrived, fellow-guests at the table d'hôte—the ladies Paille, two widows, mother and daughter; the Monecus, father and daughter; and a very small, fat, man, who was puffing like a boiler that had burst, M. Aubry-Pasteur, an ex-engineer of mines, who had made a fortune in Russia.

M. Pasteur and the Marquis were on intimate terms. He seated himself with much difficulty after some preparatory movements, circumspect and cautious, which considerably amused Christiane. Gontran sauntered away from them, in order to have a look at the other persons whom curiosity had attracted toward the knoll.

Paul Bretigny pointed out to Christiane Andermatt the views, of which they could catch glimpses in the distance. First of all, Riom made a red patch with its row of tiles along the plain; then Ennezat, Maringues, Lezoux, a heap of villages scarcely distinguishable, which only broke the wide expanse of verdure with a somber indentation here and there, and, further down, away down below, at the base of the mountains, he pretended that he could trace out Thiers.

He said, in an animated fashion: "Look, look! Just in front of my finger, exactly in front of my finger. For my part, I can see it quite distinctly."

She could see nothing, but she was not surprised at his power of vision, for he looked like a bird of prey, with his round, piercing eyes, which appeared to be as powerful as telescopes. He went on:

"The Allier flows in front of us, in the middle of that plain, but it is impossible to perceive it. It is very far off, thirty kilometers from here."

She scarcely took the trouble to glance toward the place which he indicated, for she had riveted her eyes on the rock and given it her entire attention. She was saying to herself that presently this enormous stone would no longer exist, that it would disappear in powder, and she felt herself seized with a vague pity for the stone, the pity which a little girl would feel for a broken plaything. It had been there so long, this stone; and then it was imposing—it had a picturesque look. The two men, who had by this time risen, were heaping up pebbles at the foot of it, and digging with the rapid movements of peasants working hurriedly.

The crowd gathered along the road, increasing every moment, had pushed forward to get a better view. The brats brushed against the two diggers, and kept rushing and capering round them like young animals in a state of delight; and from the elevated point at which Christiane was sitting, these people looked quite small, a crowd of insects, an anthill in confusion.

The buzz of voices ascended, now slight, scarcely noticeable, then more lively, a confused mixture of cries and human movements, but scattered through the air, evaporated already—a dust of sounds, as it were. On the knoll likewise the crowd was swelling in numbers, incessantly arriving from the village, and covering up the slope which looked down on the condemned rock.

They were distinguished from each other, as they gathered together, according to their hotels, their classes, their castes. The most clamorous portion of the assemblage was that of the actors and musicians, presided over and generaled by the conductor, Petrus Martel of the Odéon, who, under the circumstances, had given up his incessant game of billiards.

With a Panama flapping over his forehead, a black alpaca jacket covering his shoulders and allowing his big stomach to protrude in a semicircle, for he considered a waistcoat useless in the open country, the actor, with his thick mustache, assumed the airs of a commander-in-chief, and pointed out, explained, and criticised all the movements of the two Oriols. His subordinates, the comedian Lapalme, the young premier Petitnivelle, and the musicians, the maestro Saint Landri, the pianist Javel, the huge flautist Noirot, the double-bass Nicordi, gathered round him to listen. In front of them were seated three women, sheltered by three parasols, a white, a red, and a blue, which, under the sun of two o'clock, formed a strange and dazzling French flag. These were Mademoiselle Odelin, the young actress; her mother,—a mother that she had hired out, as Gontran put it,—and the female attendant of the coffee-room, three ladies who were habitual companions. The arrangement of these three parasols so as to suit the national colors was an invention of Petrus Martel, who, having noticed at the commencement of the season the blue and the white in the hands of the ladies Odelin, had made a present of the red to the coffee-room attendant.

Quite close to them, another group excited interest and observation, that of the chefs and scullions of the hotels, to the number of eight, for there was a war of rivalry between the kitchen-folk, who had attired themselves in linen jackets to make an impression on the bystanders, extending even to the scullery-maids. Standing all in a group they let the crude light of day fall on their flat white caps, presenting, at the same time, the appearance of fantastic staff-officers of lancers and a deputation of cooks.

The Marquis asked Doctor Honorat: "Where do all these people come from? I never would have imagined Enval was so thickly populated!"

"Oh! they come from all parts, from Chatel-Guyon, from Tournoel, from La Roche-Pradière, from Saint-Hippolyte. For this affair has been talked of a long time in the country, and then Père Oriol is a celebrity, an important personage on account of his influence and his wealth, besides a true Auvergnat, remaining still a peasant, working himself, hoarding, piling up gold on gold, intelligent, full of ideas and plans for his children's future."

Gontran came back, excited, his eyes sparkling.

He said, in a low tone: "Paul, Paul, pray come along with me; I'm going to show you two pretty girls; yes, indeed, nice girls, you know!"

The other raised his head, and replied: "My dear fellow, I'm in very good quarters here; I'll not budge."

"You're wrong. They are charming!" Then, in a louder tone: "But the doctor is going to tell me who they are. Two little girls of eighteen or nineteen, rustic ladies, oddly dressed, with black silk dresses that have close-fitting sleeves, some kind of uniform dresses, convent-gowns—two brunettes——"

Doctor Honorat interrupted him: "That's enough. They are Père Oriol's daughters, two pretty young girls indeed, educated at the Benedictine Convent at Clermont, and sure to make very good matches. They are two types, but simply types of our race, of the fine race of women of Auvergne, Marquis. I will show you these two little lasses——"

Gontran here slyly interposed: "You are the medical adviser of the Oriol family, doctor?"

The other appreciated this sly question, and simply responded with a "By Jove, I am!" uttered in a tone of the utmost good-humor.

The young man went on: "How did you come to win the confidence of this rich patient?"

"By ordering him to drink a great deal of good wine." And he told a number of anecdotes about the Oriols. Moreover, he was distantly related to them, and had known them for a considerable time. The old fellow, the father, quite an original, was very proud of his wine; and above all he had one vine-garden, the produce of which was reserved for the use of the family, solely for the family and their guests. In certain years they happened to empty the casks filled with the growth of this aristocratic vineyard, but in other years they scarcely succeeded in doing so. About the month of May or June, when the father saw that it would be hard to drink all that was still left, he would proceed to encourage his big son, Colosse, and would repeat: "Come on, son, we must finish it." Then they would go on pouring down their throats pints of red wine from morning till night. Twenty times during every meal, the old chap would say in a grave tone, while he held the jug over his son's glass: "We must finish it." And, as all this liquor with its mixture of alcohol heated his blood and prevented him from sleeping, he would rise up in the middle of the night, draw on his breeches, light a lantern, wake up Colosse, and off they would go to the cellar, after snatching a crust of bread each out of the cupboard, in order to steep it in their glasses, filled up again and again out of the same cask. Then, when they had swallowed so much wine that they could feel it rolling about in their stomachs, the father would tap the resounding wood of the cask to find out whether the level of the liquor had gone down.

The Marquis asked: "Are these the same people that are working at the hillock?"

"Yes, yes, exactly."

Just at that moment the two men hurried off with giant strides from the rock charged with powder, and all the crowd that surrounded them down below began to run away like a retreating army. They fled in the direction of Riom and Enval, leaving behind them by itself the huge rock on the top of the hillock covered with thin grass and pebbles, for it divided the vineyard into two sections, and its immediate surroundings had not been grubbed up yet.

The crowd assembled on the slope above, now as dense as that below, waited in trembling expectancy; and the loud voice of Petrus Martel exclaimed:

"Attention! the fuse is lit!"

Christiane shivered at the thought of what was about to happen, but the doctor murmured behind her back:

“Ho! if they left there all the fuse I saw them buying, we’ll have ten minutes of it!”

All eyes were fixed on the stone, and suddenly a dog, a little black dog, a kind of pug, was seen approaching it. He ran round it, began smelling, and no doubt, discovered a suspicious odor, for he commenced yelping as loudly as ever he could, his paws stiff, the hair on his back standing on end, his tail sticking out, and his ears erect.

A burst of laughter came from the spectators, a cruel burst of laughter; people expressed a hope that he would not keep riveted to the spot up to the time of the blast. Then voices called out to him to make him come back; some men whistled to him; they tried to hit him with stones to prevent him from going on the whole way. But the pug did not budge an inch, and kept barking furiously at the rock.

Christiane began to tremble. A horrible fear of seeing the animal disemboweled took possession of her; all her enjoyment was at an end. She cried repeatedly, with nerves unstrung, stammering, vibrating all over with anguish:

“Oh! good heavens! Oh! good heavens! it will be killed. I don’t want to look at it! I don’t want to look at it! I will not wait to see it! Come away!”

Paul Bretigny, who had been sitting by her side, arose, and, without saying one word, began to descend toward the hillock with all the speed of which his long legs were capable.

Cries of terror escaped from many lips; a panic agitated the crowd; and the pug, seeing this big man coming toward him, took refuge behind the rock. Paul pursued him; the dog ran off to the other side; and, for a minute or two, they kept rushing round the stone, now to right, now to left, as if they were playing a game of hide and seek. Seeing at last that he could not overtake the animal, the young man proceeded to reascend the slope, and the dog, seized once more with fury, renewed his barking.

Vociferations of anger greeted the return of the imprudent youth, who was quite out of breath, for people do not forgive those who excite terror in their breasts. Christiane was suffocating with emotion, her two hands pressed against her palpitating heart. She had lost her head so completely that she sobbed: “At least you are not hurt?” while Gontran cried angrily:

“He is mad, that idiot, he never does anything but tomfooleries of this kind. I never met a greater donkey!”

But the soil was now shaking; it rose in air. A formidable detonation made the entire country all around vibrate, and for a full minute thundered over the mountain, while all the echoes repeated it, like so many cannon-shots.

Christiane saw nothing but a shower of stones falling, and a high column of light clay sinking in a heap. And immediately afterward the crowd from above rushed down like a wave, uttering wild shouts. The battalion of kitchen-drudges came racing down in the direction of the knoll, leaving behind them the regiment of theatrical performers, who descended more slowly, with Petrus Martel at their head. The three parasols forming a tricolor were nearly carried away in this descent.

And all ran, men, women, peasants, and villagers. They could be seen falling, getting up again, starting on afresh, while in long procession the two streams of people, which had till now been kept back by fear, rolled along so as to knock against one another and get mixed up on the very spot where the explosion had taken place.

"Let us wait a while," said the Marquis, "till all this curiosity is satisfied, so that we may go and look in our turn."

The engineer, M. Aubry-Pasteur, who had just arisen with very great difficulty, replied:

"For my part, I am going back to the village by the footpaths. There is nothing further to keep me here."

He shook hands, bowed, and went away.

Doctor Honorat had disappeared. The party talked about him, and the Marquis said to his son:

"You have only known him three days, and all the time you have been laughing at him. You will end by offending him."

But Gontran shrugged his shoulders: "Oh! he's a wise man, a good sceptic, that doctor. I tell you in reply that he will not bother himself. When we are both alone together, he laughs at all the world and everything, commencing with his patients and his waters. I will give you a free thermal course if you ever see him annoyed by my nonsense."

Meanwhile, there was considerable agitation further down around the site of the vanished hillock. The enormous crowd, swelling, rising up, and sinking down like billows, broke out into exclamations, manifestly swayed by some emotion, some astonishing occurrence which nobody had foreseen. Andermatt, ever eager and inquisitive, was repeating:

"What is the matter with them now? What can be the matter with them?"

Gontran announced that he was going to find out, and walked off. Christiane, who had now sunk into a state of indifference, was reflecting that if the igniting substance had been only a little shorter, it would have been sufficient to have caused the death of their foolish companion or led to his being mutilated by the blasting of the rock, and all because she was afraid of a dog losing its life. She could not help thinking that he must, indeed, be very violent and passionate—this man—to expose himself to such a risk in this way without any good reason for it—simply owing to the fact that a woman who was a stranger to him had given expression to a desire.

People could be observed running along the road toward the village. The Marquis now asked, in his turn: "What is the matter with them?" And Andermatt, unable to stand it any longer, began to run down the side of the hill. Gontran, from below, made a sign to him to come on.

Paul Bretigny asked: "Will you take my arm, Madame?" She took his arm, which seemed to her as immovable as iron, and, as her feet glided along the warm grass, she leaned on it as she would have leaned on a baluster with a sense of absolute security. Gontran, who had just come back after making inquiries, exclaimed: "It is a spring. The explosion has made a spring gush out!"

And they fell in with the crowd. Then, the two young men, Paul and Gontran, moving on in front, scattered the spectators by jostling against them, and without paying any heed to their gruntings, opened a way for Christiane and her father. They walked through a chaos of sharp stones, broken, and blackened with powder, and arrived in front of a hole full of muddy water which bubbled up and then flowed away toward the river over the feet of the bystanders. Andermatt was there already, having effected a passage through the multitude by insinuating ways peculiar to himself, as Gontran used to say, and was watching with rapt attention the water escaping through the broken soil.

Doctor Honorat, facing him at the opposite side of the hole, was observing him with an air of mingled surprise and boredom.

Andermatt said to him: "It might be desirable to taste it; it is perhaps a mineral spring."

The physician returned: "No doubt it is mineral. There are any number of mineral waters here. There will soon be more springs than invalids."

The other in reply said: "But it is necessary to taste it."

The physician displayed little or no interest in the matter: "It is necessary at least to wait till we see whether it is clean."

And everyone wanted to see. Those in the second row pushed those in front almost into the muddy water. A child fell in, and caused a laugh. The Oriols, father and son, were there, contemplating gravely this unexpected phenomenon, not knowing yet what they ought to think about it. The father was a spare man, with a long, thin frame, and a bony head—the hard head of a beardless peasant; and the son, taller still, a giant, thin also, and wearing a mustache, had the look at the same time of a trooper and a vinedresser.

The bubblings of the water appeared to increase, its volume to grow larger, and it was beginning to get clearer. A movement took place among the people, and Doctor Latonne appeared with a glass in his hand. He perspired, panted, and stood quite stupefied at the sight of his brother-physician, Doctor Honorat, with one foot planted at the side of the newly discovered spring, like a general who has been the first to enter a fortress.

He asked, breathlessly: "Have you tasted it?"

"No, I am waiting to see whether 'tis clear."

Then Doctor Latonne thrust his glass into it, and drank with that solemnity of visage which experts assume when tasting wines. After that, he exclaimed, "Excellent!" which in no way compromised him, and extending the glass toward his rival said: "Do you wish to taste it?"

But Doctor Honorat, decidedly, had no love for mineral waters, for he smilingly replied:

"Many thanks! 'Tis quite sufficient that you have appreciated it. I know the taste of them."

He did know the taste of them all, and he appreciated it, too, though in quite a different fashion. Then, turning toward Père Oriol said:

"'Tisn't as good as your excellent vine-growth."

The old man was flattered. Christiane had seen enough, and wanted to go away. Her brother and Paul once more forced a path for her through the populace. She followed them, leaning on her father's arm. Suddenly she slipped and was near falling, and glancing down at her feet she saw that she had stepped on a piece of bleeding flesh, covered with black hairs and sticky with mud. It was a portion of the pug-dog, who had been mangled by the explosion and trampled underfoot by the crowd. She felt a choking sensation, and was so much moved that she could not restrain her tears. And she murmured, as she dried her eyes with her handkerchief: "Poor little animal! poor little animal!"

She wanted to know nothing more about it. She wished to go back, to shut herself up in her room. That day, which had begun so pleasantly, had ended sadly for her. Was it an omen? Her heart, shriveling up, beat with violent palpitations. They were now alone on the road, and in front of them they saw a tall hat and the two skirts of a frock-coat flapping like wings. It was Doctor Bonnefille, who had been the last to hear the news, and who was now rushing to the spot, glass in hand, like Doctor Latonne.

When he recognized the Marquis, he drew up.

"What is this I hear, Marquis? They tell me it is a spring—a mineral spring?"

"Yes, my dear doctor."

"Abundant?"

"Why, yes."

"Is it true that—that they are there?"

Gontran replied with an air of gravity: "Why, yes, certainly; Doctor Latonne has even made the analysis already."

Then Doctor Bonnefille began to run, while Christiane, a little tickled and enlivened by his face, said:

"Well, no, I am not going back yet to the hotel. Let us go and sit down in the park."

Andermatt had remained at the site of the knoll, watching the flowing of the water.

CHAPTER III.

BARGAINING

The table d'hôte was noisy that evening at the Hotel Splendid. The blasting of the hillock and the discovery of the new spring gave a brisk impetus to conversation. The diners were not numerous, however,—a score all told,—people usually taciturn and quiet, patients who, after having vainly tried all the well-known waters, had now turned to the new stations. At the end of the table occupied by the Ravenels and the Andermatts were, first, the Monecus, a little man with white hair and face and his daughter, a very pale, big girl, who sometimes rose up and went out in the middle of a meal, leaving her plate half full; fat M. Aubry-Pasteur, the ex-engineer; the Chaufours, a family in black, who might be met every day in the walks of the park behind a little vehicle which carried their deformed child, and the ladies Paille, mother and daughter, both of them widows, big and strong, strong everywhere, before and behind. "You may easily see," said Gontran, "that they ate up their husbands; that's how their stomachs got affected." It was, indeed, for a stomach affection that they had come to the station.

Further on, a man of extremely red complexion, brick-colored, M. Riquier, whose digestion was also very indifferent, and then other persons with bad complexions, travelers of that mute class who usually enter the dining-rooms of hotels with slow steps, the wife in front, the husband behind, bow as soon as they have passed the door, and then take their seats with a timid and modest air.

All the other end of the table was empty, although the plates and the covers were laid there for the guests of the future.

Andermatt talked in an animated fashion. He had spent the afternoon chatting with Doctor Latonne, giving vent in a flood of words to vast schemes with reference to Enval. The doctor had enumerated to him, with burning conviction, the wonderful qualities of his water, far superior to those of Chatel-Guyon, whose reputation nevertheless had been definitely established for the last ten years. Then, at the right, they had that hole of a place, Royat, at the height of success, and at the left, that other hole, Chatel-Guyon, which had lately been set afloat. What could they not do with Enval, if they knew how to set about it properly?

He said, addressing the engineer: "Yes, Monsieur, there's where it all is, to know the way to set about it. It is all a matter of skill, of tact, of opportunism, and of audacity. In order to establish a spa, it is necessary to know how to launch it, nothing more, and in order to launch it, it is necessary to interest the great medical body of Paris in the matter. I, Monsieur, always succeed in what I undertake, because I always seek the practical method, the only one that should determine success in every particular case with which I occupy myself; and, as long as I have not discovered it, I do nothing—I wait. It is not enough to have the water, it is necessary to get people to drink it; and to get people to drink it, it is not enough to get it cried up as unrivaled in the newspapers and elsewhere; it is necessary to know how to get this discreetly said by the only men who have influence on the public that will drink it, on the invalids whom we require, on the peculiarly credulous public that pays for drugs—in short, by the physicians. You can only address a Court of Justice through the mouths of advocates; it will only hear them, and understands only them. So you can only address the patient through the doctors—he listens only to them."

The Marquis, who greatly admired the practical common sense of his son-in-law, exclaimed:

"Ah! how true this is! Apart from this, my dear boy, you are unique for giving the right touch."

Andermatt, who was excited, went on: "There is a fortune to be made here. The country is admirable, the climate excellent. One thing alone disturbs my mind—would we have water enough for a large establishment?—for things that are only half done always miscarry. We would require a very large establishment, and consequently a great deal of water, enough of water to supply two hundred baths at the same time, with a rapid and continuous current; and the new spring added to the old one, would not supply fifty, whatever Doctor Latonne may say about it——"

M. Aubry-Pasteur interrupted him. "Oh! as for water, I will give you as much as you want of it."

Andermatt was stupefied. "You?"

"Yes, I. That astonishes you? Let me explain myself. Last year, I was here about the same time as this year, for I really find myself improved by the Enval baths. Now one morning, I lay asleep in my own room, when a stout gentleman arrived. He was the president of the governing body of the establishment. He was in a state of great agitation, and the cause of it was this: the Bonnefille Spring had lowered so much that there were some apprehensions lest it might entirely disappear. Knowing that I was a mining engineer, he had come to ask me if I could not find a means of saving the establishment.

"I accordingly set about studying the geological system of the country. You know that in each stratum of the soil original disturbances have led to different changes and conditions in the surface of the ground. The question, therefore, was to discover how the mineral water came—by what fissures—and what were the direction, the origin, and the nature of these fissures. I first inspected the establishment with great care, and, noticing in a corner an old disused pipe of a bath, I observed that it was already almost stopped up with limestone. Now the water, by depositing the salts which it contained on the coatings of the ducts, had rapidly led to an obstruction of the passage. It would inevitably happen likewise in the natural passages in the soil, this soil being granitic. So it was that the Bonnefille Spring had stopped up. Nothing more. It was necessary to get at it again farther on.

"Most people would have searched above its original point of egress. As for me, after a month of study, observation, and reasoning, I sought for and found it fifty meters lower down. And this was the explanation of the matter: I told you before that it was first necessary to determine the origin, nature, and direction of the fissures in the granite which enabled the water to spring forth. It was easy for me to satisfy myself that these fissures ran from the plain toward the mountain and not from the mountain toward the plain, inclined like a roof undoubtedly, in consequence of a depression of this plain which in breaking up had carried along with it the primitive buttresses of the mountains. Accordingly, the water, in place of descending, rose up again between the different interstices of the granitic layers. And I then discovered the cause of this unexpected phenomenon.

"Formerly the Limagne, that vast expanse of sandy and argillaceous soil, of which you can scarcely see the limits, was on a level with the first table-land of the mountains; but owing to the geological character of its lower portions, it subsided, so as to tear away the edge of the mountain, as I explained to you a moment ago. Now this immense sinking produced, at the point of separating the earth and the granite, an immense barrier of clay of great depth and impenetrable by liquids. And this is what happens: The mineral water comes from the beds of old volcanoes. That which comes from the greatest distance gets cooled on its way, and rises up perfectly cold like ordinary springs; that which comes from the volcanic beds that are nearer gushes up still warm, at varying degrees of heat, according to the distance of the subterranean fire.

"Here is the course it pursues. It is expelled from some unknown depths, up to the moment when it meets the clay barrier of the Limagne. Not being able to pass through it, and pushed on by enormous pressure, it seeks a vent. Finding then the inclined gaps of granite, it gets in there, and reascends to the point at which they reach the level of the soil. Then, resuming its original direction, it again proceeds to flow toward the plain along the ordinary bed of the streams. I may add that we do not see the hundredth part of the mineral waters of these glens. We can only discover those whose point of egress is open. As for the others, arriving as they do at the side of the fissures in the granite under a thick layer of vegetable and cultivated soil, they are lost in the earth, which absorbs them.

"From this I draw the conclusion: first, that to have the water, it is sufficient to search by following the inclination and the direction of the superimposed strips of granite; secondly, that in order to preserve it, it is enough to prevent the fissures from being stopped up by calcareous deposits, that is to say, to maintain carefully the little artificial wells by digging; thirdly, that in order to obtain the adjoining spring, it is necessary to get at it by means of a practical sounding as far as the same fissure of granite below, and not above, it being well understood that you must place yourself at the side of the barrier of clay which forces the waters to reascend. From this point of view, the spring discovered to-day is admirably situated only some meters away from this barrier. If you want to set up a new establishment, it is here you should erect it."

When he ceased speaking, there was an interval of silence.

Andermatt, ravished, said merely: "That's it! When you see the curtain drawn, the entire mystery vanishes. You are a most valuable man, M. Aubry-Pasteur."

Besides him, the Marquis and Paul Bretigny alone had understood what he was talking about. Gontran had not heard a single word. The others, with their ears and mouths open, while the engineer was talking, were simply stupefied with amazement. The ladies Paille especially, being very religious women, asked themselves if this explanation of a phenomenon ordained by God and accomplished by mysterious means had not in it something profane. The mother thought she ought to say: "Providence is very wonderful." The ladies seated at the center of the table conveyed their approval by nods of the head, disturbed also by listening to these unintelligible remarks.

M. Riquier, the brick-colored man, observed: "They may well come from volcanoes or from the moon, these Enval waters—here have I been taking them ten days, and as yet I experience no effect from them!"

M. and Madame Chaufour protested in the name of their child, who was beginning to move the right leg, a thing that had not happened during the six years they had been nursing him.

Riquier replied: "That proves, by Jove, that we have not the same ailment; it doesn't prove that the Enval water cures affections of the stomach." He seemed in a rage, exasperated by this fresh, useless experiment.

But M. Monecu also spoke in the name of his daughter, declaring that for the last eight days she was beginning to be able to retain food without being obliged to go out at every meal. And his big daughter blushed, with her nose in her plate. The ladies Paille likewise thought they had improved.

Then Riquier was vexed, and abruptly turning toward the two women said:

"Your stomachs are affected, Mesdames."

They replied together: "Why, yes, Monsieur. We can digest nothing."

He nearly leaped out of his chair, stammering: "You—you! Why, 'tis enough to look at you. Your stomachs are affected, Mesdames. That is to say, you eat too much."

Madame Paille, the mother, became very angry, and she retorted: "As for you, Monsieur, there is no doubt about it, you exhibit certainly the appearance of persons whose stomachs are destroyed. It has been well said that good stomachs make nice men."

A very thin, old lady, whose name was not known, said authoritatively: "I am sure everyone would find the waters of Enval better if the hotel chef would only bear in mind a little that he is cooking for invalids. Truly, he sends us up things that it is impossible to digest."

And suddenly the entire table agreed on the point, and indignation was expressed against the hotel-keeper, who served them with crayfish, porksteaks, salt eels, cabbage, yes, cabbage and sausages, all the most indigestible kinds of food in the world for persons for whom Doctors Bonnefille, Latonne, and Honorat had prescribed only white meats, lean and tender, fresh vegetables, and milk diet.

Riquier was shaking with fury: "Why should not the physicians inspect the table at thermal stations without leaving such an important thing as the selection of nutriment to the judgment of a brute? Thus, every day, they give us hard eggs, anchovies, and ham as side-dishes——"

M. Monecu interrupted him: "Oh! excuse me! My daughter can digest nothing well except ham, which, moreover has been prescribed for her by Mas-Roussel and Remusot."

Riquier exclaimed: "Ham! ham! why, that's poison, Monsieur."

And an interminable argument arose, which each day was taken up afresh, as to the classification of foods. Milk itself was discussed with passionate warmth. Riquier could not drink a glass of claret and milk without immediately suffering from indigestion.

Aubry-Pasteur, in answer to his remarks, irritated in his turn, observed that people questioned the properties of things which he adored:

"Why, gracious goodness, Monsieur, if you were attacked with dyspepsia and I with gastralgia, we would require food as different as the glass of the spectacles that suits short-sighted and long-sighted people, both of whom, however, have diseased eyes."

He added: "For my part I begin to choke when I swallow a glass of red wine, and I believe there is nothing worse for man than wine. All water-drinkers live a hundred years, while we——"

Gontran replied with a laugh: "Faith, without wine and without marriage, I would find life monotonous enough."

The ladies Paille lowered their eyes. They drank a considerable quantity of Bordeaux of the best quality without any water in it, and their double widowhood seemed to indicate that they had applied the same treatment to their husbands, the daughter being twenty-two and the mother scarcely forty.

But Andermatt, usually so chatty, remained taciturn and thoughtful. He suddenly asked Gontran: "Do you know where the Oriols live?"

"Yes, their house was pointed out to me a little while ago."

"Could you bring me there after dinner?"

"Certainly. It will even give me pleasure to accompany you. I shall not be sorry to have another look at the two lassies."

And, as soon as dinner was over, they went off, while Christiane, who was tired, went up with the Marquis and Paul Bretigny to spend the rest of the day in the drawing-room.

It was still broad daylight, for they dine early at thermal stations.

Andermatt took his brother-in-law's arm.

"My dear Gontran, if this old man is reasonable, and if the analysis realizes Doctor Latonne's expectations, I am probably going to try a big stroke of business here—a spa. I am going to start a spa!"

He stopped in the middle of the street, and seized his companion by both sides of his jacket.

"Ha! you don't understand, fellows like you, how amusing business is, not the business of merchants or traders, but big undertakings such as we go in for! Yes, my boy, when they are properly understood, we find in them everything that men care for—they cover, at the same time, politics, war, diplomacy, everything, everything! It is necessary to be always searching, finding, inventing, to understand everything, to foresee everything, to combine everything, to dare everything. The great battle to-day is being fought by means of money. For my part, I see in the hundred-sou pieces raw recruits in red breeches, in the twenty-franc pieces very glittering lieutenants, captains in the notes for a hundred francs, and in those for a thousand I see generals. And I fight, by heavens! I fight from morning till night against all the world, with all the world. And this is how to live, how to live on a big scale, just as the mighty lived in days of yore. We are the mighty of to-day—there you are—the only true mighty ones!

"Stop, look at that village, that poor village! I will make a town of it, yes, I will, a lovely town full of big hotels which will be filled with visitors, with elevators, with servants, with carriages, a crowd of rich folk served by a crowd of poor; and all this because it pleased me one evening to fight with Royat, which is at the right, with Chatel-Guyon, which is at the left, with Mont Doré, La Bourboule, Châteauneuf, Saint Nectaire, which are behind us, with Vichy, which is facing us. And I shall succeed because I have the means, the only means. I have seen it in one glance, just as a great general sees the weak side of an enemy. It is necessary too to know how to lead men, in our line of business, both to carry them along with us and to subjugate them.

"Good God! life becomes amusing when you can do such things. I have now three years of pleasure to look forward to with this town of mine. And then see what a chance it is to find this engineer, who told us such interesting things at dinner, most interesting things, my dear fellow. It is as clear as day, my system. Thanks to it, I can smash the old company, without even having any necessity of buying it up."

He then resumed his walk, and they quietly went up the road to the left in the direction of Chatel-Guyon.

Gontran presently observed: "When I am walking by my brother-in-law's side, I feel that the same noise disturbs his brain as that heard in the gambling rooms at Monte Carlo—that noise of gold moved about, shuffled, drawn away, raked off, lost or gained."

Andermatt did, indeed, suggest the idea of a strange human machine, constructed only for the purpose of calculating and debating about money, and mentally manipulating it. Moreover, he exhibited much vanity about his special knowledge of the world, and plumed himself on his power of estimating at one glance of his eye the actual value of anything whatever. Accordingly, he might be seen, wherever he happened to be, every moment taking up an article, examining it, turning it round, and declaring: "This is worth so much."

His wife and his brother-in-law, diverted by this mania, used to amuse themselves by deceiving him, exhibiting to him queer pieces of furniture and asking him to estimate them; and when he remained perplexed, at the sight of their unexpected finds, they would both burst out laughing like fools. Sometimes also, in the street at Paris, Gontran would stop in front of a warehouse and force him to make a calculation of an entire shop-window, or perhaps of a horse with a jolting vehicle, or else again of a luggage-van laden with household goods.

One evening, while seated at his sister's dinner-table before fashionable guests, he called on William to tell him what would be the approximate value of the Obelisk; then, when the other happened to name some figure, he would put the same question as to the Solferino Bridge, and the Arc de Triomphe de l'Étoile. And he gravely concluded: "You might write a very interesting work on the valuation of the principal monuments of the globe." Andermatt never got angry, and fell in with all his pleasantries, like a superior man sure of himself.

Gontran having asked one day: "And I—how much am I worth?" William declined to answer; then, as his brother-in-law persisted, saying: "Look here! If I should be captured by brigands, how much would you give to release me?" he replied at last: "Well, well, my dear fellow, I would give a bill." And his smile said so much that the other, a little disconcerted, did not press the matter further.

Andermatt, besides, was fond of artistic objects, and having fine taste and appreciating such things thoroughly, he skillfully collected them with that bloodhound's scent which he carried into all commercial transactions.

They had arrived in front of a house of a middle-class type. Gontran stopped him and said: "Here it is." An iron knocker hung over a heavy oaken door; they knocked, and a lean servant-maid came to open it.

The banker asked: "Monsieur Oriol?"

The woman said: "Come in."

They entered a kitchen, a big farm-kitchen, in which a little fire was still burning under a pot; then they were ushered into another part of the house, where the Oriol family was assembled.

The father was asleep, seated on one chair with his feet on another. The son, with both elbows on the table, was reading the "Petit Journal" with the spasmodic efforts of a feeble intellect always wandering; and the two girls, in the recess of the same window, were working at the same piece of tapestry, having begun it one at each end.

They were the first to rise, both at the same moment, astonished at this unexpected visit; then, big Jacques raised his head, a head congested by the pressure of his brain; then, at last, Père Oriol waked up, and took down his long legs from the second chair one after the other.

The room was bare, with whitewashed walls, a stone flooring, and furniture consisting of straw seats, a mahogany chest of drawers, four engravings by Epinal with glass over them, and big white curtains. They were all staring at each other, and the servant-maid, with her petticoat raised up to her knees, was waiting at the door, riveted to the spot by curiosity.

Andermatt introduced himself, mentioning his name as well as that of his brother-in-law, Count de Ravenel, made a low bow to the two young girls, bending his head with extreme politeness, and then calmly seated himself, adding:

"Monsieur Oriol, I came to talk to you about a matter of business. Moreover, I will not take four roads to explain myself. See here. You have just discovered a spring on your property. The analysis of this water is to be made in a few days. If it is of no value, you will understand that I will have nothing to do with it; if, on the contrary, it fulfills my anticipations, I propose to buy from you this piece of ground, and all the lands around it. Think on this. No other person but myself could make you such an offer. The old company is nearly bankrupt; it will not, therefore, have the least notion of building a new establishment, and the ill success of this enterprise will not encourage fresh attempts. Don't give me an answer to-day. Consult your family. When the analysis is known you will fix your price. If it suits me, I will say 'yes'; if it does not suit me, I will say 'no.' I never haggle for my part."

The peasant, a man of business in his own way, and sharp as anyone could be, courteously replied that he would see about it, that he felt honored, that he would think it over—and then he offered them a glass of wine.

Andermatt made no objection, and, as the day was declining, Oriol said to his daughters, who had resumed their work, with their eyes lowered over the piece of tapestry: "Let us have some light, girls."

They both got up together, passed into an adjoining room, then came back, one carrying two lighted wax-candles, the other four wineglasses without stems, glasses such as the poor use. The wax-candles were fresh looking and were garnished with red paper—placed, no doubt, by way of ornament on the young girl's mantelpiece.

Then, Colosse rose up; for only the male members of the family visited the cellar. Andermatt had an idea. "It would give me great pleasure to see your cellar. You are the principal vinedresser of the district, and it must be a very fine one."

Oriol, touched to the heart, hastened to conduct them, and, taking up one of the wax-candles, led the way. They had to pass through the kitchen again, then they got into a court where the remnant of daylight that was left enabled them to discern empty casks standing on end, big stones of giant granite in a corner pierced with a hole in the middle, like the wheels of some antique car of colossal size, a dismounted winepress with wooden screws, its brown divisions rendered smooth by wear and tear, and glittering suddenly in the light thrown by the candle on the shadows that surrounded it. Close to it, the working implements of polished steel on the ground had the glitter of arms used in warfare. All these things gradually grew more distinct, as the old man drew nearer to them with the candle in his hand, making a shade of the other.

Already they got the smell of the wine, the pounded grapes drained dry. They arrived in front of a door fastened with two locks. Oriol opened it, and quickly raising the candle above his head vaguely pointed toward a long succession of barrels standing in a row, and having on their swelling flanks a second line of smaller casks. He showed them first of all that this cellar, all on one floor, sank right into the mountain, then he explained the contents of its different casks, the ages, the nature of the various vine-crops, and their merits; then, having reached the supply reserved for the family, he caressed the cask with his hand just as one might rub the crupper of a favorite horse, and in a proud tone said:

"You are going to taste this. There's not a wine bottled equal to it—not one, either at Bordeaux or elsewhere."

For he possessed the intense passion of countrymen for wine kept in a cask.

Colosse followed him, carrying a jug, stooped down, turned the cock of the funnel, while his father cautiously held the light for him, as though he were accomplishing some difficult task requiring minute attention. The candle's flame fell directly on their faces, the father's head like that of an old attorney, and the son's like that of a peasant soldier.

Andermatt murmured in Gontran's ear: "Hey, what a fine Teniers!"

The young man replied in a whisper: "I prefer the girls."

Then they went back into the house. It was necessary, it seemed, to drink this wine, to drink a great deal of it, in order to please the two Oriols.

The lassies had come across to the table where they continued their work as if there had been no visitors. Gontran kept incessantly staring at them, asking himself whether they were twins, so closely did they resemble one another. One of them, however, was plumper and smaller, while the other was more ladylike. Their hair, dark-brown rather than black, drawn over their temples in smooth bands, gleamed with every slight movement of their heads. They had the rather heavy jaw and forehead peculiar to the people of Auvergne, cheek-bones somewhat strongly marked, but charming mouths, ravishing eyes, with brows of rare neatness, and delightfully fresh complexions. One felt, on looking at them, that they had not been brought up in this house, but in a select boarding-school, in the convent to which the daughters of the aristocracy of Auvergne are sent, and that they had acquired there the well-bred manners of cultivated young ladies.

Meanwhile, Gontran, seized with disgust before this red glass in front of him, pressed Andermatt's foot to induce him to leave. At length he rose, and they both energetically grasped the hands of the two peasants; then they bowed once more ceremoniously, the young girls each responding with a slight nod, without again rising from their seats.

As soon as they had reached the village, Andermatt began talking again.

"Hey, my dear boy, what an odd family! How manifest here is the transition from people in good society. A son's services are required to cultivate the vine so as to save the wages of a laborer,—stupid economy,—however, he discharges this function, and is one of the people. As for the girls, they are like girls of the better class—almost quite so already. Let them only make good matches, and they would pass as well as any of the women of our own class, and even much better than most of them. I am as much gratified at seeing these people as a geologist would be at finding an animal of the tertiary period."

Gontran asked: "Which do you prefer?"

"Which? How, which? Which what?"

"Of the lassies?"

"Oh! upon my honor, I haven't an idea on the subject. I have not looked at them from the standpoint of comparison. But what difference can this make to you? You have no intention to carry off one of them?"

Gontran began to laugh: "Oh! no, but I am delighted to meet for once fresh women, really fresh, fresh as women never are with us. I like looking at them, just as you like looking at a Teniers. There is nothing pleases me so much as looking at a pretty girl, no matter where, no matter of what class. These are my objects of vertu. I don't collect them, but I admire them—I admire them passionately, artistically, my friend, in the spirit of a convinced and disinterested artist. What would you have? I love this! By the bye, could you lend me five thousand francs?"

The other stopped, and murmured an "Again!" energetically.

Gontran replied, with an air of simplicity: "Always!" Then they resumed their walk.

Andermatt then said: "What the devil do you do with the money?"

"I spend it."

"Yes, but you spend it to excess."

"My dear friend, I like spending money as much as you like making it. Do you understand?"

"Very fine, but you don't make it."

"That's true. I know it. One can't have everything. You know how to make it, and, upon my word, you don't at all know how to spend it. Money appears to you no use except to get interest on it. I, on the other hand, don't know how to make it, but I know thoroughly how to spend it. It procures me a thousand things of which you don't know the name. We were cut out for brothers-in-law. We complete one another admirably."

Andermatt murmured: "What stuff! No, you sha'n't have five thousand francs, but I'll lend you fifteen hundred francs, because—because in a few days I shall, perhaps, have need of you."

Gontran rejoined: "Then I accept them on account." The other gave him a slap on the shoulder without saying anything by way of answer.

They reached the park, which was illuminated with lamps hung to the branches of the trees. The orchestra of the Casino was playing in slow time a classical piece that seemed to stagger along, full of breaks and silences, executed by the same four performers, exhausted with constant playing, morning and evening, in this solitude for the benefit of the leaves and the brook, with trying to produce the effect of twenty instruments, and tired also of never being fully paid at the end of the month. Petrus Martel always completed their remuneration, when it fell short, with hampers of wine or pints of liqueurs which the bathers might have left unconsumed.

Amid the noise of the concert could also be distinguished that of the billiard-table, the clicking of the balls and the voices calling out: "Twenty, twenty-one, twenty-two."

Andermatt and Gontran went in. M. Aubry-Pasteur and Doctor Honorat, by themselves, were drinking their coffee, at the side facing the musicians. Petrus Martel and Lapalme were playing their game with desperation; and the female attendant woke up to ask:

"What do these gentlemen wish to take?"

CHAPTER IV.

A TEST AND AN AVOWAL

Père Oriol and his son had remained for a long time chatting after the girls had gone to bed. Stirred up and excited by Andermatt's proposal, they were considering how they could inflame his desire more effectually without compromising their own interests. Like the cautious, practically-minded peasants that they were, they weighed all the chances carefully, understanding very clearly that in a country in which mineral springs gushed out along all the streams, it was not advisable to repel by an exaggerated demand this unexpected enthusiast, the like of whom they might never find again. And at the same time it would not do either to leave entirely in his hands this spring, which might, some day, yield a flood of liquid money, Royat and Chatel-Guyon serving as a precedent for them.

Therefore, they asked themselves by what course of action they could kindle into frenzy the banker's ardor; they conjured up combinations of imaginary companies covering his offers, a succession of clumsy schemes, the defects of which they felt, without succeeding in inventing more ingenious ones. They slept badly; then, in the morning, the father, having awakened first, thought in his own mind that the spring might have disappeared during the night. It was possible, after all, that it might have gone as it had come, and re-entered the earth, so that it could not be brought back. He got up in a state of unrest, seized with avaricious fear, shook his son, and told him about his alarm; and big Colosse, dragging his legs out of his coarse sheets, dressed himself in order to go out with his father, to make sure about the matter.

In any case, they would put the field and the spring in proper trim themselves, would carry off the stones, and make it nice and clean, like an animal that they wanted to sell. So they took their picks and their spades, and started for the spot side by side with great, swinging strides.

They looked at nothing as they walked on, their minds being preoccupied with the business, replying with only a single word to the "Good morning" of the neighbors and friends whom they chanced to meet. When they reached the Riom road they began to get agitated, peering into the distance to see whether they could observe the water bubbling up and glittering in the morning sun. The road was empty, white, and dusty, the river running beside it sheltered by willow-trees. Beneath one of the trees Oriol suddenly noticed two feet, then, having advanced three steps further, he recognized Père Clovis seated at the edge of the road, with his crutches lying beside him on the grass.

This was an old paralytic, well known in the district, where for the last ten years he had prowled about on his supports of stout oak, as he said himself, like a poor man made of stone.

Formerly a poacher in the woods and streams, often arrested and imprisoned, he had got rheumatic pains by his long watchings stretched on the moist grass and by his nocturnal fishings in the rivers, through which he used to wade up to his middle in water. Now he whined, and crawled about, like a crab that had lost its claws. He stumped along, dragging his right leg after him like a piece of ragged cloth. But the boys of the neighborhood, who used in foggy weather to run after the girls or the hares, declared that they used to meet Père Clovis, swift-footed as a stag, and supple as an adder, under the bushes and in the glades, and that, in short, his rheumatism was only "a dodge on the gendarmes." Colosse, especially, insisted on maintaining that he had seen him, not once, but fifty times, straining his neck with his crutches under his arms.

And Père Oriol stopped in front of the old vagabond, his mind possessed by an idea which as yet was undefined, for the brain works slowly in the thick skulls of Auvergne. He said "Good morning" to him. The other responded "Good morning." Then they spoke about the weather, the ripening of the vine, and two or three other things; but, as Colosse had gone ahead, his father with long steps hastened to overtake him.

The spring was still flowing, clear by this time, and all the bottom of the hole was red, a fine, dark red, which had arisen from an abundant deposit of iron. The two men gazed at it with smiling faces, then they proceeded to clear the soil that surrounded it, and to carry off the stones of which they made a heap. And, having found the last remains of the dead dog, they buried them with jocose remarks. But all of a sudden Père Oriol let his spade fall. A roguish leer of delight and triumph wrinkled the corners of his leathery lips and the edges of his cunning eyes, and he said to his son: "Come on, till we see."

The other obeyed. They got on the road once more, and retraced their steps. Père Clovis was still toasting his limbs and his crutches in the sun.

Oriol, drawing up before him, asked: "Do you want to earn a hundred-franc piece?"

The other cautiously refrained from answering.

The peasant said: "Hey! a hundred francs?"

Thereupon the vagabond made up his mind, and murmured: "Of course, but what am I asked to do?"

"Well, father, here's what I want you to do."

And he explained to the other at great length with tricky circumlocutions, easily understood hints, and innumerable repetitions, that, if he would consent to take a bath for an hour every day from ten to eleven in a hole which they, Colosse and he, intended to dig at the side of the spring, and to be cured at the end of a month, they would give him a hundred francs in cash.

The paralytic listened with a stupid air, and then said: "Since all the drugs haven't been able to help me, 'tisn't your water that'll cure me."

But Colosse suddenly got into a passion. "Come, my old play-actor, you're talking rubbish. I know what your disease is—don't tell me about it! What were you doing on Monday last in the Comberombe wood at eleven o'clock at night?"

The old fellow promptly answered: "That's not true."

But Colosse, firing up: "Isn't it true, you old blackguard, that you jumped over the ditch to Jean Cannezat and that you made your way along the Paulin chasm?"

The other energetically repeated: "It is not true!"

"Isn't it true that I called out to you: 'Oho, Clovis, the gendarmes!' and that you turned up the Moulinet road?"

"No, it is not."

Big Jacques, raging, almost menacing, exclaimed: "Ah! it's not true! Well, old three paws, listen! The next time I see you there in the wood at night or else in the water, I'll take a grip of you, as my legs are rather longer than your own, and I'll tie you up to some tree till morning, when we'll go and take you away, the whole village together——"

Père Oriol stopped his son; then, in a very wheedling tone: "Listen, Clovis! you can easily do the thing. We prepare a bath for you, Coloche and myself. You come there every day for a month. For that I give you, not one hundred, but two hundred francs. And then, listen! if you're cured at the end of the month, it will mean five hundred francs more. Understand clearly, five hundred in ready money, and two hundred more—that makes seven hundred. Therefore you get two hundred for taking a bath for a month and five hundred more for the curing. And listen again! Suppose the pains come back. If this happens you in the autumn, there will be nothing more for us to do, for the water will have none the less produced its effect!"

The old fellow coolly replied: "In that case I'm quite willing. If it won't succeed, we'll always see it." And the three men pressed one another's hands to seal the bargain they had concluded. Then, the two Oriols returned to their spring, in order to dig the bath for Père Clovis.

They had been working at it for a quarter of an hour, when they heard voices on the road. It was Andermatt and Doctor Latonne. The two peasants winked at one another, and ceased digging the soil.

The banker came across to them, and grasped their hands; then the entire four proceeded to fix their eyes on the water without uttering a word. It stirred about like water set in movement above a big fire, threw out bubbles and steam, then it flowed away in the direction of the brook through a tiny gutter which it had already traced out. Oriol, with a smile of pride on his lips, said suddenly: "Hey, that's iron, isn't it?"

In fact the bottom was now all red, and even the little pebbles which it washed as it flowed along seemed covered with a sort of purple mold.

Doctor Latonne replied: "Yes, but that is nothing to the purpose. We would require to know its other qualities."

The peasant observed: "Coloche and myself first drank a glass of it yesterday evening, and it has already made our bodies feel fresh. Isn't that true, son?"

The big youth replied in a tone of conviction: "Sure enough, it was very refreshing."

Andermatt remained motionless, his feet on the edge of the hole. He turned toward the physician: "We would want nearly six times this volume of water for what I would wish to do, would we not?"

"Yes, nearly."

"Do you think that we'll be able to get it?"

"Oh! as for me, I know nothing about it."

"See here! The purchase of the grounds can only be definitely effected after the soundings. It would be necessary, first of all, to have a promise of sale drawn up by a notary, once the analysis is known, but not to take effect unless the consecutive soundings give the results hoped for."

Père Oriol became restless. He did not understand. Andermatt thereupon explained to him the insufficiency of only one spring, and demonstrated to him that he could not purchase unless he found others. But he could not search for these other springs till after the signature of a promise of sale.

The two peasants appeared forthwith to be convinced that their fields contained as many springs as vine-stalks. It would be sufficient to dig for them—they would see, they would see.

Andermatt said simply: "Yes, we shall see."

But Père Oriol dipped his fingers in the water, and remarked: "Why, 'tis hot enough to boil an egg, much hotter than the Bonnefille one!"

Latonne in his turn steeped his fingers in it, and realized that this was possible.

The peasant went on: "And then it has more taste and a better taste; it hasn't a false taste, like the other. Oh! this one, I'll answer for it, is good! I know the waters of the country for the fifty years that I've seen them flowing. I never seen a finer one than this, never, never!"

He remained silent for a few seconds, and then continued: "It is not in order to puff the water that I say this!—certainly not. I would like to make a trial of it before you, a fair trial, not what your chemists make, but a trial of it on a person who has a disease. I'll bet that it will cure a paralytic, this one, so hot is it and so good to taste—I'll make a bet on it!"

He appeared to be searching his brain, then cast a look at the tops of the neighboring mountains to see whether he could discover the paralytic that he required. Not having made the discovery, he lowered his eyes to the road.

Two hundred meters away from it, at the side of the road could be distinguished the two inert legs of the vagabond, whose body was hidden by the trunk of a willow tree.

Oriol placed his hand on his forehead as a shade, and said questioningly to his son: "That isn't Père Clovis over there still?"

Colosse laughingly replied: "Yes, yes. 'Tis he—he doesn't go as quick as a hare."

Then Oriol stepped over to Andermatt's side, and with an air of serious and deep conviction: "Look here, Monchieu! Listen to me. There's a paralytic over yonder, who is well known to the doctor, a genuine one, who hasn't been seen to make a single step for the last ten years. Isn't that so, doctor?"

Latonne returned: "Oh! if you cure that fellow, I would pay a franc a glass for your water!"

Then, turning toward Andermatt: "'Tis an old fellow suffering from rheumatic gout with a sort of spasmodic contraction of the left leg and a complete paralysis of the right; in fact, I believe, an incurable."

Oriol had allowed him to talk; he resumed in a deliberate fashion: "Well, doctor, would you like to make a trial of it on him for a month? I don't say that it will succeed,—I say nothing on the matter,—I only ask to have a trial made. Hold on! Coloche and myself are going to dig a hole for the stones—well, we'll make a hole for Cloviche; he'll remain an hour there every morning, and then we'll see—there!—we'll see."

The physician murmured: "You may try. I answer confidently that you will not succeed."

But Andermatt, beguiled by the prospect of an almost miraculous cure, gladly fell in with the peasant's suggestion; and the entire four directed their steps toward the vagabond, who, all this time, had been lying motionless in the sun. The old poacher, understanding the dodge, pretended to refuse, resisted for a long time, then allowed himself to be persuaded, on the condition that Andermatt would give him two francs a day for the hour which he would spend in the water.

So the matter was settled. It was even decided that, as soon as the hole was dug, Père Clovis should take his bath that very day. Andermatt would supply him with clothes to dress himself afterward, and the two Oriols would bring him a disused shepherd's hut, which was lying in their yard, so that the invalid might shut himself in there, and change his apparel.

Then the banker and the physician returned to the village. When they reached it, they parted, the doctor going to his own house for his consultations, and Andermatt hurrying to attend on his wife, who had to come to the establishment at half past nine o'clock.

She appeared almost immediately, dressed from head to foot in pink—with a pink hat, a pink parasol, and a pink complexion, she looked like an aurora, and she descended the steps of the hotel to avoid the turn of the road with the hopping movements of a bird, as it goes from stone to stone, without opening its wing. As soon as she saw her husband, she exclaimed:

"Oh! what a pretty country it is! I am quite delighted with it."

A few bathers wandering sadly through the little park in silence turned round as she passed by, and Petrus Martel, who was smoking his pipe in his shirt-sleeves at the window of the billiard-room, called to his chum, Lapalme, sitting in a corner before a glass of white wine, and said, smacking the roof of his mouth with his tongue:

"Deuce take it, there's something sweet!"

Christiane made her way into the establishment, bowed smilingly toward the cashier, who sat at the left of the entrance-door, and saluted the ex-jailer seated at the right with a "Good morning"; then, holding out a ticket to a bath-attendant dressed like the girl in the refreshment-room, followed her into a corridor facing the doors of the bath-rooms. The lady was shown into one of them, rather large, with bare walls, furnished with a chair, a glass, and a shoe-horn, while a large oval orifice, coated, like the floor, with yellow cement, served the purposes of a bath.

The woman turned a cock like those used for making the street-gutters flow, and the water gushed through a little round grated aperture at the bottom of the bath so that it was soon full to the brim, and its overflow was diverted through a furrow sunk into the wall.

Christiane, having left her chambermaid at the hotel, declined the attendant's services in undressing, and remained there alone, saying that if she required anything, she would ring, and would do the same when she wanted her linen.

She slowly disrobed, watching as she did so the almost invisible movement of the wave gently stirring on the clear surface of the basin. When she had divested herself of all her clothing she dipped her foot in, and the pleasant warm sensation mounted to her throat; then she plunged into the tepid water first one leg, and after it the other, and sat down in the midst of this caressing heat, in this transparent bath, in this spring, which flowed over her, around her, covering her body with tiny globules all along her legs, all along her arms, and also all over her breasts. She noticed with surprise those particles of air innumerable and minute which clothed her from head to foot with an entire mail-suit of little pearls. And these pearls, so minute, flew off incessantly from her white flesh, and evaporated on the surface of the bath, driven on by others that sprung to life over her form. They sprung up over her skin, like light fruits incapable of being grasped yet charming, the fruits of this exquisite body rosy and fresh, which had generated those pearls in the water.

And Christiane felt herself so happy in it, so sweetly, so softly, so deliciously caressed and clasped by the restless wave, the living wave, the animated wave from the spring which gushed up from the depths of the basin under her legs and fled through the little opening toward the edge of the bath, that she would have liked to have remained there forever, without moving, almost without thinking. The sensation of a calm delight composed of rest and comfort, of tranquil dreamfulness, of health, of discreet joy, and silent gaiety, entered into her with the soothing warmth of this. And her spirit mused, vaguely lulled into repose by the gurgling of the overflow which was escaping—dreamed of what she would be doing by and by, of what she would be doing to-morrow, of promenades, of her father, of her husband, of her brother, and of that big boy who had made her feel slightly ill at ease since the adventure of the dog. She did not care for persons of violent tendencies.

No desire agitated her soul, calm as her heart in this grateful moist warmth, no desires save the shadowy hopes of a child, no desire of any other life, of emotion, or passion. She felt that it was well with her, and she was satisfied with the happiness of her lot.

She was suddenly startled—the door flew open; it was the Auvergnat carrying the linen. Twenty minutes had passed; it was already time for her to be dressed. It was almost a pang, almost a calamity, this awakening; she felt a longing to beg of the woman to give her a few minutes more; then she reflected that every day she would find again the same delight, and she regretfully left the bath to be wrapped in a white dressing-gown whose scorching heat felt somewhat unpleasant.

Just as she was going out, Doctor Bonnefille opened the door of his consultation-room and invited her to enter, bowing ceremoniously. He inquired about her health, felt her pulse, looked at her tongue, took note of her appetite and her digestion, asked her how she slept, and then accompanied her to the door, repeating:

"Come, come, that's right, that's right. My respects, if you please, to your father, one of the most distinguished men that I have met in my career."

At last, she got away, bored by these undesirable attentions, and at the door she saw the Marquis chatting with Andermatt, Gontran, and Paul Bretigny. Her husband, in whose head every new idea was continually buzzing, like a fly in a bottle, was relating the story of the paralytic, and wanted to go back to see whether the vagabond was taking his bath. They were about to go with him to the spot in order to please him. But Christiane very gently detained her brother, and, when they were a short distance away from the others:

"Tell me now! I wanted to talk to you about your friend; I must say I don't much care for him. Explain to me exactly what he is like."

And Gontran, who had known Paul for many years, told her about this passionate nature, uncouth, sincere, and kindly by starts. He was, according to Gontran, a clever young fellow, whose wild spirit impetuously flung itself into every new idea. Yielding to every impulse, unable to control or to direct his passions, or to fight against his feelings with the aid of reason, or to govern his life by a system based on settled convictions, he obeyed the promptings of his heart, whether they were virtuous or vicious, the moment that any desire, any thought, any emotion whatever, agitated his excitable nature.

He had already fought seven duels, as ready to insult people as to become their friend. He had been madly in love with women of every class, adored them with the same transports from the working-girl whom he picked up in the corner of some store to the actress whom he carried off, yes, carried off, on the night of a first performance, just as she was stepping into a vehicle on her way home, bearing her away in his arms in the midst of the astonished spectators, and pushing her into a carriage, which disappeared at a gallop before anyone could follow it or overtake it.

And Gontran concluded: "There you are! He is a good fellow, but a fool; very rich, moreover, and capable of anything, of anything at all, when he loses his head."

Christiane said: "What a strange perfume he carries about him! It is rather nice. What is it?"

Gontran answered: "I don't really know; he doesn't want to tell about it. I believe it comes from Russia. 'Tis the actress, his actress, she whom I cured him of this time, that gave it to him. Yes, indeed, it has a very pleasant odor."

They saw, on their way, a group of bathers and of peasants, for it was the custom every morning before breakfast to take a turn along the road.

Christiane and Gontran joined the Marquis, Andermatt, and Paul, and soon they beheld, in the place where the knoll had stood the day before, a queer-looking human head covered with a ragged felt hat, and wearing a big white beard, looking as if it had sprung up out of the ground, the head of a decapitated man, as it were, growing there like a plant. Around it, some vinedressers were looking on, amazed, impassive, the peasantry of Auvergne not being scoffers, while three tall gentlemen, visitors at second-class hotels, were laughing and joking.

Oriol and his son stood there contemplating the vagabond, who was steeped in his hole, sitting on a stone, with the water up to his chin. He might have been taken for a desperate criminal of olden times condemned to death for some unusual kind of sorcery; and he had not let go his crutches, which were by his sides in the water.

Andermatt kept repeating enthusiastically: "Bravo! bravo! there's an example which all the people in the country suffering from rheumatic pains should imitate."

And, bending toward the old man, he shouted at him as if he were deaf: "Do you feel well?"

The other, who seemed completely stupefied by this boiling water, replied: "It seems to me that I'm melting!"

But Père Oriol exclaimed: "The hotter it is, the more good it will do you."

A voice behind the Marquis said: "What is that?"

And M. Aubry-Pasteur, always puffing, stopped on his way back from his daily walk. Then Andermatt explained his experiment in curing. But the old man kept repeating: "Devil take it! how hot it is!" And he wanted to get out, asking some one to help him up. The banker succeeded eventually in calming him by promising him twenty sous more for each bath. The spectators formed a circle round the hole, in which the dirty, grayish rags were soaking wherewith this old body was covered.

A voice said: "Nice meat for broth! I wouldn't care to make soup of it!"

Another rejoined: "The meat would scarcely agree with me!"

But the Marquis observed that the bubbles of carbonic acid seemed more numerous, larger, and brighter in this new spring than in that of the baths.

The vagabond's rags were covered with them; and these bubbles rose to the surface in such abundance that the water appeared to be crossed by innumerable little chains, by an infinity of beads of exceedingly small, round diamonds, the strong midday sun making them as clear as brilliants.

Then Aubry-Pasteur burst out laughing: "Egad," said he, "I must tell you what they do at the establishment. You know they catch a spring like a bird in a kind of snare, or rather in a bell. That's what they call coaxing it. Now last year here is what happened to the spring that supplies the baths. The carbonic acid, lighter than water, was stored up to the top of the bell; then, when it was collected there in a very large quantity, it was driven back into the ducts, reascended in abundance into the baths, filled up the compartments, and all but suffocated the invalids. We have had three accidents in the course of three months. Then they consulted me again, and I invented a very simple apparatus consisting of two pipes which led off separately the liquid and the gas in the bell in order to combine them afresh immediately under the bath, and thus to reconstitute the water in its normal state while avoiding the dangerous excess of carbonic acid. But my apparatus would have cost a thousand francs. Do you know what the custodian does then? I give you a thousand guesses to find out. He bores a hole in the bell to get rid of the gas, which flies out, you understand, so that they sell you acidulated baths without any acid, or so little acid that it is not worth much. Whereas here, why just look!"

Everybody became indignant. They no longer laughed, and they cast envious looks toward the paralytic. Every bather would gladly have seized a pickax to make another hole beside that of the vagabond. But Andermatt took the engineer's arm, and they went off chatting together. From time to time Aubry-Pasteur stopped, made a show of drawing lines with his walking-stick, indicating certain points, and the banker wrote down notes in a memorandum-book.

Christiane and Paul Bretigny entered into conversation. He told her about his journey to Auvergne, and all that he had seen and experienced. He loved the country, with those warm instincts of his, with which always mingled an element of animality. He had a sensual love of nature because it excited his blood, and made his nerves and organs quiver. He said: "For my part, Madame, it seems to me as if I were open, so that everything enters into me, everything passes through me, makes me weep or gnash my teeth. Look here! when I cast a glance at that hillside facing us, that vast expanse of green, that race of trees clambering up the mountain, I feel the entire wood in my eyes; it penetrates me, takes possession of me, runs through my whole frame; and it seems to me also that I am devouring it, that it fills my being—I become a wood myself!"

He laughed, while he told her this, strained his big, round eyes, now on the wood, now on Christiane; and she, surprised, astonished, but easily impressed, felt herself devoured also, like the wood, by his great avid glance.

Paul went on: "And if you only knew what delights I owe to my sense of smell. I drink in this air through my nostrils. I become intoxicated with it; I live in it, and I feel that there is within it everything—absolutely everything. What can be sweeter? It intoxicates one more than wine; wine intoxicates the mind, but perfume intoxicates the imagination. With perfume you taste the very essence, the pure essence of things and of the universe—you taste the flowers, the trees, the grass of the fields; you can even distinguish the soul of the dwellings of olden days which sleep in the old furniture, the old carpets, the old curtains.

Listen! I am going to tell you something.

"Did you notice, when first you came here, a delicious odor, to which no other odor can be compared—so fine, so light, that it seems almost—how shall I express it?—an immaterial odor? You find it everywhere—you can seize it nowhere—you cannot discern where it comes from. Never, never has anything more divine than it arisen in my heart. Well, this is the odor of the vine in bloom. Ah! it has taken me four days to discover it. And is it not charming to think, Madame, that the vine-tree, which gives us wine, wine which only superior spirits can understand and relish, gives us, too, the most delicate and most exciting of perfumes, which only persons of the most refined sensibility can discover? And then do you recognize also the powerful smell of the chestnut-trees, the luscious savor of the acacias, the aroma of the mountains, and the grass, whose scent is so sweet, so sweet—sweeter than anyone imagines?"

She listened to these words of his in amazement, not that they were surprising so much as that they appeared so different in their nature from everything encompassing her every day. Her mind remained possessed, moved, and disturbed by them.

He kept talking uninterruptedly in a voice somewhat hollow but full of passion.

"And again, just think, do you not feel in the air, along the roads, when the day is hot, a slight savor of vanilla. Yes, am I not right? Well, that is—that is—but I dare not tell it to you!"

And now he broke into a great laugh, and waving his hand in front of him all of a sudden said: "Look there!"

A row of wagons laden with hay was coming up drawn by cows yoked in pairs. The slow-footed beasts, with their heads hung down, bent by the yoke, their horns fastened with pieces of wood, toiled painfully along; and under their skin, as it rose up and down, the bones of their legs could be seen moving. Before each team, a man in shirt-sleeves, waistcoat, and black hat, was walking with a switch in his hand, directing the pace of the animals. From time to time the driver would turn round, and, without ever hitting, would barely touch the shoulder or the forehead of a cow who would blink her big, wandering eyes, and obey the motion of his arm.

Christiane and Paul drew up to let them pass.

He said to her: "Do you feel it?"

She was amazed: "What then? That is the smell of the stable."

"Yes, it is the smell of the stable; and all these cows going along the roads—for they use no horses in this part of the country—scatter on their way that odor of the stable, which, mingled with the fine dust, gives to the wind a savor of vanilla."

Christiane, somewhat disgusted, murmured: "Oh!"

He went on: "Excuse me, at that moment, I was analyzing it like a chemist. In any case, we are, Madame, in the most seductive country, the most delightful, the most restful, that I have ever seen—a country of the golden age. And the Limagne—oh! the Limagne! But I must not talk to you about it; I want to show it to you. You shall see for yourself."

The Marquis and Gontran came up to them. The Marquis passed his arm under that of his daughter, and, making her turn round and retrace her steps, in order to get back to the hotel for breakfast, he said:

"Listen, young people! this concerns you all three. William, who goes mad when an idea comes into his head, dreams of nothing any longer but of building this new town of his, and he wants to win over to him the Oriol family. He is, therefore, anxious that Christiane should make the acquaintance of the two young girls, in order to see if they are 'possible.' But it is not necessary that the father should suspect our ruse. So I have got an idea; it is to organize a charitable fête. You, my dear, must go and see the curé; you will together hunt up two of his parishioners to make collections along with you. You understand what people you will get him to nominate, and he will invite them on his own responsibility. As for you, young men, you are going to get up a tombola at the Casino with the assistance of Petrus Martel with his company and orchestra. And if the little Oriols are nice girls, as it is said they have been well brought up at the convent, Christiane will make a conquest of them."

CHAPTER V.

DEVELOPMENTS

For eight days, Christiane wholly occupied herself with preparations for this fête. The curé, indeed, was able to find no one among his female parishioners except the Oriol girls who could be deemed worthy of collecting along with the Marquis de Ravenel's daughter; and, happy at having the opportunity of making himself prominent, he took all the necessary steps, organized everything, regulated everything, and himself invited the young girls, as if the idea had originated with him.

The inhabitants were in a state of excitement, and the gloomy bathers, finding a new topic of conversation, entertained one another at the table d'hôte with various estimates as to the possible receipts from the two portions of the fête, the sacred and the profane.

The day opened finely. It was admirable summer weather, warm and clear, with bright sunshine in the open plain and a grateful shade under the village trees. The mass was fixed for nine o'clock—a quick mass with Church music. Christiane, who had arrived before the office, in order to inspect the ornamentation of the church with garlands of flowers that had been sent from Royat and Clermont-Ferrand, consented to walk behind it. The curé, Abbé Litre, followed her accompanied by the Oriol girls, and he introduced them to her. Christiane immediately invited the young girls to luncheon. They accepted her invitation with blushes and respectful bows.

The faithful were now making their appearance. Christiane and her girls sat down on three chairs of honor reserved for them at the side of the choir, facing three other chairs, which were occupied by young lads dressed in their Sunday clothes, sons of the mayor, of the deputy, and of a municipal councilor, selected to accompany the lady-collectors and to flatter the local authorities. Everything passed off well.

The office was short. The collection realized one hundred and ten francs, which, added to Andermatt's five hundred francs, the Marquis's fifty francs, and a hundred francs contributed by Paul Bretigny, made a total of seven hundred and sixty, an amount never before reached in the parish of Enval. Then, after the conclusion of the ceremony, the Oriol girls were brought to the hotel. They appeared to be a little abashed, without any display of awkwardness, however, and scarcely uttered one word, through modesty rather than through timidity. They sat down to luncheon at the table d'hôte, and pleased the meal of all the men.

The elder the more serious of the pair, the younger the more sprightly, the elder better bred, in the common-place acceptation of the word, the younger more pleasant, they yet resembled one another as closely as two sisters possibly could.

As soon as the meal was finished, they repaired to the Casino for the lottery-drawing at the tombola, which was fixed for two o'clock.

The park, already invaded by the mixed crowd of bathers and peasants, presented the aspect of an outlandish fête.

Under their Chinese kiosque the musicians were executing a rural symphony, a work composed by Saint Landri himself. Paul, who accompanied Christiane, suddenly drew up:

"Look here!" said he, "that's pretty! He has some talent, that chap! With an orchestra, he could produce a fine effect."

Then he asked: "Are you fond of music, Madame?"

"Exceedingly."

"As for me, it overwhelms me. When I am listening to a work that I like, it seems to me first that the opening notes detach my skin from my flesh, melt it, dissolve it, cause it to disappear, and leave me like one flayed alive, under the combined attacks of the instruments. And in fact it is on my nerves that the orchestra is playing, on my nerves stripped bare, vibrating, trembling at every note. I hear it, the music, not merely with my ears, but with all the sensibility of my body quivering from head to foot. Nothing gives me such exquisite pleasure, or rather such exquisite happiness."

She smiled, and then said: "Your sensibilities are keen."

"By Jove, they are! What is the good of living if one has not keen sensibilities? I do not envy those people who wear over their hearts a tortoise's shell or a hippopotamus's hide. Those alone are happy who feel their sensations acutely, who receive them like shocks, and savor them like dainty morsels. For it is necessary to reason out all our emotions, joyous and sad, to be satiated with them, to be intoxicated with them to the most intense degree of bliss or the most extreme pitch of suffering."

She raised her eyes to look up at his face, with that sense of astonishment which she had experienced during the past eight days at all the things that he said. Indeed, during these eight days, this new friend—for, despite her repugnance toward him, on first acquaintance, he had in this short interval become her friend—was every moment shaking the tranquillity of her soul, and disturbing it as a pool of water is disturbed by flinging stones into it. And he flung stones, big stones, into this soul which had calmly slumbered until now.

Christiane's father, like all fathers, had always treated her as a little girl, to whom one ought not to say anything of a serious nature; her brother made her laugh rather than reflect; her husband did not consider it right for a man to speak of anything whatever to his wife outside the interests of their common life; and so she had hitherto lived perfectly contented, her mind steeped in a sweet torpor.

This newcomer opened her intellect with ideas which fell upon it like strokes of a hatchet. Moreover, he was one of those men who please women, all women, by his very nature, by the vibrating acuteness of his emotions. He knew how to talk to them, to tell them everything, and he made them understand everything. Incapable of continuous effort but extremely intelligent, always loving or hating passionately, speaking of everything with the ingenious ardor of a man fanatically convinced, variable as he was enthusiastic, he possessed to an excessive degree the true feminine temperament, the credulity, the charm, the mobility, the nervous sensibility of a woman, with the superior intellect, active, comprehensive, and penetrating, of a man.

Gontran came up to them in a hurry. "Come back," said he, "and give a look at the Honorat family."

They returned, and saw Doctor Honorat, accompanied by a fat, old woman in a blue dress, whose head looked like a nursery-garden, for every variety of plants and flowers were gathered together on her head.

Christiane asked in astonishment: "This is his wife, then? But she is fifteen years older than her husband."

"Yes, she is sixty-five—an old midwife whom he fell in love with between two confinements. This, however, is one of those households in which they are nagging at one another from morning till night."

They made their way toward the Casino, attracted by the exclamations of the crowd. On a large table, in front of the establishment, were displayed the lots of the tombola, which were drawn by Petrus Martel, assisted by Mademoiselle Odelin of the Odéon, a very small brunette, who also announced the numbers, with mountebank's tricks, which greatly diverted the spectators. The Marquis, accompanied by the Oriol girls and Andermatt, reappeared, and asked: "Are we to remain here? It is very noisy."

They accordingly resolved to take a walk halfway up the hill on the road from Enval to La Roche-Pradière. In order to reach it, they first ascended, one behind the other, a narrow path through vine-trees. Christiane walked on in front with a light and rapid step. Since her arrival in this neighborhood, she felt as if she existed in a new sort of way, with an active sense of enjoyment and of vitality which she had never known before. Perhaps, the baths, by improving her health, and so ridding her of that slight disturbance of the vital organs which annoyed and saddened her without any apparent cause, disposed her to perceive and to relish everything more thoroughly. Perhaps she simply felt herself animated, lashed by the presence and by the ardor of spirit of that unknown youth who had taught her how to understand. She drew a long, deep breath, as she thought of all he had said to her about the perfumes that were scattered through the atmosphere. "It is true," she mused, "that he has shown me how to feel the air." And she found again all the odors, especially that of the vine, so light, so delicate, so fleeting.

She gained the level road, and they formed themselves into groups. Andermatt and Louise Oriol, the elder girl, started first side by side, chatting about the produce of lands in Auvergne. She knew, this Auvergnat, true daughter of her sire, endowed with the hereditary instinct, all the correct and practical details of agriculture, and she spoke about them in her grave tone, in the ladylike fashion, and with the careful pronunciation which they had taught her at the convent. While listening to her, he cast a side glance at her, every now and then, and thought this little girl quite charming with her gravity of manner and her mind so full already of practical knowledge. He occasionally repeated with some surprise: "What! is the land in the Limagne worth so much as thirty thousand francs for each hectare?"[1]

"Yes, Monsieur, when it is planted with beautiful apple-trees, which supply dessert apples. It is our country which furnishes nearly all the fruit used in Paris."

Then, they turned back in order to make a more careful estimate of the Limagne, for from the road they were pursuing they could see, as far as their eyes could reach, the vast plain always covered with a light haze of blue vapor.

Christiane and Paul also halted in front of this immense veiled tract of country, so agreeable to the eye that they would have liked to remain there incessantly gazing at it. The road was bordered by enormous walnut-trees, the dense shade of which made the skin feel a refreshing sensation of coolness. It no longer ascended, but took a winding course halfway up on the slope of the hillside adorned lower down with a tapestry of vines, and then with short green herbage as far as the crest, which at this point looked rather steep.

Paul murmured: "Is it not lovely? Tell me, is it not lovely? And why does this landscape move me? Yes, why? It diffuses a charm so profound, so wide, that it penetrates to my very heart. It seems, as you gaze at this plain, that thought opens its wings, does it not? And it flies away, it soars, it passes on, it goes off there below, farther and farther, toward all the countries seen in dreams which we shall never see. Yes, see here, this is worthy of admiration because it is much more like a thing we dream of than a thing that we have seen."

She listened to him without saying anything, waiting, expectant, gathering up each of his words; and she felt herself affected without too well knowing how to explain her emotions. She caught glimpses, indeed, of other countries, blue countries, rose-hued countries, countries unlikely and marvelous, countries undiscoverable though ever sought for, which make us look upon all others as commonplace.

He went on: "Yes, it is lovely, because it is lovely. Other horizons are more striking but less harmonious. Ah! Madame, beauty, harmonious beauty! There is nothing but that in the world. Nothing exists but beauty. But how few understand it! The line of a body, of a statue, or of a mountain, the color of a painting or of that plain, the inexpressible something of the 'Joconde,' a phrase that bites you to the soul, that—nothing more—which makes an artist a creator just like God, which, therefore, distinguishes him among men. Wait! I am going to recite for you two stanzas of Baudelaire."

And he declaimed:

"Whether you come from heaven or hell I do
not care,
O Beauty, monster of splendor and terror,
yet sweet at the core,
As long as your eye, your smile, your feet
lay the infinite bare,
Unveiling a world of love that I never have
known before!

"From Satan or God, what matter, whether
angel or siren you be,
What matter if you can give, enchanting,
velvet-eyed fay,
Rhythm, perfume, and light, and be
queen of the earth for me,
And make all things less hideous, and
the sad moments fly away."

Christiane now was gazing at him, struck with wonder by his lyricism, questioning him with her eyes, not comprehending well what extraordinary meaning might be embodied in this poetry. He divined her thoughts, and was irritated at not having communicated his own enthusiasm to her, for he had recited those verses very effectively, and he resumed, with a shade of disdain:

"I am a fool to wish to force you to relish a poet of such subtle inspiration. A day will come, I hope, when you will feel those things just as I do. Women, endowed rather with intuition than comprehension, do not seize the secret and veiled purposes of art in the same way as if a sympathetic appeal had first been made to their minds."

And, with a bow, he added: "I will strive, Madame, to make this sympathetic appeal."

She did not think him impertinent, but fantastic; and moreover she did not seek any longer to understand, suddenly struck by a circumstance which she had not previously noticed: he was very elegant, though he was a little too tall and too strongly-built, with a gait so virile that one could not immediately perceive the studied refinement of his attire. And then his head had a certain brutishness about it, an incompleteness, which gave to his entire person a somewhat heavy aspect at first glance. But when one had got accustomed to his features, one found in them some charm, a charm powerful and fierce, which at moments became very pleasant according to the inflections of his voice, which always seemed veiled.

Christiane said to herself, as she observed for the first time what attention he had paid to his external appearance from head to foot: "Decidedly this is a man whose qualities must be discovered one by one."

But here Gontran came rushing toward them. He exclaimed: "Sister, I say, Christiane, wait!" And when he had overtaken them, he said to them, still laughing: "Oh! just come and listen to the younger Oriol girl! She is as droll as anything—she has wonderful wit. Papa has succeeded in putting her at her ease, and she has been telling us the most comical things in the world. Wait for them."

And they awaited the Marquis, who presently appeared with the younger of the two girls, Charlotte Oriol. She was relating with a childlike, knowing liveliness some village tales, accounts of rustic simplicity and roguery. And she imitated them with their slow movements, their grave remarks, their "fouchtras," their innumerable "bougrres," mimicking, in a fashion that made her pretty, sprightly face look charming, all the changes of their physiognomies. Her bright eyes sparkled; her rather large mouth was opened wide, displaying her white teeth; her nose, a little tip-tilted, gave her a humorous look; and she was fresh, with a flower's freshness that might make lips quiver with desire.

The Marquis, having spent nearly his entire life on his estate, in the family château where Christiane and Gontran had been brought up in the midst of rough, big Norman farmers who were occasionally invited to dine there, in accordance with custom, and whose children, companions of theirs from the period of their first communion, had been on terms of familiarity with them, knew how to talk to this little girl, already three-fourths a woman of the world, with a friendly candor which awakened at once in her a gay and self-confident assurance.

Andermatt and Louise returned after having walked as far as the village, which they did not care to enter. And they all sat down at the foot of a tree, on the grassy edge of a ditch. There they remained for a long time pleasantly chatting about everything and nothing in a torpor of languid ease. Now and then, a wagon would roll past, always drawn by the two cows whose heads were bent and twisted by the yoke, and always driven by a peasant with a shrunken frame and a big black hat on his head, guiding the animals with the end of his thin switch in the swaying style of the conductor of an orchestra.

The man would take off his hat, bowing to the Oriol girls, and they would reply with a familiar, "Good day," flung out by their fresh young voices.

Then, as the hour was growing late, they went back. As they drew near the park, Charlotte Oriol exclaimed: "Oh! the boree! the boree!" In fact, the boree was being danced to an old air well known in Auvergne.

There they were, male and female peasants stepping out, hopping, making courtesies,—turning and bowing to each other,—the women taking hold of their petticoats and lifting them up with two fingers of each hand, the men swinging their arms or holding them akimbo. The pleasant monotonous air was also dancing in the fresh evening wind; it was always the same refrain played in a very high note by the violin, and taken up in concert by the other instruments, giving a more rattling pace to the dance. And it was not unpleasant, this simple rustic music, lively and artless, keeping time as it did with this shambling country minuet.

The bathers, too, made an attempt to dance. Petrus Martel went skipping in front of little Odelin, who affected the style of a danseuse walking through a ballet, and the comic Lapalme mimicked a fantastic step round the attendant at the Casino, who seemed agitated by recollections of Bullier.

But suddenly Gontran saw Doctor Honorat dancing away with all his heart and all his limbs, and executing the classical boree like a true-blue native of Auvergne.

The orchestra became silent. All stopped. The doctor came over and bowed to the Marquis. He was wiping his forehead and puffing.

"'Tis good," said he, "to be young sometimes."

Gontran laid his hand on the doctor's shoulder, and smiling with a mischievous air: "You never told me you were married."

The physician stopped wiping his face, and gravely responded: "Yes, I am, and marred."

"What do you say?"

"I say, married and marred. Never commit that folly, young man."

"Why?"

"Why! See here! I have been married now for twenty years, and haven't got used to it yet. Every evening, when I reach home, I say to myself, 'Hold hard! this old woman is still in my house! So then she'll never go away?'" Everyone began to laugh, so serious and convinced was his tone.

But the bells of the hotel were ringing for dinner. The fête was over. Louise and Charlotte were accompanied back to their father's house; and when their new friends had left them, they commenced talking about them. Everyone thought them charming, Andermatt alone preferred the elder girl.

The Marquis said: "How pliant the feminine nature is! The mere vicinity of the paternal gold, of which they do not even know the use, has made ladies of these country girls."

Christiane, having asked Paul Bretigny: "And you, which of them do you prefer?" he murmured:

"Oh! I? I have not even looked at them. It is not they whom I prefer."

He had spoken in a very low voice; and she made no reply.

[1]A hectare is about two acres and a half.

CHAPTER VI.

ON THE BRINK

The days that followed were charming for Christiane Andermatt. She lived, light-hearted, her soul full of joy. The morning bath was her first pleasure, a delicious pleasure that made the skin tingle, an exquisite half hour in the warm, flowing water, which disposed her to feel happy all day long. She was, indeed, happy in all her thoughts and in all her desires. The affection with which she felt herself surrounded and penetrated, the intoxication of youthful life throbbing in her veins, and then again this new environment, this superb country, made for daydreams and repose, wide and odorous, enveloping her like a great caress of nature, awakened in her fresh emotions. Everything that approached, everything that touched her, continued this sensation of the morning, this sensation of a tepid bath, of a great bath of happiness wherein she plunged herself body and soul.

Andermatt, who had to leave Enval for a fortnight or perhaps a month, had gone back to Paris, having previously reminded his wife to take good care that the paralytic should not discontinue his course of treatment. So each day, before breakfast, Christiane, her father, her brother, and Paul, went to look at what Gontran called "the poor man's soup." Other bathers came there also, and they formed a circular group around the hole, while chatting with the vagabond.

He was not better able to walk, he declared, but he had a feeling as if his legs were covered with ants; and he told how these ants ran up and down, climbing as far as his thighs, and then going back again to the tips of his toes. And even at night he felt these insects tickling and biting him, so that he was deprived of sleep.

All the visitors and the peasants, divided into two camps, that of the believers and that of the sceptics, were interested in this cure.

After breakfast, Christiane often went to look for the Oriol girls, so that they might take a walk with her. They were the only members of her own sex at the station to whom she could talk or with whom she could have friendly relations, sharing a little of her confidence and asking in return for some feminine sympathy. She had at once taken a liking for the grave common sense allied with amiability which the elder girl exhibited and still more for the spirit of sly humor possessed by the younger; and it was less to please her husband than for her own amusement that she now sought the friendship of the two sisters.

They used to set forth on excursions sometimes in a landau, an old traveling landau with six seats, got from a livery-man at Riom, and at other times on foot. They were especially fond of a little wild valley near Chatel-Guyon, leading toward the hermitage of Sans-Souci. Along the narrow road, which they slowly traversed, under the pine-trees, on the bank of the little river, they would saunter in pairs, each pair chatting together. At every stage along their track, where it was necessary to cross the stream, Paul and Gontran, standing on stepping-stones in the water, seized the women each with one arm, and carried them over with a jump, so as to deposit them at the opposite side. And each of these fordings changed the order of the pedestrians. Christiane went from one to another, but found the opportunity of remaining a little while alone with Paul Bretigny either in front or in the rear.

He had no longer the same ways while in her company as in the first days of their acquaintanceship; he was less disposed to laugh, less abrupt in manner, less like a comrade, but more respectful and attentive. Their conversations, however, assumed a tone of intimacy, and the things that concerned the heart held in them the foremost place. He talked to her about sentiment and love, like a man well versed in such subjects, who had sounded the depths of women's tenderness, and who owed to them as much happiness as suffering.

She, ravished and rather touched, urged him on to confidences with an ardent and artful curiosity. All that she knew of him awakened in her a keen desire to learn more, to penetrate in thought into one of those male existences of which she had got glimpses out of books, one of those existences full of tempests and mysteries of love. Yielding to her importunities, he told her each day a little more about his life, his adventures, and his griefs, with a warmth of language which his burning memories sometimes rendered impassioned, and which the desire to please made also seductive. He opened to her gaze a world till now unknown to her, found eloquent words to express the subtleties of desire and expectation, the ravages of growing hopes, the religion of flowers and bits of ribbons, all the little objects treasured up as sacred, the enervating effect of sudden doubts, the anguish of alarming conjectures, the tortures of jealousy, and the inexpressible frenzy of the first kiss.

And he knew how to describe all these things in a very seemly fashion, veiled, poetic, and captivating. Like all men who are perpetually haunted by desire and thoughts about woman he spoke discreetly of those whom he had loved with a fever that throbbed within him still. He recalled a thousand romantic incidents calculated to move the heart, a thousand delicate circumstances calculated to make tears gather in the eyes, and all those sweet futilities of gallantry which render amorous relationships between persons of refined souls and cultivated minds the most beautiful and most entrancing experiences that can be conceived.

All these disturbing and familiar chats, renewed each day and each day more prolonged, fell on Christiane's soul like grains cast into the earth. And the charm of this country spread wide around her, the odorous air, that blue Limagne, so vast that it seemed to make the spirit expand, those extinguished volcanoes on the mountain, furnaces of the antique world serving now only to warm springs for invalids, the cool shades, the rippling music of the streams as they rushed over the stones—all this, too, penetrated the heart and the flesh of the young woman, penetrated them and softened them like a soft shower of warm rain on soil that is yet virgin, a rain that will cause to bourgeon and blossom in it the flowers of which it had received the seed.

She was quite conscious that this youth was paying court to her a little, that he thought her pretty, even more than pretty; and the desire to please him spontaneously suggested to her a thousand inventions, at the same time designing and simple, to fascinate him and to make a conquest of him.

When he looked moved, she would abruptly leave him; when she anticipated some tender allusion on his lips, she would cast toward him, ere the words were finished, one of those swift, unfathomable glances which pierce men's hearts like fire. She would greet him with soft utterances, gentle movements of her head, dreamy gestures with her hands, or sad looks quickly changed into smiles, as if to show him, even when no words had been exchanged between them, that his efforts had not been in vain.

What did she desire? Nothing. What did she expect from all this? Nothing.

She amused herself with this solely because she was a woman, because she did not perceive the danger of it, because, without foreseeing anything, she wished to find out what he would do.

And then she had suddenly developed that native coquetry which lies hidden in the veins of all feminine beings. The slumbering, innocent child of yesterday had unexpectedly waked up, subtle and keen-witted, when facing this man who talked to her unceasingly about love.

She divined the agitation that swept across his mind when he was by her side, she saw the increasing emotion that his face expressed, and she understood all the different intonations of his voice with that special intuition possessed by women who feel themselves solicited to love.

Other men had ere now paid attentions to her in the fashionable world without getting anything from her in return save the mockery of a playful young woman. Their commonplace flatteries diverted her; their looks of melancholy love filled her with merriment; and to all their manifestations of passion she responded only with derisive laughter. In the case of this man, however, she felt herself suddenly confronted with a seductive and dangerous adversary; and she had been changed into one of those clever creatures, instinctively clear-sighted, armed with audacity and coolness, who, so long as their hearts remain untrammeled, watch for, surprise, and draw men into the invisible net of sentiment.

As for him, he had, at first, thought her rather silly. Accustomed to women versed in intrigues, exercised in love just as an old soldier is in military maneuvers, skilled in all the wiles of gallantry and tenderness, he considered this simple heart commonplace, and treated it with a light disdain.

But, little by little, her ingenuousness had amused him, and then fascinated him; and yielding to his impressionable nature, he had begun to make her the object of his affectionate attentions. He knew full well that the best way to excite a pure soul was to talk incessantly about love, while exhibiting the appearance of thinking about others; and accordingly, humoring in a crafty fashion the dainty curiosity which he had aroused in her, he proceeded, under the pretense of confiding his secrets to her, to teach her what passion really meant, under the shadow of the wood.

He, too, found this play amusing, showed her, by all the little gallantries that men know how to display, the growing pleasure that he found in her society, and assumed the attitude of a lover without suspecting that he would become one in reality. And all this came about as naturally in the course of their protracted walks as it does to take a bath on a warm day, when you find yourself at the side of a river.

But, from the first moment when Christiane began to indulge in coquetry, from the time when she resorted to all the native skill of woman in beguiling men, when she conceived the thought of bringing this slave of passion to his knees, in the same way that she would have undertaken to win a game at croquet, he allowed himself to yield, this candid libertine, to the attack of this simpleton, and began to love her.

And now he became awkward, restless, nervous, and she treated him as a cat does a mouse. With another woman he would not have been embarrassed; he would have spoken out; he would have conquered by his irresistible ardor; with her he did not dare, so different did she seem from all those whom he had known. The others, in short, were women already singed by life, to whom everything might be said, with whom one could venture on the boldest appeals, murmuring close to their lips the trembling words which set the blood aflame. He knew his power, he felt that he was bound to triumph when he was able to communicate freely to the soul, the heart, the senses of her whom he loved, the impetuous desire by which he was ravaged.

With Christiane, he imagined himself by the side of a young girl, so great a novice did he consider her; and all his resources seemed paralyzed. And then he cared for her in a new sort of way, partly as a man cares for a child, and partly as he does for his betrothed. He desired her; and yet he was afraid of touching her, of soiling her, of withering her bloom. He had no longing to clasp her tightly in his arms, such as he had felt toward others, but rather to fall on his knees, to kiss her robe, and to touch gently with his lips, with an infinitely chaste and tender slowness, the little hairs about her temples, the corners of her mouth, and her eyes, her closed eyes, whose blue he could feel glancing out toward him, the charming glance awakened under the drooping lids. He would have liked to protect her against everyone and against everything, not to let her be elbowed by common people, gaze at ugly people, or go near unclean people. He would have liked to carry away the dirt of the street over which she walked, the pebbles on the roads, the brambles and the branches in the wood, to make all things easy and delicious around her, and to carry her always, so that she should never walk. And he felt annoyed because she had to talk to the other guests at the hotel, to eat the same food at the table d'hôte, and submit to all the disagreeable and inevitable little things that belong to everyday existence.

He knew not what to say to her so much were his thoughts absorbed by her; and his powerlessness to express the state of his heart, to accomplish any of the things that he wished to do, to testify to her the imperious need of devoting himself to her which burned in his veins, gave him some of the aspects of a chained wild beast, and, at the same time, made him feel a strange desire to break into sobs.

All this she perceived without completely understanding it, and felt amused by it with the malicious enjoyment of a coquette. When they had lingered behind the others, and she felt from his look that he was about to say something disquieting, she would abruptly begin to run, in order to overtake her father, and, when she got up to him, would exclaim: "Suppose we make a four-cornered game."

Four-cornered games served generally for the termination of the excursions. They looked out for a glade at the end of a wider road than usual, and they began to play like boys out for a walk.

The Oriol girls and Gontran himself took great delight in this amusement, which satisfied that incessant longing to run that is to be found in all young creatures. Paul Bretigny alone grumbled, beset by other thoughts; then, growing animated by degrees he would join in the game with more desperation than any of the others, in order to catch Christiane, to touch her, to place his hand abruptly on her shoulder or on her corsage.

The Marquis, whose indifferent and listless nature yielded in everything, as long as his rest was not disturbed, sat down at the foot of a tree, and watched his boarding-school at play, as he said. He thought this quiet life very agreeable, and the entire world perfect.

However, Paul's behavior soon alarmed Christiane. One day she even got afraid of him. One morning, they went with Gontran to the most remote part of the oddly-shaped gap which is called the End of the World. The gorge, becoming more and more narrow and winding, sank into the mountain. They climbed over enormous rocks; they crossed the little river by means of stepping-stones, and, having wheeled round a lofty crag more than fifty meters in height which entirely blocked up the cleft of the ravine, they found themselves in a kind of trench encompassed between two gigantic walls, bare as far as their summits, which were covered with trees and with verdure.

The stream formed a wide lake of bowl-like shape, and truly it was a wild-looking chasm, strange and unexpected, such as one meets more frequently in narratives than in nature. Now, on this day, Paul, gazing at the projections of the rocky eminence which barred them out from the road at the right where all pedestrians were compelled to halt, remarked that it bore traces of having been scaled. He said: "Why, we can go on farther."

Then, having clambered up the first ledge, not without difficulty, he exclaimed: "Oh! this is charming! a little grove in the water—come on, then!"

And, leaning backward, he drew Christiane up by the two hands, while Gontran, feeling his way, planted his feet on all the slight projections of the rock. The soil which had drifted down from the summit had formed on this ledge a savage and bushy garden, in which the stream ran across the roots. Another step, a little farther on, formed a new barrier of this granite corridor. They climbed it, too,—then a third; and they found themselves at the foot of an impassable wall from which fell, straight and clear, a cascade twenty meters high into a deep basin hollowed out by it, and buried under bindweeds and branches.

The cleft of the mountain had become so narrow that the two men, clinging on by their hands, could touch its sides. Nothing further could be seen, save a line of sky; nothing could be heard save the murmur of the water. It might have been taken for one of those undiscoverable retreats in which the Latin poets were wont to conceal the antique nymphs. It seemed to Christiane as if she had just intruded on the chamber of a fay.

Paul Bretigny said nothing. Gontran exclaimed: "Oh! how nice it would be if a woman white and rosy-red were bathing in that water!"

They returned. The first two shelves were as easy to descend, but the third frightened Christiane, so high and straight was it, without any visible steps. Bretigny let himself slip down the rock; then, stretching out his two arms toward her, "Jump," said he.

She would not venture. Not that she was afraid of falling, but she felt afraid of him, afraid above all of his eyes. He gazed at her with the avidity of a famished beast, with a passion which had grown ferocious; and his two hands extended toward her had such an imperious attraction for her that she was suddenly terrified and seized with a mad longing to shriek, to run away, to climb up the mountain perpendicularly to escape this irresistible appeal.

Her brother standing up behind her, cried: "Go on then!" and pushed her forward. Feeling herself falling she shut her eyes, and, caught in a gentle but powerful clasp, she felt, without seeing it, all the huge body of the young man, whose panting warm breath passed over her face. Then, she found herself on her feet once more, smiling, now that her terror had vanished, while Gontran descended in his turn.

This emotion having rendered her prudent, she took care, for some days, not to be alone with Bretigny, who now seemed to be prowling round her like the wolf in the fable round a lamb.

But a grand excursion had been planned. They were to carry provisions in the landau with six seats, and go to dine with the Oriol girls on the border of the little lake of Tazenat, which in the language of the country was called the "gour" of Tazenat, and then return at night by moonlight. Accordingly, they started one afternoon of a day of burning heat, under a devouring sun, which made the granite of the mountain as hot as the floor of an oven.

The carriage ascended the mountain-side drawn by three horses, blowing, and covered with sweat. The coachman was nodding on his seat, his head hanging down; and at the side of the road ran legions of green lizards. The heated atmosphere seemed filled with an invisible and oppressive dust of fire. Sometimes it seemed hard, unyielding, dense, as they passed through it, sometimes it stirred about and sent across their faces ardent breaths of flame in which floated an odor of resin in the midst of the long pine-wood.

Nobody in the carriage uttered a word. The three ladies, at the lower end, closed their dazzled eyes, which they shaded with their red parasols. The Marquis and Gontran, their foreheads wrapped round with handkerchiefs, had fallen asleep. Paul was looking toward Christiane, who was also watching him from under her lowered eyelids. And the landau, sending up a column of smoking white dust, kept always toiling up this interminable ascent.

When it had reached the plateau, the coachman straightened himself up, the horses broke into a trot; and they drove through a beautiful, undulating country, thickly-wooded, cultivated, studded with villages and solitary houses here and there. In the distance, at the left, could be seen the great truncated summits of the volcanoes. The lake of Tazenat, which they were going to see, had been formed by the last crater in the mountain chain of Auvergne. After they had been driving for three hours, Paul said suddenly: "Look here, the lava-currents!"

Brown rocks, fantastically twisted, made cracks in the soil at the border of the road. At the right could be seen a mountain, snub-nosed in appearance, whose wide summit had a flat and hollow look. They took a path, which seemed to pass into it through a triangular cutting; and Christiane, who was standing erect, discovered all at once, in the midst of a vast deep crater, a lovely lake, bright and round, like a silver coin. The steep slopes of the mountain, wooded at the right and bare at the left, sank toward the water, which they surrounded with a high inclosure, regular in shape. And this placid water, level and glittering, like the surface of a medal, reflected the trees on one side, and on the other the barren slope, with a clearness so complete that the edges escaped one's attention, and the only thing one saw in this funnel, in whose center the blue sky was mirrored, was a transparent, bottomless opening, which seemed to pass right through the earth, pierced from end to end up to the other firmament.

The carriage could go no farther. They got down, and took a path through the wooded side winding round the lake, under the trees, halfway up the declivity of the mountain. This track, along which only the woodcutters passed, was as green as a prairie; and, through the branches, they could see the opposite side, and the water glittering at the bottom of this mountain-lake.

Then they reached, through an opening in the wood, the very edge of the water, where they sat down upon a sloping carpet of grass, overshadowed by oak-trees.

They all stretched themselves on the green turf with sensuous and exquisite delight. The men rolled themselves about in it, plunged their hands into it; while the women, softly lying down on their sides, placed their cheeks close to it, as if to seek there a refreshing caress.

After the heat of the road, it was one of those sweet sensations so deep and so grateful that they almost amount to pure happiness.

Then once more the Marquis went to sleep; Gontran speedily followed his example. Paul began chatting with Christiane and the two young girls. About what? About nothing in particular. From time to time, one of them gave utterance to some phrase; another replied after a minute's pause, and the lingering words seemed torpid in their mouths like the thoughts within their minds.

But, the coachman having brought across to them the hamper which contained the provisions, the Oriol girls, accustomed to domestic duties in their own house, and still clinging to their active habits, quickly proceeded to unpack it, and to prepare the dinner, of which the party would by and by partake on the grass.

Paul lay on his back beside Christiane, who was in a reverie. And he murmured, in so low a tone that she scarcely heard him, so low that his words just grazed her ear, like those confused sounds that are borne on by the wind: "These are the best days of my life."

Why did these vague words move her even to the bottom of her heart? Why did she feel herself suddenly touched by an emotion such as she had never experienced before?

She was gazing through the trees at a tiny house, a hut for persons engaged in hunting and fishing, so narrow that it could barely contain one small apartment. Paul followed the direction of her glance, and said:

"Have you ever thought, Madame, what days passed together in a hut like that might be for two persons who loved one another to distraction? They would be alone in the world, truly alone, face to face! And, if such a thing were possible, ought not one be ready to give up everything in order to realize it, so rare, unseizable, and short-lived is happiness? Do we find it in our everyday life? What more depressing than to rise up without any ardent hope, to go through the same duties dispassionately, to drink in moderation, to eat with discretion, and to sleep tranquilly like a mere animal?"

She kept, all the time, staring at the little house; and her heart swelled up, as if she were going to burst into tears; for, in one flash of thought, she divined intoxicating joys, of whose existence she had no conception till that moment.

Indeed, she was thinking how sweet it would be for two to be together in this tiny abode hidden under the trees, facing that plaything of a lake, that jewel of a lake, true mirror of love! One might feel happy with nobody near, without a neighbor, without one sound of life, alone with a lover, who would pass his hours kneeling at the feet of the adored one, looking up at her, while her gaze wandered toward the blue wave, and whispering tender words in her ear, while he kissed the tips of her fingers. They would live there, amid the silence, beneath the trees, at the bottom of that crater, which would hold all their passion, like the limpid, unfathomable water, in the embrace of its firm and regular inclosure, with no other horizon for their eyes save the round line of the mountain's sides, with no other horizon for their thoughts save the bliss of loving one another, with no other horizon for their desires save kisses lingering and endless.

Were there, then, people on the earth who could enjoy days like this? Yes, undoubtedly! And why not? Why had she not sooner known that such joys exist?

The girls announced that dinner was ready. It was six o'clock already. They roused up the Marquis and Gontran in order that they might squat in Turkish fashion a short distance off, with the plates glistening beside them in the grass. The two sisters kept waiting on them, and the heedless men did not gainsay them. They ate at their leisure, flinging the cast-off pieces and the bones of the chickens into the water. They had brought champagne with them; the sudden noise of the first cork jumping up produced a surprising effect on everyone, so unusual did it appear in this solitary spot.

The day was declining; the air became impregnated with a delicious coolness. As the evening stole on, a strange melancholy fell on the water that lay sleeping at the bottom of the crater. Just as the sun was about to disappear, the western sky burst out into flame, and the lake suddenly assumed the aspect of a basin of fire. Then, when the sun had gone to rest, the horizon becoming red like a brasier on the point of being extinguished, the lake looked like a basin of blood. And suddenly above the crest of mountain, the moon nearly at its full rose up all pale in the still, cloudless firmament. Then, as the shadows gradually spread over the earth, it ascended glittering and round above the crater which was round also. It looked as if it were going to let itself drop down into the chasm; and when it had risen far up into the sky, the lake had the aspect of a basin of silver. Then, on its surface, motionless all day long, trembling movements could now be seen sometimes slow and sometimes rapid. It seemed as if some spirits skimming just above the water were drawing across it invisible veils.

It was the big fish at the bottom, the venerable carp and the voracious pike, who had come up to enjoy themselves in the moonlight.

The Oriol girls had put back all the plates, dishes, and bottles into the hamper, which the coachman came to take away. They rose up to go.

As they were passing into the path under the trees, where rays of light fell, like a silver shower, through the leaves and glittered on the grass, Christiane, who was following the others with Paul in the rear, suddenly heard a panting voice saying close to her ear: "I love you!—I love you!—I love you!"

Her heart began to beat so wildly that she was near sinking to the ground, and felt as if she could not move her limbs. Still she walked on, like one distraught, ready to turn round, her arms hanging wide and her lips tightly drawn. He had by this time caught the edge of the little shawl which she had drawn over her shoulders, and was kissing it frantically. She continued walking with such tottering steps that she no longer could feel the soil beneath her feet.

And now she emerged from under the canopy of trees, and finding herself in the full glare of the moonlight, she got the better of her agitation with a desperate effort; but, before stepping into the landau and losing sight of the lake, she half turned round to throw a long kiss with both hands toward the water, which likewise embraced the man who was following her.

On the return journey, she remained inert both in soul and body, dizzy, cramped up, as if after a fall; and, the moment they reached the hotel, she quickly rushed up to her own apartment, where she locked herself in. Even when the door was bolted and the key turned in the lock, she pressed her hand on it again, so much did she feel herself pursued and desired. Then she remained trembling in the middle of the room, which was nearly quite dark and had an empty look. The wax-candle placed on the table cast on the walls the quivering shadows of the furniture and of the curtains. Christiane sank into an armchair. All her thoughts were rushing, leaping, flying away from her so that she found it impossible to seize them, to hold them, to link them together. She felt now ready to weep, without well knowing why, broken-hearted, wretched, abandoned, in this empty room, lost in existence, just as in a forest. Where was she going, what would she do?

Breathing with difficulty, she rose up, flung open the window and the shutters in front of it, and leaned on her elbows over the balcony. The air was refreshing. In the depths of the sky, wide and empty, too, the distant moon, solitary and sad, having ascended now into the blue heights of night, cast forth a hard, cold luster on the trees and on the mountains.

The entire country lay asleep. Only the light strain of Saint Landri's violin, which he played till a late hour every night, broke the deep silence of the valley with its melancholy music. Christiane scarcely heard it. It ceased, then began again—the shrill and dolorous cry of the thin fiddlestrings.

And that moon lost in a desert sky, that feeble sound lost in the silent night, filled her heart with such a sense of solitude that she burst into sobs. She trembled and quivered to the very marrow of her bones, shaken by anguish and by the shuddering sensations of people attacked by some formidable malady; for suddenly it dawned upon her mind that she, too, was all alone in existence.

She had never realized this until to-day, and now she felt it so vividly in the distress of her soul that she imagined she was going mad.

She had a father! a brother! a husband! She loved them still, and they loved her. And here she was all at once separated from them, she had become a stranger to them as if she scarcely knew them. The calm affection of her father, the friendly companionship of her brother, the cold tenderness of her husband, appeared to her nothing any longer, nothing any longer. Her husband! This, her husband, the rosy-cheeked man who was accustomed to say to her in a careless tone, "Are you going far, dear, this morning?" She belonged to him, to this man, body and soul, by the mere force of a contract. Was this possible? Ah! how lonely and lost she felt herself! She closed her eyes to look into her own mind, into the lowest depths of her thoughts.

And she could see, as she evoked them out of her inner consciousness the faces of all those who lived around her—her father, careless and tranquil, happy as long as nobody disturbed his repose; her brother, scoffing and sceptical; her husband moving about, his head full of figures, and with the announcement on his lips, "I have just done a fine stroke of business!" when he should have said, "I love you!"

Another man had murmured that word a little while ago, and it was still vibrating in her ear and in her heart. She could see him also, this other man, devouring her with his fixed look; and, if he had been near her at that moment, she would have flung herself into his arms!

CHAPTER VII.

ATTAINMENT

Christiane, who had not gone to sleep till a very late hour, awoke as soon as the sun cast a flood of red light into her room through the window which she had left wide open. She glanced at her watch—it was five o'clock—and remained lying on her back deliciously in the warmth of the bed. It seemed to her, so active and full of joy did her soul feel, that a happiness, a great happiness, had come to her during the night. What was it? She sought to find out what it was; she sought to find out what was this new source of happiness which had thus penetrated her with delight. All her sadness of the night before had vanished, melted away, during sleep.

So Paul Bretigny loved her! How different he appeared to her from the first day! In spite of all the efforts of her memory, she could not bring back her first impression of him; she could not even recall to her mind the man introduced to her by her brother. He whom she knew to-day had retained nothing of the other, neither the face nor the bearing—nothing—for his first image had passed, little by little, day by day, through all the slow modifications which take place in the soul with regard to a being who from a mere acquaintance has come to be a familiar friend and a beloved object. You take possession of him hour by hour without suspecting it; possession of his movements, of his attitudes, of his physical and moral characteristics. He enters into you, into your eyes and your heart, by his voice, by all his gestures, by what he says and by what he thinks. You absorb him; you comprehend him; you divine him in all the meanings of his smiles and of his words; it seems at last that he belongs entirely to you, so much do you love, unconsciously still, all that is his and all that comes from him.

Then, too, it is impossible to remember what this being was like—to your indifferent eyes—when first he presented himself to your gaze. So then Paul Bretigny loved her! Christiane experienced from this discovery neither fear nor anguish, but a profound tenderness, an immense joy, new and exquisite, of being loved—of knowing that she was loved.

She was, however, a little disturbed as to the attitude that he would assume toward her and that she should preserve toward him. But, as it was a matter of delicacy for her conscience even to think of these things, she ceased to think about them, trusting to her own tact and ingenuity to direct the course of events.

She descended at the usual hour, and found Paul smoking a cigarette before the door of the hotel. He bowed respectfully to her:

"Good day, Madame. You feel well this morning?"

"Very well, Monsieur. I slept very soundly."

And she put out her hand to him, fearing lest he might hold it in his too long. But he scarcely pressed it; and they began quietly chatting as if they had forgotten one another.

And the day passed off without anything being done by him to recall his ardent avowal of the night before. He remained, on the days that followed, quite as discreet and calm; and she placed confidence in him. He realized, she thought, that he would wound her by becoming bolder; and she hoped, she firmly believed, that they might be able to stop at this delightful halting-place of tenderness, where they could love, while looking into the depths of one another's eyes, without remorse, inasmuch as they would be free from defilement.

Nevertheless, she was careful never to wander out with him alone.

Now, one evening, the Saturday of the same week in which they had visited the lake of Tazenat, as they were returning to the hotel about ten o'clock,—the Marquis, Christiane, and Paul,—for they had left Gontran playing écarté with Aubrey and Riquier and Doctor Honorat in the great hall of the Casino, Bretigny exclaimed, as he watched the moon shining through the branches:

"How nice it would be to go and see the ruins of Tournoel on a night like this!"

At this thought alone, Christiane was filled with emotion, the moon and ruins having on her the same influence which they have on the souls of all women.

She pressed the Marquis's hands. "Oh! father dear, would you mind going there?"

He hesitated, being exceedingly anxious to go to bed.

She insisted: "Just think a moment, how beautiful Tournoel is even by day! You said yourself that you had never seen a ruin so picturesque, with that great tower above the château. What must it be at night!"

At last he consented: "Well, then, let us go! But we'll only look at it for five minutes, and then come back immediately. For my part, I want to be in bed at eleven o'clock."

"Yes, we will come back immediately. It takes only twenty minutes to get there."

They set out all three, Christiane leaning on her father's arm, and Paul walking by her side.

He spoke of his travels in Switzerland, in Italy, in Sicily. He told what his impressions were in the presence of certain phenomena, his enthusiasm on seeing the summit of Monte Rosa, when the sun, rising on the horizon of this row of icy peaks, this congealed world of eternal snows, cast on each of those lofty mountain-tops a dazzling white radiance, and illumined them, like the pale beacon-lights that must shine down upon the kingdoms of the dead. Then he spoke of his emotion on the edge of the monstrous crater of Etna, when he felt himself, an imperceptible mite, many meters above the cloud line, having nothing any longer around him save the sea and the sky, the blue sea beneath, the blue sky above, and leaning over this dreadful chasm of the earth, whose breath stifled him. He enlarged the objects which he described in order to excite the young woman; and, as she listened, she panted with visions she conjured up, by a flight of imagination, of those wonderful things that he had seen.

Suddenly, at a turn of the road, they discovered Tournoel. The ancient château, standing on a mountain peak, overlooked by its high and narrow tower, letting in the light through its chinks, and dismantled by time and by the wars of bygone days, traced, upon a sky of phantoms, its huge silhouette of a fantastic manor-house.

They stopped, all three surprised. The Marquis said, at length: "Indeed, it is impressive—like a dream of Gustave Doré realized. Let us sit down for five minutes."

And he sat down on the sloping grass.

But Christiane, wild with enthusiasm, exclaimed: "Oh! father, let us go on farther! It is so beautiful! so beautiful! Let us walk to the foot, I beg of you!"

This time the Marquis refused: "No, my darling, I have walked enough; I can't go any farther. If you want to see it more closely, go on there with M. Bretigny. I will wait here for you."

Paul asked: "Will you come, Madame?"

She hesitated, seized by two apprehensions, that of finding herself alone with him, and that of wounding an honest man by having the appearance of suspecting him.

The Marquis repeated: "Go on! Go on! I will wait for you."

Then she took it for granted that her father would remain within reach of their voices, and she said resolutely: "Let us go on, Monsieur."

But scarcely had she walked on for some minutes when she felt herself possessed by a poignant emotion, by a vague, mysterious fear—fear of the ruin, fear of the night, fear of this man. Suddenly she felt her legs trembling under her, just as she felt the other night by the lake of Tazenat; they refused to bear her any further, bent under her, appeared to be sinking into the soil, where her feet remained fixed when she strove to raise them.

A large chestnut-tree, planted close to the path they had been pursuing, sheltered one side of a meadow. Christiane, out of breath just as if she had been running, let herself sink against the trunk. And she stammered: "I shall remain here—we can see very well."

Paul sat down beside her. She heard his heart beating with great emotional throbs. He said, after a brief silence: "Do you believe that we have had a previous life?"

She murmured, without having well understood his question: "I don't know. I have never thought on it."

He went on: "But I believe it—at moments—or rather I feel it. As being is composed of a soul and a body, which seem distinct, but are, without doubt, only one whole of the same nature, it must reappear when the elements which have originally formed it find themselves together for the second time. It is not the same individual assuredly, but it is the same man who comes back when a body like the previous form finds itself inhabited by a soul like that which animated him formerly. Well, I, to-night, feel sure, Madame, that I lived in that château, that I possessed it, that I fought there, that I defended it. I recognized it—it was mine, I am certain of it! And I am also certain that I loved there a woman who resembled you, and who, like you, bore the name of Christiane. I am so certain of it that I seem to see you still calling me from the top of that tower.

"Search your memory! recall it to your mind! There is a wood at the back, which descends into a deep valley. We have often walked there. You had light robes in the summer evenings, and I wore heavy armor, which clanked beneath the trees. You do not recollect? Look back, then, Christiane! Why, your name is as familiar to me as those we hear in childhood! Were we to inspect carefully all the stones of this fortress, we should find it there carved by my hand in days of yore! I declare to you that I recognize my dwelling-place, my country, just as I recognized you, you, the first time I saw you!"

He spoke in an exalted tone of conviction, poetically intoxicated by contact with this woman, and by the night, by the moon, and by the ruin.

He abruptly flung himself on his knees before Christiane, and, in a trembling voice said: "Let me adore you still since I have found you again! Here have I been searching for you a long time!"

She wanted to rise and to go away, to join her father, but she had not the strength; she had not the courage, held back, paralyzed by a burning desire to listen to him still, to hear those ravishing words entering her heart. She felt herself carried away in a dream, in the dream always hoped for, so sweet, so poetic, full of rays of moonlight and days of love.

He had seized her hands, and was kissing the ends of her finger-nails, murmuring:

"Christiane—Christiane—take me—kill me! I love you, Christiane!"

She felt him quivering, shuddering at her feet. And now he kissed her knees, while his chest heaved with sobs. She was afraid that he was going mad, and started up to make her escape. But he had risen more quickly, and seizing her in his arms he pressed his mouth against hers.

Then, without a cry, without revolt, without resistance, she let herself sink back on the grass, as if this caress, by breaking her will, had crushed her physical power to struggle. And he possessed her with as much ease as if he were culling a ripe fruit.

But scarcely had he loosened his clasp when she rose up distracted, and rushed away shuddering and icy-cold all of a sudden, like one who had just fallen into the water. He overtook her with a few strides, and caught her by the arm, whispering: "Christiane, Christiane! Be on your guard with your father!"

She walked on without answering, without turning round, going straight before her with stiff, jerky steps. He followed her now without venturing to speak to her.

As soon as the Marquis saw them, he rose up: "Hurry," said he; "I was beginning to get cold. These things are very fine to look at, but bad for one undergoing thermal treatment!"

Christiane pressed herself close to her father's side, as if to appeal to him for protection and take refuge in his tenderness.

As soon as she had re-entered her apartment, she undressed herself in a few seconds and buried herself in her bed, hiding her head under the clothes; then she wept. She wept with her face pressed against the pillow for a long, long time, inert, annihilated. She did not think, she did not suffer, she did not regret. She wept without thinking, without reflecting, without knowing why. She wept instinctively as one sings when one feels gay. Then, when her tears were exhausted, overwhelmed, paralyzed with sobbing, she fell asleep from fatigue and lassitude.

She was awakened by light taps at the door of her room, which looked out on the drawing-room. It was broad daylight, as it was nine o'clock.

"Come in," she cried.

And her husband presented himself, joyous, animated, wearing a traveling-cap and carrying by his side his little money-bag, which he was never without while on a journey.

He exclaimed: "What? You were sleeping still, my dear! And I had to awaken you. There you are! I arrived without announcing myself. I hope you are going on well. It is superb weather in Paris."

And having taken off his cap, he advanced to embrace her. She drew herself away toward the wall, seized by a wild fear, by a nervous dread of this little man, with his smug, rosy countenance, who had stretched out his lips toward her.

Then, abruptly, she offered him her forehead, while she closed her eyes. He planted there a chaste kiss, and asked: "Will you allow me to wash in your dressing-room? As no one attended on me to-day, my room was not prepared."

She stammered: "Why, certainly."

And he disappeared through a door at the end of the bed.

She heard him moving about, splashing, snorting; then he cried: "What news here? For my part, I have splendid news. The analysis of the water has given unexpected results. We can cure at least three times more patients than they can at Royat. It is superb!"

She was sitting in the bed, suffocating, her brain overwrought by this unforeseen return, which hurt her like a physical pain and gripped her like a pang of remorse. He reappeared, self-satisfied, spreading around him a strong odor of verbena. Then he sat down familiarly at the foot of the bed, and asked:

"And the paralytic? How is he going on? Is he beginning to walk? It is not possible that he is not cured with what we found in the water!"

She had forgotten all about it for several days, and she faltered: "Why, I—I believe he is beginning to walk better. Besides, I have not seen him this week. I—I am a little unwell."

He looked at her with interest, and returned: "It is true, you are a little pale. All the same, it becomes you very well. You look charming thus—quite charming."

And he drew nearer, and bending toward her was about to pass one arm into the bed under her waist.

But she made such a backward movement of terror that he remained stupefied, with his hands extended and his mouth held toward her. Then he asked: "What's the matter with you nowadays? One cannot touch you any longer. I assure you I do not intend to hurt you."

And he pressed close to her eagerly, with a glow of sudden desire in his eyes. Then she stammered:

"No—let me be—let me be! The fact is, I believe—I believe I am pregnant!"

She had said this, maddened by the mental agony she was enduring, without thinking about her words, to avoid his touch, just as she would have said: "I have leprosy, or the plague."

He grew pale in his turn, moved by a profound joy; and he merely murmured: "Already!" He yearned now to embrace her a long time, softly, tenderly, as a happy and grateful father. Then, he was seized with uneasiness.

"Is it possible?—What?—Are you sure?—So soon?"

She replied: "Yes—it is possible!"

Then he jumped about the room, and rubbing his hands, exclaimed: "Christi! Christi! What a happy day!"

There was another tap at the door. Andermatt opened it, and a chambermaid said to him: "Doctor Latonne would like to speak to Monsieur immediately."

"All right. Bring him into our drawing-room. I am going there."

He hurried away to the adjoining apartment. The doctor presently appeared. His face had a solemn look, and his manner was starched and cold. He bowed, touched the hand which the banker, a little surprised, held toward him, took a seat, and explained in the tone of a second in an affair of honor:

"A very disagreeable matter has arisen with reference to me, my dear Monsieur, and, in order to explain my conduct, I must give you an account of it. When you did me the honor to call me in to see Madame Andermatt, I hastened to come at the appointed hour; now it has transpired that, a few minutes before me, my brother-physician, the medical inspector, who, no doubt, inspires more confidence in the lady, had been sent for, owing to the attentions of the Marquis de Ravenel.

"The result of this is that, having been the second to see her I create the impression of having taken by a trick from Doctor Bonnefille a patient who already belonged to him—I create the impression of having committed an indelicate act, one unbecoming and unjustifiable from one member of the profession toward another. Now it is necessary for us to carry, Monsieur, into the exercise of our art certain precautions and unusual tact in order to avoid every collision which might lead to grave consequences. Doctor Bonnefille, having been apprised of my visit here, believing me capable of this want of delicacy, appearances being in fact against me, has spoken about me in such terms that, were it not for his age, I would have found myself compelled to demand an explanation from him. There remains for me only one thing to do, in order to exculpate myself in his eyes, and in the eyes of the entire medical body of the country, and that is to cease, to my great regret, to give my professional attentions to your wife, and to make the entire truth about this matter known, begging of you in the meantime to accept my excuses."

Andermatt replied with embarrassment:

"I understand perfectly well, doctor, the difficult situation in which you find yourself. The fault is not mine or my wife's, but that of my father-in-law, who called in M. Bonnefille without giving us notice. Could I not go to look for your brother-doctor, and tell him?——"

Doctor Latonne interrupted him: "It is useless, my dear Monsieur. There is here a question of dignity and professional honor, which I am bound to respect before everything, and, in spite of my lively regrets——"

Andermatt, in his turn, interrupted him. The rich man, the man who pays, who buys a prescription for five, ten, twenty, or forty francs, as he does a box of matches for three sous, to whom everything should belong by the power of his purse, and who only appreciates beings and objects in virtue of an assimilation of their value with that of money, of a relation, rapid and direct, established between coined metal and everything else in the world, was irritated at the presumption of this vendor of remedies on paper. He said in a stiff tone:

"Be it so, doctor. Let us stop where we are. But I trust for your own sake that this step may not have a damaging influence on your career. We shall see, indeed, which of us two shall have the most to suffer from your decision."

The physician, offended, rose up and bowing with the utmost politeness, said: "I have no doubt, Monsieur, it is I who will suffer. That which I have done to-day is very painful to me from every point of view. But I never hesitate between my interests and my conscience."

And he went out. As he emerged through the open door, he knocked against the Marquis, who was entering, with a letter in his hand. And M. de Ravenel exclaimed, as soon as he was alone with his son-in-law: "Look here, my dear fellow! this is a very troublesome thing, which has happened me through your fault. Doctor Bonnefille, hurt by the circumstance that you sent for his brother-physician to see Christiane, has written me a note couched in very dry language informing me that I cannot count any longer on his professional services."

Thereupon, Andermatt got quite annoyed. He walked up and down, excited himself by talking, gesticulated, full of harmless and noisy anger, that kind of anger which is never taken seriously. He went on arguing in a loud voice. Whose fault was it, after all? That of the Marquis alone, who had called in that pack-ass Bonnefille without giving any notice of the fact to him, though he had, thanks to his Paris physician, been informed as to the relative value of the three charlatans at Enval! And then what business had the Marquis to consult a doctor, behind the back of the husband, the husband who was the only judge, the only person responsible for his wife's health? In short, it was the same thing day after day with everything! People did nothing but stupid things around him, nothing but stupid things! He repeated it incessantly; but he was only crying in the desert, nobody understood, nobody put faith in his experience, until it was too late.

And he said, "My physician," "My experience," with the authoritative tone of a man who has possession of unique things. In his mouth the possessive pronouns had the sonorous ring of metals. And when he pronounced the words "My wife," one felt very clearly that the Marquis had no longer any rights with regard to his daughter since Andermatt had married her, to marry and to buy having the same meaning in the latter's mind.

Gontran came in, at the most lively stage of the discussion, and seated himself in an armchair with a smile of gaiety on his lips. He said nothing, but listened, exceedingly amused. When the banker stopped talking, having fairly exhausted his breath, his brother-in-law raised his hand, exclaiming:

"I request permission to speak. Here are both of you without physicians, isn't that so? Well, I propose my candidate, Doctor Honorat, the only one who has formed an exact and unshaken opinion on the water of Enval. He makes people drink it, but he would not drink it himself for all the world. Do you wish me to go and look for him? I will take the negotiations on myself."

It was the only thing to do, and they begged of Gontran to send for him immediately. The Marquis, filled with anxiety at the idea of a change of regimen and of nursing wanted to know immediately the opinion of this new physician; and Andermatt desired no less eagerly to consult him on Christiane's behalf.

She heard their voices through the door without listening to their words or understanding what they were talking about. As soon as her husband had left her, she had risen from the bed, as if from a dangerous spot, and hurriedly dressed herself, without the assistance of the chambermaid, shaken by all these occurrences.

The world appeared to her to have changed around her, her former life seemed to have vanished since last night, and people themselves looked quite different.

The voice of Andermatt was raised once more: "Hallo, my dear Bretigny, how are you getting on?"

He no longer used the word "Monsieur." Another voice could be heard saying in reply: "Why, quite well, my dear Andermatt. You only arrived, I suppose, this morning?"

Christiane, who was in the act of raising her hair over her temples, stopped with a choking sensation, her arms in the air. Through the partition, she fancied she could see them grasping one another's hands. She sat down, no longer able to hold herself erect; and her hair, rolling down, fell over her shoulders.

It was Paul who was speaking now, and she shivered from head to foot at every word that came from his mouth. Each word, whose meaning she did not seize, fell and sounded on her heart like a hammer striking a bell.

Suddenly, she articulated in almost a loud tone: "But I love him!—I love him!" as though she were affirming something new and surprising, which saved her, which consoled her, which proclaimed her innocence before the tribunal of her conscience. A sudden energy made her rise up; in one second, her resolution was taken. And she proceeded to rearrange her hair, murmuring: "I have a lover, that is all. I have a lover." Then, in order to fortify herself still more, in order to get rid of all mental distress, she determined there and then, with a burning faith, to love him to distraction, to give up to him her life, her happiness, to sacrifice everything for him, in accordance with the moral exaltation of hearts conquered but still scrupulous, that believe themselves to be purified by devotedness and sincerity.

And, from behind the wall which separated them, she threw out kisses to him. It was over; she abandoned herself to him, without reserve, as she might have offered herself to a god. The child already coquettish and artful, but still timid, still trembling, had suddenly died within her; and the woman was born, ready for passion, the woman resolute, tenacious, announced only up to this time by the energy hidden in her blue eye, which gave an air of courage and almost of bravado to her dainty white face.

She heard the door opening, and did not turn round, divining that it was her husband, without seeing him, as though a new sense, almost an instinct, had just been generated in her also.

He asked: "Will you be soon ready? We are all going presently to the paralytic's bath, to see if he is really getting better."

She replied calmly: "Yes, my dear Will, in five minutes."

But Gontran, returning to the drawing-room, was calling back Andermatt.

"Just imagine," said he; "I met that idiot Honorat in the park, and he, too, refuses to attend you for fear of the others. He talks of professional etiquette, deference, usages. One would imagine that he creates the impression of—in short, he is a fool, like his two brother-physicians. Certainly, I thought he was less of an ape than that."

The Marquis remained overwhelmed. The idea of taking the waters without a physician, of bathing for five minutes longer than necessary, of drinking one glass less than he ought, tortured him with apprehension, for he believed all the doses, the hours, and the phases of the treatment, to be regulated by a law of nature, which had made provision for invalids in causing the flow of those mineral springs, all whose mysterious secrets the doctors knew, like priests inspired and learned.

He exclaimed: "So then we must die here—we may perish like dogs, without any of these gentlemen putting himself about!"

And rage took possession of him, the rage egotistical and unreasoning of a man whose health is endangered.

"Have they any right to do this, since they pay for a license like grocers, these blackguards? We ought to have the power of forcing them to attend people, as trains can be forced to take all passengers. I am going to write to the newspapers to draw attention to the matter."

He walked about, in a state of excitement; and he went on, turning toward his son:

"Listen! It will be necessary to send for one to Royat or Clermont. We can't remain in this state."

Gontran replied, laughing: "But those of Clermont and of Royat are not well acquainted with the liquid of Enval, which has not the same special action as their water on the digestive system and on the circulatory apparatus. And then, be sure, they won't come any more than the others in order to avoid the appearance of taking the bread out of their brother-doctors' mouths."

The Marquis, quite scared, faltered: "But what, then, is to become of us?"

Andermatt snatched up his hat, saying: "Let me settle it, and I'll answer for it that we'll have the entire three of them this evening—you understand clearly, the—entire—three—at our knees. Let us go now and see the paralytic."

He cried: "Are you ready, Christiane?"

She appeared at the door, very pale, with a look of determination. Having embraced her father and her brother, she turned toward Paul, and extended her hand toward him. He took it, with downcast eyes, quivering with emotion. As the Marquis, Andermatt, and Gontran had gone on before, chatting, and without minding them, she said, in a firm voice, fixing on the young man a tender and decided glance:

"I belong to you, body and soul. Do with me henceforth what you please." Then she walked on, without giving him an opportunity of replying.

As they drew near the Oriols' spring, they perceived, like an enormous mushroom, the hat of Père Clovis, who was sleeping beneath the rays of the sun, in the warm water at the bottom of the hole. He now spent the entire morning there, having got accustomed to this boiling water which made him, he said, more lively than a yearling.

Andermatt woke him up: "Well, my fine fellow, you are going on better?"

When he had recognized his patron, the old fellow made a grimace of satisfaction: "Yes, yes, I am going on—I am going on as well as you please."

"Are you beginning to walk?"

"Like a rabbit, Mochieu—like a rabbit. I will dance a boree with my sweetheart on the first Sunday of the month."

Andermatt felt his heart beating; he repeated: "It is true, then, that you are walking?"

Père Clovis ceased jesting. "Oh! not very much, not very much. No matter—I'm getting on—I'm getting on!"

Then the banker wanted to see at once how the vagabond walked. He kept rushing about the hole, got agitated, gave orders, as if he were going to float again a ship that had foundered.

"Look here, Gontran! you take the right arm. You, Bretigny, the left arm. I am going to keep up his back. Come on! together!—one—two—three! My dear father-in-law, draw the leg toward you—no, the other, the one that's in the water. Quick, pray! I can't hold out longer. There we are—one, two—there!—ouf!"

They had put the old trickster sitting on the ground; and he allowed them to do it with a jeering look, without in any way assisting their efforts.

Then they raised him up again, and set him on his legs, giving him his crutches, which he used like walking-sticks; and he began to step out, bent double, dragging his feet after him, whining and blowing. He advanced in the fashion of a slug, and left behind him a long trail of water on the white dust of the road.

Andermatt, in a state of enthusiasm, clapped his hands, crying out as people do at theaters when applauding the actors: "Bravo, bravo, admirable, bravo!!!"

Then, as the old fellow seemed exhausted, he rushed forward to hold him up, seized him in his arms, although his clothes were streaming, and he kept repeating:

"Enough, don't fatigue yourself! We are going to put you back into your bath."

And Père Clovis was plunged once more into his hole by the four men who caught him by his four limbs and carried him carefully like a fragile and precious object.

Then, the paralytic observed in a tone of conviction: "It is good water, all the same, good water that hasn't an equal. It is worth a treasure, water like that!"

Andermatt turned round suddenly toward his father-in-law: "Don't keep breakfast waiting for me. I am going to the Oriols', and I don't know when I'll be free. It is necessary not to let these things drag!"

And he set forth in a hurry, almost running, and twirling his stick about like a man bewitched.

The others sat down under the willows, at the side of the road, opposite Père Clovis's hole.

Christiane, at Paul's side, saw in front of her the high knoll from which she had seen the rock blown up.

She had been up there that day, scarcely a month ago. She had been sitting on that russet grass. One month! Only one month! She recalled the most trifling details, the tricolored parasols, the scullions, the slightest things said by each of them! And the dog, the poor dog crushed by the explosion! And that big youth, then a stranger to her, who had rushed forward at one word uttered by her lips in order to save the animal. To-day, he was her lover! her lover! So then she had a lover! She was his mistress—his mistress! She repeated this word in the recesses of her consciousness—his mistress! What a strange word! This man, sitting by her side, whose hand she saw tearing up one by one blades of grass, close to her dress, which he was seeking to touch, this man was now bound to her flesh and to his heart, by that mysterious chain, buried in secrecy and mystery, which nature has stretched between woman and man.

With that voice of thought, that mute voice which seems to speak so loudly in the silence of troubled souls, she incessantly repeated to herself: "I am his mistress! his mistress!" How strange, how unforeseen, a thing this was!

"Do I love him?" She cast a rapid glance at him. Their eyes met, and she felt herself so much caressed by the passionate look with which he covered her, that she trembled from head to foot. She felt a longing now, a wild, irresistible longing, to take that hand which was toying with the grass, and to press it very tightly in order to convey to him all that may be said by a clasp. She let her own hand slip along her dress down to the grass, then laid it there motionless, with the fingers spread wide. Then she saw the other come softly toward it like an amorous animal seeking his companion. It came nearer and nearer; and their little fingers touched. They grazed one another at the ends gently, barely, lost one another and found one another again, like lips meeting. But this imperceptible caress, this slight contact entered into her being so violently that she felt herself growing faint as if he were once more straining her between his arms.

And she suddenly understood how a woman can belong to some man, how she no longer is anything under the love that possesses her, how that other being takes her body and soul, flesh, thought, will, blood, nerves,—all, all, all that is in her,—just as a huge bird of prey with large wings swoops down on a wren.

The Marquis and Gontran talked about the future station, themselves won over by Will's enthusiasm. And they spoke of the banker's merits, the clearness of his mind, the sureness of his judgment, the certainty of his system of speculation, the boldness of his operations, and the regularity of his character. Father-in-law and brother-in-law, in the face of this probable success, of which they felt certain, were in agreement, and congratulated one another on this alliance.

Christiane and Paul did not seem to hear, so much occupied were they with each other.

The Marquis said to his daughter: "Hey! darling, you may perhaps one day be one of the richest women in France, and people will talk of you as they do about the Rothschilds. Will has truly a remarkable, very remarkable—a great intelligence."

But a morose and whimsical jealousy entered all at once into Paul's heart.

"Let me alone now," said he, "I know it, the intelligence of all those engaged in stirring up business. They have only one thing in their heads—money! All the thoughts that we bestow on beautiful things, all the actions that we waste on our caprices, all the hours which we fling away for our distractions, all the strength that we squander on our pleasures, all the ardor and the power which love, divine love, takes from us, they employ in seeking for gold, in thinking of gold, in amassing gold! The man of intelligence lives for all the great disinterested tendernesses, the arts, love, science, travels, books; and, if he seeks money, it is because this facilitates the true pleasures of intellect and even the happiness of the heart! But they—they have nothing in their minds or their hearts but this ignoble taste for traffic! They resemble men of worth, these skimmers of life, just as much as the picture-dealer resembles the painter, as the publisher resembles the writer, as the theatrical manager resembles the dramatic poet."

He suddenly became silent, realizing that he had allowed himself to be carried away, and in a calmer voice he went on: "I don't say that of Andermatt, whom I consider a charming man. I like him a great deal, because he is a hundred times superior to all the others."

Christiane had withdrawn her hand. Paul once more stopped talking. Gontran began to laugh; and, in his malicious voice, with which he ventured to say everything, in his hours of mocking and raillery:

"In any case, my dear fellow, these men have one rare merit: that is, to marry our sisters and to have rich daughters, who become our wives."

The Marquis, annoyed, rose up: "Oh! Gontran, you are perfectly revolting."

Paul thereupon turned toward Christiane, and murmured: "Would they know how to die for one woman, or even to give her all their fortune—all—without keeping anything?"

This meant so clearly: "All I have is yours, including my life," that she was touched, and she adopted this device in order to take his hands in hers:

"Rise, and lift me up. I am benumbed from not moving."

He stood erect, seized her by the wrists, and drawing her up placed her standing on the edge of the road close to his side. She saw his mouth articulating the words, "I love you," and she quickly turned aside, to avoid saying to him in reply three words which rose to her lips in spite of her, in a burst of passion which was drawing her toward him.

They returned to the hotel. The hour for the bath was passed. They awaited the breakfast-bell. It rang, but Andermatt did not make his appearance. After taking another turn in the park, they resolved to sit down to table. The meal, although a long one, was finished before the return of the banker. They went back to sit down under the trees. And the hours stole by, one after another; the sun glided over the leaves, bending toward the mountains; the day was ebbing toward its close; and yet Will did not present himself.

All at once, they saw him. He was walking quickly, his hat in his hand, wiping his forehead, his necktie on one side, his waistcoat half open, as if after a journey, after a struggle, after a terrible and prolonged effort.

As soon as he beheld his father-in-law, he exclaimed: "Victory! 'tis done! But what a day, my friends! Ah! the old fox, what trouble he gave me!"

And immediately he explained the steps he had taken and the obstacles he had met with.

Père Oriol had, at first, shown himself so unreasonable that Andermatt was breaking off the negotiations and going away. Then the peasant called him back. The old man pretended that he would not sell his lands but would assign them to the Company with the right to resume possession of them in case of ill success. In case of success, he demanded half the profits.

The banker had to demonstrate to him, with figures on paper and tracings to indicate the different bits of land, that the fields all together would not be worth more than forty-five thousand francs at the present hour, while the expenses of the Company would mount up at one swoop to a million.

But the Auvergnat replied that he expected to benefit by the enormously increased value that would be given to his property by the erection of the establishment and hotels, and to draw his interest in the undertaking in accordance with the acquired value and not the previous value.

Andermatt had then to represent to him that the risks should be proportionate with the possible gains, and to terrify him with the apprehension of the loss.

They accordingly arrived at this agreement: Père Oriol was to assign to the Company all the grounds stretching as far as the banks of the stream, that is to say, all those in which it appeared possible to find mineral water, and in addition the top of the knoll, in order to erect there a casino and a hotel, and some vine-plots on the slope which should be divided into lots and offered to the leading physicians of Paris.

The peasant, in return for this apportionment valued at two hundred and fifty thousand francs, that is, at about four times its value, would participate to the extent of a quarter in the profits of the Company. As there was very much more land, which he did not part with, round the future establishment, he was sure, in case of success, to realize a fortune by selling on reasonable terms these grounds, which would constitute, he said, the dowry of his daughters.

As soon as these conditions had been arrived at, Will had to carry the father and the son with him to the notary's office in order to have a promise of sale drawn up defeasible in the event of their not finding the necessary water. And the drawing up of the agreement, the discussion of every point, the indefinite repetition of the same arguments, the eternal commencement over again of the same contentions, had lasted all the afternoon.

At last the matter was concluded. The banker had got his station. But he repeated, devoured by a regret: "It will be necessary for me to confine myself to the water without thinking of the questions about the land. He has been cunning, the old ape."

Then he added: "Bah! I'll buy up the old Company, and it is on that I may speculate! No matter—it is necessary that I should start this evening again for Paris."

The Marquis, astounded, cried out: "What? This evening?"

"Why, yes, my dear father-in-law, in order to get the definitive instrument prepared, while M. Aubry-Pasteur will be making excavations. It is necessary also that I should make arrangements to commence the works in a fortnight. I haven't an hour to lose. With regard to this, I must inform you that you are to constitute a portion of my board of directors in which I will need a strong majority. I give you ten shares. To you, Gontran, also I give ten shares."

Gontran began to laugh: "Many thanks, my dear fellow. I sell them back to you. That makes five thousand francs you owe me."

But Andermatt no longer felt in a mood for joking, when dealing with business of so much importance. He resumed dryly: "If you are not serious, I will address myself to another person."

Gontran ceased laughing: "No, no, my good friend, you know that I have cleared off everything with you."

The banker turned toward Paul: "My dear Monsieur, will you render me a friendly service, that is, to accept also ten shares with the rank of director?"

Paul, with a bow, replied: "You will permit me, Monsieur, not to accept this graceful offer, but to put a hundred thousand francs into the undertaking, which I consider a superb one. So then it is I who have to ask for a favor from you."

William, ravished, seized his hands. This confidence had conquered him. Besides he always experienced an irresistible desire to embrace persons who brought him money for his enterprises.

But Christiane crimsoned to her temples, pained, bruised. It seemed to her that she had just been bought and sold. If he had not loved her, would Paul have offered these hundred thousand francs to her husband? No, undoubtedly! He should not, at least, have entered into this transaction in her presence.

The dinner-bell rang. They re-entered the hotel. As soon as they were seated at table, Madame Paille, the mother, asked Andermatt:

"So you are going to set up another establishment?"

The news had already gone through the entire district, was known to everyone, it put the bathers into a state of commotion.

William replied: "Good heavens, yes! The existing one is too defective!"

And turning round to M. Aubry-Pasteur: "You will excuse me, dear Monsieur, for speaking to you at dinner of a step which I wished to take with regard to you; but I am starting again for Paris, and time presses on me terribly. Will you consent to direct the work of excavation, in order to find a volume of superior water?"

The engineer, feeling flattered, accepted the office. In five minutes everything had been discussed and settled with the clearness and precision which Andermatt imported into all matters of business. Then they talked about the paralytic. He had been seen crossing the park in the afternoon with only one walking-stick, although that morning he had used two. The banker kept repeating: "This is a miracle, a real miracle. His cure proceeds with giant strides!"

Paul, to please the husband, rejoined: "It is Père Clovis himself who walks with giant strides."

A laugh of approval ran round the table. Every eye was fixed on Will; every mouth complimented him.

The waiters of the restaurant made it their business to serve him the first, with a respectful deference, which disappeared from their faces as soon as they passed the dishes to the next guest.

One of them presented to him a card on a plate. He took it up, and read it, half aloud:

"Doctor Latonne of Paris would be happy if M. Andermatt would be kind enough to give him an interview of a few seconds before his departure."

"Tell him in reply that I have no time, but that I will be back in eight or ten days."

At the same moment, a box of flowers sent by Doctor Honorat was presented to Christiane.

Gontran laughed: "Père Bonnefille is a bad third," said he.

The dinner was nearly over. Andermatt was informed that his landau was waiting for him. He went up to look for his little bag; and when he came down again he saw half the village gathered in front of the door.

Petrus Martel came to grasp his hand, with the familiarity of a strolling actor, and murmured in his ear: "I shall have a proposal to make to you—something stunning—with reference to your undertaking."

Suddenly, Doctor Bonnefille appeared, hurrying in his usual fashion. He passed quite close to Will, and bowing very low to him as he would do to the Marquis, he said to him:

"A pleasant journey, Baron."

"That settles it!" murmured Gontran.

Andermatt, triumphant, swelling with joy and pride, pressed the hands extended toward him, thanked them, and kept repeating: "Au revoir!"

He was nearly forgetting to embrace his wife, so much was he thinking about other things. This indifference was a relief to her, and, when she saw the landau moving away on the darkening road, as the horses broke into a quick trot, it seemed to her that she had nothing more to fear from anyone for the rest of her life.

She spent the whole evening seated in front of the hotel, between her father and Paul Bretigny, Gontran having gone to the Casino, where he went every evening.

She did not want either to walk or to talk, and remained motionless, her hands clasped over her knees, her eyes lost in the darkness, languid and weak, a little restless and yet happy, scarcely thinking, not even dreaming, now and then struggling against a vague remorse, which she thrust away from her, always repeating to herself, "I love him! I love him!"

She went up to her apartment at an early hour, in order to be alone and to think. Seated in the depths of an armchair and covered with a dressing-gown which floated around her, she gazed at the stars through the window, which was left open; and in the frame of that window she evoked every minute the image of him who had conquered her. She saw him, kind, gentle, and powerful—so strong and so yielding in her presence. This man had taken herself to himself,—she felt it,—taken her forever. She was alone no longer; they were two, whose two hearts would henceforth form but one heart, whose two souls would henceforth form but one soul. Where was he? She knew not; but she knew full well that he was dreaming of her, just as she was thinking of him. At each throb of her heart she believed she heard another throb answering somewhere. She felt a desire wandering round her and fanning her cheek like a bird's wing. She felt it entering through that open window, this desire coming from him, this burning desire, which entreated her in the silence of the night.

How good it was, how sweet and refreshing to be loved! What joy to think of some one, with a longing in your eyes to weep, to weep with tenderness, and a longing also to open your arms, even without seeing him, in order to invite him to come, to stretch one's arms toward the image that presents itself, toward that kiss which your lover casts unceasingly from far or near, in the fever of his waiting.

And she stretched toward the stars her two white arms in the sleeves of her dressing-gown. Suddenly she uttered a cry. A great black shadow, striding over her balcony, had sprung up into her window.

She sprang wildly to her feet! It was he! And, without even reflecting that somebody might see them, she threw herself upon his breast.

"SHE SPRANG WILDLY TO HER FEET. IT WAS HE!"

CHAPTER VIII.

ORGANIZATION

The absence of Andermatt was prolonged. M. Aubry-Pasteur got the soil dug up. He found, in addition, four springs, which supplied the new Company with more than twice as much water as they required. The entire district, driven crazy by these searches, by these discoveries, by the great news which circulated everywhere, by the prospects of a brilliant future, became agitated and enthusiastic, talked of nothing else, and thought of nothing else. The Marquis and Gontran themselves spent their days hanging round the workmen, who were boring through the veins of granite; and they listened with increasing interest to the explanations and the lectures of the engineer on the geological character of Auvergne. And Paul and Christiane loved one another freely, tranquilly, in absolute security, without anyone suspecting anything, without anyone thinking even of spying on them, for the attention, the curiosity, and the zeal of all around them were absorbed in the future station.

Christiane acted like a young girl under the intoxication of a first love. The first draught, the first kiss, had burned, had stunned her. She had swallowed the second very quickly, and had found it better, and now again and again she raised the intoxicating cup to her lips.

Since the night when Paul had broken into her apartment, she no longer took any heed of what was happening in the world. For her, time, events, beings, no longer had any existence; there was nothing else in life save one man, he whom she loved. Henceforth, her eyes saw only him, her mind thought only of him, her hopes were fixed on him alone. She lived, went from place to place, ate, dressed herself, seemed to listen and to reply, without consciousness or thought about what she was doing. No disquietude haunted her, for no misfortune could have fallen on her. She had become insensible to everything. No physical pain could have taken hold of her flesh, as love alone could, so as to make her shudder. No moral suffering could have taken hold of her soul, paralyzed by happiness. Moreover, he, loving her with the self-abandonment which he displayed in all his attachments, excited the young woman's tenderness to distraction.

Often, toward evening, when he knew that the Marquis and Gontran had gone to the springs, he would say, "Come and look at our heaven." He called a cluster of pine-trees growing on the hillside above even the gorges their heaven. They ascended to this spot through a little wood, along a steep path, to climb which took away Christiane's breath. As their time was limited, they proceeded rapidly, and, in order that she might not be too much fatigued, he put his arm round her waist and lifted her up. Placing one hand on his shoulder, she let herself be borne along; and, from time to time, she would throw herself on his neck and place her mouth against his lips. As they mounted higher, the air became keener; and, when they reached the cluster of pine-trees, the odor of the balsam refreshed them like a breath of the sea.

They sat down under the shadowy trees, she on a grassy knoll, and he lower down, at her feet. The wind in the stems sang that sweet chant of the pine-trees which is like a wail of sorrow; and the immense Limagne, with its unseen backgrounds steeped in fog, gave them a sensation exactly like that of the ocean. Yes, the sea was there in front of them, down below. They could have no doubt of it, for they felt its breath fanning their faces.

He talked to her in the coaxing tone that one uses toward a child.

"Give me your fingers and let me eat them—they are my bonbons, mine!"

He put them one after the other into his mouth, and seemed to be tasting them with gluttonous delight.

"Oh! how nice they are!—especially the little one. I have never eaten anything better than the little one."

Then he threw himself on his knees, placed his elbows on Christiane's lap, and murmured:

"'Liane,' are you looking at me?" He called her Liane because she entwined herself around him in order to embrace him the more closely, as a plant clings around a tree. "Look at me. I am going to enter your soul."

And they exchanged that immovable, persistent glance, which seems truly to make two beings mingle with one another!

"We can only love thoroughly by thus possessing one another," he said. "All the other things of love are but foul pleasures."

And, face to face, their breaths blending into one, they sought to see one another's images in the depths of their eyes.

He murmured: "I love you, Liane. I see your adored heart."

She replied: "I, too, Paul, see your heart!"

And, indeed, they did see one another even to the depths of their hearts and souls, for there was no longer in their hearts and souls anything but a mad transport of love for one another.

He said: "Liane, your eye is like the sky. It is blue, with so many reflections, with so much clearness. It seems to me that I see swallows passing through them—these, no doubt, must be your thoughts."

And when they had thus contemplated one another for a long, long time, they drew nearer still to one another, and embraced softly with little jerks, gazing once more into each other's eyes between each kiss. Sometimes he would take her in his arms, and carry her, while he ran along the stream, which glided toward the gorges of Enval, before dashing itself into them. It was a narrow glen, where meadows and woods alternated. Paul rushed over the grass, and now and then he would raise her up high with his powerful wrists, and exclaim: "Liane, let us fly away." And with this yearning to fly away, love, their impassioned love, filled them, harassing, incessant, sorrowful. And everything around them whetted this desire of their souls, the light atmosphere—a bird's atmosphere, he said—and the vast blue horizon, in which they both would fain have taken wing, holding each other by the hand, so as to disappear above the boundless plain when the night spread its shadows across it. They would have flown thus across the hazy evening sky, never to return. Where would they have gone? They knew not; but what a glorious dream! When he had got out of breath from running while carrying her in this way, he placed her sitting on a rock in order to kneel down before her; and, kissing her ankles, he adored her, murmuring infantile and tender words.

Had they been lovers in a city, their passion, no doubt, would have been different, more prudent, more sensual, less ethereal, and less romantic. But there, in that green country, whose horizon widened the flights of the soul, alone, without anything to distract them, to attenuate their instinct of awakened love, they had suddenly plunged into a passionately poetic attachment made up of ecstasy and frenzy. The surrounding scenery, the balmy air, the woods, the sweet perfume of the fields, played for them all day and all night the music of their love—music which excited them even to madness, as the sound of tambourines and of shrill flutes drives to acts of savage unreason the dervish who whirls round with fixed intent.

One evening, as they were returning to the hotel for dinner, the Marquis said to them, suddenly: "Andermatt is coming back in four days. Matters are all arranged. We are to leave the day after his return. We have been here a long time. We must not prolong mineral water seasons too much."

They were as much taken by surprise as if they had heard the end of the world announced, and during the meal neither of them uttered a word, so much were they thinking with astonishment of what was about to happen. So then they would, in a few days, be separated and would no longer be able to see one another freely. That appeared so impossible and so extraordinary to them that they could not realize it.

Andermatt did, in fact, come back at the end of the week. He had telegraphed in order that two landaus might be sent on to him to meet the first train.

Christiane, who had not slept, tormented as she was by a strange and new emotion, a sort of fear of her husband, a fear mingled with anger, with inexplicable contempt, and a desire to set him at defiance, had risen at daybreak, and was awaiting him. He appeared in the first carriage, accompanied by three gentlemen well attired but modest in demeanor. The second landau contained four others, who seemed persons of rank somewhat inferior to the first. The Marquis and Gontran were astonished. The latter asked: "Who are these people?"

Andermatt replied: "My shareholders. We are going to establish the Company this very day, and to nominate the board of directors immediately."

He embraced his wife without speaking to her, and almost without looking at her, so preoccupied was he; and, turning toward the seven gentlemen, who were standing behind him, silent and respectful:

"Go and have breakfast, and take a walk," said he. "We'll meet again here at twelve o'clock."

They went off without saying anything, like soldiers obeying orders, and mounting the steps of the hotel one after another, they went in. Gontran, who had been watching them as they disappeared from view, asked in a very serious tone:

"Where did you find them, these 'supers' of yours?"

The banker smiled: "They are very well-to-do men, moneyed men, capitalists."

And, after a pause, he added, with a more significant smile: "They busy themselves about my affairs."

Then he repaired to the notary's office to read over again the documents, of which he had sent the originals, all prepared, some days before. There he found Doctor Latonne, with whom, moreover, he had been in correspondence, and they chatted for a long time in low tones, in a corner of the office, while the clerks' pens ran along the paper, with the buzzing noise of insects.

The meeting to establish the Company was fixed for two o'clock. The notary's study had been fitted up as if for a concert. Two rows of chairs were placed for the shareholders in front of the table, where Maître Alain was to take his seat beside his principal clerk. Maître Alain had put on his official garment in consideration of the importance of the business in hand. He was a very small man, a stuttering ball of white flesh.

Andermatt entered just as it struck two, accompanied by the Marquis, his brother-in-law, and Bretigny, and followed by the seven gentlemen, whom Gontran described as "supers." He had the air of a general. Père Oriol also made his appearance with Colosse by his side. He seemed uneasy, distrustful, as people always are when about to sign a document. The last to arrive was Doctor Latonne. He had made his peace with Andermatt by a complete submission preceded by excuses skillfully turned, and followed by an offer of his services without any reserve or restrictions.

Thereupon, the banker, feeling that he had Latonne in his power, promised him the post he longed for, of medical inspector of the new establishment.

When everyone was in the room, a profound silence reigned. The notary addressed the meeting: "Gentlemen, take your seats." He gave utterance to a few words more, which nobody could hear in the confusion caused by the moving about of the chairs.

Andermatt lifted up a chair, and placed it in front of his army, in order to keep his eye on all his supporters; then, when he was seated, he said:

"Messieurs, I need not enter into any explanations with you as to the motive that brings us together. We are going, first of all, to establish the new Company in which you have consented to become shareholders. It is my duty, however, to apprise you of a few details, which have caused us a little embarrassment. I have found it necessary, before even entering on the undertaking at all, to assure myself that we could obtain the required authority for the creation of a new establishment of public utility. This assurance I have got. What remains to be done with respect to this, I will make it my business to do. I have the Minister's promise. But another point demands my attention. We are going, Messieurs, to enter on a struggle with the old Company of the Enval waters. We shall come forth victorious in this struggle, victorious and enriched, you may be certain; but, just as in the days of old, a war cry was necessary for the combatants, we, combatants in the modern battle, require a name for our station, a name sonorous, attractive, well fashioned for advertising purposes, which strikes the ear like the note of a clarion, and penetrates the ear like a flash of lightning. Now, Messieurs, we are in Enval, and we can not unbaptize this district. One resource only is left to us. To designate our establishment, our establishment alone, by a new appellation.

"Here is what I propose to you: If our bathhouse is to be at the foot of the knoll, of which M. Oriol, here present, is the proprietor, our future Casino will be erected on the summit of this same knoll. We may, therefore, say that this knoll, this mountain—for it is a mountain, a little mountain—furnishes the site of our establishment, inasmuch as we have the foot and the top of it. Is it not, therefore, natural to call our baths the Baths of Mont Oriol, and to attach to this station, which will become one of the most important in the entire world, the name of the original proprietor? Render to Cæsar what belongs to Cæsar.

"And observe, Messieurs, that this is an excellent vocable. People will talk of 'the Mont Oriol' as they talk of 'the Mont Doré.' It fixes itself on the eye and in the ear; we can see it well; we can hear it well; it abides in us—Mont Oriol!—Mont Oriol!—The baths of Mont Oriol!"

And Andermatt made this word ring, flung it out like a ball, listening to the echo of it. He went on, repeating imaginary dialogues: "'You are going to the baths of Mont Oriol?'

"'Yes, Madame. People say they are perfect, these waters of Mont Oriol.'

"'Excellent, indeed. Besides, Mont Oriol is a delightful district.'"

And he smiled, assumed the air of people chatting to one another, altered his voice to indicate when the lady was speaking, saluted with the hand when representing the gentleman.

Then he resumed, in his natural voice: "Has anyone an objection to offer?"

The shareholders answered in chorus: "No, none."

All the "supers" applauded. Père Oriol, moved, flattered, conquered, overcome by the deep-rooted pride of an upstart peasant, began to smile while he twisted his hat about between his hands, and he made a sign of assent with his head in spite of him, a movement which revealed his satisfaction, and which Andermatt observed without pretending to see it. Colosse remained impassive, but was quite as much satisfied as his father.

Then Andermatt said to the notary: "Kindly read the instrument whereby the Company is incorporated, Maître Alain."

And he resumed his seat. The notary said to his clerk: "Go on, Marinet."

Marinet, a wretched consumptive creature, coughed, and with the intonations of a preacher, and an attempt at declamation, began to enumerate the statutes relating to the incorporation of an anonymous Company, called the Company of the Thermal Establishment of Mont Oriol at Enval with a capital of two millions.

Père Oriol interrupted him: "A moment, a moment," said he. And he drew forth from his pocket a few sheets of greasy paper, which during the past eight days had passed through the hands of all the notaries and all the men of business of the department. It was a copy of the statutes which his son and himself by this time were beginning to know by heart. Then, he slowly fixed his spectacles on his nose, raised up his head, looked out for the exact point where he could easily distinguish the letters, and said in a tone of command:

"Go on from that place, Marinet."

Colosse, having got close to his chair, also kept his eye on the paper along with his father.

And Marinet commenced over again. Then old Oriol, bewildered by the double task of listening and reading at the same time, tortured by the apprehension of a word being changed, beset also by the desire to see whether Andermatt was making some sign to the notary, did not allow a single line to be got through without stopping ten times the clerk whose elocutionary efforts he interrupted.

He kept repeating: "What did you say? What did you say there? I didn't understand—not so quick!"

Then turning aside a little toward his son: "What place is he at, Coloche?"

Coloche, more self-controlled, replied: "It's all right, father—let him go on—it's all right."

The peasant was still distrustful. With the end of his crooked finger he went on tracing on the paper the words as they were read out, muttering them between his lips; but he could not fix his attention at the same time on both matters. When he listened, he did not read, and he did not hear when he was reading. And he puffed as if he had been climbing a mountain;

he perspired as if he had been digging his vine-fields under a midday sun, and from time to time, he asked for a few minutes' rest to wipe his forehead and to take breath, like a man fighting a duel.

Andermatt, losing patience, stamped with his foot on the ground. Gontran, having noticed on a table the "Moniteur du Puy-de-Dome," had taken it up and was running his eye over it, and Paul, astride on his chair, with downcast eyes and an anxious heart, was reflecting that this little man, rosy and corpulent, sitting in front of him, was going to carry off, next day, the woman whom he loved with all his soul, Christiane, his Christiane, his fair Christiane, who was his, his entirely, nothing to anyone save him. And he asked himself whether he was not going to carry her off this very evening.

The seven gentlemen remained serious and tranquil.

At the end of an hour, it was finished. The deed was signed. The notary made out certificates for the payments on the shares. On being appealed to, the cashier, M. Abraham Levy, declared that he had received the necessary deposits. Then the company, from that moment legally constituted, was announced to be gathered together in general assembly, all the shareholders being in attendance, for the appointment of a board of directors and the election of their chairman.

All the votes with the exception of two, were recorded in favor of Andermatt's election to the post of chairman. The two dissentients—the old peasant and his son—had nominated Oriol. Bretigny was appointed commissioner of superintendence. Then, the Board, consisting of MM. Andermatt, the Marquis and the Count de Ravenel, Bretigny, the Oriols, father and son, Doctor Latonne, Abraham Levy, and Simon Zidler, begged of the remaining shareholders to withdraw, as well as the notary and his clerk, in order that they, as the governing body, might determine on the first resolutions, and settle the most important points.

Andermatt rose up again: "Messieurs, we are entering on the vital question, that of success, which we must win at any cost.

"It is with mineral waters as with everything. It is necessary to get them talked about a great deal, and continually, so that invalids may drink them.

"The great modern question, Messieurs, is that of advertising. It is the god of commerce and of contemporary industry. Without advertising there is no security. The art of advertising, moreover, is difficult, complicated, and demands a considerable amount of tact. The first persons who resorted to this new expedient employed it rudely, attracting attention by noise, by beating the big drum, and letting off cannon-shots. Mangin, Messieurs, was only a forerunner. To-day, clamor is regarded with suspicion, showy placards cause a smile, the crying out of names in the streets awakens distrust rather than curiosity. And yet it is necessary to attract public attention, and after having fixed it, it is necessary to produce conviction. The art, therefore, consists in discovering the means, the only means which can succeed, having in our possession something that we desire to sell. We, Messieurs, for our part, desire to sell water. It is by the physicians that we are to get the better of the invalids.

"The most celebrated physicians, Messieurs, are men like ourselves—who have weaknesses like us. I do not mean to convey that we can corrupt them. The reputation of the illustrious masters, whose assistance we require, places them above all suspicion of venality. But what man is there that cannot be won over by going properly to work with him? There are also women who cannot be purchased. These it is necessary to fascinate.

"Here, then, Messieurs, is the proposition which I am going to make to you, after having discussed it at great length with Doctor Latonne:

"We have, in the first place, classified in three leading groups the maladies submitted for our treatment. These are, first, rheumatism in all its forms, skin-disease, arthritis, gout, and so forth; secondly, affections of the stomach, of the intestines and of the liver; thirdly, all the disorders arising from disturbed circulation, for it is indisputable that our acidulated baths have an admirable effect on the circulation.

"Moreover, Messieurs, the marvelous cure of Père Clovis promises us miracles. Accordingly, when we have to deal with maladies which these waters are calculated to cure, we are about to make to the principal physicians who attend patients for such diseases the following proposition: 'Messieurs,' we shall say to them, 'come and see, come and see with your own eyes; follow your patients; we offer you hospitality. The country is magnificent; you require a rest after your severe labors during the winter—come! And come not to our houses, worthy professors, but to your own, for we offer you a cottage, which will belong to you, if you choose, on exceptional conditions.'"

Andermatt took breath, and went on in a more subdued tone:

"Here is how I have tried to work out this idea. We have selected six lots of land of a thousand meters each. On each of these six lots, the Bernese 'Chalets Mobiles' Company undertakes to fix one of their model buildings. We shall place gratuitously these dwellings, as elegant as they are comfortable, at the disposal of our physicians. If they are pleased with them, they need only buy the houses from the Bernese Company; as for the grounds, we shall assign them to the physicians, who are to pay us back—in invalids. Therefore, Messieurs, we obtain these multiplied advantages of covering our property with charming villas which cost us nothing, of attracting thither the leading physicians of the world and their legion of clients, and above all of convincing the eminent doctors who will very rapidly become proprietors in the district of the efficacy of our waters. As to all the negotiations necessary to bring about these results I take them upon myself, Messieurs; and I will do so, not as a speculator but as a man of the world."

Père Oriol interrupted him. The parsimony which he shared with the peasantry of Auvergne made him object to this gratuitous assignment of land.

Andermatt was inspired with a burst of eloquence. He compared the agriculturist on a large scale who casts his seed in handfuls into the teeming soil with the rapacious peasant who counts the grains and never gets more than half a harvest.

Then, as Oriol, annoyed by this language, persisted in his objections, the banker made his board divide, and shut the old man's mouth with six votes against two.

He next opened a large morocco portfolio and took out of it plans of the new establishment—the hotel and the Casino—as well as the estimates, and the most economical methods of procuring materials, which had been all prepared by the contractors, so that they might be approved of and signed before the end of the meeting. The works should be commenced by the beginning of the week after next.

The two Oriols alone wanted to investigate and discuss matters. But Andermatt, becoming irritated, said to them: "Did I ask you for money? No! Then give me peace! And, if you are not satisfied, we'll take another division on it."

Thereupon, they signed along with the remaining members of the Board; and the meeting terminated.

All the inhabitants of the place were waiting to see them going out, so intense was the excitement. The people bowed respectfully to them. As the two peasants were about to return home, Andermatt said to them:

"Do not forget that we are all dining together at the hotel. And bring your girls; I have brought them presents from Paris."

They were to meet at seven o'clock in the drawing-room of the Hotel Splendid.

It was a magnificent dinner to which the banker had invited the principal bathers and the authorities of the village. Christiane, who was the hostess, had the curé at her right, and the mayor at her left.

The conversation was all about the future establishment and the prospects of the district. The two Oriol girls had found under their napkins two caskets containing two bracelets of pearls and emeralds, and wild with delight, they talked as they had never done before, with Gontran sitting between them. The elder girl herself laughed with all her heart at the jokes of the young man, who became animated, while he talked to them, and in his own mind formed about them those masculine judgments, those judgments daring and secret, which are generated in the flesh and in the mind, at the sight of every pretty woman.

Paul did not eat, and did not open his lips. It seemed to him that his life was going to end to-night. Suddenly he remembered that just a month had glided away, day by day, since the open-air dinner by the lake of Tazenat. He had in his soul that vague sense of pain caused rather by presentiments than by grief, known to lovers alone, that sense of pain which makes the heart so heavy, the nerves so vibrating that the slightest noise makes us pant, and the mind so wretchedly sad that everything we hear assumes a somber hue so as to correspond with the fixed idea.

As soon as they had quitted the table, he went to join Christiane in the drawing-room.

"I must see you this evening," he said, "presently, immediately, since I no longer can tell when we may be able to meet. Are you aware that it is just a month to-day?"

She replied: "I know it."

He went on: "Listen! I am going to wait for you on the road to La Roche Pradière, in front of the village, close to the chestnut-trees. Nobody will notice your absence at the time. Come quickly in order to bid me adieu, since to-morrow we part."

She murmured: "I'll be there in a quarter of an hour."

And he went out to avoid being in the midst of this crowd which exasperated him.

He took the path through the vineyards which they had followed one day—the day when they had gazed together at the Limagne for the first time. And soon he was on the highroad. He was alone, and he felt alone, alone in the world. The immense, invisible plain increased still more this sense of isolation. He stopped in the very spot where they had seated themselves on the occasion when he recited Baudelaire's lines on Beauty. How far away it was already! And, hour by hour, he retraced in his memory all that had since taken place. Never had he been so happy, never! Never had he loved so distractedly, and at the same time so chastely, so devotedly. And he recalled that evening by the "gour" of Tazenat, only a month from to-day—the cool wood mellowed with a pale luster, the little lake of silver, and the big fishes that skimmed along its surface; and their return, when he saw her walking in front of him with light and shadow falling on her in turn, the moon's rays playing on her hair, on her shoulders, and on her arms through the leaves of the trees. These were the sweetest hours he had tasted in his life. He turned round to ascertain whether she might not have arrived. He did not see her, but he perceived the moon, which appeared at the horizon. The same moon which had risen for his first declaration of love had risen now for his first adieu.

A shiver ran through his body, an icy shiver. The autumn had come—the autumn that precedes the winter. He had not till now felt this first touch of cold, which pierced his frame suddenly like a menace of misfortune.

The white road, full of dust, stretched in front of him, like a river between its banks. A form at that moment rose up at the turn of the road. He recognized her at once; and he waited for her without flinching, trembling with the mysterious bliss of feeling her drawing near, of seeing her coming toward him, for him.

She walked with lingering steps, without venturing to call out to him, uneasy at not finding him yet, for he remained concealed under a tree, and disturbed by the deep silence, by the clear solitude of the earth and sky. And, before her, her shadow advanced, black and gigantic, some distance away from her, appearing to carry toward him something of her, before herself.

Christiane stopped, and the shadow remained also motionless, lying down, fallen on the road.

Paul quickly took a few steps forward as far as the place where the form of the head rounded itself on her path. Then, as if he wanted to lose no portion of her, he sank on his knees, and prostrating himself, placed his mouth on the edge of the dark silhouette. Just as a thirsty dog drinks crawling on his belly in a spring he began to kiss the dust passionately, following the outlines of the beloved shadow. In this way, he moved toward her on his hands and knees, covering with caresses the lines of her body, as if to gather up with his lips the obscure image, dear because it was hers, that lay spread along the ground.

She, surprised, a little frightened even, waited till he was at her feet before she had the courage to speak to him; then, when he had lifted up his head, still remaining on his knees, but now straining her with both arms, she asked:

"What is the matter with you, to-night?"

He replied: "Liane, I am going to lose you."

She thrust all her fingers into the thick hair of her lover, and, bending down, held back his forehead in order to kiss his eyes.

"Why lose me?" said she, smiling, full of confidence.

"Because we are going to separate to-morrow."

"We separate? For a very short time, darling."

"One never knows. We shall not again find days like those that we passed here."

"We shall have others which will be as lovely."

She raised him up, drew him under the tree, where he had been awaiting her, made him sit down close to her, but lower down, so that she might have her hand constantly in his hair; and she talked in a serious strain, like a thoughtful, ardent, and resolute woman, who loves, who has already provided against everything, who instinctively knows what must be done, who has made up her mind for everything.

"Listen, my darling. I am very free at Paris. William never bothers himself about me. His business concerns are enough for him. Therefore, as you are not married, I will go to see you. I will go to see you every day, sometimes in the morning before breakfast, sometimes in the evening, on account of the servants, who might chatter if I went out at the same hour. We can meet as often as here, even more than here, for we shall not have to fear inquisitive persons."

But he repeated with his head on her knees, and her waist tightly clasped: "Liane, Liane, I am going to lose you!"

She became impatient at this unreasonable grief, at this childish grief in this vigorous frame, while she, so fragile compared with him, was yet so sure of herself, so sure that nothing could part them.

He murmured: "If you wished it, Liane, we might fly off together, we might go far away, into a beautiful country full of flowers where we could love one another. Say, do you wish that we should go off together this evening—are you willing?"

But she shrugged her shoulders, a little nervous, a little dissatisfied, at his not having listened to her, for this was not the time for dreams and soft puerilities. It was necessary now for them to show themselves energetic and prudent, and to find out a way in which they could continue to love one another without rousing suspicion.

She said in reply: "Listen, darling! we must thoroughly understand our position, and commit no mistakes or imprudences. First of all, are you sure about your servants? The thing to be most feared is lest some one should give information or write an anonymous letter to my husband. Of his own accord, he will guess nothing. I know William well."

This name, twice repeated, all at once had an irritating effect on Paul's nerves. He said: "Oh! don't speak to me about him this evening."

She was astonished: "Why? It is quite necessary, however. Oh! I assure you that he has scarcely anything to do with me."

She had divined his thoughts. An obscure jealousy, as yet unconscious, was awakened within him. And suddenly, sinking on his knees and seizing her hands:

"Listen, Liane! What terms are you on with him?"

"Why—why—very good!"

"Yes, I know. But listen—understand me clearly. He is—he is your husband, in fact—and—and—you don't know how much I have been brooding over this for some time past—how much it torments, tortures me. You know what I mean. Tell me!"

She hesitated a few seconds, then in a flash she realized his entire meaning, and with an outburst of indignant candor:

"Oh! my darling!—can you—can you think such a thing? Oh! I am yours—do you understand?—yours alone—since I love you—oh! Paul!"

He let his head sink on the young woman's lap, and in a very soft voice, said:

"But!—after all, Liane, you know he is your husband. What will you do? Have you thought of that? Tell me! What will you do this evening or to-morrow? For you cannot—always, always say 'No' to him!"

She murmured, speaking also in a very low tone: "I have pretended to be enceinte, and—and that is enough for him. Oh! there is scarcely anything between us—Come! say no more about this, my darling. You don't know how this wounds me. Trust me, since I love you!"

He did not move, breathing hard and kissing her dress, while she caressed his face with her amorous, dainty Fingers.

But, all of a sudden, she said: "We must go back, for they will notice that we are both absent."

They embraced each other, clinging for a long time to one another in a clasp that might well have crushed their bones.

Then she rushed away so as to be back first and to enter the hotel quickly, while he watched her departing and vanishing from his sight, oppressed with sadness, as if all his happiness and all his hopes had taken flight along with her.

CHAPTER IX.

THE SPA AGAIN

The station of Enval could hardly be recognized on the first of July of the following year. On the summit of the knoll, standing between the two outlets of the valley, rose a building in the Moorish style of architecture, bearing on its front the word "Casino" in letters of gold.

A little wood had been utilized for the purpose of creating a small park on the slope facing the Limagne. Lower down, among the vines, six chalets here and there showed their façades of polished wood. On the slope facing the south, an immense structure was visible at a distance to travelers, who perceived it on their way from Riom.

This was the Grand Hotel of Mont Oriol. And exactly below it, at the very foot of the hill, a square house, simpler and more spacious, surrounded by a garden, through which ran the rivulet which flowed down from the gorges, offered to invalids the miraculous cure promised by a pamphlet of Doctor Latonne. On the façade could be read: "Thermal baths of Mont Oriol." Then, on the right wing, in smaller letters: "Hydropathy.—Stomach-washing.—Piscina with running water." And, on the left wing: "Medical institute of automatic gymnastics."

All this was white, with a fresh whiteness, shining and crude. Workmen were still occupied in completing it—house-painters, plumbers, and laborers employed in digging, although the establishment had already been a month open.

Its success, moreover, had since the start, surpassed the hopes of its founders. Three great physicians, three celebrities, Professor Mas-Roussel, Professor Cloche, and Professor Remusot, had taken the new station under their patronage, and consented to sojourn for sometime in the villas of the Bernese "Chalets Mobiles" Company, placed at their disposal by the Board intrusted with the management of the waters.

Under their influence a crowd of invalids flocked to the place. The Grand Hotel of Mont Oriol was full.

Although the baths had commenced working since the first days of June, the official opening of the station had been postponed till the first of July, in order to attract a great number of people. The fête was to commence at three o'clock with the ceremony of blessing the springs; and in the evening, a magnificent performance, followed by fireworks and a ball, would bring together all the bathers of the place, as well as those of the adjoining stations, and the principal inhabitants of Clermont-Ferrand and Riom.

The Casino on the summit of the hill was hidden from view by the flags. Nothing could be seen any longer but blue, red, white, yellow, a kind of dense and palpitating cloud; while from the tops of the gigantic masts planted along the walks in the park, huge oriflammes curled themselves in the blue sky with serpentine windings.

M. Petrus Martel, who had been appointed conductor of this new Casino, seemed to think that under this cloud of flags he had become the all-powerful captain of some fantastic ship; and he gave orders to the white-aproned waiters with the resounding and terrible voice which admirals need in order to exercise command under fire. His vibrating words, borne on by the wind, were heard even in the village.

Andermatt, out of breath already, appeared on the terrace. Petrus Martel advanced to meet him and bowed to him in a lordly fashion.

“Everything is going on well?” inquired the banker.

“Everything is going on well, my dear President.”

“If anyone wants me, I am to be found in the medical inspector’s study. We have a meeting this morning.”

And he went down the hill again. In front of the door of the thermal establishment, the overseer and the cashier, carried off also from the other Company, which had become the rival Company, but doomed without a possible contest, rushed forward to meet their master. The ex-jailer made a military salute. The other bent his head like a poor person receiving alms. Andermatt asked:

“Is the inspector here?”

The overseer replied: “Yes, Monsieur le President, all the gentlemen have arrived.”

The banker passed through the vestibule, in the midst of bathers and respectful waiters, turned to the right, opened a door, and found in a spacious apartment of serious aspect, full of books and busts of men of science, all the members of the Board at present in Enval assembled: his father-in-law the Marquis, and his brother-in-law Gontran, the Oriols, father and son, who had almost been transformed into gentlemen wearing frock-coats of such length that—with their own tallness, they looked like advertisements for a mourning-warehouse—Paul Bretigny, and Doctor Latonne.

After some rapid hand-shaking, they took their seats, and Andermatt commenced to address them:

“It remains for us to regulate an important matter, the naming of the springs. On this subject I differ entirely in opinion from the inspector. The doctor proposes to give to our three principal springs the names of the three leaders of the medical profession who are here. Assuredly, there would in this be a flattery which might touch them and win them over to us still more. But be sure, Messieurs, that it would alienate from us forever those among their distinguished professional brethren who have not yet responded to our invitation, and whom we should convince, at the cost of our best efforts and of every sacrifice, of the sovereign efficacy of our waters. Yes, Messieurs, human nature is unchangeable; it is necessary to know it and to make use of it. Never would Professors Plantureau, De Larenard, and Pascalis, to refer only to these three specialists in affections of the stomach and intestines, send their patients to be cured by the water of the Mas-Roussel Spring, the Cloche Spring, or the Remusot Spring. For these patients and the entire public would in that case be somewhat disposed to believe that it was by Professors Remusot, Cloche, and Mas-Roussel that our water and all its therapeutic properties had been discovered. There is no doubt, Messieurs, that the name of Gubler, with which the original spring at Chatel-Guyon was baptized, for a long time prejudiced against these waters, to-day in a prosperous condition, a section, at least, of the great physicians, who might have patronized it from the start.

“I accordingly propose to give quite simply the name of my wife to the spring first discovered and the names of the Mademoiselles Oriol to the other two. We shall thus have the Christiane, the Louise, and the Charlotte Springs. This suits very well; it is very nice. What do you say to it?”

His suggestion was adopted even by Doctor Latonne, who added: "We might then beg of MM. Mas-Roussel, Cloche, and Remusot to be godfathers and to offer their arms to the godmothers."

"Excellent, excellent," said Andermatt. "I am hurrying to meet them. And they will consent. I may answer for them—they will consent. Let us, therefore, reassemble at three o'clock in the church where the procession is to be formed."

And he went off at a running pace. The Marquis and Gontran followed him almost immediately. The Oriols, father and son, with tall hats on their heads, hastened to walk in their turn side by side, grave looking and all in black, on the white road; and Doctor Latonne said to Paul, who had only arrived the previous evening, to be present at the fête:

"I have detained you, Monsieur, in order to show you a thing from which I expect marvelous results. It is my medical institute of automatic gymnastics."

He took him by the arm, and led him in. But they had scarcely reached the vestibule when a waiter at the baths stopped the doctor:

"M. Riquier is waiting for his wash."

Doctor Latonne had, last year, spoken disparagingly of the stomach washings, extolled and practiced by Doctor Bonnefille, in the establishment of which he was inspector. But time had modified his opinion, and the Baraduc probe had become the great instrument of torture of the new inspector, who plunged it with an infantile delight into every gullet.

He inquired of Paul Bretigny: "Have you ever seen this little operation?"

The other replied: "No, never."

"Come on then, my dear fellow—it is very curious."

They entered the shower-bath room, where M. Riquier, the brick-colored man, who was this year trying the newly discovered springs, as he had tried, every summer, every fresh station, was waiting in a wooden armchair.

Like some executed criminal of olden times, he was squeezed and choked up in a kind of straight waistcoat of oilcloth, which was intended to preserve his clothes from stains and splashes; and he had the wretched, restless, and pained look of patients on whom a surgeon is about to operate.

As soon as the doctor appeared, the waiter took up a long tube, which had three divisions near the middle, and which had the appearance of a thin serpent with a double tail. Then the man fixed one of the ends to the extremity of a little cock communicating with the spring. The second was let fall into a glass receiver, into which would be presently discharged the liquids rejected by the patient's stomach; and the medical inspector, seizing with a steady hand the third arm of this conduit-pipe, drew it, with an air of amiability, toward M. Riquier's jaw, passed it into his mouth, and guiding it dexterously, slipped it into his throat, driving it in more and more with the thumb and index-finger, in a gracious and benevolent fashion, repeating:

"Very good! very good! very good! That will do, that will do; that will do; that will do exactly!"

M. Riquier, with staring eyes, purple cheeks, lips covered with foam, panted for breath, gasped as if he were suffocating, and had agonizing fits of coughing; and, clutching the arms of the chair, he made terrible efforts to get rid of that beastly india-rubber which was penetrating into his body.

When he had swallowed about a foot and a half of it, the doctor said: "We are at the bottom. Turn it on!"

The attendant thereupon turned on the cock, and soon the patient's stomach became visibly swollen, having been filled up gradually with the warm water of the spring.

"Cough," said the physician, "cough, in order to facilitate the descent."

In place of coughing, the poor man had a rattling in the throat, and shaken with convulsions, he looked as if his eyes were going to jump out of his head.

Then suddenly a light gurgling could be heard on the ground close to the armchair. The spout of the tube with the two passages had at last begun to work; and the stomach now emptied itself into this glass receiver where the doctor searched eagerly for the indications of catarrh and the recognizable traces of imperfect digestion.

"You are not to eat any more green peas," said he, "or salad. Oh! no salad! You cannot digest it at all. No more strawberries either! I have already repeated to you ten times, no strawberries!"

M. Riquier seemed raging with anger. He excited himself now without being able to utter a word on account of this tube, which stopped up his throat. But when, the washing having been finished, the doctor had delicately drawn out the probe from his interior, he exclaimed:

"Is it my fault if I am eating every day filth that ruins my health? Isn't it you that should watch the meals supplied by your hotel-keeper? I have come to your new cook-shop because they used to poison me at the old one with abominable food, and I am worse than ever in your big barrack of a Mont Oriol inn, upon my honor!"

The doctor had to appease him, and promised over and over again to have the invalids' food at the table d'hôte submitted beforehand to his inspection. Then, he took Paul Bretigny's arm again, and said as he led him away:

"Here are the extremely rational principles on which I have established my special treatment by the self-moving gymnastics, which we are going to inspect. You know my system of organometric medicine, don't you? I maintain that a great portion of our maladies entirely proceed from the excessive development of some one organ which encroaches on a neighboring organ, impedes its functions, and, in a little while, destroys the general harmony of the body, whence arise the most serious disturbances.

"Now, the exercise is, along with the shower-bath and the thermal treatment, one of the most powerful means of restoring the equilibrium and bringing back the encroaching parts to their normal proportions.

"But how are we to determine the man to make the exercise? There is not merely the act of walking, of mounting on horseback, of swimming or rowing—a considerable physical effort. There is also and above all a moral effort. It is the mind which determines, draws along, and sustains the body. The men of energy are men of movement. Now energy is in the soul and not in the muscles. The body obeys the vigorous will.

"It is not necessary to think, my dear friend, of giving courage to the cowardly or resolution to the weak. But we can do something else, we can do more—we can suppress mental energy, suppress moral effort and leave only physical subsisting. This moral effort, I replace with advantage by a foreign and purely mechanical force. Do you understand? No, not very well. Let us go in."

He opened a door leading into a large apartment, in which were ranged fantastic looking instruments, big armchairs with wooden legs, horses made of rough deal, articulated boards, and movable bars stretched in front of chairs fixed in the ground. And all these objects were connected with complicated machinery, which was set in motion by turning handles.

The doctor went on: "Look here. We have four principal kinds of exercise. These are walking, equitation, swimming, and rowing. Each of these exercises develops different members, acts in a special fashion. Now, we have them here—the entire four—produced by artificial means. All you have to do is to let yourself act, while thinking of nothing, and you can run, mount on horseback, swim, or row for an hour, without the mind taking any part—the slightest part in the world—in this entirely muscular work."

At that moment, M. Aubry-Pasteur entered, followed by a man whose tucked-up sleeves displayed the vigorous biceps on each arm. The engineer was as fat as ever. He was walking with his legs spread Wide apart and his arms held out from his body, While he panted for breath.

The doctor said: "You will understand by looking on at it yourself."

And addressing his patient: "Well, my dear Monsieur, what are we going to do to-day? Walking or equitation?"

M. Aubry-Pasteur, who pressed Paul's hand, replied: "I would like a little walking seated; that fatigues me less."

M. Latonne continued: "We have, in fact, walking seated and walking erect. Walking erect, while more efficacious, is rather painful. I procure it by means of pedals on which you mount and which set your legs in motion while you maintain your equilibrium by clinging to rings fastened to the wall. But here is an example of walking while seated."

The engineer had fallen back into a rocking armchair, and he placed his legs in the wooden legs with movable joints attached to this seat. His thighs, calves, and ankles were strapped down in such a way that he was unable to make any voluntary movement; then, the man with the tucked-up sleeves, seizing the handle, turned it round with all his strength. The armchair, at first, swayed to and fro like a hammock; then, suddenly, the patient's legs went out, stretching forward and bending back, advancing and returning, with extreme speed.

"He is running," said the doctor, who then gave the order: "Quietly! Go at a walking pace."

The man, turning the handle more slowly, caused the fat engineer to do the sitting walk in a more moderate fashion, which ludicrously distorted all the movements of his body.

Two other patients next made their appearance, both of them enormous, and followed also by two attendants with naked arms.

They were hoisted upon wooden horses, which, set in motion, began immediately to jump along the room, shaking their riders in an abominable manner.

"Gallop!" cried the doctor. And the artificial animals, rushing like waves and capsizing like ships, fatigued the two patients so much that they began to scream out together in a panting and pitiful tone:

"Enough! enough! I can't stand it any longer! Enough!"

The physician said in a tone of command: "Stop!" He then added: "Take breath for a little while. You will go on again in five minutes."

Paul Bretigny, who was choking with suppressed laughter, drew attention to the fact that the riders were not warm, while the handle-turners were perspiring.

"If you inverted the rôles," said he, "would it not be better?"

The doctor gravely replied: "Oh! not at all, my dear friend. We must not confound exercise and fatigue. The movement of the man who is turning the wheel is injurious, while the movement of the walker or the rider is beneficial."

But Paul noticed a lady's saddle.

"Yes," said the physician; "the evening is reserved for the other sex. The men are no longer admitted after twelve o'clock. Come, then, and look at the dry swimming."

A system of movable little boards screwed together at their ends and at their centers, stretched out in lozenge-shape or closing into squares, like that children's game which carries along soldiers who are spurred on, permitted three swimmers to be garroted and mangled at the same time.

The doctor said: "I need not extol to you the benefits of dry swimming, which does not moisten the body except by perspiration, and consequently does not expose our imaginary bather to any danger of rheumatism."

But a waiter, with a card in his hand, came to look for the doctor.

"The Duc de Ramas, my dear friend. I must leave you. Excuse me."

Paul, left there alone, turned round. The two cavaliers were trotting afresh. M. Aubry-Pasteur was walking still; and the three natives of Auvergne, with their arms all but broken and their backs cracking with thus shaking the patients on whom they were operating, were quite out of breath. They looked as if they were grinding coffee.

When he had reached the open air, Bretigny saw Doctor Honorat watching, along with his wife, the preparations for the fête. They began to chat, gazing at the flags which crowned the hill with a kind of halo.

"Is it at the church the procession is to be formed?" the physician asked his wife.

"It is at the church."

"At three o'clock?"

"At three o'clock."

"The professors will be there?"

"Yes, they will accompany the lady-sponsors."

The next persons to stop were the ladies Paille. Then, came the Monecus, father and daughter. But as he was going to breakfast alone with his friend Gontran at the Casino Café, he slowly made his way up to it. Paul, who had arrived the night before, had not had an interview with his comrade for the past month; and he was longing to tell him many boulevard stories—stories about gay women and houses of pleasure.

They remained chattering away till half past two when Petrus Martel came to inform them that people were on their way to the church.

"Let us go and look for Christiane," said Gontran.

"Let us go," returned Paul.

They found her standing on the steps of the new hotel. She had the hollow cheeks and the swarthy complexion of pregnant women; and her figure indicated a near accouchement.

"I was waiting for you," she said. "William is gone on before us. He has so many things to do to-day."

She cast toward Paul Bretigny a glance full of tenderness, and took his arm. They went quietly on their way, avoiding the stones.

She kept repeating: "How heavy I am! How heavy I am! I am no longer able to walk. I am so much afraid of falling!"

He did not reply, and carefully held her up, without seeking to meet her eyes which she turned toward him incessantly.

In front of the church, a dense crowd was awaiting them.

Andermatt cried: "At last! at last! Come, make haste. See, this is the order: two choir-boys, two chanters in surplices, the cross, the holy water, the priest, then Christiane with Professor Cloche, Mademoiselle Louise with Professor Remusot, and Mademoiselle Charlotte with Professor Mas-Roussel. Next come the members of the Board, the medical body, then the public. This is understood. Forward!"

The ecclesiastical staff thereupon left the church, taking their places at the head of the procession. Then a tall gentleman with white hair brushed back over his ears, the typical "scientist," in accordance with the academic form, approached Madame Andermatt, and saluted her with a low bow.

When he had straightened himself up again, with his head uncovered, in order to display his beautiful, scientific head, and his hat resting on his thigh with an imposing air as if he had learned to walk at the Comédie Française, and to show the people his rosette of officer of the Legion of Honor, too big for a modest man.

He began to talk: "Your husband, Madame, has been speaking to me about you just now, and about your condition which gives rise to some affectionate disquietude. He has told me about your doubts and your hesitations as to the probable moment of your delivery."

She reddened to the temples, and she murmured: "Yes, I believed that I would be a mother a very long time before the event. Now I can't tell either—I can't tell either——"

She faltered in a state of utter confusion.

A voice from behind them said: "This station has a very great future before it. I have already obtained surprising effects."

It was Professor Remusot addressing his companion, Louise Oriol. This gentleman was small, with yellow, unkempt hair, and a frock-coat badly cut, the dirty look of a slovenly savant.

Professor Mas-Roussel, who gave his arm to Charlotte Oriol, was a handsome physician, without beard or mustache, smiling, well-groomed, hardly turning gray as yet, a little fleshy, and, with his smooth, clean-shaven face, resembling neither a priest nor an actor, as was the case with Doctor Latonne.

Next came the members of the Board, with Andermatt at their head, and the tall hats of old Oriol and his son towering above them.

Behind them came another row of tall hats, the medical body of Enval, among whom Doctor Bonnefille was not included, his place, indeed, being taken by two new physicians, Doctor Black, a very short old man almost a dwarf, whose excessive piety had surprised the whole district since the day of his arrival; then a very good-looking young fellow, very much given to flirtation, and wearing a small hat, Doctor Mazelli, an Italian attached to the person of the Duc de Ramas—others said, to the person of the Duchesse.

And behind them could be seen the public, a flood of people—bathers, peasants, and inhabitants of the adjoining towns.

The ceremony of blessing the springs was very short. The Abbé Litre sprinkled them one after the other with holy water, which made Doctor Honorat say that he was going to give them new properties with chloride of sodium. Then all the persons specially invited entered the large reading-room, where a collation had been served.

Paul said to Gontran: "How pretty the little Oriol girls have become!"

"They are charming, my dear fellow."

"You have not seen M. le President?" suddenly inquired the ex-jailer overseer.

"Yes, he is over there, in the corner."

"Père Clovis is gathering a big crowd in front of the door."

Already, while moving in the direction of the springs for the purpose of having them blessed, the entire procession had filed off in front of the old invalid, cured the year before, and now again more paralyzed than ever. He would stop the visitors on the road and the last-comers as a matter of choice, in order to tell them his story:

"These waters here, you see, are no good—they cure, 'tis true, but you relapse again afterward, and after this relapse you're half a corpse. As for me, my legs were better before, and here I am now with my arms gone in consequence of the cure. And my legs, they're iron, but iron that you have to cut before it bends."

Andermatt, filled with vexation, had tried to prosecute him in a court of justice and to get him sent to jail for having depreciated the waters of Mont Oriol and having attempted extortion. But he had not succeeded in obtaining a conviction or in shutting the old fellow's mouth.

The moment he was informed that the old vagabond was babbling before the door of the establishment, he rushed out to make Clovis keep silent.

At the side of the highroad, in the center of an excited crowd, he heard angry voices. People pressed forward to listen and to see. Some ladies asked: "What is this?" Some men replied: "'Tis an invalid, whom the waters here have finished." Others believed that an infant had just been squashed. It was also said that a poor woman had got an attack of epilepsy.

Andermatt broke through the crowd, as he knew how to do, by violently pushing his little round stomach between the stomachs of other people. "It proves," Gontran remarked, "the superiority of balls to points."

Père Clovis, sitting on the ditch, whined about his pains, recounted his sufferings in a sniveling tone, while standing in front of him, and separating him from the public, the Oriols, father and son, exasperated, were hurling insults and threats at him as loudly as ever they could.

"That's not true," cried Colosse. "This fellow is a liar, a sham, a poacher, who runs all night through the wood."

But the old fellow, without getting excited, kept reiterating in a high, piercing voice which was heard above the vociferations of the two Oriols: "They've killed me, my good monchieus, they've killed me with their water. They bathed me in it by force last year. And here I am at this moment—here I am!"

Andermatt imposed silence on all, and stooping toward the impotent man, said to him, looking into the depths of his eyes: "If you are worse, it is your own fault, mind. If you listen to me, I undertake to cure you, I do, with fifteen or twenty baths at most. Come and look me up at the establishment in an hour, when the people have all gone away, my good father. In the meantime, hold your tongue."

The old fellow had understood. He became silent, then, after a pause, he answered: "I'm always willing to give it a fair trial. You'll see."

Andermatt caught the two Oriols by the arms and quickly dragged them away; while Père Clovis remained stretched on the grass between his crutches, at the side of the road, blinking his eyes under the rays of the sun.

The puzzled crowd kept pressing round him. Some gentlemen questioned him, but he did not reply, as though he had not heard or understood; and as this curiosity, futile just now, ended by fatiguing him, he began to sing, bareheaded, in a voice as false as it was shrill, an interminable ditty in an unintelligible dialect.

The crowd ebbed away gradually. Only a few children remained standing a long time in front of him, with their fingers in their noses, contemplating him.

Christiane, exceedingly tired, had gone in to take a rest. Paul and Gontran walked about through the new park in the midst of the visitors. Suddenly they saw the company of players, who had also deserted the old Casino, to attach themselves to the growing fortunes of the new.

Mademoiselle Odelin, who had become quite fashionable, was leaning as she walked on the arm of her mother, who had assumed an air of importance. M. Petitnivelle, of the Vaudeville, appeared very attentive to these ladies, who followed M. Lapalme of the Grand Theater of Bordeaux, arguing with the musicians just as of old, the maestro Saint Landri, the pianist Javel, the flautist Noirot, and the double-bass Nicordi.

On perceiving Paul and Gontran, Saint Landri rushed toward them. He had, during the winter, got a very small musical composition performed in a very small out-of-the-way theater; but the newspapers had spoken of him with a certain favor, and he now treated Massenet, Beyer, and Gounod contemptuously.

He stretched forth both hands with an outburst of friendly regard, and immediately proceeded to repeat what he had been saying to those gentlemen of the orchestra over whom he was the conductor.

"Yes, my dear friend, it is finished, finished, finished, the hackneyed style of the old school. The melodists have had their day. This is what people cannot understand. Music is a new art, melody is its first lisping. The ignorant ear loves the burden of a song. It takes a child's pleasure, a savage's pleasure in it. I may add that the ears of the people or of the ingenuous public, the simple ears, will always love little songs, airs, in a word. It is an amusement similar to that in which the frequenters of café concerts indulge. I am going to make use of a comparison in order to make myself understood. The eye of the rustic loves crude colors and glaring pictures; the eye of the intelligent representative of the middle class who is not artistic loves shades benevolently pretentious and affecting subjects; but the artistic eye, the refined eye, loves, understands, and distinguishes the imperceptible modulations of a single tone, the mysterious harmonies of light touches invisible to most people.

"It is the same with literature. Doorkeepers like romances of adventure, the middle class like novels which appeal to the feelings; while the real lovers of literature care only for the artistic books which are incomprehensible to the others. When an ordinary citizen talks music to me I feel a longing to kill him. And when it is at the opera, I ask him: 'Are you capable of telling me whether the third violin has made a false note in the overture of the third act? No. Then be silent. You have no ear. The man who does not understand, at the same time, the whole and all the instruments separately in an orchestra has no ear, and is no musician. There you are! Good night!'"

He turned round on his heel, and resumed: "For an artist all music is in a chord. Ah! my friend, certain chords madden me, cause a flood of inexpressible happiness to penetrate all my flesh. I have to-day an ear so well exercised, so finished, so matured, that I end by liking even certain false chords, just like a virtuoso whose fully-developed taste amounts to a form of depravity. I am beginning to be a vitiated person who seeks for extreme sensations of hearing. Yes, my friends, certain false notes. What delights! What perverse and profound delights! How this moves, how it shakes the nerves! how it scratches the ear—how it scratches! how it scratches!"

He rubbed his hands together rapturously, and he hummed: "You shall hear my opera—my opera—my opera. You shall hear my opera."

Gontran said: "You are composing an opera?"

"Yes, I have finished it." But the commanding voice of Petrus Martel resounded:

"You understand perfectly! A yellow rocket, and off you go!"

He was giving orders for the fireworks. They joined him, and he explained his arrangements by showing with his outstretched arm, as if he were threatening a hostile fleet, stakes of white wood on the mountain above the gorge, on the opposite side of the valley.

"It is over there that they are to be shot out. I told my pyrotechnist to be at his post at half past eight. The very moment the spectacle is over, I will give the signal from here by a yellow rocket, and then he will illuminate the opening piece."

The Marquis made his appearance: "I am going to drink a glass of water," he said.

Paul and Gontran accompanied him, and again descended the hill. On reaching the establishment, they saw Père Clovis, who had got there, sustained by the two Oriols, followed by Andermatt and by the doctor, and making, every time he trailed his legs on the ground, contortions suggestive of extreme pain.

"Let us go in," said Gontran, "this will be funny."

The paralytic was placed sitting in an armchair. Then Andermatt said to him: "Here is what I propose, old cheat that you are. You are going to be cured immediately by taking two baths a day. And the moment you walk you'll have two hundred francs."

The paralytic began to groan: "My legs, they are iron, my good Monchieu!"

Andermatt made him hold his tongue, and went on: "Now, listen! You shall again have two hundred francs every year up to the time of your death—you understand—up to the time of your death, if you continue to experience the salutary effect of our waters."

The old fellow was in a state of perplexity. The continuous cure was opposed to his plan of action. He asked in a hesitating tone: "But when—when it is closed up—this box of yours—if this should take hold of me again—I can do nothing then—I—seeing that it will be shut up—your water——"

Doctor Latonne interrupted him, and, turning toward Andermatt, said: "Excellent! excellent! We'll cure him every year. This will be even better, and will show the necessity of annual treatment, the indispensability of returning hither. Excellent—this is perfectly clear!"

But the old man repeated afresh: "It will not suit this time, my good Monchieu. My legs, they're iron, iron in bars."

A new idea sprang up in the doctor's mind: "If I got him to try a course of seated walking," he said, "I might hasten the effect of the waters considerably. It is an experiment worth trying."

"Excellent idea," returned Andermatt, adding: "Now, Père Clovis, take yourself off, and don't forget our agreement."

The old fellow went away still groaning; and, when evening came on, all the directors of Mont Oriol came back to dine, for the theatrical representation was announced to take place at half past seven.

The great hall of the new Casino was the place where they were to dine. It was capable of holding a thousand persons.

At seven o'clock the visitors who had not numbered seats presented themselves. At half past seven the hall was filled, and the curtain was raised for the performance of a vaudeville in two acts, which preceded Saint Landri's operetta, interpreted by vocalists from Vichy, who had given their services for the occasion.

Christiane in the front row, between her brother and her husband, suffered a great deal from the heat. Every moment she repeated: "I feel quite exhausted! I feel quite exhausted!"

After the vaudeville, as the operetta was opening, she was becoming ill, and turning round to her husband, said: "My dear Will, I shall have to leave. I am suffocating!"

The banker was annoyed. He was desirous above everything in the world that this fête should be a success, from start to finish, without a single hitch. He replied:

"Make every effort to hold out. I beg of you to do so! Your departure would upset everything. You would have to pass through the entire hall!"

But Gontran, who was sitting along with Paul behind her, had overheard. He leaned toward his sister: "You are too warm?" said he.

"Yes, I am suffocating."

"Good. Stay! You are going to have a laugh."

There was a window near. He slipped toward it, got upon a chair, and jumped out without attracting hardly any notice. Then he entered the café, which was perfectly empty, stretched his hand out under the bar where he had seen Petrus Martel conceal the signal-rocket, and, having filched it, he ran off to hide himself under a group of trees, and then set it on fire. The swift yellow sheaf flew up toward the clouds, describing a curve, and casting across the sky a long shower of flame-drops. Almost instantaneously a terrible detonation burst forth over the neighboring mountain, and a cluster of stars sent flying sparks through the darkness of the night.

Somebody exclaimed in the hall where the spectators were gathered, and where at the moment Saint Landri's chords were quivering: "They're letting off the fireworks!"

The spectators who were nearest to the door abruptly rose to their feet to make sure about it, and went out with light steps. All the rest turned their eyes toward the windows, but saw nothing, for they were looking at the Limagne. People kept asking: "Is it true? Is it true?"

The impatient assembly got excited, hungering above everything for simple amusements. A voice from outside announced: "It is true! The firework's are let off!"

Then, in a second everyone in the hall was standing up. They rushed toward the door; they jostled against each other; they yelled at those who obstructed their egress: "Hurry on! hurry on!"

The entire audience, in a short time, had emerged into the park. Saint Landri alone, in a state of exasperation continued beating time in front of his distracted orchestra. Meanwhile, fiery suns succeeded Roman candles in the midst of detonations.

Suddenly, a formidable voice sent forth thrice this wild exclamation: "Stop, in God's name! Stop, in God's name! Stop, in God's name!"

And, as an immense Bengal fire next illuminated the mountain and lighted up in red to the right and blue to the left, the enormous rocks and trees, Petrus Martel could be seen standing on one of the vases of imitation marble that decorated the terrace of the Casino, bareheaded, with his arms in the air, gesticulating and howling.

Then, the great illumination being extinguished, nothing could be seen any longer save the real stars. But immediately another rocket shot up, and Petrus Martel, jumping on the ground, exclaimed: "What a disaster! what a disaster! My God, what a disaster!"

And he passed through the crowd with tragic gestures, with blows of his fist in the empty air, furious stampings of his feet, always repeating: "What a disaster! My God, what a disaster!"

Christiane had taken Paul's arm to get a seat in the open air, and kept looking with delight at the rockets which ascended into the sky.

Her brother came up to her suddenly, and said: "Hey, is it a success? Do you think it is funny?"

She murmured: "What, it is you?"

"Why, yes, it is I. Is it good, hey?"

She began to laugh, finding it really amusing. But Andermatt arrived in a state of great mental distress. He did not understand how such a blow could have come. The rocket had been stolen from the bar to give the signal agreed upon. Such an infamy could only have been perpetrated by some emissary of the old Company, some agent of Doctor Bonnefille!

And he repeated: "'Tis maddening, positively maddening. Here are fireworks worth two thousand three hundred francs destroyed, entirely destroyed!"

Gontran replied: "No, my dear fellow, on a proper calculation, the loss does not mount up to more than a quarter; let us put it at a third, if you like; say seven hundred and sixty-six francs. Your guests will, therefore, have enjoyed fifteen hundred and thirty-four francs' worth of rockets. This truly is not bad."

The banker's anger turned against his brother-in-law. He caught him roughly by the arm: "Gontran, I want to talk seriously to you. Since I have a hold of you, let us take a turn in the walks. Besides, I have five minutes to spare."

Then, turning toward Christiane: "I place you in charge of our friend Bretigny, my dear; but don't remain a long time out—take care of yourself. You might catch cold, you know. Be careful! be careful!"

She murmured: "Never fear, dear."

So Andermatt carried off Gontran. When they were alone, at a little distance from the crowd, the banker stopped: "My dear fellow, 'tis about your financial position that I want to talk."

"About my financial position?"

"Yes, you know it well, your financial position."

"No. But you ought to know it for me, since you lent money to me."

"Well, yes, I do know it, and 'tis for that reason I want to talk to you."

"It seems to me, to say the least of it, that the moment is ill chosen—in the midst of a display of fireworks!"

"The moment, on the contrary, is very well chosen. I am not talking to you in the midst of a display of fireworks, but before a ball."

"Before a ball? I don't understand."

"Well, you are going to understand. Here is your position: you have nothing except debts; and you'll never have anything but debts."

Gontran gravely replied: "You tell me that a little bluntly."

"Yes, because it is necessary. Listen to me! You have eaten up the share which came to you as a fortune from your mother. Let us say no more about that."

"Let us say no more about it."

"As for your father, he possesses a yearly income of thirty thousand francs, say, a capital of about eight hundred thousand francs. Your share, later on, will, therefore, be four hundred thousand francs. Now you owe me—me, personally—one hundred and ninety thousand francs. You owe money besides to usurers."

Gontran muttered in a haughty tone: "Say, to Jews."

"Be it so, to Jews, although among the number there is a churchwarden from Saint Sulpice who made use of a priest as an intermediary between himself and you—but I will not cavil about such trifles. You owe, then, to various usurers, Israelites or Catholics, nearly as much. Let us put it at a hundred and fifty thousand at the lowest estimate. This makes a total of three hundred and forty thousand francs, on which you are paying interest, always borrowing, except with regard to mine, which you do not pay."

"That's right," said Gontran.

"So then, you have nothing more left."

"Nothing, indeed—except my brother-in-law."

"Except your brother-in-law, who has had enough of lending money to you."

"What then?"

"What then, my dear fellow? The poorest peasant living in one of these huts is richer than you."

"Exactly and next?"

"Next—next—? If your father were to die tomorrow, you would no longer have any resource to get bread—to get bread, mind you—except to take a post as a clerk in my house. And this again would only be a means of disguising the pension which I should be allowing you."

Gontran, in a tone of irritation, said: "My dear William, these things bore me. I know them, besides, just as well as you do, and, I repeat, the moment is ill chosen to remind me about them—with—with so little diplomacy."

"Allow me, let me finish. You can only extricate yourself from it by a marriage. Now, you are a wretched match, in spite of your name, which sounds well without being illustrious. In short, it is not one of those which an heiress, even a Jewish one, buys with a fortune. Therefore, we must find you a wife acceptable and rich—which is not very easy——"

Gontran interrupted him: "Give her name at once—that is the best way."

"Be it so—one of Père Oriol's daughters, whichever you prefer. And this is why I wanted to talk to you before the ball."

"And now explain yourself at greater length," returned Gontran, coldly.

"It is very simple. You see the success I have obtained at the start with this station. Now if I had in my hands, or rather if we had in our hands all the land which this cunning peasant has kept for himself, I could turn it into gold. To speak only of the vineyards which lie between the establishment and the hotel and between the hotel and the Casino, I would pay a million francs for them to-morrow—I, Andermatt. Now, these vineyards and others all round the knoll will be the dowries of these girls. The father told me so again a short time since, not without an object, perhaps. Well, if you were willing, we could do a big stroke of business there, the two of us."

Gontran muttered, with a thoughtful air: "'Tis possible. I'll think over it."

"Do think over it, my dear boy, and don't forget that I never speak of things that are not very sure, or without having given matters every consideration, and realized all the possible consequences and all the decided advantages."

But Gontran, lifting up his arm, as if he had suddenly forgotten all that his brother-in-law had been saying to him: "Look! How beautiful that is!"

The bunch of rockets flamed up, in imitation of a burning palace on which a blazing flag had inscribed on it "Mont Oriol" in letters of fire perfectly red and, right opposite to it, above the plain, the moon, red also, seemed to have come out to contemplate this spectacle. Then, when the palace, after it had been burning for some minutes, exploded like a ship which is blown up, flinging toward the wide heavens fantastic stars which burst in their turn, the moon remained all alone, calm and round, on the horizon.

The public applauded wildly, exclaiming: "Hurrah! Bravo! bravo!"

Andermatt, all of a sudden, said: "Let us go and open the ball, my dear boy. Are you willing to dance the first quadrille face to face with me?"

"Why, certainly, my dear brother-in-law."

"Who have you thought of asking to dance with you? As for me, I have bespoken the Duchesse de Ramas."

Gontran answered in a tone of indifference: "I will ask Charlotte Oriol."

They reascended. As they passed in front of the spot where Christiane was resting with Paul Bretigny, they did not notice the pair. William murmured: "She has followed my advice. She went home to go to bed. She was quite tired out to-day." And he advanced toward the ballroom which the attendants had been getting ready during the fireworks.

But Christiane had not returned to her room, as her husband supposed. As soon as she realized that she was alone with Paul she said to him in a very low tone, while she pressed his hand:

"So then you came. I was waiting for you for the past month. Every morning I kept asking myself, 'Shall I see him to-day?' and every night I kept saying to myself, 'It will be to-morrow then.' Why have you delayed so long, my love?"

He replied with some embarrassment: "I had matters to engage my attention—business."

She leaned toward him, murmuring: "It was not right to leave me here alone with them, especially in my state."

He moved his chair a little away from her.

"Be careful! We might be seen. These rockets light up the whole country around."

She scarcely bestowed a thought on it; she said: "I love you so much!" Then, with sudden starts of joy: "Ah! how happy I feel, how happy I feel at finding that we are once more together, here! Are you thinking about it? What joy, Paul! How we are going to love one another again!"

She sighed, and her voice was so weak that it seemed a mere breath.

"I feel a foolish longing to embrace you, but it is foolish—there!—foolish. It is such a long time since I saw you!"

Then, suddenly, with the fierce energy of an impassioned woman, to whom everything should give way: "Listen! I want—you understand—I want to go with you immediately to the place where we said adieu to one another last year! You remember well, on the road from La Roche Pradière?"

He replied, stupefied: "But this is senseless! You cannot walk farther. You have been standing all day. This is senseless; I will not allow it."

She had risen to her feet, and she said: "I am determined on it! If you do not accompany me, I'll go alone!"

And pointing out to him the moon which had risen: "See here! It was an evening just like this! Do you remember how you kissed my shadow?"

He held her back: "Christiane—listen—this is ridiculous—Christiane!"

She did not reply, and walked toward the descent leading to the vineyards. He knew that calm will which nothing could divert from its purpose, the graceful obstinacy of these blue eyes, of that little forehead of a fair woman that could not be stopped; and he took her arm to sustain her on her way.

"Supposing we are seen, Christiane?"

"You did not say that to me last year. And then, everyone is at the fête. We'll be back before our absence can be noticed."

It was soon necessary to ascend by the stony path. She panted, leaning with her whole weight on him, and at every step she said:

"It is good, it is good, to suffer thus!"

He stopped, wishing to bring her back. But she would not listen to him.

"No, no. I am happy. You don't understand this, you. Listen! I feel it leaping in me—our child—your child—what happiness. Give me your hand."

She did not realize that he—this man—was one of the race of lovers who are not of the race of fathers. Since he discovered that she was pregnant, he kept away from her, and was disgusted with her, in spite of himself. He had often in bygone days said that a woman who has performed the function of reproduction is no longer worthy of love. What raised him to a high pitch of tenderness was that soaring of two hearts toward an inaccessible ideal, that entwining of two souls which are immaterial—all those artificial and unreal elements which poets have associated with this passion. In the physical woman he adored the Venus whose sacred side must always preserve the pure form of sterility. The idea of a little creature which owed its birth to him, a human larva stirring in that body defiled by it and already grown ugly, inspired him with an almost unconquerable repugnance. Maternity had made this woman a brute. She was no longer the exceptional being adored and dreamed about, but the animal that reproduces its species. And even a material disgust was mingled in him with these loathings of his mind.

How could she have felt or divined this—she whom each movement of the child she yearned for attached the more closely to her lover? This man whom she adored, whom she had every day loved a little more since the moment of their first kiss, had not only penetrated to the bottom of her heart, but had given her the proof that he had also entered into the very depths of her flesh, that he had sown his own life there, that he was going to come forth from her, again becoming quite small. Yes, she carried him there under her crossed hands, himself, her good, her dear, her tenderly beloved one, springing up again in her womb by the mystery of nature. And she loved him doubly, now that she had him in two forms—the big, and the little one as yet unknown, the one whom she saw, touched, embraced, and could hear speaking to her, and the one whom she could up to this only feel stirring under her skin. They had by this time reached the road.

"You were waiting for me over there that evening," said she. And she held her lips out to him.

He kissed them, without replying, with a cold kiss.

She murmured for the second time: "Do you remember how you embraced me on the ground. We were like this—look!"

And in the hope that he would begin it all over again she commenced running to get some distance away from him. Then she stopped, out of breath, and waited, standing in the middle of the road. But the moon, which lengthened out her profile on the ground, traced there the protuberance of her swollen figure. And Paul, beholding at his feet the shadow of her pregnancy, remained unmoved at sight of it, wounded in his poetic sense with shame, exasperated that she was not able to share his feelings or divine his thoughts, that she had not sufficient coquetry, tact, and feminine delicacy to understand all the shade which give such a different complexion to circumstances; and he said to her with impatience in his voice:

"Look here, Christiane! This child's play is ridiculous."

She came back to him moved, saddened, with outstretched arms, and, flinging herself on his breast:

"Ah! you love me less. I feel it! I am sure of it!"

He took pity on her, and, encircling her head with his arms, he imprinted two long sweet kisses on her eyes.

Then in silence they retraced their steps. He could find nothing to say to her; and, as she leaned on him, exhausted by fatigue, he quickened his pace so that he might no longer feel against his side the touch of this enlarged figure. When they were near the hotel, they separated, and she went up to her own apartment.

The orchestra at the Casino was playing dance-music; and Paul went to look at the ball. It was a waltz; and they were all waltzing—Doctor Latonne with the younger Madame Paille, Andermatt with Louise Oriol, handsome Doctor Mazelli with the Duchesse de Ramas, and Gontran with Charlotte Oriol. He was whispering in her ear in that tender fashion which denotes a courtship begun; and she was smiling behind her fan, blushing, and apparently delighted.

Paul heard a voice saying behind him: "Look here! look here at M. de Ravenel whispering gallantries to my fair patient."

He added, after a pause: "And there is a pearl, good, gay, simple, devoted, upright, you know, an excellent creature. She is worth ten of the elder sister. I have known them since their childhood—these little girls. And yet the father prefers the elder one, because she is more—more like him—more of a peasant—less upright—more thrifty—more cunning—and more—more jealous. Ah! she is a good girl, all the same. I would not like to say anything bad of her; but, in spite of myself, I compare them, you understand—and, after having compared them, I judge them—there you are!"

The waltz was coming to an end; Gontran went to join his friend, and, perceiving the doctor:

"Ah! tell me now—there appears to me to be a remarkable increase in the medical body at Enval. We have a Doctor Mazelli who waltzes to perfection and an old little Doctor Black who seems on very good terms with Heaven."

But Doctor Honorat was discreet. He did not like to sit in judgment on his professional brethren.

CHAPTER X.

GONTRAN'S CHOICE

The burning question now was that of the physicians at Enval. They had suddenly made themselves the masters of the district, and absorbed all the attention and all the enthusiasm of the inhabitants. Formerly the springs flowed under the authority of Doctor Bonnefille alone, in the midst of the harmless animosities of restless Doctor Latonne and placid Doctor Honorat.

Now, it was a very different thing. Since the success planned during the winter by Andermatt had quite taken definite shape, thanks to the powerful co-operation of Professors Cloche, Mas-Roussel, and Remusot, who had each brought there a contingent of two or three hundred patients at least, Doctor Latonne, inspector of the new establishment, had become a big personage, specially patronized by Professor Mas-Roussel, whose pupil he had been, and whose deportment and gestures he imitated.

Doctor Bonnefille was scarcely ever talked about any longer. Furious, exasperated, railing against Mont Oriol, the old physician remained the whole day in the old establishment with a few old patients who had kept faithful to him.

In the minds of some invalids, indeed, he was the only person that understood the true properties of the waters; he possessed, so to speak, their secret, since he had officially administered them from the time the station was first established.

Doctor Honorat barely managed to retain his practice among the natives of Auvergne. With the moderate income he derived from this source he contented himself, keeping on good terms with everybody, and consoled himself by much preferring cards and wine to medicine. He did not, however, go quite so far as to love his professional brethren.

Doctor Latonne would, therefore, have continued to be the great soothsayer of Mont Oriol, if one morning there had not appeared a very small man, nearly a dwarf, whose big head sunk between his shoulders, big round eyes, and big hands combined to produce a very odd-looking individual. This new physician, M. Black, introduced into the district by Professor Remusot immediately excited attention by his excessive devotion. Nearly every morning, between two visits, he went into a church for a few minutes, and he received communion nearly every Sunday. The curé soon got him some patients, old maids, poor people whom he attended for nothing, pious ladies who asked the advice of their spiritual director before calling on a man of science, whose sentiments, reserve, and professional modesty, they wished to know before everything else.

Then, one day, the arrival of the Princess de Maldebourg, an old German Highness, was announced—a very fervent Catholic, who on the very evening when she first appeared in the district, sent for Doctor Black on the recommendation of a Roman cardinal. From that moment he was the fashion. It was good taste, good form, the correct thing, to be attended by him. He was the only doctor, it was said, who was a perfect gentleman—the only one in whom a woman could repose absolute confidence.

And from morning till evening this little man with the bulldog's head, who always spoke in a subdued tone in every corner with everybody, might be seen rushing from one hotel to the other. He appeared to have important secrets to confide or to receive, for he could constantly be met holding long mysterious conferences in the lobbies with the masters of the hotels, with his patients' chambermaids, with anyone who was brought into contact with the invalids. As soon as he saw any lady of his acquaintance in the street, he went straight up to her with his short, quick step, and immediately began to mumble fresh and minute directions, after the fashion of a priest at confession.

The old women especially adored him. He would listen to their stories to the end without interrupting them, took note of all their observations, all their questions, and all their wishes.

He increased or diminished each day the proportion of water to be consumed by his patients, which made them feel perfect confidence in the care taken of them by him.

"We stopped yesterday at two glasses and three-quarters," he would say; "well, to-day we shall only take two glasses and a half, and to-morrow three glasses. Don't forget! To-morrow, three glasses. I am very, very particular about it!"

And all the patients were convinced that he was very particular about it, indeed.

In order not to forget these figures and fractions of figures, he wrote them down in a memorandum-book, in order that he might never make a mistake. For the patient does not pardon a mistake of a single half-glass. He regulated and modified with equal minuteness the duration of the daily baths in virtue of principles known only to himself.

Doctor Latonne, jealous and exasperated, disdainfully shrugged his shoulders, and declared: "This is a swindler!" His hatred against Doctor Black had even led him occasionally to run down the mineral waters. "Since we can scarcely tell how they act, it is quite impossible to prescribe every day modifications of the dose, which any therapeutic law cannot regulate. Proceedings of this kind do the greatest injury to medicine."

Doctor Honorat contented himself with smiling. He always took care to forget, five minutes after a consultation, the number of glasses which he had ordered. "Two more or less," said he to Gontran in his hours of gaiety, "there is only the spring to take notice of it; and yet this scarcely incommodes it!" The only wicked pleasantry that he permitted himself on his religious brother-physician consisted in describing him as "the doctor of the Holy Sitting-Bath." His jealousy was of the prudent, sly, and tranquil kind.

He added sometimes: "Oh, as for him, he knows the patient thoroughly; and this is often better than to know the disease!"

But lo! there arrived one morning at the hotel of Mont Oriol a noble Spanish family, the Duke and Duchess of Ramas-Aldavarra, who brought with her her own physician, an Italian, Doctor Mazelli from Milan. He was a man of thirty, a tall, thin, very handsome young fellow, wearing only mustaches. From the first evening, he made a conquest of the table d'hôte, for the Duke, a melancholy man, attacked with monstrous obesity, had a horror of isolation, and desired to take his meals in the same dining-room as the other patients. Doctor Mazelli already knew by their names almost all the frequenters of the hotel; he had a kindly word for every man, a compliment for every woman, a smile even for every servant.

Placed at the right-hand side of the Duchess, a beautiful woman of between thirty-five and forty, with a pale complexion, black eyes, blue-black hair, he would say to her as each dish came round:

"Very little," or else, "No, not this," or else, "Yes, take some of that." And he would himself pour out the liquid which she was to drink with very great care, measuring exactly the proportions of wine and water which he mingled.

He also regulated the Duke's food, but with visible carelessness. The patient, however, took no heed of his advice, devoured everything with bestial voracity, drank at every meal two decanters of pure wine, then went tumbling about in a chaise for air in front of the hotel, and began whining with pain and groaning over his bad digestion.

After the first dinner, Doctor Mazelli, who had judged and weighed all around him with a single glance, went to join Gontran, who was smoking a cigar on the terrace of the Casino, told his name, and began to chat. At the end of an hour, they were on intimate terms. Next day, he got himself introduced to Christiane just as she was leaving the bath, won her good-will after ten minutes' conversation, and brought her that very day into contact with the Duchess, who no longer cared for solitude.

He kept watch over everything in the abode of the Spaniards, gave excellent advice to the chef about cooking, excellent hints to the chambermaid on the hygiene of the head in order to preserve in her mistress's hair its luster, its superb shade, and its abundance, very useful information to the coachman about veterinary medicine; and he knew how to make the hours swift and light, to invent distractions, and to pick up in the hotels casual acquaintances but always prudently chosen.

The Duchess said to Christiane, when speaking of him: "He is a wonderful man, dear Madame. He knows everything; he does everything. It is to him that I owe my figure."

"How, your figure?"

"Yes, I was beginning to grow fat, and he saved me with his regimen and his liqueurs."

Moreover, Mazelli knew how to make medicine itself interesting; he spoke about it with such ease, with such gaiety, and with a sort of light scepticism which helped to convince his listeners of his superiority.

"'Tis very simple," said he; "I don't believe in remedies—or rather I hardly believe in them. The old-fashioned medicine started with this principle—that there is a remedy for everything. God, they believe, in His divine bounty, has created drugs for all maladies, only He has left to men, through malice, perhaps, the trouble of discovering these drugs. Now, men have discovered an incalculable number of them without ever knowing exactly what disease each of them is suited for. In reality there are no remedies; there are only maladies. When a malady declares itself, it is necessary to interrupt its course, according to some, to precipitate it, according to others, by some means or another. Each school extols its own method. In the same case, we see the most antagonistic systems employed, and the most opposed kinds of medicine—ice by one and extreme heat by the other, dieting by this doctor and forced nourishment by that. I am not speaking of the innumerable poisonous products extracted from minerals or vegetables, which chemistry procures for us. All this acts, 'tis true, but nobody knows how. Sometimes it succeeds, and sometimes it kills."

And, with much liveliness, he pointed out the impossibility of certainty, the absence of all scientific basis as long as organic chemistry, biological chemistry had not become the starting-point of a new medicine. He related anecdotes, monstrous errors of the greatest physicians, and proved the insanity and the falsity of their pretended science.

"Make the body discharge its functions," said he. "Make the skin, the muscles, all the organs, and, above all, the stomach, which is the foster-father of the entire machine, its regulator and life-warehouse, discharge their functions."

He asserted that, if he liked, by nothing save regimen, he could make people gay or sad, capable of physical work or intellectual work, according to the nature of the diet which he imposed on them. He could even act on the faculties of the brain, on the memory, the imagination, on all the manifestations of intelligence. And he ended jocosely with these words:

"For my part, I nurse my patients with massage and curaçoa."

He attributed marvelous results to massage, and spoke of the Dutchman Hamstrang as of a god performing miracles. Then, showing his delicate white hands:

"With those, you might resuscitate the dead."

And the Duchess added: "The fact is that he performs massage to perfection."

He also lauded alcoholic beverages, in small proportions to excite the stomach at certain moments; and he composed mixtures, cleverly prepared, which the Duchess had to drink, at fixed hours, either before or after her meals.

He might have been seen each morning entering the Casino Café about half past nine and asking for his bottles. They were brought to him fastened with little silver locks of which he had the key. He would pour out a little of one, a little of another, slowly into a very pretty blue glass, which a very correct footman held up respectfully.

Then the doctor would give directions: "See! Bring this to the Duchess in her bath, to drink it, before she dresses herself, when coming out of the water."

And when anyone asked him through curiosity: "What have you put into it?" he would answer: "Nothing but refined aniseed-cordial, very pure curaçoa, and excellent bitters."

This handsome doctor, in a few days, became the center of attraction for all the invalids. And every sort of device was resorted to, in order to attract a few opinions from him.

When he was passing along through the walks in the park, at the hour of promenade, one heard nothing but that exclamation of "Doctor" on all the chairs where sat the beautiful women, the young women, who were resting themselves a little between two glasses of the Christiane Spring. Then, when he stopped with a smile on his lip, they would draw him aside for some minutes into the little path beside the river. At first, they talked about one thing or another; then discreetly, skillfully, coquettishly, they came to the question of health, but in an indifferent fashion as if they were touching on sundry topics.

For this medical man was not at the disposal of the public. He was not paid by them, and people could not get him to visit them at their own houses. He belonged to the Duchess, only to the Duchess. This situation even stimulated people's efforts, and provoked their desires. And, as it was whispered positively that the Duchess was jealous, very jealous, there was a desperate struggle between all these ladies to get advice from the handsome Italian doctor. He gave it without forcing them to entreat him very strenuously.

Then, among the women whom he had favored with his advice arose an interchange of intimate confidences, in order to give clear proof of his solicitude.

"Oh! my dear, he asked me questions—but such questions!"

"Very indiscreet?"

"Oh! indiscreet! Say frightful. I actually did not know what answers to give him. He wanted to know things—but such things!"

"It was the same way with me. He questioned me a great deal about my husband!"

"And me, also—together with details so—so personal! These questions are very embarrassing. However, we understand perfectly well that it is necessary to ask them."

"Oh! of course. Health depends on these minute details. As for me, he promised to perform massage on me at Paris this winter. I have great need of it to supplement the treatment here."

"Tell me, my dear, what do you intend to do in return? He cannot take fees."

"Good heavens! my idea was to present him with a scarf-pin. He must be fond of them, for he has already two or three very nice ones."

"Oh! how you embarrass me! The same notion was in my head. In that case I'll give him a ring."

And they concocted surprises in order to please him, thought of ingenious presents in order to touch him, graceful pleasantries in order to fascinate him. He became the "talk of the day," the great subject of conversation, the sole object of public attention, till the news spread that Count Gontran de Ravenel was paying his addresses to Charlotte Oriol with a view to marrying her. And this at once led to a fresh outburst of deafening clamor in Enval.

Since the evening when he had opened with her the inaugural ball at the Casino, Gontran had tied himself to the young girl's skirts. He publicly showed her all those little attentions of men who want to please without hiding their object; and their ordinary relations assumed at the same time a character of gallantry, playful and natural, which seemed likely to lead to love.

They saw one another nearly every day, for the two girls had conceived feelings of strong friendship toward Christiane, into which, no doubt, there entered a considerable element of gratified vanity. Gontran suddenly showed a disposition to remain constantly at his sister's side; and he began to organize parties for the morning and entertainments for the evening, which greatly astonished Christiane and Paul. Then they noticed that he was devoting himself to Charlotte; he gaily teased her, paid her compliments without appearing to do so, and manifested toward her in a thousand ways that tender care which tends to unite two beings in bonds of affection. The young girl, already accustomed to the free and familiar manners of this gay Parisian youth, did not at first see anything remarkable in these attentions; and, abandoning herself to the impulses of her honest and confiding heart, she began to laugh and enjoy herself with him as she might have done with a brother.

Now, she had returned home with her elder sister, after an evening party at which Gontran had several times attempted to kiss her in consequence of forfeits due by her in a game of "fly-pigeon," when Louise, who had appeared anxious and nervous for some time past, said to her in an abrupt tone:

"You would do well to be a little careful about your deportment. M. Gontran is not a suitable companion for you."

"Not a suitable companion? What has he done?"

"You know well what I mean—don't play the ninny! In the way you're going on, you would soon compromise yourself; and if you don't know how to watch over your conduct, it is my business to see after it."

Charlotte, confused, and filled with shame, faltered: "But I don't know—I assure you—I have seen nothing——"

Her sister sharply interrupted her: "Listen! Things must not go on this way. If he wants to marry you, it is for papa—for papa to consider the matter and to give an answer; but, if he only wants to trifle with you, he must desist at once!"

Then, suddenly, Charlotte got annoyed without knowing why or with what. She was indignant at her sister having taken it on herself to direct her actions and to reprimand her; and, in a trembling voice, and with tears in her eyes, she told her that she should not have interfered in what did not concern her. She stammered in her exasperation, divining by a vague but unerring instinct the jealousy that had been aroused in the embittered heart of Louise.

They parted without embracing one another, and Charlotte wept when she got into bed, as she thought over things that she had never foreseen or suspected.

Gradually her tears ceased to flow, and she began to reflect. It was true, nevertheless, that Gontran's demeanor toward her had altered. She had enjoyed his acquaintance hitherto without understanding him. She understood him now. At every turn he kept repeating to her pretty compliments full of delicate flattery. On one occasion he had kissed her hand. What were his intentions? She pleased him, but to what extent? Was it possible by any chance that he desired to marry her? And all at once she imagined that she could hear somewhere in the air, in the silent night through whose empty spaces her dreams were flitting, a voice exclaiming, "Comtesse de Ravenel."

The emotion was so vivid that she sat up in the bed; then, with her naked feet, she felt for her slippers under the chair over which she had thrown her clothes, and she went to open the window without consciousness of what she was doing, in order to find space for her hopes. She could hear what they were saying in the room below stairs, and Colosse's voice was raised: "Let it alone! let it alone! There will be time enough to see to it. Father will arrange that. There is no harm up to this. 'Tis father that will do the thing."

She noticed that the window in front of the house, just below that at which she was standing, was still lighted up. She asked herself: "Who is there now? What are they talking about?" A shadow passed over the luminous wall. It was her sister. So then, she had not yet gone to bed. Why? But the light was presently extinguished; and Charlotte began to think about other things that were agitating her heart.

She could not go to sleep now. Did he love her? Oh! no; not yet. But he might love her, since she had caught his fancy. And if he came to love her much, desperately, as people love in society, he would certainly marry her.

Born in a house of vinedressers, she had preserved, although educated in the young ladies' convent at Clermont, the modesty and humility of a peasant girl. She used to think that she might marry a notary, perhaps, or a barrister or a doctor; but the ambition to become a real lady of high social position, with a title of nobility attached to her name had never entered her mind. Even when she had just finished the perusal of some love-story, and was musing over the glimpse presented to her of such a charming prospect for a few minutes, it would speedily Vanish from her soul just as chimeras vanish. Now, here was this unforeseen, inconceivable thing, which had been suddenly conjured up by some words of her sister, apparently drawing near her after the fashion of a ship's sail driven onward by the wind.

Every time she drew breath, she kept repeating with her lips: "Comtesse de Ravenel." And the shades of her dark eyelashes, as they closed in the night, were illuminated with visions. She saw beautiful drawing-rooms brilliantly lighted up, beautiful women greeting her with smiles, beautiful carriages waiting before the steps of a château, and grand servants in livery bowing as she passed.

She felt heated in her bed; her heart was beating. She rose up a second time in order to drink a glass of water, and to remain standing in her bare feet for a few moments on the cold floor of her apartment.

Then, somewhat calmed, she ended by falling asleep. But she awakened at dawn, so much had the agitation of her heart passed into her veins.

She felt ashamed of her little room with its white walls, washed with water by a rustic glazier, her poor cotton curtains, and some straw-chairs which never quitted their place at the two corners of her chest of drawers.

She realized that she was a peasant in the midst of these rude articles of furniture which bespoke her origin. She felt herself lowly, unworthy of this handsome, mocking young fellow, whose fair hair and laughing face had floated before her eyes, had disappeared from her vision and then come back, had gradually engrossed her thoughts, and had already found a place in her heart.

Then she jumped out of bed and ran to look for her glass, her little toilette-glass, as large as the center of a plate; after that, she got into bed again, her mirror between her hands; and she looked at her face surrounded by her hair which hung loose on the white background of the pillow.

Presently she laid down on the bedclothes the little piece of glass which reflected her lineaments, and she thought how difficult it would be for such an alliance to take place, so great was the distance between them. Thereupon a feeling of vexation seized her by the throat. But immediately afterward she gazed at her image, once more smiling at herself in order to look nice, and, as she considered herself pretty, the difficulties disappeared.

When she went down to breakfast, her sister, who wore a look of irritation, asked her:

"What do you propose to do to-day?"

Charlotte replied unhesitatingly: "Are we not going in the carriage to Royat with Madame Andermatt?"

Louise returned: "You are going alone, then; but you might do something better, after what I said to you last night."

The younger sister interrupted her: "I don't ask for your advice—mind your own business!"

And they did not speak to one another again.

Père Oriol and Jacques came in, and took their seats at the table. The old man asked almost immediately: "What are you doing to-day, girls?"

Charlotte said without giving her sister time to answer: "As for me, I am going to Royat with Madame Andermatt."

The two men eyed her with an air of satisfaction; and the father muttered with that engaging smile which he could put on when discussing any business of a profitable character: "That's good! that's good!"

She was more surprised at this secret complacency which she observed in their entire bearing than at the visible anger of Louise; and she asked herself, in a somewhat disturbed frame of mind: "Can they have been talking this over all together?"

As soon as the meal was over, she went up again to her room, put on her hat, seized her parasol, threw a light cloak over her arm, and she went off in the direction of the hotel, for they were to start at half past one.

Christiane expressed her astonishment at finding that Louise had not come.

Charlotte felt herself flushing as she replied: "She is a little fatigued; I believe she has a headache."

And they stepped into the landau, the big landau with six seats, which they always used. The Marquis and his daughter remained at the lower end, while the Oriol girl found herself seated at the opposite side between the two young men.

They passed in front of Tournoel; they proceeded along the foot of the mountain, by a beautiful winding road, under the walnut and chestnut-trees. Charlotte several times felt conscious that Gontran was pressing close up to her, but was too prudent to take offense at it. As he sat at her right-hand side, he spoke with his face close to her cheek; and she did not venture to turn round to answer him, through fear of touching his mouth, which she felt already on her lips, and also through fear of his eyes, whose glance would have unnerved her.

He whispered in her ear gallant absurdities, laughable fooleries, agreeable and well-turned compliments.

Christiane scarcely uttered a word, heavy and sick from her pregnancy. And Paul appeared sad, preoccupied. The Marquis alone chatted without unrest or anxiety, in the sprightly, graceful style of a selfish old nobleman.

They got down at the park of Royat to listen to the music, and Gontran, offering Charlotte his arm, set forth with her in front. The army of bathers, on the chairs, around the kiosk, where the leader of the orchestra was keeping time with the brass instruments and the violins, watched the promenaders filing past. The women exhibited their dresses by stretching out their legs as far as the bars of the chairs in front of them, and their dainty summer head-gear made them look more fascinating.

Charlotte and Gontran sauntered through the midst of the people who occupied the seats, looking out for faces of a comic type to find materials for their pleasantries.

Every moment he heard some one saying behind them: "Look there! what a pretty girl!" He felt flattered, and asked himself whether they took her for his sister, his wife, or his mistress.

Christiane, seated between her father and Paul, saw them passing several times, and thinking they exhibited too much youthful frivolity, she called them over to her to soberize them. But they paid no attention to her, and went on vagabondizing through the crowd, enjoying themselves with their whole hearts.

She said in a whisper to Paul Bretigny: "He will finish by compromising her. It will be necessary that we should speak to him this evening when he comes back."

Paul replied: "I had already thought about it. You are quite right."

They went to dine in one of the restaurants of Clermont-Ferrand, those of Royat being no good, according to the Marquis, who was a gourmand, and they returned at nightfall.

Charlotte had become serious, Gontran having strongly pressed her hand, while presenting her gloves to her, before she quitted the table. Her young girl's conscience was suddenly troubled. This was an avowal! an advance! an impropriety! What ought she to do? Speak to him? but about what? To be offended would be ridiculous. There was need of so much tact in these circumstances. But by doing nothing, by saying nothing, she produced the impression of accepting his advances, of becoming his accomplice, of answering "yes" to this pressure of the hand.

And she weighed the situation, accusing herself of having been too gay and too familiar at Royat, thinking just now that her sister was right, that she was compromised, lost! The carriage rolled along the road. Paul and Gontran smoked in silence; the Marquis slept; Christiane gazed at the stars; and Charlotte found it hard to keep back her tears—for she had swallowed three glasses of champagne.

When they had got back, Christiane said to her father: "As it is dark, you have to see this young girl home."

The Marquis, without delay, offered her his arm, and went off with her.

Paul laid his hands on Gontran's shoulders, and whispered in his ear: "Come and have five minutes' talk with your sister and myself."

And they went up to the little drawing-room communicating with the apartments of Andermatt and his wife.

When they were seated, Christiane said: "Listen! M. Paul and I want to give you a good lecture."

"A good lecture! But about what? I'm as wise as an image for want of opportunities."

"Don't trifle! You are doing a very imprudent and very dangerous thing without thinking on it. You are compromising this young girl."

He appeared much astonished. "Who is that? Charlotte?"

"Yes, Charlotte!"

"I'm compromising Charlotte?—I?"

"Yes, you are compromising her. Everyone here is talking about it, and this evening again in the park at Royat you have been very—very light. Isn't that so, Bretigny?"

Paul answered: "Yes, Madame, I entirely share your sentiments."

Gontran turned his chair around, bestrode it like a horse, took a fresh cigar, lighted it, then burst out laughing.

"Ha! so then I am compromising Charlotte Oriol?"

He waited a few seconds to see the effect of his words, then added: "And who told you I did not intend to marry her?"

Christiane gave a start of amazement.

"Marry her? You? Why, you're mad!"

"Why so?"

"That—that little peasant girl!"

"Tra! la! la! Prejudices! Is it from your husband you learned them?"

As she made no response to this direct argument, he went on, putting both questions and answers himself:

"Is she pretty?—Yes! Is she well educated?—Yes! And more ingenuous, more simple, and more honest than girls in good society. She knows as much as another, for she can speak both English and the language of Auvergne—that makes two foreign languages. She will be as rich as any heiress of the Faubourg Saint-Germain—as it was formerly called (they are now going to christen it Faubourg Sainte-Deche)—and finally, if she is a peasant's daughter, she'll be only all the more healthy to present me with fine children. Enough!"

As he had always the appearance of laughing and jesting, Christiane asked hesitatingly: "Come! are you speaking seriously?"

"Faith, I am! She is charming, this little girl! She has a good heart and a pretty face, a genial character and a good temper, rosy cheeks, bright eyes, white teeth, ruby lips, and flowing tresses, glossy, thick, and full of soft folds. And then her vinedressing father will be as rich as Croesus, thanks to your husband, my dear sister. What more do you want? The daughter of a peasant! Well, is not the daughter of a peasant as good as any of those money-lenders' daughters who pay such high prices for dukes with doubtful titles, or any of the daughters born of aristocratic prostitution whom the Empire has given us, or any of the daughters with double sires whom we meet in society? Why, if I did marry this girl I should be doing the first wise and rational act of my life!"

Christiane reflected, then, all of a sudden, convinced, overcome, delighted, she exclaimed:

"Why, all you have said is true! It is quite true, quite right! So then you are going to marry her, my little Gontran?"

It was he who now sought to moderate her ardor. "Not so quick—not so quick—let me reflect in my turn. I only declare that, if I did marry her, I would be doing the first wise and rational act of my life. That does not go so far as saying that I will marry her; but I am thinking over it; I am studying her, I am paying her a little attention to see if I can like her sufficiently. In short, I don't answer 'yes' or 'no,' but it is nearer to 'yes' than to 'no.'"

Christiane turned toward Paul: "What do you think of it, Monsieur Bretigny?"

She called him at one time Monsieur Bretigny, and at another time Bretigny only.

He, always fascinated by the things in which he imagined he saw an element of greatness, by unequal matches which seemed to him to exhibit generosity, by all the sentimental parade in which the human heart masks itself, replied: "For my part I think he is right in this. If he likes her, let him marry her; he could not find better."

But, the Marquis and Andermatt having returned, they had to talk about other subjects; and the two young men went to the Casino to see whether the gaming-room was still open.

From that day forth Christiane and Paul appeared to favor Gontran's open courtship of Charlotte.

The young girl was more frequently invited to the hotel by Christiane, and was treated in fact as if she were already a member of the family. She saw all this clearly, understood it, and was quite delighted at it. Her little head throbbed like a drum, and went building fantastic castles in Spain. Gontran, in the meantime had said nothing definite to her; but his demeanor, all his words, the tone that he assumed with her, his more serious air of gallantry, the caress of his glance seemed every day to keep repeating to her: "I have chosen you; you are to be my wife."

And the tone of sweet affection, of discreet self-surrender, of chaste reserve which she now adopted toward him, seemed to give this answer: "I know it, and I'll say 'yes' whenever you ask for my hand."

In the young girl's family, the matter was discussed in confidential whispers. Louise scarcely opened her lips now except to annoy her with hurtful allusions, with sharp and sarcastic remarks. Père Oriol and Jacques appeared to be content.

She did not ask herself, all the same, whether she loved this good-looking suitor, whose wife she was, no doubt, destined to become. She liked him, she was constantly thinking about him; she considered him handsome, witty, elegant—she was speculating, above all, on what she would do when she was married to him.

In Enval people had forgotten the malignant rivalries of the physicians and the proprietors of springs, the theories as to the supposed attachment of the Duchess de Ramas for her doctor, all the scandals that flow along with the waters of thermal stations, in order to occupy their minds entirely with this extraordinary circumstance—that Count Gontran de Ravenel was going to marry the younger of the Oriol girls.

When Gontran thought the moment had arrived, taking Andermatt by the arm, one morning, as they were rising from the breakfast-table, he said to him: "My dear fellow, strike while the iron is hot! Here is the exact state of affairs: The little one is waiting for me to propose, without my having committed myself at all; but, you may be quite certain she will not refuse me. It is necessary to sound her father about it in such a way as to promote, at the same time, your interests and mine."

Andermatt replied: "Make your mind easy. I'll take that on myself. I am going to sound him this very day without compromising you and without thrusting you forward; and when the situation is perfectly clear, I'll talk about it."

"Capital!"

Then, after a few moments' silence, Gontran added: "Hold on! This is perhaps my last day of bachelorhood. I am going on to Royat, where I saw some acquaintances of mine the other day. I'll be back to-night, and I'll tap at your door to know the result."

He saddled his horse, and proceeded along by the mountain, inhaling the pure, genial air, and sometimes starting into a gallop to feel the keen caress of the breeze brushing the fresh skin of his cheek and tickling his mustache.

The evening-party at Royat was a jolly affair. He met some of his friends there who had brought girls along with them. They lingered a long time at supper; he returned home at a very late hour. Everyone had gone to bed in the hotel of Mont Oriol when Gontran went to tap at Andermatt's door. There was no answer at first; then, as the knocking became much louder, a hoarse voice, the voice of one disturbed while asleep, grunted from within:

"Who's there?"

"'Tis I, Gontran."

"Wait—I'm opening the door."

Andermatt appeared in his nightshirt, with puffed-up face, bristling chin, and a silk handkerchief tied round his head. Then he got back into bed, sat down in it, and with his hands stretched over the sheets:

"Well, my dear fellow, this won't do me. Here is how matters stand: I have sounded this old fox Oriol, without mentioning you, referring merely to a certain friend of mine—I have perhaps allowed him to suppose that the person I meant was Paul Bretigny—as a suitable match for one of his daughters, and I asked what dowry he would give her. He answered me by asking in his turn what were the young man's means; and I fixed the amount at three hundred thousand francs with expectations."

"But I have nothing," muttered Gontran.

"I am lending you the money, my dear fellow. If we work this business between us, your lands would yield me enough to reimburse me."

Gontran sneered: "All right. I'll have the woman and you the money."

But Andermatt got quite annoyed. "If I am to interest myself in your affairs in order that you might insult me, there's an end of it—let us say no more about it!"

Gontran apologized: "Don't get vexed, my dear fellow, and excuse me! I know that you are a very honest man of irreproachable loyalty in matters of business. I would not ask you for the price of a drink if I were your coachman; but I would intrust my fortune to you if I were a millionaire."

William, less excited, rejoined: "We'll return presently to that subject. Let us first dispose of the principal question. The old man was not taken in by my wiles, and said to me in reply: 'It depends on which of them is the girl you're talking about. If 'tis Louise, the elder one, here's her dowry.' And he enumerated for me all the lands that are around the establishment, those which are between the baths and the hotel and between the hotel and the Casino, all those, in short, which are indispensable to us, those which have for me an inestimable value. He gives, on the contrary, to the younger girl the other side of the mountain, which will be worth as much money later on, no doubt, but which is worth nothing to me. I tried in every possible way to make him modify their partition and invert the lots. I was only knocking my head against the obstinacy of a mule. He will not change; he has fixed his resolution. Reflect—what do you think of it?"

Gontran, much troubled, much perplexed, replied: "What do you think of it yourself? Do you believe that he was thinking of me in thus distributing the shares in the land?"

"I haven't a doubt of it. The clown said to himself: 'As he likes the younger one, let us take care of the bag.' He hopes to give you his daughter while keeping his best lands. And again perhaps his object is to give the advantage to the elder girl. He prefers her—who knows?—she is more like himself—she is more cunning—more artful—more practical. I believe she is a strapping lass, this one—for my part, if I were in your place, I would change my stick from one shoulder to the other."

But Gontran, stunned, began muttering: "The devil! the devil! the devil! And Charlotte's lands—you don't want them?"

Andermatt exclaimed: "I—no—a thousand times, no! I want those which are close to my baths, my hotel, and my Casino. It is very simple, I wouldn't give anything for the others, which could only be sold, at a later period, in small lots to private individuals."

Gontran kept still repeating: "The devil! the devil! the devil! here's a plaguy business! So then you advise me?"

"I don't advise you at all. I think you would do well to reflect before deciding between the two sisters."

"Yes—yes—that's true—I will reflect—I am going to sleep first—that brings counsel."

He rose up; Andermatt held him back.

"Excuse me, my dear boy!—a word or two on another matter. I may not appear to understand, but I understand very well the allusions with which you sting me incessantly, and I don't want any more of them. You reproach me with being a Jew—that is to say, with making money, with being avaricious, with being a speculator, so as to come close to sheer swindling. Now, my friend, I spend my life in lending you this money that I make—not without trouble—or rather in giving it to you. However, let that be! But there is one point that I don't admit! No, I am not avaricious. The proof of it is that I have made presents to your sister, presents of twenty thousand francs at a time, that I gave your father a Theodore Rousseau worth ten thousand francs, to which he took a fancy, and that I presented you, when you were coming here, with the horse on which you rode a little while ago to Royat. In what then am I avaricious? In not letting myself be robbed. And we are all like that among my race, and we are right, Monsieur. I want to say it to you once for all. We are regarded as misers because we know the exact value of things. For you a piano is a piano, a chair is a chair, a pair of trousers is a pair of trousers. For us also, but it represents, at the same time, a value, a mercantile value appreciable and precise, which a practical man should estimate with a single glance, not through stinginess, but in order not to countenance fraud. What would you say if a tobacconist asked you four sous for a postage-stamp or for a box of wax-matches? You would go to look for a policeman, Monsieur, for one sou, yes, for one sou—so indignant would you be! And that because you knew, by chance, the value of these two articles. Well, as for me, I know the value of all salable articles; and that indignation which would take possession of you, if you were asked four sous for a postage-stamp, I experience when I am asked twenty francs for an umbrella which is worth fifteen! I protest against the established theft, ceaseless and abominable, of merchants, servants, and coachmen. I protest against the commercial dishonesty of all your race which despises us. I give the price of a drink which I am bound to give for a service rendered, and not that which as the result of a whim you fling away without knowing why, and which ranges from five to a hundred sous according to the caprice of your temper! Do you understand?"

Gontran had risen by this time, and smiling with that refined irony which came happily from his lips:

"Yes, my dear fellow, I understand, and you are perfectly right, and so much the more right because my grandfather, the old Marquis de Ravenel, scarcely left anything to my poor father in consequence of the bad habit which he had of never picking up the change handed to him by the shopkeepers when he was paying for any article whatsoever. He thought that unworthy of a gentleman, and always gave the round sum and the entire coin."

And Gontran went out with a self-satisfied air.

CHAPTER XI.

A MUTUAL UNDERSTANDING

They were just ready to go in to dinner, on the following day, in the private dining-room of the Andermatt and Ravenel families, when Gontran opened the door announcing the "Mesdemoiselles Oriol."

They entered, with an air of constraint, pushed forward by Gontran, who laughed while he explained:

"Here they are! I have carried them both off through the middle of the street. Moreover, it excited public attention. I brought them here by force to you because I want to explain myself to Madame Louise, and could not do so in the open air."

He took from them their hats and their parasols, which they were still carrying, as they had been on their way back from a promenade, made them sit down, embraced his sister, pressed the hands of his father, of his brother-in-law, and of Paul, and then, approaching Louise Oriol once more, said:

"Here now, Mademoiselle, kindly tell me what you have against me for some time past?"

She seemed scared, like a bird caught in a net, and carried away by the hunter.

"Why, nothing, Monsieur, nothing at all! What has made you believe that?"

"Oh! everything, Mademoiselle, everything at all! You no longer come here—you no longer come in the Noah's Ark [so he had baptized the big landau]. You assume a harsh tone whenever I meet you and when I speak to you."

"Why, no, Monsieur, I assure you!"

"Why, yes, Mam'zelle, I declare to you! In any case, I don't want this to continue, and I am going to make peace with you this very day. Oh! you know I am obstinate. There's no use in your looking black at me. I'll know easily how to get the better of your hoity-toity airs, and make you be nice toward your sister, who is an angel of grace."

It was announced that dinner was ready; and they made their way to the dining-room. Gontran took Louise's arm in his. He was exceedingly attentive to her and to her sister, dividing his compliments between them with admirable tact, and remarking to the younger girl: "As for you, you are a comrade of ours—I am going to neglect you for a few days. One goes to less expense for friends than for strangers, you are aware."

And he said to the elder: "As for you, I want to bewitch you, Mademoiselle, and I warn you as a loyal foe! I will even make love to you. Ha! you are blushing—that's a good sign. You'll see that I am very nice, when I take pains about it. Isn't that so, Mademoiselle Charlotte?"

And they were both, indeed, blushing, and Louise stammered with her serious air: "Oh! Monsieur, how foolish you are!"

He replied: "Bah! you will hear many things said by others by and by in society, when you are married, which will not be long. 'Tis then they will really pay you compliments."

Christiane and Paul Bretigny expressed their approval of his action in having brought back Louise Oriol; the Marquis smiled, amused by these childish affectations. Andermatt was thinking: "He's no fool, the sly dog." And Gontran, irritated by the part which he was compelled to play, drawn by his senses toward Charlotte and by his interests toward Louise, muttered between his teeth with a sly smile in her direction: "Ah! your rascal of a father thought to play a trick upon me; but I am going to carry it with a high hand over you, my lassie, and you will see whether I won't go about it the right way!"

And he compared the two, inspecting them one after the other. Certainly, he liked the younger more; she was more amusing, more lively, with her nose tilted slightly, her bright eyes, her straight forehead, and her beautiful teeth a little too prominent in a mouth which was somewhat too wide.

However, the other was pretty, too, colder, less gay. She would never be lively or charming in the intimate relations of life; but when at the opening of a ball "the Comtesse de Ravenel" would be announced, she could carry her title well—better perhaps than her younger sister, when she got a little accustomed to it, and had mingled with persons of high birth. No matter; he was annoyed. He was full of spite against the father and the brother also, and he promised himself that he would pay them off afterward for his mischance when he was the master. When they returned to the drawing-room, he got Louise to read the cards, as she was skilled in foretelling the future. The Marquis, Andermatt, and Charlotte listened attentively, attracted, in spite of themselves, by the mystery of the unknown, by the possibility of the improbable, by that invincible credulity with reference to the marvelous which haunts man, and often disturbs the strongest minds in the presence of the silly inventions of charlatans.

Paul and Christiane chatted in the recess of an open window. For some time past she had been miserable, feeling that she was no longer loved in the same fashion; and their misunderstanding as lovers was every day accentuated by their mutual error. She had suspected this unfortunate state of things for the first time on the evening of the fête when she brought Paul along the road. But while she understood that he had no longer the same tenderness in his look, the same caress in his voice, the same passionate anxiety about her as in the days of their early love, she had not been able to divine the cause of this change.

It had existed for a long time now, ever since the day when she had said to him with a look of happiness on reaching their daily meeting-place: "You know, I believe I am really enceinte." He had felt at that moment an unpleasant little shiver running all over his skin. Then at each of their meetings she would talk to him about her condition, which made her heart dance with joy; but this preoccupation with a matter which he regarded as vexatious, ugly, and unclean clashed with his devoted exaltation about the idol that he had adored. At a later stage, when he saw her altered, thin, her cheeks hollow, her complexion yellow, he thought that she might have spared him that spectacle, and might have vanished for a few months from his sight, to reappear afterward fresher and prettier than ever, thus knowing how to make him forget this accident, or perhaps knowing how to unite to her coquettish fascinations as a mistress, another charm, the thoughtful reserve of a young mother, who only allows her baby to be seen at a distance covered up in red ribbons.

She had, besides, a rare opportunity of displaying that tact which he expected of her by spending the summer apart from him at Mont Oriol, and leaving him in Paris so that he might not see her robbed of her freshness and beauty. He had fondly hoped that she might have understood him.

But, immediately on reaching Auvergne, she had appealed to him in incessant and despairing letters so numerous and so urgent that he had come to her through weakness, through pity. And now she was boring him to death with her ungracious and lugubrious tenderness; and he felt an extreme longing to get away from her, to see no more of her, to listen no longer to her talk about love, so irritating and out of place. He would have liked to tell her plainly all that he had in his mind, to point out to her how unskillful and foolish she showed herself; but he could not bring himself to do this, and he dared not take his departure. As a result he could not restrain himself from testifying his impatience with her in bitter and hurtful words.

She was stung by them the more because, every day more ill, more heavy, tormented by all the sufferings of pregnant women, she had more need than ever of being consoled, fondled, encompassed with affection. She loved him with that utter abandonment of body and soul, of her entire being, which sometimes renders love a sacrifice without reservations and without bounds. She no longer looked upon herself as his mistress, but as his wife, his companion, his devotee, his worshiper, his prostrate slave, his chattel. For her there seemed no further need of any gallantry, coquetry, constant desire to please, or fresh indulgence between them, since she belonged to him entirely, since they were linked together by that chain so sweet and so strong—the child which would soon be born. When they were alone at the window, she renewed her tender lamentation: "Paul, my dear Paul, tell me, do you love me as much as ever?"

"Yes, certainly! Come now, you keep repeating this every day—it will end by becoming monotonous."

"Pardon me. It is because I find it impossible to believe it any longer, and I want you to reassure me; I want to hear you saying it to me forever that word which is so sweet; and, as you don't repeat it to me so often as you used to do, I am compelled to ask for it, to implore it, to beg for it from you."

"Well, yes, I love you! But let us talk of something else, I entreat of you."

"Ah! how hard you are!"

"Why, no! I am not hard. Only—only you do not understand—you do not understand that——"

"Oh! yes! I understand well that you no longer love me. If you knew how I am suffering!"

"Come, Christiane, I beg of you not to make me nervous. If you knew yourself how awkward what you are now doing is!"

"Ah! if you loved me, you would not talk to me in this way."

"But, deuce take it! if I did not love you, I would not have come."

"Listen. You belong to me now. You are mine; I am yours. There is between us that tie of a budding life which nothing can break; but will you promise me that, if one day, you should come to love me no more, you will tell me so?"

"Yes, I do promise you."

"You swear it to me?"

"I swear it to you."

"But then, all the same, we would remain friends, would we not?"

"Certainly, let us remain friends."

"On the day when you no longer regard me with love you'll come to find me and you'll say to me: 'My little Christiane, I am very fond of you, but it is not the same thing any more. Let us be friends, there! nothing but friends.'"

"That is understood; I promise it to you."

"You swear it to me?"

"I swear it to you."

"No matter, it would cause me great grief. How you adored me last year!"

A voice called out behind them: "The Duchess de Ramas-Aldavarra."

She had come as a neighbor, for Christiane held receptions each day for the principal bathers, just as princes hold receptions in their kingdoms.

Doctor Mazelli followed the lovely Spaniard with a smiling and submissive air. The two women pressed one another's hands, sat down, and commenced to chat.

Andermatt called Paul across to him: "My dear friend come here! Mademoiselle Oriol reads the cards splendidly; she has told me some astonishing things!"

He took Paul by the arm, and added: "What an odd being you are! At Paris, we never saw you, even once a month, in spite of the entreaties of my wife. Here it required fifteen letters to get you to come. And since you have come, one would think you are losing a million a day, you look so disconsolate. Come, are you hearing any matter that ruffles you? We might be able to assist you. You should tell us about it."

"Nothing at all, my dear fellow. If I haven't visited you more frequently in Paris—'tis because at Paris, you understand——"

"Perfectly—I grasp your meaning. But here, at least, you ought to be in good spirits. I am preparing for you two or three fêtes, which will, I am sure, be very successful."

"Madame Barre and Professor Cloche" were announced. He entered with his daughter, a young widow, red-haired and bold-faced. Then, almost in the same breath, the manservant called out: "Professor Mas-Roussel."

His wife accompanied him, pale, worn, with flat headbands drawn over her temples.

Professor Remusot had left the day before, after having, it was said, purchased his chalet on exceptionally favorable conditions.

The two other doctors would have liked to know what these conditions were, but Andermatt merely said in reply to them: "Oh! we have made little advantageous arrangements for everybody. If you desired to follow his example, we might see our way to a mutual understanding—we might see our way. When you have made up your mind, you can let me know, and then we'll talk about it."

Doctor Latonne appeared in his turn, then Doctor Honorat, without his wife, whom he did not bring with him. A din of voices now filled the drawing-room, the loud buzz of conversation. Gontran never left Louise Oriol's side, put his head over her shoulder in addressing her, and said with a laugh every now and again to whoever was passing near him: "This is an enemy of whom I am making a conquest."

Mazelli took a seat beside Professor Cloche's daughter. For some days he had been constantly following her about; and she had received his advances with provoking audacity.

The Duchess, who kept him well in view, appeared irritated and trembling. Suddenly she rose, crossed the drawing-room, and interrupted her doctor's confidential chat with the pretty red-haired widow, saying: "Come, Mazelli, we are going to retire. I feel rather ill at ease."

As soon as they had gone out, Christiane drew close to Paul's side, and said to him: "Poor woman! she must suffer so much!"

He asked heedlessly: "Who, pray?"

"The Duchess! You don't see how jealous she is."

He replied abruptly: "If you begin to groan over everything you can lay hold of now, you'll have no end of weeping."

She turned away, ready, indeed, to shed tears, so cruel did she find him, and, sitting down near Charlotte Oriol, who was all alone in a dazed condition, unable to comprehend the meaning of Gontran's conduct, she said to the young girl, without letting the latter realize what her words conveyed: "There are days when one would like to be dead."

Andermatt, in the midst of the doctors, was relating the extraordinary case of Père Clovis, whose legs were beginning to come to life again. He appeared so thoroughly convinced that nobody could doubt his good faith.

Since he had seen through the trick of the peasants and the paralytic, understood that he had let himself be duped and persuaded, the year before, through the sheer desire to believe in the efficacy of the waters with which he had been bitten, since, above all, he had not been able to free himself, without paying, from the formidable complaints of the old man, he had converted it into a strong advertisement, and worked it wonderfully well.

Mazelli had just come back, after having accompanied his patient to her own apartments.

Gontran caught hold of his arm: "Tell me your opinion, my good doctor. Which of the Oriol girls do you prefer?"

The handsome physician whispered in his ear: "The younger one, to love; the elder one, to marry."

"Look at that! We are exactly of the same way of thinking. I am delighted at it!"

Then, going over to his sister, who was still talking to Charlotte: "You are not aware of it? I have made up my mind that we are to visit the Puy de la Nugère on Thursday. It is the finest crater of the chain. Everyone consents. It is a settled thing."

Christiane murmured with an air of indifference: "I consent to anything you like."

But Professor Cloche, followed by his daughter, was about to take his leave, and Mazelli, offering to see them home, started off behind the young widow. In five minutes, everyone had left, for Christiane went to bed at eleven o'clock. The Marquis, Paul, and Gontran accompanied the Oriol girls. Gontran and Louise walked in front, and Bretigny, some paces behind them, felt Charlotte's arm trembling a little as it leaned on his.

They separated with the agreement: "On Thursday at eleven for breakfast at the hotel!"

On their way back they met Andermatt, detained in a corner of the park by Professor Mas-Roussel, who was saying to him: "Well, if it does not put you about, I'll come and have a chat with you to-morrow morning about that little business of the chalet."

William joined the young men to go in with them, and, drawing himself up to his brother-in-law's ear, said: "My best compliments, my dear boy! You have acted your part admirably."

Gontran, for the past two years, had been harassed by pecuniary embarrassments which had spoiled his existence. So long as he was spending the share which came to him from his mother, he had allowed his life to pass in that carelessness and indifference which he inherited from his father, in the midst of those young men, rich, blasé, and corrupted, whose doings we read about every morning in the newspapers, who belong to the world of fashion but mingle in it very little, preferring the society of women of easy virtue and purchasable hearts.

There were a dozen of them in the same set, who were to be found every night at the same café on the boulevard between midnight and three o'clock in the morning. Very well dressed, always in black coats and white waistcoats, wearing shirt-buttons worth twenty louis changed every month, and bought in one of the principal jewelers' shops, they lived careless of everything, save amusing themselves, picking up women, making them a subject of talk, and getting money by every possible means.

As the only things they had any knowledge of were the scandals of the night before, the echoes of alcoves and stables, duels and stories about gambling transactions, the entire horizon of their thoughts was shut in by these barriers. They had had all the women who were for sale in the market of gallantry, had passed them through their hands, given them up, exchanged them with one another, and talked among themselves as to their erotic qualities as they might have talked about the qualities of race-horses. They also associated with people of rank whose voluptuous habits excited comment and whose women nearly all kept up intrigues which were matters of notoriety, under the eyes of husbands indifferent or averted or closed or devoid of perception; and they passed judgment on these women as on the others, forming much the same estimate about them, save that they made a slight distinction on the grounds of birth and social position.

By dint of resorting to dodges to get the money necessary for the life which they led, outwitting usurers, borrowing on all sides, putting off tradesmen, laughing in the faces of their tailors when presented with a big bill every six months, listening to girls telling about the infamies they perpetrated in order to gratify their feminine greed, seeing systematic cheating at clubs, knowing and feeling that they were individually robbed by everyone, by servants, merchants, keepers of big restaurants and others, becoming acquainted with certain sharp practices and shady transactions in which they themselves had a hand in order to knock out a few louis, their moral sense had become blunted, used up, and their sole point of honor consisted in fighting duels when they realized that they were suspected of all the things of which they were either capable or actually guilty.

Everyone of these young roués, after some years of this existence, ended with a rich marriage, or a scandal, or a suicide, or a mysterious disappearance as complete as death. But they put their principal reliance on the rich marriage. Some trusted to their families to procure such a thing for them; others looked out themselves for it without letting it be noticed; and they had lists of heiresses just as people have lists of houses for sale. They kept their eyes fixed especially on the exotics, the Americans of the north and of the south, whom they dazzled by their "chic," by their reputation as fast men, by talk about their successes, and by the elegance of their persons. And their tradesmen also placed reliance on the rich marriage.

But this hunt after the girl with a fortune was bound to be protracted. In any case it involved inquiries, the trouble of winning a female heart, fatigues, visits, all that exercise of energy of which Gontran, careless by nature, remained utterly incapable. For a long time past, he had been saying to himself, feeling each day more keenly the unpleasantness of impecuniosity: "I must, for all that, think over it." But he did not think over it, and so he found nothing. He had been reduced to the ingenious pursuit of paltry sums, to all the questionable steps of people at the end of their resources, and, to crown all, to long sojourns in the family, when Andermatt had suddenly suggested to him the idea of marrying one of the Oriol girls.

He had, at first, said nothing through prudence, although the young girl appeared to him, at first blush, too much beneath him for him to consent to such an unequal match. But a few minutes' reflection had very speedily modified his view; and he forthwith made up his mind to make love to her in a bantering sort of way—the love-making of a spa—which would not compromise him, and would permit him to back out of it.

Thoroughly acquainted with his brother-in-law's character, he knew that this proposition must have been cogitated for a long time, and weighed and matured by him—that she meant to him a valuable prize such as it would be hard to find elsewhere.

It would cost him no trouble but that of stooping down and picking up a pretty girl, for he liked the younger sister very much, and he had often said to himself that she would be nice to associate with later on. He had accordingly selected Charlotte Oriol; and in a little time would have brought matters to the point when a regular proposal might have been made to her.

Now, as the father was bestowing on his other daughter the dowry coveted by Andermatt, Gontran had either to renounce this union or turn round to the elder sister. He felt intense dissatisfaction with this state of affairs and he had been thinking in his first moments of vexation of sending his brother-in-law to the devil and remaining a bachelor until a fresh opportunity arose. But just at that very time he found himself quite cleaned out, so that he had to ask, for his play at the Casino, a sum of twenty-five louis from Paul, after many similar loans, which he had never paid back. And again, he would have to look for a rich wife, find her, and captivate her, while without any change of place, with only a few days of attention and gallantry, he could capture the elder of the Oriol girls just as he had been able to make a conquest of the younger. In this way he would make sure in his brother-in-law of a banker whom he might render always responsible, on whom he might cast endless reproaches, and whose cash-box would always be open for him.

As for his wife, he could bring her to Paris, and there introduce her into society as the daughter of Andermatt's partner. Moreover, she bore the name of the spa, to which he would never bring her back! Never! never! in virtue of the natural law that streams do not return to their sources. She had a nice face and figure, sufficiently distinguished already to become entirely so, sufficiently intelligent to understand the ways of society, to hold her own in it, to make a good show in it, and even to do him honor. People would say: "This joker here has married a lovely girl, at whom he looks as if he were not making a bad joke of it." And he would not make a bad joke of it, in fact, for he counted on resuming by her side his bachelor existence with the money in his pockets.

So he turned toward Louise Oriol, and, taking advantage of the jealousy awakened in the skittish heart of the young girl, without being aware of it, had excited in her a coquetry which had hitherto slumbered, and a vague desire to take away from her sister this handsome lover whom people addressed as "Monsieur le Comte."

She had not said this in her own mind. She had neither thought it out nor contrived it, being surprised at their being thrown together and going off in one another's company. But when she saw him assiduous and gallant toward her, she felt from his demeanor, from his glances, and his entire attitude, that he was not enamored of Charlotte, and without trying to see beyond that, she was in a happy, joyous, almost triumphant frame of mind as she lay down to sleep.

They hesitated for a long time on the following Thursday before starting for the Puy de la Nugère. The gloomy sky and the heavy atmosphere made them anticipate rain. But Gontran insisted so strongly on going that he carried the waverers along with him. The breakfast was a melancholy affair. Christiane and Paul had quarreled the night before, without apparent cause. Andermatt was afraid that Gontran's marriage might not take place, for Père Oriol had, that very morning, spoken of him in equivocal terms. Gontran, on being informed of this, got angry and made up his mind that he would succeed. Charlotte, foreseeing her sister's triumph, without at all understanding this transfer of Gontran's affections, strongly desired to remain in the village. With some difficulty they prevailed on her to come.

Accordingly the Noah's Ark carried its full number of ordinary passengers in the direction of the high plateau which looks down on Volvic. Louise Oriol, suddenly becoming loquacious, acted as their guide along the road. She explained how the stone of Volvic, which is nothing else but the lava-current of the surrounding peaks, had helped to build all the churches and all the houses in the district—a circumstance which gives to the towns in Auvergne the dark and charred-looking aspect that they present.

She pointed out the yards where this stone was cut, showed them the molten rock that was worked as a quarry, from which was extracted the rough lava, and made them view with admiration, standing on a hilltop and bending over Volvic, the immense black Virgin who protects the town. Then they ascended toward the upper plateau, embossed with extinct volcanoes. The horses went at a walking pace over the long and toilsome road. Their path was bordered with beautiful green woods, and nobody talked any longer.

Christiane was thinking about Tazenat. It was the same carriage; they were the same persons; but their hearts were no longer the same. Everything seemed as it had been—and yet? and yet? What then had happened? Almost nothing. A little love the more on her part! A little love the less on his! Almost nothing—the invisible rent which weariness makes in an intimate attachment—oh! almost nothing—and the look in the changed eyes, because the same eyes no longer saw the same faces in the same way. What is this but a look? Almost nothing!

The coachman drew up, and said: "It is here, at the right, through that path in the wood. You have only to follow it in order to get there."

All descended, save the Marquis, who thought the weather too warm. Louise and Gontran went on in front, and Charlotte remained behind with Paul and Christiane, who found difficulty in walking. The path appeared to them long, right through the wood; then they reached a crest covered with tall grass which led by a steep ascent to the sides of the old crater. Louise and Gontran, halting when they got to the top, both looking tall and slender, had the appearance of standing in the clouds. When the others had come up with them, Paul Bretigny's enthusiastic soul was inflamed with poetic rapture.

Around them, behind them, to right, to left, they were surrounded by strange cones, decapitated, some shooting forth, others crushed into a mass, but all preserving their fantastic physiognomy of dead volcanoes. These heavy fragments of mountains with flat summits rose from south to west along an immense plateau of desolate appearance, which, itself a thousand meters above the Limagne, looked down upon it, as far as the eye could reach, toward the east and the north, on to the invisible horizon, always veiled, always blue.

The Puy de Dome, at the right, towered above all its fellows, with from seventy to eighty craters now gone to sleep. Further on were the Puy de Gravenoire, the Puy de Crouel, the Puy de la Pedge, the Puy de Sault, the Puy de Noschamps, the Puy de la Vache. Nearer, were the Puy de Come, the Puy de Jumes, the Puy de Tressoux, the Puy de Louchadière—a vast cemetery of volcanoes.

The young men gazed at the scene in amazement. At their feet opened the first crater of La Nugère, a deep grassy basin at the bottom of which could be seen three enormous blocks of brown lava, lifted up with the monster's last puff and then sunk once more into his throat as he expired, remaining there from century to century forever.

Gontran exclaimed: "As for me, I am going down to the bottom. I want to see how they give up the ghost—creatures of this sort. Come along, Mesdemoiselles, for a little run down the slope." And seizing Louise's arm, he dragged her after him. Charlotte followed them, running after them. Then, all of a sudden, she stopped, watched them as they flew along, jumping with their arms linked, and, turning back abruptly, she reascended toward Christiane and Paul, who were seated on the grass at the top of the declivity. When she reached them, she fell upon her knees, and, hiding her face in the young girl's robe she wore, she burst out sobbing.

Christiane, who understood what was the matter, and whom all the sorrows of others had, for some time past, pierced like wounds inflicted upon herself, flung her arms around the girl's neck, and, moved also by her tears, murmured: "Poor little thing! poor little thing!" The girl kept crying incessantly, and with her hands dropping listlessly to the ground, she tore up the grass unconscious of what she was doing.

Bretigny had risen up in order to avoid the appearance of having observed her, but this misery endured by a young girl, this distress of an innocent creature, filled him suddenly with indignation against Gontran. He, whom Christiane's deep anguish only exasperated, was touched to the bottom of his heart by a girl's first disillusion.

He came back, and kneeling down in his turn, in order to speak to her, said: "Come, calm yourself, I beg of you. They are going to return presently. They must not see you crying."

She sprang to her feet, scared by this idea that her sister might find her with tears in her eyes. Her throat remained choking with sobs, which she held back, which she swallowed down, which she sent back into her heart, filling it with more poignant grief. She faltered: "Yes—yes—it is over—it is nothing—it is over. Look here! It cannot be noticed now. Isn't that so? It cannot be noticed now."

Christiane wiped her cheeks with her handkerchief, then passed it also across her own. She said to Paul:

"Go, pray, and see what they are doing. We cannot see them any longer. They have disappeared under the blocks of lava. I will look after this little one, and console her."

Bretigny had again stood up, and in a trembling voice, said: "I am going there—and I'll bring them back, but it will be my affair—your brother—this very day—and he shall give me an explanation of his unjustifiable conduct, after what he said to us the other day." He began to descend, running toward the center of the crater.

Gontran, hurrying Louise along, had pulled her with all his strength over the steep side of the chasm, in order to hold her up, to sustain her, to put her out of breath, to make her dizzy, and to frighten her. She, carried along by his wild rush, attempted to stop him, gasping: "Oh! not so quickly—I'm going to fall—why, you're mad—I'm going to fall!"

They knocked against the blocks of lava, and remained standing up, both breathless. Then they walked round the crater staring at the big gaps which formed below a kind of cavern, with a double outlet.

When at the end of its life, the volcano had cast out this last mouthful of foam, unable to shoot it up to the sky as in former times, he had spat it forth, so that, thick and half-cooled, it fixed itself upon his dying lips.

"We must enter under there," said Gontran. And he pushed the young girl before him. Then, when they were in the grotto, he said: "Well, Mademoiselle, this is the moment to make a declaration to you."

She was stupefied: "A declaration—to me!"

"Why, yes, in four words—I find you charming!"

"It is to my sister you should say that!"

"Oh! you know well that I am not making a declaration to your sister."

"Come, now!"

"Look here! you would not be a woman if you did not understand that I have paid attentions to her to see what you would think of it!—and what looks you gave me on account of it. Why, you looked daggers at me! Oh! I'm quite satisfied. So then I have tried to prove to you, by all the consideration in my power, how much I thought about you."

Nobody had ever before talked to her in this way. She felt confused and delighted, her heart full of joy and pride. He went on: "I know well that I have been nasty toward your little sister. So much the worse. She is not deceived by it, never fear. You see how she remained on the hillside, how she was not inclined to follow us. Oh! she understands! she understands!"

He had caught hold of one of Louise Oriol's hands, and he kissed the ends of her fingers softly, gallantly, murmuring: "How nice you are! How nice you are!"

She, leaning against the wall of lava, heard his heart beating with emotion without uttering a word. The thought, the sole thought, which floated in her agitated mind, was one of triumph; she had got the better of her sister! But a shadow appeared at the entrance to the grotto. Paul Bretigny was looking at them. Gontran, in a natural fashion, let fall the little hand which he had been raising to his lips, and said: "Hallo! you here? Are you alone?"

"Yes. We were surprised to see you disappearing down here."

"Oh! well, let us go back. We were looking at this. Isn't it rather curious?"

Louise, flushed up to her temples, went out first, and began to reascend the slope, followed by the two young men, who were talking behind in a low tone.

Christiane and Charlotte saw them approaching, and awaited them with clasped hands.

They went back to the carriage in which the Marquis had remained, and the Noah's Ark set out again for Enval.

Suddenly, in the midst of a little forest of pine-trees the landau stopped, and the coachman began to swear. An old dead ass blocked the way.

Everyone wanted to look at it, and they got down off the carriage. He lay stretched on the blackened dust, himself discolored, and so lean that his worn skin at the places where the bones projected seemed as if it would have been burst through if the animal had not breathed forth his last sigh. The entire carcass outlined itself under the gnawed hair of his sides, and his head looked enormous—a poor-looking head, with the eyes closed, tranquil now on its bed of broken stones, so tranquil, so calm in death, that it appeared happy and surprised at this new-found rest. His big ears, now relaxed, lay like rags. Two raw wounds on his knees told how often he had fallen that very day before sinking down for the last time; and another wound on the side showed the place where his master, for years and years, had been pricking him with an iron spike attached to the end of a stick, to hasten his slow pace.

The coachman, having caught its hind legs, dragged it toward a ditch, and the neck was strained as if the dead brute were going to bray once more, to give vent to a last complaint. When this was done, the man, in a rage, muttered: "What brutes, to leave this in the middle of the road!"

No other person had said a word; they again stepped into the carriage. Christiane, heartbroken, crushed, saw all the miserable life of this animal ended thus at the side of the road: the merry little donkey with his big head, in which glittered a pair of big eyes, comical and good-tempered, with his rough hair and his long ears, gamboling about, still free, close to his mother's legs; then the first cart; the first uphill journey; the first blows; and, after that, the ceaseless and terrible walking along interminable roads, the overpowering heat of the sun, and nothing for food save a little straw, a little hay, or some branches, while all along the hard roads there was the temptation of the green meadows.

And then, again, as age came upon him, the iron spike replacing the pliant switch; and the frightful martyrdom of the animal, worn out, bereft of breath, bruised, always dragging after it excessive loads, and suffering in all its limbs, in all its old body, shabby as a beggar's cart. And then the death, the beneficent death, three paces away from the grass of the ditch, to which a man, passing by, drags it with oaths, in order to clear the road.

Christiane, for the first time, understood the wretchedness of enslaved creatures; and death appeared to her also a very good thing at times.

Suddenly they passed by a little cart, which a man nearly naked, a woman in tatters, and a lean dog were dragging along, exhausted by fatigue. The occupants of the carriage noticed that they were sweating and panting. The dog, with his tongue out, fleshless and mangy, was fastened between the wheels. There were in this cart pieces of wood picked up everywhere, stolen, no doubt, roots, stumps, broken branches, which seemed to hide other things; then over these branches rags, and on these rags a child, nothing but a head starting out through gray old scraps of cloth, a round ball with two eyes, a nose, and a mouth!

This was a family, a human family! The ass had succumbed to fatigue, and the man, without pity for his dead servant, without pushing it even into the rut, had left it in the open road, in front of any vehicles which might be coming up. Then, yoking himself in his turn with his wife in the empty shafts, they proceeded to drag it along as the beast had dragged it a short time before. They were going on. Where? To do what? Had they even a few sous? That cart—would they be dragging it forever, not being in a position to buy another animal? What would they live on? Where would they stop? They would probably die as their donkey had died.

Were they married, these beggars, or merely living together? And their child would do the same as they did, this little brute as yet unformed, concealed under sordid wrappings. Christiane was thinking on all these things; and new sensations rose up in the depths of her pitying soul. She had a glimpse of the misery of the poor.

Gontran said, all of a sudden: "I don't know why, but I would think it a delicious thing if we were all to dine together this evening at the Café Anglais. It would give me pleasure to have a look at the boulevard."

And the Marquis muttered: "Bah! we are well enough here. The new hotel is much better than the old one."

They passed in front of Tournoel. A recollection of the spot made Christiane's heart palpitate, as she recognized a certain chestnut-tree. She glanced toward Paul, who had closed his eyes, so that he did not see her meek, appealing face.

Soon they perceived two men before the carriage, two vinedressers returning from work carrying their rakes on their shoulders, and walking with the long, weary steps of laborers. The Oriol girls reddened to their very temples. It was their father and their brother, who had gone back to their vine-lands as in former times, and passed their days sweating over the soil which they had enriched, and bent double, with their buttocks in the air, kept toiling at it from morning until evening, while the fine frock-coats, carefully folded up, were at rest in the chest of drawers, and the tall hats in a press.

The two peasants bowed with a friendly smile, while everyone in the landau waved a hand in response to their "Good evening."

When they got back, just as Gontran was stepping out of the Ark to go up to the Casino, Bretigny accompanied him, and stopping on the first steps, said:

"Listen, my friend! What you're doing is not right, and I've promised your sister to speak to you about it."

"To speak about what?"

"About the way you have been acting during the last few days."

Gontran had resumed his impertinent air.

"Acting? Toward whom?"

"Toward this girl whom you are meanly jilting."

"Do you think so?"

"Yes, I do think so—and I am right in thinking so."

"Bah! you are becoming very scrupulous on the subject of jilting."

"Ah, my friend, 'tis not a question of a loose woman here, but of a young girl."

"I know that perfectly; therefore, I have not seduced her. The difference is very marked."

They went on walking together side by side. Gontran's demeanor exasperated Paul, who replied:

"If I were not your friend, I would say some very severe things to you."

"And for my part I would not permit you to say them."

"Look here, listen to me, my friend! This young girl excites my pity. She was weeping a little while ago."

"Bah! she was weeping! Why, that's a compliment to me!"

"Come, don't trifle! What do you mean to do?"

"I? Nothing!"

"Just consider! You have gone so far with her that you have compromised her. The other day you told your sister and me that you were thinking of marrying her."

Gontran stopped in his walk, and in that mocking tone through which a menace showed itself:

"My sister and you would do better not to bother yourselves about other people's love affairs. I told you that this girl pleases me well enough, and that if I happened to marry her, I would be doing a wise and reasonable act. That's all. Now it turns out that to-day I like the elder girl better. I have changed my mind. That's a thing that happens to everyone."

Then, looking him full in the face: "What is it that you do yourself when you cease to care about a woman? Do you look after her?"

Paul Bretigny, astonished, sought to penetrate the profound meaning, the hidden sense, of these words. A little feverishness also mounted into his brain. He said in a violent tone:

"I tell you again this is not a question of a hussy or a married woman, but of a young girl whom you have deceived, if not by promises, at least by your advances. That is not, mark you, the part of a man of honor!—or of an honest man!"

Gontran, pale, his voice quivering, interrupted him: "Hold your tongue! You have already said too much—and I have listened to too much of this. In my turn, if I were not your friend I—I might show you that I have a short temper. Another word, and there is an end of everything between us forever!"

Then, slowly weighing his words, and flinging them in Paul's face, he said: "I have no explanations to offer you—I might rather have to demand them from you. There is a certain kind of indelicacy of which it is not the part of a man of honor or of an honest man to be guilty—which might take many forms—from which friendship ought to keep certain people—and which love does not excuse."

All of a sudden, changing his tone, and almost jesting, he added:

“As for this little Charlotte, if she excites your pity, and if you like her, take her, and marry her. Marriage is often a solution of difficult cases. It is a solution, and a stronghold, in which one may barricade himself against desperate obstacles. She is pretty and rich! It would be very desirable for you to finish with an accident like this!—it would be amusing for us to marry here, the same day, for I certainly will marry the elder one. I tell it to you as a secret, and don’t repeat it as yet. Now don’t forget that you have less right than anyone else yourself ever to talk about integrity in matters of sentiment, and scruples of affection. And now go and look after your own affairs. I am going to look after mine. Good night!”

And suddenly turning off in another direction, he went down toward the village. Paul Bretigny, with doubts in his mind and uneasiness in his heart, returned with lingering steps to the hotel of Mont Oriol.

He tried to understand thoroughly, to recall each word, in order to determine its meaning, and he was amazed at the secret byways, shameful and unfit to be spoken of, which may be hidden in certain souls.

When Christiane asked him: “What reply did you get from Gontran?”

He faltered: “My God! he—he prefers the elder, just now. I believe he even intends to marry her—and in answer to my rather sharp reproaches he shut my mouth by allusions that are—disquieting to both of us.”

Christiane sank into a chair, murmuring: “Oh! my God! my God!”

But, as Gontran had just come in, for the bell had rung for dinner, he kissed her gaily on the forehead, asking: “Well, little sister, how do you feel now? You are not too tired?”

Then he pressed Paul’s hand, and, turning toward Andermatt, who had come in after him:

“I say, pearl of brothers-in-law, of husbands, and of friends, can you tell me exactly what an old ass dead on a road is worth?”

CHAPTER XII.

A Betrothal

Andermatt and Doctor Latonne were walking in front of the Casino on a terrace adorned with vases made of imitation marble.

"He no longer salutes me," the doctor was saying, referring to his brother-physician Bonnefille. "He is over there in his pit, like a wild-boar. I believe he would poison our springs, if he could!"

Andermatt, with his hands behind his back and his hat—a small round hat of gray felt—thrown back over his neck, so as to let the baldness above his forehead be seen, was deeply plunged in thought. At length he said:

"Oh! in three months the Company will have knuckled under. We might buy it over at ten thousand francs. It is that wretched Bonnefille who is exciting them against me, and who makes them fancy that I will give way. But he is mistaken."

The new inspector returned: "You are aware that they have shut up their Casino since yesterday. They have no one any longer."

"Yes, I am aware of it; but we have not enough of people here ourselves. They stick in too much at the hotels; and people get bored in the hotels, my dear fellow. It is necessary to amuse the bathers, to distract them, to make them think the season too short. Those staying at our Mont Oriol hotel come every evening, because they are quite near, but the others hesitate and remain in their abodes. It is a question of routes—nothing else. Success always depends on certain imperceptible causes which we ought to know how to discover. It is necessary that the routes leading to a place of recreation should be a source of recreation in themselves, the commencement of the pleasure which one will be enjoying presently.

"The ways which lead to this place are bad, stony, hard; they cause fatigue. When a route which goes to any place, to which one has a vague desire of paying a visit, is pleasant, wide, and full of shade in the daytime, easy and not too steep at night, one selects it naturally in preference to others. If you knew how the body preserves the recollection of a thousand things which the mind has not taken the trouble to retain! I believe this is how the memory of animals is constructed. Have you felt too hot when repairing to such a place? Have you tired your feet on badly broken stones? Have you found an ascent too rough, even while you were thinking of something else? If so, you will experience invincible repugnance to revisiting that spot. You were chatting with a friend; you took no notice of the slight annoyances of the journey; you were looking at nothing, remarking notice; but your legs, your muscles, your lungs, your whole body have not forgotten, and they say to the mind, when it wants to take them along the same route: 'No, I won't go; I have suffered too much there.' And the mind yields to this refusal without disputing it, submitting to this mute language of the companions who carry it along.

"So then, we want fine pathways, which comes back to saying that I require the bits of ground belonging to that donkey of a Père Oriol. But patience! Ha! with reference to that point, Mas-Roussel has become the proprietor of his own chalet on the same conditions as Remusot. It is a trifling sacrifice for which he will amply indemnify us. Try, therefore, to find out exactly what are Cloche's intentions."

"He'll do just the same thing as the others," said the physician. "But there is something else, of which I have been thinking for the last few days, and which we have completely forgotten—it is the meteorological bulletin."

"What meteorological bulletin?"

"In the big Parisian newspapers. It is indispensable, this is! It is necessary that the temperature of a thermal station should be better, less variable, more uniformly mild than that of the neighboring and rival stations. You subscribe to the meteorological bulletin in the leading organs of opinion, and I will send every evening by telegraph the atmospheric situation. I will do it in such a way that the average arrived at when the year is at an end may be higher than the best mean temperatures of the surrounding stations. The first thing that meets our eyes when we open the big newspapers are the temperatures of Vichy, of Royat, of Mont Doré, of Chatel-Guyon, and other places during the summer season, and, during the winter season, the temperatures of Cannes, Mentone, Nice, Saint Raphael. It is necessary that the weather should always be hot and always fine in these places, in order that the Parisian might say: 'Christi! how lucky the people are who go down there!'"

Andermatt exclaimed: "Upon my honor, you're right. Why have I never thought of that? I will attend to it this very day. With regard to useful things, have you written to Professors Larenard and Pascalis? There are two men I would like very much to have here."

"Unapproachable, my dear President—unless—unless they are satisfied of themselves after many trials that our waters are of a superior character. But, as far as they are concerned, you will accomplish nothing by persuasion—by anticipation."

They passed by Paul and Gontran, who had come to take coffee after luncheon. Other bathers made their appearance, especially men, for the women, on rising from the table, always went up to their rooms for an hour or two. Petrus Martel was looking after his waiters, and crying out: "A kummel, a nip of brandy, a glass of aniseed cordial," in the same rolling, deep voice which he would assume an hour later while conducting rehearsals, and giving the keynote to the young première.

Andermatt stopped a few moments for a short chat with the two young men; then he resumed his promenade by the side of the inspector.

Gontran, with legs crossed and folded arms, lolling in his chair, with the nape of his neck against the back of it, and his eyes and his cigar facing the sky, was puffing in a state of absolute contentment.

Suddenly, he asked: "Would you mind taking a turn, presently, in the valley of Sans-Souci? The girls will be there."

Paul hesitated; then, after some reflection: "Yes, I am quite willing." Then he added: "Is your affair progressing?"

"Egad, it is! Oh! I have a hold of her. She won't escape me now."

Gontran had, by this time, taken his friend into his confidence, and told him, day by day, how he was going on and how much ground he had gained. He even got him to be present, as a confederate, at his appointments, for he had managed to obtain appointments with Louise Oriol by a little bit of ingenuity.

After their promenade at the Puy de la Nugère, Christiane put an end to these excursions by not going out at all, and so rendered it more and more difficult for the lovers to meet.

Her brother, put out at first by this attitude on her part, bethought him of some means of extricating himself from this predicament. Accustomed to Parisian morals, according to which women are regarded by men of his stamp as game, the chase of which is often no easy one, he had in former days made use of many artifices in order to gain access to those for whom he had conceived a passion. He knew better than anyone else how to make use of pimps, to discover those who were accommodating through interested motives, and to determine with a single glance the men or women who were disposed to aid him in his designs.

The unconscious support of Christiane having suddenly been withdrawn from him, he had looked about him for the requisite connecting link, the "pliant nature," as he expressed it himself, whereby he could replace his sister; and his choice speedily fixed itself on Doctor Honorat's wife. Many reasons pointed at her as a suitable person. In the first place, her husband, closely associated with the Oriols, had been for the past twenty years attending this family. He had been present at the birth of the children, had dined with them every Sunday, and had entertained them at his own table every Tuesday. His wife, a fat old woman of the lower-middle class, trying to pass as a lady, full of pretension, easy to overcome through her vanity, was sure to lend both hands to every desire of the Comte de Ravenel, whose brother-in-law owned the establishment of Mont Oriol.

Besides, Gontran, who was a good judge of a go-between, had satisfied himself that this woman was naturally well adapted for the part, by merely seeing her walking through the street.

"She has the physique," was his reflection, "and when one has the physique for an employment, one has the soul required for it, too!"

Accordingly, he made his way into her abode, one day, after having accompanied her husband to his own door. He sat down, chatted, complimented the lady, and, when the dinner-bell rang, he said, as he rose up: "You have a very savory smell here. You cook better than they do at the hotel."

Madame Honorat, swelling with pride, faltered: "Good heavens! if I might make so bold—if I might make so bold, Monsieur le Comte, as——"

"If you might make so bold as what, dear Madame?"

"As to ask you to share our humble meal."

"Faith—faith, I would say 'yes.'"

The doctor, ill at ease, muttered: "But we have nothing, nothing—soup, a joint of beef, and a chicken, that's all!"

Gontran laughed: "That's quite enough for me. I accept the invitation."

And he dined at the Honorat household. The fat woman rose up, went to take the dishes out of the servant-maid's hands, in order that the latter might not spill the sauce over the tablecloth, and, in spite of her husband's impatience, insisted on attending at table herself.

The Comte congratulated her on the excellence of the cooking, on the good house she kept, on her attention to the duties of hospitality, and he left her inflamed with enthusiasm.

He returned to leave his card, accepted a fresh invitation, and thenceforth made his way constantly to Madame Honorat's house, to which the Oriol girls had paid visits frequently also for many years as neighbors and friends.

So then he spent hours there, in the midst of the three ladies, attentive to both sisters, but accentuating clearly, from day to day, his marked preference for Louise.

The jealousy that had sprung up between the girls since the time when he had begun to make love to Charlotte had assumed an aspect of spiteful hostility on the side of the elder girl and of disdain on the side of the younger. Louise, with her reserved air, imported into her reticences and her demure ways in Gontran's society much more coquetry and encouragement than the other had formerly shown with all her free and joyous unconstraint. Charlotte, wounded to the quick, concealed through pride the pain that she endured, pretended not to see or hear anything of what was happening around her, and continued her visits to Madame Honorat's house with a beautiful appearance of indifference to all these lovers' meetings. She would not remain behind at her own abode lest people might think that her heart was sore, that she was weeping, that she was making way for her sister.

Gontran, too proud of his achievement to throw a veil over it, could not keep himself from talking about it to Paul. And Paul, thinking it amusing, began to laugh. He had, besides, since the first equivocal remarks of his friend, resolved not to interfere in his affairs, and he often asked himself with uneasiness: "Can it be possible that he knows something about Christiane and me?"

He knew Gontran too well not to believe him capable of shutting his eyes to an intrigue on the part of his sister. But then, why did he not let it be understood sooner that he guessed it or was aware of it? Gontran was, in fact, one of those in whose opinion every woman in society ought to have a lover or lovers, one of those for whom the family is merely a society of mutual help, for whom morality is an attitude that is indispensable in order to veil the different appetites which nature has implanted in us, and for whom worldly honor is a front behind which amiable vices should be hidden. Moreover, if he had egged on his dear sister to marry Andermatt was it not with the vague, if not clearly-defined, idea that this Jew might be utilized, in every way, by all the family?—and he would probably have despised Christiane for being faithful to this husband of convenience, of utility, just as much as he would have despised himself for not borrowing freely from his brother-in-law's purse.

Paul pondered over all this, and it disturbed his modern Don Quixote's soul, which, in any event, was disposed toward compromise. He had, therefore, become very reserved with this enigmatic friend of his. When, accordingly, Gontran told him the use that he was making of Madame Honorat, Bretigny burst out laughing; and he had even, for some time past, allowed himself to be brought to that lady's house, and found great pleasure in chatting with Charlotte there.

The doctor's wife lent herself, with the best grace in the world, to the part she was made to play, and offered them tea about five o'clock, like the Parisian ladies, with little cakes manufactured by her own hands. On the first occasion when Paul made his way into this household, she welcomed him as if he were an old friend, made him sit down, removed his hat herself, in spite of his protests, and placed it beside the clock upon the mantelpiece. Then, eager, bustling, going from one to the other, tremendously big and fat, she asked:

"Do you feel inclined for a little dinner?"

Gontran told funny stories, joked, and laughed quite at his ease. Then, he took Louise into the recess of a window under the troubled eyes of Charlotte.

Madame Honorat, who sat chatting with Paul, said to him in a maternal tone:

"These dear children, they come here to have a few minutes' conversation with one another. 'Tis very innocent—isn't it, Monsieur Bretigny?"

"Oh! very innocent, Madame!"

When he came the next time, she familiarly addressed him as "Monsieur Paul," treating him more or less as a crony.

And from that time forth, Gontran told him, with a sort of teasing liveliness, all about the complaisant behavior of the doctor's wife, to whom he had said, the evening before: "Why do you never go out for a walk along the Sans-Souci road?"

"But we will go, M. le Comte—we will go."

"Say, to-morrow about three o'clock."

"To-morrow, about three o'clock, M. le Comte."

And Gontran explained to Paul: "You understand that in this drawing-room, I cannot say anything of a very confidential nature to the elder girl before the younger. But in the wood I can go on before or remain behind with Louise. So then you will come?"

"Yes, I have no objection."

"Let us go on then."

And they rose up, and set forth at a leisurely pace along the highroad; then, having passed through La Roche Pradière, they turned to the left and descended into the wooded glen in the midst of tangled brushwood. When they had passed the little river, they sat down at the side of the path and waited.

The three ladies soon arrived, walking in single file, Louise in front, and Madame Honorat in the rear. They exhibited surprise on both sides at having met in this way. Gontran exclaimed: "Well, now, what a good idea this was of yours to come along here!"

The doctor's wife replied: "Yes, the idea was mine."

They continued their walk. Louise and Gontran gradually quickened their steps, went on in advance, and rambled so far together that they disappeared from view at a turn of the narrow path.

The fat lady, who was breathing hard, murmured, as she cast an indulgent eye in their direction: "Bah! they're young—they have legs. As for me, I can't keep up with them."

Charlotte exclaimed: "Wait! I'm going to call them back!"

She was rushing away. The doctor's wife held her back: "Don't interfere with them, child, if they want to chat! It would not be nice to disturb them. They will come back all right by themselves."

And she sat down on the grass, under the shade of a pine-tree, fanning herself with her pocket-handkerchief. Charlotte cast a look of distress toward Paul, a look imploring and sorrowful.

He understood, and said: "Well, Mademoiselle, we are going to let Madame take a rest, and we'll both go and overtake your sister."

She answered impetuously: "Oh, yes, Monsieur."

Madame Honorat made no objection: "Go, my children, go. As for me, I'll wait for you here. Don't be too long."

And they started off in their turn. They walked quickly at first, as they could see no sign of the two others, and hoped to come up with them; then, after a few minutes, it struck them that Louise and Gontran might have turned off to the right or to the left through the wood, and Charlotte began to call them in a trembling and undecided voice. There was no response. She exclaimed: "Oh! good heavens, where can they be?"

Paul felt himself overcome once more by that profound pity, by that sympathetic tenderness toward her which had previously taken possession of him on the edge of the crater of La Nugère.

He did not know what to say to this afflicted young creature. He felt a longing, a paternal and passionate longing to take her in his arms, to embrace her, to find sweet and consoling words with which to soothe her. But what words?

She looked about on every side, searched the branches with wild glances, listening to the faintest sounds, murmuring: "I think that they are here—No, there—Do you hear nothing?"

"No, Mademoiselle, I don't hear anything. The best thing we can do is to wait here."

"Oh! heavens, no. We must find them!"

He hesitated for a few seconds, and then said to her in a low tone: "This, then, causes you much pain?"

She raised toward his her eyes, in which there was a look of wild alarm, while the gathering tears filled them with a transparent watery mist, as yet held back by the lids, over which drooped the long, brown lashes. She strove to speak, but could not, and did not venture to open her lips. But her heart swollen, choked with grief, was yearning to pour itself out.

He went on: "So then you loved him very much. He is not worthy of your love. Take heart!"

She could not restrain herself any longer, and hiding with her hands the tears that now gushed forth from her eyes, she sobbed: "No!—no!—I do not love him—he—it is too base to have acted as he did. He made a tool of me—it is too base—too cowardly—but, all the same, it does pain me—a great deal—for it is hard—very hard—oh! yes. But what grieves me most is that my sister—my sister does not care for me any longer—she who has been even more wicked than he was! I feel that she no longer cares for me—not a bit—that she hates me—I have only her—I have no one else—and I, I have done nothing!"

He only saw her ear and her neck with its young flesh sinking into the collar of her dress under the light material she wore till it was lost in the curves of her bust. And he felt himself overpowered with compassion, with sympathy, carried away by that impetuous desire of self-devotion which got the better of him every time that a woman touched his heart. And that heart of his, responsive to outbursts of enthusiasm, was excited by this innocent sorrow, agitating, ingenuous, and cruelly charming.

He stretched forth his hand toward her with an unstudied movement such as one might use in order to caress, to calm a child, and he drew it round her waist from behind over her shoulder. Then he felt her heart beaming with rapid throbs, as he might have heard the little heart of a bird that he had caught. And this beating, continuous, precipitate, sent a thrill all over his arm into his heart, accelerating its movements. And he felt those quick heart-beats coming from her and penetrating him through his flesh, his muscles, and his nerves, so that between them there was now only one heart wounded by the same pain, agitated by the same palpitation, living the same life, like clocks connected by a string at some distance from one another and made to keep time together second by second.

But suddenly she uncovered her flushed face, still tear-dimmed, quickly wiped it, and said:

"Come, I ought not to have spoken to you about this. I am foolish. Let us go back at once to Madame Honorat, and forget. Do you promise me?"

"I do promise you."

She gave him her hand. "I have confidence in you. I believe you are very honest!"

They turned back. He lifted her up in crossing the stream, just as he had lifted up Christiane, the year before. How often had he passed along this path with her in the days when he adored her! He reflected, wondering at his own changed feelings: "How short a time this passion lasted!"

Charlotte, laying a finger on his arm, murmured: "Madame Honorat is asleep. Let us sit down without making a noise."

Madame Honorat was, indeed, slumbering, with her back to a pine-tree, her handkerchief over her face and her hands crossed over her stomach. They seated themselves a few paces away from her, and refrained from speaking in order not to awaken her. Then the stillness of the wood was so profound that it became as painful to them as actual suffering. Nothing could be heard save the water gurgling over the stones, a little lower down, then those imperceptible quiverings of insects passing by, those light buzzings of flies or of other living creatures whose movements made the dead leaves flutter.

Where then were Louise and Gontran? What were they doing? All at once, the sound of their voices reached them from a distance. They were returning. Madame Honorat woke up and looked astonished.

"What! you are here again! I did not notice you coming back. And the others, have you found them?"

Paul replied: "There they are! They are coming."

They recognized Gontran's laughter. This laughter relieved Charlotte from a crushing weight, which had oppressed her mind—she could not have explained why.

They were soon able to distinguish the pair. Gontran had almost broken into a running pace, dragging by the arm the young girl, who was quite flushed. And, even before they had come up, so great a hurry was he in to tell his story, he shouted:

"You don't know what we surprised. I give you a thousand guesses to discover it! The handsome Doctor Mazelli along with the daughter of the illustrious Professor Cloche, as Will would say, the pretty widow with the red hair. Oh! yes, indeed—surprised, you understand? He was embracing her, the scamp. Oh! yes—oh! yes."

Madame Honorat, at this immoderate display of gaiety, made a dignified movement:

"Oh! M. le Comte, think of these young ladies!"

Gontran made a respectful obeisance.

"You are perfectly right, dear Madame, to recall me to the proprieties. All your inspirations are excellent."

Then, in order that they might not be all seen going back together, the two young men bowed to the ladies, and returned through the wood to the village.

"Well?" asked Paul.

"Well, I told her that I adored her and that I would be delighted to marry her."

"And she said?"

"She said, with charming discretion, 'That concerns my father. It is to him that I will give my answer.'"

"So then you are going to——"

"To intrust my ambassador Andermatt at once with the official application. And if the old boor makes any row about it, I'll compromise his daughter with a splash."

And, as Andermatt was again engaged in conversation with Doctor Latonne on the terrace of the Casino, Gontran stopped here, and immediately made his brother-in-law acquainted with the situation.

Paul went off along the road to Riom. He wanted to be alone so much did he find himself invaded by that agitation of the entire mind and body into which every meeting with a woman casts a man who is on the point of falling in love. For some time past he had felt, without quite realizing it, the penetrating and youthful fascination of this forsaken girl. He found her so nice, so good, so simple, so upright, so innocent, that from the first he had been moved by compassion for her, by that tender compassion with which the sorrows of women always inspire us. Then, when he had seen her frequently, he had allowed to bud forth in his heart that grain, that tiny grain, of tenderness which they sow in us so quickly, and which grows to such a height. And now, for the last hour especially, he was beginning to feel himself possessed, to feel within him that constant presence of the absent which is the first sign of love. He proceeded along the road, haunted by the remembrance of her glance, by the sound of her voice, by the way in which she smiled or wept, by the gait with which she walked, even by the color and the flutter of her dress. And he said to himself:

"I believe I am bitten. I know it. It is annoying, this! The best thing, perhaps, would be to go back to Paris. Deuce take it, it is a young girl! However, I can't make her my mistress."

Then, he began dreaming about it, just as he had dreamed about Christiane, the year before. How different was this one, too, from all the women he had hitherto known, born and brought up in the city, different even from those young maidens sophisticated from their childhood by the coquetry of their mothers or the coquetry which shows itself in the streets. There was in her none of the artificiality of the woman prepared for seduction, nothing studied in her words, nothing conventional in her actions, nothing deceitful in her looks. Not only was she a being fresh and pure, but she came of a primitive race; she was a true daughter of the soil at the moment when she was about to be transformed into a woman of the city.

And he felt himself stirred up, pleading for her against that vague resistance which still struggled in his breast. The forms of heroines in sentimental novels passed before his mind's eye—the creations of Walter Scott, of Dickens, and of George Sand, exciting the more his imagination, always goaded by ideal pictures of women.

Gontran passed judgment on him thus: "Paul! he is a pack-horse with a Cupid on his back. When he flings one on the ground, another jumps up in its place." But Bretigny saw that night was falling. He had been a long time walking. He returned to the village.

As he was passing in front of the new baths, he saw Andermatt and the two Oriols surveying and measuring the vinefields; and he knew from their gestures that they were disputing in an excited fashion.

An hour afterward, Will, entering the drawing-room, where the entire family had assembled, said to the Marquis: "My dear father-in-law, I have to inform you that your son Gontran is going to marry, in six weeks or two months, Mademoiselle Louise Oriol."

M. de Ravenel was startled: "Gontran? You say?"

"I say that he is going to marry in six weeks or two months, with your consent, Mademoiselle Louise Oriol, who will be very rich."

Thereupon the Marquis said simply: "Good heavens! if he likes it, I have no objection."

And the banker related how he had dealt with the old countryman. As soon as he had learned from the Comte that the young girl would consent, he wanted to obtain, at one interview, the vinedresser's assent without giving him time to prepare any of his dodges. He accordingly hurried to Oriol's house, and found him making up his accounts with great difficulty, assisted by Colosse, who was adding figures together with his fingers.

Seating himself: "I would like to drink of your excellent wine," said he.

When big Colosse had returned with the glasses and the jug brimming over, he asked whether Mademoiselle Louise had come home; then he begged of them to send for her. When she stood facing him, he rose, and, making her a low bow:

"Mademoiselle, will you regard me at this moment as a friend to whom one may say everything? Is it not so? Well, I am charged with a very delicate mission with reference to you. My brother-in-law, Comte Raoul-Olivier-Gontran de Ravenel, is smitten with you—a thing for which I commend him—and he has commissioned me to ask you, in the presence of your family, whether you will consent to become his wife."

Taken by surprise in this way, she turned toward her father her eyes, which betrayed her confusion. And Père Oriol, scared, looked at his son, his usual counselor, while Colosse looked at Andermatt, who went on, with a certain amount of pomposity:

"You understand, Mademoiselle, that I am only intrusted with this mission on the terms of an immediate reply being given to my brother-in-law. He is quite conscious of the fact that you may not care for him, and in that case he will quit this neighborhood to-morrow, never to come back to it again. I am aware, besides, that you know him sufficiently to say to me, a simple intermediary, 'I consent,' or 'I do not consent.'"

She hung down her head, and, blushing, but resolute, she faltered: "I consent, Monsieur."

Then she fled so quickly that she knocked herself against the door as she went out.

Thereupon, Andermatt sat down, and, pouring out a glass of wine after the fashion of peasants:

"Now we are going to talk about business," said he.

And, without admitting the possibility even of hesitation, he attacked the question of the dowry, relying on the declarations made to him by the vinedresser three months before. He estimated at three hundred thousand francs, in addition to expectations, the actual fortune of Gontran, and he let it be understood that if a man like the Comte de Ravenel consented to ask for the hand of Oriol's daughter, a very charming young lady in other respects, it was unquestionable that the girl's family were bound to show their appreciation of this honor by a sacrifice of money.

Then the countryman, much disconcerted, but flattered—almost disarmed, tried to make a fight for his property. The discussion was a long one. An admission on Andermatt's part had, however, rendered it easy from the start:

"We don't ask for ready money nor for bills—nothing but the lands, those which you have already indicated as forming Mademoiselle Louise's dowry, in addition to some others which I am going to point you."

The prospect of not having to pay money, that money slowly heaped together, brought into the house franc after franc, sou after sou, that good money, white or yellow, worn by the hands, the purses, the pockets, the tables of cafés, the deep drawers of old presses, that money in whose ring was told the history of so many troubles, cares, fatigues, labors, so sweet to the heart, to the eyes, to the fingers of the peasant, dearer than the cow, than the vine, than the field, than the house, that money harder to part with sometimes than life itself—the prospect of not seeing it go with the girl brought on immediately a great calm, a desire to conciliate, a secret but restrained joy, in the souls of the father and the son.

They continued the discussion, however, in order to keep a few more acres of soil. On the table was spread out a minute plan of Mont Oriol; and they marked one by one with a cross the portions assigned to Louise. It took an hour for Andermatt to secure the last two pieces. Then, in order that there might not be any deceit on one side or the other, they went over all the places on the plan. After that, they identified carefully all the slices designated by crosses, and marked them afresh.

But Andermatt got uneasy, suspecting that the two Oriols were capable of denying, at their next interview, a part of the grants to which they had consented and would seek to take back ends of vinefields, corners useful for his project; and he thought of a practical and certain means of giving definiteness to the agreement.

An idea crossed his mind, made him smile at first, then appeared to him excellent, although singular.

"If you like," said he, "we'll write it all out, so as not to forget it later on."

And as they were entering the village, he stopped before a tobacconist's shop to buy two stamped sheets of paper. He knew that the list of lands drawn up on these leaves with their legal aspect would take an almost inviolable character in the peasant's eyes, for these leaves would represent the law, always invisible and menacing, vindicated by gendarmes, fines, and imprisonment.

Then he wrote on one sheet and copied on the other:

"In pursuance of the promise of marriage exchanged between Comte Gontran de Ravenel and Mademoiselle Louise Oriol, M. Oriol, Senior, surrenders as a dowry to his daughter the lands designated below——"

And he enumerated them minutely, with the figures attached to them in the register of lands for the district.

Then, having dated and signed the document, he made Père Oriol affix his signature, after the latter had exacted in turn a written statement of the intended husband's fortune, and he went back to the hotel with the document in his pocket.

Everyone laughed at his narrative and Gontran most of all. Then the Marquis said to his son with a lofty air of dignity: "We shall both go this evening to pay a visit to this family, and I shall myself renew the application previously made by my son-in-law in order that it may be more regular."

CHAPTER XIII.

Paul Changes His Mind

Gontran made an admirable fiancé, as courteous as he was assiduous. With the aid of Andermatt's purse, he made presents to everyone; and he constantly visited the young girl, either at her own house, or that of Madame Honorat. Paul nearly always accompanied him now, in order to have the opportunity of meeting Charlotte, saying to himself, after each visit, that he would see her no more.

She had bravely resigned herself to her sister's marriage, and she referred to it with apparent unconcern, as if it did not cause her the slightest anxiety. Her character alone seemed a little altered, more sedate, less open. While Gontran was talking soft nothings to Louise in a half-whisper in a corner, Bretigny conversed with her in a serious fashion, and allowed himself to be slowly vanquished, allowed this fresh love to inundate his soul like a flowing tide. He knew what was happening to him, and gave himself up to it, thinking: "Bah! when the moment arrives. I will make my escape—that's all."

When he left her, he would go up to see Christiane, who now lay from morning till night stretched on a long chair. At the door, he could not help feeling nervous and irritated, prepared beforehand for those light quarrels to which weariness gives birth. All that she said, all that she was thinking of, annoyed him, even ere she had opened her lips. Her appearance of suffering, her resigned attitude, her looks of reproach and of supplication, made words of anger rise to his lips, which he repressed through good-breeding; and, even when by her side, he kept before his mind the constant memory, the fixed image, of the young girl whom he had just quitted.

As Christiane, tormented with seeing so little of him, overwhelmed him with questions as to how he spent his days, he invented stories, to which she listened attentively, seeking to find out whether he was thinking of some other woman. The powerlessness which she felt in herself to keep a hold on this man, the powerlessness to pour into him a little of that love with which she was tortured, the physical powerlessness to fascinate him still, to give herself to him, to win him back by caresses, since she could not regain him by the tender intimacies of love, made her suspect the worst, without knowing on what to fix her fears.

She vaguely realized that some danger was lowering over her, some great unknown danger. And she was filled with undefined jealousy, jealousy of everything—of women whom she saw passing by her window, and whom she thought charming, without even having any proof that Bretigny had ever spoken to them.

She asked of him: "Have you noticed a very pretty woman, a brunette, rather tall, whom I saw a little while ago, and who must have arrived here within the past few days?"

When he replied, "No, I don't know her," she at once jumped to the conclusion that he was lying, turned pale, and went on: "But it is not possible that you have not seen her. She appears to me very beautiful."

He was astonished at her persistency. "I assure you I have not seen her. I'll try to come across her."

She thought: "Surely it must be she!" She felt persuaded, too, on certain days, that he was hiding some intrigue in the locality, that he had sent for his mistress, an actress perhaps. And she questioned everybody, her father, her brother, and her husband, about all the women young and desirable, whom they observed in the neighborhood of Enval. If only she could have walked about, and seen for herself, she might have reassured herself a little; but the almost complete loss of motion which her condition forced upon her now made her endure an intolerable martyrdom.

When she spoke to Paul, the tone of her voice alone revealed her anguish, and intensified his nervous impatience with this love, which for him was at an end. He could no longer talk quietly about anything with her save the approaching marriage of Gontran, a subject which enabled him to pronounce Charlotte's name, and to give vent to his thoughts aloud about the young girl. And it was a mysterious source of delight to him even to hear Christiane articulating that name, praising the grace and all the qualities of this little maiden, compassionating her, regretting that her brother should have sacrificed her, and expressing a desire that some man, some noble heart, should appreciate her, love her, and marry her.

He said: "Oh! yes, Gontran acted foolishly there. She is perfectly charming, that young girl."

Christiane, without any misgiving, echoed: "Perfectly charming. She is a pearl! a piece of perfection!"

Never had she thought that a man like Paul could love a little maid like this, or that he would be likely to marry her. She had no apprehensions save of his mistresses. And it was a singular phenomenon of the heart that praise of Charlotte from Christiane's lips assumed in his eyes an extreme value, excited his love, whetted his desire, and surrounded the young girl with an irresistible attraction.

Now, one day, when he called at Madame Honorat's house to meet there the Oriol girls, they found Doctor Mazelli installed there as if he was at home. He stretched forth both hands to the two young men, with that Italian smile of his, which seemed to give away his entire heart with every word and every movement.

Gontran and he were linked by a friendship at once familiar and futile, made up of secret affinities, of hidden likenesses, of a sort of confederacy of instincts, rather than any real affection or confidence.

The Comte asked: "What about your little blonde of the Sans-Souci wood?"

The Italian smiled: "Bah! we are on terms of indifference toward one another. She is one of those women who offer everything and give nothing."

And they began to chat. The handsome physician performed certain offices for the young girls, especially for Charlotte. When addressing women, he manifested a perpetual adoration in his voice, his gestures, and his looks. His entire person, from head to foot, said to them, "I love you" with an eloquence in his attitude which never failed to win their favor. He displayed the graces of an actress, the light pirouettes of a danseuse, the supple movements of a juggler, an entire science of seduction natural and acquired, of which he constantly made use.

Paul, when returning to the hotel with Gontran, exclaimed in a tone of sullen vexation: "What does this charlatan come to that house for?"

The Comte replied quietly: "How can you ever tell when dealing with such adventurers? These sort of people slip in everywhere. This fellow must be tired of his vagabond existence, and of giving way to every caprice of his Spaniard, of whom he is rather the valet than the physician—and perhaps something more. He is looking about him. Professor Cloche's daughter was a good catch—he has failed with her, he says. The second of the Oriol girls would not be less valuable to him. He is making the attempt, feeling his way, smelling about, sounding. He would become co-proprietor of the waters, would try to knock over that idiot, Latonne, would in any case get an excellent practice here every summer for himself, which would last him over the winter. Faith! this is his plan exactly—no doubt of it!"

A dull rage, a jealous animosity, was aroused in Paul's heart. A voice exclaimed: "Hey! hey!" It was Mazelli, who had overtaken them. Bretigny said to him, with aggressive irony: "Where are you rushing so quickly, doctor? One would say that you were pursuing fortune." The Italian smiled, and, without stopping, but skipping backward, he plunged, with a mimic's graceful movement, his hands into his two pockets, quickly turned them out and showed them, both empty, holding them wide between two fingers by the ends of the seams. Then he said: "I have not got hold of it yet." And, turning on his toes, he rushed away like a man in a great hurry.

They found him again several times, on the following days, at Doctor Honorat's house, where he made himself useful to the three ladies by a thousand graceful little services, by the same clever tactics which he had no doubt adopted when dealing with the Duchess. He knew how to do everything to perfection, from paying compliments to making macaroni. He was, moreover, an excellent cook, and protecting himself from stains by means of a servant's blue apron, and wearing a chef's cap made of paper on his head, while he sang Neapolitan ditties in Italian, he did the work of a scullion, without appearing a bit ridiculous, amusing and fascinating everybody, down to the half-witted housekeeper, who said of him: "He is a marvel!"

His plans were soon obvious, and Paul no longer had any doubt that he was trying to get Charlotte to fall in love with him. He seemed to be succeeding in this. He was so profuse of flattery, so eager, so artful in striving to please, that the young girl's face had, when she looked at him, that air of contentment which indicates that the heart is gratified.

Paul, in his turn, without being even able to account to himself for his conduct, assumed the attitude of a lover, and set himself up as a rival. When he saw the doctor with Charlotte, he would come on the scene, and, with his more direct manner, exert himself to win the young girl's affections. He showed himself straightforward and sympathetic, fraternal, devoted, repeating to her, with the sincerity of a friend, in a tone so frank that one could scarcely see in it an avowal of love: "I am very fond of you; cheer up!"

Mazelli, astonished at this unexpected rivalry, had recourse to all his powers of captivation; and, when Bretigny, bitten with jealousy, that naïve jealousy which takes possession of a man when he is dealing with any woman, even without being in love with her, provided only he has taken a fancy to her—when, filled with this natural violence, he became aggressive and haughty, the other, more pliant, always master of himself, replied with sly allusions, witticisms, well-turned and mocking compliments.

It was a daily warfare which they both waged fiercely, without either of them perhaps having a well-defined object in view. They did not want to give way, like two dogs who have gained a grip of the same quarry.

Charlotte had recovered her good humor, but along with it she now exhibited a more biting waggery, a certain sphinx-like attitude, less candor in her smile and in her glance. One would have said that Gontran's desertion had educated her, prepared her for possible deceptions, disciplined, and armed her.

She played off her two admirers against one another in a sly and dexterous fashion, saying to each of them what she thought necessary, without letting the one fall foul of the other, without ever letting the one suppose that she preferred the other, laughing slightly at each of them in turn in the presence of his rival, leaving them an equal match without appearing even to take either of them seriously. But all this was done simply, in the manner of a schoolgirl rather than in that of a coquette, with that mischievous air exhibited by young girls which sometimes renders them irresistible.

Mazelli, however, seemed suddenly to be having the advantage. He had apparently become more intimate with her, as if a secret understanding had been established between them. While talking to her, he played lightly with her parasol and with one of the ribbons of her dress, which appeared to Paul, as it were, an act of moral possession, and exasperated him so much that he longed to box the Italian's ears.

But, one day, at Père Oriol's house, while Bretigny was chatting with Louise and Gontran, and, at the same time, keeping his eye fixed on Mazelli, who was telling Charlotte in a subdued voice some things that made her smile, he suddenly saw her blush with such an appearance of embarrassment as to leave no doubt for one moment on his mind that the other had spoken of love. She had cast down her eyes, and ceased to smile, but still continued listening; and Paul, who felt disposed to make a scene, said to Gontran: "Will you have the goodness to come out with me for five minutes?"

The Comte made his excuses to his betrothed, and followed his friend.

When they were in the street, Paul exclaimed: "My dear fellow, this wretched Italian must, at any cost, be prevented from inveigling this girl, who is defenseless against him."

"What do you wish me to do?"

"To warn her of the fact that he is an adventurer."

"Hey, my dear boy, those things are no concern of mine."

"After all, she is to be your sister-in-law."

"Yes, but there is nothing to show me conclusively that Mazelli has guilty designs upon her. He exhibits the same gallantry toward all women, and he has never said or done anything improper."

"Well, if you don't want to take it on yourself, I'll do it, although it concerns me less assuredly than it does you."

"So then you are in love with Charlotte?"

"I? No—but I see clearly through this blackguard's game."

"My dear fellow, you are mixing yourself up in matters of a delicate nature, and—unless you are in love with Charlotte——"

"No—I am not in love with her—but I am hunting down imposters, that's what I mean!"

"May I ask what you intend to do?"

"To thrash this beggar."

"Good! the best way to make her fall in love with him. You fight with him, and whether he wounds you, or you wound him, he will become a hero in her eyes."

"What would you do then?"

"In your place?"

"In my place."

"I would speak to the girl as a friend. She has great confidence in you. Well, I would say to her simply in a few words what these hangers-on of society are. You know very well how to say these things. You possess an eloquent tongue. And I would make her understand, first, why he is attached to the Spaniard; secondly, why he attempted to lay siege to Professor Cloche's daughter; thirdly, why, not having succeeded in this effort, he is striving, in the last place, to make a conquest of Mademoiselle Charlotte Oriol."

"Why do you not do that, yourself, who will be her brother-in-law?"

"Because—because—on account of what passed between us—come! I can't."

"That's quite right. I am going to speak to her."

"Do you want me to procure for you a private conversation with her immediately?"

"Why, yes, assuredly."

"Good! Walk about for ten minutes. I am going to carry off Louise and Mazelli, and, when you come back, you will find the other alone."

Paul Bretigny rambled along the side of the Enval gorges, thinking over the best way of opening this difficult conversation.

He found Charlotte Oriol alone, indeed, on his return, in the cold, whitewashed parlor of the paternal abode; and he said to her, as he sat down beside her: "It is I, Mademoiselle, who asked Gontran to procure me this interview with you."

She looked at him with her clear eyes: "Why, pray?"

"Oh! it is not to pay you insipid compliments in the Italian fashion. It is to speak to you as a friend—as a very devoted friend, who owes you good advice."

"Tell me what it is."

He took up the subject in a roundabout style, dwelt upon his own experience, and upon her inexperience, so as to lead gradually by discreet but explicit phrases to a reference to those adventurers who are everywhere going in quest of fortune, taking advantage with their professional skill of every ingenuous and good-natured being, man or woman, whose purses or hearts they explored.

She turned rather pale as she listened to him.

Then she said: "I understand and I don't understand. You are speaking of some one—of whom?"

"I am speaking of Doctor Mazelli."

Then, she lowered her eyes, and remained a few seconds without replying; after this, in a hesitating voice: "You are so frank that I will be the same with you. Since—since my sister's marriage has been arranged, I have become a little less—a little less stupid! Well, I had already suspected what you tell me—and I used to feel amused of my own accord at seeing him coming."

She raised her face to his as she spoke, and in her smile, in her arch look, in her little retroussé nose, in the moist and glittering brilliancy of her teeth which showed themselves between her lips, so much open-hearted gracefulness, sly gaiety, and charming frolicsomeness appeared that Bretigny felt himself drawn toward her by one of those tumultuous transports which flung him distracted with passion at the feet of the woman who was his latest love. And his heart exulted with joy because Mazelli had not been preferred to him. So then he had triumphed.

He asked: "You do not love him, then?"

"Whom? Mazelli?"

"Yes."

She looked at him with such a pained expression in her eyes that he felt thrown off his balance, and stammered, in a supplicating voice: "What?—you don't love—anyone?"

She replied, with a downward glance: "I don't know—I love people who love me."

He seized the young girl's two hands, all at once, and kissing them wildly in one of those moments of impulse in which the head loses its controlling power, and the words which rise to the lips come from the excited flesh rather than the wandering mind, he faltered:

"I!—I love you, my little Charlotte; yes, I love you!"

She quickly drew away one of her hands, and placed it on his mouth, murmuring: "Be silent!—be silent, I beg of you! It would cause me too much pain if this were another falsehood."

She stood erect; he rose up, caught her in his arms, and embraced her passionately.

A sudden noise parted them; Père Oriol had just come in, and he was gazing at them, quite scared. Then, he cried: "Ah! bougrrre! ah! bougrrre! ah! bougrrre of a savage!"

Charlotte had rushed out, and the two men remained face to face. After some seconds of agitation, Paul made an attempt to explain his position.

"My God! Monsieur—I have conducted myself—it is true—like a——"

But the old man would not listen to him. Anger, furious anger, had taken possession of him, and he advanced toward Bretigny, with clenched fists, repeating:

"Ah! bougrrre of a savage——"

Then, when they were nose to nose, he seized Paul by the collar with his knotted peasant's hands.

But the other, as tall, and strong with that superior strength acquired by the practice of athletics, freed himself with a single push from the countryman's grip, and, pushing him up against the wall:

"Listen, Père Oriol, this is not a matter for us to fight about, but to settle quietly. It is true, I was embracing your daughter. I swear to you that this is the first time—and I swear to you, too, that I desire to marry her."

The old man, whose physical excitement had subsided under the assault of his adversary, but whose anger had not yet been calmed, stuttered:

"Ha! that's how it is! You want to steal my daughter; you want my money. Bougrrre of a deceiver!"

Thereupon, he allowed all that was on his mind to escape from him in a heap of grumbling words. He found no consolation for the dowry promised with his elder girl, for his vinelands going into the hands of these Parisians. He now had his suspicions as to Gontran's want of money, Andermatt's craft, and, without forgetting the unexpected fortune which the banker brought him, he vented his bile and his secret rancor against those mischievous people who did not let him sleep any longer in peace.

One would have thought that his family and his friends were coming every night to plunder him, to rob him of everything, his lands, his springs, and his daughters. And he cast these reproaches into Paul's face, accusing him also of wanting to get hold of his property, of being a rogue, and of taking Charlotte in order to have his lands.

The other, soon losing all patience, shouted under his very nose: "Why, I am richer than you, you infernally currish old donkey. I would bring you money."

The old man listened in silence to these words, incredulous but vigilant, and then, in a milder tone, he renewed his complaints.

Paul then answered him and entered into explanations; and, believing that an obligation was imposed on him, owing to the circumstances under which he had been surprised, and for which he was solely responsible, he proposed to marry the girl without asking for any dowry.

Père Oriol shook his head and his ears, heard Paul reiterating his statements, but was unable to understand. To him this young man seemed still a pauper, a penniless wretch.

And, when Bretigny, exasperated, yelled, in his teeth: "Why, you old rascal, I have an income of more than a hundred and twenty thousand francs a year—do you understand?—three millions," the other suddenly asked: "Will you write that down on a piece of paper?"

"Yes, I will write it down!"

"And you'll sign it?"

"Yes, I will sign it."

"On a sheet of notary's paper?"

"Yes, certainly—on a sheet of notary's paper!"

Thereupon, he rose up, opened a press, took out of it two leaves marked with the Government stamp, and, seeking for the undertaking which Andermatt, a few days before, had required from him, he drew up an odd promise of marriage, in which it was made a condition that the fiancé vouched for his being worth three millions; and, at the end of it Bretigny affixed his signature.

When Paul found himself in the open air once more, he felt as if the earth no longer turned round in the same way. So then, he was engaged, in spite of himself, in spite of her, by one of those accidents, by one of those tricks of circumstance, which shut out from you every point of escape. He muttered: "What madness!" Then he reflected: "Bah! I could not have found better perhaps in all the world!"

And in his secret heart he rejoiced at this snare of destiny.

CHAPTER XIV.

Christiane's Via Crucis

The dawn of the following day brought bad news to Andermatt. He learned on his arrival at the bath-establishment that M. Aubry-Pasteur had died during the night from an attack of apoplexy at the Hotel Splendid.

In addition to the fact that the deceased was very useful to him on account of his vast scientific attainments, disinterested zeal, and attachment to the Mont Oriol station, which, in some measure, he looked upon as a daughter, it was much to be regretted that a patient who had come there to fight against a tendency toward congestion should have died exactly in this fashion, in the midst of his treatment, in the very height of the season, at the very moment when the rising spa was beginning to prove a success.

The banker, exceedingly annoyed, walked up and down in the study of the absent inspector, thinking of some device whereby this misfortune might be attributed to some other cause, such as an accident, a fall, a want of prudence, the rupture of an artery; and he impatiently awaited Doctor Latonne's arrival in order that the decease might be ingeniously certified without awakening any suspicion as to the initial cause of the fatality.

All at once, the medical inspector appeared on the scene, his face pale and indicative of extreme agitation; and, as soon as he had passed through the door, he asked: "Have you heard the lamentable news?"

"Yes, the death of M. Aubry-Pasteur."

"No, no, the flight of Doctor Mazelli with Professor Cloche's daughter."

Andermatt felt a shiver running along his skin.

"What? you tell me——"

"Oh! my dear manager, it is a frightful catastrophe, a crash!"

He sat down and wiped his forehead; then he related the facts as he got them from Petrus Martel, who had learned them directly through the professor's valet.

Mazelli had paid very marked attentions to the pretty red-haired widow, a coarse coquette, a wanton, whose first husband had succumbed to consumption, brought on, it was said, by excessive devotion to his matrimonial duties. But M. Cloche, having discovered the projects of the Italian physician, and not desiring this adventurer as a second son-in-law, violently turned him out of doors on surprising him kneeling at the widow's feet.

Mazelli, having been sent out by the door, soon re-entered through the window by the silken ladder of lovers. Two versions of the affair were current. According to the first, he had rendered the professor's daughter mad with love and jealousy; according to the second, he had continued to see her secretly, while pretending to be devoting his attention to another woman; and ascertaining finally through his mistress that the professor remained inflexible, he had carried her off, the same night, rendering a marriage inevitable, in consequence of this scandal.

Doctor Latonne rose up and, leaning his back against the mantelpiece, while Andermatt, astounded, continued walking up and down, he exclaimed:

"A physician, Monsieur, a physician to do such a thing!—a doctor of medicine!—what an absence of character!"

Andermatt, completely crushed, appreciated the consequences, classified them, and weighed them, as one does a sum in addition. They were: "First, the disagreeable report spreading over the neighboring spas and all the way to Paris. If, however, they went the right way about it, perhaps they could make use of this elopement as an advertisement. A fortnight's echoes well written and prominently printed in the newspapers would strongly attract attention to Mont Oriol. Secondly: Professor Cloche's departure an irreparable loss. Thirdly: The departure of the Duchess and the Duke de Ramas-Aldavarra, a second inevitable loss without possible compensation. In short, Doctor Latonne was right. It was a frightful catastrophe."

Then, the banker, turning toward the physician: "You ought to go at once to the Hotel Splendid, and draw up the certificate of the death of Aubry-Pasteur in such a way that no one could suspect it to be a case of congestion."

Doctor Latonne put on his hat; then just as he was leaving: "Ha! another rumor which is circulating! Is it true that your friend Paul Bretigny is going to marry Charlotte Oriol?"

Andermatt gave a start of astonishment.

"Bretigny? Come-now!—who told you that?"

"Why, as in the other case, Petrus Martel, who had it from Père Oriol himself."

"From Père Oriol?"

"Yes, from Père Oriol, who declared that his future son-in-law possessed a fortune of three millions."

William did not know what to think. He muttered: "In point of fact, it is possible. He has been rather hot on her for some time past! But in that case the whole knoll is ours—the whole knoll! Oh! I must make certain of this immediately." And he went out after the doctor in order to meet Paul before breakfast.

As he was entering the hotel, he was informed that his wife had several times asked to see him. He found her still in bed, chatting with her father and with her brother, who was looking through the newspapers with a rapid and wandering glance. She felt poorly, very poorly, restless. She was afraid, without knowing why. And then an idea had come to her, and had for some days been growing stronger in her brain, as usually happens with pregnant women. She wanted to consult Doctor Black. From the effect of hearing around her some jokes at Doctor Latonne's expense, she had lost all confidence in him, and she wanted another opinion, that of Doctor Black, whose success was constantly increasing. Fears, all the fears, all the hauntings, by which women toward the close of pregnancy are besieged, now tortured her from morning until night. Since the night before, in consequence of a dream, she imagined that the Cæsarian operation might be necessary. And she was present in thought at this operation performed on herself. She saw herself lying on her back in a bed covered with blood, while something red was being taken away, which did not move, which did not cry, and which was dead! And for ten minutes she shut her eyes, in order to witness this over again, to be present once more at her horrible and painful punishment. She had, therefore, become impressed with the notion that Doctor Black alone could tell her the truth, and she wanted him at once; she required him to examine her immediately, immediately, immediately! Andermatt, greatly agitated, did not know what answer to give her.

“But my dear child, it is difficult, having regard to my relations with Latonne it is even impossible. Listen! an idea occurs to me: I will look up Professor Mas-Roussel, who is a hundred times better than Black. He will not refuse to come when I ask him.”

But she persisted. She wanted Black, and no one else. She required to see him with his big bulldog’s head beside her. It was a longing, a wild, superstitious desire. She considered it necessary for him to see her.

Then William attempted to change the current of her thoughts:

“You haven’t heard how that intriguer Mazelli carried off Professor Cloche’s daughter the other night. They are gone away; nobody can tell where they levanted to. There’s a nice story for you!”

She was propped up on her pillow, her eyes strained with grief, and she faltered: “Oh! the poor Duchess—the poor woman—how I pity her!” Her heart had long since learned to understand that other woman’s heart, bruised and impassioned! She suffered from the same malady and wept the same tears. But she resumed: “Listen, Will! Go and find M. Black for me. I know I shall die unless he comes!”

Andermatt caught her hand, and tenderly kissed it:

“Come, my little Christiane, be reasonable—understand.”

He saw her eyes filled with tears, and, turning toward the Marquis:

“It is you that ought to do this, my dear father-in-law. As for me, I can’t do it. Black comes here every day about one o’clock to see the Princess de Maldebourg. Stop him in the passage, and send him in to your daughter. You can easily wait an hour, can you not, Christiane?”

She consented to wait an hour, but refused to get up to breakfast with the men, who passed alone into the dining-room.

Paul was there already. Andermatt, when he saw him, exclaimed: “Ah! tell me now, what is it I have been told a little while ago? You are going to marry Charlotte Oriol? It is not true, is it?”

The young man replied in a low tone, casting a restless look toward the closed door: “Good God! it is true!” Nobody having been sure of it till now, the three stared at him in amazement.

William asked: “What came over you? With your fortune, to marry—to embarrass yourself with one woman, when you have the whole of them? And then, after all, the family leaves something to be desired in the matter of refinement. It is all very well for Gontran, who hasn’t a sou!”

Bretigny began to laugh: “My father made a fortune out of flour; he was then a miller on a large scale. If you had known him, you might have said he lacked refinement. As for the young girl——”

Andermatt interrupted him: “Oh! perfect—charming—perfect—and you know—she will be as rich as yourself—if not more so. I answer for it—I—I answer for it!”

Gontran murmured: "Yes, this marriage interferes with nothing, and covers retreats. Only he was wrong in not giving us notice beforehand. How the devil was this business managed, my friend?"

Thereupon, Paul related all that had occurred with some slight modifications. He told about his hesitation, which he exaggerated, and his sudden determination on discovering from the young girl's own lips that she loved him. He described the unexpected entrance of Père Oriol, their quarrel, which he enlarged upon, the countryman's doubts concerning his fortune, and the incident of the stamped paper drawn by the old man out of the press.

Andermatt, laughing till the tears ran down his face, hit the table with his fist: "Ha! he did that over again, the stamped paper touch! It's my invention, that is!"

But Paul stammered, reddening a little: "Pray don't let your wife know about it yet. Owing to the terms which we are on at present, it is more suitable that I should announce it to her myself."

Gontran eyed his friend with an odd, good-humored smile, which seemed to say: "This is quite right, all this, quite right! That's the way things ought to end, without noise, without scandals, without any dramatic situations."

He suggested: "If you like, my dear Paul, we'll go together, after dinner, when she's up, and you will inform her of your decision."

Their eyes met, fixed, full of unfathomable thoughts, then looked in another direction. And Paul replied with an air of indifference:

"Yes, willingly. We'll talk about this presently."

A waiter from the hotel came to inform them that Doctor Black had just arrived for his visit to the Princess; and the Marquis forthwith went out to catch him in the passage. He explained the situation to the doctor, his son-in-law's embarrassment and his daughter's earnest wish, and he brought him in without resistance.

As soon as the little man with the big head had entered Christiane's apartment, she said: "Papa, leave us alone!" And the Marquis withdrew.

Thereupon, she enumerated her disquietudes, her terrors, her nightmares, in a low, sweet voice, as though she were at confession. And the physician listened to her like a priest, covering her sometimes with his big round eyes, showed his attention by a little nod of the head, murmured a "That's it," which seemed to mean, "I know your case at the end of my fingers, and I will cure you whenever I like."

When she had finished speaking, he began in his turn to question her with extreme minuteness of detail about her life, her habits, her course of diet, her treatment. At one moment he appeared to express approval with a gesture, at another to convey blame with an "Oh!" full of reservations. When she came to her great fear that the child was misplaced, he rose up, and with an ecclesiastical modesty, lightly passed his hand over the counterpane, and then remarked, "No, it's all right."

And she felt a longing to embrace him. What a good man this physician was!

He sat down at the table, took a sheet of paper, and wrote out the prescription. It was long, very long. Then he came back close to the bed, and, in an altered tone, clearly indicating that he had finished his professional and sacred duty, he began to chat. He had a deep, unctuous voice, the powerful voice of a thickset dwarf, and there were hidden questions in his most ordinary phrases. He talked about everything. Gontran's marriage seemed to interest him considerably. Then, with his ugly smile like that of an ill-shaped being:

"I have said nothing yet to you about M. Bretigny's marriage, although it cannot be a secret, for Père Oriol has told it to everybody."

A kind of fainting fit took possession of her, commencing at the end of her fingers, then invading her entire body—her arms, her breast, her stomach, her legs. She did not, however, quite understand; but a horrible fear of not learning the truth suddenly restored her powers of observation, and she faltered: "Ha! Père Oriol has told it to everybody?"

"Yes, yes. He was speaking to myself about it less than ten minutes ago. It appears that M. Bretigny is very rich, and that he has been in love with little Charlotte for some time past. Moreover, it is Madame Honorat who made these two matches. She lent her hands and her house for the meetings of the young people."

Christiane had closed her eyes. She had lost consciousness. In answer to the doctor's call, a chambermaid rushed in; then appeared the Marquis, Andermatt, and Gontran, who went to search for vinegar, ether, ice, twenty different things all equally useless. Suddenly, the young woman moved, opened her eyes, lifted up her arms, and uttered a heartrending cry, writhing in the bed. She tried to speak, and in a broken voice said:

"Oh! what pain I feel—my God!—what pain I feel—in my back—something is tearing me—Oh! my God!" And she broke out into fresh shrieks.

The symptoms of confinement were speedily recognized. Then Andermatt rushed off to find Doctor Latonne, and came upon him finishing his meal.

"Come on quickly—my wife has met with a mishap—hurry on!" Then he made use of a little deception, telling how Doctor Black had been found in the hotel at the moment of the first pains. Doctor Black himself confirmed this falsehood by saying to his brother-physician:

"I had just come to visit the Princess when I was informed that Madame Andermatt was taken ill. I hurried to her. It was time!"

But William, in a state of great excitement, his heart beating, his soul filled with alarm was all at once seized with doubts as to the competency of the two professional men, and he started off afresh, bareheaded, in order to run in the direction of Professor Mas-Roussel's house, and to entreat him to come. The professor consented to do so at once, buttoned on his frock-coat with the mechanical movement of a physician going out to pay a visit, and set forth with great, rapid strides, the eager strides of an eminent man whose presence may save a life.

When he arrived on the scene, the two other doctors, full of deference, consulted him with an air of humility, repeating together or nearly at the same time:

"Here is what has occurred, dear master. Don't you think, dear master? Isn't there reason to believe, dear master?"

Andermatt, in his turn, driven crazy with anguish at the moanings of his wife, harassed M. Mas-Roussel with questions, and also addressed him as "dear master" with wide-open mouth.

Christiane, almost naked in the presence of these men, no longer saw, noticed, or understood anything. She was suffering so dreadfully that everything else had vanished from her consciousness. It seemed to her that they were drawing from the tops of her hips along her side and her back a long saw, with blunt teeth, which was mangling her bones and muscles slowly and in an irregular fashion, with shakings, stoppages, and renewals of the operation, which became every moment more and more frightful.

When this torture abated for a few seconds, when the rendings of her body allowed her reason to come back, one thought then fixed itself in her soul, more cruel, more keen, more terrible, than her physical pain: "He was in love with another woman, and was going to marry her!"

And, in order to get rid of this pang, which was eating into her brain, she struggled to bring on once more the atrocious torment of her flesh; she shook her sides; she strained her back; and when the crisis returned again, she had, at least, lost all capacity for thought.

For fifteen hours she endured this martyrdom, so much bruised by suffering and despair that she longed to die, and strove to die in those spasms in which she writhed.

But, after a convulsion longer and more violent than the rest, it seemed to her that everything inside her body suddenly escaped from her. It was over; her pangs were assuaged, like the waves of the sea, when they are calmed; and the relief which she experienced was so intense that, for a time, even her grief became numbed. They spoke to her. She answered in a voice very weak, very low.

Suddenly, Andermatt stooped down, his face toward hers, and he said: "She will live—she is almost at the end of it. It is a girl!"

Christiane was only able to articulate: "Ah! my God!"

So then she had a child, a living child, who would grow big—a child of Paul! She felt a desire to cry out, all this fresh misfortune crushed her heart. She had a daughter. She did not want it! She would not look at it! She would never touch it!

They had laid her down again on the bed, taken care of her, tenderly embraced her. Who had done this? No doubt, her father and her husband. She could not tell. But he—where was he? What was he doing? How happy she would have felt at that moment, if only he still loved her!

The hours dragged along, following each other without any distinction between day and night so far as she was concerned, for she felt only this one thought burning into her soul: he loved another woman.

Then she said to herself all of a sudden: "What if it were false? Why should I not have known about his marriage sooner than this doctor?" After that, came the reflection that it had been kept hidden from her. Paul had taken care that she should not hear about it.

She glanced around her room to see who was there. A woman whom she did not know was keeping watch by her side, a woman of the people. She did not venture to question her. From whom, then, could she make inquiries about this matter?

The door was suddenly pushed open. Her husband entered on the tips of his toes. Seeing that her eyes were open, he came over to her.

"Are you better?"

"Yes, thanks."

"You frightened us very much since yesterday. But there is an end of the danger! By the bye, I am quite embarrassed about your case. I telegraphed to our friend, Madame Icardon, who was to have come to stay with you during your confinement, informing her about your premature illness, and imploring her to hasten down here. She is with her nephew, who has an attack of scarlet fever. You cannot, however, remain without anyone near you, without some woman who is a little—a little suitable for the purpose. Accordingly, a lady from the neighborhood has offered to nurse you, and to keep you company every day, and, faith, I have accepted the offer. It is Madame Honorat."

Christiane suddenly remembered Doctor Black's words. A start of fear shook her; and she groaned: "Oh! no—no—not she!"

William did not understand, and went on: "Listen, I know well that she is very common; but your brother has a great esteem for her; she has been of great service to him; and then it has been thrown out that she was originally a midwife, whom Honorat made the acquaintance of while attending a patient. If you take a strong dislike to her, I will send her away the next day. Let us try her at any rate. Let her come once or twice."

She remained silent, thinking. A craving to know, to know everything, entered into her, so violent that the hope of making this woman chatter freely, of tearing from her one by one the words that would rend her own heart, now filled her with a yearning to reply: "Go, go, and look for her immediately—immediately. Go, pray!"

And to this irresistible desire to know was also superadded a strange longing to suffer more intensely, to roll herself about in her misery, as she might have rolled herself on thorns, the mysterious longing, morbid and feverish, of a martyr calling for fresh pain.

So she faltered: "Yes, I have no objection. Bring me Madame Honorat."

Then, suddenly, she felt that she could not wait any longer without making sure, quite sure, of this treason; and she asked William in a voice weak as a breath:

"Is it true that M. Bretigny is getting married?"

He replied calmly: "Yes, it is true. We would have told you before this if we could have talked with you."

She continued: "With Charlotte?"

"With Charlotte."

Now William had also a fixed idea himself which from this time forth never left him—his daughter, as yet barely alive, whom every moment he was going to look at. He felt indignant because Christiane's first words were not to ask for the baby; and in a tone of gentle reproach: "Well, look here! you have not yet inquired about the little one. You are aware that she is going on very well?"

She trembled as if he had touched a living wound; but it was necessary for her to pass through all the stations of this Calvary.

"Bring her here," she said.

He vanished to the foot of the bed behind the curtain, then he came back, his face lighted up with pride and happiness, and holding in his hands, in an awkward fashion, a bundle of white linen.

He laid it down on the embroidered pillow close to the head of Christiane, who was choking with emotion, and he said: "Look here, see how lovely she is!"

She looked. He opened with two of his fingers the fine lace with which was hidden from view a little red face, so small, so red, with closed eyes, and mouth constantly moving.

And she thought, as she leaned over this beginning of being: "This is my daughter—Paul's daughter. Here then is what made me suffer so much. This—this—this is my daughter!"

Her repugnance toward the child, whose birth had so fiercely torn her poor heart and her tender woman's body had, all at once, disappeared; she now contemplated it with ardent and sorrowing curiosity, with profound astonishment, the astonishment of a being who sees her firstborn come forth from her.

Andermatt was waiting for her to caress it passionately. He was surprised and shocked, and asked: "Are you not going to kiss it?"

She stooped quite gently toward this little red forehead; and in proportion as she drew her lips closer to it, she felt them drawn, called by it. And when she had placed them upon it, when she touched it, a little moist, a little warm, warm with her own life, it seemed to her that she could not withdraw her lips from that infantile flesh, that she would leave them there forever.

Something grazed her cheek; it was her husband's beard as he bent forward to kiss her. And when he had pressed her a long time against himself with a grateful tenderness, he wanted, in his turn, to kiss his daughter, and with his outstretched mouth he gave it very soft little strokes on the nose.

Christiane, her heart shriveled up by this caress, gazed at both of them there by her side, at her daughter and at him—him!

He soon wanted to carry the infant back to its cradle.

"No," said she, "let me have it a few minutes longer, that I may feel it close to my face. Don't speak to me any more—don't move—leave us alone, and wait."

She passed one of her arms over the body hidden under the swaddling-clothes, put her forehead close to the little grinning face, shut her eyes, and no longer stirred, or thought about anything.

But, at the end of a few minutes, William softly touched her on the shoulder: "Come, my darling, you must be reasonable! No emotions, you know, no emotions!"

Thereupon, he bore away their little daughter, while the mother's eyes followed the child till it had disappeared behind the curtain of the bed.

After that, he came back to her: "Then it is understood that I am to bring Madame Honorat to you to-morrow morning, to keep you company?"

She replied in a firm tone: "Yes, my dear, you may send her to me—to-morrow morning."

And she stretched herself out in the bed, fatigued, worn out, perhaps a little less unhappy.

Her father and her brother came to see her in the evening, and told her news about the locality—the precipitate departure of Professor Cloche in search of his daughter, and the conjectures with reference to the Duchess de Ramas, who was no longer to be seen, and who was also supposed to have started on Mazelli's track. Gontran laughed at these adventures, and drew a comic moral from the occurrences:

"The history of those spas is incredible. They are the only fairylands left upon the earth! In two months more things happen in them than in the rest of the universe during the remainder of the year. One might say with truth that the springs are not mineralized but bewitched. And it is everywhere the same, at Aix, Royat, Vichy, Luchon, and also at the sea-baths, at Dieppe, Étretat, Trouville, Biarritz, Cannes, and Nice. You meet there specimens of all kinds of people, of every social grade—admirable adventures, a mixture of races and people not to be found elsewhere, and marvelous incidents. Women play pranks there with facility and charming promptitude. At Paris one resists temptation—at the waters one falls; there you are! Some men find fortune at them, like Andermatt; others find death, like Aubry-Pasteur; others find worse even than that—and get married there—like myself and Paul. Isn't it queer and funny, this sort of thing? You have heard about Paul's intended marriage—have you not?"

She murmured: "Yes; William told me about it a little while ago."

Gontran went on: "He is right, quite right. She is a peasant's daughter. Well, what of that? She is better than an adventurer's daughter or a daughter who's too short. I knew Paul. He would have ended by marrying a street-walker, provided she resisted him for six months. And to resist him it needed a jade or an innocent. He has lighted on the innocent. So much the better for him!"

Christiane listened, and every word, entering through her ears, went straight to her heart, and inflicted on her pain, horrible pain.

Closing her eyes, she said: "I am very tired. I would like to have a little rest."

They embraced her and went out.

She could not sleep, so wakeful was her mind, active and racked with harrowing thoughts. That idea that he no longer loved her at all became so intolerable that, were it not for the presence of this woman, this nurse nodding asleep in the armchair, she would have got up, opened the window, and flung herself out on the steps of the hotel. A very thin ray of moonlight penetrated through an opening in the curtains, and formed a round bright spot on the floor. She observed it; and in a moment a crowd of memories rushed together into her brain: the lake, the wood, that first "I love you," scarcely heard, so agitating, at Tournoel, and all their caresses, in the evening, beside the shadowy paths, and the road from La Roche Pradière.

Suddenly, she saw this white road, on a night when the heavens were filled with stars, and he, Paul, with his arm round a woman's waist, kissing her at every step they walked. It was Charlotte! He pressed her against him, smiled as he knew how to smile, murmured in her ear sweet words, such as he knew how to utter, then flung himself on his knees and kissed the ground in front of her, just as he had kissed it in front of herself! It was so hard, so hard for her to bear, that turning round and hiding her face in the pillow, she burst out sobbing. She almost shrieked, so much did despair rend her soul. Every beat of her heart, which jumped into her throat, which throbbed in her temples, sent forth from her one word—"Paul—Paul—Paul"—endlessly re-echoed. She stopped up her ears with her hands in order to hear nothing more, plunged her head under the sheets; but then his name sounded in the depths of her bosom with every pant of her tormented heart.

The nurse, waking up, asked of her: "Are you worse, Madame?"

Christiane turned round, her face covered with tears, and murmured: "No, I was asleep—I was dreaming—I was frightened."

Then, she begged of her to light two wax-candles, so that the ray of moonlight might be no longer visible. Toward morning, however, she slumbered.

She had been asleep for a few hours when Andermatt came in, bringing with him Madame Honorat. The fat lady, immediately adopting a familiar tone, questioned her like a doctor; then, satisfied with her answers, said: "Come, come! you're going on very nicely!" Then she took off her hat, her gloves, and her shawl, and, addressing the nurse: "You may go, my girl. You will come when we ring for you."

Christiane, already inflamed with dislike to the woman, said to her husband: "Give me my daughter for a little while."

As on the previous day, William carried the child to her, tenderly embracing it as he did so, and placed it upon the pillow. And, as on the previous day, too, when she felt close to her cheek, through the wrappings, the heat of this little stranger's body, imprisoned in linen, she was suddenly penetrated with a grateful sense of peace.

Then, all at once, the baby began to cry, screaming out in a shrill and piercing voice. "She wants nursing," said Andermatt.

He rang, and the wet-nurse appeared, a big red woman, with a mouth like an ogress, full of large, shining teeth, which almost terrified Christiane. And from the open body of her dress she drew forth a breast, soft and heavy with milk. And when Christiane beheld her daughter drinking, she felt a longing to snatch away and take back the baby, moved by a certain sense of jealousy. Madame Honorat now gave directions to the wet-nurse, who went off, carrying the baby in her arms. Andermatt, in his turn, went out, and the two women were left alone together.

Christiane did not know how to speak of what tortured her soul, trembling lest she might give way to too much emotion, lose her head, burst into tears, and betray herself. But Madame Honorat began to babble of her own accord, without having been asked a single question. When she had related all the scandalous stories that were circulating through the neighborhood, she came to the Oriol family: "They are good people," said she, "very good people. If you had known the mother, what a worthy, brave woman she was! She was worth ten women, Madame. The girls take after her, for that matter."

Then, as she was passing on to another topic, Christiane asked: "Which of the two do you prefer, Louise or Charlotte?"

"Oh! for my own part, Madame, I prefer Louise, your brother's intended wife; she is more sensible, more steady. She is a woman of order. But my husband likes the other better. Men you know, have tastes different from ours."

She ceased speaking. Christiane, whose strength was giving way, faltered: "My brother has often met his betrothed at your house."

"Oh! yes, Madame—I believe really every day. Everything was brought about at my house, everything! As for me, I let them talk, these young people, I understood the thing thoroughly. But what truly gave me pleasure was when I saw that M. Paul was getting smitten by the younger one."

Then, Christiane, in an almost inaudible voice: "Is he deeply in love with her?"

"Ah! Madame, is he in love with her? He had lost his head about her some time since. And then, when the Italian—he who ran off with Doctor Cloche's daughter—kept hanging about the girl a little, it was something worth seeing and watching—I thought they were going to fight! Ah! if you had seen M. Paul's eyes. And he looked upon her as if she were a holy Virgin, nothing less—it's a pleasant thing to see people so much in love as that!"

Thereupon, Christiane asked her about all that had taken place in her presence, about all they had said, about all they had done, about their promenades in the glen of Sans-Souci, where he had so often told her of his love for her. She put unexpected questions, which astonished the fat lady, about matters that nobody would have dreamed of, for she was constantly making comparisons; she recalled a thousand details of what had occurred the year before, all Paul's delicate gallantries, his thoughtfulness about her, his ingenious devices to please her, all that display of charming attentions and tender anxieties which on the part of a man show an imperious desire to win a woman's affections; and she wanted to find out whether he had manifested the same affectionate interest toward the other, whether he had commenced afresh this siege of a soul with the same ardor, with the same enthusiasm, with the same irresistible passion.

And every time she recognized a little circumstance, a little trait, one of those nothings which cause such exquisite bliss, one of those disquieting surprises which cause the heart to beat fast, and of which Paul was so prodigal when he loved, Christiane, as she lay prostrate in the bed, gave utterance to a little "Ah!" expressive of keen suffering.

Amazed at this strange exclamation, Madame Honorat declared more emphatically: "Why, yes. 'Tis as I tell you, exactly as I tell you. I never saw a man so much in love!"

"Has he recited verses to her?"

"I believe so indeed, Madame, and very pretty ones, too!"

And, when they had relapsed into silence, nothing more could be heard save the monotonous and soothing song of the nurse as she rocked the baby to sleep in the adjoining room.

Steps were drawing near in the corridor outside. Doctors Mas-Roussel and Latonne had come to visit their patient. They found her agitated, not quite so well as she had been on the previous day.

When they had left, Andermatt opened the door again, and without coming in: "Doctor Black would like to see you. Will you see him?"

She exclaimed, as she raised herself up in the bed: "No—no—I will not—no!"

William came over to her, looking quite astounded: "But listen to me now—it would only be right—it is his due—you ought to!"

She looked, with her wide-open eyes and quivering lips, as if she had lost her reason. She kept repeating in a piercing voice, so loud that it must have penetrated through the walls: "No!—no!—never!" And then, no longer knowing what she said, and pointing with outstretched arm toward Madame Honorat, who was standing in the center of the apartment:

"I do not want her either!—send her away!—I don't want to see her!—send her away!"

Then he rushed to his wife's side, took her in his arms, and kissed her on the forehead: "My little Christiane, be calm! What is the matter with you?—come now, be calm!"

She had by this time lost the power of raising her voice. The tears gushed from her eyes.

"Send them all away," said she, "and remain alone with me!"

He went across, in a distracted frame of mind, to the doctor's wife, and gently pushing her toward the door: "Leave us for a few minutes, pray. It is the fever—the milk-fever. I will calm her. I will look for you again by and by."

When he came back to the bedside Christiane was lying down, weeping quietly, without moving in any way, quite prostrated.

And then, for the first time in his life, he, too, began to weep.

In fact, the milk-fever had broken out during the night, and delirium supervened. After some hours of extreme excitement, the recently delivered woman suddenly began to speak.

The Marquis and Andermatt, who had resolved to remain near her, and who passed the time playing cards, counting the tricks in hushed tones, imagined that she was calling them, and, rising up, approached the bed. She did not see them; she did not recognize them. Intensely pale, on her white pillow, with her fair tresses hanging loose over her shoulders, she was gazing, with her clear blue eyes, into that unknown, mysterious, and fantastic world, in which dwell the insane.

Her hands, stretched over the bedclothes, stirred now and then, agitated by rapid and involuntary movements, tremblings, and starts.

She did not, at first, appear to be talking to anyone, but to be seeing things and telling what she saw. And the things she said seemed disconnected, incomprehensible. She found a rock too high to jump off. She was afraid of a sprain, and then she was not on intimate terms enough with the man who reached out his arms toward her. Then she spoke about perfumes. She was apparently trying to remember some forgotten phrases. "What can be sweeter? This intoxicates one like wine—wine intoxicates the mind, but perfume intoxicates the imagination. With perfume you taste the very essence, the pure essence of things and of the universe—you taste the flowers—the trees—the grass of the fields—you can even distinguish the soul of the dwellings of olden days which sleeps in the old furniture, the old carpets, and the old curtains." Then her face contracted as if she had undergone a long spell of fatigue. She was ascending a hillside slowly, heavily, and was saying to some one: "Oh! carry me once more, I beg of you. I am going to die here! I can walk no farther. Carry me as you did above the gorges. Do you remember?—how you loved me!"

Then she uttered a cry of anguish—a look of horror came into her eyes. She saw in front of her a dead animal, and she was imploring to have it taken away without giving her pain. The Marquis said in a whisper to his son-in-law: "She is thinking about an ass that we came across on our way back from La Nugère." And now she was addressing this dead beast, consoling it, telling it that she, too, was very unhappy, because she had been abandoned.

Then, on a sudden, she refused to do something required of her. She cried: "Oh! no, not that! Oh! it is you, you who want me to drag this cart!"

Then she panted, as if indeed she were dragging a vehicle along. She wept, moaned, uttered exclamations, and always, during a period of half an hour, she was climbing up this hillside, dragging after her with horrible efforts the ass's cart, beyond a doubt.

And some one was harshly beating her, for she said: "Oh! how you hurt me! At least, don't beat me! I will walk—but don't beat me any more, I entreat you! I'll do whatever you wish, but don't beat me any more!"

Then her anguish gradually abated, and all she did was to go on quietly talking in her incoherent fashion till daybreak. After that, she became drowsy, and ended by going to sleep.

Until the following day, however, her mental powers remained torpid, somewhat wavering, fleeting. She could not immediately find the words she wanted, and fatigued herself terribly in searching for them. But, after a night of rest, she completely regained possession of herself.

Nevertheless, she felt changed, as if this crisis had transformed her soul. She suffered less and thought more. The dreadful occurrences, really so recent, seemed to her to have receded into a past already far off; and she regarded them with a clearness of conception with which her mind had never been illuminated before. This light, which had suddenly dawned on her brain, and which comes to certain beings in certain hours of suffering, showed her life, men, things, the entire earth and all that it contains as she had never seen them before.

Then, more than on the evening when she had felt herself so much alone in the universe in her room, after her return from the lake of Tazenat, she looked upon herself as utterly abandoned in existence. She realized that all human beings walk along side by side in the midst of circumstances without anything ever truly uniting two persons together. She learned from the treason of him in whom she had reposed her entire confidence that the others, all the others, would never again be to her anything but indifferent neighbors in that journey short or long, sad or gay, that followed to-morrows no one could foresee.

She comprehended that even in the clasp of this man's arms, when she believed that she was intermingling with him, entering into him, when she believed that their flesh and their souls had become only one flesh and one soul, they had only drawn a little nearer to one another, so as to bring into contact the impenetrable envelopes in which mysterious nature has isolated and shut up each human creature. And she saw as well that nobody has ever been able, or ever will be able, to break through that invisible barrier which places living beings as far from each other as the stars of heaven. She divined the impotent effort, ceaseless since the first days of the world, the indefatigable effort of men and women to tear off the sheath in which their souls forever imprisoned, forever solitary, are struggling—an effort of arms, of lips, of eyes, of mouths, of trembling, naked flesh, an effort of love, which exhausts itself in kisses, to finish only by giving life to some other forlorn being.

Then an uncontrollable desire to gaze on her daughter took possession of her. She asked for it, and when it was brought to her, she begged to have it stripped, for as yet she only knew its face.

The wet-nurse thereupon unfastened the swaddling-clothes, and discovered the poor little body of the newborn infant agitated by those vague movements which life puts into these rough sketches of humanity. Christiane touched it with a timid, trembling hand, then wanted to kiss the stomach, the back, the legs, the feet, and then she stared at the child full of fantastic thoughts.

Two beings came together, loved one another with rapturous passion; and from their embrace, this being was born. It was he and she intermingled; until the death of this little child, it was he and she, living again both together; it was a little of him, and a little of her, with an unknown something which would make it different from them. It reproduced them both in the form of its body as well as in that of its mind, in its features, its gestures, its eyes, its movements, its tastes, its passions, even in the sound of its voice and its gait in walking, and yet it would be a new being!

They were separated now—he and she—forever! Never again would their eyes blend in one of those outbursts of love which make the human race indestructible. And pressing the child against her heart, she murmured: "Adieu! adieu!" It was to him that she was saying "adieu" in her baby's ear, the brave and sorrowing "adieu" of a woman who would yet have much to suffer, always, it might be, but who would know how to hide her tears.

"Ha! ha!" cried William through the half-open door. "I catch you there! Will you be good enough to give me back my daughter?"

Running toward the bed, he seized the little one in his hands already practiced in the art of handling it, and lifting it over his head, he went on repeating: "Good day, Mademoiselle Andermatt—good day, Mademoiselle Andermatt."

Christiane was thinking: "Here, then, is my husband!"

And she contemplated him, with eyes as astonished as if they were beholding him for the first, time. This was he, the man who ought to be, according to human ideas of religion, of society, the other half of her—more than that, her master, the master of her days and of her nights, of her heart and of her body! She felt almost a desire to smile, so strange did this appear to her at the moment, for between her and him no bond could ever exist, none of those bonds alas! so quickly broken, but which seem eternal, ineffably sweet, almost divine.

No remorse even came to her for having deceived him, for having betrayed him. She was surprised at this, and asked herself why it was. Why? No doubt, there was too great a difference between them, they were too far removed from one another, of races too widely dissimilar. He did not understand her at all; she did not understand him at all. And yet he was good, devoted, complaisant.

But only perhaps beings of the same shape, of the same nature, of the same moral essence can feel themselves attached to one another by the sacred bond of voluntary duty.

They dressed the baby again. William sat down.

"Listen, my darling," said he; "I don't venture to announce Doctor Black's visit to you, since you have been so nice toward myself. There is, however, one person whom I would very much like you to see—I mean Doctor Bonnefille."

Then, for the first time, she laughed, with a colorless sort of laugh, which fixed itself on her lips, without going near her heart; and she asked:

"Doctor Bonnefille! what a miracle! So then you are reconciled?"

"Why, yes! Listen! I am going to tell you, as a secret, a great bit of news. I have just bought up the old establishment. I have all the district now. Hey! what a victory. That poor Doctor Bonnefille knew it before anybody, be it understood. So then he has been sly. He came every day to obtain information as to how you were, leaving his card with a word of sympathy written on it. For my part, I responded to these advances with a single visit; and at present we are on excellent terms."

"Let him come," said Christiane, "whenever he likes. I will be glad to see him."

"Good. Thank you. I'll bring him here to you tomorrow morning. I need scarcely tell you that Paul is constantly asking me to convey to you a thousand compliments from him, and he inquires a great deal about the little one. He is very anxious to see her."

In spite of her resolutions she felt a sense of oppression. She was able, however, to say: "You will thank him on my behalf."

Andermatt rejoined: "He was very uneasy to learn whether you had been told about his intended marriage. I informed him that you had; then he asked me several times what you thought about it."

She exerted her strength to the utmost, and felt able to murmur: "You will tell him that I entirely approve of it."

William, with cruel persistency, went on: "He wishes also to know for certain what name you mean to call your daughter. I told him we were hesitating between Marguerite and Genevieve."

"I have changed my mind," said she. "I intend to call her Arlette."

Formerly, in the early days of her pregnancy, she had discussed with Paul the name which they ought to select whether for a son or for a daughter; and for a daughter they had remained undecided between Genevieve and Marguerite. She no longer wanted these two names.

William repeated: "Arlette! Arlette! That's a very nice name—you are right. For my part, I would have liked to call her Christiane, like you. I adore that name—Christiane!"

She sighed deeply: "Oh! it forebodes too much suffering to bear the name of the Crucified."

He reddened, never having dreamed of this comparison, and rising up: "Besides, Arlette is very nice. By-bye, my darling."

As soon as he had left the room, she called the wet-nurse, and directed her for the future to place the cradle beside the bed.

When the little couch in the form of a wherry, always rocking, and carrying its white curtain like a sail on its mast of twisted copper, had been rolled close to the big bed, Christiane stretched out her hand to the sleeping infant, and she said in a very hushed voice: "Go by-bye, my baby! You will never find anyone who will love you as much as I."

She passed the next few days in a state of tranquil melancholy, thinking a great deal, building up within herself a resisting soul, an energetic heart, in order to resume her life again in a few weeks. Her chief occupation now consisted in gazing into the eyes of her child, seeking to surprise in them a first look, but only seeing there two little bluish caverns invariably turned toward the sunlight coming in through the window.

And she experienced a feeling of profound sadness as she reflected that these eyes now closed in sleep would look out on the world, as she herself had looked on it, through the illusion of those secret dreamings which make the souls of young women trustful and joyous. They would love all that she had loved, the beautiful bright days, the flowers, the wood, and alas! living beings too! They would, no doubt, love a man! They would carry in their depths his image, well known, cherished, would see it when he would be far away, would be inflamed on seeing him again. And then—and then they would learn to weep! Tears, horrible tears, would flow over these little cheeks. And the frightful sufferings of love betrayed would render them unrecognizable, those poor wandering eyes which would be blue.

And she wildly embraced the child, saying to it: "Love me alone, my child!"

At length, one day, Professor Mas-Roussel, who came every morning to see her, declared: "You can soon get up for a little, Madame."

Andermatt, when the physician had left, said to his wife: "It is very unfortunate that you are not quite well, for we have a very interesting experiment to-day at the establishment. Doctor Latonne has performed a real miracle with Père Clovis by subjecting him to his system of self-moving gymnastics. Just imagine! This old vagabond is now able to walk as well as anyone. The progress of the cure, moreover, is manifest after each exhibition!"

To please him, she asked: "And are you going to have a public exhibition?"

"Yes, and no. We are having an exhibition before the medical men and a few friends."

"At what hour?"

"Three o'clock."

"Will M. Bretigny be there?"

"Yes, yes. He promised me that he would come to it. From a medical point of view, it is exceedingly curious."

"Well," she said, "as I'll just have risen myself at that time, you will ask M. Bretigny to come and see me. He will keep me company while you are looking at the experiment."

"Yes, my darling."

"You won't forget?"

"No, no. Make your mind easy."

And he went off in search of those who were to witness the exhibition.

After having been imposed upon by the Oriols at the time of the first treatment of the paralytic, he had in his turn imposed upon the credulity of invalids—so easy to get the better of, when it is a question of curing. And now he imposed upon himself with the farce of this cure, talking about it so frequently, with so much ardor and such an air of conviction that it would have been hard to determine whether he believed or disbelieved in it.

About three o'clock, all the persons whom he had induced to attend found themselves gathered together before the door of the establishment, expecting Père Clovis's arrival. He made his appearance, leaning on two walking-sticks, always dragging his legs after him, and bowing politely to everyone as he passed.

The two Oriols followed him, together with the two young girls. Paul and Gontran accompanied their intended wives.

In the great hall where the articulated instruments were fixed, Doctor Latonne was waiting, and killed time by chatting with Andermatt and Doctor Honorat.

When he saw Père Clovis, a smile of delight passed over his clean-shaven lips. He asked: "Well! how are we going on to-day?"

"Oh! all right, all right."

Petrus Martel and Saint Landri presented themselves. They wanted to satisfy their minds. The first believed; the second doubted. Behind them, people saw with astonishment Doctor Bonnefille coming up, saluting his rival, and extending his hand toward Andermatt. Doctor Black was the last to arrive.

"Well, Messieurs and Mesdemoiselles," said Doctor Latonne, as he bowed to Louise and Charlotte Oriol, "you are going to witness a very curious phenomenon. Observe first, before the experiment, this worthy fellow walking a little, but very little. Can you walk without your sticks, Père Clovis?"

"Oh! no, Mochieu!"

"Good, then let us begin."

The old fellow was hoisted on the armchair; his legs were strapped to the movable feet of the sitting-machine; then, at the command of the inspector: "Go quietly!" the attendant, with bare arms, turned the handle.

Thereupon, the right knee of the vagabond was seen rising up, stretching out, bending, then moving forward again; after that, the left knee did the same; and Père Clovis, seized with a sudden delight, began to laugh, while he repeated with his head and his long, white beard all the movements imposed on his legs.

The four physicians and Andermatt, stooping over him, examined him with the gravity of augurs, while Colosse exchanged sly winks with the old chap.

As the door had been left open, other persons kept constantly crowding in, and convinced and anxious bathers pressed forward to behold the experiment.

"Quicker!" said Doctor Latonne; and, in obedience to his command, the man who worked the handle turned it with greater energy. The old fellow's legs began to go at a running pace, and he, seized with irresistible gaiety, like a child being tickled, laughed as loudly as ever he could, moving his head about wildly. And, in the midst of his peals of laughter, he kept repeating: "What a rigolo! what a rigolo!" having, no doubt, picked up this word from the mouth of some foreigner.

Colosse, in his turn, broke out, and, stamping on the ground with his foot and striking his thighs with his hands, he exclaimed: "Ha! bougrrre of a Cloviche! bougrrre of a Cloviche!"

"Enough!" was the inspector's next command.

The vagabond was unfastened, and the physicians drew apart in order to verify the result.

Then Père Clovis was seen rising from the armchair, stepping on the ground, and walking.

He proceeded with short steps, it was true, quite bent, and grimacing from fatigue at every effort, but still he walked!

Doctor Bonnefille was the first to declare: "This is quite a remarkable case!" Doctor Black immediately improved upon his brother-physician. Doctor Honorat, alone, said nothing.

Gontran whispered in Paul's ear: "I don't understand. Look at their heads. Are they dupes or humbugs?"

But Andermatt was speaking. He told the history of this cure since the first day, the relapse, and the final recovery which was declared to be settled and absolute.

He gaily added: "If our patient goes back a little every winter, we'll cure him again every summer."

Then he pompously eulogized the waters of Mont Oriol, extolled their properties, all their properties:

"For my own part," said he; "I have had a proof of their efficacy in the case of a being who is very dear to me; and, if my family is not extinct, it is to Mont Oriol that I will owe it."

But, all at once, he had a flash of recollection. He had promised his wife a visit from Paul Bretigny. He was filled with regret for his forgetfulness, as he was most anxious to gratify her every wish. Accordingly he glanced around him, espied Paul, and coming up to him: "My dear friend, I completely forgot to tell you that Christiane is expecting you at this moment."

Bretigny said falteringly: "Me—at this moment?"

"Yes, she has got up to-day; and she desires to see you before anyone. Hurry then as quickly as possible, and excuse me."

Paul directed his steps toward the hotel, his heart throbbing with emotion. On his way he met the Marquis de Ravenel, who said to him:

"My daughter is up, and is surprised at not having seen you yet."

He halted, however, on the first steps of the staircase in order to consider what he would say to her. How would she receive him? Would she be alone? If she spoke about his marriage, what reply should he make?

Since he had heard of her confinement, he could not think about her without groaning, so uneasy did he feel; and the thought of their first meeting, every time it floated through his mind, made him suddenly redden or grow pale with anguish. He had also thought with deep anxiety of this unknown child, of which he was the father; and he remained harassed by a desire to see it, mingled with a dread of looking at it. He felt himself sunk in one of those moral foulnesses which stain a man's conscience up to the hour of his death. But he feared above all the glance of this woman, for whom his love had been so fierce and so short-lived.

Would she meet him with reproaches, with tears, or with disdain? Would she receive him, only to drive him away?

And what attitude ought he to assume toward her? Humble, crushed, suppliant, or cold? Should he explain himself or should he listen without replying? Ought he to sit down or to remain standing?

And when the child was shown to him, what should he do? What should he say? With what feeling should he appear to be agitated?

Before the door he stopped again, and at the moment when he was on the point of ringing, he noticed that his hand was trembling. However, he placed his finger on the little ivory button, and he heard the sound of the electric bell coming from the interior of the apartment.

A female servant opened the door, and admitted him. And, at the drawing-room door, he saw Christiane, at the end of the second room, lying on her long chair with her eyes fixed upon him.

These two rooms seemed to him interminable as he was passing through them. He felt himself tottering. He was afraid of knocking against the seats, and he did not venture to look down toward his feet in order to avoid lowering his eyes. She did not make a single gesture, or utter a single word. She waited till he was close beside her. Her right hand remained stretched out over her robe and her left leaned over the side of the cradle, covered all round with its curtains.

When he was three paces away from her he stopped, not knowing what best to do. The chambermaid had closed the door after him.

They were alone!

Then, he felt a longing to sink upon his knees, and implore her pardon. But she slowly raised the hand which had rested on her robe, and, extending it slightly toward him, said, "Good day," in a grave tone.

He did not venture to touch her fingers, which, however, he brushed with his lips, while he bowed to her.

She added: "Sit down." And he sat down on a lower chair, close to her feet.

He felt that he ought to speak, but he could not find a word or an idea, and he dared not even look at her. However, he ended by stammering out: "Your husband forgot to let me know that you were waiting for me; but for that, I would have come sooner."

She replied: "Oh! it matters little, since we were bound to see one another again—a little sooner—a little later!"

As she added nothing more, he hastened to say in an inquiring tone: "I hope you are getting on well by this time?"

"Thanks. As well as one can get on, after such shocks!"

She was very pale and thin, but prettier than before her confinement. Her eyes especially had gained a depth of expression which he had never seen in them before. They seemed to have acquired a darker shade, a blue less clear, less transparent, more intense. Her hands were so white that their flesh looked like that of a corpse.

She went on: "Those are hours very hard to live through. But, when one has suffered thus, one feels strong till the end of one's days."

Much affected, he murmured: "Yes; they are terrible experiences!"

She repeated, like an echo: "Terrible."

For some moments there had been light movements in the cradle—the all but imperceptible sounds of an infant awakening from sleep. Bretigny could not longer avert his gaze, preyed upon by a melancholy, morbid yearning which gradually grew stronger, tortured by the desire to behold what lived within there.

Then he observed that the curtains of the tiny bed were fastened from top to bottom with the gold pins which Christiane was accustomed to wear in her corsage. Often had he amused himself in bygone days by taking them out and pinning them again on the shoulders of his beloved, those fine pins with crescent-shaped heads. He understood what she meant; and a poignant emotion seized him, made him feel shriveled up before this barrier of golden spikes which forever separated him from this child.

A little cry, a shrill plaint arose in this white prison. Christiane quickly rocked the wherry, and in a rather abrupt tone:

"I must ask your pardon for allowing you so little time; but I must look after my daughter."

He rose, and once more kissed the hand which she extended toward him; and, as he was on the point of leaving, she said:

"I pray that you may be happy."

THE ENTIRE ORIGINAL MAUPASSANT SHORT STORIES

VOLUME I.

A STUDY BY POL. NEVEUX

"I entered literary life as a meteor, and I shall leave it like a thunderbolt." These words of Maupassant to Jose Maria de Heredia on the occasion of a memorable meeting are, in spite of their morbid solemnity, not an inexact summing up of the brief career during which, for ten years, the writer, by turns undaunted and sorrowful, with the fertility of a master hand produced poetry, novels, romances and travels, only to sink prematurely into the abyss of madness and death. . . . .

In the month of April, 1880, an article appeared in the "Le Gaulois" announcing the publication of the Soirees de Medan. It was signed by a name as yet unknown: Guy de Maupassant. After a juvenile diatribe against romanticism and a passionate attack on languorous literature, the writer extolled the study of real life, and announced the publication of the new work. It was picturesque and charming. In the quiet of evening, on an island, in the Seine, beneath poplars instead of the Neapolitan cypresses dear to the friends of Boccaccio, amid the continuous murmur of the valley, and no longer to the sound of the Pyrennean streams that murmured a faint accompaniment to the tales of Marguerite's cavaliers, the master and his disciples took turns in narrating some striking or pathetic episode of the war. And the issue, in collaboration, of these tales in one volume, in which the master jostled elbows with his pupils, took on the appearance of a manifesto, the tone of a challenge, or the utterance of a creed.

In fact, however, the beginnings had been much more simple, and they had confined themselves, beneath the trees of Medan, to deciding on a general title for the work. Zola had contributed the manuscript of the "Attaque du Moulin," and it was at Maupassant's house that the five young men gave in their contributions. Each one read his story, Maupassant being the last. When he had finished Boule de Suif, with a spontaneous impulse, with an emotion they never forgot, filled with enthusiasm at this revelation, they all rose and, without superfluous words, acclaimed him as a master.

He undertook to write the article for the Gaulois and, in cooperation with his friends, he worded it in the terms with which we are familiar, amplifying and embellishing it, yielding to an inborn taste for mystification which his youth rendered excusable. The essential point, he said, is to "unmoor" criticism.

It was unmoored. The following day Wolff wrote a polemical dissertation in the Figaro and carried away his colleagues. The volume was a brilliant success, thanks to Boule de Suif. Despite the novelty, the honesty of effort, on the part of all, no mention was made of the other stories. Relegated to the second rank, they passed without notice. From his first battle, Maupassant was master of the field in literature.

At once the entire press took him up and said what was appropriate regarding the budding celebrity. Biographers and reporters sought information concerning his life. As it was very simple and perfectly straightforward, they resorted to invention. And thus it is that at the present day Maupassant appears to us like one of those ancient heroes whose origin and death are veiled in mystery.

I will not dwell on Guy de Maupassant's younger days. His relatives, his old friends, he himself, here and there in his works, have furnished us in their letters enough valuable revelations and touching remembrances of the years preceding his literary debut. His worthy biographer, H. Edouard Maynial, after collecting intelligently all the writings, condensing and comparing them, has been able to give us some definite information regarding that early period.

I will simply recall that he was born on the 5th of August, 1850, near Dieppe, in the castle of Miromesnil which he describes in Une Vie. . . .

Maupassant, like Flaubert, was a Norman, through his mother, and through his place of birth he belonged to that strange and adventurous race, whose heroic and long voyages on tramp trading ships he liked to recall. And just as the author of "Education sentimentale" seems to have inherited in the paternal line the shrewd realism of Champagne, so de Maupassant appears to have inherited from his Lorraine ancestors their indestructible discipline and cold lucidity.

His childhood was passed at Etretat, his beautiful childhood; it was there that his instincts were awakened in the unfoldment of his prehistoric soul. Years went by in an ecstasy of physical happiness. The delight of running at full speed through fields of gorse, the charm of voyages of discovery in hollows and ravines, games beneath the dark hedges, a passion for going to sea with the fishermen and, on nights when there was no moon, for dreaming on their boats of imaginary voyages.

Mme. de Maupassant, who had guided her son's early reading, and had gazed with him at the sublime spectacle of nature, put, off as long as possible the hour of separation. One day, however, she had to take the child to the little seminary at Yvetot. Later, he became a student at the college at Rouen, and became a literary correspondent of Louis Bouilhet. It was at the latter's house on those Sundays in winter when the Norman rain drowned the sound of the bells and dashed against the window panes that the school boy learned to write poetry.

Vacation took the rhetorician back to the north of Normandy. Now it was shooting at Saint Julien l'Hospitalier, across fields, bogs, and through the woods. From that time on he sealed his pact with the earth, and those "deep and delicate roots" which attached him to his native soil began to grow. It was of Normandy, broad, fresh and virile, that he would presently demand his inspiration, fervent and eager as a boy's love; it was in her that he would take refuge when, weary of life, he would implore a truce, or when he simply wished to work and revive his energies in old-time joys. It was at this time that was born in him that voluptuous love of the sea, which in later days could alone withdraw him from the world, calm him, console him.

In 1870 he lived in the country, then he came to Paris to live; for, the family fortunes having dwindled, he had to look for a position. For several years he was a clerk in the Ministry of Marine, where he turned over musty papers, in the uninteresting company of the clerks of the admiralty.

Then he went into the department of Public Instruction, where bureaucratic servility is less intolerable. The daily duties are certainly scarcely more onerous and he had as chiefs, or colleagues, Xavier Charmes and Leon Dierx, Henry Roujon and Rene Billotte, but his office looked out on a beautiful melancholy garden with immense plane trees around which black circles of crows gathered in winter.

Maupassant made two divisions of his spare hours, one for boating, and the other for literature. Every evening in spring, every free day, he ran down to the river whose mysterious current veiled in fog or sparkling in the sun called to him and bewitched him. In the islands in the Seine between Chatou and Port-Marly, on the banks of Sartrouville and Triel he was long noted among the population of boatmen, who have now vanished, for his unwearying biceps, his cynical gaiety of good-fellowship, his unfailing practical jokes, his broad witticisms. Sometimes he would row with frantic speed, free and joyous, through the glowing sunlight on the stream; sometimes, he would wander along the coast, questioning the sailors, chatting with the ravageurs, or junk gatherers, or stretched at full length amid the irises and tansy he would lie for hours watching the frail insects that play on the surface of the stream, water spiders, or white butterflies, dragon flies, chasing each other amid the willow leaves, or frogs asleep on the lily-pads.

The rest of his life was taken up by his work. Without ever becoming despondent, silent and persistent, he accumulated manuscripts, poetry, criticisms, plays, romances and novels. Every week he docilely submitted his work to the great Flaubert, the childhood friend of his mother and his uncle Alfred Le Poittevin. The master had consented to assist the young man, to reveal to him the secrets that make chefs-d'oeuvre immortal. It was he who compelled him to make copious research and to use direct observation and who inculcated in him a horror of vulgarity and a contempt for facility.

Maupassant himself tells us of those severe initiations in the Rue Murillo, or in the tent at Croisset; he has recalled the implacable didactics of his old master, his tender brutality, the paternal advice of his generous and candid heart. For seven years Flaubert slashed, pulverized, the awkward attempts of his pupil whose success remained uncertain.

Suddenly, in a flight of spontaneous perfection, he wrote Boule de Suif. His master's joy was great and overwhelming. He died two months later.

Until the end Maupassant remained illuminated by the reflection of the good, vanished giant, by that touching reflection that comes from the dead to those souls they have so profoundly stirred. The worship of Flaubert was a religion from which nothing could distract him, neither work, nor glory, nor slow moving waves, nor balmy nights.

At the end of his short life, while his mind was still clear: he wrote to a friend: "I am always thinking of my poor Flaubert, and I say to myself that I should like to die if I were sure that anyone would think of me in the same manner."

During these long years of his novitiate Maupassant had entered the social literary circles. He would remain silent, preoccupied; and if anyone, astonished at his silence, asked him about his plans he answered simply: "I am learning my trade." However, under the pseudonym of Guy de Valmont, he had sent some articles to the newspapers, and, later, with the approval and by the advice of Flaubert, he published, in the "Republique des Lettres," poems signed by his name.

These poems, overflowing with sensuality, where the hymn to the Earth describes the transports of physical possession, where the impatience of love expresses itself in loud melancholy appeals like the calls of animals in the spring nights, are valuable chiefly inasmuch as they reveal the creature of instinct, the fawn escaped from his native forests, that Maupassant was in his early youth. But they add nothing to his glory. They are the "rhymes of a prose writer" as Jules Lemaitre said. To mould the expression of his thought according to the strictest laws, and to "narrow it down" to some extent, such was his aim. Following the example of one of his comrades of Medan, being readily carried away by precision of style and the rhythm of sentences, by the imperious rule of the ballad, of the pantoum or the chant royal, Maupassant also desired to write in metrical lines. However, he never liked this collection that he often regretted having published. His encounters with prosody had left him with that monotonous weariness that the horseman and the fencer feel after a period in the riding school, or a bout with the foils.

Such, in very broad lines, is the story of Maupassant's literary apprenticeship.

The day following the publication of "Boule de Suif," his reputation began to grow rapidly. The quality of his story was unrivalled, but at the same time it must be acknowledged that there were some who, for the sake of discussion, desired to place a young reputation in opposition to the triumphant brutality of Zola.

From this time on, Maupassant, at the solicitation of the entire press, set to work and wrote story after story. His talent, free from all influences, his individuality, are not disputed for a moment. With a quick step, steady and alert, he advanced to fame, a fame of which he himself was not aware, but which was so universal, that no contemporary author during his life ever experienced the same. The "meteor" sent out its light and its rays were prolonged without limit, in article after article, volume on volume.

He was now rich and famous . . . . He is esteemed all the more as they believe him to be rich and happy. But they do not know that this young fellow with the sunburnt face, thick neck and salient muscles whom they invariably compare to a young bull at liberty, and whose love affairs they whisper, is ill, very ill. At the very moment that success came to him, the malady that never afterwards left him came also, and, seated motionless at his side, gazed at him with its threatening countenance. He suffered from terrible headaches, followed by nights of insomnia. He had nervous attacks, which he soothed with narcotics and anesthetics, which he used freely. His sight, which had troubled him at intervals, became affected, and a celebrated oculist spoke of abnormality, asymetry of the pupils. The famous young man trembled in secret and was haunted by all kinds of terrors.

The reader is charmed at the saneness of this revived art and yet, here and there, he is surprised to discover, amid descriptions of nature that are full of humanity, disquieting flights towards the supernatural, distressing conjurations, veiled at first, of the most commonplace, the most vertiginous shuddering fits of fear, as old as the world and as eternal as the unknown. But, instead of being alarmed, he thinks that the author must be gifted with infallible intuition to follow out thus the taints in his characters, even through their most dangerous mazes. The reader does not know that these hallucinations which he describes so minutely were experienced by Maupassant himself; he does not know that the fear is in himself, the anguish of fear "which is not caused by the presence of danger, or of inevitable death, but by certain abnormal conditions, by certain mysterious influences in presence of vague dangers," the "fear of fear, the dread of that horrible sensation of incomprehensible terror."

How can one explain these physical sufferings and this morbid distress that were known for some time to his intimates alone? Alas! the explanation is only too simple. All his life, consciously or unconsciously, Maupassant fought this malady, hidden as yet, which was latent in him.

As his malady began to take a more definite form, he turned his steps towards the south, only visiting Paris to see his physicians and publishers. In the old port of Antibes beyond the causeway of Cannes, his yacht, Bel Ami, which he cherished as a brother, lay at anchor and awaited him. He took it to the white cities of the Genoese Gulf, towards the palm trees of Hyeres, or the red bay trees of Antheor.

After several tragic weeks in which, from instinct, he made a desperate fight, on the 1st of

January, 1892, he felt he was hopelessly vanquished, and in a moment of supreme clearness of intellect, like Gerard de Nerval, he attempted suicide. Less fortunate than the author of Sylvia, he was unsuccessful. But his mind, henceforth "indifferent to all unhappiness," had entered into eternal darkness.

He was taken back to Paris and placed in Dr. Meuriot's sanatorium, where, after eighteen months of mechanical existence, the "meteor" quietly passed away.

BOULE DE SUIF

For several days in succession fragments of a defeated army had passed through the town. They were mere disorganized bands, not disciplined forces. The men wore long, dirty beards and tattered uniforms; they advanced in listless fashion, without a flag, without a leader. All seemed exhausted, worn out, incapable of thought or resolve, marching onward merely by force of habit, and dropping to the ground with fatigue the moment they halted. One saw, in particular, many enlisted men, peaceful citizens, men who lived quietly on their income, bending beneath the weight of their rifles; and little active volunteers, easily frightened but full of enthusiasm, as eager to attack as they were ready to take to flight; and amid these, a sprinkling of red-breeched soldiers, the pitiful remnant of a division cut down in a great battle; somber artillerymen, side by side with nondescript foot-soldiers; and, here and there, the gleaming helmet of a heavy-footed dragoon who had difficulty in keeping up with the quicker pace of the soldiers of the line. Legions of irregulars with high-sounding names "Avengers of Defeat," "Citizens of the Tomb," "Brethren in Death"—passed in their turn, looking like banditti. Their leaders, former drapers or grain merchants, or tallow or soap chandlers—warriors by force of circumstances, officers by reason of their mustachios or their money—covered with weapons, flannel and gold lace, spoke in an impressive manner, discussed plans of campaign, and behaved as though they alone bore the fortunes of dying France on their braggart shoulders; though, in truth, they frequently were afraid of their own men—scoundrels often brave beyond measure, but pillagers and debauchees.

Rumor had it that the Prussians were about to enter Rouen.

The members of the National Guard, who for the past two months had been reconnoitering with the utmost caution in the neighboring woods, occasionally shooting their own sentinels, and making ready for fight whenever a rabbit rustled in the undergrowth, had now returned to their homes. Their arms, their uniforms, all the death-dealing paraphernalia with which they had terrified all the milestones along the highroad for eight miles round, had suddenly and marvellously disappeared.

The last of the French soldiers had just crossed the Seine on their way to Pont-Audemer, through Saint-Sever and Bourg-Achard, and in their rear the vanquished general, powerless to do aught with the forlorn remnants of his army, himself dismayed at the final overthrow of a nation accustomed to victory and disastrously beaten despite its legendary bravery, walked between two orderlies.

Then a profound calm, a shuddering, silent dread, settled on the city. Many a round-paunched citizen, emasculated by years devoted to business, anxiously awaited the conquerors, trembling lest his roasting-jacks or kitchen knives should be looked upon as weapons.

Life seemed to have stopped short; the shops were shut, the streets deserted. Now and then an inhabitant, awed by the silence, glided swiftly by in the shadow of the walls. The anguish of suspense made men even desire the arrival of the enemy.

In the afternoon of the day following the departure of the French troops, a number of uhlans, coming no one knew whence, passed rapidly through the town. A little later on, a black mass descended St. Catherine's Hill, while two other invading bodies appeared respectively on the Darnetal and the Boisguillaume roads. The advance guards of the three corps arrived at precisely the same moment at the Square of the Hotel de Ville, and the German army poured through all the adjacent streets, its battalions making the pavement ring with their firm, measured tread.

Orders shouted in an unknown, guttural tongue rose to the windows of the seemingly dead, deserted houses; while behind the fast-closed shutters eager eyes peered forth at the victors-masters now of the city, its fortunes, and its lives, by "right of war." The inhabitants, in their darkened rooms, were possessed by that terror which follows in the wake of cataclysms, of deadly upheavals of the earth, against which all human skill and strength are vain. For the same thing happens whenever the established order of things is upset, when security no longer exists, when all those rights usually protected by the law of man or of Nature are at the mercy of unreasoning, savage force. The earthquake crushing a whole nation under falling roofs; the flood let loose, and engulfing in its swirling depths the corpses of drowned peasants, along with dead oxen and beams torn from shattered houses; or the army, covered with glory, murdering those who defend themselves, making prisoners of the rest, pillaging in the name of the Sword, and giving thanks to God to the thunder of cannon—all these are appalling scourges, which destroy all belief in eternal justice, all that confidence we have been taught to feel in the protection of Heaven and the reason of man.

Small detachments of soldiers knocked at each door, and then disappeared within the houses; for the vanquished saw they would have to be civil to their conquerors.

At the end of a short time, once the first terror had subsided, calm was again restored. In many houses the Prussian officer ate at the same table with the family. He was often well-bred, and, out of politeness, expressed sympathy with France and repugnance at being compelled to take part in the war. This sentiment was received with gratitude; besides, his protection might be needful some day or other. By the exercise of tact the number of men quartered in one's house might be reduced; and why should one provoke the hostility of a person on whom one's whole welfare depended? Such conduct would savor less of bravery than of fool-hardiness. And foolhardiness is no longer a failing of the citizens of Rouen as it was in the days when their city earned renown by its heroic defenses. Last of all-final argument based on the national politeness—the folk of Rouen said to one another that it was only right to be civil in one's own house, provided there was no public exhibition of familiarity with the foreigner. Out of doors, therefore, citizen and soldier did not know each other; but in the house both chatted freely, and each evening the German remained a little longer warming himself at the hospitable hearth.

Even the town itself resumed by degrees its ordinary aspect. The French seldom walked abroad, but the streets swarmed with Prussian soldiers. Moreover, the officers of the Blue Hussars, who arrogantly dragged their instruments of death along the pavements, seemed to hold the simple townsmen in but little more contempt than did the French cavalry officers who had drunk at the same cafes the year before.

But there was something in the air, a something strange and subtle, an intolerable foreign atmosphere like a penetrating odor—the odor of invasion. It permeated dwellings and places of public resort, changed the taste of food, made one imagine one's self in far-distant lands, amid dangerous, barbaric tribes.

The conquerors exacted money, much money. The inhabitants paid what was asked; they were rich. But, the wealthier a Norman tradesman becomes, the more he suffers at having to part with anything that belongs to him, at having to see any portion of his substance pass into the hands of another.

Nevertheless, within six or seven miles of the town, along the course of the river as it flows onward to Croisset, Dieppedalle and Biessart, boat-men and fishermen often hauled to the surface of the water the body of a German, bloated in his uniform, killed by a blow from knife or club, his head crushed by a stone, or perchance pushed from some bridge into the stream below. The mud of the river-bed swallowed up these obscure acts of vengeance—savage, yet legitimate; these unrecorded deeds of bravery; these silent attacks fraught with greater danger than battles fought in broad day, and surrounded, moreover, with no halo of romance. For hatred of the foreigner ever arms a few intrepid souls, ready to die for an idea.

At last, as the invaders, though subjecting the town to the strictest discipline, had not committed any of the deeds of horror with which they had been credited while on their triumphal march, the people grew bolder, and the necessities of business again animated the breasts of the local merchants. Some of these had important commercial interests at Havre —occupied at present by the French army—and wished to attempt to reach that port by overland route to Dieppe, taking the boat from there.

Through the influence of the German officers whose acquaintance they had made, they obtained a permit to leave town from the general in command.

A large four-horse coach having, therefore, been engaged for the journey, and ten passengers having given in their names to the proprietor, they decided to start on a certain Tuesday morning before daybreak, to avoid attracting a crowd.

The ground had been frozen hard for some time-past, and about three o'clock on Monday afternoon—large black clouds from the north shed their burden of snow uninterruptedly all through that evening and night.

At half-past four in the morning the travellers met in the courtyard of the Hotel de Normandie, where they were to take their seats in the coach.

They were still half asleep, and shivering with cold under their wraps. They could see one another but indistinctly in the darkness, and the mountain of heavy winter wraps in which each was swathed made them look like a gathering of obese priests in their long cassocks. But two men recognized each other, a third accosted them, and the three began to talk. "I am bringing my wife," said one. "So am I." "And I, too." The first speaker added: "We shall not return to Rouen, and if the Prussians approach Havre we will cross to England." All three, it turned out, had made the same plans, being of similar disposition and temperament.

Still the horses were not harnessed. A small lantern carried by a stable-boy emerged now and then from one dark doorway to disappear immediately in another. The stamping of horses' hoofs, deadened by the dung and straw of the stable, was heard from time to time, and from inside the building issued a man's voice, talking to the animals and swearing at them. A faint tinkle of bells showed that the harness was being got ready; this tinkle soon developed into a continuous jingling, louder or softer according to the movements of the horse, sometimes stopping altogether, then breaking out in a sudden peal accompanied by a pawing of the ground by an iron-shod hoof.

The door suddenly closed. All noise ceased.

The frozen townsmen were silent; they remained motionless, stiff with cold.

A thick curtain of glistening white flakes fell ceaselessly to the ground; it obliterated all outlines, enveloped all objects in an icy mantle of foam; nothing was to be heard throughout the length and breadth of the silent, winter-bound city save the vague, nameless rustle of falling snow—a sensation rather than a sound—the gentle mingling of light atoms which seemed to fill all space, to cover the whole world.

The man reappeared with his lantern, leading by a rope a melancholy-looking horse, evidently being led out against his inclination. The hostler placed him beside the pole, fastened the traces, and spent some time in walking round him to make sure that the harness was all right; for he could use only one hand, the other being engaged in holding the lantern. As he was about to fetch the second horse he noticed the motionless group of travellers, already white with snow, and said to them: "Why don't you get inside the coach? You'd be under shelter, at least."

This did not seem to have occurred to them, and they at once took his advice. The three men seated their wives at the far end of the coach, then got in themselves; lastly the other vague, snow-shrouded forms clambered to the remaining places without a word.

The floor was covered with straw, into which the feet sank. The ladies at the far end, having brought with them little copper foot-warmers heated by means of a kind of chemical fuel, proceeded to light these, and spent some time in expatiating in low tones on their advantages, saying over and over again things which they had all known for a long time.

At last, six horses instead of four having been harnessed to the diligence, on account of the heavy roads, a voice outside asked: "Is every one there?" To which a voice from the interior replied: "Yes," and they set out.

The vehicle moved slowly, slowly, at a snail's pace; the wheels sank into the snow; the entire body of the coach creaked and groaned; the horses slipped, puffed, steamed, and the coachman's long whip cracked incessantly, flying hither and thither, coiling up, then flinging out its length like a slender serpent, as it lashed some rounded flank, which instantly grew tense as it strained in further effort.

But the day grew apace. Those light flakes which one traveller, a native of Rouen, had compared to a rain of cotton fell no longer. A murky light filtered through dark, heavy clouds, which made the country more dazzlingly white by contrast, a whiteness broken sometimes by a row of tall trees spangled with hoarfrost, or by a cottage roof hooded in snow.

Within the coach the passengers eyed one another curiously in the dim light of dawn.

Right at the back, in the best seats of all, Monsieur and Madame Loiseau, wholesale wine merchants of the Rue Grand-Pont, slumbered opposite each other. Formerly clerk to a merchant who had failed in business, Loiseau had bought his master's interest, and made a fortune for himself. He sold very bad wine at a very low price to the retail-dealers in the country, and had the reputation, among his friends and acquaintances, of being a shrewd rascal a true Norman, full of quips and wiles. So well established was his character as a cheat that, in the mouths of the citizens of Rouen, the very name of Loiseau became a byword for sharp practice.

Above and beyond this, Loiseau was noted for his practical jokes of every description—his tricks, good or ill-natured; and no one could mention his name without adding at once: "He's an extraordinary man—Loiseau." He was undersized and potbellied, had a florid face with grayish whiskers.

His wife-tall, strong, determined, with a loud voice and decided manner —represented the spirit of order and arithmetic in the business house which Loiseau enlivened by his jovial activity.

Beside them, dignified in bearing, belonging to a superior caste, sat Monsieur Carre-

Lamadon, a man of considerable importance, a king in the cotton trade, proprietor of three spinning-mills, officer of the Legion of Honor, and member of the General Council. During the whole time the Empire was in the ascendancy he remained the chief of the well-disposed Opposition, merely in order to command a higher value for his devotion when he should rally to the cause which he meanwhile opposed with "courteous weapons," to use his own expression.

Madame Carre-Lamadon, much younger than her husband, was the consolation of all the officers of good family quartered at Rouen. Pretty, slender, graceful, she sat opposite her husband, curled up in her furs, and gazing mournfully at the sorry interior of the coach.

Her neighbors, the Comte and Comtesse Hubert de Breville, bore one of the noblest and most ancient names in Normandy. The count, a nobleman advanced in years and of aristocratic bearing, strove to enhance by every artifice of the toilet, his natural resemblance to King Henry IV, who, according to a legend of which the family were inordinately proud, had been the favored lover of a De Breville lady, and father of her child —the frail one's husband having, in recognition of this fact, been made a count and governor of a province.

A colleague of Monsieur Carre-Lamadon in the General Council, Count Hubert represented the Orleanist party in his department. The story of his marriage with the daughter of a small shipowner at Nantes had always remained more or less of a mystery. But as the countess had an air of unmistakable breeding, entertained faultlessly, and was even supposed to have been loved by a son of Louis-Philippe, the nobility vied with one another in doing her honor, and her drawing-room remained the most select in the whole countryside—the only one which retained the old spirit of gallantry, and to which access was not easy.

The fortune of the Brevilles, all in real estate, amounted, it was said, to five hundred thousand francs a year.

These six people occupied the farther end of the coach, and represented Society—with an income—the strong, established society of good people with religion and principle.

It happened by chance that all the women were seated on the same side; and the countess had, moreover, as neighbors two nuns, who spent the time in fingering their long rosaries and murmuring paternosters and aves. One of them was old, and so deeply pitted with smallpox that she looked for all the world as if she had received a charge of shot full in the face. The other, of sickly appearance, had a pretty but wasted countenance, and a narrow, consumptive chest, sapped by that devouring faith which is the making of martyrs and visionaries.

A man and woman, sitting opposite the two nuns, attracted all eyes.

The man—a well-known character—was Cornudet, the democrat, the terror of all respectable people. For the past twenty years his big red beard had been on terms of intimate acquaintance with the tankards of all the republican cafes. With the help of his comrades and brethren he had dissipated a respectable fortune left him by his father, an old-established confectioner, and he now impatiently awaited the Republic, that he might at last be rewarded with the post he had earned by his revolutionary orgies. On the fourth of September—possibly as the result of a practical joke—he was led to believe that he had been appointed prefect; but when he attempted to take up the duties of the position the clerks in charge of the office refused to recognize his authority, and he was compelled in consequence to retire. A good sort of fellow in other respects, inoffensive and obliging, he had thrown himself zealously into the work of making an organized defence of the town. He had had pits dug in the level country, young forest trees felled, and traps set on all the roads; then at the approach of the enemy, thoroughly satisfied with his preparations, he had hastily returned to the town. He thought he might now do more good at Havre, where new intrenchments would soon be necessary.

The woman, who belonged to the courtesan class, was celebrated for an embonpoint unusual for her age, which had earned for her the sobriquet of "Boule de Suif" (Tallow Ball). Short and round, fat as a pig, with puffy fingers constricted at the joints, looking like rows of short sausages; with a shiny, tightly-stretched skin and an enormous bust filling out the bodice of her dress, she was yet attractive and much sought after, owing to her fresh and pleasing appearance. Her face was like a crimson apple, a peony-bud just bursting into bloom; she had two magnificent dark eyes, fringed with thick, heavy lashes, which cast a shadow into their depths; her mouth was small, ripe, kissable, and was furnished with the tiniest of white teeth.

As soon as she was recognized the respectable matrons of the party began to whisper among themselves, and the words "hussy" and "public scandal" were uttered so loudly that Boule de Suif raised her head. She forthwith cast such a challenging, bold look at her neighbors that a sudden silence fell on the company, and all lowered their eyes, with the exception of Loiseau, who watched her with evident interest.

But conversation was soon resumed among the three ladies, whom the presence of this girl had suddenly drawn together in the bonds of friendship—one might almost say in those of intimacy. They decided that they ought to combine, as it were, in their dignity as wives in face of this shameless hussy; for legitimized love always despises its easygoing brother.

The three men, also, brought together by a certain conservative instinct awakened by the presence of Cornudet, spoke of money matters in a tone expressive of contempt for the poor. Count Hubert related the losses he had sustained at the hands of the Prussians, spoke of the cattle which had been stolen from him, the crops which had been ruined, with the easy manner of a nobleman who was also a tenfold millionaire, and whom such reverses would scarcely inconvenience for a single year. Monsieur Carre-Lamadon, a man of wide experience in the cotton industry, had taken care to send six hundred thousand francs to England as provision against the rainy day he was always anticipating. As for Loiseau, he had managed to sell to the French commissariat department all the wines he had in stock, so that the state now owed him a considerable sum, which he hoped to receive at Havre.

And all three eyed one another in friendly, well-disposed fashion. Although of varying social status, they were united in the brotherhood of money—in that vast freemasonry made up of those who possess, who can jingle gold wherever they choose to put their hands into their breeches' pockets.

The coach went along so slowly that at ten o'clock in the morning it had not covered twelve miles. Three times the men of the party got out and climbed the hills on foot. The passengers were becoming uneasy, for they had counted on lunching at Totes, and it seemed now as if they would hardly arrive there before nightfall. Every one was eagerly looking out for an inn by the roadside, when, suddenly, the coach foundered in a snowdrift, and it took two hours to extricate it.

As appetites increased, their spirits fell; no inn, no wine shop could be discovered, the approach of the Prussians and the transit of the starving French troops having frightened away all business.

The men sought food in the farmhouses beside the road, but could not find so much as a crust of bread; for the suspicious peasant invariably hid his stores for fear of being pillaged by the soldiers, who, being entirely without food, would take violent possession of everything they found.

About one o'clock Loiseau announced that he positively had a big hollow in his stomach. They had all been suffering in the same way for some time, and the increasing gnawings of hunger had put an end to all conversation.

Now and then some one yawned, another followed his example, and each in turn, according to his character, breeding and social position, yawned either quietly or noisily, placing his hand before the gaping void whence issued breath condensed into vapor.

Several times Boule de Suif stooped, as if searching for something under her petticoats. She would hesitate a moment, look at her neighbors, and then quietly sit upright again. All faces were pale and drawn. Loiseau declared he would give a thousand francs for a knuckle of ham. His wife made an involuntary and quickly checked gesture of protest. It always hurt her to hear of money being squandered, and she could not even understand jokes on such a subject.

"As a matter of fact, I don't feel well," said the count. "Why did I not think of bringing provisions?" Each one reproached himself in similar fashion.

Cornudet, however, had a bottle of rum, which he offered to his neighbors. They all coldly refused except Loiseau, who took a sip, and returned the bottle with thanks, saying: "That's good stuff; it warms one up, and cheats the appetite." The alcohol put him in good humor, and he proposed they should do as the sailors did in the song: eat the fattest of the passengers. This indirect allusion to Boule de Suif shocked the respectable members of the party. No one replied; only Cornudet smiled. The two good sisters had ceased to mumble their rosary, and, with hands enfolded in their wide sleeves, sat motionless, their eyes steadfastly cast down, doubtless offering up as a sacrifice to Heaven the suffering it had sent them.

At last, at three o'clock, as they were in the midst of an apparently limitless plain, with not a single village in sight, Boule de Suif stooped quickly, and drew from underneath the seat a large basket covered with a white napkin.

From this she extracted first of all a small earthenware plate and a silver drinking cup, then an enormous dish containing two whole chickens cut into joints and imbedded in jelly. The basket was seen to contain other good things: pies, fruit, dainties of all sorts-provisions, in fine, for a three days' journey, rendering their owner independent of wayside inns. The necks of four bottles protruded from among the food. She took a chicken wing, and began to eat it daintily, together with one of those rolls called in Normandy "Regence."

All looks were directed toward her. An odor of food filled the air, causing nostrils to dilate, mouths to water, and jaws to contract painfully. The scorn of the ladies for this disreputable female grew positively ferocious; they would have liked to kill her, or throw, her and her drinking cup, her basket, and her provisions, out of the coach into the snow of the road below.

But Loiseau's gaze was fixed greedily on the dish of chicken. He said:

"Well, well, this lady had more forethought than the rest of us. Some people think of everything."

She looked up at him.

"Would you like some, sir? It is hard to go on fasting all day."

He bowed.

"Upon my soul, I can't refuse; I cannot hold out another minute. All is fair in war time, is it not, madame?" And, casting a glance on those around, he added:

"At times like this it is very pleasant to meet with obliging people."

He spread a newspaper over his knees to avoid soiling his trousers, and, with a pocketknife he always carried, helped himself to a chicken leg coated with jelly, which he thereupon proceeded to devour.

Then Boule le Suif, in low, humble tones, invited the nuns to partake of her repast. They both accepted the offer unhesitatingly, and after a few stammered words of thanks began to eat quickly, without raising their eyes. Neither did Cornudet refuse his neighbor's offer, and, in combination with the nuns, a sort of table was formed by opening out the newspaper over the four pairs of knees.

Mouths kept opening and shutting, ferociously masticating and devouring the food. Loiseau, in his corner, was hard at work, and in low tones urged his wife to follow his example. She held out for a long time, but overstrained Nature gave way at last. Her husband, assuming his politest manner, asked their "charming companion" if he might be allowed to offer Madame Loiseau a small helping.

"Why, certainly, sir," she replied, with an amiable smile, holding out the dish.

When the first bottle of claret was opened some embarrassment was caused by the fact that there was only one drinking cup, but this was passed from one to another, after being wiped. Cornudet alone, doubtless in a spirit of gallantry, raised to his own lips that part of the rim which was still moist from those of his fair neighbor.

Then, surrounded by people who were eating, and well-nigh suffocated by the odor of food, the Comte and Comtesse de Breville and Monsieur and Madame Carre-Lamadon endured that hateful form of torture which has perpetuated the name of Tantalus. All at once the manufacturer's young wife heaved a sigh which made every one turn and look at her; she was white as the snow without; her eyes closed, her head fell forward; she had fainted. Her husband, beside himself, implored the help of his neighbors. No one seemed to know what to do until the elder of the two nuns, raising the patient's head, placed Boule de Suif's drinking cup to her lips, and made her swallow a few drops of wine. The pretty invalid moved, opened her eyes, smiled, and declared in a feeble voice that she was all right again. But, to prevent a recurrence of the catastrophe, the nun made her drink a cupful of claret, adding: "It's just hunger —that's what is wrong with you."

Then Boule de Suif, blushing and embarrassed, stammered, looking at the four passengers who were still fasting:

"'Mon Dieu', if I might offer these ladies and gentlemen——"

She stopped short, fearing a snub. But Loiseau continued:

"Hang it all, in such a case as this we are all brothers and sisters and ought to assist each other. Come, come, ladies, don't stand on ceremony, for goodness' sake! Do we even know whether we shall find a house in which to pass the night? At our present rate of going we sha'n't be at Totes till midday to-morrow."

They hesitated, no one daring to be the first to accept. But the count settled the question. He turned toward the abashed girl, and in his most distinguished manner said:

"We accept gratefully, madame."

As usual, it was only the first step that cost. This Rubicon once crossed, they set to work with a will. The basket was emptied. It still contained a pate de foie gras, a lark pie, a piece of smoked tongue, Crassane pears, Pont-Leveque gingerbread, fancy cakes, and a cup full of pickled gherkins and onions—Boule de Suif, like all women, being very fond of indigestible things.

They could not eat this girl's provisions without speaking to her. So they began to talk, stiffly at first; then, as she seemed by no means forward, with greater freedom. Mesdames de Breville and Carre-Lamadon, who were accomplished women of the world, were gracious and tactful. The countess especially displayed that amiable condescension characteristic of great ladies whom no contact with baser mortals can sully, and was absolutely charming. But the sturdy Madame Loiseau, who had the soul of a gendarme, continued morose, speaking little and eating much.

Conversation naturally turned on the war. Terrible stories were told about the Prussians, deeds of bravery were recounted of the French; and all these people who were fleeing themselves were ready to pay homage to the courage of their compatriots. Personal experiences soon followed, and Boule le Suif related with genuine emotion, and with that warmth of language not uncommon in women of her class and temperament, how it came about that she had left Rouen.

"I thought at first that I should be able to stay," she said. "My house was well stocked with provisions, and it seemed better to put up with feeding a few soldiers than to banish myself goodness knows where. But when I saw these Prussians it was too much for me! My blood boiled with rage; I wept the whole day for very shame. Oh, if only I had been a man! I looked at them from my window—the fat swine, with their pointed helmets!—and my maid held my hands to keep me from throwing my furniture down on them. Then some of them were quartered on me; I flew at the throat of the first one who entered. They are just as easy to strangle as other men! And I'd have been the death of that one if I hadn't been dragged away from him by my hair. I had to hide after that. And as soon as I could get an opportunity I left the place, and here I am."

She was warmly congratulated. She rose in the estimation of her companions, who had not been so brave; and Cornudet listened to her with the approving and benevolent smile of an apostle, the smile a priest might wear in listening to a devotee praising God; for long-bearded democrats of his type have a monopoly of patriotism, just as priests have a monopoly of religion. He held forth in turn, with dogmatic self-assurance, in the style of the proclamations daily pasted on the walls of the town, winding up with a specimen of stump oratory in which he reviled "that besotted fool of a Louis-Napoleon."

But Boule de Suif was indignant, for she was an ardent Bonapartist. She turned as red as a cherry, and stammered in her wrath: "I'd just like to have seen you in his place—you and your sort! There would have been a nice mix-up. Oh, yes! It was you who betrayed that man. It would be impossible to live in France if we were governed by such rascals as you!"

Cornudet, unmoved by this tirade, still smiled a superior, contemptuous smile; and one felt that high words were impending, when the count interposed, and, not without difficulty, succeeded in calming the exasperated woman, saying that all sincere opinions ought to be respected. But the countess and the manufacturer's wife, imbued with the unreasoning hatred of the upper classes for the Republic, and instinct, moreover, with the affection felt by all women for the pomp and circumstance of despotic government, were drawn, in spite of themselves, toward this dignified young woman, whose opinions coincided so closely with their own.

The basket was empty. The ten people had finished its contents without difficulty amid general regret that it did not hold more. Conversation went on a little longer, though it flagged somewhat after the passengers had finished eating.

Night fell, the darkness grew deeper and deeper, and the cold made Boule de Suif shiver, in spite of her plumpness. So Madame de Breville offered her her foot-warmer, the fuel of which had been several times renewed since the morning, and she accepted the offer at once, for her feet were icy cold. Mesdames Carre-Lamadon and Loiseau gave theirs to the nuns.

The driver lighted his lanterns. They cast a bright gleam on a cloud of vapor which hovered over the sweating flanks of the horses, and on the roadside snow, which seemed to unroll as they went along in the changing light of the lamps.

All was now indistinguishable in the coach; but suddenly a movement occurred in the corner occupied by Boule de Suif and Cornudet; and Loiseau, peering into the gloom, fancied he saw the big, bearded democrat move hastily to one side, as if he had received a well-directed, though noiseless, blow in the dark.

Tiny lights glimmered ahead. It was Totes. The coach had been on the road eleven hours, which, with the three hours allotted the horses in four periods for feeding and breathing, made fourteen. It entered the town, and stopped before the Hotel du Commerce.

The coach door opened; a well-known noise made all the travellers start; it was the clanging of a scabbard, on the pavement; then a voice called out something in German.

Although the coach had come to a standstill, no one got out; it looked as if they were afraid of being murdered the moment they left their seats. Thereupon the driver appeared, holding in his hand one of his lanterns, which cast a sudden glow on the interior of the coach, lighting up the double row of startled faces, mouths agape, and eyes wide open in surprise and terror.

Beside the driver stood in the full light a German officer, a tall young man, fair and slender, tightly encased in his uniform like a woman in her corset, his flat shiny cap, tilted to one side of his head, making him look like an English hotel runner. His exaggerated mustache, long and straight and tapering to a point at either end in a single blond hair that could hardly be seen, seemed to weigh down the corners of his mouth and give a droop to his lips.

In Alsatian French he requested the travellers to alight, saying stiffly:

"Kindly get down, ladies and gentlemen."

The two nuns were the first to obey, manifesting the docility of holy women accustomed to submission on every occasion. Next appeared the count and countess, followed by the manufacturer and his wife, after whom came Loiseau, pushing his larger and better half before him.

"Good-day, sir," he said to the officer as he put his foot to the ground, acting on an impulse born of prudence rather than of politeness. The other, insolent like all in authority, merely stared without replying.

Boule de Suif and Cornudet, though near the door, were the last to alight, grave and dignified before the enemy. The stout girl tried to control herself and appear calm; the democrat stroked his long russet beard with a somewhat trembling hand. Both strove to maintain their dignity, knowing well that at such a time each individual is always looked upon as more or less typical of his nation; and, also, resenting the complaisant attitude of their companions, Boule de Suif tried to wear a bolder front than her neighbors, the virtuous women, while he, feeling that it was incumbent on him to set a good example, kept up the attitude of resistance which he had first assumed when he undertook to mine the high roads round Rouen.

They entered the spacious kitchen of the inn, and the German, having demanded the passports signed by the general in command, in which were mentioned the name, description and profession of each traveller, inspected them all minutely, comparing their appearance with the written particulars.

Then he said brusquely: "All right," and turned on his heel.

They breathed freely, All were still hungry; so supper was ordered. Half an hour was required for its preparation, and while two servants were apparently engaged in getting it ready the travellers went to look at their rooms. These all opened off a long corridor, at the end of which was a glazed door with a number on it.

They were just about to take their seats at table when the innkeeper appeared in person. He was a former horse dealer—a large, asthmatic individual, always wheezing, coughing, and clearing his throat. Follenvie was his patronymic.

He called:

"Mademoiselle Elisabeth Rousset?"

Boule de Suif started, and turned round.

"That is my name."

"Mademoiselle, the Prussian officer wishes to speak to you immediately."

"To me?"

"Yes; if you are Mademoiselle Elisabeth Rousset."

She hesitated, reflected a moment, and then declared roundly:

"That may be; but I'm not going."

They moved restlessly around her; every one wondered and speculated as to the cause of this order. The count approached:

"You are wrong, madame, for your refusal may bring trouble not only on yourself but also on all your companions. It never pays to resist those in authority. Your compliance with this request cannot possibly be fraught with any danger; it has probably been made because some formality or other was forgotten."

All added their voices to that of the count; Boule de Suif was begged, urged, lectured, and at last convinced; every one was afraid of the complications which might result from headstrong action on her part. She said finally:

"I am doing it for your sakes, remember that!"

The countess took her hand.

"And we are grateful to you."

She left the room. All waited for her return before commencing the meal. Each was distressed that he or she had not been sent for rather than this impulsive, quick-tempered girl, and each mentally rehearsed platitudes in case of being summoned also.

But at the end of ten minutes she reappeared breathing hard, crimson with indignation.

"Oh! the scoundrel! the scoundrel!" she stammered.

All were anxious to know what had happened; but she declined to enlighten them, and when the count pressed the point, she silenced him with much dignity, saying:

"No; the matter has nothing to do with you, and I cannot speak of it."

Then they took their places round a high soup tureen, from which issued an odor of cabbage. In spite of this coincidence, the supper was cheerful. The cider was good; the Loiseaus and the nuns drank it from motives of economy. The others ordered wine; Cornudet demanded beer. He had his own fashion of uncorking the bottle and making the beer foam, gazing at it as he inclined his glass and then raised it to a position between the lamp and his eye that he might judge of its color. When he drank, his great beard, which matched the color of his favorite beverage, seemed to tremble with affection; his eyes positively squinted in the endeavor not to lose sight of the beloved glass, and he looked for all the world as if he were fulfilling the only function for which he was born. He seemed to have established in his mind an affinity between the two great passions of his life—pale ale and revolution—and assuredly he could not taste the one without dreaming of the other.

Monsieur and Madame Follenvie dined at the end of the table. The man, wheezing like a broken-down locomotive, was too short-winded to talk when he was eating. But the wife was not silent a moment; she told how the Prussians had impressed her on their arrival, what they did, what they said; execrating them in the first place because they cost her money, and in the second because she had two sons in the army. She addressed herself principally to the countess, flattered at the opportunity of talking to a lady of quality.

Then she lowered her voice, and began to broach delicate subjects. Her husband interrupted her from time to time, saying:

"You would do well to hold your tongue, Madame Follenvie."

But she took no notice of him, and went on:

"Yes, madame, these Germans do nothing but eat potatoes and pork, and then pork and potatoes. And don't imagine for a moment that they are clean! No, indeed! And if only you saw them drilling for hours, indeed for days, together; they all collect in a field, then they do nothing but march backward and forward, and wheel this way and that. If only they would cultivate the land, or remain at home and work on their high roads! Really, madame, these soldiers are of no earthly use! Poor people have to feed and keep them, only in order that they may learn how to kill! True, I am only an old woman with no education, but when I see them wearing themselves out marching about from morning till night, I say to myself: When there are people who make discoveries that are of use to people, why should others take so much trouble to do harm? Really, now, isn't it a terrible thing to kill people, whether they are Prussians, or English, or Poles, or French? If we revenge ourselves on any one who injures us we do wrong, and are punished for it; but when our sons are shot down like partridges, that is all right, and decorations are given to the man who kills the most. No, indeed, I shall never be able to understand it."

Cornudet raised his voice:

"War is a barbarous proceeding when we attack a peaceful neighbor, but it is a sacred duty when undertaken in defence of one's country."

The old woman looked down:

"Yes; it's another matter when one acts in self-defence; but would it not be better to kill all the kings, seeing that they make war just to amuse themselves?"

Cornudet's eyes kindled.

"Bravo, citizens!" he said.

Monsieur Carre-Lamadon was reflecting profoundly. Although an ardent admirer of great generals, the peasant woman's sturdy common sense made him reflect on the wealth which might accrue to a country by the employment of so many idle hands now maintained at a great expense, of so much unproductive force, if they were employed in those great industrial enterprises which it will take centuries to complete.

But Loiseau, leaving his seat, went over to the innkeeper and began chatting in a low voice. The big man chuckled, coughed, sputtered; his enormous carcass shook with merriment at the pleasantries of the other; and he ended by buying six casks of claret from Loiseau to be delivered in spring, after the departure of the Prussians.

The moment supper was over every one went to bed, worn out with fatigue.

But Loiseau, who had been making his observations on the sly, sent his wife to bed, and amused himself by placing first his ear, and then his eye, to the bedroom keyhole, in order to discover what he called "the mysteries of the corridor."

At the end of about an hour he heard a rustling, peeped out quickly, and caught sight of Boule de Suif, looking more rotund than ever in a dressing-gown of blue cashmere trimmed with white lace. She held a candle in her hand, and directed her steps to the numbered door at the end of the corridor. But one of the side doors was partly opened, and when, at the end of a few minutes, she returned, Cornudet, in his shirt-sleeves, followed her. They spoke in low tones, then stopped short. Boule de Suif seemed to be stoutly denying him admission to her room. Unfortunately, Loiseau could not at first hear what they said; but toward the end of the conversation they raised their voices, and he caught a few words. Cornudet was loudly insistent.

"How silly you are! What does it matter to you?" he said.

She seemed indignant, and replied:

"No, my good man, there are times when one does not do that sort of thing; besides, in this place it would be shameful."

Apparently he did not understand, and asked the reason. Then she lost her temper and her caution, and, raising her voice still higher, said:

"Why? Can't you understand why? When there are Prussians in the house! Perhaps even in the very next room!"

He was silent. The patriotic shame of this wanton, who would not suffer herself to be caressed in the neighborhood of the enemy, must have roused his dormant dignity, for after bestowing on her a simple kiss he crept softly back to his room. Loiseau, much edified, capered round the bedroom before taking his place beside his slumbering spouse.

Then silence reigned throughout the house. But soon there arose from some remote part—it might easily have been either cellar or attic—a stertorous, monotonous, regular snoring, a dull, prolonged rumbling, varied by tremors like those of a boiler under pressure of steam. Monsieur Follenvie had gone to sleep.

As they had decided on starting at eight o'clock the next morning, every one was in the kitchen at that hour; but the coach, its roof covered with snow, stood by itself in the middle of the yard, without either horses or driver. They sought the latter in the stables, coach-houses and barns —but in vain. So the men of the party resolved to scour the country for him, and sallied forth. They found themselves in the square, with the church at the farther side, and to right and left low-roofed houses where there were some Prussian soldiers. The first soldier they saw was peeling potatoes. The second, farther on, was washing out a barber's shop. Another, bearded to the eyes, was fondling a crying infant, and dandling it on his knees to quiet it; and the stout peasant women, whose men-folk were for the most part at the war, were, by means of signs, telling their obedient conquerors what work they were to do: chop wood, prepare soup, grind coffee; one of them even was doing the washing for his hostess, an infirm old grandmother.

The count, astonished at what he saw, questioned the beadle who was coming out of the presbytery. The old man answered:

"Oh, those men are not at all a bad sort; they are not Prussians, I am told; they come from somewhere farther off, I don't exactly know where. And they have all left wives and children behind them; they are not fond of war either, you may be sure! I am sure they are mourning for the men where they come from, just as we do here; and the war causes them just as much unhappiness as it does us. As a matter of fact, things are not so very bad here just now, because the soldiers do no harm, and work just as if they were in their own homes. You see, sir, poor folk always help one another; it is the great ones of this world who make war."

Cornudet indignant at the friendly understanding established between conquerors and conquered, withdrew, preferring to shut himself up in the inn.

"They are repeopling the country," jested Loiseau.

"They are undoing the harm they have done," said Monsieur Carre-Lamadon gravely.

But they could not find the coach driver. At last he was discovered in the village cafe, fraternizing cordially with the officer's orderly.

"Were you not told to harness the horses at eight o'clock?" demanded the count.

"Oh, yes; but I've had different orders since."

"What orders?"

"Not to harness at all."

"Who gave you such orders?"

"Why, the Prussian officer."

"But why?"

"I don't know. Go and ask him. I am forbidden to harness the horses, so I don't harness them—that's all."

"Did he tell you so himself?"

"No, sir; the innkeeper gave me the order from him."

"When?"

"Last evening, just as I was going to bed."

The three men returned in a very uneasy frame of mind.

They asked for Monsieur Follenvie, but the servant replied that on account of his asthma he never got up before ten o'clock. They were strictly forbidden to rouse him earlier, except in case of fire.

They wished to see the officer, but that also was impossible, although he lodged in the inn. Monsieur Follenvie alone was authorized to interview him on civil matters. So they waited. The women returned to their rooms, and occupied themselves with trivial matters.

Cornudet settled down beside the tall kitchen fireplace, before a blazing fire. He had a small table and a jug of beer placed beside him, and he smoked his pipe—a pipe which enjoyed among democrats a consideration almost equal to his own, as though it had served its country in serving Cornudet. It was a fine meerschaum, admirably colored to a black the shade of its owner's teeth, but sweet-smelling, gracefully curved, at home in its master's hand, and completing his physiognomy. And Cornudet sat motionless, his eyes fixed now on the dancing flames, now on the froth which crowned his beer; and after each draught he passed his long, thin fingers with an air of satisfaction through his long, greasy hair, as he sucked the foam from his mustache.

Loiseau, under pretence of stretching his legs, went out to see if he could sell wine to the country dealers. The count and the manufacturer began to talk politics. They forecast the future of France. One believed in the Orleans dynasty, the other in an unknown savior—a hero who should rise up in the last extremity: a Du Guesclin, perhaps a Joan of Arc? or another Napoleon the First? Ah! if only the Prince Imperial were not so young! Cornudet, listening to them, smiled like a man who holds the keys of destiny in his hands. His pipe perfumed the whole kitchen.

As the clock struck ten, Monsieur Follenvie appeared. He was immediately surrounded and questioned, but could only repeat, three or four times in succession, and without variation, the words:

"The officer said to me, just like this: 'Monsieur Follenvie, you will forbid them to harness up the coach for those travellers to-morrow. They are not to start without an order from me. You hear? That is sufficient.'"

Then they asked to see the officer. The count sent him his card, on which Monsieur Carre-Lamadon also inscribed his name and titles. The Prussian sent word that the two men would be admitted to see him after his luncheon—that is to say, about one o'clock.

The ladies reappeared, and they all ate a little, in spite of their anxiety. Boule de Suif appeared ill and very much worried.

They were finishing their coffee when the orderly came to fetch the gentlemen.

Loiseau joined the other two; but when they tried to get Cornudet to accompany them, by way of adding greater solemnity to the occasion, he declared proudly that he would never have anything to do with the Germans, and, resuming his seat in the chimney corner, he called for another jug of beer.

The three men went upstairs, and were ushered into the best room in the inn, where the officer received them lolling at his ease in an armchair, his feet on the mantelpiece, smoking a long porcelain pipe, and enveloped in a gorgeous dressing-gown, doubtless stolen from the deserted dwelling of some citizen destitute of taste in dress. He neither rose, greeted them, nor even glanced in their direction. He afforded a fine example of that insolence of bearing which seems natural to the victorious soldier.

After the lapse of a few moments he said in his halting French:

"What do you want?"

"We wish to start on our journey," said the count.

"No."

"May I ask the reason of your refusal?"

"Because I don't choose."

"I would respectfully call your attention, monsieur, to the fact that your general in command gave us a permit to proceed to Dieppe; and I do not think we have done anything to deserve this harshness at your hands."

"I don't choose—that's all. You may go."

They bowed, and retired.

The afternoon was wretched. They could not understand the caprice of this German, and the strangest ideas came into their heads. They all congregated in the kitchen, and talked the subject to death, imagining all kinds of unlikely things. Perhaps they were to be kept as hostages —but for what reason? or to be extradited as prisoners of war? or possibly they were to be held for ransom? They were panic-stricken at this last supposition. The richest among them were the most alarmed, seeing themselves forced to empty bags of gold into the insolent soldier's hands in order to buy back their lives. They racked their brains for plausible lies whereby they might conceal the fact that they were rich, and pass themselves off as poor—very poor. Loiseau took off his watch chain, and put it in his pocket. The approach of night increased their apprehension. The lamp was lighted, and as it wanted yet two hours to dinner Madame Loiseau proposed a game of trente et un. It would distract their thoughts. The rest agreed, and Cornudet himself joined the party, first putting out his pipe for politeness' sake.

The count shuffled the cards—dealt—and Boule de Suif had thirty-one to start with; soon the interest of the game assuaged the anxiety of the players. But Cornudet noticed that

Loiseau and his wife were in league to cheat.

They were about to sit down to dinner when Monsieur Follenvie appeared, and in his grating voice announced:

"The Prussian officer sends to ask Mademoiselle Elisabeth Rousset if she has changed her mind yet."

Boule de Suif stood still, pale as death. Then, suddenly turning crimson with anger, she gasped out:

"Kindly tell that scoundrel, that cur, that carrion of a Prussian, that I will never consent—you understand?—never, never, never!"

The fat innkeeper left the room. Then Boule de Suif was surrounded, questioned, entreated on all sides to reveal the mystery of her visit to the officer. She refused at first; but her wrath soon got the better of her.

"What does he want? He wants to make me his mistress!" she cried.

No one was shocked at the word, so great was the general indignation. Cornudet broke his jug as he banged it down on the table. A loud outcry arose against this base soldier. All were furious. They drew together in common resistance against the foe, as if some part of the sacrifice exacted of Boule de Suif had been demanded of each. The count declared, with supreme disgust, that those people behaved like ancient barbarians. The women, above all, manifested a lively and tender sympathy for Boule de Suif. The nuns, who appeared only at meals, cast down their eyes, and said nothing.

They dined, however, as soon as the first indignant outburst had subsided; but they spoke little and thought much.

The ladies went to bed early; and the men, having lighted their pipes, proposed a game of ecarte, in which Monsieur Follenvie was invited to join, the travellers hoping to question him skillfully as to the best means of vanquishing the officer's obduracy. But he thought of nothing but his cards, would listen to nothing, reply to nothing, and repeated, time after time: "Attend to the game, gentlemen! attend to the game!" So absorbed was his attention that he even forgot to expectorate. The consequence was that his chest gave forth rumbling sounds like those of an organ. His wheezing lungs struck every note of the asthmatic scale, from deep, hollow tones to a shrill, hoarse piping resembling that of a young cock trying to crow.

He refused to go to bed when his wife, overcome with sleep, came to fetch him. So she went off alone, for she was an early bird, always up with the sun; while he was addicted to late hours, ever ready to spend the night with friends. He merely said: "Put my egg-nogg by the fire," and went on with the game. When the other men saw that nothing was to be got out of him they declared it was time to retire, and each sought his bed.

They rose fairly early the next morning, with a vague hope of being allowed to start, a greater desire than ever to do so, and a terror at having to spend another day in this wretched little inn.

Alas! the horses remained in the stable, the driver was invisible. They spent their time, for want of something better to do, in wandering round the coach.

Luncheon was a gloomy affair; and there was a general coolness toward Boule de Suif, for night, which brings counsel, had somewhat modified the judgment of her companions. In the cold light of the morning they almost bore a grudge against the girl for not having secretly sought out the Prussian, that the rest of the party might receive a joyful surprise when they awoke. What more simple?

Besides, who would have been the wiser? She might have saved appearances by telling the officer that she had taken pity on their distress. Such a step would be of so little consequence to her.

But no one as yet confessed to such thoughts.

In the afternoon, seeing that they were all bored to death, the count proposed a walk in the neighborhood of the village. Each one wrapped himself up well, and the little party set out, leaving behind only Cornudet, who preferred to sit over the fire, and the two nuns, who were in the habit of spending their day in the church or at the presbytery.

The cold, which grew more intense each day, almost froze the noses and ears of the pedestrians, their feet began to pain them so that each step was a penance, and when they reached the open country it looked so mournful and depressing in its limitless mantle of white that they all hastily retraced their steps, with bodies benumbed and hearts heavy.

The four women walked in front, and the three men followed a little in their rear.

Loiseau, who saw perfectly well how matters stood, asked suddenly "if that trollop were going to keep them waiting much longer in this Godforsaken spot." The count, always courteous, replied that they could not exact so painful a sacrifice from any woman, and that the first move must come from herself. Monsieur Carre-Lamadon remarked that if the French, as they talked of doing, made a counter attack by way of Dieppe, their encounter with the enemy must inevitably take place at Totes. This reflection made the other two anxious.

"Supposing we escape on foot?" said Loiseau.

The count shrugged his shoulders.

"How can you think of such a thing, in this snow? And with our wives? Besides, we should be pursued at once, overtaken in ten minutes, and brought back as prisoners at the mercy of the soldiery."

This was true enough; they were silent.

The ladies talked of dress, but a certain constraint seemed to prevail among them.

Suddenly, at the end of the street, the officer appeared. His tall, wasp-like, uniformed figure was outlined against the snow which bounded the horizon, and he walked, knees apart, with that motion peculiar to soldiers, who are always anxious not to soil their carefully polished boots.

He bowed as he passed the ladies, then glanced scornfully at the men, who had sufficient dignity not to raise their hats, though Loiseau made a movement to do so.

Boule de Suif flushed crimson to the ears, and the three married women felt unutterably humiliated at being met thus by the soldier in company with the girl whom he had treated with such scant ceremony.

Then they began to talk about him, his figure, and his face. Madame Carre-Lamadon, who had known many officers and judged them as a connoisseur, thought him not at all bad-looking; she even regretted that he was not a Frenchman, because in that case he would have made a very handsome hussar, with whom all the women would assuredly have fallen in love.

When they were once more within doors they did not know what to do with themselves. Sharp words even were exchanged apropos of the merest trifles. The silent dinner was quickly over, and each one went to bed early in the hope of sleeping, and thus killing time.

They came down next morning with tired faces and irritable tempers; the women scarcely spoke to Boule de Suif.

A church bell summoned the faithful to a baptism. Boule de Suif had a child being brought up by peasants at Yvetot. She did not see him once a year, and never thought of him; but the idea of the child who was about to be baptized induced a sudden wave of tenderness for her own, and she insisted on being present at the ceremony.

As soon as she had gone out, the rest of the company looked at one another and then drew their chairs together; for they realized that they must decide on some course of action. Loiseau had an inspiration: he proposed that they should ask the officer to detain Boule de Suif only, and to let the rest depart on their way.

Monsieur Follenvie was intrusted with this commission, but he returned to them almost immediately. The German, who knew human nature, had shown him the door. He intended to keep all the travellers until his condition had been complied with.

Whereupon Madame Loiseau's vulgar temperament broke bounds.

"We're not going to die of old age here!" she cried. "Since it's that vixen's trade to behave so with men I don't see that she has any right to refuse one more than another. I may as well tell you she took any lovers she could get at Rouen—even coachmen! Yes, indeed, madame—the coachman at the prefecture! I know it for a fact, for he buys his wine of us. And now that it is a question of getting us out of a difficulty she puts on virtuous airs, the drab! For my part, I think this officer has behaved very well. Why, there were three others of us, any one of whom he would undoubtedly have preferred. But no, he contents himself with the girl who is common property. He respects married women. Just think. He is master here. He had only to say: 'I wish it!' and he might have taken us by force, with the help of his soldiers."

The two other women shuddered; the eyes of pretty Madame Carre-Lamadon glistened, and she grew pale, as if the officer were indeed in the act of laying violent hands on her.

The men, who had been discussing the subject among themselves, drew near. Loiseau, in a state of furious resentment, was for delivering up "that miserable woman," bound hand and foot, into the enemy's power. But the count, descended from three generations of ambassadors, and endowed, moreover, with the lineaments of a diplomat, was in favor of more tactful measures.

"We must persuade her," he said.

Then they laid their plans.

The women drew together; they lowered their voices, and the discussion became general, each giving his or her opinion. But the conversation was not in the least coarse. The ladies, in particular, were adepts at delicate phrases and charming subtleties of expression to describe the most improper things. A stranger would have understood none of their allusions, so guarded was the language they employed. But, seeing that the thin veneer of modesty with which every woman of the world is furnished goes but a very little way below the surface, they began rather to enjoy this unedifying episode, and at bottom were hugely delighted —feeling themselves in their element, furthering the schemes of lawless love with the gusto of a gourmand cook who prepares supper for another.

Their gaiety returned of itself, so amusing at last did the whole business seem to them. The count uttered several rather risky witticisms, but so tactfully were they said that his audience could not help smiling. Loiseau in turn made some considerably broader jokes, but no one took offence; and the thought expressed with such brutal directness by his wife was uppermost in the minds of all: "Since it's the girl's trade, why should she refuse this man more than another?" Dainty Madame Carre-Lamadon seemed to think even that in Boule de Suif's place she would be less inclined to refuse him than another.

The blockade was as carefully arranged as if they were investing a fortress. Each agreed on the role which he or she was to play, the arguments to be used, the maneuvers to be executed. They decided on the plan of campaign, the stratagems they were to employ, and the surprise attacks which were to reduce this human citadel and force it to receive the enemy within its walls.

But Cornudet remained apart from the rest, taking no share in the plot.

So absorbed was the attention of all that Boule de Suif's entrance was almost unnoticed. But the count whispered a gentle "Hush!" which made the others look up. She was there. They suddenly stopped talking, and a vague embarrassment prevented them for a few moments from addressing her. But the countess, more practiced than the others in the wiles of the drawing-room, asked her:

"Was the baptism interesting?"

The girl, still under the stress of emotion, told what she had seen and heard, described the faces, the attitudes of those present, and even the appearance of the church. She concluded with the words:

"It does one good to pray sometimes."

Until lunch time the ladies contented themselves with being pleasant to her, so as to increase her confidence and make her amenable to their advice.

As soon as they took their seats at table the attack began. First they opened a vague conversation on the subject of self-sacrifice. Ancient examples were quoted: Judith and Holofernes; then, irrationally enough, Lucrece and Sextus; Cleopatra and the hostile generals whom she reduced to abject slavery by a surrender of her charms. Next was recounted an extraordinary story, born of the imagination of these ignorant millionaires, which told how the matrons of Rome seduced Hannibal, his lieutenants, and all his mercenaries at Capua. They held up to admiration all those women who from time to time have arrested the victorious progress of conquerors, made of their bodies a field of battle, a means of ruling, a weapon; who have vanquished by their heroic caresses hideous or detested beings, and sacrificed their chastity to vengeance and devotion.

All was said with due restraint and regard for propriety, the effect heightened now and then by an outburst of forced enthusiasm calculated to excite emulation.

A listener would have thought at last that the one role of woman on earth was a perpetual sacrifice of her person, a continual abandonment of herself to the caprices of a hostile soldiery.

The two nuns seemed to hear nothing, and to be lost in thought. Boule de Suif also was silent.

During the whole afternoon she was left to her reflections. But instead of calling her "madame" as they had done hitherto, her companions addressed her simply as "mademoiselle," without exactly knowing why, but as if desirous of making her descend a step in the esteem she had won, and forcing her to realize her degraded position.

Just as soup was served, Monsieur Follenvie reappeared, repeating his phrase of the evening before:

"The Prussian officer sends to ask if Mademoiselle Elisabeth Rousset has changed her mind."

Boule de Suif answered briefly:

"No, monsieur."

But at dinner the coalition weakened. Loiseau made three unfortunate remarks. Each was cudgeling his brains for further examples of self-sacrifice, and could find none, when the countess, possibly without ulterior motive, and moved simply by a vague desire to do homage to religion, began to question the elder of the two nuns on the most striking facts in the lives of the saints. Now, it fell out that many of these had committed acts which would be crimes in our eyes, but the Church readily pardons such deeds when they are accomplished for the glory of God or the good of mankind. This was a powerful argument, and the countess made the most of it. Then, whether by reason of a tacit understanding, a thinly veiled act of complaisance such as those who wear the ecclesiastical habit excel in, or whether merely as the result of sheer stupidity—a stupidity admirably adapted to further their designs—the old nun rendered formidable aid to the conspirator. They had thought her timid; she proved herself bold, talkative, bigoted. She was not troubled by the ins and outs of casuistry; her doctrines were as iron bars; her faith knew no doubt; her conscience no scruples. She looked on Abraham's sacrifice as natural enough, for she herself would not have hesitated to kill both father and mother if she had received a divine order to that effect; and nothing, in her opinion, could displease our Lord, provided the motive were praiseworthy. The countess, putting to good use the consecrated authority of her unexpected ally, led her on to make a lengthy and edifying paraphrase of that axiom enunciated by a certain school of moralists: "The end justifies the means."

"Then, sister," she asked, "you think God accepts all methods, and pardons the act when the motive is pure?"

"Undoubtedly, madame. An action reprehensible in itself often derives merit from the thought which inspires it."

And in this wise they talked on, fathoming the wishes of God, predicting His judgments, describing Him as interested in matters which assuredly concern Him but little.

All was said with the utmost care and discretion, but every word uttered by the holy woman in her nun's garb weakened the indignant resistance of the courtesan. Then the conversation drifted somewhat, and the nun began to talk of the convents of her order, of her Superior, of herself, and of her fragile little neighbor, Sister St. Nicephore. They had been sent for from Havre to nurse the hundreds of soldiers who were in hospitals, stricken with smallpox. She described these wretched invalids and their malady. And, while they themselves were detained on their way by the caprices of the Prussian officer, scores of Frenchmen might be dying, whom they would otherwise have saved! For the nursing of soldiers was the old nun's specialty; she had been in the Crimea, in Italy, in Austria; and as she told the story of her campaigns she revealed herself as one of those holy sisters of the fife and drum who seem designed by nature to follow camps, to snatch the wounded from amid the strife of battle, and to quell with a word, more effectually than any general, the rough and insubordinate troopers—a masterful woman, her seamed and pitted face itself an image of the devastations of war.

No one spoke when she had finished for fear of spoiling the excellent effect of her words.

As soon as the meal was over the travellers retired to their rooms, whence they emerged the following day at a late hour of the morning.

Luncheon passed off quietly. The seed sown the preceding evening was being given time to germinate and bring forth fruit.

In the afternoon the countess proposed a walk; then the count, as had been arranged beforehand, took Boule de Suif's arm, and walked with her at some distance behind the rest.

He began talking to her in that familiar, paternal, slightly contemptuous tone which men of his class adopt in speaking to women like her, calling her "my dear child," and talking down to her from the height of his exalted social position and stainless reputation. He came straight to the point.

"So you prefer to leave us here, exposed like yourself to all the violence which would follow on a repulse of the Prussian troops, rather than consent to surrender yourself, as you have done so many times in your life?"

The girl did not reply.

He tried kindness, argument, sentiment. He still bore himself as count, even while adopting, when desirable, an attitude of gallantry, and making pretty—nay, even tender—speeches. He exalted the service she would render them, spoke of their gratitude; then, suddenly, using the familiar "thou":

"And you know, my dear, he could boast then of having made a conquest of a pretty girl such as he won't often find in his own country."

Boule de Suif did not answer, and joined the rest of the party.

As soon as they returned she went to her room, and was seen no more. The general anxiety was at its height. What would she do? If she still resisted, how awkward for them all!

The dinner hour struck; they waited for her in vain. At last Monsieur Follenvie entered, announcing that Mademoiselle Rousset was not well, and that they might sit down to table. They all pricked up their ears. The count drew near the innkeeper, and whispered:

"Is it all right?"

"Yes."

Out of regard for propriety he said nothing to his companions, but merely nodded slightly toward them. A great sigh of relief went up from all breasts; every face was lighted up with joy.

"By Gad!" shouted Loiseau, "I'll stand champagne all round if there's any to be found in this place." And great was Madame Loiseau's dismay when the proprietor came back with four bottles in his hands. They had all suddenly become talkative and merry; a lively joy filled all hearts. The count seemed to perceive for the first time that Madame Carre-Lamadon was charming; the manufacturer paid compliments to the countess. The conversation was animated, sprightly, witty, and, although many of the jokes were in the worst possible taste, all the company were amused by them, and none offended—indignation being dependent, like other emotions, on surroundings. And the mental atmosphere had gradually become filled with gross imaginings and unclean thoughts.

At dessert even the women indulged in discreetly worded allusions. Their glances were full of meaning; they had drunk much. The count, who even in his moments of relaxation preserved a dignified demeanor, hit on a much-appreciated comparison of the condition of things with the termination of a winter spent in the icy solitude of the North Pole and the joy of shipwrecked mariners who at last perceive a southward track opening out before their eyes.

Loiseau, fairly in his element, rose to his feet, holding aloft a glass of champagne.

"I drink to our deliverance!" he shouted.

All stood up, and greeted the toast with acclamation. Even the two good sisters yielded to the solicitations of the ladies, and consented to moisten their lips with the foaming wine, which they had never before tasted. They declared it was like effervescent lemonade, but with a pleasanter flavor.

"It is a pity," said Loiseau, "that we have no piano; we might have had a quadrille."

Cornudet had not spoken a word or made a movement; he seemed plunged in serious thought, and now and then tugged furiously at his great beard, as if trying to add still further to its length. At last, toward midnight, when they were about to separate, Loiseau, whose gait was far from steady, suddenly slapped him on the back, saying thickly:

"You're not jolly to-night; why are you so silent, old man?"

Cornudet threw back his head, cast one swift and scornful glance over the assemblage, and answered:

"I tell you all, you have done an infamous thing!"

He rose, reached the door, and repeating: "Infamous!" disappeared.

A chill fell on all. Loiseau himself looked foolish and disconcerted for a moment, but soon recovered his aplomb, and, writhing with laughter, exclaimed:

"Really, you are all too green for anything!"

Pressed for an explanation, he related the "mysteries of the corridor," whereat his listeners were hugely amused. The ladies could hardly contain their delight. The count and Monsieur

Carre-Lamadon laughed till they cried. They could scarcely believe their ears.

"What! you are sure? He wanted——"

"I tell you I saw it with my own eyes."

"And she refused?"

"Because the Prussian was in the next room!"

"Surely you are mistaken?"

"I swear I'm telling you the truth."

The count was choking with laughter. The manufacturer held his sides. Loiseau continued:

"So you may well imagine he doesn't think this evening's business at all amusing."

And all three began to laugh again, choking, coughing, almost ill with merriment.

Then they separated. But Madame Loiseau, who was nothing if not spiteful, remarked to her husband as they were on the way to bed that "that stuck-up little minx of a Carre-Lamadon had laughed on the wrong side of her mouth all the evening."

"You know," she said, "when women run after uniforms it's all the same to them whether the men who wear them are French or Prussian. It's perfectly sickening!"

The next morning the snow showed dazzling white tinder a clear winter sun. The coach, ready at last, waited before the door; while a flock of white pigeons, with pink eyes spotted in the centres with black, puffed out their white feathers and walked sedately between the legs of the six horses, picking at the steaming manure.

The driver, wrapped in his sheepskin coat, was smoking a pipe on the box, and all the passengers, radiant with delight at their approaching departure, were putting up provisions for the remainder of the journey.

They were waiting only for Boule de Suif. At last she appeared.

She seemed rather shamefaced and embarrassed, and advanced with timid step toward her companions, who with one accord turned aside as if they had not seen her. The count, with much dignity, took his wife by the arm, and removed her from the unclean contact.

The girl stood still, stupefied with astonishment; then, plucking up courage, accosted the manufacturer's wife with a humble "Good-morning, madame," to which the other replied merely with a slight and insolent nod, accompanied by a look of outraged virtue. Every one suddenly appeared extremely busy, and kept as far from Boule de Suif as if her skirts had been infected with some deadly disease. Then they hurried to the coach, followed by the despised courtesan, who, arriving last of all, silently took the place she had occupied during the first part of the journey.

The rest seemed neither to see nor to know her—all save Madame Loiseau, who, glancing contemptuously in her direction, remarked, half aloud, to her husband:

"What a mercy I am not sitting beside that creature!"

The lumbering vehicle started on its way, and the journey began afresh.

At first no one spoke. Boule de Suif dared not even raise her eyes. She felt at once indignant with her neighbors, and humiliated at having yielded to the Prussian into whose arms they had so hypocritically cast her.

But the countess, turning toward Madame Carre-Lamadon, soon broke the painful silence:

"I think you know Madame d'Etrelles?"

"Yes; she is a friend of mine."

"Such a charming woman!"

"Delightful! Exceptionally talented, and an artist to the finger tips. She sings marvellously and draws to perfection."

The manufacturer was chatting with the count, and amid the clatter of the window-panes a word of their conversation was now and then distinguishable: "Shares—maturity—premium—time-limit."

Loiseau, who had abstracted from the inn the timeworn pack of cards, thick with the grease of five years' contact with half-wiped-off tables, started a game of bezique with his wife.

The good sisters, taking up simultaneously the long rosaries hanging from their waists, made the sign of the cross, and began to mutter in unison interminable prayers, their lips moving ever more and more swiftly, as if they sought which should outdistance the other in the race of orisons; from time to time they kissed a medal, and crossed themselves anew, then resumed their rapid and unintelligible murmur.

Cornudet sat still, lost in thought.

Ah the end of three hours Loiseau gathered up the cards, and remarked that he was hungry.

His wife thereupon produced a parcel tied with string, from which she extracted a piece of cold veal. This she cut into neat, thin slices, and both began to eat.

"We may as well do the same," said the countess. The rest agreed, and she unpacked the provisions which had been prepared for herself, the count, and the Carre-Lamadons. In one of those oval dishes, the lids of which are decorated with an earthenware hare, by way of showing that a game pie lies within, was a succulent delicacy consisting of the brown flesh of the game larded with streaks of bacon and flavored with other meats chopped fine. A solid wedge of Gruyere cheese, which had been wrapped in a newspaper, bore the imprint: "Items of News," on its rich, oily surface.

The two good sisters brought to light a hunk of sausage smelling strongly of garlic; and Cornudet, plunging both hands at once into the capacious pockets of his loose overcoat, produced from one four hard-boiled eggs and from the other a crust of bread. He removed the shells, threw them into the straw beneath his feet, and began to devour the eggs, letting morsels of the bright yellow yolk fall in his mighty beard, where they looked like stars.

Boule de Suif, in the haste and confusion of her departure, had not thought of anything, and, stifling with rage, she watched all these people placidly eating. At first, ill-suppressed wrath shook her whole person, and she opened her lips to shriek the truth at them, to overwhelm them with a volley of insults; but she could not utter a word, so choked was she with indignation.

No one looked at her, no one thought of her. She felt herself swallowed up in the scorn of these virtuous creatures, who had first sacrificed, then rejected her as a thing useless and unclean. Then she remembered her big basket full of the good things they had so greedily devoured: the two chickens coated in jelly, the pies, the pears, the four bottles of claret; and her fury broke forth like a cord that is overstrained, and she was on the verge of tears. She made terrible efforts at self-control, drew herself up, swallowed the sobs which choked her; but the tears rose nevertheless, shone at the brink of her eyelids, and soon two heavy drops coursed slowly down her cheeks. Others followed more quickly, like water filtering from a rock, and fell, one after another, on her rounded bosom. She sat upright, with a fixed expression, her face pale and rigid, hoping desperately that no one saw her give way.

But the countess noticed that she was weeping, and with a sign drew her husband's attention to the fact. He shrugged his shoulders, as if to say: "Well, what of it? It's not my fault." Madame Loiseau chuckled triumphantly, and murmured:

"She's weeping for shame."

The two nuns had betaken themselves once more to their prayers, first wrapping the remainder of their sausage in paper:

Then Cornudet, who was digesting his eggs, stretched his long legs under the opposite seat, threw himself back, folded his arms, smiled like a man who had just thought of a good joke, and began to whistle the Marseillaise.

The faces of his neighbors clouded; the popular air evidently did not find favor with them; they grew nervous and irritable, and seemed ready to howl as a dog does at the sound of a barrel-organ. Cornudet saw the discomfort he was creating, and whistled the louder; sometimes he even hummed the words:

Amour sacre de la patrie,

Conduis, soutiens, nos bras vengeurs,

Liberte, liberte cherie,

Combats avec tes defenseurs!

The coach progressed more swiftly, the snow being harder now; and all the way to Dieppe, during the long, dreary hours of the journey, first in the gathering dusk, then in the thick darkness, raising his voice above the rumbling of the vehicle, Cornudet continued with fierce obstinacy his vengeful and monotonous whistling, forcing his weary and exasperated-hearers to follow the song from end to end, to recall every word of every line, as each was repeated over and over again with untiring persistency.

And Boule de Suif still wept, and sometimes a sob she could not restrain was heard in the darkness between two verses of the song.

TWO FRIENDS

Besieged Paris was in the throes of famine. Even the sparrows on the roofs and the rats in the sewers were growing scarce. People were eating anything they could get.

As Monsieur Morissot, watchmaker by profession and idler for the nonce, was strolling along the boulevard one bright January morning, his hands in his trousers pockets and stomach empty, he suddenly came face to face with an acquaintance—Monsieur Sauvage, a fishing chum.

Before the war broke out Morissot had been in the habit, every Sunday morning, of setting forth with a bamboo rod in his hand and a tin box on his back. He took the Argenteuil train, got out at Colombes, and walked thence to the Ile Marante. The moment he arrived at this place of his dreams he began fishing, and fished till nightfall.

Every Sunday he met in this very spot Monsieur Sauvage, a stout, jolly, little man, a draper in the Rue Notre Dame de Lorette, and also an ardent fisherman. They often spent half the day side by side, rod in hand and feet dangling over the water, and a warm friendship had sprung up between the two.

Some days they did not speak; at other times they chatted; but they understood each other perfectly without the aid of words, having similar tastes and feelings.

In the spring, about ten o'clock in the morning, when the early sun caused a light mist to float on the water and gently warmed the backs of the two enthusiastic anglers, Morissot would occasionally remark to his neighbor:

"My, but it's pleasant here."

To which the other would reply:

"I can't imagine anything better!"

And these few words sufficed to make them understand and appreciate each other.

In the autumn, toward the close of day, when the setting sun shed a blood-red glow over the western sky, and the reflection of the crimson clouds tinged the whole river with red, brought a glow to the faces of the two friends, and gilded the trees, whose leaves were already turning at the first chill touch of winter, Monsieur Sauvage would sometimes smile at Morissot, and say:

"What a glorious spectacle!"

And Morissot would answer, without taking his eyes from his float:

"This is much better than the boulevard, isn't it?"

As soon as they recognized each other they shook hands cordially, affected at the thought of meeting under such changed circumstances.

Monsieur Sauvage, with a sigh, murmured:

"These are sad times!"

Morissot shook his head mournfully.

"And such weather! This is the first fine day of the year."

The sky was, in fact, of a bright, cloudless blue.

They walked along, side by side, reflective and sad.

"And to think of the fishing!" said Morissot. "What good times we used to have!"

"When shall we be able to fish again?" asked Monsieur Sauvage.

They entered a small cafe and took an absinthe together, then resumed their walk along the pavement.

Morissot stopped suddenly.

"Shall we have another absinthe?" he said.

"If you like," agreed Monsieur Sauvage.

And they entered another wine shop.

They were quite unsteady when they came out, owing to the effect of the alcohol on their empty stomachs. It was a fine, mild day, and a gentle breeze fanned their faces.

The fresh air completed the effect of the alcohol on Monsieur Sauvage. He stopped suddenly, saying:

"Suppose we go there?"

"Where?"

"Fishing."

"But where?"

"Why, to the old place. The French outposts are close to Colombes. I know Colonel Dumoulin, and we shall easily get leave to pass."

Morissot trembled with desire.

"Very well. I agree."

And they separated, to fetch their rods and lines.

An hour later they were walking side by side on the-highroad. Presently they reached the villa occupied by the colonel. He smiled at their request, and granted it. They resumed their walk, furnished with a password.

Soon they left the outposts behind them, made their way through deserted Colombes, and found themselves on the outskirts of the small vineyards which border the Seine. It was about eleven o'clock.

Before them lay the village of Argenteuil, apparently lifeless. The heights of Orgement and Sannois dominated the landscape. The great plain, extending as far as Nanterre, was empty, quite empty-a waste of dun-colored soil and bare cherry trees.

Monsieur Sauvage, pointing to the heights, murmured:

"The Prussians are up yonder!"

And the sight of the deserted country filled the two friends with vague misgivings.

The Prussians! They had never seen them as yet, but they had felt their presence in the neighborhood of Paris for months past—ruining France, pillaging, massacring, starving them. And a kind of superstitious terror mingled with the hatred they already felt toward this unknown, victorious nation.

"Suppose we were to meet any of them?" said Morissot.

"We'd offer them some fish," replied Monsieur Sauvage, with that Parisian light-heartedness which nothing can wholly quench.

Still, they hesitated to show themselves in the open country, overawed by the utter silence which reigned around them.

At last Monsieur Sauvage said boldly:

"Come, we'll make a start; only let us be careful!"

And they made their way through one of the vineyards, bent double, creeping along beneath the cover afforded by the vines, with eye and ear alert.

A strip of bare ground remained to be crossed before they could gain the river bank. They ran across this, and, as soon as they were at the water's edge, concealed themselves among the dry reeds.

Morissot placed his ear to the ground, to ascertain, if possible, whether footsteps were coming their way. He heard nothing. They seemed to be utterly alone.

Their confidence was restored, and they began to fish.

Before them the deserted Ile Marante hid them from the farther shore. The little restaurant was closed, and looked as if it had been deserted for years.

Monsieur Sauvage caught the first gudgeon, Monsieur Morissot the second, and almost every moment one or other raised his line with a little, glittering, silvery fish wriggling at the end; they were having excellent sport.

They slipped their catch gently into a close-meshed bag lying at their feet; they were filled with joy—the joy of once more indulging in a pastime of which they had long been deprived.

The sun poured its rays on their backs; they no longer heard anything or thought of anything. They ignored the rest of the world; they were fishing.

But suddenly a rumbling sound, which seemed to come from the bowels of the earth, shook the ground beneath them: the cannon were resuming their thunder.

Morissot turned his head and could see toward the left, beyond the banks of the river, the formidable outline of Mont-Valerien, from whose summit arose a white puff of smoke.

The next instant a second puff followed the first, and in a few moments a fresh detonation made the earth tremble.

Others followed, and minute by minute the mountain gave forth its deadly breath and a white puff of smoke, which rose slowly into the peaceful heaven and floated above the summit of the cliff.

Monsieur Sauvage shrugged his shoulders.

“They are at it again!” he said.

Morissot, who was anxiously watching his float bobbing up and down, was suddenly seized with the angry impatience of a peaceful man toward the madmen who were firing thus, and remarked indignantly:

“What fools they are to kill one another like that!”

“They’re worse than animals,” replied Monsieur Sauvage.

And Morissot, who had just caught a bleak, declared:

“And to think that it will be just the same so long as there are governments!”

“The Republic would not have declared war,” interposed Monsieur Sauvage.

Morissot interrupted him:

“Under a king we have foreign wars; under a republic we have civil war.”

And the two began placidly discussing political problems with the sound common sense of peaceful, matter-of-fact citizens—agreeing on one point: that they would never be free. And Mont-Valerien thundered ceaselessly, demolishing the houses of the French with its cannon balls, grinding lives of men to powder, destroying many a dream, many a cherished hope, many a prospective happiness; ruthlessly causing endless woe and suffering in the hearts of wives, of daughters, of mothers, in other lands.

“Such is life!” declared Monsieur Sauvage.

“Say, rather, such is death!” replied Morissot, laughing.

But they suddenly trembled with alarm at the sound of footsteps behind them, and, turning round, they perceived close at hand four tall, bearded men, dressed after the manner of livery servants and wearing flat caps on their heads. They were covering the two anglers with their rifles.

The rods slipped from their owners’ grasp and floated away down the river.

In the space of a few seconds they were seized, bound, thrown into a boat, and taken across to the Ile Marante.

And behind the house they had thought deserted were about a score of German soldiers.

A shaggy-looking giant, who was bestriding a chair and smoking a long clay pipe, addressed them in excellent French with the words:

“Well, gentlemen, have you had good luck with your fishing?”

Then a soldier deposited at the officer's feet the bag full of fish, which he had taken care to bring away. The Prussian smiled.

"Not bad, I see. But we have something else to talk about. Listen to me, and don't be alarmed:

"You must know that, in my eyes, you are two spies sent to reconnoitre me and my movements. Naturally, I capture you and I shoot you. You pretended to be fishing, the better to disguise your real errand. You have fallen into my hands, and must take the consequences. Such is war.

"But as you came here through the outposts you must have a password for your return. Tell me that password and I will let you go."

The two friends, pale as death, stood silently side by side, a slight fluttering of the hands alone betraying their emotion.

"No one will ever know," continued the officer. "You will return peacefully to your homes, and the secret will disappear with you. If you refuse, it means death-instant death. Choose!"

They stood motionless, and did not open their lips.

The Prussian, perfectly calm, went on, with hand outstretched toward the river:

"Just think that in five minutes you will be at the bottom of that water. In five minutes! You have relations, I presume?"

Mont-Valerien still thundered.

The two fishermen remained silent. The German turned and gave an order in his own language. Then he moved his chair a little way off, that he might not be so near the prisoners, and a dozen men stepped forward, rifle in hand, and took up a position, twenty paces off.

"I give you one minute," said the officer; "not a second longer."

Then he rose quickly, went over to the two Frenchmen, took Morissot by the arm, led him a short distance off, and said in a low voice:

"Quick! the password! Your friend will know nothing. I will pretend to relent."

Morissot answered not a word.

Then the Prussian took Monsieur Sauvage aside in like manner, and made him the same proposal.

Monsieur Sauvage made no reply.

Again they stood side by side.

The officer issued his orders; the soldiers raised their rifles.

Then by chance Morissot's eyes fell on the bag full of gudgeon lying in the grass a few feet from him.

A ray of sunlight made the still quivering fish glisten like silver. And Morissot's heart sank. Despite his efforts at self-control his eyes filled with tears.

"Good-by, Monsieur Sauvage," he faltered.

"Good-by, Monsieur Morissot," replied Sauvage.

They shook hands, trembling from head to foot with a dread beyond their mastery.

The officer cried:

"Fire!"

The twelve shots were as one.

Monsieur Sauvage fell forward instantaneously. Morissot, being the taller, swayed slightly and fell across his friend with face turned skyward and blood oozing from a rent in the breast of his coat.

The German issued fresh orders.

His men dispersed, and presently returned with ropes and large stones, which they attached to the feet of the two friends; then they carried them to the river bank.

Mont-Valerien, its summit now enshrouded in smoke, still continued to thunder.

Two soldiers took Morissot by the head and the feet; two others did the same with Sauvage. The bodies, swung lustily by strong hands, were cast to a distance, and, describing a curve, fell feet foremost into the stream.

The water splashed high, foamed, eddied, then grew calm; tiny waves lapped the shore.

A few streaks of blood flecked the surface of the river.

The officer, calm throughout, remarked, with grim humor:

"It's the fishes' turn now!"

Then he retraced his way to the house.

Suddenly he caught sight of the net full of gudgeons, lying forgotten in the grass. He picked it up, examined it, smiled, and called:

"Wilhelm!"

A white-aproned soldier responded to the summons, and the Prussian, tossing him the catch of the two murdered men, said:

"Have these fish fried for me at once, while they are still alive; they'll make a tasty dish."

Then he resumed his pipe.

THE LANCER'S WIFE

I

It was after Bourbaki's defeat in the east of France. The army, broken up, decimated, and worn out, had been obliged to retreat into Switzerland after that terrible campaign, and it was only its short duration that saved a hundred and fifty thousand men from certain death. Hunger, the terrible cold, forced marches in the snow without boots, over bad mountain roads, had caused us 'francs-tireurs', especially, the greatest suffering, for we were without tents, and almost without food, always in the van when we were marching toward Belfort, and in the rear when returning by the Jura. Of our little band that had numbered twelve hundred men on the first of January, there remained only twenty-two pale, thin, ragged wretches, when we at length succeeded in reaching Swiss territory.

There we were safe, and could rest. Everybody knows what sympathy was shown to the unfortunate French army, and how well it was cared for. We all gained fresh life, and those who had been rich and happy before the war declared that they had never experienced a greater feeling of comfort than they did then. Just think. We actually had something to eat every day, and could sleep every night.

Meanwhile, the war continued in the east of France, which had been excluded from the armistice. Besancon still kept the enemy in check, and the latter had their revenge by ravaging Franche Comte. Sometimes we heard that they had approached quite close to the frontier, and we saw Swiss troops, who were to form a line of observation between us and them, set out on their march.

That pained us in the end, and, as we regained health and strength, the longing to fight took possession of us. It was disgraceful and irritating to know that within two or three leagues of us the Germans were victorious and insolent, to feel that we were protected by our captivity, and to feel that on that account we were powerless against them.

One day our captain took five or six of us aside, and spoke to us about it, long and furiously. He was a fine fellow, that captain. He had been a sublieutenant in the Zouaves, was tall and thin and as hard as steel, and during the whole campaign he had cut out their work for the Germans. He fretted in inactivity, and could not accustom himself to the idea of being a prisoner and of doing nothing.

"Confound it!" he said to us, "does it not pain you to know that there is a number of uhlans within two hours of us? Does it not almost drive you mad to know that those beggarly wretches are walking about as masters in our mountains, when six determined men might kill a whole spitful any day? I cannot endure it any longer, and I must go there."

"But how can you manage it, captain?"

"How? It is not very difficult! Just as if we had not done a thing or two within the last six months, and got out of woods that were guarded by very different men from the Swiss. The day that you wish to cross over into France, I will undertake to get you there."

"That may be; but what shall we do in France without any arms?"

"Without arms? We will get them over yonder, by Jove!"

"You are forgetting the treaty," another soldier said; "we shall run the risk of doing the Swiss an injury, if Manteuffel learns that they have allowed prisoners to return to France."

"Come," said the captain, "those are all bad reasons. I mean to go and kill some Prussians; that is all I care about. If you do not wish to do as I do, well and good; only say so at once. I can quite well go by myself; I do not require anybody's company."

Naturally we all protested, and, as it was quite impossible to make the captain alter his mind, we felt obliged to promise to go with him. We liked him too much to leave him in the lurch, as he never failed us in any extremity; and so the expedition was decided on.

II

The captain had a plan of his own, that he had been cogitating over for some time. A man in that part of the country whom he knew was going to lend him a cart and six suits of peasants' clothes. We could hide under some straw at the bottom of the wagon, which would be loaded with Gruyere cheese, which he was supposed to be going to sell in France. The captain told the sentinels that he was taking two friends with him to protect his goods, in case any one should try to rob him, which did not seem an extraordinary precaution. A Swiss officer seemed to look at the wagon in a knowing manner, but that was in order to impress his soldiers. In a word, neither officers nor men could make it out.

"Get up," the captain said to the horses, as he cracked his whip, while our three men quietly smoked their pipes. I was half suffocated in my box, which only admitted the air through those holes in front, and at the same time I was nearly frozen, for it was terribly cold.

"Get up," the captain said again, and the wagon loaded with Gruyere cheese entered France.

The Prussian lines were very badly guarded, as the enemy trusted to the watchfulness of the Swiss. The sergeant spoke North German, while our captain spoke the bad German of the Four Cantons, and so they could not understand each other. The sergeant, however, pretended to be very intelligent; and, in order to make us believe that he understood us, they allowed us to continue our journey; and, after travelling for seven hours, being continually stopped in the same manner, we arrived at a small village of the Jura in ruins, at nightfall.

What were we going to do? Our only arms were the captain's whip, our uniforms our peasants' blouses, and our food the Gruyere cheese. Our sole wealth consisted in our ammunition, packages of cartridges which we had stowed away inside some of the large cheeses. We had about a thousand of them, just two hundred each, but we needed rifles, and they must be chassepots. Luckily, however, the captain was a bold man of an inventive mind, and this was the plan that he hit upon:

While three of us remained hidden in a cellar in the abandoned village, he continued his journey as far as Besancon with the empty wagon and one man. The town was invested, but one can always make one's way into a town among the hills by crossing the tableland till within about ten miles of the walls, and then following paths and ravines on foot. They left their wagon at Omans, among the Germans, and escaped out of it at night on foot; so as to gain the heights which border the River Doubs; the next day they entered Besancon, where there were plenty of chassepots. There were nearly forty thousand of them left in the arsenal, and General Roland, a brave marine, laughed at the captain's daring project, but let him have six rifles and wished him "good luck." There he had also found his wife, who had been through all the war with us before the campaign in the East, and who had been only prevented by illness from continuing with Bourbaki's army. She had recovered, however, in spite of the cold, which was growing more and more intense, and in spite of the numberless privations that awaited her, she persisted in accompanying her husband. He was obliged to give way to her, and they all three, the captain, his wife, and our comrade, started on their expedition.

Going was nothing in comparison to returning. They were obliged to travel by night, so as to avoid meeting anybody, as the possession of six rifles would have made them liable to suspicion. But, in spite of everything, a week after leaving us, the captain and his two men were back with us again. The campaign was about to begin.

III

The first night of his arrival he began it himself, and, under pretext of examining the surrounding country, he went along the high road.

I must tell you that the little village which served as our fortress was a small collection of poor, badly built houses, which had been deserted long before. It lay on a steep slope, which terminated in a wooded plain. The country people sell the wood; they send it down the slopes, which are called coulees, locally, and which lead down to the plain, and there they stack it into piles, which they sell thrice a year to the wood merchants. The spot where this market is held in indicated by two small houses by the side of the highroad, which serve for public houses. The captain had gone down there by way of one of these coulees.

He had been gone about half an hour, and we were on the lookout at the top of the ravine, when we heard a shot. The captain had ordered us not to stir, and only to come to him when we heard him blow his trumpet. It was made of a goat's horn, and could be heard a league off; but it gave no sound, and, in spite of our cruel anxiety, we were obliged to wait in silence, with our rifles by our side.

It is nothing to go down these coulees; one just lets one's self slide down; but it is more difficult to get up again; one has to scramble up by catching hold of the hanging branches of the trees, and sometimes on all fours, by sheer strength. A whole mortal hour passed, and he did not come; nothing moved in the brushwood. The captain's wife began to grow impatient. What could he be doing? Why did he not call us? Did the shot that we had heard proceed from an enemy, and had he killed or wounded our leader, her husband? They did not know what to think, but I myself fancied either that he was dead or that his enterprise was successful; and I was merely anxious and curious to know what he had done.

Suddenly we heard the sound of his trumpet, and we were much surprised that instead of coming from below, as we had expected, it came from the village behind us. What did that mean? It was a mystery to us, but the same idea struck us all, that he had been killed, and that the Prussians were blowing the trumpet to draw us into an ambush. We therefore returned to the cottage, keeping a careful lookout with our fingers on the trigger, and hiding under the branches; but his wife, in spite of our entreaties, rushed on, leaping like a tigress. She thought that she had to avenge her husband, and had fixed the bayonet to her rifle, and we lost sight of her at the moment that we heard the trumpet again; and, a few moments later, we heard her calling out to us:

"Come on! come on! He is alive! It is he!"

We hastened on, and saw the captain smoking his pipe at the entrance of the village, but strangely enough, he was on horseback.

"Ah! ah!" he said to us, "you see that there is something to be done here. Here I am on horseback already; I knocked over an uhlan yonder, and took his horse; I suppose they were guarding the wood, but it was by drinking and swilling in clover. One of them, the sentry at the door, had not time to see me before I gave him a sugarplum in his stomach, and then, before the others could come out, I jumped on the horse and was off like a shot.

Eight or ten of them followed me, I think; but I took the crossroads through the woods. I have got scratched and torn a bit, but here I am, and now, my good fellows, attention, and take care! Those brigands will not rest until they have caught us, and we must receive them with rifle bullets. Come along; let us take up our posts!"

We set out. One of us took up his position a good way from the village on the crossroads; I was posted at the entrance of the main street, where the road from the level country enters the village, while the two others, the captain and his wife, were in the middle of the village, near the church, whose tower served for an observatory and citadel.

We had not been in our places long before we heard a shot, followed by another, and then two, then three. The first was evidently a chassepot —one recognized it by the sharp report, which sounds like the crack of a whip—while the other three came from the lancers' carbines.

The captain was furious. He had given orders to the outpost to let the enemy pass and merely to follow them at a distance if they marched toward the village, and to join me when they had gone well between the houses. Then they were to appear suddenly, take the patrol between two fires, and not allow a single man to escape; for, posted as we were, the six of us could have hemmed in ten Prussians, if needful.

"That confounded Piedelot has roused them," the captain said, "and they will not venture to come on blindfolded any longer. And then I am quite sure that he has managed to get a shot into himself somewhere or other, for we hear nothing of him. It serves him right; why did he not obey orders?" And then, after a moment, he grumbled in his beard: "After all I am sorry for the poor fellow; he is so brave, and shoots so well!"

The captain was right in his conjectures. We waited until evening, without seeing the uhlans; they had retreated after the first attack; but unfortunately we had not seen Piedelot, either. Was he dead or a prisoner? When night came, the captain proposed that we should go out and look for him, and so the three of us started. At the crossroads we found a broken rifle and some blood, while the ground was trampled down; but we did not find either a wounded man or a dead body, although we searched every thicket, and at midnight we returned without having discovered anything of our unfortunate comrade.

"It is very strange," the captain growled. "They must have killed him and thrown him into the bushes somewhere; they cannot possibly have taken him prisoner, as he would have called out for help. I cannot understand it at all." Just as he said that, bright flames shot up in the direction of the inn on the high road, which illuminated the sky.

"Scoundrels! cowards!" he shouted. "I will bet that they have set fire to the two houses on the marketplace, in order to have their revenge, and then they will scuttle off without saying a word. They will be satisfied with having killed a man and set fire to two houses. All right. It shall not pass over like that. We must go for them; they will not like to leave their illuminations in order to fight."

"It would be a great stroke of luck if we could set Piedelot free at the same time," some one said.

The five of us set off, full of rage and hope. In twenty minutes we had got to the bottom of the coulee, and had not yet seen any one when we were within a hundred yards of the inn. The fire was behind the house, and all we saw of it was the reflection above the roof. However, we were walking rather slowly, as we were afraid of an ambush, when suddenly we heard Piedelot's well-known voice. It had a strange sound, however; for it was at the same time—dull and vibrating, stifled and clear, as if he were calling out as loud as he could with a bit of rag stuffed into his mouth. He seemed to be hoarse and gasping, and the unlucky fellow kept exclaiming: "Help! Help!"

We sent all thoughts of prudence to the devil, and in two bounds we were at the back of the inn, where a terrible sight met our eyes.

IV

Piedelot was being burned alive. He was writhing in the midst of a heap of fagots, tied to a stake, and the flames were licking him with their burning tongues. When he saw us, his tongue seemed to stick in his throat; he drooped his head, and seemed as if he were going to die. It was only the affair of a moment to upset the burning pile, to scatter the embers, and to cut the ropes that fastened him.

Poor fellow! In what a terrible state we found him. The evening before he had had his left arm broken, and it seemed as if he had been badly beaten since then, for his whole body was covered with wounds, bruises and blood. The flames had also begun their work on him, and he had two large burns, one on his loins and the other on his right thigh, and his beard and hair were scorched. Poor Piedelot!

No one knows the terrible rage we felt at this sight! We would have rushed headlong at a hundred thousand Prussians; our thirst for vengeance was intense. But the cowards had run away, leaving their crime behind them. Where could we find them now? Meanwhile, however, the captain's wife was looking after Piedelot, and dressing his wounds as best she could, while the captain himself shook hands with him excitedly, and in a few minutes he came to himself.

"Good-morning, captain; good-morning, all of you," he said. "Ah! the scoundrels, the wretches! Why, twenty of them came to surprise us."

"Twenty, do you say?"

"Yes; there was a whole band of them, and that is why I disobeyed orders, captain, and fired on them, for they would have killed you all, and I preferred to stop them. That frightened them, and they did not venture to go farther than the crossroads. They were such cowards. Four of them shot at me at twenty yards, as if I had been a target, and then they slashed me with their swords. My arm was broken, so that I could only use my bayonet with one hand."

"But why did you not call for help?"

"I took good care not to do that, for you would all have come; and you would neither have been able to defend me nor yourselves, being only five against twenty."

"You know that we should not have allowed you to have been taken, poor old fellow."

"I preferred to die by myself, don't you see! I did not want to bring you here, for it would have been a mere ambush."

"Well, we will not talk about it any more. Do you feel rather easier?"

"No, I am suffocating. I know that I cannot live much longer. The brutes! They tied me to a tree, and beat me till I was half dead, and then they shook my broken arm; but I did not make a sound. I would rather have bitten my tongue out than have called out before them.

Now I can tell what I am suffering and shed tears; it does one good. Thank you, my kind friends."

"Poor Piedelot! But we will avenge you, you may be sure!"

"Yes, yes; I want you to do that. There is, in particular, a woman among them who passes as the wife of the lancer whom the captain killed yesterday. She is dressed like a lancer, and she tortured me the most yesterday, and suggested burning me; and it was she who set fire to the wood. Oh! the wretch, the brute! Ah! how I am suffering! My loins, my arms!" and he fell back gasping and exhausted, writhing in his terrible agony, while the captain's wife wiped the perspiration from his forehead, and we all shed tears of grief and rage, as if we had been children. I will not describe the end to you; he died half an hour later, previously telling us in what direction the enemy had gone. When he was dead we gave ourselves time to bury him, and then we set out in pursuit of them, with our hearts full of fury and hatred.

"We will throw ourselves on the whole Prussian army, if it be necessary," the captain said; "but we will avenge Piedelot. We must catch those scoundrels. Let us swear to die, rather than not to find them; and if I am killed first, these are my orders: All the prisoners that you take are to be shot immediately, and as for the lancer's wife, she is to be tortured before she is put to death."

"She must not be shot, because she is a woman," the captain's wife said. "If you survive, I am sure that you would not shoot a woman. Torturing her will be quite sufficient; but if you are killed in this pursuit, I want one thing, and that is to fight with her; I will kill her with my own hands, and the others can do what they like with her if she kills me."

"We will outrage her! We will burn her! We will tear her to pieces! Piedelot shall be avenged!

"An eye for an eye, a tooth for a tooth!"

V

The next morning we unexpectedly fell on an outpost of uhlans four leagues away. Surprised by our sudden attack, they were not able to mount their horses, nor even to defend themselves; and in a few moments we had five prisoner, corresponding to our own number. The captain questioned them, and from their answers we felt certain that they were the same whom we had encountered the previous day. Then a very curious operation took place. One of us was told off to ascertain their sex, and nothing can describe our joy when we discovered what we were seeking among them, the female executioner who had tortured our friend.

The four others were shot on the spot, with their backs to us and close to the muzzles of our rifles; and then we turned our attention to the woman. What were we going to do with her? I must acknowledge that we were all of us in favor of shooting her. Hatred, and the wish to avenge Piedelot, had extinguished all pity in us, and we had forgotten that we were going to shoot a woman, but a woman reminded us of it, the captain's wife; at her entreaties, therefore, we determined to keep her a prisoner.

The captain's poor wife was to be severely punished for this act of clemency.

The next day we heard that the armistice had been extended to the eastern part of France, and we had to put an end to our little campaign. Two of us, who belonged to the neighborhood, returned home, so there were only four of us, all told: the captain, his wife, and two men.

We belonged to Besancon, which was still being besieged in spite of the armistice.

"Let us stop here," said the captain. "I cannot believe that the war is going to end like this. The devil take it! Surely there are men still left in France; and now is the time to prove what they are made of. The spring is coming on, and the armistice is only a trap laid for the Prussians. During the time that it lasts, a new army will be raised, and some fine morning we shall fall upon them again. We shall be ready, and we have a hostage—let us remain here."

We fixed our quarters there. It was terribly cold, and we did not go out much, and somebody had always to keep the female prisoner in sight.

She was sullen, and never said anything, or else spoke of her husband, whom the captain had killed. She looked at him continually with fierce eyes, and we felt that she was tortured by a wild longing for revenge. That seemed to us to be the most suitable punishment for the terrible torments that she had made Piedelot suffer, for impotent vengeance is such intense pain!

Alas! we who knew how to avenge our comrade ought to have thought that this woman would know how to avenge her husband, and have been on our guard. It is true that one of us kept watch every night, and that at first we tied her by a long rope to the great oak bench that was fastened to the wall. But, by and by, as she had never tried to escape, in spite of her hatred for us, we relaxed our extreme prudence, and allowed her to sleep somewhere else except on the bench, and without being tied. What had we to fear? She was at the end of the room, a man was on guard at the door, and between her and the sentinel the captain's wife and two other men used to lie. She was alone and unarmed against four, so there could be no danger.

One night when we were asleep, and the captain was on guard, the lancer's wife was lying more quietly in her corner than usual, and she had even smiled for the first time since she had been our prisoner during the evening. Suddenly, however, in the middle of the night, we were all awakened by a terrible cry. We got up, groping about, and at once stumbled over a furious couple who were rolling about and fighting on the ground. It was the captain and the lancer's wife. We threw ourselves on them, and separated them in a moment. She was shouting and laughing, and he seemed to have the death rattle. All this took place in the dark. Two of us held her, and when a light was struck a terrible sight met our eyes. The captain was lying on the floor in a pool of blood, with an enormous gash in his throat, and his sword bayonet, that had been taken from his rifle, was sticking in the red, gaping wound. A few minutes afterward he died, without having been able to utter a word.

His wife did not shed a tear. Her eyes were dry, her throat was contracted, and she looked at the lancer's wife steadfastly, and with a calm ferocity that inspired fear.

"This woman belongs to me," she said to us suddenly. "You swore to me not a week ago to let me kill her as I chose, if she killed my husband; and you must keep your oath. You must fasten her securely to the fireplace, upright against the back of it, and then you can go where you like, but far from here. I will take my revenge on her myself. Leave the captain's body, and we three, he, she and I, will remain here."

We obeyed, and went away. She promised to write to us to Geneva, as we were returning thither.

VI

Two days later I received the following letter, dated the day after we had left, that had been written at an inn on the high road:

"MY FRIEND: I am writing to you, according to my promise. For the moment I am at the inn, where I have just handed my prisoner over to a Prussian officer.

"I must tell you, my friend, that this poor woman has left two children in Germany. She had followed her husband, whom she adored, as she did not wish him to be exposed to the risks of war by himself, and as her children were with their grandparents. I have learned all this since yesterday, and it has turned my ideas of vengeance into more humane feelings. At the very moment when I felt pleasure in insulting this woman, and in threatening her with the most fearful torments, in recalling Piedelot, who had been burned alive, and in threatening her with a similar death, she looked at me coldly, and said:

"'What have you got to reproach me with, Frenchwoman? You think that you will do right in avenging your husband's death, is not that so?'

"'Yes,' I replied.

"'Very well, then; in killing him, I did what you are going to do in burning me. I avenged my husband, for your husband killed him.'

"'Well,' I replied, 'as you approve of this vengeance, prepare to endure it.'

"'I do not fear it.'

"And in fact she did not seem to have lost courage. Her face was calm, and she looked at me without trembling, while I brought wood and dried leaves together, and feverishly threw on to them the powder from some cartridges, which was to make her funeral pile the more cruel.

"I hesitated in my thoughts of persecution for a moment. But the captain was there, pale and covered with blood, and he seemed to be looking at me with his large, glassy eyes, and I applied myself to my work again after kissing his pale lips. Suddenly, however, on raising my head, I saw that she was crying, and I felt rather surprised.

"'So you are frightened?' I said to her.

"'No, but when I saw you kiss your husband, I thought of mine, of all whom I love.'

"She continued to sob, but stopping suddenly, she said to me in broken words and in a low voice:

"'Have you any children?'

"A shiver rare over me, for I guessed that this poor woman had some. She asked me to look in a pocketbook which was in her bosom, and in it I saw two photographs of quite young children, a boy and a girl, with those kind, gentle, chubby faces that German children have. In it there were also two locks of light hair and a letter in a large, childish hand, and beginning with German words which meant:

"'My dear little mother.

"'I could not restrain my tears, my dear friend, and so I untied her, and without venturing to look at the face of my poor dead husband, who was not to be avenged, I went with her as far as the inn. She is free; I have just left her, and she kissed me with tears. I am going upstairs to my husband; come as soon as possible, my dear friend, to look for our two bodies.'"

I set off with all speed, and when I arrived there was a Prussian patrol at the cottage; and when I asked what it all meant, I was told that there was a captain of francs-tireurs and his wife inside, both dead. I gave their names; they saw that I knew them, and I begged to be allowed to arrange their funeral.

"Somebody has already undertaken it," was the reply. "Go in if you wish to, as you know them. You can settle about their funeral with their friend."

I went in. The captain and his wife were lying side by side on a bed, and were covered by a sheet. I raised it, and saw that the woman had inflicted a similar wound in her throat to that from which her husband had died.

At the side of the bed there sat, watching and weeping, the woman who had been mentioned to me as their best friend. It was the lancer's wife.

THE PRISONERS

There was not a sound in the forest save the indistinct, fluttering sound of the snow falling on the trees. It had been snowing since noon; a little fine snow, that covered the branches as with frozen moss, and spread a silvery covering over the dead leaves in the ditches, and covered the roads with a white, yielding carpet, and made still more intense the boundless silence of this ocean of trees.

Before the door of the forester's dwelling a young woman, her arms bare to the elbow, was chopping wood with a hatchet on a block of stone. She was tall, slender, strong-a true girl of the woods, daughter and wife of a forester.

A voice called from within the house:

"We are alone to-night, Berthine; you must come in. It is getting dark, and there may be Prussians or wolves about."

"I've just finished, mother," replied the young woman, splitting as she spoke an immense log of wood with strong, deft blows, which expanded her chest each time she raised her arms to strike. "Here I am; there's no need to be afraid; it's quite light still."

Then she gathered up her sticks and logs, piled them in the chimney corner, went back to close the great oaken shutters, and finally came in, drawing behind her the heavy bolts of the door.

Her mother, a wrinkled old woman whom age had rendered timid, was spinning by the fireside.

"I am uneasy," she said, "when your father's not here. Two women are not much good."

"Oh," said the younger woman, "I'd cheerfully kill a wolf or a Prussian if it came to that."

And she glanced at a heavy revolver hanging above the hearth.

Her husband had been called upon to serve in the army at the beginning of the Prussian invasion, and the two women had remained alone with the old father, a keeper named Nicolas Pichon, sometimes called Long-legs, who refused obstinately to leave his home and take refuge in the town.

This town was Rethel, an ancient stronghold built on a rock. Its inhabitants were patriotic, and had made up their minds to resist the invaders, to fortify their native place, and, if need be, to stand a siege as in the good old days. Twice already, under Henri IV and under Louis XIV, the people of Rethel had distinguished themselves by their heroic defence of their town. They would do as much now, by gad! or else be slaughtered within their own walls.

They had, therefore, bought cannon and rifles, organized a militia, and formed themselves into battalions and companies, and now spent their time drilling all day long in the square. All-bakers, grocers, butchers, lawyers, carpenters, booksellers, chemists-took their turn at military training at regular hours of the day, under the auspices of Monsieur Lavigne, a former noncommissioned officer in the dragoons, now a draper, having married the daughter and inherited the business of Monsieur Ravaudan, Senior.

He had taken the rank of commanding officer in Rethel, and, seeing that all the young men had gone off to the war, he had enlisted all the others who were in favor of resisting an attack. Fat men now invariably walked the streets at a rapid pace, to reduce their weight and improve their breathing, and weak men carried weights to strengthen their muscles.

And they awaited the Prussians. But the Prussians did not appear. They were not far off, however, for twice already their scouts had penetrated as far as the forest dwelling of Nicolas Pichon, called Long-legs.

The old keeper, who could run like a fox, had come and warned the town. The guns had been got ready, but the enemy had not shown themselves.

Long-legs' dwelling served as an outpost in the Aveline forest. Twice a week the old man went to the town for provisions and brought the citizens news of the outlying district.

On this particular day he had gone to announce the fact that a small detachment of German infantry had halted at his house the day before, about two o'clock in the afternoon, and had left again almost immediately. The noncommissioned officer in charge spoke French.

When the old man set out like this he took with him his dogs—two powerful animals with the jaws of lions-as a safeguard against the wolves, which were beginning to get fierce, and he left directions with the two women to barricade themselves securely within their dwelling as soon as night fell.

The younger feared nothing, but her mother was always apprehensive, and repeated continually:

"We'll come to grief one of these days. You see if we don't!"

This evening she was, if possible, more nervous than ever.

"Do you know what time your father will be back?" she asked.

"Oh, not before eleven, for certain. When he dines with the commandant he's always late."

And Berthine was hanging her pot over the fire to warm the soup when she suddenly stood still, listening attentively to a sound that had reached her through the chimney.

"There are people walking in the wood," she said; "seven or eight men at least."

The terrified old woman stopped her spinning wheel, and gasped:

"Oh, my God! And your father not here!"

She had scarcely finished speaking when a succession of violent blows shook the door.

As the woman made no reply, a loud, guttural voice shouted:

"Open the door!"

After a brief silence the same voice repeated:

"Open the door or I'll break it down!"

Berthine took the heavy revolver from its hook, slipped it into the pocket of her skirt, and, putting her ear to the door, asked:

"Who are you?" demanded the young woman. "What do you want?".

"The detachment that came here the other day," replied the voice.

"My men and I have lost our way in the forest since morning. Open the door or I'll break it down!"

The forester's daughter had no choice; she shot back the heavy bolts, threw open the ponderous shutter, and perceived in the wan light of the snow six men, six Prussian soldiers, the same who had visited the house the day before.

"What are you doing here at this time of night?" she asked dauntlessly.

"I lost my bearings," replied the officer; "lost them completely. Then I recognized this house. I've eaten nothing since morning, nor my men either."

"But I'm quite alone with my mother this evening," said Berthine.

"Never mind," replied the soldier, who seemed a decent sort of fellow. "We won't do you any harm, but you must give us something to eat. We are nearly dead with hunger and fatigue."

Then the girl moved aside.

"Come in;" she said.

Then entered, covered with snow, their helmets sprinkled with a creamy-looking froth, which gave them the appearance of meringues. They seemed utterly worn out.

The young woman pointed to the wooden benches on either side of the large table.

"Sit down," she said, "and I'll make you some soup. You certainly look tired out, and no mistake."

Then she bolted the door afresh.

She put more water in the pot, added butter and potatoes; then, taking down a piece of bacon from a hook in the chimney earner, cut it in two and slipped half of it into the pot.

The six men watched her movements with hungry eyes. They had placed their rifles and helmets in a corner and waited for supper, as well behaved as children on a school bench.

The old mother had resumed her spinning, casting from time to time a furtive and uneasy glance at the soldiers. Nothing was to be heard save the humming of the wheel, the crackling of the fire, and the singing of the water in the pot.

But suddenly a strange noise—a sound like the harsh breathing of some wild animal sniffing under the door-startled the occupants of the room.

The German officer sprang toward the rifles. Berthine stopped him with a gesture, and said, smilingly:

"It's only the wolves. They are like you—prowling hungry through the forest."

The incredulous man wanted to see with his own eyes, and as soon as the door was opened he perceived two large grayish animals disappearing with long, swinging trot into the darkness.

He returned to his seat, muttering:

"I wouldn't have believed it!"

And he waited quietly till supper was ready.

The men devoured their meal voraciously, with mouths stretched to their ears that they might swallow the more. Their round eyes opened at the same time as their jaws, and as the soup coursed down their throats it made a noise like the gurgling of water in a rainpipe.

The two women watched in silence the movements of the big red beards. The potatoes seemed to be engulfed in these moving fleeces.

But, as they were thirsty, the forester's daughter went down to the cellar to draw them some cider. She was gone some time. The cellar was small, with an arched ceiling, and had served, so people said, both as prison and as hiding-place during the Revolution. It was approached by means of a narrow, winding staircase, closed by a trap-door at the farther end of the kitchen.

When Berthine returned she was smiling mysteriously to herself. She gave the Germans her jug of cider.

Then she and her mother supped apart, at the other end of the kitchen.

The soldiers had finished eating, and were all six falling asleep as they sat round the table. Every now and then a forehead fell with a thud on the board, and the man, awakened suddenly, sat upright again.

Berthine said to the officer:

"Go and lie down, all of you, round the fire. There's lots of room for six. I'm going up to my room with my mother."

And the two women went upstairs. They could be heard locking the door and walking about overhead for a time; then they were silent.

The Prussians lay down on the floor, with their feet to the fire and their heads resting on their rolled-up cloaks. Soon all six snored loudly and uninterruptedly in six different keys.

They had been sleeping for some time when a shot rang out so loudly that it seemed directed against the very walls of the house. The soldiers rose hastily. Two-then three-more shots were fired.

The door opened hastily, and Berthine appeared, barefooted and only half dressed, with her candle in her hand and a scared look on her face.

"There are the French," she stammered; "at least two hundred of them. If they find you here they'll burn the house down. For God's sake, hurry down into the cellar, and don't make a sound, whatever you do. If you make any noise we are lost."

"We'll go, we'll go," replied the terrified officer. "Which is the way?"

The young woman hurriedly raised the small, square trap-door, and the six men disappeared one after another down the narrow, winding staircase, feeling their way as they went.

But as soon as the spike of the last helmet was out of sight Berthine lowered the heavy oaken lid—thick as a wall, hard as steel, furnished with the hinges and bolts of a prison cell—shot the two heavy bolts, and began to laugh long and silently, possessed with a mad longing to dance above the heads of her prisoners.

They made no sound, inclosed in the cellar as in a strong-box, obtaining air only from a small, iron-barred vent-hole.

Berthine lighted her fire again, hung the pot over it, and prepared more soup, saying to herself:

"Father will be tired to-night."

Then she sat and waited. The heavy pendulum of the clock swung to and fro with a monotonous tick.

Every now and then the young woman cast an impatient glance at the dial-a glance which seemed to say:

"I wish he'd be quick!"

But soon there was a sound of voices beneath her feet. Low, confused words reached her through the masonry which roofed the cellar. The Prussians were beginning to suspect the trick she had played them, and presently the officer came up the narrow staircase, and knocked at the trap-door.

"Open the door!" he cried.

"What do you want?" she said, rising from her seat and approaching the cellarway.

"Open the door!"

"I won't do any such thing!"

"Open it or I'll break it down!" shouted the man angrily.

She laughed.

"Hammer away, my good man! Hammer away!"

He struck with the butt-end of his gun at the closed oaken door. But it would have resisted a battering-ram.

The forester's daughter heard him go down the stairs again. Then the soldiers came one after another and tried their strength against the trapdoor. But, finding their efforts useless, they all returned to the cellar and began to talk among themselves.

The young woman heard them for a short time, then she rose, opened the door of the house; looked out into the night, and listened.

A sound of distant barking reached her ear. She whistled just as a huntsman would, and almost immediately two great dogs emerged from the darkness, and bounded to her side. She held them tight, and shouted at the top of her voice:

"Hullo, father!"

A far-off voice replied:

"Hullo, Berthine!"

She waited a few seconds, then repeated:

"Hullo, father!"

The voice, nearer now, replied:

"Hullo, Berthine!"

"Don't go in front of the vent-hole!" shouted his daughter. "There are Prussians in the cellar!"

Suddenly the man's tall figure could be seen to the left, standing between two tree trunks.

"Prussians in the cellar?" he asked anxiously. "What are they doing?"

The young woman laughed.

"They are the same as were here yesterday. They lost their way, and I've given them free lodgings in the cellar."

She told the story of how she had alarmed them by firing the revolver, and had shut them up in the cellar.

The man, still serious, asked:

"But what am I to do with them at this time of night?"

"Go and fetch Monsieur Lavigne with his men," she replied. "He'll take them prisoners. He'll be delighted."

Her father smiled.

"So he will-delighted."

"Here's some soup for you," said his daughter. "Eat it quick, and then be off."

The old keeper sat down at the table, and began to eat his soup, having first filled two plates and put them on the floor for the dogs.

The Prussians, hearing voices, were silent.

Long-legs set off a quarter of an hour later, and Berthine, with her head between her hands, waited.

The prisoners began to make themselves heard again. They shouted, called, and beat furiously with the butts of their muskets against the rigid trap-door of the cellar.

Then they fired shots through the vent-hole, hoping, no doubt, to be heard by any German detachment which chanced to be passing that way.

The forester's daughter did not stir, but the noise irritated and unnerved her. Blind anger rose in her heart against the prisoners; she would have been only too glad to kill them all, and so silence them.

Then, as her impatience grew, she watched the clock, counting the minutes as they passed.

Her father had been gone an hour and a half. He must have reached the town by now. She conjured up a vision of him telling the story to Monsieur Lavigne, who grew pale with emotion, and rang for his servant to bring him his arms and uniform. She fancied she could bear the drum as it sounded the call to arms. Frightened faces appeared at the windows. The citizen-soldiers emerged from their houses half dressed, out of breath, buckling on their belts, and hurrying to the commandant's house.

Then the troop of soldiers, with Long-legs at its head, set forth through the night and the snow toward the forest.

She looked at the clock. "They may be here in an hour."

A nervous impatience possessed her. The minutes seemed interminable. Would the time never come?

At last the clock marked the moment she had fixed on for their arrival. And she opened the door to listen for their approach. She perceived a shadowy form creeping toward the house. She was afraid, and cried out. But it was her father.

"They have sent me," he said, "to see if there is any change in the state of affairs."

"No-none."

Then he gave a shrill whistle. Soon a dark mass loomed up under the trees; the advance guard, composed of ten men.

"Don't go in front of the vent-hole!" repeated Long-legs at intervals.

And the first arrivals pointed out the much-dreaded vent-hole to those who came after.

At last the main body of the troop arrived, in all two hundred men, each carrying two hundred cartridges.

Monsieur Lavigne, in a state of intense excitement, posted them in such a fashion as to surround the whole house, save for a large space left vacant in front of the little hole on a level with the ground, through which the cellar derived its supply of air.

Monsieur Lavigne struck the trap-door a blow with his foot, and called:

"I wish to speak to the Prussian officer!"

The German did not reply.

"The Prussian officer!" again shouted the commandant.

Still no response. For the space of twenty minutes Monsieur Lavigne called on this silent officer to surrender with bag and baggage, promising him that all lives should be spared, and that he and his men should be accorded military honors. But he could extort no sign, either of consent or of defiance. The situation became a puzzling one.

The citizen-soldiers kicked their heels in the snow, slapping their arms across their chest, as cabdrivers do, to warm themselves, and gazing at the vent-hole with a growing and childish desire to pass in front of it.

At last one of them took the risk-a man named Potdevin, who was fleet of limb. He ran like a deer across the zone of danger. The experiment succeeded. The prisoners gave no sign of life.

A voice cried:

"There's no one there!"

And another soldier crossed the open space before the dangerous vent-hole. Then this hazardous sport developed into a game. Every minute a man ran swiftly from one side to the other, like a boy playing baseball, kicking up the snow behind him as he ran. They had lighted big fires of dead wood at which to warm themselves, and the figures of the runners were illumined by the flames as they passed rapidly from the camp on the right to that on the left.

Some one shouted:

"It's your turn now, Maloison."

Maloison was a fat baker, whose corpulent person served to point many a joke among his comrades.

He hesitated. They chaffed him. Then, nerving himself to the effort, he set off at a little, waddling gait, which shook his fat paunch and made the whole detachment laugh till they cried.

"Bravo, bravo, Maloison!" they shouted for his encouragement.

He had accomplished about two-thirds of his journey when a long, crimson flame shot forth from the vent-hole. A loud report followed, and the fat baker fell face forward to the ground, uttering a frightful scream. No one went to his assistance. Then he was seen to drag himself, groaning, on all-fours through the snow until he was beyond danger, when he fainted.

He was shot in the upper part of the thigh.

After the first surprise and fright were over they laughed at him again. But Monsieur Lavigne appeared on the threshold of the forester's dwelling. He had formed his plan of attack. He called in a loud voice "I want Planchut, the plumber, and his workmen."

Three men approached.

"Take the eavestroughs from the roof."

In a quarter of an hour they brought the commandant thirty yards of pipes.

Next, with infinite precaution, he had a small round hole drilled in the trap-door; then, making a conduit with the troughs from the pump to this opening, he said, with an air of extreme satisfaction:

"Now we'll give these German gentlemen something to drink."

A shout of frenzied admiration, mingled with uproarious laughter, burst from his followers. And the commandant organized relays of men, who were to relieve one another every five minutes. Then he commanded:

"Pump!!!"

And, the pump handle having been set in motion, a stream of water trickled throughout the length of the piping, and flowed from step to step down the cellar stairs with a gentle, gurgling sound.

They waited.

An hour passed, then two, then three. The commandant, in a state of feverish agitation, walked up and down the kitchen, putting his ear to the ground every now and then to discover, if possible, what the enemy were doing and whether they would soon capitulate.

The enemy was astir now. They could be heard moving the casks about, talking, splashing through the water.

Then, about eight o'clock in the morning, a voice came from the vent-hole "I want to speak to the French officer."

Lavigne replied from the window, taking care not to put his head out too far:

"Do you surrender?"

"I surrender."

"Then put your rifles outside."

A rifle immediately protruded from the hole, and fell into the snow, then another and another, until all were disposed of. And the voice which had spoken before said:

"I have no more. Be quick! I am drowned."

"Stop pumping!" ordered the commandant.

And the pump handle hung motionless.

Then, having filled the kitchen with armed and waiting soldiers, he slowly raised the oaken trapdoor.

Four heads appeared, soaking wet, four fair heads with long, sandy hair, and one after another the six Germans emerged—scared, shivering and dripping from head to foot.

They were seized and bound. Then, as the French feared a surprise, they set off at once in two convoys, one in charge of the prisoners, and the other conducting Maloison on a mattress borne on poles.

They made a triumphal entry into Rethel.

Monsieur Lavigne was decorated as a reward for having captured a Prussian advance guard, and the fat baker received the military medal for wounds received at the hands of the enemy.

TWO LITTLE SOLDIERS

Every Sunday, as soon as they were free, the little soldiers would go for a walk. They turned to the right on leaving the barracks, crossed Courbevoie with rapid strides, as though on a forced march; then, as the houses grew scarcer, they slowed down and followed the dusty road which leads to Bezons.

They were small and thin, lost in their ill-fitting capes, too large and too long, whose sleeves covered their hands; their ample red trousers fell in folds around their ankles. Under the high, stiff shako one could just barely perceive two thin, hollow-cheeked Breton faces, with their calm, naive blue eyes. They never spoke during their journey, going straight before them, the same idea in each one's mind taking the place of conversation. For at the entrance of the little forest of Champioux they had found a spot which reminded them of home, and they did not feel happy anywhere else.

At the crossing of the Colombes and Chatou roads, when they arrived under the trees, they would take off their heavy, oppressive headgear and wipe their foreheads.

They always stopped for a while on the bridge at Bezons, and looked at the Seine. They stood there several minutes, bending over the railing, watching the white sails, which perhaps reminded them of their home, and of the fishing smacks leaving for the open.

As soon as they had crossed the Seine, they would purchase provisions at the delicatessen, the baker's, and the wine merchant's. A piece of bologna, four cents' worth of bread, and a quart of wine, made up the luncheon which they carried away, wrapped up in their handkerchiefs. But as soon as they were out of the village their gait would slacken and they would begin to talk.

Before them was a plain with a few clumps of trees, which led to the woods, a little forest which seemed to remind them of that other forest at Kermarivan. The wheat and oat fields bordered on the narrow path, and Jean Kerderen said each time to Luc Le Ganidec:

"It's just like home, just like Plounivon."

"Yes, it's just like home."

And they went on, side by side, their minds full of dim memories of home. They saw the fields, the hedges, the forests, and beaches.

Each time they stopped near a large stone on the edge of the private estate, because it reminded them of the dolmen of Locneuven.

As soon as they reached the first clump of trees, Luc Le Ganidec would cut off a small stick, and, whittling it slowly, would walk on, thinking of the folks at home.

Jean Kerderen carried the provisions.

From time to time Luc would mention a name, or allude to some boyish prank which would give them food for plenty of thought. And the home country, so dear and so distant, would little by little gain possession of their minds, sending them back through space, to the well-known forms and noises, to the familiar scenery, with the fragrance of its green fields and sea air. They no longer noticed the smells of the city. And in their dreams they saw their friends leaving, perhaps forever, for the dangerous fishing grounds.

They were walking slowly, Luc Le Ganidec and Jean Kerderen, contented and sad, haunted by a sweet sorrow, the slow and penetrating sorrow of a captive animal which remembers the days of its freedom.

And when Luc had finished whittling his stick, they came to a little nook, where every Sunday they took their meal. They found the two bricks, which they had hidden in a hedge, and they made a little fire of dry branches and roasted their sausages on the ends of their knives.

When their last crumb of bread had been eaten and the last drop of wine had been drunk, they stretched themselves out on the grass side by side, without speaking, their half-closed eyes looking away in the distance, their hands clasped as in prayer, their red-trousered legs mingling with the bright colors of the wild flowers.

Towards noon they glanced, from time to time, towards the village of Bezons, for the dairy maid would soon be coming. Every Sunday she would pass in front of them on the way to milk her cow, the only cow in the neighborhood which was sent out to pasture.

Soon they would see the girl, coming through the fields, and it pleased them to watch the sparkling sunbeams reflected from her shining pail. They never spoke of her. They were just glad to see her, without understanding why.

She was a tall, strapping girl, freckled and tanned by the open air—a girl typical of the Parisian suburbs.

Once, on noticing that they were always sitting in the same place, she said to them:

"Do you always come here?"

Luc Le Ganidec, more daring than his friend, stammered:

"Yes, we come here for our rest."

That was all. But the following Sunday, on seeing them, she smiled with the kindly smile of a woman who understood their shyness, and she asked:

"What are you doing here? Are you watching the grass grow?"

Luc, cheered up, smiled: "P'raps."

She continued: "It's not growing fast, is it?"

He answered, still laughing: "Not exactly."

She went on. But when she came back with her pail full of milk, she stopped before them and said:

"Want some? It will remind you of home."

She had, perhaps instinctively, guessed and touched the right spot.

Both were moved. Then not without difficulty, she poured some milk into the bottle in which they had brought their wine. Luc started to drink, carefully watching lest he should take more than his share. Then he passed the bottle to Jean. She stood before them, her hands on her hips, her pail at her feet, enjoying the pleasure that she was giving them. Then she went on, saying: "Well, bye-bye until next Sunday!"

For a long time they watched her tall form as it receded in the distance, blending with the background, and finally disappeared.

The following week as they left the barracks, Jean said to Luc:

"Don't you think we ought to buy her something good?"

They were sorely perplexed by the problem of choosing something to bring to the dairy maid. Luc was in favor of bringing her some chitterlings; but Jean, who had a sweet tooth, thought that candy would be the best thing. He won, and so they went to a grocery to buy two sous' worth, of red and white candies.

This time they ate more quickly than usual, excited by anticipation.

Jean was the first one to notice her. "There she is," he said; and Luc answered: "Yes, there she is."

She smiled when she saw them, and cried:

"Well, how are you to-day?"

They both answered together:

"All right! How's everything with you?"

Then she started to talk of simple things which might interest them; of the weather, of the crops, of her masters.

They didn't dare to offer their candies, which were slowly melting in Jean's pocket. Finally Luc, growing bolder, murmured:

"We have brought you something."

She asked: "Let's see it."

Then Jean, blushing to the tips of his ears, reached in his pocket, and drawing out the little paper bag, handed it to her.

She began to eat the little sweet dainties. The two soldiers sat in front of her, moved and delighted.

At last she went to do her milking, and when she came back she again gave them some milk.

They thought of her all through the week and often spoke of her: The following Sunday she sat beside them for a longer time.

The three of them sat there, side by side, their eyes looking far away in the distance, their hands clasped over their knees, and they told each other little incidents and little details of the villages where they were born, while the cow, waiting to be milked, stretched her heavy head toward the girl and mooed.

Soon the girl consented to eat with them and to take a sip of wine. Often she brought them plums pocket for plums were now ripe. Her presence enlivened the little Breton soldiers, who chattered away like two birds.

One Tuesday something unusual happened to Luc Le Ganidec; he asked for leave and did not return until ten o'clock at night.

Jean, worried and racked his brain to account for his friend's having obtained leave.

The following Friday, Luc borrowed ten sons from one of his friends, and once more asked and obtained leave for several hours.

When he started out with Jean on Sunday he seemed queer, disturbed, changed. Kerderen did not understand; he vaguely suspected something, but he could not guess what it might be.

They went straight to the usual place, and lunched slowly. Neither was hungry.

Soon the girl appeared. They watched her approach as they always did. When she was near, Luc arose and went towards her. She placed her pail on the ground and kissed him. She kissed him passionately, throwing her arms around his neck, without paying attention to Jean, without even noticing that he was there.

Poor Jean was dazed, so dazed that he could not understand. His mind was upset and his heart broken, without his even realizing why.

Then the girl sat down beside Luc, and they started to chat.

Jean was not looking at them. He understood now why his friend had gone out twice during the week. He felt the pain and the sting which treachery and deceit leave in their wake.

Luc and the girl went together to attend to the cow.

Jean followed them with his eyes. He saw them disappear side by side, the red trousers of his friend making a scarlet spot against the white road. It was Luc who sank the stake to which the cow was tethered. The girl stooped down to milk the cow, while he absent-mindedly stroked the animal's glossy neck. Then they left the pail in the grass and disappeared in the woods.

Jean could no longer see anything but the wall of leaves through which they had passed. He was unmanned so that he did not have strength to stand. He stayed there, motionless, bewildered and grieving-simple, passionate grief. He wanted to weep, to run away, to hide somewhere, never to see anyone again.

Then he saw them coming back again. They were walking slowly, hand in hand, as village lovers do. Luc was carrying the pail.

After kissing him again, the girl went on, nodding carelessly to Jean. She did not offer him any milk that day.

The two little soldiers sat side by side, motionless as always, silent and quiet, their calm faces in no way betraying the trouble in their hearts. The sun shone down on them. From time to time they could hear the plaintive lowing of the cow. At the usual time they arose to return.

Luc was whittling a stick. Jean carried the empty bottle. He left it at the wine merchant's in Bezons. Then they stopped on the bridge, as they did every Sunday, and watched the water flowing by.

Jean leaned over the railing, farther and farther, as though he had seen something in the stream which hypnotized him. Luc said to him:

“What’s the matter? Do you want a drink?”

He had hardly said the last word when Jean’s head carried away the rest of his body, and the little blue and red soldier fell like a shot and disappeared in the water.

Luc, paralyzed with horror, tried vainly to shout for help. In the distance he saw something move; then his friend’s head bobbed up out of the water only to disappear again.

Farther down he again noticed a hand, just one hand, which appeared and again went out of sight. That was all.

The boatmen who had rushed to the scene found the body that day.

Luc ran back to the barracks, crazed, and with eyes and voice full of tears, he related the accident: “He leaned—he—he was leaning —so far over—that his head carried him away—and—he—fell —he fell——”

Emotion choked him so that he could say no more. If he had only known.

FATHER MILON

For a month the hot sun has been parching the fields. Nature is expanding beneath its rays; the fields are green as far as the eye can see. The big azure dome of the sky is unclouded. The farms of Normandy, scattered over the plains and surrounded by a belt of tall beeches, look, from a distance, like little woods. On closer view, after lowering the worm-eaten wooden bars, you imagine yourself in an immense garden, for all the ancient apple-trees, as gnarled as the peasants themselves, are in bloom. The sweet scent of their blossoms mingles with the heavy smell of the earth and the penetrating odor of the stables. It is noon. The family is eating under the shade of a pear tree planted in front of the door; father, mother, the four children, and the help—two women and three men are all there. All are silent. The soup is eaten and then a dish of potatoes fried with bacon is brought on.

From time to time one of the women gets up and takes a pitcher down to the cellar to fetch more cider.

The man, a big fellow about forty years old, is watching a grape vine, still bare, which is winding and twisting like a snake along the side of the house.

At last he says: "Father's vine is budding early this year. Perhaps we may get something from it."

The woman then turns round and looks, without saying a word.

This vine is planted on the spot where their father had been shot.

It was during the war of 1870. The Prussians were occupying the whole country. General Faidherbe, with the Northern Division of the army, was opposing them.

The Prussians had established their headquarters at this farm. The old farmer to whom it belonged, Father Pierre Milon, had received and quartered them to the best of his ability.

For a month the German vanguard had been in this village. The French remained motionless, ten leagues away; and yet, every night, some of the Uhlans disappeared.

Of all the isolated scouts, of all those who were sent to the outposts, in groups of not more than three, not one ever returned.

They were picked up the next morning in a field or in a ditch. Even their horses were found along the roads with their throats cut.

These murders seemed to be done by the same men, who could never be found.

The country was terrorized. Farmers were shot on suspicion, women were imprisoned; children were frightened in order to try and obtain information. Nothing could be ascertained.

But, one morning, Father Milon was found stretched out in the barn, with a sword gash across his face.

Two Uhlans were found dead about a mile and a half from the farm. One of them was still holding his bloody sword in his hand. He had fought, tried to defend himself. A court-martial was immediately held in the open air, in front of the farm. The old man was brought before it.

He was sixty-eight years old, small, thin, bent, with two big hands resembling the claws of a crab. His colorless hair was sparse and thin, like the down of a young duck, allowing patches of his scalp to be seen. The brown and wrinkled skin of his neck showed big veins which disappeared behind his jaws and came out again at the temples. He had the reputation of being miserly and hard to deal with.

They stood him up between four soldiers, in front of the kitchen table, which had been dragged outside. Five officers and the colonel seated themselves opposite him.

The colonel spoke in French:

"Father Milon, since we have been here we have only had praise for you. You have always been obliging and even attentive to us. But to-day a terrible accusation is hanging over you, and you must clear the matter up. How did you receive that wound on your face?"

The peasant answered nothing.

The colonel continued:

"Your silence accuses you, Father Milon. But I want you to answer me! Do you understand? Do you know who killed the two Uhlans who were found this morning near Calvaire?"

The old man answered clearly

"I did."

The colonel, surprised, was silent for a minute, looking straight at the prisoner. Father Milon stood impassive, with the stupid look of the peasant, his eyes lowered as though he were talking to the priest. Just one thing betrayed an uneasy mind; he was continually swallowing his saliva, with a visible effort, as though his throat were terribly contracted.

The man's family, his son Jean, his daughter-in-law and his two grandchildren were standing a few feet behind him, bewildered and affrighted.

The colonel went on:

"Do you also know who killed all the scouts who have been found dead, for a month, throughout the country, every morning?"

The old man answered with the same stupid look:

"I did."

"You killed them all?"

"Uh huh! I did."

"You alone? All alone?"

"Uh huh!"

"Tell me how you did it."

This time the man seemed moved; the necessity for talking any length of time annoyed him visibly. He stammered:

"I dunno! I simply did it."

The colonel continued:

"I warn you that you will have to tell me everything. You might as well make up your mind right away. How did you begin?"

The man cast a troubled look toward his family, standing close behind him. He hesitated a minute longer, and then suddenly made up his mind to obey the order.

"I was coming home one night at about ten o'clock, the night after you got here. You and your soldiers had taken more than fifty ecus worth of forage from me, as well as a cow and two sheep. I said to myself: 'As much as they take from you; just so much will you make them pay back.' And then I had other things on my mind which I will tell you. Just then I noticed one of your soldiers who was smoking his pipe by the ditch behind the barn. I went and got my scythe and crept up slowly behind him, so that he couldn't hear me. And I cut his head off with one single blow, just as I would a blade of grass, before he could say 'Booh!' If you should look at the bottom of the pond, you will find him tied up in a potato-sack, with a stone fastened to it.

"I got an idea. I took all his clothes, from his boots to his cap, and hid them away in the little wood behind the yard."

The old man stopped. The officers remained speechless, looking at each other. The questioning began again, and this is what they learned.

Once this murder committed, the man had lived with this one thought: "Kill the Prussians!" He hated them with the blind, fierce hate of the greedy yet patriotic peasant. He had his idea, as he said. He waited several days.

He was allowed to go and come as he pleased, because he had shown himself so humble, submissive and obliging to the invaders. Each night he saw the outposts leave. One night he followed them, having heard the name of the village to which the men were going, and having learned the few words of German which he needed for his plan through associating with the soldiers.

He left through the back yard, slipped into the woods, found the dead man's clothes and put them on. Then he began to crawl through the fields, following along the hedges in order to keep out of sight, listening to the slightest noises, as wary as a poacher.

As soon as he thought the time ripe, he approached the road and hid behind a bush. He waited for a while. Finally, toward midnight, he heard the sound of a galloping horse. The man put his ear to the ground in order to make sure that only one horseman was approaching, then he got ready.

An Uhlan came galloping along, carrying dispatches. As he went, he was all eyes and ears. When he was only a few feet away, Father Milon dragged himself across the road, moaning: "Hilfe! Hilfe!" (Help! Help!) The horseman stopped, and recognizing a German, he thought he was wounded and dismounted, coming nearer without any suspicion, and just as he was leaning over the unknown man, he received, in the pit of his stomach, a heavy thrust from the long curved blade of the sabre. He dropped without suffering pain, quivering only in the final throes. Then the farmer, radiant with the silent joy of an old peasant, got up again, and, for his own pleasure, cut the dead man's throat. He then dragged the body to the ditch and threw it in.

The horse quietly awaited its master. Father Milon mounted him and started galloping across the plains.

About an hour later he noticed two more Uhlans who were returning home, side by side. He rode straight for them, once more crying "Hilfe! Hilfe!"

The Prussians, recognizing the uniform, let him approach without distrust. The old man passed between them like a cannon-ball, felling them both, one with his sabre and the other with a revolver.

Then he killed the horses, German horses! After that he quickly returned to the woods and hid one of the horses. He left his uniform there and again put on his old clothes; then going back into bed, he slept until morning.

For four days he did not go out, waiting for the inquest to be terminated; but on the fifth day he went out again and killed two more soldiers by the same stratagem. From that time on he did not stop. Each night he wandered about in search of adventure, killing Prussians, sometimes here and sometimes there, galloping through deserted fields, in the moonlight, a lost Uhlan, a hunter of men. Then, his task accomplished, leaving behind him the bodies lying along the roads, the old farmer would return and hide his horse and uniform.

He went, toward noon, to carry oats and water quietly to his mount, and he fed it well as he required from it a great amount of work.

But one of those whom he had attacked the night before, in defending himself slashed the old peasant across the face with his sabre.

However, he had killed them both. He had come back and hidden the horse and put on his ordinary clothes again; but as he reached home he began to feel faint, and had dragged himself as far as the stable, being unable to reach the house.

They had found him there, bleeding, on the straw.

When he had finished his tale, he suddenly lifted up his head and looked proudly at the Prussian officers.

The colonel, who was gnawing at his mustache, asked:

"You have nothing else to say?"

"Nothing more; I have finished my task; I killed sixteen, not one more or less."

"Do you know that you are going to die?"

"I haven't asked for mercy."

"Have you been a soldier?"

"Yes, I served my time. And then, you had killed my father, who was a soldier of the first Emperor. And last month you killed my youngest son, Francois, near Evreux. I owed you one for that; I paid. We are quits."

The officers were looking at each other.

The old man continued:

"Eight for my father, eight for the boy—we are quits. I did not seek any quarrel with you. I don't know you. I don't even know where you come from. And here you are, ordering me about in my home as though it were your own. I took my revenge upon the others. I'm not sorry."

And, straightening up his bent back, the old man folded his arms in the attitude of a modest hero.

The Prussians talked in a low tone for a long time. One of them, a captain, who had also lost his son the previous month, was defending the poor wretch. Then the colonel arose and, approaching Father Milon, said in a low voice:

"Listen, old man, there is perhaps a way of saving your life, it is to—"

But the man was not listening, and, his eyes fixed on the hated officer, while the wind played with the downy hair on his head, he distorted his slashed face, giving it a truly terrible expression, and, swelling out his chest, he spat, as hard as he could, right in the Prussian's face.

The colonel, furious, raised his hand, and for the second time the man spat in his face.

All the officers had jumped up and were shrieking orders at the same time.

In less than a minute the old man, still impassive, was pushed up against the wall and shot, looking smilingly the while toward Jean, his eldest son, his daughter-in-law and his two grandchildren, who witnessed this scene in dumb terror.

A COUP D'ETAT

Paris had just heard of the disaster at Sedan. A republic had been declared. All France was wavering on the brink of this madness which lasted until after the Commune. From one end of the country to the other everybody was playing soldier.

Cap-makers became colonels, fulfilling the duties of generals; revolvers and swords were displayed around big, peaceful stomachs wrapped in flaming red belts; little tradesmen became warriors commanding battalions of brawling volunteers, and swearing like pirates in order to give themselves some prestige.

The sole fact of handling firearms crazed these people, who up to that time had only handled scales, and made them, without any reason, dangerous to all. Innocent people were shot to prove that they knew how to kill; in forests which had never seen a Prussian, stray dogs, grazing cows and browsing horses were killed.

Each one thought himself called upon to play a great part in military affairs. The cafes of the smallest villages, full of uniformed tradesmen, looked like barracks or hospitals.

The town of Canneville was still in ignorance of the maddening news from the army and the capital; nevertheless, great excitement had prevailed for the last month, the opposing parties finding themselves face to face.

The mayor, Viscount de Varnetot, a thin, little old man, a conservative, who had recently, from ambition, gone over to the Empire, had seen a determined opponent arise in Dr. Massarel, a big, full-blooded man, leader of the Republican party of the neighborhood, a high official in the local masonic lodge, president of the Agricultural Society and of the firemen's banquet and the organizer of the rural militia which was to save the country.

In two weeks, he had managed to gather together sixty-three volunteers, fathers of families, prudent farmers and town merchants, and every morning he would drill them in the square in front of the town-hall.

When, perchance, the mayor would come to the municipal building, Commander Massarel, girt with pistols, would pass proudly in front of his troop, his sword in his hand, and make all of them cry: "Long live the Fatherland!" And it had been noticed that this cry excited the little viscount, who probably saw in it a menace, a threat, as well as the odious memory of the great Revolution.

On the morning of the fifth of September, the doctor, in full uniform, his revolver on the table, was giving a consultation to an old couple, a farmer who had been suffering from varicose veins for the last seven years and had waited until his wife had them also, before he would consult the doctor, when the postman brought in the paper.

M. Massarel opened it, grew pale, suddenly rose, and lifting his hands to heaven in a gesture of exaltation, began to shout at the top of his voice before the two frightened country folks:

"Long live the Republic! long live the Republic! long live the Republic!"

Then he fell back in his chair, weak from emotion.

And as the peasant resumed: "It started with the ants, which began to run up and down my legs—" Dr. Massarel exclaimed:

"Shut up! I haven't got time to bother with your nonsense. The Republic has been proclaimed, the emperor has been taken prisoner, France is saved! Long live the Republic!"

Running to the door, he howled:

"Celeste, quick, Celeste!"

The servant, affrighted, hastened in; he was trying to talk so rapidly, that he could only stammer:

"My boots, my sword, my cartridge-box and the Spanish dagger which is on my night-table! Hasten!"

As the persistent peasant, taking advantage of a moment's silence, continued, "I seemed to get big lumps which hurt me when I walk," the physician, exasperated, roared:

"Shut up and get out! If you had washed your feet it would not have happened!"

Then, grabbing him by the collar, he yelled at him:

"Can't you understand that we are a republic, you brass-plated idiot!"

But professional sentiment soon calmed him, and he pushed the bewildered couple out, saying:

"Come back to-morrow, come back to-morrow, my friends. I haven't any time to-day."

As he equipped himself from head to foot, he gave a series of important orders to his servant:

"Run over to Lieutenant Picart and to Second Lieutenant Pommel, and tell them that I am expecting them here immediately. Also send me Torchebeuf with his drum. Quick! quick!"

When Celeste had gone out, he sat down and thought over the situation and the difficulties which he would have to surmount.

The three men arrived together in their working clothes. The commandant, who expected to see them in uniform, felt a little shocked.

"Don't you people know anything? The emperor has been taken prisoner, the Republic has been proclaimed. We must act. My position is delicate, I might even say dangerous."

He reflected for a few moments before his bewildered subordinates, then he continued:

"We must act and not hesitate; minutes count as hours in times like these. All depends on the promptness of our decision. You, Picart, go to the cure and order him to ring the alarm-bell, in order to get together the people, to whom I am going to announce the news. You, Torchebeuf beat the tattoo throughout the whole neighborhood as far as the hamlets of Gerisaie and Salmare, in order to assemble the militia in the public square. You, Pommel, get your uniform on quickly, just the coat and cap. We are going to the town-hall to demand Monsieur de Varnetot to surrender his powers to me. Do you understand?"

"Yes."

"Now carry out those orders quickly. I will go over to your house with you, Pommel, since we shall act together."

Five minutes later, the commandant and his subordinates, armed to the teeth, appeared on the square, just as the little Viscount de Varnetot, his legs encased in gaiters as for a hunting party, his gun on his shoulder, was coming down the other street at double-quick time, followed by his three green-coated guards, their swords at their sides and their guns swung over their shoulders.

While the doctor stopped, bewildered, the four men entered the town-hall and closed the door behind them.

"They have outstripped us," muttered the physician, "we must now wait for reenforcements. There is nothing to do for the present."

Lieutenant Picart now appeared on the scene.

"The priest refuses to obey," he said. "He has even locked himself in the church with the sexton and beadle."

On the other side of the square, opposite the white, tightly closed town-hall, stood the church, silent and dark, with its massive oak door studded with iron.

But just as the perplexed inhabitants were sticking their heads out of the windows or coming out on their doorsteps, the drum suddenly began to be heard, and Torchebeuf appeared, furiously beating the tattoo. He crossed the square running, and disappeared along the road leading to the fields.

The commandant drew his sword, and advanced alone to half way between the two buildings behind which the enemy had intrenched itself, and, waving his sword over his head, he roared with all his might:

"Long live the Republic! Death to traitors!"

Then he returned to his officers.

The butcher, the baker and the druggist, much disturbed, were anxiously pulling down their shades and closing their shops. The grocer alone kept open.

However, the militia were arriving by degrees, each man in a different uniform, but all wearing a black cap with gold braid, the cap being the principal part of the outfit. They were armed with old rusty guns, the old guns which had hung for thirty years on the kitchen wall; and they looked a good deal like an army of tramps.

When he had about thirty men about him, the commandant, in a few words, outlined the situation to them. Then, turning to his staff: "Let us act," he said.

The villagers were gathering together and talking the matter over.

The doctor quickly decided on a plan of campaign.

"Lieutenant Picart, you will advance under the windows of this town-hall and summon Monsieur de Varnetot, in the name of the Republic, to hand the keys over to me."

But the lieutenant, a master mason, refused:

"You're smart, you are. I don't care to get killed, thank you. Those people in there shoot straight, don't you forget it. Do your errands yourself."

The commandant grew very red.

"I command you to go in the name of discipline!"

The lieutenant rebelled:

"I'm not going to have my beauty spoiled without knowing why."

All the notables, gathered in a group near by, began to laugh. One of them cried:

"You are right, Picart, this isn't the right time."

The doctor then muttered:

"Cowards!"

And, leaving his sword and his revolver in the hands of a soldier, he advanced slowly, his eye fastened on the windows, expecting any minute to see a gun trained on him.

When he was within a few feet of the building, the doors at both ends, leading into the two schools, opened and a flood of children ran out, boys from one side, girls from the ether, and began to play around the doctor, in the big empty square, screeching and screaming, and making so much noise that he could not make himself heard.

As soon as the last child was out of the building, the two doors closed again.

Most of the youngsters finally dispersed, and the commandant called in a loud voice:

"Monsieur de Varnetot!"

A window on the first floor opened and M. de Varnetot appeared.

The commandant continued:

"Monsieur, you know that great events have just taken place which have changed the entire aspect of the government. The one which you represented no longer exists. The one which I represent is taking control. Under these painful, but decisive circumstances, I come, in the name of the new Republic, to ask you to turn over to me the office which you held under the former government."

M. de Varnetot answered:

"Doctor, I am the mayor of Canneville, duly appointed, and I shall remain mayor of Canneville until I have been dismissed by a decree from my superiors. As mayor, I am in my place in the townhall, and here I stay. Anyhow, just try to get me out."

He closed the window.

The commandant returned to his troop. But before giving any information, eyeing Lieutenant Picart from head to foot, he exclaimed:

"You're a great one, you are! You're a fine specimen of manhood! You're a disgrace to the army! I degrade you."

"I don't give a——!"

He turned away and mingled with a group of townspeople.

Then the doctor hesitated. What could he do? Attack? But would his men obey orders? And then, did he have the right to do so?

An idea struck him. He ran to the telegraph office, opposite the town-hall, and sent off three telegrams:

To the new republican government in Paris.

To the new prefect of the Seine-Inferieure, at Rouen.

To the new republican sub-prefect at Dieppe.

He explained the situation, pointed out the danger which the town would run if it should remain in the hands of the royalist mayor; offered his faithful services, asked for orders and signed, putting all his titles after his name.

Then he returned to his battalion, and, drawing ten francs from his pocket, he cried: "Here, my friends, go eat and drink; only leave me a detachment of ten men to guard against anybody's leaving the town-hall."

But ex-Lieutenant Picart, who had been talking with the watchmaker, heard him; he began to laugh, and exclaimed: "By Jove, if they come out, it'll give you a chance to get in. Otherwise I can see you standing out there for the rest of your life!"

The doctor did not reply, and he went to luncheon.

In the afternoon, he disposed his men about the town as though they were in immediate danger of an ambush.

Several times he passed in front of the town-hall and of the church without noticing anything suspicious; the two buildings looked as though empty.

The butcher, the baker and the druggist once more opened up their stores.

Everybody was talking about the affair. If the emperor were a prisoner, there must have been some kind of treason. They did not know exactly which of the republics had returned to power.

Night fell.

Toward nine o'clock, the doctor, alone, noiselessly approached the entrance of the public building, persuaded that the enemy must have gone to bed; and, as he was preparing to batter down the door with a pick-axe, the deep voice of a sentry suddenly called:

"Who goes there?"

And M. Massarel retreated as fast as his legs could carry him.

Day broke without any change in the situation.

Armed militia occupied the square. All the citizens had gathered around this troop awaiting developments. Even neighboring villagers had come to look on.

Then the doctor, seeing that his reputation was at stake, resolved to put an end to the matter in one way or another; and he was about to take some measures, undoubtedly energetic ones, when the door of the telegraph station opened and the little servant of the postmistress appeared, holding in her hands two papers.

First she went to the commandant and gave him one of the despatches; then she crossed the empty square, confused at seeing the eyes of everyone on her, and lowering her head and running along with little quick steps, she went and knocked softly at the door of the barricaded house, as though ignorant of the fact that those behind it were armed.

The door opened wide enough to let a man's hand reach out and receive the message; and the young girl returned blushing, ready to cry at being thus stared at by the whole countryside.

In a clear voice, the doctor cried:

"Silence, if you please."

When the populace had quieted down, he continued proudly:

"Here is the communication which I have received from the government."

And lifting the telegram he read:

Former mayor dismissed. Inform him immediately, More orders

following.

For the sub-prefect:

SAPIN, Councillor.

He was-triumphant; his heart was throbbing with joy and his hands were trembling; but Picart, his former subordinate, cried to him from a neighboring group:

"That's all right; but supposing the others don't come out, what good is the telegram going to do you?"

M. Massarel grew pale. He had not thought of that; if the others did not come out, he would now have to take some decisive step. It was not only his right, but his duty.

He looked anxiously at the town-hall, hoping to see the door open and his adversary give in.

The door remained closed. What could he do? The crowd was growing and closing around the militia. They were laughing.

One thought especially tortured the doctor. If he attacked, he would have to march at the head of his men; and as, with him dead, all strife would cease, it was at him and him only that M. de Varnetot and his three guards would aim. And they were good shots, very good shots, as Picart had just said. But an idea struck him and, turning to Pommel, he ordered:

"Run quickly to the druggist and ask him to lend me a towel and a stick."

The lieutenant hastened.

He would make a flag of truce, a white flag, at the sight of which the royalist heart of the mayor would perhaps rejoice.

Pommel returned with the cloth and a broom-stick. With some twine they completed the flag, and M. Massarel, grasping it in both hands and holding it in front of him, again advanced in the direction of the town-hall. When he was opposite the door, he once more called: "Monsieur de Varnetot!" The door suddenly opened and M. de Varnetot and his three guards appeared on the threshold.

Instinctively the doctor stepped back; then he bowed courteously to his enemy, and, choking with emotion, he announced: "I have come, monsieur, to make you acquainted with the orders which I have received."

The nobleman, without returning the bow, answered: "I resign, monsieur, but understand that it is neither through fear of, nor obedience to, the odious government which has usurped the power." And, emphasizing every word, he declared: "I do not wish to appear, for a single day, to serve the Republic. That's all."

Massarel, stunned, answered nothing; and M. de Varnetot, walking quickly, disappeared around the corner of the square, still followed by his escort.

The doctor, puffed up with pride, returned to the crowd. As soon as he was near enough to make himself heard, he cried: "Hurrah! hurrah! Victory crowns the Republic everywhere."

There was no outburst of joy.

The doctor continued: "We are free, you are free, independent! Be proud!"

The motionless villagers were looking at him without any signs of triumph shining in their eyes.

He looked at them, indignant at their indifference, thinking of what he could say or do in order to make an impression to electrify this calm peasantry, to fulfill his mission as a leader.

He had an inspiration and, turning to Pommel, he ordered: "Lieutenant, go get me the bust of the ex-emperor which is in the meeting room of the municipal council, and bring it here with a chair."

The man presently reappeared, carrying on his right shoulder the plaster Bonaparte, and holding in his left hand a cane-seated chair.

M. Massarel went towards him, took the chair, placed the white bust on it, then stepping back a few steps, he addressed it in a loud voice:

"Tyrant, tyrant, you have fallen down in the mud. The dying fatherland was in its death throes under your oppression. Vengeful Destiny has struck you. Defeat and shame have pursued you; you fall conquered, a prisoner of the Prussians; and from the ruins of your crumbling empire, the young and glorious Republic arises, lifting from the ground your broken sword——"

He waited for applause. Not a sound greeted his listening ear. The peasants, nonplussed, kept silent; and the white, placid, well-groomed statue seemed to look at M. Massarel with its plaster smile, ineffaceable and sarcastic.

Thus they stood, face to face, Napoleon on his chair, the physician standing three feet away. Anger seized the commandant. What could he do to move this crowd and definitely to win over public opinion?

He happened to carry his hand to his stomach, and he felt, under his red belt, the butt of his revolver.

Not another inspiration, not another word cane to his mind. Then, he drew his weapon, stepped back a few steps and shot the former monarch.

The bullet made a little black hole: like a spot, in his forehead. No sensation was created. M. Massarel shot a second time and made a second hole, then a third time, then, without stopping, he shot off the three remaining shots. Napoleon's forehead was blown away in a white powder, but his eyes, nose and pointed mustache remained intact.

Then in exasperation, the doctor kicked the chair over, and placing one foot on what remained of the bust in the position of a conqueror, he turned to the amazed public and yelled: "Thus may all traitors die!"

As no enthusiasm was, as yet, visible, the spectators appearing to be dumb with astonishment, the commandant cried to the militia: "You may go home now." And he himself walked rapidly, almost ran, towards his house.

As soon as he appeared, the servant told him that some patients had been waiting in his office for over three hours. He hastened in. They were the same two peasants as a few days before, who had returned at daybreak, obstinate and patient.

The old man immediately began his explanation:

"It began with ants, which seemed to be crawling up and down my legs——"

LIEUTENANT LARE'S MARRIAGE

Since the beginning of the campaign Lieutenant Lare had taken two cannon from the Prussians. His general had said: "Thank you, lieutenant," and had given him the cross of honor.

As he was as cautious as he was brave, wary, inventive, wily and resourceful, he was entrusted with a hundred soldiers and he organized a company of scouts who saved the army on several occasions during a retreat.

But the invading army entered by every frontier like a surging sea. Great waves of men arrived one after the other, scattering all around them a scum of freebooters. General Carrel's brigade, separated from its division, retreated continually, fighting each day, but remaining almost intact, thanks to the vigilance and agility of Lieutenant Lare, who seemed to be everywhere at the same moment, baffling all the enemy's cunning, frustrating their plans, misleading their Uhlans and killing their vanguards.

One morning the general sent for him.

"Lieutenant," said he, "here is a dispatch from General de Lacere, who will be destroyed if we do not go to his aid by sunrise to-morrow. He is at Blainville, eight leagues from here. You will start at nightfall with three hundred men, whom you will echelon along the road. I will follow you two hours later. Study the road carefully; I fear we may meet a division of the enemy."

It had been freezing hard for a week. At two o'clock it began to snow, and by night the ground was covered and heavy white swirls concealed objects hard by.

At six o'clock the detachment set out.

Two men walked alone as scouts about three yards ahead. Then came a platoon of ten men commanded by the lieutenant himself. The rest followed them in two long columns. To the right and left of the little band, at a distance of about three hundred feet on either side, some soldiers marched in pairs.

The snow, which was still falling, covered them with a white powder in the darkness, and as it did not melt on their uniforms, they were hardly distinguishable in the night amid the dead whiteness of the landscape.

From time to time they halted. One heard nothing but that indescribable, nameless flutter of falling snow—a sensation rather than a sound, a vague, ominous murmur. A command was given in a low tone and when the troop resumed its march it left in its wake a sort of white phantom standing in the snow. It gradually grew fainter and finally disappeared. It was the echelons who were to lead the army.

The scouts slackened their pace. Something was ahead of them.

"Turn to the right," said the lieutenant; "it is the Ronfi wood; the chateau is more to the left."

Presently the command "Halt" was passed along. The detachment stopped and waited for the lieutenant, who, accompanied by only ten men, had undertaken a reconnoitering expedition to the chateau.

They advanced, creeping under the trees. Suddenly they all remained motionless. Around them was a dead silence. Then, quite near them, a little clear, musical young voice was heard amid the stillness of the wood.

"Father, we shall get lost in the snow. We shall never reach Blainville."

A deeper voice replied:

"Never fear, little daughter; I know the country as well as I know my pocket."

The lieutenant said a few words and four men moved away silently, like shadows.

All at once a woman's shrill cry was heard through the darkness. Two prisoners were brought back, an old man and a young girl. The lieutenant questioned them, still in a low tone:

"Your name?"

"Pierre Bernard."

"Your profession?"

"Butler to Comte de Ronfi."

"Is this your daughter?"

'Yes!'

"What does she do?"

"She is laundress at the chateau."

"Where are you going?"

"We are making our escape."

"Why?"

"Twelve Uhlans passed by this evening. They shot three keepers and hanged the gardener. I was alarmed on account of the little one."

"Whither are you bound?"

"To Blainville."

"Why?"

"Because there is a French army there."

"Do you know the way?"

"Perfectly."

"Well then, follow us."

They rejoined the column and resumed their march across country. The old man walked in silence beside the lieutenant, his daughter walking at his side. All at once she stopped.

“Father,” she said, “I am so tired I cannot go any farther.”

And she sat down. She was shaking with cold and seemed about to lose consciousness. Her father wanted to carry her, but he was too old and too weak.

“Lieutenant,” said he, sobbing, “we shall only impede your march. France before all. Leave us here.”

The officer had given a command. Some men had started off. They came back with branches they had cut, and in a minute a litter was ready. The whole detachment had joined them by this time.

“Here is a woman dying of cold,” said the lieutenant. “Who will give his cape to cover her?”

Two hundred capes were taken off. The young girl was wrapped up in these warm soldiers’ capes, gently laid in the litter, and then four’ hardy shoulders lifted her up, and like an Eastern queen borne by her slaves she was placed in the center of the detachment of soldiers, who resumed their march with more energy, more courage, more cheerfulness, animated by the presence of a woman, that sovereign inspiration that has stirred the old French blood to so many deeds of valor.

At the end of an hour they halted again and every one lay down in the snow. Over yonder on the level country a big, dark shadow was moving. It looked like some weird monster stretching itself out like a serpent, then suddenly coiling itself into a mass, darting forth again, then back, and then forward again without ceasing. Some whispered orders were passed around among the soldiers, and an occasional little, dry, metallic click was heard. The moving object suddenly came nearer, and twelve Uhlans were seen approaching at a gallop, one behind the other, having lost their way in the darkness. A brilliant flash suddenly revealed to them two hundred men lying on the ground before them. A rapid fire was heard, which died away in the snowy silence, and all the twelve fell to the ground, their horses with them.

After a long rest the march was resumed. The old man whom they had captured acted as guide.

Presently a voice far off in the distance cried out: “Who goes there?”

Another voice nearer by gave the countersign.

They made another halt; some conferences took place. It had stopped snowing. A cold wind was driving the clouds, and innumerable stars were sparkling in the sky behind them, gradually paling in the rosy light of dawn.

A staff officer came forward to receive the detachment. But when he asked who was being carried in the litter, the form stirred; two little hands moved aside the big blue army capes and, rosy as the dawn, with two eyes that were brighter than the stars that had just faded from sight, and a smile as radiant as the morn, a dainty face appeared.

“It is I, monsieur.”

The soldiers, wild with delight, clapped their hands and bore the young girl in triumph into the midst of the camp, that was just getting to arms. Presently General Carrel arrived on the scene. At nine o’clock the Prussians made an attack. They beat a retreat at noon.

That evening, as Lieutenant Lare, overcome by fatigue, was sleeping on a bundle of straw, he was sent for by the general. He found the commanding officer in his tent, chatting with the old man whom they had come across during the night. As soon as he entered the tent the general took his hand, and addressing the stranger, said:

"My dear comte, this is the young man of whom you were telling me just now; he is one of my best officers."

He smiled, lowered his tone, and added:

"The best."

Then, turning to the astonished lieutenant, he presented "Comte de Ronfi-Quedissac."

The old man took both his hands, saying:

"My dear lieutenant, you have saved my daughter's life. I have only one way of thanking you. You may come in a few months to tell me—if you like her."

One year later, on the very same day, Captain Lare and Miss Louise-Hortense-Genevieve de Ronfi-Quedissac were married in the church of St. Thomas Aquinas.

She brought a dowry of six thousand francs, and was said to be the prettiest bride that had been seen that year.

THE HORRIBLE

The shadows of a balmy night were slowly falling. The women remained in the drawing-room of the villa. The men, seated, or astride of garden chairs, were smoking outside the door of the house, around a table laden with cups and liqueur glasses.

Their lighted cigars shone like eyes in the darkness, which was gradually becoming more dense. They had been talking about a frightful accident which had occurred the night before—two men and three women drowned in the river before the eyes of the guests.

General de G——remarked:

"Yes, these things are affecting, but they are not horrible.

"Horrible, that well-known word, means much more than terrible. A frightful accident like this affects, upsets, terrifies; it does not horrify. In order that we should experience horror, something more is needed than emotion, something more than the spectacle of a dreadful death; there must be a shuddering sense of mystery, or a sensation of abnormal terror, more than natural. A man who dies, even under the most tragic circumstances, does not excite horror; a field of battle is not horrible; blood is not horrible; the vilest crimes are rarely horrible.

"Here are two personal examples which have shown me what is the meaning of horror.

"It was during the war of 1870. We were retreating toward Pont-Audemer, after having passed through Rouen. The army, consisting of about twenty thousand men, twenty thousand routed men, disbanded, demoralized, exhausted, were going to disband at Havre.

"The earth was covered with snow. The night was falling. They had not eaten anything since the day before. They were fleeing rapidly, the Prussians not being far off.

"All the Norman country, sombre, dotted with the shadows of the trees surrounding the farms, stretched out beneath a black, heavy, threatening sky.

"Nothing else could be heard in the wan twilight but the confused sound, undefined though rapid, of a marching throng, an endless tramping, mingled with the vague clink of tin bowls or swords. The men, bent, round-shouldered, dirty, in many cases even in rags, dragged themselves along, hurried through the snow, with a long, broken-backed stride.

"The skin of their hands froze to the butt ends of their muskets, for it was freezing hard that night. I frequently saw a little soldier take off his shoes in order to walk barefoot, as his shoes hurt his weary feet; and at every step he left a track of blood. Then, after some time, he would sit down in a field for a few minutes' rest, and he never got up again. Every man who sat down was a dead man.

"Should we have left behind us those poor, exhausted soldiers, who fondly counted on being able to start afresh as soon as they had somewhat refreshed their stiffened legs? But scarcely had they ceased to move, and to make their almost frozen blood circulate in their veins, than an unconquerable torpor congealed them, nailed them to the ground, closed their eyes, and paralyzed in one second this overworked human mechanism. And they gradually sank down, their foreheads on their knees, without, however, falling over, for their loins and their limbs became as hard and immovable as wood, impossible to bend or to stand upright.

"And the rest of us, more robust, kept straggling on, chilled to the marrow, advancing by a kind of inertia through the night, through the snow, through that cold and deadly country, crushed by pain, by defeat, by despair, above all overcome by the abominable sensation of abandonment, of the end, of death, of nothingness.

"I saw two gendarmes holding by the arm a curious-looking little man, old, beardless, of truly surprising aspect.

"They were looking for an officer, believing that they had caught a spy. The word 'spy' at once spread through the midst of the stragglers, and they gathered in a group round the prisoner. A voice exclaimed: 'He must be shot!' And all these soldiers who were falling from utter prostration, only holding themselves on their feet by leaning on their guns, felt all of a sudden that thrill of furious and bestial anger which urges on a mob to massacre.

"I wanted to speak. I was at that time in command of a battalion; but they no longer recognized the authority of their commanding officers; they would even have shot me.

"One of the gendarmes said: 'He has been following us for the three last days. He has been asking information from every one about the artillery.'"

I took it on myself to question this person.

"What are you doing? What do you want? Why are you accompanying the army?"

"He stammered out some words in some unintelligible dialect. He was, indeed, a strange being, with narrow shoulders, a sly look, and such an agitated air in my presence that I really no longer doubted that he was a spy. He seemed very aged and feeble. He kept looking at me from under his eyes with a humble, stupid, crafty air.

"The men all round us exclaimed.

"'To the wall! To the wall!'

"I said to the gendarmes:

"'Will you be responsible for the prisoner?'

"I had not ceased speaking when a terrible shove threw me on my back, and in a second I saw the man seized by the furious soldiers, thrown down, struck, dragged along the side of the road, and flung against a tree. He fell in the snow, nearly dead already.

"And immediately they shot him. The soldiers fired at him, reloaded their guns, fired again with the desperate energy of brutes. They fought with each other to have a shot at him, filed off in front of the corpse, and kept on firing at him, as people at a funeral keep sprinkling holy water in front of a coffin.

"But suddenly a cry arose of 'The Prussians! the Prussians!'

"And all along the horizon I heard the great noise of this panic-stricken army in full flight.

"A panic, the result of these shots fired at this vagabond, had filled his very executioners with terror; and, without realizing that they were themselves the originators of the scare, they fled and disappeared in the darkness.

"I remained alone with the corpse, except for the two gendarmes whose duty compelled them to stay with me.

"They lifted up the riddled mass of bruised and bleeding flesh.

"'He must be searched,' I said. And I handed them a box of taper matches which I had in my pocket. One of the soldiers had another box. I was standing between the two.

"The gendarme who was examining the body announced:

"'Clothed in a blue blouse, a white shirt, trousers, and a pair of shoes.'

"The first match went out; we lighted a second. The man continued, as he turned out his pockets:

"'A horn-handled pocketknife, check handkerchief, a snuffbox, a bit of pack thread, a piece of bread.'

"The second match went out; we lighted a third. The gendarme, after having felt the corpse for a long time, said:

"'That is all.'

"I said:

"'Strip him. We shall perhaps find something next his skin."

"And in order that the two soldiers might help each other in this task, I stood between them to hold the lighted match. By the rapid and speedily extinguished flame of the match, I saw them take off the garments one by one, and expose to view that bleeding bundle of flesh, still warm, though lifeless.

"And suddenly one of them exclaimed:

"'Good God, general, it is a woman!'

"I cannot describe to you the strange and poignant sensation of pain that moved my heart. I could not believe it, and I knelt down in the snow before this shapeless pulp of flesh to see for myself: it was a woman.

"The two gendarmes, speechless and stunned, waited for me to give my opinion on the matter. But I did not know what to think, what theory to adopt.

"Then the brigadier slowly drawled out:

"'Perhaps she came to look for a son of hers in the artillery, whom she had not heard from.'

"And the other chimed in:

"'Perhaps, indeed, that is so.'

"And I, who had seen some very terrible things in my time, began to cry. And I felt, in the presence of this corpse, on that icy cold night, in the midst of that gloomy plain; at the sight of this mystery, at the sight of this murdered stranger, the meaning of that word 'horror.'

"I had the same sensation last year, while interrogating one of the survivors of the Flatters Mission, an Algerian sharpshooter.

"You know the details of that atrocious drama. It is possible, however, that you are unacquainted with one of them.

"The colonel travelled through the desert into the Soudan, and passed through the immense territory of the Touaregs, who, in that great ocean of sand which stretches from the Atlantic to Egypt and from the Soudan to Algeria, are a kind of pirates, resembling those who ravaged the seas in former days.

"The guides who accompanied the column belonged to the tribe of the Chambaa, of Ouargla.

"Now, one day we encamped in the middle of the desert, and the Arabs declared that, as the spring was still some distance away, they would go with all their camels to look for water.

"One man alone warned the colonel that he had been betrayed. Flatters did not believe this, and accompanied the convoy with the engineers, the doctors, and nearly all his officers.

"They were massacred round the spring, and all the camels were captured.

"The captain of the Arab Intelligence Department at Ouargla, who had remained in the camp, took command of the survivors, spahis and sharpshooters, and they began to retreat, leaving behind them the baggage and provisions, for want of camels to carry them.

"Then they started on their journey through this solitude without shade and boundless, beneath the devouring sun, which burned them from morning till night.

"One tribe came to tender its submission and brought dates as a tribute. The dates were poisoned. Nearly all the Frenchmen died, and, among them, the last officer.

"There now only remained a few spahis with their quartermaster, Pobeguin, and some native sharpshooters of the Chambaa tribe. They had still two camels left. They disappeared one night, along with two, Arabs.

"Then the survivors understood that they would be obliged to eat each other, and as soon as they discovered the flight of the two men with the two camels, those who remained separated, and proceeded to march, one by one, through the soft sand, under the glare of a scorching sun, at a distance of more than a gunshot from each other.

"So they went on all day, and when they reached a spring each of them came to drink at it in turn, as soon as each solitary marcher had moved forward the number of yards arranged upon. And thus they continued marching the whole day, raising everywhere they passed, in that level, burnt up expanse, those little columns of dust which, from a distance, indicate those who are trudging through the desert.

"But one morning one of the travellers suddenly turned round and approached the man behind him. And they all stopped to look.

"The man toward whom the famished soldier drew near did not flee, but lay flat on the ground, and took aim at the one who was coming toward him. When he believed he was within gunshot, he fired. The other was not hit, and he continued then to advance, and levelling his gun, in turn, he killed his comrade.

"Then from all directions the others rushed to seek their share. And he who had killed the fallen man, cutting the corpse into pieces, distributed it.

"And they once more placed themselves at fixed distances, these irreconcilable allies, preparing for the next murder which would bring them together.

"For two days they lived on this human flesh which they divided between them. Then, becoming famished again, he who had killed the first man began killing afresh. And again, like a butcher, he cut up the corpse and offered it to his comrades, keeping only his own portion of it.

"And so this retreat of cannibals continued.

"The last Frenchman, Pobeguin, was massacred at the side of a well, the very night before the supplies arrived.

"Do you understand now what I mean by the horrible?"

This was the story told us a few nights ago by General de G——.

MADAME PARISSE

I was sitting on the pier of the small port of Obernon, near the village of Salis, looking at Antibes, bathed in the setting sun. I had never before seen anything so wonderful and so beautiful.

The small town, enclosed by its massive ramparts, built by Monsieur de Vauban, extended into the open sea, in the middle of the immense Gulf of Nice. The great waves, coming in from the ocean, broke at its feet, surrounding it with a wreath of foam; and beyond the ramparts the houses climbed up the hill, one after the other, as far as the two towers, which rose up into the sky, like the peaks of an ancient helmet. And these two towers were outlined against the milky whiteness of the Alps, that enormous distant wall of snow which enclosed the entire horizon.

Between the white foam at the foot of the walls and the white snow on the sky-line the little city, dazzling against the bluish background of the nearest mountain ranges, presented to the rays of the setting sun a pyramid of red-roofed houses, whose facades were also white, but so different one from another that they seemed to be of all tints.

And the sky above the Alps was itself of a blue that was almost white, as if the snow had tinted it; some silvery clouds were floating just over the pale summits, and on the other side of the gulf Nice, lying close to the water, stretched like a white thread between the sea and the mountain. Two great sails, driven by a strong breeze, seemed to skim over the waves. I looked upon all this, astounded.

This view was one of those sweet, rare, delightful things that seem to permeate you and are unforgettable, like the memory of a great happiness. One sees, thinks, suffers, is moved and loves with the eyes. He who can feel with the eye experiences the same keen, exquisite and deep pleasure in looking at men and things as the man with the delicate and sensitive ear, whose soul music overwhelms.

I turned to my companion, M. Martini, a pureblooded Southerner.

"This is certainly one of the rarest sights which it has been vouchsafed to me to admire.

"I have seen Mont Saint-Michel, that monstrous granite jewel, rise out of the sand at sunrise.

"I have seen, in the Sahara, Lake Raianechergui, fifty kilometers long, shining under a moon as brilliant as our sun and breathing up toward it a white cloud, like a mist of milk.

"I have seen, in the Lipari Islands, the weird sulphur crater of the Volcanello, a giant flower which smokes and burns, an enormous yellow flower, opening out in the midst of the sea, whose stem is a volcano.

"But I have seen nothing more wonderful than Antibes, standing against the Alps in the setting sun.

"And I know not how it is that memories of antiquity haunt me; verses of Homer come into my mind; this is a city of the ancient East, a city of the odyssey; this is Troy, although Troy was very far from the sea."

M. Martini drew the Sarty guide-book out of his pocket and read: "This city was originally a colony founded by the Phocians of Marseilles, about 340 B.C. They gave it the Greek name of Antipolis, meaning counter-city, city opposite another, because it is in fact opposite to Nice, another colony from Marseilles.

"After the Gauls were conquered, the Romans turned Antibes into a municipal city, its inhabitants receiving the rights of Roman citizenship.

"We know by an epigram of Martial that at this time——"

I interrupted him:

"I don't care what she was. I tell you that I see down there a city of the Odyssey. The coast of Asia and the coast of Europe resemble each other in their shores, and there is no city on the other coast of the Mediterranean which awakens in me the memories of the heroic age as this one does."

A footstep caused me to turn my head; a woman, a large, dark woman, was walking along the road which skirts the sea in going to the cape.

"That is Madame Parisse, you know," muttered Monsieur Martini, dwelling on the final syllable.

No, I did not know, but that name, mentioned carelessly, that name of the Trojan shepherd, confirmed me in my dream.

However, I asked: "Who is this Madame Parisse?"

He seemed astonished that I did not know the story.

I assured him that I did not know it, and I looked after the woman, who passed by without seeing us, dreaming, walking with steady and slow step, as doubtless the ladies of old walked.

She was perhaps thirty-five years old and still very beautiful, though a trifle stout.

And Monsieur Martini told me the following story:

Mademoiselle Combelombe was married, one year before the war of 1870, to Monsieur Parisse, a government official. She was then a handsome young girl, as slender and lively as she has now become stout and sad.

Unwillingly she had accepted Monsieur Parisse, one of those little fat men with short legs, who trip along, with trousers that are always too large.

After the war Antibes was garrisoned by a single battalion commanded by Monsieur Jean de Carmelin, a young officer decorated during the war, and who had just received his four stripes.

As he found life exceedingly tedious in this fortress this stuffy mole-hole enclosed by its enormous double walls, he often strolled out to the cape, a kind of park or pine wood shaken by all the winds from the sea.

There he met Madame Parisse, who also came out in the summer evenings to get the fresh air under the trees. How did they come to love each other? Who knows? They met, they looked at each other, and when out of sight they doubtless thought of each other. The image of the young woman with the brown eyes, the black hair, the pale skin, this fresh, handsome Southerner, who displayed her teeth in smiling, floated before the eyes of the officer as he continued his promenade, chewing his cigar instead of smoking it; and the image of the commanding officer, in his close-fitting coat, covered with gold lace, and his red trousers, and a little blond mustache, would pass before the eyes of Madame Parisse, when her husband, half shaven and ill-clad, short-legged and big-bellied, came home to supper in the evening.

As they met so often, they perhaps smiled at the next meeting; then, seeing each other again and again, they felt as if they knew each other. He certainly bowed to her. And she, surprised, bowed in return, but very, very slightly, just enough not to appear impolite. But after two weeks she returned his salutation from a distance, even before they were side by side.

He spoke to her. Of what? Doubtless of the setting sun. They admired it together, looking for it in each other's eyes more often than on the horizon. And every evening for two weeks this was the commonplace and persistent pretext for a few minutes' chat.

Then they ventured to take a few steps together, talking of anything that came into their minds, but their eyes were already saying to each other a thousand more intimate things, those secret, charming things that are reflected in the gentle emotion of the glance, and that cause the heart to beat, for they are a better revelation of the soul than the spoken ward.

And then he would take her hand, murmuring those words which the woman divines, without seeming to hear them.

And it was agreed between them that they would love each other without evidencing it by anything sensual or brutal.

She would have remained indefinitely at this stage of intimacy, but he wanted more. And every day he urged her more hotly to give in to his ardent desire.

She resisted, would not hear of it, seemed determined not to give way.

But one evening she said to him casually: "My husband has just gone to Marseilles. He will be away four days."

Jean de Carmelin threw himself at her feet, imploring her to open her door to him that very night at eleven o'clock. But she would not listen to him, and went home, appearing to be annoyed.

The commandant was in a bad humor all the evening, and the next morning at dawn he went out on the ramparts in a rage, going from one exercise field to the other, dealing out punishment to the officers and men as one might fling stones into a crowd,

On going in to breakfast he found an envelope under his napkin with these four words: "To-night at ten." And he gave one hundred sous without any reason to the waiter.

The day seemed endless to him. He passed part of it in curling his hair and perfuming himself.

As he was sitting down to the dinner-table another envelope was handed to him, and in it he found the following telegram:

"My Love: Business completed. I return this evening on the nine o'clock train.

PARISSE."

The commandant let loose such a vehement oath that the waiter dropped the soup-tureen on the floor.

What should he do? He certainly wanted her, that very, evening at whatever cost; and he would have her. He would resort to any means, even to arresting and imprisoning the husband. Then a mad thought struck him. Calling for paper, he wrote the following note:

MADAME: He will not come back this evening, I swear it to

you,—and I shall be, you know where, at ten o'clock. Fear nothing.

I will answer for everything, on my honor as an officer.

JEAN DE CARMELIN.

And having sent off this letter, he quietly ate his dinner.

Toward eight o'clock he sent for Captain Gribois, the second in command, and said, rolling between his fingers the crumpled telegram of Monsieur Parisse:

"Captain, I have just received a telegram of a very singular nature, which it is impossible for me to communicate to you. You will immediately have all the gates of the city closed and guarded, so that no one, mind me, no one, will either enter or leave before six in the morning. You will also have men patrol the streets, who will compel the inhabitants to retire to their houses at nine o'clock. Any one found outside beyond that time will be conducted to his home 'manu militari'. If your men meet me this night they will at once go out of my way, appearing not to know me. You understand me?"

"Yes, commandant."

"I hold you responsible for the execution of my orders, my dear captain."

"Yes, commandant."

"Would you like to have a glass of chartreuse?"

"With great pleasure, commandant."

They clinked glasses drank down the brown liquor and Captain Gribois left the room.

The train from Marseilles arrived at the station at nine o'clock sharp, left two passengers on the platform and went on toward Nice.

One of them, tall and thin, was Monsieur Saribe, the oil merchant, and the other, short and fat, was Monsieur Parisse.

Together they set out, with their valises, to reach the city, one kilometer distant.

But on arriving at the gate of the port the guards crossed their bayonets, commanding them to retire.

Frightened, surprised, cowed with astonishment, they retired to deliberate; then, after having taken counsel one with the other, they came back cautiously to parley, giving their names.

But the soldiers evidently had strict orders, for they threatened to shoot; and the two scared travellers ran off, throwing away their valises, which impeded their flight.

Making the tour of the ramparts, they presented themselves at the gate on the route to Cannes. This likewise was closed and guarded by a menacing sentinel. Messrs. Saribe and Parisse, like the prudent men they were, desisted from their efforts and went back to the station for shelter, since it was not safe to be near the fortifications after sundown.

The station agent, surprised and sleepy, permitted them to stay till morning in the waiting-room.

And they sat there side by side, in the dark, on the green velvet sofa, too scared to think of sleeping.

It was a long and weary night for them.

At half-past six in the morning they were informed that the gates were open and that people could now enter Antibes.

They set out for the city, but failed to find their abandoned valises on the road.

When they passed through the gates of the city, still somewhat anxious, the Commandant de Carmelin, with sly glance and mustache curled up, came himself to look at them and question them.

Then he bowed to them politely, excusing himself for having caused them a bad night. But he had to carry out orders.

The people of Antibes were scared to death. Some spoke of a surprise planned by the Italians, others of the landing of the prince imperial and others again believed that there was an Orleanist conspiracy. The truth was suspected only later, when it became known that the battalion of the commandant had been sent away, to a distance and that Monsieur de Carmelin had been severely punished.

Monsieur Martini had finished his story. Madame Parisse returned, her promenade being ended. She passed gravely near me, with her eyes fixed on the Alps, whose summits now gleamed rosy in the last rays of the setting sun.

I longed to speak to her, this poor, sad woman, who would ever be thinking of that night of love, now long past, and of the bold man who for the sake of a kiss from her had dared to put a city into a state of siege and to compromise his whole future.

And to-day he had probably forgotten her, if he did not relate this audacious, comical and tender farce to his comrades over their cups.

Had she seen him again? Did she still love him? And I thought: Here is an instance of modern love, grotesque and yet heroic. The Homer who should sing of this new Helen and the adventure of her Menelaus must be gifted with the soul of a Paul de Kock. And yet the hero of this deserted woman was brave, daring, handsome, strong as Achilles and more cunning than Ulysses.

MADEMOISELLE FIFI

Major Graf Von Farlsberg, the Prussian commandant, was reading his newspaper as he lay back in a great easy-chair, with his booted feet on the beautiful marble mantelpiece where his spurs had made two holes, which had grown deeper every day during the three months that he had been in the chateau of Uville.

A cup of coffee was smoking on a small inlaid table, which was stained with liqueur, burned by cigars, notched by the penknife of the victorious officer, who occasionally would stop while sharpening a pencil, to jot down figures, or to make a drawing on it, just as it took his fancy.

When he had read his letters and the German newspapers, which his orderly had brought him, he got up, and after throwing three or four enormous pieces of green wood on the fire, for these gentlemen were gradually cutting down the park in order to keep themselves warm, he went to the window. The rain was descending in torrents, a regular Normandy rain, which looked as if it were being poured out by some furious person, a slanting rain, opaque as a curtain, which formed a kind of wall with diagonal stripes, and which deluged everything, a rain such as one frequently experiences in the neighborhood of Rouen, which is the watering-pot of France.

For a long time the officer looked at the sodden turf and at the swollen Andelle beyond it, which was overflowing its banks; he was drumming a waltz with his fingers on the window-panes, when a noise made him turn round. It was his second in command, Captain Baron van Kelweinstein.

The major was a giant, with broad shoulders and a long, fan-like beard, which hung down like a curtain to his chest. His whole solemn person suggested the idea of a military peacock, a peacock who was carrying his tail spread out on his breast. He had cold, gentle blue eyes, and a scar from a swordcut, which he had received in the war with Austria; he was said to be an honorable man, as well as a brave officer.

The captain, a short, red-faced man, was tightly belted in at the waist, his red hair was cropped quite close to his head, and in certain lights he almost looked as if he had been rubbed over with phosphorus. He had lost two front teeth one night, though he could not quite remember how, and this sometimes made him speak unintelligibly, and he had a bald patch on top of his head surrounded by a fringe of curly, bright golden hair, which made him look like a monk.

The commandant shook hands with him and drank his cup of coffee (the sixth that morning), while he listened to his subordinate's report of what had occurred; and then they both went to the window and declared that it was a very unpleasant outlook. The major, who was a quiet man, with a wife at home, could accommodate himself to everything; but the captain, who led a fast life, who was in the habit of frequenting low resorts, and enjoying women's society, was angry at having to be shut up for three months in that wretched hole.

There was a knock at the door, and when the commandant said, "Come in," one of the orderlies appeared, and by his mere presence announced that breakfast was ready. In the dining-room they met three other officers of lower rank—a lieutenant, Otto von Grossling, and two sub-lieutenants, Fritz Scheuneberg and Baron von Eyrick, a very short, fair-haired man, who was proud and brutal toward men, harsh toward prisoners and as explosive as gunpowder.

Since he had been in France his comrades had called him nothing but Mademoiselle Fifi.

They had given him that nickname on account of his dandified style and small waist, which looked as if he wore corsets; of his pale face, on which his budding mustache scarcely showed, and on account of the habit he had acquired of employing the French expression, 'Fi, fi donc', which he pronounced with a slight whistle when he wished to express his sovereign contempt for persons or things.

The dining-room of the chateau was a magnificent long room, whose fine old mirrors, that were cracked by pistol bullets, and whose Flemish tapestry, which was cut to ribbons, and hanging in rags in places from sword-cuts, told too well what Mademoiselle Fifi's occupation was during his spare time.

There were three family portraits on the walls a steel-clad knight, a cardinal and a judge, who were all smoking long porcelain pipes, which had been inserted into holes in the canvas, while a lady in a long, pointed waist proudly exhibited a pair of enormous mustaches, drawn with charcoal. The officers ate their breakfast almost in silence in that mutilated room, which looked dull in the rain and melancholy in its dilapidated condition, although its old oak floor had become as solid as the stone floor of an inn.

When they had finished eating and were smoking and drinking, they began, as usual, to berate the dull life they were leading. The bottles of brandy and of liqueur passed from hand to hand, and all sat back in their chairs and took repeated sips from their glasses, scarcely removing from their mouths the long, curved stems, which terminated in china bowls, painted in a manner to delight a Hottentot.

As soon as their glasses were empty they filled them again, with a gesture of resigned weariness, but Mademoiselle Fifi emptied his every minute, and a soldier immediately gave him another. They were enveloped in a cloud of strong tobacco smoke, and seemed to be sunk in a state of drowsy, stupid intoxication, that condition of stupid intoxication of men who have nothing to do, when suddenly the baron sat up and said: "Heavens! This cannot go on; we must think of something to do." And on hearing this, Lieutenant Otto and Sub-lieutenant Fritz, who preeminently possessed the serious, heavy German countenance, said: "What, captain?"

He thought for a few moments and then replied: "What? Why, we must get up some entertainment, if the commandant will allow us." "What sort of an entertainment, captain?" the major asked, taking his pipe out of his mouth. "I will arrange all that, commandant," the baron said. "I will send Le Devoir to Rouen, and he will bring back some ladies. I know where they can be found, We will have supper here, as all the materials are at hand and; at least, we shall have a jolly evening."

Graf von Farlsberg shrugged his shoulders with a smile: "You must surely be mad, my friend."

But all the other officers had risen and surrounded their chief, saying: "Let the captain have his way, commandant; it is terribly dull here." And the major ended by yielding. "Very well," he replied, and the baron immediately sent for Le Devoir. He was an old non-commissioned officer, who had never been seen to smile, but who carried out all the orders of his superiors to the letter, no matter what they might be. He stood there, with an impassive face, while he received the baron's instructions, and then went out, and five minutes later a large military wagon, covered with tarpaulin, galloped off as fast as four horses could draw it in the pouring rain. The officers all seemed to awaken from their lethargy, their looks brightened, and they began to talk.

Although it was raining as hard as ever, the major declared that it was not so dark, and Lieutenant von Grossling said with conviction that the sky was clearing up, while Mademoiselle Fifi did not seem to be able to keep still. He got up and sat down again, and his bright eyes seemed to be looking for something to destroy. Suddenly, looking at the lady with the mustaches, the young fellow pulled out his revolver and said: "You shall not see it." And without leaving his seat he aimed, and with two successive bullets cut out both the eyes of the portrait.

"Let us make a mine!" he then exclaimed, and the conversation was suddenly interrupted, as if they had found some fresh and powerful subject of interest. The mine was his invention, his method of destruction, and his favorite amusement.

When he left the chateau, the lawful owner, Comte Fernand d'Amoys d'Uville, had not had time to carry away or to hide anything except the plate, which had been stowed away in a hole made in one of the walls. As he was very rich and had good taste, the large drawing-room, which opened into the dining-room, looked like a gallery in a museum, before his precipitate flight.

Expensive oil paintings, water colors and drawings hung against the walls, while on the tables, on the hanging shelves and in elegant glass cupboards there were a thousand ornaments: small vases, statuettes, groups of Dresden china and grotesque Chinese figures, old ivory and Venetian glass, which filled the large room with their costly and fantastic array.

Scarcely anything was left now; not that the things had been stolen, for the major would not have allowed that, but Mademoiselle Fifi would every now and then have a mine, and on those occasions all the officers thoroughly enjoyed themselves for five minutes. The little marquis went into the drawing-room to get what he wanted, and he brought back a small, delicate china teapot, which he filled with gunpowder, and carefully introduced a piece of punk through the spout. This he lighted and took his infernal machine into the next room, but he came back immediately and shut the door. The Germans all stood expectant, their faces full of childish, smiling curiosity, and as soon as the explosion had shaken the chateau, they all rushed in at once.

Mademoiselle Fifi, who got in first, clapped his hands in delight at the sight of a terra-cotta Venus, whose head had been blown off, and each picked up pieces of porcelain and wondered at the strange shape of the fragments, while the major was looking with a paternal eye at the large drawing-room, which had been wrecked after the fashion of a Nero, and was strewn with the fragments of works of art. He went out first and said with a smile: "That was a great success this time."

But there was such a cloud of smoke in the dining-room, mingled with the tobacco smoke, that they could not breathe, so the commandant opened the window, and all the officers, who had returned for a last glass of cognac, went up to it.

The moist air blew into the room, bringing with it a sort of powdery spray, which sprinkled their beards. They looked at the tall trees which were dripping with rain, at the broad valley which was covered with mist, and at the church spire in the distance, which rose up like a gray point in the beating rain.

The bells had not rung since their arrival. That was the only resistance which the invaders had met with in the neighborhood. The parish priest had not refused to take in and to feed the Prussian soldiers; he had several times even drunk a bottle of beer or claret with the hostile commandant, who often employed him as a benevolent intermediary; but it was no use to ask him for a single stroke of the bells; he would sooner have allowed himself to be shot. That was his way of protesting against the invasion, a peaceful and silent protest, the only one, he said, which was suitable to a priest, who was a man of mildness, and not of blood; and every one, for twenty-five miles round, praised Abbe Chantavoine's firmness and heroism in venturing to proclaim the public mourning by the obstinate silence of his church bells.

The whole village, enthusiastic at his resistance, was ready to back up their pastor and to risk anything, for they looked upon that silent protest as the safeguard of the national honor. It seemed to the peasants that thus they deserved better of their country than Belfort and Strassburg, that they had set an equally valuable example, and that the name of their little village would become immortalized by that; but, with that exception, they refused their Prussian conquerors nothing.

The commandant and his officers laughed among themselves at this inoffensive courage, and as the people in the whole country round showed themselves obliging and compliant toward them, they willingly tolerated their silent patriotism. Little Baron Wilhelm alone would have liked to have forced them to ring the bells. He was very angry at his superior's politic compliance with the priest's scruples, and every day begged the commandant to allow him to sound "ding-dong, ding-dong," just once, only just once, just by way of a joke. And he asked it in the coaxing, tender voice of some loved woman who is bent on obtaining her wish, but the commandant would not yield, and to console himself, Mademoiselle Fifi made a mine in the Chateau d'Uville.

The five men stood there together for five minutes, breathing in the moist air, and at last Lieutenant Fritz said with a laugh: "The ladies will certainly not have fine weather for their drive." Then they separated, each to his duty, while the captain had plenty to do in arranging for the dinner.

When they met again toward evening they began to laugh at seeing each other as spick and span and smart as on the day of a grand review. The commandant's hair did not look so gray as it was in the morning, and the captain had shaved, leaving only his mustache, which made him look as if he had a streak of fire under his nose.

In spite of the rain, they left the window open, and one of them went to listen from time to time; and at a quarter past six the baron said he heard a rumbling in the distance. They all rushed down, and presently the wagon drove up at a gallop with its four horses steaming and blowing, and splashed with mud to their girths. Five women dismounted, five handsome girls whom a comrade of the captain, to whom Le Devoir had presented his card, had selected with care.

They had not required much pressing, as they had got to know the Prussians in the three months during which they had had to do with them, and so they resigned themselves to the men as they did to the state of affairs.

They went at once into the dining-room, which looked still more dismal in its dilapidated condition when it was lighted up; while the table covered with choice dishes, the beautiful china and glass, and the plate, which had been found in the hole in the wall where its owner had hidden it, gave it the appearance of a bandits' inn, where they were supping after committing a robbery in the place. The captain was radiant, and put his arm round the women as if he were familiar with them; and when the three young men wanted to appropriate one each, he opposed them authoritatively, reserving to himself the right to apportion them justly, according to their several ranks, so as not to offend the higher powers. Therefore, to avoid all discussion, jarring, and suspicion of partiality, he placed them all in a row according to height, and addressing the tallest, he said in a voice of command:

"What is your name?" "Pamela," she replied, raising her voice. And then he said: "Number One, called Pamela, is adjudged to the commandant." Then, having kissed Blondina, the second, as a sign of proprietorship, he proffered stout Amanda to Lieutenant Otto; Eva, "the Tomato," to Sub-lieutenant Fritz, and Rachel, the shortest of them all, a very young, dark girl, with eyes as black as ink, a Jewess, whose snub nose proved the rule which allots hooked noses to all her race, to the youngest officer, frail Count Wilhelm d'Eyrick.

They were all pretty and plump, without any distinctive features, and all had a similarity of complexion and figure.

The three young men wished to carry off their prizes immediately, under the pretext that they might wish to freshen their toilets; but the captain wisely opposed this, for he said they were quite fit to sit down to dinner, and his experience in such matters carried the day. There were only many kisses, expectant kisses.

Suddenly Rachel choked, and began to cough until the tears came into her eyes, while smoke came through her nostrils. Under pretence of kissing her, the count had blown a whiff of tobacco into her mouth. She did not fly into a rage and did not say a word, but she looked at her tormentor with latent hatred in her dark eyes.

They sat down to dinner. The commandant seemed delighted; he made Pamela sit on his right, and Blondina on his left, and said, as he unfolded his table napkin: "That was a delightful idea of yours, captain."

Lieutenants Otto and Fritz, who were as polite as if they had been with fashionable ladies, rather intimidated their guests, but Baron von Kelweinstein beamed, made obscene remarks and seemed on fire with his crown of red hair. He paid the women compliments in French of the Rhine, and sputtered out gallant remarks, only fit for a low pothouse, from between his two broken teeth.

They did not understand him, however, and their intelligence did not seem to be awakened until he uttered foul words and broad expressions, which were mangled by his accent. Then they all began to laugh at once like crazy women and fell against each other, repeating the words, which the baron then began to say all wrong, in order that he might have the pleasure of hearing them say dirty things. They gave him as much of that stuff as he wanted, for they were drunk after the first bottle of wine, and resuming their usual habits and manners, they kissed the officers to right and left of them, pinched their arms, uttered wild cries, drank out of every glass and sang French couplets and bits of German songs which they had picked up in their daily intercourse with the enemy.

Soon the men themselves became very unrestrained, shouted and broke the plates and dishes, while the soldiers behind them waited on them stolidly. The commandant was the only one who kept any restraint upon himself.

Mademoiselle Fifi had taken Rachel on his knee, and, getting excited, at one moment he kissed the little black curls on her neck and at another he pinched her furiously and made her scream, for he was seized by a species of ferocity, and tormented by his desire to hurt her. He often held her close to him and pressed a long kiss on the Jewess' rosy mouth until she lost her breath, and at last he bit her until a stream of blood ran down her chin and on to her bodice.

For the second time she looked him full in the face, and as she bathed the wound, she said: "You will have to pay for, that!" But he merely laughed a hard laugh and said: "I will pay."

At dessert champagne was served, and the commandant rose, and in the same voice in which he would have drunk to the health of the Empress Augusta, he drank: "To our ladies!" And a series of toasts began, toasts worthy of the lowest soldiers and of drunkards, mingled with obscene jokes, which were made still more brutal by their ignorance of the language. They got up, one after the other, trying to say something witty, forcing themselves to be funny, and the women, who were so drunk that they almost fell off their chairs, with vacant looks and clammy tongues applauded madly each time.

The captain, who no doubt wished to impart an appearance of gallantry to the orgy, raised his glass again and said: "To our victories over hearts." and, thereupon Lieutenant Otto, who was a species of bear from the Black Forest, jumped up, inflamed and saturated with drink, and suddenly seized by an access of alcoholic patriotism, he cried: "To our victories over France!"

Drunk as they were, the women were silent, but Rachel turned round, trembling, and said: "See here, I know some Frenchmen in whose presence you would not dare say that." But the little count, still holding her on his knee, began to laugh, for the wine had made him very merry, and said: "Ha! ha! ha! I have never met any of them myself. As soon as we show ourselves, they run away!" The girl, who was in a terrible rage, shouted into his face: "You are lying, you dirty scoundrel!"

For a moment he looked at her steadily with his bright eyes upon her, as he had looked at the portrait before he destroyed it with bullets from his revolver, and then he began to laugh: "Ah! yes, talk about them, my dear! Should we be here now if they were brave?" And, getting excited, he exclaimed: "We are the masters! France belongs to us!" She made one spring from his knee and threw herself into her chair, while he arose, held out his glass over the table and repeated: "France and the French, the woods, the fields and the houses of France belong to us!"

The others, who were quite drunk, and who were suddenly seized by military enthusiasm, the enthusiasm of brutes, seized their glasses, and shouting, "Long live Prussia!" they emptied them at a draught.

The girls did not protest, for they were reduced to silence and were afraid. Even Rachel did not say a word, as she had no reply to make. Then the little marquis put his champagne glass, which had just been refilled, on the head of the Jewess and exclaimed: "All the women in France belong to us also!"

At that she got up so quickly that the glass upset, spilling the amber-colored wine on her black hair as if to baptize her, and broke into a hundred fragments, as it fell to the floor. Her lips trembling, she defied the looks of the officer, who was still laughing, and stammered out in a voice choked with rage:

"That—that—that—is not true—for you shall not have the women of France!"

He sat down again so as to laugh at his ease; and, trying to speak with the Parisian accent, he said: "She is good, very good! Then why did you come here, my dear?" She was thunderstruck and made no reply for a moment, for in her agitation she did not understand him at first, but as soon as she grasped his meaning she said to him indignantly and vehemently: "I! I! I am not a woman, I am only a strumpet, and that is all that Prussians want."

Almost before she had finished he slapped her full in the face; but as he was raising his hand again, as if to strike her, she seized a small dessert knife with a silver blade from the table and, almost mad with rage, stabbed him right in the hollow of his neck. Something that he was going to say was cut short in his throat, and he sat there with his mouth half open and a terrible look in his eyes.

All the officers shouted in horror and leaped up tumultuously; but, throwing her chair between the legs of Lieutenant Otto, who fell down at full length, she ran to the window, opened it before they could seize her and jumped out into the night and the pouring rain.

In two minutes Mademoiselle Fifi was dead, and Fritz and Otto drew their swords and wanted to kill the women, who threw themselves at their feet and clung to their knees. With some difficulty the major stopped the slaughter and had the four terrified girls locked up in a room under the care of two soldiers, and then he organized the pursuit of the fugitive as carefully as if he were about to engage in a skirmish, feeling quite sure that she would be caught.

The table, which had been cleared immediately, now served as a bed on which to lay out the lieutenant, and the four officers stood at the windows, rigid and sobered with the stern faces of soldiers on duty, and tried to pierce through the darkness of the night amid the steady torrent of rain. Suddenly a shot was heard and then another, a long way off; and for four hours they heard from time to time near or distant reports and rallying cries, strange words of challenge, uttered in guttural voices.

In the morning they all returned. Two soldiers had been killed and three others wounded by their comrades in the ardor of that chase and in the confusion of that nocturnal pursuit, but they had not caught Rachel.

Then the inhabitants of the district were terrorized, the houses were turned topsy-turvy, the country was scoured and beaten up, over and over again, but the Jewess did not seem to have left a single trace of her passage behind her.

When the general was told of it he gave orders to hush up the affair, so as not to set a bad example to the army, but he severely censured the commandant, who in turn punished his inferiors. The general had said: “One does not go to war in order to amuse one’s self and to caress prostitutes.” Graf von Farlsberg, in his exasperation, made up his mind to have his revenge on the district, but as he required a pretext for showing severity, he sent for the priest and ordered him to have the bell tolled at the funeral of Baron von Eyrick.

Contrary to all expectation, the priest showed himself humble and most respectful, and when Mademoiselle Fifi’s body left the Chateau d’Uville on its way to the cemetery, carried by soldiers, preceded, surrounded and followed by soldiers who marched with loaded rifles, for the first time the bell sounded its funeral knell in a lively manner, as if a friendly hand were caressing it. At night it rang again, and the next day, and every day; it rang as much as any one could desire. Sometimes even it would start at night and sound gently through the darkness, seized with a strange joy, awakened one could not tell why. All the peasants in the neighborhood declared that it was bewitched, and nobody except the priest and the sacristan would now go near the church tower. And they went because a poor girl was living there in grief and solitude and provided for secretly by those two men.

She remained there until the German troops departed, and then one evening the priest borrowed the baker’s cart and himself drove his prisoner to Rouen. When they got there he embraced her, and she quickly went back on foot to the establishment from which she had come, where the proprietress, who thought that she was dead, was very glad to see her.

A short time afterward a patriot who had no prejudices, and who liked her because of her bold deed, and who afterward loved her for herself, married her and made her a lady quite as good as many others.

A DUEL

The war was over. The Germans occupied France. The whole country was pulsating like a conquered wrestler beneath the knee of his victorious opponent.

The first trains from Paris, distracted, starving, despairing Paris, were making their way to the new frontiers, slowly passing through the country districts and the villages. The passengers gazed through the windows at the ravaged fields and burned hamlets. Prussian soldiers, in their black helmets with brass spikes, were smoking their pipes astride their chairs in front of the houses which were still left standing. Others were working or talking just as if they were members of the families. As you passed through the different towns you saw entire regiments drilling in the squares, and, in spite of the rumble of the carriage-wheels, you could every moment hear the hoarse words of command.

M. Dubuis, who during the entire siege had served as one of the National Guard in Paris, was going to join his wife and daughter, whom he had prudently sent away to Switzerland before the invasion.

Famine and hardship had not diminished his big paunch so characteristic of the rich, peace-loving merchant. He had gone through the terrible events of the past year with sorrowful resignation and bitter complaints at the savagery of men. Now that he was journeying to the frontier at the close of the war, he saw the Prussians for the first time, although he had done his duty on the ramparts and mounted guard on many a cold night.

He stared with mingled fear and anger at those bearded armed men, installed all over French soil as if they were at home, and he felt in his soul a kind of fever of impotent patriotism, at the same time also the great need of that new instinct of prudence which since then has, never left us. In the same railway carriage were two Englishmen, who had come to the country as sightseers and were gazing about them with looks of quiet curiosity. They were both also stout, and kept chatting in their own language, sometimes referring to their guidebook, and reading aloud the names of the places indicated.

Suddenly the train stopped at a little village station, and a Prussian officer jumped up with a great clatter of his sabre on the double footboard of the railway carriage. He was tall, wore a tight-fitting uniform, and had whiskers up to his eyes. His red hair seemed to be on fire, and his long mustache, of a paler hue, stuck out on both sides of his face, which it seemed to cut in two.

The Englishmen at once began staring at him, with smiles of newly awakened interest, while M. Dubuis made a show of reading a newspaper. He sat concealed in his corner like a thief in presence of a gendarme.

The train started again. The Englishmen went on chatting and looking out for the exact scene of different battles; and all of a sudden, as one of them stretched out his arm toward the horizon as he pointed out a village, the Prussian officer remarked in French, extending his long legs and lolling backward:

“I killed a dozen Frenchmen in that village and took more than a hundred prisoners.”

The Englishmen, quite interested, immediately asked:

“Ha! and what is the name of this village?”

The Prussian replied:

“Pharsbourg.” He added: “We caught those French scoundrels by the ears.”

And he glanced toward M. Dubuis, laughing conceitedly into his mustache.

The train rolled on, still passing through hamlets occupied by the victorious army. German soldiers could be seen along the roads, on the edges of fields, standing in front of gates or chatting outside cafes. They covered the soil like African locusts.

The officer said, with a wave of his hand:

“If I had been in command, I’d have taken Paris, burned everything, killed everybody. No more France!”

The Englishman, through politeness, replied simply:

“Ah! yes.”

He went on:

“In twenty years all Europe, all of it, will belong to us. Prussia is more than a match for all of them.”

The Englishmen, getting uneasy, no longer replied. Their faces, which had become impassive, seemed made of wax behind their long whiskers. Then the Prussian officer began to laugh. And still, lolling back, he began to sneer. He sneered at the downfall of France, insulted the prostrate enemy; he sneered at Austria, which had been recently conquered; he sneered at the valiant but fruitless defence of the departments; he sneered at the Garde Mobile and at the useless artillery. He announced that Bismarck was going to build a city of iron with the captured cannon. And suddenly he placed his boots against the thigh of M. Dubuis, who turned away his eyes, reddening to the roots of his hair.

The Englishmen seemed to have become indifferent to all that was going on, as if they were suddenly shut up in their own island, far from the din of the world.

The officer took out his pipe, and looking fixedly at the Frenchman, said:

“You haven’t any tobacco—have you?”

M. Dubuis replied:

“No, monsieur.”

The German resumed:

“You might go and buy some for me when the train stops.”

And he began laughing afresh as he added:

“I’ll give you the price of a drink.”

The train whistled, and slackened its pace. They passed a station that had been burned down; and then they stopped altogether.

The German opened the carriage door, and, catching M. Dubuis by the arm, said:

“Go and do what I told you—quick, quick!”

A Prussian detachment occupied the station. Other soldiers were standing behind wooden gratings, looking on. The engine was getting up steam before starting off again. Then M. Dubuis hurriedly jumped on the platform, and, in spite of the warnings of the station master, dashed into the adjoining compartment.

He was alone! He tore open his waistcoat, his heart was beating so rapidly, and, gasping for breath, he wiped the perspiration from his forehead.

The train drew up at another station. And suddenly the officer appeared at the carriage door and jumped in, followed close behind by the two Englishmen, who were impelled by curiosity. The German sat facing the Frenchman, and, laughing still, said:

"You did not want to do what I asked you?"

M. Dubuis replied:

"No, monsieur."

The train had just left the station.

The officer said:

"I'll cut off your mustache to fill my pipe with."

And he put out his hand toward the Frenchman's face.

The Englishmen stared at them, retaining their previous impassive manner.

The German had already pulled out a few hairs, and was still tugging at the mustache, when M. Dubuis, with a back stroke of his hand, flung aside the officer's arm, and, seizing him by the collar, threw him down on the seat. Then, excited to a pitch of fury, his temples swollen and his eyes glaring, he kept throttling the officer with one hand, while with the other clenched he began to strike him violent blows in the face. The Prussian struggled, tried to draw his sword, to clinch with his adversary, who was on top of him. But M. Dubuis crushed him with his enormous weight and kept punching him without taking breath or knowing where his blows fell. Blood flowed down the face of the German, who, choking and with a rattling in his throat, spat out his broken teeth and vainly strove to shake off this infuriated man who was killing him.

The Englishmen had got on their feet and came closer in order to see better. They remained standing, full of mirth and curiosity, ready to bet for, or against, either combatant.

Suddenly M. Dubuis, exhausted by his violent efforts, rose and resumed his seat without uttering a word.

The Prussian did not attack him, for the savage assault had terrified and astonished the officer as well as causing him suffering. When he was able to breathe freely, he said:

"Unless you give me satisfaction with pistols I will kill you."

M. Dubuis replied:

"Whenever you like. I'm quite ready."

The German said:

"Here is the town of Strasbourg. I'll get two officers to be my seconds, and there will be time before the train leaves the station."

M. Dubuis, who was puffing as hard as the engine, said to the Englishmen:

"Will you be my seconds?" They both answered together:

"Oh, yes!"

And the train stopped.

In a minute the Prussian had found two comrades, who brought pistols, and they made their way toward the ramparts.

The Englishmen were continually looking at their watches, shuffling their feet and hurrying on with the preparations, uneasy lest they should be too late for the train.

M. Dubuis had never fired a pistol in his life.

They made him stand twenty paces away from his enemy. He was asked:

"Are you ready?"

While he was answering, "Yes, monsieur," he noticed that one of the Englishmen had opened his umbrella in order to keep off the rays of the sun.

A voice gave the signal:

"Fire!"

M. Dubuis fired at random without delay, and he was amazed to see the Prussian opposite him stagger, lift up his arms and fall forward, dead. He had killed the officer.

One of the Englishmen exclaimed: "Ah!" He was quivering with delight, with satisfied curiosity and joyous impatience. The other, who still kept his watch in his hand, seized M. Dubuis' arm and hurried him in double-quick time toward the station, his fellow-countryman marking time as he ran beside them, with closed fists, his elbows at his sides, "One, two; one, two!"

And all three, running abreast rapidly, made their way to the station like three grotesque figures in a comic newspaper.

The train was on the point of starting. They sprang into their carriage. Then the Englishmen, taking off their travelling caps, waved them three times over their heads, exclaiming:

"Hip! hip! hip! hurrah!"

And gravely, one after the other, they extended their right hands to M. Dubuis and then went back and sat down in their own corner.

VOLUME II.

THE COLONEL'S IDEAS

"Upon my word," said Colonel Laporte, "although I am old and gouty, my legs as stiff as two pieces of wood, yet if a pretty woman were to tell me to go through the eye of a needle, I believe I should take a jump at it, like a clown through a hoop. I shall die like that; it is in the blood. I am an old beau, one of the old school, and the sight of a woman, a pretty woman, stirs me to the tips of my toes. There!

"We are all very much alike in France in this respect; we still remain knights, knights of love and fortune, since God has been abolished whose bodyguard we really were. But nobody can ever get woman out of our hearts; there she is, and there she will remain, and we love her, and shall continue to love her, and go on committing all kinds of follies on her account as long as there is a France on the map of Europe; and even if France were to be wiped off the map, there would always be Frenchmen left.

"When I am in the presence of a woman, of a pretty woman, I feel capable of anything. By Jove! when I feel her looks penetrating me, her confounded looks which set your blood on fire, I should like to do I don't know what; to fight a duel, to have a row, to smash the furniture, in order to show that I am the strongest, the bravest, the most daring and the most devoted of men.

"But I am not the only one, certainly not; the whole French army is like me, I swear to you. From the common soldier to the general, we all start out, from the van to the rear guard, when there is a woman in the case, a pretty woman. Do you remember what Joan of Arc made us do formerly? Come. I will make a bet that if a pretty woman had taken command of the army on the eve of Sedan, when Marshal MacMahon was wounded, we should have broken through the Prussian lines, by Jove! and had a drink out of their guns.

"It was not a Trochu, but a Sainte-Genevieve, who was needed in Paris; and I remember a little anecdote of the war which proves that we are capable of everything in presence of a woman.

"I was a captain, a simple captain, at the time, and I was in command of a detachment of scouts, who were retreating through a district which swarmed with Prussians. We were surrounded, pursued, tired out and half dead with fatigue and hunger, but we were bound to reach Bar-sur-Tain before the morrow, otherwise we should be shot, cut down, massacred. I do not know how we managed to escape so far. However, we had ten leagues to go during the night, ten leagues through the night, ten leagues through the snow, and with empty stomachs, and I thought to myself:

"'It is all over; my poor devils of fellows will never be able to do it.'

"We had eaten nothing since the day before, and the whole day long we remained hidden in a barn, huddled close together, so as not to feel the cold so much, unable to speak or even move, and sleeping by fits and starts, as one does when worn out with fatigue.

"It was dark by five o'clock, that wan darkness of the snow, and I shook my men. Some of them would not get up; they were almost incapable of moving or of standing upright; their joints were stiff from cold and hunger.

"Before us there was a large expanse of flat, bare country; the snow was still falling like a curtain, in large, white flakes, which concealed everything under a thick, frozen coverlet, a coverlet of frozen wool One might have thought that it was the end of the world.

"'Come, my lads, let us start.'

"They looked at the thick white flakes that were coming down, and they seemed to think: 'We have had enough of this; we may just as well die here!' Then I took out my revolver and said:

"'I will shoot the first man who flinches.' And so they set off, but very slowly, like men whose legs were of very little use to them, and I sent four of them three hundred yards ahead to scout, and the others followed pell-mell, walking at random and without any order. I put the strongest in the rear, with orders to quicken the pace of the sluggards with the points of their bayonets in the back.

"The snow seemed as if it were going to bury us alive; it powdered our kepis and cloaks without melting, and made phantoms of us, a kind of spectres of dead, weary soldiers. I said to myself: 'We shall never get out of this except by a miracle.'

"Sometimes we had to stop for a few minutes, on account of those who could not follow us, and then we heard nothing except the falling snow, that vague, almost undiscernible sound made by the falling flakes. Some of the men shook themselves, others did not move, and so I gave the order to set off again. They shouldered their rifles, and with weary feet we resumed our march, when suddenly the scouts fell back. Something had alarmed them; they had heard voices in front of them. I sent forward six men and a sergeant and waited.

"All at once a shrill cry, a woman's cry, pierced through the heavy silence of the snow, and in a few minutes they brought back two prisoners, an old man and a girl, whom I questioned in a low voice. They were escaping from the Prussians, who had occupied their house during the evening and had got drunk. The father was alarmed on his daughter's account, and, without even telling their servants, they had made their escape in the darkness. I saw immediately that they belonged to the better class. I invited them to accompany us, and we started off again, the old man who knew the road acting as our guide.

"It had ceased snowing, the stars appeared and the cold became intense. The girl, who was leaning on her father's arm, walked unsteadily as though in pain, and several times she murmured:

"'I have no feeling at all in my feet'; and I suffered more than she did to see that poor little woman dragging herself like that through the snow. But suddenly she stopped and said:

"'Father, I am so tired that I cannot go any further.'

"The old man wanted to carry her, but he could not even lift her up, and she sank to the ground with a deep sigh. We all gathered round her, and, as for me, I stamped my foot in perplexity, not knowing what to do, and being unwilling to abandon that man and girl like that, when suddenly one of the soldiers, a Parisian whom they had nicknamed Pratique, said:

"'Come, comrades, we must carry the young lady, otherwise we shall not show ourselves Frenchmen, confound it!'

"I really believe that I swore with pleasure. 'That is very good of you, my children,' I said; 'and I will take my share of the burden.'

"We could indistinctly see, through the darkness, the trees of a little wood on the left.

Several of the men went into it, and soon came back with a bundle of branches made into a litter.

"'Who will lend his cape? It is for a pretty girl, comrades,' Pratique said, and ten cloaks were thrown to him. In a moment the girl was lying, warm and comfortable, among them, and was raised upon six shoulders. I placed myself at their head, on the right, well pleased with my position.

"We started off much more briskly, as if we had had a drink of wine, and I even heard some jokes. A woman is quite enough to electrify Frenchmen, you see. The soldiers, who had become cheerful and warm, had almost reformed their ranks, and an old 'franc-tireur' who was following the litter, waiting for his turn to replace the first of his comrades who might give out, said to one of his neighbors, loud enough for me to hear: "'I am not a young man now, but by—-, there is nothing like the women to put courage into you!'

"We went on, almost without stopping, until three o'clock in the morning, when suddenly our scouts fell back once more, and soon the whole detachment showed nothing but a vague shadow on the ground, as the men lay on the snow. I gave my orders in a low voice, and heard the harsh, metallic sound of the cocking, of rifles. For there, in the middle of the plain, some strange object was moving about. It looked like some enormous animal running about, now stretching out like a serpent, now coiling itself into a ball, darting to the right, then to the left, then stopping, and presently starting off again. But presently that wandering shape came nearer, and I saw a dozen lancers at full gallop, one behind the other. They had lost their way and were trying to find it.

"They were so near by that time that I could hear the loud breathing of their horses, the clinking of their swords and the creaking of their saddles, and cried: 'Fire!'

"Fifty rifle shots broke the stillness of the night, then there were four or five reports, and at last one single shot was heard, and when the smoke had cleared away, we saw that the twelve men and nine horses had fallen. Three of the animals were galloping away at a furious pace, and one of them was dragging the dead body of its rider, which rebounded violently from the ground; his foot had caught in the stirrup.

"One of the soldiers behind me gave a terrible laugh and said: 'There will be some widows there!'

"Perhaps he was married. A third added: 'It did not take long!'

"A head emerged from the litter.

"'What is the matter?' she asked; 'are you fighting?'

"'It is nothing, mademoiselle,' I replied; 'we have got rid of a dozen Prussians!'

"'Poor fellows!' she said. But as she was cold, she quickly disappeared beneath the cloaks again, and we started off once more. We marched on for a long time, and at last the sky began to grow lighter. The snow became quite clear, luminous and glistening, and a rosy tint appeared in the east. Suddenly a voice in the distance cried:

"'Who goes there?'

"The whole detachment halted, and I advanced to give the countersign. We had reached the French lines, and, as my men defiled before the outpost, a commandant on horseback, whom I had informed of what had taken place, asked in a sonorous voice, as he saw the litter pass him: 'What have you in there?'

"And immediately a small head covered with light hair appeared, dishevelled and smiling, and replied:

"'It is I, monsieur.'

"At this the men raised a hearty laugh, and we felt quite light-hearted, while Pratique, who was walking by the side of the litter, waved his kepi and shouted:

"'Vive la France!' And I felt really affected. I do not know why, except that I thought it a pretty and gallant thing to say.

"It seemed to me as if we had just saved the whole of France and had done something that other men could not have done, something simple and really patriotic. I shall never forget that little face, you may be sure; and if I had to give my opinion about abolishing drums, trumpets and bugles, I should propose to replace them in every regiment by a pretty girl, and that would be even better than playing the 'Marseillaise: By Jove! it would put some spirit into a trooper to have a Madonna like that, a live Madonna, by the colonel's side."

He was silent for a few moments and then continued, with an air of conviction, and nodding his head:

"All the same, we are very fond of women, we Frenchmen!"

MOTHER SAUVAGE

Fifteen years had passed since I was at Virelogne. I returned there in the autumn to shoot with my friend Serval, who had at last rebuilt his chateau, which the Prussians had destroyed.

I loved that district. It is one of those delightful spots which have a sensuous charm for the eyes. You love it with a physical love. We, whom the country enchants, keep tender memories of certain springs, certain woods, certain pools, certain hills seen very often which have stirred us like joyful events. Sometimes our thoughts turn back to a corner in a forest, or the end of a bank, or an orchard filled with flowers, seen but a single time on some bright day, yet remaining in our hearts like the image of certain women met in the street on a spring morning in their light, gauzy dresses, leaving in soul and body an unsatisfied desire which is not to be forgotten, a feeling that you have just passed by happiness.

At Virelogne I loved the whole countryside, dotted with little woods and crossed by brooks which sparkled in the sun and looked like veins carrying blood to the earth. You fished in them for crawfish, trout and eels. Divine happiness! You could bathe in places and you often found snipe among the high grass which grew along the borders of these small water courses.

I was stepping along light as a goat, watching my two dogs running ahead of me, Serval, a hundred metres to my right, was beating a field of lucerne. I turned round by the thicket which forms the boundary of the wood of Sandres and I saw a cottage in ruins.

Suddenly I remembered it as I had seen it the last time, in 1869, neat, covered with vines, with chickens before the door. What is sadder than a dead house, with its skeleton standing bare and sinister?

I also recalled that inside its doors, after a very tiring day, the good woman had given me a glass of wine to drink and that Serval had told me the history of its people. The father, an old poacher, had been killed by the gendarmes. The son, whom I had once seen, was a tall, dry fellow who also passed for a fierce slayer of game. People called them "Les Sauvage."

Was that a name or a nickname?

I called to Serval. He came up with his long strides like a crane.

I asked him:

"What's become of those people?"

This was his story:

When war was declared the son Sauvage, who was then thirty-three years old, enlisted, leaving his mother alone in the house. People did not pity the old woman very much because she had money; they knew it.

She remained entirely alone in that isolated dwelling, so far from the village, on the edge of the wood. She was not afraid, however, being of the same strain as the men folk—a hardy old woman, tall and thin, who seldom laughed and with whom one never jested. The women of the fields laugh but little in any case, that is men's business. But they themselves have sad and narrowed hearts, leading a melancholy, gloomy life. The peasants imbibe a little noisy merriment at the tavern, but their helpmates always have grave, stern countenances. The muscles of their faces have never learned the motions of laughter.

Mother Sauvage continued her ordinary existence in her cottage, which was soon covered by the snows. She came to the village once a week to get bread and a little meat. Then she returned to her house. As there was talk of wolves, she went out with a gun upon her shoulder—her son's gun, rusty and with the butt worn by the rubbing of the hand—and she was a strange sight, the tall "Sauvage," a little bent, going with slow strides over the snow, the muzzle of the piece extending beyond the black headdress, which confined her head and imprisoned her white hair, which no one had ever seen.

One day a Prussian force arrived. It was billeted upon the inhabitants, according to the property and resources of each. Four were allotted to the old woman, who was known to be rich.

They were four great fellows with fair complexion, blond beards and blue eyes, who had not grown thin in spite of the fatigue which they had endured already and who also, though in a conquered country, had remained kind and gentle. Alone with this aged woman, they showed themselves full of consideration, sparing her, as much as they could, all expense and fatigue. They could be seen, all four of them, making their toilet at the well in their shirt-sleeves in the gray dawn, splashing with great swishes of water their pink-white northern skin, while La Mere Sauvage went and came, preparing their soup. They would be seen cleaning the kitchen, rubbing the tiles, splitting wood, peeling potatoes, doing up all the housework like four good sons around their mother.

But the old woman thought always of her own son, so tall and thin, with his hooked nose and his brown eyes and his heavy mustache which made a roll of black hair upon his lip. She asked every day of each of the soldiers who were installed beside her hearth: "Do you know where the French marching regiment, No. 23, was sent? My boy is in it."

They invariably answered, "No, we don't know, don't know a thing at all." And, understanding her pain and her uneasiness—they who had mothers, too, there at home—they rendered her a thousand little services. She loved them well, moreover, her four enemies, since the peasantry have no patriotic hatred; that belongs to the upper class alone. The humble, those who pay the most because they are poor and because every new burden crushes them down; those who are killed in masses, who make the true cannon's prey because they are so many; those, in fine, who suffer most cruelly the atrocious miseries of war because they are the feeblest and offer least resistance—they hardly understand at all those bellicose ardors, that excitable sense of honor or those pretended political combinations which in six months exhaust two nations, the conqueror with the conquered.

They said in the district, in speaking of the Germans of La Mere Sauvage:

"There are four who have found a soft place."

Now, one morning, when the old woman was alone in the house, she observed, far off on the plain, a man coming toward her dwelling. Soon she recognized him; it was the postman to distribute the letters. He gave her a folded paper and she drew out of her case the spectacles which she used for sewing. Then she read:

MADAME SAUVAGE: This letter is to tell you sad news. Your boy

Victor was killed yesterday by a shell which almost cut him in two.

I was near by, as we stood next each other in the company, and he told me about you and asked me to let you know on the same day if

anything happened to him.

I took his watch, which was in his pocket, to bring it back to you

when the war is done.

CESAIRE RIVOT,

Soldier of the 2d class, March. Reg. No. 23.

The letter was dated three weeks back.

She did not cry at all. She remained motionless, so overcome and stupefied that she did not even suffer as yet. She thought: "There's Victor killed now." Then little by little the tears came to her eyes and the sorrow filled her heart. Her thoughts came, one by one, dreadful, torturing. She would never kiss him again, her child, her big boy, never again! The gendarmes had killed the father, the Prussians had killed the son. He had been cut in two by a cannon-ball. She seemed to see the thing, the horrible thing: the head falling, the eyes open, while he chewed the corner of his big mustache as he always did in moments of anger.

What had they done with his body afterward? If they had only let her have her boy back as they had brought back her husband—with the bullet in the middle of the forehead!

But she heard a noise of voices. It was the Prussians returning from the village. She hid her letter very quickly in her pocket, and she received them quietly, with her ordinary face, having had time to wipe her eyes.

They were laughing, all four, delighted, for they brought with them a fine rabbit—stolen, doubtless—and they made signs to the old woman that there was to be something good to east.

She set herself to work at once to prepare breakfast, but when it came to killing the rabbit, her heart failed her. And yet it was not the first. One of the soldiers struck it down with a blow of his fist behind the ears.

The beast once dead, she skinned the red body, but the sight of the blood which she was touching, and which covered her hands, and which she felt cooling and coagulating, made her tremble from head to foot, and she kept seeing her big boy cut in two, bloody, like this still palpitating animal.

She sat down at table with the Prussians, but she could not eat, not even a mouthful. They devoured the rabbit without bothering themselves about her. She looked at them sideways, without speaking, her face so impassive that they perceived nothing.

All of a sudden she said: "I don't even know your names, and here's a whole month that we've been together." They understood, not without difficulty, what she wanted, and told their names.

That was not sufficient; she had them written for her on a paper, with the addresses of their families, and, resting her spectacles on her great nose, she contemplated that strange handwriting, then folded the sheet and put it in her pocket, on top of the letter which told her of the death of her son.

When the meal was ended she said to the men:

"I am going to work for you."

And she began to carry up hay into the loft where they slept.

They were astonished at her taking all this trouble; she explained to them that thus they would not be so cold; and they helped her. They heaped the stacks of hay as high as the straw roof, and in that manner they made a sort of great chamber with four walls of fodder, warm and perfumed, where they should sleep splendidly.

At dinner one of them was worried to see that La Mere Sauvage still ate nothing. She told him that she had pains in her stomach. Then she kindled a good fire to warm herself, and the four Germans ascended to their lodging-place by the ladder which served them every night for this purpose.

As soon as they closed the trapdoor the old woman removed the ladder, then opened the outside door noiselessly and went back to look for more bundles of straw, with which she filled her kitchen. She went barefoot in the snow, so softly that no sound was heard. From time to time she listened to the sonorous and unequal snoring of the four soldiers who were fast asleep.

When she judged her preparations to be sufficient, she threw one of the bundles into the fireplace, and when it was alight she scattered it over all the others. Then she went outside again and looked.

In a few seconds the whole interior of the cottage was illumined with a brilliant light and became a frightful brasier, a gigantic fiery furnace, whose glare streamed out of the narrow window and threw a glittering beam upon the snow.

Then a great cry issued from the top of the house; it was a clamor of men shouting heartrending calls of anguish and of terror. Finally the trapdoor having given way, a whirlwind of fire shot up into the loft, pierced the straw roof, rose to the sky like the immense flame of a torch, and all the cottage flared.

Nothing more was heard therein but the crackling of the fire, the cracking of the walls, the falling of the rafters. Suddenly the roof fell in and the burning carcass of the dwelling hurled a great plume of sparks into the air, amid a cloud of smoke.

The country, all white, lit up by the fire, shone like a cloth of silver tinted with red.

A bell, far off, began to toll.

The old "Sauvage" stood before her ruined dwelling, armed with her gun, her son's gun, for fear one of those men might escape.

When she saw that it was ended, she threw her weapon into the brasier. A loud report followed.

People were coming, the peasants, the Prussians.

They found the woman seated on the trunk of a tree, calm and satisfied.

A German officer, but speaking French like a son of France, demanded:

"Where are your soldiers?"

She reached her bony arm toward the red heap of fire which was almost out and answered with a strong voice:

"There!"

They crowded round her. The Prussian asked:

"How did it take fire?"

"It was I who set it on fire."

They did not believe her, they thought that the sudden disaster had made her crazy. While all pressed round and listened, she told the story from beginning to end, from the arrival of the letter to the last shriek of the men who were burned with her house, and never omitted a detail.

When she had finished, she drew two pieces of paper from her pocket, and, in order to distinguish them by the last gleams of the fire, she again adjusted her spectacles. Then she said, showing one:

"That, that is the death of Victor." Showing the other, she added, indicating the red ruins with a bend of the head: "Here are their names, so that you can write home." She quietly held a sheet of paper out to the officer, who held her by the shoulders, and she continued:

"You must write how it happened, and you must say to their mothers that it was I who did that, Victoire Simon, la Sauvage! Do not forget."

The officer shouted some orders in German. They seized her, they threw her against the walls of her house, still hot. Then twelve men drew quickly up before her, at twenty paces. She did not move. She had understood; she waited.

An order rang out, followed instantly by a long report. A belated shot went off by itself, after the others.

The old woman did not fall. She sank as though they had cut off her legs.

The Prussian officer approached. She was almost cut in two, and in her withered hand she held her letter bathed with blood.

My friend Serval added:

"It was by way of reprisal that the Germans destroyed the chateau of the district, which belonged to me."

I thought of the mothers of those four fine fellows burned in that house and of the horrible heroism of that other mother shot against the wall.

And I picked up a little stone, still blackened by the flames.

EPIPHANY

I should say I did remember that Epiphany supper during the war! exclaimed Count de Garens, an army captain.

I was quartermaster of cavalry at the time, and for a fortnight had been scouting in front of the German advance guard. The evening before we had cut down a few Uhlans and had lost three men, one of whom was that poor little Raudeville. You remember Joseph de Raudeville, of course.

Well, on that day my commanding officer ordered me to take six troopers and to go and occupy the village of Porterin, where there had been five skirmishes in three weeks, and to hold it all night. There were not twenty houses left standing, not a dozen houses in that wasps' nest. So I took ten troopers and set out about four o'clock, and at five o'clock, while it was still pitch dark, we reached the first houses of Porterin. I halted and ordered Marchas—you know Pierre de Marchas, who afterward married little Martel-Auvelin, the daughter of the Marquis de Martel-Auvelin—to go alone into the village, and to report to me what he saw.

I had selected nothing but volunteers, all men of good family. It is pleasant when on duty not to be forced to be on intimate terms with unpleasant fellows. This Marchas was as smart as possible, cunning as a fox and supple as a serpent. He could scent the Prussians as a dog can scent a hare, could discover food where we should have died of hunger without him, and obtained information from everybody, and information which was always reliable, with incredible cleverness.

In ten minutes he returned. "All right," he said; "there have been no Prussians here for three days. It is a sinister place, is this village. I have been talking to a Sister of Mercy, who is caring for four or five wounded men in an abandoned convent."

I ordered them to ride on, and we entered the principal street. On the right and left we could vaguely see roofless walls, which were hardly visible in the profound darkness. Here and there a light was burning in a room; some family had remained to keep its house standing as well as they were able; a family of brave or of poor people. The rain began to fall, a fine, icy cold rain, which froze as it fell on our cloaks. The horses stumbled against stones, against beams, against furniture. Marchas guided us, going before us on foot, and leading his horse by the bridle.

"Where are you taking us to?" I asked him. And he replied: "I have a place for us to lodge in, and a rare good one." And we presently stopped before a small house, evidently belonging to some proprietor of the middle class. It stood on the street, was quite inclosed, and had a garden in the rear.

Marchas forced open the lock by means of a big stone which he picked up near the garden gate; then he mounted the steps, smashed in the front door with his feet and shoulders, lit a bit of wax candle, which he was never without, and went before us into the comfortable apartments of some rich private individual, guiding us with admirable assurance, as if he lived in this house which he now saw for the first time.

Two troopers remained outside to take care of our horses, and Marchas said to stout Ponderel, who followed him: "The stables must be on the left; I saw that as we came in; go and put the animals up there, for we do not need them"; and then, turning to me, he said: "Give your orders, confound it all!"

This fellow always astonished me, and I replied with a laugh: "I will post my sentinels at the country approaches and will return to you here."

"How many men are you going to take?"

"Five. The others will relieve them at five o'clock in the evening."

"Very well. Leave me four to look after provisions, to do the cooking and to set the table. I will go and find out where the wine is hidden."

I went off, to reconnoitre the deserted streets until they ended in the open country, so as to post my sentries there.

Half an hour later I was back, and found Marchas lounging in a great easy-chair, the covering of which he had taken off, from love of luxury, as he said. He was warming his feet at the fire and smoking an excellent cigar, whose perfume filled the room. He was alone, his elbows resting on the arms of the chair, his head sunk between his shoulders, his cheeks flushed, his eyes bright, and looking delighted.

I heard the noise of plates and dishes in the next room, and Marchas said * to me, smiling in a contented manner: "This is famous; I found the champagne under the flight of steps outside, the brandy—fifty bottles of the very finest in the kitchen garden under a pear tree, which did not seem to me to be quite straight when I looked at it by the light of my lantern. As for solids, we have two fowls, a goose, a duck, and three pigeons. They are being cooked at this moment. It is a delightful district."

I sat down opposite him, and the fire in the grate was burning my nose and cheeks. "Where did you find this wood?" I asked. "Splendid wood," he replied. "The owner's carriage. It is the paint which is causing all this flame, an essence of punch and varnish. A capital house!"

I laughed, for I saw the creature was funny, and he went on: "Fancy this being the Epiphany! I have had a bean put into the goose dressing; but there is no queen; it is really very annoying!" And I repeated like an echo: "It is annoying, but what do you want me to do in the matter?" "To find some, of course." "Some women. Women?—you must be mad?" "I managed to find the brandy under the pear tree, and the champagne under the steps; and yet there was nothing to guide me, while as for you, a petticoat is a sure bait. Go and look, old fellow."

He looked so grave, so convinced, that I could not tell whether he was joking or not, and so I replied: "Look here, Marchas, are you having a joke with me?" "I never joke on duty." "But where the devil do you expect me to find any women?" "Where you like; there must be two or three remaining in the neighborhood, so ferret them out and bring them here."

I got up, for it was too hot in front of the fire, and Marchas went off:

"Do you want an idea?" "Yes." "Go and see the priest." "The priest? What for?" "Ask him to supper, and beg him to bring a woman with him." "The priest! A woman! Ha! ha! ha!"

But Marchas continued with extraordinary gravity: "I am not laughing; go and find the priest and tell him how we are situated, and, as he must be horribly dull, he will come. But tell him that we want one woman at least, a lady, of course, since we, are all men of the world. He is sure to know his female parishioners on the tips of his fingers, and if there is one to suit us, and you manage it well, he will suggest her to you."

"Come, come, Marchas, what are you thinking of?" "My dear Garens, you can do this quite well. It will even be very funny. We are well bred, by Jove! and we will put on our most distinguished manners and our grandest style. Tell the abbe who we are, make him laugh, soften his heart, coax him and persuade him!" "No, it is impossible."

He drew his chair close to mine, and as he knew my special weakness, the scamp continued: "Just think what a swaggering thing it will be to do and how amusing to tell about; the whole army will talk about it, and it will give you a famous reputation."

I hesitated, for the adventure rather tempted me, and he persisted: "Come, my little Garens. You are the head of this detachment, and you alone can go and call on the head of the church in this neighborhood. I beg of you to go, and I promise you that after the war I will relate the whole affair in verse in the Revue de Deux Mondes. You owe this much to your men, for you have made them march enough during the last month."

I got up at last and asked: "Where is the priest's house?" "Take the second turning at the end of the street, you will see an avenue, and at the end of the avenue you will find the church. The parsonage is beside it." As I went out, he called out: "Tell him the bill of fare, to make him hungry!"

I discovered the ecclesiastic's little house without any difficulty; it was by the side of a large, ugly brick church. I knocked at the door with my fist, as there was neither bell nor knocker, and a loud voice from inside asked: "Who is there?" To which I replied: "A quartermaster of hussars."

I heard the noise of bolts and of a key being turned, and found myself face to face with a tall priest with a large stomach, the chest of a prizefighter, formidable hands projecting from turned-up sleeves, a red face, and the look of a kind man. I gave him a military salute and said: "Good-day, Monsieur le Cure."

He had feared a surprise, some marauders' ambush, and he smiled as he replied: "Good-day, my friend; come in." I followed him into a small room with a red tiled floor, in which a small fire was burning, very different to Marchas' furnace, and he gave me a chair and said: "What can I do for you?" "Monsieur, allow me first of all to introduce myself"; and I gave him my card, which he took and read half aloud: "Le Comte de Garens."

I continued: "There are eleven of us here, Monsieur l'Abbe, five on picket duty, and six installed at the house of an unknown inhabitant. The names of the six are: Garens, myself; Pierre de Marchas, Ludovic de Ponderel, Baron d'Streillis, Karl Massouligny, the painter's son, and Joseph Herbon, a young musician. I have come to ask you, in their name and my own, to do us the honor of supping with us. It is an Epiphany supper, Monsieur le Cure, and we should like to make it a little cheerful."

The priest smiled and murmured: "It seems to me to be hardly a suitable occasion for amusing one's self." And I replied: "We are fighting during the day, monsieur. Fourteen of our comrades have been killed in a month, and three fell as late as yesterday. It is war time. We stake our life at every moment; have we not, therefore, the right to amuse ourselves freely? We are Frenchmen, we like to laugh, and we can laugh everywhere. Our fathers laughed on the scaffold! This evening we should like to cheer ourselves up a little, like gentlemen, and not like soldiers; you understand me, I hope. Are we wrong?"

He replied quickly: "You are quite right, my friend, and I accept your invitation with great pleasure." Then he called out: "Hermance!"

An old bent, wrinkled, horrible peasant woman appeared and said: "What do you want?"

"I shall not dine at home, my daughter." "Where are you going to dine then?" "With some gentlemen, the hussars."

I felt inclined to say: "Bring your servant with you," just to see Marchas' face, but I did not venture, and continued: "Do you know any one among your parishioners, male or female, whom I could invite as well?" He hesitated, reflected, and then said: "No, I do not know anybody!"

I persisted: "Nobody! Come, monsieur, think; it would be very nice to have some ladies, I mean to say, some married couples! I know nothing about your parishioners. The baker and his wife, the grocer, the—the—the—watchmaker—the—shoemaker—the—the druggist with Mrs. Druggist. We have a good spread and plenty of wine, and we should be enchanted to leave pleasant recollections of ourselves with the people here."

The priest thought again for a long time, and then said resolutely: "No, there is nobody." I began to laugh. "By Jove, Monsieur le Cure, it is very annoying not to have an Epiphany queen, for we have the bean. Come, think. Is there not a married mayor, or a married deputy mayor, or a married municipal councillor or a schoolmaster?" "No, all the ladies have gone away." "What, is there not in the whole place some good tradesman's wife with her good tradesman, to whom we might give this pleasure, for it would be a pleasure to them, a great pleasure under present circumstances?"

But, suddenly, the cure began to laugh, and laughed so violently that he fairly shook, and presently exclaimed: "Ha! ha! ha! I have got what you want, yes. I have got what you want! Ha! ha! ha! We will laugh and enjoy ourselves, my children; we will have some fun. How pleased the ladies will be, I say, how delighted they will be! Ha! ha! Where are you staying?"

I described the house, and he understood where it was. "Very good," he said. "It belongs to Monsieur Bertin-Lavaille. I will be there in half an hour, with four ladies! Ha! ha! ha! four ladies!"

He went out with me, still laughing, and left me, repeating: "That is capital; in half an hour at Bertin-Lavaille's house."

I returned quickly, very much astonished and very much puzzled. "Covers for how many?" Marchas asked, as soon as he saw me. "Eleven. There are six of us hussars, besides the priest and four ladies." He was thunderstruck, and I was triumphant. He repeated: "Four ladies! Did you say, four ladies?" "I said four women." "Real women?" "Real women." "Well, accept my compliments!" "I will, for I deserve them."

He got out of his armchair, opened the door, and I saw a beautiful white tablecloth on a long table, round which three hussars in blue aprons were setting out the plates and glasses. "There are some women coming!" Marchas cried. And the three men began to dance and to cheer with all their might.

Everything was ready, and we were waiting. We waited for nearly an hour, while a delicious smell of roast poultry pervaded the whole house. At last, however, a knock against the shutters made us all jump up at the same moment. Stout Ponderel ran to open the door, and in less than a minute a little Sister of Mercy appeared in the doorway. She was thin, wrinkled and timid, and successively greeted the four bewildered hussars who saw her enter. Behind her, the noise of sticks sounded on the tiled floor in the vestibule, and as soon as she had come into the drawing-room, I saw three old heads in white caps, following each other one by one, who came in, swaying with different movements, one inclining to the right, while the other inclined to the left. And three worthy women appeared, limping, dragging their legs behind them, crippled by illness and deformed through old age, three infirm old women, past service, the only three pensioners who were able to walk in the home presided over by Sister Saint-Benedict.

She had turned round to her invalids, full of anxiety for them, and then, seeing my quartermaster's stripes, she said to me: "I am much obliged to you for thinking of these poor women. They have very little pleasure in life, and you are at the same time giving them a great treat and doing them a great honor."

I saw the priest, who had remained in the dark hallway, and was laughing heartily, and I began to laugh in my turn, especially when I saw Marchas' face. Then, motioning the nun to the seats, I said:

"Sit down, sister; we are very proud and very happy that you have accepted our unpretentious invitation."

She took three chairs which stood against the wall, set them before the fire, led her three old women to them, settled them on them, took their sticks and shawls, which she put into a corner, and then, pointing to the first, a thin woman with an enormous stomach, who was evidently suffering from the dropsy, she said: "This is Mother Paumelle; whose husband was killed by falling from a roof, and whose son died in Africa; she is sixty years old." Then she pointed to another, a tall woman, whose head trembled unceasingly: "This is Mother Jean-Jean, who is sixty-seven. She is nearly blind, for her face was terribly singed in a fire, and her right leg was half burned off."

Then she pointed to the third, a sort of dwarf, with protruding, round, stupid eyes, which she rolled incessantly in all directions, "This is La Putois, an idiot. She is only forty-four."

I bowed to the three women as if I were being presented to some royal highnesses, and turning to the priest, I said: "You are an excellent man, Monsieur l'Abbe, to whom all of us here owe a debt of gratitude."

Everybody was laughing, in fact, except Marchas, who seemed furious, and just then Karl Massouligny cried: "Sister Saint-Benedict, supper is on the table!"

I made her go first with the priest, then I helped up Mother Paumelle, whose arm I took and dragged her into the next room, which was no easy task, for she seemed heavier than a lump of iron.

Stout Ponderel gave his arm to Mother Jean-Jean, who bemoaned her crutch, and little Joseph Herbon took the idiot, La Putois, to the dining-room, which was filled with the odor of the viands.

As soon as we were opposite our plates, the sister clapped her hands three times, and, with the precision of soldiers presenting arms, the women made a rapid sign of the cross, and then the priest slowly repeated the Benedictus in Latin. Then we sat down, and the two fowls appeared, brought in by Marchas, who chose to wait at table, rather than to sit down as a guest to this ridiculous repast.

But I cried: "Bring the champagne at once!" and a cork flew out with the noise of a pistol, and in spite of the resistance of the priest and of the kind sister, the three hussars, sitting by the side of the three invalids, emptied their three full glasses down their throats by force.

Massouligny, who possessed the faculty of making himself at home, and of being on good terms with every one, wherever he was, made love to Mother Paumelle in the drollest manner. The dropsical woman, who had retained her cheerfulness in spite of her misfortunes, answered him banteringly in a high falsetto voice which appeared as if it were put on, and she laughed so heartily at her neighbor's jokes that it was quite alarming. Little Herbon had seriously undertaken the task of making the idiot drunk, and Baron d'Streillis, whose wits were not always particularly sharp, was questioning old Jean-Jean about the life, the habits, and the rules of the hospital.

The nun said to Massouligny in consternation:

"Oh! oh! you will make her ill; pray do not make her laugh like that, monsieur. Oh! monsieur—" Then she got up and rushed at Herbon to take from him a full glass which he was hastily emptying down La Putois' throat, while the priest shook with laughter, and said to the sister: "Never mind; just this once, it will not hurt them. Do leave them alone."

After the two fowls they ate the duck, which was flanked by the three pigeons and the blackbird, and then the goose appeared, smoking, golden-brown, and diffusing a warm odor of hot, browned roast meat. La Paumelle, who was getting lively, clapped her hands; La Jean-Jean left off answering the baron's numerous questions, and La Putois uttered grunts of pleasure, half cries and half sighs, as little children do when one shows them candy. "Allow me to take charge of this animal," the cure said. "I understand these sort of operations better than most people." "Certainly, Monsieur l'Abbe," and the sister said: "How would it be to open the window a little? They are too warm, and I am afraid they will be ill."

I turned to Marchas: "Open the window for a minute." He did so; the cold outer air as it came in made the candles flare, and the steam from the goose, which the cure was scientifically carving, with a table napkin round his neck, whirl about. We watched him doing it, without speaking now, for we were interested in his attractive handiwork, and seized with renewed appetite at the sight of that enormous golden-brown bird, whose limbs fell one after another into the brown gravy at the bottom of the dish. At that moment, in the midst of that greedy silence which kept us all attentive, the distant report of a shot came in at the open window.

I started to my feet so quickly that my chair fell down behind me, and I shouted: "To saddle, all of you! You, Marchas, take two men and go and see what it is. I shall expect you back here in five minutes." And while the three riders went off at full gallop through the night, I got into the saddle with my three remaining hussars, in front of the steps of the villa, while the cure, the sister and the three old women showed their frightened faces at the window.

We heard nothing more, except the barking of a dog in the distance. The rain had ceased, and it was cold, very cold, and soon I heard the gallop of a horse, of a single horse, coming back. It was Marchas, and I called out to him: "Well?" "It is nothing; Francois has wounded an old peasant who refused to answer his challenge: 'Who goes there?' and who continued to advance in spite of the order to keep off; but they are bringing him here, and we shall see what is the matter."

I gave orders for the horses to be put back in the stable, and I sent my two soldiers to meet the others, and returned to the house. Then the cure, Marchas, and I took a mattress into the room to lay the wounded man on; the sister tore up a table napkin in order to make lint, while the three frightened women remained huddled up in a corner.

Soon I heard the rattle of sabres on the road, and I took a candle to show a light to the men who were returning; and they soon appeared, carrying that inert, soft, long, sinister object which a human body becomes when life no longer sustains it.

They put the wounded man on the mattress that had been prepared for him, and I saw at the first glance that he was dying. He had the death rattle and was spitting up blood, which ran out of the corners of his mouth at every gasp. The man was covered with blood! His cheeks, his beard, his hair, his neck and his clothes seemed to have been soaked, to have been dipped in a red tub; and that blood stuck to him, and had become a dull color which was horrible to look at.

The wounded man, wrapped up in a large shepherd's cloak, occasionally opened his dull, vacant eyes, which seemed stupid with astonishment, like those of animals wounded by a sportsman, which fall at his feet, more than half dead already, stupefied with terror and surprise.

The cure exclaimed: "Ah, it is old Placide, the shepherd from Les Moulins. He is deaf, poor man, and heard nothing. Ah! Oh, God! they have killed the unhappy man!" The sister had opened his blouse and shirt, and was looking at a little blue hole in his chest, which was not bleeding any more. "There is nothing to be done," she said.

The shepherd was gasping terribly and bringing up blood with every last breath, and in his throat, to the very depth of his lungs, they could hear an ominous and continued gurgling. The cure, standing in front of him, raised his right hand, made the sign of the cross, and in a slow and solemn voice pronounced the Latin words which purify men's souls, but before they were finished, the old man's body trembled violently, as if something had given way inside him, and he ceased to breathe. He was dead.

When I turned round, I saw a sight which was even more horrible than the death struggle of this unfortunate man; the three old women were standing up huddled close together, hideous, and grimacing with fear and horror. I went up to them, and they began to utter shrill screams, while La Jean-Jean, whose burned leg could no longer support her, fell to the ground at full length.

Sister Saint-Benedict left the dead man, ran up to her infirm old women, and without a word or a look for me, wrapped their shawls round them, gave them their crutches, pushed them to the door, made them go out, and disappeared with them into the dark night.

I saw that I could not even let a hussar accompany them, for the mere rattle of a sword would have sent them mad with fear.

The cure was still looking at the dead man; but at last he turned round to me and said:

"Oh! What a horrible thing!"

THE MUSTACHE

CHATEAU DE SOLLES,

July 30, 1883.

My Dear Lucy:

I have no news. We live in the drawing-room, looking out at the rain. We cannot go out in this frightful weather, so we have theatricals. How stupid they are, my dear, these drawing entertainments in the repertory of real life! All is forced, coarse, heavy. The jokes are like cannon balls, smashing everything in their passage. No wit, nothing natural, no sprightliness, no elegance. These literary men, in truth, know nothing of society. They are perfectly ignorant of how people think and talk in our set. I do not mind if they despise our customs, our conventionalities, but I do not forgive them for not knowing them. When they want to be humorous they make puns that would do for a barrack; when they try to be jolly, they give us jokes that they must have picked up on the outer boulevard in those beer houses artists are supposed to frequent, where one has heard the same students' jokes for fifty years.

So we have taken to Theatricals. As we are only two women, my husband takes the part of a soubrette, and, in order to do that, he has shaved off his mustache. You cannot imagine, my dear Lucy, how it changes him! I no longer recognize him-by day or at night. If he did not let it grow again I think I should no longer love him; he looks so horrid like this.

In fact, a man without a mustache is no longer a man. I do not care much for a beard; it almost always makes a man look untidy. But a mustache, oh, a mustache is indispensable to a manly face. No, you would never believe how these little hair bristles on the upper lip are a relief to the eye and good in other ways. I have thought over the matter a great deal but hardly dare to write my thoughts. Words look so different on paper and the subject is so difficult, so delicate, so dangerous that it requires infinite skill to tackle it.

Well, when my husband appeared, shaven, I understood at once that I never could fall in love with a strolling actor nor a preacher, even if it were Father Didon, the most charming of all! Later when I was alone with him (my husband) it was worse still. Oh, my dear Lucy, never let yourself be kissed by a man without a mustache; their kisses have no flavor, none whatever! They no longer have the charm, the mellowness and the snap —yes, the snap— of a real kiss. The mustache is the spice.

Imagine placing to your lips a piece of dry—or moist—parchment. That is the kiss of the man without a mustache. It is not worth while.

Whence comes this charm of the mustache, will you tell me? Do I know myself? It tickles your face, you feel it approaching your mouth and it sends a little shiver through you down to the tips of your toes.

And on your neck! Have you ever felt a mustache on your neck? It intoxicates you, makes you feel creepy, goes to the tips of your fingers. You wriggle, shake your shoulders, toss back your head. You wish to get away and at the same time to remain there; it is delightful, but irritating. But how good it is!

A lip without a mustache is like a body without clothing; and one must wear clothes, very few, if you like, but still some clothing.

I recall a sentence (uttered by a politician) which has been running in my mind for three months. My husband, who keeps up with the newspapers, read me one evening a very singular speech by our Minister of Agriculture, who was called M. Meline. He may have been superseded by this time. I do not know.

I was paying no attention, but the name Meline struck me. It recalled, I do not exactly know why, the 'Scenes de la vie de boheme'. I thought it was about some grisette. That shows how scraps of the speech entered my mind. This M. Meline was making this statement to the people of Amiens, I believe, and I have ever since been trying to understand what he meant: "There is no patriotism without agriculture!" Well, I have just discovered his meaning, and I affirm in my turn that there is no love without a mustache. When you say it that way it sounds comical, does it not?

There is no love without a mustache!

"There is no patriotism without agriculture," said M. Meline, and he was right, that minister; I now understand why.

From a very different point of view the mustache is essential. It gives character to the face. It makes a man look gentle, tender, violent, a monster, a rake, enterprising! The hairy man, who does not shave off his whiskers, never has a refined look, for his features are concealed; and the shape of the jaw and the chin betrays a great deal to those who understand.

The man with a mustache retains his own peculiar expression and his refinement at the same time.

And how many different varieties of mustaches there are! Sometimes they are twisted, curled, coquettish. Those seem to be chiefly devoted to women.

Sometimes they are pointed, sharp as needles, and threatening. That kind prefers wine, horses and war.

Sometimes they are enormous, overhanging, frightful. These big ones generally conceal a fine disposition, a kindliness that borders on weakness and a gentleness that savors of timidity.

But what I adore above all in the mustache is that it is French, altogether French. It came from our ancestors, the Gauls, and has remained the insignia of our national character.

It is boastful, gallant and brave. It sips wine gracefully and knows how to laugh with refinement, while the broad-bearded jaws are clumsy in everything they do.

I recall something that made me weep all my tears and also—I see it now—made me love a mustache on a man's face.

It was during the war, when I was living with my father. I was a young girl then. One day there was a skirmish near the chateau. I had heard the firing of the cannon and of the artillery all the morning, and that evening a German colonel came and took up his abode in our house. He left the following day.

My father was informed that there were a number of dead bodies in the fields. He had them brought to our place so that they might be buried together. They were laid all along the great avenue of pines as fast as they brought them in, on both sides of the avenue, and as they began to smell unpleasant, their bodies were covered with earth until the deep trench could be dug. Thus one saw only their heads which seemed to protrude from the clayey earth and were almost as yellow, with their closed eyes.

I wanted to see them. But when I saw those two rows of frightful faces, I thought I should faint. However, I began to look at them, one by one, trying to guess what kind of men these had been.

The uniforms were concealed beneath the earth, and yet immediately, yes, immediately, my dear, I recognized the Frenchmen by their mustache!

Some of them had shaved on the very day of the battle, as though they wished to be elegant up to the last; others seemed to have a week's growth, but all wore the French mustache, very plain, the proud mustache that seems to say: "Do not take me for my bearded friend, little one; I am a brother."

And I cried, oh, I cried a great deal more than I should if I had not recognized them, the poor dead fellows.

It was wrong of me to tell you this. Now I am sad and cannot chatter any

longer. Well, good-by, dear Lucy. I send you a hearty kiss. Long live

the mustache!

JEANNE.

MADAME BAPTISTE

The first thing I did was to look at the clock as I entered the waiting-room of the station at Loubain, and I found that I had to wait two hours and ten minutes for the Paris express.

I had walked twenty miles and felt suddenly tired. Not seeing anything on the station walls to amuse me, I went outside and stood there racking my brains to think of something to do. The street was a kind of boulevard, planted with acacias, and on either side a row of houses of varying shape and different styles of architecture, houses such as one only sees in a small town, and ascended a slight hill, at the extreme end of which there were some trees, as though it ended in a park.

From time to time a cat crossed the street and jumped over the gutters carefully. A cur sniffed at every tree and hunted for scraps from the kitchens, but I did not see a single human being, and I felt listless and disheartened. What could I do with myself? I was already thinking of the inevitable and interminable visit to the small cafe at the railway station, where I should have to sit over a glass of undrinkable beer and the illegible newspaper, when I saw a funeral procession coming out of a side street into the one in which I was, and the sight of the hearse was a relief to me. It would, at any rate, give me something to do for ten minutes.

Suddenly, however, my curiosity was aroused. The hearse was followed by eight gentlemen, one of whom was weeping, while the others were chatting together, but there was no priest, and I thought to myself:

"This is a non-religious funeral," and then I reflected that a town like Loubain must contain at least a hundred freethinkers, who would have made a point of making a manifestation. What could it be, then? The rapid pace of the procession clearly proved that the body was to be buried without ceremony, and, consequently, without the intervention of the Church.

My idle curiosity framed the most complicated surmises, and as the hearse passed me, a strange idea struck me, which was to follow it, with the eight gentlemen. That would take up my time for an hour, at least, and I accordingly walked with the others, with a sad look on my face, and, on seeing this, the two last turned round in surprise, and then spoke to each other in a low voice.

No doubt they were asking each other whether I belonged to the town, and then they consulted the two in front of them, who stared at me in turn. This close scrutiny annoyed me, and to put an end to it I went up to them, and, after bowing, I said:

"I beg your pardon, gentlemen, for interrupting your conversation, but, seeing a civil funeral, I have followed it, although I did not know the deceased gentleman whom you are accompanying."

"It was a woman," one of them said.

I was much surprised at hearing this, and asked:

"But it is a civil funeral, is it not?"

The other gentleman, who evidently wished to tell me all about it, then said: "Yes and no. The clergy have refused to allow us the use of the church."

On hearing this I uttered a prolonged "A-h!" of astonishment. I could not understand it at all, but my obliging neighbor continued:

"It is rather a long story. This young woman committed suicide, and that is the reason why she cannot be buried with any religious ceremony. The gentleman who is walking first, and who is crying, is her husband."

I replied with some hesitation:

"You surprise and interest me very much, monsieur. Shall I be indiscreet if I ask you to tell me the facts of the case? If I am troubling you, forget that I have said anything about the matter."

The gentleman took my arm familiarly.

"Not at all, not at all. Let us linger a little behind the others, and I will tell it you, although it is a very sad story. We have plenty of time before getting to the cemetery, the trees of which you see up yonder, for it is a stiff pull up this hill."

And he began:

"This young woman, Madame Paul Hamot, was the daughter of a wealthy merchant in the neighborhood, Monsieur Fontanelle. When she was a mere child of eleven, she had a shocking adventure; a footman attacked her and she nearly died. A terrible criminal case was the result, and the man was sentenced to penal servitude for life.

"The little girl grew up, stigmatized by disgrace, isolated, without any companions; and grown-up people would scarcely kiss her, for they thought that they would soil their lips if they touched her forehead, and she became a sort of monster, a phenomenon to all the town. People said to each other in a whisper: 'You know, little Fontanelle,' and everybody turned away in the streets when she passed. Her parents could not even get a nurse to take her out for a walk, as the other servants held aloof from her, as if contact with her would poison everybody who came near her.

"It was pitiable to see the poor child go and play every afternoon. She remained quite by herself, standing by her maid and looking at the other children amusing themselves. Sometimes, yielding to an irresistible desire to mix with the other children, she advanced timidly, with nervous gestures, and mingled with a group, with furtive steps, as if conscious of her own disgrace. And immediately the mothers, aunts and nurses would come running from every seat and take the children entrusted to their care by the hand and drag them brutally away.

"Little Fontanelle remained isolated, wretched, without understanding what it meant, and then she began to cry, nearly heartbroken with grief, and then she used to run and hide her head in her nurse's lap, sobbing.

"As she grew up, it was worse still. They kept the girls from her, as if she were stricken with the plague. Remember that she had nothing to learn, nothing; that she no longer had the right to the symbolical wreath of orange-flowers; that almost before she could read she had penetrated that redoubtable mystery which mothers scarcely allow their daughters to guess at, trembling as they enlighten them on the night of their marriage.

"When she went through the streets, always accompanied by her governess, as if, her parents feared some fresh, terrible adventure, with her eyes cast down under the load of that mysterious disgrace which she felt was always weighing upon her, the other girls, who were not nearly so innocent as people thought, whispered and giggled as they looked at her knowingly, and immediately turned their heads absently, if she happened to look at them.

People scarcely greeted her; only a few men bowed to her, and the mothers pretended not to see her, while some young blackguards called her Madame Baptiste, after the name of the footman who had attacked her.

"Nobody knew the secret torture of her mind, for she hardly ever spoke, and never laughed, and her parents themselves appeared uncomfortable in her presence, as if they bore her a constant grudge for some irreparable fault.

"An honest man would not willingly give his hand to a liberated convict, would he, even if that convict were his own son? And Monsieur and Madame Fontanelle looked on their daughter as they would have done on a son who had just been released from the hulks. She was pretty and pale, tall, slender, distinguished-looking, and she would have pleased me very much, monsieur, but for that unfortunate affair.

"Well, when a new sub-prefect was appointed here, eighteen months ago, he brought his private secretary with him. He was a queer sort of fellow, who had lived in the Latin Quarter, it appears. He saw Mademoiselle Fontanelle and fell in love with her, and when told of what occurred, he merely said:

"'Bah! That is just a guarantee for the future, and I would rather it should have happened before I married her than afterward. I shall live tranquilly with that woman.'

"He paid his addresses to her, asked for her hand and married her, and then, not being deficient in assurance, he paid wedding calls, as if nothing had happened. Some people returned them, others did not; but, at last, the affair began to be forgotten, and she took her proper place in society.

"She adored her husband as if he had been a god; for, you must remember, he had restored her to honor and to social life, had braved public opinion, faced insults, and, in a word, performed such a courageous act as few men would undertake, and she felt the most exalted and tender love for him.

"When she became enceinte, and it was known, the most particular people and the greatest sticklers opened their doors to her, as if she had been definitely purified by maternity.

"It is strange, but so it is, and thus everything was going on as well as possible until the other day, which was the feast of the patron saint of our town. The prefect, surrounded by his staff and the authorities, presided at the musical competition, and when he had finished his speech the distribution of medals began, which Paul Hamot, his private secretary, handed to those who were entitled to them.

"As you know, there are always jealousies and rivalries, which make people forget all propriety. All the ladies of the town were there on the platform, and, in his turn, the bandmaster from the village of Mourmillon came up. This band was only to receive a second-class medal, for one cannot give first-class medals to everybody, can one? But when the private secretary handed him his badge, the man threw it in his face and exclaimed:

"'You may keep your medal for Baptiste. You owe him a first-class one, also, just as you do me.'

"There were a number of people there who began to laugh. The common herd are neither charitable nor refined, and every eye was turned toward that poor lady. Have you ever seen a woman going mad, monsieur? Well, we were present at the sight! She got up and fell back on her chair three times in succession, as if she wished to make her escape, but saw that she could not make her way through the crowd, and then another voice in the crowd exclaimed:

"'Oh! Oh! Madame Baptiste!'

"And a great uproar, partly of laughter and partly of indignation, arose. The word was repeated over and over again; people stood on tiptoe to see the unhappy woman's face; husbands lifted their wives up in their arms, so that they might see her, and people asked:

"'Which is she? The one in blue?'

"The boys crowed like cocks, and laughter was heard all over the place.

"She did not move now on her state chair, but sat just as if she had been put there for the crowd to look at. She could not move, nor conceal herself, nor hide her face. Her eyelids blinked quickly, as if a vivid light were shining on them, and she breathed heavily, like a horse that is going up a steep hill, so that it almost broke one's heart to see her. Meanwhile, however, Monsieur Hamot had seized the ruffian by the throat, and they were rolling on the ground together, amid a scene of indescribable confusion, and the ceremony was interrupted.

"An hour later, as the Hamots were returning home, the young woman, who had not uttered a word since the insult, but who was trembling as if all her nerves had been set in motion by springs, suddenly sprang over the parapet of the bridge and threw herself into the river before her husband could prevent her. The water is very deep under the arches, and it was two hours before her body was recovered. Of course, she was dead."

The narrator stopped and then added:

"It was, perhaps, the best thing she could do under the circumstances. There are some things which cannot be wiped out, and now you understand why the clergy refused to have her taken into church. Ah! If it had been a religious funeral the whole town would have been present, but you can understand that her suicide added to the other affair and made families abstain from attending her funeral; and then, it is not an easy matter here to attend a funeral which is performed without religious rites."

We passed through the cemetery gates and I waited, much moved by what I had heard, until the coffin had been lowered into the grave, before I went up to the poor fellow who was sobbing violently, to press his hand warmly. He looked at me in surprise through his tears and then said:

"Thank you, monsieur." And I was not sorry that I had followed the funeral.

THE QUESTION OF LATIN

This subject of Latin that has been dinned into our ears for some time past recalls to my mind a story—a story of my youth.

I was finishing my studies with a teacher, in a big central town, at the Institution Robineau, celebrated through the entire province for the special attention paid there to the study of Latin.

For the past ten years, the Robineau Institute beat the imperial lycee of the town at every competitive examination, and all the colleges of the subprefecture, and these constant successes were due, they said, to an usher, a simple usher, M. Piquedent, or rather Pere Piquedent.

He was one of those middle-aged men quite gray, whose real age it is impossible to tell, and whose history we can guess at first glance. Having entered as an usher at twenty into the first institution that presented itself so that he could proceed to take first his degree of Master of Arts and afterward the degree of Doctor of Laws, he found himself so enmeshed in this routine that he remained an usher all his life. But his love for Latin did not leave him and harassed him like an unhealthy passion. He continued to read the poets, the prose writers, the historians, to interpret them and penetrate their meaning, to comment on them with a perseverance bordering on madness.

One day, the idea came into his head to oblige all the students in his class to answer him in Latin only; and he persisted in this resolution until at last they were capable of sustaining an entire conversation with him just as they would in their mother tongue. He listened to them, as a leader of an orchestra listens to his musicians rehearsing, and striking his desk every moment with his ruler, he exclaimed:

"Monsieur Lefrere, Monsieur Lefrere, you are committing a solecism! You forget the rule.

"Monsieur Plantel, your way of expressing yourself is altogether French and in no way Latin. You must understand the genius of a language. Look here, listen to me."

Now, it came to pass that the pupils of the Institution Robineau carried off, at the end of the year, all the prizes for composition, translation, and Latin conversation.

Next year, the principal, a little man, as cunning as an ape, whom he resembled in his grinning and grotesque appearance, had had printed on his programmes, on his advertisements, and painted on the door of his institution:

"Latin Studies a Specialty. Five first prizes carried off in the five classes of the lycee.

"Two honor prizes at the general examinations in competition with all the lycees and colleges of France."

For ten years the Institution Robineau triumphed in the same fashion. Now my father, allured by these successes, sent me as a day pupil to Robineau's—or, as we called it, Robinetto or Robinettino's—and made me take special private lessons from Pere Piquedent at the rate of five francs per hour, out of which the usher got two francs and the principal three francs. I was then eighteen, and was in the philosophy class.

These private lessons were given in a little room looking out on the street. It so happened that Pere Piquedent, instead of talking Latin to me, as he did when teaching publicly in the institution, kept telling me his troubles in French. Without relations, without friends, the poor man conceived an attachment to me, and poured out his misery to me.

He had never for the last ten or fifteen years chatted confidentially with any one.

"I am like an oak in a desert," he said—"'sicut quercus in solitudine'."

The other ushers disgusted him. He knew nobody in the town, since he had no time to devote to making acquaintances.

"Not even the nights, my friend, and that is the hardest thing on me. The dream of my life is to have a room with my own furniture, my own books, little things that belong to myself and which others may not touch. And I have nothing of my own, nothing except my trousers and my frock-coat, nothing, not even my mattress and my pillow! I have not four walls to shut myself up in, except when I come to give a lesson in this room. Do you see what this means—a man forced to spend his life without ever having the right, without ever finding the time, to shut himself up all alone, no matter where, to think, to reflect, to work, to dream? Ah! my dear boy, a key, the key of a door which one can lock—this is happiness, mark you, the only happiness!

"Here, all day long, teaching all those restless rogues, and during the night the dormitory with the same restless rogues snoring. And I have to sleep in the bed at the end of two rows of beds occupied by these youngsters whom I must look after. I can never be alone, never! If I go out I find the streets full of people, and, when I am tired of walking, I go into some cafe crowded with smokers and billiard players. I tell you what, it is the life of a galley slave."

I said:

"Why did you not take up some other line, Monsieur Piquedent?"

He exclaimed:

"What, my little friend? I am not a shoemaker, or a joiner, or a hatter, or a baker, or a hairdresser. I only know Latin, and I have no diploma which would enable me to sell my knowledge at a high price. If I were a doctor I would sell for a hundred francs what I now sell for a hundred sous; and I would supply it probably of an inferior quality, for my title would be enough to sustain my reputation."

Sometimes he would say to me:

"I have no rest in life except in the hours spent with you. Don't be afraid! you'll lose nothing by that. I'll make it up to you in the class-room by making you speak twice as much Latin as the others."

One day, I grew bolder, and offered him a cigarette. He stared at me in astonishment at first, then he gave a glance toward the door.

"If any one were to come in, my dear boy?"

"Well, let us smoke at the window," said I.

And we went and leaned our elbows on the windowsill looking on the street, holding concealed in our hands the little rolls of tobacco. Just opposite to us was a laundry. Four women in loose white waists were passing hot, heavy irons over the linen spread out before them, from which a warm steam arose.

Suddenly, another, a fifth, carrying on her arm a large basket which made her stoop, came out to take the customers their shirts, their handkerchiefs, and their sheets. She stopped on the threshold as if she were already fatigued; then, she raised her eyes, smiled as she saw us smoking, flung at us, with her left hand, which was free, the sly kiss characteristic of a free-and-easy working-woman, and went away at a slow place, dragging her feet as she went.

She was a woman of about twenty, small, rather thin, pale, rather pretty, with a roguish air and laughing eyes beneath her ill-combed fair hair.

Pere Piquedent, affected, began murmuring:

"What an occupation for a woman! Really a trade only fit for a horse."

And he spoke with emotion about the misery of the people. He had a heart which swelled with lofty democratic sentiment, and he referred to the fatiguing pursuits of the working class with phrases borrowed from Jean-Jacques Rousseau, and with sobs in his throat.

Next day, as we were leaning our elbows on the same window sill, the same woman perceived us and cried out to us:

"Good-day, scholars!" in a comical sort of tone, while she made a contemptuous gesture with her hands.

I flung her a cigarette, which she immediately began to smoke. And the four other ironers rushed out to the door with outstretched hands to get cigarettes also.

And each day a friendly intercourse was established between the working-women of the pavement and the idlers of the boarding school.

Pere Piquedent was really a comical sight. He trembled at being noticed, for he might lose his position; and he made timid and ridiculous gestures, quite a theatrical display of love signals, to which the women responded with a regular fusillade of kisses.

A perfidious idea came into my mind. One day, on entering our room, I said to the old usher in a low tone:

"You would not believe it, Monsieur Piquedent, I met the little washerwoman! You know the one I mean, the woman who had the basket, and I spoke to her!"

He asked, rather worried at my manner:

"What did she say to you?"

"She said to me—why, she said she thought you were very nice. The fact of the matter is, I believe, I believe, that she is a little in love with you." I saw that he was growing pale.

"She is laughing at me, of course. These things don't happen at my age," he replied.

I said gravely:

"How is that? You are all right."

As I felt that my trick had produced its effect on him, I did not press the matter.

But every day I pretended that I had met the little laundress and that I had spoken to her about him, so that in the end he believed me, and sent her ardent and earnest kisses.

Now it happened that one morning, on my way to the boarding school, I really came across her. I accosted her without hesitation, as if I had known her for the last ten years.

"Good-day, mademoiselle. Are you quite well?"

"Very well, monsieur, thank you."

"Will you have a cigarette?"

"Oh! not in the street."

"You can smoke it at home."

"In that case, I will."

"Let me tell you, mademoiselle, there's something you don't know."

"What is that, monsieur?"

"The old gentleman—my old professor, I mean—"

"Pere Piquedent?"

"Yes, Pere Piquedent. So you know his name?"

"Faith, I do! What of that?"

"Well, he is in love with you!"

She burst out laughing wildly, and exclaimed:

"You are only fooling."

"Oh! no, I am not fooling! He keeps talking of you all through the lesson. I bet that he'll marry you!"

She ceased laughing. The idea of marriage makes every girl serious. Then she repeated, with an incredulous air:

"This is humbug!"

"I swear to you, it's true."

She picked up her basket which she had laid down at her feet.

"Well, we'll see," she said. And she went away.

Presently when I had reached the boarding school, I took Pere Piquedent aside, and said:

"You must write to her; she is infatuated with you."

And he wrote a long letter, tenderly affectionate, full of phrases and circumlocutions, metaphors and similes, philosophy and academic gallantry; and I took on myself the responsibility of delivering it to the young woman.

She read it with gravity, with emotion; then she murmured:

"How well he writes! It is easy to see he has got education! Does he really mean to marry me?"

I replied intrepidly: "Faith, he has lost his head about you!"

"Then he must invite me to dinner on Sunday at the Ile des Fleurs."

I promised that she should be invited.

Pere Piquedent was much touched by everything I told him about her.

I added:

"She loves you, Monsieur Piquedent, and I believe her to be a decent girl. It is not right to lead her on and then abandon her."

He replied in a firm tone:

"I hope I, too, am a decent man, my friend."

I confess I had at the time no plan. I was playing a practical joke a schoolboy joke, nothing more. I had been aware of the simplicity of the old usher, his innocence and his weakness. I amused myself without asking myself how it would turn out. I was eighteen, and I had been for a long time looked upon at the lycee as a sly practical joker.

So it was agreed that Pere Piquedent and I should set out in a hack for the ferry of Queue de Vache, that we should there pick up Angele, and that I should take them into my boat, for in those days I was fond of boating. I would then bring them to the Ile des Fleurs, where the three of us would dine. I had inflicted myself on them, the better to enjoy my triumph, and the usher, consenting to my arrangement, proved clearly that he was losing his head by thus risking the loss of his position.

When we arrived at the ferry, where my boat had been moored since morning, I saw in the grass, or rather above the tall weeds of the bank, an enormous red parasol, resembling a monstrous wild poppy. Beneath the parasol was the little laundress in her Sunday clothes. I was surprised. She was really pretty, though pale; and graceful, though with a rather suburban grace.

Pere Piquedent raised his hat and bowed. She put out her hand toward him, and they stared at one another without uttering a word. Then they stepped into my boat, and I took the oars. They were seated side by side near the stern.

The usher was the first to speak.

"This is nice weather for a row in a boat."

She murmured:

"Oh! yes."

She dipped her hand into the water, skimming the surface, making a thin, transparent film like a sheet of glass, which made a soft plashing along the side of the boat.

When they were in the restaurant, she took it on herself to speak, and ordered dinner, fried fish, a chicken, and salad; then she led us on toward the isle, which she knew perfectly.

After this, she was gay, romping, and even rather tantalizing.

Until dessert, no question of love arose. I had treated them to champagne, and Pere Piquedent was tipsy. Herself slightly the worse, she called out to him:

"Monsieur Piquenez."

He said abruptly:

"Mademoiselle, Monsieur Raoul has communicated my sentiments to you."

She became as serious as a judge.

"Yes, monsieur."

"What is your reply?"

"We never reply to these questions!"

He puffed with emotion, and went on:

"Well, will the day ever come that you will like me?"

She smiled.

"You big stupid! You are very nice."

"In short, mademoiselle, do you think that, later on, we might—"

She hesitated a second; then in a trembling voice she said:

"Do you mean to marry me when you say that? For on no other condition, you know."

"Yes, mademoiselle!"

"Well, that's all right, Monsieur Piquedent!"

It was thus that these two silly creatures promised marriage to each other through the trick of a young scamp. But I did not believe that it was serious, nor, indeed, did they, perhaps.

"You know, I have nothing, not four sous," she said.

He stammered, for he was as drunk as Silenus:

"I have saved five thousand francs."

She exclaimed triumphantly:

"Then we can set up in business?"

He became restless.

"In what business?"

"What do I know? We shall see. With five thousand francs we could do many things. You don't want me to go and live in your boarding school, do you?"

He had not looked forward so far as this, and he stammered in great perplexity:

"What business could we set up in? That would not do, for all I know is Latin!"

She reflected in her turn, passing in review all her business ambitions.

"You could not be a doctor?"

"No, I have no diploma."

"Or a chemist?"

"No more than the other."

She uttered a cry of joy. She had discovered it.

"Then we'll buy a grocer's shop! Oh! what luck! we'll buy a grocer's shop. Not on a big scale, of course; with five thousand francs one does not go far."

He was shocked at the suggestion.

"No, I can't be a grocer. I am—I am—too well known: I only know Latin, that is all I know."

But she poured a glass of champagne down his throat. He drank it and was silent.

We got back into the boat. The night was dark, very dark. I saw clearly, however, that he had caught her by the waist, and that they were hugging each other again and again.

It was a frightful catastrophe. Our escapade was discovered, with the result that Pere Piquedent was dismissed. And my father, in a fit of anger, sent me to finish my course of philosophy at Ribaudet's school.

Six months later I took my degree of Bachelor of Arts. Then I went to study law in Paris, and did not return to my native town till two years later.

At the corner of the Rue de Serpent a shop caught my eye. Over the door were the words: "Colonial Products—Piquedent"; then underneath, so as to enlighten the most ignorant: "Grocery."

I exclaimed:

"'Quantum mutatus ab illo!'"

Piquedent raised his head, left his female customer, and rushed toward me with outstretched hands.

"Ah! my young friend, my young friend, here you are! What luck! what luck!"

A beautiful woman, very plump, abruptly left the cashier's desk and flung herself on my breast. I had some difficulty in recognizing her, she had grown so stout.

I asked:

"So then you're doing well?"

Piquedent had gone back to weigh the groceries.

"Oh! very well, very well, very well. I have made three thousand francs clear this year!"

"And what about Latin, Monsieur Piquedent?"

"Oh, good heavens! Latin, Latin, Latin—you see it does not keep the pot boiling!"

A MEETING

It was nothing but an accident, an accident pure and simple. On that particular evening the princess' rooms were open, and as they appeared dark after the brilliantly lighted parlors, Baron d'Etraille, who was tired of standing, inadvertently wandered into an empty bedroom.

He looked round for a chair in which to have a doze, as he was sure his wife would not leave before daylight. As soon as he became accustomed to the light of the room he distinguished the big bed with its azure-and-gold hangings, in the middle of the great room, looking like a catafalque in which love was buried, for the princess was no longer young. Behind it, a large bright surface looked like a lake seen at a distance. It was a large mirror, discreetly covered with dark drapery, that was very rarely let down, and seemed to look at the bed, which was its accomplice. One might almost fancy that it had reminiscences, and that one might see in it charming female forms and the gentle movement of loving arms.

The baron stood still for a moment, smiling, almost experiencing an emotion on the threshold of this chamber dedicated to love. But suddenly something appeared in the looking-glass, as if the phantoms which he had evoked had risen up before him. A man and a woman who had been sitting on a low couch concealed in the shadow had arisen, and the polished surface, reflecting their figures, showed that they were kissing each other before separating.

Baron d'Etraille recognized his wife and the Marquis de Cervigne. He turned and went away like a man who is fully master of himself, and waited till it was day before taking away the baroness; but he had no longer any thoughts of sleeping.

As soon as they were alone he said:

"Madame, I saw you just now in Princesse de Raynes' room; I need say no more, and I am not fond either of reproaches, acts of violence, or of ridicule. As I wish to avoid all such things, we shall separate without any scandal. Our lawyers will settle your position according to my orders. You will be free to live as you please when you are no longer under my roof; but, as you will continue to bear my name, I must warn you that should any scandal arise I shall show myself inflexible."

She tried to speak, but he stopped her, bowed, and left the room.

He was more astonished and sad than unhappy. He had loved her dearly during the first period of their married life; but his ardor had cooled, and now he often amused himself elsewhere, either in a theatre or in society, though he always preserved a certain liking for the baroness.

She was very young, hardly four-and-twenty, small, slight—too slight—and very fair. She was a true Parisian doll: clever, spoiled, elegant, coquettish, witty, with more charm than real beauty. He used to say familiarly to his brother, when speaking of her:

"My wife is charming, attractive, but—there is nothing to lay hold of. She is like a glass of champagne that is all froth; when you get to the wine it is very good, but there is too little of it, unfortunately."

He walked up and down the room in great agitation, thinking of a thousand things. At one moment he was furious, and felt inclined to give the marquis a good thrashing, or to slap his face publicly, in the club. But he decided that would not do, it would not be good form;

he would be laughed at, and not his rival, and this thought wounded his vanity. So he went to bed, but could not sleep. Paris knew in a few days that the Baron and Baroness d'Etraille had agreed to an amicable separation on account of incompatibility of temper. No one suspected anything, no one laughed, and no one was astonished.

The baron, however, to avoid meeting his wife, travelled for a year, then spent the summer at the seaside, and the autumn in shooting, returning to Paris for the winter. He did not meet the baroness once.

He did not even know what people said about her. In any case, she took care to respect appearances, and that was all he asked for.

He became dreadfully bored, travelled again, restored his old castle of Villebosc, which took him two years; then for over a year he entertained friends there, till at last, tired of all these so-called pleasures, he returned to his mansion in the Rue de Lille, just six years after the separation.

He was now forty-five, with a good crop of gray hair, rather stout, and with that melancholy look characteristic of those who have been handsome, sought after, and liked, but who are deteriorating, daily.

A month after his return to Paris, he took cold on coming out of his club, and had such a bad cough that his medical man ordered him to Nice for the rest of the winter.

He reached the station only a few minutes before the departure of the train on Monday evening, and had barely time to get into a carriage, with only one other occupant, who was sitting in a corner so wrapped in furs and cloaks that he could not even make out whether it was a man or a woman, as nothing of the figure could be seen. When he perceived that he could not find out, he put on his travelling cap, rolled himself up in his rugs, and stretched out comfortably to sleep.

He did not wake until the day was breaking, and looked at once at his fellow-traveller, who had not stirred all night, and seemed still to be sound asleep.

M. d'Etraille made use of the opportunity to brush his hair and his beard, and to try to freshen himself up a little generally, for a night's travel does not improve one's appearance when one has attained a certain age.

A great poet has said:

"When we are young, our mornings are triumphant!"

Then we wake up with a cool skin, a bright eye, and glossy hair.

As one grows older one wakes up in a very different condition. Dull eyes, red, swollen cheeks, dry lips, hair and beard disarranged, impart an old, fatigued, worn-out look to the face.

The baron opened his travelling case, and improved his looks as much as possible.

The engine whistled, the train stopped, and his neighbor moved. No doubt he was awake. They started off again, and then a slanting ray of sunlight shone into the carriage and on the sleeper, who moved again, shook himself, and then his face could be seen.

It was a young, fair, pretty, plump woman, and the baron looked at her in amazement. He did not know what to think. He could really have sworn that it was his wife, but wonderfully changed for the better: stouter —why she had grown as stout as he was, only it suited her much better than it did him.

She looked at him calmly, did not seem to recognize him, and then slowly laid aside her wraps. She had that quiet assurance of a woman who is sure of herself, who feels that on awaking she is in her full beauty and freshness.

The baron was really bewildered. Was it his wife, or else as like her as any sister could be? Not having seen her for six years, he might be mistaken.

She yawned, and this gesture betrayed her. She turned and looked at him again, calmly, indifferently, as if she scarcely saw him, and then looked out of the window again.

He was upset and dreadfully perplexed, and kept looking at her sideways.

Yes; it was surely his wife. How could he possibly have doubted it? There could certainly not be two noses like that, and a thousand recollections flashed through his mind. He felt the old feeling of the intoxication of love stealing over him, and he called to mind the sweet odor of her skin, her smile when she put her arms on to his shoulders, the soft intonations of her voice, all her graceful, coaxing ways.

But how she had changed and improved! It was she and yet not she. She seemed riper, more developed, more of a woman, more seductive, more desirable, adorably desirable.

And this strange, unknown woman, whom he had accidentally met in a railway carriage, belonged to him; he had only to say to her:

"I insist upon it."

He had formerly slept in her arms, existed only in her love, and now he had found her again certainly, but so changed that he scarcely knew her. It was another, and yet it was she herself. It was some one who had been born and had formed and grown since he had left her. It was she, indeed; she whom he had loved, but who was now altered, with a more assured smile and greater self-possession. There were two women in one, mingling a great part of what was new and unknown with many sweet recollections of the past. There was something singular, disturbing, exciting about it —a kind of mystery of love in which there floated a delicious confusion. It was his wife in a new body and in new flesh which lips had never pressed.

And he thought that in a few years nearly every thing changes in us; only the outline can be recognized, and sometimes even that disappears.

The blood, the hair, the skin, all changes and is renewed, and when people have not seen each other for a long time, when they meet they find each other totally different beings, although they are the same and bear the same name.

And the heart also can change. Ideas may be modified and renewed, so that in forty years of life we may, by gradual and constant transformations, become four or five totally new and different beings.

He dwelt on this thought till it troubled him; it had first taken possession of him when he surprised her in the princess' room. He was not the least angry; it was not the same woman that he was looking at —that thin, excitable little doll of those days.

What was he to do? How should he address her? and what could he say to her? Had she recognized him?

The train stopped again. He got up, bowed, and said: "Bertha, do you want anything I could bring you?"

She looked at him from head to foot, and answered, without showing the slightest surprise, or confusion, or anger, but with the most perfect indifference:

"I do not want anything—-thank you."

He got out and walked up and down the platform a little in order to recover himself, and, as it were, to recover his senses after a fall. What should he do now? If he got into another carriage it would look as if he were running away. Should he be polite or importunate? That would look as if he were asking for forgiveness. Should he speak as if he were her master? He would look like a fool, and, besides, he really had no right to do so.

He got in again and took his place.

During his absence she had hastily arranged her dress and hair, and was now lying stretched out on the seat, radiant, and without showing any emotion.

He turned to her, and said: "My dear Bertha, since this singular chance has brought up together after a separation of six years—a quite friendly separation—are we to continue to look upon each other as irreconcilable enemies? We are shut up together, tete-a-tete, which is so much the better or so much the worse. I am not going to get into another carriage, so don't you think it is preferable to talk as friends till the end of our journey?"

She answered, quite calmly again:

"Just as you please."

Then he suddenly stopped, really not knowing what to say; but as he had plenty of assurance, he sat down on the middle seat, and said:

"Well, I see I must pay my court to you; so much the better. It is, however, really a pleasure, for you are charming. You cannot imagine how you have improved in the last six years. I do not know any woman who could give me that delightful sensation which I experienced just now when you emerged from your wraps. I really could not have thought such a change possible."

Without moving her head or looking at him, she said: "I cannot say the same with regard to you; you have certainly deteriorated a great deal."

He got red and confused, and then, with a smile of resignation, he said:

"You are rather hard."

"Why?" was her reply. "I am only stating facts. I don't suppose you intend to offer me your love? It must, therefore, be a matter of perfect indifference to you what I think about you. But I see it is a painful subject, so let us talk of something else. What have you been doing since I last saw you?"

He felt rather out of countenance, and stammered:

“I? I have travelled, done some shooting, and grown old, as you see. And you?”

She said, quite calmly: “I have taken care of appearances, as you ordered me.”

He was very nearly saying something brutal, but he checked himself; and kissed his wife’s hand:

“And I thank you,” he said.

She was surprised. He was indeed diplomatic, and always master of himself.

He went on: “As you have acceded to my first request, shall we now talk without any bitterness?”

She made a little movement of surprise.

“Bitterness? I don’t feel any; you are a complete stranger to me; I am only trying to keep up a difficult conversation.”

He was still looking at her, fascinated in spite of her harshness, and he felt seized with a brutal Beside, the desire of the master.

Perceiving that she had hurt his feelings, she said:

“How old are you now? I thought you were younger than you look.”

“I am forty-five”; and then he added: “I forgot to ask after Princesse de Raynes. Are you still intimate with her?”

She looked at him as if she hated him:

“Yes, I certainly am. She is very well, thank you.”

They remained sitting side by side, agitated and irritated. Suddenly he said:

“My dear Bertha, I have changed my mind. You are my wife, and I expect you to come with me to-day. You have, I think, improved both morally and physically, and I am going to take you back again. I am your husband, and it is my right to do so."

She was stupefied, and looked at him, trying to divine his thoughts; but his face was resolute and impenetrable.

“I am very sorry,” she said, “but I have made other engagements.”

“So much the worse for you,” was his reply. “The law gives me the power, and I mean to use it.”

They were nearing Marseilles, and the train whistled and slackened speed. The baroness rose, carefully rolled up her wraps, and then, turning to her husband, said:

“My dear Raymond, do not make a bad use of this tete-a tete which I had carefully prepared. I wished to take precautions, according to your advice, so that I might have nothing to fear from you or from other people, whatever might happen. You are going to Nice, are you not?”

“I shall go wherever you go.”

"Not at all; just listen to me, and I am sure that you will leave me in peace. In a few moments, when we get to the station, you will see the Princesse de Raynes and Comtesse Henriot waiting for me with their husbands. I wished them to see as, and to know that we had spent the night together in the railway carriage. Don't be alarmed; they will tell it everywhere as a most surprising fact.

"I told you just now that I had most carefully followed your advice and saved appearances. Anything else does not matter, does it? Well, in order to do so, I wished to be seen with you. You told me carefully to avoid any scandal, and I am avoiding it, for, I am afraid—I am afraid—"

She waited till the train had quite stopped, and as her friends ran up to open the carriage door, she said:

"I am afraid"—hesitating—"that there is another reason—je suis enceinte."

The princess stretched out her arms to embrace her,—and the baroness said, painting to the baron, who was dumb with astonishment, and was trying to get at the truth:

"You do not recognize Raymond? He has certainly changed a good deal, and he agreed to come with me so that I might not travel alone. We take little trips like this occasionally, like good friends who cannot live together. We are going to separate here; he has had enough of me already."

She put out her hand, which he took mechanically, and then she jumped out on to the platform among her friends, who were waiting for her.

The baron hastily shut the carriage door, for he was too much disturbed to say a word or come to any determination. He heard his wife's voice and their merry laughter as they went away.

He never saw her again, nor did he ever discover whether she had told him a lie or was speaking the truth.

THE BLIND MAN

How is it that the sunlight gives us such joy? Why does this radiance when it falls on the earth fill us with the joy of living? The whole sky is blue, the fields are green, the houses all white, and our enchanted eyes drink in those bright colors which bring delight to our souls. And then there springs up in our hearts a desire to dance, to run, to sing, a happy lightness of thought, a sort of enlarged tenderness; we feel a longing to embrace the sun.

The blind, as they sit in the doorways, impassive in their eternal darkness, remain as calm as ever in the midst of this fresh gaiety, and, not understanding what is taking place around them, they continually check their dogs as they attempt to play.

When, at the close of the day, they are returning home on the arm of a young brother or a little sister, if the child says: "It was a very fine day!" the other answers: "I could notice that it was fine. Loulou wouldn't keep quiet."

I knew one of these men whose life was one of the most cruel martyrdoms that could possibly be conceived.

He was a peasant, the son of a Norman farmer. As long as his father and mother lived, he was more or less taken care of; he suffered little save from his horrible infirmity; but as soon as the old people were gone, an atrocious life of misery commenced for him. Dependent on a sister of his, everybody in the farmhouse treated him as a beggar who is eating the bread of strangers. At every meal the very food he swallowed was made a subject of reproach against him; he was called a drone, a clown, and although his brother-in-law had taken possession of his portion of the inheritance, he was helped grudgingly to soup, getting just enough to save him from starving.

His face was very pale and his two big white eyes looked like wafers. He remained unmoved at all the insults hurled at him, so reserved that one could not tell whether he felt them.

Moreover, he had never known any tenderness, his mother having always treated him unkindly and caring very little for him; for in country places useless persons are considered a nuisance, and the peasants would be glad to kill the infirm of their species, as poultry do.

As soon as he finished his soup he went and sat outside the door in summer and in winter beside the fireside, and did not stir again all the evening. He made no gesture, no movement; only his eyelids, quivering from some nervous affection, fell down sometimes over his white, sightless orbs. Had he any intellect, any thinking faculty, any consciousness of his own existence? Nobody cared to inquire.

For some years things went on in this fashion. But his incapacity for work as well as his impassiveness eventually exasperated his relatives, and he became a laughingstock, a sort of butt for merriment, a prey to the inborn ferocity, to the savage gaiety of the brutes who surrounded him.

It is easy to imagine all the cruel practical jokes inspired by his blindness. And, in order to have some fun in return for feeding him, they now converted his meals into hours of pleasure for the neighbors and of punishment for the helpless creature himself.

The peasants from the nearest houses came to this entertainment; it was talked about from door to door, and every day the kitchen of the farmhouse was full of people. Sometimes they placed before his plate, when he was beginning to eat his soup, some cat or dog. The animal instinctively perceived the man's infirmity, and, softly approaching, commenced eating noiselessly, lapping up the soup daintily; and, when they lapped the food rather noisily, rousing the poor fellow's attention, they would prudently scamper away to avoid the blow of the spoon directed at random by the blind man!

Then the spectators ranged along the wall would burst out laughing, nudge each other and stamp their feet on the floor. And he, without ever uttering a word, would continue eating with his right hand, while stretching out his left to protect his plate.

Another time they made him chew corks, bits of wood, leaves or even filth, which he was unable to distinguish.

After this they got tired even of these practical jokes, and the brother-in-law, angry at having to support him always, struck him, cuffed him incessantly, laughing at his futile efforts to ward off or return the blows. Then came a new pleasure—the pleasure of smacking his face. And the plough-men, the servant girls and even every passing vagabond were every moment giving him cuffs, which caused his eyelashes to twitch spasmodically. He did not know where to hide himself and remained with his arms always held out to guard against people coming too close to him.

At last he was forced to beg.

He was placed somewhere on the high-road on market-days, and as soon as he heard the sound of footsteps or the rolling of a vehicle, he reached out his hat, stammering:

"Charity, if you please!"

But the peasant is not lavish, and for whole weeks he did not bring back a sou.

Then he became the victim of furious, pitiless hatred. And this is how he died.

One winter the ground was covered with snow, and it was freezing hard. His brother-in-law led him one morning a great distance along the high road in order that he might solicit alms. The blind man was left there all day; and when night came on, the brother-in-law told the people of his house that he could find no trace of the mendicant. Then he added:

"Pooh! best not bother about him! He was cold and got someone to take him away. Never fear! he's not lost. He'll turn up soon enough tomorrow to eat the soup."

Next day he did not come back.

After long hours of waiting, stiffened with the cold, feeling that he was dying, the blind man began to walk. Being unable to find his way along the road, owing to its thick coating of ice, he went on at random, falling into ditches, getting up again, without uttering a sound, his sole object being to find some house where he could take shelter.

But, by degrees, the descending snow made a numbness steal over him, and his feeble limbs being incapable of carrying him farther, he sat down in the middle of an open field. He did not get up again.

The white flakes which fell continuously buried him, so that his body, quite stiff and stark, disappeared under the incessant accumulation of their rapidly thickening mass, and nothing was left to indicate the place where he lay.

His relatives made a pretence of inquiring about him and searching for him for about a week. They even made a show of weeping.

The winter was severe, and the thaw did not set in quickly. Now, one Sunday, on their way to mass, the farmers noticed a great flight of crows, who were whirling incessantly above the open field, and then descending like a shower of black rain at the same spot, ever going and coming.

The following week these gloomy birds were still there. There was a crowd of them up in the air, as if they had gathered from all corners of the horizon, and they swooped down with a great cawing into the shining snow, which they covered like black patches, and in which they kept pecking obstinately. A young fellow went to see what they were doing and discovered the body of the blind man, already half devoured, mangled. His wan eyes had disappeared, pecked out by the long, voracious beaks.

And I can never feel the glad radiance of sunlit days without sadly remembering and pondering over the fate of the beggar who was such an outcast in life that his horrible death was a relief to all who had known him.

INDISCRETION

They had loved each other before marriage with a pure and lofty love. They had first met on the sea-shore. He had thought this young girl charming, as she passed by with her light-colored parasol and her dainty dress amid the marine landscape against the horizon. He had loved her, blond and slender, in these surroundings of blue ocean and spacious sky. He could not distinguish the tenderness which this budding woman awoke in him from the vague and powerful emotion which the fresh salt air and the grand scenery of surf and sunshine and waves aroused in his soul.

She, on the other hand, had loved him because he courted her, because he was young, rich, kind, and attentive. She had loved him because it is natural for young girls to love men who whisper sweet nothings to them.

So, for three months, they had lived side by side, and hand in hand. The greeting which they exchanged in the morning before the bath, in the freshness of the morning, or in the evening on the sand, under the stars, in the warmth of a calm night, whispered low, very low, already had the flavor of kisses, though their lips had never met.

Each dreamed of the other at night, each thought of the other on awaking, * and, without yet having voiced their sentiments, each longing for the other, body and soul.

After marriage their love descended to earth. It was at first a tireless, sensuous passion, then exalted tenderness composed of tangible poetry, more refined caresses, and new and foolish inventions. Every glance and gesture was an expression of passion.

But, little by little, without even noticing it, they began to get tired of each other. Love was still strong, but they had nothing more to reveal to each other, nothing more to learn from each other, no new tale of endearment, no unexpected outburst, no new way of expressing the well-known, oft-repeated verb.

They tried, however, to rekindle the dwindling flame of the first love. Every day they tried some new trick or desperate attempt to bring back to their hearts the uncooled ardor of their first days of married life. They tried moonlight walks under the trees, in the sweet warmth of the summer evenings: the poetry of mist-covered beaches; the excitement of public festivals.

One morning Henriette said to Paul:

"Will you take me to a cafe for dinner?"

"Certainly, dearie."

"To some well-known cafe?"

"Of course!"

He looked at her with a questioning glance, seeing that she was thinking of something which she did not wish to tell.

She went on:

"You know, one of those cafes—oh, how can I explain myself?—a sporty cafe!"

He smiled: "Of course, I understand—you mean in one of the cafes which are commonly called bohemian."

"Yes, that's it. But take me to one of the big places, one where you are known, one where you have already supped—no—dined—well, you know—I—I—oh! I will never dare say it!"

"Go ahead, dearie. Little secrets should no longer exist between us."

"No, I dare not."

"Go on; don't be prudish. Tell me."

"Well, I—I—I want to be taken for your sweetheart—there! and I want the boys, who do not know that you are married, to take me for such; and you too—I want you to think that I am your sweetheart for one hour, in that place which must hold so many memories for you. There! And I will play that I am your sweetheart. It's awful, I know—I am abominably ashamed, I am as red as a peony. Don't look at me!"

He laughed, greatly amused, and answered:

"All right, we will go to-night to a very swell place where I am well known."

Toward seven o'clock they went up the stairs of one of the big cafes on the Boulevard, he, smiling, with the look of a conqueror, she, timid, veiled, delighted. They were immediately shown to one of the luxurious private dining-rooms, furnished with four large arm-chairs and a red plush couch. The head waiter entered and brought them the menu. Paul handed it to his wife.

"What do you want to eat?"

"I don't care; order whatever is good."

After handing his coat to the waiter, he ordered dinner and champagne. The waiter looked at the young woman and smiled. He took the order and murmured:

"Will Monsieur Paul have his champagne sweet or dry?"

"Dry, very dry."

Henriette was pleased to hear that this man knew her husband's name. They sat on the couch, side by side, and began to eat.

Ten candles lighted the room and were reflected in the mirrors all around them, which seemed to increase the brilliancy a thousand-fold. Henriette drank glass after glass in order to keep up her courage, although she felt dizzy after the first few glasses. Paul, excited by the memories which returned to him, kept kissing his wife's hands. His eyes were sparkling.

She was feeling strangely excited in this new place, restless, pleased, a little guilty, but full of life. Two waiters, serious, silent, accustomed to seeing and forgetting everything, to entering the room only when it was necessary and to leaving it when they felt they were intruding, were silently flitting hither and thither.

Toward the middle of the dinner, Henriette was well under the influence of champagne. She was prattling along fearlessly, her cheeks flushed, her eyes glistening.

"Come, Paul; tell me everything."

"What, sweetheart?"

"I don't dare tell you."

"Go on!"

"Have you loved many women before me?"

He hesitated, a little perplexed, not knowing whether he should hide his adventures or boast of them.

She continued:

"Oh! please tell me. How many have you loved?"

"A few."

"How many?"

"I don't know. How do you expect me to know such things?"

"Haven't you counted them?"

"Of course not."

"Then you must have loved a good many!"

"Perhaps."

"About how many? Just tell me about how many."

"But I don't know, dearest. Some years a good many, and some years only a few."

"How many a year, did you say?"

"Sometimes twenty or thirty, sometimes only four or five."

"Oh! that makes more than a hundred in all!"

"Yes, just about."

"Oh! I think that is dreadful!"

"Why dreadful?"

"Because it's dreadful when you think of it—all those women—and always—always the same thing. Oh! it's dreadful, just the same—more than a hundred women!"

He was surprised that she should think that dreadful, and answered, with the air of superiority which men take with women when they wish to make them understand that they have said something foolish:

"That's funny! If it is dreadful to have a hundred women, it's dreadful to have one."

"Oh, no, not at all!"

"Why not?"

"Because with one woman you have a real bond of love which attaches you to her, while with a hundred women it's not the same at all. There is no real love. I don't understand how a man can associate with such women."

"But they are all right."

"No, they can't be!"

"Yes, they are!"

"Oh, stop; you disgust me!"

"But then, why did you ask me how many sweethearts I had had?"

"Because——"

"That's no reason!"

"What were they-actresses, little shop-girls, or society women?"

"A few of each."

"It must have been rather monotonous toward the last."

"Oh, no; it's amusing to change."

She remained thoughtful, staring at her champagne glass. It was full —she drank it in one gulp; then putting it back on the table, she threw her arms around her husband's neck and murmured in his ear:

"Oh! how I love you, sweetheart! how I love you!"

He threw his arms around her in a passionate embrace. A waiter, who was just entering, backed out, closing the door discreetly. In about five minutes the head waiter came back, solemn and dignified, bringing the fruit for dessert. She was once more holding between her fingers a full glass, and gazing into the amber liquid as though seeking unknown things. She murmured in a dreamy voice:

"Yes, it must be fun!"

A FAMILY AFFAIR

The small engine attached to the Neuilly steam-tram whistled as it passed the Porte Maillot to warn all obstacles to get out of its way and puffed like a person out of breath as it sent out its steam, its pistons moving rapidly with a noise as of iron legs running. The train was going along the broad avenue that ends at the Seine. The sultry heat at the close of a July day lay over the whole city, and from the road, although there was not a breath of wind stirring, there arose a white, chalky, suffocating, warm dust, which adhered to the moist skin, filled the eyes and got into the lungs. People stood in the doorways of their houses to try and get a breath of air.

The windows of the steam-tram were open and the curtains fluttered in the wind. There were very few passengers inside, because on warm days people preferred the outside or the platforms. They consisted of stout women in peculiar costumes, of those shopkeepers' wives from the suburbs, who made up for the distinguished looks which they did not possess by ill-assumed dignity; of men tired from office-work, with yellow faces, stooped shoulders, and with one shoulder higher than the other, in consequence of, their long hours of writing at a desk. Their uneasy and melancholy faces also spoke of domestic troubles, of constant want of money, disappointed hopes, for they all belonged to the army of poor, threadbare devils who vegetate economically in cheap, plastered houses with a tiny piece of neglected garden on the outskirts of Paris, in the midst of those fields where night soil is deposited.

A short, corpulent man, with a puffy face, dressed all in black and wearing a decoration in his buttonhole, was talking to a tall, thin man, dressed in a dirty, white linen suit, the coat all unbuttoned, with a white Panama hat on his head. The former spoke so slowly and hesitatingly that it occasionally almost seemed as if he stammered; he was Monsieur Caravan, chief clerk in the Admiralty. The other, who had formerly been surgeon on board a merchant ship, had set up in practice in Courbevoie, where he applied the vague remnants of medical knowledge which he had retained after an adventurous life, to the wretched population of that district. His name was Chenet, and strange rumors were current as to his morality.

Monsieur Caravan had always led the normal life of a man in a Government office. For the last thirty years he had invariably gone the same way to his office every morning, and had met the same men going to business at the same time, and nearly on the same spot, and he returned home every evening by the same road, and again met the same faces which he had seen growing old. Every morning, after buying his penny paper at the corner of the Faubourg Saint Honore, he bought two rolls, and then went to his office, like a culprit who is giving himself up to justice, and got to his desk as quickly as possible, always feeling uneasy; as though he were expecting a rebuke for some neglect of duty of which he might have been guilty.

Nothing had ever occurred to change the monotonous order of his existence, for no event affected him except the work of his office, perquisites, gratuities, and promotion. He never spoke of anything but of his duties, either at the office, or at home—he had married the portionless daughter of one of his colleagues. His mind, which was in a state of atrophy from his depressing daily work, had no other thoughts, hopes or dreams than such as related to the office, and there was a constant source of bitterness that spoilt every pleasure that he might have had, and that was the employment of so many naval officials, tinsmiths, as they were called because of their silver-lace as first-class clerks; and every evening at dinner he discussed the matter hotly with his wife, who shared his angry feelings, and proved to their own satisfaction that it was in every way unjust to give places in Paris to men who ought properly to have been employed in the navy.

He was old now, and had scarcely noticed how his life was passing, for school had merely been exchanged for the office without any intermediate transition, and the ushers, at whom he had formerly trembled, were replaced by his chiefs, of whom he was terribly afraid. When he had to go into the rooms of these official despots, it made him tremble from head to foot, and that constant fear had given him a very awkward manner in their presence, a humble demeanor, and a kind of nervous stammering.

He knew nothing more about Paris than a blind man might know who was led to the same spot by his dog every day; and if he read the account of any uncommon events or scandals in his penny paper, they appeared to him like fantastic tales, which some pressman had made up out of his own head, in order to amuse the inferior employees. He did not read the political news, which his paper frequently altered as the cause which subsidized it might require, for he was not fond of innovations, and when he went through the Avenue of the Champs-Elysees every evening, he looked at the surging crowd of pedestrians, and at the stream of carriages, as a traveller might who has lost his way in a strange country.

As he had completed his thirty years of obligatory service that year, on the first of January, he had had the cross of the Legion of Honor bestowed upon him, which, in the semi-military public offices, is a recompense for the miserable slavery—the official phrase is, loyal services—of unfortunate convicts who are riveted to their desk. That unexpected dignity gave him a high and new idea of his own capacities, and altogether changed him. He immediately left off wearing light trousers and fancy waistcoats, and wore black trousers and long coats, on which his ribbon, which was very broad, showed off better. He got shaved every morning, manicured his nails more carefully, changed his linen every two days, from a legitimate sense of what was proper, and out of respect for the national Order, of which he formed a part, and from that day he was another Caravan, scrupulously clean, majestic and condescending.

At home, he said, "my cross," at every moment, and he had become so proud of it, that he could not bear to see men wearing any other ribbon in their button-holes. He became especially angry on seeing strange orders: "Which nobody ought to be allowed to wear in France," and he bore Chenet a particular grudge, as he met him on a tram-car every evening, wearing a decoration of one kind or another, white, blue, orange, or green.

The conversation of the two men, from the Arc de Triomphe to Neuilly, was always the same, and on that day they discussed, first of all, various local abuses which disgusted them both, and the Mayor of Neuilly received his full share of their censure. Then, as invariably happens in the company of medical men, Caravan began to enlarge on the chapter of illness, as in that manner, he hoped to obtain a little gratuitous advice, if he was careful not to show his hand. His mother had been causing him no little anxiety for some time; she had frequent and prolonged fainting fits, and, although she was ninety, she would not take care of herself.

Caravan grew quite tender-hearted when he mentioned her great age, and more than once asked Doctor Chenet, emphasizing the word doctor—although he was not fully qualified, being only an Offcier de Sante—whether he had often met anyone as old as that. And he rubbed his hands with pleasure; not, perhaps, that he cared very much about seeing the good woman last forever here on earth, but because the long duration of his mother's life was, as it were an earnest of old age for himself, and he continued:

"In my family, we last long, and I am sure that, unless I meet with an accident, I shall not die until I am very old."

The doctor looked at him with pity, and glanced for a moment at his neighbor's red face, his short, thick neck, his "corporation," as Chenet called it to himself, his two fat, flabby legs, and the apoplectic rotundity of the old official; and raising the white Panama hat from his head, he said with a snigger:

"I am not so sure of that, old fellow; your mother is as tough as nails, and I should say that your life is not a very good one."

This rather upset Caravan, who did not speak again until the tram put them down at their destination, where the two friends got out, and Chenet asked his friend to have a glass of vermouth at the Cafe du Globe, opposite, which both of them were in the habit of frequenting. The proprietor, who was a friend of theirs, held out to them two fingers, which they shook across the bottles of the counter; and then they joined three of their friends, who were playing dominoes, and who had been there since midday. They exchanged cordial greetings, with the usual question: "Anything new?" And then the three players continued their game, and held out their hands without looking up, when the others wished them "Good-night," and then they both went home to dinner.

Caravan lived in a small two-story house in Courbevaie, near where the roads meet; the ground floor was occupied by a hair-dresser. Two bed rooms, a dining-room and a kitchen, formed the whole of their apartments, and Madame Caravan spent nearly her whole time in cleaning them up, while her daughter, Marie-Louise, who was twelve, and her son, Phillip-Auguste, were running about with all the little, dirty, mischievous brats of the neighborhood, and playing in the gutter.

Caravan had installed his mother, whose avarice was notorious in the neighborhood, and who was terribly thin, in the room above them. She was always cross, and she never passed a day without quarreling and flying into furious tempers. She would apostrophize the neighbors, who were standing at their own doors, the coster-mongers, the street-sweepers, and the street-boys, in the most violent language; and the latter, to have their revenge, used to follow her at a distance when she went out, and call out rude things after her.

A little servant from Normandy, who was incredibly giddy and thoughtless, performed the household work, and slept on the second floor in the same room as the old woman, for fear of anything happening to her in the night.

When Caravan got in, his wife, who suffered from a chronic passion for cleaning, was polishing up the mahogany chairs that were scattered about the room with a piece of flannel. She always wore cotton gloves, and adorned her head with a cap ornamented with many colored ribbons, which was always tilted over one ear; and whenever anyone caught her polishing, sweeping, or washing, she used to say:

"I am not rich; everything is very simple in my house, but cleanliness is my luxury, and that is worth quite as much as any other."

As she was gifted with sound, obstinate, practical common sense, she led her husband in everything. Every evening during dinner, and afterwards when they were in their room, they talked over the business of the office for a long time, and although she was twenty years younger than he was, he confided everything to her as if she took the lead, and followed her advice in every matter.

She had never been pretty, and now she had grown ugly; in addition to that, she was short and thin, while her careless and tasteless way of dressing herself concealed her few small feminine attractions, which might have been brought out if she had possessed any taste in dress. Her skirts were always awry, and she frequently scratched herself, no matter on what part of her person, totally indifferent as to who might see her, and so persistently, that anyone who saw her might think that she was suffering from something like the itch. The only adornments that she allowed herself were silk ribbons, which she had in great profusion, and of various colors mixed together, in the pretentious caps which she wore at home.

As soon as she saw her husband she rose and said, as she kissed his whiskers:

"Did you remember Potin, my dear?"

He fell into a chair, in consternation, for that was the fourth time on which he had forgotten a commission that he had promised to do for her.

"It is a fatality," he said; "it is no good for me to think of it all day long, for I am sure to forget it in the evening."

But as he seemed really so very sorry, she merely said, quietly:

"You will think of it to-morrow, I dare say. Anything new at the office?"

"Yes, a great piece of news; another tinsmith has been appointed second chief clerk." She became very serious, and said:

"So he succeeds Ramon; this was the very post that I wanted you to have. And what about Ramon?"

"He retires on his pension."

She became furious, her cap slid down on her shoulder, and she continued:

"There is nothing more to be done in that shop now. And what is the name of the new commissioner?"

"Bonassot."

She took up the Naval Year Book, which she always kept close at hand, and looked him up.

"'Bonassot-Toulon. Born in 1851. Student Commissioner in 1871. Sub-Commissioner in 1875.' Has he been to sea?" she continued. At that question Caravan's looks cleared up, and he laughed until his sides shook.

"As much as Balin—as much as Baffin, his chief." And he added an old office joke, and laughed more than ever:

"It would not even do to send them by water to inspect the Point-du-Jour, for they would be sick on the penny steamboats on the Seine."

But she remained as serious as if she had not heard him, and then she said in a low voice, as she scratched her chin:

"If we only had a Deputy to fall back upon. When the Chamber hears everything that is going on at the Admiralty, the Minister will be turned out——"

She was interrupted by a terrible noise on the stairs. Marie-Louise and Philippe-Auguste, who had just come in from the gutter, were slapping each other all the way upstairs. Their mother rushed at them furiously, and taking each of them by an arm she dragged them into the room, shaking them vigorously; but as soon as they saw their father, they rushed up to him, and he kissed them affectionately, and taking one of them on each knee, began to talk to them.

Philippe-Auguste was an ugly, ill-kempt little brat, dirty from head to foot, with the face of an idiot, and Marie-Louise was already like her mother—spoke like her, repeated her words, and even imitated her movements. She also asked him whether there was anything fresh at the office, and he replied merrily:

"Your friend, Ramon, who comes and dines here every Sunday, is going to leave us, little one. There is a new second head-clerk."

She looked at her father, and with a precocious child's pity, she said:

"Another man has been put over your head again."

He stopped laughing, and did not reply, and in order to create a diversion, he said, addressing his wife, who was cleaning the windows:

"How is mamma, upstairs?"

Madame Caravan left off rubbing, turned round pulled her cap up, as it had fallen quite on to her back, and said with trembling lips:

"Ah! yes; let us talk about your mother, for she has made a pretty scene. Just imagine: a short time ago Madame Lebaudin, the hairdresser's wife, came upstairs to borrow a packet of starch of me, and, as I was not at home, your mother chased her out as though she were a beggar; but I gave it to the old woman. She pretended not to hear, as she always does when one tells her unpleasant truths, but she is no more deaf than I am, as you know. It is all a sham, and the proof of it is, that she went up to her own room immediately, without saying a word."

Caravan, embarrassed, did not utter a word, and at that moment the little servant came in to announce dinner. In order to let his mother know, he took a broom-handle, which always stood in a corner, and rapped loudly on the ceiling three times, and then they went into the dining-room. Madame Caravan, junior, helped the soup, and waited for the old woman, but she did not come, and as the soup was getting cold, they began to eat slowly, and when their plates were empty, they waited again, and Madame Caravan, who was furious, attacked her husband:

"She does it on purpose, you know that as well as I do. But you always uphold her."

Not knowing which side to take, he sent Marie-Louise to fetch her grandmother, and he sat motionless, with his eyes cast down, while his wife tapped her glass angrily with her knife. In about a minute, the door flew open suddenly, and the child came in again, out of breath and very pale, and said hurriedly:

"Grandmamma has fallen on the floor."

Caravan jumped up, threw his table-napkin down, and rushed upstairs, while his wife, who thought it was some trick of her mother-in-law's, followed more slowly, shrugging her shoulders, as if to express her doubt. When they got upstairs, however, they found the old woman lying at full length in the middle of the room; and when they turned her over, they saw that she was insensible and motionless, while her skin looked more wrinkled and yellow than usual, her eyes were closed, her teeth clenched, and her thin body was stiff.

Caravan knelt down by her, and began to moan.

"My poor mother! my poor mother!" he said. But the other Madame Caravan said:

"Bah! She has only fainted again, that is all, and she has done it to prevent us from dining comfortably, you may be sure of that."

They put her on the bed, undressed her completely, and Caravan, his wife, and the servant began to rub her; but, in spite of their efforts, she did not recover consciousness, so they sent Rosalie, the servant, to fetch Doctor Chenet. He lived a long way off, on the quay, going towards Suresnes, and so it was a considerable time before he arrived. He came at last, however, and, after having looked at the old woman, felt her pulse, and listened for a heart beat, he said: "It is all over."

Caravan threw himself on the body, sobbing violently; he kissed his mother's rigid face, and wept so that great tears fell on the dead woman's face like drops of water, and, naturally, Madame Caravan, junior, showed a decorous amount of grief, and uttered feeble moans as she stood behind her husband, while she rubbed her eyes vigorously.

But, suddenly, Caravan raised himself up, with his thin hair in disorder, and, looking very ugly in his grief, said:

"But—are you sure, doctor? Are you quite sure?"

The doctor stooped over the body, and, handling it with professional dexterity, as a shopkeeper might do, when showing off his goods, he said:

"See, my dear friend, look at her eye."

He raised the eyelid, and the old woman's eye appeared altogether unaltered, unless, perhaps, the pupil was rather larger, and Caravan felt a severe shock at the sight. Then Monsieur Chenet took her thin arm, forced the fingers open, and said, angrily, as if he had been contradicted:

"Just look at her hand; I never make a mistake, you may be quite sure of that."

Caravan fell on the bed, and almost bellowed, while his wife, still whimpering, did what was necessary.

She brought the night-table, on which she spread a towel and placed four wax candles on it, which she lighted; then she took a sprig of box, which was hanging over the chimney glass, and put it between the four candles, in a plate, which she filled with clean water, as she had no holy water. But, after a moment's rapid reflection, she threw a pinch of salt into the water, no doubt thinking she was performing some sort of act of consecration by doing that, and when she had finished, she remained standing motionless, and the doctor, who had been helping her, whispered to her:

"We must take Caravan away."

She nodded assent, and, going up to her husband, who was still on his knees, sobbing, she raised him up by one arm, while Chenet took him by the other.

They put him into a chair, and his wife kissed his forehead, and then began to lecture him. Chenet enforced her words and preached firmness, courage, and resignation—the very things which are always wanting in such overwhelming misfortunes—and then both of them took him by the arms again and led him out.

He was crying like a great child, with convulsive sobs; his arms hanging down, and his legs weak, and he went downstairs without knowing what he was doing, and moving his feet mechanically. They put him into the chair which he always occupied at dinner, in front of his empty soup plate. And there he sat, without moving, his eyes fixed on his glass, and so stupefied with grief, that he could not even think.

In a corner, Madame Caravan was talking with the doctor and asking what the necessary formalities were, as she wanted to obtain practical information. At last, Monsieur Chenet, who appeared to be waiting for something, took up his hat and prepared to go, saying that he had not dined yet; whereupon she exclaimed:

"What! you have not dined? Why, stay here, doctor; don't go. You shall have whatever we have, for, of course, you understand that we do not fare sumptuously." He made excuses and refused, but she persisted, and said: "You really must stay; at times like this, people like to have friends near them, and, besides that, perhaps you will be able to persuade my husband to take some nourishment; he must keep up his strength."

The doctor bowed, and, putting down his hat, he said:

"In that case, I will accept your invitation, madame."

She gave Rosalie, who seemed to have lost her head, some orders, and then sat down, "to pretend to eat," as she said, "to keep the doctor company."

The soup was brought in again, and Monsieur Chenet took two helpings. Then there came a dish of tripe, which exhaled a smell of onions, and which Madame Caravan made up her mind to taste.

"It is excellent," the doctor said, at which she smiled, and, turning to her husband, she said:

"Do take a little, my poor Alfred, only just to put something in your stomach. Remember that you have got to pass the night watching by her!"

He held out his plate, docilely, just as he would have gone to bed, if he had been told to, obeying her in everything, without resistance and without reflection, and he ate; the doctor helped himself three times, while Madame Caravan, from time to time, fished out a large piece at the end of her fork, and swallowed it with a sort of studied indifference.

When a salad bowl full of macaroni was brought in, the doctor said:

"By Jove! That is what I am very fond of." And this time, Madame Caravan helped everybody. She even filled the saucers that were being scraped by the children, who, being left to themselves, had been drinking wine without any water, and were now kicking each other under the table.

Chenet remembered that Rossini, the composer, had been very fond of that Italian dish, and suddenly he exclaimed:

"Why! that rhymes, and one could begin some lines like this:

> The Maestro Rossini
>
> Was fond of macaroni."

Nobody listened to him, however. Madame Caravan, who had suddenly grown thoughtful, was thinking of all the probable consequences of the event, while her husband made bread pellets, which he put on the table-cloth, and looked at with a fixed, idiotic stare. As he was devoured by thirst, he was continually raising his glass full of wine to his lips, and the consequence was that his mind, which had been upset by the shock and grief, seemed to become vague, and his ideas danced about as digestion commenced.

The doctor, who, meanwhile, had been drinking away steadily, was getting visibly drunk, and Madame Caravan herself felt the reaction which follows all nervous shocks, and was agitated and excited, and, although she had drunk nothing but water, her head felt rather confused.

Presently, Chenet began to relate stories of death that appeared comical to him. For in that suburb of Paris, that is full of people from the provinces, one finds that indifference towards death which all peasants show, were it even their own father or mother; that want of respect, that unconscious brutality which is so common in the country, and so rare in Paris, and he said:

"Why, I was sent for last week to the Rue du Puteaux, and when I went, I found the patient dead and the whole family calmly sitting beside the bed finishing a bottle of aniseed cordial, which had been bought the night before to satisfy the dying man's fancy."

But Madame Caravan was not listening; she was continually thinking of the inheritance, and Caravan was incapable of understanding anything further.

Coffee was presently served, and it had been made very strong to give them courage. As every cup was well flavored with cognac, it made all their faces red, and confused their ideas still more. To make matters still worse, Chenet suddenly seized the brandy bottle and poured out "a drop for each of them just to wash their mouths out with," as he termed it, and then, without speaking any more, overcome in spite of themselves, by that feeling of animal comfort which alcohol affords after dinner, they slowly sipped the sweet cognac, which formed a yellowish syrup at the bottom of their cups.

The children had fallen asleep, and Rosalie carried them off to bed. Caravan, mechanically obeying that wish to forget oneself which possesses all unhappy persons, helped himself to brandy again several times, and his dull eyes grew bright. At last the doctor rose to go, and seizing his friend's arm, he said:

"Come with me; a little fresh air will do you good. When one is in trouble, one must not remain in one spot."

The other obeyed mechanically, put on his hat, took his stick, and went out, and both of them walked arm-in-arm towards the Seine, in the starlight night.

The air was warm and sweet, for all the gardens in the neighborhood were full of flowers at this season of the year, and their fragrance, which is scarcely perceptible during the day, seemed to awaken at the approach of night, and mingled with the light breezes which blew upon them in the darkness.

The broad avenue with its two rows of gas lamps, that extended as far as the Arc de Triomphe, was deserted and silent, but there was the distant roar of Paris, which seemed to have a reddish vapor hanging over it. It was a kind of continual rumbling, which was at times answered by the whistle of a train in the distance, travelling at full speed to the ocean, through the provinces.

The fresh air on the faces of the two men rather overcame them at first, made the doctor lose his equilibrium a little, and increased Caravan's giddiness, from which he had suffered since dinner. He walked as if he were in a dream; his thoughts were paralyzed, although he felt no great grief, for he was in a state of mental torpor that prevented him from suffering, and he even felt a sense of relief which was increased by the mildness of the night.

When they reached the bridge, they turned to the right, and got the fresh breeze from the river, which rolled along, calm and melancholy, bordered by tall poplar trees, while the stars looked as if they were floating on the water and were moving with the current. A slight white mist that floated over the opposite banks, filled their lungs with a sensation of cold, and Caravan stopped suddenly, for he was struck by that smell from the water which brought back old memories to his mind. For, in his mind, he suddenly saw his mother again, in Picardy, as he had seen her years before, kneeling in front of their door, and washing the heaps of linen at her side in the stream that ran through their garden. He almost fancied that he could hear the sound of the wooden paddle with which she beat the linen in the calm silence of the country, and her voice, as she called out to him: "Alfred, bring me some soap." And he smelled that odor of running water, of the mist rising from the wet ground, that marshy smell, which he should never forget, and which came back to him on this very evening on which his mother had died.

He stopped, seized with a feeling of despair. A sudden flash seemed to reveal to him the extent of his calamity, and that breath from the river plunged him into an abyss of hopeless grief. His life seemed cut in half, his youth disappeared, swallowed up by that death. All the former days were over and done with, all the recollections of his youth had been swept away; for the future, there would be nobody to talk to him of what had happened in days gone by, of the people he had known of old, of his own part of the country, and of his past life; that was a part of his existence which existed no longer, and the rest might as well end now.

And then he saw "the mother" as she was when young, wearing well-worn dresses, which he remembered for such a long time that they seemed inseparable from her; he recollected her movements, the different tones of her voice, her habits, her predilections, her fits of anger, the wrinkles on her face, the movements of her thin fingers, and all her well-known attitudes, which she would never have again, and clutching hold of the doctor, he began to moan and weep. His thin legs began to tremble, his whole stout body was shaken by his sobs, all he could say was:

"My mother, my poor mother, my poor mother!"

But his companion, who was still drunk, and who intended to finish the evening in certain places of bad repute that he frequented secretly, made him sit down on the grass by the riverside, and left him almost immediately, under the pretext that he had to see a patient.

Caravan went on crying for some time, and when he had got to the end of his tears, when his grief had, so to say, run out, he again felt relief, repose and sudden tranquillity.

The moon had risen, and bathed the horizon in its soft light.

The tall poplar trees had a silvery sheen on them, and the mist on the plain looked like drifting snow; the river, in which the stars were reflected, and which had a sheen as of mother-of-pearl, was gently rippled by the wind. The air was soft and sweet, and Caravan inhaled it almost greedily, and thought that he could perceive a feeling of freshness, of calm and of superhuman consolation pervading him.

He actually resisted that feeling of comfort and relief, and kept on saying to himself: "My poor mother, my poor mother!" and tried to make himself cry, from a kind of conscientious feeling; but he could not succeed in doing so any longer, and those sad thoughts, which had made him sob so bitterly a shore time before, had almost passed away. In a few moments, he rose to go home, and returned slowly, under the influence of that serene night, and with a heart soothed in spite of himself.

When he reached the bridge, he saw that the last tramcar was ready to start, and behind it were the brightly lighted windows of the Cafe du Globe. He felt a longing to tell somebody of his loss, to excite pity, to make himself interesting. He put on a woeful face, pushed open the door, and went up to the counter, where the landlord still was. He had counted on creating a sensation, and had hoped that everybody would get up and come to him with outstretched hands, and say: "Why, what is the matter with you?" But nobody noticed his disconsolate face, so he rested his two elbows on the counter, and, burying his face in his hands, he murmured: "Mon Dieu! Mon Dieu!"

The landlord looked at him and said: "Are you ill, Monsieur Caravan?"

"No, my friend," he replied, "but my mother has just died."

"Ah!" the other exclaimed, and as a customer at the other end of the establishment asked for a glass of Bavarian beer, he went to attend to him, leaving Caravan dumfounded at his want of sympathy.

The three domino players were sitting at the same table which they had occupied before dinner, totally absorbed in their game, and Caravan went up to them, in search of pity, but as none of them appeared to notice him he made up his mind to speak.

"A great misfortune has happened to me since I was here," he said.

All three slightly raised their heads at the same instant, but keeping their eyes fixed on the pieces which they held in their hands.

"What do you say?"

"My mother has just died"; whereupon one of them said:

"Oh! the devil," with that false air of sorrow which indifferent people assume. Another, who could not find anything to say, emitted a sort of sympathetic whistle, shaking his head at the same time, and the third turned to the game again, as if he were saying to himself: "Is that all!"

Caravan had expected some of these expressions that are said to "come from the heart," and when he saw how his news was received, he left the table, indignant at their calmness at their friend's sorrow, although this sorrow had stupefied him so that he scarcely felt it any longer. When he got home his wife was waiting for him in her nightgown, and sitting in a low chair by the open window, still thinking of the inheritance.

"Undress yourself," she said; "we can go on talking."

He raised his head, and looking at the ceiling, said:

"But—there is nobody upstairs."

"I beg your pardon, Rosalie is with her, and you can go and take her place at three o'clock in the morning, when you have had some sleep."

He only partially undressed, however, so as to be ready for anything that might happen, and after tying a silk handkerchief round his head, he lay down to rest, and for some time neither of them spoke. Madame Caravan was thinking.

Her nightcap was adorned with a red bow, and was pushed rather to one side, as was the way with all the caps she wore, and presently she turned towards him and said:

"Do you know whether your mother made a will?"

He hesitated for a moment, and then replied:

"I—I do not think so. No, I am sure that she did not."

His wife looked at him, and she said, in a low, angry tone:

"I call that infamous; here we have been wearing ourselves out for ten years in looking after her, and have boarded and lodged her! Your sister would not have done so much for her, nor I either, if I had known how I was to be rewarded! Yes, it is a disgrace to her memory! I dare say that you will tell me that she paid us, but one cannot pay one's children in ready money for what they do; that obligation is recognized after death; at any rate, that is how honorable people act. So I have had all my worry and trouble for nothing! Oh, that is nice! that is very nice!"

Poor Caravan, who was almost distracted, kept on repeating:

"My dear, my dear, please, please be quiet."

She grew calmer by degrees, and, resuming her usual voice and manner, she continued:

"We must let your sister know to-morrow."

He started, and said:

"Of course we must; I had forgotten all about it; I will send her a telegram the first thing in the morning."

"No," she replied, like a woman who had foreseen everything; "no, do not send it before ten or eleven o'clock, so that we may have time to turn round before she comes. It does not take more than two hours to get here from Charenton, and we can say that you lost your head from grief. If we let her know in the course of the day, that will be soon enough, and will give us time to look round."

Caravan put his hand to his forehead, and, in the came timid voice in which he always spoke of his chief, the very thought of whom made him tremble, he said:

"I must let them know at the office."

"Why?" she replied. "On occasions like this, it is always excusable to forget. Take my advice, and don't let him know; your chief will not be able to say anything to you, and you will put him in a nice fix.

"Oh! yes, that I shall, and he will be in a terrible rage, too, when he notices my absence. Yes, you are right; it is a capital idea, and when I tell him that my mother is dead, he will be obliged to hold his tongue."

And he rubbed his hands in delight at the joke, when he thought of his chief's face; while upstairs lay the body of the dead old woman, with the servant asleep beside it.

But Madame Caravan grew thoughtful, as if she were preoccupied by something which she did not care to mention, and at last she said:

"Your mother had given you her clock, had she not—the girl playing at cup and ball?"

He thought for a moment, and then replied:

"Yes, yes; she said to me (but it was a long time ago, when she first came here): 'I shall leave the clock to you, if you look after me well.'"

Madame Caravan was reassured, and regained her serenity, and said:

"Well, then, you must go and fetch it out of her room, for if we get your sister here, she will prevent us from taking it."

He hesitated.

"Do you think so?"

That made her angry.

"I certainly think so; once it is in our possession, she will know nothing at all about where it came from; it belongs to us. It is just the same with the chest of drawers with the marble top, that is in her room; she gave it me one day when she was in a good temper. We will bring it down at the same time."

Caravan, however, seemed incredulous, and said:

"But, my dear, it is a great responsibility!"

She turned on him furiously.

"Oh! Indeed! Will you never change? You would let your children die of hunger, rather than make a move. Does not that chest of drawers belong to us, as she gave it to me? And if your sister is not satisfied, let her tell me so, me! I don't care a straw for your sister. Come, get up, and we will bring down what your mother gave us, immediately."

Trembling and vanquished, he got out of bed and began to put on his trousers, but she stopped him:

"It is not worth while to dress yourself; your underwear is quite enough. I mean to go as I am."

They both left the room in their night clothes, went upstairs quite noiselessly, opened the door and went into the room, where the four lighted tapers and the plate with the sprig of box alone seemed to be watching the old woman in her rigid repose, for Rosalie, who was lying back in the easy chair with her legs stretched out, her hands folded in her lap, and her head on one side, was also quite motionless, and was snoring with her mouth wide open.

Caravan took the clock, which was one of those grotesque objects that were produced so plentifully under the Empire. A girl in gilt bronze was holding a cup and ball, and the ball formed the pendulum.

“Give that to me,” his wife said, “and take the marble slab off the chest of drawers.”

He put the marble slab on his shoulder with considerable effort, and they left the room. Caravan had to stoop in the doorway, and trembled as he went downstairs, while his wife walked backwards, so as to light him, and held the candlestick in one hand, carrying the clock under the other arm.

When they were in their own room, she heaved a sigh.

“We have got over the worst part of the job,” she said; “so now let us go and fetch the other things.”

But the bureau drawers were full of the old woman’s wearing apparel, which they must manage to hide somewhere, and Madame Caravan soon thought of a plan.

“Go and get that wooden packing case in the vestibule; it is hardly worth anything, and we may just as well put it here.”

And when he had brought it upstairs they began to fill it. One by one they took out all the collars, cuffs, chemises, caps, all the well-worn things that had belonged to the poor woman lying there behind them, and arranged them methodically in the wooden box in such a manner as to deceive Madame Braux, the deceased woman’s other child, who would be coming the next day.

When they had finished, they first of all carried the bureau drawers downstairs, and the remaining portion afterwards, each of them holding an end, and it was some time before they could make up their minds where it would stand best; but at last they decided upon their own room, opposite the bed, between the two windows, and as soon as it was in its place Madame Caravan filled it with her own things. The clock was placed on the chimney-piece in the dining-room, and they looked to see what the effect was, and were both delighted with it and agreed that nothing could be better. Then they retired, she blew out the candle, and soon everybody in the house was asleep.

It was broad daylight when. Caravan opened his eyes again. His mind was rather confused when he woke up, and he did not clearly remember what had happened for a few minutes; when he did, he felt a weight at his heart, and jumped out of bed, almost ready to cry again.

He hastened to the room overhead, where Rosalie was still sleeping in the same position as the night before, not having awakened once. He sent her to do her work, put fresh tapers in the place of those that had burnt out, and then he looked at his mother, revolving in his brain those apparently profound thoughts, those religious and philosophical commonplaces which trouble people of mediocre intelligence in the presence of death.

But, as his wife was calling him, he went downstairs. She had written out a list of what had to be done during the morning, and he was horrified when he saw the memorandum:

1. Report the death at the mayor’s office. 2. See the doctor who had attended her. 3. Order the coffin. 4. Give notice at the church. 5. Go to the undertaker. 6. Order the notices of her death at the printer’s. 7. Go to the lawyer. 8. Telegraph the news to all the family.

Besides all this, there were a number of small commissions; so he took his hat and went out. As the news had spread abroad, Madame Caravan’s female friends and neighbors soon began to come in and begged to be allowed to see the body. There had been a scene between husband and wife at the hairdresser’s on the ground floor about the matter, while a customer was being shaved. The wife, who was knitting steadily, said: "Well, there is one less, and as great a miser as one ever meets with. I certainly did not care for her; but, nevertheless, I must go and have a look at her."

The husband, while lathering his patient's chin, said: "That is another queer fancy! Nobody but a woman would think of such a thing. It is not enough for them to worry you during life, but they cannot even leave you at peace when you are dead:" But his wife, without being in the least disconcerted, replied: "The feeling is stronger than I am, and I must go. It has been on me since the morning. If I were not to see her, I should think about it all my life; but when I have had a good look at her, I shall be satisfied."

The knight of the razor shrugged his shoulders and remarked in a low voice to the gentleman whose cheek he was scraping: "I just ask you, what sort of ideas do you think these confounded females have? I should not amuse myself by going to see a corpse!" But his wife had heard him and replied very quietly: "But it is so, it is so." And then, putting her knitting on the counter, she went upstairs to the first floor, where she met two other neighbors, who had just come, and who were discussing the event with Madame Caravan, who was giving them the details, and they all went together to the death chamber. The four women went in softly, and, one after the other, sprinkled the bed clothes with the salt water, knelt down, made the sign of the cross while they mumbled a prayer. Then they rose from their knees and looked for some time at the corpse with round, wide-open eyes and mouths partly open, while the daughter-in-law of the dead woman, with her handkerchief to her face, pretended to be sobbing piteously.

When she turned about to walk away whom should she perceive standing close to the door but Marie-Louise and Philippe-Auguste, who were curiously taking stock of all that was going on. Then, forgetting her pretended grief, she threw herself upon them with uplifted hands, crying out in a furious voice, "Will you get out of this, you horrid brats!"

Ten minutes later, going upstairs again with another contingent of neighbors, she prayed, wept profusely, performed all her duties, and found once more her two children, who had followed her upstairs. She again boxed their ears soundly, but the next time she paid no heed to them, and at each fresh arrival of visitors the two urchins always followed in the wake, kneeling down in a corner and imitating slavishly everything they saw their mother do.

When the afternoon came the crowds of inquisitive people began to diminish, and soon there were no more visitors. Madame Caravan, returning to her own apartments, began to make the necessary preparations for the funeral ceremony, and the deceased was left alone.

The window of the room was open. A torrid heat entered, along with clouds of dust; the flames of the four candles were flickering beside the immobile corpse, and upon the cloth which covered the face, the closed eyes, the two stretched-out hands, small flies alighted, came, went and careered up and down incessantly, being the only companions of the old woman for the time being.

Marie-Louise and Philippe-Auguste, however, had now left the house and were running up and down the street. They were soon surrounded by their playmates, by little girls especially, who were older and who were much more interested in all the mysteries of life, asking questions as if they were grown people.

"Then your grandmother is dead?" "Yes, she died yesterday evening." "What does a dead person look like?"

Then Marie began to explain, telling all about the candles, the sprig of box and the face of the corpse. It was not long before great curiosity was aroused in the minds of all the children, and they asked to be allowed to go upstairs to look at the departed.

Marie-Louise at once organized a first expedition, consisting of five girls and two boys—the biggest and the most courageous. She made them take off their shoes so that they might not be discovered. The troupe filed into the house and mounted the stairs as stealthily as an army of mice.

Once in the chamber, the little girl, imitating her mother, regulated the ceremony. She solemnly walked in advance of her comrades, went down on her knees, made the sign of the cross, moved her lips as in prayer, rose, sprinkled the bed, and while the children, all crowded together, were approaching—frightened and curious and eager to look at the face and hands of the deceased—she began suddenly to simulate sobbing and to bury her eyes in her little handkerchief. Then, becoming instantly consoled, on thinking of the other children who were downstairs waiting at the door, she ran downstairs followed by the rest, returning in a minute with another group, then a third; for all the little ragamuffins of the countryside, even to the little beggars in rags, had congregated in order to participate in this new pleasure; and each time she repeated her mother's grimaces with absolute perfection.

At length, however, she became tired. Some game or other drew the children away from the house, and the old grandmother was left alone, forgotten suddenly by everybody.

The room was growing dark, and upon the dry and rigid features of the corpse the fitful flames of the candles cast patches of light.

Towards 8 o'clock Caravan ascended to the chamber of death, closed the windows and renewed the candles. He was now quite composed on entering the room, accustomed already to regard the corpse as though it had been there for months. He even went the length of declaring that, as yet, there were no signs of decomposition, making this remark just at the moment when he and his wife were about to sit down at table. "Pshaw!" she responded, "she is now stark and stiff; she will keep for a year."

The soup was eaten in silence. The children, who had been left to themselves all day, now worn out by fatigue, were sleeping soundly on their chairs, and nobody ventured to break the silence.

Suddenly the flame of the lamp went down. Madame Caravan immediately turned up the wick, a hollow sound ensued, and the light went out. They had forgotten to buy oil. To send for it now to the grocer's would keep back the dinner, and they began to look for candles, but none were to be found except the tapers which had been placed upon the table upstairs in the death chamber.

Madame Caravan, always prompt in her decisions, quickly despatched Marie-Louise to fetch two, and her return was awaited in total darkness.

The footsteps of the girl who had ascended the stairs were distinctly heard. There was silence for a few seconds and then the child descended precipitately. She threw open the door and in a choking voice murmured: "Oh! papa, grandmamma is dressing herself!"

Caravan bounded to his feet with such precipitance that his chair fell over against the wall. He stammered out: "You say? . . . . What are you saying?"

But Marie-Louise, gasping with emotion, repeated: "Grand—grand —grandmamma is putting on her clothes, she is coming downstairs."

Caravan rushed boldly up the staircase, followed by his wife, dumfounded; but he came to a standstill before the door of the second floor, overcome with terror, not daring to enter. What was he going to see? Madame Caravan, more courageous, turned the handle of the door and stepped forward into the room.

The old woman was standing up. In awakening from her lethargic sleep, before even regaining full consciousness, in turning upon her side and raising herself on her elbow, she had extinguished three of the candles which burned near the bed. Then, gaining strength, she got off the bed and began to look for her clothes. The absence of her chest of drawers had at first worried her, but, after a little, she had succeeded in finding her things at the bottom of the wooden box, and was now quietly dressing. She emptied the plateful of water, replaced the sprig of box behind the looking-glass, and arranged the chairs in their places, and was ready to go downstairs when there appeared before her her son and daughter-in-law.

Caravan rushed forward, seized her by the hands, embraced her with tears in his eyes, while his wife, who was behind him, repeated in a hypocritical tone of voice: "Oh, what a blessing! oh, what a blessing!"

But the old woman, without being at all moved, without even appearing to understand, rigid as a statue, and with glazed eyes, simply asked: "Will dinner soon be ready?"

He stammered out, not knowing what he said:

"Oh, yes, mother, we have been waiting for you."

And with an alacrity unusual in him, he took her arm, while Madame Caravan, the younger, seized the candle and lighted them downstairs, walking backwards in front of them, step by step, just as she had done the previous night for her husband, who was carrying the marble.

On reaching the first floor, she almost ran against people who were ascending the stairs. It was the Charenton family, Madame Braux, followed by her husband.

The wife, tall and stout, with a prominent stomach, opened wide her terrified eyes and was ready to make her escape. The husband, a socialist shoemaker, a little hairy man, the perfect image of a monkey, murmured quite unconcerned: "Well, what next? Is she resurrected?"

As soon as Madame Caravan recognized them, she made frantic gestures to them; then, speaking aloud, she said: "Why, here you are! What a pleasant surprise!"

But Madame Braux, dumfounded, understood nothing. She responded in a low voice: "It was your telegram that brought us; we thought that all was over."

Her husband, who was behind her, pinched her to make her keep silent. He added with a sly laugh, which his thick beard concealed: "It was very kind of you to invite us here. We set out post haste," which remark showed the hostility which had for a long time reigned between the households. Then, just as the old woman reached the last steps, he pushed forward quickly and rubbed his hairy face against her cheeks, shouting in her ear, on account of her deafness: "How well you look, mother; sturdy as usual, hey!"

Madame Braux, in her stupefaction at seeing the old woman alive, whom they all believed to be dead, dared not even embrace her; and her enormous bulk blocked up the passageway and hindered the others from advancing. The old woman, uneasy and suspicious, but without speaking, looked at everyone around her; and her little gray eyes, piercing and hard, fixed themselves now on one and now on the other, and they were so full of meaning that the children became frightened.

Caravan, to explain matters, said: "She has been somewhat ill, but she is better now; quite well, indeed, are you not, mother?"

Then the good woman, continuing to walk, replied in a husky voice, as though it came from a distance: "It was syncope. I heard you all the while."

An embarrassing silence followed. They entered the dining-room, and in a few minutes all sat down to an improvised dinner.

Only M. Braux had retained his self-possession. His gorilla features grinned wickedly, while he let fall some words of double meaning which painfully disconcerted everyone.

But the door bell kept ringing every second, and Rosalie, distracted, came to call Caravan, who rushed out, throwing down his napkin. His brother-in-law even asked him whether it was not one of his reception days, to which he stammered out in answer: "No, only a few packages; nothing more."

A parcel was brought in, which he began to open carelessly, and the mourning announcements with black borders appeared unexpectedly. Reddening up to the very eyes, he closed the package hurriedly and pushed it under his waistcoat.

His mother had not seen it! She was looking intently at her clock which stood on the mantelpiece, and the embarrassment increased in midst of a dead silence. Turning her wrinkled face towards her daughter, the old woman, in whose eyes gleamed malice, said: "On Monday you must take me away from here, so that I can see your little girl. I want so much to see her." Madame Braux, her features all beaming, exclaimed: "Yes, mother, that I will," while Madame Caravan, the younger, who had turned pale, was ready to faint with annoyance. The two men, however, gradually drifted into conversation and soon became embroiled in a political discussion. Braux maintained the most revolutionary and communistic doctrines, his eyes glowing, and gesticulating and throwing about his arms. "Property, sir," he said, "is a robbery perpetrated on the working classes; the land is the common property of every man; hereditary rights are an infamy and a disgrace." But here he suddenly stopped, looking as if he had just said something foolish, then added in softer tones: "But this is not the proper moment to discuss such things."

The door was opened and Dr. Chenet appeared. For a moment he seemed bewildered, but regaining his usual smirking expression of countenance, he jauntily approached the old woman and said: "Aha! mamma; you are better to-day. Oh! I never had any doubt but you would come round again; in fact, I said to myself as I was mounting the staircase, 'I have an idea that I shall find the old lady on her feet once more';" and as he patted her gently on the back: "Ah! she is as solid as the Pont-Neuf, she will bury us all; see if she does not."

He sat down, accepted the coffee that was offered him, and soon began to join in the conversation of the two men, backing up Braux, for he himself had been mixed up in the Commune.

The old woman, now feeling herself fatigued, wished to retire. Caravan rushed forward. She looked him steadily in the eye and said: "You, you must carry my clock and chest of drawers upstairs again without a moment's delay." "Yes, mamma," he replied, gasping; "yes, I will do so." The old woman then took the arm of her daughter and withdrew from the room. The two Caravans remained astounded, silent, plunged in the deepest despair, while Braux rubbed his hands and sipped his coffee gleefully.

Suddenly Madame Caravan, consumed with rage, rushed at him, exclaiming: "You are a thief, a footpad, a cur! I would spit in your face! I—I —would——" She could find nothing further to say, suffocating as she was with rage, while he went on sipping his coffee with a smile.

His wife returning just then, Madame Caravan attacked her sister-in-law, and the two women—the one with her enormous bulk, the other epileptic and spare, with changed voices and trembling hands flew at one another with words of abuse.

Chenet and Braux now interposed, and the latter, taking his better half by the shoulders, pushed her out of the door before him, shouting: "Go on, you slut; you talk too much"; and the two were heard in the street quarrelling until they disappeared from sight.

M. Chenet also took his departure, leaving the Caravans alone, face to face. The husband fell back on his chair, and with the cold sweat standing out in beads on his temples, murmured: "What shall I say to my chief to-morrow?"

BESIDE SCHOPENHAUER'S CORPSE

He was slowly dying, as consumptives die. I saw him each day, about two o'clock, sitting beneath the hotel windows on a bench in the promenade, looking out on the calm sea. He remained for some time without moving, in the heat of the sun, gazing mournfully at the Mediterranean. Every now and then, he cast a glance at the lofty mountains with beclouded summits that shut in Mentone; then, with a very slow movement, he would cross his long legs, so thin that they seemed like two bones, around which fluttered the cloth of his trousers, and he would open a book, always the same book. And then he did not stir any more, but read on, read on with his eye and his mind; all his wasting body seemed to read, all his soul plunged, lost, disappeared, in this book, up to the hour when the cool air made him cough a little. Then, he got up and reentered the hotel.

He was a tall German, with fair beard, who breakfasted and dined in his own room, and spoke to nobody.

A vague, curiosity attracted me to him. One day, I sat down by his side, having taken up a book, too, to keep up appearances, a volume of Musset's poems.

And I began to look through "Rolla."

Suddenly, my neighbor said to me, in good French:

"Do you know German, monsieur?"

"Not at all, monsieur."

"I am sorry for that. Since chance has thrown us side by side, I could have lent you, I could have shown you, an inestimable thing—this book which I hold in my hand."

"What is it, pray?"

"It is a copy of my master, Schopenhauer, annotated with his own hand. All the margins, as you may see, are covered with his handwriting."

I took the book from him reverently, and I gazed at these forms incomprehensible to me, but which revealed the immortal thoughts of the greatest shatterer of dreams who had ever dwelt on earth.

And Musset's verses arose in my memory:

"Hast thou found out, Voltaire, that it is bliss to die,

And does thy hideous smile over thy bleached bones fly?"

And involuntarily I compared the childish sarcasm, the religious sarcasm of Voltaire with the irresistible irony of the German philosopher whose influence is henceforth ineffaceable.

Let us protest and let us be angry, let us be indignant, or let us be enthusiastic, Schopenhauer has marked humanity with the seal of his disdain and of his disenchantment.

A disabused pleasure-seeker, he overthrew beliefs, hopes, poetic ideals and chimeras, destroyed the aspirations, ravaged the confidence of souls, killed love, dragged down the chivalrous worship of women, crushed the illusions of hearts, and accomplished the most gigantic task ever attempted by scepticism. He spared nothing with his mocking spirit, and exhausted everything. And even to-day those who execrate him seem to carry in their own souls particles of his thought.

"So, then, you were intimately acquainted with Schopenhauer?" I said to the German.

He smiled sadly.

"Up to the time of his death, monsieur."

And he spoke to me about the philosopher and told me about the almost supernatural impression which this strange being made on all who came near him.

He gave me an account of the interview of the old iconoclast with a French politician, a doctrinaire Republican, who wanted to get a glimpse of this man, and found him in a noisy tavern, seated in the midst of his disciples, dry, wrinkled, laughing with an unforgettable laugh, attacking and tearing to pieces ideas and beliefs with a single word, as a dog tears with one bite of his teeth the tissues with which he plays.

He repeated for me the comment of this Frenchman as he went away, astonished and terrified: "I thought I had spent an hour with the devil."

Then he added:

"He had, indeed, monsieur, a frightful smile, which terrified us even after his death. I can tell you an anecdote about it that is not generally known, if it would interest you."

And he began, in a languid voice, interrupted by frequent fits of coughing.

"Schopenhauer had just died, and it was arranged that we should watch, in turn, two by two, till morning.

"He was lying in a large apartment, very simple, vast and gloomy. Two wax candles were burning on the stand by the bedside.

"It was midnight when I went on watch, together with one of our comrades. The two friends whom we replaced had left the apartment, and we came and sat down at the foot of the bed.

"The face was not changed. It was laughing. That pucker which we knew so well lingered still around the corners of the lips, and it seemed to us that he was about to open his eyes, to move and to speak. His thought, or rather his thoughts, enveloped us. We felt ourselves more than ever in the atmosphere of his genius, absorbed, possessed by him. His domination seemed to be even more sovereign now that he was dead. A feeling of mystery was blended with the power of this incomparable spirit.

"The bodies of these men disappear, but they themselves remain; and in the night which follows the cessation of their heart's pulsation I assure you, monsieur, they are terrifying.

"And in hushed tones we talked about him, recalling to mind certain sayings, certain formulas of his, those startling maxims which are like jets of flame flung, in a few words, into the darkness of the Unknown Life.

"'It seems to me that he is going to speak,' said my comrade. And we stared with uneasiness bordering on fear at the motionless face, with its eternal laugh. Gradually, we began to feel ill at ease, oppressed, on the point of fainting. I faltered:

"'I don't know what is the matter with me, but, I assure you I am not well.'

"And at that moment we noticed that there was an unpleasant odor from the corpse.

"Then, my comrade suggested that we should go into the adjoining room, and leave the door open; and I assented to his proposal.

"I took one of the wax candles which burned on the stand, and I left the second behind. Then we went and sat down at the other end of the adjoining apartment, in such a position that we could see the bed and the corpse, clearly revealed by the light.

"But he still held possession of us. One would have said that his immaterial essence, liberated, free, all-powerful and dominating, was flitting around us. And sometimes, too, the dreadful odor of the decomposed body came toward us and penetrated us, sickening and indefinable.

"Suddenly a shiver passed through our bones: a sound, a slight sound, came from the death-chamber. Immediately we fixed our glances on him, and we saw, yes, monsieur, we saw distinctly, both of us, something white pass across the bed, fall on the carpet, and vanish under an armchair.

"We were on our feet before we had time to think of anything, distracted by stupefying terror, ready to run away. Then we stared at each other. We were horribly pale. Our hearts throbbed fiercely enough to have raised the clothing on our chests. I was the first to speak:

"'Did you see?'

"'Yes, I saw.'

"'Can it be that he is not dead?'

"'Why, when the body is putrefying?'

"'What are we to do?'

"My companion said in a hesitating tone:

"'We must go and look.'

"I took our wax candle and entered first, glancing into all the dark corners in the large apartment. Nothing was moving now, and I approached the bed. But I stood transfixed with stupor and fright:

"Schopenhauer was no longer laughing! He was grinning in a horrible fashion, with his lips pressed together and deep hollows in his cheeks. I stammered out:

"'He is not dead!'

"But the terrible odor ascended to my nose and stifled me. And I no longer moved, but kept staring fixedly at him, terrified as if in the presence of an apparition.

"Then my companion, having seized the other wax candle, bent forward. Next, he touched my arm without uttering a word. I followed his glance, and saw on the ground, under the armchair by the side of the bed, standing out white on the dark carpet, and open as if to bite,

Schopenhauer's set of artificial teeth.

"The work of decomposition, loosening the jaws, had made it jump out of the mouth.

"I was really frightened that day, monsieur."

And as the sun was sinking toward the glittering sea, the consumptive German rose from his seat, gave me a parting bow, and retired into the hotel.

VOLUME III.
MISS HARRIET

There were seven of us on a drag, four women and three men; one of the latter sat on the box seat beside the coachman. We were ascending, at a snail's pace, the winding road up the steep cliff along the coast.

Setting out from Etretat at break of day in order to visit the ruins of Tancarville, we were still half asleep, benumbed by the fresh air of the morning. The women especially, who were little accustomed to these early excursions, half opened and closed their eyes every moment, nodding their heads or yawning, quite insensible to the beauties of the dawn.

It was autumn. On both sides of the road stretched the bare fields, yellowed by the stubble of wheat and oats which covered the soil like a beard that had been badly shaved. The moist earth seemed to steam. Larks were singing high up in the air, while other birds piped in the bushes.

The sun rose at length in front of us, bright red on the plane of the horizon, and in proportion as it ascended, growing clearer from minute to minute, the country seemed to awake, to smile, to shake itself like a young girl leaving her bed in her white robe of vapor. The Comte d'Etraille, who was seated on the box, cried:

"Look! look! a hare!" and he extended his arm toward the left, pointing to a patch of clover. The animal scurried along, almost hidden by the clover, only its large ears showing. Then it swerved across a furrow, stopped, started off again at full speed, changed its course, stopped anew, uneasy, spying out every danger, uncertain what route to take, when suddenly it began to run with great bounds, disappearing finally in a large patch of beet-root. All the men had waked up to watch the course of the animal.

Rene Lamanoir exclaimed:

"We are not at all gallant this morning," and; regarding his neighbor, the little Baroness de Serennes, who struggled against sleep, he said to her in a low tone: "You are thinking of your husband, baroness. Reassure yourself; he will not return before Saturday, so you have still four days."

She answered with a sleepy smile:

"How stupid you are!" Then, shaking off her torpor, she added: "Now, let somebody say something to make us laugh. You, Monsieur Chenal, who have the reputation of having had more love affairs than the Duc de Richelieu, tell us a love story in which you have played a part; anything you like."

Leon Chenal, an old painter, who had once been very handsome, very strong, very proud of his physique and very popular with women, took his long white beard in his hand and smiled. Then, after a few moments' reflection, he suddenly became serious.

"Ladies, it will not be an amusing tale, for I am going to relate to you the saddest love affair of my life, and I sincerely hope that none of my friends may ever pass through a similar experience.

"I was twenty-five years of age and was pillaging along the coast of Normandy. I call 'pillaging' wandering about, with a knapsack on one's back, from inn to inn, under the pretext of making studies and sketching landscapes. I knew nothing more enjoyable than that happy-go-lucky wandering life, in which one is perfectly free, without shackles of any kind, without care, without preoccupation, without thinking even of the morrow. One goes in any direction one pleases, without any guide save his fancy, without any counsellor save his eyes. One stops because a running brook attracts one, because the smell of potatoes frying tickles one's olfactories on passing an inn. Sometimes it is the perfume of clematis which decides one in his choice or the roguish glance of the servant at an inn. Do not despise me for my affection for these rustics. These girls have a soul as well as senses, not to mention firm cheeks and fresh lips; while their hearty and willing kisses have the flavor of wild fruit. Love is always love, come whence it may. A heart that beats at your approach, an eye that weeps when you go away are things so rare, so sweet, so precious that they must never be despised.

"I have had rendezvous in ditches full of primroses, behind the cow stable and in barns among the straw, still warm from the heat of the day. I have recollections of coarse gray cloth covering supple peasant skin and regrets for simple, frank kisses, more delicate in their unaffected sincerity than the subtle favors of charming and distinguished women.

"But what one loves most amid all these varied adventures is the country, the woods, the rising of the sun, the twilight, the moonlight. These are, for the painter, honeymoon trips with Nature. One is alone with her in that long and quiet association. You go to sleep in the fields, amid marguerites and poppies, and when you open your eyes in the full glare of the sunlight you descry in the distance the little village with its pointed clock tower which sounds the hour of noon.

"You sit down by the side of a spring which gushes out at the foot of an oak, amid a growth of tall, slender weeds, glistening with life. You go down on your knees, bend forward and drink that cold, pellucid water which wets your mustache and nose; you drink it with a physical pleasure, as though you kissed the spring, lip to lip. Sometimes, when you find a deep hole along the course of these tiny brooks, you plunge in quite naked, and you feel on your skin, from head to foot, as it were, an icy and delicious caress, the light and gentle quivering of the stream.

"You are gay on the hills, melancholy on the edge of ponds, inspired when the sun is setting in an ocean of blood-red clouds and casts red reflections or the river. And at night, under the moon, which passes across the vault of heaven, you think of a thousand strange things which would never have occurred to your mind under the brilliant light of day.

"So, in wandering through the same country where we, are this year, I came to the little village of Benouville, on the cliff between Yport and Etretat. I came from Fecamp, following the coast, a high coast as straight as a wall, with its projecting chalk cliffs descending perpendicularly into the sea. I had walked since early morning on the short grass, smooth and yielding as a carpet, that grows on the edge of the cliff. And, singing lustily, I walked with long strides, looking sometimes at the slow circling flight of a gull with its white curved wings outlined on the blue sky, sometimes at the brown sails of a fishing bark on the green sea. In short, I had passed a happy day, a day of liberty and of freedom from care.

"A little farmhouse where travellers were lodged was pointed out to me, a kind of inn, kept by a peasant woman, which stood in the centre of a Norman courtyard surrounded by a double row of beeches.

"Leaving the coast, I reached the hamlet, which was hemmed in by great trees, and I presented myself at the house of Mother Lecacheur.

"She was an old, wrinkled and stern peasant woman, who seemed always to receive customers under protest, with a kind of defiance.

“It was the month of May. The spreading apple trees covered the court with a shower of blossoms which rained unceasingly both upon people and upon the grass.

“I said: ‘Well, Madame Lecacheur, have you a room for me?’

“Astonished to find that I knew her name, she answered:

“‘That depends; everything is let, but all the same I can find out.”

“In five minutes we had come to an agreement, and I deposited my bag upon the earthen floor of a rustic room, furnished with a bed, two chairs, a table and a washbowl. The room looked into the large, smoky kitchen, where the lodgers took their meals with the people of the farm and the landlady, who was a widow.

“I washed my hands, after which I went out. The old woman was making a chicken fricassee for dinner in the large fireplace in which hung the iron pot, black with smoke.

“‘You have travellers, then, at the present time?’ said I to her.

“She answered in an offended tone of voice:

“‘I have a lady, an English lady, who has reached years of maturity. She occupies the other room.’

“I obtained, by means of an extra five sous a day, the privilege of dining alone out in the yard when the weather was fine.

“My place was set outside the door, and I was beginning to gnaw the lean limbs of the Normandy chicken, to drink the clear cider and to munch the hunk of white bread, which was four days old but excellent.

“Suddenly the wooden gate which gave on the highway was opened, and a strange lady directed her steps toward the house. She was very thin, very tall, so tightly enveloped in a red Scotch plaid shawl that one might have supposed she had no arms, if one had not seen a long hand appear just above the hips, holding a white tourist umbrella. Her face was like that of a mummy, surrounded with curls of gray hair, which tossed about at every step she took and made me think, I know not why, of a pickled herring in curl papers. Lowering her eyes, she passed quickly in front of me and entered the house.

“That singular apparition cheered me. She undoubtedly was my neighbor, the English lady of mature age of whom our hostess had spoken.

“I did not see her again that day. The next day, when I had settled myself to commence painting at the end of that beautiful valley which you know and which extends as far as Etretat, I perceived, on lifting my eyes suddenly, something singular standing on the crest of the cliff, one might have said a pole decked out with flags. It was she. On seeing me, she suddenly disappeared. I reentered the house at midday for lunch and took my seat at the general table, so as to make the acquaintance of this odd character. But she did not respond to my polite advances, was insensible even to my little attentions. I poured out water for her persistently, I passed her the dishes with great eagerness. A slight, almost imperceptible, movement of the head and an English word, murmured so low that I did not understand it, were her only acknowledgments.

“I ceased occupying myself with her, although she had disturbed my thoughts.

"At the end of three days I knew as much about her as did Madame Lecacheur herself.

"She was called Miss Harriet. Seeking out a secluded village in which to pass the summer, she had been attracted to Benouville some six months before and did not seem disposed to leave it. She never spoke at table, ate rapidly, reading all the while a small book of the Protestant propaganda. She gave a copy of it to everybody. The cure himself had received no less than four copies, conveyed by an urchin to whom she had paid two sous commission. She said sometimes to our hostess abruptly, without preparing her in the least for the declaration:

"'I love the Saviour more than all. I admire him in all creation; I adore him in all nature; I carry him always in my heart.'

"And she would immediately present the old woman with one of her tracts which were destined to convert the universe.

"In, the village she was not liked. In fact, the schoolmaster having pronounced her an atheist, a kind of stigma attached to her. The cure, who had been consulted by Madame Lecacheur, responded:

"'She is a heretic, but God does not wish the death of the sinner, and I believe her to be a person of pure morals.'

"These words, 'atheist,' 'heretic,' words which no one can precisely define, threw doubts into some minds. It was asserted, however, that this English woman was rich and that she had passed her life in travelling through every country in the world because her family had cast her off. Why had her family cast her off? Because of her impiety, of course!

"She was, in fact, one of those people of exalted principles; one of those opinionated puritans, of which England produces so many; one of those good and insupportable old maids who haunt the tables d'hote of every hotel in Europe, who spoil Italy, poison Switzerland, render the charming cities of the Mediterranean uninhabitable, carry everywhere their fantastic manias their manners of petrified vestals, their indescribable toilets and a certain odor of india-rubber which makes one believe that at night they are slipped into a rubber casing.

"Whenever I caught sight of one of these individuals in a hotel I fled like the birds who see a scarecrow in a field.

"This woman, however, appeared so very singular that she did not displease me.

"Madame Lecacheur, hostile by instinct to everything that was not rustic, felt in her narrow soul a kind of hatred for the ecstatic declarations of the old maid. She had found a phrase by which to describe her, a term of contempt that rose to her lips, called forth by I know not what confused and mysterious mental ratiocination. She said: 'That woman is a demoniac.' This epithet, applied to that austere and sentimental creature, seemed to me irresistibly droll. I myself never called her anything now but 'the demoniac,' experiencing a singular pleasure in pronouncing aloud this word on perceiving her.

"One day I asked Mother Lecacheur: 'Well, what is our demoniac about to-day?'

"To which my rustic friend replied with a shocked air:

"'What do you think, sir? She picked up a toad which had had its paw crushed and carried it to her room and has put it in her washbasin and bandaged it as if it were a man. If that is not profanation I should like to know what is!'

"On another occasion, when walking along the shore she bought a large fish which had just been caught, simply to throw it back into the sea again. The sailor from whom she had bought it, although she paid him handsomely, now began to swear, more exasperated, indeed, than if she had put her hand into his pocket and taken his money. For more than a month he could not speak of the circumstance without becoming furious and denouncing it as an outrage. Oh, yes! She was indeed a demoniac, this Miss Harriet, and Mother Lecacheur must have had an inspiration in thus christening her.

"The stable boy, who was called Sapeur, because he had served in Africa in his youth, entertained other opinions. He said with a roguish air: 'She is an old hag who has seen life.'

"If the poor woman had but known!

"The little kind-hearted Celeste did not wait upon her willingly, but I was never able to understand why. Probably her only reason was that she was a stranger, of another race; of a different tongue and of another religion. She was, in fact, a demoniac!

"She passed her time wandering about the country, adoring and seeking God in nature. I found her one evening on her knees in a cluster of bushes. Having discovered something red through the leaves, I brushed aside the branches, and Miss Harriet at once rose to her feet, confused at having been found thus, fixing on me terrified eyes like those of an owl surprised in open day.

"Sometimes, when I was working among the rocks, I would suddenly descry her on the edge of the cliff like a lighthouse signal. She would be gazing in rapture at the vast sea glittering in the sunlight and the boundless sky with its golden tints. Sometimes I would distinguish her at the end of the valley, walking quickly with her elastic English step, and I would go toward her, attracted by I know not what, simply to see her illuminated visage, her dried-up, ineffable features, which seemed to glow with inward and profound happiness.

"I would often encounter her also in the corner of a field, sitting on the grass under the shadow of an apple tree, with her little religious booklet lying open on her knee while she gazed out at the distance.

"I could not tear myself away from that quiet country neighborhood, to which I was attached by a thousand links of love for its wide and peaceful landscape. I was happy in this sequestered farm, far removed from everything, but in touch with the earth, the good, beautiful, green earth. And—must I avow it?—there was, besides, a little curiosity which retained me at the residence of Mother Lecacheur. I wished to become acquainted a little with this strange Miss Harriet and to know what transpires in the solitary souls of those wandering old English women.

"We became acquainted in a rather singular manner. I had just finished a study which appeared to me to be worth something, and so it was, as it sold for ten thousand francs fifteen years later. It was as simple, however, as two and two make four and was not according to academic rules. The whole right side of my canvas represented a rock, an enormous rock, covered with sea-wrack, brown, yellow and red, across which the sun poured like a stream of oil. The light fell upon the rock as though it were aflame without the sun, which was at my back, being visible. That was all. A first bewildering study of blazing, gorgeous light.

"On the left was the sea, not the blue sea, the slate-colored sea, but a sea of jade, greenish, milky and solid beneath the deep-colored sky.

"I was so pleased with my work that I danced from sheer delight as I carried it back to the inn. I would have liked the whole world to see it at once. I can remember that I showed it to a cow that was browsing by the wayside, exclaiming as I did so: 'Look at that, my old beauty; you will not often see its like again.'

"When I had reached the house I immediately called out to Mother Lecacheur, shouting with all my might:

"'Hullo, there! Mrs. Landlady, come here and look at this.'

"The rustic approached and looked at my work with her stupid eyes which distinguished nothing and could not even tell whether the picture represented an ox or a house.

"Miss Harriet just then came home, and she passed behind me just as I was holding out my canvas at arm's length, exhibiting it to our landlady. The demoniac could not help but see it, for I took care to exhibit the thing in such a way that it could not escape her notice. She stopped abruptly and stood motionless, astonished. It was her rock which was depicted, the one which she climbed to dream away her time undisturbed.

"She uttered a British 'Aoh,' which was at once so accentuated and so flattering that I turned round to her, smiling, and said:

"'This is my latest study, mademoiselle.'

"She murmured rapturously, comically and tenderly:

"'Oh! monsieur, you understand nature as a living thing.'

"I colored and was more touched by that compliment than if it had come from a queen. I was captured, conquered, vanquished. I could have embraced her, upon my honor.

"I took my seat at table beside her as usual. For the first time she spoke, thinking aloud:

"'Oh! I do love nature.'

"I passed her some bread, some water, some wine. She now accepted these with a little smile of a mummy. I then began to talk about the scenery.

"After the meal we rose from the table together and walked leisurely across the courtyard; then, attracted doubtless by the fiery glow which the setting sun cast over the surface of the sea, I opened the gate which led to the cliff, and we walked along side by side, as contented as two persons might be who have just learned to understand and penetrate each other's motives and feelings.

"It was one of those warm, soft evenings which impart a sense of ease to flesh and spirit alike. All is enjoyment, everything charms. The balmy air, laden with the perfume of grasses and the smell of seaweed, soothes the olfactory sense with its wild fragrance, soothes the palate with its sea savor, soothes the mind with its pervading sweetness.

"We were now walking along the edge of the cliff, high above the boundless sea which rolled its little waves below us at a distance of a hundred metres. And we drank in with open mouth and expanded chest that fresh breeze, briny from kissing the waves, that came from the ocean and passed across our faces.

"Wrapped in her plaid shawl, with a look of inspiration as she faced the breeze, the English woman gazed fixedly at the great sun ball as it descended toward the horizon. Far off in the distance a three-master in full sail was outlined on the blood-red sky and a steamship, somewhat nearer, passed along, leaving behind it a trail of smoke on the horizon. The red sun globe sank slowly lower and lower and presently touched the water just behind the motionless vessel, which, in its dazzling effulgence, looked as though framed in a flame of fire. We saw it plunge, grow smaller and disappear, swallowed up by the ocean.

"Miss Harriet gazed in rapture at the last gleams of the dying day. She seemed longing to embrace the sky, the sea, the whole landscape.

"She murmured: 'Aoh! I love—I love' I saw a tear in her eye. She continued: 'I wish I were a little bird, so that I could mount up into the firmament.'

"She remained standing as I had often before seen her, perched on the cliff, her face as red as her shawl. I should have liked to have sketched her in my album. It would have been a caricature of ecstasy.

"I turned away so as not to laugh.

"I then spoke to her of painting as I would have done to a fellow artist, using the technical terms common among the devotees of the profession. She listened attentively, eagerly seeking to divine the meaning of the terms, so as to understand my thoughts. From time to time she would exclaim:

"'Oh! I understand, I understand. It is very interesting.'

"We returned home.

"The next day, on seeing me, she approached me, cordially holding out her hand; and we at once became firm friends.

"She was a good creature who had a kind of soul on springs, which became enthusiastic at a bound. She lacked equilibrium like all women who are spinsters at the age of fifty. She seemed to be preserved in a pickle of innocence, but her heart still retained something very youthful and inflammable. She loved both nature and animals with a fervor, a love like old wine fermented through age, with a sensuous love that she had never bestowed on men.

"One thing is certain, that the sight of a bitch nursing her puppies, a mare roaming in a meadow with a foal at its side, a bird's nest full of young ones, screaming, with their open mouths and their enormous heads, affected her perceptibly.

"Poor, solitary, sad, wandering beings! I love you ever since I became acquainted with Miss Harriet.

"I soon discovered that she had something she would like to tell me, but dare not, and I was amused at her timidity. When I started out in the morning with my knapsack on my back, she would accompany me in silence as far as the end of the village, evidently struggling to find words with which to begin a conversation. Then she would leave me abruptly and walk away quickly with her springy step.

"One day, however, she plucked up courage:

"I would like to see how you paint pictures. Are you willing? I have been very curious.'

"And she blushed as if she had said something very audacious.

"I conducted her to the bottom of the Petit-Val, where I had begun a large picture.

"She remained standing behind me, following all my gestures with concentrated attention. Then, suddenly, fearing perhaps that she was disturbing me, she said: 'Thank you,' and walked away.

"But she soon became more friendly, and accompanied me every day, her countenance exhibiting visible pleasure. She carried her camp stool under her arm, not permitting me to carry it. She would remain there for hours, silent and motionless, following with her eyes the point of my brush, in its every movement. When I obtained unexpectedly just the effect I wanted by a dash of color put on with the palette knife, she involuntarily uttered a little 'Ah!' of astonishment, of joy, of admiration. She had the most tender respect for my canvases, an almost religious respect for that human reproduction of a part of nature's work divine. My studies appeared to her a kind of religious pictures, and sometimes she spoke to me of God, with the idea of converting me.

"Oh, he was a queer, good-natured being, this God of hers! He was a sort of village philosopher without any great resources and without great power, for she always figured him to herself as inconsolable over injustices committed under his eyes, as though he were powerless to prevent them.

"She was, however, on excellent terms with him, affecting even to be the confidante of his secrets and of his troubles. She would say:

"'God wills' or 'God does not will,' just like a sergeant announcing to a recruit: 'The colonel has commanded.'

"At the bottom of her heart she deplored my ignorance of the intentions of the Eternal, which she endeavored to impart to me.

"Almost every day I found in my pockets, in my hat when I lifted it from the ground, in my paintbox, in my polished shoes, standing in front of my door in the morning, those little pious tracts which she no doubt, received directly from Paradise.

"I treated her as one would an old friend, with unaffected cordiality. But I soon perceived that she had changed somewhat in her manner, though, for a while, I paid little attention to it.

"When I was painting, whether in my valley or in some country lane, I would see her suddenly appear with her rapid, springy walk. She would then sit down abruptly, out of breath, as though she had been running or were overcome by some profound emotion. Her face would be red, that English red which is denied to the people of all other countries; then, without any reason, she would turn ashy pale and seem about to faint away. Gradually, however, her natural color would return and she would begin to speak.

"Then, without warning, she would break off in the middle of a sentence, spring up from her seat and walk away so rapidly and so strangely that I was at my wits' ends to discover whether I had done or said anything to displease or wound her.

"I finally came to the conclusion that those were her normal manners, somewhat modified no doubt in my honor during the first days of our acquaintance.

"When she returned to the farm, after walking for hours on the windy coast, her long curls often hung straight down, as if their springs had been broken. This had hitherto seldom given her any concern, and she would come to dinner without embarrassment all dishevelled by her sister, the breeze.

“But now she would go to her room and arrange the untidy locks, and when I would say, with familiar gallantry, which, however, always offended her:

“‘You are as beautiful as a star to-day, Miss Harriet,’ a blush would immediately rise to her cheeks, the blush of a young girl, of a girl of fifteen.

“Then she would suddenly become quite reserved and cease coming to watch me paint. I thought, ‘This is only a fit of temper; it will blow over.’ But it did not always blow over, and when I spoke to her she would answer me either with affected indifference or with sullen annoyance.

“She became by turns rude, impatient and nervous. I never saw her now except at meals, and we spoke but little. I concluded at length that I must have offended her in some way, and, accordingly, I said to her one evening:

“‘Miss Harriet, why is it that you do not act toward me as formerly? What have I done to displease you? You are causing me much pain!’

“She replied in a most comical tone of anger:

“‘I am just the same with you as formerly. It is not true, not true,’ and she ran upstairs and shut herself up in her room.

“Occasionally she would look at me in a peculiar manner. I have often said to myself since then that those who are condemned to death must look thus when they are informed that their last day has come. In her eye there lurked a species of insanity, an insanity at once mystical and violent; and even more, a fever, an aggravated longing, impatient and impotent, for the unattained and unattainable.

“Nay, it seemed to me there was also going on within her a struggle in which her heart wrestled with an unknown force that she sought to master, and even, perhaps, something else. But what do I know? What do I know?

“It was indeed a singular revelation.

“For some time I had commenced to work, as soon as daylight appeared, on a picture the subject of which was as follows:

“A deep ravine, enclosed, surmounted by two thickets of trees and vines, extended into the distance and was lost, submerged in that milky vapor, in that cloud like cotton down that sometimes floats over valleys at daybreak. And at the extreme end of that heavy, transparent fog one saw, or, rather, surmised, that a couple of human beings were approaching, a human couple, a youth and a maiden, their arms interlaced, embracing each other, their heads inclined toward each other, their lips meeting.

“A first ray of the sun, glistening through the branches, pierced that fog of the dawn, illuminated it with a rosy reflection just behind the rustic lovers, framing their vague shadows in a silvery background. It was well done; yes, indeed, well done.

“I was working on the declivity which led to the Valley of Etretat. On this particular morning I had, by chance, the sort of floating vapor which I needed. Suddenly something rose up in front of me like a phantom; it was Miss Harriet. On seeing me she was about to flee. But I called after her, saying: 'Come here, come here, mademoiselle. I have a nice little picture for you.'

"She came forward, though with seeming reluctance. I handed her my sketch. She said nothing, but stood for a long time, motionless, looking at it, and suddenly she burst into tears. She wept spasmodically, like men who have striven hard to restrain their tears, but who can do so no longer and abandon themselves to grief, though still resisting. I sprang to my feet, moved at the sight of a sorrow I did not comprehend, and I took her by the hand with an impulse of brusque affection, a true French impulse which acts before it reflects.

"She let her hands rest in mine for a few seconds, and I felt them quiver as if all her nerves were being wrenched. Then she withdrew her hands abruptly, or, rather, snatched them away.

"I recognized that tremor, for I had felt it, and I could not be deceived. Ah! the love tremor of a woman, whether she be fifteen or fifty years of age, whether she be of the people or of society, goes so straight to my heart that I never have any hesitation in understanding it!

"Her whole frail being had trembled, vibrated, been overcome. I knew it. She walked away before I had time to say a word, leaving me as surprised as if I had witnessed a miracle and as troubled as if I had committed a crime.

"I did not go in to breakfast. I went to take a turn on the edge of the cliff, feeling that I would just as lief weep as laugh, looking on the adventure as both comic and deplorable and my position as ridiculous, believing her unhappy enough to go insane.

"I asked myself what I ought to do. It seemed best for me to leave the place, and I immediately resolved to do so.

"Somewhat sad and perplexed, I wandered about until dinner time and entered the farmhouse just when the soup had been served up.

"I sat down at the table as usual. Miss Harriet was there, eating away solemnly, without speaking to any one, without even lifting her eyes. Her manner and expression were, however, the same as usual.

"I waited patiently till the meal had been finished, when, turning toward the landlady, I said: 'Well, Madame Lecacheur, it will not be long now before I shall have to take my leave of you.'

"The good woman, at once surprised and troubled, replied in her drawling voice: 'My dear sir, what is it you say? You are going to leave us after I have become so accustomed to you?'

"I glanced at Miss Harriet out of the corner of my eye. Her countenance did not change in the least. But Celeste, the little servant, looked up at me. She was a fat girl, of about eighteen years of age, rosy, fresh, as strong as a horse, and possessing the rare attribute of cleanliness. I had kissed her at odd times in out-of-the-way corners, after the manner of travellers—nothing more.

"The dinner being at length over, I went to smoke my pipe under the apple trees, walking up and down from one end of the enclosure to the other. All the reflections which I had made during the day, the strange discovery of the morning, that passionate and grotesque attachment for me, the recollections which that revelation had suddenly called up, recollections at once charming and perplexing, perhaps also that look which the servant had cast on me at the announcement of my departure—all these things, mixed up and combined, put me now in a reckless humor, gave me a tickling sensation of kisses on the lips and in my veins a something which urged me on to commit some folly.

"Night was coming on, casting its dark shadows under the trees, when I descried Celeste, who had gone to fasten up the poultry yard at the other end of the enclosure. I darted toward her, running so noiselessly that she heard nothing, and as she got up from closing the small trapdoor by which the chickens got in and out, I clasped her in my arms and rained on her coarse, fat face a shower of kisses. She struggled, laughing all the time, as she was accustomed to do in such circumstances. Why did I suddenly loose my grip of her? Why did I at once experience a shock? What was it that I heard behind me?

"It was Miss Harriet, who had come upon us, who had seen us and who stood in front of us motionless as a spectre. Then she disappeared in the darkness.

"I was ashamed, embarrassed, more desperate at having been thus surprised by her than if she had caught me committing some criminal act.

"I slept badly that night. I was completely unnerved and haunted by sad thoughts. I seemed to hear loud weeping, but in this I was no doubt deceived. Moreover, I thought several times that I heard some one walking up and down in the house and opening the hall door.

"Toward morning I was overcome by fatigue and fell asleep. I got up late and did not go downstairs until the late breakfast, being still in a bewildered state, not knowing what kind of expression to put on.

"No one had seen Miss Harriet. We waited for her at table, but she did not appear. At length Mother Lecacheur went to her room. The English woman had gone out. She must have set out at break of day, as she was wont to do, in order to see the sun rise.

"Nobody seemed surprised at this, and we began to eat in silence.

"The weather was hot, very hot, one of those broiling, heavy days when not a leaf stirs. The table had been placed out of doors, under an apple tree, and from time to time Sapeur had gone to the cellar to draw a jug of cider, everybody was so thirsty. Celeste brought the dishes from the kitchen, a ragout of mutton with potatoes, a cold rabbit and a salad. Afterward she placed before us a dish of strawberries, the first of the season.

"As I wished to wash and freshen these, I begged the servant to go and draw me a pitcher of cold water.

"In about five minutes she returned, declaring that the well was dry. She had lowered the pitcher to the full extent of the cord and had touched the bottom, but on drawing the pitcher up again it was empty. Mother Lecacheur, anxious to examine the thing for herself, went and looked down the hole. She returned, announcing that one could see clearly something in the well, something altogether unusual. But this no doubt was bundles of straw, which a neighbor had thrown in out of spite.

"I wished to look down the well also, hoping I might be able to clear up the mystery, and I perched myself close to the brink. I perceived indistinctly a white object. What could it be? I then conceived the idea of lowering a lantern at the end of a cord. When I did so the yellow flame danced on the layers of stone and gradually became clearer. All four of us were leaning over the opening, Sapeur and Celeste having now joined us. The lantern rested on a black-and-white indistinct mass, singular, incomprehensible. Sapeur exclaimed:

"'It is a horse. I see the hoofs. It must have got out of the meadow during the night and fallen in headlong.'

"But suddenly a cold shiver froze me to the marrow. I first recognized a foot, then a leg sticking up; the whole body and the other leg were completely under water.

"I stammered out in a loud voice, trembling so violently that the lantern danced hither and thither over the slipper:

"'It is a woman! Who-who-can it be? It is Miss Harriet!'

"Sapeur alone did not manifest horror. He had witnessed many such scenes in Africa.

"Mother Lecacheur and Celeste began to utter piercing screams and ran away.

"But it was necessary to recover the corpse of the dead woman. I attached the young man securely by the waist to the end of the pulley rope and lowered him very slowly, watching him disappear in the darkness. In one hand he held the lantern and a rope in the other. Soon I recognized his voice, which seemed to come from the centre of the earth, saying:

"'Stop!'

"I then saw him fish something out of the water. It was the other leg. He then bound the two feet together and shouted anew:

"'Haul up!'

"I began to wind up, but I felt my arms crack, my muscles twitch, and I was in terror lest I should let the man fall to the bottom. When his head appeared at the brink I asked:

"'Well?' as if I expected he had a message from the drowned woman.

"We both got on the stone slab at the edge of the well and from opposite sides we began to haul up the body.

"Mother Lecacheur and Celeste watched us from a distance, concealed from view behind the wall of the house. When they saw issuing from the hole the black slippers and white stockings of the drowned person they disappeared.

"Sapeur seized the ankles, and we drew up the body of the poor woman. The head was shocking to look at, being bruised and lacerated, and the long gray hair, out of curl forevermore, hanging down tangled and disordered.

"'In the name of all that is holy! how lean she is,' exclaimed Sapeur in a contemptuous tone.

"We carried her into the room, and as the women did not put in an appearance I, with the assistance of the stable lad, dressed the corpse for burial.

"I washed her disfigured face. Under the touch of my finger an eye was slightly opened and regarded me with that pale, cold look, that terrible look of a corpse which seems to come from the beyond. I braided as well as I could her dishevelled hair and with my clumsy hands arranged on her head a novel and singular coiffure. Then I took off her dripping wet garments, baring, not without a feeling of shame, as though I had been guilty of some profanation, her shoulders and her chest and her long arms, as slim as the twigs of a tree.

"I next went to fetch some flowers, poppies, bluets, marguerites and fresh, sweet-smelling grass with which to strew her funeral couch.

"I then had to go through the usual formalities, as I was alone to attend to everything. A letter found in her pocket, written at the last moment, requested that her body be buried in the village in which she had passed the last days of her life. A sad suspicion weighed on my heart. Was it not on my account that she wished to be laid to rest in this place?

"Toward evening all the female gossips of the locality came to view the remains of the defunct, but I would not allow a single person to enter. I wanted to be alone, and I watched beside her all night.

"I looked at the corpse by the flickering light of the candles, at this unhappy woman, unknown to us all, who had died in such a lamentable manner and so far away from home. Had she left no friends, no relations behind her? What had her infancy been? What had been her life? Whence had she come thither alone, a wanderer, lost like a dog driven from home? What secrets of sufferings and of despair were sealed up in that unprepossessing body, in that poor body whose outward appearance had driven from her all affection, all love?

"How many unhappy beings there are! I felt that there weighed upon that human creature the eternal injustice of implacable nature! It was all over with her, without her ever having experienced, perhaps, that which sustains the greatest outcasts to wit, the hope of being loved once! Otherwise why should she thus have concealed herself, fled from the face of others? Why did she love everything so tenderly and so passionately, everything living that was not a man?

"I recognized the fact that she believed in a God, and that she hoped to receive compensation from the latter for all the miseries she had endured. She would now disintegrate and become, in turn, a plant. She would blossom in the sun, the cattle would browse on her leaves, the birds would bear away the seeds, and through these changes she would become again human flesh. But that which is called the soul had been extinguished at the bottom of the dark well. She suffered no longer. She had given her life for that of others yet to come.

"Hours passed away in this silent and sinister communion with the dead. A pale light at length announced the dawn of a new day; then a red ray streamed in on the bed, making a bar of light across the coverlet and across her hands. This was the hour she had so much loved. The awakened birds began to sing in the trees.

"I opened the window to its fullest extent and drew back the curtains that the whole heavens might look in upon us, and, bending over the icy corpse, I took in my hands the mutilated head and slowly, without terror or disgust, I imprinted a kiss, a long kiss, upon those lips which had never before been kissed."

Leon Chenal remained silent. The women wept. We heard on the box seat the Count d'Atraille blowing his nose from time to time. The coachman alone had gone to sleep. The horses, who no longer felt the sting of the whip, had slackened their pace and moved along slowly. The drag, hardly advancing at all, seemed suddenly torpid, as if it had been freighted with sorrow.

[Miss Harriet appeared in Le Gaulois, July 9, 1883, under the title of Miss Hastings. The story was later revised, enlarged; and partly reconstructed. This is what De Maupassant wrote to Editor Havard March 15, 1884, in an unedited letter, in regard to the title of the story that was to give its name to the volume:

"I do not believe that Hastings is a bad name, inasmuch as it is known all over the world, and recalls the greatest facts in English history. Besides, Hastings is as much a name as Duval is with us.

"The name Cherbuliez selected, Miss Revel, is no more like an English name than like a Turkish name. But here is another name as English as Hastings, and more euphonious; it is Miss Harriet.
I will ask you therefore to substitute Harriet for Hastings."

It was in regard to this very tittle that De Maupassant had a disagreement with Audran and Boucheron director of the Bouffes Parisiens in October, 1890. They had given this title to an operetta about to be played at the Bouffes. It ended however, by their ceding to De Maupassant, and the title of the operetta was changed to Miss Helyett.]

LITTLE LOUISE ROQUE

The former soldier, Mederic Rompel, familiarly called Mederic by the country folks, left the post office of Roily-le-Tors at the usual hour. After passing through the village with his long stride, he cut across the meadows of Villaume and reached the bank of the Brindille, following the path along the water's edge to the village of Carvelin, where he commenced to deliver his letters. He walked quickly, following the course of the narrow river, which frothed, murmured and boiled in its grassy bed beneath an arch of willows.

Mederic went on without stopping, with only this thought in his mind: "My first letter is for the Poivron family, then I have one for Monsieur Renardet; so I must cross the wood."

His blue blouse, fastened round his waist by a black leather belt, moved in a quick, regular fashion above the green hedge of willow trees, and his stout stick of holly kept time with his steady tread.

He crossed the Brindille on a bridge consisting of a tree trunk, with a handrail of rope, fastened at either end to a stake driven into the ground.

The wood, which belonged to Monsieur Renardet, the mayor of Carvelin and the largest landowner in the district, consisted of huge old trees, straight as pillars and extending for about half a league along the left bank of the stream which served as a boundary to this immense dome of foliage. Alongside the water large shrubs had grown up in the sunlight, but under the trees one found nothing but moss, thick, soft and yielding, from which arose, in the still air, an odor of dampness and of dead wood.

Mederic slackened his pace, took off his black cap adorned with red lace and wiped his forehead, for it was by this time hot in the meadows, though it was not yet eight o'clock in the morning.

He had just recovered from the effects of the heat and resumed his quick pace when he noticed at the foot of a tree a knife, a child's small knife. When he picked it up he discovered a thimble and also a needlecase not far away.

Having taken up these objects, he thought: "I'll entrust them to the mayor," and he resumed his journey, but now he kept his eyes open, expecting to find something else.

All of a sudden he stopped short, as if he had struck against a wooden barrier. Ten paces in front of him lay stretched on her back on the moss a little girl, perfectly nude, her face covered with a handkerchief. She was about twelve years old.

Meredic advanced on tiptoe, as if he apprehended some danger, and he glanced toward the spot uneasily.

What was this? No doubt she was asleep. Then he reflected that a person does not go to sleep naked at half-past seven in the morning under the cool trees. So, then, she must be dead, and he must be face to face with a crime. At this thought a cold shiver ran through his frame, although he was an old soldier. And then a murder was such a rare thing in the country, and, above all, the murder of a child, that he could not believe his eyes. But she had no wound-nothing save a spot of blood on her leg. How, then, had she been killed?

He stopped close to her and gazed at her, while he leaned on his stick. Certainly he must know her, for he knew all the inhabitants of the district; but, not being able to get a look at her face, he could not guess her name. He stooped forward in order to take off the handkerchief which covered her face, then paused, with outstretched hand, restrained by an idea that occurred to him.

Had he the right to disarrange anything in the condition of the corpse before the official investigation? He pictured justice to himself as a kind of general whom nothing escapes and who attaches as much importance to a lost button as to the stab of a knife in the stomach. Perhaps under this handkerchief evidence could be found to sustain a charge of murder; in fact, if such proof were there it might lose its value if touched by an awkward hand.

Then he raised himself with the intention of hastening toward the mayor's residence, but again another thought held him back. If the little girl were still alive, by any chance, he could not leave her lying there in this way. He sank on his knees very gently, a little distance from her, through precaution, and extended his hand toward her foot. It was icy cold, with the terrible coldness of death which leaves us no longer in doubt. The letter carrier, as he touched her, felt his heart in his mouth, as he said himself afterward, and his mouth parched. Rising up abruptly, he rushed off under the trees toward Monsieur Renardet's house.

He walked on faster than ever, with his stick under his arm, his hands clenched and his head thrust forward, while his leathern bag, filled with letters and newspapers, kept flapping at his side.

The mayor's residence was at the end of the wood which served as a park, and one side of it was washed by the Brindille.

It was a big square house of gray stone, very old, and had stood many a siege in former days, and at the end of it was a huge tower, twenty metres high, rising out of the water.

From the top of this fortress one could formerly see all the surrounding country. It was called the Fox's tower, without any one knowing exactly why; and from this appellation, no doubt, had come the name Renardet, borne by the owners of this fief, which had remained in the same family, it was said, for more than two hundred years. For the Renardets formed part of the upper middle class, all but noble, to be met with so often in the province before the Revolution.

The postman dashed into the kitchen, where the servants were taking breakfast, and exclaimed:

"Is the mayor up? I want to speak to him at once."

Mederic was recognized as a man of standing and authority, and they understood that something serious had happened.

As soon as word was brought to Monsieur Renardet, he ordered the postman to be sent up to him. Pale and out of breath, with his cap in his hand, Mederic found the mayor seated at a long table covered with scattered papers.

He was a large, tall man, heavy and red-faced, strong as an ox, and was greatly liked in the district, although of an excessively violent disposition. Almost forty years old and a widower for the past six months, he lived on his estate like a country gentleman. His choleric temperament had often brought him into trouble from which the magistrates of Roily-le-Tors, like indulgent and prudent friends, had extricated him. Had he not one day thrown the conductor of the diligence from the top of his seat because he came near running over his retriever, Micmac? Had he not broken the ribs of a gamekeeper who abused him for having, gun in hand, passed through a neighbor's property? Had he not even caught by the collar the sub-prefect, who stopped over in the village during an administrative circuit, called by Monsieur Renardet an electioneering circuit, for he was opposed to the government, in accordance with family traditions.

The mayor asked:

"What's the matter now, Mederic?"

"I found a little girl dead in your wood."

Renardet rose to his feet, his face the color of brick.

"What do you say—a little girl?"

"Yes, m'sieu, a little girl, quite naked, on her back, with blood on her, dead—quite dead!"

The mayor gave vent to an oath:

"By God, I'd make a bet it is little Louise Roque! I have just learned that she did not go home to her mother last night. Where did you find her?"

The postman described the spot, gave full details and offered to conduct the mayor to the place.

But Renardet became brusque:

"No, I don't need you. Send the watchman, the mayor's secretary and the doctor to me at once, and resume your rounds. Quick, quick, go and tell them to meet me in the wood."

The letter carrier, a man used to discipline, obeyed and withdrew, angry and grieved at not being able to be present at the investigation.

The mayor, in his turn, prepared to go out, took his big soft hat and paused for a few seconds on the threshold of his abode. In front of him stretched a wide sward, in which were three large beds of flowers in full bloom, one facing the house and the others at either side of it. Farther on the outlying trees of the wood rose skyward, while at the left, beyond the Brindille, which at that spot widened into a pond, could be seen long meadows, an entirely green flat sweep of country, intersected by trenches and hedges of pollard willows.

To the right, behind the stables, the outhouses and all the buildings connected with the property, might be seen the village, which was wealthy, being mainly inhabited by cattle breeders.

Renardet slowly descended the steps in front of his house, and, turning to the left, gained the water's edge, which he followed at a slow pace, his hand behind his back. He walked on, with bent head, and from time to time glanced round in search of the persons he had sent for.

When he stood beneath the trees he stopped, took off his hat and wiped his forehead as Mederic had done, for the burning sun was darting its fiery rays on the earth. Then the mayor resumed his journey, stopped once more and retraced his steps. Suddenly, stooping down, he steeped his handkerchief in the stream that glided along at his feet and spread it over his head, under his hat. Drops of water flowed down his temples over his ears, which were always purple, over his strong red neck, and made their way, one after the other, under his white shirt collar.

As nobody had appeared, he began tapping with his foot, then he called out:

"Hello! Hello!"

A voice at his right answered:

"Hello! Hello!"

And the doctor appeared under the trees. He was a thin little man, an ex-military surgeon, who passed in the neighborhood for a very skillful practitioner. He limped, having been wounded while in the service, and had to use a stick to assist him in walking.

Next came the watchman and the mayor's secretary, who, having been sent for at the same time, arrived together. They looked scared, and hurried forward, out of breath, walking and running alternately to hasten their progress, and moving their arms up and down so vigorously that they seemed to do more work with them than with their legs.

Renardet said to the doctor:

"You know what the trouble is about?"

"Yes, a child found dead in the wood by Mederic."

"That's quite correct. Come on!"

They walked along, side by side, followed by the two men.

Their steps made no sound on the moss. Their eyes were gazing ahead in front of them.

Suddenly the doctor, extending his arm, said:

"See, there she is!"

Far ahead of them under the trees they saw something white on which the sun gleamed down through the branches. As they approached they gradually distinguished a human form lying there, its head toward the river, the face covered and the arms extended as though on a crucifix.

"I am fearfully warm," said the mayor, and stooping down, he again soaked his handkerchief in the water and placed it round his forehead.

The doctor hastened his steps, interested by the discovery. As soon as they were near the corpse, he bent down to examine it without touching it. He had put on his pince-nez, as one does in examining some curious object, and turned round very quietly.

He said, without rising:

"Violated and murdered, as we shall prove presently. This little girl, moreover, is almost a woman—look at her throat."

The doctor lightly drew away the handkerchief which covered her face, which looked black, frightful, the tongue protruding, the eyes bloodshot. He went on:

"By heavens! She was strangled the moment the deed was done."

He felt her neck.

"Strangled with the hands without leaving any special trace, neither the mark of the nails nor the imprint of the fingers. Quite right. It is little Louise Roque, sure enough!"

He carefully replaced the handkerchief.

"There's nothing for me to do. She's been dead for the last hour at least. We must give notice of the matter to the authorities."

Renardet, standing up, with his hands behind his back, kept staring with a stony look at the little body exposed to view on the grass. He murmured:

"What a wretch! We must find the clothes."

The doctor felt the hands, the arms, the legs. He said:

"She had been bathing no doubt. They ought to be at the water's edge."

The mayor thereupon gave directions:

"Do you, Principe" (this was his secretary), "go and find those clothes for me along the stream. You, Maxime" (this was the watchman), "hurry on toward Rouy-le-Tors and bring with you the magistrate with the gendarmes. They must be here within an hour. You understand?"

The two men started at once, and Renardet said to the doctor:

"What miscreant could have done such a deed in this part of the country?"

The doctor murmured:

"Who knows? Any one is capable of that. Every one in particular and nobody in general. No matter, it must be some prowler, some workman out of employment. Since we have become a Republic we meet only this kind of person along the roads."

Both of them were Bonapartists.

The mayor went on:

"Yes, it can only be a stranger, a passer-by, a vagabond without hearth or home."

The doctor added, with the shadow of a smile on his face:

"And without a wife. Having neither a good supper nor a good bed, he became reckless. You can't tell how many men there may be in the world capable of a crime at a given moment. Did you know that this little girl had disappeared?"

And with the end of his stick he touched one after the other the stiffened fingers of the corpse, resting on them as on the keys of a piano.

"Yes, the mother came last night to look for me about nine o'clock, the child not having come home at seven to supper. We looked for her along the roads up to midnight, but we did not think of the wood. However, we needed daylight to carry out a thorough search."

"Will you have a cigar?" said the doctor.

"Thanks, I don't care to smoke. This thing affects me so."

They remained standing beside the corpse of the young girl, so pale on the dark moss. A big blue fly was walking over the body with his lively, jerky movements. The two men kept watching this wandering speck.

The doctor said:

"How pretty it is, a fly on the skin! The ladies of the last century had good reason to paste them on their faces. Why has this fashion gone out?"

The mayor seemed not to hear, plunged as he was in deep thought.

But, all of a sudden, he turned round, surprised by a shrill noise. A woman in a cap and blue apron was running toward them under the trees. It was the mother, La Roque. As soon as she saw Renardet she began to shriek:

"My little girl! Where's my little girl?" so distractedly that she did not glance down at the ground. Suddenly she saw the corpse, stopped short, clasped her hands and raised both her arms while she uttered a sharp, heartrending cry—the cry of a wounded animal. Then she rushed toward the body, fell on her knees and snatched away the handkerchief that covered the face. When she saw that frightful countenance, black and distorted, she rose to her feet with a shudder, then sinking to the ground, face downward, she pressed her face against the ground and uttered frightful, continuous screams on the thick moss.

Her tall, thin frame, with its close-clinging dress, was palpitating, shaken with spasms. One could see her bony ankles and her dried-up calves covered with coarse blue stockings shaking horribly. She was digging the soil with her crooked fingers, as though she were trying to make a hole in which to hide herself.

The doctor, much affected, said in a low tone:

"Poor old woman!"

Renardet felt a strange sensation. Then he gave vent to a sort of loud sneeze, and, drawing his handkerchief from his pocket, he began to weep internally, coughing, sobbing and blowing his nose noisily.

He stammered:

"Damn—damn—damned pig to do this! I would like to see him guillotined."

Principe reappeared with his hands empty. He murmured:

"I have found nothing, M'sieu le Maire, nothing at all anywhere."

The mayor, alarmed, replied in a thick voice, drowned in tears:

"What is that you could not find?"

"The little girl's clothes."

"Well—well—look again, and find them—or you 'll have to answer to me."

The man, knowing that the mayor would not brook opposition, set forth again with hesitating steps, casting a timid side glance at the corpse.

Distant voices were heard under the trees, a confused sound, the noise of an approaching crowd, for Mederic had, in the course of his rounds, carried the news from door to door. The people of the neighborhood, dazed at first, had gossiped about it in the street, from one threshold to another. Then they gathered together. They talked over, discussed and commented on the event for some minutes and had now come to see for themselves.

They arrived in groups, a little faltering and uneasy through fear of the first impression of such a scene on their minds. When they saw the body they stopped, not daring to advance, and speaking low. Then they grew bolder, went on a few steps, stopped again, advanced once more, and presently formed around the dead girl, her mother, the doctor and Renardet a close circle, restless and noisy, which crowded forward at the sudden impact of newcomers. And now they touched the corpse. Some of them even bent down to feel it with their fingers. The doctor kept them back. But the mayor, waking abruptly out of his torpor, flew into a rage, and seizing Dr. Labarbe's stick, flung himself on his townspeople, stammering:

"Clear out—clear out—you pack of brutes—clear out!"

And in a second the crowd of sightseers had fallen back two hundred paces.

Mother La Roque had risen to a sitting posture and now remained weeping, with her hands clasped over her face.

The crowd was discussing the affair, and young lads' eager eyes curiously scrutinized this nude young form. Renardet perceived this, and, abruptly taking off his coat, he flung it over the little girl, who was entirely hidden from view beneath the large garment.

The secretary drew near quietly. The wood was filled with people, and a continuous hum of voices rose up under the tangled foliage of the tall trees.

The mayor, in his shirt sleeves, remained standing, with his stick in his hands, in a fighting attitude. He seemed exasperated by this curiosity on the part of the people and kept repeating:

"If one of you come nearer I'll break his head just as I would a dog's."

The peasants were greatly afraid of him. They held back. Dr. Labarbe, who was smoking, sat down beside La Roque and spoke to her in order to distract her attention. The old woman at once removed her hands from her face and replied with a flood of tearful words, emptying her grief in copious talk. She told the whole story of her life, her marriage, the death of her man, a cattle drover, who had been gored to death, the infancy of her daughter, her wretched existence as a widow without resources and with a child to support. She had only this one, her little Louise, and the child had been killed—killed in this wood. Then she felt anxious to see her again, and, dragging herself on her knees toward the corpse, she raised up one corner of the garment that covered her; then she let it fall again and began wailing once more. The crowd remained silent, eagerly watching all the mother's gestures.

But suddenly there was a great commotion at the cry of "The gendarmes! the gendarmes!"

Two gendarmes appeared in the distance, advancing at a rapid trot, escorting their captain and a little gentleman with red whiskers, who was bobbing up and down like a monkey on a big white mare.

The watchman had just found Monsieur Putoin, the magistrate, at the moment when he was mounting his horse to take his daily ride, for he posed as a good horseman, to the great amusement of the officers.

He dismounted, along with the captain, and pressed the hands of the mayor and the doctor, casting a ferret-like glance on the linen coat beneath which lay the corpse.

When he was made acquainted with all the facts, he first gave orders to disperse the crowd, whom the gendarmes drove out of the wood, but who soon reappeared in the meadow and formed a hedge, a big hedge of excited and moving heads, on the other side of the stream.

The doctor, in his turn, gave explanations, which Renardet noted down in his memorandum book. All the evidence was given, taken down and commented on without leading to any discovery. Maxime, too, came back without having found any trace of the clothes.

This disappearance surprised everybody; no one could explain it except on the theory of theft, and as her rags were not worth twenty sous, even this theory was inadmissible.

The magistrate, the mayor, the captain and the doctor set to work searching in pairs, putting aside the smallest branch along the water.

Renardet said to the judge:

"How does it happen that this wretch has concealed or carried away the clothes, and has thus left the body exposed, in sight of every one?"

The other, crafty and sagacious, answered:

"Ha! ha! Perhaps a dodge? This crime has been committed either by a brute or by a sly scoundrel. In any case, we'll easily succeed in finding him."

The noise of wheels made them turn their heads round. It was the deputy magistrate, the doctor and the registrar of the court who had arrived in their turn. They resumed their search, all chatting in an animated fashion.

Renardet said suddenly:

"Do you know that you are to take luncheon with me?"

Every one smilingly accepted the invitation, and the magistrate, thinking that the case of little Louise Roque had occupied enough attention for one day, turned toward the mayor.

"I can have the body brought to your house, can I not? You have a room in which you can keep it for me till this evening?"

The other became confused and stammered:

"Yes—no—no. To tell the truth, I prefer that it should not come into my house on account of—on account of my servants, who are already talking about ghosts in—in my tower, in the Fox's tower. You know—I could no longer keep a single one. No—I prefer not to have it in my house."

The magistrate began to smile.

"Good! I will have it taken at once to Roily for the legal examination." And, turning to his deputy, he said:

"I can make use of your trap, can I not?"

"Yes, certainly."

They all came back to the place where the corpse lay. Mother La Roque, now seated beside her daughter, was holding her hand and was staring right before her with a wandering, listless eye.

The two doctors endeavored to lead her away, so that she might not witness the dead girl's removal, but she understood at once what they wanted to do, and, flinging herself on the body, she threw both arms round it. Lying on top of the corpse, she exclaimed:

"You shall not have it—it's mine—it's mine now. They have killed her for me, and I want to keep her—you shall not have her——"

All the men, affected and not knowing how to act, remained standing around her. Renardet fell on his knees and said to her:

"Listen, La Roque, it is necessary, in order to find out who killed her. Without this, we could not find out. We must make a search for the man in order to punish him. When we have found him we'll give her up to you. I promise you this."

This explanation bewildered the woman, and a feeling of hatred manifested itself in her distracted glance.

"So then they'll arrest him?"

"Yes, I promise you that."

She rose up, deciding to let them do as they liked, but when the captain remarked:

"It is surprising that her clothes were not found," a new idea, which she had not previously thought of, abruptly entered her mind, and she asked:

"Where are her clothes? They're mine. I want them. Where have they been put?"

They explained to her that they had not been found. Then she demanded them persistently, crying and moaning.

"They're mine—I want them. Where are they? I want them!"

The more they tried to calm her the more she sobbed and persisted in her demands. She no longer wanted the body, she insisted on having the clothes, as much perhaps through the unconscious cupidity of a wretched being to whom a piece of silver represents a fortune as through maternal tenderness.

And when the little body, rolled up in blankets which had been brought out from Renardet's house, had disappeared in the vehicle, the old woman standing under the trees, sustained by the mayor and the captain, exclaimed:

"I have nothing, nothing, nothing in the world, not even her little cap —her little cap."

The cure, a young priest, had just arrived. He took it on himself to accompany the mother, and they went away together toward the village. The mother's grief was modified by the sugary words of the clergyman, who promised her a thousand compensations. But she kept repeating: "If I had only her little cap." This idea now dominated every other.

Renardet called from the distance:

"You will lunch with us, Monsieur l'Abbe—in an hour's time."

The priest turned his head round and replied:

"With pleasure, Monsieur le Maire. I'll be with you at twelve."

And they all directed their steps toward the house, whose gray front, with the large tower built on the edge of the Brindille, could be seen through the branches.

The meal lasted a long time. They talked about the crime. Everybody was of the same opinion. It had been committed by some tramp passing there by mere chance while the little girl was bathing.

Then the magistrates returned to Rouy, announcing that they would return next day at an early hour. The doctor and the cure went to their respective homes, while Renardet, after a long walk through the meadows, returned to the wood, where he remained walking till nightfall with slow steps, his hands behind his back.

He went to bed early and was still asleep next morning when the magistrate entered his room. He was rubbing his hands together with a self-satisfied air.

"Ha! ha! You are still sleeping! Well, my dear fellow, we have news this morning."

The mayor sat up in his bed.

"What, pray?"

"Oh! Something strange. You remember well how the mother clamored yesterday for some memento of her daughter, especially her little cap? Well, on opening her door this morning she found on the threshold her child's two little wooden shoes. This proves that the crime was perpetrated by some one from the district, some one who felt pity for her. Besides, the postman, Mederic, brought me the thimble, the knife and the needle case of the dead girl. So, then, the man in carrying off the clothes to hide them must have let fall the articles which were in the pocket. As for me, I attach special importance to the wooden shoes, as they indicate a certain moral culture and a faculty for tenderness on the part of the assassin. We will, therefore, if you have no objection, go over together the principal inhabitants of your district."

The mayor got up. He rang for his shaving water and said:

"With pleasure, but it will take some time, and we may begin at once."

M. Putoin sat astride a chair.

Renardet covered his chin with a white lather while he looked at himself in the glass. Then he sharpened his razor on the strop and continued:

"The principal inhabitant of Carvelin bears the name of Joseph Renardet, mayor, a rich landowner, a rough man who beats guards and coachmen—"

The examining magistrate burst out laughing.

"That's enough. Let us pass on to the next."

"The second in importance is Pelledent, his deputy, a cattle breeder, an equally rich landowner, a crafty peasant, very sly, very close-fisted on every question of money, but incapable in my opinion of having perpetrated such a crime."

"Continue," said M. Putoin.

Renardet, while proceeding with his toilet, reviewed the characters of all the inhabitants of Carvelin. After two hours' discussion their suspicions were fixed on three individuals who had hitherto borne a shady reputation—a poacher named Cavalle, a fisherman named Paquet, who caught trout and crabs, and a cattle drover named Clovis. II

The search for the perpetrator of the crime lasted all summer, but he was not discovered. Those who were suspected and arrested easily proved their innocence, and the authorities were compelled to abandon the attempt to capture the criminal.

But this murder seemed to have moved the entire country in a singular manner. There remained in every one's mind a disquietude, a vague fear, a sensation of mysterious terror, springing not merely from the impossibility of discovering any trace of the assassin, but also and above all from that strange finding of the wooden shoes in front of La Roque's door the day after the crime. The certainty that the murderer had assisted at the investigation, that he was still, doubtless, living in the village, possessed all minds and seemed to brood over the neighborhood like a constant menace.

The wood had also become a dreaded spot, a place to be avoided and supposed to be haunted.

Formerly the inhabitants went there to spend every Sunday afternoon. They used to sit down on the moss at the feet of the huge tall trees or walk along the water's edge watching the trout gliding among the weeds. The boy's used to play bowls, hide-and-seek and other games where the ground had been cleared and levelled, and the girls, in rows of four or five, would trip along, holding one another by the arms and screaming songs with their shrill voices. Now nobody ventured there for fear of finding some corpse lying on the ground.

Autumn arrived, the leaves began to fall from the tall trees, whirling round and round to the ground, and the sky could be seen through the bare branches. Sometimes, when a gust of wind swept over the tree tops, the slow, continuous rain suddenly grew heavier and became a rough storm that covered the moss with a thick yellow carpet that made a kind of creaking sound beneath one's feet.

And the sound of the falling leaves seemed like a wail and the leaves themselves like tears shed by these great, sorrowful trees, that wept in the silence of the bare and empty wood, this dreaded and deserted wood where wandered lonely the soul, the little soul of little Louise Roque.

The Brindille, swollen by the storms, rushed on more quickly, yellow and angry, between its dry banks, bordered by two thin, bare, willow hedges.

And here was Renardet suddenly resuming his walks under the trees. Every day, at sunset, he came out of his house, descended the front steps slowly and entered the wood in a dreamy fashion, with his hands in his pockets, and paced over the damp soft moss, while a legion of rooks from all the neighboring haunts came thither to rest in the tall trees and then flew off like a black cloud uttering loud, discordant cries.

Night came on, and Renardet was still strolling slowly under the trees; then, when the darkness prevented him from walking any longer, he would go back to the house and sink into his armchair in front of the glowing hearth, stretching his damp feet toward the fire.

One morning an important bit of news was circulated through the district; the mayor was having his wood cut down.

Twenty woodcutters were already at work. They had commenced at the corner nearest to the house and worked rapidly in the master's presence.

And each day the wood grew thinner, losing its trees, which fell down one by one, as an army loses its soldiers.

Renardet no longer walked up, and down. He remained from morning till night, contemplating, motionless, with his hands behind his back, the slow destruction of his wood. When a tree fell he placed his foot on it as if it were a corpse. Then he raised his eyes to the next with a kind of secret, calm impatience, as if he expected, hoped for something at the end of this slaughter.

Meanwhile they were approaching the place where little Louise Roque had been found. They came to it one evening in the twilight.

As it was dark, the sky being overcast, the woodcutters wanted to stop their work, putting off till next day the fall of an enormous beech tree, but the mayor objected to this and insisted that they should at once lop and cut down this giant, which had sheltered the crime.

When the lopper had laid it bare and the woodcutters had sapped its base, five men commenced hauling at the rope attached to the top.

The tree resisted; its powerful trunk, although notched to the centre, was as rigid as iron. The workmen, all together, with a sort of simultaneous motion, strained at the rope, bending backward and uttering a cry which timed and regulated their efforts.

Two woodcutters standing close to the giant remained with axes in their grip, like two executioners ready to strike once more, and Renardet, motionless, with his hand on the trunk, awaited the fall with an uneasy, nervous feeling.

One of the men said to him:

"You are too near, Monsieur le Maire. When it falls it may hurt you."

He did not reply and did not move away. He seemed ready to catch the beech tree in his open arms and to cast it on the ground like a wrestler.

All at once, at the base of the tall column of wood there was a rent which seemed to run to the top, like a painful shock; it bent slightly, ready to fall, but still resisting. The men, in a state of excitement, stiffened their arms, renewed their efforts with greater vigor, and, just as the tree came crashing down, Renardet suddenly made a forward step, then stopped, his shoulders raised to receive the irresistible shock, the mortal shock which would crush him to the earth.

But the beech tree, having deviated a little, only rubbed against his loins, throwing him on his face, five metres away.

The workmen dashed forward to lift him up. He had already arisen to his knees, stupefied, with bewildered eyes and passing his hand across his forehead, as if he were awaking from an attack of madness.

When he had got to his feet once more the men, astonished, questioned him, not being able to understand what he had done. He replied in faltering tones that he had been dazed for a moment, or, rather, he had been thinking of his childhood days; that he thought he would have time to run under the tree, just as street boys rush in front of vehicles driving rapidly past; that he had played at danger; that for the past eight days he felt this desire growing stronger within him, asking himself each time a tree began to fall whether he could pass beneath it without being touched. It was a piece of stupidity, he confessed, but every one has these moments of insanity and these temptations to boyish folly.

He made this explanation in a slow tone, searching for his words, and speaking in a colorless tone.

Then he went off, saying:

"Till to-morrow, my friends-till to-morrow."

As soon as he got back to his room he sat down at his table which his lamp lighted up brightly, and, burying his head in his hands, he began to cry.

He remained thus for a long time, then wiped his eyes, raised his head and looked at the clock. It was not yet six o'clock.

He thought:

"I have time before dinner."

And he went to the door and locked it. He then came back, and, sitting down at his table, pulled out the middle drawer. Taking from it a revolver, he laid it down on his papers in full view. The barrel of the firearm glittered, giving out gleams of light.

Renardet gazed at it for some time with the uneasy glance of a drunken man. Then he rose and began to pace up and down the room.

He walked from one end of the apartment to the other, stopping from time to time, only to pace up and down again a moment afterward. Suddenly he opened the door of his dressing-room, steeped a towel in the water pitcher and moistened his forehead, as he had done on the morning of the crime.

Then he, began walking up and down again. Each time he passed the table the gleaming revolver attracted his glance, tempted his hand, but he kept watching the clock and reflected:

"I have still time."

It struck half-past six. Then he took up the revolver, opened his mouth wide with a frightful grimace and stuck the barrel into it as if he wanted to swallow it. He remained in this position for some seconds without moving, his finger on the trigger. Then, suddenly seized with a shudder of horror, he dropped the pistol on the carpet.

He fell back on his armchair, sobbing:

"I cannot. I dare not! My God! my God! How can I have the courage to kill myself?'"

There was a knock at the door. He rose up, bewildered. A servant said:

"Monsieur's dinner is ready."

He replied:

"All right. I'm coming down."

Then he picked up the revolver, locked it up again in the drawer and looked at himself in the mirror over the mantelpiece to see whether his face did not look too much troubled. It was as red as usual, a little redder perhaps. That was all. He went down and seated himself at table.

He ate slowly, like a man who wants to prolong the meal, who does not want to be alone.

Then he smoked several pipes in the hall while the table was being cleared. After that he went back to his room.

As soon as he had locked himself in he looked, under the bed, opened all the closets, explored every corner, rummaged through all the furniture. Then he lighted the candles on the mantelpiece, and, turning round several times, ran his eye all over the apartment with an anguish of terror that distorted his face, for he knew well that he would see her, as he did every night—little Louise Roque, the little girl he had attacked and afterward strangled.

Every night the odious vision came back again. First he seemed to hear a kind of roaring sound, such as is made by a threshing machine or the distant passage of a train over a bridge. Then he commenced to gasp, to suffocate, and he had to unbutton his collar and his belt. He moved about to make his blood circulate, he tried to read, he attempted to sing. It was in vain. His thoughts, in spite of himself, went back to the day of the murder and made him begin it all over again in all its most secret details, with all the violent emotions he had experienced from the first minute to the last.

He had felt on rising that morning, the morning of the horrible day, a little dizziness and headache, which he attributed to the heat, so that he remained in his room until breakfast time.

After the meal he had taken a siesta, then, toward the close of the afternoon, he had gone out to breathe the fresh, soothing breeze under the trees in the wood.

But, as soon as he was outside, the heavy, scorching air of the plain oppressed him still more. The sun, still high in the heavens, poured down on the parched soil waves of burning light. Not a breath of wind stirred the leaves. Every beast and bird, even the grasshoppers, were silent. Renardet reached the tall trees and began to walk over the moss where the Brindille produced a slight freshness of the air beneath the immense roof of branches. But he felt ill at ease. It seemed to him that an unknown, invisible hand was strangling him, and he scarcely thought of anything, having usually few ideas in his head. For the last three months only one thought haunted him, the thought of marrying again. He suffered from living alone, suffered from it morally and physically. Accustomed for ten years past to feeling a woman near him, habituated to her presence every moment, he had need, an imperious and perplexing need of such association. Since Madame Renardet's death he had suffered continually without knowing why, he had suffered at not feeling her dress brushing past him, and, above all, from no longer being able to calm and rest himself in her arms. He had been scarcely six months a widower and he was already looking about in the district for some young girl or some widow he might marry when his period of mourning was at an end.

He had a chaste soul, but it was lodged in a powerful, herculean body, and carnal imaginings began to disturb his sleep and his vigils. He drove them away; they came back again; and he murmured from time to time, smiling at himself:

"Here I am, like St. Anthony."

Having this special morning had several of these visions, the desire suddenly came into his breast to bathe in the Brindille in order to refresh himself and cool his blood.

He knew of a large deep pool, a little farther down, where the people of the neighborhood came sometimes to take a dip in summer. He went there.

Thick willow trees hid this clear body of water where the current rested and went to sleep for a while before starting on its way again. Renardet, as he appeared, thought he heard a light sound, a faint plashing which was not that of the stream on the banks. He softly put aside the leaves and looked. A little girl, quite naked in the transparent water, was beating the water with both hands, dancing about in it and dipping herself with pretty movements. She was not a child nor was she yet a woman. She was plump and developed, while preserving an air of youthful precocity, as of one who had grown rapidly. He no longer moved, overcome with surprise, with desire, holding his breath with a strange, poignant emotion. He remained there, his heart beating as if one of his sensuous dreams had just been realized, as if an impure fairy had conjured up before him this young creature, this little rustic Venus, rising from the eddies of the stream as the real Venus rose from the waves of the sea.

Suddenly the little girl came out of the water, and, without seeing him, came over to where he stood, looking for her clothes in order to dress herself. As she approached gingerly, on account of the sharp-pointed stones, he felt himself pushed toward her by an irresistible force, by a bestial transport of passion, which stirred his flesh, bewildered his mind and made him tremble from head to foot.

She remained standing some seconds behind the willow tree which concealed him from view. Then, losing his reason entirely, he pushed aside the branches, rushed on her and seized her in his arms. She fell, too terrified to offer any resistance, too terror-stricken to cry out. He seemed possessed, not understanding what he was doing.

He woke from his crime as one wakes from a nightmare. The child burst out weeping.

"Hold your tongue! Hold your tongue!" he said. "I'll give you money."

But she did not hear him and went on sobbing.

"Come now, hold your tongue! Do hold your tongue! Keep quiet!" he continued.

She kept shrieking as she tried to free herself. He suddenly realized that he was ruined, and he caught her by the neck to stop her mouth from uttering these heartrending, dreadful screams. As she continued to struggle with the desperate strength of a being who is seeking to fly from death, he pressed his enormous hands on the little throat swollen with screaming, and in a few seconds he had strangled her, so furiously did he grip her. He had not intended to kill her, but only to make her keep quiet.

Then he stood up, overwhelmed with horror.

She lay before him, her face bleeding and blackned. He was about to rush away when there sprang up in his agitated soul the mysterious and undefined instinct that guides all beings in the hour of danger.

He was going to throw the body into the water, but another impulse drove him toward the clothes, which he made into a small package. Then, as he had a piece of twine in his pocket, he tied it up and hid it in a deep portion of the stream, beneath the trunk of a tree that overhung the Brindille.

Then he went off at a rapid pace, reached the meadows, took a wide turn in order to show himself to some peasants who dwelt some distance away at the opposite side of the district, and came back to dine at the usual hour, telling his servants all that was supposed to have happened during his walk.

He slept, however, that night; he slept with a heavy, brutish sleep like the sleep of certain persons condemned to death. He did not open his eyes until the first glimmer of dawn, and he waited till his usual hour for riding, so as to excite no suspicion.

Then he had to be present at the inquiry as to the cause of death. He did so like a somnambulist, in a kind of vision which showed him men and things as in a dream, in a cloud of intoxication, with that sense of unreality which perplexes the mind at the time of the greatest catastrophes.

But the agonized cry of Mother Roque pierced his heart. At that moment he had felt inclined to cast himself at the old woman's feet and to exclaim:

"I am the guilty one!"

But he had restrained himself. He went back, however, during the night to fish up the dead girl's wooden shoes, in order to place them on her mother's threshold.

As long as the inquiry lasted, as long as it was necessary to lead justice astray he was calm, master of himself, crafty and smiling. He discussed quietly with the magistrates all the suppositions that passed through their minds, combated their opinions and demolished their arguments. He even took a keen and mournful pleasure in disturbing their investigations, in embroiling their ideas, in showing the innocence of those whom they suspected.

But as soon as the inquiry was abandoned he became gradually nervous, more excitable than he had been before, although he mastered his irritability. Sudden noises made him start with fear; he shuddered at the slightest thing and trembled sometimes from head to foot when a fly alighted on his forehead. Then he was seized with an imperious desire for motion, which impelled him to take long walks and to remain up whole nights pacing up and down his room.

It was not that he was goaded by remorse. His brutal nature did not lend itself to any shade of sentiment or of moral terror. A man of energy and even of violence, born to make war, to ravage conquered countries and to massacre the vanquished, full of the savage instincts of the hunter and the fighter, he scarcely took count of human life. Though he respected the Church outwardly, from policy, he believed neither in God nor the devil, expecting neither chastisement nor recompense for his acts in another life. His sole belief was a vague philosophy drawn from all the ideas of the encyclopedists of the last century, and he regarded religion as a moral sanction of the law, the one and the other having been invented by men to regulate social relations. To kill any one in a duel, or in war, or in a quarrel, or by accident, or for the sake of revenge, or even through bravado would have seemed to him an amusing and clever thing and would not have left more impression on his mind than a shot fired at a hare; but he had experienced a profound emotion at the murder of this child. He had, in the first place, perpetrated it in the heat of an irresistible gust of passion, in a sort of tempest of the senses that had overpowered his reason. And he had cherished in his heart, in his flesh, on his lips, even to the very tips of his murderous fingers a kind of bestial love, as well as a feeling of terrified horror, toward this little girl surprised by him and basely killed. Every moment his thoughts returned to that horrible scene, and, though he endeavored to drive this picture from his mind, though he put it aside with terror, with disgust, he felt it surging through his soul, moving about in him, waiting incessantly for the moment to reappear.

Then, as evening approached, he was afraid of the shadow falling around him. He did not yet know why the darkness seemed frightful to him, but he instinctively feared it, he felt that it was peopled with terrors. The bright daylight did not lend itself to fears. Things and beings were visible then, and only natural things and beings could exhibit themselves in the light of day. But the night, the impenetrable night, thicker than walls and empty; the infinite night, so black, so vast, in which one might brush against frightful things; the night, when one feels that a mysterious terror is wandering, prowling about, appeared to him to conceal an unknown threatening danger, close beside him.

What was it?

He knew ere long. As he sat in his armchair, rather late one evening when he could not sleep, he thought he saw the curtain of his window move. He waited, uneasily, with beating heart. The drapery did not stir; then, all of a sudden, it moved once more. He did not venture to rise; he no longer ventured to breathe, and yet he was brave. He had often fought, and he would have liked to catch thieves in his house.

Was it true that this curtain did move? he asked himself, fearing that his eyes had deceived him. It was, moreover, such a slight thing, a gentle flutter of drapery, a kind of trembling in its folds, less than an undulation caused by the wind.

Renardet sat still, with staring eyes and outstretched neck. He sprang to his feet abruptly, ashamed of his fear, took four steps, seized the drapery with both hands and pulled it wide apart. At first he saw nothing but darkened glass, resembling plates of glittering ink. The night, the vast, impenetrable night, stretched beyond as far as the invisible horizon. He remained standing in front of this illimitable shadow, and suddenly he perceived a light, a moving light, which seemed some distance away.

Then he put his face close to the window pane, thinking that a person looking for crabs might be poaching in the Brindille, for it was past midnight, and this light rose up at the edge of the stream, under the trees. As he was not yet able to see clearly, Renardet placed his hands over his eyes, and suddenly this light became an illumination, and he beheld little Louise Roque naked and bleeding on the moss. He recoiled, frozen with horror, knocked over his chair and fell over on his back. He remained there some minutes in anguish of mind; then he sat up and began to reflect. He had had a hallucination—that was all, a hallucination due to the fact that a night marauder was walking with a lantern in his hand near the water's edge. What was there astonishing, besides, in the circumstance that the recollection of his crime should sometimes bring before him the vision of the dead girl?

He rose from the ground, swallowed a glass of wine and sat down again. He was thinking:

"What am I to do if this occurs again?"

And it would occur; he felt it; he was sure of it. Already his glance was drawn toward the window; it called him; it attracted him. In order to avoid looking at it, he turned his chair round. Then he took a book and tried to read, but it seemed to him that he presently heard something stirring behind him, and he swung round his armchair on one foot.

The curtain was moving again; unquestionably, it moved this time. He could no longer have any doubt about it.

He rushed forward and grasped it so violently that he pulled it down with its pole. Then he eagerly glued his face to the glass. He saw nothing. All was black outside, and he breathed with the joy of a man whose life has just been saved.

Then he went back to his chair and sat down again, but almost immediately he felt a longing to look out once more through the window. Since the curtain had fallen down, the window made a sort of gap, fascinating and terrible, on the dark landscape. In order not to yield to this dangerous temptation, he undressed, blew out the light and closed his eyes.

Lying on his back motionless, his skin warm and moist, he awaited sleep. Suddenly a great gleam of light flashed across his eyelids. He opened them, believing that his dwelling was on fire. All was black as before, and he leaned on his elbow to try to distinguish the window which had still for him an unconquerable attraction. By dint of, straining his eyes he could perceive some stars, and he rose, groped his way across the room, discovered the panes with his outstretched hands, and placed his forehead close to them. There below, under the trees, lay the body of the little girl gleaming like phosphorus, lighting up the surrounding darkness.

Renardet uttered a cry and rushed toward his bed, where he lay till morning, his head hidden under the pillow.

From that moment his life became intolerable. He passed his days in apprehension of each succeeding night, and each night the vision came back again. As soon as he had locked himself up in his room he strove to resist it, but in vain. An irresistible force lifted him up and pushed him against the window, as if to call the phantom, and he saw it at once, lying first in the spot where the crime was committed in the position in which it had been found.

Then the dead girl rose up and came toward him with little steps just as the child had done when she came out of the river. She advanced quietly, passing straight across the grass and over the bed of withered flowers. Then she rose up in the air toward Renardet's window. She came toward him as she had come on the day of the crime. And the man recoiled before the apparition—he retreated to his bed and sank down upon it, knowing well that the little one had entered the room and that she now was standing behind the curtain, which presently moved. And until daybreak he kept staring at this curtain with a fixed glance, ever waiting to see his victim depart.

But she did not show herself any more; she remained there behind the curtain, which quivered tremulously now and then.

And Renardet, his fingers clutching the clothes, squeezed them as he had squeezed the throat of little Louise Roque.

He heard the clock striking the hours, and in the stillness the pendulum kept ticking in time with the loud beating of his heart. And he suffered, the wretched man, more than any man had ever suffered before.

Then, as soon as a white streak of light on the ceiling announced the approaching day, he felt himself free, alone at last, alone in his room; and he went to sleep. He slept several hours—a restless, feverish sleep in which he retraced in dreams the horrible vision of the past night.

When he went down to the late breakfast he felt exhausted as after unusual exertion, and he scarcely ate anything, still haunted as he was by the fear of what he had seen the night before.

He knew well, however, that it was not an apparition, that the dead do not come back, and that his sick soul, his soul possessed by one thought alone, by an indelible remembrance, was the only cause of his torture, was what brought the dead girl back to life and raised her form before his eyes, on which it was ineffaceably imprinted. But he knew, too, that there was no cure, that he would never escape from the savage persecution of his memory, and he resolved to die rather than to endure these tortures any longer.

Then he thought of how he would kill himself, It must be something simple and natural, which would preclude the idea of suicide. For he clung to his reputation, to the name bequeathed to him by his ancestors; and if his death awakened any suspicion people's thoughts might be, perhaps, directed toward the mysterious crime, toward the murderer who could not be found, and they would not hesitate to accuse him of the crime.

A strange idea came into his head, that of allowing himself to be crushed by the tree at the foot of which he had assassinated little Louise Roque. So he determined to have the wood cut down and to simulate an accident. But the beech tree refused to crush his ribs.

Returning to his house, a prey to utter despair, he had snatched up his revolver, and then did not dare to fire it.

The dinner bell summoned him. He could eat nothing, and he went upstairs again. And he did not know what to do. Now that he had escaped the first time, he felt himself a coward. Presently he would be ready, brave, decided, master of his courage and of his resolution; now he was weak and feared death as much as he did the dead girl.

He faltered:

"I dare not venture it again—I dare not venture it."

Then he glanced with terror, first at the revolver on the table and next at the curtain which hid his window. It seemed to him, moreover, that something horrible would occur as soon as his life was ended. Something? What? A meeting with her, perhaps. She was watching for him; she was waiting for him; she was calling him; and it was in order to seize him in her turn, to draw him toward the doom that would avenge her, and to lead him to die, that she appeared thus every night.

He began to cry like a child, repeating:

"I will not venture it again—I will not venture it."

Then he fell on his knees and murmured:

"My God! my God!" without believing, nevertheless, in God. And he no longer dared, in fact, to look at his window, where he knew the apparition was hiding, nor at his table, where his revolver gleamed. When he had risen up he said:

"This cannot last; there must be an end of it"

The sound of his voice in the silent room made a chill of fear pass through his limbs, but as he could not bring himself to come to a determination, as he felt certain that his finger would always refuse to pull the trigger of his revolver, he turned round to hide his head under the bedclothes and began to reflect.

He would have to find some way in which he could force himself to die, to play some trick on himself which would not permit of any hesitation on his part, any delay, any possible regrets. He envied condemned criminals who are led to the scaffold surrounded by soldiers. Oh! if he could only beg of some one to shoot him; if after confessing his crime to a true friend who would never divulge it he could procure death at his hand. But from whom could he ask this terrible service? From whom? He thought of all the people he knew. The doctor? No, he would talk about it afterward, most probably. And suddenly a fantastic idea entered his mind. He would write to the magistrate, who was on terms of close friendship with him, and would denounce himself as the perpetrator of the crime. He would in this letter confess everything, revealing how his soul had been tortured, how he had resolved to die, how he had hesitated about carrying out his resolution and what means he had employed to strengthen his failing courage. And in the name of their old friendship he would implore of the other to destroy the letter as soon as he had ascertained that the culprit had inflicted justice on himself. Renardet could rely on this magistrate; he knew him to be true, discreet, incapable of even an idle word. He was one of those men who have an inflexible conscience, governed, directed, regulated by their reason alone.

Scarcely had he formed this project when a strange feeling of joy took possession of his heart. He was calm now. He would write his letter slowly, then at daybreak he would deposit it in the box nailed to the outside wall of his office; then he would ascend his tower to watch for the postman's arrival; and when the man in the blue blouse had gone away, he would cast himself head foremost on the rocks on which the foundations rested, He would take care to be seen first by the workmen who had cut down his wood. He could climb to the projecting stone which bore the flagstaff displayed on festivals, He would smash this pole with a shake and carry it along with him as he fell.

Who would suspect that it was not an accident? And he would be killed outright, owing to his weight and the height of the tower.

Presently he got out of bed, went over to the table and began to write. He omitted nothing, not a single detail of the crime, not a single detail of the torments of his heart, and he ended by announcing that he had passed sentence on himself, that he was going to execute the criminal, and begged his friend, his old friend, to be careful that there should never be any stain on his memory.

When he had finished this letter he saw that the day had dawned.

He closed, sealed it and wrote the address. Then he descended with light steps, hurried toward the little white box fastened to the outside wall in the corner of the farmhouse, and when he had thrown into it this letter, which made his hand tremble, he came back quickly, drew the bolts of the great door and climbed up to his tower to wait for the passing of the postman, who was to bear away his death sentence.

He felt self-possessed now. Liberated! Saved!

A cold dry wind, an icy wind passed across his face. He inhaled it eagerly with open mouth, drinking in its chilling kiss. The sky was red, a wintry red, and all the plain, whitened with frost, glistened under the first rays of the sun, as if it were covered with powdered glass.

Renardet, standing up, his head bare, gazed at the vast tract of country before him, the meadows to the left and to the right the village whose chimneys were beginning to smoke in preparation for the morning meal. At his feet he saw the Brindille flowing amid the rocks, where he would soon be crushed to death. He felt new life on that beautiful frosty morning. The light bathed him, entered his being like a new-born hope. A thousand recollections assailed him, recollections of similar mornings, of rapid walks on the hard earth which rang beneath his footsteps, of happy days of shooting on the edges of pools where wild ducks sleep. All the good things that he loved, the good things of existence, rushed to his memory, penetrated him with fresh desires, awakened all the vigorous appetites of his active, powerful body.

And he was about to die! Why? He was going to kill himself stupidly because he was afraid of a shadow-afraid of nothing! He was still rich and in the prime of life. What folly! All he needed was distraction, absence, a voyage in order to forget.

This night even he had not seen the little girl because his mind was preoccupied and had wandered toward some other subject. Perhaps he would not see her any more? And even if she still haunted him in this house, certainly she would not follow him elsewhere! The earth was wide, the future was long.

Why should he die?

His glance travelled across the meadows, and he perceived a blue spot in the path which wound alongside the Brindille. It was Mederic coming to bring letters from the town and to carry away those of the village.

Renardet gave a start, a sensation of pain shot through his breast, and he rushed down the winding staircase to get back his letter, to demand it back from the postman. Little did it matter to him now whether he was seen, He hurried across the grass damp from the light frost of the previous night and arrived in front of the box in the corner of the farmhouse exactly at the same time as the letter carrier.

The latter had opened the little wooden door and drew forth the four papers deposited there by the inhabitants of the locality.

Renardet said to him:

"Good-morrow, Mederic."

"Good-morrow, Monsieur le Maire."

"I say, Mederic, I threw a letter into the box that I want back again. I came to ask you to give it back to me."

"That's all right, Monsieur le Maire—you'll get it."

And the postman raised his eyes. He stood petrified at the sight of Renardet's face. The mayor's cheeks were purple, his eyes were anxious and sunken, with black circles round them, his hair was unbrushed, his beard untrimmed, his necktie unfastened. It was evident that he had not been in bed.

The postman asked:

"Are you ill, Monsieur le Maire?"

The other, suddenly comprehending that his appearance must be unusual, lost countenance and faltered:

"Oh! no-oh! no. Only I jumped out of bed to ask you for this letter. I was asleep. You understand?"

He said in reply:

"What letter?"

"The one you are going to give back to me."

Mederic now began to hesitate. The mayor's attitude did not strike him as natural. There was perhaps a secret in that letter, a political secret. He knew Renardet was not a Republican, and he knew all the tricks and chicanery employed at elections.

He asked:

"To whom is it addressed, this letter of yours?"

"To Monsieur Putoin, the magistrate—you know, my friend, Monsieur Putoin!"

The postman searched through the papers and found the one asked for. Then he began looking at it, turning it round and round between his fingers, much perplexed, much troubled by the fear of either committing a grave offence or of making an enemy of the mayor.

Seeing his hesitation, Renardet made a movement for the purpose of seizing the letter and snatching it away from him. This abrupt action convinced Mederic that some important secret was at stake and made him resolve to do his duty, cost what it may.

So he flung the letter into his bag and fastened it up, with the reply:

"No, I can't, Monsieur le Maire. As long as it is for the magistrate, I can't."

A dreadful pang wrung Renardet's heart and he murmured:

"Why, you know me well. You are even able to recognize my handwriting. I tell you I want that paper."

"I can't."

"Look here, Mederic, you know that I'm incapable of deceiving you—I tell you I want it."

"No, I can't."

A tremor of rage passed through Renardet's soul.

"Damn it all, take care! You know that I never trifle and that I could get you out of your job, my good fellow, and without much delay, either, And then, I am the mayor of the district, after all; and I now order you to give me back that paper."

The postman answered firmly:

"No, I can't, Monsieur le Maire."

Thereupon Renardet, losing his head, caught hold of the postman's arms in order to take away his bag; but, freeing himself by a strong effort, and springing backward, the letter carrier raised his big holly stick. Without losing his temper, he said emphatically:

"Don't touch me, Monsieur le Maire, or I'll strike. Take care, I'm only doing my duty!"

Feeling that he was lost, Renardet suddenly became humble, gentle, appealing to him like a whimpering child:

"Look here, look here, my friend, give me back that letter and I'll recompense you—I'll give you money. Stop! stop! I'll give you a hundred francs, you understand—a hundred francs!"

The postman turned on his heel and started on his journey.

Renardet followed him, out of breath, stammering:

"Mederic, Mederic, listen! I'll give you a thousand francs, you understand—a thousand francs."

The postman still went on without giving any answer.

Renardet went on:

"I'll make your fortune, you understand—whatever you wish—fifty thousand francs—fifty thousand francs for that letter! What does it matter to you? You won't? Well, a hundred thousand—I say—a hundred thousand francs. Do you understand? A hundred thousand francs—a hundred thousand francs."

The postman turned back, his face hard, his eye severe:

"Enough of this, or else I'll repeat to the magistrate everything you have just said to me."

Renardet stopped abruptly. It was all over. He turned back and rushed toward his house, running like a hunted animal.

Then, in his turn, Mederic stopped and watched his flight with stupefaction. He saw the mayor reenter his house, and he waited still, as if something astonishing were about to happen.

In fact, presently the tall form of Renardet appeared on the summit of the Fox's tower. He ran round the platform like a madman. Then he seized the flagstaff and shook it furiously without succeeding in breaking it; then, all of a sudden, like a diver, with his two hands before him, he plunged into space.

Mederic rushed forward to his assistance. He saw the woodcutters going to work and called out to them, telling them an accident had occurred. At the foot of the walls they found a bleeding body, its head crushed on a rock. The Brindille surrounded this rock, and over its clear, calm waters could be seen a long red thread of mingled brains and blood.

THE DONKEY

There was not a breath of air stirring; a heavy mist was lying over the river. It was like a layer of cotton placed on the water. The banks themselves were indistinct, hidden behind strange fogs. But day was breaking and the hill was becoming visible. In the dawning light of day the plaster houses began to appear like white spots. Cocks were crowing in the barnyard.

On the other side of the river, hidden behind the fogs, just opposite Frette, a slight noise from time to time broke the dead silence of the quiet morning. At times it was an indistinct plashing, like the cautious advance of a boat, then again a sharp noise like the rattle of an oar and then the sound of something dropping in the water. Then silence.

Sometimes whispered words, coming perhaps from a distance, perhaps from quite near, pierced through these opaque mists. They passed by like wild birds which have slept in the rushes and which fly away at the first light of day, crossing the mist and uttering a low and timid sound which wakes their brothers along the shores.

Suddenly along the bank, near the village, a barely perceptible shadow appeared on the water. Then it grew, became more distinct and, coming out of the foggy curtain which hung over the river, a flatboat, manned by two men, pushed up on the grass.

The one who was rowing rose and took a pailful of fish from the bottom of the boat, then he threw the dripping net over his shoulder. His companion, who had not made a motion, exclaimed: "Say, Mailloche, get your gun and see if we can't land some rabbit along the shore."

The other one answered: "All right. I'll be with you in a minute." Then he disappeared, in order to hide their catch.

The man who had stayed in the boat slowly filled his pipe and lighted it. His name was Labouise, but he was called Chicot, and was in partnership with Maillochon, commonly called Mailloche, to practice the doubtful and undefined profession of junk-gatherers along the shore.

They were a low order of sailors and they navigated regularly only in the months of famine. The rest of the time they acted as junk-gatherers. Rowing about on the river day and night, watching for any prey, dead or alive, poachers on the water and nocturnal hunters, sometimes ambushing venison in the Saint-Germain forests, sometimes looking for drowned people and searching their clothes, picking up floating rags and empty bottles; thus did Labouise and Maillochon live easily.

At times they would set out on foot about noon and stroll along straight ahead. They would dine in some inn on the shore and leave again side by side. They would remain away for a couple of days; then one morning they would be seen rowing about in the tub which they called their boat.

At Joinville or at Nogent some boatman would be looking for his boat, which had disappeared one night, probably stolen, while twenty or thirty miles from there, on the Oise, some shopkeeper would be rubbing his hands, congratulating himself on the bargain he had made when he bought a boat the day before for fifty francs, which two men offered him as they were passing.

Maillochon reappeared with his gun wrapped up in rags. He was a man of forty or fifty, tall and thin, with the restless eye of people who are worried by legitimate troubles and of hunted animals. His open shirt showed his hairy chest, but he seemed never to have had any more hair on his face than a short brush of a mustache and a few stiff hairs under his lower lip. He was bald around the temples. When he took off the dirty cap that he wore his scalp seemed to be covered with a fluffy down, like the body of a plucked chicken.

Chicot, on the contrary, was red, fat, short and hairy. He looked like a raw beefsteak. He continually kept his left eye closed, as if he were aiming at something or at somebody, and when people jokingly cried to him, "Open your eye, Labouise!" he would answer quietly: "Never fear, sister, I open it when there's cause to."

He had a habit of calling every one "sister," even his scavenger companion.

He took up the oars again, and once more the boat disappeared in the heavy mist, which was now turned snowy white in the pink-tinted sky.

"What kind of lead did you take, Maillochon?" Labouise asked.

"Very small, number nine; that's the best for rabbits."

They were approaching the other shore so slowly, so quietly that no noise betrayed them. This bank belongs to the Saint-Germain forest and is the boundary line for rabbit hunting. It is covered with burrows hidden under the roots of trees, and the creatures at daybreak frisk about, running in and out of the holes.

Maillochon was kneeling in the bow, watching, his gun hidden on the floor. Suddenly he seized it, aimed, and the report echoed for some time throughout the quiet country.

Labouise, in a few strokes, touched the beach, and his companion, jumping to the ground, picked up a little gray rabbit, not yet dead.

Then the boat once more disappeared into the fog in order to get to the other side, where it could keep away from the game wardens.

The two men seemed to be riding easily on the water. The weapon had disappeared under the board which served as a hiding place and the rabbit was stuffed into Chicot's loose shirt.

After about a quarter of an hour Labouise asked: "Well, sister, shall we get one more?"

"It will suit me," Maillochon answered.

The boat started swiftly down the current. The mist, which was hiding both shores, was beginning to rise. The trees could be barely perceived, as through a veil, and the little clouds of fog were floating up from the water. When they drew near the island, the end of which is opposite Herblay, the two men slackened their pace and began to watch. Soon a second rabbit was killed.

Then they went down until they were half way to Conflans. Here they stopped their boat, tied it to a tree and went to sleep in the bottom of it.

From time to time Labouise would sit up and look over the horizon with his open eye. The last of the morning mist had disappeared and the large summer sun was climbing in the blue sky.

On the other side of the river the vineyard-covered hill stretched out in a semicircle. One house stood out alone at the summit. Everything was silent.

Something was moving slowly along the tow-path, advancing with difficulty. It was a woman dragging a donkey. The stubborn, stiff-jointed beast occasionally stretched out a leg in answer to its companion's efforts, and it proceeded thus, with outstretched neck and ears lying flat, so slowly that one could not tell when it would ever be out of sight.

The woman, bent double, was pulling, turning round occasionally to strike the donkey with a stick.

As soon as he saw her, Labouise exclaimed: "Say, Mailloche!"

Mailloche answered: "What's the matter?"

"Want to have some fun?"

"Of course!"

"Then hurry, sister; we're going to have a laugh."

Chicot took the oars. When he had crossed the river he stopped opposite the woman and called:

"Hey, sister!"

The woman stopped dragging her donkey and looked.

Labouise continued: "What are you doing—going to the locomotive show?"

The woman made no reply. Chicot continued:

"Say, your trotter's prime for a race. Where are you taking him at that speed?"

At last the woman answered: "I'm going to Macquart, at Champioux, to have him killed. He's worthless."

Labouise answered: "You're right. How much do you think Macquart will give you for him?"

The woman wiped her forehead on the back of her hand and hesitated, saying: "How do I know? Perhaps three francs, perhaps four."

Chicot exclaimed: "I'll give you five francs and your errand's done! How's that?"

The woman considered the matter for a second and then exclaimed: "Done!"

The two men landed. Labouise grasped the animal by the bridle. Maillochon asked in surprise:

"What do you expect to do with that carcass?"

Chicot this time opened his other eye in order to express his gaiety. His whole red face was grinning with joy. He chuckled: "Don't worry, sister. I've got my idea."

He gave five francs to the woman, who then sat down by the road to see what was going to happen. Then Labouise, in great humor, got the gun and held it out to Maillochon, saying: "Each one in turn; we're going after big game, sister. Don't get so near or you'll kill it right away! You must make the pleasure last a little."

He placed his companion about forty paces from the victim. The ass, feeling itself free, was trying to get a little of the tall grass, but it was so exhausted that it swayed on its legs as if it were about to fall.

Maillochon aimed slowly and said: "A little pepper for the ears; watch, Ghicot!" And he fired.

The tiny shot struck the donkey's long ears and he began to shake them in order to get rid of the stinging sensation. The two men were doubled up with laughter and stamped their feet with joy. The woman, indignant, rushed forward; she did not want her donkey to be tortured, and she offered to return the five francs. Labouise threatened her with a thrashing and pretended to roll up his sleeves. He had paid, hadn't he? Well, then, he would take a shot at her skirts, just to show that it didn't hurt. She went away, threatening to call the police. They could hear her protesting indignantly and cursing as she went her way.

Maillochon held out the gun to his comrade, saying: "It's your turn, Chicot."

Labouise aimed and fired. The donkey received the charge in his thighs, but the shot was so small and came from such a distance that he thought he was being stung by flies, for he began to thrash himself with his tail.

Labouise sat down to laugh more comfortably, while Maillochon reloaded the weapon, so happy that he seemed to sneeze into the barrel. He stepped forward a few paces, and, aiming at the same place that his friend had shot at, he fired again. This time the beast started, tried to kick and turned its head. At last a little blood was running. It had been wounded and felt a sharp pain, for it tried to run away with a slow, limping, jerky gallop.

Both men darted after the beast, Maillochon with a long stride, Labouise with the short, breathless trot of a little man. But the donkey, tired out, had stopped, and, with a bewildered look, was watching his two murderers approach. Suddenly he stretched his neck and began to bray.

Labouise, out of breath, had taken the gun. This time he walked right up close, as he did not wish to begin the chase over again.

When the poor beast had finished its mournful cry, like a last call for help, the man called: "Hey, Mailloche! Come here, sister; I'm going to give him some medicine." And while the other man was forcing the animal's mouth open, Chicot stuck the barrel of his gun down its throat, as if he were trying to make it drink a potion. Then he said: "Look out, sister, here she goes!"

He pressed the trigger. The donkey stumbled back a few steps, fell down, tried to get up again and finally lay on its side and closed its eyes: The whole body was trembling, its legs were kicking as if it were, trying to run. A stream of blood was oozing through its teeth. Soon it stopped moving. It was dead.

The two men went along, laughing. It was over too quickly; they had not had their money's worth. Maillochon asked: "Well, what are we going to do now?"

Labouise answered: "Don't worry, sister. Get the thing on the boat; we're going to have some fun when night comes."

They went and got the boat. The animal's body was placed on the bottom, covered with fresh grass, and the two men stretched out on it and went to sleep.

Toward noon Labouise drew a bottle of wine, some bread and butter and raw onions from a hiding place in their muddy, worm-eaten boat, and they began to eat.

When the meal was over they once more stretched out on the dead donkey and slept. At nightfall Labouise awoke and shook his comrade, who was snoring like a buzzsaw. "Come on, sister," he ordered.

Maillochon began to row. As they had plenty of time they went up the Seine slowly. They coasted along the reaches covered with water-lilies, and the heavy, mud-covered boat slipped over the lily pads and bent the flowers, which stood up again as soon as they had passed.

When they reached the wall of the Eperon, which separates the Saint-Germain forest from the Maisons-Laffitte Park, Labouise stopped his companion and explained his idea to him. Maillochon was moved by a prolonged, silent laugh.

They threw into the water the grass which had covered the body, took the animal by the feet and hid it behind some bushes. Then they got into their boat again and went to Maisons-Laffitte.

The night was perfectly black when they reached the wine shop of old man Jules. As soon as the dealer saw them he came up, shook hands with them and sat down at their table. They began to talk of one thing and another. By eleven o'clock the last customer had left and old man Jules winked at Labouise and asked: "Well, have you got any?"

Labouise made a motion with his head and answered: "Perhaps so, perhaps not!"

The dealer insisted: "Perhaps you've not nothing but gray ones?"

Chicot dug his hands into his flannel shirt, drew out the ears of a rabbit and declared: "Three francs a pair!"

Then began a long discussion about the price. Two francs sixty-five and the two rabbits were delivered. As the two men were getting up to go, old man Jules, who had been watching them, exclaimed:

"You have something else, but you won't say what."

Labouise answered: "Possibly, but it is not for you; you're too stingy."

The man, growing eager, kept asking: "What is it? Something big? Perhaps we might make a deal."

Labouise, who seemed perplexed, pretended to consult Maillochon with a glance. Then he answered in a slow voice: "This is how it is. We were in the bushes at Eperon when something passed right near us, to the left, at the end of the wall. Mailloche takes a shot and it drops. We skipped on account of the game people. I can't tell you what it is, because I don't know. But it's big enough. But what is it? If I told you I'd be lying, and you know, sister, between us everything's above-board."

Anxiously the man asked: "Think it's venison?"

Labouise answered: "Might be and then again it might not! Venison?—uh! uh!—might be a little big for that! Mind you, I don't say it's a doe, because I don't know, but it might be."

Still the dealer insisted: "Perhaps it's a buck?"

Labouise stretched out his hand, exclaiming: "No, it's not that! It's not a buck. I should have seen the horns. No, it's not a buck!"

"Why didn't you bring it with you?" asked the man.

"Because, sister, from now on I sell from where I stand. Plenty of people will buy. All you have to do is to take a walk over there, find the thing and take it. No risk for me."

The innkeeper, growing suspicious, exclaimed "Supposing he wasn't there!"

Labouise once more raised his hand and said:

"He's there, I swear!—first bush to the left. What it is, I don't know. But it's not a buck, I'm positive. It's for you to find out what it is. Twenty-five francs, cash down!"

Still the man hesitated: "Couldn't you bring it?"

Maillochon exclaimed: "No, indeed! You know our price! Take it or leave it!"

The dealer decided: "It's a bargain for twenty francs!"

And they shook hands over the deal.

Then he took out four big five-franc pieces from the cash drawer, and the two friends pocketed the money. Labouise arose, emptied his glass and left. As he was disappearing in the shadows he turned round to exclaim: "It isn't a buck. I don't know what it is!—but it's there. I'll give you back your money if you find nothing!"

And he disappeared in the darkness. Maillochon, who was following him, kept punching him in the back to express his joy.

MOIRON

As we were still talking about Pranzini, M. Maloureau, who had been attorney general under the Empire, said: "Oh! I formerly knew a very curious affair, curious for several reasons, as you will see.

"I was at that time imperial attorney in one of the provinces. I had to take up the case which has remained famous under the name of the Moiron case.

"Monsieur Moiron, who was a teacher in the north of France, enjoyed an excellent reputation throughout the whole country. He was a person of intelligence, quiet, very religious, a little taciturn; he had married in the district of Boislinot, where he exercised his profession. He had had three children, who had died of consumption, one after the other. From this time he seemed to bestow upon the youngsters confided to his care all the tenderness of his heart. With his own money he bought toys for his best scholars and for the good boys; he gave them little dinners and stuffed them with delicacies, candy and cakes: Everybody loved this good man with his big heart, when suddenly five of his pupils died, in a strange manner, one after the other. It was supposed that there was an epidemic due to the condition of the water, resulting from drought; they looked for the causes without being able to discover them, the more so that the symptoms were so peculiar. The children seemed to be attacked by a feeling of lassitude; they would not eat, they complained of pains in their stomachs, dragged along for a short time, and died in frightful suffering.

"A post-mortem examination was held over the last one, but nothing was discovered. The vitals were sent to Paris and analyzed, and they revealed the presence of no toxic substance.

"For a year nothing new developed; then two little boys, the best scholars in the class, Moiron's favorites, died within four days of each other. An examination of the bodies was again ordered, and in both of them were discovered tiny fragments of crushed glass. The conclusion arrived at was that the two youngsters must imprudently have eaten from some carelessly cleaned receptacle. A glass broken over a pail of milk could have produced this frightful accident, and the affair would have been pushed no further if Moiron's servant had not been taken sick at this time. The physician who was called in noticed the same symptoms he had seen in the children. He questioned her and obtained the admission that she had stolen and eaten some candies that had been bought by the teacher for his scholars.

"On an order from the court the schoolhouse was searched, and a closet was found which was full of toys and dainties destined for the children. Almost all these delicacies contained bits of crushed glass or pieces of broken needles!

"Moiron was immediately arrested; but he seemed so astonished and indignant at the suspicion hanging over him that he was almost released. How ever, indications of his guilt kept appearing, and baffled in my mind my first conviction, based on his excellent reputation, on his whole life, on the complete absence of any motive for such a crime.

"Why should this good, simple, religious man have killed little children, and the very children whom he seemed to love the most, whom he spoiled and stuffed with sweet things, for whom he spent half his salary in buying toys and bonbons?

"One must consider him insane to believe him guilty of this act. Now, Moiron seemed so normal, so quiet, so rational and sensible that it seemed impossible to adjudge him insane.

"However, the proofs kept growing! In none of the candies that were bought at the places where the schoolmaster secured his provisions could the slightest trace of anything suspicious be found.

"He then insisted that an unknown enemy must have opened his cupboard with a false key in order to introduce the glass and the needles into the eatables. And he made up a whole story of an inheritance dependent on the death of a child, determined on and sought by some peasant, and promoted thus by casting suspicions on the schoolmaster. This brute, he claimed, did not care about the other children who were forced to die as well.

"The story was possible. The man appeared to be so sure of himself and in such despair that we should undoubtedly have acquitted him, notwithstanding the charges against him, if two crushing discoveries had not been made, one after the other.

"The first one was a snuffbox full of crushed glass; his own snuffbox, hidden in the desk where he kept his money!

"He explained this new find in an acceptable manner, as the ruse of the real unknown criminal. But a mercer from Saint-Marlouf came to the presiding judge and said that a gentleman had several times come to his store to buy some needles; and he always asked for the thinnest needles he could find, and would break them to see whether they pleased him. The man was brought forward in the presence of a dozen or more persons, and immediately recognized Moiron. The inquest revealed that the schoolmaster had indeed gone into Saint-Marlouf on the days mentioned by the tradesman.

"I will pass over the terrible testimony of children on the choice of dainties and the care which he took to have them eat the things in his presence, and to remove the slightest traces.

"Public indignation demanded capital punishment, and it became more and more insistent, overturning all objections.

"Moiron was condemned to death, and his appeal was rejected. Nothing was left for him but the imperial pardon. I knew through my father that the emperor would not grant it.

"One morning, as I was working in my study, the visit of the prison almoner was announced. He was an old priest who knew men well and understood the habits of criminals. He seemed troubled, ill at ease, nervous. After talking for a few minutes about one thing and another, he arose and said suddenly: 'If Moiron is executed, monsieur, you will have put an innocent man to death.'

"Then he left without bowing, leaving me behind with the deep impression made by his words. He had pronounced them in such a sincere and solemn manner, opening those lips, closed and sealed by the secret of confession, in order to save a life.

"An hour later I left for Paris, and my father immediately asked that I be granted an audience with the emperor.

"The following day I was received. His majesty was working in a little reception room when we were introduced. I described the whole case, and I was just telling about the priest's visit when a door opened behind the sovereign's chair and the empress, who supposed he was alone, appeared. His majesty, Napoleon, consulted her. As soon as she had heard the matter, she exclaimed: 'This man must be pardoned. He must, since he is innocent.'

"Why did this sudden conviction of a religious woman cast a terrible doubt in my mind?

"Until then I had ardently desired a change of sentence. And now I suddenly felt myself the toy, the dupe of a cunning criminal who had employed the priest and confession as a last means of defence.

“I explained my hesitancy to their majesties. The emperor remained undecided, urged on one side by his natural kindness and held back on the other by the fear of being deceived by a criminal; but the empress, who was convinced that the priest had obeyed a divine inspiration, kept repeating: ‘Never mind! It is better to spare a criminal than to kill an innocent man!’ Her advice was taken. The death sentence was commuted to one of hard labor.

“A few years later I heard that Moiron had again been called to the emperor’s attention on account of his exemplary conduct in the prison at Toulon and was now employed as a servant by the director of the penitentiary.

“For a long time I heard nothing more of this man. But about two years ago, while I was spending a summer near Lille with my cousin, De Larielle, I was informed one evening, just as we were sitting down to dinner, that a young priest wished to speak to me.

“I had him shown in and he begged me to come to a dying man who desired absolutely to see me. This had often happened to me in my long career as a magistrate, and, although I had been set aside by the Republic, I was still often called upon in similar circumstances. I therefore followed the priest, who led me to a miserable little room in a large tenement house.

“There I found a strange-looking man on a bed of straw, sitting with his back against the wall, in order to get his breath. He was a sort of skeleton, with dark, gleaming eyes.

“As soon as he saw me, he murmured: ‘Don’t you recognize me?’

“‘No.’

“‘I am Moiron.’

“I felt a shiver run through me, and I asked ‘The schoolmaster?’

“‘Yes.’

“‘How do you happen to be here?’

“‘The story is too long. I haven’t time to tell it. I was going to die and that priest was brought to me—and as I knew that you were here I sent for you. It is to you that I wish to confess—since you were the one who once saved my life.’

“His hands clutched the straw of his bed through the sheet and he continued in a hoarse, forcible and low tone: ‘You see—I owe you the truth—I owe it to you—for it must be told to some one before I leave this earth.

“‘It is I who killed the children—all of them. I did it—for revenge!

“‘Listen. I was an honest, straightforward, pure man—adoring God—this good Father—this Master who teaches us to love, and not the false God, the executioner, the robber, the murderer who governs the earth. I had never done any harm; I had never committed an evil act. I was as good as it is possible to be, monsieur.

“‘I married and had children, and I loved them as no father or mother ever loved their children. I lived only for them. I was wild about them. All three of them died! Why? why? What had I done? I was rebellious, furious; and suddenly my eyes were opened as if I were waking up out of a sleep. I understood that God is bad. Why had He killed my children? I opened my eyes and saw that He loves to kill. He loves only that, monsieur. He gives life but to destroy it! God, monsieur, is a murderer! He needs death every day. And He makes it of every variety, in order the better to be amused. He has invented sickness and accidents in order to give Him diversion all through the months and the years; and when He grows tired of this, He has epidemics, the plague, cholera, diphtheria, smallpox, everything possible! But this does not satisfy Him; all these things are too similar; and so from time to time He has wars, in order to see two hundred thousand soldiers killed at once, crushed in blood and in the mud, blown apart, their arms and legs torn off, their heads smashed by bullets, like eggs that fall on the ground.

"'But this is not all. He has made men who eat each other. And then, as men become better than He, He has made beasts, in order to see men hunt them, kill them and eat them. That is not all. He has made tiny little animals which live one day, flies who die by the millions in one hour, ants which we are continually crushing under our feet, and so many, many others that we cannot even imagine. And all these things are continually killing each other and dying. And the good Lord looks on and is amused, for He sees everything, the big ones as well as the little ones, those who are in the drops of water and those in the other firmaments. He watches them and is amused. Wretch!

"'Then, monsieur, I began to kill children. I played a trick on Him. He did not get those. It was not He, but I! And I would have killed many others, but you caught me. There!

"'I was to be executed. I! How He would have laughed! Then I asked for a priest, and I lied. I confessed to him. I lied and I lived.

"'Now, all is over. I can no longer escape from Him. I no longer fear Him, monsieur; I despise Him too much.'

"This poor wretch was frightful to see as he lay there gasping, opening an enormous mouth in order to utter words which could scarcely be heard, his breath rattling, picking at his bed and moving his thin legs under a grimy sheet as though trying to escape.

"Oh! The mere remembrance of it is frightful!

"'You have nothing more to say?' I asked.

"'No, monsieur.'

"'Then, farewell.'

"'Farewell, monsieur, till some day——'

"I turned to the ashen-faced priest, whose dark outline stood out against the wall, and asked: 'Are you going to stay here, Monsieur l'Abbe?'

"'Yes.'

"Then the dying man sneered: 'Yes, yes, He sends His vultures to the corpses.'

"I had had enough of this. I opened the door and ran away."

THE DISPENSER OF HOLY WATER

He lived formerly in a little house beside the high road outside the village. He had set up in business as a wheelwright, after marrying the daughter of a farmer of the neighborhood, and as they were both industrious, they managed to save up a nice little fortune. But they had no children, and this caused them great sorrow. Finally a son was born, whom they named Jean. They both loved and petted him, enfolding him with their affection, and were unwilling to let him be out of their sight.

When he was five years old some mountebanks passed through the country and set up their tent in the town hall square.

Jean, who had seen them pass by, made his escape from the house, and after his father had made a long search for him, he found him among the learned goats and trick dogs, uttering shouts of laughter and sitting on the knees of an old clown.

Three days later, just as they were sitting down to dinner, the wheelwright and his wife noticed that their son was not in the house. They looked for him in the garden, and as they did not find him, his father went out into the road and shouted at the top of his voice, "Jean!"

Night came on. A brown vapor arose making distant objects look still farther away and giving them a dismal, weird appearance. Three tall pines, close at hand, seemed to be weeping. Still there was no reply, but the air appeared to be full of indistinct sighing. The father listened for some time, thinking he heard a sound first in one direction, then in another, and, almost beside himself, he ran, out into the night, calling incessantly "Jean! Jean!"

He ran along thus until daybreak, filling the, darkness with his shouts, terrifying stray animals, torn by a terrible anguish and fearing that he was losing his mind. His wife, seated on the stone step of their home, sobbed until morning.

They did not find their son. They both aged rapidly in their inconsolable sorrow. Finally they sold their house and set out to search together.

They inquired of the shepherds on the hillsides, of the tradesmen passing by, of the peasants in the villages and of the authorities in the towns. But their boy had been lost a long time and no one knew anything about him. He had probably forgotten his own name by this time and also the name of his village, and his parents wept in silence, having lost hope.

Before long their money came to an end, and they worked out by the day in the farms and inns, doing the most menial work, eating what was left from the tables, sleeping on the ground and suffering from cold. Then as they became enfeebled by hard work no one would employ them any longer, and they were forced to beg along the high roads. They accosted passers-by in an entreating voice and with sad, discouraged faces; they begged a morsel of bread from the harvesters who were dining around a tree in the fields at noon, and they ate in silence seated on the edge of a ditch. An innkeeper to whom they told their story said to them one day:

"I know some one who had lost their daughter, and they found her in Paris."

They at once set out for Paris.

When they entered the great city they were bewildered by its size and by the crowds that they saw. But they knew that Jean must be in the midst of all these people, though they did not know how to set about looking for him. Then they feared that they might not recognize him, for he was only five years old when they last saw him.

They visited every place, went through all the streets, stopping whenever they saw a group of people, hoping for some providential meeting, some extraordinary luck, some compassionate fate.

They frequently walked at haphazard straight ahead, leaning one against the other, looking so sad and poverty-stricken that people would give them alms without their asking.

They spent every Sunday at the doors of the churches, watching the crowds entering and leaving, trying to distinguish among the faces one that might be familiar. Several times they thought they recognized him, but always found they had made a mistake.

In the vestibule of one of the churches which they visited the most frequently there was an old dispenser of holy Water who had become their friend. He also had a very sad history, and their sympathy for him had established a bond of close friendship between them. It ended by them all three living together in a poor lodging on the top floor of a large house situated at some distance, quite on the outskirts of the city, and the wheelwright would sometimes take his new friend's place at the church when the latter was ill.

Winter came, a very severe winter. The poor holy water sprinkler died and the parish priest appointed the wheelwright, whose misfortunes had come to his knowledge, to replace him. He went every morning and sat in the same place, on the same chair, wearing away the old stone pillar by continually leaning against it. He would gaze steadily at every man who entered the church and looked forward to Sunday with as much impatience as a schoolboy, for on that day the church was filled with people from morning till night.

He became very old, growing weaker each day from the dampness of the church, and his hope oozed away gradually.

He now knew by sight all the people who came to the services; he knew their hours, their manners, could distinguish their step on the stone pavement.

His interests had become so contracted that the entrance of a stranger in the church was for him a great event. One day two ladies came in; one was old, the other young—a mother and daughter probably. Behind them came a man who was following them. He bowed to them as they came out, and after offering them some holy water, he took the arm of the elder lady.

"That must be the fiance of the younger one," thought the wheelwright. And until evening he kept trying to recall where he had formerly seen a young man who resembled this one. But the one he was thinking of must be an old man by this time, for it seemed as if he had known him down home in his youth.

The same man frequently came again to walk home with the ladies, and this vague, distant, familiar resemblance which he could not place worried the old man so much that he made his wife come with him to see if she could help his impaired memory.

One evening as it was growing dusk the three strangers entered together. When they had passed the old man said:

"Well, do you know him?"

His wife anxiously tried to ransack her memory. Suddenly she said in a low tone:

"Yes—yes—but he is darker, taller, stouter and is dressed like a gentleman, but, father, all the same, it is your face when you were young!"

The old man started violently.

It was true. He looked like himself and also like his brother who was dead, and like his father, whom he remembered while he was yet young. The old couple were so affected that they could not speak. The three persons came out and were about to leave the church.

The man touched his finger to the holy water sprinkler. Then the old man, whose hand was trembling so that he was fairly sprinkling the ground with holy water, exclaimed:

"Jean!"

The young man stopped and looked at him.

He repeated in a lower tone:

"Jean!"

The two women looked at them without understanding.

He then said for the third time, sobbing as he did so:

"Jean!"

The man stooped down, with his face close to the old man's, and as a memory of his childhood dawned on him he replied:

"Papa Pierre, Mamma Jeanne!"

He had forgotten everything, his father's surname and the name of his native place, but he always remembered those two words that he had so often repeated: "Papa Pierre, Mamma Jeanne."

He sank to the floor, his face on the old man's knees, and he wept, kissing now his father and then his mother, while they were almost breathless from intense joy.

The two ladies also wept, understanding as they did that some great happiness had come to pass.

Then they all went to the young man's house and he told them his history. The circus people had carried him off. For three years he traveled with them in various countries. Then the troupe disbanded, and one day an old lady in a chateau had paid to have him stay with her because she liked his appearance. As he was intelligent, he was sent to school, then to college, and the old lady having no children, had left him all her money. He, for his part, had tried to find his parents, but as he could remember only the two names, "Papa Pierre, Mamma Jeanne," he had been unable to do so. Now he was about to be married, and he introduced his fiancee, who was very good and very pretty.

When the two old people had told their story in their turn he kissed them once more. They sat up very late that night, not daring to retire lest the happiness they had so long sought should escape them again while they were asleep.

But misfortune had lost its hold on them and they were happy for the rest of their lives.

A PARRICIDE

The lawyer had presented a plea of insanity. How could anyone explain this strange crime otherwise?

One morning, in the grass near Chatou, two bodies had been found, a man and a woman, well known, rich, no longer young and married since the preceding year, the woman having been a widow for three years before.

They were not known to have enemies; they had not been robbed. They seemed to have been thrown from the roadside into the river, after having been struck, one after the other, with a long iron spike.

The investigation revealed nothing. The boatmen, who had been questioned, knew nothing. The matter was about to be given up, when a young carpenter from a neighboring village, Georges Louis, nicknamed "the Bourgeois," gave himself up.

To all questions he only answered this:

"I had known the man for two years, the woman for six months. They often had me repair old furniture for them, because I am a clever workman."

And when he was asked:

"Why did you kill them?"

He would obstinately answer:

"I killed them because I wanted to kill them."

They could get nothing more out of him.

This man was undoubtedly an illegitimate child, put out to nurse and then abandoned. He had no other name than Georges Louis, but as on growing up he became particularly intelligent, with the good taste and native refinement which his acquaintances did not have, he was nicknamed "the Bourgeois," and he was never called otherwise. He had become remarkably clever in the trade of a carpenter, which he had taken up. He was also said to be a socialist fanatic, a believer in communistic and nihilistic doctrines, a great reader of bloodthirsty novels, an influential political agitator and a clever orator in the public meetings of workmen or of farmers.

His lawyer had pleaded insanity.

Indeed, how could one imagine that this workman should kill his best customers, rich and generous (as he knew), who in two years had enabled him to earn three thousand francs (his books showed it)? Only one explanation could be offered: insanity, the fixed idea of the unclassed individual who reeks vengeance on two bourgeois, on all the bourgeoisie, and the lawyer made a clever allusion to this nickname of "The Bourgeois," given throughout the neighborhood to this poor wretch. He exclaimed:

"Is this irony not enough to unbalance the mind of this poor wretch, who has neither father nor mother? He is an ardent republican. What am I saying? He even belongs to the same political party, the members of which, formerly shot or exiled by the government, it now welcomes with open arms this party to which arson is a principle and murder an ordinary occurrence.

"These gloomy doctrines, now applauded in public meetings, have ruined this man. He has heard republicans—even women, yes, women—ask for the blood of M. Gambetta, the blood of M. Grevy; his weakened mind gave way; he wanted blood, the blood of a bourgeois!

"It is not he whom you should condemn, gentlemen; it is the Commune!"

Everywhere could be heard murmurs of assent. Everyone felt that the lawyer had won his case. The prosecuting attorney did not oppose him.

Then the presiding judge asked the accused the customary question:

"Prisoner, is there anything that you wish to add to your defense?"

The man stood up.

He was a short, flaxen blond, with calm, clear, gray eyes. A strong, frank, sonorous voice came from this frail-looking boy and, at the first words, quickly changed the opinion which had been formed of him.

He spoke loud in a declamatory manner, but so distinctly that every word could be understood in the farthest corners of the big hall:

"Your honor, as I do not wish to go to an insane asylum, and as I even prefer death to that, I will tell everything.

"I killed this man and this woman because they were my parents.

"Now, listen, and judge me.

"A woman, having given birth to a boy, sent him out, somewhere, to a nurse. Did she even know where her accomplice carried this innocent little being, condemned to eternal misery, to the shame of an illegitimate birth; to more than that—to death, since he was abandoned and the nurse, no longer receiving the monthly pension, might, as they often do, let him die of hunger and neglect!

"The woman who nursed me was honest, better, more noble, more of a mother than my own mother. She brought me up. She did wrong in doing her duty. It is more humane to let them die, these little wretches who are cast away in suburban villages just as garbage is thrown away.

"I grew up with the indistinct impression that I was carrying some burden of shame. One day the other children called me a 'b——'. They did not know the meaning of this word, which one of them had heard at home. I was also ignorant of its meaning, but I felt the sting all the same.

"I was, I may say, one of the cleverest boys in the school. I would have been a good man, your honor, perhaps a man of superior intellect, if my parents had not committed the crime of abandoning me.

"This crime was committed against me. I was the victim, they were the guilty ones. I was defenseless, they were pitiless. Their duty was to love me, they rejected me.

"I owed them life—but is life a boon? To me, at any rate, it was a misfortune. After their shameful desertion, I owed them only vengeance. They committed against me the most inhuman, the most infamous, the most monstrous crime which can be committed against a human creature.

"A man who has been insulted, strikes; a man who has been robbed, takes back his own by force. A man who has been deceived, played upon, tortured, kills; a man who has been slapped, kills; a man who has been dishonored, kills. I have been robbed, deceived, tortured, morally slapped, dishonored, all this to a greater degree than those whose anger you excuse.

"I revenged myself, I killed. It was my legitimate right. I took their happy life in exchange for the terrible one which they had forced on me.

"You will call me parricide! Were these people my parents, for whom I was an abominable burden, a terror, an infamous shame; for whom my birth was a calamity and my life a threat of disgrace? They sought a selfish pleasure; they got an unexpected child. They suppressed the child. My turn came to do the same for them.

"And yet, up to quite recently, I was ready to love them.

"As I have said, this man, my father, came to me for the first time two years ago. I suspected nothing. He ordered two pieces of furniture. I found out, later on, that, under the seal of secrecy, naturally, he had sought information from the priest.

"He returned often. He gave me a lot of work and paid me well. Sometimes he would even talk to me of one thing or another. I felt a growing affection for him.

"At the beginning of this year he brought with him his wife, my mother. When she entered she was trembling so that I thought her to be suffering from some nervous disease. Then she asked for a seat and a glass of water. She said nothing; she looked around abstractedly at my work and only answered 'yes' and 'no,' at random, to all the questions which he asked her. When she had left I thought her a little unbalanced.

"The following month they returned. She was calm, self-controlled. That day they chattered for a long time, and they left me a rather large order. I saw her three more times, without suspecting anything. But one day she began to talk to me of my life, of my childhood, of my parents. I answered: 'Madame, my parents were wretches who deserted me.' Then she clutched at her heart and fell, unconscious. I immediately thought: 'She is my mother!' but I took care not to let her notice anything. I wished to observe her.

"I, in turn, sought out information about them. I learned that they had been married since last July, my mother having been a widow for only three years. There had been rumors that they had loved each other during the lifetime of the first husband, but there was no proof of it. I was the proof—the proof which they had at first hidden and then hoped to destroy.

"I waited. She returned one evening, escorted as usual by my father. That day she seemed deeply moved, I don't know why. Then, as she was leaving, she said to me: 'I wish you success, because you seem to me to be honest and a hard worker; some day you will undoubtedly think of getting married. I have come to help you to choose freely the woman who may suit you. I was married against my inclination once and I know what suffering it causes. Now I am rich, childless, free, mistress of my fortune. Here is your dowry.'

"She held out to me a large, sealed envelope.

"I looked her straight in the eyes and then said: 'Are you my mother?'

"She drew back a few steps and hid her face in her hands so as not to see me. He, the man, my father, supported her in his arms and cried out to me: 'You must be crazy!'

"I answered: 'Not in the least. I know that you are my parents. I cannot be thus deceived. Admit it and I will keep the secret; I will bear you no ill will; I will remain what I am, a carpenter.'

"He retreated towards the door, still supporting his wife who was beginning to sob. Quickly I locked the door, put the key in my pocket and continued: 'Look at her and dare to deny that she is my mother.'

"Then he flew into a passion, very pale, terrified at the thought that the scandal, which had so far been avoided, might suddenly break out; that their position, their good name, their honor might all at once be lost. He stammered out: 'You are a rascal, you wish to get money from us! That's the thanks we get for trying to help such common people!'

"My mother, bewildered, kept repeating: 'Let's get out of here, let's get out!'

"Then, when he found the door locked, he exclaimed: 'If you do not open this door immediately, I will have you thrown into prison for blackmail and assault!'

"I had remained calm; I opened the door and saw them disappear in the darkness.

"Then I seemed to have been suddenly orphaned, deserted, pushed to the wall. I was seized with an overwhelming sadness, mingled with anger, hatred, disgust; my whole being seemed to rise up in revolt against the injustice, the meanness, the dishonor, the rejected love. I began to run, in order to overtake them along the Seine, which they had to follow in order to reach the station of Chaton.

"I soon caught up with them. It was now pitch dark. I was creeping up behind them softly, that they might not hear me. My mother was still crying. My father was saying: 'It's all your own fault. Why did you wish to see him? It was absurd in our position. We could have helped him from afar, without showing ourselves. Of what use are these dangerous visits, since we can't recognize him?'

"Then I rushed up to them, beseeching. I cried:

"'You see! You are my parents. You have already rejected me once; would you repulse me again?'

"Then, your honor, he struck me. I swear it on my honor, before the law and my country. He struck me, and as I seized him by the collar, he drew from his pocket a revolver.

"The blood rushed to my head, I no longer knew what I was doing, I had my compass in my pocket; I struck him with it as often as I could.

"Then she began to cry: 'Help! murder!' and to pull my beard. It seems that I killed her also. How do I know what I did then?

"Then, when I saw them both lying on the ground, without thinking, I threw them into the Seine.

"That's all. Now sentence me."

The prisoner sat down. After this revelation the case was carried over to the following session. It comes up very soon. If we were jurymen, what would we do with this parricide?

BERTHA

Dr. Bonnet, my old friend—one sometimes has friends older than one's self—had often invited me to spend some time with him at Riom, and, as I did not know Auvergne, I made up my mind to visit him in the summer of 1876.

I arrived by the morning train, and the first person I saw on the platform was the doctor. He was dressed in a gray suit, and wore a soft, black, wide-brimmed, high-crowned felt hat, narrow at the top like a chimney pot, a hat which hardly any one except an Auvergnat would wear, and which reminded one of a charcoal burner. Dressed like that, the doctor had the appearance of an old young man, with his spare body under his thin coat, and his large head covered with white hair.

He embraced me with that evident pleasure which country people feel when they meet long-expected friends, and, stretching out his arm, he said proudly:

"This is Auvergne!" I saw nothing before me except a range of mountains, whose summits, which resembled truncated cones, must have been extinct volcanoes.

Then, pointing to the name of the station, he said:

"Riom, the fatherland of magistrates, the pride of the magistracy, and which ought rather to be the fatherland of doctors."

"Why?" I, asked.

"Why?" he replied with a laugh. "If you transpose the letters, you have the Latin word 'mori', to die. That is the reason why I settled here, my young friend."

And, delighted at his own joke, he carried me off, rubbing his hands.

As soon as I had swallowed a cup of coffee, he made me go and see the town. I admired the druggist's house, and the other noted houses, which were all black, but as pretty as bric-a-brac, with their facades of sculptured stone. I admired the statue of the Virgin, the patroness of butchers, and he told me an amusing story about this, which I will relate some other time, and then Dr. Bonnet said to me:

"I must beg you to excuse me for a few minutes while I go and see a patient, and then I will take you to Chatel-Guyon, so as to show you the general aspect of the town, and all the mountain chain of the Puy-de-Dome before lunch. You can wait for me outside; I shall only go upstairs and come down immediately."

He left me outside one of those old, gloomy, silent, melancholy houses, which one sees in the provinces, and this one appeared to look particularly sinister, and I soon discovered the reason. All the large windows on the first floor were boarded half way up. The upper part of them alone could be opened, as if one had wished to prevent the people who were locked up in that huge stone box from looking into the street.

When the doctor came down again, I told him how it struck me, and he replied:

"You are quite right; the poor creature who is living there must never see what is going on outside. She is a madwoman, or rather an idiot, what you Normans would call a Niente. It is a miserable story, but a very singular pathological case at the same time. Shall I tell you?"

I begged him to do so, and he continued:

"Twenty years ago the owners of this house, who were my patients, had a daughter who was like all other girls, but I soon discovered that while her body became admirably developed, her intellect remained stationary.

"She began to walk very early, but she could not talk. At first I thought she was deaf, but I soon discovered that, although she heard perfectly, she did not understand anything that was said to her. Violent noises made her start and frightened her, without her understanding how they were caused.

"She grew up into a superb woman, but she was dumb, from an absolute want of intellect. I tried all means to introduce a gleam of intelligence into her brain, but nothing succeeded. I thought I noticed that she knew her nurse, though as soon as she was weaned, she failed to recognize her mother. She could never pronounce that word which is the first that children utter and the last which soldiers murmur when they are dying on the field of battle. She sometimes tried to talk, but she produced nothing but incoherent sounds.

"When the weather was fine, she laughed continually, and emitted low cries which might be compared to the twittering of birds; when it rained she cried and moaned in a mournful, terrifying manner, which sounded like the howling of a dog before a death occurs in a house.

"She was fond of rolling on the grass, as young animals do, and of running about madly, and she would clap her hands every morning, when the sun shone into her room, and would insist, by signs, on being dressed as quickly as possible, so that she might get out.

"She did not appear to distinguish between people, between her mother and her nurse, or between her father and me, or between the coachman and the cook. I particularly liked her parents, who were very unhappy on her account, and went to see them nearly every day. I dined with them quite frequently, which enabled me to remark that Bertha (they had called her Bertha) seemed to recognize the various dishes, and to prefer some to others. At that time she was twelve years old, but as fully formed in figure as a girl of eighteen, and taller than I was. Then the idea struck me of developing her greediness, and by this means of cultivating some slight power of discrimination in her mind, and to force her, by the diversity of flavors, if not to reason, at any rate to arrive at instinctive distinctions, which would of themselves constitute a kind of process that was necessary to thought. Later on, by appealing to her passions, and by carefully making use of those which could serve our purpose, we might hope to obtain a kind of reaction on her intellect, and by degrees increase the unconscious action of her brain.

"One day I put two plates before her, one of soup, and the other of very sweet vanilla cream. I made her taste each of them successively, and then I let her choose for herself, and she ate the plate of cream. In a short time I made her very greedy, so greedy that it appeared as if the only idea she had in her head was the desire for eating. She perfectly recognized the various dishes, and stretched out her hands toward those that she liked, and took hold of them eagerly, and she used to cry when they were taken from her. Then I thought I would try and teach her to come to the dining-room when the dinner bell rang. It took a long time, but I succeeded in the end. In her vacant intellect a vague correlation was established between sound and taste, a correspondence between the two senses, an appeal from one to the other, and consequently a sort of connection of ideas—if one can call that kind of instinctive hyphen between two organic functions an idea—and so I carried my experiments further, and taught her, with much difficulty, to recognize meal times by the clock.

"It was impossible for me for a long time to attract her attention to the hands, but I succeeded in making her remark the clockwork and the striking apparatus. The means I employed were very simple; I asked them not to have the bell rung for lunch, and everybody got up and went into the dining-room when the little brass hammer struck twelve o'clock, but I found great difficulty in making her learn to count the strokes. She ran to the door each time she heard the clock strike, but by degrees she learned that all the strokes had not the same value as far as regarded meals, and she frequently fixed her eyes, guided by her ears, on the dial of the clock.

"When I noticed that, I took care every day at twelve, and at six o'clock, to place my fingers on the figures twelve and six, as soon as the moment she was waiting for had arrived, and I soon noticed that she attentively followed the motion of the small brass hands, which I had often turned in her presence.

"She had understood! Perhaps I ought rather to say that she had grasped the idea. I had succeeded in getting the knowledge, or, rather, the sensation, of the time into her, just as is the case with carp, who certainly have no clocks, when they are fed every day exactly at the same time.

"When once I had obtained that result all the clocks and watches in the house occupied her attention almost exclusively. She spent her time in looking at them, listening to them, and in waiting for meal time, and once something very funny happened. The striking apparatus of a pretty little Louis XVI clock that hung at the head of her bed having got out of order, she noticed it. She sat for twenty minutes with her eyes on the hands, waiting for it to strike ten, but when the hands passed the figure she was astonished at not hearing anything; so stupefied was she, indeed, that she sat down, no doubt overwhelmed by a feeling of violent emotion such as attacks us in the face of some terrible catastrophe. And she had the wonderful patience to wait until eleven o'clock in order to see what would happen, and as she naturally heard nothing, she was suddenly either seized with a wild fit of rage at having been deceived and imposed upon by appearances, or else overcome by that fear which some frightened creature feels at some terrible mystery, and by the furious impatience of a passionate individual who meets with some obstacle; she took up the tongs from the fireplace and struck the clock so violently that she broke it to pieces in a moment.

"It was evident, therefore, that her, brain did act and calculate, obscurely it is true, and within very restricted limits, for I could never succeed in making her distinguish persons as she distinguished the time; and to stir her intellect, it was necessary to appeal to her passions, in the material sense of the word, and we soon had another, and alas! a very terrible proof of this!

"She had grown up into a splendid girl, a perfect type of a race, a sort of lovely and stupid Venus. She was sixteen, and I have rarely seen such perfection of form, such suppleness and such regular features. I said she was a Venus; yes, a fair, stout, vigorous Venus, with large, bright, vacant eyes, which were as blue as the flowers of the flax plant; she had a large mouth with full lips, the mouth of a glutton, of a sensualist, a mouth made for kisses. Well, one morning her father came into my consulting room with a strange look on his face, and, sitting down without even replying to my greeting, he said:

"'I want to speak to you about a very serious matter. Would it be possible—would it be possible for Bertha to marry?'

"'Bertha to marry! Why, it is quite impossible!'

"'Yes, I know, I know,' he replied. 'But reflect, doctor. Don't you think—perhaps—we hoped—if she had children—it would be a great shock to her, but a great happiness, and—who knows whether maternity might not rouse her intellect?'

"I was in a state of great perplexity. He was right, and it was possible that such a new situation, and that wonderful instinct of maternity, which beats in the hearts of the lower animals as it does in the heart of a woman, which makes the hen fly at a dog's jaws to defend her chickens, might bring about a revolution, an utter change in her vacant mind, and set the motionless mechanism of her thoughts in motion. And then, moreover, I immediately remembered a personal instance. Some years previously I had owned a spaniel bitch who was so stupid that I could do nothing with her, but when she had had puppies she became, if not exactly intelligent, yet almost like many other dogs who had not been thoroughly broken.

"As soon as I foresaw the possibility of this, the wish to get Bertha married grew in me, not so much out of friendship for her and her poor parents as from scientific curiosity. What would happen? It was a singular problem. I said in reply to her father:

"'Perhaps you are right. You might make the attempt, but you will never find a man to consent to marry her.'

"'I have found somebody,' he said, in a low voice.

"I was dumfounded, and said: 'Somebody really suitable? Some one of your own rank and position in society?'

"'Decidedly,' he replied.

"'Oh! And may I ask his name?'

"'I came on purpose to tell you, and to consult you. It is Monsieur Gaston du Boys de Lucelles.'

"I felt inclined to exclaim: 'The wretch!' but I held my tongue, and after a few moments' silence I said:

"'Oh! Very good. I see nothing against it.'

"The poor man shook me heartily by the hand.

"'She is to be married next month,' he said.

"Monsieur Gaston du Boys de Lucelles was a scapegrace of good family, who, after having spent all that he had inherited from his father, and having incurred debts in all kinds of doubtful ways, had been trying to discover some other means of obtaining money, and he had discovered this method. He was a good-looking young fellow, and in capital health, but fast; one of that odious race of provincial fast men, and he appeared to me to be as suitable as anyone, and could be got rid of later by making him an allowance. He came to the house to pay his addresses and to strut about before the idiot girl, who, however, seemed to please him. He brought her flowers, kissed her hands, sat at her feet, and looked at her with affectionate eyes; but she took no notice of any of his attentions, and did not make any distinction between him and the other persons who were about her.

"However, the marriage took place, and you may guess how my curiosity was aroused. I went to see Bertha the next day to try and discover from her looks whether any feelings had been awakened in her, but I found her just the same as she was every day, wholly taken up with the clock and dinner, while he, on the contrary, appeared really in love, and tried to rouse his wife's spirits and affection by little endearments and such caresses as one bestows on a kitten. He could think of nothing better.

"I called upon the married couple pretty frequently, and I soon perceived that the young woman knew her husband, and gave him those eager looks which she had hitherto only bestowed on sweet dishes.

"She followed his movements, knew his step on the stairs or in the neighboring rooms, clapped her hands when he came in, and her face was changed and brightened by the flames of profound happiness and of desire.

"She loved him with her whole body and with all her soul to the very depths of her poor, weak soul, and with all her heart, that poor heart of some grateful animal. It was really a delightful and innocent picture of simple passion, of carnal and yet modest passion, such as nature had implanted in mankind, before man had complicated and disfigured it by all the various shades of sentiment. But he soon grew tired of this ardent, beautiful, dumb creature, and did not spend more than an hour during the day with her, thinking it sufficient if he came home at night, and she began to suffer in consequence. She used to wait for him from morning till night with her eyes on the clock; she did not even look after the meals now, for he took all his away from home, Clermont, Chatel-Guyon, Royat, no matter where, as long as he was not obliged to come home.

"She began to grow thin; every other thought, every other wish, every other expectation, and every confused hope disappeared from her mind, and the hours during which she did not see him became hours of terrible suffering to her. Soon he ceased to come home regularly of nights; he spent them with women at the casino at Royat and did not come home until daybreak. But she never went to bed before he returned. She remained sitting motionless in an easy-chair, with her eyes fixed on the hands of the clock, which turned so slowly and regularly round the china face on which the hours were painted.

"She heard the trot of his horse in the distance and sat up with a start, and when he came into the room she got up with the movements of an automaton and pointed to the clock, as if to say: 'Look how late it is!'

"And he began to be afraid of this amorous and jealous, half-witted woman, and flew into a rage, as brutes do; and one night he even went so far as to strike her, so they sent for me. When I arrived she was writhing and screaming in a terrible crisis of pain, anger, passion, how do I know what? Can one tell what goes on in such undeveloped brains?

"I calmed her by subcutaneous injections of morphine, and forbade her to see that man again, for I saw clearly that marriage would infallibly kill her by degrees.

"Then she went mad! Yes, my dear friend, that idiot went mad. She is always thinking of him and waiting for him; she waits for him all day and night, awake or asleep, at this very moment, ceaselessly. When I saw her getting thinner and thinner, and as she persisted in never taking her eyes off the clocks, I had them removed from the house. I thus made it impossible for her to count the hours, and to try to remember, from her indistinct reminiscences, at what time he used to come home formerly. I hope to destroy the recollection of it in time, and to extinguish that ray of thought which I kindled with so much difficulty.

"The other day I tried an experiment. I offered her my watch; she took it and looked at it for some time; then she began to scream terribly, as if the sight of that little object had suddenly awakened her memory, which was beginning to grow indistinct. She is pitiably thin now, with hollow and glittering eyes, and she walks up and down ceaselessly, like a wild beast in its cage; I have had gratings put on the windows, boarded them up half way, and have had the seats fixed to the floor so as to prevent her from looking to see whether he is coming.

"Oh! her poor parents! What a life they must lead!"

We had got to the top of the hill, and the doctor turned round and said to me:

"Look at Riom from here."

The gloomy town looked like some ancient city. Behind it a green, wooded plain studded with towns and villages, and bathed in a soft blue haze, extended until it was lost in the distance. Far away, on my right, there was a range of lofty mountains with round summits, or else cut off flat, as if with a sword, and the doctor began to enumerate the villages, towns and hills, and to give me the history of all of them. But I did not listen to him; I was thinking of nothing but the madwoman, and I only saw her. She seemed to be hovering over that vast extent of country like a mournful ghost, and I asked him abruptly:

"What has become of the husband?"

My friend seemed rather surprised, but after a few moments' hesitation, he replied:

"He is living at Royat, on an allowance that they made him, and is quite happy; he leads a very fast life."

As we were slowly going back, both of us silent and rather low-spirited, an English dogcart, drawn by a thoroughbred horse, came up behind us and passed us rapidly. The doctor took me by the arm.

"There he is," he said.

I saw nothing except a gray felt hat, cocked over one ear above a pair of broad shoulders, driving off in a cloud of dust.

THE PATRON

We never dreamed of such good fortune! The son of a provincial bailiff, Jean Marin had come, as do so many others, to study law in the Quartier Latin. In the various beer-houses that he had frequented he had made friends with several talkative students who spouted politics as they drank their beer. He had a great admiration for them and followed them persistently from cafe to cafe, even paying for their drinks when he had the money.

He became a lawyer and pleaded causes, which he lost. However, one morning he read in the papers that one of his former comrades of the Quartier had just been appointed deputy.

He again became his faithful hound, the friend who does the drudgery, the unpleasant tasks, for whom one sends when one has need of him and with whom one does not stand on ceremony. But it chanced through some parliamentary incident that the deputy became a minister. Six months later Jean Marin was appointed a state councillor.

He was so elated with pride at first that he lost his head. He would walk through the streets just to show himself off, as though one could tell by his appearance what position he occupied. He managed to say to the shopkeepers as soon as he entered a store, bringing it in somehow in the course of the most insignificant remarks and even to the news vendors and the cabmen:

"I, who am a state councillor—"

Then, in consequence of his position as well as for professional reasons and as in duty bound through being an influential and generous man, he felt an imperious need of patronizing others. He offered his support to every one on all occasions and with unbounded generosity.

When he met any one he recognized on the boulevards he would advance to meet them with a charmed air, would take their hand, inquire after their health, and, without waiting for any questions, remark:

"You know I am state councillor, and I am entirely at your service. If I can be of any use to you, do not hesitate to call on me. In my position one has great influence."

Then he would go into some cafe with the friend he had just met and ask for a pen and ink and a sheet of paper. "Just one, waiter; it is to write a letter of recommendation."

And he wrote ten, twenty, fifty letters of recommendation a day. He wrote them to the Cafe Americain, to Bignon's, to Tortoni's, to the Maison Doree, to the Cafe Riche, to the Helder, to the Cafe Anglais, to the Napolitain, everywhere, everywhere. He wrote them to all the officials of the republican government, from the magistrates to the ministers. And he was happy, perfectly happy.

One morning as he was starting out to go to the council it began to rain. He hesitated about taking a cab, but decided not to do so and set out on foot.

The rain came down in torrents, swamping the sidewalks and inundating the streets. M. Marin was obliged to take shelter in a doorway. An old priest was standing there—an old priest with white hair. Before he became a councillor M. Marin did not like the clergy. Now he treated them with consideration, ever since a cardinal had consulted him on an important matter. The rain continued to pour down in floods and obliged the two men to take shelter in the porter's lodge so as to avoid getting wet. M. Marin, who was always itching to talk so as to let people know who he was, remarked:

"This is horrible weather, Monsieur l'Abbe."

The old priest bowed:

"Yes indeed, sir, it is very unpleasant when one comes to Paris for only a few days."

"Ah! You come from the provinces?"

"Yes, monsieur. I am only passing through on my journey."

"It certainly is very disagreeable to have rain during the few days one spends in the capital. We officials who stay here the year round, we think nothing of it."

The priest did not reply. He was looking at the street where the rain seemed to be falling less heavily. And with a sudden resolve he raised his cassock just as women raise their skirts in stepping across water.

M. Marin, seeing him start away, exclaimed:

"You will get drenched, Monsieur l'Abbe. Wait a few moments longer; the rain will be over."

The good man stopped irresistibly and then said:

"But I am in a great hurry. I have an important engagement."

M. Marin seemed quite worried.

"But you will be absolutely drenched. Might I ask in which direction you are going?"

The priest appeared to hesitate. Then he said:

"I am going in the direction of the Palais Royal."

"In that case, if you will allow me, Monsieur l'Abbe, I will offer you the shelter of my umbrella: As for me, I am going to the council. I am a councillor of state."

The old priest raised his head and looked at his neighbor and then exclaimed:

"I thank you, monsieur. I shall be glad to accept your offer."

M. Marin then took his arm and led him away. He directed him, watched over him and advised him.

"Be careful of that stream, Monsieur l'Abbe. And be very careful about the carriage wheels; they spatter you with mud sometimes from head to foot. Look out for the umbrellas of the people passing by; there is nothing more dangerous to the eyes than the tips of the ribs. Women especially are unbearable; they pay no heed to where they are going and always jab you in the face with the point of their parasols or umbrellas. And they never move aside for anybody. One would suppose the town belonged to them. They monopolize the pavement and the street. It is my opinion that their education has been greatly neglected."

And M. Marin laughed.

The priest did not reply. He walked along, slightly bent over, picking his steps carefully so as not to get mud on his boots or his cassock.

M. Marin resumed:

"I suppose you have come to Paris to divert your mind a little?"

The good man replied:

"No, I have some business to attend to."

"Ali! Is it important business? Might I venture to ask what it is? If I can be of any service to you, you may command me."

The priest seemed embarrassed. He murmured:

"Oh, it is a little personal matter; a little difficulty with—with my bishop. It would not interest you. It is a matter of internal regulation—an ecclesiastical affair."

M. Marin was eager.

"But it is precisely the state council that regulates all those things. In that case, make use of me."

"Yes, monsieur, it is to the council that I am going. You are a thousand times too kind. I have to see M. Lerepere and M. Savon and also perhaps M. Petitpas."

M. Marin stopped short.

"Why, those are my friends, Monsieur l'Abbe, my best friends, excellent colleagues, charming men. I will speak to them about you, and very highly. Count upon me."

The cure thanked him, apologizing for troubling him, and stammered out a thousand grateful promises.

M. Marin was enchanted.

"Ah, you may be proud of having made a stroke of luck, Monsieur l'Abbe. You will see—you will see that, thanks to me, your affair will go along swimmingly."

They reached the council hall. M. Marin took the priest into his office, offered him a chair in front of the fire and sat down himself at his desk and began to write.

"My dear colleague, allow me to recommend to you most highly a venerable and particularly worthy and deserving priest, M. L'Abbe——"

He stopped and asked:

"Your name, if you please?"

"L'Abbe Ceinture."

"M. l'Abbe Ceinture, who needs your good office in a little matter which he will communicate to you.

"I am pleased at this incident which gives me an opportunity, my dear colleague——"

And he finished with the usual compliments.

When he had written the three letters he handed them to his protege, who took his departure with many protestations of gratitude.

M. Marin attended to some business and then went home, passed the day quietly, slept well, woke in a good humor and sent for his newspapers.

The first he opened was a radical sheet. He read:

"OUR CLERGY AND OUR GOVERNMENT OFFICIALS

"We shall never make an end of enumerating the misdeeds of the clergy. A certain priest, named Ceinture, convicted of conspiracy against the present government, accused of base actions to which we will not even allude, suspected besides of being a former Jesuit, metamorphosed into a simple priest, suspended by a bishop for causes that are said to be unmentionable and summoned to Paris to give an explanation of his conduct, has found an ardent defender in the man named Marin, a councillor of state, who was not afraid to give this frocked malefactor the warmest letters of recommendation to all the republican officials, his colleagues.

"We call the, attention of the ministry to the unheard of attitude of this councillor of state——"

M. Marin bounded out of bed, dressed himself and hastened to his colleague, Petitpas, who said to him:

"How now? You were crazy to recommend to me that old conspirator!"

M. Marin, bewildered, stammered out:

"Why no—you see—I was deceived. He looked such an honest man. He played me a trick—a disgraceful trick! I beg that you will sentence him severely, very severely. I am going to write. Tell me to whom I should write about having him punished. I will go and see the attorney-general and the archbishop of Paris—yes, the archbishop."

And seating himself abruptly at M. Petitpas' desk, he wrote:

"Monseigneur, I have the honor to bring to your grace's notice the fact that I have recently been made a victim of the intrigues and lies of a certain Abbe Ceinture, who imposed on my kind-heartedness.

"Deceived by the representations of this ecclesiastic, I was led——"

Then, having signed and sealed his letter, he turned to his colleague and exclaimed:

"See here; my dear friend, let this be a warning to you never to recommend any one again."

THE DOOR

“Bah!” exclaimed Karl Massouligny, “the question of complaisant husbands is a difficult one. I have seen many kinds, and yet I am unable to give an opinion about any of them. I have often tried to determine whether they are blind, weak or clairvoyant. I believe that there are some which belong to each of these categories.

“Let us quickly pass over the blind ones. They cannot rightly be called complaisant, since they do not know, but they are good creatures who cannot see farther than their nose. It is a curious and interesting thing to notice the ease with which men and women can, be deceived. We are taken in by the slightest trick of those who surround us, by our children, our friends, our servants, our tradespeople. Humanity is credulous, and in order to discover deceit in others, we do not display one-tenth the shrewdness which we use when we, in turn, wish to deceive some one else.

“Clairvoyant husbands may be divided into three classes: Those who have some interest, pecuniary, ambitious or otherwise, in their wife’s having love affairs. These ask only to safeguard appearances as much as possible, and they are satisfied.

“Next come those who get angry. What a beautiful novel one could write about them!

“Finally the weak ones! Those who are afraid of scandal.

“There are also those who are powerless, or, rather, tired, who flee from the duties of matrimony through fear of ataxia or apoplexy, who are satisfied to see a friend run these risks.

“But I once met a husband of a rare species, who guarded against the common accident in a strange and witty manner.

“In Paris I had made the acquaintance of an elegant, fashionable couple. The woman, nervous, tall, slender, courted, was supposed to have had many love adventures. She pleased me with her wit, and I believe that I pleased her also. I courted her, a trial courting to which she answered with evident provocations. Soon we got to tender glances, hand pressures, all the little gallantries which precede the final attack.

“Nevertheless, I hesitated. I consider that, as a rule, the majority of society intrigues, however short they may be, are not worth the trouble which they give us and the difficulties which may arise. I therefore mentally compared the advantages and disadvantages which I might expect, and I thought I noticed that the husband suspected me.

“One evening, at a ball, as I was saying tender things to the young woman in a little parlor leading from the big hall where the dancing was going on, I noticed in a mirror the reflection of some one who was watching me. It was he. Our looks met and then I saw him turn his head and walk away.

“I murmured: ‘Your husband is spying on us.’

“She seemed dumbfounded and asked: ‘My husband?’

“‘Yes, he has been watching us for some time:

“‘Nonsense! Are you sure?’

“‘Very sure.’

"'How strange! He is usually extraordinarily pleasant to all my friends.'

"'Perhaps he guessed that I love you!'

"'Nonsense! You are not the first one to pay attention to me. Every woman who is a little in view drags behind her a herd of admirers.'

"'Yes. But I love you deeply.'

"'Admitting that that is true, does a husband ever guess those things?'

"'Then he is not jealous?'

"'No-no!'

"She thought for an instant and then continued: 'No. I do not think that I ever noticed any jealousy on his part.'

"'Has he never watched you?'

"'No. As I said, he is always agreeable to my friends.'

"From that day my courting became much more assiduous. The woman did not please me any more than before, but the probable jealousy of her husband tempted me greatly.

"As for her, I judged her coolly and clearly. She had a certain worldly charm, due to a quick, gay, amiable and superficial mind, but no real, deep attraction. She was, as I have already said, an excitable little being, all on the surface, with rather a showy elegance. How can I explain myself? She was an ornament, not a home.

"One day, after taking dinner with her, her husband said to me, just as I was leaving: 'My dear friend' (he now called me 'friend'), 'we soon leave for the country. It is a great pleasure to my wife and myself to entertain people whom we like. We would be very pleased to have you spend a month with us. It would be very nice of you to do so.'

"I was dumbfounded, but I accepted.

"A month later I arrived at their estate of Vertcresson, in Touraine. They were waiting for me at the station, five miles from the chateau. There were three of them, she, the husband and a gentleman unknown to me, the Comte de Morterade, to whom I was introduced. He appeared to be delighted to make my acquaintance, and the strangest ideas passed through my mind while we trotted along the beautiful road between two hedges. I was saying to myself: 'Let's see, what can this mean? Here is a husband who cannot doubt that his wife and I are on more than friendly terms, and yet he invites me to his house, receives me like an old friend and seems to say: "Go ahead, my friend, the road is clear!"'

"Then I am introduced to a very pleasant gentleman, who seems already to have settled down in the house, and—and who is perhaps trying to get out of it, and who seems as pleased at my arrival as the husband himself.

"Is it some former admirer who wishes to retire? One might think so. But, then, would these two men tacitly have come to one of these infamous little agreements so common in society? And it is proposed to me that I should quietly enter into the pact and carry it out. All hands and arms are held out to me. All doors and hearts are open to me.

"And what about her? An enigma. She cannot be ignorant of everything. However—however—Well, I cannot understand it.

"The dinner was very gay and cordial. On leaving the table the husband and his friend began to play cards, while I went out on the porch to look at the moonlight with madame. She seemed to be greatly affected by nature, and I judged that the moment for my happiness was near. That evening she was really delightful. The country had seemed to make her more tender. Her long, slender waist looked pretty on this stone porch beside a great vase in which grew some flowers. I felt like dragging her out under the trees, throwing myself at her feet and speaking to her words of love.

"Her husband's voice called 'Louise!'

"'Yes, dear.'

"'You are forgetting the tea.'

"'I'll go and see about it, my friend.'

"We returned to the house, and she gave us some tea. When the two men had finished playing cards, they were visibly tired. I had to go to my room. I did not get to sleep till late, and then I slept badly.

"An excursion was decided upon for the following afternoon, and we went in an open carriage to visit some ruins. She and I were in the back of the vehicle and they were opposite us, riding backward. The conversation was sympathetic and agreeable. I am an orphan, and it seemed to me as though I had just found my family, I felt so at home with them.

"Suddenly, as she had stretched out her foot between her husband's legs, he murmured reproachfully: 'Louise, please don't wear out your old shoes yourself. There is no reason for being neater in Paris than in the country.'

"I lowered my eyes. She was indeed wearing worn-out shoes, and I noticed that her stockings were not pulled up tight.

"She had blushed and hidden her foot under her dress. The friend was looking out in the distance with an indifferent and unconcerned look.

"The husband offered me a cigar, which I accepted. For a few days it was impossible for me to be alone with her for two minutes; he was with us everywhere. He was delightful to me, however.

"One morning he came to get me to take a walk before breakfast, and the conversation happened to turn on marriage. I spoke a little about solitude and about how charming life can be made by the affection of a woman. Suddenly he interrupted me, saying: 'My friend, don't talk about things you know nothing about. A woman who has no other reason for loving you will not love you long. All the little coquetries which make them so exquisite when they do not definitely belong to us cease as soon as they become ours. And then—the respectable women—that is to say our wives—are—are not—in fact do not understand their profession of wife. Do you understand?'

"He said no more, and I could not guess his thoughts.

"Two days after this conversation he called me to his room quite early, in order to show me a collection of engravings. I sat in an easy chair opposite the big door which separated his apartment from his wife's, and behind this door I heard some one walking and moving, and I was thinking very little of the engravings, although I kept exclaiming: 'Oh, charming! delightful! exquisite!'

"He suddenly said: 'Oh, I have a beautiful specimen in the next room. I'll go and get it.'

"He ran to the door quickly, and both sides opened as though for a theatrical effect.

"In a large room, all in disorder, in the midst of skirts, collars, waists lying around on the floor, stood a tall, dried-up creature. The lower part of her body was covered with an old, worn-out silk petticoat, which was hanging limply on her shapeless form, and she was standing in front of a mirror brushing some short, sparse blond hairs. Her arms formed two acute angles, and as she turned around in astonishment I saw under a common cotton chemise a regular cemetery of ribs, which were hidden from the public gaze by well-arranged pads.

"The husband uttered a natural exclamation and came back, closing the doors, and said: 'Gracious! how stupid I am! Oh, how thoughtless! My wife will never forgive me for that!'

"I already felt like thanking him. I left three days later, after cordially shaking hands with the two men and kissing the lady's fingers. She bade me a cold good-by."

Karl Massouligny was silent. Some one asked: "But what was the friend?"

"I don't know—however—however he looked greatly distressed to see me leaving so soon."

A SALE

The defendants, Cesaire-Isidore Brument and Prosper-Napoleon Cornu, appeared before the Court of Assizes of the Seine-Inferieure, on a charge of attempted murder, by drowning, of Mme. Brument, lawful wife of the first of the aforenamed.

The two prisoners sat side by side on the traditional bench. They were two peasants; the first was small and stout, with short arms, short legs, and a round head with a red pimply face, planted directly on his trunk, which was also round and short, and with apparently no neck. He was a raiser of pigs and lived at Cacheville-la-Goupil, in the district of Criquetot.

Cornu (Prosper-Napoleon) was thin, of medium height, with enormously long arms. His head was on crooked, his jaw awry, and he squinted. A blue blouse, as long as a shirt, hung down to his knees, and his yellow hair, which was scanty and plastered down on his head, gave his face a worn-out, dirty look, a dilapidated look that was frightful. He had been nicknamed "the cure" because he could imitate to perfection the chanting in church, and even the sound of the serpent. This talent attracted to his cafe—for he was a saloon keeper at Criquetot—a great many customers who preferred the "mass at Cornu" to the mass in church.

Mme. Brument, seated on the witness bench, was a thin peasant woman who seemed to be always asleep. She sat there motionless, her hands crossed on her knees, gazing fixedly before her with a stupid expression.

The judge continued his interrogation.

"Well, then, Mme. Brument, they came into your house and threw you into a barrel full of water. Tell us the details. Stand up."

She rose. She looked as tall as a flag pole with her cap which looked like a white skull cap. She said in a drawling tone:

"I was shelling beans. Just then they came in. I said to myself, 'What is the matter with them? They do not seem natural, they seem up to some mischief.' They watched me sideways, like this, especially Cornu, because he squints. I do not like to see them together, for they are two good-for-nothings when they are in company. I said: 'What do you want with me?' They did not answer. I had a sort of mistrust——"

The defendant Brument interrupted the witness hastily, saying:

"I was full."

Then Cornu, turning towards his accomplice said in the deep tones of an organ:

"Say that we were both full, and you will be telling no lie."

The judge, severely:

"You mean by that that you were both drunk?"

Brument: "There can be no question about it."

Cornu: "That might happen to anyone."

The judge to the victim: "Continue your testimony, woman Brument."

"Well, Brument said to me, 'Do you wish to earn a hundred sous?' 'Yes,' I replied, seeing that a hundred sous are not picked up in a horse's tracks. Then he said: 'Open your eyes and do as I do,' and he went to fetch the large empty barrel which is under the rain pipe in the corner, and he turned it over and brought it into my kitchen, and stuck it down in the middle of the floor, and then he said to me: 'Go and fetch water until it is full.'

"So I went to the pond with two pails and carried water, and still more water for an hour, seeing that the barrel was as large as a vat, saving your presence, m'sieu le president.

"All this time Brument and Cornu were drinking a glass, and then another glass, and then another. They were finishing their drinks when I said to them: 'You are full, fuller than this barrel.' And Brument answered me. 'Do not worry, go on with your work, your turn will come, each one has his share.' I paid no attention to what he said as he was full.

"When the barrel was full to the brim, I said: 'There, that's done.'

"And then Cornu gave me a hundred sous, not Brument, Cornu; it was Cornu gave them to me. And Brument said: 'Do you wish to earn a hundred sous more?' 'Yes,' I said, for I am not accustomed to presents like that. Then he said: 'Take off your clothes!

"'Take off my clothes?'

"'Yes,' he said.

"'How many shall I take off?'

"'If it worries you at all, keep on your chemise, that won't bother us.'

"A hundred sous is a hundred sous, and I have to undress myself; but I did not fancy undressing before those two good-for-nothings. I took off my cap, and then my jacket, and then my skirt, and then my sabots. Brument said, 'Keep on your stockings, also; we are good fellows.'

"And Cornu said, too, 'We are good fellows.'

"So there I was, almost like mother Eve. And they got up from their chairs, but could not stand straight, they were so full, saving your presence, M'sieu le president.

"I said to myself: 'What are they up to?'

"And Brument said: 'Are you ready?'

"And Cornu said: 'I'm ready!'

"And then they took me, Brument by the head, and Cornu by the feet, as one might take, for instance, a sheet that has been washed. Then I began to bawl.

"And Brument said: 'Keep still, wretched creature!'

"And they lifted me up in the air and put me into the barrel, which was full of water, so that I had a check of the circulation, a chill to my very insides.

"And Brument said: 'Is that all?'

"Cornu said: 'That is all.'

"Brument said: 'The head is not in, that will make a difference in the measure.'

"Cornu said: 'Put in her head.'

"And then Brument pushed down my head as if to drown me, so that the water ran into my nose, so that I could already see Paradise. And he pushed it down, and I disappeared.

"And then he must have been frightened. He pulled me out and said: 'Go and get dry, carcass.'

"As for me, I took to my heels and ran as far as M. le cure's. He lent me a skirt belonging to his servant, for I was almost in a state of nature, and he went to fetch Maitre Chicot, the country watchman who went to Criquetot to fetch the police who came to my house with me.

"Then we found Brument and Cornu fighting each other like two rams.

"Brument was bawling: 'It isn't true, I tell you that there is at least a cubic metre in it. It is the method that was no good.'

"Cornu bawled: 'Four pails, that is almost half a cubic metre. You need not reply, that's what it is.'

"The police captain put them both under arrest. I have no more to tell."

She sat down. The audience in the court room laughed. The jurors looked at one another in astonishment. The judge said:

"Defendant Cornu, you seem to have been the instigator of this infamous plot. What have you to say?"

And Cornu rose in his turn.

"Judge," he replied, "I was full."

The Judge answered gravely:

"I know it. Proceed."

"I will. Well, Brument came to my place about nine o'clock, and ordered two drinks, and said: 'There's one for you, Cornu.' I sat down opposite him and drank, and out of politeness, I offered him a glass. Then he returned the compliment and so did I, and so it went on from glass to glass until noon, when we were full.

"Then Brument began to cry. That touched me. I asked him what was the matter. He said: 'I must have a thousand francs by Thursday.' That cooled me off a little, you understand. Then he said to me all at once: 'I will sell you my wife.'

"I was full, and I was a widower. You understand, that stirred me up. I did not know his wife, but she was a woman, wasn't she? I asked him: 'How much would you sell her for?'

"He reflected, or pretended to reflect. When one is full one is not very clear-headed, and he replied: 'I will sell her by the cubic metre.'

"That did not surprise me, for I was as drunk as he was, and I knew what a cubic metre is in my business. It is a thousand litres, that suited me.

"But the price remained to be settled. All depends on the quality. I said: 'How much do you want a cubic metre?'

"He answered: 'Two thousand francs.'

"I gave a bound like a rabbit, and then I reflected that a woman ought not to measure more than three hundred litres. So I said: 'That's too dear.'

"He answered: 'I cannot do it for less. I should lose by it.'

"You understand, one is not a dealer in hogs for nothing. One understands one's business. But, if he is smart, the seller of bacon, I am smarter, seeing that I sell them also. Ha, Ha, Ha! So I said to him: 'If she were new, I would not say anything, but she has been married to you for some time, so she is not as fresh as she was. I will give you fifteen hundred francs a cubic metre, not a sou more. Will that suit you?'

"He answered: 'That will do. That's a bargain!'

"I agreed, and we started out, arm in arm. We must help each other in this world.

"But a fear came to me: 'How can you measure her unless you put her into the liquid?'

"Then he explained his idea, not without difficulty for he was full. He said to me: 'I take a barrel, and fill it with water to the brim. I put her in it. All the water that comes out we will measure, that is the way to fix it.'

"I said: 'I see, I understand. But this water that overflows will run away; how are you going to gather it up?'

"Then he began stuffing me and explained to me that all we should have to do would be to refill the barrel with the water his wife had displaced as soon as she should have left. All the water we should pour in would be the measure. I supposed about ten pails; that would be a cubic metre. He isn't a fool, all the same, when he is drunk, that old horse.

"To be brief, we reached his house and I took a look at its mistress. A beautiful woman she certainly was not. Anyone can see her, for there she is. I said to myself: 'I am disappointed, but never mind, she will be of value; handsome or ugly, it is all the same, is it not, monsieur le president?' And then I saw that she was as thin as a rail. I said to myself: 'She will not measure four hundred litres.' I understand the matter, it being in liquids.

"She told you about the proceeding. I even let her keep on her chemise and stockings, to my own disadvantage.

"When that was done she ran away. I said: 'Look out, Brument! she is escaping.'

"He replied: 'Do not be afraid. I will catch her all right. She will have to come back to sleep, I will measure the deficit.'

"We measured. Not four pailfuls. Ha, Ha, Ha!"

The witness began to laugh so persistently that a gendarme was obliged to punch him in the back. Having quieted down, he resumed:

"In short, Brument exclaimed: 'Nothing doing, that is not enough.' I bawled and bawled, and bawled again, he punched me, I hit back. That would have kept on till the Day of judgment, seeing we were both drunk.

"Then came the gendarmes! They swore at us, they took us off to prison. I want damages."

He sat down.

Brument confirmed in every particular the statements of his accomplice. The jury, in consternation, retired to deliberate.

At the end of an hour they returned a verdict of acquittal for the defendants, with some severe strictures on the dignity of marriage, and establishing the precise limitations of business transactions.

Brument went home to the domestic roof accompanied by his wife.

Cornu went back to his business.

THE IMPOLITE SEX

Madame de X. to Madame de L.

ETRETAT, Friday.

My Dear Aunt:

I am coming to see you without anyone knowing it. I shall be at Les Fresnes on the 2d of September, the day before the hunting season opens, as I do not want to miss it, so that I may tease these gentlemen. You are too good, aunt, and you will allow them, as you usually do when there are no strange guests, to come to table, under pretext of fatigue, without dressing or shaving for the occasion.

They are delighted, of course, when I am not present. But I shall be there and will hold a review, like a general, at dinner time; and, if I find a single one of them at all careless in dress, no matter how little, I mean to send them down to the kitchen with the servants.

The men of to-day have so little consideration for others and so little good manners that one must be always severe with them. We live indeed in an age of vulgarity. When they quarrel, they insult each other in terms worthy of longshoremen, and, in our presence, they do not conduct themselves even as well as our servants. It is at the seaside that you see this most clearly. They are to be found there in battalions, and you can judge them in the lump. Oh! what coarse beings they are!

Just imagine, in a train, a gentleman who looked well, as I thought at first sight, thanks to his tailor, carefully took off his boots in order to put on a pair of old shoes! Another, an old man who was probably some wealthy upstart (these are the most ill-bred), while sitting opposite to me, had the delicacy to place his two feet on the seat quite close to me. This is a positive fact.

At the watering-places the vulgarity is unrestrained. I must here make one admission—that my indignation is perhaps due to the fact that I am not accustomed to associate, as a rule, with the sort of people one comes across here, for I should be less shocked by their manners if I had the opportunity of observing them oftener. In the office of the hotel I was nearly thrown down by a young man who snatched the key over my head. Another knocked against me so violently without begging my pardon or lifting his hat, coming away from a ball at the Casino, that it gave me a pain in the chest. It is the same way with all of them. Watch them addressing ladies on the terrace; they scarcely ever bow. They merely raise their hands to their headgear. But, indeed, as they are all more or less bald, it is the best plan.

But what exasperates and disgusts me particularly is the liberty they take of talking in public, without any kind of precaution, about the most revolting adventures. When two men are together, they relate to each other, in the broadest language and with the most abominable comments really horrible stories, without caring in the slightest degree whether a woman's ear is within reach of their voices. Yesterday, on the beach, I was forced to leave the place where I was sitting in order not to be any longer the involuntary confidante of an obscene anecdote, told in such immodest language that I felt just as humiliated as indignant at having heard it. Would not the most elementary good-breeding teach them to speak in a lower tone about such matters when we are near at hand. Etretat is, moreover, the country of gossip and scandal. From five to seven o'clock you can see people wandering about in quest of scandal, which they retail from group to group. As you remarked to me, my dear aunt, tittle-tattle is the mark of petty individuals and petty minds. It is also the consolation of women who are no longer loved or sought after. It is enough for me to observe the women who are fondest of gossiping to be persuaded that you are quite right.

The other day I was present at a musical evening at the Casino, given by a remarkable artist, Madame Masson, who sings in a truly delightful manner. I took the opportunity of applauding the admirable Coquelin, as well as two charming vaudeville performers, M——and Meillet. I met, on this occasion, all the bathers who were at the beach. It is no great distinction this year.

Next day I went to lunch at Yport. I noticed a tall man with a beard, coming out of a large house like a castle. It was the painter, Jean Paul Laurens. He is not satisfied apparently with imprisoning the subjects of his pictures, he insists on imprisoning himself.

Then I found myself seated on the shingle close to a man still young, of gentle and refined appearance, who was reading poetry. But he read it with such concentration, with such passion, I may say, that he did not even raise his eyes towards me. I was somewhat astonished and asked the proprietor of the baths, without appearing to be much concerned, the name of this gentleman. I laughed to myself a little at this reader of rhymes; he seemed behind the age, for a man. This person, I thought, must be a simpleton. Well, aunt, I am now infatuated about this stranger. Just fancy, his name is Sully Prudhomme! I went back and sat down beside him again so as to get a good look at him. His face has an expression of calmness and of penetration. Somebody came to look for him, and I heard his voice, which is sweet and almost timid. He would certainly not tell obscene stories aloud in public or knock up against ladies without apologizing. He is assuredly a man of refinement, but his refinement is of an almost morbid, sensitive character, I will try this winter to get an introduction to him.

I have no more news, my dear aunt, and I must finish this letter in

haste, as the mail will soon close. I kiss your hands and your cheeks.

Your devoted niece,

BERTHE DE X.

P. S.—I should add, however, by way of justification of French politeness, that our fellow-countrymen are, when travelling, models of good manners in comparison with the abominable English, who seem to have been brought up in a stable, so careful are they not to discommode themselves in any way, while they always discommode their neighbors.

Madame de L. to Madame de X.

LES FRESNES, Saturday.

My Dear Child:

Many of the things you have said to me are very sensible, but that does not prevent you from being wrong. Like you, I used formerly to feel very indignant at the impoliteness of men, who, as I supposed, constantly treated me with neglect; but, as I grew older and reflected on everything, putting aside coquetry, and observing things without taking any part in them myself, I perceived this much—that if men are not always polite, women are always indescribably rude.

We imagine that we should be permitted to do anything, my darling, and at the same time we consider that we have a right to the utmost respect, and in the most flagrant manner we commit actions devoid of that elementary good-breeding of which you speak so feelingly.

I find, on the contrary, that men consider us much more than we consider them. Besides, darling, men must needs be, and are, what we make them. In a state of society, where women are all true gentlewomen, all men would become gentlemen.

Come now; just observe and reflect.

Look at two women meeting in the street. What an attitude each assumes towards the other! What disparaging looks! What contempt they throw into each glance! How they toss their heads while they inspect each other to find something to condemn! And, if the footpath is narrow, do you think one woman would make room for another, or would beg pardon as she sweeps by? Never! When two men jostle each other by accident in some narrow lane, each of them bows and at the same time gets out of the other's way, while we women press against each other stomach to stomach, face to face, insolently staring each other out of countenance.

Look at two women who are acquaintances meeting on a staircase outside the door of a friend's drawing-room, one of them just leaving, the other about to go in. They begin to talk to each other and block up all the landing. If anyone happens to be coming up behind them, man or woman, do you imagine that they will put themselves half an inch out of their way? Never! never!

I was waiting myself, with my watch in my hands, one day last winter at a certain drawing-room door. And, behind me, two gentlemen were also waiting without showing any readiness, as I did, to lose their temper. The reason was that they had long grown accustomed to our unconscionable insolence.

The other day, before leaving Paris, I went to dine with no less a person than your husband, in the Champs Elysees, in order to enjoy the fresh air. Every table was occupied. The waiter asked us to wait and there would soon be a vacant table.

At that moment I noticed an elderly lady of noble figure, who, having paid for her dinner, seemed on the point of going away. She saw me, scanned me from head to foot, and did not budge. For more than a quarter of an hour she sat there, immovable, putting on her gloves, and calmly staring at those who were waiting like myself. Now, two young men who were just finishing their dinner, having seen me in their turn, hastily summoned the waiter, paid what they owed, and at once offered me their seats, even insisting on standing while waiting for their change. And, bear in mind, my fair niece, that I am no longer pretty, like you, but old and white-haired.

It is we, you see, who should be taught politeness, and the task would be such a difficult one that Hercules himself would not be equal to it. You speak to me about Etretat and about the people who indulged in "tittle-tattle" along the beach of that delightful watering-place. It is a spot now lost to me, a thing of the past, but I found much amusement therein days gone by.

There were only a few of us, people in good society, really good society, and a few artists, and we all fraternized. We paid little attention to gossip in those days.

As we had no monotonous Casino, where people only gather for show, where they whisper, where they dance stupidly, where they succeed in thoroughly boring one another, we sought some other way of passing our evenings pleasantly. Now, just guess what came into the head of one of our husbands? Nothing less than to go and dance each night in one of the farm-houses in the neighborhood.

We started out in a group with a street-organ, generally played by Le Poittevin, the painter, with a cotton nightcap on his head. Two men carried lanterns. We followed in procession, laughing and chattering like a pack of fools.

We woke up the farmer and his servant-maids and farm hands. We got them to make onion soup (horror!), and we danced under the apple trees, to the sound of the barrel-organ. The cocks waking up began to crow in the darkness of the out-houses; the horses began prancing on the straw of their stables. The cool air of the country caressed our cheeks with the smell of grass and of new-mown hay.

How long ago it is! How long ago it is! It is thirty years since then!

I do not want you, my darling, to come for the opening of the hunting

season. Why spoil the pleasure of our friends by inflicting on them

fashionable toilettes on this day of vigorous exercise in the country?

This is the way, child, that men are spoiled. I embrace you. Your old

aunt,

GENEVIEVE DE L.

A WEDDING GIFT

For a long time Jacques Bourdillere had sworn that he would never marry, but he suddenly changed his mind. It happened suddenly, one summer, at the seashore.

One morning as he lay stretched out on the sand, watching the women coming out of the water, a little foot had struck him by its neatness and daintiness. He raised his eyes and was delighted with the whole person, although in fact he could see nothing but the ankles and the head emerging from a flannel bathrobe carefully held closed. He was supposed to be sensual and a fast liver. It was therefore by the mere grace of the form that he was at first captured. Then he was held by the charm of the young girl's sweet mind, so simple and good, as fresh as her cheeks and lips.

He was presented to the family and pleased them. He immediately fell madly in love. When he saw Berthe Lannis in the distance, on the long yellow stretch of sand, he would tingle to the roots of his hair. When he was near her he would become silent, unable to speak or even to think, with a kind of throbbing at his heart, and a buzzing in his ears, and a bewilderment in his mind. Was that love?

He did not know or understand, but he had fully decided to have this child for his wife.

Her parents hesitated for a long time, restrained by the young man's bad reputation. It was said that he had an old sweetheart, one of these binding attachments which one always believes to be broken off and yet which always hold.

Besides, for a shorter or longer period, he loved every woman who came within reach of his lips.

Then he settled down and refused, even once, to see the one with whom he had lived for so long. A friend took care of this woman's pension and assured her an income. Jacques paid, but he did not even wish to hear of her, pretending even to ignore her name. She wrote him letters which he never opened. Every week he would recognize the clumsy writing of the abandoned woman, and every week a greater anger surged within him against her, and he would quickly tear the envelope and the paper, without opening it, without reading one single line, knowing in advance the reproaches and complaints which it contained.

As no one had much faith in his constancy, the test was prolonged through the winter, and Berthe's hand was not granted him until the spring. The wedding took place in Paris at the beginning of May.

The young couple had decided not to take the conventional wedding trip, but after a little dance for the younger cousins, which would not be prolonged after eleven o'clock, in order that this day of lengthy ceremonies might not be too tiresome, the young pair were to spend the first night in the parental home and then, on the following morning, to leave for the beach so dear to their hearts, where they had first known and loved each other.

Night had come, and the dance was going on in the large parlor. 'The two had retired into a little Japanese boudoir hung with bright silks and dimly lighted by the soft rays of a large colored lantern hanging from the ceiling like a gigantic egg. Through the open window the fresh air from outside passed over their faces like a caress, for the night was warm and calm, full of the odor of spring.

They were silent, holding each other's hands and from time to time squeezing them with all their might. She sat there with a dreamy look, feeling a little lost at this great change in her life, but smiling, moved, ready to cry, often also almost ready to faint from joy, believing the whole world to be changed by what had just happened to her, uneasy, she knew not why, and feeling her whole body and soul filled with an indefinable and delicious lassitude.

He was looking at her persistently with a fixed smile. He wished to speak, but found nothing to say, and so sat there, expressing all his ardor by pressures of the hand. From time to time he would murmur: "Berthe!" And each time she would raise her eyes to him with a look of tenderness; they would look at each other for a second and then her look, pierced and fascinated by his, would fall.

They found no thoughts to exchange. They had been left alone, but occasionally some of the dancers would cast a rapid glance at them, as though they were the discreet and trusty witnesses of a mystery.

A door opened and a servant entered, holding on a tray a letter which a messenger had just brought. Jacques, trembling, took this paper, overwhelmed by a vague and sudden fear, the mysterious terror of swift misfortune.

He looked for a longtime at the envelope, the writing on which he did not know, not daring to open it, not wishing to read it, with a wild desire to put it in his pocket and say to himself: "I'll leave that till to-morrow, when I'm far away!" But on one corner two big words, underlined, "Very urgent," filled him with terror. Saying, "Please excuse me, my dear," he tore open the envelope. He read the paper, grew frightfully pale, looked over it again, and, slowly, he seemed to spell it out word for word.

When he raised his head his whole expression showed how upset he was. He stammered: "My dear, it's—it's from my best friend, who has had a very great misfortune. He has need of me immediately—for a matter of life or death. Will you excuse me if I leave you for half an hour? I'll be right back."

Trembling and dazed, she stammered: "Go, my dear!" not having been his wife long enough to dare to question him, to demand to know. He disappeared. She remained alone, listening to the dancing in the neighboring parlor.

He had seized the first hat and coat he came to and rushed downstairs three steps at a time. As he was emerging into the street he stopped under the gas-jet of the vestibule and reread the letter. This is what it said:

SIR: A girl by the name of Ravet, an old sweetheart of yours, it

seems, has just given birth to a child that she says is yours. The

mother is about to die and is begging for you. I take the liberty to

write and ask you if you can grant this last request to a woman who

seems to be very unhappy and worthy of pity.

Yours truly, DR. BONNARD.

When he reached the sick-room the woman was already on the point of death. He did not recognize her at first. The doctor and two nurses were taking care of her. And everywhere on the floor were pails full of ice and rags covered with blood. Water flooded the carpet; two candles were burning on a bureau; behind the bed, in a little wicker crib, the child was crying, and each time it would moan the mother, in torture, would try to move, shivering under her ice bandages.

She was mortally wounded, killed by this birth. Her life was flowing from her, and, notwithstanding the ice and the care, the merciless hemorrhage continued, hastening her last hour.

She recognized Jacques and wished to raise her arms. They were so weak that she could not do so, but tears coursed down her pallid cheeks. He dropped to his knees beside the bed, seized one of her hands and kissed it frantically. Then, little by little, he drew close to the thin face, which started at the contact. One of the nurses was lighting them with a candle, and the doctor was watching them from the back of the room.

Then she said in a voice which sounded as though it came from a distance: "I am going to die, dear. Promise to stay to the end. Oh! don't leave me now. Don't leave me in my last moments!"

He kissed her face and her hair, and, weeping, he murmured: "Do not be uneasy; I will stay."

It was several minutes before she could speak again, she was so weak. She continued: "The little one is yours. I swear it before God and on my soul. I swear it as I am dying! I have never loved another man but you —promise to take care of the child."

He was trying to take this poor pain-racked body in his arms. Maddened by remorse and sorrow, he stammered: "I swear to you that I will bring him up and love him. He shall never leave me."

Then she tried to kiss Jacques. Powerless to lift her head, she held out her white lips in an appeal for a kiss. He approached his lips to respond to this piteous entreaty.

As soon as she felt a little calmer, she murmured: "Bring him here and let me see if you love him."

He went and got the child. He placed him gently on the bed between them, and the little one stopped crying. She murmured: "Don't move any more!" And he was quiet. And he stayed there, holding in his burning hand this other hand shaking in the chill of death, just as, a while ago, he had been holding a hand trembling with love. From time to time he would cast a quick glance at the clock, which marked midnight, then one o'clock, then two.

The physician had returned. The two nurses, after noiselessly moving about the room for a while, were now sleeping on chairs. The child was asleep, and the mother, with eyes shut, appeared also to be resting.

Suddenly, just as pale daylight was creeping in behind the curtains, she stretched out her arms with such a quick and violent motion that she almost threw her baby on the floor. A kind of rattle was heard in her throat, then she lay on her back motionless, dead.

The nurses sprang forward and declared: "All is over!"

He looked once more at this woman whom he had so loved, then at the clock, which pointed to four, and he ran away, forgetting his overcoat, in the evening dress, with the child in his arms.

After he had left her alone the young wife had waited, calmly enough at first, in the little Japanese boudoir. Then, as she did not see him return, she went back to the parlor with an indifferent and calm appearance, but terribly anxious. When her mother saw her alone she asked: "Where is your husband?" She answered: "In his room; he is coming right back."

After an hour, when everybody had questioned her, she told about the letter, Jacques' upset appearance and her fears of an accident.

Still they waited. The guests left; only the nearest relatives remained. At midnight the bride was put to bed, sobbing bitterly. Her mother and two aunts, sitting around the bed, listened to her crying, silent and in despair. The father had gone to the commissary of police to see if he could obtain some news.

At five o'clock a slight noise was heard in the hall. A door was softly opened and closed. Then suddenly a little cry like the mewing of a cat was heard throughout the silent house.

All the women started forward and Berthe sprang ahead of them all, pushing her way past her aunts, wrapped in a bathrobe.

Jacques stood in the middle of the room, pale and out of breath, holding an infant in his arms. The four women looked at him, astonished; but Berthe, who had suddenly become courageous, rushed forward with anguish in her heart, exclaiming: "What is it? What's the matter?"

He looked about him wildly and answered shortly:

"I—I have a child and the mother has just died."

And with his clumsy hands he held out the screaming infant.

Without saying a word, Berthe seized the child, kissed it and hugged it to her. Then she raised her tear-filled eyes to him, asking: "Did you say that the mother was dead?" He answered: "Yes—just now—in my arms. I had broken with her since summer. I knew nothing. The physician sent for me."

Then Berthe murmured: "Well, we will bring up the little one."

THE RELIC

"To the Abbe Louis d'Ennemare, at Soissons.

"My Dear Abbe.

"My marriage with your cousin is broken off in the most stupid way, all on account of an idiotic trick which I almost involuntarily played my intended. In my perplexity I turn to you, my old school chum, for you may be able to help me out of the difficulty. If you can, I shall be grateful to you until I die.

"You know Gilberte, or, rather, you think you know her, but do we ever understand women? All their opinions, their ideas, their creeds, are a surprise to us. They are all full of twists and turns, cf the unforeseen, of unintelligible arguments, of defective logic and of obstinate ideas, which seem final, but which they alter because a little bird came and perched on the window ledge.

"I need not tell you that your cousin is very religious, as she was brought up by the White (or was it the Black?) Ladies at Nancy. You know that better than I do, but what you perhaps do not know is, that she is just as excitable about other matters as she is about religion. Her head flies away, just as a leaf is whirled away by the wind; and she is a true woman, or, rather, girl, for she is moved or made angry in a moment, starting off at a gallop in affection, just as she does in hatred, and returning in the same manner; and she is pretty—as you know, and more charming than I can say—as you will never know.

"Well, we became engaged, and I adored her, as I adore her still, and she appeared to love me.

"One evening, I received a telegram summoning me to Cologne for a consultation, which might be followed by a serious and difficult operation, and as I had to start the next morning, I went to wish Gilberte good-by, and tell her why I could not dine with them on Wednesday, but would do so on Friday, the day of my return. Ah! Beware of Fridays, for I assure you they are unlucky!

"When I told her that I had to go to Germany, I saw that her eyes filled with tears, but when I said I should be back very soon, she clapped her hands, and said:

"'I am very glad you are going, then! You must bring me back something; a mere trifle, just a souvenir, but a souvenir that you have chosen for me. You must guess what I should like best, do you hear? And then I shall see whether you have any imagination.'

"She thought for a few moments, and then added:

"'I forbid you to spend more than twenty francs on it. I want it for the intention, and for a remembrance of your penetration, and not for its intrinsic value:

"And then, after another moment's silence, she said, in a low voice, and with downcast eyes:

"'If it costs you nothing in money, but is something very ingenious and pretty, I will—I will kiss you.'

"The next day I was in Cologne. It was a case of a terrible accident, which had plunged a whole family into despair, and a difficult amputation was necessary. They lodged me in the house; I might say, they almost locked me up, and I saw nobody but people in tears, who almost deafened me with their lamentations; I operated on a man who appeared to be in a moribund state, and who nearly died under my hands, and with whom I remained two nights; and then, when I saw that there was a chance of his recovery, I drove to the station. I had, however, made a mistake in the trains, and I had an hour to wait, and so I wandered about the streets, still thinking of my poor patient, when a man accosted me. I do not know German, and he was totally ignorant of French, but at last I made out that he was offering me some relics. I thought of Gilberte, for I knew her fanatical devotion, and here was my present ready to hand, so I followed the man into a shop where religious objects were for sale, and I bought a small piece of a bone of one of the Eleven Thousand Virgins.

"The pretended relic was inclosed in a charming old silver box, and that determined my choice, and, putting my purchase into my pocket, I went to the railway station, and so on to Paris.

"As soon as I got home, I wished to examine my purchase again, and on taking hold of it, I found that the box was open, and the relic missing! I searched in vain in my pocket, and turned it inside out; the small bit of bone, which was no bigger than half a pin, had disappeared.

"You know, my dear little Abbe, that my faith is not very fervent, but, as my friend, you are magnanimous enough to put up with my lukewarmness, and to leave me alone, and to wait for the future, so you say. But I absolutely disbelieve in the relics of secondhand dealers in piety, and you share my doubts in that respect. Therefore, the loss of that bit of sheep's carcass did not grieve me, and I easily procured a similar fragment, which I carefully fastened inside my jewel-box, and then I went to see my intended.

"As soon as she saw me, she ran up to me, smiling and eager, and, said to me:

"'What have you brought me?'

"I pretended to have forgotten, but she did not believe me, and I made her beg, and even beseech me. But when I saw that she was devoured by curiosity, I gave her the sacred silver box. She appeared overjoyed.

"'A relic! Oh! A relic!'

"And she kissed the box passionately, so that I was ashamed of my deception. She was not quite satisfied, however, and her uneasiness soon turned to terrible fear, and looking straight into my eyes, she said:

"'Are you sure-that it is genuine?'

"'Absolutely certain.'

"'How can you be so certain?'

"I was trapped; for to say that I had bought it of a man in the streets would be my destruction. What was I to say? A wild idea struck me, and I said, in a low, mysterious voice:

"'I stole it for you.'

"She looked at me with astonishment and delight in her large eyes.

"'Oh! You stole it? Where?'

"'In the cathedral; in the very shrine of the Eleven Thousand Virgins.'

"Her heart beat with pleasure, and she murmured:

"'Oh! Did you really do that-for me? Tell me-all about it!'

"That was the climax; I could not retract what I had said. I made up a fanciful story; with precise details: I had given the custodian of the building a hundred francs to be allowed to go about the building by myself; the shrine was being repaired, but I happened to be there at the breakfast hour of the workmen and clergy; by removing a small panel, I had been enabled to seize a small piece of bone (oh! so small), among a quantity of others (I said a quantity, as I thought of the amount that the remains of the skeletons of eleven thousand virgins must produce). Then I went to a goldsmith's and bought a casket worthy of the relic; and I was not sorry to let her know that the silver box cost me five hundred francs.

"But she did not think of that; she listened to me, trembling, in an ecstasy, and whispering: 'How I love you!' she threw herself into my arms.

"Just note this: I had committed sacrilege for her sake. I had committed a theft; I had violated a church; I had violated a shrine; violated and stolen holy relics, and for that she adored me, thought me perfect, tender, divine. Such is woman, my dear Abbe, every woman.

"For two months I was the most admirable of lovers. In her room, she had made a kind of magnificent chapel in which to keep this bit of mutton chop, which, as she thought, had made me commit that divine love-crime, and she worked up her religious enthusiasm in front of it every morning and evening. I had asked her to keep the matter secret, for fear, as I said, that I might be arrested, condemned, and given over to Germany, and she kept her promise.

"Well, at the beginning of the summer, she was seized with an irresistible desire to see the scene of my exploit, and she teased her father so persistently (without telling him her secret reason), that he took her to Cologne, but without telling me of their trip, according to his daughter's wish.

"I need not tell you that I had not seen the interior of the cathedral. I do not know where the tomb (if there be a tomb) of the Eleven Thousand Virgins is; and then, it appears, it is unapproachable, alas!

"A week afterward, I received ten lines, breaking off our engagement, and then an explanatory letter from her father, whom she had, somewhat late, taken into her confidence.

"At the sight of the shrine, she had suddenly seen through my trickery and my lie, and at the same time discovered my real innocence of any crime. Having asked the keeper of the relics whether any robbery had been committed, the man began to laugh, and pointed out to them how impossible such a crime was. But, from the moment that I had not plunged my profane hand into venerable relics, I was no longer worthy of my fair-haired, sensitive betrothed.

"I was forbidden the house; I begged and prayed in vain; nothing could move the fair devotee, and I became ill from grief. Well, last week, her cousin, Madame d'Arville, who is your cousin also, sent me word that she should like to see me, and when I called, she told me on what conditions I might obtain my pardon, and here they are. I must bring her a relic, a real, authentic relic of some virgin and martyr, certified to be such by our Holy Father, the

Pope, and I am going mad from embarrassment and anxiety.

"I will go to Rome, if needful, but I cannot call on the Pope unexpectedly, to tell him my stupid misadventure; and, besides, I doubt whether they allow private individuals to have relics. Could not you give me an introduction to some cardinal, or even to some French prelate who possesses some remains of a female saint? Or, perhaps, you may have the precious object she wants in your collection?

"Help me out of my difficulty, my dear Abbe, and I promise you that I will be converted ten years sooner than I otherwise should be!

"Madame d'Arville, who takes the matter seriously, said to me the other day:

"'Poor Gilberte will never marry.'

"My dear old schoolmate, will you allow your cousin to die the victim of a stupid piece of subterfuge on my part? Pray prevent her from being virgin eleven thousand and one.

"Pardon me, I am unworthy, but I embrace you, and love you with all my heart.

"Your old friend,

"HENRI FONTAL."

VOLUME IV.
THE MORIBUND

The warm autumn sun was beating down on the farmyard. Under the grass, which had been cropped close by the cows, the earth soaked by recent rains, was soft and sank in under the feet with a soggy noise, and the apple trees, loaded with apples, were dropping their pale green fruit in the dark green grass.

Four young heifers, tied in a line, were grazing and at times looking toward the house and lowing. The fowls made a colored patch on the dung-heap before the stable, scratching, moving about and cackling, while two roosters crowed continually, digging worms for their hens, whom they were calling with a loud clucking.

The wooden gate opened and a man entered. He might have been forty years old, but he looked at least sixty, wrinkled, bent, walking slowly, impeded by the weight of heavy wooden shoes full of straw. His long arms hung down on both sides of his body. When he got near the farm a yellow cur, tied at the foot of an enormous pear tree, beside a barrel which served as his kennel, began at first to wag his tail and then to bark for joy. The man cried:

"Down, Finot!"

The dog was quiet.

A peasant woman came out of the house. Her large, flat, bony body was outlined under a long woollen jacket drawn in at the waist. A gray skirt, too short, fell to the middle of her legs, which were encased in blue stockings. She, too, wore wooden shoes, filled with straw. The white cap, turned yellow, covered a few hairs which were plastered to the scalp, and her brown, thin, ugly, toothless face had that wild, animal expression which is often to be found on the faces of the peasants.

The man asked:

"How is he gettin' along?"

The woman answered:

"The priest said it's the end—that he will never live through the night."

Both of them went into the house.

After passing through the kitchen, they entered a low, dark room, barely lighted by one window, in front of which a piece of calico was hanging. The big beams, turned brown with age and smoke, crossed the room from one side to the other, supporting the thin floor of the garret, where an army of rats ran about day and night.

The moist, lumpy earthen floor looked greasy, and, at the back of the room, the bed made an indistinct white spot. A harsh, regular noise, a difficult, hoarse, wheezing breathing, like the gurgling of water from a broken pump, came from the darkened couch where an old man, the father of the peasant woman, was dying.

The man and the woman approached the dying man and looked at him with calm, resigned eyes.

The son-in-law said:

"I guess it's all up with him this time; he will not last the night."

The woman answered:

"He's been gurglin' like that ever since midday." They were silent. The father's eyes were closed, his face was the color of the earth and so dry that it looked like wood. Through his open mouth came his harsh, rattling breath, and the gray linen sheet rose and fell with each respiration.

The son-in-law, after a long silence, said:

"There's nothing more to do; I can't help him. It's a nuisance, just the same, because the weather is good and we've got a lot of work to do."

His wife seemed annoyed at this idea. She reflected a few moments and then said:

"He won't be buried till Saturday, and that will give you all day tomorrow."

The peasant thought the matter over and answered:

"Yes, but to-morrow I'll have to invite the people to the funeral. That means five or six hours to go round to Tourville and Manetot, and to see everybody."

The woman, after meditating two or three minutes, declared:

"It isn't three o'clock yet. You could begin this evening and go all round the country to Tourville. You can just as well say that he's dead, seem' as he's as good as that now."

The man stood perplexed for a while, weighing the pros and cons of the idea. At last he declared:

"Well, I'll go!"

He was leaving the room, but came back after a minute's hesitation:

"As you haven't got anythin' to do you might shake down some apples to bake and make four dozen dumplings for those who come to the funeral, for one must have something to cheer them. You can light the fire with the wood that's under the shed. It's dry."

He left the room, went back into the kitchen, opened the cupboard, took out a six-pound loaf of bread, cut off a slice, and carefully gathered the crumbs in the palm of his hand and threw them into his mouth, so as not to lose anything. Then, with the end of his knife, he scraped out a little salt butter from the bottom of an earthen jar, spread it on his bread and began to eat slowly, as he did everything.

He recrossed the farmyard, quieted the dog, which had started barking again, went out on the road bordering on his ditch, and disappeared in the direction of Tourville.

As soon as she was alone, the woman began to work. She uncovered the meal-bin and made the dough for the dumplings. She kneaded it a long time, turning it over and over again, punching, pressing, crushing it. Finally she made a big, round, yellow-white ball, which she placed on the corner of the table.

Then she went to get her apples, and, in order not to injure the tree with a pole, she climbed up into it by a ladder. She chose the fruit with care, only taking the ripe ones, and gathering them in her apron.

A voice called from the road:

"Hey, Madame Chicot!"

She turned round. It was a neighbor, Osime Favet, the mayor, on his way to fertilize his fields, seated on the manure-wagon, with his feet hanging over the side. She turned round and answered:

"What can I do for you, Maitre Osime?"

"And how is the father?"

She cried:

"He is as good as dead. The funeral is Saturday at seven, because there's lots of work to be done."

The neighbor answered:

"So! Good luck to you! Take care of yourself."

To his kind remarks she answered:"

"Thanks; the same to you."

And she continued picking apples.

When she went back to the house, she went over to look at her father, expecting to find him dead. But as soon as she reached the door she heard his monotonous, noisy rattle, and, thinking it a waste of time to go over to him, she began to prepare her dumplings. She wrapped up the fruit, one by one, in a thin layer of paste, then she lined them up on the edge of the table. When she had made forty-eight dumplings, arranged in dozens, one in front of the other, she began to think of preparing supper, and she hung her kettle over the fire to cook potatoes, for she judged it useless to heat the oven that day, as she had all the next day in which to finish the preparations.

Her husband returned at about five. As soon as he had crossed the threshold he asked:

"Is it over?"

She answered:

"Not yet; he's still gurglin'."

They went to look at him. The old man was in exactly the same condition. His hoarse rattle, as regular as the ticking of a clock, was neither quicker nor slower. It returned every second, the tone varying a little, according as the air entered or left his chest.

His son-in-law looked at him and then said:

"He'll pass away without our noticin' it, just like a candle."

They returned to the kitchen and started to eat without saying a word. When they had swallowed their soup, they ate another piece of bread and butter. Then, as soon as the dishes were washed, they returned to the dying man.

The woman, carrying a little lamp with a smoky wick, held it in front of her father's face. If he had not been breathing, one would certainly have thought him dead.

The couple's bed was hidden in a little recess at the other end of the room. Silently they retired, put out the light, closed their eyes, and soon two unequal snores, one deep and the other shriller, accompanied the uninterrupted rattle of the dying man.

The rats ran about in the garret.

The husband awoke at the first streaks of dawn. His father-in-law was still alive. He shook his wife, worried by the tenacity of the old man.

"Say, Phemie, he don't want to quit. What would you do?"

He knew that she gave good advice.

She answered:

"You needn't be afraid; he can't live through the day. And the mayor won't stop our burying him to-morrow, because he allowed it for Maitre Renard's father, who died just during the planting season."

He was convinced by this argument, and left for the fields.

His wife baked the dumplings and then attended to her housework.

At noon the old man was not dead. The people hired for the day's work came by groups to look at him. Each one had his say. Then they left again for the fields.

At six o'clock, when the work was over, the father was still breathing. At last his son-in-law was frightened.

"What would you do now, Phemie?"

She no longer knew how to solve the problem. They went to the mayor. He promised that he would close his eyes and authorize the funeral for the following day. They also went to the health officer, who likewise promised, in order to oblige Maitre Chicot, to antedate the death certificate. The man and the woman returned, feeling more at ease.

They went to bed and to sleep, just as they did the preceding day, their sonorous breathing blending with the feeble breathing of the old man.

When they awoke, he was not yet dead.

Then they began to be frightened. They stood by their father, watching him with distrust, as though he had wished to play them a mean trick, to deceive them, to annoy them on purpose, and they were vexed at him for the time which he was making them lose.

The son-in-law asked:

"What am I goin' to do?"

She did not know. She answered:

"It certainly is annoying!"

The guests who were expected could not be notified. They decided to wait and explain the case to them.

Toward a quarter to seven the first ones arrived. The women in black, their heads covered with large veils, looking very sad. Then men, ill at ease in their homespun coats, were coming forward more slowly, in couples, talking business.

Maitre Chicot and his wife, bewildered, received them sorrowfully, and suddenly both of them together began to cry as they approached the first group. They explained the matter, related their difficulty, offered chairs, bustled about, tried to make excuses, attempting to prove that everybody would have done as they did, talking continually and giving nobody a chance to answer.

They were going from one person to another:

"I never would have thought it; it's incredible how he can last this long!"

The guests, taken aback, a little disappointed, as though they had missed an expected entertainment, did not know what to do, some remaining seated others standing. Several wished to leave. Maitre Chicot held them back:

"You must take something, anyhow! We made some dumplings; might as well make use of 'em."

The faces brightened at this idea. The yard was filling little by little; the early arrivals were telling the news to those who had arrived later. Everybody was whispering. The idea of the dumplings seemed to cheer everyone up.

The women went in to take a look at the dying man. They crossed themselves beside the bed, muttered a prayer and went out again. The men, less anxious for this spectacle, cast a look through the window, which had been opened.

Madame Chicot explained her distress:

"That's how he's been for two days, neither better nor worse. Doesn't he sound like a pump that has gone dry?"

When everybody had had a look at the dying man, they thought of the refreshments; but as there were too many people for the kitchen to hold, the table was moved out in front of the door. The four dozen golden dumplings, tempting and appetizing, arranged in two big dishes, attracted the eyes of all. Each one reached out to take his, fearing that there would not be enough. But four remained over.

Maitre Chicot, his mouth full, said:

"Father would feel sad if he were to see this. He loved them so much when he was alive."

A big, jovial peasant declared:

"He won't eat any more now. Each one in his turn."

This remark, instead of making the guests sad, seemed to cheer them up. It was their turn now to eat dumplings.

Madame Chicot, distressed at the expense, kept running down to the cellar continually for cider. The pitchers were emptied in quick succession. The company was laughing and talking loud now. They were beginning to shout as they do at feasts.

Suddenly an old peasant woman who had stayed beside the dying man, held there by a morbid fear of what would soon happen to herself, appeared at the window and cried in a shrill voice:

"He's dead! he's dead!"

Everybody was silent. The women arose quickly to go and see. He was indeed dead. The rattle had ceased. The men looked at each other, looking down, ill at ease. They hadn't finished eating the dumplings. Certainly the rascal had not chosen a propitious moment. The Chicots were no longer weeping. It was over; they were relieved.

They kept repeating:

"I knew it couldn't 'last. If he could only have done it last night, it would have saved us all this trouble."

Well, anyhow, it was over. They would bury him on Monday, that was all, and they would eat some more dumplings for the occasion.

The guests went away, talking the matter over, pleased at having had the chance to see him and of getting something to eat.

And when the husband and wife were alone, face to face, she said, her face distorted with grief:

"We'll have to bake four dozen more dumplings! Why couldn't he have made up his mind last night?"

The husband, more resigned, answered:

"Well, we'll not have to do this every day."

THE GAMEKEEPER

It was after dinner, and we were talking about adventures and accidents which happened while out shooting.

An old friend, known to all of us, M. Boniface, a great sportsman and a connoisseur of wine, a man of wonderful physique, witty and gay, and endowed with an ironical and resigned philosophy, which manifested itself in caustic humor, and never in melancholy, suddenly exclaimed:

"I know a story, or rather a tragedy, which is somewhat peculiar. It is not at all like those which one hears of usually, and I have never told it, thinking that it would interest no one.

"It is not at all sympathetic. I mean by that, that it does not arouse the kind of interest which pleases or which moves one agreeably.

"Here is the story:

"I was then about thirty-five years of age, and a most enthusiastic sportsman.

"In those days I owned a lonely bit of property in the neighborhood of Jumieges, surrounded by forests and abounding in hares and rabbits. I was accustomed to spending four or five days alone there each year, there not being room enough to allow of my bringing a friend with me.

"I had placed there as gamekeeper, an old retired gendarme, a good man, hot-tempered, a severe disciplinarian, a terror to poachers and fearing nothing. He lived all alone, far from the village, in a little house, or rather hut, consisting of two rooms downstairs, with kitchen and store-room, and two upstairs. One of them, a kind of box just large enough to accommodate a bed, a cupboard and a chair, was reserved for my use.

"Old man Cavalier lived in the other one. When I said that he was alone in this place, I was wrong. He had taken his nephew with him, a young scamp about fourteen years old, who used to go to the village and run errands for the old man.

"This young scapegrace was long and lanky, with yellow hair, so light that it resembled the fluff of a plucked chicken, so thin that he seemed bald. Besides this, he had enormous feet and the hands of a giant.

"He was cross-eyed, and never looked at anyone. He struck me as being in the same relation to the human race as ill-smelling beasts are to the animal race. He reminded me of a polecat.

"He slept in a kind of hole at the top of the stairs which led to the two rooms.

"But during my short sojourns at the Pavilion—so I called the hut —Marius would give up his nook to an old woman from Ecorcheville, called Celeste, who used to come and cook for me, as old man Cavalier's stews were not sufficient for my healthy appetite.

"You now know the characters and the locality. Here is the story:

"It was on the fifteenth of October, 1854—I shall remember that date as long as I live.

"I left Rouen on horseback, followed by my dog Bock, a big Dalmatian hound from Poitou, full-chested and with a heavy jaw, which could retrieve among the bushes like a Pont-

Andemer spaniel.

"I was carrying my satchel slung across my back and my gun diagonally across my chest. It was a cold, windy, gloomy day, with clouds scurrying across the sky.

"As I went up the hill at Canteleu, I looked over the broad valley of the Seine, the river winding in and out along its course as far as the eye could see. To the right the towers of Rouen stood out against the sky, and to the left the landscape was bounded by the distant slopes covered with trees. Then I crossed the forest of Roumare and, toward five o'clock, reached the Pavilion, where Cavalier and Celeste were expecting me.

"For ten years I had appeared there at the same time, in the same manner; and for ten years the same faces had greeted me with the same words:

"'Welcome, master! We hope your health is good.'

"Cavalier had hardly changed. He withstood time like an old tree; but Celeste, especially in the past four years, had become unrecognizable.

"She was bent almost double, and, although still active, when she walked her body was almost at right angles to her legs.

"The old woman, who was very devoted to me, always seemed affected at seeing me again, and each time, as I left, she would say:

"'This may be the last time, master.'

"The sad, timid farewell of this old servant, this hopeless resignation to the inevitable fate which was not far off for her, moved me strangely each year.

"I dismounted, and while Cavalier, whom I had greeted, was leading my horse to the little shed which served as a stable, I entered the kitchen, which also served as dining-room, followed by Celeste.

"Here the gamekeeper joined us. I saw at first glance that something was the matter. He seemed preoccupied, ill at ease, worried.

"I said to him:

"'Well, Cavalier, is everything all right?'

"He muttered:

"'Yes and no. There are things I don't like.'

"I asked:

"'What? Tell me about it.'

"But he shook his head.

"'No, not yet, monsieur. I do not wish to bother you with my little troubles so soon after your arrival.'

"I insisted, but he absolutely refused to give me any information before dinner. From his expression, I could tell that it was something very serious.

“Not knowing what to say to him, I asked:

“‘How about game? Much of it this year?’

“‘Oh, yes! You’ll find all you want. Thank heaven, I looked out for that.’

“He said this with so much seriousness, with such sad solemnity, that it was really almost funny. His big gray mustache seemed almost ready to drop from his lips.

“Suddenly I remembered that I had not yet seen his nephew.

“‘Where is Marius? Why does he not show himself?’

“The gamekeeper started, looking me suddenly in the face:

“Well, monsieur, I had rather tell you the whole business right away; it’s on account of him that I am worrying.’

“‘Ah! Well, where is he?’

“‘Over in the stable, monsieur. I was waiting for the right time to bring him out.’

“‘What has he done?’

“‘Well, monsieur——’

“The gamekeeper, however, hesitated, his voice altered and shaky, his face suddenly furrowed by the deep lines of an old man.

“He continued slowly:

“‘Well, I found out, last winter, that someone was poaching in the woods of Roseraies, but I couldn’t seem to catch the man. I spent night after night on the lookout for him. In vain. During that time they began poaching over by Ecorcheville. I was growing thin from vexation. But as for catching the trespasser, impossible! One might have thought that the rascal was forewarned of my plans.

“‘But one day, while I was brushing Marius’ Sunday trousers, I found forty cents in his pocket. Where did he get it?

“‘I thought the matter over for about a week, and I noticed that he used to go out; he would leave the house just as I was coming home to go to bed—yes, monsieur.

“‘Then I started to watch him, without the slightest suspicion of the real facts. One morning, just after I had gone to bed before him, I got right up again, and followed him. For shadowing a man, there is nobody like me, monsieur.

“‘And I caught him, Marius, poaching on your land, monsieur; he my nephew, I your keeper!

“‘The blood rushed to my head, and I almost killed him on the spot, I hit him so hard. Oh! yes, I thrashed him all right. And I promised him that he would get another beating from my hand, in your presence, as an example.

“‘There! I have grown thin from sorrow. You know how it is when one is worried like that. But tell me, what would you have done? The boy has no father or mother, and I am the last one of his blood; I kept him, I couldn't drive him out, could I?

"'I told him that if it happened again I would have no more pity for him, all would be over. There! Did I do right, monsieur?'

"I answered, holding out my hand:

"'You did well, Cavalier; you are an honest man.'

"He rose.

"'Thank you, monsieur. Now I am going to fetch him. I must give him his thrashing, as an example.'

"I knew that it was hopeless to try and turn the old man from his idea. I therefore let him have his own way.

"He got the rascal and brought him back by the ear.

"I was seated on a cane chair, with the solemn expression of a judge.

"Marius seemed to have grown; he was homelier even than the year before, with his evil, sneaking expression.

"His big hands seemed gigantic.

"His uncle pushed him up to me, and, in his soldierly voice, said:

"'Beg the gentleman's pardon.'

"The boy didn't say a word.

"Then putting one arm round him, the former gendarme lifted him right off the ground, and began to whack him with such force that I rose to stop the blows.

"The boy was now howling: 'Mercy! mercy! mercy! I promise——'

"Cavalier put him back on the ground and forced him to his knees:

"'Beg for pardon,' he said.

"With eyes lowered, the scamp murmured:

"'I ask for pardon!'

"Then his uncle lifted him to his feet, and dismissed him with a cuff which almost knocked him down again.

"He made his escape, and I did not see him again that evening.

"Cavalier appeared overwhelmed.'

"'He is a bad egg,' he said.

"And throughout the whole dinner, he kept repeating:

"'Oh! that worries me, monsieur, that worries me.'

"I tried to comfort him, but in vain.

"I went to bed early, so that I might start out at daybreak.

"My dog was already asleep on the floor, at the foot of my bed, when I put out the light.

"I was awakened toward midnight by the furious barking of my dog Bock. I immediately noticed that my room was full of smoke. I jumped out of bed, struck a light, ran to the door and opened it. A cloud of flames burst in. The house was on fire.

"I quickly closed the heavy oak door and, drawing on my trousers, I first lowered the dog through the window, by means of a rope made of my sheets; then, having thrown out the rest of my clothes, my game-bag and my gun, I in turn escaped the same way.

"I began to shout with all my might: 'Cavalier! Cavalier! Cavalier!'

"But the gamekeeper did not wake up. He slept soundly like an old gendarme.

"However, I could see through the lower windows that the whole ground-floor was nothing but a roaring furnace; I also noticed that it had been filled with straw to make it burn readily.

"Somebody must purposely have set fire to the place!

"I continued shrieking wildly: 'Cavalier!'

"Then the thought struck me that the smoke might be suffocating him. An idea came to me. I slipped two cartridges into my gun, and shot straight at his window.

"The six panes of glass shattered into the room in a cloud of glass. This time the old man had heard me, and he appeared, dazed, in his nightshirt, bewildered by the glare which illumined the whole front of his 'house.

"I cried to him:

"'Your house is on fire! Escape through the window! Quick! Quick!'

"The flames were coming out through all the cracks downstairs, were licking along the wall, were creeping toward him and going to surround him. He jumped and landed on his feet, like a cat.

"It was none too soon. The thatched roof cracked in the middle, right over the staircase, which formed a kind of flue for the fire downstairs; and an immense red jet jumped up into the air, spreading like a stream of water and sprinkling a shower of sparks around the hut. In a few seconds it was nothing but a pool of flames.

"Cavalier, thunderstruck, asked:

"'How did the fire start?'

"I answered:

"'Somebody lit it in the kitchen.'

"He muttered:

"'Who could have started the fire?'

"And I, suddenly guessing, answered:

"'Marius!'

"The old man understood. He stammered:

"'Good God! That is why he didn't return.'

"A terrible thought flashed through my mind. I cried:

"'And Celeste! Celeste!'

"He did not answer. The house caved in before us, forming only an enormous, bright, blinding brazier, an awe-inspiring funeral-pile, where the poor woman could no longer be anything but a glowing ember, a glowing ember of human flesh.

"We had not heard a single cry.

"As the fire crept toward the shed, I suddenly bethought me of my horse, and Cavalier ran to free it.

"Hardly had he opened the door of the stable, when a supple, nimble body darted between his legs, and threw him on his face. It was Marius, running for all he was worth.

"The man was up in a second. He tried to run after the wretch, but, seeing that he could not catch him, and maddened by an irresistible anger, yielding to one of those thoughtless impulses which we cannot foresee or prevent, he picked up my gun, which was lying on the ground. near him, put it to his shoulder, and, before I could make a motion, he pulled the trigger without even noticing whether or not the weapon was loaded.

"One of the cartridges which I had put in to announce the fire was still intact, and the charge caught the fugitive right in the back,—throwing him forward on the ground, bleeding profusely. He immediately began to claw the earth with his hands and with his knees, as though trying to run on all fours like a rabbit who has been mortally wounded, and sees the hunter approaching.

"I rushed forward to the boy, but I could already hear the death-rattle. He passed away before the fire was extinguished, without having said a word.

"Cavalier, still in his shirt, his legs bare, was standing near us, motionless, dazed.

"When the people from the village arrived, my gamekeeper was taken away, like an insane man.

"I appeared at the trial as witness, and related the facts in detail, without changing a thing. Cavalier was acquitted. He disappeared that very day, leaving the country.

"I have never seen him since.

"There, gentlemen, that is my story."

THE STORY OF A FARM GIRL

PART I

As the weather was very fine, the people on the farm had hurried through their dinner and had returned to the fields.

The servant, Rose, remained alone in the large kitchen, where the fire was dying out on the hearth beneath the large boiler of hot water. From time to time she dipped out some water and slowly washed her dishes, stopping occasionally to look at the two streaks of light which the sun threw across the long table through the window, and which showed the defects in the glass.

Three venturesome hens were picking up the crumbs under the chairs, while the smell of the poultry yard and the warmth from the cow stall came in through the half-open door, and a cock was heard crowing in the distance.

When she had finished her work, wiped down the table, dusted the mantelpiece and put the plates on the high dresser close to the wooden clock with its loud tick-tock, she drew a long breath, as she felt rather oppressed, without exactly knowing why. She looked at the black clay walls, the rafters that were blackened with smoke and from which hung spiders' webs, smoked herrings and strings of onions, and then she sat down, rather overcome by the stale odor from the earthen floor, on which so many things had been continually spilled and which the heat brought out. With this there was mingled the sour smell of the pans of milk which were set out to raise the cream in the adjoining dairy.

She wanted to sew, as usual, but she did not feel strong enough, and so she went to the door to get a mouthful of fresh air, which seemed to do her good.

The fowls were lying on the steaming dunghill; some of them were scratching with one claw in search of worms, while the cock stood up proudly in their midst. When he crowed, the cocks in all the neighboring farmyards replied to him, as if they were uttering challenges from farm to farm.

The girl looked at them without thinking, and then she raised her eyes and was almost dazzled at the sight of the apple trees in blossom. Just then a colt, full of life and friskiness, jumped over the ditches and then stopped suddenly, as if surprised at being alone.

She also felt inclined to run; she felt inclined to move and to stretch her limbs and to repose in the warm, breathless air. She took a few undecided steps and closed her eyes, for she was seized with a feeling of animal comfort, and then she went to look for eggs in the hen loft. There were thirteen of them, which she took in and put into the storeroom; but the smell from the kitchen annoyed her again, and she went out to sit on the grass for a time.

The farmyard, which was surrounded by trees, seemed to be asleep. The tall grass, amid which the tall yellow dandelions rose up like streaks of yellow light, was of a vivid, fresh spring green. The apple trees cast their shade all round them, and the thatched roofs, on which grew blue and yellow irises, with their sword-like leaves, steamed as if the moisture of the stables and barns were coming through the straw. The girl went to the shed, where the carts and buggies were kept. Close to it, in a ditch, there was a large patch of violets, whose fragrance was spread abroad, while beyond the slope the open country could be seen, where grain was growing, with clumps of trees in places, and groups of laborers here and there, who looked as small as dolls, and white horses like toys, who were drawing a child's cart, driven by a man as tall as one's finger.

She took up a bundle of straw, threw it into the ditch and sat down upon it. Then, not feeling comfortable, she undid it, spread it out and lay down upon it at full length on her back, with both arms under her head and her legs stretched out.

Gradually her eyes closed, and she was falling into a state of delightful languor. She was, in fact, almost asleep when she felt two hands on her bosom, and she sprang up at a bound. It was Jacques, one of the farm laborers, a tall fellow from Picardy, who had been making love to her for a long time. He had been herding the sheep, and, seeing her lying down in the shade, had come up stealthily and holding his breath, with glistening eyes and bits of straw in his hair.

He tried to kiss her, but she gave him a smack in the face, for she was as strong as he, and he was shrewd enough to beg her pardon; so they sat down side by side and talked amicably. They spoke about the favorable weather, of their master, who was a good fellow, then of their neighbors, of all the people in the country round, of themselves, of their village, of their youthful days, of their recollections, of their relations, who had left them for a long time, and it might be forever. She grew sad as she thought of it, while he, with one fixed idea in his head, drew closer to her.

"I have not seen my mother for a long time," she said. "It is very hard to be separated like that," and she directed her looks into the distance, toward the village in the north which she had left.

Suddenly, however, he seized her by the neck and kissed her again, but she struck him so violently in the face with her clenched fist that his nose began to bleed, and he got up and laid his head against the stem of a tree. When she saw that, she was sorry, and going up to him, she said: "Have I hurt you?" He, however, only laughed. "No, it was a mere nothing; only she had hit him right on the middle of the nose. What a devil!" he said, and he looked at her with admiration, for she had inspired him with a feeling of respect and of a very different kind of admiration which was the beginning of a real love for that tall, strong wench. When the bleeding had stopped, he proposed a walk, as he was afraid of his neighbor's heavy hand, if they remained side by side like that much longer; but she took his arm of her own accord, in the avenue, as if they had been out for an evening's walk, and said: "It is not nice of you to despise me like that, Jacques." He protested, however. No, he did not despise her. He was in love with her, that was all.

"So you really want to marry me?" she asked.

He hesitated and then looked at her sideways, while she looked straight ahead of her. She had fat, red cheeks, a full bust beneath her cotton jacket; thick, red lips; and her neck, which was almost bare, was covered with small beads of perspiration. He felt a fresh access of desire, and, putting his lips to her ear, he murmured: "Yes, of course I do."

Then she threw her arms round his neck and kissed him till they were both out of breath. From that moment the eternal story of love began between them. They plagued one another in corners; they met in the moonlight beside the haystack and gave each other bruises on the legs, under the table, with their heavy nailed boots. By degrees, however, Jacques seemed to grow tired of her; he avoided her, scarcely spoke to her, and did not try any longer to meet her alone, which made her sad and anxious; and soon she found that she was enceinte.

At first she was in a state of consternation, but then she got angry, and her rage increased every day because she could not meet him, as he avoided her most carefully. At last, one night, when every one in the farmhouse was asleep, she went out noiselessly in her petticoat, with bare feet, crossed the yard and opened the door of the stable where Jacques was lying in a large box of straw above his horses. He pretended to snore when he heard her coming, but she knelt down by his side and shook him until he sat up.

"What do you want?" he then asked her. And with clenched teeth, and trembling with anger, she replied: "I want—I want you to marry me, as you promised." But he only laughed and replied: "Oh! if a man were to marry all the girls with whom he has made a slip, he would have more than enough to do."

Then she seized him by the throat, threw him or his back, so that he could not get away from her, and, half strangling him, she shouted into his face:

"I am enceinte, do you hear? I am enceinte!"

He gasped for breath, as he was almost choked, and so they remained, both of them, motionless and without speaking, in the dark silence, which was only broken by the noise made by a horse as he, pulled the hay out of the manger and then slowly munched it.

When Jacques found that she was the stronger, he stammered out: "Very well, I will marry you, as that is the case." But she did not believe his promises. "It must be at once," she said. "You must have the banns put up." "At once," he replied. "Swear solemnly that you will." He hesitated for a few moments and then said: "I swear it, by Heaven!"

Then she released her grasp and went away without another word.

She had no chance of speaking to him for several days; and, as the stable was now always locked at night, she was afraid to make any noise, for fear of creating a scandal. One morning, however, she saw another man come in at dinner time, and she said: "Has Jacques left?" "Yes;" the man replied; "I have got his place."

This made her tremble so violently that she could not take the saucepan off the fire; and later, when they were all at work, she went up into her room and cried, burying her head in the bolster, so that she might not be heard. During the day, however, she tried to obtain some information without exciting any suspicion, but she was so overwhelmed by the thoughts of her misfortune that she fancied that all the people whom she asked laughed maliciously. All she learned, however, was that he had left the neighborhood altogether.

PART II

Then a cloud of constant misery began for her. She worked mechanically, without thinking of what she was doing, with one fixed idea in her head:

"Suppose people were to know."

This continual feeling made her so incapable of reasoning that she did not even try to think of any means of avoiding the disgrace that she knew must ensue, which was irreparable and drawing nearer every day, and which was as sure as death itself. She got up every morning long before the others and persistently tried to look at her figure in a piece of broken looking-glass, before which she did her hair, as she was very anxious to know whether anybody would notice a change in her, and, during the day, she stopped working every few minutes to look at herself from top to toe, to see whether her apron did not look too short.

The months went on, and she scarcely spoke now, and when she was asked a question, did not appear to understand; but she had a frightened look, haggard eyes and trembling hands, which made her master say to her occasionally: "My poor girl, how stupid you have grown lately."

In church she hid behind a pillar, and no longer ventured to go to confession, as she feared to face the priest, to whom she attributed superhuman powers, which enabled him to read people's consciences; and at meal times the looks of her fellow servants almost made her faint with mental agony; and she was always fancying that she had been found out by the cowherd, a precocious and cunning little lad, whose bright eyes seemed always to be watching her.

One morning the postman brought her a letter, and as she had never received one in her life before she was so upset by it that she was obliged to sit down. Perhaps it was from him? But, as she could not read, she sat anxious and trembling with that piece of paper, covered with ink, in her hand. After a time, however, she put it into her pocket, as she did not venture to confide her secret to any one. She often stopped in her work to look at those lines written at regular intervals, and which terminated in a signature, imagining vaguely that she would suddenly discover their meaning, until at last, as she felt half mad with impatience and anxiety, she went to the schoolmaster, who told her to sit down and read to her as follows:

"MY DEAR DAUGHTER: I write to tell you that I am very ill. Our neighbor, Monsieur Dentu, begs you to come, if you can.

"From your affectionate mother,

"CESAIRE DENTU, Deputy Mayor."

She did not say a word and went away, but as soon as she was alone her legs gave way under her, and she fell down by the roadside and remained there till night.

When she got back, she told the farmer her bad news, and he allowed her to go home for as long as she liked, and promised to have her work done by a charwoman and to take her back when she returned.

Her mother died soon after she got there, and the next day Rose gave birth to a seven-months child, a miserable little skeleton, thin enough to make anybody shudder, and which seemed to be suffering continually, to judge from the painful manner in which it moved its poor little hands, which were as thin as a crab's legs; but it lived for all that. She said she was married, but could not be burdened with the child, so she left it with some neighbors, who promised to take great care of it, and she went back to the farm.

But now in her heart, which had been wounded so long, there arose something like brightness, an unknown love for that frail little creature which she had left behind her, though there was fresh suffering in that very love, suffering which she felt every hour and every minute, because she was parted from her child. What pained her most, however, was the mad longing to kiss it, to press it in her arms, to feel the warmth of its little body against her breast. She could not sleep at night; she thought of it the whole day long, and in the evening, when her work was done, she would sit in front of the fire and gaze at it intently, as people do whose thoughts are far away.

They began to talk about her and to tease her about her lover. They asked her whether he was tall, handsome and rich. When was the wedding to be and the christening? And often she ran away to cry by herself, for these questions seemed to hurt her like the prick of a pin; and, in order to forget their jokes, she began to work still more energetically, and, still thinking of her child, she sought some way of saving up money for it, and determined to work so that her master would be obliged to raise her wages.

By degrees she almost monopolized the work and persuaded him to get rid of one servant girl, who had become useless since she had taken to working like two; she economized in the bread, oil and candles; in the corn, which they gave to the chickens too extravagantly, and in the fodder for the horses and cattle, which was rather wasted. She was as miserly about her master's money as if it had been her own; and, by dint of making good bargains, of getting high prices for all their produce, and by baffling the peasants' tricks when they offered anything for sale, he, at last, entrusted her with buying and selling everything, with the direction of all the laborers, and with the purchase of provisions necessary for the household; so that, in a short time, she became. indispensable to him. She kept such a strict eye on everything about her that, under her direction, the farm prospered wonderfully, and for five miles around people talked of "Master Vallin's servant," and the farmer himself said everywhere: "That girl is worth more than her weight in gold."

But time passed by, and her wages remained the same. Her hard work was accepted as something that was due from every good servant, and as a mere token of good will; and she began to think rather bitterly that if the farmer could put fifty or a hundred crowns extra into the bank every month, thanks to her, she was still only earning her two hundred francs a year, neither more nor less; and so she made up her mind to ask for an increase of wages. She went to see the schoolmaster three times about it, but when she got there, she spoke about something else. She felt a kind of modesty in asking for money, as if it were something disgraceful; but, at last, one day, when the farmer was having breakfast by himself in the kitchen, she said to him, with some embarrassment, that she wished to speak to him particularly. He raised his head in surprise, with both his hands on the table, holding his knife, with its point in the air, in one, and a piece of bread in the other, and he looked fixedly at, the girl, who felt uncomfortable under his gaze, but asked for a week's holiday, so that she might get away, as she was not very well. He acceded to her request immediately, and then added, in some embarrassment himself:

"When you come back, I shall have something to say to you myself."

PART III

The child was nearly eight months old, and she did not recognize it. It had grown rosy and chubby all over, like a little roll of fat. She threw herself on it, as if it had been some prey, and kissed it so violently that it began to scream with terror; and then she began to cry herself, because it did not know her, and stretched out its arms to its nurse as soon as it saw her. But the next day it began to know her, and laughed when it saw her, and she took it into the fields, and ran about excitedly with it, and sat down under the shade of the trees; and then, for the first time in her life, she opened her heart to somebody, although he could not understand her, and told him her troubles; how hard her work was, her anxieties and her hopes, and she quite tired the child with the violence of her caresses.

She took the greatest pleasure in handling it, in washing and dressing it, for it seemed to her that all this was the confirmation of her maternity; and she would look at it, almost feeling surprised 'that it was hers, and would say to herself in a low voice as she danced it in her arms: "It is my baby, it's my baby."

She cried all the way home as she returned to the farm and had scarcely got in before her master called her into his room; and she went, feeling astonished and nervous, without knowing why.

"Sit down there," he said. She sat down, and for some moments they remained side by side, in some embarrassment, with their arms hanging at their sides, as if they did not know what to do with them, and looking each other in the face, after the manner of peasants.

The farmer, a stout, jovial, obstinate man of forty-five, who had lost two wives, evidently felt embarrassed, which was very unusual with him; but, at last, he made up his mind, and began to speak vaguely, hesitating a little, and looking out of the window as he talked. "How is it, Rose," he said, "that you have never thought of settling in life?" She grew as pale as death, and, seeing that she gave him no answer, he went on: "You are a good, steady, active and economical girl; and a wife like you would make a man's fortune."

She did not move, but looked frightened; she did not even try to comprehend his meaning, for her thoughts were in a whirl, as if at the approach of some great danger; so, after waiting for a few seconds, he went on: "You see, a farm without a mistress can never succeed, even with a servant like you." Then he stopped, for he did not know what else to say, and Rose looked at him with the air of a person who thinks that he is face to face with a murderer and ready to flee at the slightest movement he may make; but, after waiting for about five minutes, he asked her: "Well, will it suit you?" "Will what suit me, master?" And he said quickly: "Why, to marry me, by Heaven!"

She jumped up, but fell back on her chair, as if she had been struck, and there she remained motionless, like a person who is overwhelmed by some great misfortune. At last the farmer grew impatient and said: "Come, what more do you want?" She looked at him, almost in terror, then suddenly the tears came into her eyes and she said twice in a choking voice: "I cannot, I cannot!" "Why not?" he asked. "Come, don't be silly; I will give you until tomorrow to think it over."

And he hurried out of the room, very glad to have got through with the matter, which had troubled him a good deal, for he had no doubt that she would the next morning accept a proposal which she could never have expected and which would be a capital bargain for him, as he thus bound a woman to his interests who would certainly bring him more than if she had the best dowry in the district.

Neither could there be any scruples about an unequal match between them, for in the country every one is very nearly equal; the farmer works with his laborers, who frequently become masters in their turn, and the female servants constantly become the mistresses of the establishments without its making any change in their life or habits.

Rose did not go to bed that night. She threw herself, dressed as she was, on her bed, and she had not even the strength to cry left in her, she was so thoroughly dumfounded. She remained quite inert, scarcely knowing that she had a body, and without being at all able to collect her thoughts, though, at moments, she remembered something of what had happened, and then she was frightened at the idea of what might happen. Her terror increased, and every time the great kitchen clock struck the hour she broke out in a perspiration from grief. She became bewildered, and had the nightmare; her candle went out, and then she began to imagine that some one had cast a spell over her, as country people so often imagine, and she felt a mad inclination to run away, to escape and to flee before her misfortune, like a ship scudding before the wind. An owl hooted; she shivered, sat up, passed her hands over her face, her hair, and all over her body, and then she went downstairs, as if she were walking in her sleep. When she got into the yard she stooped down, so as not to be seen by any prowling scamp, for the moon, which was setting, shed a bright light over the fields. Instead of opening the gate she scrambled over the fence, and as soon as she was outside she started off. She went on straight before her, with a quick, springy trot, and from time to time she unconsciously uttered a piercing cry. Her long shadow accompanied her, and now and then some night bird flew over her head, while the dogs in the farmyards barked as they heard her pass; one even jumped over the ditch, and followed her and tried to bite her, but she turned round and gave such a terrible yell that the frightened animal ran back and cowered in silence in its kennel.

The stars grew dim, and the birds began to twitter; day was breaking. The girl was worn out and panting; and when the sun rose in the purple sky, she stopped, for her swollen feet refused to go any farther; but she saw a pond in the distance, a large pond whose stagnant water looked like blood under the reflection of this new day, and she limped on slowly with her hand on her heart, in order to dip both her feet in it. She sat down on a tuft of grass, took off her heavy shoes, which were full of dust, pulled off her stockings and plunged her legs into the still water, from which bubbles were rising here and there.

A feeling of delicious coolness pervaded her from head to foot, and suddenly, while she was looking fixedly at the deep pool, she was seized with dizziness, and with a mad longing to throw herself into it. All her sufferings would be over in there, over forever. She no longer thought of her child; she only wanted peace, complete rest, and to sleep forever, and she got up with raised arms and took two steps forward. She was in the water up to her thighs, and she was just about to throw her self in when sharp, pricking pains in her ankles made her jump back, and she uttered a cry of despair, for, from her knees to the tips of her feet, long black leeches were sucking her lifeblood, and were swelling as they adhered to her flesh. She did not dare to touch them, and screamed with horror, so that her cries of despair attracted a peasant, who was driving along at some distance, to the spot. He pulled off the leeches one by one, applied herbs to the wounds, and drove the girl to her master's farm in his gig.

She was in bed for a fortnight, and as she was sitting outside the door on the first morning that she got up, the farmer suddenly came and planted himself before her. "Well," he said, "I suppose the affair is settled isn't it?" She did not reply at first, and then, as he remained standing and looking at her intently with his piercing eyes, she said with difficulty: "No, master, I cannot." He immediately flew into a rage.

"You cannot, girl; you cannot? I should just like to know the reason why?" She began to cry, and repeated: "I cannot." He looked at her, and then exclaimed angrily: "Then I suppose you have a lover?" "Perhaps that is it," she replied, trembling with shame.

The man got as red as a poppy, and stammered out in a rage: "Ah! So you confess it, you slut! And pray who is the fellow? Some penniless, half-starved ragamuffin, without a roof to his head, I suppose? Who is it, I say?" And as she gave him no answer, he continued: "Ah! So you will not tell me. Then I will tell you; it is Jean Baudu?"—"No, not he," she exclaimed. "Then it is Pierre Martin?"—"Oh! no, master."

And he angrily mentioned all the young fellows in the neighborhood, while she denied that he had hit upon the right one, and every moment wiped her eyes with the corner of her blue apron. But he still tried to find it out, with his brutish obstinacy, and, as it were, scratching at her heart to discover her secret, just as a terrier scratches at a hole to try and get at the animal which he scents inside it. Suddenly, however, the man shouted: "By George! It is Jacques, the man who was here last year. They used to say that you were always talking together, and that you thought about getting married."

Rose was choking, and she grew scarlet, while her tears suddenly stopped and dried up on her cheeks, like drops of water on hot iron, and she exclaimed: "No, it is not he, it is not he!" "Is that really a fact?" asked the cunning peasant, who partly guessed the truth; and she replied, hastily: "I will swear it; I will swear it to you—" She tried to think of something by which to swear, as she did not venture to invoke sacred things, but he interrupted her: "At any rate, he used to follow you into every corner and devoured you with his eyes at meal times. Did you ever give him your promise, eh?"

This time she looked her master straight in the face. "No, never, never; I will solemnly swear to you that if he were to come to-day and ask me to marry him I would have nothing to do with him." She spoke with such an air of sincerity that the farmer hesitated, and then he continued, as if speaking to himself: "What, then? You have not had a misfortune, as they call it, or it would have been known, and as it has no consequences, no girl would refuse her master on that account. There must be something at the bottom of it, however."

She could say nothing; she had not the strength to speak, and he asked her again: "You will not?" "I cannot, master," she said, with a sigh, and he turned on his heel.

She thought she had got rid of him altogether and spent the rest of the day almost tranquilly, but was as exhausted as if she had been turning the thrashing machine all day in the place of the old white horse, and she went to bed as soon as she could and fell asleep immediately. In the middle of the night, however, two hands touching the bed woke her. She trembled with fear, but immediately recognized the farmer's voice, when he said to her: "Don't be frightened, Rose; I have come to speak to you." She was surprised at first, but when he tried to take liberties with her she understood and began to tremble violently, as she felt quite alone in the darkness, still heavy from sleep, and quite unprotected, with that man standing near her. She certainly did not consent, but she resisted carelessly struggling against that instinct which is always strong in simple natures and very imperfectly protected by the undecided will of inert and gentle races. She turned her head now to the wall, and now toward the room, in order to avoid the attentions which the farmer tried to press on her, but she was weakened by fatigue, while he became brutal, intoxicated by desire.

They lived together as man and wife, and one morning he said to her: "I have put up our banns, and we will get married next month."

She did not reply, for what could she say? She did not resist, for what could she do?

PART IV

She married him. She felt as if she were in a pit with inaccessible sides from which she could never get out, and all kinds of misfortunes were hanging over her head, like huge rocks, which would fall on the first occasion. Her husband gave her the impression of a man whom she had robbed, and who would find it out some day or other. And then she thought of her child, who was the cause of her misfortunes, but who was also the cause of all her happiness on earth, and whom she went to see twice a year, though she came back more unhappy each time.

But she gradually grew accustomed to her life, her fears were allayed, her heart was at rest, and she lived with an easier mind, though still with some vague fear floating in it. And so years went on, until the child was six. She was almost happy now, when suddenly the farmer's temper grew very bad.

For two or three years he seemed to have been nursing some secret anxiety, to be troubled by some care, some mental disturbance, which was gradually increasing. He remained sitting at table after dinner, with his head in his hands, sad and devoured by sorrow. He always spoke hastily, sometimes even brutally, and it even seemed as if he had a grudge against his wife, for at times he answered her roughly, almost angrily.

One day, when a neighbor's boy came for some eggs, and she spoke rather crossly to him, as she was very busy, her husband suddenly came in and said to her in his unpleasant voice: "If that were your own child you would not treat him so." She was hurt and did not reply, and then she went back into the house, with all her grief awakened afresh; and at dinner the farmer neither spoke to her nor looked at her, and he seemed to hate her, to despise her, to know something about the affair at last. In consequence she lost her composure, and did not venture to remain alone with him after the meal was over, but left the room and hastened to the church.

It was getting dusk; the narrow nave was in total darkness, but she heard footsteps in the choir, for the sacristan was preparing the tabernacle lamp for the night. That spot of trembling light, which was lost in the darkness of the arches, looked to Rose like her last hope, and with her eyes fixed on it, she fell on her knees. The chain rattled as the little lamp swung up into the air, and almost immediately the small bell rang out the Angelus through the increasing mist. She went up to him, as he was going out.

"Is Monsieur le Cure at home?" she asked. "Of course he is; this is his dinnertime." She trembled as she rang the bell of the parsonage. The priest was just sitting down to dinner, and he made her sit down also. "Yes, yes, I know all about it; your husband has mentioned the matter to me that brings you here." The poor woman nearly fainted, and the priest continued: "What do you want, my child?" And he hastily swallowed several spoonfuls of soup, some of which dropped on to his greasy cassock. But Rose did not venture to say anything more, and she got up to go, but the priest said: "Courage."

And she went out and returned to the farm without knowing what she was doing. The farmer was waiting for her, as the laborers had gone away during her absence, and she fell heavily at his feet, and, shedding a flood of tears, she said to him: "What have you got against me?"

He began to shout and to swear: "What have I got against you? That I have no children, by—. When a man takes a wife it is not that they may live alone together to the end of their days. That is what I have against you. When a cow has no calves she is not worth anything, and when a woman has no children she is also not worth anything."

She began to cry, and said: "It is not my fault! It is not my fault!" He grew rather more gentle when he heard that, and added: "I do not say that it is, but it is very provoking, all the same."

PART V

From that day forward she had only one thought: to have a child another child; she confided her wish to everybody, and, in consequence of this, a neighbor told her of an infallible method. This was, to make her husband drink a glass of water with a pinch of ashes in it every evening. The farmer consented to try it, but without success; so they said to each other: "Perhaps there are some secret ways?" And they tried to find out. They were told of a shepherd who lived ten leagues off, and so Vallin one day drove off to consult him. The shepherd gave him a loaf on which he had made some marks; it was kneaded up with herbs, and each of them was to eat a piece of it, but they ate the whole loaf without obtaining any results from it.

Next, a schoolmaster unveiled mysteries and processes of love which were unknown in the country, but infallible, so he declared; but none of them had the desired effect. Then the priest advised them to make a pilgrimage to the shrine at Fecamp. Rose went with the crowd and prostrated herself in the abbey, and, mingling her prayers with the coarse desires of the peasants around her, she prayed that she might be fruitful a second time; but it was in vain, and then she thought that she was being punished for her first fault, and she was seized by terrible grief. She was wasting away with sorrow; her husband was also aging prematurely, and was wearing himself out in useless hopes.

Then war broke out between them; he called her names and beat her. They quarrelled all day long, and when they were in their room together at night he flung insults and obscenities at her, choking with rage, until one night, not being able to think of any means of making her suffer more he ordered her to get up and go and stand out of doors in the rain until daylight. As she did not obey him, he seized her by the neck and began to strike her in the face with his fists, but she said nothing and did not move. In his exasperation he knelt on her stomach, and with clenched teeth, and mad with rage, he began to beat her. Then in her despair she rebelled, and flinging him against the wall with a furious gesture, she sat up, and in an altered voice she hissed: "I have had a child, I have had one! I had it by Jacques; you know Jacques. He promised to marry me, but he left this neighborhood without keeping his word."

The man was thunderstruck and could hardly speak, but at last he stammered out: "What are you saying? What are you saying?" Then she began to sob, and amid her tears she continued: "That was the reason why I did not want to marry you. I could not tell you, for you would have left me without any bread for my child. You have never had any children, so you cannot understand, you cannot understand!"

He said again, mechanically, with increasing surprise: "You have a child? You have a child?"

"You took me by force, as I suppose you know? I did not want to marry you," she said, still sobbing.

Then he got up, lit the candle, and began to walk up and down, with his arms behind him. She was cowering on the bed and crying, and suddenly he stopped in front of her, and said: "Then it is my fault that you have no children?" She gave him no answer, and he began to walk up and down again, and then, stopping again, he continued: "How old is your child?" "Just six," she whispered. "Why did you not tell me about it?" he asked. "How could I?" she replied, with a sigh.

He remained standing, motionless. "Come, get up," he said. She got up with some difficulty, and then, when she was standing on the floor, he suddenly began to laugh with the hearty laugh of his good days, and, seeing how surprised she was, he added: "Very well, we will go and fetch the child, as you and I can have none together."

She was so scared that if she had had the strength she would assuredly have run away, but the farmer rubbed his hands and said: "I wanted to adopt one, and now we have found one. I asked the cure about an orphan some time ago."

Then, still laughing, he kissed his weeping and agitated wife on both cheeks, and shouted out, as though she could not hear him: "Come along, mother, we will go and see whether there is any soup left; I should not mind a plateful."

She put on her petticoat and they went downstairs; and while she was kneeling in front of the fireplace and lighting the fire under the saucepan, he continued to walk up and down the kitchen with long strides, repeating:

"Well, I am really glad of this; I am not saying it for form's sake, but I am glad, I am really very glad."

THE WRECK

It was yesterday, the 31st of December.

I had just finished breakfast with my old friend Georges Garin when the servant handed him a letter covered with seals and foreign stamps.

Georges said:

"Will you excuse me?"

"Certainly."

And so he began to read the letter, which was written in a large English handwriting, crossed and recrossed in every direction. He read them slowly, with serious attention and the interest which we only pay to things which touch our hearts.

Then he put the letter on the mantelpiece and said:

"That was a curious story! I've never told you about it, I think. Yet it was a sentimental adventure, and it really happened to me. That was a strange New Year's Day, indeed! It must have been twenty years ago, for I was then thirty and am now fifty years old.

"I was then an inspector in the Maritime Insurance Company, of which I am now director. I had arranged to pass New Year's Day in Paris—since it is customary to make that day a fete—when I received a letter from the manager, asking me to proceed at once to the island of Re, where a three-masted vessel from Saint-Nazaire, insured by us, had just been driven ashore. It was then eight o'clock in the morning. I arrived at the office at ten to get my advices, and that evening I took the express, which put me down in La Rochelle the next day, the 31st of December.

"I had two hours to wait before going aboard the boat for Re. So I made a tour of the town. It is certainly a queer city, La Rochelle, with strong characteristics of its own streets tangled like a labyrinth, sidewalks running under endless arcaded galleries like those of the Rue de Rivoli, but low, mysterious, built as if to form a suitable setting for conspirators and making a striking background for those old-time wars, the savage heroic wars of religion. It is indeed the typical old Huguenot city, conservative, discreet, with no fine art to show, with no wonderful monuments, such as make Rouen; but it is remarkable for its severe, somewhat sullen look; it is a city of obstinate fighters, a city where fanaticism might well blossom, where the faith of the Calvinists became enthusiastic and which gave birth to the plot of the 'Four Sergeants.'

"After I had wandered for some time about these curious streets, I went aboard the black, rotund little steamboat which was to take me to the island of Re. It was called the Jean Guiton. It started with angry puffings, passed between the two old towers which guard the harbor, crossed the roadstead and issued from the mole built by Richelieu, the great stones of which can be seen at the water's edge, enclosing the town like a great necklace. Then the steamboat turned to the right.

"It was one of those sad days which give one the blues, tighten the heart and take away all strength and energy and force-a gray, cold day, with a heavy mist which was as wet as rain, as cold as frost, as bad to breathe as the steam of a wash-tub.

"Under this low sky of dismal fog the shallow, yellow, sandy sea of all practically level beaches lay without a wrinkle, without a movement, without life, a sea of turbid water, of greasy water, of stagnant water. The Jean Guiton passed over it, rolling a little from habit, dividing the smooth, dark blue water and leaving behind a few waves, a little splashing, a slight swell, which soon calmed down.

"I began to talk to the captain, a little man with small feet, as round as his boat and rolling in the same manner. I wanted some details of the disaster on which I was to draw up a report. A great square-rigged three-master, the Marie Joseph, of Saint-Nazaire, had gone ashore one night in a hurricane on the sands of the island of Re.

"The owner wrote us that the storm had thrown the ship so far ashore that it was impossible to float her and that they had to remove everything which could be detached with the utmost possible haste. Nevertheless I must examine the situation of the wreck, estimate what must have been her condition before the disaster and decide whether all efforts had been used to get her afloat. I came as an agent of the company in order to give contradictory testimony, if necessary, at the trial.

"On receipt of my report, the manager would take what measures he might think necessary to protect our interests.

"The captain of the Jean Guiton knew all about the affair, having been summoned with his boat to assist in the attempts at salvage.

"He told me the story of the disaster. The Marie Joseph, driven by a furious gale lost her bearings completely in the night, and steering by chance over a heavy foaming sea—'a milk-soup sea,' said the captain—had gone ashore on those immense sand banks which make the coasts of this country look like limitless Saharas when the tide is low.

"While talking I looked around and ahead. Between the ocean and the lowering sky lay an open space where the eye could see into the distance. We were following a coast. I asked:

"'Is that the island of Re?'

"'Yes, sir.'

"And suddenly the captain stretched his right hand out before us, pointed to something almost imperceptible in the open sea, and said:

"'There's your ship!'

"'The Marie Joseph!'

"'Yes.'

"I was amazed. This black, almost imperceptible speck, which looked to me like a rock, seemed at least three miles from land.

"I continued:

"'But, captain, there must be a hundred fathoms of water in that place.'

"He began to laugh.

"'A hundred fathoms, my child! Well, I should say about two!'

"He was from Bordeaux. He continued:

"'It's now nine-forty, just high tide. Go down along the beach with your hands in your pockets after you've had lunch at the Hotel du Dauphin, and I'll wager that at ten minutes to three, or three o'clock, you'll reach the wreck without wetting your feet, and have from an hour and three-quarters to two hours aboard of her; but not more, or you'll be caught. The faster the sea goes out the faster it comes back. This coast is as flat as a turtle! But start away at ten minutes to five, as I tell you, and at half-past seven you will be again aboard of the Jean Guiton, which will put you down this same evening on the quay at La Rochelle.'

"I thanked the captain and I went and sat down in the bow of the steamer to get a good look at the little city of Saint-Martin, which we were now rapidly approaching.

"It was just like all small seaports which serve as capitals of the barren islands scattered along the coast—a large fishing village, one foot on sea and one on shore, subsisting on fish and wild fowl, vegetables and shell-fish, radishes and mussels. The island is very low and little cultivated, yet it seems to be thickly populated. However, I did not penetrate into the interior.

"After breakfast I climbed across a little promontory, and then, as the tide was rapidly falling, I started out across the sands toward a kind of black rock which I could just perceive above the surface of the water, out a considerable distance.

"I walked quickly over the yellow plain. It was elastic, like flesh and seemed to sweat beneath my tread. The sea had been there very lately. Now I perceived it at a distance, escaping out of sight, and I no longer could distinguish the line which separated the sands from ocean. I felt as though I were looking at a gigantic supernatural work of enchantment. The Atlantic had just now been before me, then it had disappeared into the sands, just as scenery disappears through a trap; and I was now walking in the midst of a desert. Only the feeling, the breath of the salt-water, remained in me. I perceived the smell of the wrack, the smell of the sea, the good strong smell of sea coasts. I walked fast; I was no longer cold. I looked at the stranded wreck, which grew in size as I approached, and came now to resemble an enormous shipwrecked whale.

"It seemed fairly to rise out of the ground, and on that great, flat, yellow stretch of sand assumed wonderful proportions. After an hour's walk I at last reached it. It lay upon its side, ruined and shattered, its broken bones showing as though it were an animal, its bones of tarred wood pierced with great bolts. The sand had already invaded it, entering it by all the crannies, and held it and refused to let it go. It seemed to have taken root in it. The bow had entered deep into this soft, treacherous beach, while the stern, high in air, seemed to cast at heaven, like a cry of despairing appeal, the two white words on the black planking, Marie Joseph.

"I climbed upon this carcass of a ship by the lowest side; then, having reached the deck, I went below. The daylight, which entered by the stove-in hatches and the cracks in the sides, showed me dimly long dark cavities full of demolished woodwork. They contained nothing but sand, which served as foot-soil in this cavern of planks.

"I began to take some notes about the condition of the ship. I was seated on a broken empty cask, writing by the light of a great crack, through which I could perceive the boundless stretch of the strand. A strange shivering of cold and loneliness ran over my skin from time to time, and I would often stop writing for a moment to listen to the mysterious noises in the derelict: the noise of crabs scratching the planking with their crooked claws; the noise of a thousand little creatures of the sea already crawling over this dead body or else boring into the wood.

"Suddenly, very near me, I heard human voices. I started as though I had seen a ghost. For a second I really thought I was about to see drowned men rise from the sinister depths of the hold, who would tell me about their death. At any rate, it did not take me long to swing myself on deck. There, standing by the bows, was a tall Englishman with three young misses. Certainly they were a good deal more frightened at seeing this sudden apparition on the abandoned three-master than I was at seeing them. The youngest girl turned and ran, the two others threw their arms round their father. As for him, he opened his mouth—that was the only sign of emotion which he showed.

"Then, after several seconds, he spoke:

"'Mosieu, are you the owner of this ship?'

"'I am.'

"'May I go over it?'

"'You may.'

"Then he uttered a long sentence in English, in which I only distinguished the word 'gracious,' repeated several times.

"As he was looking for a place to climb up I showed him the easiest way, and gave him a hand. He climbed up. Then we helped up the three girls, who had now quite recovered their composure. They were charming, especially the oldest, a blonde of eighteen, fresh as a flower, and very dainty and pretty! Ah, yes! the pretty Englishwomen have indeed the look of tender sea fruit. One would have said of this one that she had just risen out of the sands and that her hair had kept their tint. They all, with their exquisite freshness, make you think of the delicate colors of pink sea-shells and of shining pearls hidden in the unknown depths of the ocean.

"She spoke French a little better than her father and acted as interpreter. I had to tell all about the shipwreck, and I romanced as though I had been present at the catastrophe. Then the whole family descended into the interior of the wreck. As soon as they had penetrated into this sombre, dimly lit cavity they uttered cries of astonishment and admiration. Suddenly the father and his three daughters were holding sketch-books in their hands, which they had doubtless carried hidden somewhere in their heavy weather-proof clothes, and were all beginning at once to make pencil sketches of this melancholy and weird place.

"They had seated themselves side by side on a projecting beam, and the four sketch-books on the eight knees were being rapidly covered with little black lines which were intended to represent the half-opened hulk of the Marie Joseph.

"I continued to inspect the skeleton of the ship, and the oldest girl talked to me while she worked.

"They had none of the usual English arrogance; they were simple honest hearts of that class of continuous travellers with which England covers the globe. The father was long and thin, with a red face framed in white whiskers, and looking like a living sandwich, a piece of ham carved like a face between two wads of hair. The daughters, who had long legs like young storks, were also thin-except the oldest. All three were pretty, especially the tallest.

"She had such a droll way of speaking, of laughing, of understanding and of not understanding, of raising her eyes to ask a question (eyes blue as the deep ocean), of stopping her drawing a moment to make a guess at what you meant, of returning once more to work, of saying 'yes' or 'no'—that I could have listened and looked indefinitely.

"Suddenly she murmured:

"'I hear a little sound on this boat.'

"I listened and I immediately distinguished a low, steady, curious sound. I rose and looked out of the crack and gave a scream. The sea had come up to us; it would soon surround us!

"We were on deck in an instant. It was too late. The water circled us about and was running toward the coast at tremendous speed. No, it did not run, it glided, crept, spread like an immense, limitless blot. The water was barely a few centimeters deep, but the rising flood had gone so far that we no longer saw the vanishing line of the imperceptible tide.

"The Englishman wanted to jump. I held him back. Flight was impossible because of the deep places which we had been obliged to go round on our way out and into which we should fall on our return.

"There was a minute of horrible anguish in our hearts. Then the little English girl began to smile and murmured:

"'It is we who are shipwrecked.'

"I tried to laugh, but fear held me, a fear which was cowardly and horrid and base and treacherous like the tide. All the danger which we ran appeared to me at once. I wanted to shriek: 'Help!' But to whom?

"The two younger girls were clinging to their father, who looked in consternation at the measureless sea which hedged us round about.

"The night fell as swiftly as the ocean rose—a lowering, wet, icy night.

"I said:

"'There's nothing to do but to stay on the ship:

"The Englishman answered:

"'Oh, yes!'

"And we waited there a quarter of an hour, half an hour, indeed I don't know how long, watching that creeping water growing deeper as it swirled around us, as though it were playing on the beach, which it had regained.

"One of the young girls was cold, and we went below to shelter ourselves from the light but freezing wind that made our skins tingle.

"I leaned over the hatchway. The ship was full of water. So we had to cower against the stern planking, which shielded us a little.

"Darkness was now coming on, and we remained huddled together. I felt the shoulder of the little English girl trembling against mine, her teeth chattering from time to time. But I also felt the gentle warmth of her body through her ulster, and that warmth was as delicious to me as a kiss. We no longer spoke; we sat motionless, mute, cowering down like animals in a ditch when a hurricane is raging. And, nevertheless, despite the night, despite the terrible and increasing danger, I began to feel happy that I was there, glad of the cold and the peril, glad of the long hours of darkness and anguish that I must pass on this plank so near this dainty, pretty little girl.

"I asked myself, 'Why this strange sensation of well-being and of joy?'

"Why! Does one know? Because she was there? Who? She, a little unknown English girl? I did not love her, I did not even know her. And for all that, I was touched and conquered. I wanted to save her, to sacrifice myself for her, to commit a thousand follies! Strange thing! How does it happen that the presence of a woman overwhelms us so? Is it the power of her grace which enfolds us? Is it the seduction of her beauty and youth, which intoxicates one like wine?

"Is it not rather the touch of Love, of Love the Mysterious, who seeks constantly to unite two beings, who tries his strength the instant he has put a man and a woman face to face?

"The silence of the darkness became terrible, the stillness of the sky dreadful, because we could hear vaguely about us a slight, continuous sound, the sound of the rising tide and the monotonous plashing of the water against the ship.

"Suddenly I heard the sound of sobs. The youngest of the girls was crying. Her father tried to console her, and they began to talk in their own tongue, which I did not understand. I guessed that he was reassuring her and that she was still afraid.

"I asked my neighbor:

"'You are not too cold, are you, mademoiselle?'

"'Oh, yes. I am very cold.'

"I offered to give her my cloak; she refused it.

"But I had taken it off and I covered her with it against her will. In the short struggle her hand touched mine. It made a delicious thrill run through my body.

"For some minutes the air had been growing brisker, the dashing of the water stronger against the flanks of the ship. I raised myself; a great gust of wind blew in my face. The wind was rising!

"The Englishman perceived this at the same time that I did and said simply:

"'This is bad for us, this——'

"Of course it was bad, it was certain death if any breakers, however feeble, should attack and shake the wreck, which was already so shattered and disconnected that the first big sea would carry it off.

"So our anguish increased momentarily as the squalls grew stronger and stronger. Now the sea broke a little, and I saw in the darkness white lines appearing and disappearing, lines of foam, while each wave struck the Marie Joseph and shook her with a short quiver which went to our hearts.

"The English girl was trembling. I felt her shiver against me. And I had a wild desire to take her in my arms.

"Down there, before and behind us, to the left and right, lighthouses were shining along the shore—lighthouses white, yellow and red, revolving like the enormous eyes of giants who were watching us, waiting eagerly for us to disappear. One of them in especial irritated me. It went out every thirty seconds and it lit up again immediately. It was indeed an eye, that one, with its lid incessantly lowered over its fiery glance.

"From time to time the Englishman struck a match to see the hour; then he put his watch back in his pocket. Suddenly he said to me, over the heads of his daughters, with tremendous gravity:

"'I wish you a happy New Year, Mosieu.'

"It was midnight. I held out my hand, which he pressed. Then he said something in English, and suddenly he and his daughters began to sing 'God Save the Queen,' which rose through the black and silent air and vanished into space.

"At first I felt a desire to laugh; then I was seized by a powerful, strange emotion.

"It was something sinister and superb, this chant of the shipwrecked, the condemned, something like a prayer and also like something grander, something comparable to the ancient 'Ave Caesar morituri te salutant.'

"When they had finished I asked my neighbor to sing a ballad alone, anything she liked, to make us forget our terrors. She consented, and immediately her clear young voice rang out into the night. She sang something which was doubtless sad, because the notes were long drawn out and hovered, like wounded birds, above the waves.

"The sea was rising now and beating upon our wreck. As for me, I thought only of that voice. And I thought also of the sirens. If a ship had passed near by us what would the sailors have said? My troubled spirit lost itself in the dream! A siren! Was she not really a siren, this daughter of the sea, who had kept me on this worm-eaten ship and who was soon about to go down with me deep into the waters?

"But suddenly we were all five rolling on the deck, because the Marie Joseph had sunk on her right side. The English girl had fallen upon me, and before I knew what I was doing, thinking that my last moment was come, I had caught her in my arms and kissed her cheek, her temple and her hair.

"The ship did not move again, and we, we also, remained motionless.

"The father said, 'Kate!' The one whom I was holding answered 'Yes' and made a movement to free herself. And at that moment I should have wished the ship to split in two and let me fall with her into the sea.

"The Englishman continued:

"'A little rocking; it's nothing. I have my three daughters safe.'

"Not having seen the oldest, he had thought she was lost overboard!

"I rose slowly, and suddenly I made out a light on the sea quite close to us. I shouted; they answered. It was a boat sent out in search of us by the hotelkeeper, who had guessed at our imprudence.

"We were saved. I was in despair. They picked us up off our raft and they brought us back to Saint-Martin.

"The Englishman began to rub his hand and murmur:

"'A good supper! A good supper!'

"We did sup. I was not gay. I regretted the Marie Joseph.

"We had to separate the next day after much handshaking and many promises to write. They departed for Biarritz. I wanted to follow them.

"I was hard hit. I wanted to ask this little girl to marry me. If we had passed eight days together, I should have done so! How weak and incomprehensible a man sometimes is!

"Two years passed without my hearing a word from them. Then I received a letter from New York. She was married and wrote to tell me. And since then we write to each other every year, on New Year's Day. She tells me about her life, talks of her children, her sisters, never of her husband! Why? Ah! why? And as for me, I only talk of the Marie Joseph. That was perhaps the only woman I have ever loved—no—that I ever should have loved. Ah, well! who can tell? Circumstances rule one. And then—and then—all passes. She must be old now; I should not know her. Ah! she of the bygone time, she of the wreck! What a creature! Divine! She writes me her hair is white. That caused me terrible pain. Ah! her yellow hair. No, my English girl exists no longer. How sad it all is!"

THEODULE SABOT'S CONFESSION

When Sabot entered the inn at Martinville it was a signal for laughter. What a rogue he was, this Sabot! There was a man who did not like priests, for instance! Oh, no, oh, no! He did not spare them, the scamp.

Sabot (Theodule), a master carpenter, represented liberal thought in Martinville. He was a tall, thin man, with gray, cunning eyes, and thin lips, and wore his hair plastered down on his temples. When he said: "Our holy father, the pope" in a certain manner, everyone laughed. He made a point of working on Sunday during the hour of mass. He killed his pig each year on Monday in Holy Week in order to have enough black pudding to last till Easter, and when the priest passed by, he always said by way of a joke: "There goes one who has just swallowed his God off a salver."

The priest, a stout man and also very tall, dreaded him on account of his boastful talk which attracted followers. The Abbe Maritime was a politic man, and believed in being diplomatic. There had been a rivalry between them for ten years, a secret, intense, incessant rivalry. Sabot was municipal councillor, and they thought he would become mayor, which would inevitably mean the final overthrow of the church.

The elections were about to take place. The church party was shaking in its shoes in Martinville.

One morning the cure set out for Rouen, telling his servant that he was going to see the archbishop. He returned in two days with a joyous, triumphant air. And everyone knew the following day that the chancel of the church was going to be renovated. A sum of six hundred francs had been contributed by the archbishop out of his private fund. All the old pine pews were to be removed, and replaced by new pews made of oak. It would be a big carpentering job, and they talked about it that very evening in all the houses in the village.

Theodule Sabot was not laughing.

When he went through the village the following morning, the neighbors, friends and enemies, all asked him, jokingly:

"Are you going to do the work on the chancel of the church?"

He could find nothing to say, but he was furious, he was good and angry.

Ill-natured people added:

"It is a good piece of work; and will bring in not less than two or three per cent. profit."

Two days later, they heard that the work of renovation had been entrusted to Celestin Chambrelan, the carpenter from Percheville. Then this was denied, and it was said that all the pews in the church were going to be changed. That would be well worth the two thousand francs that had been demanded of the church administration.

Theodule Sabot could not sleep for thinking about it. Never, in all the memory of man, had a country carpenter undertaken a similar piece of work. Then a rumor spread abroad that the cure felt very grieved that he had to give this work to a carpenter who was a stranger in the community, but that Sabot's opinions were a barrier to his being entrusted with the job.

Sabot knew it well. He called at the parsonage just as it was growing dark. The servant told him that the cure was at church. He went to the church.

Two attendants on the altar of the Virgin, two sour old maids, were decorating the altar for the month of Mary, under the direction of the priest, who stood in the middle of the chancel with his portly paunch, directing the two women who, mounted on chairs, were placing flowers around the tabernacle.

Sabot felt ill at ease in there, as though he were in the house of his greatest enemy, but the greed of gain was gnawing at his heart. He drew nearer, holding his cap in his hand, and not paying any attention to the "demoiselles de la Vierge," who remained standing startled, astonished, motionless on their chairs.

He faltered:

"Good morning, monsieur le cure."

The priest replied without looking at him, all occupied as he was with the altar:

"Good morning, Mr. Carpenter."

Sabot, nonplussed, knew not what to say next. But after a pause he remarked:

"You are making preparations?"

Abbe Maritime replied:

"Yes, we are near the month of Mary."

"Why, why," remarked Sabot and then was silent. He would have liked to retire now without saying anything, but a glance at the chancel held him back. He saw sixteen seats that had to be remade, six to the right and eight to the left, the door of the sacristy occupying the place of two. Sixteen oak seats, that would be worth at most three hundred francs, and by figuring carefully one might certainly make two hundred francs on the work if one were not clumsy.

Then he stammered out:

"I have come about the work."

The cure appeared surprised. He asked:

"What work?"

"The work to be done," murmured Sabot, in dismay.

Then the priest turned round and looking him straight in the eyes, said:

"Do you mean the repairs in the chancel of my church?"

At the tone of the abbe, Theodule Sabot felt a chill run down his back and he once more had a longing to take to his heels. However, he replied humbly:

"Why, yes, monsieur le cure."

Then the abbe folded his arms across his large stomach and, as if filled with amazement, said:

"Is it you—you—you, Sabot—who have come to ask me for this . . . You—the only irreligious man in my parish! Why, it would be a scandal, a public scandal! The archbishop would give me a reprimand, perhaps transfer me."

He stopped a few seconds, for breath, and then resumed in a calmer tone: "I can understand that it pains you to see a work of such importance entrusted to a carpenter from a neighboring parish. But I cannot do otherwise, unless—but no—it is impossible—you would not consent, and unless you did, never."

Sabot now looked at the row of benches in line as far as the entrance door. Christopher, if they were going to change all those!

And he asked:

"What would you require of me? Tell me."

The priest, in a firm tone replied:

"I must have an extraordinary token of your good intentions."

"I do not say—I do not say; perhaps we might come to an understanding," faltered Sabot.

"You will have to take communion publicly at high mass next Sunday," declared the cure.

The carpenter felt he was growing pale, and without replying, he asked:

"And the benches, are they going to be renovated?"

The abbe replied with confidence:

"Yes, but later on."

Sabot resumed:

"I do not say, I do not say. I am not calling it off, I am consenting to religion, for sure. But what rubs me the wrong way is, putting it in practice; but in this case I will not be refractory."

The attendants of the Virgin, having got off their chairs had concealed themselves behind the altar; and they listened pale with emotion.

The cure, seeing he had gained the victory, became all at once very friendly, quite familiar.

"That is good, that is good. That was wisely said, and not stupid, you understand. You will see, you will see."

Sabot smiled and asked with an awkward air:

"Would it not be possible to put off this communion just a trifle?"

But the priest replied, resuming his severe expression:

"From the moment that the work is put into your hands, I want to be assured of your conversion."

Then he continued more gently:

"You will come to confession to-morrow; for I must examine you at least twice."

"Twice?" repeated Sabot.

"Yes."

The priest smiled.

"You understand perfectly that you must have a general cleaning up, a thorough cleansing. So I will expect you to-morrow."

The carpenter, much agitated, asked:

"Where do you do that?"

"Why—in the confessional."

"In—that box, over there in the corner? The fact is—is—that it does not suit me, your box."

"How is that?"

"Seeing that—seeing that I am not accustomed to that, and also I am rather hard of hearing."

The cure was very affable and said:

"Well, then! you shall come to my house and into my parlor. We will have it just the two of us, tete-a-tete. Does that suit you?"

"Yes, that is all right, that will suit me, but your box, no."

"Well, then, to-morrow after the days work, at six o'clock."

"That is understood, that is all right, that is agreed on. To-morrow, monsieur le cure. Whoever draws back is a skunk!"

And he held out his great rough hand which the priest grasped heartily with a clap that resounded through the church.

Theodule Sabot was not easy in his mind all the following day. He had a feeling analogous to the apprehension one experiences when a tooth has to be drawn. The thought recurred to him at every moment: "I must go to confession this evening." And his troubled mind, the mind of an atheist only half convinced, was bewildered with a confused and overwhelming dread of the divine mystery.

As soon as he had finished his work, he betook himself to the parsonage. The cure was waiting for him in the garden, reading his breviary as he walked along a little path. He appeared radiant and greeted him with a good-natured laugh.

"Well, here we are! Come in, come in, Monsieur Sabot, no one will eat you."

And Sabot preceded him into the house. He faltered:

"If you do not mind I should like to get through with this little matter at once."

The cure replied:

"I am at your service. I have my surplice here. One minute and I will listen to you."

The carpenter, so disturbed that he had not two ideas in his head, watched him as he put on the white vestment with its pleated folds. The priest beckoned to him and said:

"Kneel down on this cushion."

Sabot remained standing, ashamed of having to kneel. He stuttered:

"Is it necessary?"

But the abbe had become dignified.

"You cannot approach the penitent bench except on your knees."

And Sabot knelt down.

"Repeat the confiteor," said the priest.

"What is that?" asked Sabot.

"The confiteor. If you do not remember it, repeat after me, one by one, the words I am going to say." And the cure repeated the sacred prayer, in a slow tone, emphasizing the words which the carpenter repeated after him. Then he said:

"Now make your confession."

But Sabot was silent, not knowing where to begin. The abbe then came to his aid.

"My child, I will ask you questions, since you don't seem familiar with these things. We will take, one by one, the commandments of God. Listen to me and do not be disturbed. Speak very frankly and never fear that you may say too much.

"'One God alone, thou shalt adore,

And love him perfectly.'

"Have you ever loved anything, or anybody, as well as you loved God? Have you loved him with all your soul, all your heart, all the strength of your love?"

Sabot was perspiring with the effort of thinking. He replied:

"No. Oh, no, m'sieu le cure. I love God as much as I can. That is —yes—I love him very much. To say that I do not love my children, no—I cannot say that. To say that if I had to choose between them and God, I could not be sure. To say that if I had to lose a hundred francs for the love of God, I could not say about that. But I love him well, for sure, I love him all the same." The priest said gravely "You must love Him more than all besides." And Sabot, meaning well, declared "I will do what I possibly can, m'sieu le cure." The abbe resumed:

"'God's name in vain thou shalt not take

Nor swear by any other thing.'

"Did you ever swear?"

"No-oh, that, no! I never swear, never. Sometimes, in a moment of anger, I may say sacre nom de Dieu! But then, I never swear."

"That is swearing," cried the priest, and added seriously:

"Do not do it again.

"'Thy Sundays thou shalt keep

In serving God devoutly.'

"What do you do on Sunday?"

This time Sabot scratched his ear.

"Why, I serve God as best I can, m'sieu le cure. I serve him—at home. I work on Sunday."

The cure interrupted him, saying magnanimously:

"I know, you will do better in future. I will pass over the following commandments, certain that you have not transgressed the two first. We will take from the sixth to the ninth. I will resume:

"'Others' goods thou shalt not take

Nor keep what is not thine.'

"Have you ever taken in any way what belonged to another?"

But Theodule Sabot became indignant.

"Of course not, of course not! I am an honest man, m'sieu le cure, I swear it, for sure. To say that I have not sometimes charged for a few more hours of work to customers who had means, I could not say that. To say that I never add a few centimes to bills, only a few, I would not say that. But to steal, no! Oh, not that, no!"

The priest resumed severely:

"To take one single centime constitutes a theft. Do not do it again.

'False witness thou shalt not bear,

Nor lie in any way.'

"Have you ever told a lie?"

"No, as to that, no. I am not a liar. That is my quality. To say that I have never told a big story, I would not like to say that. To say that I have never made people believe things that were not true when it was to my own interest, I would not like to say that. But as for lying, I am not a liar."

The priest simply said:

"Watch yourself more closely." Then he continued:

"'The works of the flesh thou shalt not desire

Except in marriage only.'

"Did you ever desire, or live with, any other woman than your wife?"

Sabot exclaimed with sincerity:

"As to that, no; oh, as to that, no, m'sieu le Cure. My poor wife, deceive her! No, no! Not so much as the tip of a finger, either in thought or in act. That is the truth."

They were silent a few seconds, then, in a lower tone, as though a doubt had arisen in his mind, he resumed:

"When I go to town, to say that I never go into a house, you know, one of the licensed houses, just to laugh and talk and see something different, I could not say that. But I always pay, monsieur le cure, I always pay. From the moment you pay, without anyone seeing or knowing you, no one can get you into trouble."

The cure did not insist, and gave him absolution.

Theodule Sabot did the work on the chancel, and goes to communion every month.

THE WRONG HOUSE

Quartermaster Varajou had obtained a week's leave to go and visit his sister, Madame Padoie. Varajou, who was in garrison at Rennes and was leading a pretty gay life, finding himself high and dry, wrote to his sister saying that he would devote a week to her. It was not that he cared particularly for Mme. Padoie, a little moralist, a devotee, and always cross; but he needed money, needed it very badly, and he remembered that, of all his relations, the Padoies were the only ones whom he had never approached on the subject.

Pere Varajou, formerly a horticulturist at Angers, but now retired from business, had closed his purse strings to his scapegrace son and had hardly seen him for two years. His daughter had married Padoie, a former treasury clerk, who had just been appointed tax collector at Vannes.

Varajou, on leaving the train, had some one direct him to the house of his brother-in-law, whom he found in his office arguing with the Breton peasants of the neighborhood. Padoie rose from his seat, held out his hand across the table littered with papers, murmured, "Take a chair. I will be at liberty in a moment," sat down again and resumed his discussion.

The peasants did not understand his explanations, the collector did not understand their line of argument. He spoke French, they spoke Breton, and the clerk who acted as interpreter appeared not to understand either.

It lasted a long time, a very long time. Varajou looked at his brother-in-law and thought: "What a fool!" Padoie must have been almost fifty. He was tall, thin, bony, slow, hairy, with heavy arched eyebrows. He wore a velvet skull cap with a gold cord vandyke design round it. His look was gentle, like his actions. His speech, his gestures, his thoughts, all were soft. Varajou said to himself, "What a fool!"

He, himself, was one of those noisy roysterers for whom the greatest pleasures in life are the cafe and abandoned women. He understood nothing outside of these conditions of existence.

A boisterous braggart, filled with contempt for the rest of the world, he despised the entire universe from the height of his ignorance. When he said: "Nom d'un chien, what a spree!" he expressed the highest degree of admiration of which his mind was capable.

Having finally got rid of his peasants, Padoie inquired:

"How are you?"

"Pretty well, as you see. And how are you?"

"Quite well, thank you. It is very kind of you to have thought of coming to see us."

"Oh, I have been thinking of it for some time; but, you know, in the military profession one has not much freedom."

"Oh, I know, I know. All the same, it is very kind of you."

"And Josephine, is she well?"

"Yes, yes, thank you; you will see her presently." "Where is she?"

"She is making some calls. We have a great many friends here; it is a very nice town."

"I thought so."

The door opened and Mme. Padoie appeared. She went over to her brother without any eagerness, held her cheek for him to kiss, and asked:

"Have you been here long?"

"No, hardly half an hour."

"Oh, I thought the train would be late. Will you come into the parlor?"

They went into the adjoining room, leaving Padoie to his accounts and his taxpayers. As soon as they were alone, she said:

"I have heard nice things about you!"

"What have you heard?"

"It seems that you are behaving like a blackguard, getting drunk and contracting debts."

He appeared very much astonished.

"I! never in the world!"

"Oh, do not deny it, I know it."

He attempted to defend himself, but she gave him such a lecture that he could say nothing more.

She then resumed:

"We dine at six o'clock, and you can amuse yourself until then. I cannot entertain you, as I have so many things to do."

When he was alone he hesitated as to whether he should sleep or take a walk. He looked first at the door leading to his room and then at the hall door, and decided to go out. He sauntered slowly through the quiet Breton town, so sleepy, so calm, so dead, on the shores of its inland bay that is called "le Morbihan." He looked at the little gray houses, the occasional pedestrians, the empty stores, and he murmured:

"Vannes is certainly not gay, not lively. It was a sad idea, my coming here."

He reached the harbor, the desolate harbor, walked back along a lonely, deserted boulevard, and got home before five o'clock. Then he threw himself on his bed to sleep till dinner time. The maid woke him, knocking at the door.

"Dinner is ready, sir:"

He went downstairs. In the damp dining-room with the paper peeling from the walls near the floor, he saw a soup tureen on a round table without any table cloth, on which were also three melancholy soup-plates.

M. and Mme. Padoie entered the room at the same time as Varajou. They all sat down to table, and the husband and wife crossed themselves over the pit of their stomachs, after which Padoie helped the soup, a meat soup. It was the day for pot-roast.

After the soup, they had the beef, which was done to rags, melted, greasy, like pap. The officer ate slowly, with disgust, weariness and rage.

Mme. Padoie said to her husband:

"Are you going to the judge's house this evening?"

"Yes, dear."

"Do not stay late. You always get so tired when you go out. You are not made for society, with your poor health."

She then talked about society in Vannes, of the excellent social circle in which the Padoies moved, thanks to their religious sentiments.

A puree of potatoes and a dish of pork were next served, in honor of the guest. Then some cheese, and that was all. No coffee.

When Varajou saw that he would have to spend the evening tete-a-tete with his sister, endure her reproaches, listen to her sermons, without even a glass of liqueur to help him to swallow these remonstrances, he felt that he could not stand the torture, and declared that he was obliged to go to the police station to have something attended to regarding his leave of absence. And he made his escape at seven o'clock.

He had scarcely reached the street before he gave himself a shake like a dog coming out of the water. He muttered:

"Heavens, heavens, heavens, what a galley slave's life!"

And he set out to look for a cafe, the best in the town. He found it on a public square, behind two gas lamps. Inside the cafe, five or six men, semi-gentlemen, and not noisy, were drinking and chatting quietly, leaning their elbows on the small tables, while two billiard players walked round the green baize, where the balls were hitting each other as they rolled.

One heard them counting:

"Eighteen-nineteen. No luck. Oh, that's a good stroke! Well played! Eleven. You should have played on the red. Twenty. Froze! Froze! Twelve. Ha! Wasn't I right?"

Varajou ordered:

"A demi-tasse and a small decanter of brandy, the best." Then he sat down and waited for it.

He was accustomed to spending his evenings off duty with his companions, amid noise and the smoke of pipes. This silence, this quiet, exasperated him. He began to drink; first the coffee, then the brandy, and asked for another decanter. He now wanted to laugh, to shout, to sing, to fight some one. He said to himself:

"Gee, I am half full. I must go and have a good time."

And he thought he would go and look for some girls to amuse him. He called the waiter:

"Hey, waiter."

"Yes, sir."

"Tell me, where does one amuse oneself here?"

The man looked stupid, and replied:

"I do not know, sir. Here, I suppose!"

"How do you mean here? What do you call amusing oneself, yourself?"

"I do not know, sir, drinking good beer or good wine."

"Ah, go away, dummy, how about the girls?"

"The girls, ah! ah!"

"Yes, the girls, where can one find any here?"

"Girls?"

"Why, yes, girls!"

The boy approached and lowering his voice, said: "You want to know where they live?"

"Why, yes, the devil!"

"You take the second street to the left and then the first to the right. It is number fifteen."

"Thank you, old man. There is something for you."

"Thank you, sir."

And Varajou went out of the cafe, repeating, "Second to the left, first to the right, number 15." But at the end of a few seconds he thought, "second to the left yes. But on leaving the cafe must I walk to the right or the left? Bah, it cannot be helped, we shall see."

And he walked on, turned down the second street to the left, then the first to the right and looked for number 15. It was a nice looking house, and one could see behind the closed blinds that the windows were lighted up on the first floor. The hall door was left partly open, and a lamp was burning in the vestibule. The non-commissioned officer thought to himself:

"This looks all right."

He went in and, as no one appeared, he called out:

"Hallo there, hallo!"

A little maid appeared and looked astonished at seeing a soldier. He said:

"Good-morning, my child. Are the ladies upstairs?"

"Yes, sir."

"In the parlor?"

"Yes, sir."

"May I go up?"

"Yes, sir."

"The door opposite the stairs?"

"Yes, sir."

He ascended the stairs, opened a door and saw sitting in a room well lighted up by two lamps, a chandelier, and two candelabras with candles in them, four ladies in evening dress, apparently expecting some one.

Three of them, the younger ones, remained seated, with rather a formal air, on some crimson velvet chairs; while the fourth, who was about forty-five, was arranging some flowers in a vase. She was very stout, and wore a green silk dress with low neck and short sleeves, allowing her red neck, covered with powder, to escape as a huge flower might from its corolla.

The officer saluted them, saying:

"Good-day, ladies."

The older woman turned round, appeared surprised, but bowed.

"Good-morning, sir."

He sat down. But seeing that they did not welcome him eagerly, he thought that possibly only commissioned officers were admitted to the house, and this made him uneasy. But he said:

"Bah, if one comes in, we can soon tell."

He then remarked:

"Are you all well?"

The large lady, no doubt the mistress of the house, replied:

"Very well, thank you!"

He could think of nothing else to say, and they were all silent. But at last, being ashamed of his bashfulness, and with an awkward laugh, he said:

"Do not people have any amusement in this country? I will pay for a bottle of wine."

He had not finished his sentence when the door opened, and in walked Padoie dressed in a black suit.

Varajou gave a shout of joy, and rising from his seat, he rushed at his brother-in-law, put his arms round him and waltzed him round the room, shouting:

"Here is Padoie! Here is Padoie! Here is Padoie!"

Then letting go of the tax collector he exclaimed as he looked him in the face:

"Oh, oh, oh, you scamp, you scamp! You are out for a good time, too. Oh, you scamp! And my sister! Are you tired of her, say?"

As he thought of all that he might gain through this unexpected situation, the forced loan, the inevitable blackmail, he flung himself on the lounge and laughed so heartily that the piece of furniture creaked all over.

The three young ladies, rising simultaneously, made their escape, while the older woman retreated to the door looking as though she were about to faint.

And then two gentlemen appeared in evening dress, and wearing the ribbon of an order. Padoie rushed up to them.

"Oh, judge—he is crazy, he is crazy. He was sent to us as a convalescent. You can see that he is crazy."

Varajou was sitting up now, and not being able to understand it all, he guessed that he had committed some monstrous folly. Then he rose, and turning to his brother-in-law, said:

"What house is this?"

But Padoie, becoming suddenly furious, stammered out:

"What house—what—what house is this? Wretch—scoundrel—villain—what house, indeed? The house of the judge—of the judge of the Supreme Court—of the Supreme Court—of the Supreme Court—Oh, oh—rascal! —rascal!—rascal!"

THE DIAMOND NECKLACE

The girl was one of those pretty and charming young creatures who sometimes are born, as if by a slip of fate, into a family of clerks. She had no dowry, no expectations, no way of being known, understood, loved, married by any rich and distinguished man; so she let herself be married to a little clerk of the Ministry of Public Instruction.

She dressed plainly because she could not dress well, but she was unhappy as if she had really fallen from a higher station; since with women there is neither caste nor rank, for beauty, grace and charm take the place of family and birth. Natural ingenuity, instinct for what is elegant, a supple mind are their sole hierarchy, and often make of women of the people the equals of the very greatest ladies.

Mathilde suffered ceaselessly, feeling herself born to enjoy all delicacies and all luxuries. She was distressed at the poverty of her dwelling, at the bareness of the walls, at the shabby chairs, the ugliness of the curtains. All those things, of which another woman of her rank would never even have been conscious, tortured her and made her angry. The sight of the little Breton peasant who did her humble housework aroused in her despairing regrets and bewildering dreams. She thought of silent antechambers hung with Oriental tapestry, illumined by tall bronze candelabra, and of two great footmen in knee breeches who sleep in the big armchairs, made drowsy by the oppressive heat of the stove. She thought of long reception halls hung with ancient silk, of the dainty cabinets containing priceless curiosities and of the little coquettish perfumed reception rooms made for chatting at five o'clock with intimate friends, with men famous and sought after, whom all women envy and whose attention they all desire.

When she sat down to dinner, before the round table covered with a tablecloth in use three days, opposite her husband, who uncovered the soup tureen and declared with a delighted air, "Ah, the good soup! I don't know anything better than that," she thought of dainty dinners, of shining silverware, of tapestry that peopled the walls with ancient personages and with strange birds flying in the midst of a fairy forest; and she thought of delicious dishes served on marvellous plates and of the whispered gallantries to which you listen with a sphinxlike smile while you are eating the pink meat of a trout or the wings of a quail.

She had no gowns, no jewels, nothing. And she loved nothing but that. She felt made for that. She would have liked so much to please, to be envied, to be charming, to be sought after.

She had a friend, a former schoolmate at the convent, who was rich, and whom she did not like to go to see any more because she felt so sad when she came home.

But one evening her husband reached home with a triumphant air and holding a large envelope in his hand.

"There," said he, "there is something for you."

She tore the paper quickly and drew out a printed card which bore these words:

The Minister of Public Instruction and Madame Georges Ramponneau

request the honor of M. and Madame Loisel's company at the palace of

the Ministry on Monday evening, January 18th.

Instead of being delighted, as her husband had hoped, she threw the invitation on the table crossly, muttering:

"What do you wish me to do with that?"

"Why, my dear, I thought you would be glad. You never go out, and this is such a fine opportunity. I had great trouble to get it. Every one wants to go; it is very select, and they are not giving many invitations to clerks. The whole official world will be there."

She looked at him with an irritated glance and said impatiently:

"And what do you wish me to put on my back?"

He had not thought of that. He stammered:

"Why, the gown you go to the theatre in. It looks very well to me."

He stopped, distracted, seeing that his wife was weeping. Two great tears ran slowly from the corners of her eyes toward the corners of her mouth.

"What's the matter? What's the matter?" he answered.

By a violent effort she conquered her grief and replied in a calm voice, while she wiped her wet cheeks:

"Nothing. Only I have no gown, and, therefore, I can't go to this ball. Give your card to some colleague whose wife is better equipped than I am."

He was in despair. He resumed:

"Come, let us see, Mathilde. How much would it cost, a suitable gown, which you could use on other occasions—something very simple?"

She reflected several seconds, making her calculations and wondering also what sum she could ask without drawing on herself an immediate refusal and a frightened exclamation from the economical clerk.

Finally she replied hesitating:

"I don't know exactly, but I think I could manage it with four hundred francs."

He grew a little pale, because he was laying aside just that amount to buy a gun and treat himself to a little shooting next summer on the plain of Nanterre, with several friends who went to shoot larks there of a Sunday.

But he said:

"Very well. I will give you four hundred francs. And try to have a pretty gown."

The day of the ball drew near and Madame Loisel seemed sad, uneasy, anxious. Her frock was ready, however. Her husband said to her one evening:

"What is the matter? Come, you have seemed very queer these last three days."

And she answered:

"It annoys me not to have a single piece of jewelry, not a single ornament, nothing to put on. I shall look poverty-stricken. I would almost rather not go at all."

"You might wear natural flowers," said her husband. "They're very stylish at this time of year. For ten francs you can get two or three magnificent roses."

She was not convinced.

"No; there's nothing more humiliating than to look poor among other women who are rich."

"How stupid you are!" her husband cried. "Go look up your friend, Madame Forestier, and ask her to lend you some jewels. You're intimate enough with her to do that."

She uttered a cry of joy:

"True! I never thought of it."

The next day she went to her friend and told her of her distress.

Madame Forestier went to a wardrobe with a mirror, took out a large jewel box, brought it back, opened it and said to Madame Loisel:

"Choose, my dear."

She saw first some bracelets, then a pearl necklace, then a Venetian gold cross set with precious stones, of admirable workmanship. She tried on the ornaments before the mirror, hesitated and could not make up her mind to part with them, to give them back. She kept asking:

"Haven't you any more?"

"Why, yes. Look further; I don't know what you like."

Suddenly she discovered, in a black satin box, a superb diamond necklace, and her heart throbbed with an immoderate desire. Her hands trembled as she took it. She fastened it round her throat, outside her high-necked waist, and was lost in ecstasy at her reflection in thc mirror.

Then she asked, hesitating, filled with anxious doubt:

"Will you lend me this, only this?"

"Why, yes, certainly."

She threw her arms round her friend's neck, kissed her passionately, then fled with her treasure.

The night of the ball arrived. Madame Loisel was a great success. She was prettier than any other woman present, elegant, graceful, smiling and wild with joy. All the men looked at her, asked her name, sought to be introduced. All the attaches of the Cabinet wished to waltz with her. She was remarked by the minister himself.

She danced with rapture, with passion, intoxicated by pleasure, forgetting all in the triumph of her beauty, in the glory of her success, in a sort of cloud of happiness comprised of all this homage, admiration, these awakened desires and of that sense of triumph which is so sweet to woman's heart.

She left the ball about four o'clock in the morning. Her husband had been sleeping since midnight in a little deserted anteroom with three other gentlemen whose wives were enjoying the ball.

He threw over her shoulders the wraps he had brought, the modest wraps of common life, the poverty of which contrasted with the elegance of the ball dress. She felt this and wished to escape so as not to be remarked by the other women, who were enveloping themselves in costly furs.

Loisel held her back, saying: "Wait a bit. You will catch cold outside. I will call a cab."

But she did not listen to him and rapidly descended the stairs. When they reached the street they could not find a carriage and began to look for one, shouting after the cabmen passing at a distance.

They went toward the Seine in despair, shivering with cold. At last they found on the quay one of those ancient night cabs which, as though they were ashamed to show their shabbiness during the day, are never seen round Paris until after dark.

It took them to their dwelling in the Rue des Martyrs, and sadly they mounted the stairs to their flat. All was ended for her. As to him, he reflected that he must be at the ministry at ten o'clock that morning.

She removed her wraps before the glass so as to see herself once more in all her glory. But suddenly she uttered a cry. She no longer had the necklace around her neck!

"What is the matter with you?" demanded her husband, already half undressed.

She turned distractedly toward him.

"I have—I have—I've lost Madame Forestier's necklace," she cried.

He stood up, bewildered.

"What!—how? Impossible!"

They looked among the folds of her skirt, of her cloak, in her pockets, everywhere, but did not find it.

"You're sure you had it on when you left the ball?" he asked.

"Yes, I felt it in the vestibule of the minister's house."

"But if you had lost it in the street we should have heard it fall. It must be in the cab."

"Yes, probably. Did you take his number?"

"No. And you—didn't you notice it?"

"No."

They looked, thunderstruck, at each other. At last Loisel put on his clothes.

"I shall go back on foot," said he, "over the whole route, to see whether I can find it."

He went out. She sat waiting on a chair in her ball dress, without strength to go to bed, overwhelmed, without any fire, without a thought.

Her husband returned about seven o'clock. He had found nothing.

He went to police headquarters, to the newspaper offices to offer a reward; he went to the cab companies—everywhere, in fact, whither he was urged by the least spark of hope.

She waited all day, in the same condition of mad fear before this terrible calamity.

Loisel returned at night with a hollow, pale face. He had discovered nothing.

"You must write to your friend," said he, "that you have broken the clasp of her necklace and that you are having it mended. That will give us time to turn round."

She wrote at his dictation.

At the end of a week they had lost all hope. Loisel, who had aged five years, declared:

"We must consider how to replace that ornament."

The next day they took the box that had contained it and went to the jeweler whose name was found within. He consulted his books.

"It was not I, madame, who sold that necklace; I must simply have furnished the case."

Then they went from jeweler to jeweler, searching for a necklace like the other, trying to recall it, both sick with chagrin and grief.

They found, in a shop at the Palais Royal, a string of diamonds that seemed to them exactly like the one they had lost. It was worth forty thousand francs. They could have it for thirty-six.

So they begged the jeweler not to sell it for three days yet. And they made a bargain that he should buy it back for thirty-four thousand francs, in case they should find the lost necklace before the end of February.

Loisel possessed eighteen thousand francs which his father had left him. He would borrow the rest.

He did borrow, asking a thousand francs of one, five hundred of another, five louis here, three louis there. He gave notes, took up ruinous obligations, dealt with usurers and all the race of lenders. He compromised all the rest of his life, risked signing a note without even knowing whether he could meet it; and, frightened by the trouble yet to come, by the black misery that was about to fall upon him, by the prospect of all the physical privations and moral tortures that he was to suffer, he went to get the new necklace, laying upon the jeweler's counter thirty-six thousand francs.

When Madame Loisel took back the necklace Madame Forestier said to her with a chilly manner:

"You should have returned it sooner; I might have needed it."

She did not open the case, as her friend had so much feared. If she had detected the substitution, what would she have thought, what would she have said? Would she not have taken Madame Loisel for a thief?

Thereafter Madame Loisel knew the horrible existence of the needy. She bore her part, however, with sudden heroism. That dreadful debt must be paid. She would pay it. They dismissed their servant; they changed their lodgings; they rented a garret under the roof.

She came to know what heavy housework meant and the odious cares of the kitchen. She washed the dishes, using her dainty fingers and rosy nails on greasy pots and pans. She washed the soiled linen, the shirts and the dishcloths, which she dried upon a line; she carried the slops down to the street every morning and carried up the water, stopping for breath at every landing. And dressed like a woman of the people, she went to the fruiterer, the grocer, the butcher, a basket on her arm, bargaining, meeting with impertinence, defending her miserable money, sou by sou.

Every month they had to meet some notes, renew others, obtain more time.

Her husband worked evenings, making up a tradesman's accounts, and late at night he often copied manuscript for five sous a page.

This life lasted ten years.

At the end of ten years they had paid everything, everything, with the rates of usury and the accumulations of the compound interest.

Madame Loisel looked old now. She had become the woman of impoverished households—strong and hard and rough. With frowsy hair, skirts askew and red hands, she talked loud while washing the floor with great swishes of water. But sometimes, when her husband was at the office, she sat down near the window and she thought of that gay evening of long ago, of that ball where she had been so beautiful and so admired.

What would have happened if she had not lost that necklace? Who knows? who knows? How strange and changeful is life! How small a thing is needed to make or ruin us!

But one Sunday, having gone to take a walk in the Champs Elysees to refresh herself after the labors of the week, she suddenly perceived a woman who was leading a child. It was Madame Forestier, still young, still beautiful, still charming.

Madame Loisel felt moved. Should she speak to her? Yes, certainly. And now that she had paid, she would tell her all about it. Why not?

She went up.

"Good-day, Jeanne."

The other, astonished to be familiarly addressed by this plain good-wife, did not recognize her at all and stammered:

"But—madame!—I do not know—You must have mistaken."

"No. I am Mathilde Loisel."

Her friend uttered a cry.

"Oh, my poor Mathilde! How you are changed!"

"Yes, I have had a pretty hard life, since I last saw you, and great poverty—and that because of you!"

"Of me! How so?"

"Do you remember that diamond necklace you lent me to wear at the ministerial ball?"

"Yes. Well?"

"Well, I lost it."

"What do you mean? You brought it back."

"I brought you back another exactly like it. And it has taken us ten years to pay for it. You can understand that it was not easy for us, for us who had nothing. At last it is ended, and I am very glad."

Madame Forestier had stopped.

"You say that you bought a necklace of diamonds to replace mine?"

"Yes. You never noticed it, then! They were very similar."

And she smiled with a joy that was at once proud and ingenuous.

Madame Forestier, deeply moved, took her hands.

"Oh, my poor Mathilde! Why, my necklace was paste! It was worth at most only five hundred francs!"

THE MARQUIS DE FUMEROL

Roger de Tourneville was whiffing a cigar and blowing out small clouds of smoke every now and then, as he sat astride a chair amid a party of friends. He was talking.

"We were at dinner when a letter was brought in which my father opened. You know my father, who thinks that he is king of France ad interim. I call him Don Quixote, because for twelve years he has been running a tilt against the windmill of the Republic, without quite knowing whether it was in the cause of the Bourbons or the Orleanists. At present he is bearing the lance in the cause of the Orleanists alone, because there is no one else left. In any case, he thinks himself the first gentleman of France, the best known, the most influential, the head of the party; and as he is an irremovable senator, he thinks that the thrones of the neighboring kings are very insecure.

"As for my mother, she is my father's soul, she is the soul of the kingdom and of religion, and the scourge of all evil-thinkers.

"Well, a letter was brought in while we were at dinner, and my father opened and read it, and then he said to mother: 'Your brother is dying.' She grew very pale. My uncle was scarcely ever mentioned in the house, and I did not know him at all; all I knew from public talk was, that he had led, and was still leading, a gay life. After having spent his fortune in fast living, he was now in small apartments in the Rue des Martyrs.

"An ancient peer of France and former colonel of cavalry, it was said that he believed in neither God nor devil. Not believing, therefore, in a future life he had abused the present life in every way, and had become a live wound in my mother's heart.

"'Give me that letter, Paul,' she said, and when she read it, I asked for it in my turn. Here it is:

'Monsieur le Comte, I think I ought to let you know that your

brother-in-law, the Comte Fumerol, is going to die. Perhaps you

would like to make some arrangements, and do not forget I told you.

Your servant,

'MELANIE.'

"'We must take counsel,' papa murmured. 'In my position, I ought to watch over your brother's last moments.'

"Mamma continued: 'I will send for Abbe Poivron and ask his advice, and then I will go to my brother with the abbe and Roger. Remain here, Paul, for you must not compromise yourself; but a woman can, and ought to do these things. For a politician in your position, it is another matter. It would be a fine thing for one of your opponents to be able to bring one of your most laudable actions up against you.' 'You are right,' my father said. 'Do as you think best, my dear wife.'

"A quarter of an hour, later, the Abbe Poivron came into the drawing-room, and the situation was explained to him, analyzed and discussed in all its bearings. If the Marquis de Fumerol, one of the greatest names in France, were to die without the ministrations of religion, it would assuredly be a terrible blow to the nobility in general, and to the Count de Tourneville in particular, and the freethinkers would be triumphant. The liberal newspapers would sing songs of victory for six months; my mother's name would be dragged through the mire and brought into the prose of Socialistic journals, and my father's name would be smirched. It was impossible that such a thing should be.

"A crusade was therefore immediately decided upon, which was to be led by the Abbe Poivron, a little, fat, clean, priest with a faint perfume about him, a true vicar of a large church in a noble and rich quarter.

"The landau was ordered and we all three set out, my mother, the cure and I, to administer the last sacraments to my uncle.

"It had been decided first of all we should see Madame Melanie who had written the letter, and who was most likely the porter's wife, or my uncle's servant, and I dismounted, as an advance guard, in front of a seven-story house and went into a dark passage, where I had great difficulty in finding the porter's den. He looked at me distrustfully, and I said:

"'Madame Melanie, if you please.' 'Don't know her!' 'But I have received a letter from her.' 'That may be, but I don't know her. Are you asking for a lodger?' 'No, a servant probably. She wrote me about a place.' 'A servant?—a servant? Perhaps it is the marquis'. Go and see, the fifth story on the left.'

"As soon as he found I was not asking for a doubtful character he became more friendly and came as far as the corridor with me. He was a tall, thin man with white whiskers, the manners of a beadle and majestic gestures.

"I climbed up a long spiral staircase, the railing of which I did not venture to touch, and I gave three discreet knocks at the left-hand door on the fifth story. It opened immediately, and an enormous dirty woman appeared before me. She barred the entrance with her extended arms which she placed against the two doorposts, and growled:

"'What do you want?' 'Are you Madame Melanie?' 'Yes.' 'I am the Visconte de Tourneville.' 'Ah! All right! Come in.' 'Well, the fact is, my mother is downstairs with a priest.' 'Oh! All right; go and bring them up; but be careful of the porter.'

"I went downstairs and came up again with my mother, who was followed by the abbe, and I fancied that I heard other footsteps behind us. As soon as we were in the kitchen, Melanie offered us chairs, and we all four sat down to deliberate.

"'Is he very ill?' my mother asked. 'Oh! yes, madame; he will not be here long.' 'Does he seem disposed to receive a visit from a priest?' 'Oh! I do not think so.' 'Can I see him?' 'Well—yes madame—only —only—those young ladies are with him.' 'What young ladies?' 'Why—why—his lady friends, of course.' 'Oh!' Mamma had grown scarlet, and the Abbe Poivron had lowered his eyes.

"The affair began to amuse me, and I said: 'Suppose I go in first? I shall see how he receives me, and perhaps I shall be able to prepare him to receive you.'

"My mother, who did not suspect any trick, replied: 'Yes, go, my dear.' But a woman's voice cried out: 'Melanie!'

"The servant ran out and said: 'What do you want, Mademoiselle Claire?' 'The omelette; quickly.' 'In a minute, mademoiselle.' And coming back to us, she explained this summons.

"They had ordered a cheese omelette at two o'clock as a slight collation. And she at once began to break the eggs into a salad bowl, and to whip them vigorously, while I went out on the landing and pulled the bell, so as to formally announce my arrival. Melanie opened the door to me, and made me sit down in an ante-room, while she went to tell my uncle that I had come; then she came back and asked me to go in, while the abbe hid behind the door, so that he might appear at the first signal.

"I was certainly very much surprised at the sight of my uncle, for he was very handsome, very solemn and very elegant, the old rake.

"Sitting, almost lying, in a large armchair, his legs wrapped in blankets, his hands, his long, white hands, over the arms of the chair, he was waiting for death with the dignity of a patriarch. His white beard fell on his chest, and his hair, which was also white, mingled with it on his cheeks.

"Standing behind his armchair, as if to defend him against me, were two young women, who looked at me with bold eyes. In their petticoats and morning wrappers, with bare arms, with coal black hair twisted in a knot on the nape of their neck, with embroidered, Oriental slippers, which showed their ankles and silk stockings, they looked like the figures in some symbolical painting, by the side of the dying man. Between the easy-chair and the bed, there was a table covered with a white cloth, on which two plates, two glasses, two forks and two knives, were waiting for the cheese omelette which had been ordered some time before of Melanie.

"My uncle said in a weak, almost breathless, but clear voice:

"'Good-morning, my child; it is rather late in the day to come and see me; our acquaintanceship will not last long.' I stammered out, 'It was not my fault, uncle:' 'No; I know that,' he replied. 'It is your father and mother's fault more than yours. How are they?' 'Pretty well, thank you. When they heard that you were ill, they sent me to ask after you.' 'Ah! Why did they not come themselves?'

"I looked up at the two girls and said gently: 'It is not their fault if they could not come, uncle. But it would be difficult for my father, and impossible for my mother to come in here.' The old man did not reply, but raised his hand toward mine, and I took the pale, cold hand and held it in my own.

"The door opened, Melanie came in with the omelette and put it on the table, and the two girls immediately sat down at the table, and began to eat without taking their eyes off me. Then I said: 'Uncle, it would give great pleasure to my mother to embrace you.' 'I also,' he murmured, 'should like——' He said no more, and I could think of nothing to propose to him, and there was silence except for the noise of the plates and that vague sound of eating.

"Now, the abbe, who was listening behind the door, seeing our embarrassment, and thinking we had won the game, thought the time had come to interpose, and showed himself. My uncle was so stupefied at sight of him that at first he remained motionless; and then he opened his mouth as if he meant to swallow up the priest, and shouted to him in a strong, deep, furious voice: 'What are you doing here?'

"The abbe, who was used to difficult situations, came forward into the room, murmuring: 'I have come in your sister's name, Monsieur le Marquis; she has sent me. She would be happy, monsieur—'

"But the marquis was not listening. Raising one hand, he pointed to the door with a proud, tragic gesture, and said angrily and breathing hard: 'Leave this room—go out—robber of souls. Go out from here, you violator of consciences. Go out from here, you pick-lock of dying men's doors!'

"The abbe retreated, and I also went to the door, beating a retreat with the priest; the two young women, who had the best of it, got up, leaving their omelette only half eaten, and went and stood on either side of my uncle's easy-chair, putting their hands on his arms to calm him, and to protect him against the criminal enterprises of the Family, and of Religion.

"The abbe and I rejoined my mother in the kitchen, and Melanie again offered us chairs. 'I knew quite well that this method would not work; we must try some other means, otherwise he will escape us.' And they began deliberating afresh, my mother being of one opinion and the abbe of another, while I held a third.

"We had been discussing the matter in a low voice for half an hour, perhaps, when a great noise of furniture being moved and of cries uttered by my uncle, more vehement and terrible even than the former had been, made us all four jump up.

"Through the doors and walls we could hear him shouting: 'Go out—out —rascals—humbugs, get out, scoundrels—get out—get out!'

"Melanie rushed in, but came back immediately to call me to help her, and I hastened in. Opposite to my uncle, who was terribly excited by anger, almost standing up and vociferating, stood two men, one behind the other, who seemed to be waiting till he should be dead with rage.

"By his ridiculous long coat, his long English shoes, his manners of a tutor out of a position, his high collar, white necktie and straight hair, his humble face of a false priest of a bastard religion, I immediately recognized the first as a Protestant minister.

"The second was the porter of the house, who belonged to the reformed religion and had followed us, and having seen our defeat, had gone to fetch his own pastor, in hopes that he might meet a better reception. My uncle seemed mad with rage! If the sight of the Catholic priest, of the priest of his ancestors, had irritated the Marquis de Fumerol, who had become a freethinker, the sight of his porter's minister made him altogether beside himself. I therefore took the two men by the arm and threw them out of the room so roughly that they bumped against each other twice, between the two doors which led to the staircase; and then I disappeared in my turn and returned to the kitchen, which was our headquarters in order to take counsel with my mother and the abbe.

"But Melanie came back in terror, sobbing out:

"'He is dying—he is dying—come immediately—he is dying.'

"My mother rushed out. My uncle had fallen to the ground, and lay full length along the floor, without moving. I fancy he was already dead. My mother was superb at that moment! She went straight up to the two girls who were kneeling by the body and trying to raise it up, and pointing to the door with irresistible authority, dignity and majesty, she said: 'Now it is time for you to leave the room.'

"And they went out without a word of protest. I must add, that I was getting ready to turn them out as unceremoniously as I had done the parson and the porter.

"Then the Abbe Poivron administered the last sacraments to my uncle with all the customary prayers, and remitted all his sins, while my mother sobbed as she knelt near her brother. Suddenly, however, she exclaimed: 'He recognized me; he pressed my hand; I am sure he recognized me!!!—and that he thanked me! Oh, God, what happiness!'

"Poor mamma! If she had known or guessed for whom those thanks were intended!

"They laid my uncle on his bed; he was certainly dead this time.

"'Madame,' Melanie said, 'we have no sheets to bury him in; all the linen belongs to these two young ladies,' and when I looked at the omelette which they had not finished, I felt inclined to laugh and to cry at the same time. There are some humorous moments and some humorous situations in life, occasionally!

"We gave my uncle a magnificent funeral, with five speeches at the grave. Baron de Croiselles, the senator, showed in admirable terms that God always returns victorious into well-born souls which have temporarily been led into error. All the members of the Royalist and Catholic party followed the funeral procession with the enthusiasm of victors, as they spoke of that beautiful death after a somewhat troublous life."

Viscount Roger ceased speaking; his audience was laughing. Then somebody said: "Bah! That is the story of all conversions in extremis."

THE TRIP OF LE HORLA

On the morning of July 8th I received the following telegram: “Fine day. Always my predictions. Belgian frontier. Baggage and servants left at noon at the social session. Beginning of manoeuvres at three. So I will wait for you at the works from five o’clock on. Jovis.”

At five o’clock sharp I entered the gas works of La Villette. It might have been mistaken for the colossal ruins of an old town inhabited by Cyclops. There were immense dark avenues separating heavy gasometers standing one behind another, like monstrous columns, unequally high and, undoubtedly, in the past the supports of some tremendous, some fearful iron edifice.

The balloon was lying in the courtyard and had the appearance of a cake made of yellow cloth, flattened on the ground under a rope. That is called placing a balloon in a sweep-net, and, in fact, it appeared like an enormous fish.

Two or three hundred people were looking at it, sitting or standing, and some were examining the basket, a nice little square basket for a human cargo, bearing on its side in gold letters on a mahogany plate the words: Le Horla.

Suddenly the people began to stand back, for the gas was beginning to enter into the balloon through a long tube of yellow cloth, which lay on the soil, swelling and undulating like an enormous worm. But another thought, another picture occurs to every mind. It is thus that nature itself nourishes beings until their birth. The creature that will rise soon begins to move, and the attendants of Captain Jovis, as Le Horla grew larger, spread and put in place the net which covers it, so that the pressure will be regular and equally distributed at every point.

The operation is very delicate and very important, for the resistance of the cotton cloth of which the balloon is made is figured not in proportion to the contact surface of this cloth with the net, but in proportion to the links of the basket.

Le Horla, moreover, has been designed by M. Mallet, constructed under his own eyes and made by himself. Everything had been made in the shops of M. Jovis by his own working staff and nothing was made outside.

We must add that everything was new in this balloon, from the varnish to the valve, those two essential parts of a balloon. Both must render the cloth gas-proof, as the sides of a ship are waterproof. The old varnishes, made with a base of linseed oil, sometimes fermented and thus burned the cloth, which in a short time would tear like a piece of paper.

The valves were apt to close imperfectly after being opened and when the covering called “cataplasme” was injured. The fall of M. L’Hoste in the open sea during the night proved the imperfection of the old system.

The two discoveries of Captain Jovis, the varnish principally, are of inestimable value in the art of ballooning.

The crowd has begun to talk, and some men, who appear to be specialists, affirm with authority that we shall come down before reaching the fortifications. Several other things have been criticized in this novel type of balloon with which we are about to experiment with so much pleasure and success.

It is growing slowly but surely. Some small holes and scratches made in transit have been discovered, and we cover them and plug them with a little piece of paper applied on the cloth while wet. This method of repairing alarms and mystifies the public.

While Captain Jovis and his assistants are busy with the last details, the travellers go to dine in the canteen of the gas-works, according to the established custom.

When we come out again the balloon is swaying, enormous and transparent, a prodigious golden fruit, a fantastic pear which is still ripening, covered by the last rays of the setting sun. Now the basket is attached, the barometers are brought, the siren, which we will blow to our hearts' content, is also brought, also the two trumpets, the eatables, the overcoats and raincoats, all the small articles that can go with the men in that flying basket.

As the wind pushes the balloon against the gasometers, it is necessary to steady it now and then, to avoid an accident at the start.

Captain Jovis is now ready and calls all the passengers.

Lieutenant Mallet jumps aboard, climbing first on the aerial net between the basket and the balloon, from which he will watch during the night the movements of Le Horla across the skies, as the officer on watch, standing on starboard, watches the course of a ship.

M. Etierine Beer gets in after him, then comes M. Paul Bessand, then M. Patrice Eyries and I get in last.

But the basket is too heavy for the balloon, considering the long trip to be taken, and M. Eyries has to get out, not without great regret.

M. Joliet, standing erect on the edge of the basket, begs the ladies, in very gallant terms, to stand aside a little, for he is afraid he might throw sand on their hats in rising. Then he commands:

"Let it loose," and, cutting with one stroke of his knife the ropes that hold the balloon to the ground, he gives Le Horla its liberty.

In one second we fly skyward. Nothing can be heard; we float, we rise, we fly, we glide. Our friends shout with glee and applaud, but we hardly hear them, we hardly see them. We are already so far, so high! What? Are we really leaving these people down there? Is it possible? Paris spreads out beneath us, a dark bluish patch, cut by its streets, from which rise, here and there, domes, towers, steeples, then around it the plain, the country, traversed by long roads, thin and white, amidst green fields of a tender or dark green, and woods almost black.

The Seine appears like a coiled snake, asleep, of which we see neither head nor tail; it crosses Paris, and the entire field resembles an immense basin of prairies and forests dotted here and there by mountains, hardly visible in the horizon.

The sun, which we could no longer see down below, now reappears as though it were about to rise again, and our balloon seems to be lighted; it must appear like a star to the people who are looking up. M. Mallet every few seconds throws a cigarette paper intospace and says quietly: "We are rising, always rising," while Captain Jovis, radiant with joy, rubs his hands together and repeats: "Eh? this varnish? Isn't it good?"

In fact, we can see whether we are rising or sinking only by throwing a cigarette paper out of the basket now and then. If this paper appears to fall down like a stone, it means that the balloon is rising; if it appears to shoot skyward the balloon is descending.

The two barometers mark about five hundred meters, and we gaze with enthusiastic admiration at the earth we are leaving and to which we are not attached in any way; it looks like a colored map, an immense plan of the country. All its noises, however, rise to our ears very distinctly, easily recognizable. We hear the sound of the wheels rolling in the streets, the snap of a whip, the cries of drivers, the rolling and whistling of trains and the laughter of small boys running after one another. Every time we pass over a village the noise of children's voices is heard above the rest and with the greatest distinctness. Some men are calling us; the locomotives whistle; we answer with the siren, which emits plaintive, fearfully shrill wails like the voice of a weird being wandering through the world.

We perceive lights here and there, some isolated fire in the farms, and lines of gas in the towns. We are going toward the northwest, after roaming for some time over the little lake of Enghien. Now we see a river; it is the Oise, and we begin to argue about the exact spot we are passing. Is that town Creil or Pontoise—the one with so many lights? But if we were over Pontoise we could see the junction of the Seine and the Oise; and that enormous fire to the left, isn't it the blast furnaces of Montataire? So then we are above Creil. The view is superb; it is dark on the earth, but we are still in the light, and it is now past ten o'clock. Now we begin to hear slight country noises, the double cry of the quail in particular, then the mewing of cats and the barking of dogs. Surely the dogs have scented the balloon; they have seen it and have given the alarm. We can hear them barking all over the plain and making the identical noise they make when baying at the moon. The cows also seem to wake up in the barns, for we can hear them lowing; all the beasts are scared and moved before the aerial monster that is passing.

The delicious odors of the soil rise toward us, the smell of hay, of flowers, of the moist, verdant earth, perfuming the air-a light air, in fact, so light, so sweet, so delightful that I realize I never was so fortunate as to breathe before. A profound sense of well-being, unknown to me heretofore, pervades me, a well-being of body and spirit, composed of supineness, of infinite rest, of forgetfulness, of indifference to everything and of this novel sensation of traversing space without any of the sensations that make motion unbearable, without noise, without shocks and without fear.

At times we rise and then descend. Every few minutes Lieutenant Mallet, suspended in his cobweb of netting, says to Captain Jovis: "We are descending; throw down half a handful." And the captain, who is talking and laughing with us, with a bag of ballast between his legs, takes a handful of sand out of the bag and throws it overboard.

Nothing is more amusing, more delicate, more interesting than the manoeuvring of a balloon. It is an enormous toy, free and docile, which obeys with surprising sensitiveness, but it is also, and before all, the slave of the wind, which we cannot control. A pinch of sand, half a sheet of paper, one or two drops of water, the bones of a chicken which we had just eaten, thrown overboard, makes it go up quickly.

A breath of cool, damp air rising from the river or the wood we are traversing makes the balloon descend two hundred metres. It does not vary when passing over fields of ripe grain, and it rises when it passes over towns.

The earth sleeps now, or, rather, men sleep on the earth, for the beasts awakened by the sight of our balloon announce our approach everywhere. Now and then the rolling of a train or the whistling of a locomotive is plainly distinguishable. We sound our siren as we pass over inhabited places; and the peasants, terrified in their beds, must surely tremble and ask themselves if the Angel Gabriel is not passing by.

A strong and continuous odor of gas can be plainly observed. We must have encountered a current of warm air, and the balloon expands, losing its invisible blood by the escape-valve, which is called the appendix, and which closes of itself as soon as the expansion ceases.

We are rising. The earth no longer gives back the echo of our trumpets; we have risen almost two thousand feet. It is not light enough for us to consult the instruments; we only know that the rice paper falls from us like dead butterflies, that we are rising, always rising. We can no longer see the earth; a light mist separates us from it; and above our head twinkles a world of stars.

A silvery light appears before us and makes the sky turn pale, and suddenly, as if it were rising from unknown depths behind the horizon below us rises the moon on the edge of a cloud. It seems to be coming from below, while we are looking down upon it from a great height, leaning on the edge of our basket like an audience on a balcony. Clear and round, it emerges from the clouds and slowly rises in the sky.

The earth no longer seems to exist, it is buried in milky vapors that resemble a sea. We are now alone in space with the moon, which looks like another balloon travelling opposite us; and our balloon, which shines in the air, appears like another, larger moon, a world wandering in the sky amid the stars, through infinity. We no longer speak, think nor live; we float along through space in delicious inertia. The air which is bearing us up has made of us all beings which resemble itself, silent, joyous, irresponsible beings, intoxicated by this stupendous flight, peculiarly alert, although motionless. One is no longer conscious of one's flesh or one's bones; one's heart seems to have ceased beating; we have become something indescribable, birds who do not even have to flap their wings.

All memory has disappeared from our minds, all trouble from our thoughts; we have no more regrets, plans nor hopes. We look, we feel, we wildly enjoy this fantastic journey; nothing in the sky but the moon and ourselves! We are a wandering, travelling world, like our sisters, the planets; and this little world carries five men who have left the earth and who have almost forgotten it. We can now see as plainly as in daylight; we look at each other, surprised at this brightness, for we have nothing to look at but ourselves and a few silvery clouds floating below us. The barometers mark twelve hundred metres, then thirteen, fourteen, fifteen hundred; and the little rice papers still fall about us.

Captain Jovis claims that the moon has often made balloons act thus, and that the upward journey will continue.

We are now at two thousand metres; we go up to two thousand three hundred and fifty; then the balloon stops: We blow the siren and are surprised that no one answers us from the stars.

We are now going down rapidly. M. Mallet keeps crying: "Throw out more ballast! throw out more ballast!" And the sand and stones that we throw over come back into our faces, as if they were going up, thrown from below toward the stars, so rapid is our descent.

Here is the earth! Where are we? It is now past midnight, and we are crossing a broad, dry, well-cultivated country, with many roads and well populated.

To the right is a large city and farther away to the left is another. But suddenly from the earth appears a bright fairy light; it disappears, reappears and once more disappears. Jovis, intoxicated by space, exclaims: "Look, look at this phenomenon of the moon in the water. One can see nothing more beautiful at night!"

Nothing indeed can give one an idea of the wonderful brightness of these spots of light which are not fire, which do not look like reflections, which appear quickly here or there and immediately go out again. These shining lights appear on the winding rivers at every turn, but one hardly has time to see them as the balloon passes as quickly as the wind.

We are now quite near the earth, and Beer exclaims:—"Look at that! What is that running over there in the fields? Isn't it a dog?" Indeed, something is running along the ground with great speed, and this something seems to jump over ditches, roads, trees with such ease that we could not understand what it might be. The captain laughed: "It is the shadow of our balloon. It will grow as we descend."

I distinctly hear a great noise of foundries in the distance. And, according to the polar star, which we have been observing all night, 'and which I have so often watched and consulted from the bridge of my little yacht on the Mediterranean, we are heading straight for Belgium.

Our siren and our two horns are continually calling. A few cries from some truck driver or belated reveler answer us. We bellow: "Where are we?" But the balloon is going so rapidly that the bewildered man has not even time to answer us. The growing shadow of Le Horla, as large as a child's ball, is fleeing before us over the fields, roads and woods. It goes along steadily, preceding us by about a quarter of a mile; and now I am leaning out of the basket, listening to the roaring of the wind in the trees and across the harvest fields. I say to Captain Jovis: "How the wind blows!"

He answers: "No, those are probably waterfalls." I insist, sure of my ear that knows the sound of the wind, from hearing it so often whistle through the rigging. Then Jovis nudges me; he fears to frighten his happy, quiet passengers, for he knows full well that a storm is pursuing us.

At last a man manages to understand us; he answers: "Nord!" We get the same reply from another.

Suddenly the lights of a town, which seems to be of considerable size, appear before us. Perhaps it is Lille. As we approach it, such a wonderful flow of fire appears below us that I think myself transported into some fairyland where precious stones are manufactured for giants.

It seems that it is a brick factory. Here are others, two, three. The fusing material bubbles, sparkles, throws out blue, red, yellow, green sparks, reflections from giant diamonds, rubies, emeralds, turquoises, sapphires, topazes. And near by are great foundries roaring like apocalyptic lions; high chimneys belch forth their clouds of smoke and flame, and we can hear the noise of metal striking against metal.

"Where are we?"

The voice of some joker or of a crazy person answers: "In a balloon!"

"Where are we?"

"At Lille!"

We were not mistaken. We are already out of sight of the town, and we see Roubaix to the right, then some well-cultivated, rectangular fields, of different colors according to the crops, some yellow, some gray or brown. But the clouds are gathering behind us, hiding the moon, whereas toward the east the sky is growing lighter, becoming a clear blue tinged with red. It is dawn. It grows rapidly, now showing us all the little details of the earth, the trains, the brooks, the cows, the goats. And all this passes beneath us with surprising speed. One hardly has time to notice that other fields, other meadows, other houses have already disappeared. Cocks are crowing, but the voice of ducks drowns everything. One might think the world to be peopled, covered with them, they make so much noise.

The early rising peasants are waving their arms and crying to us: "Let yourselves drop!" But we go along steadily, neither rising nor falling, leaning over the edge of the basket and watching the world fleeing under our feet.

Jovis sights another city far off in the distance. It approaches; everywhere are old church spires. They are delightful, seen thus from above. Where are we? Is this Courtrai? Is it Ghent?

We are already very near it, and we see that it is surrounded by water and crossed in every direction by canals. One might think it a Venice of the north. Just as we are passing so near to a church tower that our long guy-rope almost touches it, the chimes begin to ring three o'clock. The sweet, clear sounds rise to us from this frail roof which we have almost touched in our wandering course. It is a charming greeting, a friendly welcome from Holland. We answer with our siren, whose raucous voice echoes throughout the streets.

It was Bruges. But we have hardly lost sight of it when my neighbor, Paul Bessand, asks me: "Don't you see something over there, to the right, in front of us? It looks like a river."

And, indeed, far ahead of us stretches a bright highway, in the light of the dawning day. Yes, it looks like a river, an immense river full of islands.

"Get ready for the descent," cried the captain. He makes M. Mallet leave his net and return to the basket; then we pack the barometers and everything that could be injured by possible shocks. M. Bessand exclaims: "Look at the masts over there to the left! We are at the sea!"

Fogs had hidden it from us until then. The sea was everywhere, to the left and opposite us, while to our right the Scheldt, which had joined the Moselle, extended as far as the sea, its mouths vaster than a lake.

It was necessary to descend within a minute or two. The rope to the escape-valve, which had been religiously enclosed in a little white bag and placed in sight of all so that no one would touch it, is unrolled, and M. Mallet holds it in his hand while Captain Jovis looks for a favorable landing.

Behind us the thunder was rumbling and not a single bird followed our mad flight.

"Pull!" cried Jovis.

We were passing over a canal. The basket trembled and tipped over slightly. The guy-rope touched the tall trees on both banks. But our speed is so great that the long rope now trailing does not seem to slow down, and we pass with frightful rapidity over a large farm, from which the bewildered chickens, pigeons and ducks fly away, while the cows, cats and dogs run, terrified, toward the house.

Just one-half bag of ballast is left. Jovis throws it overboard, and Le Horla flies lightly across the roof.

The captain once more cries: "The escape-valve!"

M. Mallet reaches for the rope and hangs to it, and we drop like an arrow. With a slash of a knife the cord which retains the anchor is cut, and we drag this grapple behind us, through a field of beets. Here are the trees.

"Take care! Hold fast! Look out for your heads!"

We pass over them. Then a strong shock shakes us. The anchor has taken hold.

"Look out! Take a good hold! Raise yourselves by your wrists. We are going to touch ground."

The basket does indeed strike the earth. Then it flies up again. Once more it falls and bounds upward again, and at last it settles on the ground, while the balloon struggles madly, like a wounded beast.

Peasants run toward us, but they do not dare approach. They were a long time before they decided to come and deliver us, for one cannot set foot on the ground until the bag is almost completely deflated.

Then, almost at the same time as the bewildered men, some of whom showed their astonishment by jumping, with the wild gestures of savages, all the cows that were grazing along the coast came toward us, surrounding our balloon with a strange and comical circle of horns, big eyes and blowing nostrils.

With the help of the accommodating and hospitable Belgian peasants, we were able in a short time to pack up all our material and carry it to the station at Heyst, where at twenty minutes past eight we took the train for Paris.

The descent occurred at three-fifteen in the morning, preceding by only a few seconds the torrent of rain and the blinding lightning of the storm which had been chasing us before it.

Thanks to Captain Jovis, of whom I had heard much from my colleague, Paul Ginisty—for both of them had fallen together and voluntarily into the sea opposite Mentone—thanks to this brave man, we were able to see, in a single night, from far up in the sky, the setting of the sun, the rising of the moon and the dawn of day and to go from Paris to the mouth of the Scheldt through the skies.

[This story appeared in "Figaro" on July 16, 1887, under the title:

"From Paris to Heyst."]

FAREWELL!

The two friends were getting near the end of their dinner. Through the cafe windows they could see the Boulevard, crowded with people. They could feel the gentle breezes which are wafted over Paris on warm summer evenings and make you feel like going out somewhere, you care not where, under the trees, and make you dream of moonlit rivers, of fireflies and of larks.

One of the two, Henri Simon, heaved a deep sigh and said:

"Ah! I am growing old. It's sad. Formerly, on evenings like this, I felt full of life. Now, I only feel regrets. Life is short!"

He was perhaps forty-five years old, very bald and already growing stout.

The other, Pierre Carnier, a trifle older, but thin and lively, answered:

"Well, my boy, I have grown old without noticing it in the least. I have always been merry, healthy, vigorous and all the rest. As one sees oneself in the mirror every day, one does not realize the work of age, for it is slow, regular, and it modifies the countenance so gently that the changes are unnoticeable. It is for this reason alone that we do not die of sorrow after two or three years of excitement. For we cannot understand the alterations which time produces. In order to appreciate them one would have to remain six months without seeing one's own face —then, oh, what a shock!

"And the women, my friend, how I pity the poor beings! All their joy, all their power, all their life, lies in their beauty, which lasts ten years.

"As I said, I aged without noticing it; I thought myself practically a youth, when I was almost fifty years old. Not feeling the slightest infirmity, I went about, happy and peaceful.

"The revelation of my decline came to me in a simple and terrible manner, which overwhelmed me for almost six months—then I became resigned.

"Like all men, I have often been in love, but most especially once.

"I met her at the seashore, at Etretat, about twelve years ago, shortly after the war. There is nothing prettier than this beach during the morning bathing hour. It is small, shaped like a horseshoe, framed by high white cliffs, which are pierced by strange holes called the 'Portes,' one stretching out into the ocean like the leg of a giant, the other short and dumpy. The women gather on the narrow strip of sand in this frame of high rocks, which they make into a gorgeous garden of beautiful gowns. The sun beats down on the shores, on the multicolored parasols, on the blue-green sea; and all is gay, delightful, smiling. You sit down at the edge of the water and you watch the bathers. The women come down, wrapped in long bath robes, which they throw off daintily when they reach the foamy edge of the rippling waves; and they run into the water with a rapid little step, stopping from time to time for a delightful little thrill from the cold water, a short gasp.

"Very few stand the test of the bath. It is there that they can be judged, from the ankle to the throat. Especially on leaving the water are the defects revealed, although water is a powerful aid to flabby skin.

"The first time that I saw this young woman in the water, I was delighted, entranced. She stood the test well. There are faces whose charms appeal to you at first glance and delight you instantly. You seem to have found the woman whom you were born to love. I had that feeling and that shock.

"I was introduced, and was soon smitten worse than I had ever been before. My heart longed for her. It is a terrible yet delightful thing thus to be dominated by a young woman. It is almost torture, and yet infinite delight. Her look, her smile, her hair fluttering in the wind, the little lines of her face, the slightest movement of her features, delighted me, upset me, entranced me. She had captured me, body and soul, by her gestures, her manners, even by her clothes, which seemed to take on a peculiar charm as soon as she wore them. I grew tender at the sight of her veil on some piece of furniture, her gloves thrown on a chair. Her gowns seemed to me inimitable. Nobody had hats like hers.

"She was married, but her husband came only on Saturday, and left on Monday. I didn't cencern myself about him, anyhow. I wasn't jealous of him, I don't know why; never did a creature seem to me to be of less importance in life, to attract my attention less than this man.

"But she! how I loved her! How beautiful, graceful and young she was! She was youth, elegance, freshness itself! Never before had I felt so strongly what a pretty, distinguished, delicate, charming, graceful being woman is. Never before had I appreciated the seductive beauty to be found in the curve of a cheek, the movement of a lip, the pinkness of an ear, the shape of that foolish organ called the nose.

"This lasted three months; then I left for America, overwhelmed with sadness. But her memory remained in me, persistent, triumphant. From far away I was as much hers as I had been when she was near me. Years passed by, and I did not forget her. The charming image of her person was ever before my eyes and in my heart. And my love remained true to her, a quiet tenderness now, something like the beloved memory of the most beautiful and the most enchanting thing I had ever met in my life.

"Twelve years are not much in a lifetime! One does not feel them slip by. The years follow each other gently and quickly, slowly yet rapidly, each one is long and yet so soon over! They add up so rapidly, they leave so few traces behind them, they disappear so completely, that, when one turns round to look back over bygone years, one sees nothing and yet one does not understand how one happens to be so old. It seemed to me, really, that hardly a few months separated me from that charming season on the sands of Etretat.

"Last spring I went to dine with some friends at Maisons-Laffitte.

"Just as the train was leaving, a big, fat lady, escorted by four little girls, got into my car. I hardly looked at this mother hen, very big, very round, with a face as full as the moon framed in an enormous, beribboned hat.

"She was puffing, out of breath from having been forced to walk quickly. The children began to chatter. I unfolded my paper and began to read.

"We had just passed Asnieres, when my neighbor suddenly turned to me and said:

"'Excuse me, sir, but are you not Monsieur Garnier?'

"'Yes, madame.'

"Then she began to laugh, the pleased laugh of a good woman; and yet it was sad.

"'You do not seem to recognize me.'

"I hesitated. It seemed to me that I had seen that face somewhere; but where? when? I answered:

"'Yes—and no. I certainly know you, and yet I cannot recall your name.'

"She blushed a little:

"'Madame Julie Lefevre.'

"Never had I received such a shock. In a second it seemed to me as though it were all over with me! I felt that a veil had been torn from my eyes and that I was going to make a horrible and heartrending discovery.

"So that was she! That big, fat, common woman, she! She had become the mother of these four girls since I had last her. And these little beings surprised me as much as their mother. They were part of her; they were big girls, and already had a place in life. Whereas she no longer counted, she, that marvel of dainty and charming gracefulness. It seemed to me that I had seen her but yesterday, and this is how I found her again! Was it possible? A poignant grief seized my heart; and also a revolt against nature herself, an unreasoning indignation against this brutal, infarious act of destruction.

"I looked at her, bewildered. Then I took her hand in mine, and tears came to my eyes. I wept for her lost youth. For I did not know this fat lady.

"She was also excited, and stammered:

"'I am greatly changed, am I not? What can you expect—everything has its time! You see, I have become a mother, nothing but a good mother. Farewell to the rest, that is over. Oh! I never expected you to recognize me if we met. You, too, have changed. It took me quite a while to be sure that I was not mistaken. Your hair is all white. Just think! Twelve years ago! Twelve years! My oldest girl is already ten.'

"I looked at the child. And I recognized in her something of her mother's old charm, but something as yet unformed, something which promised for the future. And life seemed to me as swift as a passing train.

"We had reached. Maisons-Laffitte. I kissed my old friend's hand. I had found nothing but the most commonplace remarks. I was too much upset to talk.

"At night, alone, at home, I stood in front of the mirror for a long time, a very long time. And I finally remembered what I had been, finally saw in my mind's eye my brown mustache, my black hair and the youthful expression of my face. Now I was old. Farewell!"

THE WOLF

This is what the old Marquis d'Arville told us after St. Hubert's dinner at the house of the Baron des Ravels.

We had killed a stag that day. The marquis was the only one of the guests who had not taken part in this chase. He never hunted.

During that long repast we had talked about hardly anything but the slaughter of animals. The ladies themselves were interested in bloody and exaggerated tales, and the orators imitated the attacks and the combats of men against beasts, raised their arms, romanced in a thundering voice.

M. d Arville talked well, in a certain flowery, high-sounding, but effective style. He must have told this story frequently, for he told it fluently, never hesitating for words, choosing them with skill to make his description vivid.

Gentlemen, I have never hunted, neither did my father, nor my grandfather, nor my great-grandfather. This last was the son of a man who hunted more than all of you put together. He died in 1764. I will tell you the story of his death.

His name was Jean. He was married, father of that child who became my great-grandfather, and he lived with his younger brother, Francois d'Arville, in our castle in Lorraine, in the midst of the forest.

Francois d'Arville had remained a bachelor for love of the chase.

They both hunted from one end of the year to the other, without stopping and seemingly without fatigue. They loved only hunting, understood nothing else, talked only of that, lived only for that.

They had at heart that one passion, which was terrible and inexorable. It consumed them, had completely absorbed them, leaving room for no other thought.

They had given orders that they should not be interrupted in the chase for any reason whatever. My great-grandfather was born while his father was following a fox, and Jean d'Arville did not stop the chase, but exclaimed: "The deuce! The rascal might have waited till after the view —halloo!"

His brother Francois was still more infatuated. On rising he went to see the dogs, then the horses, then he shot little birds about the castle until the time came to hunt some large game.

In the countryside they were called M. le Marquis and M. le Cadet, the nobles then not being at all like the chance nobility of our time, which wishes to establish an hereditary hierarchy in titles; for the son of a marquis is no more a count, nor the son of a viscount a baron, than a son of a general is a colonel by birth. But the contemptible vanity of today finds profit in that arrangement.

My ancestors were unusually tall, bony, hairy, violent and vigorous. The younger, still taller than the older, had a voice so strong that, according to a legend of which he was proud, all the leaves of the forest shook when he shouted.

When they were both mounted to set out hunting, it must have been a superb sight to see those two giants straddling their huge horses.

Now, toward the midwinter of that year, 1764, the frosts were excessive, and the wolves became ferocious.

They even attacked belated peasants, roamed at night outside the houses, howled from sunset to sunrise, and robbed the stables.

And soon a rumor began to circulate. People talked of a colossal wolf with gray fur, almost white, who had eaten two children, gnawed off a woman's arm, strangled all the watch dogs in the district, and even come without fear into the farmyards. The people in the houses affirmed that they had felt his breath, and that it made the flame of the lights flicker. And soon a panic ran through all the province. No one dared go out any more after nightfall. The darkness seemed haunted by the image of the beast.

The brothers d'Arville determined to find and kill him, and several times they brought together all the gentlemen of the country to a great hunt.

They beat the forests and searched the coverts in vain; they never met him. They killed wolves, but not that one. And every night after a battue the beast, as if to avenge himself, attacked some traveller or killed some one's cattle, always far from the place where they had looked for him.

Finally, one night he stole into the pigpen of the Chateau d'Arville and ate the two fattest pigs.

The brothers were roused to anger, considering this attack as a direct insult and a defiance. They took their strong bloodhounds, used to pursue dangerous animals, and they set off to hunt, their hearts filled with rage.

From dawn until the hour when the empurpled sun descended behind the great naked trees, they beat the woods without finding anything.

At last, furious and disgusted, both were returning, walking their horses along a lane bordered with hedges, and they marvelled that their skill as huntsmen should be baffled by this wolf, and they were suddenly seized with a mysterious fear.

The elder said:

"That beast is not an ordinary one. You would say it had a mind like a man."

The younger answered:

"Perhaps we should have a bullet blessed by our cousin, the bishop, or pray some priest to pronounce the words which are needed."

Then they were silent.

Jean continued:

"Look how red the sun is. The great wolf will do some harm to-night."

He had hardly finished speaking when his horse reared; that of Franqois began to kick. A large thicket covered with dead leaves opened before them, and a mammoth beast, entirely gray, jumped up and ran off through the wood.

Both uttered a kind of grunt of joy, and bending over the necks of their heavy horses, they threw them forward with an impulse from all their body, hurling them on at such a pace, urging them, hurrying them away, exciting them so with voice and with gesture and with spur that the experienced riders seemed to be carrying the heavy beasts between their thighs and to bear them off as if they were flying.

Thus they went, plunging through the thickets, dashing across the beds of streams, climbing the hillsides, descending the gorges, and blowing the horn as loud as they could to attract their people and the dogs.

And now, suddenly, in that mad race, my ancestor struck his forehead against an enormous branch which split his skull; and he fell dead on the ground, while his frightened horse took himself off, disappearing in the gloom which enveloped the woods.

The younger d'Arville stopped quick, leaped to the earth, seized his brother in his arms, and saw that the brains were escaping from the wound with the blood.

Then he sat down beside the body, rested the head, disfigured and red, on his knees, and waited, regarding the immobile face of his elder brother. Little by little a fear possessed him, a strange fear which he had never felt before, the fear of the dark, the fear of loneliness, the fear of the deserted wood, and the fear also of the weird wolf who had just killed his brother to avenge himself upon them both.

The gloom thickened; the acute cold made the trees crack. Francois got up, shivering, unable to remain there longer, feeling himself growing faint. Nothing was to be heard, neither the voice of the dogs nor the sound of the horns-all was silent along the invisible horizon; and this mournful silence of the frozen night had something about it terrific and strange.

He seized in his immense hands the great body of Jean, straightened it, and laid it across the saddle to carry it back to the chateau; then he went on his way softly, his mind troubled as if he were in a stupor, pursued by horrible and fear-giving images.

And all at once, in the growing darkness a great shape crossed his path. It was the beast. A shock of terror shook the hunter; something cold, like a drop of water, seemed to glide down his back, and, like a monk haunted of the devil, he made a great sign of the cross, dismayed at this abrupt return of the horrible prowler. But his eyes fell again on the inert body before him, and passing abruptly from fear to anger, he shook with an indescribable rage.

Then he spurred his horse and rushed after the wolf.

He followed it through the copses, the ravines, and the tall trees, traversing woods which he no longer recognized, his eyes fixed on the white speck which fled before him through the night.

His horse also seemed animated by a force and strength hitherto unknown. It galloped straight ahead with outstretched neck, striking against trees, and rocks, the head and the feet of the dead man thrown across the saddle. The limbs tore out his hair; the brow, beating the huge trunks, spattered them with blood; the spurs tore their ragged coats of bark. Suddenly the beast and the horseman issued from the forest and rushed into a valley, just as the moon appeared above the mountains. The valley here was stony, inclosed by enormous rocks.

Francois then uttered a yell of joy which the echoes repeated like a peal of thunder, and he leaped from his horse, his cutlass in his hand.

The beast, with bristling hair, the back arched, awaited him, its eyes gleaming like two stars. But, before beginning battle, the strong hunter, seizing his brother, seated him on a rock, and, placing stones under his head, which was no more than a mass of blood, he shouted in the ears as if he was talking to a deaf man: "Look, Jean; look at this!"

Then he attacked the monster. He felt himself strong enough to overturn a mountain, to bruise stones in his hands. The beast tried to bite him, aiming for his stomach; but he had seized the fierce animal by the neck, without even using his weapon, and he strangled it gently, listening to the cessation of breathing in its throat and the beatings of its heart. He laughed, wild with joy, pressing closer and closer his formidable embrace, crying in a delirium of joy, "Look, Jean, look!" All resistance ceased; the body of the wolf became limp. He was dead.

Francois took him up in his arms and carried him to the feet of the elder brother, where he laid him, repeating, in a tender voice: "There, there, there, my little Jean, see him!"

Then he replaced on the saddle the two bodies, one upon the other, and rode away.

He returned to the chateau, laughing and crying, like Gargantua at the birth of Pantagruel, uttering shouts of triumph, and boisterous with joy as he related the death of the beast, and grieving and tearing his beard in telling of that of his brother.

And often, later, when he talked again of that day, he would say, with tears in his eyes: "If only poor Jean could have seen me strangle the beast, he would have died content, that I am sure!"

The widow of my ancestor inspired her orphan son with that horror of the chase which has transmitted itself from father to son as far down as myself.

The Marquis d'Arville was silent. Some one asked:

"That story is a legend, isn't it?"

And the story teller answered:

"I swear to you that it is true from beginning to end."

Then a lady declared, in a little, soft voice

"All the same, it is fine to have passions like that."

THE INN

Resembling in appearance all the wooden hostelries of the High Alps situated at the foot of glaciers in the barren rocky gorges that intersect the summits of the mountains, the Inn of Schwarenbach serves as a resting place for travellers crossing the Gemini Pass.

It remains open for six months in the year and is inhabited by the family of Jean Hauser; then, as soon as the snow begins to fall and to fill the valley so as to make the road down to Loeche impassable, the father and his three sons go away and leave the house in charge of the old guide, Gaspard Hari, with the young guide, Ulrich Kunsi, and Sam, the great mountain dog.

The two men and the dog remain till the spring in their snowy prison, with nothing before their eyes except the immense white slopes of the Balmhorn, surrounded by light, glistening summits, and are shut in, blocked up and buried by the snow which rises around them and which envelops, binds and crushes the little house, which lies piled on the roof, covering the windows and blocking up the door.

It was the day on which the Hauser family were going to return to Loeche, as winter was approaching, and the descent was becoming dangerous. Three mules started first, laden with baggage and led by the three sons. Then the mother, Jeanne Hauser, and her daughter Louise mounted a fourth mule and set off in their turn and the father followed them, accompanied by the two men in charge, who were to escort the family as far as the brow of the descent. First of all they passed round the small lake, which was now frozen over, at the bottom of the mass of rocks which stretched in front of the inn, and then they followed the valley, which was dominated on all sides by the snow-covered summits.

A ray of sunlight fell into that little white, glistening, frozen desert and illuminated it with a cold and dazzling flame. No living thing appeared among this ocean of mountains. There was no motion in this immeasurable solitude and no noise disturbed the profound silence.

By degrees the young guide, Ulrich Kunsi, a tall, long-legged Swiss, left old man Hauser and old Gaspard behind, in order to catch up the mule which bore the two women. The younger one looked at him as he approached and appeared to be calling him with her sad eyes. She was a young, fairhaired little peasant girl, whose milk-white cheeks and pale hair looked as if they had lost their color by their long abode amid the ice. When he had got up to the animal she was riding he put his hand on the crupper and relaxed his speed. Mother Hauser began to talk to him, enumerating with the minutest details all that he would have to attend to during the winter. It was the first time that he was going to stay up there, while old Hari had already spent fourteen winters amid the snow, at the inn of Schwarenbach.

Ulrich Kunsi listened, without appearing to understand and looked incessantly at the girl. From time to time he replied: "Yes, Madame Hauser," but his thoughts seemed far away and his calm features remained unmoved.

They reached Lake Daube, whose broad, frozen surface extended to the end of the valley. On the right one saw the black, pointed, rocky summits of the Daubenhorn beside the enormous moraines of the Lommern glacier, above which rose the Wildstrubel. As they approached the Gemmi pass, where the descent of Loeche begins, they suddenly beheld the immense horizon of the Alps of the Valais, from which the broad, deep valley of the Rhone separated them.

In the distance there was a group of white, unequal, flat, or pointed mountain summits, which glistened in the sun; the Mischabel with its two peaks, the huge group of the

Weisshorn, the heavy Bruneggehorn, the lofty and formidable pyramid of Mount Cervin, that slayer of men, and the Dent-Blanche, that monstrous coquette.

Then beneath them, in a tremendous hole, at the bottom of a terrific abyss, they perceived Loeche, where houses looked as grains of sand which had been thrown into that enormous crevice that is ended and closed by the Gemmi and which opens, down below, on the Rhone.

The mule stopped at the edge of the path, which winds and turns continually, doubling backward, then, fantastically and strangely, along the side of the mountain as far as the almost invisible little village at its feet. The women jumped into the snow and the two old men joined them. "Well," father Hauser said, "good-by, and keep up your spirits till next year, my friends," and old Hari replied: "Till next year."

They embraced each other and then Madame Hauser in her turn offered her cheek, and the girl did the same.

When Ulrich Kunsi's turn came, he whispered in Louise's ear, "Do not forget those up yonder," and she replied, "No," in such a low voice that he guessed what she had said without hearing it. "Well, adieu," Jean Hauser repeated, "and don't fall ill." And going before the two women, he commenced the descent, and soon all three disappeared at the first turn in the road, while the two men returned to the inn at Schwarenbach.

They walked slowly, side by side, without speaking. It was over, and they would be alone together for four or five months. Then Gaspard Hari began to relate his life last winter. He had remained with Michael Canol, who was too old now to stand it, for an accident might happen during that long solitude. They had not been dull, however; the only thing was to make up one's mind to it from the first, and in the end one would find plenty of distraction, games and other means of whiling away the time.

Ulrich Kunsi listened to him with his eyes on the ground, for in his thoughts he was following those who were descending to the village. They soon came in sight of the inn, which was, however, scarcely visible, so small did it look, a black speck at the foot of that enormous billow of snow, and when they opened the door Sam, the great curly dog, began to romp round them.

"Come, my boy," old Gaspard said, "we have no women now, so we must get our own dinner ready. Go and peel the potatoes." And they both sat down on wooden stools and began to prepare the soup.

The next morning seemed very long to Kunsi. Old Hari smoked and spat on the hearth, while the young man looked out of the window at the snow-covered mountain opposite the house.

In the afternoon he went out, and going over yesterday's ground again, he looked for the traces of the mule that had carried the two women. Then when he had reached the Gemmi Pass, he laid himself down on his stomach and looked at Loeche.

The village, in its rocky pit, was not yet buried under the snow, from which it was sheltered by the pine woods which protected it on all sides. Its low houses looked like paving stones in a large meadow from above. Hauser's little daughter was there now in one of those gray-colored houses. In which? Ulrich Kunsi was too far away to be able to make them out separately. How he would have liked to go down while he was yet able!

But the sun had disappeared behind the lofty crest of the Wildstrubel and the young man returned to the chalet. Daddy Hari was smoking, and when he saw his mate come in he proposed a game of cards to him, and they sat down opposite each other, on either side of the table. They played for a long time a simple game called brisque and then they had supper and went to bed.

The following days were like the first, bright and cold, without any fresh snow. Old Gaspard spent his afternoons in watching the eagles and other rare birds which ventured on those frozen heights, while Ulrich returned regularly to the Gemmi Pass to look at the village. Then they played cards, dice or dominoes and lost and won a trifle, just to create an interest in the game.

One morning Hari, who was up first, called his companion. A moving, deep and light cloud of white spray was falling on them noiselessly and was by degrees burying them under a thick, heavy coverlet of foam. That lasted four days and four nights. It was necessary to free the door and the windows, to dig out a passage and to cut steps to get over this frozen powder, which a twelve hours' frost had made as hard as the granite of the moraines.

They lived like prisoners and did not venture outside their abode. They had divided their duties, which they performed regularly. Ulrich Kunsi undertook the scouring, washing and everything that belonged to cleanliness. He also chopped up the wood while Gaspard Hari did the cooking and attended to the fire. Their regular and monotonous work was interrupted by long games at cards or dice, and they never quarrelled, but were always calm and placid. They were never seen impatient or ill-humored, nor did they ever use hard words, for they had laid in a stock of patience for their wintering on the top of the mountain.

Sometimes old Gaspard took his rifle and went after chamois, and occasionally he killed one. Then there was a feast in the inn at Schwarenbach and they revelled in fresh meat. One morning he went out as usual. The thermometer outside marked eighteen degrees of frost, and as the sun had not yet risen, the hunter hoped to surprise the animals at the approaches to the Wildstrubel, and Ulrich, being alone, remained in bed until ten o'clock. He was of a sleepy nature, but he would not have dared to give way like that to his inclination in the presence of the old guide, who was ever an early riser. He breakfasted leisurely with Sam, who also spent his days and nights in sleeping in front of the fire; then he felt low-spirited and even frightened at the solitude, and was seized by a longing for his daily game of cards, as one is by the craving of a confirmed habit, and so he went out to meet his companion, who was to return at four o'clock.

The snow had levelled the whole deep valley, filled up the crevasses, obliterated all signs of the two lakes and covered the rocks, so that between the high summits there was nothing but an immense, white, regular, dazzling and frozen surface. For three weeks Ulrich had not been to the edge of the precipice from which he had looked down on the village, and he wanted to go there before climbing the slopes which led to Wildstrubel. Loeche was now also covered by the snow and the houses could scarcely be distinguished, covered as they were by that white cloak.

Then, turning to the right, he reached the Loemmern glacier. He went along with a mountaineer's long strides, striking the snow, which was as hard as a rock, with his iron-pointed stick, and with his piercing eyes he looked for the little black, moving speck in the distance, on that enormous, white expanse.

When he reached the end of the glacier he stopped and asked himself whether the old man had taken that road, and then he began to walk along the moraines with rapid and uneasy steps. The day was declining, the snow was assuming a rosy tint, and a dry, frozen wind blew in rough gusts over its crystal surface. Ulrich uttered a long, shrill, vibrating call. His voice sped through the deathlike silence in which the mountains were sleeping; it reached the distance, across profound and motionless waves of glacial foam, like the cry of a bird across the waves of the sea. Then it died away and nothing answered him.

He began to walk again. The sun had sunk yonder behind the mountain tops, which were still purple with the reflection from the sky, but the depths of the valley were becoming gray, and suddenly the young man felt frightened. It seemed to him as if the silence, the cold, the solitude, the winter death of these mountains were taking possession of him, were going to stop and to freeze his blood, to make his limbs grow stiff and to turn him into a motionless and frozen object, and he set off running, fleeing toward his dwelling. The old man, he thought, would have returned during his absence. He had taken another road; he would, no doubt, be sitting before the fire, with a dead chamois at his feet. He soon came in sight of the inn, but no smoke rose from it. Ulrich walked faster and opened the door. Sam ran up to him to greet him, but Gaspard Hari had not returned. Kunsi, in his alarm, turned round suddenly, as if he had expected to find his comrade hidden in a corner. Then he relighted the fire and made the soup, hoping every moment to see the old man come in. From time to time he went out to see if he were not coming. It was quite night now, that wan, livid night of the mountains, lighted by a thin, yellow crescent moon, just disappearing behind the mountain tops.

Then the young man went in and sat down to warm his hands and feet, while he pictured to himself every possible accident. Gaspard might have broken a leg, have fallen into a crevasse, taken a false step and dislocated his ankle. And, perhaps, he was lying on the snow, overcome and stiff with the cold, in agony of mind, lost and, perhaps, shouting for help, calling with all his might in the silence of the night.. But where? The mountain was so vast, so rugged, so dangerous in places, especially at that time of the year, that it would have required ten or twenty guides to walk for a week in all directions to find a man in that immense space. Ulrich Kunsi, however, made up his mind to set out with Sam if Gaspard did not return by one in the morning, and he made his preparations.

He put provisions for two days into a bag, took his steel climbing iron, tied a long, thin, strong rope round his waist, and looked to see that his iron-shod stick and his axe, which served to cut steps in the ice, were in order. Then he waited. The fire was burning on the hearth, the great dog was snoring in front of it, and the clock was ticking, as regularly as a heart beating, in its resounding wooden case. He waited, with his ears on the alert for distant sounds, and he shivered when the wind blew against the roof and the walls. It struck twelve and he trembled: Then, frightened and shivering, he put some water on the fire, so that he might have some hot coffee before starting, and when the clock struck one he got up, woke Sam, opened the door and went off in the direction of the Wildstrubel. For five hours he mounted, scaling the rocks by means of his climbing irons, cutting into the ice, advancing continually, and occasionally hauling up the dog, who remained below at the foot of some slope that was too steep for him, by means of the rope. It was about six o'clock when he reached one of the summits to which old Gaspard often came after chamois, and he waited till it should be daylight.

The sky was growing pale overhead, and a strange light, springing nobody could tell whence, suddenly illuminated the immense ocean of pale mountain summits, which extended for a hundred leagues around him. One might have said that this vague brightness arose from the snow itself and spread abroad in space. By degrees the highest distant summits assumed a delicate, pink flesh color, and the red sun appeared behind the ponderous giants of the Bernese Alps.

Ulrich Kunsi set off again, walking like a hunter, bent over, looking for tracks, and saying to his dog: "Seek, old fellow, seek!"

He was descending the mountain now, scanning the depths closely, and from time to time shouting, uttering aloud, prolonged cry, which soon died away in that silent vastness. Then he put his ear to the ground to listen. He thought he could distinguish a voice, and he began to run and shouted again, but he heard nothing more and sat down, exhausted and in despair. Toward midday he breakfasted and gave Sam, who was as tired as himself, something to eat also, and then he recommenced his search.

When evening came he was still walking, and he had walked more than thirty miles over the mountains. As he was too far away to return home and too tired to drag himself along any further, he dug a hole in the snow and crouched in it with his dog under a blanket which he had brought with him. And the man and the dog lay side by side, trying to keep warm, but frozen to the marrow nevertheless. Ulrich scarcely slept, his mind haunted by visions and his limbs shaking with cold.

Day was breaking when he got up. His legs were as stiff as iron bars and his spirits so low that he was ready to cry with anguish, while his heart was beating so that he almost fell over with agitation, when he thought he heard a noise.

Suddenly he imagined that he also was going to die of cold in the midst of this vast solitude, and the terror of such a death roused his energies and gave him renewed vigor. He was descending toward the inn, falling down and getting up again, and followed at a distance by Sam, who was limping on three legs, and they did not reach Schwarenbach until four o'clock in the afternoon. The house was empty and the young man made a fire, had something to eat and went to sleep, so worn out that he did not think of anything more.

He slept for a long time, for a very long time, an irresistible sleep. But suddenly a voice, a cry, a name, "Ulrich!" aroused him from his profound torpor and made him sit up in bed. Had he been dreaming? Was it one of those strange appeals which cross the dreams of disquieted minds? No, he heard it still, that reverberating cry-which had entered his ears and remained in his flesh-to the tips of his sinewy fingers. Certainly somebody had cried out and called "Ulrich!" There was somebody there near the house, there could be no doubt of that, and he opened the door and shouted, "Is it you, Gaspard?" with all the strength of his lungs. But there was no reply, no murmur, no groan, nothing. It was quite dark and the snow looked wan.

The wind had risen, that icy wind that cracks the rocks and leaves nothing alive on those deserted heights, and it came in sudden gusts, which were more parching and more deadly than the burning wind of the desert, and again Ulrich shouted: "Gaspard! Gaspard! Gaspard." And then he waited again. Everything was silent on the mountain.

Then he shook with terror and with a bound he was inside the inn, when he shut and bolted the door, and then he fell into a chair trembling all over, for he felt certain that his comrade had called him at the moment he was expiring.

He was sure of that, as sure as one is of being alive or of eating a piece of bread. Old Gaspard Hari had been dying for two days and three nights somewhere, in some hole, in one of those deep, untrodden ravines whose whiteness is more sinister than subterranean darkness. He had been dying for two days and three nights and he had just then died, thinking of his comrade. His soul, almost before it was released, had taken its flight to the inn where Ulrich was sleeping, and it had called him by that terrible and mysterious power which the spirits of the dead have to haunt the living. That voiceless soul had cried to the worn-out soul of the sleeper; it had uttered its last farewell, or its reproach, or its curse on the man who had not searched carefully enough.

And Ulrich felt that it was there, quite close to him, behind the wall, behind the door which he had just fastened. It was wandering about, like a night bird which lightly touches a lighted window with his wings, and the terrified young man was ready to scream with horror. He wanted to run away, but did not dare to go out; he did not dare, and he should never dare to do it in the future, for that phantom would remain there day and night, round the inn, as long as the old man's body was not recovered and had not been deposited in the consecrated earth of a churchyard.

When it was daylight Kunsi recovered some of his courage at the return of the bright sun. He prepared his meal, gave his dog some food and then remained motionless on a chair, tortured at heart as he thought of the old man lying on the snow, and then, as soon as night once more covered the mountains, new terrors assailed him. He now walked up and down the dark kitchen, which was scarcely lighted by the flame of one candle, and he walked from one end of it to the other with great strides, listening, listening whether the terrible cry of the other night would again break the dreary silence outside. He felt himself alone, unhappy man, as no man had ever been alone before! He was alone in this immense desert of Snow, alone five thousand feet above the inhabited earth, above human habitation, above that stirring, noisy, palpitating life, alone under an icy sky! A mad longing impelled him to run away, no matter where, to get down to Loeche by flinging himself over the precipice; but he did not even dare to open the door, as he felt sure that the other, the dead man, would bar his road, so that he might not be obliged to remain up there alone:

Toward midnight, tired with walking, worn out by grief and fear, he at last fell into a doze in his chair, for he was afraid of his bed as one is of a haunted spot. But suddenly the strident cry of the other evening pierced his ears, and it was so shrill that Ulrich stretched out his arms to repulse the ghost, and he fell backward with his chair.

Sam, who was awakened by the noise, began to howl as frightened dogs do howl, and he walked all about the house trying to find out where the danger came from. When he got to the door, he sniffed beneath it, smelling vigorously, with his coat bristling and his tail stiff, while he growled angrily. Kunsi, who was terrified, jumped up, and, holding his chair by one leg, he cried: "Don't come in, don't come in, or I shall kill you." And the dog, excited by this threat, barked angrily at that invisible enemy who defied his master's voice. By degrees, however, he quieted down and came back and stretched himself in front of the fire, but he was uneasy and kept his head up and growled between his teeth.

Ulrich, in turn, recovered his senses, but as he felt faint with terror, he went and got a bottle of brandy out of the sideboard, and he drank off several glasses, one after anther, at a gulp. His ideas became vague, his courage revived and a feverish glow ran through his veins.

He ate scarcely anything the next day and limited himself to alcohol, and so he lived for several days, like a drunken brute. As soon as he thought of Gaspard Hari, he began to drink again, and went on drinking until he fell to the ground, overcome by intoxication. And there he remained lying on his face, dead drunk, his limbs benumbed, and snoring loudly. But scarcely had he digested the maddening and burning liquor than the same cry, "Ulrich!" woke him like a bullet piercing his brain, and he got up, still staggering, stretching out his hands to save himself from falling, and calling to Sam to help him. And the dog, who appeared to be going mad like his master, rushed to the door, scratched it with his claws and gnawed it with his long white teeth, while the young man, with his head thrown back drank the brandy in draughts, as if it had been cold water, so that it might by and by send his thoughts, his frantic terror, and his memory to sleep again.

In three weeks he had consumed all his stock of ardent spirits. But his continual drunkenness only lulled his terror, which awoke more furiously than ever as soon as it was impossible for him to calm it. His fixed idea then, which had been intensified by a month of drunkenness, and which was continually increasing in his absolute solitude, penetrated him like a gimlet. He now walked about the house like a wild beast in its cage, putting his ear to the door to listen if the other were there and defying him through the wall. Then, as soon as he dozed, overcome by fatigue, he heard the voice which made him leap to his feet.

At last one night, as cowards do when driven to extremities, he sprang to the door and opened it, to see who was calling him and to force him to keep quiet, but such a gust of cold wind blew into his face that it chilled him to the bone, and he closed and bolted the door again immediately, without noticing that Sam had rushed out. Then, as he was shivering with cold, he threw some wood on the fire and sat down in front of it to warm himself, but suddenly he started, for somebody was scratching at the wall and crying. In desperation he called out: "Go away!" but was answered by another long, sorrowful wail.

Then all his remaining senses forsook him from sheer fright. He repeated: "Go away!" and turned round to try to find some corner in which to hide, while the other person went round the house still crying and rubbing against the wall. Ulrich went to the oak sideboard, which was full of plates and dishes and of provisions, and lifting it up with superhuman strength, he dragged it to the door, so as to form a barricade. Then piling up all the rest of the furniture, the mattresses, palliasses and chairs, he stopped up the windows as one does when assailed by an enemy.

But the person outside now uttered long, plaintive, mournful groans, to which the young man replied by similar groans, and thus days and nights passed without their ceasing to howl at each other. The one was continually walking round the house and scraped the walls with his nails so vigorously that it seemed as if he wished to destroy them, while the other, inside, followed all his movements, stooping down and holding his ear to the walls and replying to all his appeals with terrible cries. One evening, however, Ulrich heard nothing more, and he sat down, so overcome by fatigue, that he went to sleep immediately and awoke in the morning without a thought, without any recollection of what had happened, just as if his head had been emptied during his heavy sleep, but he felt hungry, and he ate.

The winter was over and the Gemmi Pass was practicable again, so the Hauser family started off to return to their inn. As soon as they had reached the top of the ascent the women mounted their mule and spoke about the two men whom they would meet again shortly. They were, indeed, rather surprised that neither of them had come down a few days before, as soon as the road was open, in order to tell them all about their long winter sojourn. At last, however, they saw the inn, still covered with snow, like a quilt. The door and the window were closed, but a little smoke was coming out of the chimney, which reassured old Hauser. On going up to the door, however, he saw the skeleton of an animal which had been torn to pieces by the eagles, a large skeleton lying on its side.

They all looked close at it and the mother said:

"That must be Sam," and then she shouted: "Hi, Gaspard!" A cry from the interior of the house answered her and a sharp cry that one might have thought some animal had uttered it. Old Hauser repeated, "Hi, Gaspard!" and they heard another cry similar to the first.

Then the three men, the father and the two sons, tried to open the door, but it resisted their efforts. From the empty cow-stall they took a beam to serve as a battering-ram and hurled it against the door with all their might. The wood gave way and the boards flew into splinters. Then the house was shaken by a loud voice, and inside, behind the side board which was overturned, they saw a man standing upright, with his hair falling on his shoulders and a beard descending to his breast, with shining eyes, and nothing but rags to cover him. They did not recognize him, but Louise Hauser exclaimed:

"It is Ulrich, mother." And her mother declared that it was Ulrich, although his hair was white.

He allowed them to go up to him and to touch him, but he did not reply to any of their questions, and they were obliged to take him to Loeche, where the doctors found that he was mad, and nobody ever found out what had become of his companion.

Little Louise Hauser nearly died that summer of decline, which the physicians attributed to the cold air of the mountains.

VOLUME V.

MONSIEUR PARENT

George's father was sitting in an iron chair, watching his little son with concentrated affection and attention, as little George piled up the sand into heaps during one of their walks. He would take up the sand with both hands, make a mound of it, and put a chestnut leaf on top. His father saw no one but him in that public park full of people.

The sun was just disappearing behind the roofs of the Rue Saint-Lazare, but still shed its rays obliquely on that little, overdressed crowd. The chestnut trees were lighted up by its yellow rays, and the three fountains before the lofty porch of the church had the appearance of liquid silver.

Monsieur Parent, accidentally looking up at the church clock, saw that he was five minutes late. He got up, took the child by the arm, shook his dress, which was covered with sand, wiped his hands, and led him in the direction of the Rue Blanche. He walked quickly, so as not to get in after his wife, and the child could not keep up with him. He took him up and carried him, though it made him pant when he had to walk up the steep street. He was a man of forty, already turning gray, and rather stout. At last he reached his house. An old servant who had brought him up, one of those trusted servants who are the tyrants of families, opened the door to him.

"Has madame come in yet?" he asked anxiously.

The servant shrugged her shoulders:

"When have you ever known madame to come home at half-past six, monsieur?"

"Very well; all the better; it will give me time to change my things, for I am very warm."

The servant looked at him with angry and contemptuous pity. "Oh, I can see that well enough," she grumbled. "You are covered with perspiration, monsieur. I suppose you walked quickly and carried the child, and only to have to wait until half-past seven, perhaps, for madame. I have made up my mind not to have dinner ready on time. I shall get it for eight o'clock, and if, you have to wait, I cannot help it; roast meat ought not to be burnt!"

Monsieur Parent pretended not to hear, but went into his own room, and as soon as he got in, locked the door, so as to be alone, quite alone. He was so used now to being abused and badly treated that he never thought himself safe except when he was locked in.

What could he do? To get rid of Julie seemed to him such a formidable thing to do that he hardly ventured to think of it, but it was just as impossible to uphold her against his wife, and before another month the situation would become unbearable between the two. He remained sitting there, with his arms hanging down, vaguely trying to discover some means to set matters straight, but without success. He said to himself: "It is lucky that I have George; without him I should-be very miserable."

Just then the clock struck seven, and he started up. Seven o'clock, and he had not even changed his clothes. Nervous and breathless, he undressed, put on a clean shirt, hastily finished his toilet, as if he had been expected in the next room for some event of extreme importance, and went into the drawing-room, happy at having nothing to fear. He glanced at the newspaper, went and looked out of the window, and then sat down again, when the door opened, and the boy came in, washed, brushed, and smiling. Parent took him up in his arms and kissed him passionately; then he tossed him into the air, and held him up to the ceiling, but soon sat down again, as he was tired with all his exertion. Then, taking George on his knee, he made him ride a-cock-horse. The child laughed and clapped his hands and shouted with pleasure, as did his father, who laughed until his big stomach shook, for it amused him almost more than it did the child.

Parent loved him with all the heart of a weak, resigned, ill-used man. He loved him with mad bursts of affection, with caresses and with all the bashful tenderness which was hidden in him, and which had never found an outlet, even at the early period of his married life, for his wife had always shown herself cold and reserved.

Just then Julie came to the door, with a pale face and glistening eyes, and said in a voice which trembled with exasperation: "It is half-past seven, monsieur."

Parent gave an uneasy and resigned look at the clock and replied: "Yes, it certainly is half-past seven."

"Well, my dinner is quite ready now."

Seeing the storm which was coming, he tried to turn it aside. "But did you not tell me when I came in that it would not be ready before eight?"

"Eight! what are you thinking about? You surely do not mean to let the child dine at eight o'clock? It would ruin his stomach. Just suppose that he only had his mother to look after him! She cares a great deal about her child. Oh, yes, we will speak about her; she is a mother! What a pity it is that there should be any mothers like her!"

Parent thought it was time to cut short a threatened scene. "Julie," he said, "I will not allow you to speak like that of your mistress. You understand me, do you not? Do not forget it in the future."

The old servant, who was nearly choked with surprise, turned and went out, slamming the door so violently after her that the lustres on the chandelier rattled, and for some seconds it sounded as if a number of little invisible bells were ringing in the drawing-room.

Eight o'clock struck, the door opened, and Julie came in again. She had lost her look of exasperation, but now she put on an air of cold and determined resolution, which was still more formidable.

"Monsieur," she said, "I served your mother until the day of her death, and I have attended to you from your birth until now, and I think it may be said that I am devoted to the family." She waited for a reply, and Parent stammered:

"Why, yes, certainly, my good Julie."

"You know quite well," she continued, "that I have never done anything for the sake of money, but always for your sake; that I have never deceived you nor lied to you, that you have never had to find fault with me—"

"Certainly, my good Julie."

"Very well, then, monsieur; it cannot go on any longer like this. I have said nothing, and left you in your ignorance, out of respect and liking for you, but it is too much, and every one in the neighborhood is laughing at you. Everybody knows about it, and so I must tell you also, although I do not like to repeat it. The reason why madame comes in at any time she chooses is that she is doing abominable things."

He seemed stupefied and not to understand, and could only stammer out:

"Hold your tongue; you know I have forbidden you——"

But she interrupted him with irresistible resolution. "No, monsieur, I must tell you everything now. For a long time madame has been carrying on with Monsieur Limousin. I have seen them kiss scores of times behind the door. Ah! you may be sure that if Monsieur Limousin had been rich, madame would never have married Monsieur Parent. If you remember how the marriage was brought about, you would understand the matter from beginning to end."

Parent had risen, and stammered out, his face livid: "Hold your tongue —hold your tongue, or——"

She went on, however: "No, I mean to tell you everything. She married you from interest, and she deceived you from the very first day. It was all settled between them beforehand. You need only reflect for a few moments to understand it, and then, as she was not satisfied with having married you, as she did not love you, she has made your life miserable, so miserable that it has almost broken my heart when I have seen it."

He walked up and down the room with hands clenched, repeating: "Hold your tongue—hold your tongue——" For he could find nothing else to say. The old servant, however, would not yield; she seemed resolved on everything.

George, who had been at first astonished and then frightened at those angry voices, began to utter shrill screams, and remained behind his father, with his face puckered up and his mouth open, roaring.

His son's screams exasperated Parent, and filled him with rage and courage. He rushed at Julie with both arms raised, ready to strike her, exclaiming: "Ah! you wretch. You will drive the child out of his senses." He already had his hand on her, when she screamed in his face:

"Monsieur, you may beat me if you like, me who reared you, but that will not prevent your wife from deceiving you, or alter the fact that your child is not yours——"

He stopped suddenly, let his arms fall, and remained standing opposite to her, so overwhelmed that he could understand nothing more.

"You need only to look at the child," she added, "to know who is its father! He is the very image of Monsieur Limousin. You need only look at his eyes and forehead. Why, a blind man could not be mistaken in him."

He had taken her by the shoulders, and was now shaking her with all his might. "Viper, viper!" he said. "Go out the room, viper! Go out, or I shall kill you! Go out! Go out!"

And with a desperate effort he threw her into the next room. She fell across the table, which was laid for dinner, breaking the glasses. Then, rising to her feet, she put the table between her master and herself. While he was pursuing her, in order to take hold of her again, she flung terrible words at him.

"You need only go out this evening after dinner, and come in again immediately, and you will see! You will see whether I have been lying! Just try it, and you will see." She had reached the kitchen door and escaped, but he ran after her, up the back stairs to her bedroom, into which she had locked herself, and knocking at the door, he said:

"You will leave my house this very instant!"

"You may be certain of that, monsieur," was her reply. "In an hour's time I shall not be here any longer."

He then went slowly downstairs again, holding on to the banister so as not to fall, and went back to the drawing-room, where little George was sitting on the floor, crying. He fell into a chair, and looked at the child with dull eyes. He understood nothing, knew nothing more; he felt dazed, stupefied, mad, as if he had just fallen on his head, and he scarcely even remembered the dreadful things the servant had told him. Then, by degrees, his mind, like muddy water, became calmer and clearer, and the abominable revelations began to work in his heart.

He was no longer thinking of George. The child was quiet now and sitting on the carpet; but, seeing that no notice was being taken of him, he began to cry. His father ran to him, took him in his arms, and covered him with kisses. His child remained to him, at any rate! What did the rest matter? He held him in his arms and pressed his lips to his light hair, and, relieved and composed, he whispered:

"George—my little George—my dear little George——" But he suddenly remembered what Julie had said! Yes, she had said that he was Limousin's child. Oh! it could not be possible, surely. He could not believe it, could not doubt, even for a moment, that he was his own child. It was one of those low scandals which spring from servants' brains! And he repeated: "George—my dear little George." The youngster was quiet again, now that his father was fondling him.

Parent felt the warmth of the little chest penetrate through his clothes, and it filled him with love, courage, and happiness; that gentle warmth soothed him, fortified him and saved him. Then he put the small, curly head away from him a little, and looked at it affectionately, still repeating: "George! Oh, my little George!" But suddenly he thought:

"Suppose he were to resemble Limousin, after all!" He looked at him with haggard, troubled eyes, and tried to discover whether there was any likeness in his forehead, in his nose, mouth, or cheeks. His thoughts wandered as they do when a person is going mad, and his child's face changed in his eyes, and assumed a strange look and improbable resemblances.

The hall bell rang. Parent gave a bound as if a bullet had gone through him. "There she is," he said. "What shall I do?" And he ran and locked himself up in his room, to have time to bathe his eyes. But in a few moments another ring at the bell made him jump again, and then he remembered that Julie had left, without the housemaid knowing it, and so nobody would go to open the door. What was he to do? He went himself, and suddenly he felt brave, resolute, ready for dissimulation and the struggle. The terrible blow had matured him in a few moments. He wished to know the truth, he desired it with the rage of a timid man, and with the tenacity of an easy-going man who has been exasperated.

Nevertheless, he trembled. Does one know how much excited cowardice there often is in boldness? He went to the door with furtive steps, and stopped to listen; his heart beat furiously. Suddenly, however, the noise of the bell over his head startled him like an explosion. He seized the lock, turned the key, and opening the door, saw his wife and Limousin standing before him on the stairs.

With an air of astonishment, which also betrayed a little irritation, she said:

“So you open the door now? Where is Julie?”

His throat felt tight and his breathing was labored as he tried to. reply, without being able to utter a word.

“Are you dumb?” she continued. “I asked you where Julie is?”

“She—she—has—gone——” he managed to stammer.

His wife began to get angry. “What do you mean by gone? Where has she gone? Why?”

By degrees he regained his coolness. He felt an intense hatred rise up in him for that insolent woman who was standing before him.

“Yes, she has gone altogether. I sent her away.”

“You have sent away Julie? Why, you must be mad.”

“Yes, I sent her away because she was insolent, and because—because she was ill-using the child.”

“Julie?”

“Yes—Julie.”

“What was she insolent about?”

“About you.”

“About me?”

“Yes, because the dinner was burnt, and you did not come in.”

“And she said——”

“She said—offensive things about you—which I ought not which I could not listen to——”

“What did she, say?”

“It is no good repeating them.”

“I want to hear them.”

“She said it was unfortunate for a man like me to be married to a woman like you, unpunctual, careless, disorderly, a bad mother, and a bad wife.”

The young woman had gone into the anteroom, followed by Limousin, who did not say a word at this unexpected condition of things. She shut the door quickly, threw her cloak on a chair, and going straight up to her husband, she stammered out:

“You say? You say? That I am——”

Very pale and calm, he replied: “I say nothing, my dear. I am simply repeating what Julie said to me, as you wanted to know what it was, and I wish you to remark that I turned her off just on account of what she said.”

She trembled with a violent longing to tear out his beard and scratch his face. In his voice and manner she felt that he was asserting his position as master. Although she had nothing to say by way of reply, she tried to assume the offensive by saying something unpleasant. "I suppose you have had dinner?" she asked.

"No, I waited for you."

She shrugged her shoulders impatiently. "It is very stupid of you to wait after half-past seven," she said. "You might have guessed that I was detained, that I had a good many things to do, visits and shopping,"

And then, suddenly, she felt that she wanted to explain how she had spent her time, and told him in abrupt, haughty words that, having to buy some furniture in a shop a long distance off, very far off, in the Rue de Rennes, she had met Limousin at past seven o'clock on the Boulevard Saint-Germain, and that then she had gone with him to have something to eat in a restaurant, as she did not like to go to one by herself, although she was faint with hunger. That was how she had dined with Limousin, if it could be called dining, for they had only some soup and half a chicken, as they were in a great hurry to get back.

Parent replied simply: "Well, you were quite right. I am not finding fault with you."

Then Limousin, who, had not spoken till then, and who had been half hidden behind Henriette, came forward and put out his hand, saying: "Are you very well?"

Parent took his hand, and shaking it gently, replied: "Yes, I am very well."

But the young woman had felt a reproach in her husband's last words. "Finding fault! Why do you speak of finding fault? One might think that you meant to imply something."

"Not at all," he replied, by way of excuse. "I simply meant that I was not at all anxious although you were late, and that I did not find fault with you for it."

She, however, took the high hand, and tried to find a pretext for a quarrel. "Although I was late? One might really think that it was one o'clock in the morning, and that I spent my nights away from home."

"Certainly not, my dear. I said late because I could find no other word. You said you should be back at half-past six, and you returned at half-past eight. That was surely being late. I understand it perfectly well. I am not at all surprised, even. But—but—I can hardly use any other word."

"But you pronounce them as if I had been out all night."

"Oh, no-oh, no!"

She saw that he would yield on every point, and she was going into her own room, when at last she noticed that George was screaming, and then she asked, with some feeling: "What is the matter with the child?"

"I told you that Julie had been rather unkind to him."

"What has the wretch been doing to him?"

"Oh nothing much. She gave him a push, and he fell down."

She wanted to see her child, and ran into the dining room, but stopped short at the sight of the table covered with spilt wine, with broken decanters and glasses and overturned saltcellars. "Who did all that mischief?" she asked.

"It was Julie, who——" But she interrupted him furiously:

"That is too much, really! Julie speaks of me as if I were a shameless woman, beats my child, breaks my plates and dishes, turns my house upside down, and it appears that you think it all quite natural."

"Certainly not, as I have got rid of her."

"Really! You have got rid of her! But you ought to have given her in charge. In such cases, one ought to call in the Commissary of Police!"

"But—my dear—I really could not. There was no reason. It would have been very difficult——"

She shrugged her shoulders disdainfully. "There! you will never be anything but a poor, wretched fellow, a man without a will, without any firmness or energy. Ah! she must have said some nice things to you, your Julie, to make you turn her off like that. I should like to have been here for a minute, only for a minute." Then she opened the drawing-room door and ran to George, took him into her arms and kissed him, and said: "Georgie, what is it, my darling, my pretty one, my treasure?"

Then, suddenly turning to another idea, she said: "But the child has had no dinner? You have had nothing to eat, my pet?"

"No, mamma."

Then she again turned furiously upon her husband. "Why, you must be mad, utterly mad! It is half-past eight, and George has had no dinner!"

He excused himself as best he could, for he had nearly lost his wits through the overwhelming scene and the explanation, and felt crushed by this ruin of his life. "But, my dear, we were waiting for you, as I did not wish to dine without you. As you come home late every day, I expected you every moment."

She threw her bonnet, which she had kept on till then, into an easy-chair, and in an angry voice she said: "It is really intolerable to have to do with people who can understand nothing, who can divine nothing and do nothing by themselves. So, I suppose, if I were to come in at twelve o'clock at night, the child would have had nothing to eat? Just as if you could not have understood that, as it was after half-past seven, I was prevented from coming home, that I had met with some hindrance!"

Parent trembled, for he felt that his anger was getting the upper hand, but Limousin interposed, and turning toward the young woman, said:

"My dear friend, you, are altogether unjust. Parent could not guess that you would come here so late, as you never do so, and then, how could you expect him to get over the difficulty all by himself, after having sent away Julie?"

But Henriette was very angry, and replied:

"Well, at any rate, he must get over the difficulty himself, for I will not help him," she replied. "Let him settle it!" And she went into her own room, quite forgetting that her child had not had anything to eat.

Limousin immediately set to work to help his friend. He picked up the broken glasses which strewed the table and took them out, replaced the plates and knives and forks, and put the child into his high chair, while Parent went to look for the chambermaid to wait at table. The girl came in, in great astonishment, as she had heard nothing in George's room, where she had been working. She soon, however, brought in the soup, a burnt leg of mutton, and mashed potatoes.

Parent sat by the side of the child, very much upset and distressed at all that had happened. He gave the boy his dinner, and endeavored to eat something himself, but he could only swallow with an effort, as his throat felt paralyzed. By degrees he was seized with an insane desire to look at Limousin, who was sitting opposite to him, making bread pellets, to see whether George was like him, but he did not venture to raise his eyes for some time. At last, however, he made up his mind to do so, and gave a quick, sharp look at the face which he knew so well, although he almost fancied that he had never examined it carefully. It looked so different to what he had imagined. From time to time he looked at Limousin, trying to recognize a likeness in the smallest lines of his face, in the slightest features, and then he looked at his son, under the pretext of feeding him.

Two words were sounding in his ears: "His father! his father! his father!" They buzzed in his temples at every beat of his heart. Yes, that man, that tranquil man who was sitting on the other side of the table, was, perhaps, the father of his son, of George, of his little George. Parent left off eating; he could not swallow any more. A terrible pain, one of those attacks of pain which make men scream, roll on the ground, and bite the furniture, was tearing at his entrails, and he felt inclined to take a knife and plunge it into his stomach. He started when he heard the door open. His wife came in. "I am hungry," she said; "are not you, Limousin?"

He hesitated a little, and then said: "Yes, I am, upon my word." She had the leg of mutton brought in again. Parent asked himself "Have they had dinner? Or are they late because they have had a lovers' meeting?"

They both ate with a very good appetite. Henriette was very calm, but laughed and joked. Her husband watched her furtively. She had on a pink teagown trimmed with white lace, and her fair head, her white neck and her plump hands stood out from that coquettish and perfumed dress as though it were a sea shell edged with foam.

What fun they must be making of him, if he had been their dupe since the first day! Was it possible to make a fool of a man, of a worthy man, because his father had left him a little money? Why could one not see into people's souls? How was it that nothing revealed to upright hearts the deceits of infamous hearts? How was it that voices had the same sound for adoring as for lying? Why was a false, deceptive look the same as a sincere one? And he watched them, waiting to catch a gesture, a word, an intonation. Then suddenly he thought: "I will surprise them this evening," and he said:

"My dear, as I have dismissed Julie, I will see about getting another girl this very day. I will go at once to procure one by to-morrow morning, so I may not be in until late."

"Very well," she replied; "go. I shall not stir from here. Limousin will keep me company. We will wait for you." Then, turning to the maid, she said: "You had better put George to bed, and then you can clear away and go up to your room."

Parent had got up; he was unsteady on his legs, dazed and bewildered, and saying, "I shall see you again later on," he went out, holding on to the wall, for the floor seemed to roll like a ship. George had been carried out by his nurse, while Henriette and Limousin went into the drawing-room.

As soon as the door was shut, he said: "You must be mad, surely, to torment your husband as you do?"

She immediately turned on him: "Ah! Do you know that I think the habit you have got into lately, of looking upon Parent as a martyr, is very unpleasant?"

Limousin threw himself into an easy-chair and crossed his legs. "I am not setting him up as a martyr in the least, but I think that, situated as we are, it is ridiculous to defy this man as you do, from morning till night."

She took a cigarette from the mantelpiece, lighted it, and replied: "But I do not defy him; quite the contrary. Only he irritates me by his stupidity, and I treat him as he deserves."

Limousin continued impatiently: "What you are doing is very foolish! I am only asking you to treat your husband gently, because we both of us require him to trust us. I think that you ought to see that."

They were close together: he, tall, dark, with long whiskers and the rather vulgar manners of a good-looking man who is very well satisfied with himself; she, small, fair, and pink, a little Parisian, born in the back room of a shop, half cocotte and half bourgeoise, brought up to entice customers to the store by her glances, and married, in consequence, to a simple, unsophisticated man, who saw her outside the door every morning when he went out and every evening when he came home.

"But do you not understand; you great booby," she said, "that I hate him just because he married me, because he bought me, in fact; because everything that he says and does, everything that he thinks, acts on my nerves? He exasperates me every moment by his stupidity, which you call his kindness; by his dullness, which you call his confidence, and then, above all, because he is my husband, instead of you. I feel him between us, although he does not interfere with us much. And then—-and then! No, it is, after all, too idiotic of him not to guess anything! I wish he would, at any rate, be a little jealous. There are moments when I feel inclined to say to him: 'Do you not see, you stupid creature, that Paul is my lover?'

"It is quite incomprehensible that you cannot understand how hateful he is to me, how he irritates me. You always seem to like him, and you shake hands with him cordially. Men are very extraordinary at times."

"One must know how to dissimulate, my dear."

"It is no question of dissimulation, but of feeling. One might think that, when you men deceive one another, you like each other better on that account, while we women hate a man from the moment that we have betrayed him."

"I do not see why one should hate an excellent fellow because one is friendly with his wife."

"You do not see it? You do not see it? You all of you are wanting in refinement of feeling. However, that is one of those things which one feels and cannot express. And then, moreover, one ought not. No, you would not understand; it is quite useless! You men have no delicacy of feeling."

And smiling, with the gentle contempt of an impure woman, she put both her hands on his shoulders and held up her lips to him. He stooped down and clasped her closely in his arms, and their lips met. And as they stood in front of the mantel mirror, another couple exactly like them embraced behind the clock.

They had heard nothing, neither the noise of the key nor the creaking of the door, but suddenly Henriette, with a loud cry, pushed Limousin away with both her arms, and they saw Parent looking at them, livid with rage, without his shoes on and his hat over his forehead. He looked at each, one after the other, with a quick glance of his eyes and without moving his head. He appeared beside himself. Then, without saying a word, he threw himself on Limousin, seized him as if he were going to strangle him, and flung him into the opposite corner of the room so violently that the other lost his balance, and, beating the air with his hand, struck his head violently against the wall.

When Henriette saw that her husband was going to murder her lover, she threw herself on Parent, seized him by the neck, and digging her ten delicate, rosy fingers into his neck, she squeezed him so tightly, with all the vigor of a desperate woman, that the blood spurted out under her nails, and she bit his shoulder, as if she wished to tear it with her teeth. Parent, half-strangled and choking, loosened his hold on Limousin, in order to shake off his wife, who was hanging to his neck. Putting his arms round her waist, he flung her also to the other end of the drawing-room.

Then, as his passion was short-lived, like that of most good-tempered men, and his strength was soon exhausted, he remained standing between the two, panting, worn out, not knowing what to do next. His brutal fury had expended itself in that effort, like the froth of a bottle of champagne, and his unwonted energy ended in a gasping for breath. As soon as he could speak, however, he said:

"Go away—both of you—immediately! Go away!"

Limousin remained motionless in his corner, against the wall, too startled to understand anything as yet, too frightened to move a finger; while Henriette, with her hands resting on a small, round table, her head bent forward, her hair hanging down, the bodice of her dress unfastened, waited like a wild animal which is about to spring. Parent continued in a stronger voice: "Go away immediately. Get out of the house!"

His wife, however, seeing that he had got over his first exasperation grew bolder, drew herself up, took two steps toward him, and, grown almost insolent, she said: "Have you lost your head? What is the matter with you? What is the meaning of this unjustifiable violence?"

But he turned toward her, and raising his fist to strike her, he stammered out: "Oh—oh—this is too much, too much! I heard everything! Everything—do you understand? Everything! You wretch—you wretch! You are two wretches! Get out of the house, both of you! Immediately, or I shall kill you! Leave the house!"

She saw that it was all over, and that he knew everything; that she could not prove her innocence, and that she must comply. But all her impudence had returned to her, and her hatred for the man, which was aggravated now, drove her to audacity, made her feel the need of bravado, and of defying him, and she said in a clear voice: "Come, Limousin; as he is going to turn me out of doors, I will go to your lodgings with you."

But Limousin did not move, and Parent, in a fresh access of rage, cried out: "Go, will you? Go, you wretches! Or else—or else——" He seized a chair and whirled it over his head.

Henriette walked quickly across the room, took her lover by the arm, dragged him from the wall, to which he appeared fixed, and led him toward the door, saying: "Do come, my friend—you see that the man is mad. Do come!"

As she went out she turned round to her husband, trying to think of something that she could do, something that she could invent to wound him to the heart as she left the house, and an idea struck her, one of those venomous, deadly ideas in which all a woman's perfidy shows itself, and she said resolutely: "I am going to take my child with me."

Parent was stupefied, and stammered: "Your—your—child? You dare to talk of your child? You venture—you venture to ask for your child—after-after—Oh, oh, that is too much! Go, you vile creature! Go!"

She went up to him again, almost smiling, almost avenged already, and defying him, standing close to him, and face to face, she said: "I want my child, and you have no right to keep him, because he is not yours—do you understand? He is not yours! He is Limousin's!"

And Parent cried out in bewilderment: "You lie—you lie—worthless woman!"

But she continued: "You fool! Everybody knows it except you. I tell you, this is his father. You need only look at him to see it."

Parent staggered backward, and then he suddenly turned round, took a candle, and rushed into the next room; returning almost immediately, carrying little George wrapped up in his bedclothes. The child, who had been suddenly awakened, was crying from fright. Parent threw him into his wife's arms, and then, without speaking, he pushed her roughly out toward the stairs, where Limousin was waiting, from motives of prudence.

Then he shut the door again, double-locked and bolted it, but had scarcely got back into the drawing-room when he fell to the floor at full length.

Parent lived alone, quite alone. During the five weeks that followed their separation, the feeling of surprise at his new life prevented him from thinking much. He had resumed his bachelor life, his habits of lounging, about, and took his meals at a restaurant, as he had done formerly. As he wished to avoid any scandal, he made his wife an allowance, which was arranged by their lawyers. By degrees, however, the thought of the child began to haunt him. Often, when he was at home alone at night, he suddenly thought he heard George calling out "Papa," and his heart would begin to beat, and he would get up quickly and open the door, to see whether, by chance, the child might have returned, as dogs or pigeons do. Why should a child have less instinct than an animal? On finding that he was mistaken, he would sit down in his armchair again and think of the boy. He would think of him for hours and whole days. It was not only a moral, but still more a physical obsession, a nervous longing to kiss him, to hold and fondle him, to take him on his knees and dance him. He felt the child's little arms around his neck, his little mouth pressing a kiss on his beard, his soft hair tickling his cheeks, and the remembrance of all those childish ways made him suffer as a man might for some beloved woman who has left him. Twenty or a hundred times a day he asked himself the question whether he was or was not George's father, and almost before he was in bed every night he recommenced the same series of despairing questionings.

He especially dreaded the darkness of the evening, the melancholy feeling of the twilight.

Then a flood of sorrow invaded his heart, a torrent of despair which seemed to overwhelm him and drive him mad. He was as afraid of his own thoughts as men are of criminals, and he fled before them as one does from wild beasts. Above all things, he feared his empty, dark, horrible dwelling and the deserted streets, in which, here and there, a gas lamp flickered, where the isolated foot passenger whom one hears in the distance seems to be a night prowler, and makes one walk faster or slower, according to whether he is coming toward you or following you.

And in spite of himself, and by instinct, Parent went in the direction of the broad, well-lighted, populous streets. The light and the crowd attracted him, occupied his mind and distracted his thoughts, and when he was tired of walking aimlessly about among the moving crowd, when he saw the foot passengers becoming more scarce and the pavements less crowded, the fear of solitude and silence drove him into some large cafe full of drinkers and of light. He went there as flies go to a candle, and he would sit down at one of the little round tables and ask for a "bock," which he would drink slowly, feeling uneasy every time a customer got up to go. He would have liked to take him by the arm, hold him back, and beg him to stay a little longer, so much did he dread the time when the waiter should come up to him and say sharply: "Come, monsieur, it is closing time!"

He thus got into the habit of going to the beer houses, where the continual elbowing of the drinkers brings you in contact with a familiar and silent public, where the heavy clouds of tobacco smoke lull disquietude, while the heavy beer dulls the mind and calms the heart. He almost lived there. He was scarcely up before he went there to find people to distract his glances and his thoughts, and soon, as he felt too lazy to move, he took his meals there.

After every meal, during more than an hour, he sipped three or four small glasses of brandy, which stupefied him by degrees, and then his head drooped on his chest, he shut his eyes, and went to sleep. Then, awaking, he raised himself on the red velvet seat, straightened his waistcoat, pulled down his cuffs, and took up the newspapers again, though he had already seen them in the morning, and read them all through again, from beginning to end. Between four and five o'clock he went for a walk on the boulevards, to get a little fresh air, as he used to say, and then came back to the seat which had been reserved for him, and asked for his absinthe. He would talk to the regular customers whose acquaintance he had made. They discussed the news of the day and political events, and that carried him on till dinner time; and he spent the evening as he had the afternoon, until it was time to close. That was a terrible moment for him when he was obliged to go out into the dark, into his empty room full of dreadful recollections, of horrible thoughts, and of mental agony. He no longer saw any of his old friends, none of his relatives, nobody who might remind him of his past life. But as his apartments were a hell to him, he took a room in a large hotel, a good room on the ground floor, so as to see the passers-by. He was no longer alone in that great building. He felt people swarming round him, he heard voices in the adjoining rooms, and when his former sufferings tormented him too much at the sight of his bed, which was turned down, and of his solitary fireplace, he went out into the wide passages and walked up and down them like a sentinel, before all the closed doors, and looked sadly at the shoes standing in couples outside them, women's little boots by the side of men's thick ones, and he thought that, no doubt, all these people were happy, and were sleeping in their warm beds. Five years passed thus; five miserable years. But one day, when he was taking his usual walk between the Madeleine and the Rue Drouot, he suddenly saw a lady whose bearing struck him. A tall gentleman and a child were with her, and all three were walking in front of him. He asked himself where he had seen them before, when suddenly he recognized a movement of her hand; it was his wife, his wife with Limousin and his child, his little George.

His heart beat as if it would suffocate him, but he did not stop, for he wished to see them, and he followed them. They looked like a family of the better middle class. Henriette was leaning on Paul's arm, and speaking to him in a low voice, and looking at him sideways occasionally. Parent got a side view of her and recognized her pretty features, the movements of her lips, her smile, and her coaxing glances. But the child chiefly took up his attention. How tall and strong he was! Parent could not see his face, but only his long, fair curls. That tall boy with bare legs, who was walking by his mother's side like a little man, was George. He saw them suddenly, all three, as they stopped in front of a shop. Limousin had grown very gray, had aged and was thinner; his wife, on the contrary, was as young looking as ever, and had grown stouter. George he would not have recognized, he was so different from what he had been formerly.

They went on again and Parent followed them. He walked on quickly, passed them, and then turned round, so as to meet them face to face. As he passed the child he felt a mad longing to take him into his arms and run off with him, and he knocked against him as if by accident. The boy turned round and looked at the clumsy man angrily, and Parent hurried away, shocked, hurt, and pursued by that look. He went off like a thief, seized with a horrible fear lest he should have been seen and recognized by his wife and her lover. He went to his cafe without stopping, and fell breathless into his chair. That evening he drank three absinthes. For four months he felt the pain of that meeting in his heart. Every night he saw the three again, happy and tranquil, father, mother, and child walking on the boulevard before going in to dinner, and that new vision effaced the old one. It was another matter, another hallucination now, and also a fresh pain. Little George, his little George, the child he had so much loved and so often kissed, disappeared in the far distance, and he saw a new one, like a brother of the first, a little boy with bare legs, who did not know him! He suffered terribly at that thought. The child's love was dead; there was no bond between them; the child would not have held out his arms when he saw him. He had even looked at him angrily.

Then, by degrees he grew calmer, his mental torture diminished, the image that had appeared to his eyes and which haunted his nights became more indistinct and less frequent. He began once more to live nearly like everybody else, like all those idle people who drink beer off marble-topped tables and wear out their clothes on the threadbare velvet of the couches.

He grew old amid the smoke from pipes, lost his hair under the gas lights, looked upon his weekly bath, on his fortnightly visit to the barber's to have his hair cut, and on the purchase of a new coat or hat as an event. When he got to his cafe in a new hat he would look at himself in the glass for a long time before sitting down, and take it off and put it on again several times, and at last ask his friend, the lady at the bar, who was watching him with interest, whether she thought it suited him.

Two or three times a year he went to the theatre, and in the summer he sometimes spent his evenings at one of the open-air concerts in the Champs Elysees. And so the years followed each other slow, monotonous, and short, because they were quite uneventful.

He very rarely now thought of the dreadful drama which had wrecked his life; for twenty years had passed since that terrible evening. But the life he had led since then had worn him out. The landlord of his cafe would often say to him: "You ought to pull yourself together a little, Monsieur Parent; you should get some fresh air and go into the country. I assure you that you have changed very much within the last few months." And when his customer had gone out be used to say to the barmaid: "That poor Monsieur Parent is booked for another world; it is bad never to get out of Paris. Advise him to go out of town for a day occasionally; he has confidence in you. Summer will soon be here; that will put him straight."

And she, full of pity and kindness for such a regular customer, said to Parent every day: "Come, monsieur, make up your mind to get a little fresh air. It is so charming in the country when the weather is fine. Oh, if I could, I would spend my life there!"

By degrees he was seized with a vague desire to go just once and see whether it was really as pleasant there as she said, outside the walls of the great city. One morning he said to her:

"Do you know where one can get a good luncheon in the neighborhood of Paris?"

"Go to the Terrace at Saint-Germain; it is delightful there!"

He had been there formerly, just when he became engaged. He made up his mind to go there again, and he chose a Sunday, for no special reason, but merely because people generally do go out on Sundays, even when they have nothing to do all the week; and so one Sunday morning he went to Saint-Germain. He felt low-spirited and vexed at having yielded to that new longing, and at having broken through his usual habits. He was thirsty; he would have liked to get out at every station and sit down in the cafe which he saw outside and drink a "bock" or two, and then take the first train back to Paris. The journey seemed very long to him. He could remain sitting for whole days, as long as he had the same motionless objects before his eyes, but he found it very trying and fatiguing to remain sitting while he was being whirled along, and to see the whole country fly by, while he himself was motionless.

However, he found the Seine interesting every time he crossed it. Under the bridge at Chatou he saw some small boats going at great speed under the vigorous strokes of the bare-armed oarsmen, and he thought: "There are some fellows who are certainly enjoying themselves!" The train entered the tunnel just before you get to the station at Saint-Germain, and presently stopped at the platform. Parent got out, and walked slowly, for he already felt tired, toward the Terrace, with his hands behind his back, and when he got to the iron balustrade, stopped to look at the distant horizon. The immense plain spread out before him vast as the sea, green and studded with large villages, almost as populous as towns. The sun bathed the whole landscape in its full, warm light. The Seine wound like an endless serpent through the plain, flowed round the villages and along the slopes. Parent inhaled the warm breeze, which seemed to make his heart young again, to enliven his spirits, and to vivify his blood, and said to himself:

"Why, it is delightful here."

Then he went on a few steps, and stopped again to look about him. The utter misery of his existence seemed to be brought into full relief by the intense light which inundated the landscape. He saw his twenty years of cafe life—dull, monotonous, heartbreaking. He might have traveled as others did, have gone among foreigners, to unknown countries beyond the sea, have interested himself somewhat in everything which other men are passionately devoted to, in arts and science; he might have enjoyed life in a thousand forms, that mysterious life which is either charming or painful, constantly changing, always inexplicable and strange. Now, however, it was too late. He would go on drinking "bock" after "bock" until he died, without any family, without friends, without hope, without any curiosity about anything, and he was seized with a feeling of misery and a wish to run away, to hide himself in Paris, in his cafe and his lethargy! All the thoughts, all the dreams, all the desires which are dormant in the slough of stagnating hearts had reawakened, brought to life by those rays of sunlight on the plain.

Parent felt that if he were to remain there any longer he should lose his reason, and he made haste to get to the Pavilion Henri IV for lunch, to try and forget his troubles under—the influence of wine and alcohol, and at any rate to have some one to speak to.

He took a small table in one of the arbors, from which one can see all the surrounding country, ordered his lunch, and asked to be served at once. Then some more people arrived and sat down at tables near him. He felt more comfortable; he was no longer alone. Three persons were eating luncheon near him. He looked at them two or three times without seeing them clearly, as one looks at total strangers. Suddenly a woman's voice sent a shiver through him which seemed to penetrate to his very marrow. "George," it said, "will you carve the chicken?"

And another voice replied: "Yes, mamma."

Parent looked up, and he understood; he guessed immediately who those people were! He should certainly not have known them again. His wife had grown quite white and very stout, an elderly, serious, respectable lady, and she held her head forward as she ate for fear of spotting her dress, although she had a table napkin tucked under her chin. George had become a man. He had a slight beard, that uneven and almost colorless beard which adorns the cheeks of youths. He wore a high hat, a white waistcoat, and a monocle, because it looked swell, no doubt. Parent looked at him in astonishment. Was that George, his son? No, he did not know that young man; there could be nothing in common between them. Limousin had his back to him, and was eating; with his shoulders rather bent.

All three of them seemed happy and satisfied; they came and took luncheon in the country at well-known restaurants. They had had a calm and pleasant existence, a family existence in a warm and comfortable house, filled with all those trifles which make life agreeable, with affection, with all those tender words which people exchange continually when they love each other. They had lived thus, thanks to him, Parent, on his money, after having deceived him, robbed him, ruined him! They had condemned him, the innocent, simple-minded, jovial man, to all the miseries of solitude, to that abominable life which he had led, between the pavement and a bar-room, to every mental torture and every physical misery! They had made him a useless, aimless being, a waif in the world, a poor old man without any pleasures, any prospects, expecting nothing from anybody or anything. For him, the world was empty, because he loved nothing in the world. He might go among other nations, or go about the streets, go into all the houses in Paris, open every room, but he would not find inside any door the beloved face, the face of wife or child which smiles when it sees you. This idea worked upon him more than any other, the idea of a door which one opens, to see and to embrace somebody behind it.

And that was the fault of those three wretches! The fault of that worthless woman, of that infamous friend, and of that tall, light-haired lad who put on insolent airs. Now he felt as angry with the child as he did with the other two. Was he not Limousin's son? Would Limousin have kept him and loved him otherwise? Would not Limousin very quickly have got rid of the mother and of the child if he had not felt sure that it was his, positively his? Does anybody bring up other people's children? And now they were there, quite close to him, those three who had made him suffer so much.

Parent looked at them, irritated and excited at the recollection of all his sufferings and of his despair, and was especially exasperated at their placid and satisfied looks. He felt inclined to kill them, to throw his siphon of Seltzer water at them, to split open Limousin's head as he every moment bent it over his plate, raising it again immediately.

He would have his revenge now, on the spot, as he had them under his hand. But how? He tried to think of some means, he pictured such dreadful things as one reads of in the newspapers occasionally, but could not hit on anything practical. And he went on drinking to excite himself, to give himself courage not to allow such an opportunity to escape him, as he might never have another.

Suddenly an idea struck him, a terrible idea; and he left off drinking to mature it. He smiled as he murmured: "I have them, I have them! We will see; we will see!"

They finished their luncheon slowly, conversing with perfect unconcern. Parent could not hear what they were saying, but he saw their quiet gestures. His wife's face especially exasperated him. She had assumed a haughty air, the air of a comfortable, devout woman, of an unapproachable, devout woman, sheathed in principles, iron-clad in virtue. They paid their bill and got up from table. Parent then noticed Limousin. He might have been taken for a retired diplomat, for he looked a man of great importance, with his soft white whiskers, the tips of which touched his coat collar.

They walked away. Parent rose and followed them. First they went up and down the terrace, and calmly admired the landscape, and then they went into the forest. Parent followed them at a distance, hiding himself so as not to excite their suspicion too soon.

Parent came up to them by degrees, breathing hard with emotion and fatigue, for he was unused to walking now. He soon came up to them, but was seized with fear, an inexplicable fear, and he passed them, so as to turn round and meet them face to face. He walked on, his heart beating, feeling that they were just behind him now, and he said to himself: "Come, now is the time. Courage! courage! Now is the moment!"

He turned round. They were all three sitting on the grass, at the foot of a huge tree, and were still chatting. He made up his mind, and walked back rapidly; stopping in front of them in the middle of the road, he said abruptly, in a voice broken by emotion:

"It is I! Here I am! I suppose you did not expect me?"

They all three stared at this man, who seemed to be insane. He continued:

"One would suppose that you did not know me again. Just look at me! I am Parent, Henri Parent. You thought it was all over, and that you would never see me again. Ah! but here I am once more, you see, and now we will have an explanation."

Henriette, terrified, hid her face in her hands, murmuring: "Oh! Good heavens!"

Seeing this stranger, who seemed to be threatening his mother, George sprang up, ready to seize him by the collar. Limousin, thunderstruck, looked in horror at this apparition, who, after gasping for breath, continued:

"So now we will have an explanation; the proper moment has come! Ah! you deceived me, you condemned me to the life of a convict, and you thought that I should never catch you!"

The young man took him by the shoulders and pushed him back.

"Are you mad?" he asked. "What do you want? Go on your way immediately, or I shall give you a thrashing!"

"What do I want?" replied Parent. "I want to tell you who these people are."

George, however, was in a rage, and shook him; and was even going to strike him.

"Let me go," said Parent. "I am your father. There, see whether they recognize me now, the wretches!"

The young man, thunderstruck, unclenched his fists and turned toward his mother. Parent, as soon as he was released, approached her.

"Well," he said, "tell him yourself who I am! Tell him that my name is Henri Parent, that I am his father because his name is George Parent, because you are my wife, because you are all three living on my money, on the allowance of ten thousand francs which I have made you since I drove you out of my house. Will you tell him also why I drove you out? Because I surprised you with this beggar, this wretch, your lover! Tell him what I was, an honorable man, whom you married for money, and whom you deceived from the very first day. Tell him who you are, and who I am——"

He stammered and gasped for breath in his rage. The woman exclaimed in a heartrending voice:

"Paul, Paul, stop him; make him be quiet! Do not let him say this before my son!"

Limousin had also risen to his feet. He said in a very low voice: "Hold your tongue! Hold your tongue! Do you understand what you are doing?"

"I quite know what I am doing," resumed Parent, "and that is not all. There is one thing that I will know, something that has tormented me for twenty years." Then, turning to George, who was leaning against a tree in consternation, he said:

"Listen to me. When she left my house she thought it was not enough to have deceived me, but she also wanted to drive me to despair. You were my only consolation, and she took you with her, swearing that I was not your father, but, that he was your father. Was she lying? I do not know. I have been asking myself the question for the last twenty years." He went close up to her, tragic and terrible, and, pulling away her hands, with which she had covered her face, he continued:

"Well, now! I call upon you to tell me which of us two is the father of this young man; he or I, your husband or your lover. Come! Come! tell us."

Limousin rushed at him. Parent pushed him back, and, sneering in his fury, he said: "Ah! you are brave now! You are braver than you were that day when you ran downstairs because you thought I was going to murder you. Very well! If she will not reply, tell me yourself. You ought to know as well as she. Tell me, are you this young fellow's father? Come! Come! Tell me!"

He turned to his wife again. "If you will not tell me, at any rate tell your son. He is a man, now, and he has the right to know who his father is. I do not know, and I never did know, never, never! I cannot tell you, my boy."

He seemed to be losing his senses; his voice grew shrill and he worked his arms about as if he had an epileptic 'fit.

"Come! . . . Give me an answer. She does not know . . . I will make a bet that she does not know . . . No . . . she does not know, by Jove! Ha! ha! ha! Nobody knows . . . nobody . . . How can one know such things?

"You will not know either, my boy, you will not know any more than I do . . . never. . . . Look here . . . Ask her you will find that she does not know . . . I do not know either . . . nor does he, nor do you, nobody knows. You can choose . . . You can choose . . . yes, you can choose him or me. . . Choose.

"Good evening . . . It is all over. If she makes up her mind to tell you, you will come and let me know, will you not? I am living at the Hotel des Continents . . . I should be glad to know . . . Good evening . . . I hope you will enjoy yourselves very much . . ."

And he went away gesticulating, talking to himself under the tall trees, in the quiet, the cool air, which was full of the fragrance of growing plants. He did not turn round to look at them, but went straight on, walking under the stimulus of his rage, under a storm of passion, with that one fixed idea in his mind. All at once he found himself outside the station. A train was about to start and he got in. During the journey his anger calmed down, he regained his senses and returned to Paris, astonished at his own boldness, full of aches and pains as if he had broken some bones. Nevertheless, he went to have a "bock" at his brewery.

When she saw him come in, Mademoiselle Zoe asked in surprise: "What! back already? are you tired?"

"Yes—yes, I am tired . . . very tired . . . You know, when one is not used to going out. . . I've had enough of it. I shall not go into the country again. It would have been better to have stayed here. For the future, I shall not stir out."

She could not persuade him to tell her about his little excursion, much as she wished to.

For the first time in his life he got thoroughly drunk that night, and had to be carried home.

QUEEN HORTENSE

In Argenteuil she was called Queen Hortense. No one knew why. Perhaps it was because she had a commanding tone of voice; perhaps because she was tall, bony, imperious; perhaps because she governed a kingdom of servants, chickens, dogs, cats, canaries, parrots, all so dear to an old maid's heart. But she did not spoil these familiar friends; she had for them none of those endearing names, none of the foolish tenderness which women seem to lavish on the soft fur of a purring cat. She governed these beasts with authority; she reigned.

She was indeed an old maid—one of those old maids with a harsh voice and angular motions, whose very soul seems to be hard. She never would stand contradiction, argument, hesitation, indifference, laziness nor fatigue. She had never been heard to complain, to regret anything, to envy anyone. She would say: "Everyone has his share," with the conviction of a fatalist. She did not go to church, she had no use for priests, she hardly believed in God, calling all religious things "weeper's wares."

For thirty years she had lived in her little house, with its tiny garden running along the street; she had never changed her habits, only changing her servants pitilessly, as soon as they reached twenty-one years of age.

When her dogs, cats and birds would die of old age, or from an accident, she would replace them without tears and without regret; with a little spade she would bury the dead animal in a strip of ground, throwing a few shovelfuls of earth over it and stamping it down with her feet in an indifferent manner.

She had a few friends in town, families of clerks who went to Paris every day. Once in a while she would be invited out, in the evening, to tea. She would inevitably fall asleep, and she would have to be awakened, when it was time for her to go home. She never allowed anyone to accompany her, fearing neither light nor darkness. She did not appear to like children.

She kept herself busy doing countless masculine tasks—carpentering, gardening, sawing or chopping wood, even laying bricks when it was necessary.

She had relatives who came to see her twice a year, the Cimmes and the Colombels, her two sisters having married, one of them a florist and the other a retired merchant. The Cimmes had no children; the Colombels had three: Henri, Pauline and Joseph. Henri was twenty, Pauline seventeen and Joseph only three.

There was no love lost between the old maid and her relatives.

In the spring of the year 1882 Queen Hortense suddenly fell sick. The neighbors called in a physician, whom she immediately drove out. A priest then having presented himself, she jumped out of bed, in order to throw him out of the house.

The young servant, in despair, was brewing her some tea.

After lying in bed for three days the situation appeared so serious that the barrel-maker, who lived next door, to the right, acting on advice from the doctor, who had forcibly returned to the house, took it upon himself to call together the two families.

They arrived by the same train, towards ten in the morning, the Colombels bringing little Joseph with them.

When they got to the garden gate, they saw the servant seated in the chair against the wall, crying.

The dog was sleeping on the door mat in the broiling sun; two cats, which looked as though they might be dead, were stretched out in front of the two windows, their eyes closed, their paws and tails stretched out at full length.

A big clucking hen was parading through the garden with a whole regiment of yellow, downy chicks, and a big cage hanging from the wall and covered with pimpernel, contained a population of birds which were chirping away in the warmth of this beautiful spring morning.

In another cage, shaped like a chalet, two lovebirds sat motionless side by side on their perch.

M. Cimme, a fat, puffing person, who always entered first everywhere, pushing aside everyone else, whether man or woman, when it was necessary, asked:

"Well, Celeste, aren't things going well?"

The little servant moaned through her tears:

"She doesn't even recognize me any more. The doctor says it's the end."

Everybody looked around.

Mme. Cimme and Mme. Colombel immediately embraced each other, without saying a word. They looked very much alike, having always worn their hair in Madonna bands, and loud red French cashmere shawls.

Cimme turned to his brother-in-law, a pale, sallow-complexioned, thin man, wasted by stomach complaints, who limped badly, and said in a serious tone of voice:

"Gad! It was high time."

But no one dared to enter the dying woman's room on the ground floor. Even Cimme made way for the others. Colombel was the first to make up his mind, and, swaying from side to side like the mast of a ship, the iron ferule of his cane clattering on the paved hall, he entered.

The two women were the next to venture, and M. Cimmes closed the procession.

Little Joseph had remained outside, pleased at the sight of the dog.

A ray of sunlight seemed to cut the bed in two, shining just on the hands, which were moving nervously, continually opening and closing. The fingers were twitching as though moved by some thought, as though trying to point out a meaning or idea, as though obeying the dictates of a will. The rest of the body lay motionless under the sheets. The angular frame showed not a single movement. The eyes remained closed.

The family spread out in a semi-circle and, without a word, they began to watch the contracted chest and the short, gasping breathing. The little servant had followed them and was still crying.

At last Cimme asked:

"Exactly what did the doctor say?"

The girl stammered:

"He said to leave her alone, that nothing more could be done for her."

But suddenly the old woman's lips began to move. She seemed to be uttering silent words, words hidden in the brain of this dying being, and her hands quickened their peculiar movements.

Then she began to speak in a thin, high voice, which no one had ever heard, a voice which seemed to come from the distance, perhaps from the depths of this heart which had always been closed.

Cimme, finding this scene painful, walked away on tiptoe. Colombel, whose crippled leg was growing tired, sat down.

The two women remained standing.

Queen Hortense was now babbling away, and no one could understand a word. She was pronouncing names, many names, tenderly calling imaginary people.

"Come here, Philippe, kiss your mother. Tell me, child, do you love your mamma? You, Rose, take care of your little sister while I am away. And don't leave her alone. Don't play with matches!"

She stopped for a while, then, in a louder voice, as though she were calling someone: "Henriette!" then waited a moment and continued:

"Tell your father that I wish to speak to him before he goes to business." And suddenly: "I am not feeling very well to-day, darling; promise not to come home late. Tell your employer that I am sick. You know, it isn't safe to leave the children alone when I am in bed. For dinner I will fix you up a nice dish of rice. The little ones like that very much. Won't Claire be happy?"

And she broke into a happy, joyous laugh, such as they had never heard: "Look at Jean, how funny he looks! He has smeared jam all over his face, the little pig! Look, sweetheart, look; isn't he funny?"

Colombel, who was continually lifting his tired leg from place to place, muttered:

"She is dreaming that she has children and a husband; it is the beginning of the death agony."

The two sisters had not yet moved, surprised, astounded.

The little maid exclaimed:

"You must take off your shawls and your hats! Would you like to go into the parlor?"

They went out without having said a word. And Colombel followed them, limping, once more leaving the dying woman alone.

When they were relieved of their travelling garments, the women finally sat down. Then one of the cats left its window, stretched, jumped into the room and on to Mme. Cimme's knees. She began to pet it.

In the next room could be heard the voice of the dying woman, living, in this last hour, the life for which she had doubtless hoped, living her dreams themselves just when all was over for her.

Cimme, in the garden, was playing with little Joseph and the dog, enjoying himself in the whole hearted manner of a countryman, having completely forgotten the dying woman.

But suddenly he entered the house and said to the girl:

"I say, my girl, are we not going to have luncheon? What do you ladies wish to eat?"

They finally agreed on an omelet, a piece of steak with new potatoes, cheese and coffee.

As Mme. Colombel was fumbling in her pocket for her purse, Cimme stopped her, and, turning to the maid: "Have you got any money?"

She answered:

"Yes, monsieur."

"How much?"

"Fifteen francs."

"That's enough. Hustle, my girl, because I am beginning to get very hungry:"

Mme. Cimme, looking out over the climbing vines bathed in sunlight, and at the two turtle-doves on the roof opposite, said in an annoyed tone of voice:

"What a pity to have had to come for such a sad occasion. It is so nice in the country to-day."

Her sister sighed without answering, and Colombel mumbled, thinking perhaps of the walk ahead of him:

"My leg certainly is bothering me to-day:"

Little Joseph and the dog were making a terrible noise; one was shrieking with pleasure, the other was barking wildly. They were playing hide-and-seek around the three flower beds, running after each other like mad.

The dying woman continued to call her children, talking with each one, imagining that she was dressing them, fondling them, teaching them how to read: "Come on! Simon repeat: A, B, C, D. You are not paying attention, listen—D, D, D; do you hear me? Now repeat—"

Cimme exclaimed: "Funny what people say when in that condition."

Mme. Colombel then asked:

"Wouldn't it be better if we were to return to her?"

But Cimme dissuaded her from the idea:

"What's the use? You can't change anything. We are just as comfortable here."

Nobody insisted. Mme. Cimme observed the two green birds called love-birds. In a few words she praised this singular faithfulness and blamed the men for not imitating these animals. Cimme began to laugh, looked at his wife and hummed in a teasing way: "Tra-la-la, tra-la-la" as though to cast a good deal of doubt on his own, Cimme's, faithfulness:

Colombel was suffering from cramps and was rapping the floor with his cane.

The other cat, its tail pointing upright to the sky, now came in.

They sat down to luncheon at one o'clock.

As soon as he had tasted the wine, Colombel, for whom only the best of Bordeaux had been prescribed, called the servant back:

"I say, my girl, is this the best stuff that you have in the cellar?"

"No, monsieur; there is some better wine, which was only brought out when you came."

"Well, bring us three bottles of it."

They tasted the wine and found it excellent, not because it was of a remarkable vintage, but because it had been in the cellar fifteen years. Cimme declared:

"That is regular invalid's wine."

Colombel, filled with an ardent desire to gain possession of this Bordeaux, once more questioned the girl:

"How much of it is left?"

"Oh! Almost all, monsieur; mamz'elle never touched it. It's in the bottom stack."

Then he turned to his brother-in-law:

"If you wish, Cimme, I would be willing to exchange something else for this wine; it suits my stomach marvellously."

The chicken had now appeared with its regiment of young ones. The two women were enjoying themselves throwing crumbs to them.

Joseph and the dog, who had eaten enough, were sent back to the garden.

Queen Hortense was still talking, but in a low, hushed voice, so that the words could no longer be distinguished.

When they had finished their coffee all went in to observe the condition of the sick woman. She seemed calm.

They went outside again and seated themselves in a circle in the garden, in order to complete their digestion.

Suddenly the dog, who was carrying something in his mouth, began to run around the chairs at full speed. The child was chasing him wildly. Both disappeared into the house.

Cimme fell asleep, his well-rounded paunch bathed in the glow of the shining sun.

The dying woman once more began to talk in a loud voice. Then suddenly she shrieked.

The two women and Colombel rushed in to see what was the matter. Cimme, waking up, did not budge, because, he did not wish to witness such a scene.

She was sitting up, with haggard eyes. Her dog, in order to escape being pursued by little Joseph, had jumped up on the bed, run over the sick woman, and entrenched behind the pillow, was looking down at his playmate with snapping eyes, ready to jump down and begin the game again. He was holding in his mouth one of his mistress' slippers, which he had torn to pieces and with which he had been playing for the last hour.

The child, frightened by this woman who had suddenly risen in front of him, stood motionless before the bed.

The hen had also come in, and frightened by the noise, had jumped up on a chair and was wildly calling her chicks, who were chirping distractedly around the four legs of the chair.

Queen Hortense was shrieking:

"No, no, I don't want to die, I don't want to! I don't want to! Who will bring up my children? Who will take care of them? Who will love them? No, I don't want to!—I don't——"

She fell back. All was over.

The dog, wild with excitement, jumped about the room, barking.

Colombel ran to the window, calling his brother-in-law:

"Hurry up, hurry up! I think that she has just gone."

Then Cimme, resigned, arose and entered the room, mumbling

"It didn't take as long as I thought it would!"

TIMBUCTOO

The boulevard, that river of humanity, was alive with people in the golden light of the setting sun. The whole sky was red, blinding, and behind the Madeleine an immense bank of flaming clouds cast a shower of light the whole length of the boulevard, vibrant as the heat from a brazier.

The gay, animated crowd went by in this golden mist and seemed to be glorified. Their faces were gilded, their black hats and clothes took on purple tints, the patent leather of their shoes cast bright reflections on the asphalt of the sidewalk.

Before the cafes a mass of men were drinking opalescent liquids that looked like precious stones dissolved in the glasses.

In the midst of the drinkers two officers in full uniform dazzled all eyes with their glittering gold lace. They chatted, happy without asking why, in this glory of life, in this radiant light of sunset, and they looked at the crowd, the leisurely men and the hurrying women who left a bewildering odor of perfume as they passed by.

All at once an enormous negro, dressed in black, with a paunch beneath his jean waistcoat, which was covered with charms, his face shining as if it had been polished, passed before them with a triumphant air. He laughed at the passers-by, at the news venders, at the dazzling sky, at the whole of Paris. He was so tall that he overtopped everyone else, and when he passed all the loungers turned round to look at his back.

But he suddenly perceived the officers and darted towards them, jostling the drinkers in his path. As soon as he reached their table he fixed his gleaming and delighted eyes upon them and the corners of his mouth expanded to his ears, showing his dazzling white teeth like a crescent moon in a black sky. The two men looked in astonishment at this ebony giant, unable to understand his delight.

With a voice that made all the guests laugh, he said:

"Good-day, my lieutenant."

One of the officers was commander of a battalion, the other was a colonel. The former said:

"I do not know you, sir. I am at a loss to know what you want of me."

"Me like you much, Lieutenant Vedie, siege of Bezi, much grapes, find me."

The officer, utterly bewildered, looked at the man intently, trying to refresh his memory. Then he cried abruptly:

"Timbuctoo?"

The negro, radiant, slapped his thigh as he uttered a tremendous laugh and roared:

"Yes, yes, my lieutenant; you remember Timbuctoo, ya. How do you do?"

The commandant held out his hand, laughing heartily as he did so. Then Timbuctoo became serious. He seized the officer's hand and, before the other could prevent it, he kissed it, according to negro and Arab custom. The officer embarrassed, said in a severe tone:

"Come now, Timbuctoo, we are not in Africa. Sit down there and tell me how it is I find you here."

Timbuctoo swelled himself out and, his words falling over one another, replied hurriedly:

"Make much money, much, big restaurant, good food; Prussians, me, much steal, much, French cooking; Timbuctoo cook to the emperor; two thousand francs mine. Ha, ha, ha, ha!"

And he laughed, doubling himself up, roaring, with wild delight in his glances.

When the officer, who understood his strange manner of expressing himself, had questioned him he said:

"Well, au revoir, Timbuctoo. I will see you again."

The negro rose, this time shaking the hand that was extended to him and, smiling still, cried:

"Good-day, good-day, my lieutenant!"

He went off so happy that he gesticulated as he walked, and people thought he was crazy.

"Who is that brute?" asked the colonel.

"A fine fellow and a brave soldier. I will tell you what I know about him. It is funny enough.

"You know that at the commencement of the war of 1870 I was shut up in Bezieres, that this negro calls Bezi. We were not besieged, but blockaded. The Prussian lines surrounded us on all sides, outside the reach of cannon, not firing on us, but slowly starving us out.

"I was then lieutenant. Our garrison consisted of soldier of all descriptions, fragments of slaughtered regiments, some that had run away, freebooters separated from the main army, etc. We had all kinds, in fact even eleven Turcos [Algerian soldiers in the service of France], who arrived one evening no one knew whence or how. They appeared at the gates of the city, exhausted, in rags, starving and dirty. They were handed over to me.

"I saw very soon that they were absolutely undisciplined, always in the street and always drunk. I tried putting them in the police station, even in prison, but nothing was of any use. They would disappear, sometimes for days at a time, as if they had been swallowed up by the earth, and then come back staggering drunk. They had no money. Where did they buy drink and how and with what?

"This began to worry me greatly, all the more as these savages interested me with their everlasting laugh and their characteristics of overgrown frolicsome children.

"I then noticed that they blindly obeyed the largest among them, the one you have just seen. He made them do as he pleased, planned their mysterious expeditions with the all-powerful and undisputed authority of a leader. I sent for him and questioned him. Our conversation lasted fully three hours, for it was hard for me to understand his remarkable gibberish. As for him, poor devil, he made unheard-of efforts to make himself intelligible, invented words, gesticulated, perspired in his anxiety, mopping his forehead, puffing, stopping and abruptly beginning again when he thought he had found a new method of explaining what he wanted to say.

"I gathered finally that he was the son of a big chief, a sort of negro king of the region around Timbuctoo. I asked him his name. He repeated something like 'Chavaharibouhalikranafotapolara.' It seemed simpler to me to give him the name of his native place, 'Timbuctoo.' And a week later he was known by no other name in the garrison.

"But we were all wildly anxious to find out where this African ex-prince procured his drinks. I discovered it in a singular manner.

"I was on the ramparts one morning, watching the horizon, when I perceived something moving about in a vineyard. It was near the time of vintage, the grapes were ripe, but I was not thinking of that. I thought that a spy was approaching the town, and I organized a complete expedition to catch the prowler. I took command myself, after obtaining permission from the general.

"I sent out by three different gates three little companies, which were to meet at the suspected vineyard and form a cordon round it. In order to cut off the spy's retreat, one of these detachments had to make at least an hour's march. A watch on the walls signalled to me that the person I had seen had not left the place. We went along in profound silence, creeping, almost crawling, along the ditches. At last we reached the spot assigned.

"I abruptly disbanded my soldiers, who darted into the vineyard and found Timbuctoo on hands and knees travelling around among the vines and eating grapes, or rather devouring them as a dog eats his sop, snatching them in mouthfuls from the vine with his teeth.

"I wanted him to get up, but he could not think of it. I then understood why he was crawling on his hands and knees. As soon as we stood him on his feet he began to wabble, then stretched out his arms and fell down on his nose. He was more drunk than I have ever seen anyone.

"They brought him home on two poles. He never stopped laughing all the way back, gesticulating with his arms and legs.

"This explained the mystery. My men also drank the juice of the grapes, and when they were so intoxicated they could not stir they went to sleep in the vineyard. As for Timbuctoo, his love of the vineyard was beyond all belief and all bounds. He lived in it as did the thrushes, whom he hated with the jealous hate of a rival. He repeated incessantly: 'The thrushes eat all the grapes, captain!'

"One evening I was sent for. Something had been seen on the plain coming in our direction. I had not brought my field-glass and I could not distinguish things clearly. It looked like a great serpent uncoiling itself—a convoy. How could I tell?

"I sent some men to meet this strange caravan, which presently made its triumphal entry. Timbuctoo and nine of his comrades were carrying on a sort of altar made of camp stools eight severed, grinning and bleeding heads. The African was dragging along a horse to whose tail another head was fastened, and six other animals followed, adorned in the same manner.

"This is what I learned: Having started out to the vineyard, my Africans had suddenly perceived a detachment of Prussians approaching a village. Instead of taking to their heels, they hid themselves, and as soon as the Prussian officers dismounted at an inn to refresh themselves, the eleven rascals rushed on them, put to flight the lancers, who thought they were being attacked by the main army, killed the two sentries, then the colonel and the five officers of his escort.

"That day I kissed Timbuctoo. I saw, however, that he walked with difficulty and thought he was wounded. He laughed and said:

"'Me provisions for my country.'

"Timbuctoo was not fighting for glory, but for gain. Everything he found that seemed to him to be of the slightest value, especially anything that glistened, he put in his pocket. What a pocket! An abyss that began at his hips and reached to his ankles. He had retained an old term used by the troopers and called it his 'profonde,' and it was his 'profonde' in fact.

"He had taken the gold lace off the Prussian uniforms, the brass off their helmets, detached their buttons, etc., and had thrown them all into his 'profonde,' which was full to overflowing.

"Each day he pocketed every glistening object that came beneath his observation, pieces of tin or pieces of silver, and sometimes his contour was very comical.

"He intended to carry all that back to the land of ostriches, whose brother he might have been, this son of a king, tormented with the longing to gobble up all objects that glistened. If he had not had his 'profonde' what would he have done? He doubtless would have swallowed them.

"Each morning his pocket was empty. He had, then, some general store where his riches were piled up. But where? I could not discover it.

"The general, on being informed of Timbuctoo's mighty act of valor, had the headless bodies that had been left in the neighboring village interred at once, that it might not be discovered that they were decapitated. The Prussians returned thither the following day. The mayor and seven prominent inhabitants were shot on the spot, by way of reprisal, as having denounced the Prussians.

"Winter was here. We were exhausted and desperate. There were skirmishes now every day. The famished men could no longer march. The eight 'Turcos' alone (three had been killed) remained fat and shiny, vigorous and always ready to fight. Timbuctoo was even getting fatter. He said to me one day:

"'You much hungry; me good meat.'

"And he brought me an excellent filet. But of what? We had no more cattle, nor sheep, nor goats, nor donkeys, nor pigs. It was impossible to get a horse. I thought of all this after I had devoured my meat. Then a horrible idea came to me. These negroes were born close to a country where they eat human beings! And each day such a number of soldiers were killed around the town! I questioned Timbuctoo. He would not answer. I did not insist, but from that time on I declined his presents.

"He worshipped me. One night snow took us by surprise at the outposts. We were seated, on the ground. I looked with pity at those poor negroes shivering beneath this white frozen shower. I was very cold and began to cough. At once I felt something fall on me like a large warm quilt. It was Timbuctoo's cape that he had thrown on my shoulders.

"I rose and returned his garment, saying:

"'Keep it, my boy; you need it more than I do.'

"'Non, my lieutenant, for you; me no need. Me hot, hot!'

"And he looked at me entreatingly.

"'Come, obey orders. Keep your cape; I insist,' I replied.

"He then stood up, drew his sword, which he had sharpened to an edge like a scythe, and holding in his other hand the large cape which I had refused, said:

"'If you not keep cape, me cut. No one cape.'

"And he would have done it. So I yielded.

"Eight days later we capitulated. Some of us had been able to escape, the rest were to march out of the town and give themselves up to the conquerors.

"I went towards the exercising ground, where we were all to meet, when I was dumfounded at the sight of a gigantic negro dressed in white duck and wearing a straw hat. It was Timbuctoo. He was beaming and was walking with his hands in his pockets in front of a little shop where two plates and two glasses were displayed.

"'What are you doing?' I said.

"'Me not go. Me good cook; me make food for Colonel Algeria. Me eat Prussians; much steal, much.'

"There were ten degrees of frost. I shivered at sight of this negro in white duck. He took me by the arm and made me go inside. I noticed an immense flag that he was going to place outside his door as soon as we had left, for he had some shame."

I read this sign, traced by the hand of some accomplice

"'ARMY KITCHEN OF M. TIMBUCTOO,

"'Formerly Cook to H. M. the Emperor.

"'A Parisian Artist. Moderate Prices.'

"In spite of the despair that was gnawing at my heart, I could not help laughing, and I left my negro to his new enterprise.

"Was not that better than taking him prisoner?

"You have just seen that he made a success of it, the rascal.

"Bezieres to-day belongs to the Germans. The 'Restaurant Timbuctoo' is the beginning of a retaliation."

TOMBSTONES

The five friends had finished dinner, five men of the world, mature, rich, three married, the two others bachelors. They met like this every month in memory of their youth, and after dinner they chatted until two o'clock in the morning. Having remained intimate friends, and enjoying each other's society, they probably considered these the pleasantest evenings of their lives. They talked on every subject, especially of what interested and amused Parisians. Their conversation was, as in the majority of salons elsewhere, a verbal rehash of what they had read in the morning papers.

One of the most lively of them was Joseph de Bardon, a celibate living the Parisian life in its fullest and most whimsical manner. He was not a debauche nor depraved, but a singular, happy fellow, still young, for he was scarcely forty. A man of the world in its widest and best sense, gifted with a brilliant, but not profound, mind, with much varied knowledge, but no true erudition, ready comprehension without true understanding, he drew from his observations, his adventures, from everything he saw, met with and found, anecdotes at once comical and philosophical, and made humorous remarks that gave him a great reputation for cleverness in society.

He was the after dinner speaker and had his own story each time, upon which they counted, and he talked without having to be coaxed.

As he sat smoking, his elbows on the table, a petit verre half full beside his plate, half torpid in an atmosphere of tobacco blended with steaming coffee, he seemed to be perfectly at home. He said between two whiffs:

"A curious thing happened to me some time ago."

"Tell it to us," they all exclaimed at once.

"With pleasure. You know that I wander about Paris a great deal, like book collectors who ransack book stalls. I just look at the sights, at the people, at all that is passing by and all that is going on.

"Toward the middle of September—it was beautiful weather—I went out one afternoon, not knowing where I was going. One always has a vague wish to call on some pretty woman or other. One chooses among them in one's mental picture gallery, compares them in one's mind, weighs the interest with which they inspire you, their comparative charms and finally decides according to the influence of the day. But when the sun is very bright and the air warm, it takes away from you all desire to make calls.

"The sun was bright, the air warm. I lighted a cigar and sauntered aimlessly along the outer boulevard. Then, as I strolled on, it occurred to me to walk as far as Montmartre and go into the cemetery.

"I am very fond of cemeteries. They rest me and give me a feeling of sadness; I need it. And, besides, I have good friends in there, those that one no longer goes to call on, and I go there from time to time.

"It is in this cemetery of Montmartre that is buried a romance of my life, a sweetheart who made a great impression on me, a very emotional, charming little woman whose memory, although it causes me great sorrow, also fills me with regrets—regrets of all kinds. And I go to dream beside her grave. She has finished with life.

"And then I like cemeteries because they are immense cities filled to overflowing with inhabitants. Think how many dead people there are in this small space, think of all the generations of Parisians who are housed there forever, veritable troglodytes enclosed in their little vaults, in their little graves covered with a stone or marked by a cross, while living beings take up so much room and make so much noise —imbeciles that they are!

"Then, again, in cemeteries there are monuments almost as interesting as in museums. The tomb of Cavaignac reminded me, I must confess without making any comparison, of the chef d'oeuvre of Jean Goujon: the recumbent statue of Louis de Breze in the subterranean chapel of the Cathedral of Rouen. All modern and realistic art has originated there, messieurs. This dead man, Louis de Breze, is more real, more terrible, more like inanimate flesh still convulsed with the death agony than all the tortured corpses that are distorted to-day in funeral monuments.

"But in Montmartre one can yet admire Baudin's monument, which has a degree of grandeur; that of Gautier, of Murger, on which I saw the other day a simple, paltry wreath of immortelles, yellow immortelles, brought thither by whom? Possibly by the last grisette, very old and now janitress in the neighborhood. It is a pretty little statue by Millet, but ruined by dirt and neglect. Sing of youth, O Murger!

"Well, there I was in Montmartre Cemetery, and was all at once filled with sadness, a sadness that is not all pain, a kind of sadness that makes you think when you are in good health, 'This place is not amusing, but my time has not come yet.'

"The feeling of autumn, of the warm moisture which is redolent of the death of the leaves, and the weakened, weary, anaemic sun increased, while rendering it poetical, the sensation of solitude and of finality that hovered over this spot which savors of human mortality.

"I walked along slowly amid these streets of tombs, where the neighbors do not visit each other, do not sleep together and do not read the newspapers. And I began to read the epitaphs. That is the most amusing thing in the world. Never did Labiche or Meilhac make me laugh as I have laughed at the comical inscriptions on tombstones. Oh, how much superior to the books of Paul de Kock for getting rid of the spleen are these marble slabs and these crosses where the relatives of the deceased have unburdened their sorrow, their desires for the happiness of the vanished ones and their hope of rejoining them—humbugs!

"But I love above all in this cemetery the deserted portion, solitary, full of great yews and cypresses, the older portion, belonging to those dead long since, and which will soon be taken into use again; the growing trees nourished by the human corpses cut down in order to bury in rows beneath little slabs of marble those who have died more recently.

"When I had sauntered about long enough to refresh my mind I felt that I would soon have had enough of it and that I must place the faithful homage of my remembrance on my little friend's last resting place. I felt a tightening of the heart as I reached her grave. Poor dear, she was so dainty, so loving and so white and fresh—and now—if one should open the grave—

"Leaning over the iron grating, I told her of my sorrow in a low tone, which she doubtless did not hear, and was moving away when I saw a woman in black, in deep mourning, kneeling on the next grave. Her crape veil was turned back, uncovering a pretty fair head, the hair in Madonna bands looking like rays of dawn beneath her sombre headdress. I stayed.

"Surely she must be in profound grief. She had covered her face with her hands and, standing there in meditation, rigid as a statue, given up to her grief, telling the sad rosary of her remembrances within the shadow of her concealed and closed eyes, she herself seemed like a dead person mourning another who was dead. All at once a little motion of her back, like a flutter of wind through a willow, led me to suppose that she was going to cry. She wept softly at first, then louder, with quick motions of her neck and shoulders. Suddenly she uncovered her eyes. They were full of tears and charming, the eyes of a bewildered woman, with which she glanced about her as if awaking from a nightmare. She looked at me, seemed abashed and hid her face completely in her hands. Then she sobbed convulsively, and her head slowly bent down toward the marble. She leaned her forehead on it, and her veil spreading around her, covered the white corners of the beloved tomb, like a fresh token of mourning. I heard her sigh, then she sank down with her cheek on the marble slab and remained motionless, unconscious.

"I darted toward her, slapped her hands, blew on her eyelids, while I read this simple epitaph: 'Here lies Louis-Theodore Carrel, Captain of Marine Infantry, killed by the enemy at Tonquin. Pray for him.'

"He had died some months before. I was affected to tears and redoubled my attentions. They were successful. She regained consciousness. I appeared very much moved. I am not bad looking, I am not forty. I saw by her first glance that she would be polite and grateful. She was, and amid more tears she told me her history in detached fragments as well as her gasping breath would allow, how the officer was killed at Tonquin when they had been married a year, how she had married him for love, and being an orphan, she had only the usual dowry.

"I consoled her, I comforted her, raised her and lifted her on her feet. Then I said:

"'Do not stay here. Come.'

"'I am unable to walk,' she murmured.

"'I will support you.'

"'Thank you, sir; you are good. Did you also come to mourn for some one?'

"'Yes, madame.'

"'A dead friend?'

"'Yes, madame.'

"'Your wife?'

"'A friend.'

"'One may love a friend as much as they love their wife. Love has no law.'

"'Yes, madame.'

"And we set off together, she leaning on my arm, while I almost carried her along the paths of the cemetery. When we got outside she faltered:

"'I feel as if I were going to be ill.'

"'Would you like to go in anywhere, to take something?'

"'Yes, monsieur.'

"I perceived a restaurant, one of those places where the mourners of the dead go to celebrate the funeral. We went in. I made her drink a cup of hot tea, which seemed to revive her. A faint smile came to her lips. She began to talk about herself. It was sad, so sad to be always alone in life, alone in one's home, night and day, to have no one on whom one can bestow affection, confidence, intimacy.

"That sounded sincere. It sounded pretty from her mouth. I was touched. She was very young, perhaps twenty. I paid her compliments, which she took in good part. Then, as time was passing, I suggested taking her home in a carriage. She accepted, and in the cab we sat so close that our shoulders touched.

"When the cab stopped at her house she murmured: 'I do not feel equal to going upstairs alone, for I live on the fourth floor. You have been so good. Will you let me take your arm as far as my own door?'

"I agreed with eagerness. She ascended the stairs slowly, breathing hard. Then, as we stood at her door, she said:

"'Come in a few moments so that I may thank you.'

"And, by Jove, I went in. Everything was modest, even rather poor, but simple and in good taste.

"We sat down side by side on a little sofa and she began to talk again about her loneliness. She rang for her maid, in order to offer me some wine. The maid did not come. I was delighted, thinking that this maid probably came in the morning only, what one calls a charwoman.

"She had taken off her hat. She was really pretty, and she gazed at me with her clear eyes, gazed so hard and her eyes were so clear that I was terribly tempted. I caught her in my arms and rained kisses on her eyelids, which she closed suddenly.

"She freed herself and pushed me away, saying:

"'Have done, have done.'

"But I next kissed her on the mouth and she did not resist, and as our glances met after thus outraging the memory of the captain killed in Tonquin, I saw that she had a languid, resigned expression that set my mind at rest.

"I became very attentive and, after chatting for some time, I said:

"'Where do you dine?'

"'In a little restaurant in the neighborhood:

"'All alone?'

"'Why, yes.'

"'Will you dine with me?'

"'Where?'

"'In a good restaurant on the Boulevard.'

"She demurred a little. I insisted. She yielded, saying by way of apology to herself: 'I am so lonely—so lonely.' Then she added:

"'I must put on something less sombre, and went into her bedroom. When she reappeared she was dressed in half-mourning, charming, dainty and slender in a very simple gray dress. She evidently had a costume for the cemetery and one for the town.

"The dinner was very enjoyable. She drank some champagne, brightened up, grew lively and I went home with her.

"This friendship, begun amid the tombs, lasted about three weeks. But one gets tired of everything, especially of women. I left her under pretext of an imperative journey. She made me promise that I would come and see her on my return. She seemed to be really rather attached to me.

"Other things occupied my attention, and it was about a month before I thought much about this little cemetery friend. However, I did not forget her. The recollection of her haunted me like a mystery, like a psychological problem, one of those inexplicable questions whose solution baffles us.

"I do not know why, but one day I thought I might possibly meet her in the Montmartre Cemetery, and I went there.

"I walked about a long time without meeting any but the ordinary visitors to this spot, those who have not yet broken off all relations with their dead. The grave of the captain killed at Tonquin had no mourner on its marble slab, no flowers, no wreath.

"But as I wandered in another direction of this great city of the dead I perceived suddenly, at the end of a narrow avenue of crosses, a couple in deep mourning walking toward me, a man and a woman. Oh, horrors! As they approached I recognized her. It was she!

"She saw me, blushed, and as I brushed past her she gave me a little signal, a tiny little signal with her eye, which meant: 'Do not recognize me!' and also seemed to say, 'Come back to see me again, my dear!'

"The man was a gentleman, distingue, chic, an officer of the Legion of Honor, about fifty years old. He was supporting her as I had supported her myself when we were leaving the cemetery.

"I went my way, filled with amazement, asking myself what this all meant, to what race of beings belonged this huntress of the tombs? Was she just a common girl, one who went to seek among the tombs for men who were in sorrow, haunted by the recollection of some woman, a wife or a sweetheart, and still troubled by the memory of vanished caresses? Was she unique? Are there many such? Is it a profession? Do they parade the cemetery as they parade the street? Or else was she only impressed with the admirable, profoundly philosophical idea of exploiting love recollections, which are revived in these funereal places?

"And I would have liked to know whose widow she was on that special day."

MADEMOISELLE PEARL

I

What a strange idea it was for me to choose Mademoiselle Pearl for queen that evening!

Every year I celebrate Twelfth Night with my old friend Chantal. My father, who was his most intimate friend, used to take me round there when I was a child. I continued the custom, and I doubtless shall continue it as long as I live and as long as there is a Chantal in this world.

The Chantals lead a peculiar existence; they live in Paris as though they were in Grasse, Evetot, or Pont-a-Mousson.

They have a house with a little garden near the observatory. They live there as though they were in the country. Of Paris, the real Paris, they know nothing at all, they suspect nothing; they are so far, so far away! However, from time to time, they take a trip into it. Mademoiselle Chantal goes to lay in her provisions, as it is called in the family. This is how they go to purchase their provisions:

Mademoiselle Pearl, who has the keys to the kitchen closet (for the linen closets are administered by the mistress herself), Mademoiselle Pearl gives warning that the supply of sugar is low, that the preserves are giving out, that there is not much left in the bottom of the coffee bag. Thus warned against famine, Mademoiselle Chantal passes everything in review, taking notes on a pad. Then she puts down a lot of figures and goes through lengthy calculations and long discussions with Mademoiselle Pearl. At last they manage to agree, and they decide upon the quantity of each thing of which they will lay in a three months' provision; sugar, rice, prunes, coffee, preserves, cans of peas, beans, lobster, salt or smoked fish, etc., etc. After which the day for the purchasing is determined on and they go in a cab with a railing round the top and drive to a large grocery store on the other side of the river in the new sections of the town.

Madame Chantal and Mademoiselle Pearl make this trip together, mysteriously, and only return at dinner time, tired out, although still excited, and shaken up by the cab, the roof of which is covered with bundles and bags, like an express wagon.

For the Chantals all that part of Paris situated on the other side of the Seine constitutes the new quarter, a section inhabited by a strange, noisy population, which cares little for honor, spends its days in dissipation, its nights in revelry, and which throws money out of the windows. From time to time, however, the young girls are taken to the Opera-Comique or the Theatre Francais, when the play is recommended by the paper which is read by M. Chantal.

At present the young ladies are respectively nineteen and seventeen. They are two pretty girls, tall and fresh, very well brought up, in fact, too well brought up, so much so that they pass by unperceived like two pretty dolls. Never would the idea come to me to pay the slightest attention or to pay court to one of the young Chantal ladies; they are so immaculate that one hardly dares speak to them; one almost feels indecent when bowing to them.

As for the father, he is a charming man, well educated, frank, cordial, but he likes calm and quiet above all else, and has thus contributed greatly to the mummifying of his family in order to live as he pleased in stagnant quiescence. He reads a lot, loves to talk and is readily affected. Lack of contact and of elbowing with the world has made his moral skin very tender and sensitive. The slightest thing moves him, excites him, and makes him suffer.

The Chantals have limited connections carefully chosen in the neighborhood. They also exchange two or three yearly visits with relatives who live in the distance.

As for me, I take dinner with them on the fifteenth of August and on Twelfth Night. That is as much one of my duties as Easter communion is for a Catholic.

On the fifteenth of August a few friends are invited, but on Twelfth Night I am the only stranger.

Well, this year, as every former year, I went to the Chantals' for my Epiphany dinner.

According to my usual custom, I kissed M. Chantal, Madame Chantal and Mademoiselle Pearl, and I made a deep bow to the Misses Louise and Pauline. I was questioned about a thousand and one things, about what had happened on the boulevards, about politics, about how matters stood in Tong-King, and about our representatives in Parliament. Madame Chantal, a fat lady, whose ideas always gave me the impression of being carved out square like building stones, was accustomed to exclaiming at the end of every political discussion: "All that is seed which does not promise much for the future!" Why have I always imagined that Madame Chantal's ideas are square? I don't know; but everything that she says takes that shape in my head: a big square, with four symmetrical angles. There are other people whose ideas always strike me as being round and rolling like a hoop. As soon as they begin a sentence on any subject it rolls on and on, coming out in ten, twenty, fifty round ideas, large and small, which I see rolling along, one behind the other, to the end of the horizon. Other people have pointed ideas—but enough of this.

We sat down as usual and finished our dinner without anything out of the ordinary being said. At dessert the Twelfth Night cake was brought on. Now, M. Chantal had been king every year. I don't know whether this was the result of continued chance or a family convention, but he unfailingly found the bean in his piece of cake, and he would proclaim Madame Chantal to be queen. Therefore, I was greatly surprised to find something very hard, which almost made me break a tooth, in a mouthful of cake. Gently I took this thing from my mouth and I saw that it was a little porcelain doll, no bigger than a bean. Surprise caused me to exclaim:

"Ah!" All looked at me, and Chantal clapped his hands and cried: "It's Gaston! It's Gaston! Long live the king! Long live the king!"

All took up the chorus: "Long live the king!" And I blushed to the tip of my ears, as one often does, without any reason at all, in situations which are a little foolish. I sat there looking at my plate, with this absurd little bit of pottery in my fingers, forcing myself to laugh and not knowing what to do or say, when Chantal once more cried out: "Now, you must choose a queen!"

Then I was thunderstruck. In a second a thousand thoughts and suppositions flashed through my mind. Did they expect me to pick out one of the young Chantal ladies? Was that a trick to make me say which one I prefer? Was it a gentle, light, direct hint of the parents toward a possible marriage? The idea of marriage roams continually in houses with grown-up girls, and takes every shape and disguise, and employs every subterfuge. A dread of compromising myself took hold of me as well as an extreme timidity before the obstinately correct and reserved attitude of the Misses Louise and Pauline. To choose one of them in preference to the other seemed to me as difficult as choosing between two drops of water; and then the fear of launching myself into an affair which might, in spite of me, lead me gently into matrimonial ties, by means as wary and imperceptible and as calm as this insignificant royalty—the fear of all this haunted me.

Suddenly I had an inspiration, and I held out to Mademoiselle Pearl the symbolical emblem. At first every one was surprised, then they doubtless appreciated my delicacy and discretion, for they applauded furiously. Everybody was crying: "Long live the queen! Long live the queen!"

As for herself, poor old maid, she was so amazed that she completely lost control of herself; she was trembling and stammering: "No—no—oh! no—not me—please—not me—I beg of you——"

Then for the first time in my life I looked at Mademoiselle Pearl and wondered what she was.

I was accustomed to seeing her in this house, just as one sees old upholstered armchairs on which one has been sitting since childhood without ever noticing them. One day, with no reason at all, because a ray of sunshine happens to strike the seat, you suddenly think: "Why, that chair is very curious"; and then you discover that the wood has been worked by a real artist and that the material is remarkable. I had never taken any notice of Mademoiselle Pearl.

She was a part of the Chantal family, that was all. But how? By what right? She was a tall, thin person who tried to remain in the background, but who was by no means insignificant. She was treated in a friendly manner, better than a housekeeper, not so well as a relative. I suddenly observed several shades of distinction which I had never noticed before. Madame Chantal said: "Pearl." The young ladies: "Mademoiselle Pearl," and Chantal only addressed her as "Mademoiselle," with an air of greater respect, perhaps.

I began to observe her. How old could she be? Forty? Yes, forty. She was not old, she made herself old. I was suddenly struck by this fact. She fixed her hair and dressed in a ridiculous manner, and, notwithstanding all that, she was not in the least ridiculous, she had such simple, natural gracefulness, veiled and hidden. Truly, what a strange creature! How was it I had never observed her before? She dressed her hair in a grotesque manner with little old maid curls, most absurd; but beneath this one could see a large, calm brow, cut by two deep lines, two wrinkles of long sadness, then two blue eyes, large and tender, so timid, so bashful, so humble, two beautiful eyes which had kept the expression of naive wonder of a young girl, of youthful sensations, and also of sorrow, which had softened without spoiling them.

Her whole face was refined and discreet, a face the expression of which seemed to have gone out without being used up or faded by the fatigues and great emotions of life.

What a dainty mouth! and such pretty teeth! But one would have thought that she did not dare smile.

Suddenly I compared her to Madame Chantal! Undoubtedly Mademoiselle Pearl was the better of the two, a hundred times better, daintier, prouder, more noble. I was surprised at my observation. They were pouring out champagne. I held my glass up to the queen and, with a well-turned compliment, I drank to her health. I could see that she felt inclined to hide her head in her napkin. Then, as she was dipping her lips in the clear wine, everybody cried: "The queen drinks! the queen drinks!" She almost turned purple and choked. Everybody was laughing; but I could see that all loved her.

As soon as dinner was over Chantal took me by the arm. It was time for his cigar, a sacred hour. When alone he would smoke it out in the street; when guests came to dinner he would take them to the billiard room and smoke while playing. That evening they had built a fire to celebrate Twelfth Night; my old friend took his cue, a very fine one, and chalked it with great care; then he said:

"You break, my boy!"

He called me "my boy," although I was twenty-five, but he had known me as a young child.

I started the game and made a few carroms. I missed some others, but as the thought of Mademoiselle Pearl kept returning to my mind, I suddenly asked:

"By the way, Monsieur Chantal, is Mademoiselle Pearl a relative of yours?"

Greatly surprised, he stopped playing and looked at me:

"What! Don't you know? Haven't you heard about Mademoiselle Pearl?"

"No."

"Didn't your father ever tell you?"

"No."

"Well, well, that's funny! That certainly is funny! Why, it's a regular romance!"

He paused, and then continued:

"And if you only knew how peculiar it is that you should ask me that to-day, on Twelfth Night!"

"Why?"

"Why? Well, listen. Forty-one years ago to day, the day of the Epiphany, the following events occurred: We were then living at Roily-le-Tors, on the ramparts; but in order that you may understand, I must first explain the house. Roily is built on a hill, or, rather, on a mound which overlooks a great stretch of prairie. We had a house there with a beautiful hanging garden supported by the old battlemented wall; so that the house was in the town on the streets, while the garden overlooked the plain. There was a door leading from the garden to the open country, at the bottom of a secret stairway in the thick wall—the kind you read about in novels. A road passed in front of this door, which was provided with a big bell; for the peasants, in order to avoid the roundabout way, would bring their provisions up this way.

"You now understand the place, don't you? Well, this year, at Epiphany, it had been snowing for a week. One might have thought that the world was coming to an end. When we went to the ramparts to look over the plain, this immense white, frozen country, which shone like varnish, would chill our very souls. One might have thought that the Lord had packed the world in cotton to put it away in the storeroom for old worlds. I can assure you that it was dreary looking.

"We were a very numerous family at that time my father, my mother, my uncle and aunt, my two brothers and four cousins; they were pretty little girls; I married the youngest. Of all that crowd, there are only three of us left: my wife, I, and my sister-in-law, who lives in

Marseilles. Zounds! how quickly a family like that dwindles away! I tremble when I think of it! I was fifteen years old then, since I am fifty-six now.

"We were going to celebrate the Epiphany, and we were all happy, very happy! Everybody was in the parlor, awaiting dinner, and my oldest brother, Jacques, said: 'There has been a dog howling out in the plain for about ten minutes; the poor beast must be lost.'

"He had hardly stopped talking when the garden bell began to ring. It had the deep sound of a church bell, which made one think of death. A shiver ran through everybody. My father called the servant and told him to go outside and look. We waited in complete silence; we were thinking of the snow which covered the ground. When the man returned he declared that he had seen nothing. The dog kept up its ceaseless howling, and always from the same spot.

"We sat down to dinner; but we were all uneasy, especially the young people. Everything went well up to the roast, then the bell began to ring again, three times in succession, three heavy, long strokes which vibrated to the tips of our fingers and which stopped our conversation short. We sat there looking at each other, fork in the air, still listening, and shaken by a kind of supernatural fear.

"At last my mother spoke: 'It's surprising that they should have waited so long to come back. Do not go alone, Baptiste; one of these gentlemen will accompany you.'

"My Uncle Francois arose. He was a kind of Hercules, very proud of his strength, and feared nothing in the world. My father said to him: 'Take a gun. There is no telling what it might be.'

"But my uncle only took a cane and went out with the servant.

"We others remained there trembling with fear and apprehension, without eating or speaking. My father tried to reassure us: 'Just wait and see,' he said; 'it will be some beggar or some traveller lost in the snow. After ringing once, seeing that the door was not immediately opened, he attempted again to find his way, and being unable to, he has returned to our door.'

"Our uncle seemed to stay away an hour. At last he came back, furious, swearing: 'Nothing at all; it's some practical joker! There is nothing but that damned dog howling away at about a hundred yards from the walls. If I had taken a gun I would have killed him to make him keep quiet.'

"We sat down to dinner again, but every one was excited; we felt that all was not over, that something was going to happen, that the bell would soon ring again.

"It rang just as the Twelfth Night cake was being cut. All the men jumped up together. My Uncle, Francois, who had been drinking champagne, swore so furiously that he would murder it, whatever it might be, that my mother and my aunt threw themselves on him to prevent his going. My father, although very calm and a little helpless (he limped ever since he had broken his leg when thrown by a horse), declared, in turn, that he wished to find out what was the matter and that he was going. My brothers, aged eighteen and twenty, ran to get their guns; and as no one was paying any attention to me I snatched up a little rifle that was used in the garden and got ready to accompany the expedition.

"It started out immediately. My father and uncle were walking ahead with Baptiste, who was carrying a lantern. My brothers, Jacques and Paul, followed, and I trailed on behind in spite of the prayers of my mother, who stood in front of the house with her sister and my cousins.

"It had been snowing again for the last hour, and the trees were weighted down. The pines were bending under this heavy, white garment, and looked like white pyramids or enormous sugar cones, and through the gray curtains of small hurrying flakes could be seen the lighter bushes which stood out pale in the shadow. The snow was falling so thick that we could hardly see ten feet ahead of us. But the lantern threw a bright light around us. When we began to go down the winding stairway in the wall I really grew frightened. I felt as though some one were walking behind me, were going to grab me by the shoulders and carry me away, and I felt a strong desire to return; but, as I would have had to cross the garden all alone, I did not dare. I heard some one opening the door leading to the plain; my uncle began to swear again, exclaiming: 'By—-! He has gone again! If I can catch sight of even his shadow, I'll take care not to miss him, the swine!'

"It was a discouraging thing to see this great expanse of plain, or, rather, to feel it before us, for we could not see it; we could only see a thick, endless veil of snow, above, below, opposite us, to the right, to the left, everywhere. My uncle continued:

"'Listen! There is the dog howling again; I will teach him how I shoot. That will be something gained, anyhow.'

"But my father, who was kind-hearted, went on:

"'It will be much better to go on and get the poor animal, who is crying for hunger. The poor fellow is barking for help; he is calling like a man in distress. Let us go to him.'

"So we started out through this mist, through this thick continuous fall of snow, which filled the air, which moved, floated, fell, and chilled the skin with a burning sensation like a sharp, rapid pain as each flake melted. We were sinking in up to our knees in this soft, cold mass, and we had to lift our feet very high in order to walk. As we advanced the dog's voice became clearer and stronger. My uncle cried: 'Here he is!' We stopped to observe him as one does when he meets an enemy at night.

"I could see nothing, so I ran up to the others, and I caught sight of him; he was frightful and weird-looking; he was a big black shepherd's dog with long hair and a wolf's head, standing just within the gleam of light cast by our lantern on the snow. He did not move; he was silently watching us.

"My uncle said: 'That's peculiar, he is neither advancing nor retreating. I feel like taking a shot at him.'

"My father answered in a firm voice: 'No, we must capture him.'

"Then my brother Jacques added: 'But he is not alone. There is something behind him."

"There was indeed something behind him, something gray, impossible to distinguish. We started out again cautiously. When he saw us approaching the dog sat down. He did not look wicked. Instead, he seemed pleased at having been able to attract the attention of some one.

"My father went straight to him and petted him. The dog licked his hands. We saw that he was tied to the wheel of a little carriage, a sort of toy carriage entirely wrapped up in three or four woolen blankets. We carefully took off these coverings, and as Baptiste approached his lantern to the front of this little vehicle, which looked like a rolling kennel, we saw in it a little baby sleeping peacefully.

"We were so astonished that we couldn't speak.

"My father was the first to collect his wits, and as he had a warm heart and a broad mind, he stretched his hand over the roof of the carriage and said: 'Poor little waif, you shall be one of us!' And he ordered my brother Jacques to roll the foundling ahead of us. Thinking out loud, my father continued:

"'Some child of love whose poor mother rang at my door on this night of Epiphany in memory of the Child of God.'

"He once more stopped and called at the top of his lungs through the night to the four corners of the heavens: 'We have found it!' Then, putting his hand on his brother's shoulder, he murmured: 'What if you had shot the dog, Francois?'

"My uncle did not answer, but in the darkness he crossed himself, for, notwithstanding his blustering manner, he was very religious.

"The dog, which had been untied, was following us.

"Ah! But you should have seen us when we got to the house! At first we had a lot of trouble in getting the carriage up through the winding stairway; but we succeeded and even rolled it into the vestibule.

"How funny mamma was! How happy and astonished! And my four little cousins (the youngest was only six), they looked like four chickens around a nest. At last we took the child from the carriage. It was still sleeping. It was a girl about six weeks old. In its clothes we found ten thousand francs in gold, yes, my boy, ten thousand francs!—which papa saved for her dowry. Therefore, it was not a child of poor people, but, perhaps, the child of some nobleman and a little bourgeoise of the town—or again—we made a thousand suppositions, but we never found out anything-never the slightest clue. The dog himself was recognized by no one. He was a stranger in the country. At any rate, the person who rang three times at our door must have known my parents well, to have chosen them thus.

"That is how, at the age of six weeks, Mademoiselle Pearl entered the Chantal household.

"It was not until later that she was called Mademoiselle Pearl. She was at first baptized 'Marie Simonne Claire,' Claire being intended, for her family name.

"I can assure you that our return to the diningroom was amusing, with this baby now awake and looking round her at these people and these lights with her vague blue questioning eyes.

"We sat down to dinner again and the cake was cut. I was king, and for queen I took Mademoiselle Pearl, just as you did to-day. On that day she did not appreciate the honor that was being shown her.

"Well, the child was adopted and brought up in the family. She grew, and the years flew by. She was so gentle and loving and minded so well that every one would have spoiled her abominably had not my mother prevented it.

"My mother was an orderly woman with a great respect for class distinctions. She consented to treat little Claire as she did her own sons, but, nevertheless, she wished the distance which separated us to be well marked, and our positions well established. Therefore, as soon as the child could understand, she acquainted her with her story and gently, even tenderly, impressed on the little one's mind that, for the Chantals, she was an adopted daughter, taken in, but, nevertheless, a stranger. Claire understood the situation with peculiar intelligence and with surprising instinct; she knew how to take the place which was allotted her, and to keep it with so much tact, gracefulness and gentleness that she often brought tears to my father's eyes. My mother herself was often moved by the passionate gratitude and timid devotion of this dainty and loving little creature that she began calling her: 'My daughter.' At times, when the little one had done something kind and good, my mother would raise her spectacles on her forehead, a thing which always indicated emotion with her, and she would repeat: 'This child is a pearl, a perfect pearl!' This name stuck to the little Claire, who became and remained for us Mademoiselle Pearl."

II

M. Chantal stopped. He was sitting on the edge of the billiard table, his feet hanging, and was playing with a ball with his left hand, while with his right he crumpled a rag which served to rub the chalk marks from the slate. A little red in the face, his voice thick, he was talking away to himself now, lost in his memories, gently drifting through the old scenes and events which awoke in his mind, just as we walk through old family gardens where we were brought up and where each tree, each walk, each hedge reminds us of some occurrence.

I stood opposite him leaning against the wall, my hands resting on my idle cue.

After a slight pause he continued:

"By Jove! She was pretty at eighteen—and graceful—and perfect. Ah! She was so sweet—and good and true—and charming! She had such eyes—blue-transparent—clear—such eyes as I have never seen since!"

He was once more silent. I asked: "Why did she never marry?"

He answered, not to me, but to the word "marry" which had caught his ear: "Why? why? She never would—she never would! She had a dowry of thirty thousand francs, and she received several offers—but she never would! She seemed sad at that time. That was when I married my cousin, little Charlotte, my wife, to whom I had been engaged for six years."

I looked at M. Chantal, and it seemed to me that I was looking into his very soul, and I was suddenly witnessing one of those humble and cruel tragedies of honest, straightforward, blameless hearts, one of those secret tragedies known to no one, not even the silent and resigned victims. A rash curiosity suddenly impelled me to exclaim:

"You should have married her, Monsieur Chantal!"

He started, looked at me, and said:

"I? Marry whom?"

"Mademoiselle Pearl."

"Why?"

"Because you loved her more than your cousin."

He stared at me with strange, round, bewildered eyes and stammered:

“I loved her—I? How? Who told you that?”

“Why, anyone can see that—and it’s even on account of her that you delayed for so long your marriage to your cousin who had been waiting for you for six years.”

He dropped the ball which he was holding in his left hand, and, seizing the chalk rag in both hands, he buried his face in it and began to sob. He was weeping with his eyes, nose and mouth in a heartbreaking yet ridiculous manner, like a sponge which one squeezes. He was coughing, spitting and blowing his nose in the chalk rag, wiping his eyes and sneezing; then the tears would again begin to flow down the wrinkles on his face and he would make a strange gurgling noise in his throat. I felt bewildered, ashamed; I wanted to run away, and I no longer knew what to say, do, or attempt.

Suddenly Madame Chantal’s voice sounded on the stairs. “Haven’t you men almost finished smoking your cigars?”

I opened the door and cried: “Yes, madame, we are coming right down.”

Then I rushed to her husband, and, seizing him by the shoulders, I cried: “Monsieur Chantal, my friend Chantal, listen to me; your wife is calling; pull yourself together, we must go downstairs.”

He stammered: “Yes—yes—I am coming—poor girl! I am coming—tell her that I am coming.”

He began conscientiously to wipe his face on the cloth which, for the last two or three years, had been used for marking off the chalk from the slate; then he appeared, half white and half red, his forehead, nose, cheeks and chin covered with chalk, and his eyes swollen, still full of tears.

I caught him by the hands and dragged him into his bedroom, muttering: “I beg your pardon, I beg your pardon, Monsieur Chantal, for having caused you such sorrow—but—I did not know—you—you understand.”

He squeezed my hand, saying: “Yes—yes—there are difficult moments.”

Then he plunged his face into a bowl of water. When he emerged from it he did not yet seem to me to be presentable; but I thought of a little stratagem. As he was growing worried, looking at himself in the mirror, I said to him: “All you have to do is to say that a little dust flew into your eye and you can cry before everybody to your heart’s content.”

He went downstairs rubbing his eyes with his handkerchief. All were worried; each one wished to look for the speck, which could not be found; and stories were told of similar cases where it had been necessary to call in a physician.

I went over to Mademoiselle Pearl and watched her, tormented by an ardent curiosity, which was turning to positive suffering. She must indeed have been pretty, with her gentle, calm eyes, so large that it looked as though she never closed them like other mortals. Her gown was a little ridiculous, a real old maid’s gown, which was unbecoming without appearing clumsy.

It seemed to me as though I were looking into her soul, just as I had into Monsieur Chantal’s; that I was looking right from one end to the other of this humble life, so simple and devoted. I felt an irresistible longing to question her, to find out whether she, too, had loved him; whether she also had suffered, as he had, from this long, secret, poignant grief, which one cannot see, know, or guess, but which breaks forth at night in the loneliness of the dark room. I was watching her, and I could observe her heart beating under her waist, and I wondered whether this sweet, candid face had wept on the soft pillow and she had sobbed, her whole body shaken by the violence of her anguish.

I said to her in a low voice, like a child who is breaking a toy to see what is inside: "If you could have seen Monsieur Chantal crying a while ago it would have moved you."

She started, asking: "What? He was weeping?"

"Ah, yes, he was indeed weeping!"

"Why?"

She seemed deeply moved. I answered:

"On your account."

"On my account?"

"Yes. He was telling me how much he had loved you in the days gone by; and what a pang it had given him to marry his cousin instead of you."

Her pale face seemed to grow a little longer; her calm eyes, which always remained open, suddenly closed so quickly that they seemed shut forever. She slipped from her chair to the floor, and slowly, gently sank down as would a fallen garment.

I cried: "Help! help! Mademoiselle Pearl is ill."

Madame Chantal and her daughters rushed forward, and while they were looking for towels, water and vinegar, I grabbed my hat and ran away.

I walked away with rapid strides, my heart heavy, my mind full of remorse and regret. And yet sometimes I felt pleased; I felt as though I had done a praiseworthy and necessary act. I was asking myself: "Did I do wrong or right?" They had that shut up in their hearts, just as some people carry a bullet in a closed wound. Will they not be happier now? It was too late for their torture to begin over again and early enough for them to remember it with tenderness.

And perhaps some evening next spring, moved by a beam of moonlight falling through the branches on the grass at their feet, they will join and press their hands in memory of all this cruel and suppressed suffering; and, perhaps, also this short embrace may infuse in their veins a little of this thrill which they would not have known without it, and will give to those two dead souls, brought to life in a second, the rapid and divine sensation of this intoxication, of this madness which gives to lovers more happiness in an instant than other men can gather during a whole lifetime!

THE THIEF

While apparently thinking of something else, Dr. Sorbier had been listening quietly to those amazing accounts of burglaries and daring deeds that might have been taken from the trial of Cartouche. "Assuredly," he exclaimed, "assuredly, I know of no viler fault nor any meaner action than to attack a girl's innocence, to corrupt her, to profit by a moment of unconscious weakness and of madness, when her heart is beating like that of a frightened fawn, and her pure lips seek those of her tempter; when she abandons herself without thinking of the irremediable stain, nor of her fall, nor of the morrow.

"The man who has brought this about slowly, viciously, who can tell with what science of evil, and who, in such a case, has not steadiness and self-restraint enough to quench that flame by some icy words, who has not sense enough for two, who cannot recover his self-possession and master the runaway brute within him, and who loses his head on the edge of the precipice over which she is going to fall, is as contemptible as any man who breaks open a lock, or as any rascal on the lookout for a house left defenceless and unprotected or for some easy and dishonest stroke of business, or as that thief whose various exploits you have just related to us.

"I, for my part, utterly refuse to absolve him, even when extenuating circumstances plead in his favor, even when he is carrying on a dangerous flirtation, in which a man tries in vain to keep his balance, not to exceed the limits of the game, any more than at lawn tennis; even when the parts are inverted and a man's adversary is some precocious, curious, seductive girl, who shows you immediately that she has nothing to learn and nothing to experience, except the last chapter of love, one of those girls from whom may fate always preserve our sons, and whom a psychological novel writer has christened 'The Semi-Virgins.'

"It is, of course, difficult and painful for that coarse and unfathomable vanity which is characteristic of every man, and which might be called 'malism', not to stir such a charming fire, difficult to act the Joseph and the fool, to turn away his eyes, and, as it were, to put wax into his ears, like the companions of Ulysses when they were attracted by the divine, seductive songs of the Sirens, difficult only to touch that pretty table covered with a perfectly new cloth, at which you are invited to take a seat before any one else, in such a suggestive voice, and are requested to quench your thirst and to taste that new wine, whose fresh and strange flavor you will never forget. But who would hesitate to exercise such self-restraint if, when he rapidly examines his conscience, in one of those instinctive returns to his sober self in which a man thinks clearly and recovers his head, he were to measure the gravity of his fault, consider it, think of its consequences, of the reprisals, of the uneasiness which he would always feel in the future, and which would destroy the repose and happiness of his life?

"You may guess that behind all these moral reflections, such as a graybeard like myself may indulge in, there is a story hidden, and, sad as it is, I am sure it will interest you on account of the strange heroism it shows."

He was silent for a few moments, as if to classify his recollections, and, with his elbows resting on the arms of his easy-chair and his eyes looking into space, he continued in the slow voice of a hospital professor who is explaining a case to his class of medical students, at a bedside:

"He was one of those men who, as our grandfathers used to say, never met with a cruel woman, the type of the adventurous knight who was always foraging, who had something of the scamp about him, but who despised danger and was bold even to rashness. He was ardent in the pursuit of pleasure, and had an irresistible charm about him, one of those men in whom we excuse the greatest excesses as the most natural things in the world. He had run through all his money at gambling and with pretty girls, and so became, as it were, a soldier of fortune. He amused himself whenever and however he could, and was at that time quartered at Versailles.

"I knew him to the very depths of his childlike heart, which was only too easily seen through and sounded, and I loved him as some old bachelor uncle loves a nephew who plays him tricks, but who knows how to coax him. He had made me his confidant rather than his adviser, kept me informed of his slightest pranks, though he always pretended to be speaking about one of his friends, and not about himself; and I must confess that his youthful impetuosity, his careless gaiety, and his amorous ardor sometimes distracted my thoughts and made me envy the handsome, vigorous young fellow who was so happy at being alive, that I had not the courage to check him, to show him the right road, and to call out to him: 'Take care!' as children do at blind man's buff.

"And one day, after one of those interminable cotillons, where the couples do not leave each other for hours, and can disappear together without anybody thinking of noticing them, the poor fellow at last discovered what love was, that real love which takes up its abode in the very centre of the heart and in the brain, and is proud of being there, and which rules like a sovereign and a tyrannous master, and he became desperately enamored of a pretty but badly brought up girl, who was as disquieting and wayward as she was pretty.

"She loved him, however, or rather she idolized him despotically, madly, with all her enraptured soul and all her being. Left to do as she pleased by imprudent and frivolous parents, suffering from neurosis, in consequence of the unwholesome friendships which she contracted at the convent school, instructed by what she saw and heard and knew was going on around her, in spite of her deceitful and artificial conduct, knowing that neither her father nor her mother, who were very proud of their race as well as avaricious, would ever agree to let her marry the man whom she had taken a liking to, that handsome fellow who had little besides vision, ideas and debts, and who belonged to the middle-class, she laid aside all scruples, thought of nothing but of becoming his, no matter what might be the cost.

"By degrees, the unfortunate man's strength gave way, his heart softened, and he allowed himself to be carried away by that current which buffeted him, surrounded him, and left him on the shore like a waif and a stray.

"They wrote letters full of madness to each other, and not a day passed without their meeting, either accidentally, as it seemed, or at parties and balls. She had yielded her lips to him in long, ardent caresses, which had sealed their compact of mutual passion."

The doctor stopped, and his eyes suddenly filled with tears, as these former troubles came back to his mind; and then, in a hoarse voice, he went on, full of the horror of what he was going to relate:

"For months he scaled the garden wall, and, holding his breath and listening for the slightest noise, like a burglar who is going to break into a house, he went in by the servants' entrance, which she had left open, slunk barefoot down a long passage and up the broad staircase, which creaked occasionally, to the second story, where his sweetheart's room was, and stayed there for hours.

"One night, when it was darker than usual, and he was hurrying lest he should be later than the time agreed on, he knocked up against a piece of furniture in the anteroom and upset it. It so happened that the girl's mother had not gone to sleep, either because she had a sick headache, or else because she had sat up late over some novel, and, frightened at that unusual noise which disturbed the silence of the house, she jumped out of bed, opened the door, saw some one indistinctly running away and keeping close to the wall, and, immediately thinking that there were burglars in the house, she aroused her husband and the servants by her frantic screams. The unfortunate man understood the situation; and, seeing what a terrible fix he was in, and preferring to be taken for a common thief to dishonoring his adored one's name, he ran into the drawing-room, felt on the tables and what-nots, filled his pockets at random with valuable bric-a-brac, and then cowered down behind the grand piano, which barred the corner of a large room.

"The servants, who had run in with lighted candles, found him, and, overwhelming him with abuse, seized him by the collar and dragged him, panting and apparently half dead with shame and terror, to the nearest police station. He defended himself with intentional awkwardness when he was brought up for trial, kept up his part with the most perfect self-possession and without any signs of the despair and anguish that he felt in his heart, and, condemned and degraded and made to suffer martyrdom in his honor as a man and a soldier—he was an officer—he did not protest, but went to prison as one of those criminals whom society gets rid of like noxious vermin.

"He died there of misery and of bitterness of spirit, with the name of the fair-haired idol, for whom he had sacrificed himself, on his lips, as if it had been an ecstatic prayer, and he intrusted his will 'to the priest who administered extreme unction to him, and requested him to give it to me. In it, without mentioning anybody, and without in the least lifting the veil, he at last explained the enigma, and cleared himself of those accusations the terrible burden of which he had borne until his last breath.

"I have always thought myself, though I do not know why, that the girl married and had several charming children, whom she brought up with the austere strictness and in the serious piety of former days!"

CLAIR DE LUNE

Abbe Marignan's martial name suited him well. He was a tall, thin priest, fanatic, excitable, yet upright. All his beliefs were fixed, never varying. He believed sincerely that he knew his God, understood His plans, desires and intentions.

When he walked with long strides along the garden walk of his little country parsonage, he would sometimes ask himself the question: "Why has God done this?" And he would dwell on this continually, putting himself in the place of God, and he almost invariably found an answer. He would never have cried out in an outburst of pious humility: "Thy ways, O Lord, are past finding out."

He said to himself: "I am the servant of God; it is right for me to know the reason of His deeds, or to guess it if I do not know it."

Everything in nature seemed to him to have been created in accordance with an admirable and absolute logic. The "whys" and "becauses" always balanced. Dawn was given to make our awakening pleasant, the days to ripen the harvest, the rains to moisten it, the evenings for preparation for slumber, and the dark nights for sleep.

The four seasons corresponded perfectly to the needs of agriculture, and no suspicion had ever come to the priest of the fact that nature has no intentions; that, on the contrary, everything which exists must conform to the hard demands of seasons, climates and matter.

But he hated woman—hated her unconsciously, and despised her by instinct. He often repeated the words of Christ: "Woman, what have I to do with thee?" and he would add: "It seems as though God, Himself, were dissatisfied with this work of His." She was the tempter who led the first man astray, and who since then had ever been busy with her work of damnation, the feeble creature, dangerous and mysteriously affecting one. And even more than their sinful bodies, he hated their loving hearts.

He had often felt their tenderness directed toward himself, and though he knew that he was invulnerable, he grew angry at this need of love that is always vibrating in them.

According to his belief, God had created woman for the sole purpose of tempting and testing man. One must not approach her without defensive precautions and fear of possible snares. She was, indeed, just like a snare, with her lips open and her arms stretched out to man.

He had no indulgence except for nuns, whom their vows had rendered inoffensive; but he was stern with them, nevertheless, because he felt that at the bottom of their fettered and humble hearts the everlasting tenderness was burning brightly—that tenderness which was shown even to him, a priest.

He felt this cursed tenderness, even in their docility, in the low tones of their voices when speaking to him, in their lowered eyes, and in their resigned tears when he reproved them roughly. And he would shake his cassock on leaving the convent doors, and walk off, lengthening his stride as though flying from danger.

He had a niece who lived with her mother in a little house near him. He was bent upon making a sister of charity of her.

She was a pretty, brainless madcap. When the abbe preached she laughed, and when he was angry with her she would give him a hug, drawing him to her heart, while he sought unconsciously to release himself from this embrace which nevertheless filled him with a sweet pleasure, awakening in his depths the sensation of paternity which slumbers in every man.

Often, when walking by her side, along the country road, he would speak to her of God, of his God. She never listened to him, but looked about her at the sky, the grass and flowers, and one could see the joy of life sparkling in her eyes. Sometimes she would dart forward to catch some flying creature, crying out as she brought it back: "Look, uncle, how pretty it is! I want to hug it!" And this desire to "hug" flies or lilac blossoms disquieted, angered, and roused the priest, who saw, even in this, the ineradicable tenderness that is always budding in women's hearts.

Then there came a day when the sexton's wife, who kept house for Abbe Marignan, told him, with caution, that his niece had a lover.

Almost suffocated by the fearful emotion this news roused in him, he stood there, his face covered with soap, for he was in the act of shaving.

When he had sufficiently recovered to think and speak he cried: "It is not true; you lie, Melanie!"

But the peasant woman put her hand on her heart, saying: "May our Lord judge me if I lie, Monsieur le Cure! I tell you, she goes there every night when your sister has gone to bed. They meet by the river side; you have only to go there and see, between ten o'clock and midnight."

He ceased scraping his chin, and began to walk up and down impetuously, as he always did when he was in deep thought. When he began shaving again he cut himself three times from his nose to his ear.

All day long he was silent, full of anger and indignation. To his priestly hatred of this invincible love was added the exasperation of her spiritual father, of her guardian and pastor, deceived and tricked by a child, and the selfish emotion shown by parents when their daughter announces that she has chosen a husband without them, and in spite of them.

After dinner he tried to read a little, but could not, growing more and, more angry. When ten o'clock struck he seized his cane, a formidable oak stick, which he was accustomed to carry in his nocturnal walks when visiting the sick. And he smiled at the enormous club which he twirled in a threatening manner in his strong, country fist. Then he raised it suddenly and, gritting his teeth, brought it down on a chair, the broken back of which fell over on the floor.

He opened the door to go out, but stopped on the sill, surprised by the splendid moonlight, of such brilliance as is seldom seen.

And, as he was gifted with an emotional nature, one such as had all those poetic dreamers, the Fathers of the Church, he felt suddenly distracted and moved by all the grand and serene beauty of this pale night.

In his little garden, all bathed in soft light, his fruit trees in a row cast on the ground the shadow of their slender branches, scarcely in full leaf, while the giant honeysuckle, clinging to the wall of his house, exhaled a delicious sweetness, filling the warm moonlit atmosphere with a kind of perfumed soul.

He began to take long breaths, drinking in the air as drunkards drink wine, and he walked along slowly, delighted, marveling, almost forgetting his niece.

As soon as he was outside of the garden, he stopped to gaze upon the plain all flooded with the caressing light, bathed in that tender, languishing charm of serene nights. At each moment was heard the short, metallic note of the cricket, and distant nightingales shook out their scattered notes—their light, vibrant music that sets one dreaming, without thinking, a music made for kisses, for the seduction of moonlight.

The abbe walked on again, his heart failing, though he knew not why. He seemed weakened, suddenly exhausted; he wanted to sit down, to rest there, to think, to admire God in His works.

Down yonder, following the undulations of the little river, a great line of poplars wound in and out. A fine mist, a white haze through which the moonbeams passed, silvering it and making it gleam, hung around and above the mountains, covering all the tortuous course of the water with a kind of light and transparent cotton.

The priest stopped once again, his soul filled with a growing and irresistible tenderness.

And a doubt, a vague feeling of disquiet came over him; he was asking one of those questions that he sometimes put to himself.

"Why did God make this? Since the night is destined for sleep, unconsciousness, repose, forgetfulness of everything, why make it more charming than day, softer than dawn or evening? And why does this seductive planet, more poetic than the sun, that seems destined, so discreet is it, to illuminate things too delicate and mysterious for the light of day, make the darkness so transparent?

"Why does not the greatest of feathered songsters sleep like the others? Why does it pour forth its voice in the mysterious night?

"Why this half-veil cast over the world? Why these tremblings of the heart, this emotion of the spirit, this enervation of the body? Why this display of enchantments that human beings do not see, since they are lying in their beds? For whom is destined this sublime spectacle, this abundance of poetry cast from heaven to earth?"

And the abbe could not understand.

But see, out there, on the edge of the meadow, under the arch of trees bathed in a shining mist, two figures are walking side by side.

The man was the taller, and held his arm about his sweetheart's neck and kissed her brow every little while. They imparted life, all at once, to the placid landscape in which they were framed as by a heavenly hand. The two seemed but a single being, the being for whom was destined this calm and silent night, and they came toward the priest as a living answer, the response his Master sent to his questionings.

He stood still, his heart beating, all upset; and it seemed to him that he saw before him some biblical scene, like the loves of Ruth and Boaz, the accomplishment of the will of the Lord, in some of those glorious stories of which the sacred books tell. The verses of the Song of Songs began to ring in his ears, the appeal of passion, all the poetry of this poem replete with tenderness.

And he said unto himself: "Perhaps God has made such nights as these to idealize the love of men."

He shrank back from this couple that still advanced with arms intertwined. Yet it was his niece. But he asked himself now if he would not be disobeying God. And does not God permit love, since He surrounds it with such visible splendor?

And he went back musing, almost ashamed, as if he had intruded into a temple where he had, no right to enter.

Milton Keynes UK
Ingram Content Group UK Ltd.
UKHW040635100823
426486UK00037B/66

9 789358 372151